D1037281

In Volume 2 of Columbia's c[...] anthology of modern Japane[...] thoughtfully selected and caref[...] readings portray the vast changes that have transformed Japanese culture since the end of the Pacific War. Beginning with the Allied Occupation in 1945 and concluding with the early twenty-first century, these stories, poems, plays, and essays reflect Japan's heady transition from poverty to prosperity, its struggle with conflicting ideologies and political beliefs, and the growing influence of popular culture on the country's artistic and intellectual traditions.

Organized chronologically and by genre within each period, readings include fiction by Hayashi Fumiko and Ōe Kenzaburō; poems by Ayukawa Nobuo, Katsura Nobuko, and Saitō Fumi; plays by Mishima Yukio and Shimizu Kunio; and a number of essays, among them Etō Jun on Natsume Sōseki and his brilliant novel *Kokoro* (*The Heart of Things*), and Kawabata Yasunari on the shape of his literary career and the enduring influence of classical Japanese literature.

Some authors train a keen eye on the contemporary world, while others address the historical past and its relationship to modern culture. Some adopt an even broader scope and turn to European models for inspiration, while others look inward, exploring psychological and sexual terrain in new, often daring ways. Spanning almost six decades, this anthology provides a thorough introduction to a profound period of creative activity.

CONTINUED ON BACK FLAP

The Columbia Anthology of Modern Japanese Literature

VOLUME 2

MODERN ASIAN LITERATURE

The Columbia Anthology of Modern Japanese Literature

VOLUME 2:
FROM 1945 TO THE PRESENT

Edited by J. Thomas Rimer and Van C. Gessel

*With Additional Selections by Amy Vladeck Heinrich
and Hiroaki Sato, Poetry Editors*

COLUMBIA UNIVERSITY

NEW YORK

WINGATE UNIVERSITY LIBRARY

Columbia University Press wishes to express its appreciation for assistance given
by the Pushkin Fund toward the cost of publishing this book.

Columbia University Press
Publishers Since 1893

New York   Chichester, West Sussex

Copyright © 2007 Columbia University Press

All rights reserved

Library of Congress Cataloging-in-Publication Data
The Columbia anthology of modern Japanese literature / edited by J. Thomas Rimer and
Van C. Gessel.
p. cm. — (Modern Asian literature)
Includes bibliographical references.
Contents: v. 1. From restoration to occupation, 1868–1945—
v. 2. From 1945 to the present
ISBN 0-231-11860-0 (vol. 1, cloth : alk. paper)
ISBN 0-231-13804-0 (vol. 2, cloth : alk. paper)
1. Japanese literature—1868—Translations into English.
I. Rimer, J. Thomas.   II. Gessel, Van C.   III. Series.
PL782.E1C55 2005
895.6'4408—dc22
2004056206

∞

Columbia University Press books are printed on permanent and durable acid-free paper.

Printed in the United States of America

c 10 9 8 7 6 5 4 3 2

WINGATE UNIVERSITY LIBRARY

CONTENTS

PREFACE

An anthology can look only backward. Even in the process of assembling and editing this collection, which has taken us several years, other, newer works of high merit have appeared, and older ones have asserted fresh claims to be included as well. For *The Columbia Anthology of Modern Japanese Literature*, we have attempted to assemble a series of works from the 1870s to the present. The issues at stake here, however, are complex. To many readers, the written word as a primary and privileged means to engage with the "deep sense of self that comes from the act of reading, in a true spirit,"[1] now seems to be in the process of being replaced by the culture of the electronic image. In contrast, most of what is contained in this anthology moves the reader backward from what might be termed a postmodern stance toward those decades before the rise of the electronic media. We have provided what we hope is a representative sample of works that convey, for their authors and their readers alike, the thoughts and feelings that only the culture of the printed word can offer.

We cannot say that no contemporary Japanese literature of scope and ambition is now being written and read. The newest works included here have been composed with a level of skill, sophistication, and purpose as appropriate to the current moment as any of the works were that came before them.

---

1. For this quotation in context, see Paul W. Kroll, "Recent Anthologies of Chinese Literature in Translation," *Journal of Asian Studies* 61 (2002): 997.

Whatever the level of young people's interest in Japanese *manga* (comics) and video games may be, literature, as opposed to simple entertainment, often remains the best way to grapple with the problems, and ironies, of the present generation in Japan. Indeed, we have assembled this anthology because we believe that it provides a relevant, resonant experience of Japanese culture not otherwise available.

The students and other readers who use this book will find a generous sampling of the literary corpus of Japan since the 1870s, Japan's so-called modern period. The intellectual sketch map that this book provides needs to be absorbed before moving on to a higher engagement with the texts, theories, and multitudinous disciplinary readings that belong to Japanese (or any other) literature. Just as attempts to allow students to "perform" in a foreign language are doomed to failure unless they have been given a basic vocabulary and a sense of the grammar, so an intelligent study of literature requires that students have a body of texts to discuss.

Other anthologies of what is generally termed "modern Japanese literature" have preceded this one, and surely many others will follow. One difference, however, between this volume and some of the earlier collections is related to the evolving view of both Japanese and foreign scholars as to what constitutes "literature." Many of the earlier collections sought, consciously or unconsciously, to privilege the long and elegant aesthetic traditions of Japan as they were transformed and manifested anew in modern works. For several generations, this view of Japanese literature prevailed and perhaps culminated in the awarding of the Nobel Prize for Literature to Kawabata Yasunari in 1968. By common consent, some of the greatest twentieth-century Japanese literary works can be categorized in this fashion. But many other kinds of writing, ranging from detective stories to political accounts—always valued by Japanese readers but neglected by translators in the early postwar decades—can now be sampled here.

In addition, our own definition of what constitutes literature extends beyond the prose fictional narrative. In this book, we also have included poetry, in both its traditional and its modern forms, as well as representative play texts and essays. But one shortcoming of this anthology—an inevitable one, in our view—is the absence of longer works of prose fiction, simply for reasons of space. It would be a serious misrepresentation of the period, however, if readers thought that some of the most significant writers of the past hundred years—Natsume Sōseki, Shiga Naoya, Tanizaki Jun'ichirō, Shimazaki Tōson, Mishima Yukio, Ōe Kenzaburō, and so many others—wrote only short pieces. In a few cases here, we provide excerpts from longer works as a way of calling attention to their importance, from both a literary and a historical point of view. The bibliography at the end of this volume lists a variety of the longer works that have been translated into English.

The items that we have chosen for this book reflect the convictions and enthusiasms of both of us as editors. We have attempted to chronicle a long native tradition's encounter with and response to the newly introduced writings of Western nations. Japanese writers of the modern age—which begins with the opening of the country to the West in the late 1860s—were conscious of the weight of their own traditions. But they also were inspired by the different approaches to writing they discovered in Western literature, first made available to them at the end of the nineteenth century.

Consequently, the history of modern literature in Japan is largely the story of the interactions between the native tradition and the imported forms and styles, in every genre of writing. The Meiji period (1868–1912) was a time of grand experiment in literature, and since then the pendulum has swung back and forth as writers have tried to imitate what they saw in Western drama, fiction, and poetry or, alternatively, to hang on to what they regarded as the essence of their past.

For the two centuries preceding the opening of Japan to the West, native literary traditions had been developing inside the boundaries of what Donald Keene called a "world within walls."[2] In the early seventeenth century, the new Tokugawa military regime sealed off the country to virtually all foreign interaction, prohibited Japanese citizens from leaving the islands, and wiped out the vestiges of the initial Western influence by expelling the Catholic missionaries and "reconverting" the swelling Japanese Christian population through brutal torture—all in the name of preserving domestic tranquillity and social stability. Although poetry, drama, and the prose narrative flourished early in the seclusion period—the *haiku* of Bashō, the new dramatic forms of *kabuki* and the puppet theater, and the detached, witty stories of Saikaku—by the mid-nineteenth century the literary pond, bereft of outlets and with all fresh streams dammed off, had become increasingly stagnant. It was, to paraphrase Bashō's famous verse, time for a new frog to jump into the old pond.

The "black ships" of Commodore Matthew Perry that came steaming into Edo Bay in the summer of 1853 started in motion the ripple effect that stirred the waters of this isolated pond and opened new vistas to writers of every persuasion. One of the most influential intellectual imports in these early years was the literature of Europe and, later, of the United States. Over a hundred-year period, starting with the founding of the Meiji era in 1868, the Japanese literary scene became a kind of experimental laboratory in which many new ingredients were brought in from foreign suppliers—new notions of the self; theories of romanticism and naturalism, democracy and individual freedom, gender and social equality; the rights of the working class; modernism and postmodernism; an *après guerre* existentialism in tandem with a dedicated Marxist

---

2. Donald Keene's thorough and evocative treatment of the period can be found in his book by that title, *World Within Walls: Japanese Literature of the Pre-modern Era, 1600–1867* (New York: Columbia University Press, 1999). Those wishing to read translated examples of works of literature from this period will enjoy Haruo Shirane's *Early Modern Japanese Literature: An Anthology, 1600–1900* (New York: Columbia University Press, 2002).

INTRODUCTION

VAN C. GESSEL

The works of Japanese literature in volume 2 of *The Columbia Anthology of Modern Japanese Literature* span six decades, during which Japan moved from a war-demolished wasteland to one of the world's leading economic and political powers. Given this rapid and dramatic transformation, it should not be surprising to discover that Japanese literature similarly evolved and diversified, speeding through "movements" and styles and tones as frequently as Toyota or Honda vehicles sped through model changes.

In the middle of the twentieth century, the Japanese lived lives sometimes eerily parallel to those of their grandparents in the early Meiji period (1868–1912). In both instances, an abrupt, traumatic encounter with Western civilization left the Japanese feeling inferior, demoralized, and prepared to jettison the values that had sustained their lives and culture. The black ships of Commodore Matthew Perry forced open the doors of the isolated nation, and the introduction of Western material culture and ideas compelled the Japanese to try to become more "like," and therefore more competitive with, the foreign powers. At the end of the Pacific War, it was not black ships but silver bombers that leveled much of the defeated nation and prepared for the very first foreign occupation of Japan and the only time that the country surrendered both its hegemony and its identity. During the Meiji period, Japan's leaders often willingly—albeit sometimes randomly—changed key institutions and attitudes in order to modernize the country and preserve its national identity. But under the direction of General Douglas MacArthur, a complete reformation of Japanese social structures—however much such changes may have seemed later to harmonize with the will of the Japanese people themselves—was imposed with paternalistic zeal on a devastated enemy state.

Although Japan made a pact of military convenience with Germany during World War II, the two countries' postwar literary responses to their near annihilation could not have been less closely allied. Postwar German writers relentlessly revisited issues of communal guilt for the country's Nazi atrocities, and the rejuvenation of the German psyche seems to have hinged on the people's acceptance of responsibility. In contrast, the Japanese people shifted the blame for the catastrophically ill-thought war effort onto the shoulders of their nation's military leaders. Whether this was a reflection of unchallenged political propaganda or an evasion of individual responsibility, nonetheless very few literary works produced in the first years after the defeat placed the burden of guilt on the people themselves. We should note, however, that despite its commitment to the freedom of speech, the Allied Occupation policy set limits on what Japanese writers could publish right after the war. That is, they could not criticize the Occupation's edicts; they were forbidden to write in any detail about the atomic bombing of Hiroshima and Nagasaki; and they were not allowed to depict American soldiers in the company of Japanese women.

After the emperor announced Japan's unconditional surrender, the people were not sure whether the Japanese nation would survive. Millions of Japanese had perished during the long years of warfare that had begun in China in the early 1930s. At the end of the Pacific War, more than a million Japanese troops were stationed overseas, throughout China and the South Pacific, and there was no indication when they might, if ever, return to their homes and families— if, indeed, their homes and families had withstood the ravages of fire and atomic bombs. Indeed, some soldiers were rounded up by Soviet forces and taken to prison camps in Siberia, never to be heard from again. Still others went into hiding in the jungles of Southeast Asia, some of whom have resurfaced over the years since then. In any case, Japan in August 1945 was teetering on the brink of collapse, humiliated and fearful that widespread retaliation by the occupying forces would destroy the remainder of their culture.

EARLY POSTWAR LITERATURE, 1945 TO 1970

The predominant image of Japan's postwar literature is that of the controlling male. Despite being so forcefully etched into prewar literature in the form of self-narrated autobiographical "fictions" (*shi-shōsetsu*), it was forever shattered by the experiences of war and defeat. Indeed, Japan's military loss is depicted as "humanity lost," which is also the literal meaning of the title of Dazai Osamu's novel *Ningen shikkaku* (1948, trans. by Donald Keene in 1957 as *No Longer Human*), which was published shortly before the author committed suicide. The death of the male persona is ubiquitous, whereas women are presented as survivors who continue to live, with scarcely any hope, only because there is no other choice available to them.

An arresting image comes from "The Magic Chalk" (Mahō no chōku), a story published in 1950 by a new writer, Abe Kōbō, in which a starving artist discovers in his bare apartment a piece of red chalk that performs an unusual miracle: any object that he draws on his walls becomes real. He of course starts drawing, and then gorging himself on, sumptuous foods. Then he grows more ambitious and decides to re-create the world to suit his own tastes by sketching a door. When he opens it, he is certain that he will see beyond it a new, happier, more egalitarian society that will accept him as he is. But when he opens the door, he is greeted by nothingness. The only thing in sight is a plain horizon line, and he must create his mental utopia line by line, piece by piece. But the task is too daunting for him, and his last conscious act is to draw a naked woman on the wall to satisfy his less-than-lofty material yearnings.[1] Two companion pieces to this story, "The Red Cocoon" (Akai mayu, 1950) and "The Flood" (Kōzui, 1950), open this volume of the anthology.

In the late 1940s and early 1950s, the Japanese moral landscape resembled the theme of this story. Destroyed by the war and defeat, Japan had a wealth of possibilities and options for its recovery. But nothing was clear yet, nothing hinting at the kind of nation Japan would become. Its writers, perhaps reflecting more closely at this time the mental attitudes of the entire nation than in any previous or subsequent period, were hesitant to commit themselves to any particular philosophy, having been so recently betrayed by the propaganda from their own political leadership. MacArthur and the Occupation authorities clearly intended to make over Japan in the image of the American democratic model, and yet one of the Supreme Commander's earliest and boldest decisions was to free from jail all the key Marxist political leaders who had been imprisoned by the Japanese militarists for more than a decade. Thus, communism and a more nativized form of socialism became viable, if not fully comprehended, possibilities for many intellectuals in the postwar years.

In stories that earlier would have been somber self-examinations, existential despair alternates with existential hope, with sardonic irony often seeping in. Shiina Rinzō, the first postwar writer to display an affinity for Kierkegaard and Sartre, became a Christian in 1950 and twelve years later wrote "The Go-Between" (Baishakunin), in which the last thing his Christian protagonist wants is to become an intercessory sacrifice in a nasty family squabble.

In the first decade or so after 1945, many writers depicted the utter desolation of the Japanese landscape, both physical and spiritual. In Noma Hiroshi's "A Red Moon in Her Face" (Kao no naka no akai tsuki, 1947), a man's and a woman's

---

1. A translation of this story into English by Alison Kibrick appears in *The Shōwa Anthology: Modern Japanese Short Stories*, vol. 1, 1929–1961, ed. Van C. Gessel and Tomone Matsumoto (Tokyo: Kodansha International, 1985), 63–75.

experiences of war were so different that the notion of trying to share them comes to seem absurd. In Yasuoka Shōtarō's masochistically humorous "Prized Possessions" (Aigan, 1952), a father, returning as only a fragment of his former self because of his war experience, can do no more to keep his family from starving than stuff his borrowed lodging with rabbits that he hopes will produce wool for coats, with the bitter humor that the members of his family start to look like rabbits just as the bottom falls out of the wool market when the rabbits are reaching maturity.

Other writers of Yasuoka's generation—known as the "third generation of new authors" (daisan no shinjin) because they began writing after the wave of Marxist and existential writings had crested—replaced the "lost father" with a forgiving maternal character who accepted the weaknesses of their protagonists and shielded them from punishment. This theme peaked in the writings of a renowned Japanese Christian author, Endō Shūsaku. Endō published one of the most acclaimed postwar novels in 1966: Silence (Chinmoku, trans. 1969). Set in the era of Christian persecution in the early seventeenth century in Japan, it is a moving meditation on the meaning of faith in a brutal world, a theme that resonated even among Endō's Marxist literary rivals. At the same time, Silence is an examination of how forgiveness often can come through the love of a mother or, in this case, a maternal God. Endō pursues the same theme in "Mothers" (Haha naru mono, 1969, trans. 1984), a story of Japanese Christians who went underground to avoid torture and death.

As Japan's male writers were portraying compassionate women willing to accept the men who had proved to be unfit defenders of the nation, the female voice resurfaced, in part because Japanese women no longer had to look to their absent or absent-minded fathers and husbands for validation. The first female author to take a place in the male-dominated literary establishment was Enchi Fumiko, whose work exhibits both an attachment to the classical poetic dreamworld of The Tale of Genji and (partly because of a desperately unhappy marriage) an almost sadistic yearning to even the score against men by holding them accountable for the centuries of oppressive behavior toward women. In her groundbreaking novel The Waiting Years (Onnazaka, 1957, trans. 1971), Enchi returns to her grandmother's era to tell a tale of a strong, virtuous wife who shatters her philandering husband's ego by requesting on her deathbed that her ashes be scattered over the ocean rather than placed with his in the family crypt. Enchi's story "Skeletons of Men" (Otoko no hone, 1956, trans. 1988) uses similar materials and also suggests that the basic natures of men and women do not change over time.

By the mid-1950s, a kind of domestic calm had settled over the literature, although this often was a deceptive veneer that concealed an underlying anxiety. The protagonist in Shōno Junzō's "Evenings at the Pool" (Pūrusaido shōkei, 1954) is a typical Japanese "salaryman" whose marriage is thrown into turmoil when he loses his job yet continues to leave his house at the same time as he had for work so that his busybody neighbors will not know. On those days when the rush-hour train is less appealing, he can always go to the nearby pool and just . . . float.

The lifting of the wartime censorship attracted new writers and liberated established ones, many of whom had become well known before the war. For example, Tanizaki Jun'ichirō spent the war years in virtual silence, although he continued to work on the novel that appeared in finished form in 1948: his masterpiece, *The Makioka Sisters* (*Sasameyuki*, trans. 1957). Kawabata Yasunari produced a self-styled "elegy to the lost Japan" in his novel of old age, *The Sound of the Mountain* (*Yama no oto*, 1952, trans. 1970). Even though much of his postwar work was structurally and stylistically uneven, Kawabata worked ceaselessly on behalf of younger writers. And as an international vice president of the P.E.N. Club, the important international writers' association, he was able for the first time to bring the attention of global readers to modern Japanese literature, by hosting a meeting of the association in Tokyo in 1957 and helping promote the translation of Japanese literary works into a variety of foreign languages. Translations of his own work and of that of Tanizaki and the younger Mishima Yukio and Abe Kōbō created something of a "golden age" in the internationalization of Japanese literature and in 1968 helped Kawabata win the first Nobel Prize in Literature awarded to a Japanese author.

Kawabata's brightest disciple, Mishima Yukio, was a gifted but demonized writer who retold in his story "Patriotism" (*Yūkoku*, 1960, trans. 1966) the true story of a failed army uprising in February 1936. It turned out to be a prescient forecast of his own sensational death by *harakiri* in 1970.

If, indeed, the literature produced after the war was more settled, certainly the most placid writer of all was Ibuse Masuji, a man with such extraordinary faith in the restorative powers of nature that he was able to write a powerful documentary novel about the bombing of Hiroshima, *Black Rain* (*Kuroi ame*, 1966, trans. 1969), as well as such warmly amusing pastoral works as the story included here, "Old Ushitora" (*Ushitora jiisan*, 1950, trans. 1971). Another writer who seemed able to maintain a sense of equilibrium despite all the chaos around him was Inoue Yasushi, many of whose works are set in ancient China and along the Silk Road and who also produced many affecting pieces like "The Rhododendrons of Hira" (*Hira no shakunage*, 1950, trans. 1979).

In the 1960s, as Japan began to accelerate toward its subsequent "economic miracle," several more women authors made their debuts. Ariyoshi Sawako, represented in this volume by "The Village of Eguchi" (*Eguchi no sato*, 1958, trans. 1971), published several popular novels, many of which deal with the challenges faced by contemporary Japanese women. Her novel *Kōkotsu no hito* (literally, "a man in rapture," 1972, trans. in 1984 as *The Twilight Years*) created a significant stir in Japanese society. Focused on a single family—and particularly on a working mother who is forced by convention to care for her husband's demented father until his death—the novel sparked a debate in the Japanese Diet over the nation's lagging preparations to provide government-sponsored care for a rapidly graying society. It sold more copies than did any other novel published in Japan since the Meiji Restoration.

Other women finding their artistic voices during this period include Kanai

Mieko, represented here by her brief tale of identity confusion, "Homecoming" (Kikan, 1970); Kurahashi Yumiko, an experimental writer who uses Greek mythology in her story "To Die at the Estuary" (Kakō ni shisu, 1971, trans. 1977); and Kōno Taeko, whose sadomasochistic fantasies—often involving the torture and murder of both young and older men—seem like excursions into the subconscious where frustrations can be acted out without destroying the fabric of everyday life. Kōno is represented in this volume by another story of fantasy, "Final Moments" (Saigo no toki, 1966, trans. 1996), which is aimed at bringing some measure of meaning into a woman's life with the threat of imminent death.

Poets and playwrights of the early postwar period expressed, in both traditional and modern, Westernized forms, their own responses to recent traumas. Often the playwrights blended the two, as in Kinoshita Junji's *Twilight Crane* (*Yūzuru*, 1949) and Mishima Yukio's modern nō play, *Yuya* (1955). Both use classical themes in contemporary settings. In reverse, Betsuyaku Minoru recasts a familiar Western story in a Japanese context in *The Little Match Girl* (*Matchi-uri no shōjo*, 1966, trans. 1992).

TOWARD A CONTEMPORARY LITERATURE, 1971 TO THE PRESENT

Perhaps the easiest way to describe the differences between the literature written in Japan in the 1970s and that at the beginning of the twenty-first century is to compare the titles of the acceptance speeches delivered in Stockholm by the only two Japanese writers who have, to date, received the Nobel Prize for Literature. Kawabata Yasunari entitled his 1968 speech "Japan, the Beautiful, and Myself" (Utsukushii Nihon no watashi; this volume contains a complete translation).[2] When Ōe Kenzaburō received the award in 1995, he acknowledged his predecessor in the title of his speech, "Japan, the Ambiguous, and Myself" (Aimai na Nihon no watashi, also included in this volume), and described the shift in Japanese society from an "exotic" Asian civilization to a highly cosmopolitan, Westernized Asian culture.[3] The ambiguous in contemporary Japanese writing may be that much of it has no sense of place, of time, and of moral focus. In that respect, the current literature shares much more with the literature of other advanced industrialized nations. Often a translation into English can be distinguished as a Japanese work only because the names of the characters (if, indeed, any names are given at all) sound Japanese. Otherwise, it could have been written anywhere.

Similarly, Japanese authors of today seldom look back to classical roots. For

---

2. The title of this speech is nearly impossible to translate. Literally it means something like "I who am a part of beautiful Japan."

3. Its similarly indecisive title means "I who am a part of ambivalent Japan."

example, when Kojima Nobuo, author of the story "The Smile" (Bishō, 1954), included in this volume, was asked to name his favorite work of "classical Japanese literature," he did not, as the generation before him surely would have done, cite *The Tale of Genji* or the poetry of court and cloister. Instead, he selected Natsume Sōseki's *The Gate* (*Mon*, trans. 1972), written in 1910! Perhaps the most creative description of the widespread deracination of contemporary Japanese literature was that by Mishima Yukio (who gave the ironically arid title *The Sea of Fertility* [*Hōjō no umi*, 1966–1971, trans. 1972–1975] to the tetralogy he published before his suicide). Mishima referred to the writing of his colleague Abe Kōbō as lacking the "high humidity content" of previous Japanese authors.

More frequently now than ever before, Japan's writers view their country from the outside, for many have spent months, even years, living abroad. In Kaikō Takeshi's story of cultural ambivalence, "The Crushed Pellet" (Tama kudakeru, 1978), Japan is regarded as a stifling destination to a wanderer who has spent much of his time outside his native land. As he sits on the airplane taking him back to his homeland, he feels a layer of "fungus" begin to grow on his skin. The central character in Kanai Mieko's brief story "Homecoming" (Kikan, 1970) loses both her sense of location and her identity (a fate she shares with the solo actress who dominates the stage in Inoue Hisashi's extraordinary play *Makeup* [*Keshō*, 1983]). Even in a science-fiction story like Hoshi Shin'ichi's "He-y, Come on Ou-t!" (O-i, dete ko-i, 1978), the subtle implication is that modern society pays a toxic price for its technological advances.

Nakagami Kenji, whose story "The Wind and the Light" (Sōmoku, 1975) is in this volume, distanced himself even further from the mainstream of his country's society. Most of his stories are set either in the "alley" of outcasts who have never found a home in Japan's rigidly stratified social hierarchy or in the mystical mountains of the Kumano region, where quotidian reality is transcended by means of magic and acts of antisocial violence. Tsushima Yūko, the daughter of Dazai Osamu, wanders into the realm of hallucination in her autobiographical story "That One Glimmering Point of Light" (Hikarikagayaku itten o, 1988), in which a single mother weighed down with nurturing and providing for her children refuses to accept the "rational" conclusions of society after her young son inexplicably dies in their bathtub.

The most popular Japanese writers in both Japan and overseas as this volume goes to press are Murakami Haruki and Yoshimoto Banana.[4] Murakami's stories regularly appear in the *New Yorker*, and Yoshimoto's American publisher proclaimed a virtual "Bananamania" when her novella *Kitchen* appeared in English translation. Although it is still too early to make a final judgment, it seems unlikely that either of these writers will be able to sustain an enduring

---

4. She reportedly chose the pen name "Banana" because it looked better in the Japanese phonetic alphabet than "Pineapple" did.

readership or reputation. The uneasy, confused worlds they examine through postmodern lenses have limited attraction, and their prose styles—like the people and places they depict—lack the aesthetic beauty and flavor (and "humidity") found in the works of earlier writers. The fact that so many readers flock to them, however, demonstrates that some people will never stop searching for creative, imaginative works that help illuminate, divert, reassure, and even stimulate. Indeed, people have always read for the same reasons: to be introduced to new worlds, to move outside themselves and gain a perspective not their own, and to become—in even the most limited sense—like the god described by C. S. Lewis in his space adventure novel *Perelandra*—as one who "can think of all, and all different."[5]

---

5. C. S. Lewis, *Perelandra*, Scribner Paperback Fiction (1944; reprint, New York: Scribner, 1996), 61.

Chapter 5

EARLY POSTWAR LITERATURE, 1945 TO 1970

With the end of World War II in 1945, Japanese literature seemed to take, in the eyes of both writers and readers, a number of new and potentially creative turns.

To some extent, of course, a new generation had come to the fore. Some of the older masters, like Kawabata Yasunari and Tanizaki Jun'ichirō, continued to write and, indeed, produced some of their best work after 1945. But other important prewar figures, such as Shiga Naoya, remained virtually silent. Along with those older writers who began to publish new works, several younger novelists, poets, and playwrights now appeared, many of them part of a generation with personal experiences of the war. Some of these writers regarded their experiences as tragic or nihilistic, whereas others found sardonic elements in them.

In addition, Japan's writers were faced with a topic they never before could have imagined, the atomic bombing of Hiroshima and Nagasaki in 1945. For several decades, the horror of those events provided a thematic grounding for much of their writing. In addition, during the twenty-five years from 1945 to 1970, at least three main currents could be found in the literature.

The first current was a resumption of the contact with contemporary developments in Western literature. During the decade or more of war, Japanese writers' and intellectuals' contacts with their counterparts in Europe diminished and then virtually disappeared altogether. Now, however, their enthusiasm for contemporary literature from abroad, particularly from France, was renewed. These

She seems kind. The wind of hope blows through the neighborhood of my heart. My heart becomes a flag that spreads out flat and flutters in the wind. I smile, too. Like a real gentleman, I say:

"Excuse me, but this isn't my house by any chance?"

The woman's face abruptly hardens. "What? Who are you?"

About to explain, all of a sudden I can't. I don't know what I should explain. How can I make her understand that it's not a question now of who I am? Getting a little desperate, I say:

"Well, if you think this isn't my house, will you please prove it to me?"

"My god. . . ." The woman's face is frightened. That gets me angry.

"If you have no proof, it's all right for me to think it's mine."

"But this is my house."

"What does that matter? Just because you say it's yours doesn't mean it's not mine. That's so."

Instead of answering, the woman turns her face into a wall and shuts the window. That's the true form of a woman's smiling face. It's always this transformation that gives away the incomprehensible logic by which, because something belongs to someone, it does not belong to me.

But, why . . . why does everything belong to someone else and not to me? Even if it isn't mine, can't there be just one thing that doesn't belong to anyone?

Sometimes, I have delusions. That the concrete pipes on construction sites or in storage yards are my house. But they're already on the way to belonging to somebody. Because they become someone else's, they disappear without any reference to my wishes or interest in them. Or they turn into something that is clearly not my house.

Well then, how about park benches? They'd be fine, of course. If they were really my house, and if only he didn't come and chase me off them with his stick. . . . Certainly they belong to everybody, not to anybody. But he says:

"Hey, you, get up. This bench belongs to everybody. It doesn't belong to anybody, least of all you. Come on, start moving. If you don't like it, you can spend the night in the basement lockup at the precinct house. If you stop anyplace else, no matter where, you'll be breaking the law."

The Wandering Jew—is that who I am?

The sun is setting. I keep walking.

A house . . . houses that don't disappear, turn into something else, that stand on the ground and don't move. Between them, the cleft that keeps changing, that doesn't have any one face that stays the same . . . the street. On rainy days, it's like a paint-loaded brush, on snowy days it becomes just the width of the tire ruts, on windy days it flows like a conveyor belt. I keep walking. I can't understand why I don't have a house, and so I can't even hang myself.

Hey, who's holding me around the ankle? If it's the rope for hanging, don't get so excited, don't be in such a hurry. But that's not what it is. It's a sticky silk thread. When I grab it and pull it, the end's in a split between the upper and sole of my shoe. It keeps getting longer and longer, slippery-like. This is weird: My curiosity makes me keep pulling it in. Then something even weirder happens. I'm slowly leaning over. I can't stand up at a right angle to the ground. Has the earth's axis tilted or the gravitational force changed direction?

A thud. My shoe drops off and hits the ground. I see what's happening. The earth's axis hasn't tilted, one of my legs has gotten shorter. As I pull at the thread, my leg rapidly gets shorter and shorter. Like the elbow of a frayed jacket unraveling, my leg's unwinding. The thread, like the fiber of a snake gourd, is my disintegrating leg.

I can't take one more step. I don't know what to do. I keep on standing. In my hand that doesn't know what to do either, my leg that has turned into a silk thread starts to move by itself. It crawls out smoothly. The tip, without any help from my hand, unwinds itself and like a snake starts wrapping itself around me. When my left leg's all unwound, the thread switches as natural as you please to my right leg. In a little while, the thread has wrapped my whole body in a bag. Even then, it doesn't stop but unwinds me from the hips to the chest, from the chest to the shoulders, and as it unwinds it strengthens the bag from inside. In the end, I'm gone.

Afterward, there remained a big empty cocoon.

Ah, now at last I can rest. The evening sun dyes the cocoon red. This, at least, is my house for sure, which nobody can keep me out of. The only trouble is now that I have a house, there's no "I" to return to it.

Inside the cocoon, time stopped. Outside, it was dark, but inside the cocoon it was always evening. Illumined from within, it glowed red with the colors of sunset. This outstanding peculiarity was bound to catch his sharp policeman's eye. He spotted me, the cocoon, lying between the rails of the crossing. At first he was angry, but soon changing his mind about this unusual find, he put me into his pocket. After tumbling around in there for a while, I was transferred to his son's toy box.

THE FLOOD (KŌZUI)

Translated by Lane Dunlop

A certain poor but honest philosopher, to study the laws of the universe, took a telescope up to the roof of his tenement and pursued the movements of the heavenly bodies. As always, he seemed unable to discover more than a few meaningless shooting stars and the stars in their usual positions. It was not that he was bored or anything, but he happened to turn his telescope casually on the earth. An upside-down road dangled in front of his nose. A similarly inverted worker appeared, walking backward along the road. Righting these images in his head, and returning them to their usual relationship, the philosopher adjusted the lens and followed the worker's movements. Under the wide-bore lens, the interior of the worker's little head was transparent. The reason was that the worker, on his way back from the night shift at the factory, had nothing in his head but fatigue.

However, the persevering philosopher, not turning the lens aside because of that, continued to follow the worker's progress. The philosopher's patience was soon rewarded. Suddenly, the following changes took place in the worker.

The outline of the worker's body unexpectedly grew blurred. Melting from the feet up, the figure knelt slimily and dissolved. Only the clothes, cap, and shoes remained, in a mass of fleshy liquid. Finally, completely fluid, it spread out flat on the ground.

The liquefied worker quietly began to flow toward lower ground. He flowed into a pothole. Then he crawled out of it. This movement of the liquid worker, in defiance of the laws of hydrodynamics, amazed the philosopher so much that he almost dropped the telescope. Flowing onward, the worker, when he came up against a roadside fence, crawled up it just like a snail gliding on its membrane, and disappeared from view over the fence. The philosopher, taking his eye from the telescope, heaved a deep sigh. The next day, he announced to the world the coming of a great flood.

Actually, everywhere in the world, the liquefaction of workers and poor people had begun. Particularly remarkable were the group liquefactions. In a large factory, the machinery would suddenly stop. The workers, deliquescing all at once, would form a single mass of liquid that flowed in a stream under the door or, crawling up the wall, flowed out the window. Sometimes the process was reversed: after the workers had turned into liquid, only the machinery, in the deserted factory, would senselessly continue running and in the end break down. In addition, breakouts from prisons due to the mass liquefaction of the prisoners and small floods caused by the liquefaction of whole populations of farm villages were reported one after another in the newspapers.

The liquefaction of human beings, not limited to this kind of phenomenal abnormality, occasioned confusion in a variety of ways. Perfect crimes owing to the liquefaction of the criminal increased dramatically. Law and order were threatened. The police, secretly mobilizing the physicists, began an investigation of the properties of this water. But the liquid, completely ignoring the scientific laws of fluids, merely plunged the physicists into ludicrous confusion. Although to the touch it was in no way different from ordinary water, at times it displayed a strong surface tension like mercury and could retain its shape like amoebae, so that not only could it crawl, as indicated before, from a low to a higher place, but after blending perfectly with its fellow liquefied people and other natural liquids, at some impulse or other it could also separate itself into its original volume. Again, conversely, it sometimes displayed a weak surface tension like that of alcohol. At such times, it had an extraordinary power of permeation vis-à-vis all solids. E.g., at times, probably in relation to differences in its use, with the same kind of paper it could either have absolutely no effect or could dissolve it chemically.

The liquefied human beings were also able to freeze or evaporate. Their freezing and evaporation points were various. Sleighs running over thick ice would be swallowed up horse and all by the suddenly melted ice; front-runners in skating contests would abruptly vanish. Again, swimming pools would suddenly freeze in midsummer, sealing up girls who'd been swimming in them in frozen poses in the ice. The liquid human beings crawled up mountains, mixed with rivers, crossed oceans, evaporated into clouds and fell as rain, so that they spread all over the world. One could never tell what kind of thing was going to happen when and where. Chemistry experiments became well-nigh impossible. The boilers of steam engines, because of an admixture of liquid people, became completely unserviceable. No matter how much they were stoked, no pressure built up. Or all of a sudden the liquid people would violently expand and explode the boiler. Fish and plants that had a vital relationship to water were in a state of chaos beyond description. In every field of biology, transformations difficult to calculate, and destructions, had begun. Apples rolled around warbling snatches of melody; rice-stalks burst with a noise like firecrackers. Especially serious were the effects on human beings who had not yet deliquesced, and in particular on rich people.

One morning, the owner of a big factory drowned in a cup of coffee as soon as he put his lips to the cup. Another industrialist drowned in a glass of whiskey, An extreme example was a drowning in a single drop of eyewash. These seem like things scarcely to be believed, but they all happened.

As these facts were reported, many rich people contracted hydrophobia in the true sense of the word. A certain high government official made the following confession: "When I'm about to drink, I look at the water in the glass and already it does not seem like water to me. In short, it is a liquidized mineral, a harmful substance that is impossible to digest. If I took a mouthful, I am positive I would immediately get sick. I'm instantly invaded by tragic fears."

Even if dysphagia were not present, this was plainly hydrophobia. Everywhere, there were instances of old ladies who fainted away at the mere sight of water. Yet antirabies vaccine did no good whatsoever.

By now, from one end of the world to the other, invisible voices were mingling in a chorus crying doom by a great flood. But the newspapers, at first publishing the following reasons, strenuously denied those rumors:

a) This year's rainfall, both regional and global, is below the annual average.
b) All rivers reported to have flooded have not exceeded the seasonal variation for a normal year.
c) No meteorological or geological abnormalities have been served.

These were the facts. But it was also a fact that the flood had already started. This contradiction caused general social unrest. It was already clear to everyone that this was no ordinary flood. Presently even the newspapers were forced to acknowledge the reality of the flood. But in their usual optimistic tone, they reiterated that this was due to some cosmic accident, was no more than temporary, and would soon end of its own accord. However, the flood, spreading daily, engulfed many villages and towns, many flatlands and low hills were submerged by the liquid people, and the people of status, the people of wealth, began a competitive stampede for refuge in the uplands and mountain districts. Although realizing that that kind of thing was useless against the liquid people who climbed even walls, they were unable to think of anything else to do.

Finally, even the presidents and prime ministers admitted the urgency of the situation. Proclamations were issued, saying that in order to save humanity from extinction in this flood it was necessary to mobilize all spiritual and material resources and expedite the building of great dams and dikes. Tens of thousands of workers, for that purpose, were rounded up for compulsory labor. Whereupon the newspapers also, suddenly changing their attitude, chimed in with the proclamations and praised their high morality and sense of public duty. But just about everybody, including the presidents and prime ministers, knew that those proclamations were nothing more than proclamations for the sake of proclamations. Dikes and such, against the liquid people, being no more than Newtonian dynamics against quantum dynamics, were completely ineffectual. Not only that, but the workers constructing the dikes were rapidly turning into liquid this side of the dikes. The "personal items" pages of the newspapers were awash with notices of missing persons. But, true to character, the newspapers dealt with such disappearances simply as effects rather than causes of the flood. In regard to the contradictory nature of the flood and its essential cause, they maintained a resolute silence, refusing even to mention the subject.

At this time, there was a scientist who proposed that the liquid that had covered the earth be volatilized by means of nuclear energy. The governments, speedily indicating their approval, pledged their full-scale assistance. But when they tried to begin, what became clear, rather than various difficulties, was the impossibility of the project. Because of the liquefaction of human beings, which was accelerating at geometrical progression, there were not enough workers for adequate replacements. Also, liquefaction was already occurring among the scientists. Furthermore, the parts factories were steadily being destroyed and engulfed by the waters. Harassed by problems of reorganization and reconstruction, governments could not predict when the production of vital nuclear equipment would begin.

Unrest and distress swept the world. People were turning into mummies from dehydration, emitting gasping, rattling noises each time they breathed.

There was just one person who was calm and happy. This was the optimistic and wily Noah. Noah, from his experience with the previous flood, without getting agitated or panicky, diligently worked on his ark. When he thought that the future of the human race was being entrusted to him and his family alone, he was even able to step himself in a religious exaltation.

Presently, when the flood approached his house, Noah, accompanied by his family and domestic animals, boarded the ark. Immediately, the liquid people started to crawl up the sides of the boat. Noah berated them in a loud voice.

"Hey! Whose boat do you think this is? I am Noah. This is Noah's Ark. Make no mistake about it. Go on, get out of here!"

But to think that the liquid, which was no longer human, could understand his words was clearly a hasty conclusion and a miscalculation. For liquid, there are only concerns of liquid. The next minute, the ark filled up with liquid and the living creatures drowned. The derelict ark drifted at the mercy of the wind.

In this manner, humanity perished in the Second Flood. But, if you could have looked at the street corners and under the trees of the villages at the bottom of the now-peaceful waters, you would have seen a glittering substance starting to crystallize. Probably around the invisible core of the supersaturated liquid people.

AGAWA HIROYUKI

Agawa Hiroyuki (b. 1920) served as an information officer in the Japanese Imperial Navy during World War II. He began his writing career soon after being repatriated to his demolished hometown of Hiroshima, an experience he describes in the following autobiographical story, "From Age to Age" (Nennen saisai, 1946). Indeed, much of Agawa's work deals with the war, including the destruction of Hiroshima in *Devil's Heritage* (*Ma no isan*, 1953, trans. 1973) and the kamikaze pilots in *Grave Marker in the Clouds* (*Kumo no bohyō*, 1955). His most enduring works are the three sensitive, interpretive biographies of the "liberal trio" of Japanese naval admirals who argued against going to war with the United States: *Yamamoto Isoroku* (1969, trans. in 1979 as *The Reluctant Admiral*), *Yonai Mitsumasa* (1978), and *Inoue Seibi* (1986).

FROM AGE TO AGE (NENNEN SAISAI)

Translated by Eric P. Cunningham

I

With a jolt, the train carrying the repatriated servicemen slowly began to move. Neither the bell nor the steam whistle sounded. As dusk approached, a fine, fog-like drizzle trickled down the glass of the passenger car windows. The men, faces covered with grime, rode through the gloomy twilight, piled into the car along with their luggage. The lights in the car were out. Michio and his fellow passengers all were navy men returning from Shanghai. Since landing, it had been a dizzying number of hours of being rushed along with shouts of "Run!" and "Hurry up!" by foreign troops carrying sticks and dripping with rain and sweat through DDT disinfections, baggage inspections, ID processing, money

"What, are you kidding? No, that's OK."

The petty officer, smiling, flicked his cigarette into the sea. Leaning over the rails, Michio could see the blue waves collapsing into white foam as it flowed through the blades of the shining brass port screw. Whenever the stern rose, the propellers would race wildly in midair.

The night they entered port at Hakata, Michio took off his lieutenant's collar devices and shoulder boards and threw them into the water. The insignia, wrapped in a piece of white paper and a *bentō* wrapper, disappeared into the silent, oil-covered waves.

When he opened his eyes, the train was proceeding as before through the pitch black night.

It was almost over, but somehow he didn't feel like he was really home. He thought he should be gripped by a stronger sense of happiness, but more than anything else, he felt indifferent. Perhaps it was because he had just been so busy.

Images of his father in Hiroshima came to him. Hiroshima. Even Shaohai, a tramp at the collection center in Shanghai, knew about the atomic bomb in Hiroshima. Both his mother, with her bad eyes, and his half-paralyzed father were so old. He could not even hope that they were alive. He wondered whether maybe his sister and nephew had survived. After the war ended, whenever he got the chance, he looked carefully at pictures and newspapers. Little by little his heart grew darker, and quite naturally he became disconsolate.

The train passed through the Kanmon tunnel. Michio slept a little more. How long had he slept? As the train lurched to a halt and his eyes suddenly opened, he saw that they were at a small station in Yamaguchi Prefecture. The clock said it was about three o'clock in the morning. On the far side of the tracks, a station employee was engrossed in stealing from a shipment of miso stacked beneath the platform lights. Perhaps he was going to have the miso for dinner. The people in the car, now awake, broke out laughing. The laughter woke up others.

"Hey, conductor, why don't you turn the lights off?"

"Come on, take some more! If you're going to steal, you might as well make it worth your while!"

The employee looked over at the repatriates' train and, laughing embarrassedly, stopped taking the miso and disappeared. The rain had stopped at some point, and from the wet window, the station stood out with remarkable clarity and brightness.

The train started moving. Michio gloomily fell back to sleep.

The next time he woke up, he could already see the black shadows of Itsukushima, and the sky was becoming lighter. A petty officer from Kure woke up quickly and cheerfully got ready to get off the train.

"My folks don't have any idea that I'm back. My mom'll be cooking by the back door right about now. I can't wait to sneak up from behind and surprise her!" he said happily, gnawing on a piece of hardtack.

"It must be pretty nice to have folks waiting for you at home," Michio said.

"Don't be so pessimistic. You're not going to know anything until you get back and see for yourself."

"I think I have a pretty good idea already."

As Hiroshima drew closer, dawn was breaking, and the men, all roused from their sleep, looked out the window, earnestly preparing themselves for their encounter with the devastation of the atomic bomb. It was the first time they would see the changed face of their home.

"Where the hell is home?" Michio wondered. "I don't have the slightest idea." Eventually, the inevitable moment arrived. He had no idea what kind of environment he was being thrown into, and although he felt anxious, he was not in the least bit fearful. He wasn't sure how he would actually react after he confirmed that his parents were dead, but he decided to behave calmly, as if it were a foregone conclusion.

III

Passing Hatsukaichi and Itsukaichi, the train drew closer to the outskirts of Hiroshima.

"Look, there're plenty of houses here, aren't there? Don't worry, sir," said a petty officer from Osaka.

"This isn't even Hiroshima, you fool."

As expected, as soon as they passed through Koi, the evidence of the destruction suddenly appeared. The first impression, which lasted for some time, was that of a few remaining houses thinly scattered about, giving the landscape the appearance of a place that had been hit by a massive earthquake. After that, there was nothing. Looking at fields to the left and right of the tracks, the scorched plain continued without end. An American magazine he had seen in Shanghai used the words "atomic desert," and that's exactly what it seemed like. Michio gulped, staring at the drastic changes to the streets of his home.

"Whereabouts is your house?"

"Hold on a second. Just a little farther and you can see it, on the left-hand side, just after we cross the second bridge."

Hoping against hope, Michio became excited. The train drew around a gentle curve. It crossed the bridge.

"Well that's lovely."

He calmed himself down as much as he could. There was nothing there. From the northern to the southern edges, the neighborhood was an undifferentiated expanse of burned field. The remains of buildings that long ago could not be seen from the trains now appeared, isolated and distant from one another. The panorama of spindly, charred, drooping trees was eerie. The other men, sympathetic, remained silent.

"Well, at least the grain's growing," somebody said. It was true. After the scorching, the grain was growing tall. Somehow it brought some cheer.

"At any rate, I better get ready to get off." With a thud, he sat back down in the seat. There was no way out but through the window. The train entered the station.

"Hiroshima, Hiroshima . . . changing trains . . . some delays. . . . Everyone . . . now more than ever . . . for the good of our country." In the middle of the clamor, the voice over the loudspeaker was broken but audible.

"Well, Commander, Wakada, Hiratani, Ebihara. Good-bye. Take care, and good-bye."

It was awful leaving them. Without looking back, he went down the stairs, almost at a run.

"Lieutenant Kagawa, if you ever need anything, just come to my house. If you get off at Yano Station, just ask somebody. They'll tell you where to go!" said the petty officer from Kure.

"Thanks, but I really wouldn't want to impose on you."

He and the petty officer parted ways.

IV

There was a police box in front of the station. Upon seeing it, Michio's feelings of insecurity grew stronger.

"Uh—I just came back from China, and I'm trying to find out if my family is—alive or dead—I was wondering if you could tell me where the city office is now?"

The patrolman appeared to have little interest. "It's in the same place it used to be."

"Um—I noticed that K village in Hakushima is—well, it's obviously not there anymore."

It was something he had just seen. The policeman looked as though it couldn't have concerned him in the least.

"You said it. It's obviously not there."

There was nothing to do but start walking. And so, not really knowing where his destination lay, his feet headed by instinct in the direction of the burned ruins of his house. He hoisted his trunk onto his shoulders, hooked his duffel bag with his arm, and walked, breaking out in a sweat almost instantly. He couldn't walk very fast. The road had changed so much that he couldn't tell if it was the way he used to always go or if he had gotten lost. There were barracks standing in various places along the way. There were signs saying things like "Taishū Diner," "Sweet Bean Soup, five yen," "Ersatz Noodles, five yen." In vacant lots here and there, grain was growing. He walked from place to place, absorbing what he saw.

There was fresh greenery, wet with the morning dew. The sky was very clear. All over the place, trees that had turned into charcoal were still standing. He thought they resembled the corpses of incinerated humans.

It was early in the morning, and from time to time, he crossed the paths of people who looked like they were going to work. As if by prearrangement, they all had scuffed and ripped-up shoes and carried knapsacks over their shoulders. At the first sight of Michio, people would look down and head the other way without uttering so much as a word. From afar, a woman about twenty-seven or twenty-eight years old carrying a backpack approached. Her hair was cut short, and she was wearing soiled Western clothes. He had the feeling he had seen her somewhere before. The woman looked back at him. As they passed each other, they both stopped. They remembered each other. They were classmates from elementary school.

"Whaa—Kagawa san! What are you doing? Where are you coming from just now?"

He couldn't quite remember her name.

"I've just come back from China. Um—maybe you know something about my family?"

"Oh dear, no. I did see your sister some time back. She was fine. She didn't have a scratch on her."

At least his sister was definitely all right. He felt better.

"Are my parents dead?"

"Your parents . . ." she paused. "Mother? Oh, Mother?"

Her mother was walking up a short distance behind her. It cheered him up to see an old friend from school. She didn't appear to be married. Although she had once been someone with prospects, she seemed to have become aged by the disappointment of failed expectations.

"Mother, this is Kagawa san. He says he just got back from China. Do you remember what became of his parents?"

If they were dead, he wanted to know as soon as possible.

"Hmmm. Well, now. I can't imagine how you must have suffered, but I think you'll be happy to know that both your parents are doing quite well. Congratulations. The other day—well, actually it was some time ago, I saw your mother at the rice distribution center."

"What? Really? They're really alive?"

"They certainly are. Just as sure as I'm standing here. Now, I think, they're over in A village, in Ushida. Down the riverbank road from your old house, the Tanis have built a barracks, and they're living there. You ought to stop by and ask them where your home is."

"My god! They're alive!"

He laughed out loud, like a child in possession of a wonderful secret. There were no words to express the gratitude he felt.

"Well, you take care now. Your mother is going to be so happy!"

Even as she was speaking, he dashed off. He couldn't stop laughing out loud.

As instructed, he went to the home of his relatives, the Tanis, and learned that his grandfather, the family patriarch, had died instantly on the day of the atomic attack. With only women and children left, the family was living in a barracks. He heard a number of different things. His sister and nephew were definitely safe. His brother in Manchuria had been relocated to Beijing a month earlier. He somehow felt that he had been blessed. A little cousin loaded his baggage on a cart and told Michio he would lead him to the house, and he was very grateful. He and the boy set out on the riverbank road. At the remains of a house, two stone lanterns and a toilet stood in their proper places, looking very strange and isolated. A glass bottle was stretched and twisted like taffy. A bridge going over the river was bent into the shape of a V, but according to the boy, the damage was not caused by the atomic blast but, rather, by the subsequent flood.

"Do you ever go to your aunt's house to visit?"

"Nope," the boy, said shaking his head. "Auntie has bad eyes, so she can't get around, you know. My mom said I shouldn't go over there so much."

"Hey, I'll take the bags now, so you run up ahead and tell your aunt I'm coming, OK?"

The boy nodded earnestly and took off running. He stopped, ran back, and told Michio the way to follow. Then he started off again.

V

"Oh my goodness! Oh dear, Oh dear!! I couldn't believe what the lad said when he came in! You've come home? You've really come home?"

His mother came out of the house, taking off her glasses. "Come in! Come in! Take off your shoes! Oh my goodness!"

"You're alive. Mother, you're really alive!"

"You better believe I am! Oh my goodness!" As she spoke, she turned her head away and cried. The paper door opened, and he saw his dad in front of the *kotatsu*.

"Papa, he's home! He made it!"

His father, who appeared immobile, began to crawl in Michio's direction. He continued to stare at his son, speechless.

"Oh—Oh—" he cried. Without his false teeth, and his mouth hanging open, his expression was fearful. "Oo—oo—oo," he sobbed, emitting a long groan. Michio's nephew Hiroshi came flying down from upstairs.

"Welcome home, Uncle Michi! I knew you'd come back. I went to the station every day, and I stopped everybody who looked like he might be a soldier coming home. But Grandma and Grandpa said there was no way you could be alive."

His parents were weeping, and he didn't know where to look, so he just nodded to Hiroshi, saying, "It's all right. Everything's all right." His mother continued to sob profusely.

"At first we thought you were all right, but when we didn't hear from you for half a year and all our letters were returned, we thought you must have died somewhere."

"Mother was so worried, but I knew you were all right. Even in the papers we saw that a lot of people were coming home," his father said, shaking as he wiped away his tears with his sleeve. Without his teeth, his breath whistled, and he seemed very old.

"Oh, I was fine the whole time, but over the last seven months, I've been worried that you and Mom had passed away, and I had resigned myself to the fact that you were gone. I had no idea what to do . . . get off at Hiroshima? Go back home to the grave at Yamaguchi? Go to Tokyo first and then come back and look for bones? How can it be that you're alive? It's like a dream; it's just like a dream."

His dad kept crying in a childlike voice. His mom wept, holding her apron up to her face. Only Hiroshi seemed happy.

"I'll get you a robe!" he said.

He ran to the closet and pulled on the clothes basket. Then stopping, his face contorted, and he collapsed on the basket.

"What's wrong? What's the matter?" Michio said. He too felt like crying, but he couldn't shed any tears.

Saying, "OK, that's enough. . . . It's OK, pull yourself together," he put his hand on Hiroshi's shoulder. Hiroshi suddenly pushed it off and ran out onto the veranda. Taking up a broom, he pretended to sweep and began to cry again. Unable to say much, Michio pushed open the shoji and went out on the veranda. In front of the veranda was a small garden, with grain and beans, and they were growing vigorously.

"Well I guess it's a lie that you can't live seventy years. Doesn't the grain look good?"

His father seemed to have brightened somewhat.

"Do you think you could help me pull out some of the weeds? I can't get around much these days, and they're not growing very well."

He looked out at the grain growing in the plot. Father had been unable to get around easily lately. Lamenting the fact that he couldn't do yard work, he had taken to complaining a little.

Hiroshi and Mother seemed to enjoy helping out, and somehow it helped Mother relax. "Well, I'll make breakfast. The miso's boiling." "So what have you been doing?"

"Well, you know Hiroshima High School? It's in Otake now. I'm taking the tests, but I'm nervous. Having the radio nearby is really a nuisance. I can't get any studying done, listening to dumb songs like 'Come, Come, Everybody.' So Michi, how did you get home, on an LST? A navy ship?"

"The ship I took home was the *Liberty*. Mother, what have you been doing with yourself?"

She told him that his brother would be repatriated from northern China soon and that his sister's family was living in Tokyo. In the space of an hour, all his worries vanished like smoke. The Tani boy went home without anybody's noticing.

Sitting down at the breakfast table and enjoying the warmth of the miso soup, he felt enormously pleased about everything that was happening.

"Look at all this. I don't think there is as fortunate a family anywhere in Hiroshima," he said.

"It's so true, it's so true. I don't believe that just because we have lost our house and clothing in the fires that we have been reduced to nothing. Thank goodness, we somehow have food to eat and now you're back . . . there is nothing for us to say. I give thanks to the Lord Buddha every day."

"But Mother, it's easy to say that, but if you don't know anything about the new money—all our savings are frozen, and there is nothing for sale in the stores. You seem pretty unconcerned, but you're still in a tough spot."

"I know what you're saying. I have a thousand yen in new money, you know."

Michio laughed. It had been weeks since he had had miso soup, and the fresh pickles were really delicious. He drank cup after cup of the aromatic tea.

"Michi, were you a coolie after the war? Did they beat you? What kind of stuff did you eat?"

Hiroshi asked questions about the things in which only he was interested.

"Did you buy that trunk over there?"

"I bought that when I was posted overseas. I'll open it now. I thought it would be nice to bring some stuff with me."

The things he packed were Shanghai rice, canned food, soap, and a bag of candy, all wrapped individually in dirty shirts. "One bag has two thousand yen worth of candy. Seems pretty stupid, doesn't it? But if I had known everybody was all right, I would have bought a lot more. Of course, I am not trying to force anybody to eat candy."

"Wow, two thousand yen worth of candy. Can we try one?"

"Which one, which one?"

Papa stuck his hand out. Hiroshi unwrapped the gold paper and stuck it in his grandfather's mouth. The toothless jaw chewed laboriously.

"Eat them up everybody, and don't leave any. I don't want any. Let me tell you about the prices in Shanghai. It cost seventy yen to ride a train. Special passes went for fourteen thousand."

"What a strange place!"

Mama and Hiroshi laughed.

"Son, if there is anything you want to eat, let me know, all right? For dinner I have almost half a liter of red beans, so maybe we can have some red beans and rice."

"That sounds great. Anything would be great, but that sounds delicious, so sure. Let's get some oysters and trout—maybe some *shiokara*—I feel like eating until I burst."

"Well, trout is probably impossible, but they sell oysters at the black market in front of the station. After you've rested a while, maybe you can go out and buy some."

"It would be a good idea to telegraph Tokyo, too. I'll go with you," Hiroshi said.

"OK, let's go shopping. We'll buy everything in sight and then come back and have a feast!"

"Hey, now don't go and spend all your money all at once just because you've got a mind to. You'll only regret it later. This isn't the old days, you know."

Papa was about to launch into one of his famous speeches, and Michio didn't mind a bit. His mother started clearing the dishes. When she extended her arm, he noticed the pus from an ugly burn wound.

"Mother, what's that scar?"

"Oh, this one?"

On the morning of the atomic attack, his mother had been facing the window looking at a newspaper. Without warning, there was a blinding blue flash, and a wind came out of nowhere, knocking the house askew and throwing her some distance. The glasses she was wearing from her cataract operation flew off.

"Papa, Papa," she called, and from somewhere his voice replied, "Hey, I'm over here." When she looked at her kimono, she noticed that it was on fire from the shoulder to the sleeve. She quickly ripped it off and got rid of it. At the time she didn't understand why, but the atomic bomb's radiation caused the fire to break out.

"That's where the burn scar came from. For a long time it festered, and it started to smell really bad," Mama said.

Changing his sticky shirt and taking off his navy uniform jacket, Michio left the house with Hiroshi; the two took a shopping basket with them. The rain from last night had dried up, and the bright sunlight of the late March day fell on the road he had taken just a little while before. He felt as cheerful as he could possibly feel. The water in the storm drains flowed like a small river and made a gurgling sound. He started chanting a war tune.

"Invincible warships, on wings of victory, rule the waves . . ."

"Hey Michi, if you sing songs like that these days you're going to get clobbered," Hiroshi laughed. Michio laughed, too. Listening to Hiroshi talk as they walked along, Michio realized that he had lost more friends, family, and teachers than he had fingers on both hands.

"Uncle Michio, are you going to get married?"

"Well—"

"I'll tell you what. You marry a girl from Hiroshima, and you'll probably have kids with one eye and three legs."

"Oh, stop it!"

"I'm serious! People say that kids are coming out all deformed or like vegetables."

"Who knows, maybe I'll get a wife."

"My mom is really looking forward to that. She says she wants a little sister, and I'd like a young aunt, too."

"My sister said that?"

"Yeah, I think all she lives for is to see you get married to some cute girl. But if you marry an ugly one, she's going to give you hell."

"Don't be silly!"

They both laughed. At the post office in front of the station, they sent two or three telegrams. At the market they bought oysters, sea cucumber, beef, and onions and rode the train home. It was a neighborhood where you could see little but barracks and a few trees, but the trains ran frequently.

"Hey! Hey! Lady! What happened to your ticket? You better pay up before you get off. I'm living on rice gruel, you know!"

Listening to the motorman, it occurred to him that he was having a good time.

VI

Michio had been in Hiroshima a week. During that time he took Hiroshi to go low-tide shellfish digging at Ushina, and they brought back two liters of littlenecks and clams, which they gave to Mother, who was very pleased. Michio was getting over his fatigue and starting to settle down. His military lifestyle was starting to recede into the distant past, and he was thinking that he had better be getting on his way to Tokyo. When he told his mother this, she responded, a little disappointedly, "You still have plenty of time to use your repatriate's ticket, don't you?" But she didn't stop him. Hiroshi's entrance exam was coming up soon.

One day, he went to the Tani house for a combination of family business and pleasure.

"Michi, you have to stay here a little longer and help take care of the family."

"I know, but I have to get a job, too," he said noncommittally.

"At least take your mother out for an afternoon. Because of your father's physical condition, she doesn't get outside much."

The words stunned him. It occurred to him that Mother had not even walked to the old house in a long time. Her eyes were bad, and what's more, she couldn't leave Father alone for an instant. He suddenly felt very sorry for her.

"I've decided to leave the day after tomorrow," he announced.

"Is that so? I think it would be better for you to go a little later. I hear that Tokyo has a pretty bad food shortage," Mother remarked. Father and Hiroshi were unhappy to hear that Michio was leaving too, but they didn't try to stop him, either.

"Mother, if we have nice weather like this tomorrow, I'm going to take you out to look at the cherry blossoms. What do you say?"

"By all means, take her out! Your mother has been working hard for a long time. Go out, have a nice picnic, and take your time coming back," Father said from the side.

"Oh dear! Flower viewing? I can't really go by myself, but it would be wonderful to go with someone, wouldn't it?"

"Look, Hiroshi can watch Papa for half a day, can't he?"

"Who, me? Just say the word. Go out and enjoy yourself. There's nothing to worry about."

"That's right. Don't worry about me. I can take care of myself," Father added, even though there was no way he could take care of himself.

That evening, Michio went to the sandal shop on the corner and picked up four eggs. At home, he placed them carefully on the bookcase.

"Wow, that's great, Uncle Michi, taking Grandma flower viewing. I mean really great."

"What, you're jealous because you want to go, too?"

"No, that's not what I mean at all."

"Oh stop, you're embarrassing yourself!" said Papa's voice from somewhere in the house.

"What do you mean embarrassing myself? Whenever I see somebody do something decent, I just like to show a little appreciation; that's all."

"That's very nice, Hiroshi. Your compassion is very admirable," Mother said.

"See? So pretty soon you'll give me some money and let me go to Miyajima, right?"

"Sure, as long as you pass your exams."

Before long, everybody went to bed. The next morning it was cool, and the weather was good. Michio woke up and picked weeds out of the grain. He could hear his parents discussing something.

"I always tell you not to put my chamber pot on the dresser, don't I? I feel like it's going to fall off."

"I know but it's dangerous leaving it on the tatami, so I put it up here. I can't see very well, and with Michio and Hiroshi banging around—I don't know how many times they've turned it over with their carrying on."

"OK, fine, put it where you want! I just don't know why you hate consulting me about these things."

"Well, you don't have to say such hateful things to me. I'll put it down here!"

"NO! Up there is fine!"

Michio felt miserable. When he was finished weeding, he went into the kitchen to wash his hands. His mother was breaking twigs for the fire.

"Papa gets kind of bent out of shape over things, doesn't he? Look, I really don't want to make him any worse than he is."

"Aren't you cooking the rice?"

". . ."

"Mama, aren't you making the lunches?"

"Maybe we should just cancel the flower viewing today."

"I don't get it."

"Oh, I'll waste half a day, then I'll just have that much more to do when I come home, and walking is going to make my corns hurt . . ."

"Well, if that's what you want, but—it's really a shame."

Michio walked aimlessly about the garden and sat on the veranda, staring at the soybean flowers and a butterfly that was making its way across the yard.

"What are you doing?" asked Hiroshi, who had stepped out from the toilet. "Grandma's in a pretty rotten mood."

"It seems like she and Grandpa had words again."

"Yep."

"What about the cherry blossoms?"

"It's off."

"That's too bad." Hiroshi made an unhappy face.

"She'll change her mind before too long. She always does."

"You think so? I guess she hasn't changed much."

As if on cue, in a few moments there were signs of Mother in the kitchen hanging pots and boiling water. Hiroshi poked Michio. Michio, feigning ignorance, wandered into the kitchen.

"Well, maybe we should go after all," she said.

"OK, we have to make lunch fast."

"I can be done in half an hour."

The sliding door opened, and Papa called.

"Hey, hey!"

"What is it?"

"I need a little favor."

"You have to pee?"

"Yeah." While his pot was being taken away, Papa added, "Well, if you're going, you'd better go quick. It's almost noon."

"Well you say that, but if I don't get your lunches made, you're going to be all upset, right?"

Michio showed Hiroshi the eggs on the shelf.

"You didn't have to buy eggs. I think we still have some."

"That's fine. We'll take these two and go. Later on, you and Grandpa can boil these and eat them for lunch."

VII

Skylarks sang high and low in the wheat fields. Crossing over a crooked bridge, the breeze from the stream felt a little cold. The water was clear and blue. The sunlight breaking over the rippling wavelets was as beautiful as he had ever remembered it. *Hae*, between nine and twelve centimeters long, were swimming. From time to time they would turn quickly and flash their silver bellies.

"Mama, look! *Hae*!"

"Really? Where?"

"Over there, in that deep spot, where the water is still."

Mama leaned over the rail to get a close look at the water.

"I can't see them. They're big ones, are they?"

"Some are twelve centimeters long."

"Really? I wish we could catch one."

"Too bad we don't have any fishing gear. Well, let's go."

They walked along the path that had been worn into the bank. Pieces of metal and broken shards that had yet to be cleaned up were scattered all over both sides of the stream, and amid the debris, grain grew tall along the paths leading to the ruins of houses. Here and there they could see the flowers of rape-seed plants. Toward the south, surprisingly close to them, they could see burned-out buildings.

From the trunk of an ancient cherry tree grew a giant bough that had broken nearly in half. It dangled to the ground, covered with a profusion of blossoms.

"That must have been snapped by the atomic blast, huh?"

"I think you're right. Even broken like that, it still flowers so beautifully. Do you think you could break a twig off for me? I'd like to bring it home and show it to Papa."

"There's more over where we're going."

"Really? Well, even so, could you break a couple of twigs off for me?"

"I think this must be somebody's private cherry tree. It wouldn't be right to break it. There's plenty over there, I'm sure of it."

"Really?"

With his mother thus reassured, they resumed their slow, toddler-like pace. Michio, counting his steps, walked alongside his mother. In the vicinity of a prewar army engineer corps base, they saw a cherry tree that belonged to the grounds of a nursing home.

"Can you see it? It's in full bloom!"

"I can see it all right. It's really blooming beautifully."

"There's nobody here. In the old days, it used to get so crowded, though."

"Now things go at such a slow pace. People don't even want to come out flower viewing."

"Let's go down here."

Michio took his mother's hand and went down toward the grass. A little foot-path continued through a small grove of cherries planted along the undulating course of the river. Vegetables and grain were growing in various spots in the meadow. The path became narrower, and just to the right was the water, so walking became especially difficult for Mother.

"Are you all right?"

"I'm all right."

Her sandals were worn down and slick.

"Are you sure you're all right?"

"It's a little hard to walk. I'm a little scared, I guess."

"I was wrong to bring you out. Let's go back the way we came."

"Even if we head back, I'm not sure I can make it."

"I'll help you along."

With a heave, Michio picked up his mother's light frame and carried her up to the road on the riverbank. She took off her sandals and had on only her socks. After walking along the good road as far as the cherry grove, they went back down toward the riverside. The limbs overhead were nine-parts flowers covering the sky with the pale color of cherry blossoms. The trees were old ones that had been around since his childhood. Some peach trees mixed among the cherry trees also were blooming. The peaches were beautiful and looked delicious enough to eat.

"Do you want to eat here?"

"Let's. Do we have anything to sit on?"

Michio had brought along a small floor table. Beneath the cluster of cherry blossoms, there were no signs of other people. They sat down at the little table and listened to the water lapping against a log stuck in the stream. When the wind blew, the blossoms scattered a little. Mother took out an old pipe and smoked two bowls of tobacco. Michio had forgotten to bring his cigarettes, so he borrowed some of his mother's tobacco.

"Here, have some."

They spread out some newspaper and opened up the two lunch boxes. Bugs flew over and descended on the sesame oil–covered rice. The oyster tempura and boiled *konyaku* was remarkably tasty.

"I brought a chunk of your father's favorite brown sugar," Mama said, tearing the wrapper in half and putting a crystal of sugar on it.

"Here, I brought two eggs."

Mother said she didn't like raw eggs; at any rate, she insisted that she couldn't eat them, so Michio slurped up the two eggs by himself. As they sat, the breeze off the river was cold. When their meal was finished, the two stood up and began to follow the road home. All the lower branches had been broken off, and the high ones were unreachable, so they weren't able to get the branches that they had wanted to bring home. Blossoms fell down on Mother's white hair.

"Shall we go home through Nishinakacho?"

A white road went straight through the ruins. At a corner, a beggar was selling newspapers and magazines, using small stones as paperweights.

"Do you want to buy something?" he asked.

After looking at two or three magazines, Michio bought a copy of *Asahi Graph*. It was the first magazine he had purchased since being home. Opening the cover, he saw a photograph of some plum flowers in bloom. The bottom half of the picture showed that the flowers were growing at the site of what apparently were some bombed-out Tokyo ruins. The upper right section of the picture showed a white, crumbling, three-story building. Beneath the blossoms an elderly man and three women were digging in the soil. On the left margin were printed the words of a Tang-dynasty poem:

> Year by year, from age to age, the flowers remain the same
> From age to age, year by year, people come and go

"Mother, look at this."

A distant look came over Mother's eyes as she stared at length at the photo.

"The flowers are really blooming—at a burned-out house, too. And people are working in the fields."

When they left the river plain, the wind stopped, and the warm rays of the sun fell on Michio's and his mother's shoulders.

ARIYOSHI SAWAKO

Ariyoshi Sawako's (1931–1984) many writings show two concerns. The first is her deep personal affection for the Japanese artistic tradition, and the second is her strong sense of social issues, particularly regarding the role of women in society, the theme of two of her most widely admired novels: *The River Ki* (*Ki no kawa*, 1959) and *The Doctor's Wife* (*Hanaoka seishū no tsuma*, 1966). Her early story "The Village of Eguchi" (Eguchi no sato, 1958) combines a bit of both concerns.

THE VILLAGE OF EGUCHI (EGUCHI NO SATO)

Translated by Yukio Sawa and Herbert Glazer

I

For Father Gounod, Sunday no longer had the aura of holiness of the Lord's Day. After celebrating two morning Masses, one at six-thirty and one at nine-thirty, he had to attend, in succession, short meetings of the Young Men's Association, the Society of St. Mary, and the Church Committee. Most of the time he could barely eat breakfast, and occasionally he had to forgo lunch altogether. Japanese Catholics appeared to him to be particularly fervent. At church meetings they sit with their rows of flat faces, praising God, praying to Mary, and complaining how difficult life was for a Catholic in Japan. Father Gounod doubted that Japanese Catholics had any human aspects apart from their Catholicism. And when he saw them continually talking about their faith many times more fervently than he their priest, it made his stomach contract all the more until his hunger became unbearable.

On an unexpectedly cool Sunday in late summer, Father Gounod as usual had been impatiently attending the regular Sunday meetings of his church members. The meeting room in the rectory made it easy to endure the heat of the summer; it was as if the heat of the previous weeks was unreal, and as a consequence the young men and women stayed longer than usual. It seemed strange to Father Gounod that men and women of this age should hold separate meetings and not make much effort to associate with one another in some organization of their own, and he could not understand their wasting their valuable

Sundays attending meetings in a dreary rectory. He sometimes wondered whether these young people had sweethearts, but on seeing their blank expressions and hearing their colorless chatter, he realized that even if they did fall in love and were goaded on by their friends, it was hardly likely that they would have the courage to run off and get married.

As he expected, the meeting of the Church Committee dragged on longer than that of the young people. Mr. Nozoe, a senior member of the church, and Mrs. Sakurai were both criticizing their former priest, and they admonished Father Gounod not to repeat his mistakes.

"Father, it seems to me that your sermon was somewhat shorter," said Mrs. Sakurai.

"Yes, today's sermon ended much earlier than I had expected," said Mr. Nozoe. "It lasted only seven and one-half minutes," he added.

Amazed, Father Gounod stared at both of them. He recalled from his younger days that the longer were the sermons of the priest at Mass, the more boring and annoying they were to him. When he was a student in theology school, he kept thinking that after he became ordained, he would wind up his sermons rapidly and allow his congregation to leave as early as possible. And these people were indicating that the Japanese believers did not welcome this.

After the committee members left, Father Gounod rushed to the kitchen for the lunch that old Matsutani had prepared for him. Glancing at his watch, he noticed that it was after one o'clock. He had picked up his fork and was about to lift some rice from the bowl when he heard someone at the gate loudly calling his name.

"Father! Father! My aunt is in critical condition. Please prepare to administer the final sacrament. Please come immediately." The speech was stiff and formal.

Since time was of the essence, Father Gounod prepared to leave immediately and jumped into the car waiting for him. He prayed silently that the flies in the kitchen would not alight on the white rice he had left behind uneaten.

Thinking that the patient whom he was attending was about to pass away momentarily, Father Gounod administered the final sacrament in about a minute. People around him were quite shocked and asked how it was possible for him to have finished so soon. After giving some thought to the way in which they expressed themselves in Japanese, he concluded that they were implying that his rapid performance did not adequately reflect the importance of the sacrament.

Unavoidably the priest felt obliged to recite part of the breviary for that day before he could leave the hospital twenty minutes later. The dying believer had a happy expression on her face as she made the sign of the cross on her chest, but the priest felt that she would somehow recover from her illness and leave the hospital in a few days.

En route to the rectory from the hospital, he observed that on every street in

Tokyo there seemed to be either road-repairing or subway construction going on. On his return he found neglected in a corner of the kitchen the rice and miso soup as he had left them. On hearing Father Gounod noisily charge back into the room, the surprised flies flew away as if they did not want him to see that they had been licking his rice.

But old Matsutani, wiping the kitchen cupboard with a damp rag, heartlessly told him that waiting for him in the sanctuary was a believer who had come to have an infant baptized, and so Father Gounod could not even raise his fork. Since an infant had no power of resistance to disease, there was no knowing when and how it might suddenly die. Therefore this kind of baptism should be administered as rapidly as the final sacrament, if asked.

He was reciting "In the name of the Father, the Son, and the Holy Ghost, I baptize thee" and had just made the sign of the cross with holy water over the infant's face when he suddenly felt dizzy. He rushed out of the sanctuary thanking God that he had not been born a cannibal.

It was after three when he finally got around to eating his cold rice and miso soup. He again thanked God this time that he was too hungry to feel unhappy about having to eat strange Japanese food, and wiping his mouth with his handkerchief he went to his room to relax. However, no matter how hard he wiped, he still could not get rid of the taste of the miso soup and the yellow radish pickles he had eaten for the first time that day. Removing a bottle of White Horse Scotch that he had hidden behind the bookshelf, he drank a slug directly from the bottle. How fragrant was the scent of the whisky, he thought. Since Mrs. Sakurai had disapprovingly told him of some of the previous priests drinking saké, Father Gounod made it a rule to keep everything alcoholic safely hidden from the eyes of his parishioners.

Having eaten a starchy meal and not knowing what to do with his weariness, he sank into the swivel chair in front of his desk and began to amuse himself by kicking the floor and propelling himself from side to side, maintaining his balance by sticking out his stomach. All that remained for him to do that day was to check the amount in the collection box which had been passed around at Mass by a young man who acted as an attendant. He had already recited one-third of the breviary in the hospital, so he lazily stretched his arms, expecting to spend the rest of the day comfortably. He began to think of visiting the Foreign Missionary Club that night, where he had not been for some time, and of eating a rich dish. He enjoyed thinking about eating things which he couldn't come by easily. Arousing himself from his reverie, he picked up the notebook on which "Holy Day Contributions" was written and tried to finish off the work that remained for him to do. The notebook also contained the financial records of the Young Men's Association.

The amount collected at the first Mass at six-thirty was 483 yen. The priest was pleased, as this exceeded the previous week's collection of 475 yen. Naturally, some of the faithful actually preferred the shorter sermon. However, when he came to the section in which the amount collected at the nine o'clock Mass was indicated, he couldn't help rubbing his eyes in disbelief—1,490 yen! He looked again, but it was certainly 1,490 yen. The total amount collected that day showed 1,973 yen, so the 1,490-yen figure was not an error.

Even though Father Gounod's church was in Tokyo, it was located in what was called a suburban slum area, and as a result his congregation consisted mostly of workshop laborers, their wives and children, and no more than about ten families who had saved a little money in running small home factories. Consequently the average individual contribution at Sunday Mass was 10 yen, although there were some who unconcernedly gave nothing and some, feeling they had committed a sinful act, occasionally contributed a 100-yen note. Under such circumstances the total collected at both Masses rarely exceeded 1,000 yen.

Father Gounod folded his arms. Since he had preached exactly the same sermon at both Masses, it was hardly likely that only those who particularly attended the second Mass were so impressed as to loosen their purse-strings. His parishioners were not the type to shell out large bills just because they heard a seven and one-half minute sermon. Then he thought perhaps the 1,000-yen note was thrown in by someone who had committed a serious crime and, being reluctant to confess, threw in the 1,000-yen note. But he could not by any stretch of the imagination picture any of those who regularly attended Mass committing a serious crime, even by accident. It would have been difficult for him to recognize one unfamiliar face among the hundred attendees. Was there a nonbeliever who came to church for the first time that day—? As he thought about this possibility, one thing did occur to him.

It was after the nine o'clock Mass, just before ten, while he was on his way back to the rectory from the sanctuary with his assistant. His attention was attracted to a group of children who had run out of the church and were staring curiously in the direction of the gate, where he inadvertently noticed a woman getting into a large elegant car. Father Gounod halted unconsciously. He could only see her back, and as he had been away from secular life for a long time, he was struck by the beauty of the Japanese style clothes she was wearing. The India ink chrysanthemum design on her wisteria-blue short-coat stood out clearly, especially on the lower half of the coat, the shoulder, and the left sleeve; and her gold embroidered sash shone with a subdued brilliance. Although he understood little of color schemes, he could not help admiring the beautiful harmony of the colors and the design. She was already seated in the car when he saw her suddenly straighten up for fear of getting her sash out of shape. Her profile was even more beautiful than her kimono. She raised a filmy linen handkerchief to her nose and said something to the driver while at the same instant, with her other hand, she lightly touched the back of her hair. All of her movements had an air of grace about them which the women he had seen in church never exhibited. Gounod stood staring at her until the car drove away.

"Father!"

His trance was broken by Mrs. Sakurai. She had just returned from home where she had gone for breakfast after the six-thirty Mass.

As he pictured the sight of that beautiful woman folding a 1,000-yen note into a small rectangular shape and delicately placing it in the collection box, he became convinced that she must have been the person responsible for the large donation. He did not try to find out who she was. Even if he had, he thought that it would be difficult for a foreigner like himself to understand Japanese ways, and besides, he considered it unlikely that she would visit his church again. Nevertheless, Father Gounod felt for the first time a deep glow of satisfaction on the holy day. How pleasing it was to see an attractive woman and how beautiful was the Japanese kimono.

"God bless her 1,000-yen note and her future," he prayed silently. He had already made up his mind not to go to the Foreign Missionary Association but just to pay his respects over the telephone. His state of mind at that moment was such that he considered he would be overindulging himself to have a fine meal the same Sunday on which he saw a beautiful woman.

II

On the following Friday night, Mr. Nozoe, the Church Committee member, pressed the doorbell of the rectory. He apologized for having come unexpectedly when Father Gounod let him in. After showing him to the drawing room, the priest asked him the reason for his visit. Mr. Nozoe replied repeatedly that he hoped that the sermon on the coming Sunday would be amply long. Father Gounod felt uncomfortable as he assured Mr. Nozoe on his departure that his sermon would be plenty long. Father Gounod was just now beginning to understand why this church, which in theory could be administered equally well by a Japanese priest, had been placed under the Foreign Missionary Association. The believers were too zealous. Nothing their priests did satisfied them, and so they made a practice of appealing directly to the bishop, who was head of the district, requesting replacements. After receiving numerous complaints, the bishop had come to feel that the situation was intolerable and, as a result, had assigned to the head of the Foreign Missionary Association the responsibility for administering that church.

Father Gounod tried very hard to think of some way in which he could implant the concept of tolerance in the minds of these people. How easy it was to admonish the idle to work hard, but he found it more difficult to those who worked hard to relax and engage in some form of recreation. It annoyed him that he, a priest whose duty it was to lead the faithful, was being embarrassed by their excessive zeal.

Nevertheless, since it was unethical for a priest to go back on his word, whatever the reason, he felt obliged to spend all of Saturday evening drafting his sermon for the next morning. He mused that it was regrettable there existed no biblical passage praising the virtue of the idle, so he decided to avoid as much as possible giving his congregation the impression that he was reading to them directly from the Bible, and thus he proceeded to write a sermon which did not quote scripture directly but which used homely examples to illustrate biblical injunctions. He thought of first making a draft in his native language, then translating it into Japanese, and finally rehearsing it; in addition to which he considered reading it aloud to estimate how long it would run when he delivered it in church the next morning, but he gave up the whole idea as being rather silly.

The next morning, as he mounted the pulpit, he carefully looked around the sanctuary. Satisfied that Mr. Nozoe and Mrs. Sakurai were present, he began to speak in fluent Japanese, intending to tire them with his overly long sermon. Although he had been in Japan but a year and a half, he had been studying Japanese since his theology-school days, which, coupled with the fact that he was gifted with an exceptional aptitude for languages, resulted in his speaking with an air of complete confidence. After he had spoken for fifteen minutes, he noticed that Mr. Nozoe's eyes were closed, and he seemed to be napping. So Father Gounod raised his voice unnecessarily and shouted a passage from the Bible. As he had anticipated, Mr. Nozoe, surprised by this unexpected outburst, suddenly stirred and adjusted his thick spectacles for the aged.

Mrs. Sakurai was listening attentively and nodding her head in approval. When Father Gounod saw her simple honest face exuding faith, he felt strangely as if he were committing a crime. That flat Japanese face, he discovered, can produce a sense of uneasiness in others.

Father Gounod sighed and continued his preaching on the tolerant spirit of Jesus Christ. Because his sermon was in a language not his own, the same simple words were repeated, and thus it was necessary for him to use stress in order to change expression. This sermon, which began quite brilliantly only to drag on to a dull finish, may have made his parishioners, who had liked or had been accustomed to the simple lucid style of previous sermons, feel rather uncomfortable.

Extremely tired after finishing his sermon, which lasted about thirty minutes, he went and knelt at the altar. How good it was, he thought, to have spoken for a long time in a loud voice. The essence of the sermon was firmly embedded in his heart, and he felt that his preaching had reflected this. He thanked God for having given him this opportunity through Mr. Nozoe. He decided that in future sermons, he would make the cultivation of a spirit of tolerance toward others his principal theme.

When he came to the same sermon at the second Mass, he had lost his feeling of self-consciousness, and his state of mind was as serene as if he were reciting the Lord's Prayer. This time it did not occur to him to observe the reaction of his congregation, and as the words flowed from his mouth, he was neither elated nor depressed. In his preaching he repeatedly emphasized, in a calm manner, that the spirit of love was the spirit of tolerance and that this was one of the most fundamental principles of Catholicism.

As he reached the end of his sermon, Father Gounod noticed sitting in a remote seat in a back row of the church, that same woman in beautiful Japanese dress who had been present the previous week and who had left in a luxury car. Although Father Gounod recognized her, this time he did not lose his composure, and he calmly continued to watch her while finishing his sermon. He had been hoping she would come again, and now he felt relieved.

It was twenty minutes past ten when Father Gounod left the sanctuary to return to the rectory to change his clothes. As usual, there were the Young Men's Association, the Society of St. Mary, and the Church Committee meetings to attend. Fearing that the speeches in these meetings would be as long as his sermon, he hurriedly changed into his black suit and went out to fulfill his obligation of smiling farewell to each of his parishioners as he left for home.

He was not without hope that he would see her, and then when he glanced toward the gate and saw her standing there, watching the crowd coming out of the church, and shyly looking up at the church bulletin board, he advanced directly toward her.

His first duty was to worship God; his second duty was to preach to the faithful; and his third duty was to be a missionary of the Lord. But should there be someone who is religious-minded, he should open his door and welcome him. Should there be someone who hesitates at the gate, he should advance and invite him to enter.

She was surprised when she suddenly saw the tall Father Gounod standing in front of her. However, she seemed friendly by nature and she smiled uncertainly. Her smile was that of someone confused: shy but affable and charming.

"You were here last week, too, weren't you?" Father Gounod said in ungrammatical Japanese, as he broadly returned her smile.

"Uh-hun," she nodded and then corrected herself.

"Yes."

Father Gounod also nodded as he repeated the word "yes" in Japanese, and they understood each other. He pointed to the schedule of catechism lessons on the church bulletin board.

"Won't you please try to come at this hour?"

The woman nodded obediently, but when she noticed the lessons were given in the evening, she indicated that it was difficult for her to go out at that time.

"Perhaps you would prefer some time in the morning?"

"Mm . . ."

Seeing that she was somewhat hesitant, Father Gounod did not pursue the matter. He didn't believe in being persistent or attempting to use persuasion in such situations, so he changed the subject.

"Do you live near here?"

He was hoping indirectly to obtain some indication of the reason for her un-expected appearance in church the previous week.

Without disclosing her present address, she simply stated that she did not live in the area but that her late mother used to live in that neighborhood. It had been seven days before, when she was returning home after attending thirty-fifth-day memorial services for her mother,[1] that she'd heard the hymn being sung which had attracted her to the church gate. Mixed with her desire to pray for the soul of her dead mother was a slight feeling of curiosity; then looking up at Father Gounod, she said shyly, "It was a very unusual feeling."

"Was it really? I am pleased to hear it," he gently reassured her. Father Gounod grasped that the Lord had been revealed to this woman.

"Father! We are all waiting!"

One of the young men from the Young Men's Association was calling to him, and thus, with regret, he had to bid the woman farewell.

"Please feel free to return at any time," he said politely.

The woman bowed. "Thank you so much." Her face was wreathed in smiles.

While he was attending the meeting of the Young Men's Association, he thought of her and recalled the old saw about how the ideal life for a Western man consisted in having a Japanese wife and eating Chinese food. He had been in Japan only a short time, but now for the first time he felt that he truly under-stood the meaning of those words.

The man of God was seen in two lights by the Japanese people. There were either the stares of the curious directed at the man dressed in a priest's garb and clerical collar or the stern looks of the believers. Indeed, they were extremely stern. To them, the priest was sanctified by his holy calling and was not to be al-lowed to draw a human breath, even during a respite from his labors.

During that day's meeting of the Young Men's Association, Father Gounod was asked to provide a motto for the recently organized labor union at the steel workshop where most of them were working. They didn't go into detail but sim-ply indicated that they felt that the satisfaction derived from a hard day's work was God-given, and thus they wished to follow as their guiding principle a moral precept which went back to the Middle Ages, namely, that every man should obey his employer as long as he provides him with a day of worship for the Lord.

"The leaders of the Central Labor Union are all Communists," they interjected.

This revelation forced Father Gounod to explain to them that communism and Catholicism were fundamentally opposed doctrines. The young men lis-tened with some fascination, their faces all showing exactly the same reaction.

---

1. Buddhist memorial services for the dead are held on the thirty-fifth day (as well as on a number of other fixed days) after a death.

III

Father Gounod was reflecting on the fact that recently Sunday's events had come to be foretold by the events of the preceding Friday. What happened was that he was visited on Friday evening by three men representing the laborers of the workshop in which some of the young men of the church were employed. One of them was a radical, and the moment he saw Father Gounod, he challenged him.

"Does Catholicism support the capitalists? Does it wish to hasten the destruction of Labor?"

The theorist member of the three intervened and politely explained to Father Gounod the reason for their visit. There was a depressed atmosphere in their workshop because management felt that the current recession threatened the continued survival of the small-scale company, and in an attempt to tide the company over the difficult period, it had decided to lay off a number of workers and to delay the payment of salaries. Faced with this crisis, the union leaders wanted to present a united front in opposition to the moves taken by management, but their plan was undermined by a number of workers who would not go along with the majority, and some of these dissidents secretly communicated with management.

"They are all members of the Catholic Church," the radical said angrily.

Father Gounod looked puzzled. "That's strange. How come these Catholics don't join with the rest of you?"

"That's what we came here to find out," replied the radical impatiently.

The activist member of the delegation, who had been silent up to that time, glared at the priest. "I hear that the Church forbids its subjects to engage in union activities."

"What makes you think that?" Father Gounod was still puzzled.

The radical and activist jumped to their feet, their faces red with anger, but the theorist who was sitting between them calmly began to explain in detail as he had done before. "I know it's difficult for a foreigner like yourself to understand."

Starting out with a description of the living conditions of Tokyo laborers, he showed the priest statistics which illustrated how the recession would affect their standard of living. Thus, he explained, he was at a loss to understand why the Catholics would not join their fellow-workers in an effort to save this situation.

Then the radical spoke up again. "What can Christ do when times are difficult? There is no excuse for Christ obstructing the collective action of the fraternity of men." All the while the activist continued to glare at the priest maliciously.

"Would you be willing to return on Sunday, the day after tomorrow?" Father Gounod wanted them to attend the nine o'clock Mass. "Perhaps the Catholic young men from your workshop will show up."

They listened to this man of few words with his deep-set sad blue eyes and then left, each with a different personal reaction to the priest.

When he came back to his room and was finally alone, Father Gounod stood before his large desk, closed his eyes, and pressed his hands to his forehead. He could picture the exceptionally pale rigid faces of the members of the church's Young Men's Association. At that moment he thought if he were a Japanese non-believer, he would be tempted to press a red-hot iron to their bellies.

A few minutes later, Father Gounod found himself kneeling in the darkness of the sanctuary. The movement of his lips indicated he was chanting the breviary. The strong vitality of his features was reflected by the red oil-lamp which burned continuously on the altar.

All that night the electric light shone in the priest's room. Old Matsutani, who had gotten up late at night to go to the lavatory, noticed it and, thinking that the priest had forgotten to turn it off, opened the door only to stop short when he found Father Gounod earnestly writing something in his notebook. Quietly making his way back to his room, old Matsutani was convinced that the priest was engaged in some effort to combat the Communists who had visited the rectory earlier that evening, and as he prayed for God's blessing on Father Gounod, he felt a keen sense of pleasure in this unspoken secret communication between the old sheep and his shepherd.

Sunday was a clear day. During the course of the Mass Father Gounod mounted the pulpit and began to preach. "How nice a day it is today. There is a blue sky which God has given to all of us, the children, the young, and the old. And so our Lord shows us that he always wishes to treat us equally."

His voice was resonant as he spoke in fluent Japanese indicating that he probably had rehearsed his sermon a number of times. At first the audience was somewhat surprised and then attracted by the vigor of his delivery.

"Recently each Sunday I have preached on the spirit of tolerance, but it must be understood that this is something that should exist among men in their relation with one another; it does not necessarily follow that our Lord exhibits this same spirit of tolerance toward man. He sometimes severely condemns man for sins committed in human affairs. And when does the Lord condemn man? It is when man has lost the spirit of love."

The congregation was at a loss to understand why Father Gounod's tone was so severe. They listened somewhat blankly in amazement.

Again it was a long sermon, lasting thirty minutes. This time, far from napping, Mr. Nozoe was blinking nervously and Mrs. Sakurai, with her eyes closed, looked as if she had fainted from a deep emotional experience.

"Today the Young Men's Association and the Society of St. Mary will meet jointly." Father Gounod had already spoken when something occurred to him as the result of his having seen his three visitors of the previous Friday sitting side by side in one of the center pews.

When he came into the courtyard after having changed into his usual black suit, the three men were confronting some of the young men of the church. It was difficult for Father Gounod to make out what they were saying, as he was unable to understand the rapid speech used between native Japanese.

"You fool!"

"It serves you right!"

As he caught some of what the radical was saying, the activist suddenly punched one of the young men of the church. The young man who had been knocked down looked up palely and began to talk back. A crowd consisting of worshipers who had just come out of the church and some people who had been passing by in front of the church began to gather at a distance.

Father Gounod left the crowd and approached the beautiful woman who had once again made her appearance that day.

"Good morning," he said smilingly.

She acknowledged his greeting with a slightly embarrassed smile and pointed to the incident.

"What's happening?"

"Some wild fellow flailing away."

"Oh, my! Is he a member of the church?"

The priest replied sadly. "The man who was punched is a church member." He then turned the subject back to her.

"For your benefit, I am thinking of scheduling the catechism lesson for Sunday morning beginning about this time."

"Oh! That's just what I was thinking of asking you if you would do."

Leading the woman back to the church, Father Gounod forced his way through the crowd into the center of the activity. He shouted to make himself heard.

"The joint meeting of the Young Men's Association and the Society of St. Mary will begin shortly. Let's assemble."

He dispersed the crowd, then went up to his three visitors of the previous Friday, and said politely, "I am glad to see you here."

"Oh, I want to beg your pardon," the theorist replied apologetically.

Father Gounod bowed to him once again. "Won't you consider coming and talking to the young people of the church? I, too, have something about which I want to talk with you."

Father Gounod then turned toward the two comrades of the theorist and, with a calm expression on his face, indicated resolutely that he wanted them to leave.

The meeting that day was unusually high-spirited due to the presence of many young people who rarely attended meetings of the Young Men's Association or the Society of St. Mary. Their interest might have been aroused by the punching incident in the churchyard, but Father Gounod surmised that the reason for their coming to the meeting was more basic. He thought that it was the opportunity for the young men and young women to get together. The priest was pleased to see so many new healthy young faces in addition to the usual group of pallid men who were always embracing their prayer-books.

He introduced the theorist to them. "As some of you saw a short time ago, just because he was a Catholic, one of your young men was assaulted by a nonbeliever. I believe that this young man is going to talk to you about that incident." It was hardly likely that there would be any applause.

The theorist scratched his head, stood up, and began to speak. "First of all, I want to explain why it happened."

In contrast to Protestant denominations, wherein emphasis is placed on the sermon, it is the Mass which is of primary importance in the Catholic Church, and thus Catholics have the advantage of being able to listen even to dull sermons without getting bored. It was with this attitude that the young people listened to the speech of the theorist. There were no jeers, interruptions, or applause as the speaker finished telling his story with a sad expression on his face. Finally a young man in the audience spoke up.

"He deserved to be punched."

It went without saying that he was not regular member of the Young Men's Association.

"It's ridiculous for a person not to join the labor union just because he is a Catholic. As a Catholic myself, I consider that attitude too stupid to get angry about. It was not a true believer who was punched. The fool, who deserved to be punched, just happened to be a Catholic."

The theorist brightened up. "Yes, I see. I understand."

Although most of those present tended to ignore the foolish young man who had been punched, one of the congregation, who still could not understand, spoke up faintly in a squeaky voice, "But Father said . . ."

Without taking time to get up from his chair, Father Gounod immediately interrupted. "Your priest's responsibility is to preach to you concerning the relationship between God and man, and that is all! The problems which arise in the relationship between man and man, as a matter of course, must be solved by man himself. You must understand that your priest rejects materialism only in the relationship between God and man. The church never stands in the way of men working together in a spirit of love. Never! Because God expects man to live!"

Having combined the meetings of the Young Men's Association and the Society of St. Mary, Father Gounod then thought secretly that he would be able to have his breakfast during the free hour, but inevitably the Lord seemed to compel him to go hungry on Sundays. After leaving the meeting-room, he remembered that he had left that beautiful woman in the drawing room by the entrance, and he resigned himself to his fate.

"How is it going?"

When he called out to her, she stood up and showed him that she had been reading *The Lives of the Saints*. She looked like a grade school child showing her homework to her teacher.

"I have read this far," she indicated. Before he hurriedly left her there to go to the meeting, he had stacked on the table the Bible, *The Bible Story*, Cate-

chism, and *The Lives of the Saints* and had said, "Please read anything you find interesting."

Prior to his beginning her first catechism lesson, Father Gounod had to ask her name, as a minimum of information about her.

"I am Sakai Satoko," she replied.

"Well, Miss Sakai."

"Yes?"

"Please read the first page."

"Yes, sir."

"For what purpose was man born into this world?"

"The reason why man was born into this world was to know our Lord, love Him, serve Him, and eventually to obtain happiness in heaven."

The tall foreigner and the lovely petite Japanese woman proceeded to read repetitively in the question-and-answer format of the catechism.

As they were reading, Father Gounod asked, "Do you understand?"

Sakai Satoko answered timidly, "Yes," but the priest said, "No, there is more to understanding than just these words."

Somewhat surprised, she raised her head.

"It is the heart, which we also call the soul, that is most important. Words exist to convey the concept of the soul."

"Yes, without expecting to, I suddenly felt that way when I came to church for the first time."

Just before departing, she left something wrapped in paper with Father Gounod. Hurrying back to the meeting-room for the Church Committee meeting, he opened it unintentionally and out fell a neatly folded 1,000-yen note. What made her leave it? In any event she was the first nonbeliever ever to pay tuition for a catechism lesson. Father Gounod wondered who she could possibly be.

That day Father Gounod made a rather radical proclamation in the meeting of the virtuous looking adults of his Church Committee. "Henceforth I intend that the Church Committee shall meet once a month."

The reaction was immediate. Everyone seemed equally displeased. Mr. Nozoe, acting as the committee representative, asked Father Gounod for his reason.

Father Gounod kept folding and unfolding Sakai's 1,000-yen note. "The congregation between God and man takes place at least once a week. This the Church decided. I believe that it is sufficient for the gathering of men alone to meet once a month." Having made this pronouncement, he obstinately remained silent.

IV

On the desk of Bishop Ayabe, Father Gounod's superior, there lay a pile of written complaints from worshipers in Father Gounod's congregation. Members of the Church Committee came to see the bishop to obtain his advice. However, he perfunctorily told them that he had placed the responsibility for their church in the hands of the Foreign Missionary Association, and consequently, since it was up to the head of the Foreign Missionary Association, Bishop Rogendorf, to hear their complaints and deal with them, he only promised to convey their sentiments to Bishop Rogendorf.

When he was asked over the telephone by the Foreign Missionary Association about the complaints it had received indicating he had assembled a number of his congregation and allowed a Communist to make a speech before them, Father Gounod replied, "That Communist recently came to Mass." Although he really could not tell whether or not the labor union theorist and the others were Communists, he thought he might just as well go along with the label which his temporizing believers had seen fit to apply to them. With only this explanation the Association was satisfied that it understood Father Gounod's intentions.

Lamenting the fact that the relationship between the Foreign Missionary Association and the ordinary Catholic was as loose as has been indicated, the members of the Church Committee decided to counsel Father Gounod once again. Needless to say, Mr. Nozoe and Mrs. Sakurai took the lead. However, Father Gounod replied harshly that the congregation must obey its priest, a successor of Peter.

"But Father, our former priest never combined the Young Men's Association with the Society of St. Mary," said Mrs. Sakurai.

"That may have been so, but I am going to combine them."

"In other churches, these two groups operate independently," she insisted.

"Is that so! Well in this church they will operate together."

No matter how long the Church Committee argued, it was to no avail. All their arguments were dismissed in this offhand way.

One day in the Church Committee meeting, Mrs. Sakurai challenged Father Gounod in a shrill voice. "Father, do you intend to christen a geisha?"

"A geisha?" Father Gounod vacantly pondered her statement.

"Yes, a geisha! The geisha from Yanagibashi attends catechism lessons, doesn't she?"

Thus it was that about six months after she had first appeared in the church, the identity of Sakai Satoko was finally disclosed. Father Gounod was struck with wonder at the thought of Sakai Satoko being a geisha. From what Mrs. Sakurai told him, it seemed that Satoko came from a poor family of that town and, being rather good-looking, had been sold to a geisha house. She had begun her training in the lower ranks and was now ranked among the first class.

"Oh, did you say Yanagibashi?" Mr. Nozoe pressed forward. When he heard her name, he said admiringly, "So she's *the* Kofumi." Judging from Mr. Nozoe's admiration, she was probably a well-known geisha.

Mrs. Sakurai went on to explain that her middle daughter and grandchild had been visiting her, and when they went to Sunday Mass together for the first time in a long time, her daughter happened to meet Sakai Satoko, who had been a primary school classmate of hers.

"Instantly I told her to be silent. If a thing like this were to get around, it would be a disgrace to our church."

"Why is that?" asked Father Gounod.

Mrs. Sakurai puffed out her chest. "But Father, don't you understand? She's a geisha!"

"What's so disgraceful about being a geisha?" he asked.

Mrs. Sakurai blushed. The priest watched blotches of color appear on her dried-out cheeks.

Some other members of the Church Committee stepped forward in place of Mrs. Sakurai to explain the sort of life led by a geisha, but as Father Gounod listened with an extremely serious expression on his face, a slight feeling of vague apprehension began to steal over them.

"In short, her way of life includes the act of prostitution. Otherwise it would hardly be possible for her to be so gaily dressed and to live in such a showy way. Furthermore, any geisha who is ranked as she is, among the first class, must of necessity have a wealthy patron to enable her to retain her fame. The reason why the antiprostitution law was not applied to the geisha world was that the geisha had many customers among politicians."

"Father, the life she is leading is contrary to the Sixth and Ninth Commandments. 'Thou shalt not commit adultery' and 'Thou shalt not covet thy neighbor's spouse,' " Mrs. Sakurai continued.

They drew closer to him and asked whether he could possibly christen a geisha who had broken these two Commandments.

"Didn't she tell you herself that she was a geisha?"

"No, she didn't, because I didn't ask."

"Does she want to be christened?" asked Mr. Nozoe.

"Yes, she has recently indicated that she wishes to be christened."

Mrs. Sakurai spoke up in her shrill voice. "Well, Father, how are you going to deal with the matter?"

Now that Father Gounod knew that Sakai Satoko was a geisha, it seemed obvious when he remembered her grace, sensitivity, and the facial expression which he had rarely seen in the Japanese. In spite of the fact that he knew she was a prostitute, he still was not disappointed in her. After all, he had already gone through the catechism lessons with her and had explained in detail both the Sixth and Ninth Commandments. Even after she knew what Catholicism prohibited, she had still exhibited a desire to be christened and so he thought that she must have come to some decision.

"Well, Father, has she said that she intends to give up being a geisha?"

"I don't know what her intentions are. Since she didn't say she was a geisha, obviously she couldn't have told me she intends to give it up."

"You will, of course, find out whether or not she intends to give it up."

"Why?" asked Father Gounod critically. "It is up to me to decide whom I will permit to be baptized."

After a lengthy silence, Mr. Nozoe spoke up. "Well, I don't think she is about to quit."

When asked why, he replied that each time he saw her on Sunday, she was extremely well-dressed. A geisha who has reached the stage where she is thinking of retiring usually shows some sign of fading, but in her case there was no such sign. Furthermore, seeing as how she was the Kofumi of Yanagibashi, renowned for her beauty and skill in the dance, it was extremely likely that she had as her patron some prominent figure.

Although she was listening intently, Mrs. Sakurai felt obliged to interject some critical remarks. "You're very familiar with that sort of thing, aren't you?"

Mr. Nozoe became flustered and began to make excuses, "Oh, no! It's just that I happened to hear these things when I was invited out socially to a restaurant."

"In any event," Mrs. Sakurai looked up at Father Gounod as she prepared to leave, "there are, needless to say, many aspects of life in Japan today which are not in accordance with the teachings of Catholicism. It is particularly true in the case of a foreigner that there are many things which he can hardly be expected to understand. I hope that you will not find yourself in any difficulty."

That night Father Gounod prayed for a long time in the deserted sanctuary. He was not at all disturbed by the fact that Sakai Satoko was a geisha. He was praying to God for guidance in making Mrs. Sakurai into a true Catholic.

It was unlikely that she would understand, even if he told her the story of Jesus, who, on pointing to a prostitute, said, "Whosoever be without sin, let him strike her." For the priest, Mrs. Sakurai, who was convinced she was well versed in Catholicism, was a more difficult sheep to lead than someone who scarcely knew anything about Catholicism.

V

One day in late autumn, six months later, Father Gounod had been invited to dinner by the head of the district, Bishop Rogendorf. It was Friday evening, and the fried flatfish lying in his plate reminded him of how long he had been away from sirloin steak. How sick he was of obeying the injunction against eating meat on Friday in a country where the people ate fish and vegetables almost every day.

After they had talked about various subjects, the bishop casually changed the topic of conversation to church matters.

"By the way, I hear that there is a geisha in your church," he said with a slight smile on his face.

"Yes, there is, among those who seek the truth."

Now, thought Father Gounod, he was about to be interrogated as a result of those written complaints, and the anguish he felt as he looked up at the bishop was harder to bear than that which he felt when he saw the flatfish in his plate. But the next question was friendly and understanding. "Is she beautiful?"

His spirits raised, Father Gounod replied, "Yes, she is, very beautiful."

Mrs. Sakurai, despite her saying that she didn't want knowledge of this situation to become widespread, had, on her own the following week, stirred up the women of the church who had then gone to see Father Gounod, but the priest would not, in any event, have been so hasty as to christen someone who had been studying the catechism for only six months.

It was his practice to wait quietly for Sakai Satoko, open the Bible when she arrived, and then talk with her about the significance of the Mass or the lives of the saints, and only once did he pry into her personal life.

"Are you married?"

"Why do you want to be christened?"

He considered her answer to this question remarkable.

"I feel a bond between myself and the church. It is as if my mother were calling to me. I have had this feeling ever since I first came to church by accident that day I was returning from thirty-fifth-day memorial services for my mother. I believe in everything you say, Father, and I believe that everything written in your books is true."

"*Go-en ga aru*—there is a bond." The bishop and priest softly repeated these words to themselves in Japanese. Was there any difference in feeling between these words and the words "divine revelation" in the catechism?

"Her background includes neither Buddhism nor atheism. Of all the believers and nonbelievers in my church I consider her to have the purest most honest soul. And . . ."

"And what?" the bishop urged.

Father Gounod regretted that he was unable to re-evoke the mood she inspired. "I don't know what the situation might have been at some other church, but to have had the opportunity to welcome her to my present church every week has been a blessing of the Lord."

Father Gounod confessed to the bishop that Sakai Satoko had been a consolation to him in his efforts to enrich the narrow faith of his congregation.

"A written report of the investigation into her background has been placed in my hands," the bishop said.

Father Gounod assumed that the bishop did not refer to its contents because it probably described the fact that she had a patron and her life as a geisha. He could do nothing but reply sadly, "I must admit that it was prepared and sent to you by a member of my congregation." This admission made the sweet dessert he was eating taste bitter to his tongue. He recalled the scene in the churchyard when one of the young men of his congregation had been knocked down by a nonbeliever. How impossible it was even to imagine the same scene with Sakai Satoko punching Mrs. Sakurai.

After Father Gounod had been observing Satoko for a year, he realized that she neither questioned nor was ashamed of her present life. She was the geisha

Kofumi to the very bone. Such an unusual concept of morality had been drummed into her head since childhood that she could not possibly imagine that having a patron went against the Sixth and Ninth Commandments.

"To save her we must eliminate the geisha quarters. But as long as we are not in a position to make a clean sweep of the politicians who allow the geisha to exist, how can we refuse a geisha who wants to be christened?"

Bishop Rogendorf stood up and patted Father Gounod on the back. "We'll have make you run for office under the Japanese Socialist banner."

"How about my running as a candidate of the Communist Party?"

"If they would have you, it would be much more effective."

The two priests looked solemn as they jokingly made these remarks.

After being jostled about in a tram and bus for about an hour, Father Gounod finally arrived at the church, where old Matsutani informed him that Mr. Nozoe had collapsed as the result of high blood pressure and his condition was very serious.

"I telephoned the Foreign Missionary Association but was told that you had just left. . . ."

Saying nothing, Father Gounod prepared sacramental oil and rushed from the rectory. Fortunately a small dusty taxi just happened to be passing by the gate.

Rushing in, he saw a Japanese priest just leaving Mr. Nozoe's room after having administered the final sacrament of extreme unction. Since it happened so suddenly, a priest from the nearest church had been called when it was learned that Father Gounod was away. The doctor had already left.

Among the utterly despondent family of the deceased, it was Mr. Nozoe's second son who appeared to be taking charge of everything. On seeing Father Gounod, he immediately went to him and talked with him about making the arrangements for the funeral. The priest remembered him as the young man who had defended union activity by Catholics, and as Father Gounod quietly knelt at the dead man's bedside, he contrasted the son's attitude with that of his father, who had been obsessed with the idea that the Communist Party was synonymous with the devil and who had persistently criticized Father Gounod for allowing a Communist to make a speech before the young people of the church.

"Lord, may he rest in peace and may Thy eternal light shine upon him."

As he uttered the last phrase of this prayer recited after the soul has departed from the body, the priest keenly felt the existence of divine providence.

The sudden death of Mr. Nozoe following directly on his strained meeting with the bishop left Father Gounod completely exhausted, but he soon had to go out again that day. The geisha of Yanagibashi were holding their annual dance performance at a mid-town Tokyo theater. Sakai Satoko had left him a ticket. "Father, you must come, please?" she had insisted.

It was at this time that of her own volition she first revealed to him her true identity, and Father Gounod, being deeply moved, wanted to go and see her, from the bottom of his heart: so he promised. He remembered that when he had told Bishop Rogendorf about it, the bishop looked disappointed and said that he had someone to interview at the time of the show. Father Gounod looked at his watch and, seeing that he would arrive in time for the performance even if he took a tram, suddenly felt somewhat relieved. It was because he had taken a tram rather than a taxi returning from the meeting with the bishop that he had been unable to be with Mr. Nozoe during his last moments, and so it was somehow not right to take a taxi to go to a theater.

Although he had to wait for a fairly long time, finally both a tram and a bus appeared, and when he arrived at the theater, he found that he still had time before Kofumi went on. He bought a thick program, which was luxuriously printed in color, sat down on a sofa in the lobby, and began to turn the pages.

Under the title "Saigyō in the Rain Shower" were listed the names of the performers Kofumi and Hanaka. Regretting that he had not brought a dictionary, Father Gounod tried to learn something about the dance performance beforehand by reading the outline in the program. To get some idea of the meaning, he had to continually reread those sections which contained words he did not understand.

He had a good seat, H23, in the eighth row center. Around Father Gounod the air was filled with the scent of wealthy people, even a slight indication of which he had never noticed in his church. He was reminded of how the young people who prayed in a corner of his church could not even go to a movie theater on Sundays because their life was so hard, and this place he was in now made him wonder if it too was located in the same Japan. On his right there were three middle-aged women sitting together. Judging from their conversation, they seemed to be the wives of company directors, and the priest wondered how they had the nerve to cheerfully look forward to enjoying the dancing of geisha. The curtain rose on "Saigyō in the Rain Shower." Hanaka began her dance in the role of the priest Saigyō, wearing a wig parted in the middle, and Kofumi, wearing the Shimada coiffure and an India ink print–skirted white costume, danced the role of a courtesan. The stage contained only a single dignified folding screen before which their dances were performed in simple costumes.

To the accompaniment of the samisen, the song taken from the celebrated nō drama flowed from the mouths of the geisha who were seated in rows on either side of the stage.

> At evening's twilight in the village of Eguchi,
> Having cast away all worldly desires,
> Standing under the eaves of a brothel,
> Unable to bear the drenching shower,
> When he asked a night's lodging,
> The harlot who seemed to be the mistress of the brothel

Sakai Satoko, wearing a large linen shawl with a satin figured pattern, was completely transformed into the courtesan of Eguchi. Her thickly powdered white face contrasting with the redness of the rouge on her lips and the corners of her eyes and the blackness of her eyebrows made her beauty much more apparent.

The scene arrived in which the courtesan who gave the priest Saigyō a room for the night told about herself.

> Blossoming in the morning of Spring,
> Reddening in the evening of Autumn,
> The colorful mountain's floral attire.
> Men court her, desire aroused by moon and snow,
> Though their bed is sad. . . .

Despite his careful reading of the plot, Father Gounod was unable to appreciate Kofumi's wonderful performance as the ordinary Japanese spectators were able to do, since he was not very familiar with the movements of Japanese dancing; but just as she had submissively melted into Catholicism, he now found himself attracted openheartedly to her dancing as a whole. It seemed to him that he was not seeing the dancing of a courtesan but was watching Sakai Satoko in the village of Eguchi. When Hanaka, who played the priest Saigyō, came to dance the scene in which she prayed to the Bodhisattva Fugen, who appeared to her in the human form of the dancing courtesan, Father Gounod forgot completely the plot of "Saigyō in the Rain Shower." Watching the dancing figure of Kofumi waving a folding fan, his life of that year passed before him. As he had told Rogendorf, how rich his life had become since she first appeared. He resolved to thank the Lord for His blessings and to repay them.

ENCHI FUMIKO

Enchi Fumiko (1905–1986) was the daughter of a famous scholar of the Japanese language, Ueda Kazutoshi, as well as a historian of literature in her own right. Her prose examines the feminine psyche using a knowledge of Japanese classical literature, making her translation into modern Japanese of the great Heian classic *The Tale of Genji* (*Genji monogatari*) particularly admired, as are a number of her novels. The story translated here, "Skeletons of Men" (Otoko no hone, 1956), is thematically tied to her most famous novel, *The Waiting Years* (*Onnazaka*, 1957). In it, Enchi weaves together several layers of narrative to present the stor(ies) of a manipulative man and the women in his life who are almost overcome with jealousy.

SKELETONS OF MEN (OTOKO NO HONE)

Translated by Susan Matisoff

"Nice sash. Did you find it at Itoki too?" I asked, gazing at the old, heavy brocade obi Mikanagi Shizuko was wearing. A performance of the play *Kinuta* on the Kanze nō stage had just ended, while in the seat in front of me Shizuko continued jotting with a pencil in a little notebook, apparently drafting a poem.

"This? You like it?" she asked, still writing.

"Yes. When did you buy it?"

Shizuko was a scholar of classical literature and a poet, one of my closest friends. She had a taste for wearing antique dyed goods and often checked out the high-class used clothing shops in the back streets near Asakusa. I supposed this was one of those obi, but I'd come to an overly hasty conclusion.

"Unfortunately, this isn't something I bought. It's a keepsake from my mother. I'd kept it since the time she died, and then last month, on the third anniversary of her death, I remembered it. It's not the sort of thing to keep tucked away in the bottom of a chest forever. It's a bit conservative, but since I thought I'd try wearing it some time, I took out the lining. Even though the material is so thick, it had two layers of stiff cotton padding inside . . . so heavy . . . so very heavy."

As she spoke, Shizuko looked down and lightly tapped the obi with her fingers to show me.

"Really this obi wasn't my mother's; it belonged to her mother. It's a second-generation family keepsake. And since it seems to be from when my grandmother was rather young, it's really a long-lived sash."

"A hundred years, goodness, could it be?" I said, fingering the edge of the bow, tied small and tight on Shizuko's slender back. Tiny chrysanthemums and maples were embroidered densely on the navy blue background, and the brocade had a firm, yet pliant, feel. It was attractive and filled me with a sense of happiness tinged with nostalgia.

"It's probably from around the late 1870s. Nothing much by way of an antique, but old for something handed down within a family. Somehow when clothing gets to be this old, it almost seems to take on a life of its own. I've been thinking about quite a lot of things lately. I've been manipulated by the spirit of this sash."

Seeing my dubious expression when she mentioned the spirit of the sash, Shizuko smiled at me and said, "Later." The story I am about to write is what Shizuko revealed to me, bit by bit, as we ate supper in a restaurant off the Ginza on our way home that evening.

On a leaden afternoon in December while relaxing after assembling a selection of poems for a magazine, Shizuko took the heavy obi into her late husband's studio and sat on the sofa. Using scissors she began undoing the stitching of the seam in the heavy cloth. Over the years, the finely stitched silk thread had become absorbed into the cloth as if it were a part of the brocade itself. The only way to unravel it was to lift it stitch by stitch with the points of the scissors. Simply to unravel about two feet near the center of the seam took quite a while.

Rain had continued on and off since morning, and as she worked, the sky became even darker and more oppressive. After clearing away the unraveled threads, Shizuko opened the window a little for ventilation and found that rain, so fine it was invisible, had started to soak the leaves of the *yatsude* plants. If it went on like this, dusk would arrive without the day ever having become light, she thought, as she felt about with her hand thrust inside the partially undone obi. She grasped an inside corner and, nursing the stiff material along, pulled the right half inside out, lining and all. The colored threads on the densely embroidered background of the outside rose to the surface on the inside; their deep reds, creamy yellows, and purples, like satin, provided an unexpectedly gaudy luster. Once she had pulled the other half out the same way, the entire sash was inside out, just as when it was sewed. Now she could remove its lining.

Then Shizuko noticed the tip of what appeared to be thin wastepaper poking out from between the two layers of lining where the stitching had been removed. Idly pulling it out, she discovered that what had seemed a single sheet was actually the corner of a surprisingly long letter on rolled-up paper.

Startled, Shizuko picked it up and, in that instant, suddenly felt that this was probably the last testament of her grandmother Ritsu. Ritsu surely had held many secrets that she did not wish to reveal to others but couldn't bear to keep stored away only in her heart. Yet when Shizuko looked hesitantly at the rolled letter, she saw written on the outside in a faltering hand the words "Chise's blood letter." This evidently was Ritsu's handwriting.

"Blood letter" was a strange expression, and Shizuko hesitated for a moment, but the letter was hardly something to be tossed out without examination. Contrary to her expectations, the inner contents were written in ordinary ink. The text was done in formal calligraphy and in an old-fashioned, unpunctuated epistolary style that was quite difficult to read. Moreover, the ink wasn't very dark, making matters even harder. Shizuko read the letter, unconsciously mumbling while taking in the meaning little by little as she pieced the words together.

The phraseology was neither testament nor memoir. Clearly it was a woman's love letter to some man. It seemed to have been written in agony by a woman who was trying to rekindle the flames of passion in the breast of a man who had cast her aside. Ceaselessly she protested her affection, but with threatening phrases interspersed, like stabs of a dagger: "If you do not answer this letter, I do not know what will become of me" or "Suppose I become even more upset and say or do unthinkable things: that might damage your status."

It wasn't clear just what the position of the letter's author, Chise, might have been—a wife or a mistress—but in any case it appeared that she was also involved with some other man. Something written toward the end had made Ritsu append the notation "blood letter":

So that my words might penetrate your icy heart, I secretly cut myself in the thigh and squeezed out some blood, dissolved it in with the ink, and wrote this letter. I could have written the full length of this in blood alone, but I figured that might put you off and keep you from reading right through, beginning to end. So I chose this inconspicuous method. If you think this is a lie, look at the letter with bright noonday sun shining through, and you'll recognize the color of blood mixed in with the ink. Since you were raised in a samurai family, you're not likely to confuse blood for rouge.

When Shizuko read these lines, she felt as if a freezing hand had clasped her wrist. She didn't actually hold it to the light, and in the cold, rainy twilight, the very shapes of the characters themselves were scarcely visible.

Shizuko hadn't any idea of the identity of Chise, and yet she did have some understanding of the circumstances leading her grandmother Ritsu to hide this letter away inside her obi. Ritsu had often confided in her daughter about the lifelong torment she suffered because of her husband's love affairs and self-indulgence. And the daughter had eventually passed these stories on to her own grown daughter, Shizuko.

Ritsu's husband, Sagane Yoshimitsu, had been a samurai receiving a small stipend from the Hosokawa domain; but at the beginning of the modern era he had come up to Tokyo and become a government official. Apparently rather smart and courageous, he became a high official in the Metropolitan Police Department after holding a sequence of posts in the provinces. In the period just before the promulgation of the constitution, he prospered as a gentleman-official. He also managed to acquire sufficient wealth to live out his life in luxury following his retirement.

Considering that the better part of the Sagane family wealth was in Tokyo real estate, it seemed likely that he had taken advantage of his position while a government official, buying up much of the property at low rates. Of course Sagane wasn't the only one who did this; this scheme for amassing wealth seemed to be employed by virtually every member of the newly risen class of government authorities.

Sagane was one of the so-called nouveau riche bureaucrats who had risen from rural samurai families. As he was handsome, a bracing speaker, and shrewd in financial matters, he had been involved in many amorous affairs ever since he was a young man. In his own household he was extremely self-centered and an incorrigible husband for his wife, Ritsu, who, like him, had grown up in Kyushu.

A high-class Shimbashi district geisha had apparently become so attracted to him that she offered her services gratis, and the principal of a private school, a woman scholar of exceptional education for those times, was constantly writing love poems for him. Ritsu was confronted right and left with rivals with whom she could not compete. It took her immense effort to avoid arousing the ire of her autocratic husband.

For a time Yoshimitsu had been intimate with a married woman, though her precise status wasn't clear. Even though she had a spouse, it evidently took great efforts on Yoshimitsu's part to sever their connections, and even Ritsu knew only half the story. Perhaps Chise, the author of this letter, was that woman. Maybe she had sent her letter in an attempt to get through to Yoshimitsu, charging with blood the futility of her unquenchable love.

It wasn't clear just what had become of their relationship, but as Yoshimitsu suffered no social setback, the resentment felt by the author of the letter seemed to have finally settled down to her simply crying herself to sleep at night. With a bitter smile, Shizuko reflected that the heartless malice of a man pursued by a woman he's grown tired of—his stubborn coldness, his comical haste to take flight—is a scene from the human drama that had remained utterly unchanged from past to present.

"So, what did you do with the letter? Did you sew it back into the obi?"

Shizuko shook her head vigorously in response to my question.

After reading it, she left it overnight in a drawer of the desk in her husband's studio, but she felt so constantly unsettled thinking of it that the next day she made up her mind, took it out into the back garden, and burned it along with some fallen leaves.

The old, thin rolled paper turned to ashes all too soon, leaving no trace of the woman's passionate attachment that had been hidden away in the lining of the obi for several decades. But before burning it, Shizuko had looked at it, letting the bright daylight shine through, and just as the letter said, there was a faded red color faintly mixed in with the ink. The traces were particularly clear at places where the brush had started to run dry after writing several characters continuously.

Ritsu had kept these words by her body throughout her life, sewn into her sash; and Shizuko was moved to reflect more deeply on her grandmother's emotions than on the letter writer's feelings of frustration.

Ritsu ended her days still married to Yoshimitsu, dying some ten years before him. But from their middle years, they were husband and wife in name alone. Yoshimitsu's personal needs were taken care of by his young mistress Shiga, and the couple treated each other as virtual strangers.

Yoshimitsu had two mistresses, both of them living in the family home. At some point one of them got married and went off elsewhere. Yoshimitsu was more than thirty years her senior, but Shiga, who had been purchased as an innocent young girl, served him as the only man throughout her whole life and remained in his household until his death.

Yoshimitsu had terrible fears of deteriorating health stemming from his youthful excesses. Starting in middle age he rarely ventured out, carrying on the life of a feudal lord in his grand mansion. It was an existence in which a woman like Shiga—both servant and nurse—was utterly indispensable.

When Shizuko was a little girl, taken along by her mother to her grandfather's house at New Year's time, the mistress whom everyone referred to as "O-Shiga san" would appear, busying herself with Shizuko's care, helping her change clothes or preparing her food. Thinking back on it, Shiga was probably not yet forty then. But she was sensitive to cold and wore heavily padded clothes that rounded her back. And she tended to push her hands wearily into the ends of her sleeves. Shiga always created a tired, dull impression, and in the child's eyes, there was nothing beautiful about her.

Grandfather Yoshimitsu always sat facing the front of the parlor, supported by a back rest and with his legs wrapped in a blanket. Winter or summer, this was his unchanging posture. By his side he kept an array of boric acid eye-wash, mouthwash, a spittoon, and the like, and he was able to supply all his needs just as he sat there.

With his high cheekbones and long face, he resembled Yamagata Aritomo;[1] and there was a certain haughtiness in the way he consciously withdrew from his surroundings and remained in one place all day long, unmoving. His wife and his mistress, his sons and his servants meekly obeyed the orders of their aging master. The grandfather acted kindly enough toward his daughter's child, Shizuko, whom he saw only occasionally. He would give her things she specially liked to eat, buy her gifts, and make a fuss over her. But with her child's heart, Shizuko was never able to feel at ease with the frightening qualities she sensed behind her grandfather's apparent gentleness. She never knew any real affection for him.

Shizuko became interested in her grandfather long after his death. When she considered how gloomy and constrained the lives of both Ritsu and Shiga had been in the environment of Yoshimitsu's forceful exertion of his own will, she felt she couldn't just forget all about Yoshimitsu. The stories of the Sagane family that had been passed down to Shizuko were all from Ritsu's point of view. But for Shiga, too, life must have been stifling. No matter how affectionately Yoshimitsu treated Shiga, and no matter how distant the relationship between him and Ritsu, Shiga endured many long years with Ritsu, the legal wife, like a heavy weight pressing down on her head. To the child Shizuko's undiscerning eyes, Shiga had seemed like a moody, exhausted old cat. Perhaps that was a true portrait of her.

Shizuko had no way of knowing how the scars caused by Chise's love for Yoshimitsu might have healed in later years. But it was an absolute certainty that Ritsu and Shiga experienced the smoldering fires of a kind of living hell on account of Yoshimitsu. Yoshimitsu had grown up in Kyushu with its powerful traditions of male dominance and female suppression. He was probably quite unaware of the suffering he caused by keeping two women under one roof in a state of constant contention. On the contrary, he may well have taken undue pleasure in sensing the way they effectively kept each other in check.

Neither Ritsu nor Shiga, nor even Shizuko's mother, opposed Yoshimitsu's lack of compassion. But his granddaughter Shizuko had begun to feel that his conduct was unforgivable. The evil of this man, whose treatment of women

---

1. Yamagata Aritomo (1838–1922) was one of the leaders of the Meiji Restoration.

was so devoid of sympathy, who would so easily break a woman, and the dispositions of the women who learned nothing from that treatment but went on loving the man all the while they were being broken—both images tugged simultaneously at Shizuko like an insoluble puzzle.

When Shizuko was a girl, her mother was rather sickly, and during her frequent illnesses her grandmother Ritsu often came to stay and would sleep with Shizuko. At those times, as they lay in bed together, Ritsu would tell Shizuko old-fashioned tales like the story of *Ko Atsumori* or *Matsuyama Kagami*. Among these tales was the story of Ishidōmaru's father before he entered the priesthood.

> Ishidōmaru's father was called Katō Saemon Shigeuji, and he was the governor of Kyushu. He had two beautiful women, his wife and his mistress, living together in his house. Katō Saemon Shigeuji was delighted by how well the two of them got along together.
>
> But one day, as he was strolling about in his garden, he noticed the scent of aloes emanating from the women's quarters. Then he heard an uncanny noise, and when he crept up and peered inside, he saw his wife and mistress together. They had fallen into a deep sleep while playing a game of go, one leaning on her armrest, the other face down on the game board. Their black hair was standing on end, and the tips had turned into serpents that glared at each other with inflamed eyes. The serpents were undulating, intertwined, spitting flame-like tongues and biting at each other.
>
> As he looked at them, Shigeuji realized the evil of his ways and recognized the terrible hidden jealousy between the women. Immediately he abandoned his household and entered the priesthood.

This was probably a story that grew out of Hinayana Buddhism or from some Chinese legend. And when Shizuko thought back on it after she was grown, she imagined the emotions Ritsu had felt in telling this story to her granddaughter. She could envision how, just as an author introduces emotions into a plot, Ritsu, for all her self-control, was including her own emotions in the telling of this story.

Through the blind attachment of the two women, Katō Saemon came to recognize the truth of impermanence. That was the plot of a religious tale, and it was affecting enough, but most men, in real life, wouldn't actually take up priestly practice because of something like seeing women's hair turned into snakes. Certainly Sagane Yoshimitsu had been one those hard-hearted fellows. Still, the women also seemed to have harbored abundant foolish desires to dance like puppets manipulated by the strings of this nasty fellow's conniving heart.

Some ten days after she had reduced the blood letter to ashes, Shizuko set off for the Tama cemetery, a place she hadn't visited in years. She had kept meaning to go sometime soon after the end of the war but had found neither the time nor the mental leisure and hadn't gotten around to it. Now she was setting off to sweep her grandfather's long-neglected grave. It was Chise's blood letter, of course, that had finally got her moving.

It was a sunny afternoon, but with the New Year's festivities fast approaching, there was hardly anyone to be seen in the suburban graveyard. In the broad, clear sky, the lofty treetops of red pines rustled in the breeze, making a dry sound. The scene was refreshing. Grave plots were arrayed right and left along a broad path, and here and there on the grounds were azaleas and nandina bamboo mixed in among the evergreens, their bright foliage glowing even this late in the year.

The Sagane family plot, in section five, looked long unvisited. In the basin before the gravestone there was nothing but some wind-tossed dry pine needles, not even a trace of wilted flowers. Shizuko washed the grave with water she had brought in a bucket from a tea stall and put some flowers in the vase. As she squatted there, with her hands pressed together in prayer and her eyes tightly closed, the memory of the day some twenty years earlier when they had put her grandfather's bones to rest here came back to life.

The stonemason was waiting with the slab lifted off the front of the grave. After removing it from a plain wooden box, her uncle placed the white porcelain urn containing her grandfather's ashes in the grave's Chinese chest. He put it next to Ritsu's urn, which had been placed there previously. The interior of the Chinese chest was rather spacious, intended as a burial receptacle for several generations, and a number of other urns were visible, clustered in a corner.

Dressed in a formal black crested kimono and with a quartz rosary around her wrist, Shiga was there along with the family. After the ceremony they all walked back to the tea stall, chatting in groups of twos and threes as they followed the broad path bordered with swaying pines trees, which were then nowhere near as tall as now. Even now Shizuko couldn't help remembering that day Shiga had looked splendidly beautiful, even though she was well over fifty and dressed in mourning.

When she was young, Shiga's glossy jet black hair was extremely thick and grew from a perfectly even hairline. She had hated it when people told her that she looked like the girls pictured in cloth collages on the festive battledores for New Year's games of shuttlecock. Even in her old age it hadn't turned white, and on that day she had done it up in a style with the front of her somewhat thinned hair softly puffed out. On her supple, small-boned body, she was wearing her kimono with the neckband somewhat loose, and though her obi was tied rather low, the undercord around her waist was pulled tight, raising a corner of her hem and giving the kimono skirt the smooth trim appearance called "willow-hipped." It was a stylish look, calling to mind precisely the image of a turn-of-the century concubine, like a high-class geisha who somehow retained an appearance of innocence.

"Dear old Shiga's looking terribly alluring today, isn't she? She's really at home in a black-crested kimono. The young folks pale by comparison, don't you think?" One of Shizuko's elder cousins, much the young man-about-town, said this, tapping Shizuko on the shoulder playfully; and in truth, all those young ladies with their tidily arranged neckbands did look quite unprepossessing in comparison to Shiga.

It came about naturally with the death of Sagane Yoshimitsu that Shiga was finally able to emerge from the shadowy position she'd been kept in all her life, but by that time Shiga herself had reached an age that afforded her no prospects of love or marriage. For good or ill, it had been Shiga's life to be raised by Yoshimitsu and to have grown old with him.

Before her grandfather's possessions were to be divided up, Shizuko's mother was summoned to her ancestral home to sort through his clothing. Shiga was by her side, and with the palm of her hand, she lovingly stroked an indigo-striped garment that Yoshimitsu used to wear when he went out.

"My master liked this. He wore it often. It really suited him well, even when he'd grown old," she said to Shizuko's mother.

Then Shizuko's mother gazed with amazement as, despite her advanced age, Shiga's large round eyes moistened and filled with tears.

"Well, after all, since they'd been together so long, it seems she did feel that he cared for her and she wasn't bothered by the difference in their ages. She didn't show the least hint of relief over his passing," Shizuko's mother told her.

Shiga had never had any children. She was given enough stock certificates to allow her to manage independently and was set up living with her niece in a Sagane family rental house. But just before the war became severe, she died of pneumonia. Shizuko was away from Tokyo at the time, so she couldn't even go to pay her last respects, but in all likelihood Shiga's bones were interred here in this grave as one of the Sagane family, right along with the urns of Yoshimitsu and Ritsu.

When she imagined the bones of Ritsu and Shiga flanking Yoshimitsu's bones, Shizuko thought once again of her grandmother's bedtime story about Ishidōmaru's father. But then, when they've turned to white ash that could pass for asbestos, stuff that rustles dryly in a porcelain urn, the physical attributes of wife or mistress, man or woman, have long since been lost.

Who knew what end in life had finally come to Chise, the author of the blood letter? Her words alone lived on for some sixty or seventy years sewn inside Ritsu's obi, and knowledge of the passionate attachment that she could not suppress was transmitted to Shizuko. That blood letter was definitely written by Chise, but somehow Ritsu must have had similar feelings. To Shizuko this seemed the reason why instead of destroying and discarding it on the spot, as one might expect, she sewed it into the lining of her obi, keeping it to survive for so long, hidden from the light of day.

Perhaps when Shizuko burned up the letter, the attachments felt by both Chise and Ritsu met their blazing conclusion together.

"Shizuko, I suspect there's something more to your story," I said when I'd heard her out.

"Oh, you're sharp. Couldn't you just let it go at that?" Shizuko smiled vaguely.

"You must have visited Minami's grave. I'm sure his grave is there, too."

Minami was an elder cousin of Shizuko's husband, a diplomat with whom she'd had an affair after her husband's death. Put in mind of the charms of nasty men by Shizuko's story of her grandfather, I'd been taking in her story and associating the better part of it with the Minami affair.

Of course she didn't write a blood letter, but when she and Minami parted company and he was leaving to assume a post in Europe, she pursued him, following him to the port at Shimonoseki, and finally returned without meeting up with him. I'd heard the whole story. That impetuous behavior was atypical of Shizuko. Minami died during the war at his foreign post.

Shizuko reddened about the eyes and blinked, looking a bit embarrassed. She said that she'd supposed I would think of Minami while she was telling her story, but she'd thought I'd keep quiet about it.

After visiting her grandfather's grave, carrying another bunch of flowers in her bucket, Shizuko went looking for Minami's grave, which was a good way back in the cemetery. She was relying on the map she had consulted in the cemetery office. Even when she'd gotten fairly close to his grave, she couldn't find it and inadvertently started over to the grave of someone else with the same surname.

"It was like the plot of 'Mistaken Judgment,'"[2] said Shizuko, smiling brightly.

When she finally found Minami's grave and put her flowers in the vase, Shizuko felt relieved. As she stood there bowing deeply, the white bones beneath the grave seemed to fade dimly, and it was as if the haze congealed into the form of Minami.

The sun slipped behind the clouds and a strong wind came up. Some sort of bird cried boisterously in the top of the lone tree, straight and tall as a cryptomeria, that stood by Minami's grave.

ENDŌ SHŪSAKU

At the age of ten, Endō Shōsaku (1923–1996) was baptized into the Catholic Church, primarily to please his mother. Moreover, he often described his literary career as an attempt to "retailor the Western-style suit of clothing" in which his mother had dressed him. Not surprisingly, Endō shared with many of his war-generation contemporaries a concern for the weakling who is compelled to renounce his personal beliefs. But he stood virtually alone in his quest to locate—in

---

2. "Mistaken Judgment" was a *rakugo* vaudeville skit.

such powerful novels as *Silence* (*Chinmoku*, 1966) and *Deep River* (*Fukai kawa*, 1993), as well as in the following story, "Mothers" (Haha naru mono, 1969)—spiritual solace for his suffering characters, a solace that takes the form of a forgiving Christ figure who shares with them the pains of mortal existence.

MOTHERS (HAHA NARU MONO)

Translated by Van C. Gessel

I reached the dock at nightfall.

The ferryboat had not yet arrived. I peered over the low wall of the quay. Small gray waves laden with refuse and leaves licked at the jetty like a puppy quietly lapping up water. A single truck was parked in the vacant lobby of the dock; beyond the lot stood two warehouses. A man had lit a bonfire in front of one of the warehouses; the red flames flickered.

In the waiting room, five or six local men wearing high boots sat patiently on benches, waiting for the ticket booth to open. At their feet were dilapidated trunks and boxes loaded with fish. I also noticed several cages packed full of chickens. The birds thrust their long necks through the wire mesh and writhed as though in pain. The men sat quietly on the benches, occasionally glancing in my direction.

I felt as though I had witnessed a scene like this in some Western painting. But I couldn't recall who had sketched it or when I had seen it.

The lights on the broad gray shore of the island across the water twinkled faintly. Somewhere a dog was howling, but I couldn't tell whether it was over on the island or here on my side of the bay.

Gradually some of the lights which I had thought belonged to the island began to move. I finally realized that they belonged to the ferryboat that was heading this way. At last the ticket booth opened, and the men got up from the benches and formed a queue. When I lined up behind them, the smell of fish was overpowering. I had heard that most of the people on the island mixed farming with fishing.

Their faces all looked the same. Their eyes seemed sunken, perhaps because of the protruding cheekbones; their faces were void of expression as if they were afraid of something. In short, dishonesty and dread had joined together to mold the faces of these islanders. Perhaps I felt that way because of the preconceived notions I had about the island I was about to visit. Throughout the Edo period, the residents of the island had suffered through poverty, hard, grinding labor, and religious persecution.

After some time I boarded the ferryboat, which soon pulled away from the harbor. Only three trips a day connected the island with the Kyushu mainland. Until just two years before, boats had made the crossing only twice a day, once in the morning and once in the evening.

It was, in fact, little more than a large motor launch and had no seats. The passengers stood between bicycles and fish crates and old trunks, exposed to the chilling sea winds that blew through the windows. Had this been Tokyo, some passengers would undoubtedly have complained at the conditions, but here no one said a word. The only sound was the grinding of the boat's engine; even the chickens in the cages at our feet did not utter a peep. I jabbed at some of the chickens with the toe of my shoe. A look of fear darted across their faces. They looked just like the men from the waiting room, and I had to smile.

The wind whipped up; the sea was dark, and the waves black. I tried several times to light a cigarette, but the wind extinguished my match at every attempt. The unlit cigarette grew damp from my lips, and finally I hurled it overboard . . . though the winds may very well have blown it back onto the boat. The weariness of the twelve-hour bus ride from Nagasaki overcame me. I was stiff from the small of my back to my shoulders. I closed my eyes and listened to the droning of the engine.

Several times, out on the pitch black ocean, the pounding of the engine grew suddenly faint. In an instant it would surge up again, only to slacken once more. I listened to that process repeat itself several times before I opened my eyes again. The lights of the island were directly ahead.

"Hello!" a voice called. "Is Watanabe there? Throw the line!"

There was a dull, heavy thud as the line was thrown to the quay.

I got off after the locals had disembarked. The cold night wind bore the smells of fish and of the sea. Just beyond the dock gate stood five or six shops selling dried fish and local souvenirs. I had heard that the best-known local product was a dried flying fish called *ago*. A man dressed in boots and wearing a jacket stood in front of the shops. He watched me closely as I stepped through the gate, then came up to me and said, "Sensei, thank you for coming all this way. The church sent me to meet you."

He bowed to me an embarrassing number of times, then tried to wrest my suitcase from my hands. No matter how often I refused, he would not let go of it. The palms that brushed against my hand were as solid and large as the root of a tree. They were not like the soft, damp hands of the Tokyo Christians that I knew so well.

I tried to walk beside him, but he stubbornly maintained a distance of one pace behind me. I remembered that he had called me "sensei," and I felt bewildered. If the church people persisted in addressing me in terms of respect, the locals might be put on their guard against me.

The smell of fish that permeated the harbor trailed persistently after us. That odor seemed to have embedded itself in the low-roofed houses and the narrow road over the course of many years. Off to my left, across the sea, the lights of Kyushu now shone faintly in the darkness.

"How is the father?" I asked. "I came as soon as I got his letter . . ."

But there was no answer from behind. I tried to detect whether I had done something to offend him, but that did not appear to be the case. Perhaps he was just diffident and determined not to engage in idle chatter. Or possibly, after long years of experience, the people of this island had concluded that the best way to protect themselves was to avoid imprudent conversation.

I had met their priest in Tokyo. He had come up from Kyushu to attend a meeting just after I had published a novel about the Christian era in Japan. I went up and introduced myself to him. He, too, had the deep-set eyes and the prominent cheekbones of the island's fishermen. Bewildered perhaps to be in Tokyo among all the notable clerics and nuns, his face tightened and he said very little when I spoke to him. In that sense, he was very much like the man who was now carrying my suitcase.

"Do you know Father Fukabori?" I had asked the priest. A year earlier, I had taken a bus to a fishing village an hour from Nagasaki. There I met the village priest, Father Fukabori, who was from the Urakami district. Not only did he teach me how to deep-sea fish, he also provided me with considerable assistance in my research. The purpose of my visit had been to visit the *kakure*, descendants of some of the original Christian converts in the seventeenth century who had, over the space of many years, gradually corrupted the religious practices. Father Fukabori took me to the homes of several of the *kakure*, who still stubbornly refused to be reconverted to Catholicism. As I have said, the faith of the *kakure* Christians over the long years of national isolation had drifted far from true Christianity and had embraced elements of Shinto, Buddhism, and local superstition. Because of this, one of the missions of the church in this region, ever since the arrival of Father Petitjean in the Meiji period [1868–1912], was the reconversion of the *kakure* who were scattered throughout the Gotō and Ikitsuki islands.

"He let me stay at his church." I continued to grasp for threads of conversation, but the priest clutched his glass of juice tightly and muttered only monosyllabic responses.

"Are there any *kakure* in your parish?"

"Yes."

"They're starting to show up on television these days, and they look a little happier now that they're making some money out of it. The old man that Father Fukabori introduced me to was just like an announcer on a variety show. Is it easy to meet the *kakure* on your island?"

"No, it's very difficult."

Our conversation broke off there, and I moved on in search of more congenial company.

Yet to my surprise, a month ago I received a letter from this artless country priest. It opened with the customary Catholic "Peace of the Lord" salutation and went on to say that he had persuaded some of the *kakure* who lived in his parish to show me their religious icons and copies of their prayers. His handwriting was surprisingly fluent.

I looked back at the man walking behind me and asked, "Are there any *kakure* around here?"

He shook his head. "No, they all live in the mountains."

Half an hour later we reached the church. A man dressed in a black cassock, his hands clasped behind him, stood at the doorway. Beside him was a young man with a bicycle.

Since I had already met the priest—though only once—I greeted him casually, but he looked somewhat perplexed and glanced at the other two men. I had been thoughtless. I had forgotten that unlike Tokyo or Osaka, in this district the priest was like a village headman or, in some cases, as highly respected as a feudal lord.

"Jirō, go and tell Mr. Nakamura that the sensei has arrived," he ordered. With a deep bow the young man climbed on his bicycle and disappeared into the darkness.

"Which way is the *kakure* village?" I asked. The priest pointed in the opposite direction to that from which I had come. I couldn't see any lights, perhaps because the mountains obstructed my view. In the age of persecution, to escape the eyes of the officials, the *kakure* Christians had settled as much as possible in secluded mountain fastnesses or on inaccessible coastlines. Undoubtedly that was the case here. We'll have to walk quite a way tomorrow, I thought, surveying my own rather fragile body. Seven years before, I had undergone chest surgery, and though I had recovered, I still had little faith in my physical strength.

I dreamed of my mother. In my dream I had just been brought out of the operating theater and was sprawled out on my bed like a corpse. A rubber tube connected to an oxygen tank was thrust into my nostril, and intravenous needles pierced my right arm and leg, carrying blood from the transfusion bottles dangling over my bed.

Although I should have been half-unconscious, through the languid weight of the anesthetic I recognized the gray shadow that held my hand. It was my mother. Strangely, neither my wife nor any of the doctors was in the room.

I have had that dream many times. Frequently I wake up unable to distinguish dream from reality and lie in a daze on my bed until I realize with a sigh that I am not in the hospital where I spent three years, but in my own home.

I have not told my wife about that dream. She was the one who watched over me through every night after each of my three operations, and I felt remorseful that my wife did not even seem to exist in my dreams. The main reason I said nothing to her, however, was my distasteful realization that the firm bonds between my mother and myself—stronger than even I had suspected—continued to link us some twenty years after her death, even in my dreams.

I know little about psychoanalysis, so I have no idea exactly what this dream means. In it, I cannot actually see my mother's face. Nor are her movements distinct. When I reflect back on the dream, the figure seems to be my mother, but I cannot positively say that it is. But it most definitely is not my wife or any kind of nurse or attendant, or even a doctor.

So far as my memory serves me, I can recollect no experience in my youth when I lay ill in bed with my mother holding my hand. Normally the image of my mother that pops into my mind is the figure of a woman who lived her life fervently.

When I was five years old, we were living in Dairen in Manchuria in connection with my father's work. I can still vividly recall the icicles that hung down past the windows of our tiny house like the teeth of a fish. The sky is overcast, and it looks as if it will begin to snow at any moment, but the snow never comes. In a nine-by-twelve room, my mother is practicing the violin. For hours on end she practices the same melody over and over again. With the violin wedged under her chin, her face is hard, stonelike, and her eyes are fixed on a single point in space as she seems to be trying to isolate that one true note somewhere in the void. Unable to find that elusive note, she heaves a sigh; her irritation mounts, and she continues to scrape the bow across the strings. The brownish calluses on her chin were familiar to me. They had formed when she was still a student at the music academy and had kept her violin tucked constantly under her chin. The tips of her fingers, too, were as hard to the touch as pebbles, the result of the many thousands of times she had pressed down on the strings in her quest for that one note.

The image of my mother in my school days—that image within my heart was of a woman abandoned by her husband. She sits like a stone statue on the sofa in that dark room at nightfall in Dairen. As a child I could not bear to see her struggling so to endure her grief. I sat near her, pretending to do my homework but concentrating every nerve in my body on her. Because I could not fathom the complex situation, I was all the more affected by the picture of her suffering, her hand pressed against her forehead. I was in torment, not knowing what I should do.

Those dismal days stretched from autumn into winter. Determined not to see her sitting in that darkened room, I walked home from school as slowly as I could. I followed the old White Russian who sold Russian bread everywhere he went. Around sunset I finally turned toward home, kicking pebbles along the side of the road.

One day, when my father had taken me out on one of our rare walks together, he said suddenly, "Your mother . . . she's going back to Japan on an important errand. . . . Would you like to go with her?"

Detecting a grown-up's lie, I grunted, "Uh-huh" and went on walking along behind him in silence, kicking at every rock I could find. The following month, with financial assistance from her older sister in Kobe, my mother took me back to Japan.

And then my mother during my middle-school days. Though I have various memories of her, they all congeal on one spot. Just as she had once played her violin in search of the one true note, she subsequently adopted a stern, solitary life in quest of the one true religion. On wintry mornings, at the frozen fissure of dawn, I often noticed a light in her room. I knew what she was doing in there. She was fingering the beads of her rosary and praying. Eventually she would take me with her on the first Hankyō-line train of the day and set out for Mass. On the deserted train I slouched back in my seat and pretended to be rowing a boat. But occasionally I would open my eyes and see my mother's fingers gliding along those rosary beads.

In the darkness, I opened my eyes to the sound of rain. I dressed hurriedly and ran from my bungalow to the brick chapel across the way.

The chapel was almost too ornate for this beggarly island village. The previous evening, the priest had told me that the village Christians had worked for two years to erect this chapel, hauling the stones and cutting the wood themselves. They say that three hundred years ago, the faithful also built churches with their own hands to please the foreign missionaries. That custom has been passed down undiluted on this remote island off Kyushu.

In the dimly lit chapel knelt three peasant women in their work attire, with white cloths covering their heads. There were also two men in working clothes. Since the nave was bereft of kneelers or benches, they each knelt on straw mats to offer up their prayers. One had the impression that as soon as Mass was over, they would pick up their hoes and head straight for the fields or the sea. At the altar, the priest turned his sunken eyes toward the tiny congregation, lifted up the chalice with both hands, and intoned the prayer of Consecration. The light from the candles illuminated the text of the large Latin missal. I thought of my mother. I couldn't help but feel that this chapel somehow resembled the church she and I had attended thirty years before.

When we stepped outside after Mass, the rain had stopped but a dense fog had settled in. The direction in which the *kakure* village lay was shrouded in a milky haze; the silhouettes of trees hovered like ghosts amid the fog.

"It doesn't look like you'll be able to set out in all this fog," the priest muttered from behind me, rubbing his hands together. "The mountain roads are very slippery. You'd better spend the day resting yourself. Why don't you go tomorrow?"

He proposed a tour of the Christian graves in his village for the afternoon. Since the *kakure* district lay deep in the mountains, it would be no easy matter for even a local resident to make the climb, and with only one lung I certainly did not have the strength to walk there in the dense, soaking mist.

Through breaks in the fog, the ocean appeared, black and cold. Not a single boat had ventured out. Even from where I stood, I could make out the frothy white fangs of the waves.

I had breakfast with the priest and went to lie down in the six-mat room that had been provided for me. In bed I reread a book about the history of this region. A thin rain began to fall; its sound, like shifting sands, deepened the solitude within my room, which was bare except for a bus timetable tacked to the wall. Suddenly I wanted to go back to Tokyo.

According to the historical documents, the persecution of Christians in this area commenced in 1607 and was at its fiercest between 1615 and 1617.

Father Pedro de San Dominico
Matthias
Francisco Gorosuke

Miguel Shin'emon
Dominico Kisuke

This list includes only the names of the priests and monks who were martyred in the village in 1615. No doubt there were many more nameless peasants and fisherwomen who gave up their lives for the faith. In the past, as I devoted my free time to reading the history of Christian martyrdoms in Japan, I formulated within my mind an audacious theory. My hypothesis is that these public executions might have been carried out as warnings to the leaders of each village rather than to each individual believer. This will, of course, never be anything more than my own private conjecture so long as the historical records offer no supportive evidence. But I can't help feeling that the faithful in those days, rather than deciding individually whether to die for the faith or to apostatize, were instead bowing to the will of the entire community.

It has been my long-held supposition that because the sense of community, based on blood relationships, was so much stronger among villagers in those days, it was not left up to individuals to determine whether they would endure persecution or succumb. Instead this matter was decided by the village as a whole. In other words, the officials, knowing that they would be exterminating their labor force if they executed an entire community that stubbornly clung to its faith, would only kill selected representatives of the village. In cases where there was no choice but apostasy, the villagers would renounce their beliefs en masse to ensure the preservation of the community. That, I felt, was the fundamental distinction between Japanese Christian martyrdoms and the martyrs in foreign lands.

The historical documents clearly indicate that in former times, nearly fifteen hundred Christians lived on this ten- by three-and-a-half-kilometer island. The most active proselytizer on the island in those days was the Portuguese father Camillo Constanzo, who was burned at the stake on the beach of Tabira in 1622. They say that even after the fire was lit and his body was engulfed in black smoke, the crowd could hear him singing the Laudate Dominum. When he finished singing, he cried "Holy! Holy!" five times and breathed his last.

Peasants and fishermen found to be practicing Christianity were executed on a craggy islet—appropriately named the Isle of Rocks—about a half hour from here by rowboat. They were bound hand and foot, taken to the top of the sheer precipice of the island, and hurled to their deaths. At the height of the persecutions, the number of believers killed on the Isle of Rocks never fell below ten per month, according to contemporary reports. To simplify matters, the officers would sometimes bind several prisoners together in a rush mat and toss them into the frigid seas. Virtually none of the bodies of these martyrs was ever recovered.

I read over the grisly history of the island's martyrs until past noon. The drizzling rain continued to fall.

At lunchtime the priest was nowhere to be seen. A sunburned, middle-aged woman with jutting cheekbones served my meal. I judged her to be the wife of some fisherman, but in the course of conversation, I learned to my surprise that she was a nun who had devoted herself to a life of celibate service. The image I had always fostered of nuns was limited to those women I often saw in Tokyo with their peculiar black robes. This woman told me about the order of sisters in this area, known in the local jargon as "The Servants' Quarters." The order, to which she belonged, practiced communal living, worked in the fields the same as the other farm women, looked after children at the nursery school, and tended the sick in the hospital.

"Father went on his motorcycle to Mount Fudō. He said he'd be back around three o'clock." Her eyes shifted toward the rain-splattered window. "With this awful weather, you must be terribly bored, Sensei. Jirō from the office said he'd be by soon to show you the Christian graves."

Jirō was the young man with the bicycle who had been standing beside the priest when I arrived the previous night.

Just as she predicted, Jirō appeared soon after I had finished lunch and invited me to accompany him. He even brought along a pair of boots for me to wear.

"I didn't think you'd want to get your shoes all muddy."

He apologized that the boots were so old, bowing his head so incessantly that I was embarrassed.

"I'm ashamed to make you ride in a truck like this," he added.

As we drove along the streets in his little van, I found that the mental picture I had drawn the previous night was accurate. All the houses were squat, and the village reeked of fish. At the dock, about ten small boats were preparing to go to sea. The only buildings made of reinforced concrete were the village office and the primary school. Even the "main street" gave way to thatched-roofed farmhouses after less than five minutes. The telephone poles were plastered with rain-soaked advertisements for a strip show. They featured a picture of a nude woman cupping her breasts; the show bore the dreadful title "The Sovereign of Sex."

"Father is heading a campaign to stop these shows in the village."

"But I'll bet the young men spend all their free time there. Even the young Christians . . ."

My attempt at humor fell on deaf ears as Jirō tightened his grip on the steering wheel. I quickly changed the subject.

"About how many Christians are there on the island now?"

"I think around a thousand."

In the seventeenth century, the number had been calculated at fifteen hundred, meaning a loss of about one-third since that time.

"And how many *kakure*?"

"I'm really not sure. I imagine they get fewer in number every year. Only the old people stick to their practices. The young ones say the whole thing's ridiculous."

Jirō related an interesting story. In spite of frequent encouragement from the priests and believers, the *kakure* had refused to reconvert to Catholicism. They claimed that it was their brand of Christianity which had been handed down from their ancestors, making it the true original faith; they further insisted that the Catholicism brought back to Japan in the Meiji period was a reformed religion. Their suspicions were confirmed by the modern attire of the priests, which differed radically from that of the padres they had been told about over the generations.

"And so one French priest had a brilliant idea. He dressed up like one of the padres from those days and went to visit the *kakure*."

"What happened?"

"The *kakure* admitted he looked a lot like the real thing, but something was wrong. They just couldn't believe him!"

I sensed a degree of contempt toward the *kakure* in Jirō's tale, but I laughed aloud anyway. Surely the French priest who went to all the trouble of dressing up like a friar from the seventeenth century had had a sense of humor about him. The story seemed somehow exhilaratingly typical of this island.

Once we left the village, the gray road extended out along the coast. Mountains pressed in from our left, the ocean to our right. The waters churned, a leaden color, and when I rolled down the window an inch, a gust of rainy wind pelted my face.

Jirō stopped his truck in the shelter of a windbreak and held out an umbrella for me. The earth was sandy, dotted here and there with growths of tiny pine shrubs. The Christian graveyard lay at the crest of a sand-dune perched precariously over the ocean. It hardly deserved to be called a graveyard. The single stone marker was so tiny that even I could have lifted it with a little effort, and a good third of it was buried beneath the sand. The face of the stone was bleached gray by the wind and rain; all that I could make out was a cross that seemed to have been scratched into the rock with some object, and the Roman letters "M" and "R." Those two characters suggested a name like "Maria," and I wondered if the Christian buried here might have been a woman.

I had no idea why this solitary grave had been dug in a spot so far removed from the village. Perhaps some relative had quietly moved it to this inconspicuous location after the exterminations. Or possibly, during the persecution, this woman had been executed on this very beach.

A choppy sea stretched out beyond this forsaken Christian grave. The gusts pounding the windbreak sounded like electric wires chafing together. In the offing I could see a tiny black island, the Isle of Rocks where Christians from this district had been strung together like beads and hurled into the waters below.

I learned how to lie to my mother.

As I think back on it now, I suppose my lies must have sprung from some sort of complex I had about her. This woman, who had been driven to seek consolation in religion after being abandoned by her husband, had redirected the fervor she had once expended in search of the one true violin note toward a quest for the one true God. I can comprehend that zeal now, but as a child it suffocated me.

The more she compelled me to share her faith, the more I fought her oppressive power, the way a drowning child struggles against the pressure of the water.

One of my friends at school was a boy called Tamura. His father ran a brothel at Nishinomiya. He always had a filthy bandage wound about his neck, and he was often absent from school; I suppose he must have had tuberculosis even then. He had very few friends and was constantly mocked by the conscientious students. Certainly part of the reason I latched onto him was a desire to get back at my strict mother.

The first time I smoked a cigarette under Tamura's tutelage, I felt as though I was committing a horrid sin. Behind the archery range at school, Tamura, sensitive to every noise around us, stealthily pulled a crumpled cigarette pack from the pocket of his school uniform.

"You can't inhale deeply right at first. Try just a little puff at a time."

I hacked, choked by the piercing smoke that filled my nose and throat. At that moment, my mother's face appeared before me. It was her face as she prayed with her rosary in the predawn darkness. I took a deeper drag on the cigarette to exorcise this vision.

Another thing I learned from Tamura was going to movies on my way home from school. I slipped into the darkened Niban Theater near the Nishinomiya Hanshin Station, following Tamura like a criminal. The smell from the toilet filled the auditorium. Amid the sounds of crying babies and the coughs of old men, I listened to the monotonous gyrations of the movie projector. My whole mind was absorbed with thoughts of what my mother would be doing just then.

"Let's go home."

Over and over I pressed Tamura to leave, until finally he snarled angrily, "Stop pestering me! Go home by yourself, then!"

When we finally went outside, the Hanshin train that sped past us was carrying workers back to their homes.

"You've got to stop being so scared of your mother." Tamura shrugged his shoulders derisively. "Just make up a good excuse."

After we parted, I walked along the deserted road, trying to think up a convincing lie. I hadn't come up with one until I stepped through the doorway.

"We had some extra classes today," I caught my breath and blurted out. "They said we have to start preparing for entrance exams." When it was obvious that my mother had believed me, a pain clutched at my chest even as I experienced an inner feeling of satisfaction.

To be quite honest, I had no true religious faith whatsoever. Although I attended church at my mother's insistence, I merely cupped my hands together and made as if to pray while inwardly my mind roamed over empty landscapes. I recalled scenes from the many movies I seen with Tamura, and I even thought about the photographs of naked women he had shown me one day. Inside the chapel the faithful stood or knelt in response to the prayers of the priest reciting the Mass. The more I tried to restrain my fantasies, the more they flooded into my brain with mocking clarity.

I truly could not understand why my mother believed in such a religion. The words of the priest, the stories in the Bible, the Crucifix—they all seemed like intangible happenings from a past that had nothing to do with us. I doubted the sincerity of the people who gathered there each Sunday to clasp their hands in prayer even as they scolded their children and cleared their throats. Sometimes I would regret such thoughts and feel apologetic toward my mother. And I prayed that if there was a God, He would grant me a believing heart. But there was no reason to think that such a plea would change how I felt.

Finally I stopped going to morning Mass altogether. My excuse was that I had to study for my entrance exams. I felt not the slightest qualms when after that, I lay in bed listening to my mother's footsteps as she set out alone for church each winter morning. By then she had already begun to complain of heart spasms. Eventually I stopped going to church even on Sundays, though out of consideration for my mother's feelings I left the house and then slipped away to pass my time wandering around the bustling shopping center at Nishinomiya or staring at the advertisements in front of the movie theaters.

Around that time mother often had trouble breathing. Sometimes, just walking down the street, she would stop suddenly and clutch her chest, her face twisted into an ugly grimace. I ignored her. A sixteen-year-old boy could not imagine what it was to fear death. The attacks passed quickly, and she was back to normal within five minutes, so I assumed it was nothing serious. In reality, her many years of torment and weariness had worn out her heart. Even so, she still got up at five o'clock every morning and, dragging her heavy legs, walked to the station down the deserted road. The church was two stops away on the train.

One Saturday, unable to resist the temptation, I decided to play truant from school and got off the train near an amusement district. I left my school bag at a coffee shop that Tamura and I had begun to frequent. I still had quite a bit of time before the film started. In my pocket I carried a one-yen note I had taken from my mother's purse several days earlier. Somewhere along the way I had picked up the habit of dipping into her wallet. I sat through several movies until sunset, then returned home with a look of innocence on my face.

When I opened the door, I was surprised to see my mother standing there. She stared at me without saying a word. Then slowly her face contorted, and tears trickled down her twisted cheeks. It seems she had found out everything through a phone call from my school. She wept softly in the room adjoining mine until late into the night. I stuck my fingers in my ears, trying to block out the sound, but somehow it insinuated itself into my eardrums. Thoughts of a convenient lie to get me out of this situation left me little room for remorse.

Afterward, Jirō took me to the village office. While I was examining some local artifacts, sunlight began to warm the windows. I glanced up and saw that the rain had finally stopped.

"You can see a few more of these if you go over to the school." Mr. Nakamura, a deputy official in the village, stood beside me with a worried expression on his face, as though it were his personal responsibility that there was nothing here worth looking at. The only displays at the village office and the elementary school were of some earthenware fragments from remote antiquity, dug up by the teachers at the school. They had none of the *kakure* relics that I was eager to examine.

"Don't you have any *kakure* rosaries or crosses?"

Mr. Nakamura shook his head with embarrassed regret. "Those people like to keep things to themselves. You'll just have to go there yourself. They're a bunch of eccentrics, if you ask me."

His words were filled with the same contempt for the *kakure* that I had detected in Jirō's remarks.

Jirō, having observed the weather conditions, returned to the village office and announced cheerfully, "It's cleared up. We'll be able to go tomorrow for sure. Would you like to go and see the Isle of Rocks now?"

When we had visited the Christian grave, I had especially asked to see the Isle of Rocks.

Mr. Nakamura made a quick phone call to the fishermen's union. Village offices can be useful at such times; the union was more than willing to provide us with a small motorboat.

I borrowed a mackintosh from Mr. Nakamura. He accompanied Jirō and me to the dock, where a fisherman had the boat waiting. A mat had been laid in the wet bilges for us to sit on. In the murky waters that slopped around our feet floated the tiny silver body of a dead fish.

With a buzz from the motor, the boat set out into the still rough seas, vibrating ever more fiercely. It was invigorating to ride the crest of a wave, but each time we sank into a trough, I felt as though my stomach were cramping.

"The fishing's good at the Isle of Rocks," Nakamura commented. "We often go there on holidays. Do you fish, Sensei?"

When I shook my head, he gave me a disappointed look and began boasting to Jirō and the fisherman about the large sea bream he had once caught.

The spray drenched my mackintosh. The chill of the sea winds rendered me speechless. The surface of the water, which had started out gray, was now a dark, cold-looking black. I thought of the Christians who had been hurled into these waters four centuries before. If I had been born in such a time, I would not have had the strength to endure such a punishment. Suddenly I thought of my mother. I saw myself strolling around the entertainment district at Nishinomiya, then telling lies to my mother.

The little island drew closer. True to its name, it was composed entirely of craggy rocks, the very crest of which was crowned with a scant growth of vegetation. In response to a question from me, Mr. Nakamura reported that aside from occasional visits by officials of the Ministry of Postal Services, the island was used by the villagers only as a place from which to fish.

Ten or so crows squawked hoarsely as they hovered over the top of the islet. Their calls pierced the wet gray sky, giving the scene an eerie, desolate air. Now we had a clear view of the cracks and fissures in the rocks. The waves beat against the crags with a roar, spewing up white spray.

I asked to see the spot from which the Christians were cast into the sea, but neither Jirō nor Nakamura knew where it was. Most likely there had not been one particular location; the faithful had probably been thrown down from any convenient place.

"It's frightening even to think about it."

"It's impossible to imagine nowadays."

Evidently the thoughts that had been running through my head had not even occurred to my two Catholic companions.

"There's lots of bats in these caves. When you get up close, you can hear them shrieking."

"They're strange creatures. They fly so fast, and yet they never bump into anything. I hear they've got something like radar."

"Well, Sensei, shall we take a walk around and then go back?"

The island from which we had come was being pounded by white surf. The rain clouds split open, and we had a clear view of the mountain slopes in the distance.

Mr. Nakamura, pointing toward the mountains as the priest had done the previous evening, said, "That's where the *kakure* village is."

"Nowadays I suppose they don't keep to themselves like they used to, do they?"

"As a matter of fact, they do. We had one working as a janitor at the school. Shimomura was his name. He was from the *kakure* village. But I didn't much care for him. There wasn't anything to talk to him about."

The two men explained that the Catholics on the island were hesitant about associating with the *kakure* or intermarrying with them. Their reluctance seemed to have more to do with psychological conflicts than with religious differences. Even now the *kakure* married their own kind; if they did otherwise, they would not be able to preserve their faith. This custom reinforced their conviction that they were a peculiar people.

On the breast of those mountains half concealed in mist, the *kakure* Christians had sustained their religious faith for three hundred years, guarding their secret institutions from outsiders, as was done in all the *kakure* villages, by appointing people to such special village posts as "Waterworks Official," "Watchman," "Greeter," and "Ombudsman." From grandfather to father and from father to son, their formal prayers were passed through the generations, and their objects of worship were concealed behind the dark Buddhist altars. My eyes searched the mountain slope for that isolated village, as though I were gazing at some forsaken landscape. But of course it was impossible to spot it from there.

"Sensei, why are you interested in such a strange group of people?" Nakamura asked me in amazement. My reply was noncommittal.

One clear autumn day, I bought some chrysanthemums and set out for the cemetery. My mother's grave is in a Catholic cemetery in Fuchū. I can't begin to count the number of times I have made the journey to that graveyard since my school days. In the past, the road was surrounded by groves of chestnut and buckeye trees and fields of wheat; in the spring it was a pleasant path for a leisurely stroll. But now it is a busy thoroughfare crowded with all manner of shops. Even the stone carver's little hut that once stood all by itself at the entrance to the cemetery has turned into a solid one-story building.

Memories flood my mind each time I visit that place. I went to pay my respects the day I graduated from the university. The day before I was due to board a ship for France to continue my studies, I again made the journey there. It was the first spot I visited when I fell ill and had to return to Japan. I was careful to visit the grave on the day I was married and on the day I went into the hospital. Sometimes I make the pilgrimage without telling anyone, not even my wife. It is the spot where I conduct private conversations with my mother. In the depths of my heart lurks a desire not to be disturbed even by those who are close to me. I make my way down the path. A statue of the Holy Mother stands in the center of the graveyard, surrounded by a tidy row of stone markers belonging to the graves of foreign nuns who have been buried here in Japan. Branching out from this center point are white crosses and gravestones. A bright sun and a peaceful silence hover over each of the graves.

Mother's grave is small. My heart constricts whenever I look at that tiny grave marker. I pluck the wild grasses that surround it. With buzzing wings, insects swarm around me as I work in solitude. There is no other sound.

As I pour a ladle of water into the flower vase, I think (as I always do) of the day my mother died. The memory is a painful one for me. I was not with her when she collapsed in the hallway from a heart attack, nor was I beside her when she died. I was at Tamura's house, doing something that would have made her weep had she seen it.

Tamura had pulled a sheaf of postcards wrapped in newspaper from his desk drawer. And he smiled that thin smile he always wore when he was about to teach me something.

"These aren't like the phony ones they sell around here."

There were something like ten photographs inside the newspaper wrapping. Their edges were yellow and faded. The dark figure of a man was stretched out on top of the white body of a woman. She had a look as though of pain on her face. I caught my breath and flipped through the pictures one after another.

"Lecher! You've seen enough, haven't you?" Tamura cackled.

Their telephone rang, and after it was answered, we heard footsteps approaching. Hurriedly Tamura stuffed the photographs into his drawer. A woman's voice called my name.

"You must go home right away! Your mother's had an attack!"

"What's up?" Tamura asked.

"I don't know." I was still glancing at the drawer. "How did she know I was here?"

I was less concerned about her attack than the fact that she knew I was at Tamura's. She had forbidden me to go there after she found out that Tamura's father ran a whorehouse. It was not unusual for her to have to go to bed with heart palpitations, but if she took the white pills (I've forgotten the name) that the doctor gave her, the attack was always brought under control.

I made my way slowly along the back streets still warmed by the bright sun. Rusted scraps of metal were piled up in a field marked with a "For Sale" sign. Beside the field was a small factory. I didn't know what they manufactured there, but a dull, heavy, pounding noise was repeated regularly inside the building. A man came riding toward me on a bicycle, but he stopped beside the dusty, weed-covered field and began to urinate.

My house came into view. The window to my room was half-open, the way it always was. Neighborhood children were playing in front of the house. Everything was normal, and there was no sign that anything unusual had happened. The priest from our church was standing at the front door.

"Your mother . . . died just a few moments ago." He spoke each word softy and clearly. Even a mindless middle-school student like myself could tell that he was struggling to suppress the emotion in his voice. Even a mindless middle-school student like myself could sense the criticism in his voice.

In the back room, my mother's body was surrounded by neighbors and people from the church, sitting with stooped shoulders. No one turned to look at me; no one spoke a word to me. I knew from the stiffness of their backs that they all were condemning me.

Mother's face was white as milk. A shadow of pain still lingered between her brows. Her expression reminded me of the look on the face of the woman in the photographs I had just been examining. Only then did I realize what I had done, and I wept.

I finish pouring the water from the bucket and put the chrysanthemums into the vase that is part of the gravestone. The insects that have been buzzing about my face now cluster around the flowers. The earth beneath which my mother lies is the dark soil peculiar to the Musashi Plain. At some point, I too will be buried here, and as in my youth, I will be living alone again with my mother.

I had not given Mr. Nakamura a satisfactory answer when he asked me why I was interested in the *kakure*.

Public curiosity about the *kakure* has increased recently. This "hidden" religion is an ideal subject for investigation by those doing research in comparative religion. NHK, the national educational television channel, has done several features on the *kakure* of Gotō and Ikitsuki, and many of the foreign priests of my acquaintance come to visit the *kakure* whenever they are in Nagasaki. But I am interested in the *kakure* for only one reason—because they are the offspring of apostates. Like their ancestors, they cannot utterly abandon their faith; instead, they live out their lives consumed by remorse and dark guilt and shame.

I was first drawn to these descendants of apostates after I had written a novel set in the Christian era. Sometimes I catch a glimpse of myself in these *kakure*, people who have had to lead lives of duplicity, lying to the world and never revealing their true feelings to anyone. I, too, have a secret that I have never told anyone and that I will carry within myself until the day I die.

That evening I drank saké with the Father, Jirō, and Mr. Nakamura. The nun who had served me lunch brought out a large tray stacked with raw sea urchins and abalone. The local saké was too sweet for someone like myself who drinks only the dry variety, but the sea urchins were so fresh they made the Nagasaki ones seem almost stale. The rain had let up earlier, but it began to pour again. Jirō got drunk and began to sing.

> Oh, let us go, let us go
> To the Temple of Paradise, let us go,
> Oh, oh.
> They call it the Temple of Paradise,
> They say it is spacious and grand.
> But whether it is large or small
> Is really up to my heart.

I knew the song. When I'd visited Hirado two years before, the Christians there had taught it to me. The melody was complicated and impossible to remember, but as I listened to Jirō's plaintive singing, I thought of the dark expressions on the faces of the *kakure*. Protruding cheekbones and sunken eyes that seemed to be fixed on a single point in space. Perhaps, as they waited through the long years of national isolation for the boats of the missionaries that might never return, they muttered this song to themselves.

"Mr. Takaishi on Mount Fudō—his cow died. It was a good old cow." The priest was unlike the man I had met at the party in Tokyo. With a cup or so of saké in him, he was flushed down to his neck as he spoke to Mr. Nakamura. Over the course of the day, he and Jirō had perhaps ceased to regard me as an outsider. Gradually I warmed to this countrified priest, so unlike the swaggering prelates of Tokyo.

"Are there any *kakure* on Mount Fudō?" I asked.

"None. Everyone there belongs to our parish." He thrust out his chest a bit as he spoke, and Jirō and Nakamura nodded solemnly. I had noticed that morning how these people seemed to look down upon the *kakure* and regard them with contempt.

"There's nothing we can do about them. They won't have anything to do with us. Those people behave like some kind of secret society."

The *kakure* of Gotō and Ikitsuki were no longer as withdrawn as those on this island. Here even the Catholics appeared to be wary of the secretiveness of the *kakure*. But Jirō and Mr. Nakamura had *kakure* among their ancestors. It was rather amusing that the two of them now seemed to be oblivious of that fact.

"What exactly do they worship?"

"What do they worship? Well, it's no longer true Christianity." The priest sighed in consternation. "It's a form of superstition."

They gave me another interesting piece of information. The Catholics on the island celebrate Christmas and Easter according to the Western calendar, but the *kakure* secretly continue to observe the same festivals according to the old lunar calendar.

"Once when I went up the mountain, I found them all gathered together on the sly. Later I asked around and discovered they were celebrating their Easter."

After Nakamura and Jirō left, I returned to my room. My head felt feverish, perhaps due to the saké, and I opened the window. The ocean was pounding like a drum. Darkness had spread thickly in all directions. It seemed to me that the drumming of the waves deepened the darkness and the silence. I have spent nights in many different places, but I have never known a night as fathomless as this.

I was moved beyond words as I reflected on the many long years that the *kakure* on this island would have listened to the sound of this ocean. They were the offspring of traitors who had abandoned their religious beliefs because of the fear of death and the infirmities of their flesh. Scorned by the officials and by the Buddhist laity, the *kakure* had moved to Gotō, to Ikitsuki, and here to this island. Nevertheless, they had been unable to cast off the teachings of their ancestors, nor did they have the courage to defend their faith boldly like the martyrs of old. They had lived amid their shame ever since.

Over the years, that shame had shaped the unique features of their faces. They were all the same—the four or five men who had ridden with me on the ferryboat, Jirō, and Mr. Nakamura. Occasionally a look of duplicity mingled with cowardice would dart across their faces.

Although there were minor differences between the *kakure* village organizations on this island and those in the settlements on Gotō or Ikitsuki, in each village the role of the priest was filled either by the "Watchman" or the "Village Elder." The latter would teach the people the essential prayers and important festival days. Baptism was administered to newly born infants by the "Waterworks Official." In some villages the positions of "Village Elder" and "Waterworks Official" were assumed by the same individual. In many instances these offices had been passed down through the patriarchal line for many generations. On Ikitsuki I had observed a case where units of organization had been established for every five households.

In front of the officials, the *kakure* had, of course, pretended to be practicing Buddhists. They belonged to their own parish temples and had their names recorded as Buddhist believers in the religious registry.

Like their ancestors, at certain times they were forced to trample on the *fumie*

in the presence of the authorities. On the days when they had trodden on the sa-
cred image, they returned to their villages filled with remorse over their own
cowardice and filthiness, and there they scourged themselves with ropes woven
of fibers, which they called "*tempensha.*" The word originally meant "whip" and
was derived from their misinterpretation of the Portuguese word for "scourge." I
have seen one of these "*tempensha*" at the home of a Tokyo scholar of the Chris-
tian era. It was made from forty-six strands of rope, woven together, and did in
fact cause a considerable amount of pain when I struck my wrist with it. The
kakure had flogged their bodies with such whips.

Even this act of penitence did not assuage their guilt. The humiliation and
anxiety of a traitor do not simply evaporate. The relentless gaze of their martyred
comrades and the missionaries who had guided them continued to torment
them from afar. No matter how diligently they tried, they could not be rid of
those accusing eyes. Their prayers are therefore unlike the awkwardly translated
Catholic invocations of the present day; rather, they are filled with faltering ex-
pressions of grief and phrases imploring forgiveness. These prayers, uttered from
the stammering mouths of illiterate *kakure*, all sprang from the midst of their hu-
miliation. "Santa Maria, Mother of God, be merciful to us sinners in the hour of
death." "We beseech thee, as we weep and moan in this vale of tears. Intercede
for us, and turn eyes filled with mercy upon us."

As I listened to the thrashing of the sea in the darkness, I thought of the
kakure, finished with their labors in the fields and their fishing upon the waters,
muttering these prayers in their rasping voices. They could only pray that the
mediation of the Holy Mother would bring forgiveness of their frailties. For to
the *kakure*, God was a stern paternal figure, and as a child asks its mother to in-
tercede with its father, the *kakure* prayed for the Virgin Mary to intervene on
their behalf. Faith in Mary was particularly strong among the *kakure*, and I con-
cluded that their weakness had also prompted them to worship a figure that was
a composite of the Holy Mother and Kannon, the Buddhist Goddess of Mercy.

I could not sleep even after I crawled into bed. As I lay beneath the thin cov-
erlet, I tried to sing the words of the song that Jirō had performed that evening,
but I couldn't remember them.

I had a dream. It seemed that my operation was over and I had just been
wheeled back to my room; I lay back on the bed like a dead man. A rubber tube
connected to an oxygen tank was thrust into my nostril, and transfusion needles
from the plasma bottles hung over my bed had been inserted into my right arm
and leg. My consciousness should have been blurred, but I recognized the gray-
ish shadow that clutched my hand. It was my mother, and she was alone with
me in my hospital room. There were no doctors; not even my wife.

I saw my mother in other places, too. As I walked over a bridge at dusk, her
face would sometimes appear suddenly in the gathering clouds overhead. Oc-
casionally I would be in a bar, talking with the hostesses; when the conversa-
tion broke off and a sense of empty meaninglessness stole across my heart, I
would feel my mother's presence beside me. As I bent over my work desk late

in the night, I would abruptly sense her standing behind me. She seemed to be peering over my shoulder at the movements of my pen. I had strictly forbidden my children and even my wife to disturb me while I was working, but strangely it did not bother me to have my mother there. I felt no irritation whatsoever.

At such times, the figure of my mother that appeared to me was not the impassioned woman who had played her violin in search of the one perfect note. Nor was it the woman who had groped for her rosary each morning on the first Hankyū-line train, deserted except for the conductor. It was, rather, a figure of my mother with her hands joined in front of her, watching me from behind with a look of gentle sorrow in her eyes.

I must have built up that image of my mother within myself the way a translucent pearl is gradually formed inside an oyster shell. For I have no concrete memory of ever seeing my mother look at me with that weary, plaintive expression.

I now know how that image came to be formed. I superimposed on her face that of a statue of "Mater Dolorosa," the Holy Mother of Sorrows, which my mother used to own.

After my mother's death, people came to take away her kimonos and obis and other possessions, one after another. They claimed to be sharing out mementos of my mother, but to my young eyes, my aunts seemed to be going through the drawers of her dresser like shoppers rifling through goods in a department store. Yet they paid no attention to her most valued possessions—the old violin, the well-used prayer book she had kept for so many years, and the rosary with a string that was ready to break. And among the items my aunts had left behind was that cheap statue of the Holy Mother, the sort sold at every church.

Once my mother was dead, I took those few precious things with me in a box every time I moved from one lodging-house to another. Eventually the strings on the violin snapped and cracks formed in the wood. The cover was torn off her prayer book. And the statue of Mary was burned in an air raid in the winter of 1945.

The sky was a stunning blue the morning after the air raid. Charred ruins stretched from Yotsuya to Shinjuku, and all around, the embers were still smoldering. I crouched down in the remains of my apartment building in Yotsuya and picked through the ashes with a stick, pulling out broken bowls and a dictionary that had only a few unburned pages left. Eventually I struck something hard. I reached into the still warm ashes with my hand and pulled out the broken upper half of that statue. The plaster was badly scorched, and the plain face was even uglier than before. Today, with the passage of time the facial features have grown vaguer. After I was married, my wife once dropped the statue. I repaired it with glue, with the result that the expression on the face is all the more indistinct.

When I went into hospital, I placed the statue in my room. After the first operation failed and I began my second year in hospital, I had reached the end of my rope both financially and emotionally. The doctors had all but given up hope for my recovery, and my income had dissolved to nothing.

At night, beneath the dim lights, I would often stare from my bed at the face of the Holy Mother. For some reason her face seemed sad, and she appeared to be returning my gaze. It was unlike any Western painting or sculpture of the Mother of God that I had ever seen. Its face was cracked from age and from the air raid, and it was missing its nose; where the face had once been, only sorrow remained. When I studied in France, I saw scores of statues and portraits of the "Mater Dolorosa," but this memento of my mother had lost all traces of its origins. Only that sorrow lingered.

At some point I must have blended together the look on my mother's face and the expression on that statue. At times the face of the Holy Mother of Sorrows seemed to resemble my mother's face when she died. I still remember clearly how she looked laid out on top of her quilt, with that shadow of pain etched into her brow.

Only once did I ever tell my wife about my mother appearing to me. The one time I did say something, she gave some sort of reply, but a look of evident displeasure flickered on her face.

There was fog everywhere.

The squawking of crows could be heard in the mist, so we knew that the village was near at hand. With my reduced lung capacity, it was quite a struggle to make it all this way. The mountain path was very steep, but my greatest difficulty was that the boots which Jirō had lent me kept slipping in the sticky clay.

Even so, Mr. Nakamura explained, we were having an easier time of it than in the old days. Back then—and we couldn't see it now because of the fog—there had been just one mountain path to the south, and it had taken half a day to reach the village. The resourceful kakure had deliberately chosen such a remote location for their village in order to avoid surveillance by the officials.

There were terraced fields on both sides of the path, and the black silhouettes of trees emerged from the fog. The shrieking of the crows grew louder. I remembered the flock of crows that had circled the summit of the Isle of Rocks on the previous day.

Mr. Nakamura called out to a mother and child working in the fields. The mother removed the towel that covered her face and bowed to him politely.

"Kawahara Kikuichi's house is just down this way, isn't it?" Nakamura asked. "There's a sensei from Tokyo here who'd like to talk to him."

The woman's child gawked at me curiously until his mother scolded him, at which point he charged off into the field.

It had been Mr. Nakamura's sensible suggestion that we bring along a bottle of saké from the village as a gift for Mr. Kawahara. Jirō had carried it for me on our trek, but at this point I took it from him and followed the two men into the village. A radio was playing a popular song. Some of the houses had motorcycles parked in their sheds.

"All the young people want to get out of this place."

"Do they come to town?"

"No, a lot of them go to work in Sasebo or Hirado. I suppose it's hard for them to find work on the island when they're known as children of the *kakure*."

The crows were still following us along the road. They settled on the thatched roof of a house and cawed. It was as if they were warning the villagers of our arrival.

The house of Kawahara Kikuichi was somewhat larger than the others in the village, with a tiled roof and a giant camphor tree growing at the back. A single look at the house and it was obvious Kikuichi was the "Village Elder," the individual who performed the role of priest in this community.

Leaving me outside, Mr. Nakamura went into the house and negotiated with the family for a few minutes. The child we had seen in the field watched us from a distance, his hands thrust into trousers that had half fallen down. I glanced at him and realized that his bare feet were covered with mud. The crows squawked again.

I turned to Jirō. "It looks as though he doesn't want to meet us."

"Oh, no. With Mr. Nakamura talking to him, everything will be just fine," he reassured me.

Finally an agreement was reached. When I stepped inside the earthen entranceway, a woman was staring at me from the dark interior. I held out the bottle of saké and told her it was a small token of my gratitude, but there was no response.

Inside the house it was incredibly dark. The weather was partly to blame, but it was so dark I had the feeling it would be little different on a clear day. And there was a peculiar smell.

Kawahara Kikuichi was a man of about sixty. He never looked directly at me but always kept his fearful eyes focused on some other spot in the room as he spoke. His replies were truncated, and he gave the impression that he wanted us to leave as soon as possible. Each time the conversation faltered, my eyes shifted to different corners of the room, to the stone mortar in the entranceway, to the straw matting, or to the sheaves of straw. I was searching for the characteristic staff that belonged to the "Village Elder" and for the place where they had concealed their icons.

The Village Elder's staff was something only he was allowed to possess. When he went to perform baptisms, he carried a staff made of oak; to drive evil spirits from a home, he used a silverberry staff. His staff was never made from bamboo. Clearly these staffs were an imitation of the croziers carried by priests in the Christian age.

I searched carefully, but I was unable to locate either a staff or the closet where the icons were hidden away. Eventually I was able to hear the prayers handed down to Kikuichi from his ancestors, but the hesitant expressions of grief and the pleas for forgiveness were like every other *kakure* supplication I had heard.

"We beseech thee, as we weep and moan in this vale of tears." As he intoned the melody, Kikuichi stared into space. "Intercede for us, and turn eyes filled with mercy upon us." Like the song Jirō had crooned the previous evening, this was just a string of clumsy phrases addressed as an appeal to someone.

"As we weep and moan in this vale of tears . . ." I repeated Kikuichi's words, trying to commit the tune to memory.

"We beseech thee . . ."

"We beseech thee."

". . . Turn eyes filled with mercy . . ."

"Turn eyes filled with mercy . . ."

In the back of my mind was an image of the *kakure* returning to their village one night each year after being forced to trample on the *fumie* and pay their respects at the Buddhist altars. Back in their darkened homes, they recited these words of prayer. "Intercede for us, and turn eyes filled with mercy upon us. . . ."

The crows shrieked. For a few moments we were all silent, staring out at the thick mist that drifted past the veranda. A wind must have got up, for the milky fog swirled by more quickly than before.

"Could you perhaps show me your . . . your altar icons?" I stammered through my request, but Kikuichi's eyes remained fixed in another direction, and he gave no answer. The term "altar icons" is not Christian jargon, of course, but refers more generally to the Buddhist deities which are worshiped in an inner room of the house. Among the *kakure*, however, the object to which they prayed was concealed in the most inconspicuous part of the house; to deceive the officials, they referred to these images as their "altar icons." Even today, when they have full freedom of worship, they do not like to show these images to nonbelievers. Many of them believe that they defile their hidden icons by displaying them to outsiders.

Mr. Nakamura was somewhat firmer in his request. "He's come all the way from Tokyo. Why don't you show them to him?"

Finally Kikuichi stood up.

We followed him through the entranceway. The eyes of the woman in the darkened room were riveted on our movements.

"Watch your head!" Jirō called out from behind as we entered the inner room. The door was so low we had to bend over in order to go in. The tiny room, darker than the entranceway, was filled with the musty smells of straw and potatoes. Straight ahead of us was a small Buddhist altar decorated with a candle. This was certainly a decoy. Kikuichi's eyes shifted to the left. Two pale blue curtains hung there, though I had not noticed them when we came through the door. Rice cakes and a white bottle of offertory wine had been placed on the altar stand. Kikuichi's wrinkled hand slowly drew aside the curtains. Gradually the sections of an ocher-colored hanging scroll were revealed to us.

Behind us, Jirō sighed, "It's just a picture."

A drawing of the Holy Mother cradling the Christ child—no, it was a picture of a farm woman holding a nursing baby. The robes worn by the child were a pale indigo, while the mother's kimono was painted a murky yellow. It was clear from the inept brushwork and composition that the picture had been painted many years before by one of the local *kakure*. The farm woman's kimono was open, exposing her breast. Her obi was knotted at the front, adding to the impression that she was dressed in the rustic apparel of a worker in the fields. The face was like that of every woman on the island. It was the face of a woman who gives suckle to her child even as she plows the fields and mends the fishing nets. I was suddenly reminded of the woman earlier who had removed the towel from her face and bowed to Mr. Nakamura.

Jirō had a mocking smile on his face. Mr. Nakamura was pretending to look serious, but I knew that inside he was laughing.

Still, for some time I could not take my eyes off that clumsily drawn face. These people had joined their gnarled hands together and offered up supplications for forgiveness to this portrait of a mother. Within me there welled up the feeling that their intent had been identical to mine. Many long years ago, missionaries had crossed the seas to bring the teachings of God the Father to this land. But when the missionaries had been expelled and the churches demolished, the Japanese *kakure*, over the space of many years, stripped away all those parts of the religion that they could not embrace, and the teachings of God the Father were gradually replaced by a yearning after a Mother—a yearning which lies at the very heart of Japanese religion. I thought of my own mother. She stood again at my side, an ashen-colored shadow. She was not playing the violin or clutching her rosary now. Her hands were joined in front of her, and she stood gazing at me with a touch of sorrow in her eyes.

The fog had started to dissipate when we left the village, and far in the distance we could see the dark ocean. The wind seemed to have stirred up the sea again. I could not see the Isle of Rocks. The mist was even thicker in the valley. From somewhere in the trees that rose up through the mist, crows cried out. "In this vale of tears, intercede for us; and turn eyes filled with mercy upon us." I hummed the melody of the prayer that I had just learned from Kikuichi. I muttered the supplication that the *kakure* continually intoned.

"How ridiculous! Sensei, it must have been a terrible disappointment to have them show you something so stupid." As we left the village, Jirō apologized to me over and over, as though he were personally responsible for the whole thing. Mr. Nakamura, who had picked up a tree branch along the way to use as a walking stick, walked ahead of us in silence. His back was stiff. I couldn't imagine what he was thinking.

HANIYA YUTAKA

Before the war, Haniya Yutaka (1910–1997) was imprisoned for his Marxist leanings, which he combined with his commitment to the avant-garde to produce a series of difficult but highly accomplished stories and longer works of fiction.

Although much admired in Japan, few of Haniya's works have been translated into English, perhaps because of their conceptual sophistication and linguistic difficulty. His story "The Black Horse Out of the Darkness" (Yami no naka no kuroi uma, 1970) is a good example of his complex and elevated style.

THE BLACK HORSE OUT OF THE DARKNESS
(YAMI NO NAKA NO KUROI UMA)

Translated by William J. Tyler

Total darkness. . . . I have spent hour upon hour lying awake late at night because of a stubborn case of insomnia, which I nurse like a chronic illness. If anything, the hours I spend enveloped in total darkness now consume the better part of each and every night. It is a time of terrible frustration when I must lie still, scarcely making a sound when I breathe, and biting down hard, I ruminate on the inexpressible nature of my unhappiness. As I lie in bed, I reach out, and toying with the little bit of space directly in front of me, I seek to dispel something of the anxiety I feel. Yet what stretches before me is wrapped—nay, drenched—in a darkness so deep that it is surely of the same consistency as the darkness at the end of the universe—or, insofar as the imagination can conceive it, a distance that is billions of light-years away. As I peer endlessly into the total darkness, how I wish my hairy, apelike hand had the power to grab hold of it and throttle it by the neck! That's how much I have come to loathe this time at night. Yet I also know it is during these cursed hours, when all is held in silent abeyance, that I am able to delve into myself and explore who I am. These are the hours when my teeth begin their long, slow grind, and I dig deep down inside to find something within myself. They are—well, let me put it this way—my hours of "quiet mastication."

I have come to believe we human beings by nature are divided into two types, diurnal and nocturnal. As for the former, diurnals are all movement and progress. In other words, their spiritual window is set so that they are open to the future, which resides alongside the present like a neighbor who lives next door. The latter are, by contrast, different in nearly every way. Nocturnals never tire of looking at chaos and nothingness, which stretch so far into the distance that no one can hope to see where they end. They are relentless in looking back at the past or ahead to the future. Let my mind start to ruminate in the boundless, black lacquer depths of the night, and my thoughts take off, running on and on like chaos in its primal state, which has no end.

Isn't that because thinking in the dark is far different from thinking during the day, when the bright light of the sun invariably illuminates a figure or provides a diagram that defines who we are? Nocturnal thoughts have no definition and no end. They reach back to a primal beginning or forward to the future, both of which sink into endless darkness by virtue of being amorphous and far away. In short, nocturnal ruminations sooner or later arrive at a point of origination or an ultimate pole of no certifiable shape. Moreover, that is when they turn into a single particle of dust that may or may not possess a marker identifiable as "the self." In the end, they simply disintegrate and disappear, becoming indistinguishable from the four great elements of earth, water, fire, and wind and leaving no visible trace of having existed. That's how it is with nocturnal thoughts as a general rule.

It is also in such moments that I experience a strange and mysterious vertigo. It fills me with not only terror but also the pleasure of knowing I have returned at long last to the place from whence we all began. It is a state of mind like the deep sleep of an innocent child. It is the sweet feeling of ecstasy that comes when, in nodding off, one drifts into the arms of what I choose to call "a quiet nothingness."

It is true. Nocturnals have a dark core of denial at the center of their being. They wallow in the poison of their own vehement self-rejection, and as a result, they become empty and hollow. They are like an old tree rotting from the inside. Although the trunk may appear to be solid, by and by the tree falls soundlessly in the forest. But what saves them from becoming totally static and inert is the sense of mysterious awe and discovery they detect in the midst of chaos and nothingness on the far side of darkness. That's the critical difference. A sense of awe and discovery—along with no shortage of the feelings of sweet ecstasy they find so seductive and full of flavor—are what keeps them in pursuit of the infinitely infinite.

The hours I spend fine-tuning my thoughts in a room impervious to a single ray of light are, as I said before, my hours of quiet mastication. In truth, I experience terrible frustration at having to confront something so incredibly vast and impenetrable. Nonetheless, if I permit my feelings of frustration to combine with those of sweet ecstasy, I find I have the ingredients for creating a powerfully harmonious brew. Yes, add ecstasy, and I have the makings of "a stiff cocktail, rigorously stirred."

Very well, then. Because darkness is the source of my ruminations on mastication and infinity, I know there are many kinds of darkness residing inside me, each with its own particular set of meanings. For right now, though, I shall confine myself to jotting down my thoughts on darkness of the philosophical type. It's the type that, having imbibed existence to the full, returns to stasis even as it starts to move forward again.

In the middle of the night, when I am lost in thought behind the four gray walls of my room, I am often visited by a vision of a black horse. He comes to me out of the distant void, galloping across the dark winter night and soundlessly entering my quarters. Per usual, I am a stubborn insomniac. I have only to keep my eyes shut and my ears carefully attuned to the darkness to know he has arrived. He is standing by the edge of the school ground next door. There, at the far end of the ground is a fan-shaped athletic field, which is the source of much shrieking and shouting during the day. I can tell he has stopped in his tracks, and tossing his mane in the air, he has turned momentarily to look over his shoulder at the black, empty space from which he emerged. And then, without making a sound, he thrusts his head and front legs through the bars on the grillwork that covers the square-shaped window above my head. He passes through the wall of the house as if it was transparent and steps toward me. Right from the start I have been holding my breath, and there he is in the dark, inches from my face. Suddenly he turns into a toy horse that is small enough to sit in the palm of my hand—only to flit past me and disappear like a black phantom in a dream.

What difference did it make if my eyes happened to be open or closed at that moment or whether I moved or not, given the way the darkness thickly clung to me? What I knew for certain was this: a black horse came riding out of the distant void. As it entered the dark space directly in front of my eyes, it transformed itself into a toy model of the real thing. It even rested for a moment in the palm of my hand. I am certain of it because the composition of the entire scene is still fresh in my mind. There I was, lying on my side like a man half-dead. I was scarcely breathing as I watched the horse. How shall I put it?—I was like the man in Blake's illustration who is visited and then abandoned by celestial spirits. The black horse out of the darkness had come to me in a vision. He had flitted past my face and then disappeared before my very eyes. After he was gone, all that remained was the tension in the air. Even that lasted only a few seconds.

As I lay in bed in the middle of the night unable to sleep, my eyes more awake than ever, I decided to conduct "a clinical experiment" on myself. It was an experiment with the nature of feeling and consciousness, and I, its subject. To tell the truth, I hardly ever pay attention to my physical body. By and large I am content to let it lie on its side in the grasses of darkness without ever bothering to think about it. But now a totally unanticipated event had occurred between the little horse and me. It happened just as he grazed past me in the dark, and his face was within inches of my own.

It happened when he was a toy horse in the palm of my hand. In that instant he cast a sidelong glance at me as his eyes moved into my line of sight. His head was exactly five inches from mine. As the two of us came eye to eye, I felt something white-hot. It struck me like a beam of light. I had no idea what it was, but I felt certain the look of eternal and incurable despair on my face—brought on by the thought of not seeing the likes of him again—had coalesced and become one with the look of profound compassion he directed at me. Put together they generated light, or what I choose to call "the light born of boundless resignation and of boundless peace of mind." I instinctively reached out and tried to touch it, although I can't say why. And as I did, the tail of the horse, which had been waving back and forth in front of me, brushed against my hand in the darkness. All of a sudden, it lifted me into the air, and I found myself clinging to it for dear life. I was like a wind sock blowing horizontally in the wind. I rose higher and higher, and we headed slowly into the pitch black void. That was when I had another unbelievable, brilliant inspiration. "Never let go," I told myself. "Because this is the way to reach 'the end of darkness.'"

Was a dark nebula acting as my guiding star? By nature I am wont to immerse myself in endless darkness, via leaps of fantasy or manipulations of logic. I have been determined to reach the end of darkness, no matter what. It has been my *idée fixe* that, like the green longings of childhood, has been a part of my life for as long as I can remember. "Here's your chance at last." All I had to do was to get beyond the incredibly vast stretch of outer space that I refer to privately as "the obi of Venus." If only I could find a way across this great divide that separates us from the universe. If only I could access the eternal dark room on the other side of it. I would be able to see for the first time—and with unmatched precision— the true face of every misconception recorded in *The Universe's History of Misconceived Ideas*. I was convinced of it.

Let me evoke the following scene: there is a spirit dwelling at the bottom of the earth. He is a troll and a hunchback who hunkers in the dark, keeping his treasures hidden so no one can see them. He is constantly on guard. As he watches the surface of the earth from below, he speaks to no one and wears a bizarre look on his face. He can see all the explorers moving on the earth's crust, as well as every attempt they make to peer into the blackness under their feet. What the troll sees is a veritable kaleidoscope of misconceived ideas! As he watches them dig in the bright light of day, he sees both those who miss the mark by only the finest line, as well as those who dig in earnest but are hopelessly wide of the mark.

In fact, my analogy can be applied to a whole range of contrasts: the dark room where the mysterious observer lies versus the bright world outside, the pitch black future where the mysterious troll hides versus today here on earth, or the end of darkness toward which my black horse is striding versus this place here and now. These dichotomies are the reason why I'm determined to reach the other side of the universe and have a good look at the history of misconceived ideas.

. . . And now, at long last my black pony is about to carry me across the threshold to "the obi of Venus."

A ring rotates around Venus's big, black belt, glowing like a crown studded with countless, tiny lights. Even a distant glimpse of Venus's girdle is enough to dazzle one awake. The ring is like a giant wheel. As it slowly turns on its axis, the spokes shift inside from to one side to the other like a bundle of arrows, and the tips of the spokes are like sparks darting across the ground when a firecracker is set off on a summer night. Spin any object hard enough, and particles of light will fly from it as the object gains centrifugal force. Moreover, when it slows to a set speed, it sends out long, tapering tentacles of light that look like blue flowers. As the flowers on Venus's obi reached out to touch us, they looked like fireworks ignited in a dark place. They lifted their heads, exploded, and turned into many different shapes. At first I thought it was the speed with which the horse traveled that caused the blue arms to rush after us. . . .

The situation in space and in my room are virtually analogous, but it wasn't speed that had made it possible for the black horse to enter my room by passing through its gray walls. Lo and behold, it was his shape, which not only befitted a black space but also expanded exponentially to fill it. But how could I have known?—everything in the room was shrouded in darkness. Even as the horse expanded with incredible velocity, I had no way of telling. Only when we reached outer space, where the arms of light in the ring revolving around Venus's obi provided a clear-cut comparison, could I see how rapidly he was growing. And no, it wasn't on account of the blue arms that burst into color or how madly they rushed at us. I knew I was right because the ring around Venus's obi was suddenly gone from sight. By now what had glowed like a crown with countless little lights was no more than a glimmer that receded farther and farther into the distance.

I could hardly believe my eyes. In no time we had made our way across the incredibly broad, black band of Venus's obi! Given that outer space is so vast and we were moving through it every which way, I simply decided the obi of Venus was without limit and had no end. "That's how," I told myself, "its black band had given birth to the concept of 'eternity.'"

Only after the last glimmer of light from the entrance to the obi had receded from sight did I realize we'd arrived at the point in the universe that is total nothingness and complete cessation. "I know this is it. Surely this is the end of darkness." I felt I was right to the very bottom of my soul. And now that we were there at last, there was one more thing I needed to know. It was a question that I had readied in advance of getting here someday. "It's the darkness. Tell me about the dark," I asked out loud. "Is it 'the critique of light'? Or is it the 'last misconceived idea in life'?"

The reply that came from the darkness was strange and unsettling. It was an echo without an echo and an answer without an answer.

Because what I saw for the first time was I'd become as large as the universe itself. For no one can reach the end of the universe without expanding to match its size. Likewise, that explained why my silent sidekick of the black pony had also grown to such unparalleled dimensions. I was wrong in thinking of speed as the key element that permitted us to whiz past the crown of lights at the threshold to the obi of Venus. To the contrary. Only by drawing everything inside myself and immersing myself in it all was I able to expand without end. And that was what I continued to do.

But back to my question. Which is it? Am I the one inside the dark of the black horse? Or is it the other way around, and the black horse is inside me, casting sidelong glances at my face and watching each and every one of my thoughts from the interior of a darkness that is also himself? Just as one part of me invariably gives rise to another, I have made up my mind to stay here and stare at the darkness until I see it generate light. In the meantime, there is only one thing about which I am absolutely certain. The horse stands next to the troll hunkered in the dark, and he is staring straight at the space in front of himself. And there, in the space where despair and compassion coalesce, the look in his eyes is filled with a boundless peace of mind that arises from a boundless sense of resignation. For surely the one who has transported me far beyond the obi of Venus to the very end of darkness is he, and he alone—this black horse who plumbs the deep meaning of the dark.

HAYASHI FUMIKO

Hayashi Fumiko (1903–1951) was one of the most remarkable writers of her generation, and her creative work spanned both the prewar and postwar periods. The daughter of an itinerant peddler, Hayashi was raised in poverty, and her early works record her struggles to eke out a living in difficult and sometimes harrowing circumstances. These early experiences gave her a strong sense of compassion for the poor, and those in her later years, for those ordinary citizens who suffered because of the deprivations of war. Her characters, whatever the complexity of their personal circumstances, often show remarkable resilience and self-respect. Her story "Blindfold Phoenix" (Mekakushi hōō, 1950), composed late in her life, looks at the vagaries of old age as lived in occupied Japan.

BLINDFOLD PHOENIX (MEKAKUSHI HŌŌ)

Translated by Lane Dunlop

Turning his eyes clogged with mucus toward the garden, Kenkichi gazed at the flowers. In full bloom, they seemed to be laughing excitedly together. Nearly six hundred pots of "May azaleas" were in rows along the garden shelves.

Yesterday, a foreigner's car passing by on the road stopped outside the hedge. A soldier, his face flushed, got out and looked at the rows of potted plants for a while. Then he opened the gate and briskly entered the garden. Gesturing as if to say "they're beautiful," he walked among the shelves, studying each plant. When he came to one, nicknamed "Passing Shower," he stopped. The petals, white, were crinkled like fine crepe silk, with speckles of pale vermilion here and there. Now was the very best time to see it. All along the branches, the flowers had bloomed in profusion. The soldier, although very enthusiastic about it, could not make himself understood to Kenkichi. Taking out his wallet, he seemed to be telling Kenkichi to take as many bills from it as he pleased. In his incomprehensible language, he seemed to be praising the "Passing Shower" to the skies. Kenkichi, shaking his head, refused. This plant is not for sale, he wanted to say. I have put my whole into it, my very soul. Seeing the old man shake his head, the soldier, looking disappointed, went out into the street again. Following him out, Kenkichi gazed in the direction in which the car had gone. Most likely it was headed for Iya.

Looking at the "Passing Shower" in its pot, Kenkichi thought: Since the foreigner liked it so much, I should have given it to him. —He went into the garden. A mist was flowing through it. This morning, the Benkei was in flawless full bloom as if it were in an insanely good humor. Its large blossoms, with fleshy, vermilion-colored petals, did not have a single insect on them. Putting his hand to the flower, Kenkichi gazed at it entranced. The drops of evening dew on the petals were like the pleasurable awakening of the flower, he thought. Displaying all its charms, the Benkei seemed to lean against him coquettishly. Outside the hedge, two young men, peering in at the array of flowers, went by. These days, dealers in black market leaf tobacco could be seen even out here.

At the approach to this village of Hakuchi, about six kilometers from Awa-Ikeda, a yellow signboard with sideways writing in the Roman alphabet had been put up. Every now and then, magnificent vehicles of the Occupation forces rolled through the village. Although Kenkichi had heard that Japan had lost the war, the fact of defeat had no effect on his own life. The world did not seem to *him* as though it had utterly changed.

Then, taking the portable earthenware stove out to the front of the garden, he kindled a fire in it. The smoke, wavering in all directions, flowed out. The indescribably fresh fragrance of spring titillated Kenkichi's nostrils. He loved this kind of morning calm, undisturbed by people. Picking out the bits of burned charcoal with his bare fingers, he tossed them onto the flames and put on the teakettle. Gradually, beams of soft sunlight were filtering through the trees. The sky had paled to a bright, whitish blue.

For Kenkichi, who had wandered all over Japan for sixty years, no place felt so comfortable to him as this, his native village. He was now seventy-eight. Leading an idle existence, just like a dog or cat, he had put up this house with his own hands. In the single six-mat room, a morning glory had been trained to grow on the wall by his pillow. It was his pride and joy. But the room always smelled of the privy. Putting in an ornamental alcove on the west side of the room, he'd hung up an inexpensive lithograph of a Buddhist picture scroll there. The alcove posts were made of the bamboo for which this part of the country is known, but having been improperly seasoned, they were beginning to show vertical cracks. Instead of tatami, he had laid down thin straw mats. The bed was perpetually unmade. It had been seven years since he had built this little house for himself.

Throwing open the veranda rain shutters, he brought the small earthenware stove into the room. When he sat down on his bedding, a burst of glittering sunlight fell across the plant shelves in the garden. The flowers seemed alive with color. The purple-bordered Sukeroku, although already displaying the colors of its demise, in Kenkichi's eyes was still fresh and innocent looking. Perhaps because he'd skimped just a little this year on oil-cake fertilizer, the life span of the flowers seemed somehow briefer. Stepping down into the garden again, Kenkichi looked closely at the Sukeroku's petals. A little ladybug had crawled into the many-folded, translucently freckled heart of the flower. With a pair of handmade bamboo tweezers, Kenkichi picked out the ladybug and crushed it beneath his straw sandal.

"Old man. Good morning. . . ."

O-Yasu of the Fishing Hole, unusually gussied up, was passing by the garden on her way somewhere. "Won't you go with me?" Kenkichi, his eyes narrowed, looked at her. "Where are you going?" When she had come to the edge of the veranda and sat down, O-Yasu wrinkled up her nose at the pervasive smell of the privy. "Elder brother has been repatriated. I'm on my way to Awa-Ikeda to meet him." Although he'd heard of O-Yasu's "elder brother," Kenkichi had no memory of him.

After sixty years of wandering around the country, Kenkichi had come back to this village of Hakuchi in his seventy-first year. He had been eleven when he'd left the village. It had been a long vagabondage, more than half a century. He didn't know the villagers well, even by sight. Because he had returned with two cartloads of potted azaleas from Osaka, he'd been nicknamed "Old Man Flowerpot." —To enter the village, you had to cross over a long bridge. Hakuchi was situated on a triangular patch of land that led toward the Iyo Highway. The broad Yoshino River flowed past the approach to the village. The combination restaurant and inn called "The Fishing Hole" stood on the bank of the river. "The Fishing Hole" was the villagers' name for the place. By the blackboard fence of the entrance was a signboard inscribed with characters that said: "The Pavilion of Brocade Spray." The old man who was the inn's proprietor was the younger brother of the old man of the flowerpots. Kenkichi was the oldest of the three brothers, the offspring of the village carpenter. Yōjirō, the proprietor of "The Pavilion of Brocade Spray," had been born after Kenkichi had left home. Sixty years had passed without the brothers meeting each other. Coming back after those sixty years, Kenkichi had brought with him the masses of potted azaleas as a sort of homecoming gift. It was summer. The very next day, carefully putting out the straw-wrapped flowerpots one by one around the Pavilion's miniature lake and clearing a plot in front of the stonemason's, Kenkichi began to put up plant shelves. Being a carpenter's son, he had good instincts in such matters. In less than a week, the shelves for the azaleas were finished. When they'd taken the straw off the pots, the waitresses from the Pavilion brought them to the shelves. Among those waitresses, Kenkichi's eye had happened to fall on the diminutive O-Yasu. A plump woman, like a freshly pounded rice cake, O-Yasu wasn't much on looks. Most likely it was her gentle disposition that attracted Kenkichi. Taken with this girl who might have been his own granddaughter, whenever he had some errand Kenkichi always used O-Yasu. The teetery, lanky Kenkichi and the maidenly, petite O-Yasu made a strange pair. But whether or not anyone had guessed what was in Kenkichi's heart, even when O-Yasu and he went down to the dry, white riverbed for walks, it excited no gossip among the villagers. —One day in early September, the two had walked upstream along the riverbed. Reflecting the light thrown off by the white, sandy bed on either side, the river's deep current clearly mirrored in its surface the shadows of the mountainside. From the hushed, dusky thickets, a late-season nightingale sang out every now and then. As the riverbed narrowed, the scent of water hovered all the more densely in the air. The scene sank into an even deeper quietness. O-Yasu, who was wearing wooden clogs, seemed to be having a hard time making her way over the pebbles and rocks of the riverbed. As she walked, O-Yasu clung to and dangled from Kenkichi's arm. "How old are you?" Kenkichi abruptly asked. "Why, how old do I look?" O-Yasu looked up at the tall Kenkichi. Apparently Kenkichi's set of false teeth had been badly fitted, for each time he spoke they made a sound like crockery. "Eighteen?" O-Yasu suddenly giggled. "I'm twenty-one." At the year's end, O-Yasu had intended to go on leave from the Fishing Hole and marry Masa san of the barber shop. But this summer, she told Kenkichi, he had departed for the front. Everything had been left up in the air. As O-Yasu clutched his arm, Kenkichi gently felt around with his fingertips the area beneath her sash. O-Yasu, seemingly quite used to that sort of thing, was singing to herself in a low voice popular songs and the like. Sitting down on a big rock, Kenkichi lighted his long, slender Japanese pipe. Picking up some pebbles, O-Yasu tossed them at the quiet surface of the water. None of her tosses went very far. A hazy cloud of insects wavered annoyingly to and fro in front of their eyes. Kenkichi could remember nothing of the past, only what was in front of his eyes. O-Yasu, throwing pebbles like a child, was unbearably adorable. "Old man, don't you have a wife or children?" Although her teeth were yellow, O-Yasu's skin was white. She was beautiful. Kenkichi did not answer. He was afraid that if he told her about his six wives, he would lose her friendship. Among those six wives was one whose death Kenkichi had caused. It was forty years ago.

At the time, he'd been a contractor for railroad ties in Sendai. After becoming intimate with a geisha from Ishinomaki, he had lived a desperate life of passion with her for about two years. Finally the couple decided to throw themselves into the sea at Matsushima. The woman died. Kenkichi was rescued. The woman was twenty-four, with weak lungs. Now that forty years had passed, Kenkichi had no memory of her face. But even now, at night, Kenkichi sometimes felt a vague fear of the woman's ghost. It was not that he had seen any suspicious apparitions, but late at night he would suddenly awake, gasping for breath, as if his shoulders were being pressed down. And sometimes he would hear a rustle of silk as if someone were standing by his pillow. Although he had seen nothing with his own eyes, he was oppressed by what he'd heard and felt from such ghostly manifestations. Eventually he became unable to fall asleep unless a light was burning brightly in the room. After the geisha, he had had other wives, from all of whom he had separated forever. He had no news of any of them. Some of the wives he had hated. Some were disagreeable. Some whom he had parted from in tears. All of them, now, had faded out of Kenkichi's memory. —When he'd run away from home at eleven, crossing over from Muya to Awaji on the ferry, Kenkichi had gotten a job in a sesame oil extraction plant in Fukura. Midway across the tidal straits of Naruto, there had been a terrible storm. The blue waves, in choppy patterns that resembled nothing so much as a cabbage field, had churned up whirlpools. Having heard in his mother's bedtime stories about the great naval battle in this area between the rival Heike and Genji clans and how the princesses of the defeated Heike had leaped into this sea of Naruto in their scarlet formal divided skirts, Kenkichi had retained a vivid memory of the whirlpools of Naruto at the time he left home. His job at the sesame oil extraction plant, where he'd worked stark naked in the vats, hadn't lasted two years. Fleeing to the Tennozan District of Osaka, he fell into an existence of virtual poverty. But when he'd run away from Hakuchi, Kenkichi had brought along a carpenter's plane. Rummaging in each house's trash cans, he would collect old wooden sandals and skillfully fashion them into memorial tablets, selling them cheap to the altar utensil shops in the temple district. Back in those days, in front of the Umeda railway station, Japanese sweet shops, restaurants, and cheap hotels were lined up close together. Kenkichi had only the memory of a neighborhood of weather-darkened wooden houses and shops. Sometimes he would steal a pair of high-heeled sandals that had been washed and set out to dry and make them into memorial sculptures, complete with a lotus calyx. When he'd sold about four of them, he would go to one of the food shops in front of Umeda Station. There he would have sushi, which sent up fragrant steam from its basket. As he ate, he would marvel at there being such delicious food in this world. Strips of fried egg, shrimp, and oak mushrooms were served on top of the hot vinegared rice.

When he'd collected the sandals, Kenkichi would hollow out the holes where scraps of thong still clung, and assiduously whittle them down to flattish memorial tablets. If it were a high-heeled clog, the middle part would be thick and well suited to carving out a lotus calyx. Most of the clogs he found were made of pawlonia wood.

Either he would sleep in Umeda Station, or in hot weather, as the nightwatch boy of the billiards parlor, he would line up some chairs and sleep on them. When Kenkichi was a boy, the city of Osaka had considerable glamour. Alongside the station was a bathhouse that catered to the guests of the inns. Once, at the request of the stoker when he delivered some coal there, Kenkichi went out in the dog days of August to help weed the paddies of a farmer in Kawachi. After five days or so, though, he'd been fired. Although he was given all the rice he could eat, he never pulled out the weeds properly; instead, as if caressing them, he gently removed the stems from the mud. "You really know how to do your job, don't you?" he was sarcastically complimented by the exasperated farmer. Of course, it was no easy task weeding out the paddies in the sweltering August heat. Kenkichi had been glad to get back to Osaka. Through an employment agency, he got a job as a delivery boy with an ice company. Every day, he would push a large wagon around the streets making deliveries. At one house he was given an iced bean-jam bun as a reward. He thought the bean jam was especially delicious at that house.

Kenkichi changed jobs many times. Each time he changed his job, he also changed his name. When he was working at a rice-candy store in Tamatsukuri, he went by the name Umeda Tamatsukuri—that kind of thing. Kenkichi hadn't even bothered to go for his draft physical. When he was twenty-two or twenty-three, he'd gotten a job as a performer at a theater in Fukuchi-yama, which featured a combination of movie and vaudeville show popular at the time. Tall and awkward, he hadn't been much of a hit. But it was there that he had met the actress Umezu Keiko and had his first affair. Umezu Keiko had been two or three years past thirty.

O-Yasu, who had been singing popular songs and marches to herself, abruptly turned around toward Kenkichi. "Old man, I wonder if you could lend me some money . . ." Caught by surprise, Kenkichi said: "I might lend you some money, but what do you need it for?" "Elder brother is going to the front soon. So I'll need around fifty yen." Kenkichi wondered whether it had to do with her marriage to Masa san of the barber shop at the year's end.

In a low voice, as if he were joking, Kenkichi said: "If you would just once be nice to this old man, I might lend you the money." O-Yasu, giggling, replied, "Yes, I will."

Two or three days later, O-Yasu had neatly coaxed fifty yen out of Kenkichi. But she hadn't particularly enjoyed being "nice" to the old man.

Shortly afterward, Kenkichi started to build a house for himself next to the plant shelves. Apart from hiring a helper to carry the wood and tiles, he did everything himself, from the kneading of the mud for the walls to the splitting of the bamboo for the laths. It was all done by hand, right down to the shutters and translucent paper doors. He'd also installed opaque paper doors. The villagers who came to watch were startled by the morning glory that he trained to grow up the wall of the parlor, and by the privy hole that he made through the wall to the cesspool. Although one could say it was the laziness of an old man, it was surely the first time that a privy had been built into the parlor, the gossip ran. Even if it was all right in winter, in summer it would be a breeding place for flies and maggots. If nothing else, the stench alone would be unendurable, it was thought. In winter and summer, however, Kenkichi stuck twigs of cedar in among the tendrils of the morning glory. Every morning, he would change the fragrant-smelling sprigs, so that the cedar was always fresh and verdant among the blossoms.

O-Yasu could not tell how much money old man Kenkichi had. He didn't seem to have a post-office savings account, and she hadn't heard of any dealings he'd had with the bank. For about two years, O-Yasu had continued her peculiar relationship with Kenkichi. Little by little, though, the times had turned harsh. Losing her job as a waitress, O-Yasu had left the Fishing Hole and gone to find work in Osaka.

At the end of the year before the year the war ended, Yōjirō of the Fishing Hole died of a heart attack. His wife, Tomi, a longtime sufferer from rheumatism, let the place run down after his death. It was taken over by a tobacco factory in Aka-Ikeda as a hostelry for its employees. At the end of the war, the proprietress, Tomi, also died, and her adopted daughter Chiyo inherited the Fishing Hole. As a woman who had gone to Tokyo and worked for a while at a restaurant in Tsukiji, Chiyo had a ready eye for the opportunities of postwar economic conditions. Having a boat built so that customers could fish for freshwater trout, she remodeled the parlor in the latest Tokyo style. And over time, she hired two or three waitresses. —One day, the second year after the war, O-Yasu suddenly reappeared in the village of Hakuchi. Her color had darkened, and she had lost a lot of weight. One would not have recognized her as the O-Yasu of the past.

O-Yasu was surprised to learn that old man Kenkichi was still alive, hale and hearty. Remembering their intimacy of the past, she went to visit him in his solitary house.

Even though his eyes were dim and he had grown hard of hearing, Kenkichi seemed extremely lively. Black hairs were still mingled among the gray. In the middle of the room, a table had been placed with an inexpensive little terrestrial globe on it. His bed, as always, was unmade, and cedar twigs were still stuck in among the morning glories. From the ceiling, entirely blackened with soot, an electric cord dangled, white with accumulated dust. The plant shelves were even bigger than they'd been in the past. Also the hedge had been replaced by a board fence.

From the stonemason's out front, unchanged from the past, came the sound of his mallet as he chiseled his gravestones. When he saw O-Yasu, Kenkichi stood up and came over from the far side of the table. For a moment, he simply stared at her. Perhaps because his memories of O-Yasu, whom he hadn't seen in four years, had become tenuous, he didn't seem to recognize her at first. In a loud voice, O-Yasu announced: "It's Yasu. The Yasu who went away to Osaka. Old man, do you remember who I am?" She was shouting. Finally Kenkichi—did he remember her?—grinning ear from ear, put on a pot of tea for her. Even though it was a cold day in February, the smell of the privy hovered in the room. How can he stand living in such a place, O-Yasu thought. Even the tea he served her smelled of the privy.

Even when O-Yasu told him how her rented house had burned down in an air raid, Kenkichi merely said, "Oh, is that so?" He was the same old disinterested Kenkichi she'd known during the war. "How old are you now?" Kenkichi asked her. "Oh, I'm already an old woman. I'm twenty-six." Indeed, O-Yasu seemed to have aged. Since she had never been good-looking, even during her young heyday of fair-skinned plumpness, O-Yasu had looked older than her age. Now that she had grown lean and dark complected, she looked like a mature woman of thirty. She had made up her lips crimson red and was wearing Western-style clothes. But they were the artless attire of a country bus conductor.

Stepping up onto the step into the house, O-Yasu advanced toward the table.

On this side of it was something that looked like a half-carved memorial tablet. It was an impressive piece of work. O-Yasu remembered hearing stories from Kenkichi about how in the old days he had made memorial tablets out of wooden clogs and sold them.

Afterward, O-Yasu resumed her former relationship with Kenkichi. Now, however, rather than the full-fledged sexual intercourse of the past, Kenkichi simply stroked the soles of O-Yasu's feet. In her waitress days, O-Yasu had slept with many men. But perhaps because she had never been made love to in such a strange way, for the first time in her life she had the curious feeling that she was being deprived of her virginity. There even were times when Kenkichi licked the soles of O-Yasu's feet. Was this what was called an eccentric habit? Whatever, it was the most that Kenkichi was capable of.

Occasionally, O-Yasu would coax spending money out of Kenkichi. Now that she had returned to her native village of Hakuchi and had settled down in her old nest, perhaps because of the waters of the Yoshino River, O-Yasu's skin became fair and white again. Little by little, she put on weight. Kenkichi was very fond of O-Yasu. He even thought that when the summons from hell came, it would be good to leave all his shelves of azaleas to O-Yasu. But sometimes he would change his mind. When he went to bed with the lamp brightly burning and woke up in a fright in the middle of the night, O-Yasu would seem very dear to him, and he would think that he should leave her not only the azaleas but all the things he'd hidden away as well. But then when dawn came, he would completely forget about O-Yasu and not feel like leaving her anything. Recently, when Kenkichi lay awake in bed, he had often gotten up and worked on his own memorial tablet. —One night, this kind of thing happened. It was shortly after O-Yasu had come back from Osaka. The two having gotten together again, she would sneak over at bedtime, spend a little time with Kenkichi, and return to the Fishing Hole. Late on one of those nights, Kenkichi was awakened by knocking on the rain shutters. Thinking that O-Yasu had come back, he listened intently. The shutters were smoothly slid all the way open. There, by the translucent paper door that opened on to the veranda, someone seemed to be standing and peering inside. Kenkichi lay absolutely still. The paper door smoothly slid open. A figure in a red kimono—he could not tell whether it was a man or a woman—glided past the head of the bed. Maybe this is the messenger from hell, come to fetch me, Kenkichi thought.

The figure was looking backward, so that Kenkichi could not see its face. The skirts of its kimono trailed far behind it. There was a rustling sound—*pasa, pasa*—as of silk. Although Kenkichi was not in the least bit frightened, he shut his eyes tightly. The sounds the figure made as it moved about cut through the stagnant air of the room. There was one sound—*ku-u, ku-u*—as if it were clearing its throat. Something on the table fell over with a clatter. Soon the apparition began to walk around on top of Kenkichi's bedding. Although it was weightless, walking on the quilt with no pressure, the sensation of being walked on made Kenkichi go all numb. From outside the house—was it raining?—there was a streaming sound, *za-a, za-a,* like a torrential downpour. Kenkichi opened his eyes. It was pitch dark.

With the lantern out, it was as if he'd been dragged into the depths of a bottomless swamp. It was a weird, scary feeling. There was a sound as if someone were sewing a tatami mat. Kenkichi, burrowing into his bedcovers, prayed to the Buddha for forgiveness. His breath seemed about to stop. He had the feeling that any minute now the ghost would crawl into the bed alongside him. Kenkichi remembered the woman for whose death he had been responsible forty years ago. It was as if the spirit of the woman with whom he had failed to die in the sea off Matsushima Island had come for him. After the woman's death, Kenkichi hadn't felt the slightest affection for her memory. Until the moment of their attempted love-suicide, as if driven to it, he had thought of nothing but dying. But once he had survived, it was unpleasant even to think about the woman.

The next morning, Kenkichi could not for the life of him decide whether the apparition of the night before had been a ghost or a dream. Going over to the Fishing Hole, he tried asking the women there if it had rained last night, but they all agreed that it had not. There did not seem to have been any power failure. Saying it must have been an evil spirit after all, Kenkichi asked Chiyo to let O-Yasu come and stay with him for a few nights. Smiling, Chiyo summoned O-Yasu in a loud voice.

"Please go and take care of the old man. He says he feels lonely unless you're there."

Inasmuch as nobody envied her her relationship with Kenkichi, O-Yasu felt embarrassed about it. From that night, her bedcovers in her arms, she went to stay with Kenkichi. But her co-workers all laughed at her behind her back. Poor Yasu, they said, she has to keep Old Man Piss Pot company.

But even O-Yasu could stick it out at Kenkichi's place for only four or five nights. Kenkichi had taken to intoning the *nenbutsu* in bed, invariably in the middle of the night. Abruptly getting out of bed, stark naked, he would grope his way over to the table and sit down in front of it. His eyes heavy lidded with sleep, he would mutter some syllables of the prayer formula. The old man's nakedness reminded O-Yasu of a skeleton. The thin, dried-out, yellowish brown skin was no more than a bag for his bones. Even more pathetic, the sad old testicles that hung down between his thighs like a dirty scrap of cloth seemed comical to O-Yasu. She gazed vaguely at the naked old man seated in the formal prayer posture. There even were wrinkles on his stomach, on his chest. His shoulders seemed hung up like a bone rack from which the rest of the body was suspended. Folded under him, his legs, nothing but skin and bones, left an opening between the emaciated thighs. Wouldn't he catch his death of cold, O-Yasu wondered.

Slowly getting to his feet, Kenkichi took down the sacred picture from the ornamental alcove and stroked the wall. Getting out of bed, O-Yasu held him in her arms as she gathered his nightclothes around him. —Four or five days later, making it her excuse that the room reeked of the privy, O-Yasu refused to go any more to Kenkichi's.

She didn't tell anyone about his getting up out of bed stark naked in the middle of the night to pray. In her heart of hearts, she thought that the old man was not long for this world. That was the kind of feeling she had about him.

Time passed. It was May.

Word came from his relatives in Iya that Masa san of the barber shop had been repatriated from Siberia. Today was the day that he was due to arrive in Awa-Ikeda. Given leave from the proprietress Chiyo, O-Yasu had dolled herself up and was on her way to welcome him.

Kenkichi had a broad smile on his face. And yet . . . O-Yasu, having merrily primped herself like this, did not give him a good feeling. If she were to marry the repatriated Masa san, his own relationship with O-Yasu would be over. Already there were not even memories to console him.

"You're certainly made up to kill. . . ."

"Yes. Today's the day of Masa san's homecoming. . . ."

"Are you happy about it?"

"Happy? Of course I'm happy. It's a matter of human feeling."

Not saying anything, Kenkichi had gone out to the rows of plant shelves and was examining the hearts of the flowers. "Old man," O-Yasu, as if dazzled, called out. "What?" "Come over here." There was a flirtatious note in her loud summons. Sulkily, Kenkichi came back to the veranda. O-Yasu thought for a moment, and then, putting her lips to Kenkichi's ear, said: "Masa san got dyed red, so I don't know whether I'm marrying him or not." Kenkichi did not understand what O-Yasu meant by "got dyed red." On his terrestrial globe, the territory of Russia was a rose pink color. He couldn't tell what Masa san had been up to getting himself dyed red. Kenkichi had never even met Masa san. "He's come back with radical ideas, so they say it'll be better if we just leave things as they are for the time being. Even so, Masa san is a good person. I like him. They say he was in the southern part of Siberia, in a place with some tongue-twisting name, like Krasnobodusk. . . . I'm told he had a photograph of me with him. That made me want to go and welcome him. Until I see him, I won't know whether or not we're getting married. I'm already a disreputable old maid, so it doesn't matter who I marry. But if Masa san says he doesn't mind, I'm thinking I might marry him. . . ." Puffing on his Japanese pipe, its tiny bowl stuffed with shredded tobacco, Kenkichi thought about Masa san's "radical ideas." He didn't understand what was meant by the term, but he supposed it might be something like the hot blood of youth. Whatever it was, it was all right. Just like a river, the hot blood of life flowed rapidly, a never-failing stream. That vigor would eventually wear away, weather away into an aged, smelly creature like himself. Yet even so, in the faraway past, even I had hot blood in my veins, Kenkichi thought. I haven't passed through this world without doing anything. Back in the old days, when he was a public works contractor and the money was coming in like nobody's business, his student houseboy had often recited Chinese poems for Kenkichi. "The sagacious horse, returning home, now gallops, now flies. . . ." Man's life passed like the shadow of a bird. Even the hot blood of youth soon cooled into age. Under the watchful eyes of his wife and children, a man became a money-grubbing captive in the prison of domesticity. Finally, his clear purposes fallen into confusion, he died. . . . That was the story of life. No doubt "radical ideas" and hot blood were different somehow, but it was no great matter. Kenkichi just couldn't accept the way that O-Yasu had gotten herself all gussied up. Didn't she feel any nostalgia for the truly human relationship they had developed, the indescribably refined intimacy and absence of constraint? With an old person's willfulness, Kenkichi grew angry at O-Yasu.

For her part, O-Yasu remembered that night when she had seen the old man naked, skinny, a mere skeleton. She'd been shocked by the dirty thing between his thighs.

O-Yasu took pleasure in imagining what kind of person the as-yet-unseen Masa had become. Just the thought that he was a man who had kept her photograph under the distant skies of Siberia made her heart dance. If she remembered correctly, this year Masa san would be twenty-eight. Although he had a solid, squarely built physique, Masa san's fingers were soft and cold.

"Old man, I'm going now. I'll be back." Kenkichi pinched the brim of his ancient straw hat. O-Yasu wanted unbearably to be on her way. Life is short, but there are many things in the heart, a proverb said. Kenkichi could not bring himself to give up O-Yasu. Had even taking care of the azaleas become a tedious chore? From some time back, a hornet had been hovering about the flower shelves with its peculiar high-pitched drone. If the stamens and pistils were damaged, the flower would soon wither away. Going around to the back of the house, Kenkichi brought out his bamboo broom. Swishing it, he chased away the hornet dancing over the flowers. The hornet, a burnished golden color, vanished into the bright sky. When Kenkichi stared up at the sky, from out of nowhere, like a flung pebble, another hornet dive-bombed the flowers, leveling off just above them. Brandishing the broom, Kenkichi drove the hornet away with several brisk passes. But this time, some pure white flowers went flying, too. With a violent clatter, one of the unglazed earthenware pots toppled from the shelf and smashed into pieces on the ground. It was a flower that had had two or three days of life left. Of the variety of azalea called "Double Phoenix," a large flower like a lily, it bloomed like a flowering of sea spray. Getting down on his hands and knees, Kenkichi gathered up the scattered flower petals. The hornet continued to circle slowly above the flower shelf. Somewhere a turtledove was singing. Clutching the flower petals, Kenkichi stayed there on the ground, without getting up.

HIRABAYASHI TAIKO

Hirabayashi Taiko (1905–1972) began her writing career in 1926 as a member of the anarchist movement. Then, in 1937 and 1938 she was imprisoned because of her associations with the Communist Party (although she was never a member herself), and she contracted tuberculosis in jail. With the end of the war and an improvement in her health, Hirabayashi was able to begin writing again. Her later works are generally autobiographical and often critical of society and government. In 1946 the adoption by Hirabayashi and her husband of his younger brother's daughter provided the background to "Demon Goddess" (Kishimojin, 1946), the work translated here.

The title of the story is based on the legend of Kishimojin (Kishibojin), an ogress who devoured children. The Buddha tried to reason with Kishimojin, pointing out that as the mother of ten thousand children herself, she should understand the love of a parent for a child. When she still did not stop, the Buddha kidnapped her youngest and favorite child and hid him in his begging bowl. Finally Kishimojin repented her ways, becoming the deity of safe delivery and the guardian of children.

DEMON GODDESS (KISHIMOJIN)

Translated by Rebecca Copeland

"Just as wide as it is short! What curious things children wear." Keiko scrutinized the garment for the first time as she undressed Yoshiko. That morning when changing the child out of her nightgown, she had mistakenly put the little dress on backward, letting the girl out to play like that.

"You don't mean to tell me that there's a pocket on the back of that dress!" The wife next door had sounded the alarm from where she knelt gathering greens for the morning's soup.

"Oh dear! Ha, ha, ha!" Keiko had no choice but to laugh. Yet she felt a fissure had opened in her heart, allowing a glimpse into her feelings. She was more than a little embarrassed.

Unforeseen circumstances had brought Yoshiko into her life. Although Keiko had accepted the little girl with open arms, the suddenness of the child's arrival had left her little time to prepare. She lacked a mother's basic knowledge about children's clothing, and she had no ideas about child rearing. In fact, it would hardly be an exaggeration to say that Keiko was like a blank sheet of paper as yet unmarked by maternal love. Each new movement that this small creature made, each new expression, came to her as a fresh discovery. A spark of wonder would ignite in her heart—just a brief flash really, the kind made by striking flints, but a spark nonetheless—and this thrilled Keiko.

Keiko took Yoshiko's dress by the hem and pulled it over the little girl's head. Before she picked up the warm washcloth to scrub the child from head to toe, she absentmindedly squeezed the girl's arms and patted her thighs. The soft, supple skin on Yoshiko's arms and legs reminded Keiko of the flesh of calves and lambs. She recalled the delicate, almost insubstantial flavor of their meat. Keiko had been raised with animals; they had been part of her life ever since she could remember. Now, whenever she tried to understand children, she found it most expedient to think of them in terms of animal young.

Yoshiko squirmed and squealed so happily under Keiko's touch that she very nearly wet herself. Finally, when she could stand the tickling no longer, she shouted, "I'm cold!"

"Oh? Well then, let's get started."

Keiko unfolded the warm cloth, and holding the girl's fruitlike face in one hand, began to wash her with the other. The child's sparkling eyes were more lustrous than the finest, most highly polished mirror. They were pretty, Keiko reasoned, because being still brand-new, they had not reflected much of humanity. Her tiny nipples were like summer grapes. Keiko imagined how the glands and nerves, as slender as silk threads, were sleeping inside, ripe with the promise of bloom. Those perky little buds would not alter their shape but swell to maturity like pumpkins on the vine.

The child's belly button was dewy and soft and seemed to suggest that the point of connection between mother and child had not yet withered and dried. It was not dead but was growing still with a life of its own, separate from the girl's body. Keiko was compelled to recall her own raisin of a belly button. She felt that it spoke vividly of the distance now between herself and her own mother.

When she had finished washing Yoshiko, she pulled the dress back over her head. Yoshiko hopped off toward the living room on one foot. Her pink cheeks glistened in the sunlight that filled the blue sky and poured in through the window.

From the very first, Keiko had been aware that the eyes she focused on Yoshiko were almost too unclouded. Most mothers are myopic when it comes to their own children; they are as nearsighted as a barnyard hen. Maternal instinct spews forth a fog that blurs everything in sight. Keiko could not help but laugh at this myopia, yet at the same time she yearned to make it hers. Suppose a child were carelessly to relieve himself on the floor, right there by the dinner table. All the adults would scowl in disgust, but the child's mother would no doubt blurt out proudly, "My, what a healthy stool! And such good color!" Keiko found the prospect of ever becoming such a mother terrifying . . . but also appealing. Even so, it seemed her vision was just too powerful, too clear to permit her to be pulled out to that foggy sea.

How does love grow? The only point of reference Keiko had was the love she shared with her husband, even though the relationship between a man and a woman could hardly be compared with that between a mother and child. She and her husband, Yoshizo, had come together twenty years ago for no particular reason and without so much as the slightest pressure. Like a lock and key they had fit smoothly together, a single unit, and thus had plunged into the sea of love, a sea far deeper than any mere ocean.

The more sophisticated a lock's inner mechanisms are, the easier it is to close. So it was with Keiko and Yoshizo. An impartial observer would no doubt claim that a variety of circumstances had led them to each other. But it would be difficult to determine who was first attracted to whom, who pushed and who pulled.

The participants themselves could recall only a sudden bolt of lightning. When they had come to their senses, they already were deep at sea.

There had been no lightning between Keiko and Yoshiko. Even so, whenever she stroked the little girl's short silky hair, Keiko would tell herself that this was no cause for concern. She knew from experience that like all things in life, human relationships take form through one of two processes: the slow process, like the path up a gently sloping hill, and the sudden process, a sharp spurt of water. She wondered whether the love she shared with Yoshiko wasn't taking the slow path up the gentle slope. Her love for Yoshiko and her love for her husband were of different colors, different shapes. And that was as it should be, Keiko felt.

To tell the truth, when she was young, Keiko had ventured down the rainbow paths her dreams had unfurled. She had struck out bravely over fields and mountains where no one else had gone, living the fullest breadth of a woman's life.

Once, she had fallen ill. Her lover had been thrown in jail, and she herself had ended up in a home for the indigent. She remembered laying her head on the hard pillow and weeping hot tears. Then again there had been a time when, with the piety of a magician seeking to gain all by casting all away, she had taken advantage of the nihilism sweeping the country with its darkness and despair, handling the men dealt to her by fate as if they were so many cards. Emboldened by her pose, she had pushed open the doors of a great bank, where even men had faltered, and had demanded money that by rights was not hers to have. At that point she felt the same thirst for life that Sophia Perovskaya must have felt.[1] She, a simple Oriental woman, had accomplished without a moment's fear what the great Western philosopher had longed for when he said: "I want to experience ten thousand lifetimes in the course of one."[2]

But Keiko was now nearing forty and, with it, the crest of life. This was not to suggest that the spring of womanhood that had once gushed within her was soon to run dry. Yet Keiko could hear a fervent voice telling her: "You have lived the breadth of a woman's life, now plumb its depths with similar passion." It was just at this point, just as Keiko stood at the crossroads of indecision, that Yoshiko had entered her life, filling the void.

When she was younger, insensitive people would tell her that she should adopt a child from some family overburdened with offspring. Sensing an ulterior motive at work, she would turn to the person and say, "Really? Well, I don't know. My house is so small, where do you suppose I could keep it? Do you think I could keep it out in the yard?"

But Keiko had left that perverse, affected nature of hers far behind. Now,

----

1. Sophia Perovskaya (1853–1881) was a Russian revolutionary executed for her involvement in a plot against Czar Alexander II.

2. Quoted from Goethe's *Faust*.

like an oyster that diligently transforms into a pearl whatever foreign object has been thrust into its shell, Keiko was determined to devote herself to Yoshiko. And yet a foreign object is, after all, a foreign object.

It had been Keiko's idea to place a little futon between hers and her husband's where Yoshiko could sleep. When she first told Yoshizo of her plan, his face lit up like a common fishmonger's, just as Keiko knew it would, and he began to pontificate on sleeping "snug as bugs in a rug." Keiko had known what to expect, but even so she could not help but turn away, her face puckered with distaste. These all were new experiences for her, and she responded to them much as if she were a blank sheet of paper suddenly splashed with ink. She had wanted to channel her emotions into a mental image of the three of them sleeping together, before Yoshizo had launched into his hackneyed exposition of "bugs in rugs!" How should she judge the sensibility of the person who had first coined this phrase? Was the phrase meant to be so ridiculously domestic? Or was it the exact description of a sweetly beguiling scene? Keiko thought about it briefly and then came up with a version that best answered her needs.

The tiny household she shared with her husband was not really any different from those of other families in the surrounding tenements. And yet when she spread their futons out side by side to sleep "snug as bugs," just as the saying had it, Keiko felt strangely awkward, as if embarrassed by her actions. And it wasn't the child sandwiched between them who seemed out of place. It was her husband there on the other side. She felt as if she were seeing him for the first time.

Having been in nonstop motion all day long, the child's arms and legs now glowed with warmth like little pocket heaters. They refused to remain covered. No sooner did Keiko tuck the blankets around the girl than Yoshiko would wiggle and squirm, and there she'd be sprawled across the tatami again, imprinting the weave of the matting on her forehead.

Children, Keiko had recently discovered, became vastly heavier after they were asleep—all the world like magical creatures in a fairy tale. The sleeping Yoshiko was so limp she dangled heavily from Keiko's arms as if half her body had turned to liquid.

In the pitch black of night, Keiko became aware of her husband's arm lying near hers, sensing his warmth in the languid sensuality of her half-sleep state. Having the child between them, like a neutral zone in a battlefield, was a new experience for them both. Even before going to bed, they had been aware of the novelty. Keiko imagined groggily that the mood still had them it its grip. Now that they had donned the guise of "Mother" and "Father," they would have to reconsider their identities as husband and wife. But this was something that all couples, from all walks of life, must surely face when they first become parents.

Keiko moved her own arm toward the thick, heavy arm she was so used to grasping. Yet what met her touch was soft and velvety. Yoshiko! Keiko was shocked by her mistake.

It wasn't just the fact that she had been mistaken. On other occasions, when her instinctive response might prove correct, would she still be able to control her sensuality, distinguishing appropriately between Yoshiko and her husband? For years her husband had been the only physical presence in her life. Apparently, long habit had rendered her incapable of responding to any physical contact except as an overture from him. Perhaps it was selfishness on her part; perhaps it was willfulness; perhaps it was even a deformity in her nature—but from the very beginning, Keiko's heart had come equipped with room for only one. There was little she could do to alter that fact now.

"Shall it be my husband or the child? I've space for only one." This was all she could think, and it made her sad.

Today, like all the other days, Keiko took the warm water she had heated in the large kettle and began to wash Yoshiko. Various emotions swept over her in various shades of intensity. She was now storing up knowledge of Yoshiko in her heart, little by little, a fact that produced an ecstasy in Keiko that far surpassed the ecstasy of love.

She had had barely a fortnight in which to gather the feelings and facts that other mothers could acquire at a leisurely pace, from the day they first learned of their pregnancy until their children reached Yoshiko's age. From a distance Keiko watched herself trying greedily to catch up.

"Mommy!"

Yoshiko would call out to Keiko like that from time to time for no apparent reason. It was as though she had suddenly remembered something. Each time Keiko would be mildly alarmed, fearing her unpreparedness had been found out. But that voice!

The pure timbre of the child's voice would have put the finest songbird to shame.

"Um, yes? What is it?"

Keiko's own voice seemed rusty in comparison and somehow clumsy. She was amused that she snapped to attention whenever Yoshiko called, like a plebe at roll call. But she couldn't help herself.

Whenever she heard the child call out to her, Keiko's answer would be nothing more than an echo of the girl's voice. Once Yoshiko heard her mother's response, she would peer up at Keiko with bright eyes, trying to confirm what she had heard. Her gaze flew with the sharpness of a hornet, leaving Keiko stunned. Keiko would try to return the child's gaze, but the eyes looking down and those looking up never quite connected. The realization left Keiko full of shame.

Keiko suddenly recalled how the novelist Arishima Takeo had taken the age-old proverb "You understand the debt to your parents only when you become one" and had altered it to "You understand your debt to your child only when you have one." The former, as implausible as it was, had never applied to Keiko, and the other adage did not agree with her experience either. However carefully Keiko thought about it, she could believe only that children served the purpose of intermediaries and little else: They take you by the hand and lead you to "something"—a something for which Keiko felt the deepest reverence. That was why she felt such awe as well as shame in the presence of children.

And what was this "something" to which a child will lead you? Keiko could not put her finger on it exactly; it was too vague a concept. For want of a better word, she referred to it as a third entity, something beyond parent and child. All she could say was that it had caused her breasts, woman that she was, to swell like rising bread and had opened a window onto a new and bracing wisdom, a wisdom that she had never known existed.

Keiko began to rub the warm washcloth over Yoshiko's body, as she always did, working her way gradually to the space between the little girl's plump thighs. Her pretty little private parts reminded Keiko of a half-ripe peach cleft in two by a perfect line. Lately Keiko had grown determined to increase her understanding of the child's body, believing that it was her right, even her duty, as a novice mother. But even she doubted that her rights permitted her to go so far as to illuminate this particular feature of the child's anatomy. And yet every time she ran the washcloth along the little girl's legs, she was enthralled by the way the tiny peach would split open at the cleft with each movement the girl made. The red flesh inside, unfurled like a bolt of silk, formed a half-opened mouth. Here, Keiko realized, was the essence of that which was "woman," an essence she longed to explore. Having no reason to be reserved with this slip of a girl, she could explore to her heart's content.

For a woman of Keiko's age still not to know the basic facts about female physiology would seem impossible. But it was true. Here she was—while regarding it a disgrace to use a word without knowing the proper way to write it, she still had no idea where her own urine came from, despite the thousands of times she had urinated in her lifetime. It was nothing short of ridiculous. And yet it was society's odd notion of common sense that kept this kind of knowledge from women, even from women like Keiko.

"Yoshiko dear, it's dirty here. We'll have to wash you here today, OK?"

Keiko pressed the washcloth against the girl's thighs, trying to force a little leeway between her legs.

"No! It tickles!" Yoshiko clamped her legs together with surprising strength.

"Now stop misbehaving! I'm going to wash here today."

"No," Yoshiko would not be persuaded, and with her legs held tightly together, she refused to budge. Her resistance was so intractable that Keiko felt it must be born of some innate female instinct for self-protection. It was, in fact, awe inspiring. Caught completely off guard, Keiko had been laid bare before the fierceness of the girl's denial. Backing off now with an idiotic look on her face, she began to chuckle stupidly, peering into Yoshiko's eyes.

"Well then, Yoshiko dear, I'll give you something nice . . . something that starts with 'P.'"

Keiko was disgusted with herself for stooping to such a trick. She was quickly losing what little pride she had left.

"Please open up . . . just a little, OK? Please, Yoshiko."

"No! You're stupid!"

And with this exchange they both stripped away the thin layer of emotion they had stored up between them—feelings of parent for child and child for parent. They emerged to confront each other with the naked faces of strangers.

"I'm going to wash you here. Mommy has to!"

With a perverse strength, Keiko thrust her hands between Yoskiko's legs and roughly pried them apart just as if they were chopsticks. Yoshiko reeled and then burst into tears as she tumbled to the wooden floor. Keiko gazed down at the wet floorboards, her eyes opened wide as if she had just awoken.

Yoshiko's violent sobs lashed the ears of this idiot mother like an icy wind. Keiko did not try to comfort the girl but dejectedly turned her gaze inward.

"For my own self-fulfillment . . . for my fulfillment as a woman . . . is it necessary to sacrifice this innocent child? How much more blood must be spilled?"

According to an old proverb, a woman born in the Year of the Fiery Horse will devour her husband. Even though she was not born in the Year of the Fiery Horse, women like Keiko possess an animal's will to live. Tethered as they are, they eat and eat whatever is in their reach—devouring poisonous grasses along with the sweet—and thus they strain to grow. But more prevalent still are those who, so afraid they'll eat all there is to eat until not a blade of grass remains, never even test the limits of their ropes.

Keiko was suddenly reminded of the child-eating goddess Kishimojin, and realizing that she, too, should declare herself by that name, she was beset by loneliness.

HOTTA YOSHIE

In bad health as a young man during the war, Hotta Yoshie (1918–1998) was never conscripted but worked in China after 1945 for several years, an experience that brought his strong political consciousness to bear on his numerous writings. In 1951 he won the Akutagawa Prize for his novel *Solitude in the Square* (*Hiroba no kodoku*), which deals with the reactions of intellectuals from various countries to the Korean War. Much of Hotta's fiction centers on the loneliness and solitude of postwar life. His *Shadow Pieces* (*Kage no bubun*, 1952) juxtaposes three interlocking visions of life in the difficult aftermath of the war, the first of which, "The Old Man" (Rōjin), is included here.

THE OLD MAN (RŌJIN)

Translated by P. G. O'Neill

It was already a year since a fresh war had begun in Korea, but the neighborhood where the old man lived showed no sign that even the previous war had come to an end. In the first place, there were his clothes: an old patched army jacket and a pair of American G.I. trousers which he had obtained from a prostitute living at the same place. The background against which the old man searched for cigarette ends with the tottering step of a battered clockwork doll was the city of Tokyo; but he would hardly have looked out of place if he had been set down instead in a dense forest in Upper Burma where the luxuriant growth of vegetation had suddenly sucked in the smell of death. He carried a haversack slung across from each shoulder. One, which contained prepared food as seldom as the haversacks of those miserable soldiers in Burma, had in it only an old tin can he used as a cup, a box of matches and a tattered towel he had picked up somewhere, chopsticks, a newspaper to wrap any special find such as a bit of discarded food that looked as if it might keep, and a pencil stolen from a cycle-racing tipster at the same lodging-house. At this welfare hostel, stealing was as unremarkable as it was in the army. The place where the old man slept was in a row of perhaps more than a hundred so-called welfare hostels, but such a description could lead to their being confused with establishments in countries with thorough-going social security systems. To be exact, his had the long name of "The Heavenly Curtain Hotel's House of Hope, The Fortieth Welfare Hostel in trust to, and under the management of, the Greater Tokyo Federation of Non-luxury Hotel Associations," but in case this leads anyone to take it yet again for one of the fine establishments just mentioned, it should be pointed out that the Heavenly Curtain Hotel's House of Hope was the sort of place that really did rely on curtains to shut out the heavens. That is to say, it was like a rectangular box with sides made from boards only a fraction the thickness of those formerly used for barracks, from the top of which hastily tarred army tenting looked skyward. One could think of it as a big apple box dragged up from a drain where it had lain until sodden. This "house" had only one room, and virtually all those who lodged there, from the old man down, had somewhere on them khaki clothing or equipment from the last war. The gate pillars—by which is meant two slender poles supporting a board with the long-winded name of the place—were topped by two rusty and crumbling steel helmets as if they marked the graves of unknown war dead. Six years after the end of the war the upper levels of society had led the way in gradually casting off wartime clothing. Already, along such streets as the Ginza, the only people with anything military about them were the soldiers and police of the Occupation, and beggars, scavengers and the like. It was as if all signs of the previous war had been ironed away until the solitary crumpled spot that remained was the welfare hostel of the Heavenly Curtain Hotel. Standing side by side with all the other buildings in the street, the misshapen rectangle of this wooden lodging-house sheltered men and women with dull, deeply puffy faces. The old man thought the whole quarter probably held about ten thousand people. All who came there were under some great pressure. People whose lifelong work had been torn from them by such great pressure gathered there from all parts of the country. More and more of them seem to be coming again, thought the old man.

Standing between the helmeted gateposts, he looked up at the sky. It would be about seven o'clock in the morning. It was already terribly hot. As the drops of light snatched up the moisture, the boarding began to buckle, and from time to time, even the metal sheeting creaked free from its nails. The open drain had completely dried up; but the smell from it remained unchanged, no matter what. With it came, as ever, the stink of rotting leather and fish-based vitamin foods to fill the air all around.

The old man suddenly tried to think what he had had to eat the night before but, as always, his memory was far from clear. With shoulders bent and head down, he began to walk. For thirteen yen he bought a pound of steamed potatoes from the cheerful woman who did them as a sideline to a book-lending business, and walked on chewing them with his front teeth into pieces small enough to be washed down with drinks of water. The old man might resign himself to the loss of almost all his back teeth, but one of the things which troubled him was what he would do if his front teeth fell out too. If he were now to lose his front teeth as well, he would no longer be able to carry on his trade. That is, he would no longer be able to sell his rubber brushes.

Even though the war had been left behind in his particular quarter of Asakusa, there was certainly no reason for even this old man to have to eat steamed potatoes all day at a time of such great recovery from the devastation of war and such abundance that it was already possible to start a new war. The twenty-five yen which a set meal would have cost him was there in his haversack. But today he had something special in mind, and this required him to take care of all the one hundred and twelve yen which the bag contained.

On the afternoon of the previous day, the old man had been chewing bread as he sheltered from the heat beneath some shady trees in the Rokku district of Asakusa that had somehow escaped the fires. He had been reading a newspaper that a young man had thrown away. The name or date of the paper did not matter to him. For so long now, since days that had all but faded from his memory, a newspaper had been something with war on the first page, money-making on the second, death on the third, and gardening and women's affairs on the fourth. Medically speaking, he might be suffering from amnesic senility or some such thing, thought the old man, but what good would it do him even if he did know the exact name of his illness? He had also decided for himself that he was probably about sixty-five years old, but it was not likely to matter very much even if he was not.

It would certainly be wrong, however, to assume from this that the old man had lost interest in things generally. In all probability, he read newspapers more avidly than anyone else in the hostel. His small steel-rimmed glasses were seldom anything but bright. In the newspapers the old man was searching for himself, for his past. If he saw an article about a fire in Hachiōji, off he would go all the way to Hachiōji. If it said that there had been a raid on a gang running an illicit still in Fukagawa, he would go to Fukagawa. If there was a murder in Kawasaki, he would set off for Kawasaki. The old man was searching for himself and, above all, for his birthplace. If he found it, he intended to leave the stinking welfare hostel and settle in his native town or village; and after setting up a house of his own, to make a living and then to die there.

Now in the newspaper he had read the previous day was an article telling how, at the bathing beach of the town of Y in the Shōnan region, two young women had killed themselves in a love suicide. Reading it made him suddenly feel, in his usual way, that perhaps he had been born in a seaside town. In any case, it had been a long time since he had seen the blue of the sea, and his trade invariably prospered in towns where there had been some such misfortune as a love suicide, murder, or fire. His trade, as mentioned before, consisted of making a speech and then selling rubber brushes, but in places that were still heavily veiled in the shadow of death, his speeches brought him enough to pay for his bed and a meal even if he sold no brushes at all. It was certainly very pleasant to get money just for making a speech. When he did so, he felt like a priest or a member of the Diet. Then he would wonder whether he had not perhaps been a politician. The old man was well aware that the people in the welfare hostel and everyone else treated him as if he were mad; and it did not upset him in the least. If he were allowed a touch of madness which brought him money just to make a speech, was it not more profitable to be mad? He sometimes thought so.

The old man's plan for this particular day was to go to the beach in the town of Y where the love suicides had taken place. If he took a tram direct from the stop in the quarter where his lodgings were, it would take him as far as Tokyo Station in about an hour. But he had never yet boarded at the local stop, for he liked to walk. He liked to wander leisurely along, particularly when he first left the lodging-house; he would think then about who and what he had been, and who and what he was. Even though his memory was imperfect, it was not as if his mind was completely shut off by a curtain of unbroken whiteness. The curtain had any number of holes through which he could sometimes peep into dimly lit places that seemed to belong to his past. Only the previous day he had come to a sudden stop when, having finished with the newspaper, he had stood up and, keeping to the shade of the trees, had come out in front of the Rokku fairground with its roundabouts. Although not a child was riding on them, the wooden horses were going round and round to the tune of a forty- or fifty-year-old song called "The Beauty of Nature," and then to the music of a children's song, "The Sunset Glow." As he gazed at them blankly, another small hole suddenly appeared in the white curtain of his mind, and through it two fragments came back to him: "18th April" and "the bombing." It was unusual for a number to emerge, but he was at a loss to know how the two things linked up together or what their connection was with the roundabout and the old songs. He still had other things which seemed to be bits of his memory, but none of them tied up with any of the others. The small holes in the curtain remained quite separate. Into them went parallel rays of dark light to fall on the past for which the old man was searching, and from them, at times, came sounds like mad laughter.

Nothing had any connection with anything else, but the old man felt no pain when this fact confronted him. Were not wars almost the only things that followed on one after the other? The outside world in general was running on smoothly and, thanks to this, his own inner inconsequences did not trouble him at all. The old man felt that, strangely enough, life had probably become a little easier since war began in Korea a year ago this summer. It seemed, too, that more people now listened to his speeches. When he left the welfare hostel in the mornings, therefore, the old man took great pains over his dress. This involved no more than putting on the things he needed to appear in public, but what required most care was his nose. The old man's nose had no side to the right nostril. On that side there was no flesh covering the bone. His nostrils were thus uneven, the one with the other. The forty-year-old prostitute who always slept on the mat next to the old man's at the welfare hostel had prattled on about it sometimes, talking knowingly of how she was sure it must have been syphilis that had made his nose like that, and of how she had heard that they could cure anything by bringing on a high fever and supposed it was that that had made him funny in the head, when the high fever damaged his mind so that he could not remember anything. At night his nose sometimes itched unbearably when a white powder was breathed out around his imperfect nostril; and it was this alone, his very own nose, which caused him endless trouble. That morning, for example, he had carefully wiped away the white powder, cut off with a penknife a prong from one of his stock of brushes, and fitted this exquisitely hand-wrought nosepiece into the part that he lacked. Then, securing it top and bottom by means of elastic bands round the back of his head and neck, he had set out.

He walked down to the River Sumida and there waited for the tram. As he waited, he repeated softly to himself the name which he had decided on was his own and the words of his speech, putting himself into the right frame of mind for his lecture tour. Today was, after all, a special occasion, for he was off to the beach where there were sure to be tens of thousands of people. It was the sea for him today. Foreigners would no doubt be there too. In short, there would probably be any number of people who would understand what was written on the sandwich-boards he carried. Since the boards hung down front and back, the old man disliked riding in very crowded trams, and it was because of this that he let them go by one after the other.

The scavengers who had left the welfare hostel while it was still dark to clear up the streets of Asakusa came back one after the other. All of them greeted the old man as they passed. In reply he would give a quick lift of his bony chin and raise his right hand. The reason why he offered only such a cursory greeting was partly because the boards front and back and his home-made nose prevented him from moving very suddenly, but the truth of it was that the old man had no liking for these people. They made it impossible to enjoy a good night's sleep in the hostel, however much one earned. What he disliked most about them was the incessant noise they made all night long with a sustained clatter of clogs or shoes as they discarded them at the entrance, for all the world like a centipede back from a journey.

A crowd of them came along. Adjusting the glasses that had slipped down his nose, the old man nodded and, gripping his bamboo stick in his left hand like a soldier with a sword, threw out his chest. When acquaintances happened to pass him at times like this, his right hand went naturally toward his army cap, and he would think that perhaps he had once been a soldier. A high-ranking one, of course—a general or something like that. Even his name would tell him that he belonged to a military family. . . .

With a clatter of boards, the old man climbed into the tram and heard a voice say,

"Hey, look at old grandpa here!"

It was a rasping voice, so peculiarly rasping that it carried no mirth. Indeed, it would only be a slight extravagance to say that there was a strange sadness about it. The old man always felt sorry for people who laughed at him, especially if they were young. Turning round he saw two young toughs in striped shirts. As the old man glared at the one who had spoken, he suddenly hunched his shoulders like a foreigner and said to his companion, "What does it say? Hey, look! 'The only speech-making beggar in Japan,' it says. 'The product of a defeated country. King of the gutter,' it says. Heh!"

Perhaps the rest of the wording given on the boards should be added for reference. There followed an English version of the phrases the tough had just read. It went: LOOK AT THE ONLY ONE BEGGAR, WHO IS THE GREATEST PRODUCT OF THE DEFEATED JAPAN. This part was written in big block capitals; the remainder was written in thin letters which filled every inch of the two-foot-square boards: "Listen!—to the tragic story of man's existence told by the Japanese Jean Valjean, in a Japan that is struggling along a hard and stormy path. Listen to his own songs and monologues, to his tales of popular morality, religion, and philosophy . . ."

IBUSE MASUJI

Ibuse Masuji (1898–1993) had a long and successful career as a writer. Born in a small village near Hiroshima, he often drew on his memories of life in the countryside to create some of his most memorable characters. During the war, when Ibuse was in his middle years, he wrote a number of stories about life in wartime, culminating in his novel *Black Rain* (*Kuroi ame*, 1966), which, for many readers around the world, remains the supreme literary description of the atomic bombing of Hiroshima. His story "Old Ushitora" (Ushitora jiisan, 1950) deals with life in the countryside, marked by Ibuse's special brand of humor and compassion.

OLD USHITORA (USHITORA JIISAN)

Translated by John Bester

The Kasumigamori district of our village is divided into eastern and western sections by a winding road that passes through the village's very center. A river, also winding, tangles with the road as it runs down the valley. The people in the next village of Yaburodani, farther up the stream, must pass along the main road through Kasumigamori whenever they visit any other village, for Yaburo-dani is surrounded on three sides by steep hills, the only side lying open being that facing Kasumigamori. Yaburodani, in short, is the village at the farthest end of the valley. When Kasumigamori children spot a child from Yaburodani passing through, they often cry out teasingly, "Old back of beyond!"

In Yaburodani, there lives an old man called Grandpa Ushitora. His real name is Torakichi, but since the first half of his given name means "tiger," and since he is a past master of the art of rearing bulls, someone once dubbed him Ushitora, "Ox-tiger"—two animals that stand adjacent in the Japanese zodiac—and the name stuck. His main occupation is providing bulls for breeding pur-poses. He also has a sharp eye, of course, for distinguishing between a good animal and a bad one. He can buy what seems an exceedingly ordinary calf and rear it into a fine, well-built bull. Cattle dealers from other parts often ask Grandpa the best way to raise cattle, but he invariably denies any special knowl-edge of such things.

A while ago, at a grand cattle show held jointly by two prefectures, Grandpa Ushitora's three bulls won awards. First, second, and third prizes all went to bulls entered by the old man. For the prizegiving ceremony, a representative came from the regional branch of a leading Osaka newspaper and took two photo-graphs of the old man for publication, he said, in the regional edition. First he told Grandpa to smile and took a photo of him with his mouth open, thus reveal-ing the gaps in his teeth; then he took another showing the old man stroking the head of the bull that had won first prize.

The same newspaperman also asked Grandpa some questions. "I wonder, now," he said, "if you'd list your essential conditions for raising cattle? Of course, there's love for the animal, which I imagine is an indispensable item. And then, I suppose, one needs to be thoroughly versed in the habits of cattle. But isn't there some secret formula or other? This is a very important matter where stock-breeding is concerned, so I'd be grateful if you'd let us hear some of your ideas."

At a loss for a reply and with a large number of people looking on, Grandpa stood in some embarrassment.

"Now, Grandpa," spoke up an official from the stockbreeding section of the prefectural office, "surely there's some formula, some trick of the trade, isn't there?"

Grandpa thought for a long time and finally turned to the newspaperman.

"Trick of the trade—" he began, "now, I wouldn't know about that. One thing, though, is this: all the time, I treat my bulls as though I'd never kept a bull before. When I take them round with me, or cut grass for them, or put grass in their stalls, or clear away their dirty straw for them, or when I'm scraping them down with the brush, I take care of them as though I'd never done it before in my whole life."

All this the man from the newspaper branch took down on paper, nodding to himself all the while.

The newspaperman, who though young seemed to have an appetite for the unusual, went so far as to ask the old man the names of the three prizewinning animals. The winner of the first prize, having been bought at a place called Chiya, was known, it seemed, as "the Chiya bull." The winner of the second prize, which had been bought as a calf from a man called Heisaku who lived in Kasumigamori, was called "the bull bought at Heisaku's." The third prizewinner had been bought when still a calf at the monthly cattle market and was known accordingly as "the bull bought at the market."

Such commonplace names were not, apparently, to the newspaperman's taste.

"Look here, Grandpa," he began in a discontented tone, "can't you find them some names with a more pastoral flavor? What we're really after is names with more local color—something with a more rustic touch, something that makes people long for their innocent childhood days. How would it be if you gave them some other names? 'Wild Cherry,' for example—that suggests the wild cherry blooming deep in the hills. Or 'Volga,' which suggests the boatman hauling his barge up the river, or 'Oak,' with its suggestion of fresh green leaves. Wouldn't you care to rename them, now, in honor of the occasion?"

The newspaperman was undoubtedly a kindhearted man or he would hardly, from the outset, have felt like writing an article about animals with such boorish names as "the bull bought at Heisaku's."

"Very well, then," said Grandpa, who saw no need to object, "I'll take advantage of that kind thought of yours. But I'd be much obliged if you'd just say those names again?"

"Wild Cherry . . . Volga . . . Oak." Grandpa repeated them to himself over and over again until they were firmly fixed in his mind. The winners of the first and second prizes were dubbed "Wild Cherry" and "Volga" respectively. The third prizewinner was named "Oak."

On his arrival back in Yaburodani, Grandpa notified his son of the change. His son, however, was highly embarrassed. The names, he declared, sounded like the names of coffee shops; just to hear them was enough to set his teeth on edge. The neighbors got wind of the disagreement but were obliged to admit, even so, that Grandpa's bulls had acquired a new dignity.

The newspaper reported the cattle show in the local news column of the regional edition, where it was dismissed in a meager three or four lines. All it said, in fact, was that Grandpa Ushitora's bulls had won prizes. Nevertheless, the same report brought a definite increase in the number of people who came to him to have their cows serviced. Hitherto, Grandpa had gone round the neighboring villages with his bulls, providing service at any house where a cow happened to be in heat. His bulls had always had a good reputation, and most farmers were already accustomed to rely on them to service their cows when necessary. Occasionally, a farmer would bring a cow specially to Grandpa's place, but since Grandpa's son objected strongly to the mating taking place at their home, Grandpa would go and call on the client later, taking the bull with him. His son, Tōkichi by name, was only a humble charcoal burner, but he could not agree, he declared, to his own father permitting such indelicate behavior; his whole being revolted against the idea. He even told the neighbors that if his father broke the taboo it would mean a severing of relations between parent and child.

Tōkichi had two children, a boy and a girl. Two years previously, when the boy had started at primary school, Tōkichi had made Grandpa stop taking his bulls about their own village. He felt sorry for the child, he said, because the other children at school looked at him oddly.

At first, Grandpa had told his son not to be so fussy.

"Now if you were a schoolteacher," he said, "I might listen to you. As it is, though, you're just a plain charcoal burner, so I'd be obliged if you'd be a bit less severe about what I do."

There is no family in the village that does not keep cattle, and some of the other schoolchildren themselves came from families that had their cows serviced as the occasion required. Why, Grandpa demanded, should those children take exception to his grandson just because his grandfather took his bulls around? It was not as though a man who kept bulls for breeding was a kind of pimp; if anything, he was closer to a doctor. Tōkichi replied that it was because Grandpa took money for servicing the cows that the child felt so awkward. Anyway, he asked him to give it up for his child's sake; and Grandpa, for the sake of his beloved grandson, agreed to give up providing service at least in their own village.

In the event, getting Grandpa's name in the papers was, in a way, the source of all the trouble in Grandpa's family. Every week or ten days, an average of two people began to turn up at Grandpa's place, bringing cows in heat. Grandpa pleaded an unwritten family rule as his excuse for refusing, but even so some clients would complain indignantly that he was hardhearted in turning them down when they had come such a long way. Some even made sarcastic remarks about people who put on airs. When his son was at home, Grandpa would send them away, saying he would call on them with the bull later. More often than not, however, his son was away at the charcoal-burning kiln. Then, things were different; if a client came, Grandpa would choose a moment when his son's wife and his grandson were not looking to take the client and his cow into the woods, then take the bull to them a little later.

Even this ruse, though, was bound to be detected if repeated too often. One day, his son Tōkichi learned the truth from a charcoal buyer and came home in a towering rage. As soon as the evening meal was over and the two children were asleep, Tōkichi set about picking a quarrel with his wife.

"I simply don't understand," he declared. "I don't understand how he could give them such damn silly names in the first place. 'Volga'! 'Oak'! I told you, too, that you weren't ever to use such disgusting names. But you did, and now even the children do the same. It's enough to break up the whole family!"

At the sink in the kitchen, his wife, seeing storm clouds in the offing, went on washing the dishes in silence.

"A fine thing I heard today from the charcoal buyer!" he went on. "I never heard anything so shameful! But the truth always comes out in the end. He takes his bulls off into the woods on the quiet and mates them there for money. And you knew all the time, woman, but pretended you didn't! Mating cattle without telling people, it's immoral—it's adulterous, that's what it is!"

"I won't keep quiet any longer," Grandpa broke in, flinging to the ground half-made one of the straw sandals that he worked on at night to supplement their income. "'Break up the whole family,' indeed! 'Adultery'! I don't know how you can talk such nonsense. What's adulterous about mating a couple of cows, I'd like to know? You'd probably tell a man he'd committed adultery if he saw a pair of dragonflies coupling in the woods."

"Whether it was in the woods or in the cowshed, I can't say," Tōkichi retorted. "I'm talking about something different. To mate them furtively and charge money for it, that's what's so degrading. If some outsider wants to bring his bulls to the cows, I couldn't care less. But not to know the distinction between the two things is awful. It's filthy! Ever since I was a kid I've had to suffer because of this same thing. That's why I became a charcoal burner. 'Oak'! 'Volga'! The very sound of them makes me want to throw up! I'm clearing out."

"What d'you mean 'makes you want to throw up'?" demanded Grandpa. "Oak and Volga, I'll have you know, are a fine pair of bulls. And I'm an expert with cattle. My name was in the papers. If you don't like it here, you can get out. The more I put up with you, the more you take advantage of it. Clear out, then!"

Tōkichi, who was sitting cross-legged at the edge of the raised floor in the kitchen, shot to his feet and went off round the front. His wife chased after him but got no farther than the front entrance before turning back again. She knew perfectly well, either way, that Tōkichi's destination would only be the charcoal burners' hut.

Grandpa was beside himself with rage.

"He can please himself what he does! I'm going off round the neighboring villages with my bulls. I'm clearing out this instant. I've been patient enough. You, girl, you can tell Tōkichi that I've left this house for good. You can tell him that from me!"

True to his word, Grandpa set about making preparations for a tour of the villages.

This was the first time that Tōkichi's wife had witnessed such a serious quarrel between father and son. Minor differences of opinion there had often been, but the old man had always given in immediately and things had gone no further. This time it was different. Tōkichi had never used such harsh language to the old man before. Nor had the old man ever shouted at Tōkichi in such a loud voice. Tōkichi's wife was at a loss how to handle things.

"Grandpa, do try and calm yourself. Please!" she begged, making a clumsy attempt to bow with her forehead to the floor. "I'm apologizing for him, aren't I?"

"I don't want to hear it! I can take so much and no more. You tell Tōkichi that!"

Grandpa put on his long rubber boots. After that, he only had to fasten his wicker basket on his back and he was ready for the journey. Inside the basket there were two nosebags, blankets, sickles large and small, whetstones, a bamboo basket, brushes and a few other things.

The bulls were already bedded down for the night, but Grandpa led all three of them out of the cowshed. He would leave Oak, he decided, with Gosuke, a neighbor who was fond of cattle, and take the other two with him. Since the end of the last century, local regulations had forbidden lone cattle dealers to take more than two adult beasts about with them at a time. Besides, Oak was the youngest of the three; older bulls are liable to use their horns on human beings if beaten or struck—not, of course, that such a thing was likely at Gosuke's. The only animal Gosuke had was a calf, but he had four sons, so there would be no shortage of labor to look after Oak the bull. Children on country farms soon make friends with cattle, which also serve as playthings for them.

Gosuke was still up, busy at work making buckshot, with his working gear scattered about the unfloored part of the house. He made the shot by melting lead and dropping it into cold water, each drop becoming a shot as it cooled. He was also a hunter, and would start making shot in his spare time before the summer was out, then sell it to other hunters and use the proceeds to buy his own cartridges.

"Gosuke, I don't like to ask you, but could you look after Oak for me? I'll go halves with you on the money I get for mating him if you like." Grandpa was still so excited that he offered to split the proceeds without even pausing to do his mental arithmetic first.

"What are you talking about, Grandpa? Oak? You're not serious!"

"Yes I am. Something's happened to me that I just can't stomach. Something very serious has happened to me."

Gosuke opened the door leading into the house. "Hey, stop that clatter!" he called to his wife, who was busily plying a hand mill in the kitchen. "How can we talk about important things with that row going on?"

Grandpa refrained from relating the bald facts and gave a rather romanticized version of the story instead. For personal reasons, he was setting out, this very instant, on a tour with his bulls. He would come back from time to time to fetch Oak for mating with a cow, but he refused ever to set foot in his own house. That was why he wanted Gosuke to look after Oak. This was definitely not a passing whim, nor was he doing it because he anticipated any failing in Oak's powers. He was rather weighed down at the moment, perhaps, by the uncertainty of existence.

Gosuke, who had been listening with a rather suspicious air, seemed to change his attitude at this and began to speak in serious tones.

"Ah, I see," he said. "I think I know that feeling. I have to kill living creatures myself, you know, when I go hunting. It must have been some fate that brought you here. . . . Right, leave him with me! He's my responsibility."

"He's in your hands, then. I've got him here outside the gate."

Following the custom among horse and cattle dealers, they clapped hands together three times to set the seal on the agreement.

Gosuke put Oak in the cowshed and chopped up some fodder for him. His wife held up a bicycle lamp for him so that he could see what he was doing. "Why don't we enter him in the cattle show next year?" she said gaily. "I wonder if there's a prize goes with it? Yon see, the name of the person entering him would be different, wouldn't it?"

"Shut your silly mouth, woman!" said Gosuke.

Grandpa Ushitora shone the flashlight round the cowshed. Oak was already lying on his side on the straw. The calf that had been there all the time was standing in a corner of the shed.

Gosuke and his wife saw Grandpa off up the slope back to the road. The old man was still angry about his son, but he managed to tell the story of his ginger and the moles, which had no bearing on his present situation at all. Twenty years previously, he had planted some ginger, but moles had eaten the whole lot. Gosuke responded by telling how, as a child, he had seen a stray dog running by with a mole in its mouth.

Back on the main road, Grandpa Ushitora set off, with Wild Cherry in front of him and Volga behind. The moon was not up yet but the sky was full of stars, and he began to feel rather easier in his mind. The clopping of the bulls' hooves and the sound of the stream running down the valley were not, after all, especially depressing. By the time a crooked moon rose above the hills, he had already reached Kasumigamori.

Grandpa let his bulls lead him to a house where they might call and not be unwelcome. Wild Cherry could always find, by some kind of sixth sense, a house where there was a cow in heat. Perhaps it was his sense of smell, or perhaps he heard the faintest of distant lowings that told him whether it was the right time for the cow and where she was. Or perhaps he just had a general idea of what was happening from frequent experience in the past.

"Off you go," said Grandpa. "Good hunting!" He flung the rope up onto Wild Cherry's back and let the great animal lead the way.

Wild Cherry quickened his pace slightly and gave two great, mournful bellows. In response, the lowing of a cow came across the river from the general area of the wayside shrine in the eastern section of the village. It was the cow at Shuzō's place, just opposite the shrine. Wild Cherry had forgotten his reputation for finding a cow by his sixth sense and relied on her cries to lead him to her.

"Cunning beast!" grumbled Grandpa, with something like complacency, as he followed after him.

From time to time, Wild Cherry and Shuzō's cow on the other side of the river lowed to each other as though they had some secret understanding. Even Volga gave a bellow. Halfway along the narrow road from the main road to the eastern section of the village there was a narrow, earth-covered bridge. Beneath it, by the side of a still pool, stood a great shell-shaped rock. By night, without a moon, the bridge would have been dangerous, but Wild Cherry crossed it without the slightest hesitation and pressed ahead until finally he stopped in front of the cowshed at Shuzō's.

The cow in the cowshed was setting up a great commotion, snorting heavily and jabbing upward at the crosspieces on the door with its horns in an attempt to open the door from the inside. Every year, she went into heat in an alarming fashion, but the previous year she had been serviced twice without producing any calves. That year too she had already been serviced once without result. She might well be a barren cow. Barren or no, her spells in heat were something terrible and set her rampaging about in great excitement.

Grandpa took his two bulls round by the outbuilding and tethered them separately to persimmon trees.

"Who is it?" demanded Shuzō, hastening out of the entrance to see what the commotion was about. In the light of the moon, he soon made out Grandpa Ushitora and his bulls.

"Well, Grandpa Ushitora!" he exclaimed. "Doing your round of the villages? You came at just the right time. My cow's been lowing all the time, and terribly restless. I came out to the cowshed any number of times to see what was up with her. There didn't seem to be anything I could do. But then you turned up. Talk about a fairy godmother!"

"I don't like to turn up late at night like this, without letting you know . . ."

"Eh? Late at night? Don't be silly. Just look at that cow of mine. Look how restless she is, poor thing! And it's embarrassing with the neighbors, too, the way she gets excited when she's in heat."

Shuzō turned out the light he held in his hand.

Grandpa tied the cow in the shed on a short tether so that she could not jump about, then drove Wild Cherry into the shed. The mating was all over in a flash. To make sure that things took properly, Grandpa rubbed the cow's back for her. Then he drove Wild Cherry and Volga into the stable, which stood empty, and left them feeding on some sweet-potato runners that Shuzō had put in the manger for them.

Shuzō was in his forties and lived alone. He had no children. If he wanted so much as a cup of tea, he had to struggle to light the fire for himself beneath the kettle, filling the whole kitchen with smoke in the process. His wife had died the year before. Nothing could be done about that, Shuzō said; what really hurt was that people recently had begun to gossip about the cow. She was a typical barren female with sex on the brain, they said. The year before, he had had her serviced twice by Ushitora's bulls to no avail, so this year he had taken her to a place called the O.K. Breeders, a good twelve miles away. That did not take either. To make matters worse, every time she was in heat she bellowed and threw herself about as though she were half crazy, and had twice broken down the door of the cowshed during the night and run away.

The first time, the course she had taken was clear in every detail the next morning. She had fled to the rock garden at the Tsuruyas' nearby, where she had relieved herself on a rock covered with green moss. From there, she had gone on to the house of a widow who had a bull, and had stamped up and down in front of the cowshed. The widow's eldest son, drawn outside by the noise, had attempted to capture the offending animal, only to see it make off, swifter than any horse, in the direction of the Ashishina district of the village.

The next morning, Shuzō discovered the door of his cowshed smashed and the cow gone. Uproar ensued. Before long, news came from the Tsuruyas. A cow unknown had disgraced itself on a rock in their garden and made a clean sweep of the strips of giant radish hung out to dry over the veranda. Unless she was caught as soon as possible and given a dose of bicarbonate of soda, the dried radish would swell up in her stomach and choke her to death when she ruminated.

Pale at the thought of the terrible loss that threatened, Shuzō set off in search of the cow on his bicycle. Fortunately, he soon found her, tethered to a persimmon tree in one of the terraced fields on a hillside at Ashishina. She was only a cow, it was true, but to have created such a public disturbance, especially over a display of carnal lust, was disgraceful.

The second time she had run away had been on the twenty-first day following her servicing at the O.K. Breeders. On that occasion, she had run a full twelve miles in the middle of the night and gone back to the O.K. Breeders. As soon as Shuzō found in the morning that his cow had gone, he guessed where she was and went to the O.K. Breeders on his bicycle to fetch her back. Even a cow, he had reasoned, must cherish a rather special feeling for the partner made familiar from experience. Fortunately enough, his shot in the dark had hit the mark. Any delay, and the cow would almost certainly have been made off with by someone else.

She was a troublesome cow, indeed. Even so, Shuzō was fond of her and was determined, he said, to see her blessed with children. To have a calf would, he was convinced, put an end to her carnal preoccupations. Even while he was drinking tea in the kitchen, Shuzō got up two or three times to go and peer into the cowshed.

"Will it take or won't it?" said Shuzō anxiously. "I wonder. . . . If it doesn't take this time, do you think it means she's barren?"

Such a question was not for Grandpa to answer; it was the province of the vet, after a proper examination.

They went to bed, their quilts laid out side by side on the floor, but Shuzō got up yet again to go and look in the cowshed. The cow was lying on her belly with her legs folded beneath her, peacefully dribbling as she ruminated. Even after he was back in bed, Shuzō started talking to Grandpa again. If a mating was not successful, it was natural for anybody's cow to go into heat again and there was no need for Shuzō to worry so much. If it wasn't successful this time, he said, he was afraid the cow would get excited and start rampaging and bellowing almost immediately. It humiliated him in the eyes of the neighbors. They would get the idea that her owner was the same way. He would willingly provide a bull for her just to keep her quiet; in fact, if that was the only purpose, any seedy animal from the nearest place at hand would do. And yet, for a man of his age and living alone to provide such a service was hardly respectable.

Grandpa himself had once been asked by a circus to provide just that kind of service. Twenty years previously, a cattle market had been established in Kasumigamori, and one of the committee members had invited a circus to the village for the opening ceremonies. The circus was made up of a dozen or so men and women who brought with them two horses, one cow, and a dog, and its performances consisted of putting the animals through various acts to make the audience laugh. Grandpa had been summoned to bring a bull to the circus.

The booths for the performances, simple affairs of frames covered with straw matting, had been set up on the dry riverbed in Kasumigamori. Arriving there with his bull, Grandpa was met by a large man in dark glasses, who looked like the manager of the circus and who asked him to do something about his cow, which was in heat. It didn't matter whether she got pregnant or not, he said, so long as she cooled off. To fill such an order was hardly going to increase the reputation of a cattle breeder. Then, to top it all, the man who seemed to be the manager asked him outright to see, if possible, that the bull didn't make her pregnant. "Damn fool," thought Grandpa, and went straight home again with his bull.

Unfortunately, the wrong story had got about. The tale that spread around was that old Ushitora, the cattle breeder, had put his bull to the circus cow to get her off heat rather than with calf: a bovine brothel, said people snidely. In a day or two, everyone had heard the story, not only in Kasumigamori but in Yaburodani and all the other villages round about. The net result was that Grandpa became a laughing stock, while the circus cow enjoyed an enormous vogue. The general impression seemed to be that she was in some way a seductive, flirty type of cow. Thanks to this, the circus had a considerable attendance, but on Grandpa's side his son Tōkichi, who was still at primary school, was ostracized by the other children for quite a while afterward. On more than a few occasions, Tōkichi came home from school crying. Tōkichi had never forgotten how he had suffered at that time; that was why, even now, he was still oversensitive where breeding was concerned.

"Really, it's a nasty business," concluded Grandpa Ushitora. "You could go on fretting about it forever. Let's go to sleep," said Shuzō.

The next morning, Grandpa woke up early. It was a fine day. Before breakfast, he went to the water mill to buy rice bran. On the way back, he dropped in at a shop where they processed bean curd and bought some of the sediment left after making the curd. Everything was intended as fodder for the bulls, but he set a little of the sediment aside and had Shuzō mix it with the rice for their breakfast.

Grandpa had just finished breakfast when he had a visitor. It was Uchida from Kasumigamori, who had found out somehow where he was. Then, almost immediately afterward, he had another visitor. This time it was the former priest of the Myōkendō shrine in the western section of the village. Both of them, by strange coincidence, brought presents of sweet potatoes for the bulls, and asked him to bring his bulls for mating with their cows.

When Grandpa led the two bulls out of the stable, both Uchida and Myō-kendō, as he was still known, asked to have the servicing done by Wild Cherry. Wild Cherry, however, was not for use for some time to come. Even with a bull in the prime of life, it is normal to mate him with no more than seventy to seventy-five cows in a year. Grandpa had always made it a rule to put Wild Cherry to work five times a month, and to get the other two bulls to help out with the rest.

The Myōkendō priest was much taken with Wild Cherry. "When all's said and done, you can't beat a Chiya bull," he said. "This one's the best of the bunch. A good, substantial animal!"

His companion Uchida also praised Wild Cherry to the point where Grandpa began to get embarrassed. His praises sounded so much like flattery designed for the ears of Wild Cherry himself that Shuzō interrupted him.

"Praise him as much as you like, the animal couldn't care less," he said. "If you praise him too much it sounds barefaced, like some marriage go-between talking."

"Well! So my cow's not the only one that gives trouble," said Myōkendō, making a sly reference to the unconventional behavior of Shuzō's own cow.

Grandpa received his payment from Shuzō, and got back onto the main road with his two bulls. Uchida and Myōkendō followed in their wake, vying with each other all the while in praising the way that Wild Cherry walked, the gloss of his coat, and so on. His appearance was, indeed, so fine that even the non-expert would have noticed it. He was massive and handsomely built, whether seen from the front or the side. His dewlap hung in ample folds from his chin and down his chest, as though the surplus weight of his body were overflowing into it. Viewed from the rear, his gait had a ponderous assurance. His thighs were pleasingly plump, his hips square-set, and his coat gleamed a dazzling black as he walked. His horns rose straight and even, glossy black at the tips and matt black at the base, as though they had been dipped water.

Uchida and Myōkendō were each trying to let the other take precedence in having his cows serviced. There were another five days before Wild Cherry would be fit to use.

"No, after you," said Uchida. "My cow's only two years old. Whoever heard of a youngster taking precedence over someone older from the same village? My cow must certainly take second place because of her age, quite apart from anything else."

"No, no. *You* first. My cow's so shy, you wouldn't believe it. Last year, now, we had the bull brought twice, but she behaved as though nothing was up at all. This time too, I expect it'll take time."

After much give-and-take, it was finally agreed that Uchida's cow should be serviced first. Myōkendō's cow might or might not be bashful, but the fact was that Grandpa had taken his bull there twice the previous year, only to find that he had met his match. Myōkendō's cow had not given Wild Cherry—then still known as "the Chiya bull"—so much as a second glance. Slowly, as though she had all the time in the world, she had put herself out of his reach, though she bellowed all the while as though she was off her head, with bloodshot eyes and every other physical sign of being in heat. Having given birth to twin calves two years previously, she ought not to have objected to the mating, but for some reason or other she rejected his advances on both occasions.

Myōkendō, watching the proceedings, had grown desperate. "Come on," he had scolded her, "get some life into you! None of your airs and graces!" The second time, too, he had scolded her in the same way, afraid that the fee he paid was going to be wasted. Possibly the timing had been wrong on both occasions; most cows go into heat between twenty-one and twenty-eight days after parturition and are in heat every third or fourth week thereafter, but the period is a bare one and a half days, and even then, the first half day is the best.

Once the servicing of Uchida's cow was over, Grandpa went to cut grass on the embankment of the pond below the temple, then took Wild Cherry alone down to the river in the valley. He made him walk about in the shallows and washed him all over with a brush, then wiped the drops off him with a towel. He even cleaned the dirt off his hooves. Then he took the bull's hooves one at a time on his knee, and was scraping the underside with a sickle to improve their appearance when a voice hailed him:

"Well, Grandpa Ushitora! Haven't seen you for a long time! Cleaning his hooves, I see. A cow's hooves are surprisingly soft, aren't they?"

It was the younger brother of the previous head of the Tsuruya family. He carried a fishing rod, with a fisherman's creel in his hand, and his trousers were soaked through up to the knees. He was already in his early fifties, and the sideburns below his white hat were flecked with gray. Some thirty years ago, he had gone to Tokyo to study but had dropped out of school and, disqualified thereby from obtaining a job with a decent firm or government office, was said to have been making a living writing novels. For nearly two years during the war, he had brought his large family to stay with the Tsuruyas in order to escape the air raids. Even then, he had gone fishing in the river every day throughout the summer. When one of the neighbors greeted him with a "Hello! Going fishing?" he would reply "Off to work!" thus doing his own reputation a good deal of harm. This time—again, it seemed, with the purpose of tiding over a financially thin time—he had brought his son, who was on vacation. One could hardly expect much, at any rate, of a man who abandoned his birthplace and went off to knock around in foreign parts. To say that a bull's hard hooves were surprisingly soft was hardly a compliment. . . .

"It all depends on how you use the sickle," said Grandpa, giving him little encouragement, and went on paring.

"They say cows like being scratched here, don't they?" went on the Tsuruyas' visitor, pinching at Wild Cherry's dewlap. "In the Kantō area they call this part the 'hangskin,' you know. What would the cattle dealers in these parts call it?"

"We call it the 'hanging.' The *throat* hanging.'"

"Is that so? The 'hanging,' eh? And how do you tell a cow's age? I hear there are all kinds of complicated ways of telling it, by the proportion of deciduous teeth to permanent teeth, or the extent to which the permanent teeth have been eroded. . . ."

"We here, we just look to see how many teeth it's cut, if a young animal. With an older animal, we look to see how much it's worn down its second teeth."

As soon as Grandpa had finished paring the bull's hooves, the Tsuruyas' visitor went down under the bridge and started fishing. Soon Grandpa appeared up on the bridge leading his bull, whereupon he hailed him again from below.

"Grandpa—perhaps I shouldn't bring this up now, but they do say you've left home. Somebody tipped me off about it a while back. But you know, Grandpa, traveling about never got anybody anywhere!"

He might almost have been talking about himself.

That night, Grandpa got Uchida to put him up. The next day, he took his bulls down to the broad, dry riverbed about two and a half miles downstream and turned them loose there. At nights he stayed at the general store near the bus stop; the owner was a distant relative. The store had a two-story outbuilding at the back, with a window looking out over the riverbed, which was convenient for keeping an eye on the bulls. The next day, and the following one, he slept on the second floor of the outbuilding; and all the while, as he watched over the animals, he tried hard to keep thoughts of his son's willfulness out of his head, so that the bulls too could take their ease and relax.

On the fifth day, he set out early in the morning with his two bulls and went to the Myōkendō shrine in Kasumigamori. The cow there still showed no change, but the next morning she was definitely in heat. Contrary to Myōkendō's prediction made the other day, the cow proved neither bashful nor retiring. If anything, she was rather forward. When Wild Cherry came lumbering into the cowshed, she simply stood there motionless, as though stuffed.

That night, Grandpa put up with Myōkendō. With the latter's approval, he drove the two bulls into the outbuilding, which was all but empty, and gave them their nosebags with sweet potatoes in them. He opened the two windows high up in the walls as wide as possible.

Myōkendō's place stood on a piece of high ground, an offshoot of the hills. It had originally been a shrine dedicated to the Bodhisattva Myōken, but, since the war, serving the gods and Buddhas was no longer a profitable sideline, so the place had ceased to be a temple, and Myōkendō had returned to secular life as a farmer pure and simple. The hall that had housed the statue, the priest's living quarters, the cowsheds, and the outbuildings all stood side by side in a line, with a rocky cliff behind them. The remaining three sides formed a steep slope of red clay sparsely dotted with pine trees, with a narrow path winding up the slope. The site was quite well protected, in fact, but some intuition warned Grandpa that he should fasten the door of the outbuilding with nails.

Myōkendō laid out quilts for Grandpa in the very center of what had been the shrine and hung a mosquito net over it for him. He also opened up all the shutters, so that there was a pleasant breeze.

Grandpa was already in bed when Myōkendō came to worship before the statue of Myōken that still stood in the sanctuary at the back of the hall. Grandpa was just dozing off but woke up again.

"Well, well, Myōkendō," he said. "Time for prayers, eh? You mustn't mind if I go to sleep."

"Go ahead, go ahead. You know—it doesn't really pay to do this nowadays, but even so I say the sutras every ten days."

He lit a small candle in the candlestick standing on the altar. Then, rubbing his prayer beads between his palms, he said:

"Sorry to bother you, then. Afraid the sutras will disturb your sleep rather, but I'll start the service if you don't mind." And he started chanting the sacred scripture. It was quite impossible for Grandpa to go to sleep, but to get out of bed seemed rather too pointed, so he lay still and did nothing.

The sutra-reading over, Myōkendō apologized to Grandpa again.

"Sorry to bother you again, but I'll give the drum a bang while I'm about it, if you don't mind. I expect you can hear this drum way over in Yaburodani, can't you?"

"Yes, we can hear it at night over in my place."

"You know, it just doesn't feel right unless I give this a bang. Just to let people know we have the faith, you see. . . ."

He started beating the drum. He beat it with a fine abandon and at the same time began chanting in a loud voice. It occurred to Grandpa, though he disapproved of his own thoughts, that if Myōkendō went at it like that, there must surely be the occasional person who came with offerings in a sudden fit of generosity. He could not help having this idea, so unpleasantly jarring was the sound. The noise must have stopped without his realizing it, however, for he soon fell asleep.

The next morning, disaster struck. Immediately on rising, Grandpa went straight to the outbuilding, where he found the door open and both bulls gone.

"Oh, my God!" cried Grandpa, stamping his foot, and set off at a run for the former priest's living quarters. Shouting he knew not what at the top of his voice, he pounded on the door. The commotion roused Myōkendō, who was still in bed. As soon as he heard the grave news, he started bawling at his wife, too, to get up. She came out wearing nothing but a nether garment, only to be yelled at angrily by Myōkendō. "Idiot! Loose woman! Go and get some clothes on!"

Marks on the outbuilding door suggested that the nails holding it fast had been pulled out with pliers or some similar instrument. In the unfloored downstairs section, only a single pile of cow dung was to be seen, and quite a few of the sweet potatoes were still left in the nosebags. Someone had apparently led them away the previous night against their will, before they had got far into their potatoes.

"As I see things, this is what happened," said Grandpa. "The thief must have come during the night. It must be someone who knows this place well. That's how I see things."

"Right, right," said Myōkendō. "They almost certainly came while I was banging the drum. Must know how the land lies, eh?"

The former priest and Grandpa followed the tracks left by the bulls in the soil. Here and there on the surface of the red clay, hoofprints were visible.

"There were two of them!"

Myōkendō and Grandpa followed the tracks to the back of the shed. On the narrow road leading down from the garden, there were confused imprints of cattle hooves. At the very bottom of the road, there were footprints of rubber-soled socks and military boots, left in the sand that had been washed down by the rain.

"Three of them must have worked together. Perhaps as many as four. Odd way to go about things," said Myōkendō peevishly.

The hoofprints disappeared after crossing the earth-covered bridge over the river in the valley. An embankment covered with green grass led along the river from the end of the bridge. The culprits seemed to have taken the bulls along it, but the grass grew too thickly for footprints to be distinguishable.

"We have to report it at the police station at any rate, so I'll go downstream," said Myōkendō. "You go and look upstream."

"I don't think the thieves will have got very far. If a cow in heat bellows, Wild Cherry bellows back, doesn't he? So keep your ears open for any cow that calls."

Grandpa was just setting off along the path by the river when Myōkendō added: "And don't forget—it's important to ask around for any information likely to be useful."

The green grass that covered the path was wet with morning dew. From time to time, he noticed that the grass had been trodden down, hut it seemed unlikely that cattle had passed that way. He hurried along the track straight along by the river. Eventually, it gave onto the main road. The question was whether or not there were any signs of cattle having passed that point.

The sun had not yet risen. The raised path along the river had been constructed to prevent flooding. The righthand side, overlooking the river, was faced with stones, while on the left a row of plum trees stretched for a good three or four hundred yards. The path led onto the main road at the point where the trees ended. Here, there was another earth-covered bridge, and at one end of the bridge stood a water mill, now deserted and tumbledown. Grandpa went back and forth across the bridge, hoping to find any tracks left by the bulls on the road, but found nothing that looked at all likely. He even opened the wooden door of the water mill. Once there had been an incident in which a young man from another village stole a cow from our village, slaughtered it secretly in the water mill, and discarded the bones at the back of the building.

Grandpa went inside and struck a match. The earthen floor was empty save for three millstones, on one of which lay a bunch of withered plum branches, left there, probably, by children at play. He looked out at the back and found a man there, fishing.

"Well, good morning!" said the other, looking up at Grandpa. It was the Tsuruyas' visitor again.

"Good morning," said Grandpa politely.

"You're an early riser, Grandpa. I was here fishing before it got light this morning. Caught quite a lot. Nice river you've got here in this valley."

"Glad you like it. . . . By the way, have you seen anybody go by with some bulls?"

But just then, someone came across the bridge on a bicycle, calling to Grandpa as he came. It was Uchida, who was wearing a cotton night kimono that stopped at his knees, pins high rubber boots.

"I just got the alarm from Myōkendō," he said. "Dreadful shock. No idea, he says, where the bulls have gone. We split up and rushed off in different directions to look for them. If we get wind of the criminal, the signal is two strokes on the fire bell."

"No sign of the bulls going along the main road, I suppose?"

"Nothing," said Uchida. "Nor where the path on the downstream side leads into the main road. Not so much as a chicken feather, let alone a hoofprint."

If the thief had made his escape along the main road with the bulls, he could only have taken them by truck, but there were no truck marks on the road either. The thief, Uchida said, might have fled into the hills. But the hills surrounding Kasumigamori slope up steeply from the back of the village, and it would be hard going to take refuge in them with cattle on one's hands. Even the road upstream came to a dead halt at Yaburodani.

"If they fled into the hills, they must still be lying low there. I wish a cow in a stall somewhere would give a call for a bull."

Cupping his hands, Grandpa imitated the sound of a bull lowing. The Tsuruyas' visitor gave up his fishing and produced a similar imitation. He gave his imitation with great gusto, in a much louder voice than Grandpa, then said:

"No reply. . . . You know, Grandpa, you really shouldn't have left home. Just supposing, now—only supposing, of course—that it was your own son Tōkichi who'd stolen the bulls. It would make a nice ending to the story, wouldn't it? If Tōkichi were back home with the bulls now, it would mean an end to your wanderings, wouldn't it, Grandpa? Or perhaps I'm a bit indiscreet to go making such predictions. Not that it's anything more than my wishful thinking, of course. . . ."

Grandpa could not have cared less whether it was indiscreet or not. Without even replying he made off at once, leaving Uchida to follow after him, pushing his bicycle as he came.

INOUE YASUSHI

Inoue Yasushi (1907–1991) was one of the most distinguished postwar novelists, well known both in Japan and abroad for his poetic and often austere historical novels, particularly *The Roof Tile of Tenpyō* (*Tenpyō no iraka*, 1957), which deals with the arrival of Buddhism in Japan. Less well known abroad are Inoue's works of fiction set in the modern period, such as "The Rhododendrons of Hira" (Hira no shakunage, 1950), translated here and one of his finest.

THE RHODODENDRONS OF HIRA (HIRA NO SHAKUNAGE)

Translated by Edward G. Seidensticker

How quickly time passes. It is five years since I was last here at Katada. Five years have gone by since that spring, the spring of 1944, when we had begun to see that the war was not going well. It seems like many years ago, and it seems like yesterday. Sometimes I think I am less sensitive to time than I once was. When I was young it was different. In the *Anatomy Magazine* last month someone called me a vigorous old gentleman of eighty. I am not, though. I still have two years to go, but I suppose I must strike people as an "old gentleman." I don't like that expression. There is something a little too warm and mellow about it. I would much rather be called an old scholar. Miike Shuntarō, old scholar.

"There are more famous spots for viewing Lake Biwa than you can count on your fingers," the owner of this inn used to say, "but there is no place along the entire lake shore that is better than Katada for viewing Mount Hira." In particular, he liked to boast that no view of Hira could compare with the one from the northeast room of the Reihōkan Inn itself. Indeed the Reihōkan, "Inn of the Holy Mount," takes its name from the fact that Hira viewed from here looks its grandest and most god-like. The view is not like that from Hikone, with Hira sweeping the horizon east to west, the very essence of the great mountain mass; but from here it has a dignity and character you do not find in ordinary mountains. Calmly enfolding those deep valleys, the summit more often than not hidden in clouds, it sweeps down to plant its foot solidly on the shore of the lake. There is no denying its beauty.

How long has the old innkeeper been dead, I wonder. Twenty years?—no, longer. The second time I came here, over the Keisuke affair, he was already paralyzed and had trouble speaking, and it must have been very soon afterward, possibly two or three months, that I had notice of his death. He seemed like a worn-out old man to me then, but he could not have been over seventy. Already I have lived almost ten years longer than he did.

Nothing in the inn has changed. I was twenty-four or twenty-five when I first came here. Fifty years have somehow gone by since I first sat in this room. It is strange for a house to have gone unchanged for fifty years. The young owner is the image of his father, and he sits in the same dark office off the hall, his expressions and his mannerisms exactly like the old man's. The landscape painting in the musty alcove here and the statue under it might for all I know be the ones that were here then. Everything has changed at home. Furniture, people, the way people think. I know of nothing that has not changed. A steady change, from year to year, from month to month—from moment to moment and from second to second, it might be better to say. There cannot be many houses where change is so constant. It is intolerable. I put a chair out on the veranda and I can be sure that in an hour it will be facing another direction.

What a calm, quiet place this is! And how many years has it been since I was last able to relax so completely? The scholar's hour. I sit on the veranda with no one watching me. I look at the lake. I look at Hira. No one runs a malicious eye toward me, no brassy voices jar on my nerves. If I want a cup of tea I clap for the maid. Probably if I were not to clap I would see no one until time for dinner. I do not hear a radio. Or a phonograph or a piano. I do not hear that shrill voice of Haruko's or the voices of those wild grandchildren. Or Hiroyuki's voice—he has become a little insolent these last few years.

In any case, they must be quite upset by now, probably in an uproar because I disappeared without a word. I have stopped going out alone as I have grown older, never knowing when the worst might happen. And now I have been missing for more than five hours. Even Haruko will be upset. "The old man has disappeared, the old man has disappeared," she'll be saying in that shrill voice as she hunts around the neighborhood and asks whether anyone has seen me. Hiroyuki will have been called home from the office, but, being Hiroyuki, he'll not have wanted to call the police or tell the relatives. He'll have telephoned people and found not a trace of me, and he'll be pacing the floor with a sour expression on his face. But he's a worrier. Maybe he'll have called at least his brother and sister. Sadamitsu will have come from the university, and he'll be at my desk drinking tea and scowling to show how much he resents having been bothered. Kyōko will have hurried over from Kitano. Sadamitsu and Kyōko never show their faces unless something like this happens. I suppose they are busy, but it wouldn't hurt them now and then to come around and bring a little candy or fruit to the only parent they have left. For six months or a year on end they would forget all about me if I didn't remind them, that's how little the two of them know of their duty as children.

Let them worry until tomorrow. Tomorrow at noon I'll be back as if I had never been away. I still have my rights, even if I am seventy-eight. I can go out alone if I want to. I have the rights that are so fashionable these days. I don't see why it should be wrong for me to go out without telling everyone. I used to be a good drinker in my younger days, and I would spend a night here and a night there without saying a word to Misa. Sometimes I would stay away for three or four nights running, and not once did I call up the house, as Hiroyuki is always doing, to say I wouldn't be home. Haruko has him under her thumb. He's too soft with her and he's too soft with the children. I don't like it at all.

I don't suppose, though, that we'll get by without a quarrel when I do go back tomorrow. This is what I mean, this is why it wears me out so to take care of him, Haruko will say in a voice loud enough for Sadamitsu and Kyōko to hear. And since Haruko is Haruko, she might even throw herself down and weep for them, just to make herself amply disagreeable. The others will have to tell me too how they stayed awake the whole night worrying. But I won't say a word. I'll just look quietly from face to face, and I'll march into my study. Hiroyuki will follow me. He'll put on a sober expression, and tell me that they'd rather not have any more of my perverseness in the future. "How old do you think you are?" he'll say. "Think of your age. We can't have you doing this sort of thing. It doesn't look good." And he'll tell me how peevish and irritable I'm becoming. Let him talk. I won't say a word. I won't say a word, and I'll look at the photograph on the wall of Professor Schalbe, at those quiet eyes, filled with gentleness and charity. When I have calmed myself, I'll open my notebook and go to work on Part Nine of *Arteriensystem der Japaner*. My pen will run on.

"Im Jahre 1896 bin ich in der Anatomie und Anthropologie mit einer Anschauung hervorgetreten, indem ich behauptete . . ." ("In the year 1896 I came forth with new views in anatomy and anthropology. I held that . . .") They won't have any idea what I've written. None of them will understand that in this preface shines the immortal glory of Miike Shuntarō, scholar. Hiroyuki couldn't understand a word of it if he tried. I don't know how many years of German he had in school, but there are few who are as good at forgetting as Hiroyuki is. Sadamitsu is translating Goethe, and I suppose he might be able to read it. But then maybe he can't read anything except Goethe—he's been that way since he was very young. You can't be sure even about his Goethe. I know nothing of Goethe the writer, but I suppose Sadamitsu has succeeded in making his Goethe hard to live with. Goethe the poet can't have wanted as much as Sadamitsu does to have everything his way, refusing even to see his father and his brother and sister. All Sadamitsu knows about is Goethe, and he doesn't care whether his own father is alive or dead. He can have no idea, not the slightest, of the meaning, the scholarly value, of this study of the Japanese circulatory system, this modest but important work in non-osseous anthropology. When it comes to Hiroyuki—the others too, Haruko, Kyōko, Kyōko's husband Takatsu— I suppose the view is that a hundred-yen bill is more important than a line of my writing. They're proud enough for all that of the vulgar prestige that goes with my name, member of the Japan Academy, recipient of the X Prize, Dean of the Q University Medical School. They haul my name out in public so often that I'm almost ashamed for them. That is very well. Let them, if they like. But if it is such an honor to be my children, they might make an effort to understand me, they might be a little more considerate.

Possibly Yokoya and Sugiyama at the university have been told that I'm missing. They'll wonder if I've gone away to die. Will they think I've decided to kill myself out of disgust with the times, or will they think I don't want to live any longer because my research is not going as well as it might? If Keisuke were living, he at least might understand. Looking at me with those clean, gentle eyes, he would come nearer than anyone to understanding. He was my eldest son. He grew up when I was living in a tenement, and he was sensitive to things as the others have never been. Even to his father it was plain that he was unusually subtle and discerning.

If pressed, though, I would have to admit that I did not like Keisuke as well as the others. He never was near me, he never climbed on my knee, maybe because I was studying in Germany during the years when he began to take notice of the world. I can't help thinking, though, that if Keisuke were alive he would understand. He would eye me coolly, but he would arrange somehow to make me feel a little less unhappy.

But I won't kill myself. *The Arterial System of the Japanese* has yet to be finished. The work that I shall not finish if I live to be a hundred, the arduous and thankless work that no one can continue when I die, is waiting for me. My life is irreplaceable, and only I in all the world know its value. Very probably—I may be the only person in the world. In 1909 at the Anthropological Congress in Berlin, Professor Cracci said he placed a higher value on Miike the scholar than even Miike did, and he hoped that Miike would be kind to himself. The calmest and cleanest words of praise I have ever heard, and they were for me. But Professor Cracci is dead. So are Sakura and Iguchi. Sakura and Iguchi saw the value of my work, it seemed, but they were remarkable men themselves. It's been a very long time now since the academic world last heard of them, splendid though their work was. Probably I'm the only person left who can see it for what it was.

Why did I suddenly want to come to Katada? The impulse seems strange indeed. I wanted more than I can say to be in the northwest room of the Reihōkan looking at the lake. I wanted so much to look up from the lake to Hira that I could not control myself. It was the matter of the money that set me off, of course, but my real reason had nothing to do with such trivia.

Yesterday I asked Hiroyuki for the twelve thousand yen they had from selling part of the stock of paper I had stored in the basement at the university. Hiroyuki gave me a sour, twisted look. He sees to most of my expenses, and, life not being easy these days, it no doubt seemed natural that the money from my paper should go to him. But I couldn't agree. The paper was for publishing Volume Three of what is literally my life's work, *Arteriensystem der Japaner.* It is paper that I would not trade for anything in the world, paper that I bought during the war with money I somehow managed to scrape together, and stored at the university when it seemed that we would be bombed. It is not like paper that would go into publishing worthless novels or dictionaries. The result of fifty years' labor by Miike Shuntarō, founder of non-osseous anthropology, printed, and, if the times were but normal, distributed to every university and every library in the world. It is not just ordinary paper. It is paper on which my life, turned to several million words of German, should be printed. I wanted to put the money away in my desk, so that I could go on with my work feeling at least the slight repose it would bring. Though I have been poor all my life, I have never let myself feel poor. I have had to borrow, but I have bought what I wanted, and eaten what I wanted, and I have drunk each day as though saké were meant to swim in. Is it really possible to be poor and at the same time a scholar? People who have never been scholars cannot judge.

I let word slip out about the paper, and Hiroyuki and Haruko set their eyes on it. If I had said nothing, they could hardly have had ideas about making money from my paper.

It's my money. I won't have them laying their hands on a single yen of it. So I said to Hiroyuki. I was not being unpleasant and I was not being selfish. I was only saying what I meant.

"You might be a little more cooperative, Father," Hiroyuki said, and with that I lost my temper.

If he had come and asked me humbly for the money, I might have reconsidered on the spot. "We're having a hard time of it, Father," he might have said. "Forgive us for asking, but could you let us have part of the money?" I might not have given up as much as half of it, but I would have let him have possibly a fifth.

Haruko poked her head in from the dining room: "Father is right. It's his money. It would be best to give it to him, every last cent of it." She was polite in a very icy way.

"That's right. It's my money. I won't have it being wasted on candy for those children."

Hiroyuki snorted. Let him snort—I don't care if he is my son, that sort of double-dealing is intolerable. If Misa were alive, I would not be driven to this. Misa tended to be weak, though, and toward the end she was taking their part. I could not depend on her. But when it came to money from paper that was to go into my work she would not have given in easily. I feel sure of that.

What happened this morning only made matters worse. I was at my desk, ready to begin work, when Haruko came in with a roll of bills, twelve thousand yen. That was very well, but she didn't have to say what she did: "You're getting to be very fond of money, aren't you, Father?"

I am not fond of money. I am seventy-eight years old, and I have lived a life of honest poverty with my studies. I have had nothing besides scholarship. If I had wanted money, I would have become a clinician, and presently I would have opened my own practice, and by now I would be a rich man. I would not have spent my time prodding corpses in a dark laboratory, begging rich businessmen for donations, writing books in foreign languages and not selling a copy. Haruko was as wrong as she could be. There's a limit to this obtuseness. Having to live in such a vulgar atmosphere, in the house of an ordinary office worker with not the slightest scholarly ties, and, the times being what they are, having to depend on his insignificant salary, how can I rest easy without money of my own, however little it may be, tucked away in my desk? I can't relax with my work. And they seem to resent the fact that I don't turn over my pension to help pay household expenses. But if I were to do that, where would I find the money to pay the students who help me? That pension is all the money I have for my research. Isn't it really going too far when a son sets his eye on his own father's pension?

I did not answer Haruko. I did not want to dirty my mouth with a single word. I took the twelve thousand yen from her, and counted it with quivering hands, bill by bill, right under her eyes. It was exactly right: a hundred twenty bills.

"Very well. You may go now," I said.

I sat for a time at my desk. I made myself a bowl of tea. I held the old Hagi tea bowl (it was left on my seventieth birthday by a student who did not give his name—I like both the bowl and the student, whoever he was) at my chest, and tilted it so that the rich green foam trailed off down the side.

I looked out at the garden. Beyond the shrubbery I saw a slovenly figure in Western clothes coming in from the gate. It was the manager of the Ōmoriya Dry Goods Store. I had seen him two or three times before. Probably Haruko was selling another kimono. She brought her clothes with her when she was married, and she can sell them if she likes. We are not that hard up yet, however. If we were, we could stop those piano lessons for Yōichi. What possible good does it do to spend a lot of money giving piano lessons to a twelve-year-old boy who has no real talent? And how annoying that piano is! Music is for a genius to give his life to. The painting lessons for Keiko, who is only eight, are the same. Complete, absolute waste! They talk about "educating the sensibilities." Educating the sensibilities! Education of the sensibilities is a far different thing. How can they educate the sensibilities without teaching a decent respect for scholarship?

The useless expenses on the children are one example, but there are plenty of others. Haruko was saying the other day that she had her shoes shined at Shijō, and it cost her twenty yen. Shocking! But did Hiroyuki reprimand her for it? By no means. He said that he himself had his shoes shined in front of Kyō-goku. It cost him thirty yen, but the shoe-shine boys at Kyōgoku were politer and more thorough. An able-bodied man and woman hiring someone to shine their shoes! What can one possibly say?

And then they complain that they have trouble making ends meet, and they sell their clothes. Their whole way of thinking is riddled with inconsistencies. If the husband drank, if he drank like a fish, and that made it hard to pay the bills, I would understand. My life as a matter of fact has been a succession of days when drinking made it hard to pay the bills. Research and liquor. The dissecting room and the bar. But the money I spent on liquor was different, even if you must call it waste. I would never economize on liquor to have my shoes shined. I would probably go on drinking even if I had to shine someone else's shoes. Liquor is one of my basic needs. Like my research, it makes its demands and there is no putting it off.

As I heard the man from the Ōmoriya ringing the door bell, I got up and changed clothes. Across my chest I strung the decoration I am most fond of, the little Order of the Red Cross, First Degree, given to me by the Polish government.

With the beginning of Part Nine and a German dictionary in my brief case, I stepped down from the veranda into the garden. I first put the twelve thousand yen in an outside pocket, then moved it to my breast pocket. I cut across the garden and went out through the back gate. Perhaps because I was angry, my knee joint creaked at each step.

I walked slowly out to the streetcar track, where I was lucky enough to stop a taxi. I asked how much the fare would be to Katada. It would be possibly two hundred yen, I thought, but the driver, who could not have been more than eighteen or nineteen, said two thousand. I was furious. My hands shook. The driver spun the wheel as though he thought me a complete fool, but I called after him. "All right, take me to Katada." He turned around and opened the door from inside. In the old days a driver would have climbed out to open the door.

The taxi shook violently. "This will never do," I said to myself. I told the driver to slow down. I closed my eyes, folded my arms, and hunched my shoulders, contracting the exposed surface of my heart to lessen the burden on it. The shaking subsided as we moved out of Kyoto and onto the concrete surface of the Ōtsu highway. Over the pass at Keage and down into Yamashina and Ōtsu. From Ōtsu the road turned north along the lake-shore, and Hira lay before us. Ah, Hira! my heart sang. I had almost unconsciously told the driver that I wanted to go to Katada, and the impulse had not been wrong. I did indeed want to see Lake Biwa, and Hira. I wanted to stand on the veranda of the Reihōkan, all by myself, and look at the quiet waters of Lake Biwa and at Mount Hira beyond until I was content.

I was twenty-five when I first saw Hira. Some years before, I had come upon a copy of *Picture News*, a magazine but recently founded. I was still a high school student in Tokyo, and the magazine belonged to my landlady's daughter. The frontispiece, in the violet tint popular then, was captioned "The Rhododendrons of Hira."

I remember the picture vividly even now. It was taken from the summit of Hira, with a corner of Lake Biwa like a mirror far below. Down over the steep slope, broken here and there by a boulder, stretched a brilliant field of mountain rhododendrons. A sort of astonishment swept over me, I have no idea why. A volatile, ether-like excitement stirred a corner of my heart. Carefully I studied the picture of the rhododendrons of Hira.

I said to myself that someday I would stand on the little steamer, depicted in a circular inset on the same page, that several times each day made its way from hamlet to hamlet up the lake coast; and, looking up at the jagged lines of Hira, I would climb to exactly the spot on the peak from which the picture was taken. I do not know how to explain it, but I was quite sure that the day would come. It would come. Without fail. My heart had made its decision, shall we say—in any case, I felt not the slightest doubt.

And I thought too that the day when I would climb Hira would be a lonely day for me. How shall I describe it? A day when I had to be moving, when no one understood me. "Solitary" is a convenient word. Or perhaps "despairing" will do. Solitary, despairing. In general I dislike such dandyisms, but I can't help thinking that here they fit the case. On a day of solitude and despair, I would climb to the summit of Hira, where the mountain rhododendrons would be in bloom, and I would lie down by myself and sleep under the heavily scented clusters of flowers. That day would come. It had to come. My confidence, as I look back on it, seems so passive that I find it hard to understand, but at the time it moved into my heart as the most proper and acceptable thing in the world. So it was that I first came to know of Hira.

Some years later I saw not a picture but the real Hira. I was twenty-five, I think. It was the end of the year after I graduated from the Imperial University, and I was lecturing at the Okayama Medical College. That would make it 1896. An angel of death was with me in those days. Everyone goes through some such period when he is young, and life hardly seems worth living. Keisuke was twenty-five when he died so senselessly. If he had lived through the crisis, he would probably have had tens of years ahead of him. Spineless, irresolute Keisuke—but the angel of death that was after him may have been a stronger one than mine. What a fool he was, though—and yet one couldn't help feeling sorry for him. If he were alive today—the fool, the fool. The unspeakable fool. When I think of Keisuke, my temper quite gets the better of me.

The angel of death that followed me when I was twenty-five was a simpler one than Keisuke's. I had doubts about the meaning of my existence, and I thought of ending it, that was all. I had not yet come upon my life's work, non-osseous anthropology. I can see now that my heart was full of chinks. I was saturated in religion and philosophy as no student of the natural sciences should be. It was some years later that Fujimura Masao threw himself over Kegon Falls, but every student who went into philosophy and such was at some time or other threatened by much the same angel of death. "The truth is exhausted in one word, 'incomprehensible' "—it was a strange age, and we seriously thought such thoughts. A strange age, when the youth of the nation was lost in meditation on problems of life and death.

Winter vacation came. I went straight to Kyoto with a Zen text under my arm, and into the Tenryō-ji temple at Saga. There, with an old sage for my master, I threw myself into Zen meditation. Almost every night I sat on the veranda of the main hall. Sometimes I went out to sit on a boulder by the lake, which was covered each night with a thin sheet of ice. When we finished the all-night services celebrating the Buddha's enlightenment, I was staggering with exhaustion. I can see now that there was nothing in the world the matter with me but a bad case of nerves from malnutrition and overwork and lack of sleep.

It was the morning of the twenty-second or twenty-third of December, whichever day the winter solstice was that year. As soon as the services were over, I left the Tenryū-ji and started for Ōtsu. I suppose it was about eight o'clock in the morning. The tree stumps in the temple precincts were covered lightly with snow, and it was a cold morning even for Saga, a morning to freeze the nose and ears. In my cotton priest's robe, my bare feet slipped into sandals, I walked as fast as I could through Kitano and the main part of Kyoto, and on to Ōtsu, not once stopping to rest, over the road I took today. I remember that a light snow was falling when I passed the Kaneyo restaurant in Yamashina. I was nearly fainting with hunger.

Why do you suppose I went to Ōtsu? The details are no longer very clear in my mind. It would be a distortion to say that I was attracted to Hira by the picture I had seen in *Picture News* years before. Probably I started out with a vague intention of finding a place on the shore of the lake to die. Or possibly I simply moved toward the lake like a sleepwalker, and as I looked out over the water the thought of dying came to me.

It was a very cold day. At Ōtsu I turned and walked up the lake, the angel of death with me. On my right the cold water stretched motionless, on and on. Now and then a few birds started up from among the reeds near the shore.

In front of me was Mount Hiei, and to the left and far beyond soared a line of peaks white with snow, their beauty a revelation. I was used to the gentler lines of the mountains around Saga with their scattered groves of trees, and the harsh, grand beauty of these mountains was a change to make me wonder that the word "mountain" could cover both. I must have asked a peddler along the way—in any case I knew that the range before me was Hira. Now and then I stopped to look at Hira, and the angel of death looked with me. I was held captive by those jagged lines stretching off into the distance, almost god-like.

It was evening when I reached the Floating Hall in Katada. From time to time through the day a few flakes of snow had fallen. Now it began snowing in earnest, and the air was dense with snowflakes. I stood for a long time under the eaves of the Floating Hall. The surface of the lake was cut off from view. I took out my purse and undid the strings with freezing fingers, and one five-yen bill fell out. With that clutched in my hand I stepped into the wide hall of an inn by the lake. It was a fairly imposing place, but somehow it suggested a country post-inn—the Reihōkan.

A middle-aged man with close-cropped hair was warming himself in the office. I shoved the five-yen bill at him and asked him to let me stay the night. He said I should pay in the morning, and when I made him take it he looked at me curiously. He was suddenly very kind. A maid fifteen or sixteen years old brought hot water, and as I sat down on the sill, rolled up the skirt of my robe, and soaked my toes, red and numb from the cold, I felt a little like a human being again. I was given this room, the best one in the Reihōkan. It was already so dark that I had to have a light.

I said not a word. I ate what the innkeeper's wife gave me, and, taking up my position before the alcove, I began my Zen meditations again. I had decided that the next day I would jump over the cliff beside the Floating Hall. I wondered with some disquiet whether my five-foot self would sink quietly, as a rock sinks. My drowned form at the bottom of the lake came before my eyes time after time, and I felt that I was seeing a particularly heroic death.

It was as quiet as the hall of the Tenryū-ji. The night was bitterly cold, and the slightest movement brought new stabs of cold. I sat in meditation for I do not know how many hours. Toward dawn I came to myself. I was thoroughly exhausted. I got up and went to the toilet, and then lay down to rest. Bedding had been laid out in a corner of the room, but I did not touch it. Instead I lay on the floor with my arm for a pillow. I thought I would doze off for an hour or two until daylight.

At that moment a piercing, throat-splitting scream filled the air. The cry of a night bird possibly? I raised my head and looked around, but the night was as quiet as before. I was composing myself for sleep when the same scream came a second time, from under the veranda, it seemed, almost below my head. I got up, lit a lantern, went out to the veranda, and slid open the outside door. The light reached only the eaves. I could see nothing beyond. Fine snowflakes fell steadily into the narrow circle. As I leaned over the railing and tried to see into the darkness under the veranda, the scream came again, louder than before; and from directly below me, where the cliff fell away to the lake, a bird flew up with a terrible beating of wings, almost near enough to brush my cheek. I could not see it, but those wings, flying off into the snowy darkness over the lake, sounded with a violence that struck me to the heart. I stood for a time almost reeling.

The terrible energy, shall we call it the vital force, in one night bird took me so by surprise that my angel of death left me.

The next day, in heavy snow, I walked back alive to Kyoto.

I did not see Hira from Katada again until the time of the Keisuke affair. The date I cannot forget: the fall of 1926.

It was the year I became dean of the medical school, and I was fifty-five. The years from then until I retired at sixty were years of rankling unpleasantness. The Keisuke affair, Misa's death a year later, Hiroyuki's marriage and Kyōko's, both of which displeased me intensely. Then there was Sadamitsu's drift toward radicalism, and as dean of the medical school I was little more than an errand boy, forced to give up what was most important to me, my research. Each day added a new irritation.

The Keisuke affair came quite without warning. A call from R University, and Misa went to see what the difficulty was. Keisuke had been expelled because of trouble with some woman. I could not believe my ears when Misa came into my study and told me. Keisuke had always had a weak strain in him, and we had had to put him in R University, a private school without much standing, because his grades were below average; but there was something boyish about him; he had a quietness and docility lacking in the other children. I had always thought him a model of good behavior. But I suppose he showed a different face to other people, and he had proceeded to get some tramp of an eighteen-year-old waitress pregnant.

I thought the affair might just possibly have found its way into the papers, and when I opened my evening paper, there indeed it was, headlined "Student

Indecencies" or something equally trite. The story of Keisuke's misbehavior, quite new to me, was told in some detail. "The son of an important educator, a dean in a certain university," the article said, giving a fictitious name that would suggest mine immediately. My standing as an educator was gone. That was very well. I had never considered myself an educator anyway. I am only a scholar. But the boy's conduct, so unbecoming in a student, was most distressing to me as a father, the only father he had, after all. I had more trouble later when Sadamitsu turned radical, but that incident at least had its redeeming features. There was not one detail I could console myself with in the Keisuke affair.

I did not leave my study until Keisuke came home later that night. I heard him in the dining room, talking to Misa in that wheedling way of his. He seemed to be eating. I could hear a clatter of dishes.

I walked down the hall and slid open the door to the dining room. Keisuke's student uniform was unbuttoned and the white lining was in full view. The sight of him there quite at his ease, with Misa to serve him, was too much for me.

"Get out of here. I won't have the likes of you around the house."

Keisuke pulled himself up. His soft eyes were turned to the floor.

I shouted at him again. "Get out of here! Get out!"

He quietly left the room and went upstairs.

I did not think he would really leave the house, but at about nine o'clock, when Misa went upstairs to look for him, he was gone.

From the next day Misa refused to eat. I thought little about the matter, however. Keisuke being Keisuke, I was sure that he would be crawling home very soon.

I have no idea how she was able to learn so much, but Misa reported that the girl, in spite of her youth, was a formidable creature indeed. She had already had one child, and she had had no trouble in making a plaything of Keisuke.

"Whether he was the deceiver or the deceived," I answered, "the end result was the same."

Just as I had expected, a telephone call came from Keisuke. It was the third day after he had left home. Quite by accident I was looking for medical magazines in the next room, where my books were stored. I thought there was something very strange about Hiroyuki's smothered voice. I went out to the veranda, where he and Misa were whispering to each other, and asked if the call hadn't been from Keisuke. Neither of them answered for a time, but Hiroyuki finally admitted that it had been. They had apparently meant to tell me nothing. Keisuke, it seemed, was staying with the woman at the Lakeside Hotel in Sakamoto, and Hiroyuki was to take him money.

The next afternoon, brushing aside Misa's misgivings, I went by taxi to the Lakeside Hotel. I asked at the desk to have Keisuke called, and a minute or two later there was a slapping of sandals on the wide staircase before me, and a young girl appeared. Her hair was cut in bangs after the schoolgirl fashion. She wore a cheap kimono tied with a narrow reddish obi. Careless, childish if you will—in any case it was an odd way to be dressed. She came halfway downstairs and threw a glance in my direction, and when she saw who it was her expression quickly changed. She stared at me for a moment with wide, round eyes, then turned and ran back upstairs with a lightness that made me think of a squirrel. It was hard to believe that she was pregnant.

Another minute passed and a worried-looking Keisuke came down. I went with him into the lobby, where we sat facing each other over a table. I handed him the money he had asked for.

"You are to go home today. You are not to go out of the house for the time being. You are not to see that woman again. Misa will take care of her."

"But . . ." Keisuke hesitated.

"You are to go home today," I said again.

Keisuke asked me to let him think the matter over until the next day. I was so furious that I shook, but I could say nothing. There seemed to be a wedding reception somewhere in the hotel, and people in formal clothes were giving us vaguely curious glances. I stood up.

"Very well. You have your choice. Either that worthless woman or your own father."

I ordered him to come to Katada with his answer by noon the next day.

"Yes, sir," Keisuke said quietly. "I'm sorry to have bothered you." He turned and went back upstairs. I had the man at the desk call the Reihōkan—Katada was not far away—and presently I stepped from the taxi and was back at this inn for the first time in thirty years. The Keisuke affair had exhausted me mentally and physically. The next day was Sunday, and I looked forward to a good rest.

The innkeeper came up to my room. He had aged, but I could still see in his face the face of thirty years before. I telephoned the house in Kyoto to tell Misa briefly what had happened. How many years since I had last spent a quiet evening alone, reading nothing and writing nothing? It was a little early for duck, but the fish from the lake was very good. I slept beautifully.

There was a telephone call from Kyoto at ten the next morning as I was sitting down to breakfast. The voice over the wire was not Misa's usual voice.

"Word has come from the hotel that Keisuke and the woman drowned themselves in the lake this morning. Please go to Sakamoto at once. We are just leaving the house."

I was stunned. What had the fool done? He had taken the woman and discarded me. That was very well. But did he have to pick such an unpleasant way to answer his own father?

I did not go to Sakamoto.

At about three Hiroyuki came to the inn. I was sitting on the veranda in a rattan chair, and I looked up to see Hiroyuki glaring at me, his face pale and grim.

"Don't you feel the least bit sorry for him?"

"Of course I do. I would feel sorry for anyone who could be such a fool."

"They haven't found the bodies yet. All sorts of people have been helping, and you ought to show your face." He threw the words out, and turned to leave. He had come all the way to my inn just to say that.

About an hour later Misa came, with Kyōko and Takatsu, who was then Kyō-ko's fiancé. Misa came into the room and started toward me as though she wanted to throw herself at my feet. Then she reconsidered and sat down in a corner, silent and motionless, her face buried in her hands. I knew that she was trying very hard to keep from sobbing.

"Maybe they will come up before evening," Takatsu said. He meant the bodies.

I disliked having him around at such a time. I had of course been opposed from the start to his marrying Kyōko. His father, the most successful or possibly the second most successful businessman in Osaka, was an uncultured upstart who cared less than nothing for scholarship. His sneering arrogance thoroughly displeased me. "I think I can see to the money for your publishing," he said the first time I met him. Misa and the children visited his house once, and I gather that the power of money swept them off their feet. "The house is enormous, and the living room is magnificent, and he has a country house at Yase and another at Takarazuka," and so on and so on—I found the liveliness most distasteful.

That was not all. The son, Takatsu himself, had been in France for three years, but all he could talk about was the Louvre. He didn't study when he was in France and he didn't drink. All he did was wander around looking at pictures, though he was no painter. He frittered away his time. And up he came to Kyoto every Sunday, rain or snow, without waiting to see whether we would let him marry Kyōko. He's a sort I will never understand. When I said I was opposed to the marriage, Kyōko burst into tears. I was incensed. I asked how the others felt, and I found that all of them, Misa and the children, took Kyōko's part. Takatsu had apparently made a good impression on everyone but me. Neither Keisuke nor Hiroyuki had any interest in scholarship, and Sadamitsu was not to be depended upon, and I thought that at the very least I would have Kyōko marry some fine young man prepared to devote his life to scholarship. But now I was forced to give up that hope too.

In any case, I was most unhappy to see Takatsu pushing his way into an important Miike family conference, even before the wedding date had been set.

"Kyōko can go back to Sakamoto. I want to talk to her mother alone," I said.

Kyōko and Takatsu had the people at the inn make them a lunch, and called a taxi, and in general raised a commotion suggesting that the whole affair was a picnic for them.

When they had left and the room was quiet, I thought I would like to say something comforting to Misa, but instead I found myself scolding her.

"It's your fault that Keisuke has come to this. You spoiled him."

Misa sat with her head bowed, her face in her hands, so still that she might have been dead.

"Hiroyuki, and Kyōko too. All of them are worthless. I have stood all I can."

Misa got up and staggered to the veranda. She put one hand to her forehead and, leaning against a pillar, looked at me. Only one time in her life did Misa look into my eyes in that quiet way. After a time she sank to the floor as though her legs would no longer support her.

"I think at least half the fault is yours. What have you ever done for the children?"

She usually had so little to say that her talkativeness made me wonder whether the affair might not have deranged her.

"You were away in Germany when Keisuke was small. You went for three years and you stayed eight. The last five years you sent no word either to us or to the ministry. I don't think you can imagine how terrible those years were for us."

It was as Misa said. I saved the money the Ministry of Education had given me for three years' study and stayed eight years. I had no wife and no children and no house. I lived in a cheap room and ate black bread, and I kept my eye trained on scholarship, that distant eminence, lofty as the Alps. Otherwise I would not have been able to do the work I am doing today.

Misa went on. "Research, research, you say, and you have no Sundays and no holidays. When you have spare time you prod your corpses. And when you come home you say you're tired of the smell of corpses and you start drinking. You never even smile when you're drinking, and you go on writing away at that German. What have you done for the children? Have you even once looked at a report card? Have you once taken them to the zoo? You've sacrificed the children and me to that research of yours."

That I should have to hear this from Misa, who had helped me with my research through the long years of poverty, never once stopping to pamper herself!

I wanted no more of her complaining. "That's enough. I sacrificed myself too," I said.

I was staring absently at the lake, as I had been all the hours since breakfast. When I raised my eyes from the lake, there was Hira, wrapped in the deep colors of autumn, spreading its quiet form grandly before me, as if to embrace me.

"I'm going, back to the hotel," said Misa coldly. She stood up and turned to leave. "I don't know what happened yesterday, but I imagine the boy died cursing you."

Perhaps she had wept herself out. Her eyes were dry, and her face was strangely composed as she arranged her shawl. She almost snatched up her bundles, and she turned her back abruptly and marched from the room as if she meant never to come back to me.

An inexpressible feeling of loneliness came over me. That will do, I said to myself, and stood up. I sat down again. I did not know what it was that would do.

I called the desk and asked for a notebook. I had not thought of him in years, but I sat down to draft a letter to Tanio Kaigetsu. Tanio Kaigetsu was neither an anatomist nor an anthropologist. For seven years I studied under Professor Schalbe at Strassburg, doing research principally on birthmarks, but also laying the foundation for my life's work, non-osseous anthropology. Afterward I spent a year at the Leyden Museum—actually it was something of a detour for me—measuring the crania of some thousand Filipinos. A bar run by a Japanese woman was the congregating place for Japanese scholars in Leyden, and it was there that I met Tanio Kaigetsu.

He was a priest, a rather unusual priest, who was studying Sanskrit, also at the Leyden Museum. He was a little older than I, and he was a good toper—that expression fitted Tanio Kaigetsu perfectly. I was much taken with his dashing, lighthearted way of drinking. Even when he was drinking, his mind was on scholarship. I knew nothing about his research, and doubtless he knew nothing about mine, but we were exactly suited for each other. We both knew the dignity of scholarship, and we respected each other as scholars. When I left Leyden, Tanio Kaigetsu said he wanted to give me the most valuable farewell present he could. He would like to know what I needed. "Let me have your body to dissect when you die," I said.

Kaigetsu took out pen and paper on the spot, and wrote down his testament. "I give my body to the anatomist Miike Shuntarō." To his own copy he added an injunction: "My relatives are not to challenge the validity of this testament."

I had not seen Kaigetsu since I said goodbye to him in the doorway of the Leyden Museum in 1912. I knew, however, that he had come back to Japan some years after me and that he was alive and well, the resident priest in a little temple somewhere in the mountains. I was sure if I asked at the university someone would know the address of Tanio Kaigetsu, obscure old scholar of Buddhism.

I thought to get through the day by writing to Kaigetsu. The promise he had given me, I almost felt, was the only promise I had left in the world. It was the only bit of human intercourse, the only incident in my relations with mankind, in which I could have confidence.

But I sat there with pen in hand, not knowing how to begin. It seemed immeasurably difficult to communicate the warm, flowing human affection I felt for Kaigetsu after years of neglect.

I laid down my pen and looked out. The surface of the lake was aglow in the autumn twilight. Far to the east some dozens of boats were floating motionless, like fallen leaves. Keisuke and that girl—I could only think of the woman who had died with Keisuke, the woman I had seen halfway down the stairs at the Lakeside Hotel, as a young girl—the boats clustered there, I said to myself, are perhaps looking for the bodies of Keisuke and that girl.

I did not write to Kaigetsu. Instead I sat on the veranda, with the lake for my partner, trying to endure, to resist. When night came, I went back into the room and sat rigid before the desk. Now and then I stood up and looked east over the lake. There in the same spot, on into the night, were those dozens of little boats, like lights strung out for decoration.

The third and most recent time I saw Hira from the Reihōkan was in the darkest days Japan has known. My heart, the heart of the nation, was plunged into a darkness that held not a fragment of hope.

We did not know when the air raids would begin, and every day the newspapers and radios were shouting at people to leave the cities. With the war situation growing worse, blackness hung ready to envelop the country. It was then, in the spring of 1944, that I was brought to Katada by Atsuko, Haruko's youngest sister. Atsuko was in her fifth year of high school. Nearly twenty years had gone by since the Keisuke affair.

I was alone in the Kyoto house with only a maid. At the beginning of the year, Hiroyuki had been transferred to the Kanazawa branch of his company, and Haruko and the four children had gone with him. I say that he was transferred. Actually Hiroyuki himself had wanted very much to flee the city and the bombings, and the initiative had been his. For a man with four children, the oldest of them only eleven, I suppose this was most natural.

It apparently bothered both Hiroyuki and Haruko to leave an old man alone in Kyoto. Although they persisted in trying to make me go with them, I would have none of it. I suppose they took my refusal for the stubbornness of the old, but it was not. My work was important to me. No one, however long he argued, could pry me loose from my desk.

Hiroyuki said that my research depended on my life, but for me it was the opposite: my life depended on my research. My work was everything, and I could not proceed with my work away from the university. I had to go to the anatomy laboratory, and I could not be cut off from the libraries. If I were to leave Kyoto, my work would stop.

I could go on with my research only as long as I lived, Hiroyuki said. To me, at seventy-three, the matter was more urgent. Every morning as I sat down and began to write, a picture of my own circulatory system would float before my eyes. I knew that my veins had so degenerated that they would crumble between the fingers like scraps of biscuit. Even had there been no war, I would have been in a race against death. Each day lived was so much gained. If things progressed smoothly, I would be ninety-three when I finished *The Arterial System of the Japanese*. I knew therefore that I could never expect to see the end of my work, and I wanted to get out the last chapter and the last sentence I could. I worked out a plan for publishing in successive volumes, each part to be sent around to the printer's as it was finished. The times were such, however, that I could not be sure when the printer would close shop.

And even if by good luck I should succeed in having several volumes published, the possibility of sending them abroad was as good as gone. I had thought, through the good offices of the German consulate in Kobe, at least to send my work to universities in the Axis countries, but it seemed that the war in Europe had succeeded in denying my last wish.

I sat at my desk those days literally begrudging the passage of each minute. I must write, and if I wrote, everything would somehow be all right. Years, tens of years after my death, by whatever devious course, my work would come to be recognized in the academic world for what it was. It would become a rock that would not wear away. Scholars would follow in my footsteps and non-osseous anthropology would be brought to maturity. So I thought, so I believed, as I drove myself on.

For all that, I often dreamed I saw my manuscript licked by flames, blazing up and dancing into the heavens with the smoke. Each time I had the dream I awoke to find my eyes wet with tears.

There was a small second-hand bookshop near the university that I used to dread going by. I knew that buried under layers of dust in one corner of the shop was a manuscript on the topography of Kyoto. I do not know who the author was, but the manuscript was written neatly in the old style on Japanese paper. It may or may not have been of value. In any case there it was, laboriously put together by someone, and, for nearly three years after I first noticed it, lying in the same corner of that bookshop, held together by a thin cord. I could not bear to think that the manuscript of *The Arterial System of the Japanese*, with its hundreds of illustrations, might have in store for it the fate of that unhappy work on Kyoto topography. I would think, as I passed, of the dark destiny that might be lying in wait for my work, and a feeling of utter desolation would come over me.

Every Sunday Atsuko came up from Ashiya. To comfort an old man working alone, she always brought wrapped in a kerchief some bread she said she had baked herself, and laid it carefully on my desk with two or three apples. Apples were not easy to find in those days.

I became rather fond of the seventeen-year-old Atsuko. There was something modest and withdrawn about her, quite the opposite of Haruko's gaudiness, and yet she was bright and open. I am not capable of affection for my grandchildren, but I felt a strange warmth, a father's affection almost, for a girl who was not even one of the family. Atsuko for her part seemed to like the old man well enough.

I was walking in the garden that morning. Generally I went to work immediately after breakfast, but that morning was different. I paced the garden fretfully. The spring sun found its way through the trees to warm the earth, but I felt only a rough, harsh chill that could not be called simple anger or loneliness. I could think of nothing to do for myself but walk around the garden.

The Imperial Culture Awards had been announced with much fanfare that morning. Six men from the humanities and the natural sciences had been awarded the Culture Medal, the highest honor the nation can give its scholars.

I stared for a time at the photographs of the recipients, each with a medal on his chest, and I thought how I too would like to have a medal. I thought how I would like to be thus commended, to have my achievements written of, to have centered on me the respect and interest and understanding of the country and the people. I had never in my life envied anyone for worldly honors, but just this once, I thought, I would like to feel the weight of popular acclaim on my thin shoulders.

Was not my work greater than the work of these six men? I laid the newspaper down, went to my study, and sat at my desk. I stood up again and went out to the garden. Was my work not worth a national commendation, in all probability the last it could expect? Was my work not fit to be praised by the government, admired and respected by the people, protected? I wanted honor, now, today, I thought, however slight the honor might be. However subdued the acclaim, I wanted something to turn to.

The name Miike Shuntarō must be inscribed on men's hearts. Every last individual must be made to see the value of Miike Shuntarō's work. But there I was, at the end of my life, with the country on the verge of collapse. My thousands of pages of manuscript must be given up to no one could foresee what fate. Perhaps they would go up in smoke before my work could be recognized for what it was. Professor Schalbe—the name of the man to whom I owed so much came to my lips, and tears came to my eyes.

There was a telephone call from the administrative office at the university. The university was to give a reception the next day for Dr. K, one of the six honored scholars, and it would be appreciated if I could say a few words of congratulation on behalf of the professors emeritus. I refused.

Not five minutes later there was a call from Professor Yokoya, one of my students, with the same request.

"I have no time to write messages of congratulations about other people," I said. "I have more than enough work of my own to fill my time. I am at an age when no one need be surprised if I die tomorrow."

Yokoya was very polite and did not press the point.

I had no sooner hung up than there was a call from a newspaper reporter. He wanted a few remarks on one of the medal holders.

"I am interested in nothing except my own work. It was good of you to call, but it will not be worth your trouble to see me." With that I hung up. Since I would of course be having more calls, I left the receiver off the hook.

I went down into the garden again. For very little reason, I was overcome with a mixture of anger and sorrow and loneliness. As I paced the garden, Atsuko came in through the shrubbery. She was dressed in the drab, baggy trousers that were standard, and her face, with its young smile, was like a flower (she was indeed a flower to me then). She took out a few groceries she said had been sent by her family.

"Would you like to go to Lake Biwa?" she asked.

"Lake Biwa?" I was a little startled.

"Let's go to Lake Biwa and have a boat ride."

Even in wartime, the warmth of spring seemed to stir the young to more than everyday brightness. I found myself strangely unresisting.

"Very well. Will you take me to Lake Biwa?"

I can do nothing else today, but I can at least do what this girl wants me to. I can at least follow her—such, if I am to put them honestly, were my feelings.

We let train after train pass until finally one came with a few empty seats. We rode to Ōtsu. It was nearly twenty years since the Keisuke affair. While I was in the university and even after I retired I had chances enough to go to Ōtsu for banquets and such, but with the Keisuke affair I had come to dislike Lake Biwa and I avoided the place.

But now, brought to the lake again by Atsuko, I saw only its beauty. Time is a fearful thing. The pain of the Keisuke affair had quite faded away. The surface of the lake shimmered like fish-scales spread out in the noonday sun. Atsuko had said she wanted a boat ride, and indeed there were little rowboats and sailboats scattered over the lake. Here at least the shadow of war did not seem to fall.

As I looked out and saw Hira rising from the water, I suddenly wanted to go to Katada. A steamer was leaving just then, and the two of us climbed aboard.

A half hour later we were in Katada. We rested for a time at the Reihōkan. I saw no one I knew from the innkeeper's family, the place apparently being occupied by a single sullen maid. The windows along the hall were broken, and the inn was plainly run-down, as indeed inns were everywhere.

Atsuko helped me into a boat not far from the pier where the steamer had come in. It was my first ride in a rowboat. She borrowed a thin cushion from the boathouse for me, and showed me how to hold the sides of the boat.

There was not another boat in sight as we floated out over the water. Atsuko arched her back and strained at the oars. Perspiration broke out on her face.

"Are you enjoying yourself?" she asked.

I was in fact less than delighted, with the spray from the oars hitting me in the face and my life entrusted to a flimsy little boat.

"Thoroughly," I said. I forbade her to go into deep water, however. Cherries were blooming along the shore. The April sun carried just a touch of chill, and the clear air, free from the dust of the city, had not yet taken on the sourness of summer. Hira was beautiful.

A fish jumped up near the boat. "A fish," said Atsuko, turning to gaze with wide eyes. She slapped industriously with the oars and pulled the boat to the spot where the fish had been. I suddenly thought of the girl I had seen for but an instant halfway down the stairs at the Lakeside Hotel, the girl who had died with Keisuke. There was a trace of her in Atsuko. The exaggerated, childish surprise at the fish, the quick agility with which Atsuko brought the boat around—whatever it was, a giddiness came over me as the images of Atsuko and the girl merged. Perhaps the girl too was fresh and clean like Atsuko. Strangely, I no longer felt angry at the girl who had taken Keisuke. Rather I was conscious of something very like affection for her, an affection which I could not feel for Keisuke himself.

I stared down into the water that buried everything, the water into which Keisuke and the girl had sunk. I pushed my hand down the side of the boat. The water slid through five thin old fingers, colder than I would have expected it to be.

Atsuko is gone. Much too soon, she died in the typhus epidemic at the end of the war. Misa is gone. Kyōko's father-in-law, whom I so disliked, is dead too. Tanio Kaigetsu died the year the war ended. Good people and bad, they all are gone.

When Kaigetsu died there was a query from the Tanio family on the matter of the dissection, and it would seem therefore that Kaigetsu still meant to honor his promise of thirty years before. The times being what they were, however, there was little I could do. I finally had to let the contract I had made with Kaigetsu in Leyden come to nothing.

It is drawing on toward evening, and the wind from the lake is chilly. It is especially chilly at the collar and knees. Here it is May, and I feel as if I should be wearing wool. The roaring in my ears is especially strong today. Exactly as if the wind were blowing. And indeed the wind has grown stronger.

I suppose the house will be in a turmoil by now. It will be good for them all. It will bring them to their senses. Maybe Yokoya and Sugiyama at the university have been told of the crisis, and the two of them have come running to hear the worst about their old benefactor, their faces suggesting suitable concern. They cut a considerable swathe as professors at the university, but have they inherited in the slightest degree my qualities as a scholar? They seem to have no real understanding for my work. "Professor Miike, Professor Miike," they say with great shows of respect when I am around. You would think they could find better things to do. No doubt it is "old fogey, old fogey" when I am out of sight—I feel quite certain it is. I remember well enough how those two were during the war. "Let's get the university out in the country, let's get the students organized for the war effort." Off they went and forgot all about their studies. I didn't say anything then, but I saw their limitations as scholars, and I was very sad. Whatever they are, they cannot be called scholars.

Little waves are breaking around the rickety pier where Atsuko rented her boat. There are ripples all over the lake, I see now. The white flags waving from the masts have probably been forgotten. Someone should have taken them in. I have found it more and more annoying these last years to see things that should be put away and are not. Everything has to be where it belongs. In the old days I was not so fussy. The people in the house have made me what I am. Unless I speak to her time after time, Haruko does nothing about the laundry I see from my study, and Hiroyuki leaves stamped and addressed letters lying on his desk for days on end. Kyōko and Sadamitsu too are partly to blame. And it is not only the family. The people at the university are as bad.

A year has gone by since I asked for a short report on the lymph gland, and it was the youngest research student of them all who finally came around with an interim report.

I don't want to think about anything. To think is to exhaust yourself. I don't want to think about anything except *The Arterial System of the Japanese.* I have wasted a day on trivialities, and I must work tonight. Work, work, Miike Shuntarō, old scholar, must go on with his work while he lives. Tonight I must write explanations for the illustrations to Part Nine, or if not the full explanations at least the headings. Yes, and I must ask the maid to bring saké so that I can have a drink when I've finished work and am ready for bed. Two hundred grams of good saké, in a carefully washed decanter. Work that I could once have finished in an hour now takes a day, sometimes even two days or three. Growing old is a terrible thing.

Fifty years ago when I was in this room I thought only of dying. Youth has no sense of values. Today I want to live even one day more. Professor Schalbe is dead, and Professor Yamaoka of Tokyo is dead. I am sure that neither was ready to die. Both must have wanted to live and work even a day longer. Tanio Kaigetsu too. It was his great ambition to compile a Sanskrit dictionary, but he does not seem to have lived to finish it. Priests and ministers I suppose have their own special views on life and death—but Kaigetsu was not a priest. He was a scholar. It was precisely because he was a scholar among scholars that I liked and admired him. I don't think Kaigetsu was ready to die. Enlightenment, they call it, but I suspect that enlightenment is in the last analysis a convenient refuge for the lazy. Man was meant to work furiously to the end. Why else was he created? Not to bask in the sun, surely. Not just to be happy.

I wanted to see Hira today. I wanted to see Hira so much that I could not help myself. I sent Haruko from the room and tried to control my annoyance. I made myself a bowl of tea, but the rancor was still there. As I drank from that Hagi bowl and set it on my knee, the image of Hira floated before me. By the time the man from the Ōmoriya was ringing the doorbell my mind was made up. Hira was calling me with a strength I could not resist. I have been sitting here half a day now, and I have looked at Hira enough. The face of Hira, so deep and rich in the daylight, has these last few minutes grown pale, and the sky outlining it has become almost too bright. Another hour and Hira will have melted back into the darkness.

The azaleas were beautiful today as we came past Keage. Possibly, since they belong to the same family, the rhododendrons are in bloom at the summit of Hira. Somewhere high on that slope, the white flowers are blooming. The great white clusters spread over the face of the mountain. Ah, how much more at peace I would be if I could lie there at the summit under those scented clusters! To lie with my legs stretched out and to look up into the night sky—I am happier even at the thought of it. There and only there, I somehow feel, is what could rock me and lull me, give me peace. I should have gone up there, at least once. It is too late now. It is no longer possible for me to climb mountains.

I have less chance of climbing Hira than of finishing *The Arterial System of the Japanese*.

On the snowy day when I came here in a cotton priest's robe, and at the time of the Keisuke affair, and when I went rowing with Atsuko, I saw Hira. My eye was on Hira. But I did not have the slightest desire to climb it. Why? Because the season was wrong? No, not that. Perhaps until now I have not had the qualifications. That is the point, I am sure of it.

Long ago, as I looked at the picture of the rhododendrons of Hira, I thought that the day must come when I would climb to the top. Perhaps the day was today. But today, however much I may want to, I cannot climb Hira.

Well, back into the room. I must hurry through dinner and get on with my work. How many years has it been since I last had a quiet evening away from the voices of the children? A bell is ringing somewhere. Or is an old man's ear imagining things? But I do hear a bell, behind the roaring in my ears. No, it is my imagination. I was working in a German mountain lodge (I had gone there to prepare a paper for a discussion with Dr. Steda of the red bones he had found in Siberia), and I heard the cowbells ringing. What a lovely sound it was. Perhaps something has made me hear it again, in my memory, from those tens of years ago.

Hurry with dinner, please. I have work to do. I must go back into the world of red veins, into the coral grove.

ISHIKAWA JUN

Ishikawa Jun (1899–1987), an admirer and a translator of André Gide's fiction, considered himself a modernist and used some of Gide's literary techniques to create his first great success in 1936, the novel *Boddhisatva* (*Fugen*). But it was not until after the war that Ishikawa truly came into his own as a writer. One of his postwar successes was "The Jesus of the Ruins" (Yakeato no Iesu, 1946), a cogent rendering of the atmosphere of early postwar Japan.

THE JESUS OF THE RUINS (YAKEATO NO IESU)

Translated by William J. Tyler

Under the blazing sky of a hot summer sun, amidst choking dirt and dust, a cluster of makeshift stalls has sprung from the land, and like a weed that grows in a dump, it has sent out its tendrils to cover the earth. The stands are partitioned by screens made of reeds, each pressing so hard upon the next there is scarcely room to breathe, let alone move. And as for the occupants, if there are those who flog their various and sundry household goods by simply setting them out on the ground, and those who spread kimonos or things to wear across tables, by far the vast majority are people with food to sell. They operate out of their carts, openly taking out white rice and serving it to the public in defiance of the law.

"Last chance! Last chance!" they cry. "Today's the last day! Tomorrow's too late."

The faces of the men turn beet red under the broiling rays of the sun as they shout at the top of their lungs, and oily beads of sweat drip from their brows. And, to the chorus of the men's voices, the women vendors add their ear-splitting cries, the noisy crescendo of the marketplace rising to a fever pitch. The spectacle of so many people furiously shrieking and shouting is a powerful, even frightful sight. Indeed it is a scene that is almost bloodthirsty in its relentlessness.

For today is July 31, 1946, and come tomorrow, the first of August, official notice has been served that the market is to be closed for good. Everyone stands on the brink of being put out of business.

And, even if that were not the case—

This is Tokyo's Ueno, the most pugnacious part of town, where tempers and nostrils flare, and every inch of territory—even the space under a train trestle—is guarded jealously. Yes, it is just the sort of place where, not so very long ago, there was a bloody row in which the locals took on the gendarmes of the law.

It is also what comes in the wake of wax and its fire: a city in ruins, the burnt-out shell of a metropolis. Its creatures have hatched out of the debris, and now they survive by the sheer tenacity with which they came into the world and by which they cling to life.

In truth, they live as though in their original naked state, all looking alike and possessed of nothing more than the shirt on their backs. Yes, were it not for the flimsiness of the fabric one could hardly discern male from female, the men identifiable only by the tattoos visible on their shoulders and backs; the women, by the rounded swell of their chests.

Each lurks within the shadow of his or her reed stall, hiding there and harboring a unique brand of venom. For the denizens of the marketplace are as ready as ever to reach into the crowd and sink their teeth into a potential customer. Indeed they have so devised the business of selling food that they need only to rattle a plate to make the cheapest of yen notes fly forth from someone's tired pocket. It is like a trap or a clever springlike device in which the clatter of dishes sets up a hollow sound that echoes all the way down to the pit of the empty stomach of every customer and makes him or her want to eat.

Yet look at the customers—

They too are not about to be outdone, each and every one a perfect match for the hawkers. Wild-eyed and frantic, the whites of their eyes all bloodshot, they too are poised, their mouths lunging for food almost before there is time to race into a booth and polish off a filthy plate in a single gulp.

The business of the marketplace is the transactions of beasts, the winners in the game of profit and loss being decided in a single bite. It is a dog-eat-dog world; and no matter how much one creature feeds or is fed upon, the time never comes when either party announces he or she has had enough. No, it appears there will never be a time in which they will lift their heads and, momentarily studying the sky, decide to take a breather.

No, it appears there will never be a moment when a cool breeze might arise from one quarter or the other.

A man slaps a pound of sardines on what passes for a grill and lets the fish sizzle. The sardines are already red around the eye, and a sheet of corrugated metal is no great shakes as a griddle. Nonetheless, the foul, rancid smell that fills the air when the oily fish hits the hot metal—an odor rank enough to turn the stomach of any ordinary mortal—appears only to whet the vulgar appetites of the crowd, and all the more shamelessly. The great unwashed come running, and like flies, they swarm over the stall.

Yet real flies know better, and fearing the heat of the flame, they keep their distance, content merely to buzz about noisily. They head downwind of the breeze that carries the smell of the oily sardines and the stench of the sweaty crowd, and they decide to settle on the stall next door. Alighting atop the dark, round, and uncovered objects that have been set out on the counter for sale, they swarm over them and turn them completely black. . . .

Aside from the woman who works at the stand, no one is about. Apparently there has been a momentary lull in her business. . . .

"Get 'em while they're still nice and warm! Fresh *o-musubi*. That's right. *O-musubi* for only ten yen apiece. And made from polished rice too!"

Were it not for her verbal advertisement, who would have known what it was she had for sale? Sure enough, the dark, round objects set out on the counter were *o-musubi*. They were balls of rice, and each had been wrapped in a thin sheet of dried seaweed.

Yet the seaweed had none of the sheen or crinkle of a reliable brand. It was of a cheap, inferior sort that, when pressed against the warm, moist surface of a ball of freshly steamed rice, merely went limp and looked more like wilted *shiso* leaves than seaweed. Moreover, it was torn in spots, and as a result, the rice showed through the tears. The rice was white all right, just as the woman had loudly proclaimed in her promise of polished rice, but once the grains had dried out and started to stick together, they looked as though they had been glued in place. There was no trace—nay, not even a lingering whiff—of the steam or the heart-warming smell that arises when freshly cooked rice is scooped from the pot and pressed into firmly shaped balls.

To the contrary, were there any suggestion of steaminess—and the feeling of fecundity that fills the air when one lifts the lid from a tub of freshly steamed rice—surely it was not to be found enveloping the *o-musubi* that had been set out for sale. No, it emanated instead from the woman who sold them. . . .

Just how old is she, anyway?

All that can be said with certainty is she had yet to acquire any real age in life and was still very much a young woman. She had filled out, the flesh on her limbs radiating with the voluptuousness of youth, its heat almost palpable as it glowed on her sunburnt skin. And through the peachlike fuzz that covered her arms and legs shone the blush of the crimson that coursed so richly through her veins and that, in rising to the surface, brought to her complexion its fresh and healthy fragrance. Her arms and legs were full, almost bursting with an excess of energy; and when she threw back her head and shoulders with a defiant look, her breasts flashed like the tips of pointed daggers as they pressed against the fabric of her sliplike chemise.

She had hiked up the hem of her already short skirt as she sat in the booth, and without the slightest hint of shame, she lifted one leg and let it rest on the other in full view of the crowd. It was a pose that seemed to suggest she was inciting her own body and, by egging it on, aroused herself to a state of sexual desire.

Yet, really, was there any other position for her to assume, given a body so free of strain or artifice? There she was, arrayed in her most natural mode of expression, even to the point of looking almost base or ugly. She made one think. Given a world in which the physical nature of human beings was allowed to manifest itself regardless of its surroundings, just how far might we go in letting ourselves give expression to the inner chemistry of our bodies? Why, wouldn't naked desire want to push us way to the fore and make itself known to the world in the same sort of wild and uncivilized way in which the girl presented herself here? In short, wouldn't debauchery come to constitute a new and wholesome morality? And flesh, a new and competing source of illumination and enlightenment in the world? For so intense was the glow of the girl and her body, and so blinding was its glaze when it struck the eye that even the sun at high noon began to pale by comparison. Yes, even a force as powerful as the sun assumed an artificial hue and looked almost sedate in its hazy efflorescence. . . .

From time to time the woman belted out her cry, hawking her wares, but her voice never assumed the cutthroat and gangsterlike tone of her male competitors. They were professional salesmen, and they had learned how to make their sales pitch sound like an adult throwing a temper tantrum. By contrast, the woman's cry remained unabashedly her own, and by virtue of that fact, it was natural, and it revealed a lingering touch of innocence.

"Step right up and get a freshly made *o-musubi*. Only ten yen apiece. . . ."

Just then a commotion broke out in the stall next-door that was selling sardines. The crowd began to stir.

"You filthy . . ."

"Don't touch me. Yeah, you. You heard me. Don't even get near me. Keep your dirty paws to yourself."

"Get out of here. Get the hell out of here, and I mean now."

The crowd was thrown into an agitated state, with everyone shouting at once. A man came rushing over to the stall. He was dressed in a pair of shorts and military boots. He appeared to be a patrolman who had been hired by the market to keep an eye on things.

"You're back, huh? I thought I told you to clear out," he said in a gruff voice. "You don't listen, do ya?"

"Hell, you're so filthy; who'd want to lay a hand on you? All right, you'll stay out of here from now on, or you'll be as good as dead if I find you around here again. Got it? 'Cuz I'll bash your head in. Now git the hell outta here."

The man in the boots might as well have been driving off a stray dog, his voice having become a veritable hiss. Words were a powerful whip that he used to lash at his victim.

Yet what shot from the torrent of abuse that the man rained upon the ground—yes, what shot our from the stall or, more precisely, from between the legs of the customers standing there—was surely no dog.

It was a boy.

A living, breathing human being.

And insofar as appellations of gender or age may apply, yes, he was male . . . and a child . . . in short, just a boy.

Yet, in point of fact, he defied description. Here was a creature for whom there was no proper name, because the taxonomy of his kind had yet to be invented. . . .

It was as though an old suit of clothes had been abandoned by the wayside. It had gotten dirty and foul from lying in the dirt, but then one day who should come along but some wild and crazy sprite. The sprite took a liking to the clothes, quickly donning them, upon which the old suit suddenly sprang to life. Yes, there it was, a set of rags, and it was standing on its own two feet. Fanned by the breeze, it began to walk about, acting ever so much like a human being who was out for a stroll.

Behold, the boy was black as the sludge in a ditch, and it was impossible to tell at a glance where the ragged edge of his clothes ended and the flesh underneath began. He was so caked in dirt and filth, he looked as if he were covered in scales. To make matters worse, his head and face were covered in unspeakable boils. The boils oozed with pus that, baked to a crust in the terrible heat of the sun, had dried and begun to reek with an awful smell. Indeed, the stench was so potent that it seemed to reach out and attack one's nostrils. Even those who worked in the marketplace had begun to complain, and surely they had never been known to flinch at the thought of handling anything foul or rotten. . . . Not even the immovable object of the man in the military boots was unfazed. He too could hardly bear to stand next to the boy.

So that, while the former soldier sounded tough, and his voice rumbled like a resonating gong, he contented himself with taking a few steps back and motioning for the boy to get moving.

Yet in backing off and simply using threats instead of actually taking the boy in hand, he suggested by his manner that, were there a cowering dog in the marketplace, surely it was none other than himself. And, like a dog that is easily frightened by the specter of whatever lurks in the shadows, it appeared he had decided to confine his barking to a safe distance.

What was it about the boy? He had only to step into the center of the thoroughfare, and a look of sheer panic spread across the faces in the crowd. It was a reaction shared by all—one read it in the eyes of vendor and passerby alike. Every man and woman was on guard, knees bent, their bodies ready to spring into action at a moment's notice. But, somehow, like the hireling in the military boots, their legs failed them. It seemed as though they were powerless to move. Whatever had caused each and every one of them to assume an unexpectedly frozen pose, and with a conformity that was universal?

Fear. It goes by no other name. Albeit a lawless mob, this was a crowd that knew trouble when they saw it coming their way.

True, it had been a while since they experienced what it was like to live in fear and trepidation of something far more powerful than themselves. They had known the feeling, but they had driven all thought of it from their minds, and now they acted as though the terrors of the not so distant past had never really happened. Why, if one tried counting, back only a mere five years, to a date as close in time as 1941, and asked them to recall the events of their lives in those fateful Shōwa years, surely that was to ask them to cross a mental divide that, in terms of its historical significance, measured not five but a full five thousand years!

Besides, now that they had lost their way in a land ravaged by war and fire, and they had wandered into the labyrinth of the marketplace that grew out of the ruins, what need did they have to think of the past, anyway? It was as if no one had survived from the last century and, no, there had never been an era in the history of modern Japan when people had paraded about smugly wearing the look of His Majesty's loyal subjects—when the land had been populated by a race of so-called Neo-Confucian gentlemen who were only too happy to be of unquestioning service to the empire. No, not a soul from that day and age appeared to be alive. They had all vanished—down to every last man, woman, and child.

They were errant seeds, their feet planted on the spot where they happened to land. They had sprouted out of the ground, and with the force of a weed that reaches maturity overnight, they were now fully grown. They were the "new leaf" that had been turned over. They were the "newly created society." They were all of the new this-and-that touted in the press of late. They were billed as a "brand-new" product: the local specialty and the showcase item of today's "new moment in history."

Such were the people milling about the marketplace. Down to a man they had the look of moral delinquents and social outlaws who knew no yesterday and know no tomorrow. And as for what Heaven might have to say, they cared not a whit—for they feared it no more. The business at hand here on earth was making money and the art of making money lay in their skill at duping their neighbors. By taking advantage of people and their ignorance, they knew how to skin them alive and make a hearty meal of them. Yes, their fellow human beings were to be the source of their sustenance.

Besides, no one had been appointed as the new leader for them to follow and serve, and since the old calendar of imperial events and obligations was now no longer in force, what difference did it make whose reign it was or what was today's date?

Likewise, if one did not recognize the law, then why give a damn about rules and regulations, anyway? Or care about whomever it was who claimed the right to enforce them? If it is not one official line, then surely it is another. To hell with them all, the faces in the crowd seemed to say, their nostrils flaring defiantly. Yet, in spite of all their talk and bravura, what did one find when the time came for these people to get down in the dust and hammer out a price for their goods? Namely, that everything was contraband. In short, in the entire lot of food and clothes and whatever else they have for sale on just about any street corner in the city, there is not a single item worthy of being called bona fide or legitimate. What's more, the currency with which these goods are bought and sold is of equally dubious value, since the government bureaucrats who manufacture the money do not hesitate to mint more and more stacks of devalued yen notes. . . .

Consequently, for all the talk of "the new ways of living" and "the dawning awareness of newly emergent peoples," what is it really worth? Is it something truly new and genuine? No, not in the least. So much for talk of "the contemporary lifestyle" and "the modern consciousness." For in point of fact people have yet to take one step beyond the here and now, and the most quotidian prescriptions of what they think life is about. It appears that, just as in the last century, they are still self-absorbed in the lusty appetites of their baser emotions, and their lives are consumed by the myriad transactions that are part and parcel of running a business and making a living. There has been no change. Only now, by being caught in the throes of being busier than ever before, they have failed to ask what the all-important and much touted "today" really means. Today marks, in fact, the end of time as we have known it heretofore.

But, alas, this precious moment is about to slip away, and it will be already too late when people look up and finally take notice. They will come to their senses only to find that the surface of reality is as unbroken as it was before, the fabric of their lives looking as though, no, there had never been a hole in it—no, it had never been rent or torn. Everything would remain the same, as if there had never been any change after all. The damned hole—the spot, the little rip, the "oh-did-I-do-that?" cigarette burn—that by virtue of its foolish and irritating presence challenges us and allows time to enter into our lives would be gone forever. . . .

But, suddenly, standing there in the void was the boy, catching everyone at an unguarded moment. Dirty, foul-smelling, and glowing with an otherworldly black sheen, he revealed himself in all of his ugly glory. He stood in the midst of the squalor and stench of the marketplace, and he outshone it in his filthiness. He arrested every eye; and in his doing so, did not the denizens of this lowly place—these vulgar and undaunted types who never flinched in the face of anything—secretly turn inward and, taking a long look at themselves and the state in which they lived, suddenly realize they were no different? Startled at the mirror image of their own ugliness, they shuddered. And as each inwardly raised a bootless cry for help, a great shock wave passed through the multitude.

One could hardly bear to look at the boy because of the unspeakable rags and boils that covered him. Still, there was nothing about his person, neither in his posture or his deportment, that spoke of the beggar or the petty thief. Nor was there any sign of physical illness, mental imbalance, or other infirmity. No, there were none of these, although, given the circumstances, he might well become a bank robber . . . or a murderer . . . or whatever monstrosity one might care to imagine.

Yet given—hmm—the comparatively normal shape of whatever part of his face was visible through the sea of pus and boils—and the correctness with which he carried himself, keeping his back straight as a rod—and the way his shoulders had begun to fill out, it appeared he possessed a surprisingly solid physique. One guessed his age was somewhere between ten and fifteen. In short, he was at the peak of his growing years. The healthy development of his bones and the lack of any malformation in the extremities served to insure his growth into a healthy, unstunted adult male.

Still, there remained something physically soft and supple about him. No doubt his boyishness accounted for the touch of arrogance that he gave off as he walked down the street. He thrust out his chest. He never looked back. And he paid no heed to the crowd as it swirled around him. "Why all the fuss?" his body seemed to say, as he moved silently and singularly through the throng, his gaze coolly fixed on a point far in the distance. He was like an actor who makes his grand entrance down the ramp, gliding to the center of the stage with the greatest of ease. How calm and collected he was! Surely it was by no mean feat that he carried himself with such aplomb, and doubtless the naturalness of his step derived in great measure from his profound sense of self-reliance. He depended on no one; and without such confidence, he should not have been able to make his feet advance so adroitly. As for whither he came or where he was going, that was something no one knew.

But then, the marketplace was a recent development, and no one knew where any of the people here had come from or to what tribe, or subspecies, they belonged. They simply milled about with no apparent direction. Some moved one way; the others, another. Thus, when a lone boy—a boy possessed of

an air of authority and looking ever so assured of his ultimate destination—
stepped into their midst, the mere lightness of his step was reason enough to
bring a startled look to their faces. How nimble he was on his feet! Indeed so
great was the impression he had made on the crowd, people were immune to
further surprise. By now they would not have been fazed in the least were he,
like a specter that appears momentarily in broad daylight, to snap his fingers
and with equal suddenness—poof!—vanish into thin air.

But then, something unexpected happened.

Paying no more heed to the sardines on the grill, the boy turned from the
stall and started into the crowd. But just as he was about to make his exit and it
appeared to all eyes that he would disappear into thin air, suddenly he reeled
about, and darting past the reed partition, he shot into the neighboring stall.
From seemingly nowhere, he produced a brand-new crisp and seamless ten-yen
note and slapped it on the counter.

Seizing one of the rice balls that was black with the flies that had settled on
it, he opened his mouth and bit into it, flies and all. His hand moved so fast that
no one could intervene, and by the time the woman at the stall started to her
feet, shouting something in shocked surprise, the merchandise had already
been consumed.

And now, with the same lightning speed, the boy directed the thrust of his
hand toward the woman. As she started to stand, he flew at her, his body danc-
ing wildly toward her, and he pushed her back against the bench. Grabbing at
her, he reached for the exposed flesh of her thighs, and making it the object of
his embrace, he attacked it with the same determination with which he had
sunk his teeth into the o-musubi ball of rice. As his face smacked full force
against the side of the woman's leg, it made a slapping sound loud enough that
it could be heard beyond the confines of the stall. Crying out in shock and pain,
the woman jumped up and tried to free herself.

"What do you think you're doing? Damn you, you little brat. . . ."

But the boy was not about to give up, no matter how hard she struggled to
disengage herself.

By now the man in the military boots had come running. This time he was
brandishing a long, thin bamboo stick.

"Damn you, you little beast. . . ."

Yet the fact that the man did no more than curse suggested, once again, the
sight of the boy's boils and dirty rags kept him at bay; and holding himself at
arm's length, he merely leapt about, circling the pair and letting the woman
bear the brunt of having to contend with the boy. By doing no more than lash-
ing the air with the bamboo stick and making it crack like a whip, not only did
he avoid having to touch the boy but—by not laying a hand on him—he also
saved himself the trouble of pulling the two apart.

The bodies of the boy and the woman were united as one, and as their entwined form emerged from the stall and spilled into the street, they teetered back and forth, ready at any moment to fall to the ground.

But then their bodies shifted, and suddenly the pair came crashing headlong in this—or shall I say *my?*—direction. It just so happened I was standing in front of the adjoining stall at that very moment. The stall next to the woman's was run by a seller of sweets and candies, but the candyman could be persuaded to reach into the false bottom of the kerosene drum that held his wares to produce a pack or two of contraband cigarettes. I had prevailed upon him, and I had just now lit a match and was about to light one of the cigarettes I had purchased.

I was in danger, of course; and I immediately adopted a stance of being ready to grab hold of and roll with the lump of flesh as it tumbled toward me. Otherwise, I would be crushed underneath when the boy and the woman toppled to the ground.

A single lump—or clump—of flesh had been formed by the union of the two bodies. I had to think fast, and making a quick decision, I chose to embrace the half where the skin would be soft and pleasant to the touch rather than the half covered in rags and boils and pus and, no doubt, lice. Yes, how much better to latch onto the gentler part. . . .

What I mean is—and I am embarrassed to say this—but from the time I had approached the booth of the candyman, I too had seen the meaty thighs of the woman's legs, and I could think of nothing else. I was mesmerized: yet no matter how much I might be overcome by the sight of a beautiful pair of legs, never—no, never—would I throw caution to the winds and rush forth to embrace them in full view of the public as the boy had just now done. No, it was something I simply could not do, and the reason lies solely in the fact I do not possess one iota of the spunk and courage demonstrated by this young man. It is just that simple. . . .

Yet, given the unexpected stroke of good luck that was now about to come tumbling my way, what need had I to be shy about standing in the shadow of the boy's glory? By basking in the virtuous light of his courageousness, why not make happenstance the happy occasion in which I saw to the fulfillment of my basest desires? Yes, it was terrible of me. And as if that were not vile enough, let me add that the thought occurred to me to be even nefarious enough to push the boy aside and attempt to take the woman solely for myself. Once he was out of the way, I could direct my attention to her backside and seize her from the rear. . . .

But punishment was about to be meted out to me right on the spot. For no sooner did I find myself unable to check the motion of the woman's body by use of my passive strength than, believe it or not, her powerful hips came flying my way, and with a high-spirited upper cut, she sent me sailing through the air. It was with a resounding thud that I found myself thrown to the ground.

My knees and elbows were badly scraped. I bit back the pain, and when at last I managed to get to my feet, I found the boy was now nowhere in sight. He had vanished without so much as a shadow or trace of his former presence. As for the woman, she was shouting at the top of her lungs about something or other that I found impossible to comprehend. She was livid as hell, and the force of her anger—as well as the heat of her glare—was clearly directed at me. Standing alongside her was the man in the military boots, slashing at the air with his bamboo stick. He was intent upon intimidating me into submission, as he towered over me and sought to block any avenue of escape.

I gathered from what the woman said that, in the confusion of the moment, the light from the tip of my cigarette had somehow or other pressed against her back, and it had burned a huge hole in her blouse. Yes, a hole . . . a singed spot . . . a cigarette burn. . . .

A crowd had formed. It was in a nasty mood, and it was clear I was the object of its anger. People assumed I had been the one who had grabbed the woman by the leg and attacked her. (Actually, it is true that I had been party to the whole sordid affair.)

My face turned bright red. My embarrassment was due in part to being at the center of a crowd in broad daylight, but I also shuddered at the thought of what new indignity was about to come my way. Driven by the desire to flee as fast as I could, I scanned the wall of people lined up in front of me. Aiming for the weakest build and the least attentive face, I saw my opening and charged headlong. I shunted the man aside, and weaving my way through the now disordered ranks of the crowd, I ran like mad. I was desperate to get outside the marketplace.

Just beyond the narrow confines of the market lay a broad avenue where streetcars ran. I kept running until I reached it. Only then did I stop to catch my breath. I turned around and looked behind me. To my great relief, I could see that no one had come in pursuit.

Yet when I looked once more in the direction of the streetcar tracks, I realized everyone was staring at me. There was a look of stern disapproval on every face.

No wonder. I was covered in mud from the top of my head to the tip of my toes. My elbows and knees were scraped and bloodied from where I had fallen on the ground. Moreover, one adopts a certain air on entering the marketplace, and I had yet to shed it. I must have looked bizarre and out-of-place.

By nature I am a proud and vain sort of person who spends much of his time and energy keeping up appearances. Even on the occasion when I have rubbed shoulders with the shameless types who populate the marketplace or I have been smitten by the sight, for example, of a pair of good-looking legs like the ones on the woman at the o-musubi stand, I have always been careful not to reveal the slightest suggestion of anything vulgar or base in the way I present myself. I have put on airs, inasmuch as one can these days. By making myself appear ever so prim and proper, I have advertised myself to the world as a paragon of refinement.

Yet once things had reached this pretty pass, what did I have to say for myself? I looked worse than the most shameless denizen of the marketplace. I was an outcast who ranks as the lowest of the low.

But forget the revealing light of day. Forget the eyes that stared at me in rebuke. They are hardly worth mentioning, even if it is true that I felt totally embarrassed. More important, what did I have to say for myself? What excuse could I offer to assuage my own wounded sense of pride? My vanity was hurt at the thought of how utterly difficult it was for me to speak to my own defense. What was there to say on my own behalf?

I brushed the dirt from my clothes. I wiped the blood from my scratches. I tied the laces of my shoes. And, feigning an air of nonchalance, I started to walk away. But my feet would not cooperate. They were clumsy and would not move with the ease that I demanded of them.

And speaking of feet, how was it that the boy managed to move with such composure when he made his way among the blackguards of the market? How deftly, how subtly—or, rather, how boldly and with what unfettered grace—he parted the crowd as he passed through it! From what distant reach of heaven or what bowel deep in the earth had he come? For surely he had been sent to the marketplace on a divine mission, had he not? He had come to this newly created site, and it was here that he made himself manifest to its people. "I am the progenitor of a new race that shall plant its seed and flourish in this vast and empty plain." That was what he seemed to say—just as he also threatened to push from the ring any contender who dared to step forward to challenge his authority over the arena of the marketplace.

For who else was prepared to stand side by side with the naked camp of the poor and outcast? Who else but the boy would succor the multitudes who knew no law and who were dressed only in the garments of their naked shame? Is it not written that the Messiah is always with the poor and the oppressed, and that God loves those who do not know the Law? If such is the case, might it not be that the young boy stood far closer to the divine than one might think? Might it just not be the case that he ranks among the very first of men—that, yea, he is to be the leader of a new breed of humankind that dwells in the place of ruin and sends out its tendrils to cover the earth? Indeed it may very well be the case that he has been singled out to play the role of the Son of Man who is come to save us. The signs are all unclear, and I feel uncertain in going so far as to suggest he has been chosen as our lord and savior, as the name Christ implies. Yet surely I am not wide of the mark in saying he is at least our Jesus, and a very human Jesus at that. Yes, am I not on target in calling him "the Jesus of the ruins"? "The Jesus of the Burnt-Out Shell of Japan."

I never cease to be amazed that the denizens of the marketplace are a tight-lipped lot who keep their mouths shut and have little to say. But how much more so in the case of the boy! He is doubly silent, what with never having uttered a single word. Come to think of it, I suspect it is his acts that are his true words. They are his sole means of communication.

What's more, were we to examine each and every act he has undertaken and how he has sought to express himself in each and every case—be it the act of "hand over a sardine," or the gesture of "gimme a rice ball," or the feat in "let me at her thighs"—inevitably we would find in each and every instance they are cast in the imperative voice. His acts are commands and, inasmuch as each and every one of them is delivered like an order from on high, surely they possess some sort of deeper, theological meaning. Doubtless they speak of things that are comprehended only by theologians and the like, and which we vulgar mortals cannot hope to grasp.

Truly, the boy's every act is a metaphor and has parallels to be found in the words and deeds of Jesus of Nazareth. Indeed, were someone to observe the boy's daily comings and goings in detail and then go so far as to write them down and compile a permanent record, would we not have before us a new set of teachings on life in the promised land that constitutes no less a testament than Jesus' Sermon on the Mount?

Yes, now that I thought of it, it seemed to me the boy possessed great majesty, his physical appearance notwithstanding. It is no ordinary mortal who can stand before the world adorned in robes so thoroughly tattered and a body so encrusted with boils, pus, and, no doubt, lice too. It takes the authority of a king and, even then, only the most regal and stately of rulers. I too have been stirred by the secret desire to transform myself into something more impressive, to take my vulgar body and garb it in the best of fashion; and I have suffered not inconsiderably, my sense of pride and vanity wounded, given my current lack of means. In fact, it appears the day when I shall be able to don the raiments of a king and be arrayed in splendor is a time that not only has not come but also seems so distant in the future that I may never see it.

In the meantime, then, for me at least, the enemy is this Jesus.

And if in our tug-of-war for the woman at the o-musubi stand the worst disaster to befall me was to scrape a hand or a knee, what of it? My losses were light. It is probably best that I forget the entire matter and not dwell on it. At last I began to calm down and pull myself together.

By the time I had cooled off, I had walked as far as Ueno Hirokōji. I stood at the broad intersection there and waited for a streetcar headed for Yanaka, a section of Ueno that was not far away. Yet when there was no sign that a car would be coming along, and it looked as if I would have to wait quite a while, I decided to go on foot. The quickest route to Yanaka lay over Ueno Hill. The grounds of the Tōshōgu Shrine were atop the long incline. I could cut through the shrine precincts and then head down the other side of the hill to Yanaka. Indeed, going to Yanaka had been the reason I had set out this morning and the reason I had come all the way to Ueno.

It was only the other day that I had been to Yanaka on another errand. As I was walking back to Ueno, I happened to pass a temple that is the grave site of Dazai Shundai, a noted scholar of the Confucian classics who lived in the Edo period. Both the temple and the surrounding neighborhood had been lucky during the war, and they had escaped the terrible fires that had ravaged so much of Tokyo. The rows of houses that line the streets of Yanaka looked much as they had when they were originally built.

I entered the temple grounds through the main gate, and skirting around the main sanctuary, I headed for the cemetery in the rear. That I should do this— namely, decide on the spur of the moment to stop and take a look at Shundai's grave—had nothing to do, of course, with anything so conventional as wishing to pay my respects to Shundai by washing the headstone of his grave. To tell the truth, I have no reason whatsoever to mourn the man buried there, because, when it comes to the matter of Confucianism and the study of its texts and its teachings, I consider myself a total outsider. In fact, I could care less about them or for that matter anything about Dazai Shundai and his school of Neo-Confucian scholarship. I do not even think much of the personality of the man as it is recorded in the history books. Frankly speaking, Dazai Shundai is a figure altogether alien to me and my interests.

What had arrested my eye was the memorial stone erected at the site of his grave or, more important, the inscription that had been done in brush and then carved onto the stone. In short, my interest in Shundai lay solely in his epitaph. Both the words of the memorial and the characters in which they were written came from the pen of no less a figure than Hattori Nankaku, the greatest master of Chinese verse as it was practiced in Japan in the eighteenth century. It is Nankaku who is to be credited with having laid the foundation for the great revival of interest in Chinese poetry and belles lettres that flourished among the citizens of the city of Edo; and, as a latter-day child of that time and place, I count myself fortunate to be an heir—however distant—to the great literary tradition that he fostered. When it comes to the spirit of Nankaku and his works, I consider myself neither stranger nor alien.

That the arts and letters flourished and witnessed a great renaissance in the city of Edo in the mid- and late eighteenth century during the three successive eras known as Meiwa, An'ei, and Tenmei and that the writing of poetry reached an unprecedented degree of sophistication in the form of the "Tenmei Style" was due in no small part to the efforts of Nankaku, who, several decades in advance of anyone else in Japan, set about disseminating to the general public a knowledge and appreciation of the verse of the great masters of the T'ang dynasty. It was to the works of the T'ang that the practitioners of Tenmei poetry and prose turned for their inspiration, and there can be no question that the Chinese verse produced in Tenmei—albeit a distant echo of an earlier, far greater age— owes a considerable debt to T'ang poetry for its own thoroughly fashionable, cosmopolitan, and altogether up-to-date air. I dare say the spirit of the T'ang masters has become the fundamental source for all of the subsequent literary scholarship in Japan that is worthy of the accolade of "modern" or "sophisticated."

Fortunately, the memorial tablet had escaped damage in the war, and Nankaku's inscription was perfectly intact. Yet even in surviving the flames when so much else was in ruins, given the amnesia of the times, thought of it had slipped from public memory, and the tablet was now in danger of falling into oblivion. Yes, as far as the world was concerned, it was almost as though it no longer existed. For my part I wished to do something to preserve the words of Nankaku's memorial before it became too late and they were lost for all time. The day that I happened upon Shundai's grave, I made a mental note to myself to return. This time I would be prepared, and I would take a rubbing from the stone. I had set a date, and I had readied the necessary materials.

The day circled on my calendar is, of course, none other than today. And here I was. I was ready, and I was on my way. As a matter of fact, in one hand I held a small cloth bundle. Wrapped inside the bundle were rubbing paper and ink as well as two hard rolls that will have to suffice as my lunch for today's outing.

A rubbing is, to be sure, a nullity and an imperfection. For once the paper is pulled from the stone, it becomes nothing more than a secondhand acquaintance with a lost age—a pale copy, yea a mere tracing, taken from the annals of the history of arts and letters.

Yet even a leftover has a life of its own, does it not? And weren't there plenty of cracks in the walls of my temporary and ever-so-humble abode? And wasn't a rubbing just the thing to keep up appearances and paper over the worst holes in my life?

Now, where were we? I know—I was making my way up Ueno Hill and was about to reach Kiyomizu Hall, the first of the outbuildings at Tōshōgu Shrine, when I happened for no particular reason to turn around and look behind me.

Who should I see following me up the hill but the boy from the marketplace! He was still several blocks away, but it was clear he was headed in my direction.

No, there was no mistaking him. It was the boy all right. He was dressed in rags, and his face was covered in boils.

Yet what need had I to pay attention to him now that I had gotten back to the business that brought me here in the first place? I had already wasted too much time loitering on the way. Besides, from the top of a broad and open space like Ueno Hill, the boy did not look much like Jesus. He had changed, and curiously enough, here on "Mount Ueno" he lost the Jesus-like aura that had come so naturally to him when he had moved through the crowd in the marketplace. Here, he was simply a lone animal on the prowl for its supper. No longer the progenitor of a new race, he had become instead—in the words of the New Testament—the sole survivor of a generation of swine who, possessed by the devil, had flung themselves over a precipice and perished in the waters below. He alone had survived and was left to wander along the side of the mountain or by the edge of the sea. That was how he looked, and whatever fascination he may have held for me initially was now gone. I turned away. I paid him no mind and pressed on about my business.

This far up Ueno Hill there were no shops set out with things to sell, and only rarely did I encounter anyone who was out for a stroll. There was no danger of being tempted by the sight of a pair of women's legs here, however wanton and frivolous my thoughts might be.

As I passed through the torii that gave entrance to the shrine precincts, I turned around once more and casually looked behind me.

Sure enough. There he was. The enemy was behind me, but this time he had narrowed the distance, and now it was only a matter of his being ten or fifteen yards away. There was no question about it. He was following me.

What I saw was the face of the enemy, and the look on it was no joke. No longer the last of a dying breed of swine, the boy had become a wolf thirsty for blood.

There was a murderous glint in his eye. His teeth, which were exposed for me to see, glistened in the sun. Even the pustules on his face were flush with the red glow that comes from having imbibed the blood of prey recently taken. The rags that stuck to his skin bristled like the hairs on the back of a wolf. His eyes, his mouth, his face—they all spoke of the powerful thirst for the hunt.

But why of all people had the enemy set his sights on me? Did he hold a grudge because of the incident at the marketplace? I saw no reason why he should. I could care less about it. Or was he out to waylay me and take my money? Yes, I had a wallet, which I carried shoved deep inside my pocket. But, as for its contents, they were so negligible as to be hardly worth the trouble.

Or was he simply out for blood? Were that the case, he would have even less to chew on, given the fact that I am probably more anemic than the undernourished condition of my wallet. . . .

Yet the logic of a human may not be that of a wolf, and what made sense to me may not have been equally comprehensible to the boy. Whatever the case, it was all too apparent—the fearsome reality of it was now staring me squarely in the face—that the enemy, having stalked me this far, was ready to pounce.

I tried to remain calm. I told myself to slow down and walk as nonchalantly as possible.

By now I had reached the front of the Tōshōgu Shrine. There was no more need to turn around and look. I knew the enemy was closing in. It was only a matter of time before he would strike. I could feel him behind me, the poised energy of imminent attack tangible against the tensing muscles in my neck and shoulders. No one else was in sight. There were a few large trees here and there, but they did not amount to anything that one could rely on for cover. The sun beat down as relentlessly as ever. I was soaked to the skin. I felt as though I were swimming in an oily pool of sweat.

At last I came to the rear of the shrine. If only I could make it to the path that led down the other side of the hill, at least there would be houses in the neighborhood. But it was already too late. With a precision that was almost painful, my ears registered every move the enemy made, be it the sound of his labored breathing or the grinding and gnashing of his teeth. He was only a few feet away. In one flying leap, he would be on top of me, sinking his teeth into the nape of my neck. That is just how close he was.

I began to panic. I tried to reach the row of houses up ahead. Yet, by quickening my pace, I merely drove myself farther into the open—and right into the enemy's trap.

It was a field where tufts of weeds grew out of the red clay soil—or just the perfect place for the site of a bloodletting. At least I knew not to cry out or to break into a mad dash. The enemy would jump on me for sure.

Yet wasn't I equally foolish in doing nothing? The enemy had me cornered no matter what, and he was about to go for the jugular. The time in which I might have suddenly spun around and adopted a stance of engaging him head-on had long since passed, however. All that I had in my hand was the small cloth bundle. And inside was only the broadsheet of paper on which I planned to trace a pale copy of a lost, great age from the history of the art of poetry.

Alas, a blank sheet of paper is far too transparent and insubstantial a thing to be of much use in times like these. And here I was calling upon it to serve as a weapon in mortal combat with a wolf. How could it possibly prevail against a vicious set of claws and teeth? I was trapped, and I was desperate.

When I came to the biggest tree I could find, I decided to turn and confront the enemy. As I spun around, he too made his move and came lunging at me.

Yes, what kicked the earth and came flying through the air, only to crash on top of me, was a hideous clod—a sickening, foul-smelling clump—of rags and boils and pus and, no doubt, even lice. I raised my hands in front of me in order to break the full force of his attack. I felt his claws . . . I felt his teeth . . . as they tore into me. I heard my shirt rip. I felt his nails dig into the flesh of my arms.

Everything became an incoherent blur after that. We had become a single, solidified mass that fell down and rolled across the ground. Yes, I had become one with the hideous clump of rags and boils and pus and, no doubt, even lice.

The struggle went back and forth in total silence, but at last I was able to grab hold of the boy's wrists and hold him down. His hands were as powerful as they were agile, but I also discovered to my surprise how soft they were to the touch. Yes, his skin was as fine as could be. His hands had the texture of a youth somewhere between the ages of ten and fifteen.

How I did it I shall never know, but by summoning forth, the last ounce of life left in my body, I managed to get a lockhold on the boy, and I succeeded in pressing his arms to the ground. There, staring me straight in the eye, was the face of the enemy. Yes, it was a dirty face covered in pus and sweat and grime. It was a tormented face too—a face that had been twisted out of shape as the boy, gasping for air, struggled to catch his breath.

And in the split second when I stared at him and he at me, his face being right there before my eyes, I felt a terrible shudder pass through the core of my entire being. It was an experience bordering well-nigh on ecstasy.

For what had I seen? No, it was not the dirty face of a boy or the mangy head of a wolf. No, it was not a face that belonged to just any man either. To the contrary; it was the incarnation of the pain that had etched itself upon Veronica's veil. It was the living, suffering face of Jesus of Nazareth as he made his way along the road to Calvary. I knew it immediately, the recognition of it having come to me in a piercing flash of insight.

The boy was Jesus, the Son of Man; and he was also Christ, the King and Messiah. Surely the enemy had been sent to bring me this message of salvation.

I know that I am unworthy, and as a person without so much as a single redeeming merit, I rank among the lowest of the low. Nonetheless, by virtue of possessing at least a touch of the coarse and common disposition that is enchanted, if only in passing, by the sight of a good-looking pair of legs such as those on the woman at the o-musubi stand, had I not revealed something of my true self and thereby found favor with God? And had not God therefore sent me his bearer of the good tidings of the gospel? My hands and feet began to shake in fear and awe of what had happened to me.

And in that unguarded moment, the enemy slipped his wrist free from my hand and delivered a powerful uppercut to my jaw. I fell flat on my back.

And, in that selfsame second, I saw the small cloth bundle fly through the air and land on the spot next to where my head hit the ground. The bundle fell apart, spilling its contents. Out came the paper, so crumpled it was now hopelessly bent out of shape. Out came the two pieces of hardtack, which rolled in the dirt.

The boy scooped up the bread; and then, grabbing the paper, he threw it, dirt and all, right in my face. With that, he was off. He headed over the hill and disappeared.

When afterward I got to my feet, I found there were teeth and fingernail marks the length of my arms and legs. And when I went to brush the dirt from my pants, I reached into my pocket and found it was empty. My wallet was gone.

The following morning, I left my apartment and set out once more to the marketplace in Ueno. Perhaps it was the aftereffect of having worked up a sweat in a fight the day before, but I felt curiously refreshed. Even my head felt somehow revitalized, my thinking having become a bit more clear and tidy. And, as for the unfinished business of taking a rubbing from the memorial stone in Yanaka, I gave it nary a second thought.

No, it was because I was in hopes of seeing the face of Jesus one more time that I made my way to the marketplace. And if in passing the o-musubi stand I also happened to catch sight of the woman with the good-looking legs, so much the better. Yes, if only I might have one more chance . . . that was the sort of outrageous thought that I had in mind.

But overnight the topography of the marketplace had been altered forever.

"Closed effective August 1."

That was the official edict, although it was probably no more reliable than many of the pronouncements issued by officialdom.

But, astonishingly enough, this time it was being put into effect.

The area had been cordoned off along the street where the streetcars ran. Ropes stretched from one corner to the next across the alleys that gave access to the interior, and two or three military policemen dressed in white summer uniforms were stationed at the corner of each alleyway.

So blank was their stare and so firmly were their feet planted to the spot, they looked like stakes or pylons that had been hammered into the ground. There was a fixity to them that suggested they would not be moved nor just anyone be allowed to pass through.

A crowd had gathered a short distance away By craning their necks and struggling to peer down the alleys, people were trying to see what had happened to the quarter. I too mixed in, and by peeping around the erect, white pylons at the entryway to the marketplace, I managed to find a gap through which I could see inside.

The center of the market area was completely deserted. It was now a cold, white desert, and there was no indication—nay, not even the shadow—of anyone moving about. It was as though the earth had opened up and swallowed the river of the great unwashed that had flowed through the streets and stalls of the marketplace until only yesterday.

Alas, never again would I have the means whereby I might see the face of Jesus or the good-looking pair of legs on the woman at the *o-musubi* stand! Indeed were it not for the wound marks of the boy's teeth and nails that remained so vividly and freshly imprinted upon my arms and legs, I might have thought the events of the previous day were altogether too unreal to believe. Yes, without solid evidence to the contrary, I might have been tempted to think it had all been a dream—the work of an aberrant figure who, by forcing his way into my fantasies, had come to attack me.

Until only yesterday stands had lined the alleys of the marketplace like a wall. But what about today?

All that remained along either side of the streets were the long, empty rows of stalls constructed of flimsy reed screens. Stretching as far as the eye could see, they resembled a huge stable equipped with countless berths and mangers. But it was a horseless livery. Not a horse was in sight.

Peering still farther inside, one saw an open space. It looked freshly swept. It was as if someone had taken a stiff broom and given it a vigorous sweeping.

Still, the surface was marked by a spot here and there. It was as though something had traipsed across it and left behind its traces. They were the marks of an unidentified being that had walked upon the face of the earth and left its telltale imprint. As a matter of fact, the traces looked ever so much like footsteps— yea, even hoofprints—that a strange creature, having wandered into the desert, left as its tracks in the sand.

KANAI MIEKO

Kanai Mieko (b. 1947) was a precocious author who began publishing at the age of nineteen. Using graphic and fantastic elements, she often uses deconstructionist and postmodern techniques to explore her unusual subject matter. Her story translated here, "Homecoming" (Kikan, 1970), is one of many in which the characters, no longer certain of their own identities, struggle to cope with the growing complexities of contemporary life.

HOMECOMING (KIKAN)

Translated by Van C. Gessel

When she returned from her long journey, a young man came up to her and announced that he had come to the station to meet her. She was very surprised and said to the young man, "I think you must have the wrong person."

"No, I don't. I know all about you. Your husband is ill and couldn't come to pick you up, so I've come in his place. Your husband has been very worried about you," the man said, and then like a magician, he reached into his pocket and with an elegant flourish pulled out a large red silk handkerchief that he used to wipe the sweat from his brow.

"My goodness," the young man sighed, "it is hot, isn't it? Here, let me take your bag for you."

She repeated what she had said before: "I'm sure you must think I'm someone else. You did get my name right, but I don't have a husband. And besides, nobody knew that I was coming back today. I've got to be going; I'm in a hurry."

The young man smiled, his face all but vocally saying, "You're teasing me with such a serious face," and gestured for her to hand him her suitcase. "Your husband is ill, and he wants to see you right away. You received the telegram while you were away (I can tell you what it said; I'm the one who went to the telegraph office, so I remember it well. It said: 'RETURN IMMEDIATELY I LOVE YOU ALWAYS ETERNALLY, YOUR HUSBAND'), and we got your reply last night. It read: 'ARRIVE TWO P.M. ON SEVENTH, YOUR LOVE.' And so here I am to meet you. Your husband described you, so I recognized you at once. Black hair, black eyes, skin that should be tanned by the seaside sun. . . . I think the image your husband described was right on the mark! I knew you at a single glance!"

"I have no idea what you're talking about! The person you're looking for is somebody else. I didn't receive a telegram from my husband and didn't send a reply. How could I? I'm single. I don't have a husband!"

The young man finally seemed to realize that this was no ordinary situation. With a baffled look, he stammered, "Isn't your address 446 N-machi?" Although she didn't know why, it infuriated her to have her address announced to her, and in one breath she rattled off: "Yes, it is, but that's a pretty crummy way to trick someone. Going to all the trouble to look up my address—what are you, a police dog?"

Startled by her demeanor, he quickly replied, "You're the one who needs to stop this nonsense. Your husband is waiting for you at your home at 446 N-machi. He didn't want me to tell you this, but he has an incurable disease. So for you to claim that you're single, even if it's a joke, is disgusting!"

She was at a loss, unable to grasp what was happening. This fellow was telling her that a man with an incurable disease who claimed to be her husband was at her house at 446 N-machi and that he would love her for eternity! Having never been married or even engaged, how was it that she had a husband, and why was it that he was waiting at her house in N-machi? Her head began to throb, and she started wondering whether she had gone mad or perhaps lost her memory. She felt nauseated, and a feverish chill shook her body as if she had suddenly been propelled into the middle of a nightmare.

"In any case," she announced peremptorily to the man, "446 N-machi is my house, so I'm going to go home. Then everything will be perfectly clear. Because it is absolutely certain that I do not have a husband. Either I've gone crazy, or else you're the one who's crazy!"

She climbed into the young man's car, not uttering a word as they drove to her house. There was much she had to consider, but she didn't know where to begin. What exactly had happened while she had been gone? A young man she'd never seen before suddenly shows up, and then he starts talking about her husband, and even worse, he claims that her husband is in bed with an incurable disease and wants to see her.

It was an odd feeling. When they opened the door to her house (actually, after the man rang the bell, a young woman who appeared to be a nurse opened it from inside), a repulsive odor made her sick to her stomach. She went with the young man into the living room and sat down on the couch. There was no question that this was in fact her house; everything was as she had left it when she set off on her trip. Only one thing was different: there was an unfamiliar silver picture frame on her table with a photograph inside it. It was a snapshot of a man and a woman sitting in chairs on a terrace, with the sea lit by the evening sun and a cloudy sky as the backdrop. The couple glowed almost imperceptibly in the backlighting of the setting sun. The man was looking straight ahead, and the woman's face was concealed under a large white hat. Their bodies were pressed together, the man's arm around her shoulders, and one of her hands rested on his leg. She picked up the photograph and stared at it. She was about to ask the young man who these people were, but she realized that the answer was a foregone conclusion. He would surely say, "This is a photograph taken on your honeymoon." And in fact, that is precisely what he said to her as she looked at the picture: "It's a photograph from your honeymoon."

She twisted her lip and said, "So you're claiming this woman is me? That's ridiculous. I've never seen this woman before, and I have never laid eyes on this man!"

The young man peered at her hard, a look of astonishment on his face. "Come now! You're completely exhausted. And I'm sure you're not feeling well. You'll come to your senses if you just get some rest." Evidently he had decided to ignore her assertions.

"Stop it! I'm not going to be fooled by these preposterous tricks. It's true that the woman in this picture does somehow resemble me. But you use such nasty tricks. Hmmph! Her face is hidden by this large hat, isn't it? If you think I'm going to be fooled by that, you're sadly mistaken. Let me see the man you claim is my husband. I'll be more than happy to tell him that I've never seen him before and to get the hell out of here!"

Restraining her anger, she spoke with a quavering voice. Although she had no idea what this absurd situation might mean, fueled by rage she was determined to drive these people from her house. She stood up from the couch, glaring straight at the young man, and said, "Fine, take me to him! Surely he's not using my bedroom?"

Her overbearing tone caught him off guard, and he guided her to the room where the man he had called her husband was sleeping. It was, in fact, her bedroom, and her eyes swam in anger at their audacity. When she entered the room, that peculiar odor took her breath away. The man lying in her bed lifted his head, smiled weakly, and said "You came back. I knew you'd come back. You can't betray our love. I forgive you for everything. I love you."

She shuddered with revulsion, and choking from the foul stench that seemed somehow to emanate from the man's afflicted body, she said, "Who are you? Just who are you?"

"Your eternal lover." He answered in a feeble, almost imperceptible voice, but she heard him clearly. He slowly closed his eyes, the smile still floating on his lips. Those were his final words. With a smile on his face, he died.

KITA MORIO

Kita Morio (b. 1927) is the pen name of a son of Saitō Mokichi, a psychiatrist and arguably the leading *tanka* poet of the modern age. (Some of Saitō's poems are included in volume 1 of this anthology.) Saitō's son Kita appears to have decided to become a writer even before he completed his medical degree at Tōhoku University. A literary schizophrenia is evident in his work, which is divided almost evenly between serious fiction influenced by Thomas Mann and lighthearted essays based on Kita's many world travels. His most admired novel, *The House of Nire* (*Nireke no hitobito*, 1964), is a chronicle of three generations in a family much like his own, over the decades leading up to World War II. The work included here is an excerpt from *Doctor Manbo at Sea* (*Dokutoru Manbo kōkaiki*, 1960), the most popular of Kita's humorous works and based on his own experiences as a doctor aboard a Fisheries Agency ship.

DOCTOR MANBO AT SEA (DOKUTORU MANBO KŌKAIKI)

Translated by Ralph F. McCarthy

Betrayed by My Country in Deutschland

Because the wind whips across the Bay of Biscay at right angles to the sea lanes, even the largest ships have trouble in stormy weather there—or so I've heard. We, however, had smooth sailing all the way, and even as we approached the English Channel the sea was a soft, gently sinuous green. Having read the horrifying descriptions of winter on the Atlantic in Monsarrat's *The Cruel Sea*, I'd been expecting the worst, but so far it hadn't been bad at all. The sky was a clear, pale blue, the horizon wavered in a lazy, smoky haze, and a score of sea gulls flapped along at the stern of the ship and seemed willing to follow us anywhere. The wind was awfully cold, though.

We passed through the Straits of Dover at midnight. I strolled out on deck and was dazzled by what I saw: a galaxy of shifting, blinking lights afloat in the darkness. Several vessels were cruising right alongside us. Outlined by the lamps on their sides and masts, they looked like fabulous, enchanted castles. Others, scattered in the distance, were visible only as single spots of light. Ships were everywhere—ahead of us, behind us, to the left and right—and the parade of lights suggested a mighty flotilla on the move. The radar screen, someone said, indicated forty-two vessels within a twelve-mile radius.

Even as I watched, we began to pick up speed and pull away from the ships beside us. The *Shoyo Maru*'s top speed was a respectable thirteen knots, but since leaving Japan, though we'd been overtaken and passed any number of times, we had yet to leave anyone in our wake. Now, seeing the lights of ship after ship fall behind, I was so thrilled I let out a whoop of triumph. It was, however, only for safety's sake that the other ships were moving so slowly, and our pilot was also promptly ordered to reduce speed and hang with the pack.

Two days later, in the early afternoon of February 1, we reached the mouth of the River Elbe. Boats and small ships were everywhere plying the muddy waters. The sky was clear and the sun shone brightly, but the cold wind blowing on deck seemed to cut to the bone. The Elbe is so wide that even after we'd entered its waters we couldn't see either bank, and it wasn't until evening that I first laid eyes on Germany—a dark and barren winter forest stretching as far as I could see.

By the time we docked at the pier in Hamburg it was quite late. I wanted to go ashore immediately, but we had to await permission. Two or three ladies stood on the other side of the steel screen at customs. I heard one of them, a blonde, mutter a single word of Japanese: "*Samui!*" She was right, of course—it was very cold—and they finally left, having apparently given up on us coming ashore. A thin man with a sharply hooked nose then came alongside the ship and held out a smudged and wrinkled piece of paper upon which someone had penciled—in Japanese—an advertisement for his bar ("Good wine, good women, good atmosphere, reasonable prices"). Once we'd looked at the paper, he asked us to give it back.

We waited for quite some time before being rewarded with the news that we wouldn't be permitted to go ashore that night.

Next morning a thick fog hung in the cold air. The deck was frozen and slippery, and white frost clung to all the rigging. The fog seemed like tiny, delicate particles of ice floating in the air. Looking up, I saw the faint white glow of the sun, shining so weakly that when a particularly heavy layer of fog rolled overhead, it disappeared altogether. Thomas Mann once described the winter sun as a mere outline beyond stratus clouds, and I was pleased to be able to witness that effect for myself. I'd once seen something similar in Japan, through a dense fog enveloping the peak of Mount Yari, but this German sun seemed even smaller and more forlorn.

Freezing, gloomy weather like this was to follow us all the way to France.

I had advanced some money to Ingeborg Bendt, a German psychologist and follower of Ernst Kretschmer who'd previously lived in Japan, with the intention of having her pay me back in marks. Having this extra cash would make my stay in Germany considerably more enjoyable as it would allow me to ride the trains and lodge in inns and whatnot without being unduly concerned about expense. I hoped to have her send the money to Mr. Y., a Japanese acquaintance of both Fraulein Bendt and my friend A., and had asked A. for a letter of introduction. My only aim was to get the cash, but Mr. Y. was an extraordinarily hospitable gentleman who ended up looking after me the entire time I was in Germany. Typically, I took full advantage of his kindness, the only drawback being that it prevented me from accumulating experiences in my own blundering way. Thanks to Mr. Y., I was able to talk on the telephone to Fraulein Bendt, who was staying in Berlin. A dedicated Japanophile, she was still writing articles and lecturing about the psychology of my countrymen. I half expected her to have forgotten the language, but her Japanese was, in fact, better than ever; no doubt she was still hitting the books with characteristic indefatigability.

She invited me to visit Berlin, and when Mr. Y. also strongly urged me to see that city it began to seem an awfully good idea. I wanted especially to have a look, however brief, at East Berlin, particularly after seeing all the posters on the streets of Hamburg which demanded in large, bold letters that the Brandenburg Gate be reopened. But while getting to Berlin would be easy enough, getting back out could, I was given to understand, be a bit difficult, what with all the refugees from East Germany and other questionable types forever trying to leave. Mr. Y. said seaman's papers would hardly be considered adequate identification, so we called the Japanese consulate. The consulate, however, said they would grant permission only to government officials.

Not satisfied, in other words, with rejecting my application to study overseas, the Japanese government was now practically inviting me to plot an insurrection by trying to restrict my movements abroad. Later, in Lübeck, I purchased a number of "instant" sweepstake tickets in a selfless attempt to add to my country's foreign currency reserves. When I really set my mind to it, I invariably win at this sort of thing, but none of the tickets I bought in Lübeck paid off. Obviously, the mixed feelings I'd acquired toward the Japanese government had destroyed my concentration.

West Germany, by the way, is up to its ears in foreign currency reserves. Yet, according to Mr. Y., seventy percent of the sugar consumed in Germany is produced from domestic sugar beets; beet sugar is placed on the table even in places like the dining room in the cellar of the Rathaus. "Try that in Japan," he said. "You could plant half of Hokkaido with sugar beets and get the government to promote consumption, but even the poorest people would be too proud to buy anything but cane sugar."

I hate to say it, but German cooking isn't very good. One sometimes gets the impression that great pains have been taken to make the stuff taste awful. There are, of course, tasty dishes, but your tongue is likely to be rendered insensitive before you find them. In a restaurant at the station, I found myself longing for something familiar and ordered Wiener schnitzel, expecting a meal along the lines of the pork cutlets you get in Japan. What I was served, however, didn't bear the slightest resemblance to anything I'd ever seen before. The potatoes are as good as they're reputed to be, but you're served a great mound of the things on a separate plate, mixed with green beans, and it's altogether more than anyone can possibly eat. Disliking the idea of being considered wasteful by German waiters, I did my best to clean the plate but finally laid down my fork in surrender. To give credit where credit is due, though, the wurst you buy at stand-up counters is actually quite a treat. Served steaming hot, slapped with mustard, and washed down with beer, these sausages make an excellent and inexpensive meal.

One thing I wanted at all costs to get my hands on was a gas pistol. In many countries one can buy what's known as an alarm gun—a heavy, exact replica of a Colt that makes a convincing bang—but those that fire gas pellets are sold only in Germany. A German student I once met who visited Japan on a trip around the world had one of these. He claimed that in a remote part of India he'd fired it at a policeman with whom he'd had an altercation, and the cop had dropped like a sack of potatoes. "What happened to him?" I asked. "Was he all right?" The student shrugged and said he hadn't waited around to find out. This lad, by the way, like most of his peers, was fiercely opposed to communism. Many Germans his age have relatives who died or otherwise suffered at the hands of Russian soldiers (in areas once occupied by the Russians, in fact, to ask a woman about the last days of the war is to violate a strict social taboo), so their hatred of Reds is based on something much more visceral and inexorable than mere ideology.

At any rate, I didn't necessarily want to exterminate policemen, but I did buy a gas pistol the first chance I had. Mr. Y., who had taken me to the gun shop, gave me look of fatherly concern and said something about my certainly having a taste for the, er, unusual.

When I got back to the pier with my purchase, a boy of seven or eight looked up at me and said, "Kapitan?"

"No," I told him, "I'm the doctor."

"For that ship?"

"Yes."

The little tyke asked me to introduce him to the captain and announced that he was going to ride back to Japan with us. "I can pay for it," he said.

I asked him where he lived, and he said, "Japan." Thinking my German had failed me, I rephrased the question.

"Where is your house?"

"In Japan."

I took the kid to my cabin and gave him some caramel and chewing gum. Children are not spoiled and fussed over in Europe as they are in Japan, and this was obviously quite a treat for him. He romped about the cabin, stuffed his cheeks with five pieces of gum at once, and generally went wild. Unaccustomed to addressing anyone with the familiar *du*, I kept calling the boy *Sie*—the difference being more or less equivalent to that between *omae* and *anata* in Japanese—and every time I did, his eyes would take on a glazed, vacant look, and communication would falter. I mentioned this to A. when I got back to Japan.

"It's the same with dogs," he said. "Call them *'omae'* and they bark and wag their tails. But if you look at a dog and say *'anata,'* he just stares back at you goggle-eyed."

I was able to spend only one day in Lübeck, the old town where Thomas Mann was born. The house Mann lived in—the prototype for the house in his novel *Buddenbrooks*—still stands, and I wanted very much to see it. Mann was, of course, the premier writer of this century, but he is not as widely read in Germany today as I'd imagined (though, admittedly, my reverence for the man tends to blow things out of proportion). Toward the end of his life, Arthur Schopenhauer is said to have lamented the "extraordinary ignorance" of the German people and to confess to a feeling of shame at being a citizen of that country, but it wasn't until I met Germans who told me that Thomas Mann "wasn't really German, you know," that I got some inkling of what he was talking about.

Having just received my money from Fraulein Bendt, I was feeling like a full-fledged tourist the morning I set out for Lübeck. I took a taxi to the central station in Hamburg and, following Thomas Mann's example, tipped the driver generously. *"Tausend Danke,"* he called after me. *"Gute Reise."* In the station I shunned the cheap food stands and plopped myself down at a secluded table in the second-floor restaurant. I was about to order a bottle of expensive wine when the idea of being so profligate with my precious marks suddenly seemed like madness; I opted instead for Wiener schnitzel and beer.

I did splurge on the beer, however, drinking several glasses, and was feeling no pain by the time I got up, over-tipped the waiter, and strolled downstairs to the wicket. In a pleasantly hazy frame of mind, I asked the man to tell me which was my platform. He glanced at my ticket, grabbed my arm, pointed, and gestured that I should run like hell. This was no time for my Thomas Mann act. I sprinted the fifty meters or so in nothing flat and dove aboard the double-decker train, wheezing and snorting and stone cold sober, just as it started to move.

There's something about traveling alone through an unfamiliar land that sets the soul tingling. It's even better if you have no fixed destination and no clear idea of where you are at any given moment, which is precisely the case of the protagonist of Mann's very short—and, for him, rather romantic—story, "The Wardrobe." It was, therefore, almost with a sense of regret that I got off the train in Lübeck.

I caught a taxi in front of the station and was disappointed to find that Mann's house is by no means what one could call a landmark. All I knew was that it was somewhere behind the Rathaus, but that put me one up on the driver. I abandoned the cab and asked a plump elderly lady sitting on a bench in front of the Rathaus and, contrary to my expectations, she knew exactly where the house was. "It's on that corner right over there," she said, pointing. It was something of a let-down to have the mystery solved so quickly, but I set off for the indicated corner, eyeing the schoolgirls as I went. I half expected to run into one like *Tonio Kröger*'s lovely blonde Inge of the laughing blue eyes, but, not surprisingly, none of the girls came close.

I reached the corner, looked around, decided it must be the next corner, and pushed off again. Halfway down the block I stopped in a bookstore. I'd noticed in Hamburg that whenever I entered one of these establishments, a salesperson would immediately approach and begin pestering me. Here, too, a saleslady lost no time in making her presence felt. Not knowing how else to respond in the face of such high-pressure tactics, I purchased a copy of Karl Jaspers' *Die Atombombe und die Zukunft des Menschen*, a grim, imposing tome I'd noticed in the store window. Not that I'd ever be able to read the damned thing. As she rang up my purchase, I casually asked the saleslady about Mann's residence, and she told me it was, indeed, on the corner I'd just left. I wobbled, bewildered, back to square one, but still didn't see any buildings that could possibly have been the *Buddenbrooks* house. A man on the corner gave me a long, complicated set of directions, speaking so rapidly that I hardly understood a word, and sent me toddling off toward a nebulous spot some blocks away. When I finally realized that I'd been misled, I asked a fourth informant, an old man shuffling arthritically down the street. The name Thomas Mann seemed to mean nothing to him—he cocked his head and hemmed and hawed. I tried to escape, but he clamped onto my arm, leaving me little choice but to shuffle along beside him. I was dejectedly wondering where I'd end up this time when I realized we were back at the original corner. The ancient one aimed his crooked finger at a small office building. I looked at the place dubiously before noticing, beneath a sign reading "Volksbank," a plaque inscribed with a brief description of the history of the *Buddenbrooks* house. It pays to respect the elderly.

The house was an unremarkable building of plain white stone, likely to disappoint any devoted reader of *Buddenbrooks*. The inconspicuous plaque was inscribed with three or four lines, which explained that the house had been built in 1758 and belonged to the Mann family from 1841 to 1891. A friend of mine who'd visited here just after the war had said nothing of this plaque, nor had I ever read any mention of it, so I assume it was placed there after Mann's death. An air of brick buildings flanked the house. To the left, bird cages hung in the display window of a seed store called "Michael Samen"; the building on the right housed a grocery.

I loitered on the pavement awhile wallowing in Weltschmerz. It was growing late; the bells of the church behind me started their plangent, solemn tolling, and twilight began its slow descent. As I retreated toward the Rathaus, down the narrow streets so redolent of the Middle Ages, I was again aware of the faint, furtive hope of coming face to face with the blue eyes and golden hair I'd dreamed of more than ten years before, when I first read *Tonio Kröger*. But, of course, as Tonio himself reflected, "Such things do not happen in this world."

How I wanted to spend the night in this town! Here, surely, I would have been able to find some room to fit and sustain the nostalgic, melancholy mood I'd slipped into; each winding lane and each gabled house seemed familiar to me. But, in fact, I was so pressed for time that even a leisurely walk back to the station was out of the question. I hailed a cab in front of the Rathaus. "When is spring in Japan?" the driver asked me, and it grieves me to admit that he hadn't even asked my nationality. I replied that it began in April or so. "It's the same as here, then," he said. "You should see those fields over there in the spring. Full of flowers." My answer had been less than precise, of course; spring in Tokyo arrives a good month earlier than in Lübeck.

It was dark when I reached Hamburg. I took care of some business on the ship and at about ten o'clock set out for the famed St. Pauli Strasse. This was to be my last night in Hamburg, and I wanted to make the most of every moment. Passing up the Zillertal, the enormous beer hall to which Mr. Y. had taken me the previous evening, I started at one end of the street and worked my way down, stopping at every bar I saw. In only one did I stay long enough to drink a beer; the others I merely popped into and, after a quick look around, out of. In the ninth or tenth bar, a waiter rushed up to greet me. I tried to fend him off by saying I was only looking for some friends, but to my surprise he told me they were here waiting. "Right this way, sir," he said, and I followed him, curious, to a table in the back, where I found the third engineer—the poor fellow who'd nearly died of a toothache—and another man from the ship. They were drinking beer, and seated next to each was an attractive young woman. There appeared to be something of a communication problem, and when the girls heard me speak a few words of German, they treated me like a hero home from the front. One of them was exactly my type, and I decided to join the party.

After a few beers I was in high spirits and called for a bottle of Rhine wine. An elderly sommelier appeared with the list, grinning from ear to ear, as if my asking for wine was simply the most wonderful thing that had ever happened to him. In Germany all the waiters—even the most insolent, oleaginous punks—are referred to as "Herr Ober," but this was a man who obviously deserved the title. He was short and solidly built, glabrous as an egg, and his face was creased with softly curved lines that suggested infinite gentility. Wary of being swept up in the rapture my request for wine had occasioned in him, I tactlessly blurted out my primary concern—that it not be very expensive. Without the slightest change in attitude, however, he pointed out a name toward the bottom of the list and asked if he might venture to suggest . . . ? I nodded. He glided away and returned bearing a bottle, offered me a taste, poured, and shimmered off again, all with the same air of deferential ecstasy—a far cry from those waiters who slouch against the wall and watch you with a sneer that seems to ask, "Why don't you swallow your fork and die?"

The two girls scribbled their names in *katakana* for us but couldn't speak Japanese at all. A telephone sat on the table at each booth in this bar to allow the customer to ring up any lady he fancied and invite her to join him. I had no opportunity to experiment with the system, however, since the one I fancied was sitting right before me. She and I later went off alone to a nightclub some-where. A band composed entirely of English girls was playing; we drank more wine and I ended up jitterbugging my partner across the floor with all the passion and grace of a whirling dervish.

She told me she'd once lived with an Indo-Chinese man and that she now had a Japanese lover, a sailor who came to Hamburg once every six months. She also showed me snapshots of herself with a peculiar-looking old Japanese cod-ger, but made it clear that it was business, not love, that had brought them to-gether. At some point, well in my cups, I found myself unable to say anything except how beautiful she was, how her eyes were like shining stars, her lips like honey, and so on and so forth. I would never be able to say such things in Japa-nese, of course, but in German it all sounded—to me, at least—like sheer po-etry. One is again reminded of the masterful subtlety of Thomas Mann, who in *The Magic Mountain* has Hans Castorp confess his bizarre love for Clavdia Chauchat in French.

But back to the subject of my jitterbugging. Now, as I write this, I am as frail as a helpless old dotard, and it amazes me to recall the human tornado I must have resembled that night. Were I to try to duplicate those spins and gy-rations now, my spine would probably crack and splinter. I whipped myself into such a frenzy, in fact, that I suffered a sort of temporary amnesia. Of what happened after we left the nightclub, not even a fragment—not one slender shard—remains.

KOJIMA NOBUO

After Kojima Nobuo (1915–2006) was drafted into the army and served in China, the subject of most of his postwar writings became satires of his experiences in the military and of the confusion and disillusionment felt by soldiers returning from the war. In that regard, his attitude was different from that in the work of Agawa Hiroyuki, who sometimes used the same themes. Kojima's story "The Smile" (Bishō, 1954) is a characteristic portrayal of the psychological burdens of a war veteran.

THE SMILE (BISHŌ)

Translated by Lawrence Rogers

The other day a local paper ran a picture taken at a swimming class for children who've had polio. The caption under it referred to "a smiling father in the pool." I was that smiling, apparently happy father. I'd been getting the word out to my friends and acquaintances about the class for some time, so everyone congratulated me when the photo appeared in the paper.

1

I saw my son for the first time when I returned home from the war. I'd been gone for four years. I was oppressed by the sense that rather than simply being my *son*, he was more my *sickly son*. When I returned to where my family had been evacuated during the war, he was not in the shack that served as a home but was playing outside. Instead of calling for him, I went out to look for this son I'd never laid eyes on as though I were looking for hidden treasure. I'd seen only pictures of him when he was a baby, so in searching for my four-year-old son, it was obviously better that I look for someone who resembled me rather than rely on my recollection of him in a photograph, and as it turned out, I was able to find this boy who looked like me. He already walked with a limp then, his right heel up off the ground. My wife told me that was because his injured big toe hadn't yet healed and said she'd been taking him to a masseuse.

That seemed implausible to me. If his big toe hurt, you could hardly expect him to walk on it intentionally, heel in the air. That was perfectly obvious to me, and in my mind I told myself over and over what a disaster it was and even said as much, yet I went day after day telling myself that the next day when he got up, a miracle will have occurred and he wouldn't limp anymore. There was no room for pity for the boy quite yet, for I was gripped by doubt: was I really meeting my obligations as a father? Yet I once carried him on my back almost eight miles along a mountain road down to the nearest train station and, from there, gone one hour by train, getting then on another train and taking him to the Red Cross hospital in Nagoya. There was a suspension bridge on the mountain road that crossed a deep gorge, and when I looked down at the water roaring far below me, I almost passed out. When we got to the other side my wife spoke.

"I used to go to Gifu for provisions with this boy on my back. I'd close my eyes and pray and think of you before I started across. Then I'd sing the song that goes 'the pure white foothills of Fuji' as I crossed. I've no idea why I sang that song, but oddly enough, it gave me courage."

That time with me, however, she hadn't sung, despite what she'd just told me. My wife and I took turns carrying the boy along the long road, and each time we set him down, we'd sit down and rest a bit and feed him. My mind was at ease, for I felt I was doing my duty, and I enjoyed it, and my wife seemed happy somehow, and by doing this I was earning my own self-respect.

At the Red Cross hospital we took him to General Medicine. All they did was put a compress on him. After we came home, the boy soon lost the ability to hold chopsticks in his right hand. He couldn't hold them no matter how much I scolded him. Before long he started to stutter. Sensitive to stuttering, my dismay was complete, for there could be no more indisputable proof that he was *my* son. Until that moment I'd felt that he was my wife's boy, and since I'd been brooding over his affliction day after day, that he was "our sickly son," but when he began to stutter I was stopped cold in my tracks.

My father stuttered; when I was a child I was cured of my stuttering, though even now I can't say the cure was completely successful. If I'm angry with my wife, for example, my stuttering is something fierce, so much so that she's the one who is struck speechless. My son probably inherited this predisposition to the wretched affliction from me, or most certainly picked up my speech mannerisms and was soon stuttering after I returned and had quarreled with my wife several times.

In that sense as well, my son has been a sickly son. Stutterer or not, of course, it would be a truly sad situation for any father, yet on the whole, feelings of pity for him have been beyond me. I've thought a good deal about this. Neither my mother nor my father ever treated me coldly, and I've acted the same way toward them. When you get right down to it, I don't think I've been such a cold fish as a human being. They did make overblown gestures at suicide, often when they were sick and frustrated at the lack they perceived in the way they were being nursed and at having to be dependent on such care. Father's was directed at Mother and Mother's at my older sister. Father walked to the persimmon tree in the back carrying a kimono sash cord. He was probably waiting for me to stop him. Mother tried to jump out a second-story window. She also anticipated my stopping her. I went and wrapped my arms around them, arriving neither too soon nor too late. Had I acted then out of duty? No, I had raged at their sicknesses and wept at how they must have felt. My parents, in fact, also were angered by their afflictions, but I sensed that their desire to confront them, to play the fool within the human drama, was the stronger emotion.

2

A year after we moved to Gifu, we knew that it was infantile paralysis, but to be cured the patient must receive a spinal injection within two months of contracting the disease, after which the only treatment is massage—which you also have to leave to a specialist. But since my son had both a bad leg and a bad arm, it was cerebral, for which from day one there is no cure. This is also what they told me at the Red Cross hospital. They had not been able to come up with a diagnosis at the local prefectural hospital. When I heard from the doctors that it was too late, I felt immensely relieved, as though a weight had been lifted from my shoulders. I no longer felt responsible, I told my wife, and if responsibility didn't lie with the disease, it was the responsibility of the war, which had led to his malnourishment, and if the war were to blame, I asked her, shouldn't we be thankful simply that he survived? I'd said it less to console my wife than to affirm my own sense of deliverance. After I'd told her this, I often took the child out to play. I observed myself when I didn't do it. I found that to me it was less a matter of pitying and lamenting the child's disability as he walked than taking my son out and demonstrating that I was equal to being stared at. It was my intention thereby to compensate for the feebleness of the love I felt for him.

As I had anticipated, when the two of us, father and son, went for a walk, passersby would inevitably turn and look at us. I discovered that people walking toward us didn't look until they were passing, that when they came precisely abreast of us they looked hard at the child and then turned back to stare.

"Don't let their staring get to you," I often told my son as we walked, "Daddy's with you." I wonder, though, if in the final analysis, it was really my intention to raise the child's spirits. I'd return home exhausted from these emotional ordeals.

I'd take him to ride the horizontal swinging log at the playground.

"Ready? Get on."

If I'd taken him with the actual intention of having him ride the log, I'd have done it when no one was watching, and I certainly would have set him on it with the greatest care and held him there. Yet not only did I not help my fearful son, who would look anxiously up at me, I would simply stand there and stare at him as he limped toward the log, his right hand twisted behind him.

"Don't worry. Get on."

I must instill courage in this crippled boy if he is to brave the raging sea of life.

This was what I chose to think as I swung the log vigorously. I knew just how repulsive an expression the boy would have on his face as he cried. He'd look not simply like one of our family who was crying. He'd have that lopsided, contorted expression characteristic of the infirm.

One day an old woman I'd never laid eyes on before caught me in the act.

"You there!" she called out in the local dialect. A look at her angry face made me, curiously, fiercely angry myself.

Is he your kid? Do you think I'd do this if he were someone else's kid? I handed him a toy I'd spent my last yen on. I felt such rage toward this old woman who had seen deep into my heart that I could have knocked her down. When my agitation subsided, however, I felt so wretched I wanted to take my son in my arms and plunge from the bridge over the Nagara River. And I realized that in this respect I was indisputably my mother's son.

I was aware that the reason I felt no love for my son was a consequence of my not personally taking part in raising the boy myself, and it was for this reason, I concluded, that I'd have to take a hand in disciplining him. Yet the fact is, it's not simply a matter of not loving my son. I *despise* him for his disability. When I think about this hapless child, I'm absolutely overwhelmed.

My wife scolds the child, forgetting he's crippled. Then at night she'll cry in bed, back turned to me. I, on the other hand, scold the boy *because* he is crippled. In that sense, I find my wife's mentality the more frightening.

My wife was in bed for a good while with morning sickness. The boy has to urinate a lot. (Another thing that comes from his affliction.) After I woke him one night, the boy was starting to pass water as he stood on the futon. I knocked him down, took hold of his rigid body by his legs, and carried him to the roof eaves at the window. I savored a pleasant numbing sensation as I did so. I don't deny, of course, that I was a kind of devil at the time, yet I felt I myself was quelling an imp. (I despise the devil of deformity.) I took the board-rigid body and tossed it on the futon as one would a stick. I then began spanking the boy as one would beat a drum.

The war had ended recently and I was utterly exhausted, and my wife had lain in bed for more than a month, able to hold nothing down. She was not going to make it if the fetus wasn't aborted immediately. I was waiting for my wife to stop me, at which point she came flying at me. I grabbed her by the throat. She kicked me in the stomach, and I fell backward. For the first time since I'd known her, she reviled me as she lay face down on the floor with the violent, rough sort of language only men use.

"What the hell are you doing?!"

I'm sure that's what she said. How could my wife, whose upbringing was better than mine, use language like that? Shocked at this unexpected outburst, I was able to regain my composure.

What the hell are you doing?!

Turning these words over and over again in my mind, I took care of the futon. I then put the boy to bed. (In a little while, he had forgotten what I'd done to him and was asleep. I don't know whether this is symptomatic of his disease.) I put a cold compress on my wife's forehead and sat where I was for a long while. We were staying on the second floor of an inn, so everyone had seen what I'd done.

I knew I had to consider how it was that such a cruel act had come into my head. All during my long and frenzied life in the military I'd lived an even-tempered existence and had never even touched another person. Why had I, having thus responded to military life, done something like this? If I'm capable of this sort of thing, I must be cautious about myself.

Shall I join a church?
Shall I undertake spiritual training?
Shall I hold myself in check with other actions?

By other actions I mean such things as suddenly starting to dust with a duster when I get excited, or sweep with a broom, or run outside. But perhaps before I'm able to do any of those things, I'll beat him with the duster, knock him over with jabs from the broom, or beat him and flee. As for faith and spiritual training, it would doubtless be a simple matter to cast either aside, since whether to contemplate faith or to throw it over would be entirely up to me. Yet it also seemed to me that at the least, my intentions are perhaps the better for it while I'm in this frame of mind. And thanks to this incident, my wife's morning sickness disappeared completely.

I often found myself musing silently as I stood behind my wife, who would be doing the laundry.

I wonder what I should do.

I wanted to have the confidence to retrieve my own mild temperament. My wife was trying to teach the boy to count. He was old enough to go to kindergarten but simply couldn't get beyond four, so I calmed her down and took over the task.

"After four comes five. Five."

I repeated the number for him with uncommon gentleness.

"You have to go easy with him. OK, are we ready, son? It's one, two, three, four, five. Five."

"One, two, three, four . . ."

He fell silent after he reached four.

"It's five! It's no big deal!" I said, recalling as I spoke that the boy was a stutterer.

"Now, son, is it that you can't *say* it, that you know what it is but you can't say it? Which is it? Which? You don't know? You can't say it? Tell me. Which?"

The boy started to snicker.

My hand betrayed my heart and in a flash was on its way to his cheek.

"You think its funny? Laugh at this!"

Stop my hand.

What the hell are you doing?!

His snickering didn't stop after I hit him, but the tears finally began to flow. His hand over his little thing, his whole body began to shake. It had come to this because my son had abruptly started to snicker at a time when he shouldn't have, when I was groping about for answers: Is his slow-wittedness inborn? Is it due to the polio? Or is he incapable of counting because he stutters? And in fact the boy laughed because he was unhappy. Perhaps there's something wrong with his brain.

My wife had a daughter, the baby who almost didn't get born, who in her birth availed herself of my son's victimhood. After she was born, I was astonished at the common, everyday love residing in my own heart. Just imagining this baby contracting polio made my head swim. And I realized for the very first time, and with a sense of wonder, that for a child not to be a cripple is the normal state of affairs.

Until my daughter was born, I vaguely sensed that there were an awful lot of kids who weren't disabled. It's just like marveling at the longevity of others when one's own relatives and friends are dropping all around you. Because I didn't want to look at normal children, I simply had an unfocused feeling—that boy is normal; our child should also be in good health—that there are a lot of healthy ones. This was because it was too painful for me to look at other children and I so avoided it. When my son entered kindergarten, it was inevitable that I should fear he would be ignored by the other children and that I would have to go and see for myself.

There I was blinded by the sight of all the normal children and unable to keep my eyes open. I knew that in two or three days, these children would bring their cunning and wit into play and would be showing us their imitations of my son's walk and how he talks. There's a chance he might not even realize that he's being made fun of. *But I'll be damned if I'll take him out of kindergarten.*

As I watched, I could see him laughing happily. And because he was laughing, he was losing his turn on the swing to the other children. When he caught sight of me in the distance, he limped quickly toward me, his right hand upraised as though carrying a flag. I was waiting for him to tumble over, and sure enough, he had taken a spill by the time he got to me. I waited for him to get up. He came nearer, a frown on his face. I didn't take him back to the swing but sent him back by himself. I briefly observed him with a casual air as I stood behind the other children, then bellowed at the children in a voice that reverberated over the kindergarten grounds, castigating them for not getting on the swing in proper order. I continued my scrutiny, agitated as a bear, my breathing labored.

In kindergarten my son was pushed off a bench and broke his arm. My wife was sickly and couldn't go out, so I'd put the two children in the baby buggy and make the trips to the orthopedist. By that time we had moved to a small country town.

It seemed to me I heard voices coming from behind the glass doors of the houses in town.

He's going by again with them in the baby buggy. He wants to show off the girl.

The boy's arm is in a sling, but the truth is, it's polio. It was treated too late. The parents are to blame.

He likes going to the orthopedist. He likes it because it's an honest-to-god hospital.

The bone setting turned out poorly. The splint was removed too early, which dislocated the rigid muscle. I went off to Tokyo with him to talk to an old friend who was at Tokyo University Hospital. We went through the wards, and he introduced me to a number of specialists in the field.

"The muscle is already formed, you see. We could fix the dislocation surgically, but you have to remember this is infantile paralysis. He might end up even worse off."

After I'd said good-bye to my friend and left the hospital, I was exhilarated, as though I'd made a suicide pact and then discovered that I, and I alone, had had the good fortune to survive. As I was walking toward the Ochanomizu train station, a woman called out to me.

"Did your little boy have polio? Poor baby! There's little hope he'll get better, is there."

My self-centered exhilaration evaporated utterly at the sound of this well-meaning stranger's voice, and my wife's face rose before me.

"What would you like?" I asked my son, who had his eyes glued to the window, looking outside as we rode the train back. "Daddy will buy it for you."

He shook his head and smiled.

"I wanna go home right away."

"You do? Were you scared?"

"Uh-huh."

My son had wept in the hospital, his naked body rigid. Quite naturally, he's heard me tell doctors the same story over and over again. I've gradually gotten better at telling them about his polio. I've already created a plausible legend, as opposed to the simple facts.

Or perhaps it would be better to say I've created an environment in which the response is inevitable.

"Nothing can be done, I'm afraid."

This time, in a large city hospital, he'd climbed up onto the X-ray table by himself to be confronted by a ring of musing doctors. He'd stood there like a defendant in the dock.

"You want to get well, son?" I asked him absurdly on the train. I'd hoped he would be unaware of even the existence of wellness and sickness. His response to this was merely to smile. I wanted to know what the smile meant. Whenever I saw his smile, I felt like a sumo wrestler suddenly thrown out of the ring. And simultaneously, there began to lurk somewhere inside me a hideous something that knew I could do anything to this boy, that anything would be allowed.

"Why are you laughing, son? You get a funny feeling when you think? Surely it's not because you're happy, is it?"

Still smiling, my son lowered his eyes, then stealing a glance at the other pas-

sengers, he went from merely smiling to actually snickering. What had pro-
voked his suppressed laughter were the exaggerated gestures and conversation
of several young blackmarketeers who were joking and fooling around in our
car. Not surprisingly, my son and I don't get through to each other. The reason
we don't—is it my fault, or in the end, is it due to his sickness?—is something
I'm attempting to divine in my son's naive, afflicted head.

"Polio is the problem," I told my wife when I returned home. I played with
my daughter as I talked, not looking at my wife full in the face. "The disloca-
tion has nothing to do with it. And the dislocation certainly seems to be the re-
sult of the polio. It probably has nothing to do with his fall at kindergarten."

My wife's eyes suddenly opened wide. It was as though she were looking not
at me but at something huge behind me. I looked away from her.

"That's not true at all! He dislocated it because he fell. Because you had him
go to kindergarten, even though I was so opposed to it. We're certainly not go-
ing to stay in a town that has a kindergarten like that. They weren't even watch-
ing when he was shoved. The polio didn't cripple him. He's got everything
exactly where it should be. The dislocation is what's crippling him. That's what
it is. And it's the poor child who has to suffer!"

She burst into tears.

My wife despised the town, though in reality it seemed to me that I was the
only one she was mad at. Driven on by that anger, we came to Tokyo.

3

My son, older, but still misshapen, was soon big enough to go to school. We
came to Tokyo and discovered that in the big city, people weren't as concerned
about the boy's affliction as those in a small town were, since you could find dis-
abled kids everywhere if you put your mind to it. Whenever I discovered a child
who'd had polio, I'd tell my wife right away. On days when I had that to talk
about, I quickly came home. I also came across children who had to walk with
crutches. There was no timidity in the faces of such children, and they had the
unaffected air of those who are used to being looked at, even though they did
walk off to one side.

He's better off than that kid. Imagine how his parents must feel!

I once watched one going along an arrow-straight riverside road on the out-
skirts of town until he was out of sight.

And I was quick to bring home stories I'd heard at work or from friends who
worked elsewhere, about people who'd had polio and yet did regular work like
everyone else.

Gradually my wife was taken in by my strategy.

"The candy store owner was in hysterics," she told me one day. "The boy
tells me that everyone in the household comes running out to see him when he
goes there. And then he wins another prize."

Unobserved, I followed my son to the store to appraise the situation myself. I assumed it must be due to the goodwill of the candy store owner or my wife's hopeless fantasizing. I returned home dumbstruck with admiration. He again had won something. I no longer felt any need to sound out my wife. Even if she were doing something to help things along, it was doubtless because she herself was now sure of the outcome. I, for my part, have decided to believe that this is how it will always turn out.

The child's right hand interferes with his left. It moves about like a snake, independent of his will. It blocks his one healthy hand, and when it comes to rest on his desk, it tears up any papers there, willy-nilly. Except when he's asleep, the hand is in constant motion and you can never tell what it's going to do. Because of this, the boy restrains the hand by keeping it hooked onto a pocket, which he'll abruptly rip.

"It's really a problem, this darned hand," he complains shrilly to no one in particular. He chastises his mischievous right hand. I recalled what a doctor once told me.

"We could stop it from moving around like that with brain surgery. The only problem is, it would never move again."

"You're right," his mother said, "you're ripping your pockets is really a problem." She had beaten me at my own game, and I was staggered. I was forced to respond.

"C'mon boy, try and wrap your fingers around Daddy's."

My boy's fingers wrapped themselves around mine with an aberrant force that tore at my heart. I pushed back hard against his palm and fingers.

"Ah! That feels good! It feels real good!"

The boy squealed in delight as I pushed even harder. Only a portion of the nerves in his arm and fingers was alive, and it was now ignoring the dead nerves and doing as it damned well pleased. The muscles were being taunted, and they, in turn, were complaining to the nerves. Their complaints were being acknowledged.

How very happy my impulsive malice had made the boy. I remembered a passage I'd read in a novel about a field hospital. In order to recover the use of fingers left on a hand that a bullet had raised havoc with, a patient had to submit to some one hundred painful lashes of a whiplike leather device.

"Will I really get movement back this way?" asked the patient, a major.

"That is a photograph of someone who was successfully treated," said the doctor, pointing coldly. "That is why I have the photo on the wall. You must trust me."

The leather whip was an amalgam of the doctor's good and evil intentions. It occurred to me that I, too, in my own way, might find it necessary to sustain, or try to sustain, this evil intent.

Even so, I was outraged at my wife's stupidity, her falling into my trap, her cornering me, but when I do walk along the street and see people with their children, I'm filled with concern for my boy and hurry home and, after shouting at my wife for no good reason, start to push on his fingers. Thus my wife was now completely reassured.

"What's the matter with your right hand? Pick up the chopsticks."

At mealtimes I doggedly harassed him about the hand. For this trivial lifting of a pair of chopsticks, my son assumed the strained expression of a man lifting a half-ton stone.

"Try to hold it, even if you can't. Understand? There's no other way to do it. I'll push on your hand again."

I let out an ear-splitting scream. It was directed at my wife. Or perhaps it was not. I struck a hectoring posture for both of us, for me and for my wife, in the face of an unseen observer, one that some might liken to God himself.

"It's a fact," my wife said. "He's getting lazy, this boy."

"Getting lazy? He certainly isn't. It's not the boy who's getting lazy."

"And who are you saying is lazy?"

"I d-dunno who. I d-dunno wh-who." I was shaking with rage and couldn't talk.

I took my son out into the yard.

"You're gonna catch the ball. Use your right hand as much as possible. I won't m-m-make it easy for you."

When I saw my son run gleefully into the yard with the ball, I knew what it was I was up to. How fine it would be, I thought, if at a time like this, I were a nice man from the neighborhood gazing on the charming scene from atop the bluff and shedding a tear or two, and not the father of this boy.

4

I'd recently read an article in the paper about a special swimming class for those who've had polio, to be held in the YWCA's indoor pool. It said the class, sponsored by the Red Cross, would be undertaken as an experiment and that each of eighty polio victims from throughout Tokyo would have their own instructor.

(Given the fact that there would be a swimming class for polio victims, I, his father, had no option but to go.)

It was with a heavy heart I entertained the thought. I've never missed such an article. Just as I'd watched him at the kindergarten and had watched myself being looked at when I put the boy in the baby buggy, I'd been on the lookout for this sort of article. My wife had decided that I was overjoyed at being able to take part. And because she'd come to that conclusion, I had no choice but to go.

They say that America leads in the treatment of this affliction, and I've even heard speculation that it's been on the increase since the American Occupation.

The article said that the class would be conducted by a doctor who had returned from America, bringing with him a dozen or so instructors he had personally trained.

As the class began and all those disabled by this same disease came together under one roof, I had the feeling that all the polio victims that I'd sought out in my walks were gathered right there before me. There actually were children I remembered seeing before. Absurdly enough, the less severe the child's case, the more puffed up with pride the mother and father were, and faint though they were, I could nonetheless see proud smiles playing about their lips. I wondered how in the world I looked. *That* was my greater concern, not my son.

I suddenly noticed that my son was paying no attention to what the director and the other speakers were saying, to their speeches of encouragement, but was looking around at the other crippled boys in his row, as though he were about to launch into some tomfoolery with them at any moment, even though he was now in his fifth year in grammar school. I pulled on his bad right hand.

"Put it in your pocket," I said, pinching him hard.

"Ow! That hurts!"

He at least had that much sensation left in his hand. I'd known that, of course, but hadn't thought he'd yell out like that.

All eyes fell on me.

Well, am I the only one who does this sort of thing?

I am a evil person to do it. I am an irredeemable villain.

As I thought this to myself, I struck a protective pose, putting my arms around my son. I forced myself to lift my face.

I watched from the stands as my son was left to bob about by himself in the pool. Few pools could have been as noisy as this one. The children swimming weren't chattering away, however. It was their instructors who were talking. They would explain something, show their charges how to float, play the fool, praise the children. As I watched, it struck me that somehow it might be the instructors who were abnormal, brimming as they were with an exaggerated sense of their own benevolence. This flood of goodness almost made my head spin.

An instructor took my son in his arms and placed him in the water as though he were a newborn being given his first bath. The instructor, a college student, didn't get into the water ahead of him.

The director saw this.

"Not like that!"

I was near the director and felt the impulse to make an excuse for the youth in spite of myself, but the director's back was turned to me as though in rebuff.

I realized that it was best not to say anything. My son was full of cheer, as though revived in the water, and frolicked about, laughing. As I looked on his artless, ungainly face, I wanted to call out to him.

Don't be too proud of yourself! You're a sick boy!

I didn't know how to deal with my feelings if I were to continue watching, so I closed my eyes, moving not a muscle, but even then I could hear his shouts of joy. I couldn't very well put my hands over my ears, so I let my head hang down between the bleacher seats, staying absolutely still.

"Excuse me, sir. You, sir, the father of this child."

The director was calling me. Flustered, I picked up a towel and ran to the edge of the pool.

"Your father will take good care of you."

"The student's just a part-time worker," I said, surprised at my own words.

"What's 'part-time' mean?" my son asked me.

I'd been avoiding the director, but now he approached me and suggested I get in the water with my boy.

"You can learn a bit too."

Learn?

What can I learn? Might I learn something about restraint?

Doing as I was told, I put on a pair of trunks and got into the pool, but I lacked the confidence to go near my son. For reasons not entirely clear to even me, I went over to the most seriously disabled lad. He was a middle school student. The upper half of his body was that of a superbly conditioned adult, but his legs were as spindly as bamboo. It was obvious he couldn't stand even in the water. When he lay face up he had no trouble floating because his lower extremities were so light.

He was first to smile as I approached him, and when the instructor let go of his hands, he paddled and moved forward slightly.

"I did it! I swam!" he said, looking at me as the instructor supported him in the water. He then swam over to me. He bumped into me hard. This was something I had anticipated, however.

"Well done!" I said, holding his strange, pathetic body in my arms. Yet I could feel the rage in my heart. For the youth with his crippled body, entirely dependent on me, was trembling with delight. In the water, surrounded by the stands as I was, however, I was compelled to smile, and moving my facial muscles, I told him again and again how well he had done. My mouth told him so, but I felt like someone involved in a conspiracy, and maintaining the deception was sheer torture.

I looked around at my own boy. It was just not possible for me to see him as my own flesh and blood anymore. There seemed to be not enough room for me between the instructor and my son. Besides, if I went to him it would probably cause him to sink, and this after all the effort he'd put into floating. These thoughts ran through my mind as I stood there blankly, unable to move.

"Excuse me sir! Sir!" Someone was calling to me. Startled, I turned around.

"Excuse me!" The voice was coming from outside of the pool. "Smile, please! Turn your head this way a bit more."

Ensnared, I smiled in spite of myself. There was a bright flash in front of me.

"Sir! Sir! Excuse me. Do you think this experiment is working out? What is your opinion?"

My interlocutor grabbed my arm and pulled me over to the side of the pool. "I think it is." *For a father the likes of me.*

That day I let my boy take a chance on the million-yen lottery at the Ochano-mizu train station in the city.

For me, the words my wife spoke so many years ago now resonated with my voice and the voice of the director.

What the hell are you doing?!

I'm the one in the photo of "a smiling father" that was in the paper the other day.

KŌNO TAEKO

Kōno Taeko (b. 1926) spent her adolescence working as a conscript in a military-run factory. After the war, she found work in a government office but struggled for several years with ill health. Kōno's first important story, "Toddler Hunting" (Yōjigari), appeared in 1961. Two years later, she was awarded the Akutagawa Prize for the story "Crabs" (Kani). Kōno's work, heavily influenced by the vision of human desire fleshed out in the work of Tanizaki Jun'ichirō, is filled with the sadomasochistic dreams of women who rage against their female roles and maternal instincts. The story translated here, "Final Moments" (Saigo no toki, 1966), reveals the thought processes of a woman confronting the possibility of death.

FINAL MOMENTS (SAIGO NO TOKI)

Translated by Lucy North

She had to die at some point, she could accept that; and to die in that particular way might even be her fate. But so suddenly, so quickly—Noriko couldn't begin to face the possibility.

"Give me a few days," she begged.

"You mean you want time to get used to the idea," a voice said.

"Who ever 'gets used' to dying?" she retorted. "I'm not an old lady—not terminally ill: I'm middle-aged. I'm healthy—and nothing is wrong with my mind, as far as I know. And anyway, there's not a drop of samurai blood in my veins: I know I won't want to let go of life—I'll be exceptionally unwilling—unless you manage to kill me on your very first try."

"I thought you said you believed in spirits."

"I do. But that doesn't mean I'm happy to die!"

"Well, that's better than not believing at all."

"I don't know if I agree with you. Spirits and ghosts are probably powerless creatures, you know. I know they're supposed to be able to influence humans—to be able to read their minds, and so on. But they don't have physical power over people, or objects; I don't think they can even see them. And what happens when from the other side they try to reach people whose minds are insensitive and who don't react? Or who are too sensitive, so they overreact? I'm sure lines get crossed all the time: it must be easy for a ghost to get frustrated, and lose interest. Besides, after a while, seeing into people's minds must get quite boring and annoying. And aren't ghosts supposed to be bundles of irritation and resentment? No, I dread dying all the more when I think of such an eternally painful existence. If anything, I envy people who can believe in nothingness after death."

Then she cried out: "Oh, I wish that my spirit could stay with my body forever! Or at least that when I die, my spirit would go too!" She so fiercely wanted this that for a moment she forgot about the reprieve.

"Anyway, the point is," she resumed, "I don't want to die. I have to, I know, but you could at least give me some extra time."

"You can't get out of it, you know."

"I know. That's exactly why I'm asking. I only need two or three days. . . ."

"Out of the question."

"But it's not as though I was born in a matter of seconds. How can I just suddenly die? There are so many things I have to take care of before I . . ."

"Such as?"

"Look at me," she said, holding the edges of her kimono sleeves as she spread her arms out. "You can't expect me to die like this. I was on my way to a friend's funeral. I wouldn't have dressed like this if I'd known."

"That's good enough—better than house slippers and an apron."

"But this is black—the color of the dead!"

"The color of the dead is white. Oh, you're right, so is black. But so much the better—think how impressed everybody'll be by your wearing black: they'll think you died very tastefully, in a mood of calmness and acceptance."

"But that's the last thing I want! I don't want to give the impression I went calmly and peacefully!"

"Well, what would you wear to show them you held out to your very last breath?"

"I don't know! I need time. Time to think about it, time to change."

"All right. You have a day to get ready."

"Can't you make it two?"

"What difference will that make? One day, and no more."

Noriko looked at her wristwatch—1:17. The ticking seconds were suddenly very loud to her ears.

"I expect you here in exactly twenty-four hours," the voice said.

The ticking grew even louder. At 1:17 tomorrow, Noriko thought, trembling, she would probably still be alive—but by 1:30 or 1:40, she'd be dead. The fatal time was getting closer by the minute, and once it came, she would never experience that time, or any time of day, ever again.

"Can't you make it twenty-six hours?" she pleaded.

The tiny hand continued on its way round the watch dial. Seconds were passing; already it was 1:19.

"All right—3:19 tomorrow!"

Noriko bowed, and began hurrying away.

"So you're not going to the funeral, after all?" the voice said, behind her. "Your friend's ghost will be sad—don't you care?"

Noriko didn't pause to look back, but walked even more quickly toward home.

As Noriko turned off the street for the road to her house, the red public telephone in front of the corner bread shop caught her eye. She went over, dialed the number of her husband Asari's office and, staring blankly at the broken cradle for the receiver, listened to the urgent ringing. It would seem odd, she reflected, if she asked straight out when he was coming home. First she'd pretend to consult him about how much money to take to the funeral as a condolence gift.

The switchboard operator came on the line.

"Mr. Asari in sales, please," Noriko said.

"Who shall I say is calling?"

Noriko was silent,

"Who is calling, please!" the operator repeated, her voice rising. Noriko cut the connection, and replaced the receiver.

Arriving home, she unlocked the front door and turning the knob to go in, her eyes fell on the yellow milk-bottle box by the step's wooden wainscoting. Its lid was half up, propped on the two empties from breakfast. After tomorrow, she reflected, one bottle would be enough. Her habit was to attach her order for the milkman to an empty bottle with a rubber band whenever Asari went away on business, or the two of them took a trip. "Please leave one bottle till such-and-such a date," she would write; or "Please cease deliveries until further notice."

It occurred to her as she went inside and slipped off her sandals that she should write a note before she forgot, telling the milkman, "Starting the day after tomorrow, please leave one bottle only." Taking a ballpoint pen from the letter rack, she sat down at the dinner table and searched in her bag for the condolence envelope. She found an unmarked part of the envelope and, after taking out the money, tore off a rectangular strip.

"Dear Milkman," she wrote. "Thank you for delivering the milk every day. From the day after tomorrow . . ." But here she paused. She intended to take proper leave of her husband but discreetly, without his actually being aware of it. If she put this note on the bottle now, and Asari saw it, she'd destroy her whole plan. No, it would have to wait till tomorrow morning, after her husband had left the house.

Any number of things would have to be put off until her husband departed tomorrow: the key, for example, there on the tatami next to her purse. Whenever she left the house knowing he might return before she did, she hid it on her way out in the drainpipe by the kitchen door. On occasion, she forgot, and

Asari was locked out. That must not happen tomorrow, but she couldn't attend to it until she left for the very last time.

Noriko tore another strip off the envelope. After scribbling *key*, and *milkman*, she folded it up in her powderpuff box on the low table before her mirror. She would definitely open that tomorrow.

She untied her obi and took off her kimono. After changing into a sweater and skirt, she threw open all the windows as well as the connecting doors between the parlor, the living room, and the corridor. A fresh breeze and spring sunshine flooded the rooms of the small house. She wondered: should she leave her kimono out for a while? But according to her watch it was already nearly two o'clock. If she wasted energy on tasks like that—and she had scarcely worn it anyway—she wouldn't get anything important done by the deadline tomorrow. She would only regret it, so she started to fold up the kimono. She glanced at the undergarments lying beside it, her hands moving busily. She could put those things in the garbage, she thought. It would all be collected tomorrow.

Once the kimono had been tidied away, she took the neck band off her chemise, wrapped it and her other undergarments in newspaper, and stuffed them all in a large plastic bag. Everything she had to discard could go in the bag. The garbage truck would come at eleven—the underwear she changed out of tomorrow morning could be thrown away, too. She took some freshly washed underwear from the wardrobe and laid them ready on the quilt in the closet. On second thought, she didn't want to leave her worn nightgown lying around to be found. She wrapped the nightgown she'd worn last night in a newspaper, put it in the bag, and chose a fresh one for tonight—this one would go in too, eventually. She placed some clean underwear and a pair of pajamas for Asari on the quilt. Opening the other closet door, she took out pillows and changed their cases. From the bottom half of the closet, she dragged out the two folded futons to strip off their sheets. Then she put them both back, set two clean sheets on top, and closed the closet.

She would have to do something with that, she realized, eyeing the mound of dirty clothes at her feet. But laundry would be a waste of precious time now. The man from the cleaner's might come round tomorrow. . . . But then again, he might not. True, she could always call to tell him to come and collect it, but there was no guarantee she would be there to receive him.

"I have to get everything sorted out—as soon as I can," Noriko told herself.

They had six sets of sheets and pillowcases, the extra set for guests. Surely it would be all right to throw these two sets away; she wasn't going to be around any more. She stuffed them in the plastic bag. Asari's pajamas, however, made her hesitate: he only had three pairs. But she discarded these, to save time. And noticing her tabi, which she'd worn with the kimono, she added them to the bag—by now, it was filled to bursting.

There was no risk of Asari noticing a garbage bag, and even if he did, he would hardly check its contents. Noriko tied it up, carried it out through the kitchen door, and deposited it next to the plastic trash bin. Countless other things still had to be thrown away, but unfortunately, they'd have to wait, like the key and the note for the milkman, until tomorrow.

Noriko went upstairs. She tore a piece of paper from a pad in Asari's desk to make a list of things to dispose of.

"My pillowcase," she wrote, "sheets; nightdress; and today's clothes (skirt and sweater)." Then, under a separate heading for Asari, she wrote, "underwear." After thinking for a while, she added, "socks and handkerchief." But then, where was she going to hide this list? Some place that wouldn't catch Asari's eye, but where she would see it once he had gone, before the garbage truck came by. The harder Noriko tried to think of a place, the more elusive it became. Well, for the time being she could conceal it in her can of dried sardines: she'd open that up tomorrow, to make miso soup for breakfast. True, Asari would still be home; but she could move it somewhere else then, and in any case, a better spot might still occur to her.

As she made her way down to the kitchen, Noriko was still pondering what to wear when she left home for the last time tomorrow. She was determined to die in a way that clearly showed her will to live. She was even more set on leaving traces of the most appalling death agony. It would be best if blood spewed out, if it left the most gruesome stains. She would struggle to her very last breath, thrashing about horribly with her arms and legs, slipping and rolling in her blood, smearing it everywhere. . . . Come to think of it, blood would never have shown up against the black kimono she'd been wearing this morning. Thank goodness she hadn't had to go dressed in that.

Noriko recalled a white outfit that she had had made two years before. The fabric seemed slightly yellowed; she hadn't worn it once this season. But it was basically still the same color. It would set the blood off nicely. But then she remembered: white was a color for the dead. One more minute, and she would have opted for what she least desired. Well, the only other garment that would do, considering the season, was her beige suit. A simple jersey skirt and jacket, she hardly ever wore it. She knew the suit would be in the wardrobe, but she opened the door just to make sure.

Yes, there it was: it would contrast shockingly with the blood. A purple winter suit was also hanging there, as well as a raincoat, an overcoat, a light green spring suit, and a folded blouse sharing its hanger with a cardigan. None had been cleaned since she last wore them; these clothes would have to be thrown away too. Come to think of it, there was also the shoe cupboard in the hall—she would only need one pair now. But all the other shoes, sandals, and rain clogs had been kicked off and thrown inside. She didn't want to leave them in that state. But Asari also used the wardrobe and the shoe cabinet, and again, he might notice if she cleared them out too soon.

Noriko headed toward the kitchen—*wardrobe* and *shoe cabinet* had to be added to the list in the dried sardine can—but halfway there, she stopped in her tracks. I must not forget, she told herself firmly, that I was the mistress of this household. If I get rid of everything, the house will look like a place left by a daughter who has run away to get married, or a maid who has stolen everything and gone off. She retraced her steps, draped a tortoiseshell necklace over the beige suit on its hanger, and closed the wardrobe. On her way back down the front hall, she let herself glance inside the shoe cupboard. Her brown shoes, and several pairs of Asari's were, all of them, clean enough.

Cutting down the number of her tasks was a relief, but the next moment it occurred to her that she would never have thought of such things if she hadn't started preparing her outfit for tomorrow. If she didn't keep her wits about her, she thought anxiously, she would forget so many things—she would die without completing important tasks. . . . The more she worried, the more impossible it became to keep track of where one task ended and another began.

Already it was nearly three o'clock. The front door of the bathhouse was just being thrown open. Noriko imagined selecting one of the wooden basins stacked just inside the bathing area, and hearing its hollow echo as she set it down in front of a deserted row of faucets. The afternoon sun would stream in through the high white-framed windows and reflect off the bottom of the tub. . . . Her very last bath, Noriko thought. She wanted to hear the clap of the wooden basin; she wanted to see the sunlight hit the tub.

But there was still a much more important task: she hurried upstairs, opened a closet, and from behind some cushions at the bottom removed a wicker basket. She took out of it Asari's three yukata. She replaced the basket and cushions. Standing up, she looked at the yukata in her arms: one more month, she thought, and it would be time to wear these. Asari would be sure to find them if she put them in the chest of drawers downstairs, with his underwear. And then it occurred to her that it might be nice to leave him a little message in one of these yukata. That way he'd discover it one summer evening, the first time he put it on. Yes, she wanted to whisper just a few words to her husband.

Noriko laid the yukata down, and sitting at Asari's desk, took out some writing paper and a pen. She contemplated the garments on the tatami, and the yukata-clad figure of Asari rose to mind—not on his way out to the bath, nor on his way back, but off to see a movie, on one of his evenings of not drinking.

Every ten days or so, Asari would declare, as he was changing out of his work clothes, "Tonight, I'll do without." This was his way of saying that he wouldn't have any drinks with dinner. When Noriko replied with comments like "Great!" or "I'm impressed!" he'd snap back: "I didn't say I wouldn't have any later!" On the other hand, if she only said, "I see," or "All right," he'd look hurt and resentful, and accuse her of indifference. Whatever she said on the nights he tried not to drink put him in a foul mood. She remembered infuriating him one evening: he'd asked her where the hammer was, and she'd told him to go and look in the saké cupboard. On these evenings, Asari always felt the need for some distraction, and often ended up at their local movie theater. He hardly ever invited her, but then she didn't particularly want to go. If anything, she felt relief when he told her that he was going out, after a short supper without saké or beer; she would busily help him get ready. The tense set of his shoulders as he left showed that he was fuming about having said he wouldn't drink. Rather than money she would put books of movie tickets in his yukata sleeve, so he would not be tempted on the way home. She felt sorry for him, but she also found the whole thing a little amusing.

Noriko gripped the pen.

"Good evening, dear," she wrote. "So you've put on your yukata. You must be feeling cool and comfortable. Are you on your way to the Shōwa Cinema? Perhaps they're showing one of your favorite sexy comedies tonight."

She signed her name, folded the note twice, then slipped it into the sleeve of the yukata on the top of the pile—a navy blue one with white horizontal stripes made up of small circles like sliced macaroni.

But the prospect of greeting her husband from his yukata sleeve after her death like this made her want to give him a winter surprise too—perhaps from the pocket of his overcoat. She took up the pen again.

"It's gotten so cold, hasn't it!" she wrote on the next sheet of paper: "I expect you'll stop off for a drink on your way home tonight. Here's a little pocket money, from my own secret supply. Well, I wish that were true. You always said, didn't you, that I was no good at saving—that's why you could trust me. Well, you were right, dear: this is only household expense money, plus the condolence gift for my friend's funeral, which in the end I didn't attend. You're fussy enough about money—except when it comes to drink—to have been wondering what became of this small sum. Didn't I see you, the other day, rummaging around in the chest of drawers for it? I'm glad you finally have it—sorry there's no interest. Well, say hello to your friends for me. . . ."

She would have to remember to enclose the money with the note. She tore that page off the pad, set it on the desk, and took up her pen again. It did cross her mind that perhaps she should be writing her will rather than these little notes. But no, she decided, that could wait; it wasn't as if she could forget that. If she began to run out of time, a simple letter of testament to Asari would suffice. These messages were much more precious, at least in her opinion.

"So you're off on a business trip?" She would put this one in his suitcase: "You really are devoted to your job. Should I come with you? Or shall I stay home? Well, maybe I will stay. I should look after our house, after all. Well, when you are leaving, don't forget me—that way, you'll remember to shut off the gas and lock up. Have a safe trip."

She should next appear, she decided, from their bundle of New Year's cards. Asari would look them over again, before writing his own cards for the coming year. "I hope that you will marry again, and that your new wife will make you happy," she would write. "You won't be seeing me any more now. This is good-bye forever," and with these words, she would disappear from his life.

But it occurred to her, as she finished writing, that Asari might very well re-marry *before* the year was out. Even if she could count on surprising him from his yukata sleeve, there was every chance that an appearance from his overcoat pocket might bring her face to face not with Asari, but with his new wife.

A widower, just past forty, with a steady job and no children (even if he drank too much and wasn't likely to be promoted), Asari wouldn't have much difficulty in finding a new partner. He'd probably remarry as soon as he could, Noriko thought. He hadn't had much luck with wives, as her own death would shortly prove; and she was his second. From what she knew of his past and personality, though, bad luck would not make him give up on marriage altogether. He wouldn't search high and low trying to find the perfect partner this time either; he would get married again, not because he couldn't bear being single, but simply because there was no reason not to.

When Asari had first met Noriko, about eight years ago, he had been quite open about having already been married once. His wife had affected traditional tastes, he said. Their marriage hadn't lasted long; they had divorced three or four years before. Noriko hadn't any idea of the woman's name or her age: Asari had gotten a completely new family register drawn up when he married her.

Noriko knew, because he had told her himself, that he had had several affairs after his divorce, before meeting her. It seemed he'd even lived with one woman. When Noriko first moved in, she came across all sorts of feminine accessories among his things: a bright red fountain pen, a set of automatic pencils, a little wickerwork purse, a lady's scarf. . . . They were mostly imported, hardly likely belongings of a woman with traditional tastes. Asari didn't seem particularly bothered that she discovered them; and Noriko herself had been quite unconcerned. She'd even appropriated some, though the fountain pen she was using now was Asari's.

Once, a year or two after they were married, Noriko, looking for wrapping paper, had discovered a department store package with a mailing label on it. It had been sent to Asari at the address where he had lived with his first wife. Though he'd told Noriko he had been divorced for three or four years before meeting her, it had been postmarked just the year prior.

"Would you like to see what I've found?" she asked, showing it to him.

"Where did that come from?" he asked, staring at the address label.

"It must bring back memories," Noriko teased. "It was in the closet, with the wrapping paper."

"That's strange. I wonder how it got there."

"It is strange, isn't it?" Noriko pointed at the postmark: "Especially this."

Asari didn't seem to know what to say.

"Oh, I remember," he said, suddenly reassured. "Look. My brother sent it to me."

"Oh yes. He was in Hakata by then, wasn't he."

"I'd been too busy to tell him I'd moved. . . . So he mailed it to my old place."

"And then?"

"And then it was forwarded. I got it here."

Noriko started to laugh. "So it was in the mail for years?" she asked. "The post office forwarded it three years later? Don't worry—it's all right. I'll let it go."

"You're just like the secret police," Asari said, scowling. He returned the package to her with a show of indifference.

Noriko suspected, judging from the quantity and type of items left behind, that they had belonged to the woman Asari had lived with for a while after his divorce. If so, since he'd been divorced later than he'd originally said, he must have married and divorced one woman, lived with another, and then married her—all in a short space of time.

But she didn't think Asari had actually been unfaithful: true, there'd been signs that he had been dragged off certain places by disreputable friends a couple of times. Maybe she'd let herself be fooled, but she basically trusted him.

And this trust might account for Noriko never having felt any jealousy about the women in his past. She herself had had a lover before meeting Asari, though they'd broken up completely. The fact was, neither had a right to object to the other's past—and anyway those relationships weren't worth getting upset about.

If anything, Noriko felt a certain intimacy with Asari's first wife as well as with the imported accessories owner, which only increased when she learned that he had been involved with all three in such quick succession. She came to think of the three of them as some harem in a primitive land, all sharing the same husband and coexisting in harmony.

Asari must have sensed her feelings: "Hey, Noriko," he would say, showing her some little thing he had come across. "Look what I found—would you like it?" He didn't go so far as to say that it had belonged to a woman with whom he had been involved; but he didn't have to, it was obvious.

"Oh, yes," she would say, gratefully, "Give it to me." And the truth was that she'd also been gratified by the discovery of the package with that mailing label.

Noriko now started to feel that same sort of intimacy toward Asari's future women: surely his third wife wouldn't object to meeting her amid Asari's things. The two of them might enjoy reading her messages together. The new wife might even declare that, of the three women in his past, she liked her, Noriko, best of all.

Thinking this, Noriko wanted to send a little note to Asari's wife-to-be. Since he hadn't discarded the packaging or the other woman's things around the house, he would probably be just as lax preparing for his third spouse. Noriko didn't worry that her note wouldn't be found.

"Hello, how do you do? I'm so glad to meet you. I've been wanting to have a chat. There are so many things I'd like to share with you.

"Perhaps I should start by telling you the bad things about Asari. He won't buy you anything, you know, unless you ask him a thousand times. As you must have realized, he's very tight with money and for some reason, he's particularly stingy about our clothes. He's very clever in the way he gets out of it: 'Don't buy that,' he'll say. 'Let's shop around and get something that really suits you.' So you must make him buy you as many clothes as you can—get him to buy you what he didn't buy me.

"Also, please help yourself to any of my things, though I doubt they'll be of much use to you. I used his other women's belongings—I'd love it if you did the same with mine."

Realizing that Asari might again renew his family register for his third marriage, and that her name would mean nothing to his new spouse, Noriko signed the note: "From the deceased wife."

She tore off the page, and left it on the desk with the other notes. Later she would put it in the crate of her summer glassware. She took up the pen again and started another note: "Well, I see that you are now quite settled in. I'm very happy to see you being so good to him. I hope you won't spare any effort to see to his every need. . . ."

Writing this, a picture began to form in Noriko's mind of the way Asari and his well-settled-in wife would live. The living room would be much more cramped—cramped and untidy. They would have rented the second floor to an office worker and Asari's desk would have been brought down, and all sorts of objects would be piled on top of it, and around it. One of his wife's soiled workaday kimonos would hang on the wall. The table would be laid with food, a strange combination—curry and then squid cooked with radish in soy sauce. Asari and his wife would be eating in silence, their eyes on the television.

"This singer looks like our lodger," the wife would say.

Asari would not reply.

"Oh, speaking of the lodger," she would continue, "I think he's going to get married soon. Something tells me."

"What makes you say that?"

"I don't know. Just something. He's got his nerve—staying on all this time, paying the same rent. You can tell he's a hick."

"You were the one who wanted to rent it out."

"Well, we need the money, don't we, if we're going to build a house. We'll never do it on your salary."

"The rent doesn't make that much difference, does it?"

"Every little bit helps. We couldn't hope to buy a house without it. Look how little you earn. And you like to drink."

Asari, who that night would be abstaining, would grimace, his chopsticks moving, his eyes on the screen, but his wife would continue, undeterred.

"You know how much last month's liquor bill was? Eight thousand yen!"

"So what!" Asari would snap, finally facing her, and a violent altercation would ensue.

But a few hours later, in the bedroom, the wife would say: "You know, the sooner we have our own house, the better."

And Asari would reply: "Well, I probably can't even find a plot of land within an hour and a half of work."

Noriko had never grumbled about Asari's meager salary. They had no children, after all, and she'd been able to make ends meet. It was true that they were only renting. Asari was always regaling her with grand plans about the dream house he would build for them in the future, and so she'd stopped even thinking about owning their own place. As a result, both of them seemed tacitly resigned to renting for the rest of their days.

In other words, Noriko realized, she had never, not once, broached the subject of owning their own house. Was it appropriate, then, to consider themselves "husband and wife"? She found herself forced to look at her life with him in a new light. She went back to the letter she was writing.

"Thinking about it now," she wrote, "maybe Asari and I weren't really married, after all. Maybe we were only lovers who happened to end up living together. Legally speaking, we were married; we lived together for six years—a record for Asari; and we loved each other, or so I like to think. But I have a feeling that we lived together the way lovers do, not like a husband and wife. People often say that couples who don't have sex can't really be married, but it's in the opposite sense that we weren't really married. I would guess that some of those other couples were more truly husband and wife than we were.

"You will try, won't you, to be really married. Please let him experience this—contrary to appearances, he never has before. . . .

"Why do I say we were not husband and wife? Well . . ."

Noriko let the pen fall from her hands. The truth of her life with Asari was bearing down upon her so closely, she had a hard time assimilating it.

Yes—that was right, Noriko admitted, still lost in thought. They hadn't been husband and wife; they had simply chosen to live together. Sometimes they were like brother and sister, each in turn playing the older sibling, and at other times like parent and child. But they had never been husband and wife. Their life together hadn't been what marriage is supposed to be.

Yet as Noriko looked back over her relationship with Asari, her strongest impression was of their happiness. And so was it really that important, not having been husband and wife? She couldn't help being disturbed, though, by having been all this time under the illusion that they were truly married.

They were both at fault for not becoming a true married couple, it seemed to her: perhaps they simply hadn't bothered. Of course, they hadn't been young when they met; Asari had been married before; and they didn't have any children. But all these factors didn't get at the root of the trouble. Their dispositions—Asari nonchalantly giving her former lovers' belongings, and her eager appropriations— she wasn't certain, but Noriko suspected their dispositions were somehow to blame. All she knew now was that all sorts of evidence was suddenly assailing her that their marriage had been a sham.

All the time they'd been together, Noriko had seen to Asari's every need—if he washed his face, she'd be there to hand him a towel. Every day he had a choice of clean underclothes, a variety of dishes to eat, and freshly aired sheets and futon. She tolerated his drinking, hardly ever losing patience with his coming home late after an evening out, in his cups, and still eager to hit the bottle; or when he got so drunk that he was throwing up and kept her awake all night. She never sulked the next morning. Asari, who didn't seem to know what a hangover was, would get up looking reinvigorated, and just at the sight of him she would feel refreshed. Far from discouraging him when he wanted to go out for drinks with his friends, she let him have all the spare money.

But now she knew a wife wouldn't have been so tolerant or devoted. A husband returns in a drunken stupor in the middle of night—a real wife would be angry the next day, and resentful, and refuse to speak to him. He'd have to sit there, suffering a terrible hangover, in silence. Perhaps more than his constitution played into Asari's freedom from hangovers.

Had she been a wife, she would never have given Asari all their money when he went out drinking: she'd been more like a doting mother spoiling her son. Of course, the roles were often reversed, and she was the daughter looking after the house for her father.

Sometimes, toward the end of the month, she'd ask Asari in the morning: "Can I have some money?"

"You've run out?"

"Yes, I have."

"You've got to be more careful. Well, on my way back home tonight I can buy meat or something—or we can eat out." Asari would search in his pocket, and leave two hundred yen: "This should do for lunch."

She had no interest in hoarding up the monthly household account money, the passion of so many wives, and he didn't have affairs, but didn't both these facts really mean they were united only by love and nothing else? If they'd loved each other as husband and wife, surely, he would have been thrilled by the prospect of love affairs, and she by hoarding money.

And they never fought—there just didn't seem to be anything worth fighting about. True, she thought he was stingy; she'd written as much to his next wife. But perhaps she'd exaggerated, hoping to get a taste of conjugality. All in all, their life was extremely calm and harmonious. Except, of course, when Asari got terribly drunk, or irritable because he was trying not to drink. They had been happy. She hadn't assumed for the rest of their days they would never know any sorrow. But it had never crossed her mind that she'd find herself rethinking their relationship in the final moments of her life.

"I'm home," Asari called, opening the front door. She went out into the hall.

"There's an odd letter in our mailbox," he added, with a wave toward the front gate. He threw the evening paper, which she'd forgotten to bring in, at her feet. Slipping on some sandals, Noriko pushed past him taking off his shoes, ran out, and opened the mailbox flap to find the red-topped salt shaker inside.

"You didn't do it?" Asari asked, as she hurried back in with the shaker. He stopped unknotting his tie and mimed sprinkling salt on himself.

Noriko's parents had taught her the custom of shaking salt over oneself before going inside the house after a funeral. Her mother and father never forgot this act of purification. She remembered one summer evening her mother had called from the front door: "I'm home. . . . Can someone bring me the salt?" She'd been on her way to the theater that night, not a funeral: Noriko had gone out to the hall. Her mother's face was deadly pale.

"Where's the salt? Quickly," her mother had repeated. Noriko brought a jar of coarse salt from the kitchen. Her mother scattered handful after handful over her shoulders and around the hem of her kimono. When she finally entered the house and sat down, she explained that a young woman had committed suicide by throwing herself in front of the train.

"She was about your age," her mother had told Noriko, then just twenty. "Not married, apparently. It was so awful, I couldn't look. But I heard them saying, 'That's a leg,' and 'That's an arm,' and 'There's a lump of flesh.' And such a smell . . ."

It was probably the memory of that incident which caused Noriko to carry on the salt ritual herself. Her mother's white face at the door, the young woman her same age whose body had been turned into lumps of flesh in the space of a second. . . . Her mother's ghastly expression made Noriko imagine she might be possessed by a ghost. The look was gone by the time she came inside and Noriko could see her in the light. But who could tell whether, had she come straight in, that thing might not have come in too, and still be hovering in the air?

Whenever Asari returned from a funeral, Noriko would have him wait at the door as she hurried to fetch the salt. "Don't bother. It's silly," he would say, coming straight in to remove his shoes. But Noriko would insist on taking him back outside and shaking salt over him. Her parents had always used coarse salt, which wasn't available these days, so Noriko made do with the ordinary table variety, though it left something to be desired.

One day as she sprinkled him with salt, Asari had asked her: "What'll happen if you die before I do? Will you shake salt down on me from somewhere in the sky when I come back from your funeral?"

Whenever Noriko knew that she'd have to purify herself, she would leave the salt shaker in the mailbox as she set out—as she had done today.

"I must have forgotten," she told Asari, putting it back on the dinner table, and forcing a smile. "Which do you want first: dinner or a bath?"

"What would you prefer?" Asari said, adjusting the front panels of his kimono before tying his sash.

"I don't mind either way."

"I'll go later, then—I'm starved." He added: "Tonight, I'll do without."

But Noriko didn't want him not drinking tonight: the last thing she wanted was for him to go off to the Shōwa. On the other hand, if he stayed home, he'd only get irritable, and it would be even worse if he started after dinner: he might get very drunk.

"Well," she replied, "feel free to change your mind." This was her habitual response these days when he announced that he'd do without. But tonight she chose to say this for a special reason: she wanted him to drink, not too much, just enough so he'd stay and talk with her.

In the end, Asari did break his resolution—not through weakness, but at her suggestion.

"Would you mind if I had a beer, though?" Noriko asked, using the same embarrassed tone Asari adopted if he changed his mind. "I'm really thirsty."

"All right," he said. He grinned. "Since it's a request from someone who rarely indulges, I'll make an exception and have some too."

"But we'll have to go at my pace."

"What do you mean, your pace?"

"You know what I mean."

"Whatever you say."

Noriko brought over the bottle, and Asari reached out to open it.

"Let me do the honors," he said. "Now, you can purify yourself with beer, since you forgot the salt."

Noriko silently gazed at the filling glass. Asari stopped when it was half full.

"Is that all I get?"

"I'll give you some more in a minute. You're not a drinker, after all."

Noriko took the bottle from him, poured his beer, and by the time she'd set it down, he was already swigging. "Aren't we going to toast, since I so rarely indulge?" she asked.

"Oh, that's right." But all he did was put down his glass and seize his chopsticks.

Noriko took a sip.

"How old was your friend who died?" Asari asked.

"My age."

"An old lady like that?" Asari covered his mouth, pretending that had slipped out. "Who let her get behind the wheel?"

"She gave me a ride once."

"That was stupid. You've got to be more careful. What if you'd been in the car when she had the accident? You'd have died, and I'd have had nobody to sprinkle salt over me after funerals."

Noriko picked up her glass, and drank a little beer.

"It was safer then. She had a sticker in the window that said 'I just got my license. Thank you for your cooperation.'"

"People don't pay any attention to those stickers."

"No, but that's how careful she was."

"Anyway, I don't want you to ever get in a car with a woman driver."

"You don't mind if the driver's a man? Even on a very long long trip?"

"I'm serious."

"I know."

"I hope so. But you know, going so unexpectedly like that—I think that'd be the worst."

"So you'd rather I came and said goodbye?"

"I meant if *I* died. Well, it would be pretty bad if you did, too. . .. ."

"You think so? Tell me, what would you want to take care of before you died? Do you have a mistress?"

"Possibly. Actually, at one time I thought a lot about what would happen if I did die unexpectedly. Right after I got out of school my father died, and my mother divided up the family property for the children. Some land was bought for me in Setagaya—Mother planned on my building a house there, and moving in with me when I got married, but it was years before I did marry, and in the meantime I sold the land and squandered all the money."

"You've told me this story."

"But she never knew. Every time I went home, my mother would tell me to go ahead, get married and build my own house, she'd help me financially. And then prices went up. I'd sold the land when it was cheap, and there wasn't any left. Back then, you know, I really drank—I don't drink at all now in comparison— I ended up not being able to pay the rent. I brought all my things to the pawn shop, my suitcases and trunks were empty. Once, I counted up the tickets from the pawn shop, you now, and I had eighteen. But I kept hitting the bottle. Sometimes I'd wake up on a bench in some train station: what would happen if I died now, I'd wonder. Those pawn tickets would loom up before my eyes. I couldn't stand the thought of Mother finding out I drank the land away, debts piled up, and had nothing but a stack of pawn tickets. I'd have to get rid of those tickets, I'd have to have time for that, at least, I'd tell myself."

"What would you do if you were going to die now?"

"Well, first of all, this, I suppose." Asari raised his glass, and gulped down some beer.

Noriko picked up hers. It was nearly empty. As she drank, the foam on the top sank down to the crystal bottom, the bubbles dispersing. Asari's face, the size of a bean, came into view.

"Want some more?" he asked.

Noriko held out her glass, and as he started pouring, she warned, "Oh, not too much."

"You were complaining a minute ago how little I gave you," replied Asari, deliberately taking his time complying.

Noriko took two sips in a row. Her glass was more than half full.

"You sure you're all right?"

She paused. "Yes," she answered, glass in hand, and the next moment, she finished it off. Pretending to be engaged in draining it to the last drop, she immersed herself again in that distant, miniature, cheerful world sparkling in the bottom of her glass. Seated at a cute little table scattered with dishes, Asari looked small enough to hold in the palm of her hand. What would he do, she wondered, if she told him she only had a few hours to live? Would he kill her before 3:19 tomorrow, with his own hands?

"I see what you're doing," said Asari, who was copying her. "You look so tiny."

"So do you. It's pretty, isn't it?" And then, after a pause, she asked: "Tell me, did you ever think of leaving any notes behind for people to read after you died?"

"No." Asari put down his glass and Noriko did the same. "My only hope was that my mother would die, so she wouldn't see me end so miserably. That was my one try at filial piety. Now," he changed the subject: "How about some saké?"

Usually he found it difficult to stop once he got onto saké.

"If we're going at my pace," replied Noriko, "that's it, I think. But we could eat. How do you feel?"

"That's fine with me," Asari acquiesced, mildly.

As they ate dinner, Noriko asked: "I wonder how we'll turn out, growing old together, you and I."

"What do you mean, how we'll turn out?"

"You know, how we'll lead our lives."

"Same as we do now, I'd guess."

"You mean like young newlyweds, or like friends who get together over a cup of tea—for the next twenty, thirty years?"

That's not a true married life, she wanted to say. But Asari seemed oblivious.

"What a great way of putting it!" was his reply.

He glanced at the clock above the cupboard. "Guess what—it's not too late for the movie at the Shōwa. I don't mind taking you, if you'd like to go."

Taking the ticket book from the letter rack, he flipped open the red cover. "Only one left. Want to buy me another booklet and use one yourself?"

Noriko said yes.

They set out, walking along close to the hedges that lined the neighborhood roads. In the gardens they could see light from the houses, soft lights that spoke of spring evenings. These houses all looked so peaceful and assured to Noriko's eyes. In the past, she had once been terribly lonely after being abandoned by her first lover, and she remembered that the light from other people's windows had always looked so warm and inviting. When she returned to her lodgings and switched on the light in her small bare room, she would think that nobody, not even a person dying of cold and hunger, would look with envy and longing at her window. Now, as she strolled along with Asari, she wondered about the light from their living room window. Did it glow, calm and confident, like these? Or was it the weaker, uncertain kind that shines from an inn or dormitory?

They reached the shopping district and crossed the railway tracks. The Shōwa Cinema was a small theater beyond the station, specializing in foreign films.

"Hmm, I wonder what's playing," Asari said aloud to himself, looking at the movie stills in the window: a western and an Italian film, apparently.

"One book of tickets, please," Noriko said, handing over the 500-yen note she'd tucked into her sash.

"I thought you were going to buy me a few," Asari grumbled next to her.

They went inside and as Asari opened the door, Noriko made out lines of backs ranged in all the seats. But when her eyes gradually adjusted to the darkness, she saw several empty places near the front.

"Let's go over there," Asari said. Crouching, he headed down the aisle. Once seated, they looked up at the screen: the Italian film was playing. A shot of a peaceful country village in beautiful muted colors; then a train station; and in the next scene appeared a woman, obviously recovering from a serious illness, accompanied by her husband: they were leaving a health spa. Not long after they got home, a visitor came, a friend of the husband. From what the men said when the woman was out of the room it became clear that the marriage was no longer passionate—in fact the couple hardly felt anything for each other any more.

Not like herself and Asari, Noriko thought: they still felt strongly about each other. Not one day passed without her being aware of his heart beating, and it was surely the same for him. Yet she did wonder about the kind of light shining out of their home. A legal bond, cohabitation, sex, and love were supposed to be the four pillars of marriage. But they don't alone suffice—any more than four pillars constitute a house. Neither of them had bothered to do any work on their four pillars, it seemed to her. They hadn't put a roof over them; they hadn't even painted the walls—the things that would keep a house up when a pillar got wobbly. But their marriage had nothing supporting it. Their life together only amounted to a simple succession of days.

In other words, she reflected, they hadn't known the hardship or the happiness of true conjugal life. But if only they'd been aware that they were lovers, and not husband and wife, and lived out their relationship as it really was, their experience might have been totally different. True, they might have been ostracized, and they would have lost their easy tranquillity—but they might also have felt a keener, more intense kind of joy.

If she did write a letter to Asari before her death, Noriko told herself, she'd have to be honest with him. "What I regret," she would say, "is dying without ever finding out what our relationship might have been, had we tried to be husband and wife—or known that we were, in fact, simply lovers living together."

The movie was still depicting the husband and wife becoming more and more estranged. One or the other would occasionally attempt a reconciliation, but each time both felt betrayed and ended up feeling more hopeless than ever.

"Your wife will never get better unless you encourage her more," the husband's friend told him. The husband immediately followed this advice.

"You look wonderful this morning," he said to her. "Your cheeks are so rosy. The worst must be over by now."

The wife took this as a sign of his impatience with her weak condition and forced herself to pretend that she did feel better: At this, her husband said that since she was doing so well, he would be able to take her to a party he'd been invited to the following week.

A few days later, their little boy ran a fever. They both nursed him through the night.

"Mummy and Daddy are here, sonny," the husband told the boy, his arm around her shoulders.

"Darling," the wife said, addressing their son. "How many days do you want to stay out of school? Daddy can do everything; if he can cure people, maybe he can arrange for you to be ill as long as you like."

The man's arm fell from her shoulders.

"I want to get better quickly," the son said.

"All right. I'll make you get well very soon."

On the day of the party, the wife came into her husband's room, dressed up and ready to go out. He had forgotten all about the party, and hurriedly started shaving.

Despite how badly they got along, there were no fights: only short ironic exchanges between this husband and wife showed how distant their hearts and minds had become. And so the days passed, without any incident that might have led to divorce.

Noriko turned her now heavy head to look at Asari sitting beside her. His eyes fixed on the screen, his face was bathed in its light. Would he understand if she told him she didn't think they had ever truly been married? They were nothing like the couple in the movie. But their bond of simple love and affection had allowed them to interpret each other's words in purely positive ways—the way that he had taken it as a compliment when she said at dinner they were half like newlyweds and half like friends visiting over a cup of tea. The couple in the movie drifted farther apart because they always interpreted each other's words negatively; but she was Asari's accomplice in a similar sort of crime, continually inferring only good things in what was said, without really listening.

She could imagine the way he would reply if she did say to him, "Please listen to me. I'm wondering now if it's a good thing that we've never had a fight."

"It is a good thing!" he would say. "Trust me. I know." And the urge to tell him what she wanted to say would fade, just as it did for the screen couple who never bothered to explain any true state of mind. . . .

They got home just past ten o'clock, after staying to watch the western.

"I think I'll go take a bath," said Asari.

Noriko stopped herself from saying she'd go too.

"That's good—see you when you get back."

When he left the house, she went upstairs, sat at the desk, and took out some paper.

"I must tell you that if I had to die now, I would have regrets and disappointments," she wrote.

She went on to describe her fears that, even though they had been legally married and lived under the same roof, united in mind and body, they hadn't been a married couple. After listing her reasons, she continued:

Today, waiting for the bus on my way to the funeral, I looked at my watch: it was just past one o'clock. At that time the day before yesterday, my friend was still alive. She'd eaten lunch, and left the house, just as I had. The thought of death was probably the furthest thing from her mind. When I imagined her driving, without the faintest idea of what was going to happen, I got so frightened that the ticking of my watch scared me. As you said, it must be the worst thing to die unexpectedly. My friend would have had so many things to do, had she known her fate—if she could only have had one more day. . . . That idea made me think about what I would do if I had to die tomorrow afternoon. I didn't stop thinking about it, even after I'd come home. I started to wonder about your next marriage, which I imagined as something quite different from our own; and then that made me reflect on our life together.

My dear, our choice was either to become husband and wife in the true sense or consciously live out the relationship that we have—simply a man and a woman who love each other. And I want us to do one or the other now—even if it brings conflict and pain. What I don't want is to continue to believe that we're living a married life when we're not. . . .

And you know, when I do finally die, I think I would like a few final moments. Because even if they bring on other regrets and disappointments, at least I'll be able to feel that I've lived my life fully.

In any case, I'm sure I won't regret my friend's death making me reflect on the life I've led with you.

As soon as Asari came back, Noriko said that it was her turn.

"What? You didn't go yet?" he asked. "We could have gone together."

"Only we would have had to lock up the house again," Noriko replied, gathering her toiletries.

"There's an odd letter in our mailbox," she called back to him, the moment she was out the door.

No sooner had Noriko put her shoes in the bathhouse locker and taken the key, than the outside light over the entrance was turned off. A few people remained in the changing area, putting on their clothes: only one other person was undressing.

"Good night," a woman called as she was leaving to the girl tidying up the baskets.

Wooden pails lay scattered over the bathing area tiles. Four or five women, at some distance from each other, were washing themselves, and one started to wash her hair. That's nice, Noriko told herself, stretching out in the tub. Thanks to her, she could take her time.

At that moment, over on the men's side of the bathhouse, someone started whistling. It was a straightforward happy tune, a children's song from a well-known musical. Whoever it was, he was whistling very exuberantly.

Noriko tried to conjure up a picture of the man who was whistling. Perhaps he was a young manual laborer from one of the better factories—maybe he had worked overtime tonight. His shift finally over, all that he had to do now was go home and sleep, without a care for tomorrow. . . . That was why he could be so happy-go-lucky, whistling. As Noriko listened, he came to the end of the song, managing the instrumental part with skill. Then, he started all over again with even more enthusiasm. Noriko felt her own heart ease and lift.

KURAHASHI YUMIKO

Like many writers in the early postwar period, Kurahashi Yumiko (b. 1935) was interested in the work of Sartre and Camus, electing not to write the kind of naturalistic fiction that was still popular. After what some critics have described as a series of violent experiments, Kurahashi displays a later calmer and more mature style in "To Die at the Estuary" (Kakō ni shisu, 1971), from a collection of five novellas based on themes suggested by Greek tragedies, in this case Sophocles' *Oedipus at Colonus.*

TO DIE AT THE ESTUARY (KAKŌ NI SHISU)

Translated by Dennis Keene

The rains had ended, and as the couple came out of the station swallows were flying in a clear summer sky. The plaza in front of the station was much larger now, and the old man, Takayanagi, looked up at the high buildings that enclosed it and remarked that the town had certainly changed.

"But it must be thirty years since you were here, Father," Asako said. As she opened a parasol to shield him from the fierce rays of the sun, she seemed too young to be his daughter. They were more like grandfather and granddaughter. Asako was too young in her white dress and white shoes, her face flushed and shining like a fruit that has drunk in the summer's sun. But in the air-conditioned coolness of the taxi her cheeks returned to their usual porcelain white. Her head poised on her slender neck hardly turned as her long eyes seemed to be carefully observing the rows of houses that passed by on both sides. Takayanagi looked at the profile of his young daughter, and for a moment had the feeling that he was looking at the face of someone quite unknown to him. He told himself that it was the face of a young woman who was both his daughter and his granddaughter.

Asako turned toward him and asked:

"Is it all right to go directly there?"

"Of course. Nagasawa seems to have taken care of everything. All we have to do is move in."

Takayanagi had been thinking for some years now of acquiring a house in his hometown and spending a few months of each year there. But since he disliked the bother of going down himself to look for a house or arrange to have one built, he had simply asked two or three people he knew to buy one for him if anything suitable turned up. His only specific requirement was that it be east of the town, on the northern bank of the river near the estuary. He intended to die there. This year such a house had been found. Formerly it was part of a restaurant, but the management had changed hands, the large annex with its own spacious garden had been converted into a hotel catering to short-time couples, and only the pleasantly small main building had been put up for sale. Takayanagi decided to buy it, and entrusted the whole business to an old classmate he had known since their primary-school days, a Doctor Nagasawa, who had retired and left the practice to his son.

The taxi turned toward a bridge and ascended a steep rise, then swung left and drove for some time down an embankment road that ran along the river. The river itself could not yet be seen. It was hidden from view by a great many buildings, mostly inns or restaurants.

When the driver found the house it turned out to be surrounded by a bamboo fence, and the gateway, though small, was in the old style with a roof over it. The name "Takayanagi" had already been put up. Nagasawa had arrived before them and was waiting. He came out onto the veranda and pointed out the various trees and shrubs in the garden.

"That's crape myrtle, that's paulownia, and that tall one's quite rare, aralia or something, and then there's loquat and rhododendron, all transplanted from the old garden. All but the pagoda tree."

Since a garden was not relevant to the purposes of the "hotel," that space was now wholly occupied by the so-called new building.

"But, I don't know, there doesn't seem to be any life in them. And it's not just because they were transplanted either. The air's pretty bad around here—you can blame it on the weird thing they've put up over there."

The embankment wall along the river blocked the view, but from the upstairs windows they saw an astounding sight extending along both sides of the river right down to the sea. Takayanagi gasped. It seemed unreal, as if his eyes had filmed over or he had gone blind and was suffering from a hallucination. This was a place he had grown up with, a place seen again and again in his dreams as he grew old. The river flowed through the town and here where it suddenly widened and emptied into the sea there should have been a wasteland, the remains of what was once a delta, tussocks of grass springing from sandy earth, and then, projecting from it into the sea, a long sandbar like a tongue with ripples washing gently over it. As a boy he would run among the summer grasses, or in spring dig into the soft sand bottom for shells. In summer the boys of the town would swim farther upstream, but when the tide was going out Takayanagi would often make his way down with the current, under one bridge after the other, swimming down almost to where it met the sea. Then when his body caught against the sand of this island he would lie there like a boat run aground, the sun burning down upon the deck of his back, and wait for the returning tide. At last the salt water would flow back from the sea and the current begin to turn. As he swam upstream again with the current the sharp spines of a flathead sometimes cut his legs.

Now most of the estuary had been filled in, and on this reclaimed land an oil refinery and chemical plant had been built, a glittering mass of silver storage tanks and pipes. To the old man it look like a metal fortress, and yet he also thought that this was perhaps as it should be, perhaps it was even the kind of sight one ought to see at the end of a long journey. As an old man he had not intended to seek here what he had known as a boy. The sentimentality for such a quest, the addiction to seeking what might or might not be found, had all left him. But the sight that lay spread out before his eyes was so far beyond his experience that its very remoteness, the remoteness now of the whole estuary, made it seem an abode of the gods. Was this the setting he required for ending his days? If it was, Takayanagi accepted it.

His daughter looked at him with anxious, troubled eyes. Takayanagi did not like people to commiserate with him.

"Now that's really something. Unexpected, but most imposing."

"But it's so awful," Asako said plaintively, adding, "isn't it, Father?" in an almost accusing tone of voice. Takayanagi kept his face turned firmly away from her, looking fixedly at the black river and the silvery plant.

"That's what I wrote about in my letter the other day, and, well, there it is."

Takayanagi could not recall anything of the sort in Nagasawa's letter. Had he read it and just not been able to take it in? Or was his memory slipping? Whichever it was he felt irritated with himself.

"That's right, you did," he replied. "I must say I didn't expect a change on quite this scale, though. But it's not a bad thing. If the town can attract enterprises like that it must be prospering."

"This neighborhood's about the bleakest place in town now. Still, it's where you wanted to be, so here you are. About the only place old people can tolerate anymore is that residential section north of the castle."

Asako was silently looking at the sea beyond the plant. It was the height of summer, and the burning sun and the smoke belching out from the chimneys of the plant gave a cloudy whiteness to the sky. Perhaps it was only imagination, but the wind blowing in off the sea seemed to smell of hydrogen sulfide.

She smiled. "Anyway, we're near the sea. You can smell the sea breeze."

Could it come from the sea? Late that first night Takayanagi heard a kind of reverberation he found difficult to identify. Surely it was not the break and flow of the sea; it was more like a trembling within the earth itself. The sound came from the direction of the plant. Could it be the hum of machines working through the night, or the roar of something burning? The plant made relatively little noise, nothing disturbing. With all its tanks and pipes it was indeed plant-like, a vegetable growth. Perhaps there was some saplike fluid circulating ceaselessly throughout it. The old man decided it was that kind of sound.

He became aware that Asako too was lying with her eyes open as if straining to listen. He told her it was probably the noise from the plant.

"I don't hear anything like that," she replied. "Aren't you just imagining it, Father?"

"You're young, you see. There are strange sounds you don't hear when you're young. You start to hear them as you get older."

As death approaches, he had meant to say, but decided not to. Then he heard something like the cries of a woman coming from the hotel next door. That was what Asako must have been trying to catch.

She seemed unable to sleep because of the heat. Having kicked the light bed-clothes off, she now lay rigidly on her back. The swelling outlines of her breasts showed, as if she were holding her breath.

"How old are you, Asako?"

"Nineteen," she answered, lying there looking up at the ceiling, her eyes open, unmoving.

"That's young. Too young. About the right age for my granddaughter," he said in a slightly odd tone of voice.

He was thinking that in fact Asako could be called his granddaughter although she did not know it. But this was something he could not tell her now. Asako had her life to live, and if one thread of that irrelevant past were loosened the whole thing would unravel in confusion, foulness, and blood. If she were covered by that filth and horror perhaps she would die of suffocation.

He thought how little she knew about her mother. When Asako was only five years old her mother had gone insane and hanged herself. She probably did not even recall the nature of her mother's death. Her mother's insanity had begun as no more than a form of neurosis. He had merely let it take its course, left his own wife to suffer and wind herself up within a cocoon of madness. Her suicide could be attributed to the birth of a child that was not his. That child was Asako, and the man who fathered her was Shuji, supposedly his own younger brother but in fact his son. Thus legally Asako was his daughter while in reality she was his granddaughter.

He felt he would tell her all this sometime, perhaps even in the near future. By "sometime" he meant just before he died, and Takayanagi had decided that his own death would occur when the gods called him, whether from heaven or earth or from the sea, or even from such sacred ground, such an abode of the gods, as this metallic fortress in the estuary. That reverberation he had heard coming from somewhere deep in the night was perhaps a voice audible only to a man anticipating it. When the time came he too would enter the company of the gods. Then would not he himself be able to proclaim with the voice of a god the truth of those people who remained after him, the truth of what they were? He felt a small, nervous lift of excitement at the thought.

Asako must have got up before him.

The old man was aware of this while still half in his dream, a dream he had been drowning in since dawn, struggling as it came upon him like the rising tide. Perhaps it was fatigue from the journey, but the dream was as oppressive as if he were floundering in filthy sewage water. His hands felt inordinately heavy, their movements dull. He seemed to be trying to swim toward someone he wanted to meet.

It was someone out of his childhood, a blind beggar who lived beneath one of the bridges. Actually, the man did not beg; it was only because he lived in such a place that the children called him a beggar. His blindness too seemed appropriate to a beggar, someone crippled or disfigured; and so he became the undeserved object of their mockery and contempt. However he was not just a failure living out the rest of his days under the archway of a bridge. Takayanagi had learned from his father that the blind man was the descendant of feudal lords, the son of a former governor of this province, and even now, living in this makeshift hut with only the underside of a bridge for a ceiling, he was still being looked after by the present governor in some indirect way. His father had also told him that the man's condition was the result of a dreadful crime he had committed, but more than that he had not learned.

In his dream Takayanagi was a boy again, swimming at the rear of the blind beggar's hut. In the shadow of the bridge the water would be cold and dark, a place the boys of the town avoided, but in his dream the young Takayanagi swam as if paddling his way through the amniotic waters of the womb. Looking up at the rafters and crossbeams of the bridge, he saw that they were swarming with bats. He hid behind one of the slime-covered supports and peered into the old blind man's hovel. He had only seen the place from the front before, from the road that ran down below the bridge. Now, viewed from the back, it was unmistakably a beggar's hovel, filled with an almost obscene disorder. It was as if one were looking inside the belly of a wild animal. The blind man's daughter was at the rear of the hovel washing some indescribably filthy clothes. The boy strenuously raised his head from the surface of the river to avoid drinking its water muddied by menstrual blood and dissolving excrement, and as he did so the girl noticed him there and gave him a brilliant smile. Then the image changed to that of his smiling, young, beautiful stepmother.

There the dream broke off momentarily, and Takayanagi wondered if it was a repetition of something he had actually experienced in the past. He decided it was not.

At first he had not known that the blind beggar had a daughter. Then he heard from older boys that the old man made his daughter attract customers, whatever that meant, and his feelings of hatred and contempt for him became all the more violent. He thought it just that the old beggar be so scorned.

At the height of summer, either as they were on their way home from a swim or because that day they were bored with swimming, the boys would seek another kind of sport, and begin attacking this blind beggar. In their minds he was a hideous, evil monster which should be hunted out and destroyed. They would pass before his hovel shouting insults, sometimes even throwing stones. Once the old man was sitting crosslegged outside the door, like a wooden Buddha, and the boys found this even more provoking. Dreaming again, suddenly Taka-yanagi was in the lead and had hurled a stone. Although he took no proper aim his stone flew straight at that face, but at the last moment the blind old man made a slight movement of the head and dodged it. Then he stood up. Despite his thin-ness his size was astonishing. As he approached them with the stiff, faltering steps of some evil effigy come to life, the boys let out a cry of fear and scattered in all di-rections. Takayanagi fled too, but as hard as he ran, whenever he looked back there was this giant figure with its dark, mysterious, magnificent blind counte-nance, stumbling and coming after him, stumbling, and coming after him. . . .

The cry seemed to have stuck in his throat, and as old Takayanagi tried to cough it out, he must have actually uttered a kind of cry. Asako heard it and was now at his bedside, anxiously calling him.

"Father!"

"What time is it?" he asked.

"It's past eight."

The upstairs room was exposed to full sun from the east and it was unpleas-ant to lie there in bed on a summer morning.

"We'd better have an air conditioner put in," he said.

"That place next door must have them in every room, and they seemed to be making quite a noise last night. Maybe that's what disturbed you."

Probably that was the sound he had thought was coming from the plant. Asako should have said so last night. He felt irritable.

"An air conditioner wouldn't bother me. It's not being able to sleep that I can't stand. Let's have one on each floor."

He felt the heat more than most and he intended to ignore Asako's complaint that air conditioning is bad for one's health.

Asako tied the apron strings at the back of her neck, and said:

"It seems easier to put up with the heat here than in Tokyo, even though we're farther south. There's the breeze off the sea, for one thing." Then she added: "But this morning there doesn't seem to be any breeze at all. Perhaps it's what they call the morning calm."

When she brought breakfast in from the kitchen she still seemed cheerful.

"Have you seen the kitchen? It's enormous, with all sorts of gadgets left be-hind; more like living in a restaurant than in a house. If we had a proper cook we could set ourselves up in business tomorrow."

There was vinegared cucumber, sliced very thin. Then, what he often ate here as a boy, long eggplants, fried. Apparently a greengrocer had turned up early that morning, making the rounds in a covered truck. Asako guessed it was because there were so many inns and restaurants in the area. Takayanagi had awakened with a good appetite.

"I seem to have had a bad dream last night," he said abruptly, and Asako stopped eating in surprise, her chopsticks poised in the air.

"In my dream I was a boy again. I threw a stone at a blind beggar and he got angry and came after me, on and on after me. He was an old man who'd built a sort of hut under the bridge down the river, and although we never really saw him beg, we boys used to torment him and call him a beggar. He lived alone with his daughter—a pretty girl, if you looked at her, probably a little older than you. Do you know that novel by George Sand, *La Petite Fadette*?"

"Yes. It's one of the village novels."

"Well, think of the girl in that and you'll get some idea what she was like. There was something very pure and graceful about her, and in the way she dressed and carried herself."

"How old were you at the time, Father?"

"Thirteen, maybe fourteen. Anyway it was after my voice changed, so I was certainly old enough to feel an attraction to her."

Saying nothing to Asako, he thought of how the girl had been taken by his father as his second wife. When Takayanagi grew into a young man he slept with this woman who had become his mother. He had been driven by the idea that it was something he had to do, in order to fulfill the prophecy made about him, and the remembrance of those days in hell was as vivid as ever.

"It would be nice if Grandmother could live with us in this house."

Asako's remark brought him back to the present. Why did she say that? What was she thinking? She could hardly know where his stepmother had come from or what she had done. Could it be that at some time she had suddenly understood everything? Perhaps it was merely because such a thought had crossed his mind, but as she lifted the teapot, her head turned a little away from him, there seemed to be a cloud shadowing her face, as if she knew some dark secret.

But that was impossible. Asako could only have heard it from his stepmother, and she was not the kind of woman who would talk about things like that.

"Why did you mention your grandmother?" he asked, as if expecting an answer.

"While you were talking about that old man and his daughter they seemed like you and me, Father, living here alone, and it made me sad. But then I remembered that we still had Grandmother."

"Are you lonely then, being alone with me?"

Asako shook her head firmly.

"You should have gone to college."

"I don't want to. Living with you has nothing to do with it."

"Then you should think about getting married. Nineteen's not too early."

"When I feel like it I will, and not give you a second thought."

There was a night of heavy rain and thunder as if the rains were back again. Then next morning came the burning heat of true summer. Takayanagi spent that morning in the now air-conditioned room reading the *Hōjōki* and occasionally looking out at the garden whose plants had come back to life.

While he was still going to the office he had liked to read, regretting that he could not spend more time on books; sometimes he would even read the new foreign novels that Asako bought. Yet lately, now that he had the time for it, he found his interest in reading had waned. He had lost patience with the loquacious, effeminate meanderings of intellectually and spiritually empty prose. Certainly he found confessional writing particularly irritating. He had once told Asako he would be happy to give her his whole library, but perhaps because Asako herself was no great reader, or because she was not possessive about books, she had merely smiled and let the matter go.

However, the *Hōjōki* was among the few books he kept by his side, to take up whenever he felt so inclined. It said only what needed to be said, and said it in a man's voice, a voice free of weakness or ornamentation. Takayanagi valued it as an example of the way a man should speak at the end of his life. Nothing was known of how Kamo no Chōmei had lived after writing this work, nor of how he had met his death. If, in the midst of writing, he had laid down his brush because he realized he understood nothing, Takayanagi accepted this silence as right. If he himself had come to that realization, then it would be good to die in ignorance and silence. The struggle of youth lay bare all the ugly realities of one's being and was something he could do without.

Later that morning old Nagasawa came to see him. He brought his only grandson, Takashi, and wanted advice on how to get the young man into a certain private university in Tokyo, since Takayanagi was on its board of governors. Takayanagi listened agreeably, and made a note in his memo book. Then he asked Nagasawa about the young man's record in school. It was good.

"With grades like that there should be no problem about admission whether I try to clear the way or not. The size of any donation to the university has nothing to do with it. You could pay out as much as you liked, but if the grades were too low even the chairman of the board couldn't help you."

The young man listened calmly to this conversation about himself, nodding from time to time, but showing no sign of embarrassment or of trying to make a good impression.

When Nagasawa's business was finished, Asako served them ceremonial tea. She was wearing a summer kimono and her face was lightly made up. As she set the tea bowl before Takashi, she permitted herself a cold, restrained smile.

Nagasawa mentioned that the young man was studying the nō dance, the simpler kind that does not require costume.

"He's been under Mr. Miura since last year."

"That's the Komparu school, isn't it?" Takayanagi asked the young man. "What are you practicing at the moment?"

"*Tamura.*"

"You enjoy your lessons, do you?"

Takashi looked as if he was not sure how to reply.

"I admire your grandson," said Takayanagi. "He manages to avoid saying more than needs to be said. That's good. His grandfather tends to be garrulous, perhaps a sign of old age."

"I've never known what to say to these taunts of yours."

"No offense intended, believe me. Just speaking the truth."

"That's why I've never known what to say."

Asako served a light lunch neatly arranged on bamboo ware with leaves folded in half-moon shapes.

"To judge from this sparse elegance, the girl seems to be playing at tea ceremony," Takayanagi said, but Nagasawa paid the appropriate compliments.

Asako saw the guests off as far as the gate. When she came back she laughed and said:

"That boy Takashi certainly is odd."

"What's he done?"

"He was just getting in the car when he got all the way out again and asked me what character I used for my name."

"Don't say that didn't please you."

"I really wouldn't know."

Takayanagi felt a sudden chill. A boy had now invaded their lives as he had invaded the lives of the old blind man and his daughter, and the thought troubled him.

At night one could see the fire of waste gas burning at the top of a towerlike chimney of the refinery. It was like a giant blazing candle, but Asako said it looked like a devil's tongue, weird and repulsive.

"A very literary sentiment. But I suppose you could say that about the way I see it. In fact, to me it looks like a torch set on holy ground, a sacred flame offered to the gods."

"Do you really see that as a place for gods to be living?"

"Gods, or at least some kind of spirits, used to live there in the past. They were spirits of women's hatred."

Successive generations of inbred feudal lords will produce some abnormal individuals; and an ugly tale of one of them, of the wholesale abduction and torturing to death of the town's maidens, was still told in this castle town. The corpses had been buried in that wasteland, it was said; but some years later there was an earthquake, followed by a tidal wave that washed the skeletons away, the floodwaters carrying the bones off and finally depositing them on the banks of the castle moat, where they lay scattered like dead white flowers. After that the grove of pines on the shore facing the wasteland became notorious as a place where women went to hang themselves.

"They used to say that if a woman who had grown weary of her life went near the pine grove, ghosts would appear in every tree in the form of a human head larger than you could put your arms around, and they would dangle there giving off a sulphurous light, crying together, calling. That tale goes back two hundred years."

"I wonder if anything of the grove is left?"

"I shouldn't think so. They seem to have built a landing stage for oil tankers in that area."

"Then there's nowhere for the ghosts to live, is there?" she asked in all seriousness.

"I don't suppose there is. But when you consider that a refinery now stands where there was only wasteland, rank grass blown by the sea wind, perhaps those evil spirits have changed into benevolent ones ensuring the prosperity of the place. They must be pleased to be living in such up-to-date surroundings."

As a boy he had heard something of the kind from the blind man, although of course there had been no mention of oil refineries. The old man had said that the vengeful spirits of the murdered women or women suicides only awaited the ceremony of prayer to be joyfully apotheosized into guardian deities. Occasionally the old man would also speak of the future of certain individuals.

Probably that was why the people of the town came to think of him as a fortuneteller. When the boy heard some of the local wives talking about going to the old man to have their fortunes told, he suddenly felt well disposed toward him. He would explain to the other boys that this was no beggar but a practitioner of the ancient art of divination. Still, the old man had never been seen with a bundle of divination rods, nor, being blind, could he have read anyone's palm. Later when the boy became his friend, he had several opportunities to witness what happened. The old man simply remained silent and let his visitor speak. A woman who wanted her fortune told would talk on and on about herself, working up to a plea for some divine revelation. Then the old blind man would utter a dreadful rebuke, a kind of scolding—he might even spit out harsh, merciless words as if putting a curse on her—and he would angrily drive the visitor away from his door.

"All I tell people who come here is how worthless they are. Coming to a place like this and depending on a stranger only proves it. But to gain the power to know your own worthlessness can be a form of help. First I listen to what the person has to say, and in what he says all that he is appears to me, and I know that one so weak cannot decide his own fate. Then I utter certain words that seem not to come from a human mouth. In that way the fates of various people are determined."

"Then you must be a prophet," the boy Takayanagi said, but the old man shook his head severely.

"I am no prophet. There is no resemblance between me and the prophets of the Old Testament. You should think of the words that come from my mouth more as an oracle, the ambiguous words of the gods."

Later on it was to be the words of the old man uttered to him just before he died that were to determine his life. Among them were words declaring that he would couple with his mother. When Takayanagi had done exactly as foretold, he had intended it all to be through the power of his own will. Now that very exercise of the will seemed predetermined by the words of the old man.

Old Takayanagi looked at the burning fire, at what Asako had called the devil's tongue, and sipped hot coffee she had just made for him from fresh-ground beans.

"Grandmother really loves coffee," she suddenly said.

"Yes, she does," Takayanagi replied, noticing that this was the second time Asako had mentioned his stepmother.

"She can't get proper coffee like this in that old people's home, but she still gulps down lots of instant coffee even though she complains how awful it tastes."

Last year he had had his stepmother, Aya, permanently placed in a home for the aged in the resort area of Izu, a hundred miles southwest of Tokyo. To Asako this was simply getting rid of her. Takayanagi had cut off his relatives like a doctor amputating useless limbs. He had done so with Asako's elder sister, Kyoko, when he married her off, and Kyoko herself, though she visited home once with her first-born child, had in recent years made no attempt to keep in touch except for an occasional telephone call to Asako. Takayanagi never mentioned her name. And long before that, when Asako was born, he got rid of Shuji by sending him abroad. Asako would not know about that.

"Do you often go to visit your grandmother?"

"Yes. Two or three times a month."

Since the unknown visits had been so frequent, she sounded as if she had boldly made up her mind to confess. In the way she spoke, and in the way she held her shoulders, he sensed a direct criticism of himself.

"Is she well?"

"Yes."

"She's well in her head too? After all, she's past seventy. She isn't getting senile and saying anything funny, is she?"

"She seems perfectly all right. She doesn't go on about the old days like most elderly people. She watches television a lot, and seems to remember things that happened recently, as if she had more interest in the present than in the past."

He was impressed by Asako's precise view of old age. For a person lapsing into second childhood, recent impressions were the first to disappear from memory, with only ancient recollections persisting oddly. Takayanagi had been afraid that it was of such ancient events that young Asako might have been told again and again on her visits.

"In that case she shouldn't be causing any trouble, so now is hardly the time to take her out of there. When she's finally going to die all we can do is to put her in the right hospital. There seems to be no question of her ever living with us again. Both Mother and I are people who have nothing left to do but die, and we separated so that we could die on our own, apart from each other. Mother's the sort of person with the strength to do that. You shouldn't bother your head so much with the affairs of old people. That goes for my affairs as well."

He felt his words were too harsh, but he had no intention of retracting them or softening them in any way. That was how he truly felt, and as he got older he found he had no wish to say anything more than was required to express his thoughts.

Asako looked straight back at him with tears in her eyes, but then lowered her long eyelashes. Her face was reflected in the glass windowpane, over the image of the burning fire, gold-colored flames tinged with red. It was as if Asako's hair were on fire.

"There's a fireworks display tonight."

Apparently Takashi had come to invite Asako out to see it. Takayanagi said he himself didn't care to go wandering about at night, but he urged Asako to let him take her. She hesitated, saying she had to get his dinner, but asked Takashi if he wouldn't mind waiting twenty or thirty minutes. Then she started setting the table and hastily preparing what was available. At last she went to put on a little makeup.

Meanwhile Takashi sat in one of the wicker chairs on the upstairs veranda, and Takayanagi in the other.

He had no idea what one talked about with a boy of seventeen or eighteen, but brought up the question of student revolt, which had recently spread from the universities to the high schools. At Takashi's own high school it seemed there were signs of trouble among the students, egged on by various "rebel" teachers.

"So you're a bit concerned about the All-Out Offensive, or whatever it's called, are you?" Takayanagi said, tempted to make fun of him.

"It gets on my nerves," the boy replied. "The Student Left bunch is no good, but the ones who really irritate me are the teachers. That's not the way to do things."

"You mean these 'rebel' teachers?"

"They're the worst, of course. They're making a first-class mess of things."

Asako had changed into a light summer kimono.

"We're ready to go then?" Takashi asked.

"Yes," Asako replied stiffly, not looking in his direction.

"Hurry up and go, you two. It seems to have started already."

The noise of rockets exploding one after the other rattled the glass windows. It was Asako, rather than Takashi, who seemed most eager to leave.

"Well then, with your permission, sir, I'll take her to see it."

Takashi looked slightly over-intense as he bowed to Takayanagi, and then turned his eyes urgently toward the girl.

"We can go down here if you like, and walk along the riverbank," Takashi suggested, as they descended the steps from the first bridge.

It was high tide, and the river, swollen with black water, had risen almost to the level of the path. There were pools of water in places where the asphalt had crumbled and caved in. Presumably it had once been a favorite promenade, now abandoned and allowed to fall into disrepair as the river grew dirtier and dirtier. Asako sometimes had to squeeze right up against the embankment wall to avoid the water, wondering to herself if this could be the same river in which her father used to swim.

"Some people have taken boats out," she said.

"We can go in a boat if you like. But the river smells especially bad at high tide."

"I'd rather just stroll along like this."

"The main display is farther up the river. An awful lot of people will be going to see it, so we probably can't get very close. Anyway we'll go as far as we can."

By the time they reached the third bridge, it was indeed crowded with sightseers both on the river path and on the bridge itself. The display was at its peak and the fireworks exploded continuously, unfolding and spraying out above their heads in chrysanthemumlike patterns. Sparks of flame fell like occasional drops of rain.

"We mustn't get separated in the crush," Asako said, and grasped Takashi's hand. From then on, jostled by the crowd, they only tried to get away to some place with fewer people. There was no hope of reaching the wooden grounds of the shrine across the river, where one would have the best view of the final set piece. The smell of acetylene lamps from the special night stalls mingled with the sweaty odor of the crowd.

They crossed the bridge and went down an incline into the main road, where streetcars were running. There was a smart little coffee shop with white walls, and as they went in Asako released his hand. Wiping her palm and fingers with the hot towel, she said:

"All the feeling seems to have gone out of the fingers of this hand."

"It was like gripping a practice sword with all one's might."

"You do *kendō* too?"

"Until last year, I was captain of the school team."

Asako looked intently at him. Unlike most present-day young men, he wore his hair cropped short, and the lines of his face were simple and clear-cut, with no surplus fat. It was like looking at a very large dog which had intelligently pricked up its ears. That is the kind of dog I rather like, she thought. But what she said was:

"I have the feeling we've known each other before, like brother and sister."

"Then I'd be your younger brother," he said seriously.

"And that would make me your respected elder sister, I suppose, though I can't say I feel much like one. Still, I could hardly be younger than you."

"I can't help feeling, well, as if you're a good deal older. For example, you might be my young stepmother, something like that. Maybe that's because I don't have a mother."

"I don't have a mother either. She went out of her mind and killed herself when I was five."

"Then let's not talk about our mothers."

"Sorry. Anyway it's not very nice when you start calling me your stepmother. What a thing to say!"

"But your father's the same age as my grandfather, isn't he? So while you're a daughter I'm a grandson, and that seems odd to me."

"I'm too young for his daughter, that's all."

"But he's only sixty, and you're nineteen, which means he was forty-one when you were born. There's nothing so unusual about that, is there?"

"I'm only thinking out loud, and if you don't like it you don't have to listen, but the truth is I have a feeling I'm not really my father's daughter. Father sometimes looks at me as if he's looking at an object, or a kind of mysterious moving thing, a strange animal, you might say. When there's a real blood connection between people it doesn't matter how hard you are to each other; even if you loathe one another the way close relatives sometimes do, there's still a kind of softness there, a feeling that deep down, essentially, one forgives the other. Father doesn't have that feeling for me. When he looks at me as he does, staring right into me, I get a really desperate feeling that I don't know who I am anymore. I suppose that makes me start imagining I'm not his child. And sometimes I think I must know who I am, even if it means cutting Father open to find out; I work myself up like that. I suppose I'm possessed by an evil spirit." She smiled at Takashi, though with unhappiness in her eyes.

"There are good spirits as well as evil ones—white magic, you know. But I can't help feeling there is something remote in you, as if you were living in a world of spirits."

"That's how I feel about my father and grandmother, as if they're not really human. I don't know quite what it is about them, but it's as if they've done things no normal person could do, and yet have gone on living as calmly as ever. After Mother died they brought me up like that."

"Is your grandmother still alive?"

"Yes, but Father's stuck her in an old people's home in Izu, and it doesn't look as if he'll even go to see her before she dies. I've been going there two or three times a month, trying to worm something out of her. It's not that I like her or feel sorry for her, I just think I might be able to learn a secret about myself."

Asako leaned over the table, propping her cheek with her bare arms, and looked up wickedly at Takashi.

"Do you know Racine's *Phèdre*? The heroine's the same Phaedra who turns up in Greek tragedies and legends. One of my fantasies is that Grandmother and Father are like Phaedra and Hippolytus."

"And what was there between them?"

"Phaedra was the young queen of Theseus, but she was cursed by Aphrodite so that she fell in love with her stepson Hippolytus. Grandmother was grandfather's second wife. There's only twelve or thirteen years difference between her and my father."

"Did she tell you anything about this?"

"No. It's just my intuition. But you only have to watch the two of them together. You can feel a link between them, they're still bound by a psychological connection ever since the physical one. You know that warning system where an infrared ray you can't see makes a bell ring when you cross it? Something like that."

"Then you could be the child of your father and grandmother?"

"I've suspected that, but thinking about it I had to laugh. Grandmother would have been seventy-three, less nineteen, that's fifty-four when I was born."

Asako asked Takashi the time. It was still before eight, but she began worrying about her father. Also, she was hungry.

"I'd like to see you again," she said quietly, almost submissively.

"Next time I'll bring the car, and we can go for a drive."

Takashi's voice was unfaltering but a little strained.

When Asako got home the front door was locked. Fortunately she had the spare key in her bag. At first she thought her father might already be in bed, but it seemed too early for that, since he was in the habit of staying up later than most people his age. The air conditioner had been left on, and that was the only sound in the house, like a human voice quietly intoning away. The house was chilly. Suddenly she had a premonition that her father had died, perhaps had taken his own life. Her blood ran cold.

Takayanagi was nowhere in the house. She could not believe he had merely gone for a walk, to see the fireworks or to stroll around town; possibly, it occurred to her, he had gone in search of a place to die. She went upstairs and glanced over his Japanese writing desk, but there was only his tobacco tray and his tea things, all tidily arranged. A few books were piled on the small shelf at the side of the *tokonoma,* and on top of them lay a clothbound notebook. It bulged slightly since he had left his fountain pen between its pages and she found herself opening it. The first words she read were:

My property. Two-thirds Asako. Rest disposed as law requires.

And then:

Other things to write besides will.
What blind man said. Oracle. How fulfilled.
About Aya. Masayo, Shuji: my children, made brother and sister.
About Junko and Shuji. Asako: my grandchild, made child.
Dealing with Shuji.
Junko's illness, suicide.

For Asako these were words whose connections she could not grasp. Aya was her grandmother, and Masayo and Shuji her aunt and uncle. Junko was her own mother. A network of threads seemed to hold all these names together in a horrifying set of interrelations, but the panic of knowing she was reading what she should not read—apparently rough notes for her father's will—kept her from making any sense of it. Perhaps her father had heard voices calling him, a summons to death, had been drawn outside, and was now wandering along the estuary. If that was so, she could do nothing about it. The thought seemed to give her a mooring, like a ship's anchor finally touching the bottom of the sea. Regaining her wits at last, she telephoned Nagasawa.

A woman answered, a maid or nurse probably, then Nagasawa came on.

"I think my father . . ."

"That's right, he's here. Hold on and I'll call him."

She felt the strength drain from her, and began to cry.

"Father, couldn't you have—"

"Nagasawa invited me over to watch the fireworks, and we had a little something to drink. I'm fine, on top of the world. Stop sniveling. I'll get home all right, so don't worry. You needn't wait up. How did your date with Takashi go? Did you enjoy yourself? You're home early enough, anyway!"

He seemed fairly drunk, talking with rare exuberance. As she listened, the tears ran down her face.

"Come home as soon as you can, please," she said, sounding as if her nose was blocked up.

Asako went downstairs and saw that the dinner she had prepared earlier for her father lay untouched. She started to eat, but noticed that she was totally unaware of what she was eating; she had only a sense of her own empty nothingness. Even her body seemed unreal to her. She sat like a puppet awaiting the return of its master. She hoped that her father, her master, would come home soon. But if he never came home again, perhaps the puppet would develop the strength to move of its own will. When she understood that somewhere within her was a desire for her father's death she felt a truly physical chill. She got up and turned off the air conditioner.

She started to think about the notebook, but did not feel like touching it again.

Takayanagi was a good drinker, but out of practice; obviously he had overindulged. The next morning he remembered only patches of what had happened. It must have been Takashi that drove him home, but his telephone conversation with Asako was hard to recall. Again, he had no idea what he said to her as she was putting him to bed. Perhaps he had even told her some acid truth that would eat its way into her mind. Still if his drunkenness was enough to loosen his tongue, it could just as well have made him drop off immediately to sleep.

He had got up that morning at his usual hour, but of course with no appetite. After drinking a little cold vegetable juice Asako made for him, he went upstairs again and stretched out in the wicker chair. When he moved his head the room seemed to sway. He thought he might be getting sick.

He rested the clothbound notebook on his stomach, opened it, and looked indifferently at the notes he had scribbled in it after Asako went out last night. Now they bored him; he did not feel like adding any details under the various headings. Hearing Asako come upstairs, he hurriedly closed it and slipped it between some magazines and the *Hōjōki* on his desk. She brought him a glass dish of sliced white peaches. She sat in the rocking chair opposite him as he ate. Takayanagi usually sat in that chair himself, but this morning had prudently chosen the more stable wicker chair with the footrest.

"Don't you think it's a good idea to turn off this air conditioner and open the windows?" she said. "There's plenty of breeze up here. And in summer it's surely more pleasant to let your skin perspire a little."

"All right then," Takayanagi agreed.

From time to time Asako talked like a housewife running a family, and since he found it tiresome to argue with her he would usually do what she said. And this morning, what with his hangover, he did feel very, very weak. For Asako's benefit he was acting the part of an old man on the verge of his second childhood. At least he felt sure he was only acting, although Asako might not see it that way.

She opened the window and let in an extremely warm breeze, in place of the cool artificial one.

"Now that feels good, doesn't it?"

He closed his eyes. As he lay there limp in the chair, devoid of all strength, suddenly the sensation of floating on his back down river with the current came vividly to him. He could hear the sound of water beating behind his ears, and even feel the burning rays of the sun on his eyelids.

"This is how I used to float down the river."

"What *are* you talking about, Father?" Asako said sharply.

"That river has died. There's nothing alive in it now, nothing swimming, not even a dog. How about asking Takashi along and going for a swim in the sea?"

"Do you mean yourself as well, Father?"

"I certainly do. I swam off the west coast of Izu only two or three years ago. If the beach slopes out gently, I won't have to worry about being carried out of my depth."

"We'd better ask Dr. Nagasawa first."

"That old fraud! Anyway, he was a gynecologist. Spent most of his time giving illegal abortions, from before the war, apparently."

Takayanagi opened his eyes. Asako was rocking back and forth in the chair opposite him, her face hidden by the magazine she was holding, a woman's magazine with an actress on its cover. Her bare knees shone like two white peaches. As she sank deeper into the chair her short skirt revealed the insides of her thighs. She seemed absorbed in her magazine, unaware that he was looking at her. Finally she let one of her slippers drop and crossed her legs. As he watched her legs rising and falling with the movement of the chair he found that he was being aroused by the sight, and closed his eyes again.

He had lost his virility years ago and what he had come to desire in women was the same as when he was a virgin; his desire had again taken on an abstract form with no carnal purpose behind it. Even the powerful attraction he felt toward the thighs and calves of young girls was a kind of regression to his boyhood. Then he had been obsessed by the legs alone, as if cut off from the rest of the body, independent living things. The sight of attractive legs made him wish to possess only them, and because he knew that was impossible he would feel a deep, sorrowful pain. The blind man's daughter had legs that aroused that pain.

Toward the end of spring the boy would often go with Aya down to the estuary to search for clams and shells. Her legs would be bared to the thighs, and to look at them like that from behind would make him unhappy. He thought of them as the legs of a goddess, but he kept the thought to himself. As the goddess's legs became wet and sandy the boy would feel a strange, ambivalent lust for them.

He wondered if Asako's legs were those of a goddess, and he opened his eyes to see. Perhaps he was too close, but Asako's crossed legs looked unexpectedly strong and sensuous.

She abruptly laid her magazine aside and stood up.

"I'll make some tea."

As he watched her walking barefoot across the room he saw that she had indeed the slim legs of most girls nowadays. The legs of a goddess should be a little fuller, more rounded.

"Lead me by the hand," the old blind man said.

During his afternoon sleep Takayanagi had returned to his boyhood again, and his hand was in the inhumanly strong grip of the old man's huge hand.

They were not by the hut under the bridge but in the center of the wasteland in the estuary. The blind man lived in a new hut now among the rank grasses of the wasteland. The bridge had been rebuilt, and the old man and his daughter expelled from the town; Takayanagi's father, at the request of the governor, had given them this hut built for workmen on land which had previously been used by his company for storing timber. From then on, the boys saw little of the old man, who somehow was no longer called "the beggar." For Takayanagi he had the aura of a recluse possessed of a wisdom beyond the merely human. Now that the boy's voice had broken he had drifted away from his former friends, and he would often go to visit the old man in what he thought of as the "grass hut" in which wise men and poets of old had lived. It was on such a visit that the old man had taken the boy's hand and said he wanted to walk.

In that grip the boy felt a mysterious power. If fate assumes the heavy shape of powerful men, then it seemed to have become this blind old man and it was taking the boy by the hand. Although entrusting his hand to the boy, the old man walked quite freely and easily among the summer grasses, almost like an ordinary person. There was none of the stumbling, clumsy movement of the usual blind man being led; rather, the boy felt like a small boat being towed in the wake of a large ship.

They went down into a hollow which was enclosed by a crumbling L-shaped stone wall. Tall, wild yellow spirea was in flower, and pink convolvulus straggled over the stone wall.

"It is dark here. What place is this?" asked the old man.

"It's a place people always told us to stay away from. Long ago a mad lord in the castle used to torture women to death and then have their corpses thrown away here. They say if you come here your arms and legs will rot and fall off, or you'll fall asleep and your flesh will melt away till there's only a skeleton left. Lots of other horrible things, too."

"And do you believe all that?"

"No. Children often come here to explore. When I was little I came any number of times with my friends. But I was the only one who dared to climb over the wall and come right in."

The boy spoke with pride. "I'm not afraid of superstitions. Anyway, nothing happened to me afterward."

"You mean nothing's happened yet. You don't know what's going to happen now, do you? You don't even know that something is going to happen."

"Don't try to frighten me!" Takayanagi had meant to say it jokingly, but he was aware that a whine had crept into his voice. Perhaps the old man intended to strangle him. To conceal his terror he tried to apply his mind to other things. But even this attempt would be discernible to the old man, not with his blind eyes but with those other eyes he had. The boy turned to look at him, but silhouetted against the sun in the west, the old man was only a black shape, the incarnation of darkness. What was this man then? The boy realized that he knew nothing of him. All that he had been told—that he was a blind beggar, a tramp who practiced fortunetelling, the descendant of feudal lords—all of it was of no use in answering the question of what he really was.

"There is nothing to fear," the old man said. "We shall have a long talk. The sun is still high. But first, find me a place to sit."

The boy seated the old man at a shaded spot on the crumbling wall. He himself sat close by, on a stone about the size of a human head.

"This is a bad place, a place of terror. The earth here has drunk in blood. It is still haunted by evil spirits, although this could not be known to ordinary folk. But the spirits gathered here are like flabby entrails, the shapeless ghosts of inferior souls. They possess little power; enough, perhaps, to create miasmas to disturb the mind of some weak-spirited person from time to time, but no more than that. There is nothing to be anxious about."

"I don't believe in such things, but I wouldn't be afraid, anyway. I don't believe in any superhuman power. That's why I've brought you to a place other people won't come near."

"I wasn't brought by you. It was I who brought you here. You seem to trust too much in the power of your own free will."

"I refuse to believe in any gods or fates, in anything that surpasses the power of man!" Takayanagi shouted.

That shout must have broken his dream. As his head surfaced into the present, old Takayanagi realized he had been sweating in his sleep. The afternoon breeze was blowing in from the estuary, but it was the heat from the roof clogging the room like raw cotton that gave the real feeling of high summer. As a boy he had felt that same heat among the summer grasses on the wasteland.

He looked down into the garden full of burning sunlight. The trees and shrubs seemed dusty and shrunken, enduring the heat. On the opposite bank the oil refinery glittered, casting back the full rays of the sun, as if at close range one might hear the crackle of burning metal.

Takayanagi was wearing a lemon-colored polo shirt, rather bright for an old

man, and its heavy terrycloth had made him sweat. But a little natural perspira-
tion felt pleasant in the heat of the day.

"Yes, the sun is still high."

He spoke quietly to himself, looking up at the sky with its thin haze of smoke,
and tried to reconstruct the dialogue with the blind man. He became the old
blind man and asked his boyhood self:

"So you really don't believe that anything surpasses man?"

"Man is the measure of all things."

"But aren't there things you can't measure with your human yardstick? Like
me, for example? Look at me."

The old man turned his head, exposing his face to the sun. The boy had
never looked straight at those blind eyes. Perhaps he had always managed to
avoid looking because he knew unconsciously that he could not bear to see
them. He had not thought the old man was blinded by cataract or glaucoma or
an infection, and he had not wanted to think there were more terrible ways in
which a man could lose his sight.

The old man had no eyes. The boy could not tell if they had been gouged
out or destroyed, or even if he had never had eyes. Now there were only two
holes, and around them the skin was mysteriously wrinkled and scarred as if it
had been burned. No eyelids moved. It was like looking at the remains of a vol-
cano which had erupted once and was now silent.

"I burned out these eyes with red-hot iron rods," the old man had said in a low
voice. "It was the rage within me. Not because I had looked upon what I should not
have seen, my own evil deeds. Nor was it because I could no longer bear to look
upon misfortune. I had believed that these eyes could see all things, and because
they had not seen what they should have seen, I destroyed them in the wildness of
my rage. But that, too, was mere foolishness. I had meant to gouge out my shame,
and now my shame is only made visible. These scars are the signs of my defeat.
What defeated me was a power that surpasses the power of man. These are words
you dislike, but it was the power of the gods. Certainly what I call the gods is no
more than a word men use. And yet it is also certain that they sway men in what
they do. Men use the word 'god' for what sways them, guessing at the source of that
power against which they themselves are so powerless. By good fortune most men
live their lives without ever hearing the voices of the gods. They live like puppets
unaware of what moves them. There are mechanical puppets who believe they
move only by their own free will, all unaware of the clockwork mechanism inside
them, and of the beings who placed it there. But I was different. At least I was
aware of the mechanism set within me to make me move as I did. Call that mecha-
nism fate, if you will. It is constructed from the words of the gods. Once a man
took those words apart to show me their terrible meaning. Do you understand?
That man was as I am now, an old beggar. Yet I am hardly as old as you think. I
look older than my years because I grappled with the machine, used it harshly, and
these are my scars. Be that as it may, this beggar who prophesied my fate was also
blind. I think he had cast away his sight so as not to see what need not be seen, and

see only what men do not see. What he said to me was, 'While you remain in the light of the sun you will murder your father and couple with the mother who gave you birth. Help will come to you only after you have lost the light of the sun.'"

The old man paused, his face turned as if in pursuit of the sun journeying westward. The sky darkened. The piled-up cumulus clouds seemed ready to descend. A moist wind presaging a thunderstorm began to rustle the summer grasses.

"Remember this well. This will happen to you."

The boy tensed, and gooseflesh stood out on his body. Could the old man be referring to him? Or was he only repeating the words of the other blind man? The old man perceived that the boy was going to stand up, and stretched out a hand to restrain him.

"Wait. There is more to be said. These things happened long, long ago. The same things may have happened countless times since then. Probably they will go on happening over and over. While men use language, links are made, one link of horror fitting into the next, and a chain is formed. Why was I caught in one link of that chain, in one round circle of it? Because the gods had chosen me. Because they had decided to set this mechanism, this hell, within me. What other explanation can there be? I went against the gods: I tried to smash the mechanism. I would outwit their machine: I would spit their words back in their faces. I had been told what I would do in the future. Very well, but my will was free, and so the ability to do otherwise was mine. I used all my power in order that the prophecy, the words the gods had let me hear, should never be realized. I ran away from my father and mother. I was the wisest of all men; about things human, about those things of which man is the measure, there was nothing I could not understand. I succeeded in many endeavors. But let me be brief; there is little time left. In one thing only I did not succeed: escaping the mechanism of the gods. Finally I did all as had been foretold. I killed a drunkard in self-defense, and so killed my father. I married his widow, my mother. Children were born to us, all cruelly deformed except my youngest daughter. A priest told me I was being punished for having committed evil, an obvious judgment; but because I wanted to know what evil, and why, I began studying the question on who I was and what I had done. To be truthful, it amounted to no more than an intensive gathering of testimonials about myself. Who was I? A man who had killed his father and taken his mother to wife, that was all. But that equation had already been worked out for me. I had only worked it out again for myself by an enormous and elaborate procedure I referred to as 'self-awareness'; I had shown that the solution of the equation was unmistakably correct. Now you may wonder if these things happened because I already knew the solution, and constructed the equation accordingly. In other words, although I claim I killed my father and coupled with my mother in all ignorance, surely the truth is that these acts had been foretold, and I committed them knowing that I had to. Or can we say that it was simply coincidental, all done in perfect ignorance? If that is so, I am no more than the victim of a calamity. I myself, this wretched man, was merely used by the gods for their diversion. But the gods had already pronounced my fate. Surely, the gods had chosen *me*, a man to whom they could reveal everything, a man who would oppose their plan but who would eventually surrender to them of his own free will, carrying out that plan to the letter. I *was* that kind of man, I knew all and was an accomplice of the gods, but my eyes, those eyes of which I had been so proud, were not able to discern it. Then in my rage I burned out my eyes and saw for the first time. Yet even that had already been prophesied. Do you remember? The blind beggar said that help would come when I had lost the light of the sun. Losing the light of the sun meant losing my eyes. And was it not said in the very first words of the prophecy that all this would happen while I remained in the light of the sun? The whole prophecy was true, and until I knew its meaning I had to perform one foul act after another until I finally destroyed my eyes. Can it be that the gods thought I was a man who would immediately grasp that meaning? If so, the gods overestimated me, since such perception is beyond human ability. Probably they were pleased that I was foolish enough to act the part of their accomplice to the very end. In that case there must be some recompense for me. And that time is now approaching. . . ."

The sky grew darker and darker, and there was thunder in the distance.

Takayanagi got up from his wicker chair, opened his notebook, and wrote down the words that the blind man must then have said.

Losing the light of the sun meant that I should come to see what I had not seen until then. That did not mean myself. The question of who I am myself is not worthy of consideration. I am nothing but myself. What I first saw was the shape of those beings who had controlled all that I had done. Also I saw the intimate relation between those beings and myself. That was part of the help to come to me; but ultimate help lies somewhere far beyond knowledge and wisdom. Casting away my sight has meant losing the light of the sun, but, more than that, I am to go where the light of the sun cannot be seen. The ultimate help the gods will grant me as my final reward is no more, and no less, than death. This is what the prophesy had been telling me from the very beginning.

"You have some eccentric ideas."

Nagasawa repeated it as their car arrived at the beach inn. Takashi was driving with Asako at his side, and the two old men in the back seat.

"I don't insist on swimming. The main object is to have a few drinks at this inn, whatever it's called, and then take a little nap in the sea breeze."

"We'd both be well advised to avoid the cold water. No point reminding ourselves we're no longer young."

The shore was full of rocks, and from early August the sea became so rough that people stopped coming to swim. A few boys were ducking underwater in search of sea urchins and shells, and a woman in a flowery dress holding a parasol was walking along the rocky shore. She stepped gingerly from one rock to the next as if they felt burning hot to the soles of her bare feet.

"Was this beach always so deserted?" Takayanagi asked as they looked out from the inn.

Nagasawa shook his head. "I'm afraid I don't remember. I only came here once, and that was half a century ago."

"People tend to use the beach on the other side of that point," said Takashi, who had already stripped to his swimming trunks. "They've put up a hotel and a marina recently, and lots of people go. It's always been like this here, so I don't suppose it will change."

Asako put on her bathing suit in the next room, came in again briefly, and went down to the beach with Takashi to have a swim before lunch.

For some time the image of his daughter sliding open the door and appearing there almost naked in what was presumably a "bikini" remained with Takayanagi. Being indoors she had seemed particularly white and naked. Perhaps she had done it on purpose, wanting to show herself off. Takayanagi disliked senseless exhibitionism. Nor did he like those preposterous huge round sunglasses she was wearing.

"That gave me quite a shock. At first I thought some film star had turned up." Nagasawa also seemed taken aback by the girl's audacity, and he followed the two of them with his eyes as they made their way down to the beach.

"I didn't think she was that sort," Takayanagi said, looking rather shaken.

"But it's because she's young, I suppose. Young people will do things we can't understand."

"She's grown up into a fine girl. It's all very well for her to be properly dressed, keeping herself under control, and that suits her, too; but so does that bikini, doesn't it? Anyway, my grandson's old enough to be very interested in her."

"And she's old enough to be interested in him, I expect. But she's had nothing to do with men, and I doubt if she thinks of Takashi that way."

"I can't make out Takashi either. I don't know if he's peculiarly mature for his age or if he's still a complete child. Whichever it is, young people nowadays don't seem to go through adolescence the way we did, with pimples and all the rest. I suppose they stay children longer. Yet they can do things with a reckless nerve we grownups don't have."

"That's because they're children. Those two are probably playing with each other now like little children playing doctor."

Nagasawa gave an embarrassed grunt and started looking nervously out of the open window.

Takayanagi thought of the blind man's daughter and what they had done together in the shadow of the breakwater. Probably that too had been a kind of playing doctor. He must have been fourteen or fifteen, and she would have been twenty-six or -seven. He was already equipped for penetrating her, but he had somehow been unable to do it. In the sea nearby were many large crabs swimming about with their spatulate legs. Her body was wet with spray, and he felt like one of those crabs as he slowly clambered over her. But when he tried to kiss her lips she suddenly struck him in the face.

Then Takayanagi's father had taken her and made her his new mother. When he was twenty it was she who had tried to kiss him, and he had slapped her with his open hand. Aya reminded him that she had once fended him off.

"They're taking their time," Nagasawa said.

"Shall we start without them? The children can have lunch later." Taka-yanagi called the maid. "It won't be much more than ordinary fisherman's fare, but at least everything will be good and fresh."

It was indeed. Though not very attractively served, all the seafood, starting with lobster and sliced raw turbot, had a sweet fresh flavor with a strong scent of the ocean. The saké was drawn straight from the cask, and they drank it cold out of aromatic cedar cups.

The wind bells hanging above the veranda tinkled in the sea breeze, over the sound of the waves. Occasionally there was the rustle of pine branches brushing against the wooden eaves. As the saké went to their heads the colors of sky and sea became indistinguishable. The clouds crossing the sky were like ships with white sails.

"It's a good feeling, just on the verge of being drunk. Makes you forget you're going to die."

"With your constitution you needn't think about that for another ten years," replied Nagasawa, his face now red.

"It has nothing to do with my constitution. There are voices that only I shall hear, and when they call me it will be good-by to all this. I don't think it will be very long till I hear them, coming from where the river flows into the sea."

"You've had too much to drink; I can't imagine what you're talking about. If you don't mind I think I'll have a little . . ." Nagasawa lay back with his arm as a pillow and went to sleep.

Takayanagi peered beyond the narrow stretch of sandy beach to the shallow in-shore sea with its many rocks, trying to make out the figures of Asako and Takashi. The one with the orange cap swimming between the rocks seemed to be Asako. As the waves broke they scattered a foam of white lace over that speck of orange.

Asako and Takashi ran with long, loping strides across the scorching sand. When they came under the shade of the pine trees the needles pricked the soles of their bare feet. At the bottom of stone steps leading up to a shrine on the hill there was a small wayside shop, sheltered by screens of marsh reeds, where an old woman was selling licorice water and old-style fizzy lemonade.

"Rustic, isn't it?" said Asako, sitting on the wide bench covered with straw matting provided for customers. "I suppose licorice water is different from arrow-root water."

"I suppose so," Takashi replied.

"When I was a child I used to drink something like this, dogtooth violet dis-solved in hot sugar water, I think. That was mostly in summer, or when I was sick. I had a weak stomach."

"Sweet saké would taste good right now."

"I even drank it in winter, when I was in Kyoto and used to go up into the hills, to Takao and then down to Sagano. Can I have a bottle of fizz too?"

"You're going to have both?"

"Certainly. You don't often find these things anymore. Drinking fizz is really quite poetic: bubbles bubbling up and up, what bliss! This will be only my third bottle in my whole life."

"It's past twelve-thirty. We'd better be getting back. They're probably waiting for us, and ready for lunch."

"Waiting for us!" Asako exclaimed, stretching her white neck to drain the lemonade. "Those two will have started long ago, and they'll have had enough saké to forget all about us. Let's go for another swim."

Asako pulled the hood of her beach coat over her head, put on the huge sunglasses that seemed to project some distance from her face, and walked off, waving a cheerful good-bye to the old woman squatting in her shop.

"Asako," Takashi called, and ran after her.

"My head feels a little strange," she said, almost singing the words.

"Has something happened between you and your father?"

"Only that I've had a good look at his notebook on the sly. I read all of it. 'Losing the light of the sun meant that I should come to see what I had not seen until then. . . . Casting away my sight has meant losing the light of the sun, but, more than that, I am to go where the light of the sun cannot be seen. The ultimate help the gods will grant me as my final reward is no more, and no less, than death.' Can you make anything of that, Takashi? I can't. All I understand is that Father is thinking about death, but this talk about gods is like talking about strangers from an unknown country. What sort of arrangement has he made with these gods, anyway? He'll be saved by them when he loses the light of the sun, which means going blind; then he'll be able to see what the gods see; and finally he'll die and go where there is no sun. That seems to be his salvation. But Father's not blind; he's got wonderful eyesight, doesn't even need reading glasses. Of course it must mean that this 'I' isn't Father at all, but that blind beggar he's talked about. Maybe he's writing a novel with the blind man as narrator."

Asako went on wondering aloud as they walked along the water's edge until they reached an old boat that had been washed halfway up on the shore. The hull seemed rotten, but the bare wood inside was bone dry. She put her foot on the edge of the boat and swarms of sea lice scurried under the hull.

Asako stretched herself out in the boat with her head at its bow.

"I want to get a tan."

"If you get too sunburned you may have a sunstroke. Especially with that fair skin of yours."

She covered her forehead and eyes with her straw hat. Takashi got into the boat too and, placing his hands on either side of her as if about to start doing push-ups, lowered his face toward hers.

"Asako!" he said.

She laid her finger across her mouth, motioning him to be silent. Then she raised her body slightly, flipped her hands behind her back, and untied the thin strip of cloth covering her breasts. The small, swelling breasts were even whiter than the surrounding skin, like the full orb of the moon at the height of day. The sun burned down on her flesh, and as it drank in the heat it seemed to be changing into some other, warmer substance.

Takashi gazed at her breasts like a well-trained dog sitting patiently looking at its dinner. Suddenly be knelt down reverently, as if performing some kind of ceremonious courtesy, and pressed his hands against the small, firm, rounded breasts. As he did so her flesh seemed to melt and flow, becoming as soft as ripe melon, and something like the butt of a pencil poked up under his hands. He put his mouth to it, a nipple that had pushed up its little towerlike head.

Asako lay dead still, looking up at the sun through her straw hat, letting the boy's lips and hands move at will. Only when the hat was brushed off and his mouth sought hers did she squirm violently and push him away.

As they walked back, trailing their shadows across the sand, Takashi said:

"I was going to tell you something in the boat, but I stopped."

"Tell me now."

"I heard from my grandfather recently that your grandmother—your father's stepmother, that is—was the daughter of that man who lived under the bridge."

"The blind beggar's daughter, you mean?" she replied in an even tone. "I knew that."

"Father, there's something I want to talk to you about," Asako said after breakfast.

These past few days Takayanagi had spent most of his time drinking with Nagasawa. Asako had never hesitated to warn him to restrain himself, but now she let him do exactly as he pleased. Takayanagi thought she might be watching a weak, senile old fool destroying himself.

"Sister telephoned."

"Ah, Masayo phoned, did she?" he said, then realized with a shock his mistake. Masayo was Takayanagi's child by his stepmother, and thus in fact Asako's elder sister; but she had been registered as the child of Takayanagi's father, which made her officially his own sister and Asako's aunt.

Asako seemed quite unconcerned.

"No; *my* sister," she corrected him, explaining that Kyoko wanted to come and stay with them for a week or so at the end of the month, bringing the children.

"So it's all arranged," he said with a forced smile.

"No, it's not. Naturally they'll only come if you don't object."

"Naturally. And naturally they all mean to stay in this house, I suppose."

"Yes." Asako shrugged. "I said myself I didn't really think that was possible."

"You needn't have bothered."

He spoke as if trying to hold down something rising within him.

"Don't bother saying what needn't be said. If people want to come, let them."

"Then it's all right?"

"I'll tell her myself. Tonight. And I'll tell her I probably won't be here."

"Are you going back to Tokyo?"

"I don't know," he said, and then, in a pleasanter tone: "There are other places."

He stood up and looked toward the oil refinery in the estuary.

"Aren't you going to switch off the air conditioner and open the windows?"

"The smoke from the factory chimneys smells too awful," she said.

Later Asako reappeared wearing cotton pants that were ragged around the ankles, as if the cuffs had been savagely ripped off.

"Just going for a drive with Takashi."

"That's a pretty funny get-up. Won't your legs be too hot in pants?"

"The car's air-conditioned. This way I won't catch cold."

He wondered if Asako and Takashi had become lovers since that trip to the beach. But surely they were too young to fall in love. He couldn't imagine what kind of emotional life two such children could have. None, probably; no passion, no soul: just two innocent little animals frisking about.

Takayanagi himself as a boy had had no soul, and hence no possibility of emotional rapport with Aya. Then when he reached young manhood he made this goddess his woman by virtually raping her. When he did that, his actions had been guided by the old blind man's words. Indeed, Takayanagi and Aya confided in each other only when Aya herself confessed that she had always intended to make her father's words come true.

Masayo and Shuji had been born; then his father had died of cancer. Takayanagi had meant to tell him the truth of his illness, but Aya stopped him, saying his father was too weak to bear such knowledge. When a man has one foot in the grave there is no point in flogging him to death.

"My father never prophesied that the two of us would kill him," she had said.

"I wonder."

"Then why didn't we?" Aya watched to see if his expression would change, and smiled.

"Don't expect us to act out the plot of a tragedy. We betrayed my father to the limit of our powers. Your own father was more than human, and so he could bring about atrocities on a grander scale. He seems like someone out of an ancient myth."

Takayanagi decided to record that in his notebook too, and went to the low cupboard and took out the small metal box in which he kept it. The box was unlocked. Ever since he had been going out so often he had been careful to keep the notebook locked in that box. If he had forgotten to lock it, Asako would certainly have read his notebook. He did not trust her.

Distracted, he forgot what he had intended to write. He sat down in the wicker chair, opened his notebook in front of him, and tried to concentrate on it. After a while he closed the notebook again.

"It's no good, I can't bring it to mind," he muttered to himself.

Perhaps all the things he had meant to bring to mind had vanished in the same way. When you no longer know anything, it is best to lay down your pen. No need to go on stringing one irrelevant word after another, only to end with Asako reading it on the sly.

He got up, wrapped the notebook in newspaper, tied the parcel firmly, and called a taxi. As he waited for it he looked at his reflection in the mirror and grinned. He had put on dark glasses and was wearing a brick-red polo shirt; except for the fact that his close-cropped hair was half gray, he looked absurdly young for his age, rather like a rich middle-aged American with thick, bronzed forearms, coming ashore from his yacht.

"Just take me down toward the refinery," he told the taxi driver. "You can go as slow as you like."

"It's pretty bleak around there, sir," the driver said, looking dubious. "Nothing much to see."

"That's all right. I used to play in the field there when I was a boy, and before I go back to Tokyo I want to see how it's changed. When you get to the mouth of the river, turn off along the ocean and you'll come to a pine forest. About that far will do."

"The pine forest near the river? A lot of it's gone now, and it'll take a good ten minutes to get to where it starts."

"That's all right."

The taxi crossed a new bridge that had been built downstream, the estuary opening out in sweeping curves to their left, and ran along the fence of the refinery. The rough concrete embankment wall that kept the estuary from view seemed to go on forever, like the wall of an enormous prison.

"It does seem awfully desolate around here."

"Well, it's mostly tanks and pipes."

Under the burning midday sun there was no sign of workers in this landscape, and the plant seemed like a vast, barren metal graveyard. No buses or trucks were on the road, though occasionally they passed a bus stop. Takayanagi decided that this was truly an abode of the gods, but refrained from saying anything to the driver. He had the car stop at a place where the embankment wall was low, intending to climb up to look at the sea. And he had something to throw away.

The top of the embankment wall was almost over his head. Takayanagi placed the newspaper-wrapped notebook on the wall, stepped back a few paces to gather momentum, and then dashed forward and tried to scramble up it. His failure only made him determined to keep on trying. Just as he managed to get one leg on top the driver came bellowing after him, and leaped nimbly up on the wall, grabbing hold of his arm in an almost threatening way.

"Don't get any funny ideas, now!"

Apparently he had thought Takayanagi was going to do away with himself.

"No, no, I only want to throw this into the ocean, that's all." Takayanagi pointed to the paper parcel. The driver picked up the parcel, and seemed relieved. "You see? No human limbs or anything. I'm just throwing it away to keep it out of my child's hands."

"Ah. Some of those dirty pictures, is it? Or maybe a book?"

"Something like that."

The surface of the water seemed surprisingly far below. No waves broke against the wall as the dark, purplish water ebbed and flowed. The sandbar that had stretched out like a long tongue must have ended around here, but there was no sign of it anywhere.

"It must be pretty deep here."

"Pretty deep, I guess. There's a landing stage for tankers a bit farther on, and the whole sea bottom must have been dug out around here."

At that, Takayanagi hurled his parcel out into the sea. It sank into the turbid water and vanished.

Going back to the car, they set off again, and immediately arrived at the landing stage. No oil tankers were there, only a black dredging barge at work. The driver asked if he wanted to get out and take a look, but Takayanagi told him to go straight on. Finally they arrived at the pine forest.

"There's nothing but miles of pine trees from here. It's not much of a coast for scenery."

It was the same kind of pine forest you found throughout this region, the same uninhabited shore. No children swimming, no fishing boats out, a landscape unrelated to human life stretching on into the distance. But at a fork in the unpaved road they saw a car parked among the trees.

"Doing it in the car's all the rage lately," the driver said, turning to grin at Takayanagi. "There's a couple up to something in that car."

"I didn't notice," said Takayanagi, in a tired voice.

"Somebody saw us," Asako said.

"No one who'd recognize us, anyway."

"That was a taxi. Isn't it odd for a taxi to go by out here? Maybe Father has been following us to see what we're up to."

"You're imagining things. Are you really afraid of your father?"

"I'm afraid all right, anyone would be. The more you try to find out about him the less you can understand him."

"Shall we get out of the car?" Takashi asked. "In a place like this we could go for a swim naked."

"No thanks. It gives me the creeps, all that empty sea and pebbly beach, and no one anywhere along the shore. If there was someone else in the water I wouldn't mind going in."

"I'll go in, and be that someone."

"Stop it."

Asako put her arms around his neck and pulled him down, curling herself up in the awkwardly narrow space of the seat. Since she would not allow him to kiss her mouth, he fondled her breasts. She had slipped buckskin shoes on over her bare feet, and a white ankle revealed below the ragged fringe of her cotton pants attracted his attention. Grasping her foot, he pressed his lips to that ankle, then to her calf. When he pulled off her shoe and rested his cheek against the small, deeply arched sole of her foot he was aware of a faint odor of new leather and rubber.

At the same time Asako groped for his hard, tautly erect penis. When she took hold of it he closed his eyes and became quite still. Asako thought to herself he was behaving like a surgical patient under an anesthetic. As she toyed with his penis, rubbing it between her palm and fingers, she felt as if she had a big dog on its back, with all four paws in the air.

An afternoon thunderstorm had been threatening, and as they crossed the bridge at the mouth of the estuary, large drops of rain began to beat on the roof of the car. Asako was driving them back. Near her house Takashi said:

"I don't think I want to stop in at your place today."

"We're not going to my place. We're going to finish what we just left off." She was looking straight ahead, expressionless, and drove on past the house and turned in through the gateway of the hotel next door. She put on her big round sunglasses, then smiled quickly at Takashi as if making some sort of signal to him.

"Here?" said Takashi, putting on his own sunglasses. "You really have tremendous nerve, Asako. I don't know how you do it."

The strange darkness of the sky made Takayanagi uneasy, unable to settle down, and he wondered if perhaps he shouldn't take a quick bath. He got the bath ready, and as he was sitting soaking quietly in the wooden tub a sudden haze seemed to descend, inside the house as well as outside. He got out of the tub and hastily dried himself, peering into the garden, where a violent rain was beating down. He closed the shutters and went upstairs. The rain seemed to dash against the overhanging eaves, and he decided to have a drink as he watched it through the window. He went to get the little cask of saké and wooden cup he had received as a parting gift from the inn he had visited with Nagasawa.

The surface of the river looked as if it were being flailed by bundles of silver threads. From time to time misty clouds raced over it. The estuary and sea beyond had faded behind the rain, dissolving and mingling with the black clouds into such darkness that the landscape seemed not of this world. He wondered if there were an entrance to a sunless world over there, and as the lightning began to flash he knew it to be the same landscape he had seen that time as a boy.

The old blind man stood up.

"Now I must go."

As he spoke, large drops of rain began to strike his face and neck. The boy took his hand to lead him back to the hut, but the old man stared walking in the opposite direction.

"Where are you going?"

"Come with me. I want you to bear witness."

Holding the boy's hand in his own, which felt like a hand carved out of hard wood, he walked toward the sea.

The rain began falling heavily, and thunder was approaching. He wanted to warn the old man that he might be struck by lightning, but the old man only walked faster and faster, so fast and sure that one could hardly imagine him to be blind, pushing his way through thick clusters of swamp lilies until they reached the sandy spur. Here a large tongue of soft, watery sand stretched out toward the sea. Eaten away at the edges by the incoming waves, porous with the myriad little holes drilled by the rain, the sand became softer the farther one went. Walking in bare feet felt like walking on something fleshy, something very like a tongue in fact. The boy stopped in fear. If they went any farther they might be sucked down into that mud. The old man let go his hand.

"You can watch from here. You must not come with me. And listen: If you don't watch right until the end, if you move before it's over, something terrible will happen to you. You understand? You don't need to worry about me. The voices are calling me. The voices are telling me that it is time to go with them, that I am not to keep them waiting any longer. Truly I have lived too long; I have kept them waiting a long time. The stupidity of what I have done . . ."

The boy understood where the old man was going. But what would the entrance to the country of death be like? Because he wanted to see it, the boy forgot his fear.

After two or three steps the old man turned.

"Don't come," he shouted. "It is not the time for you to come. When you go back, tell my daughter: 'You will couple with your own son and give birth to his child.' Tell her that. I have already told you what will happen to you, and that is what will happen. But you are not to go mad. Stay sane."

As the old man walked on, he seemed to grow larger and larger, ignoring the laws of perspective. The shoal of sand seemed endless, since the old man never sank beneath the waves. But the rain was heavy and the black clouds hung low, and at last he was about to be obliterated by that strange darkness. At that moment the old man was enveloped in a glow of purplish white light, and there was a bursting sound as of something being rent apart.

A great peal of thunder shook the house and made Takayanagi spill his drink. Lightning must have struck nearby, since the lamp had gone out. Already a little drunk, he wondered vaguely if the same kind of thunderbolt had fallen on the old man.

"What did happen then?" he asked himself.

The blind old man had been struck by lightning and had died. Man dies and returns to nothingness. But perhaps that old man had become more than man, had gone to some actual place. That thought still held Takayanagi in its grasp; and he found himself imagining that he might do the same. He laughed at his own stupidity and poured himself another drink.

His eyes seemed to have misted over, and he saw Asako emerge from the haze. She was soaked to the skin. Her disordered hair was dripping wet and clung to her face.

"What's happened to you? You're all drenched like some poor little beggar girl."

The blind man's daughter had looked like that as she came running through the rain that time. While he told her exactly what had happened she had said nothing but merely nodded her head. She had made no attempt to look for the body. Even after they were back in the hut and she was hanging his shirt and trousers up to dry she had still not wept.

"Are you crying?" he asked Asako, looking into her eyes. She shook her head, knelt down, and pressed her wet face against his lap. Barefoot, in those ragged pants, she was more like some little vagrant urchin clinging to him. He lifted the strands of wet hair from her neck. How she could go out in that sort of get-up with a boyfriend, and one younger than herself, he could not begin to understand. What was going on in her head? She must be emotionally empty, like a deserted wasteland, like an animal; and so she had gone off to romp like some little wild animal. The driver's words, "doing it in the car," came back to him.

Asako raised her head. Her eyes had become hard and glinting, uncanny-looking, like a wolf's eyes. Before Takayanagi could speak his mouth was stopped by the girl's lips. With a feeling of horror as if he were being savaged by an animal gone wild, he felt her lips on his. He thought he felt her hot tongue. Wondering what on earth was wrong with the girl, he put his arm around her slender shoulders, and noticed the frailty of her flesh.

Asako drew her face away from his and buried it in his chest.

"Am I your daughter?" she said. "I've read your notebook, you see."

Takayanagi gave a grunt of pain. The pressure on his chest was making it hard to breathe.

"If you've read it, you've read it. But such things have no meaning. All pure fantasy, something I ought to know better than to indulge in at my time of life."

"Who am I then?"

"You must decide that for yourself."

"But I can't. I must hear it from you."

"You are my daughter."

"So you are my true father, are you? As long as I can be sure of that."

"That's right. But what's happened to you today? I seem to be looking at some crazy girl. Was it Takashi?"

"No. He hasn't even kissed me. I don't think I'll see him anymore. I'll go away from here with you. We'll leave tomorrow."

"Will we?" he said, laughing at her now. "Even if you feel like playing the pathetic, grief-stricken heroine, I don't think I'll be leaving here, at least for the time being."

"But Sister's coming with the children."

"They can come. I said so this morning, didn't I? I've simply changed my own plans and will be here for the rest of the summer."

"I'm going to be awfully busy," Asako said, half sobbing and half laughing.

"You like Kyoko and the children, do you?"

"Not really. Only I'm not strong inside the way you are, Father, and I think it's nice to have relations, even if you don't particularly like them. Grandmother too."

"I can see you've been wanting to say that."

By the time Asako had taken her bath and put on her bathrobe the rain had stopped.

"There'll probably be a rainbow," she said, leaning out of the window. She could not see a rainbow.

The sun over the western hills lit up the rows of storage tanks glowing red above the black estuary.

MATSUMOTO SEICHŌ

Matsumoto Seichō (1909–1992) began work as a commercial artist and then in the 1950s turned to writing mystery novels. He quickly became the most highly regarded such novelist in Japan, a reputation he sustained throughout his long career. Seichō eventually developed an international following as well, since several of his novels, among them *Points and Lines* (*Ten to sen*, 1958) and *Inspector Imanishi Investigates* (*Suna no utsuwa*, 1968), as well as some of his short stories, have been translated. "The Stakeout" (Harikomi), included here, was written in 1955.

THE STAKEOUT (HARIKOMI)

Translated by Daniel Zoll

1

Detectives Yuki and Shimo'oka boarded the westbound train at Yokohama. They chose not to get on at Tokyo Station because they were afraid of being seen by some reporter. The train was scheduled to depart at 9:30 P.M. Both men had gone home from the police station to prepare for the trip, then had taken a commuter train to Yokohama Station, where they met.

As they had expected, the seats in the third-class cars were all taken, and many people were standing. Spreading out a newspaper in the aisle, they sat down to spend the night. Sleep was impossible.

Shimo'oka finally got a seat at Kyoto, Yuki at Osaka.

The sun rose. Its autumn rays filtered through the windows, warming the seats. Oblivious to all, the two men slept.

Yuki vaguely recalled hearing the cities of Okayama and Onomichi announced, but he was not fully awake until they reached the vicinity of Hiroshima. Outside, the sun shed weak red rays on the ocean.

"We sure slept," said Shimo'oka, laughing. The first to wake up, he had just returned from the washroom and sat smoking a cigarette. They bought box lunches at Iwakuni and ate a meal that was neither lunch nor dinner.

"You get off pretty soon," Yuki said.

"Right. The station after next." The ocean, which had been in constant view from the window, had darkened, and the flickering lights on the offshore islands had gained in intensity. This was the first time either man had come so far on an assignment.

"You've still got a long way to go, eh?" Shimo'oka looked Yuki in the face.

"Yeah," mumbled Yuki, looking away. A lighthouse beacon blinked on and off.

Shimo'oka got off at a lonely station called Ogōri. There he would switch to a branch line and proceed to another small town. He stood at the window of Yuki's car until it began to move, then waved goodbye. "Take care of yourself!" he shouted. Yuki was moved by an indescribable loneliness as he watched his companion's figure dwindle on the darkened platform of the unfamiliar little station.

Yuki was on his way to Kyushu. After crossing by ferry to Moji, he would continue by train for another three hours. That was what Shimo'oka had meant when he said Yuki still had a long way to go. His words were meant to show his sympathy for a colleague who faced not just a long journey but a tough assignment at the end of it.

Once he was alone, Yuki took out a paperback edition of foreign poetry in translation and began to read. Having been dubbed "the young man of letters" by the other detectives in the department, he never read in their presence.

The crime had occurred a month earlier in Tokyo's Meguro Ward. Someone had broken into the house of a company executive, killed him, and fled with some money. At first there were no clues to the culprit's identity, and the investigation made little progress. Then suddenly three days ago they had had a break: A man stopped for questioning by an officer on patrol turned out to be the culprit. A twenty-eight-year-old laborer named Yamada, he was working in a construction camp. At first Yamada insisted that he had acted alone, and the story was written up that way in the newspapers. Then two days ago he had changed his story. He now claimed he had had an accomplice.

"The job was my idea, but he's the one who killed him. His name's Ishii Kyūichi. We were in the same camp."

When investigation revealed that Yamada and Ishii had indeed been working together, the police ran a check on Ishii. He was from a rural area in Yamaguchi Prefecture, and a number of siblings and other relatives were still living there. He was thirty years old, a bachelor. Three years ago he had left his hometown and come to Tokyo. At first he had worked as a live-in clerk in a store, but after losing that job, apparently he had done a variety of things. He had worked as a day laborer and had sold blood. He had joined the construction camp only recently.

"He's the quiet type. Said he hated Tokyo. There was something wrong with his lungs, but he used to laugh and say it didn't matter because he was going to kill himself anyway. He kept saying he wanted to go home, but hell, he didn't have the money. At the camp you barely make enough to eat."

Immediately they had alerted the police in Ishii's hometown, who reported that there was no sign of his having returned. Still, chances were good that he would show up in the area. It was decided to send someone from Tokyo to the town to offer assistance. This was standard procedure. Shimo'oka had drawn the assignment.

Yamada had had more to say about Ishii. "He once told me he'd been dreaming about his old girlfriend. I asked him what had happened to her, and he said she was married and living in Kyushu. Said he even knew her address. That's all. He didn't tell me her name or anything else about her."

That information, however, they were able to obtain from the police in Ishii's hometown, to whom they had wired an inquiry on the off chance that the local police might know something. The police there had checked on the woman. They said that indeed she and Ishii had been lovers, but that a year after he had run off to Tokyo she had gone to Kyushu to marry. The local police provided them with her name and the name and address of the man she had married.

The Tokyo detectives were of two opinions. One group held that Ishii had been unable to forget the woman and that he would probably turn up in the vicinity of her home. The other group argued that it was unlikely that he would still be in love with the woman after all this time—especially now that she was married and living in Kyushu.

Yuki belonged to the former group. He could not forget that Ishii had been seeing his former lover in his dreams, that he had lung trouble, and that he had said he wanted to kill himself. In some ways the crime smacked of hopeless desperation. Yuki thought about this man who had come to Tokyo to get ahead but had lost his job, worked as a day laborer, sold blood, taken a job as a construction worker, and finally contracted a lung disease and lost all hope.

"Ishii may be planning to commit suicide somewhere. If so, he's sure to try to see the woman first."

Few of the other detectives shared Yuki's opinion, but his chief reluctantly went along with him. It was decided that Shimo'oka would go to Ishii's hometown, Yuki to Kyushu.

Although the newspapers knew that Yamada had been arrested for the crime, they had not been informed that he had implicated Ishii. The local papers had once broken a story about a case under investigation in Tokyo, as a result of which the suspect had got a three-hour head start on the police and eluded them. The case remained unsolved. Having learned from this experience, the police had decided to keep Ishii's existence a secret. Hence Yuki and Shimo'oka's concern with leaving Tokyo unobserved.

2

Late that night Yuki arrived in S City and checked into an inn across the street from the station. He was exhausted from the trip, but after a good night's sleep he felt his old self again.

The first thing he did the next morning was go to the local police station, where he met the police chief. Yuki handed the chief a sealed envelope containing documents on the case, including a letter requesting the cooperation of the local police.

The chief called in a subordinate. They promised their full cooperation and offered to assign as many men to the case as the Tokyo detective wanted. Yuki turned them down. He had come merely to introduce himself. He thanked them for their offer and said he would ask for their help when the time came. Then he left. Yuki had his own ideas about how to proceed.

Before leaving, he had cautioned both the police chief and the subordinate. "Make sure the local papers don't hear about the case. She's a married woman now and has no connection with Ishii. The last thing she needs is for him to show up. It'd be a shame if the papers got hold of the story and wrecked a happy home."

The woman's husband knew nothing. Most likely she had never told him about Ishii. That was fine. They were leading a good, peaceful life. In family life the woman had found security. If her husband and others found out that a dangerous criminal, a man she had once known, might try to see her, what would they think? The past would rear its ugly head and might well destroy her.

Yuki walked through the town. It was a quiet rural town, too small to have streetcars. A number of canals ran through it.

Such and such *banchi*, so and so *chō*, S City. Yokokawa Sentarō and Sadako. It was the address and name of the woman and her husband. The house was on a back street. It was a one-story building with a low fence around it. The name plate at the entrance read "Yokokawa." The husband worked at a local bank. The house was appropriately small and neat looking. On closer inspection, Yuki noticed a piece of paper with the family members' names on it attached to the mailbox: Sentarō, Sadako, Ryūichi, Kimiko, Sadaji. She was the man's second wife.

Nothing stirred in the house.

Yuki looked around. Across the street was a small, inconspicuous inn with a sign reading "Hizen'ya." Perfect.

The Yokokawa house could be seen clearly from the second story of the inn. Inside the fence, cosmos bloomed in profusion. The garden was small but well kept, and there were several bonsai. Yokokawa's hobby, no doubt. Secondary eaves obstructed the view of the interior of the house, but the edge of one room and the veranda could be seen.

Yuki decided to take a room at the inn immediately. Having received only a meager sum to cover expenses, he was grateful that it was an inexpensive inn.

The detective opened the opaque shōji panel covering the window of his room a crack and sat down. He never took his eyes off the house.

A woman wearing a smock came into view. She spread some bedding on the veranda to air. Yuki watched her intently. She was twenty-seven or twenty-eight and of medium build. Her eyes were big and bright. Sadako, he thought. She looked to him like a typical housewife. Nothing about her hinted that she had once been someone's lover.

A boy of about six appeared and began clinging to the woman. Probably their youngest. He and his stepmother seemed to get along well. Yuki could not hear what they were talking about. To the casual observer, it was a family scene as tranquil as the quiet autumn sun.

Apparently the woman had not been contacted by Ishii. If she had been, surely she wouldn't be so calm, the detective reasoned.

It neared noon. Sadako brought a knitting machine over near the veranda and began knitting some yarn. Head down, she moved her arm intently. All Yuki could hear was the clatter of the machine.

About one o'clock a boy of fifteen or sixteen and a girl of twelve or thirteen came home from school. The older stepson and the stepdaughter. Sadako stopped knitting and disappeared into the house. Probably fixing lunch. After a little while she reappeared. Returning to the machine, she knitted for more than an hour. The older boy left with a baseball glove in his hand, and his sister went out to play, too.

Sadako went to get a magazine and sat there looking at it. Instead of reading it, however, she seemed to be searching for something in its appendix, perhaps a knitting pattern. Occasionally she would stop to look carefully and thought-fully at something in the appendix.

After that, she disappeared into the house and did not reappear until around four. Shopping basket in hand, she left through the rear of the house and came out to the road. Most likely on her way to buy something for dinner. Yuki could see her face clearly. Her features were good but rather expressionless, and her clothes made her look older than her age. Somehow she lacked vitality.

Forty minutes later she returned home. In the basket was something wrapped in newspaper. She carried a small bottle of saké in one hand. Apparently her husband drank.

The husband got home just before six o'clock. He was thin and extremely tall. He appeared to have a habit of looking down when he walked, for he had round shoulders. Yuki only had a moment to look at him, but he noticed that the man had high cheekbones and that his face was wrinkled. He ducked as he entered the front door.

There was a considerable difference in their ages. The husband had to be around fifty. And he had three children. Why would a young woman getting married for the first time choose a man like that? Or was it her past that had consigned her to such a marriage? Such were the thoughts that crossed the detective's mind.

When the maid brought his dinner in to him, Yuki sounded her out. "I've been staring out the window all day killing time. The woman in the house over there with the cosmos sure works hard, doesn't she?"

"Shame on you! So you've set your sights on the lady across the street, have you?" The maid laughed. "She *is* a good wife, isn't she? Especially for a second wife. Good looking and good natured. Maybe I shouldn't say this, but she's really too good for that Yokokawa."

"Why do you say that?" Yuki immediately asked her.

"Why, he's forty-eight—twenty years older than her! A real tightwad, too. They say he holds the purse strings in the family. Gives her a hundred yen each morning before he leaves for the bank. When she first moved in, there was a lock on the rice bin. Supposedly he'd measure her out a certain amount for meals each day. They say he himself drinks saké in the evenings, but he's never once let his wife go to a movie."

"They can't be very happily married, then, can they?"

"She's so good natured they never quarrel. And she really loves the stepchildren. You won't find many women like that."

3

Yokokawa left for the bank at 8:20 the next morning, his tall, gaunt form hunched over as he walked. Yuki caught a glimpse of his profile: With its knitted eyebrows and deeply chiseled wrinkles, it was the face of a difficult man.

Sadako came out to the gate and paused there a moment as she saw him off. The morning sun seemed to bleach her face white. Was it the detective's imagination that she looked tired? She seemed so dispassionate that he could hardly believe she had had anything to do with Ishii. The two school-age children had already left.

She began to clean the house—the rooms, the corridor, the entrance, the garden. It took a full two hours. Perhaps her miserly husband was a stickler for cleanliness, too. Still, all things considered, it was as peaceful a household as any.

The mailman came at ten o'clock. After tossing two or three pieces of mail into the mailbox, he continued on his way. Would one of them destroy the family's tranquillity? The white corner of a letter protruded from the mailbox. Yuki's curiosity was aroused, but he could not check the contents of the mailbox without permission. He would need a search warrant.

Just how would Ishii go about getting in touch with her? By letter? By telegram? By messenger? There was no telephone in the house. Would he summon

Sadako to a nearby phone? Or would he visit her in person? Yuki formed a number of hypotheses in his mind.

While tidying up the garden, Sadako came over to the mailbox and removed its contents. She stood there a moment, looking at the return address on a letter. It did not seem to interest her. There was one postcard. Yuki held his breath as Sadako read it intently. When she had finished, she went back inside the house. Nothing appeared to be wrong. She began hanging up the wash. Apparently the card was not from Ishii.

Then she knitted. The youngest child, who had been playing outside, came home. The other two children got back from school about one o'clock. Lunch. Sadako was out of sight as she cleaned up after the meal. At four o'clock she emerged again, shopping basket in hand, and left for the market. Definitely not in high spirits. She returned about forty minutes later and went inside the house, no doubt to prepare dinner. Shortly before six her tall, stoop-shouldered husband got home from work. He was looking as difficult as usual.

The sun went down. An orange light shone brightly on the shōji. A radio was on. Perhaps it belonged to a neighbor. From time to time a silhouette moved across the shōji. It was a serene family scene. Yuki felt the melancholy peculiar to travelers as thoughts of his own family back in Tokyo flooded his mind.

At about nine o'clock Sadako shut the rain shutters. Apparently this was another of her duties. The house went dark. Yuki could make out the cosmos by the fence. A peaceful if not cheerful family was going to bed. It was the end of another uneventful day.

A new day dawned. At precisely 8:20 Yokokawa left through the gate, his tall form bent forward as he walked. His wife started cleaning. Ten o'clock. Yuki held his breath as the mailman approached. Today, however, he passed by without stopping. Knitting. The children returned from school at two o'clock.

At four Sadako left for the market. Slightly before six the tall man came walking slowly home. Obviously he always got home at this time.

Nothing happened. The end of still another uneventful day.

Yuki stretched out on the floor, lost in thought. He was beginning to have misgivings; perhaps he had been wrong.

He recalled the words of the detectives who had taken issue with his hypothesis: Would a man still be in love with a woman he had parted from three years before, even though she had married? Maybe they were right.

But Ishii had made up his mind to die. There were no other women in his life. He was on the run. Yuki could not discount the possibility that he would come to see this woman.

After all, he told himself, it had only been three days. Ishii must have tens of thousands of yen with him. The victim, in need of cash, had withdrawn a sizable sum from the bank on the very day of the robbery. His two assailants had taken that. Ishii might be holed up somewhere for the time being, but he was sure to try to see Sadako before his money ran out. He knew her address. He had remarked that he had been seeing the woman in his dreams—wasn't that a sign that she still meant something to him? A loser, on the run, Ishii must be longing to bask in the warmth of a woman's affection if only for a few minutes. Yuki was fairly sure his hunch was right. Even so, he was bothered by a lurking fear that he would be proved wrong.

Yuki toyed with the idea of going over to see Sadako when she was alone and explaining the situation to her, but he quickly abandoned that tack. It was highly unlikely that someone in her position would be willing to cooperate with the police. In cases like this, it was not unusual for the woman to help the criminal escape.

Morning again. At 8:20 her husband left for work. Cleaning. Once again the mailman passed the house by. Knitting. The wash. Shopping. A little before six her husband came home. By now it was a familiar routine. Perhaps their life was peaceful and uneventful precisely because it was so humdrum. At any rate, it wouldn't be long before Ishii showed up and threw their world out of kilter.

The fourth day passed uneventfully.

On the fifth day, too, her husband left for work right on time, and Sadako monotonously did the cleaning, the wash, and the knitting. Convinced that it was the lull before the storm, Yuki was barely able to control his anxiety.

The weather was beautiful. The sun shone brightly on the little-traveled street. It was a lackluster, sleepy sort of town with thatch-roofed houses here and there along its streets. On the road below Yuki's window a couple of townspeople stood chatting. A post office employee rode up on a bicycle and visited several houses to collect post office life-insurance premiums. Next a man wearing a suit and toting a briefcase went from door to door. Probably collecting money or selling something. He visited the Yokokawa house as well. If he was a salesman, he didn't stand a chance. Sadako, given a mere hundred yen a day by her stingy husband, was in no position to buy anything. Sure enough, the man left almost immediately. He strolled on down the street and turned the corner.

Three boys walked past, talking loudly. Because they spoke in the local dialect, Yuki could not catch much of what they were saying, but he was struck by the singsong intonation of their speech. Someone would pass by every twenty minutes or so.

It was so monotonous that the detective's eyelids began to grow heavy.

Sadako came out. She was wearing a white smock, but Yuki noticed that her skirt was not the usual color. She had changed her sweater, too. He looked down at his wristwatch: 10:50. It was unlikely that she was on her way to the market. It was too early for that.

Yuki rushed down the stairs. He paid for each night's lodging in advance so that he could leave the inn at a moment's notice.

It was Ishii, he thought. In the detective's mind flashed the image of the man in the suit, the money collector or salesman who had just left.

4

By the time Yuki stepped into the street, Sadako was out of sight. He set off at a fast clip, confident that he would soon overtake her.

He was wrong. The road branched in three directions. Along the road to the right he could see the marketplace. Having seen Sadako leave for the market wearing a smock each afternoon, Yuki automatically associated the smock with the market. Without a moment's hesitation he took the road to the right.

In the market, there were a number of narrow roads lined with shops. Women milled about, some in white smocks. Yuki searched frantically, but there was no sign of Sadako.

Upset, he stopped someone and asked the way to the station. The directions were hard to understand.

When the detective finally reached the station, he instinctively made his way to the timetable. It was now 11:20. The last upbound train had left an hour ago. He was relieved. Slowly he walked around the station, checking out the waiting room and elsewhere: no sign of her. Except for some children playing, the waiting room was empty. The next train was not due for another hour.

Yuki walked out to the square in front of the station. A flock of pigeons was gathered there in a patch of sunlight. He stuck a cigarette in his mouth.

A bus arrived, disgorged its passengers, and sped off. As Yuki followed it with his eyes, he noticed a bus terminal across the way with three buses lined up. The buses were white, with a neat red stripe down the side.

Why hadn't it occurred to him? Yuki hurried over to the terminal.

Lines of people waited to board the buses. The detective quickly ran his eyes over the crowd. She wasn't there. He walked over to the ticket booth, a sleek glass cubicle. Three or four conductors and drivers sat next to it chatting. Yuki produced one of his cards. "What's the destination of the bus that just left?"

"Shirasaki," answered a man who appeared to be the conductors' supervisor. Looking at the card, he stiffened slightly as he spoke.

"Did a woman wearing a smock get on?" Actually the detective was not at all sure that she would still have had the smock on.

"Hmm . . ." The supervisor walked over to where the conductors were sitting to ask. The ticket seller hadn't noticed.

The supervisor returned with a woman conductor in tow. Yuki could tell from her expression what her answer would be.

"Yes, I saw a woman wearing a smock get on the bus that just left for Shirasaki. But the person with her made her take it off," the woman said.

"The person with her? Was it a man or a woman?" He fixed her with a sharp gaze.

"It was a man."

"What did he look like?"

"Well, I didn't pay that much attention to him. I think he was around thirty. He had on a suit—navy blue, I think."

"Right, a navy blue suit. And he was carrying a briefcase, right?"

"Yes, he was. Not black—brown."

Right.

"You wouldn't happen to know how far they were going?"

She didn't.

"What time does the bus reach the end of the line?"

"Twelve forty-five."

Yuki looked at his watch. It was five to twelve. If he hired a car and told the driver to step on it, he might be able to overtake the bus before it reached Shirasaki.

Returning to the station, Yuki got into a taxi. He told the driver to follow the bus route to Shirasaki.

It was a wide, well-surfaced road. Once outside the city, rice fields opened up on either side, and mountains could be seen in the distance. The road was lined with sumac, their leaves a gorgeous red.

Before long the plain narrowed, and the road began to climb into the foothills. The woods were filled with the red of sumac. They passed several villages. Finally they arrived in the small town of Shirasaki. The bus was already parked there, and its driver and conductor were resting nearby. The passengers had disembarked and were nowhere in sight.

Yuki approached the driver and conductor. "You had a couple on your bus, a man about thirty with a navy blue suit and a brown briefcase, and a woman twenty-seven or twenty-eight. Do you remember where you let them off?"

"He must mean them," the driver said to the conductor, tossing his cigarette on the ground. The conductor, a young woman, nodded.

"They got off at Kusakari. It's five stops back." She explained that the reason they remembered was that someone on the bus had noticed the couple heading up the road for a hot spring in the mountains instead of toward the village and had broken up the bus with a lewd remark. She added that there was a bus that went directly to the hot spring from S City but that you could get there by coming over the mountain, too.

Yuki went over to the post office and wired the S police station for assistance.

5

The road climbed gently into the hills. Fallen leaves were piled high on both sides. Maples added a splash of scarlet to the forest's creamy yellow.

Yuki walked up the road. Now that he knew the couple's destination, there was no need to hurry. They had walked up the road, so he would do the same. After all, he had no way of knowing where he might run into them. Anyway, simply knowing where they were headed put his mind at ease.

According to his watch it was one thirty. Autumn sun or not, he was sweating as he made his way up the mountain road. He encountered no other people. The cries of the shrikes were piercing.

Cedars and Japanese cypress were plentiful, together with *shide* and camellia trees and various grasses. A mountain wisteria had entwined itself around a huge camphor tree. High in the tree's branches hung an *akebi* vine.

At the unfamiliar sound of a crow's cry, Yuki looked up and saw a flock of birds hopping about in the branches of the trees. He saw that they were Korean magpies, not crows.

As he neared the top of the hill, the view unfolded around him. In the distance behind him lay the plain. The rice had been harvested, and the fields had turned dark. Scattered over the fields were stacks of bundled rice.

By the road stood a signboard that read "Kawakita Hot Spring." Below that were the names of three inns: Hishūya, Yūunkan, and Matsu'urakan. Yuki paused a moment to consider which of the inns the two would have chosen.

The road began to go downhill. He was in the midst of rolling hills. The pampas grass sparkled in disarray. Tall mountains were so close one could make out the furrows on their slopes.

Suddenly a shot rang out. The sound tore through the clear mountain air, reverberating in the forest and hills.

Yuki jumped, "Damn!" he blurted out without thinking. He turned in the direction of the shot, but his feet refused to move. For some reason he expected to hear a second shot. It did not come. Started, the birds flew off as one.

Since when did Ishii have a gun? Certainly he would not have had much trouble buying one with all the money he carried. Yuki felt foolish for having overlooked this possibility.

But which of the two had the muzzle been pointed at? At the woman? At Ishii himself? The reason Yuki had immediately expected to hear a second report was that he imagined that after killing the woman Ishii would aim the gun at his own chest and pull the trigger. With just one shot, however, the detective had no way of knowing which of the two had been shot.

Yuki left the road he had been following and began walking down a path. Ahead of him was a thick growth of dead shrubbery and a grove of bare trees of various kinds. He was pretty sure the shot had come from inside the grove.

Just then he heard footsteps coming toward him. He tried to hide in the shrubbery, but before he could do so, a setter came bounding toward him. When the animal saw him, it stopped and began barking. Someone called to the dog. A moment later a figure emerged from the grove. It was a middle-aged man in a leather hunting outfit. He had a gun slung over his shoulder.

"Sorry about that." The man in the hunting suit scolded his dog.

Yuki breathed a sigh of relief. As the hunter began to walk away, the detective called after him. "Excuse me. Did you happen to see a man and woman? The man was wearing a navy blue suit and carrying a briefcase."

The man eyed Yuki suspiciously.

"It's all right, I'm a policeman."

With that, the man nodded. "Yes, I saw them. They were walking by the edge of the grove. The fellow was dressed just like you said."

Yuki thanked the man, who silently walked off leading his dog. He hurried through to the other side of the grove. The couple were not there.

Yuki thought it curious that he had expected to hear two shots. Granted, he had been afraid that Ishii would kill himself. But the thought of his committing double suicide with a lover had never entered Yuki's mind. The possibility had dawned on him only as he found himself waiting for a second shot.

Now that he thought about it, there was indeed a distinct possibility that Ishii would commit double suicide. Having resigned himself to the thought of dying, he might very well want a woman to accompany him to the other world. By no means was it far-fetched to assume that Sadako would be the woman he chose. Yuki felt he had no choice but to modify his theory that Ishii had come merely to say goodbye to the woman.

There were several farmhouses near the spot where Yuki emerged from the grove. An old lady with a child on her back was standing nearby, eyeing him dubiously. He asked her if she had seen the couple. "They went that way," she said, pointing.

The road they had taken led deeper into the forest. When Yuki finally emerged from the trees, the road started up a gently sloping hill. The hill was covered with bare trees, which obstructed his view. He would not have been surprised to see a rabbit dart across the road.

Voices could be heard approaching. It was three village boys carrying firewood on their backs.

"They were walking by the reservoir," the boys told Yuki.

A reservoir! Yuki's heart skipped a beat. He hurried down a path in the direction the boys had indicated.

Finally he spied the couple in the distance. They sat on the bank of what must be the reservoir, though he could not see the water, beneath the outstretched limbs of some sumac trees ablaze with autumn tints. The navy blue of the man's suit and the orange of the woman's sweater merged in a single blob of color.

Taking care not to be seen, Yuki inched closer to them, sinking down into the tall, dry grass. The voices of the pair did not carry that far.

The woman's body lay languidly across the man's knees. Again and again he pressed his face down on hers. Laughing, she encircled his neck with her arms.

The woman in Sadako had come alive. No longer was she the tired, unemotional housewife. At that moment she was free of her bonds—the stingy, disagreeable husband who was twenty years her senior, her three stepchildren. She clung to Ishii, oblivious to everything else.

Yuki lay back in the grass and looked up at the sky. It was a clear blue sky dotted with small clouds. Since he could not have a cigarette, he contented himself with savoring the fragrance of the fallen leaves.

After several minutes he lifted his head. The two were standing. The woman had gone around behind the man and was picking grass off his suit. Then she took out a comb and began combing his hair.

They began walking. The woman carried the man's brown briefcase in one hand. Her other arm was entwined in his. She leaned against him as she walked.

This was not the tired-looking Sadako that Yuki had been observing for five days. She was a different person altogether. It was as if someone had breathed new life into her. She was bursting with vitality. She was a woman aflame.

In the end, Yuki was unable to approach Ishii. Something held him back.

6

The Kawakita Hot Spring was a small mountain resort with just four or five inns. The stream to its rear was the source of the river that flowed through S City. The bus route direct from S City to the resort ran along this river. Yuki stood by the side of the road and stared at the river while he smoked a cigarette. If he tired of the view, he decided, he would sit down and take out his book of poetry.

An old jeep approached from the direction of S City. Yuki raised his hand. A half-dozen detectives from the S police station got out of the jeep.

"Thanks for coming," Yuki said to the men.

"You must be Detective Yuki. Sorry it took us so long to get here. Where's our man?" The detective who spoke was the oldest in the group, a man with big eyes. Yuki pointed to the inn in front of them. "Here. They just went inside." The sign in front of the inn read "Matsu'urakan."

"Shall we take him now?"

"He'll be in the bath now. There's a woman with him."

"Living it up, eh—some nerve." The other detectives laughed.

"She's not involved. And she's not his mistress. Leave her to me." Looking puzzled, the detectives remained silent.

The men took up their positions, two in front of the inn and two in back, near the stream.

Yuki and two other detectives went inside. The detective with big eyes whispered something in the ear of the man at the front desk. Visibly shaken, the man stood up immediately and quietly asked them to follow him. The maids, sensing something out of the ordinary, looked uneasy as they watched the group leave the desk.

They entered a room.

"He's in the bath now," the manager explained. "The woman is in the women's bath."

The brown briefcase sat in the decorative alcove beneath an inexpensive hanging scroll. Yuki picked it up and handed it to the detectives without opening it. A navy blue suit hung in the closet. Yuki quickly emptied its pockets of their contents and wrapped them in a handkerchief, which he also gave to the detectives. He found no weapons. He then left the room and walked down a well-polished corridor toward the bath.

From the opposite direction approached a man of about thirty. He was wearing the padded kimono the inn provided for guests, and he carried a towel. The hall was too narrow for two people to pass abreast. Yuki pressed his back against the wall to let the man by. Apparently taking the detective for an employee of the inn, the man nonchalantly started to walk past. His hair was neatly parted, and steam rose from his face.

"Ishii." The detective called his name. The man whirled around in surprise. Yuki grabbed one of his wrists. "Ishii Kyūichi. That's right, isn't it?" Even before he had finished uttering the words, he had snapped a pair of handcuffs on the man's wrists. For an instant it looked as though Ishii would put up a fight, but instead he merely dropped his head.

"Here, I've got a warrant for your arrest."

"I see," muttered Ishii without bothering to look at the document in the detective's hand. Steam was still rising from his now-ashen face. Yuki held Ishii close to him as the two returned to the room.

The detective with big eyes, who was waiting inside, stood up. "Well!"

Yuki had the men take Ishii away. He remained in the room alone. Lighting up a cigarette, he gazed at the scroll in the alcove for a while, then glanced at his watch: 4:50. It would be more than an hour before Sadako's tall, stoop-shouldered, beetle-brewed husband came plodding home.

The door of the room slid open. It was Sadako. She was surprised to see a strange man sitting there; she seemed to think she had the wrong room. In the inn's kimono she looked like a different person still, this one warm and voluptuous.

"Ma'am," said Yuki. Sadako's expression changed. He handed her his card.

"We had Ishii accompany us to the police station. Why don't you take the bus back home right now. If you leave right away, you'll be back before your husband gets home."

Unable to speak, Sadako stood rooted to the spot, her eyes fixed straight ahead. She was breathing heavily.

It would take her a while to change her clothes, Yuki thought. He turned his back on her and opened the shōji.

As he stared at the stream below, thoughts flowed through his mind: For a few brief hours this woman has truly lived. Tonight she will return to her round-shouldered, stingy husband and her three stepchildren. And tomorrow, as she sits at the knitting machine, her face will offer no hint of the passion that smolders in her breast.

MISHIMA YUKIO

Mishima Yukio (1925–1970) is one of Japan's best-known and most widely translated postwar authors. A prolific writer, Mishima produced many novels, plays, and essays, many of them available in translation in a number of European languages. Mishima's interest in the physical body and right-wing politics continued until his death by suicide in 1970. Accordingly, many of these concerns are reflected in his short story "Patriotism" (Yūkoku, 1960), which was filmed, with Mishima playing the leading role.

PATRIOTISM (YŪKOKU)

Translated by Geoffrey W. Sargent

1

On the twenty-eighth of February, 1936 (on the third day, that is, of the February 26 Incident), Lieutenant Shinji Takeyama of the Konoe Transport Battalion—profoundly disturbed by the knowledge that his closest colleagues had been with the mutineers from the beginning, and indignant at the imminent prospect of Imperial troops attacking Imperial troops—took his officer's sword and ceremonially disemboweled himself in the eight-mat room of his private residence in the sixth block of Aoba-chō, in Yotsuya Ward. His wife, Reiko, followed him, stabbing herself to death. The lieutenant's farewell note consisted of one sentence: "Long live the Imperial Forces." His wife's, after apologies for her unfilial conduct in thus preceding her parents to the grave, concluded: "The day which, for a soldier's wife, had to come, has come. . . ." The last moments of this heroic and dedicated couple were such as to make the gods themselves weep. The lieutenant's age, it should be noted, was thirty-one, his wife's twenty-three; and it was not half a year since the celebration of their marriage.

2

Those who saw the bride and bridegroom in the commemorative photograph—perhaps no less than those actually present at the lieutenant's wedding—had exclaimed in wonder at the bearing of this handsome couple. The lieutenant, majestic in military uniform, stood protectively beside his bride, his right hand resting upon his sword, his officer's cap held at his left side. His expression was severe, and his dark brows and wide-gazing eyes well conveyed the clear integrity of youth. For the beauty of the bride in her white over-robe no comparisons were adequate. In the eyes, round beneath soft brows, in the slender, finely shaped nose, and in the full lips, there was both sensuousness and refinement.

One hand, emerging shyly from a sleeve of the over-robe, held a fan, and the tips of the fingers, clustering delicately, were like the bud of a moonflower.

After the suicide, people would take out this photograph and examine it, and sadly reflect that too often there was a curse on these seemingly flawless unions. Perhaps it was no more than imagination, but looking at the picture after the tragedy it almost seemed as if the two young people before the gold-lacquered screen were gazing, each with equal clarity, at the deaths which lay before them.

Thanks to the good offices of their go-between, Lieutenant General Ozeki, they had been able to set themselves up in a new home at Aoba-chō in Yotsuya. "New home" is perhaps misleading. It was an old three-room rented house backing onto a small garden. As neither the six- nor the four-and-a-half-mat room downstairs was favored by the sun, they used the upstairs eight-mat room as both bedroom and guest room. There was no maid, so Reiko was left alone to guard the house in her husband's absence.

The honeymoon trip was dispensed with on the grounds that these were times of national emergency. The two of them had spent the first night of their marriage at this house. Before going to bed, Shinji, sitting erect on the floor with his sword laid before him, had bestowed upon his wife a soldierly lecture. A woman who had become the wife of a soldier should know and resolutely accept that her husband's death might come at any moment. It could be tomorrow. It could be the day after. But, no matter when it came—he asked—was she steadfast in her resolve to accept it? Reiko rose to her feet, pulled open a drawer of the cabinet, and took out what was the most prized of her new possessions, the dagger her mother had given her. Returning to her place, she laid the dagger without a word on the mat before her, just as her husband had laid his sword. A silent understanding was achieved at once, and the lieutenant never again sought to test his wife's resolve.

In the first few months of her marriage Reiko's beauty grew daily more radiant, shining serene like the moon after rain.

As both were possessed of young, vigorous bodies, their relationship was passionate. Nor was this merely a matter of the night. On more than one occasion, returning home straight from maneuvers, and begrudging even the time it took to remove his mud-splashed uniform, the lieutenant had pushed his wife to the floor almost as soon as he had entered the house. Reiko was equally ardent in her response. For a little more or a little less than a month, from the first night of their marriage Reiko knew happiness, and the lieutenant, seeing this, was happy too.

Reiko's body was white and pure, and her swelling breasts conveyed a firm and chaste refusal; but, upon consent, those breasts were lavish with their intimate, welcoming warmth. Even in bed these two were frighteningly and awesomely serious. In the very midst of wild, intoxicating passions, their hearts were sober and serious.

By day the lieutenant would think of his wife in the brief rest periods between training; and all day long, at home, Reiko would recall the image of her husband. Even when apart, however, they had only to look at the wedding photograph for their happiness to be once more confirmed. Reiko felt not the slightest surprise that a man who had been a complete stranger until a few months ago should now have become the sun about which her whole world revolved.

All these things had a moral basis, and were in accordance with the Education Rescript's injunction that "husband and wife should be harmonious." Not once did Reiko contradict her husband, nor did the lieutenant ever find reason to scold his wife. On the god shelf below the stairway, alongside the tablet from the Great Ise Shrine, were set photographs of their Imperial Majesties, and regularly every morning, before leaving for duty, the lieutenant would stand with his wife at this hallowed place and together they would bow their heads low. The offering water was renewed each morning, and the sacred sprig of *sasaki* was always green and fresh. Their lives were lived beneath the solemn protection of the gods and were filled with an intense happiness which set every fiber in their bodies trembling.

3

Although Lord Privy Seal Saitō's house was in their neighborhood, neither of them heard any noise of gunfire on the morning of February 26. It was a bugle, sounding muster in the dim, snowy dawn, when the ten-minute tragedy had already ended, which first disrupted the lieutenant's slumbers. Leaping at once from his bed, and without speaking a word, the lieutenant donned his uniform, buckled on the sword held ready for him by his wife, and hurried swiftly out into the snow-covered streets of the still darkened morning. He did not return until the evening of the twenty-eighth.

Later, from the radio news, Reiko learned the full extent of this sudden eruption of violence. Her life throughout the subsequent two days was lived alone, in complete tranquillity, and behind locked doors.

In the lieutenant's face, as he hurried silently out into the snowy morning, Reiko had read the determination to die. If her husband did not return, her own decision was made: she too would die. Quietly she attended to the disposition of her personal possessions. She chose her sets of visiting kimonos as keepsakes for friends of her schooldays, and she wrote a name and address on the stiff paper wrapping in which each was folded. Constantly admonished by her husband never to think of the morrow, Reiko had not even kept a diary and was now denied the pleasure of assiduously rereading her record of the happiness of the past few months and consigning each page to the fire as she did so. Ranged across the top of the radio were a small china dog, a rabbit, a squirrel, a bear, and a fox. There were also a small vase and a water pitcher. These comprised Reiko's one and only collection. But it would hardly do, she imagined, to give such things as keepsakes. Nor again would it be quite proper to ask specifically for them to be included in the coffin. It seemed to Reiko, as these thoughts passed through her mind, that the expressions on the small animals' faces grew even more lost and forlorn.

Reiko took the squirrel in her hand and looked at it. And then, her thoughts turning to a realm far beyond these childlike affections, she gazed up into the distance at the great sunlike principle which her husband embodied. She was ready, and happy, to he hurtled along to her destruction in that gleaming sun chariot—but now, for these few moments of solitude, she allowed herself to luxuriate in this innocent attachment to trifles. The time when she had genuinely loved these things, however, was long past. Now she merely loved the memory of having once loved them, and their place in her heart had been filled by more intense passions, by a more frenzied happiness. . . . For Reiko had never, even to herself, thought of those soaring joys of the flesh as a mere pleasure. The February cold, and the icy touch of the china squirrel, had numbed Reiko's slender fingers; yet, even so, in her lower limbs, beneath the ordered repetition of the pattern which crossed the skirt of her trim *meisen* kimono, she could feel now, as she thought of the lieutenant's powerful arms reaching out toward her, a hot moistness of the flesh which defied the snows.

She was not in the least afraid of the death hovering in her mind. Waiting alone at home, Reiko firmly believed that everything her husband was feeling or thinking now, his anguish and distress, was leading her—just as surely as the power in his flesh—to a welcome death. She felt as if her body could melt away with ease and be transformed to the merest fraction of her husband's thought.

Listening to the frequent announcements on the radio, she heard the names of several of her husband's colleagues mentioned among those of the insurgents. This was news of death. She followed the developments closely, wondering anxiously, as the situation became daily more irrevocable, why no Imperial ordinance was sent down, and watching what had at first been taken as a movement to restore the nation's honor come gradually to be branded with the infamous name of mutiny. There was no communication from the regiment. At any moment, it seemed, fighting might commence in the city streets, where the remains of the snow still lay.

Toward sundown on the twenty-eighth Reiko was startled by a furious pounding on the front door. She hurried downstairs. As she pulled with fumbling fingers at the bolt, the shape dimly outlined beyond the frosted-glass panel made no sound, but she knew it was her husband. Reiko had never known the bolt on the sliding door to be so stiff. Still it resisted. The door just would not open.

In a moment, almost before she knew she had succeeded, the lieutenant was standing before her on the cement floor inside the porch, muffled in a khaki greatcoat, his top boots heavy with slush from the street. Closing the door behind him, he returned the bolt once more to its socket. With what significance, Reiko did not understand.

"Welcome home."

Reiko bowed deeply, but her husband made no response. As he had already unfastened his sword and was about to remove his greatcoat, Reiko moved around behind to assist. The coat, which was cold and damp and had lost the odor of horse dung it normally exuded when exposed to the sun, weighed heavily upon her arm. Draping it across a hanger, and cradling the sword and leather belt in her sleeves, she waited while her husband removed his top boots and then followed behind him into the "living room." This was the six-mat room downstairs.

Seen in the clear light from the lamp, her husband's face, covered with a heavy growth of bristle, was almost unrecognizably wasted and thin. The cheeks were hollow, their luster and resilience gone. In his normal good spirits he would have changed into old clothes as soon as he was home and have pressed her to get supper at once, but now he sat before the table still in his uniform, his head drooping dejectedly. Reiko refrained from asking whether she should prepare the supper.

After an interval the lieutenant spoke.

"I knew nothing. They hadn't asked me to join. Perhaps out of consideration, because I was newly married. Kanō, and Homma too, and Yamaguchi."

Reiko recalled momentarily the faces of high-spirited young officers, friends of her husband, who had come to the house occasionally as guests.

"There may be an Imperial ordinance sent down tomorrow. They'll be posted as rebels, I imagine. I shall be in command of a unit with orders to attack them. I can't do it. It's impossible to do a thing like that."

He spoke again.

"They've taken me off guard duty, and I have permission to return home for one night. Tomorrow morning, without question, I must leave to join the attack. I can't do it, Reiko."

Reiko sat erect with lowered eyes. She understood clearly that her husband had spoken of his death. The lieutenant was resolved. Each word, being rooted in death, emerged sharply and with powerful significance against this dark, unmovable background. Although the lieutenant was speaking of his dilemma, already there was no room in his mind for vacillation.

However, there was a clarity, like the clarity of a stream fed from melting snows, in the silence which rested between them. Sitting in his own home after the long two-day ordeal, and looking across at the face of his beautiful wife, the lieutenant was for the first time experiencing true peace of mind. For he had at once known, though she said nothing, that his wife divined the resolve which lay beneath his words.

"Well, then . . ." The lieutenant's eyes opened wide. Despite his exhaustion they were strong and clear, and now for the first time they looked straight into the eyes of his wife. "Tonight I shall cut my stomach."

Reiko did not flinch.

Her round eyes showed tension, as taut as the clang of a bell.

"I am ready," she said. "I ask permission to accompany you."

The lieutenant felt almost mesmerized by the strength in those eyes. His words flowed swiftly and easily, like the utterances of a man in delirium, and it was beyond his understanding how permission in a matter of such weight could be expressed so casually.

"Good. We'll go together. But I want you as a witness, first, for my own suicide. Agreed?"

When this was said a sudden release of abundant happiness welled up in both their hearts. Reiko was deeply affected by the greatness of her husband's trust in her. It was vital for the lieutenant, whatever else might happen, that there should be no irregularity in his death. For that reason there had to be a witness. The fact that he had chosen his wife for this was the first mark of his trust. The second, and even greater mark, was that though he had pledged that they should die together he did not intend to kill his wife first—he had deferred her death to a time when he would no longer be there to verify it. If the lieutenant had been a suspicious husband, he would doubtless, as in the usual suicide pact, have chosen to kill his wife first.

When Reiko said, "I ask permission to accompany you," the lieutenant felt these words to be the final fruit of the education which he had himself given his wife, starting on the first night of their marriage, and which had schooled her, when the moment came, to say what had to be said without a shadow of hesitation. This flattered the lieutenant's opinion of himself as a self-reliant man. He was not so romantic or conceited as to imagine that the words were spoken spontaneously, out of love for her husband.

With happiness welling almost too abundantly in their hearts, they could not help smiling at each other. Reiko felt as if she had returned to her wedding night.

Before her eyes was neither pain nor death. She seemed to see only a free and limitless expanse opening out into vast distances.

"The water is hot. Will you take your bath now?"

"Ah yes, of course."

"And supper . . . ?"

The words were delivered in such level, domestic tones that the lieutenant came near to thinking, for the fraction of a second, that everything had been a hallucination.

"I don't think we'll need supper. But perhaps you could warm some saké?"

"As you wish."

As Reiko rose and took a *tanzen* gown from the cabinet for after the bath, she purposely directed her husband's attention to the opened drawer. The lieutenant rose, crossed to the cabinet, and looked inside. From the ordered array of paper wrappings he read, one by one, the addresses of the keepsakes. There was no grief in the lieutenant's response to this demonstration of heroic resolve. His heart was filled with tenderness. Like a husband who is proudly shown the childish purchases of a young wife, the lieutenant, overwhelmed by affection, lovingly embraced his wife from behind and implanted a kiss upon her neck.

Reiko felt the roughness of the lieutenant's unshaven skin against her neck. This sensation, more than being just a thing of this world, was for Reiko almost the world itself, but now—with the feeling that it was soon to be lost forever—it had freshness beyond all her experience. Each moment had its own vital strength, and the senses in every corner of her body were reawakened. Accepting her husband's caresses from behind, Reiko raised herself on the tips of her toes, letting the vitality seep through her entire body.

"First the bath, and then, after some saké . . . lay out the bedding upstairs, will you?"

The lieutenant whispered the words into his wife's ear. Reiko silently nodded.

Flinging off his uniform, the lieutenant went to the bath. To faint background noises of slopping water Reiko tended the charcoal brazier in the living room and began the preparations for warming the saké.

Taking the *tanzen*, a sash, and some underclothes, she went to the bathroom to ask how the water was. In the midst of a coiling cloud of steam the lieutenant was sitting cross-legged on the floor, shaving, and she could dimly discern the rippling movements of the muscles on his damp, powerful back as they responded to the movement of his arms.

There was nothing to suggest a time of any special significance. Reiko, going busily about her tasks, was preparing side dishes from odds and ends in stock. Her hands did not tremble. If anything, she managed even more efficiently and smoothly than usual. From time to time, it is true, there was a strange throbbing deep within her breast. Like distant lightning, it had a moment of sharp intensity and then vanished without trace. Apart from that, nothing was in any way out of the ordinary.

The lieutenant, shaving in the bathroom, felt his warmed body miraculously healed at last of the desperate tiredness of the days of indecision and filled—in spite of the death which lay ahead—with pleasurable anticipation. The sound of his wife going about her work came to him faintly. A healthy physical craving, submerged for two days, reasserted itself.

The lieutenant was confident there had been no impurity in that joy they had experienced when resolving upon death. They had both sensed at that moment—though not, of course, in any clear and conscious way—that those permissible pleasures which they shared in private were once more beneath the protection of Righteousness and Divine Power, and of a complete and unassailable morality. On looking into each other's eyes and discovering there an honorable death, they had felt themselves safe once more behind steel walls which none could destroy, encased in an impenetrable armor of Beauty and Truth. Thus, so far from seeing any inconsistency or conflict between the urges of his flesh and the sincerity of his patriotism, the lieutenant was even able to regard the two as parts of the same thing.

Thrusting his face close to the dark, cracked, misted wall mirror, the lieutenant shaved himself with great care. This would be his death face. There must be no unsightly blemishes. The clean-shaven face gleamed once more with a youthful luster, seeming to brighten the darkness of the mirror. There was a certain elegance, he even felt, in the association of death with this radiantly healthy face.

Just as it looked now, this would become his death face! Already, in fact, it had half departed from the lieutenant's personal possession and had become the bust above a dead soldier's memorial. As an experiment he closed his eyes tight. Everything was wrapped in blackness, and he was no longer a living, seeing creature.

Returning from the bath, the traces of the shave glowing faintly blue beneath his smooth cheeks, he seated himself beside the now well-kindled charcoal brazier. Busy though Reiko was, he noticed, she had found time lightly to touch up her face. Her cheeks were gay and her lips moist. There was no shadow of sadness to be seen. Truly, the lieutenant felt, as he saw this mark of his young wife's passionate nature, he had chosen the wife he ought to have chosen.

As soon as the lieutenant had drained his saké cup he offered it to Reiko. Reiko had never before tasted saké, but she accepted without hesitation and sipped timidly.

"Come here," the lieutenant said.

Reiko moved to her husband's side and was embraced as she leaned backward across his lap. Her breast was in violent commotion, as if sadness, joy, and the potent saké were mingling and reacting within her. The lieutenant looked down into his wife's face. It was the last face he would see in this world, the last face he would see of his wife. The lieutenant scrutinized the face minutely, with the eyes of a traveler bidding farewell to splendid vistas which he will never revisit. It was a face he could not tire of looking at—the features regular yet not cold, the lips lightly closed with a soft strength. The lieutenant kissed those lips, unthinkingly. And suddenly, though there was not the slightest distortion of the face into the unsightliness of sobbing, he noticed that tears were welling slowly from beneath the long lashes of the closed eyes and brimming over into a glistening stream.

When, a little later, the lieutenant urged that they should move to the upstairs bedroom, his wife replied that she would follow after taking a bath. Climbing the stairs alone to the bedroom, where the air was already warmed by the gas heater, the lieutenant lay down on the bedding with arms outstretched and legs apart. Even the time at which he lay waiting for his wife to join him was no later and no earlier than usual.

He folded his hands beneath his head and gazed at the dark boards of the ceiling in the dimness beyond the range of the standard lamp. Was it death he was now waiting for? Or a wild ecstasy of the senses? The two seemed to overlap, almost as if the object of this bodily desire was death itself. But, however that might be, it was certain that never before had the lieutenant tasted such total freedom.

There was the sound of a car outside the window. He could hear the screech of its tires skidding in the snow piled at the side of the street. The sound of its horn re-echoed from near-by walls. . . . Listening to these noises he had the feeling that this house rose like a solitary island in the ocean of a society going as restlessly about its business as ever. All around, vastly and untidily, stretched the country for which he grieved. He was to give his life for it. But would that great country, with which he was prepared to remonstrate to the extent of destroying himself, take the slightest heed of his death? He did not know; and it did not matter. His was a battlefield without glory, a battlefield where none could display deeds of valor: it was the front line of the spirit.

Reiko's footsteps sounded on the stairway. The steep stairs in this old house creaked badly. There were fond memories in that creaking, and many a time, while waiting in bed, the lieutenant had listened to its welcome sound. At the thought that he would hear it no more he listened with intense concentration, striving for every corner of every moment of this precious time to be filled with the sound of those soft footfalls on the creaking stairway. The moments seemed transformed to jewels, sparkling with inner light.

Reiko wore a Nagoya sash about the waist of her *yukata*, but as the lieutenant reached toward it, its redness sobered by the dimness of the light, Reiko's hand moved to his assistance and the sash fell away, slithering swiftly to the floor. As she stood before him, still in her *yukata*, the lieutenant inserted his hands through the side slits beneath each sleeve, intending to embrace her as she was; but at the touch of his finger tips upon the warm naked flesh, and as the armpits closed gently about his hands, his whole body was suddenly aflame.

In a few moments the two lay naked before the glowing gas heater.

Neither spoke the thought, but their hearts, their bodies, and their pounding breasts blazed with the knowledge that this was the very last time. It was as if the words "The Last Time" were spelled out, in invisible brushstrokes, across every inch of their bodies.

The lieutenant drew his wife close and kissed her vehemently. As their tongues explored each other's mouths, reaching out into the smooth, moist interior, they felt as if the still-unknown agonies of death had tempered their senses to the keenness of red-hot steel. The agonies they could not yet feel, the distant pains of death, had refined their awareness of pleasure.

"This is the last time I shall see your body," said the lieutenant. "Let me look at it closely." And, tilting the shade on the lampstand to one side, he directed the rays along the full length of Reiko's outstretched form.

Reiko lay still with her eyes closed. The light from the low lamp clearly revealed the majestic sweep of her white flesh. The lieutenant, not without a touch of egocentricity, rejoiced that he would never see this beauty crumble in death.

At his leisure, the lieutenant allowed the unforgettable spectacle to engrave itself upon his mind. With one hand he fondled the hair, with the other he softly stroked the magnificent face, implanting kisses here and there where his eyes lingered. The quiet coldness of the high, tapering forehead, the closed eyes with their long lashes beneath faintly etched brows, the set of the finely shaped nose, the gleam of teeth glimpsed between full, regular lips, the soft cheeks and the small, wise chin . . . these things conjured up in the lieutenant's mind the vision of a truly radiant death face, and again and again he pressed his lips tight against the white throat—where Reiko's own hand was soon to strike—and the throat reddened faintly beneath his kisses. Returning to the mouth he laid his lips against it with the gentlest of pressures, and moved them rhythmically over Reiko's with the light rolling motion of a small boat. If he closed his eyes, the world became a rocking cradle.

Wherever the lieutenant's eyes moved his lips faithfully followed. The high, swelling breasts, surmounted by nipples like the buds of a wild cherry, hardened as the lieutenant's lips closed about them. The arms flowed smoothly downward from each side of the breast, tapering toward the wrists, yet losing nothing of their roundness or symmetry, and at their tips were those delicate fingers which had held the fan at the wedding ceremony. One by one, as the lieutenant kissed them, the fingers withdrew behind their neighbor as if in shame. . . . The natural hollow curving between the bosom and the stomach carried in its lines a suggestion not only of softness but of resilient strength, and while it gave forewarning of the rich curves spreading outward from here to the hips it had, in itself, an appearance only of restraint and proper discipline. The whiteness and richness of the stomach and hips was like milk brimming in a great bowl, and the sharply shadowed dip of the navel could have been the fresh impress of a raindrop, fallen there that very moment. Where the shadows gathered more thickly, hair clustered, gentle and sensitive, and as the agitation mounted in the now no longer passive body there hung over this region a scent like the smoldering of fragrant blossoms, growing steadily more pervasive.

At length, in a tremulous voice, Reiko spoke.

"Show me. . . . Let me look too, for the last time."

Never before had he heard from his wife's lips so strong and unequivocal a request. It was as if something which her modesty had wished to keep hidden to the end had suddenly burst its bonds of constraint. The lieutenant obediently lay back and surrendered himself to his wife. Lithely she raised her white, trembling body, and—burning with an innocent desire to return to her husband what he had done for her—placed two white fingers on the lieutenant's eyes, which gazed fixedly up at her, and gently stroked them shut.

Suddenly overwhelmed by tenderness, her cheeks flushed by a dizzying uprush of emotion, Reiko threw her arms about the lieutenant's close-cropped head. The bristly hairs rubbed painfully against her breast, the prominent nose was cold as it dug into her flesh, and his breath was hot. Relaxing her embrace, she gazed down at her husband's masculine face. The severe brows, the closed eyes, the splendid bridge of the nose, the shapely lips drawn firmly together . . . the blue, clean-shaven cheeks reflecting the light and gleaming smoothly. Reiko kissed each of these. She kissed the broad nape of the neck, the strong, erect shoulders, the powerful chest with its twin circles like shields and its russet nipples. In the armpits, deeply shadowed by the ample flesh of the shoulders and chest, a sweet and melancholy odor emanated from the growth of hair, and in the sweetness of this odor was contained, somehow, the essence of young death. The lieutenant's naked skin glowed like a field of barley, and everywhere the muscles showed in sharp relief, converging on the lower abdomen about the small, unassuming navel. Gazing at the youthful, firm stomach, modestly covered by a vigorous growth of hair, Reiko thought of it as it was soon to be, cruelly cut by the sword, and she laid her head upon it, sobbing in pity, and bathed it with kisses.

At the touch of his wife's tears upon his stomach the lieutenant felt ready to endure with courage the cruelest agonies of his suicide.

What ecstasies they experienced after these tender exchanges may well be imagined. The lieutenant raised himself and enfolded his wife in a powerful embrace, her body now limp with exhaustion after her grief and tears. Passionately they held their faces close, rubbing cheek against cheek. Reiko's body was trembling. Their breasts, moist with sweat, were tightly joined, and every inch of the young and beautiful bodies had become so much one with the other that it seemed impossible there should ever again be a separation. Reiko cried out. From the heights they plunged into the abyss, and from the abyss they took wing and soared once more to dizzying heights. The lieutenant panted like the regimental standard-bearer on a route march. . . . As one cycle ended, almost immediately a new wave of passion would be generated, and together—with no trace of fatigue—they would climb again in a single breathless movement to the very summit.

4

When the lieutenant at last turned away, it was not from weariness. For one thing, he was anxious not to undermine the considerable strength he would need in carrying out his suicide. For another, he would have been sorry to mar the sweetness of these last memories by overindulgence.

Since the lieutenant had clearly desisted, Reiko too, with her usual compliance, followed his example. The two lay naked on their backs, with fingers interlaced, staring fixedly at the dark ceiling. The room was warm from the heater, and even when the sweat had ceased to pour from their bodies they felt no cold. Outside, in the hushed night, the sounds of passing traffic had ceased. Even the noises of the trains and streetcars around Yotsuya station did not penetrate this far. After echoing through the region bounded by the moat, they were lost in the heavily wooded park fronting the broad driveway before Akasaka Palace. It was hard to believe in the tension gripping this whole quarter, where the two factions of the bitterly divided Imperial Army now confronted each other, poised for battle.

Savoring the warmth glowing within themselves, they lay still and recalled the ecstasies they had just known. Each moment of the experience was relived. They remembered the taste of kisses which had never wearied, the touch of naked flesh, episode after episode of dizzying bliss. But already, from the dark boards of the ceiling, the face of death was peering down. These joys had been final, and their bodies would never know them again. Not that joy of this intensity—and the same thought had occurred to them both—was ever likely to be re-experienced, even if they should live on to old age.

The feel of their fingers intertwined—this too would soon be lost. Even the wood-grain patterns they now gazed at on the dark ceiling boards would be taken from them. They could feel death edging in, nearer and nearer. There could be no hesitation now. They must have the courage to reach out to death themselves, and to seize it.

"Well, let's make our preparations," said the lieutenant. The note of determination in the words was unmistakable, but at the same time Reiko had never heard her husband's voice so warm and tender.

After they had risen, a variety of tasks awaited them.

The lieutenant, who had never once before helped with the bedding, now cheerfully slid back the door of the closet, lifted the mattress across the room by himself, and stowed it away inside.

Reiko turned off the gas heater and put away the lamp standard. During the lieutenant's absence she had arranged this room carefully, sweeping and dusting it to a fresh cleanness, and now—if one overlooked the rosewood table drawn into one corner—the eight-mat room gave all the appearance of a reception room ready to welcome an important guest.

"We've seen some drinking here, haven't we? With Kano and Homma and Noguchi . . ."

"Yes, they were great drinkers, all of them."

"We'll be meeting them before long, in the other world. They'll tease us, I imagine, when they find I've brought you with me."

Descending the stairs, the lieutenant turned to look back into this calm, clean room, now brightly illuminated by the ceiling lamp. There floated across his mind the faces of the young officers who had drunk there, and laughed, and innocently bragged. He had never dreamed then that he would one day cut open his stomach in this room.

In the two rooms downstairs husband and wife busied themselves smoothly and serenely with their respective preparations. The lieutenant went to the toilet, and then to the bathroom to wash. Meanwhile Reiko folded away her husband's padded robe, placed his uniform tunic, his trousers, and a newly cut bleached loincloth in the bathroom, and set out sheets of paper on the living-room table for the farewell notes. Then she removed the lid from the writing box and began rubbing ink from the ink tablet. She had already decided upon the wording of her own note.

Reiko's fingers pressed hard upon the cold gilt letters of the ink tablet, and the water in the shallow well at once darkened, as if a black cloud had spread across it. She stopped thinking that this repeated action, this pressure from her fingers, this rise and fall of faint sound, was all and solely for death. It was a routine domestic task, a simple paring away of time until death should finally stand before her. But somehow, in the increasingly smooth motion of the tablet rubbing on the stone, and in the scent from the thickening ink, there was unspeakable darkness.

Neat in his uniform, which he now wore next to his skin, the lieutenant emerged from the bathroom. Without a word he seated himself at the table, bolt upright, took a brush in his hand, and stared undecidedly at the paper before him.

Reiko took a white silk kimono with her and entered the bathroom. When she reappeared in the living room, clad in the white kimono and with her face lightly made up, the farewell note lay completed on the table beneath the lamp. The thick black brushstrokes said simply:

"Long Live the Imperial Forces—Army Lieutenant Takeyama Shinji."

While Reiko sat opposite him writing her own note, the lieutenant gazed in silence, intensely serious, at the controlled movement of his wife's pale fingers as they manipulated the brush.

With their respective notes in their hands—the lieutenant's sword strapped to his side, Reiko's small dagger thrust into the sash of her white kimono—the two of them stood before the god shelf and silently prayed. Then they put out all the downstairs lights. As he mounted the stairs the lieutenant turned his head and gazed back at the striking, white-clad figure of his wife, climbing behind him, with lowered eyes, from the darkness beneath.

The farewell notes were laid side by side in the alcove of the upstairs room. They wondered whether they ought not to remove the hanging scroll, but since it had been written by their go-between, Lieutenant General Ozeki, and consisted, moreover, of two Chinese characters signifying "Sincerity," they left it where it was. Even if it were to become stained with splashes of blood, they felt that the lieutenant general would understand.

The lieutenant, sitting erect with his back to the alcove, laid his sword on the floor before him.

Reiko sat facing him, a mat's width away. With the rest of her so severely white the touch of rouge on her lips seemed remarkably seductive.

Across the dividing mat they gazed intently into each other's eyes. The lieutenant's sword lay before his knees. Seeing it, Reiko recalled their first night and was overwhelmed with sadness. The lieutenant spoke, in a hoarse voice:

"As I have no second to help me I shall cut deep. It may look unpleasant, but please do not panic. Death of any sort is a fearful thing to watch. You must not be discouraged by what you see. Is that all right?"

"Yes."

Reiko nodded deeply.

Looking at the slender white figure of his wife the lieutenant experienced a bizarre excitement. What he was about to perform was an act in his public capacity as a soldier, something he had never previously shown his wife. It called for a resolution equal to the courage to enter battle; it was a death of no less degree and quality than death in the front line. It was his conduct on the battlefield that he was now to display.

Momentarily the thought led the lieutenant to a strange fantasy. A lonely death on the battlefield, a death beneath the eyes of his beautiful wife . . . in the sensation that he was now to die in these two dimensions, realizing an impossible union of them both, there was sweetness beyond words. This must be the very pinnacle of good fortune, he thought. To have every moment of his death observed by those beautiful eyes—it was like being borne to death on a gentle, fragrant breeze. There was some special favor here. He did not understand precisely what it was, but it was a domain unknown to others: a dispensation granted to no one else had been permitted to himself. In the radiant, bridelike figure of his white-robed wife the lieutenant seemed to see a vision of all those things he had loved and for which he was to lay down his life—the Imperial Household, the Nation, the Army Flag. All these, no less than the wife who sat before him, were presences observing him closely: with clear and never-faltering eyes.

Reiko too was gazing intently at her husband, so soon to die, and she thought that never in this world had she seen anything so beautiful. The lieutenant always looked well in uniform, but now, as he contemplated death with severe brows and firmly closed lips, he revealed what was perhaps masculine beauty at its most superb.

"It's time to go," the lieutenant said at last.

Reiko bent her body low to the mat in a deep bow. She could not raise her face. She did not wish to spoil her make-up with tears, but the tears could not be held back.

When at length she looked up she saw hazily through the tears that her husband had wound a white bandage around the blade of his now unsheathed sword, leaving five or six inches of naked steel showing at the point.

Resting the sword in its cloth wrapping on the mat before him, the lieutenant rose from his knees, resettled himself cross-legged, and unfastened the hooks of his uniform collar. His eyes no longer saw his wife. Slowly, one by one, he undid the flat brass buttons. The dusky brown chest was revealed, and then the stomach. He unclasped his belt and undid the buttons of his trousers. The pure whiteness of the thickly coiled loincloth showed itself. The lieutenant pushed the cloth down with both hands, further to ease his stomach, and then reached for the white-bandaged blade of his sword. With his left hand he massaged his abdomen, glancing downward as he did so.

To reassure himself on the sharpness of his sword's cutting edge the lieutenant folded back the left trouser flap, exposing a little of his thigh, and lightly drew the blade across the skin. Blood welled up in the wound at once, and several streaks of red trickled downward, glistening in the strong light.

It was the first time Reiko had ever seen her husband's blood, and she felt a violent throbbing in her chest. She looked at her husband's face. The lieutenant was looking at the blood with calm appraisal. For a moment—though thinking at the same time that it was hollow comfort—Reiko experienced a sense of relief.

The lieutenant's eyes fixed his wife with an intense, hawk-like stare. Moving the sword around to his front, he raised himself slightly on his hips and let the upper half of his body lean over the sword point. That he was mustering his whole strength was apparent from the angry tension of the uniform at his shoulders. The lieutenant aimed to strike deep into the left of his stomach. His sharp cry pierced the silence of the room.

Despite the effort he had himself put into the blow, the lieutenant had the impression that someone else had struck the side of his stomach agonizingly with a thick rod of iron. For a second or so his head reeled and he had no idea what had happened. The five or six inches of naked point had vanished completely into his flesh, and the white bandage, gripped in his clenched fist, pressed directly against his stomach.

He returned to consciousness. The blade had certainly pierced the wall of the stomach, he thought. His breathing was difficult, his chest thumped violently, and in some far deep region, which he could hardly believe was a part of himself, a fearful and excruciating pain came welling up as if the ground had split open to disgorge a boiling stream of molten rock. The pain came suddenly nearer, with terrifying speed. The lieutenant bit his lower lip and stifled an instinctive moan.

Was this *seppuku?*—he was thinking. It was a sensation of utter chaos, as if the sky had fallen on his head and the world was reeling drunkenly. His will power and courage, which had seemed so robust before he made the incision, had now dwindled to something like a single hairlike thread of steel, and he was assailed by the uneasy feeling that he must advance along this thread, clinging to it with desperation. His clenched fist had grown moist. Looking down, he saw that both his hand and the cloth about the blade were drenched in blood. His loincloth too was dyed a deep red. It struck him as incredible that, amidst this terrible agony, things which could be seen could still be seen, and existing things existed still.

The moment the lieutenant thrust the sword into his left side and she saw the deathly pallor fall across his face, like an abruptly lowered curtain, Reiko had to struggle to prevent herself from rushing to his side. Whatever happened, she must watch. She must be a witness. That was the duty her husband had laid upon her. Opposite her, a mat's space away, she could clearly see her husband biting his lip to stifle the pain. The pain was there, with absolute certainty, before her eyes. And Reiko had no means of rescuing him from it.

The sweat glistened on her husband's forehead. The lieutenant closed his eyes, and then opened them again, as if experimenting. The eyes had lost their luster, and seemed innocent and empty like the eyes of a small animal.

The agony before Reiko's eyes burned as strong as the summer sun, utterly remote from the grief which seemed to be tearing herself apart within. The pain grew steadily in stature, stretching upward. Reiko felt that her husband had already become a man in a separate world, a man whose whole being had been resolved into pain, a prisoner in a cage of pain where no hand could reach out to him. But Reiko felt no pain at all. Her grief was not pain. As she thought about this, Reiko began to feel as if someone had raised a cruel wall of glass high between herself and her husband.

Ever since her marriage her husband's existence had been her own existence, and every breath of his had been a breath drawn by herself. But now, while her husband's existence in pain was a vivid reality, Reiko could find in this grief of hers no certain proof at all of her own existence.

With only his right hand on the sword the lieutenant began to cut sideways across his stomach. But as the blade became entangled with the entrails it was pushed constantly outward by their soft resilience; and the lieutenant realized that it would be necessary, as he cut, to use both hands to keep the point pressed deep into his stomach. He pulled the blade across. It did not cut as easily as he had expected. He directed the strength of his whole body into his right hand and pulled again. There was a cut of three or four inches.

The pain spread slowly outward from the inner depths until the whole stomach reverberated. It was like the wild clanging of a bell. Or like a thousand bells which jangled simultaneously at every breath he breathed and every throb of his pulse, rocking his whole being. The lieutenant could no longer stop himself from moaning. But by now the blade had cut its way through to below the navel, and when he noticed this he felt a sense of satisfaction, and a renewal of courage.

The volume of blood had steadily increased, and now it spurted from the wound as if propelled by the beat of the pulse. The mat before the lieutenant was drenched red with splattered blood, and more blood overflowed onto it from pools which gathered in the folds of the lieutenant's khaki trousers. A spot, like a bird, came flying across to Reiko and settled on the lap of her white silk kimono.

By the time the lieutenant had at last drawn the sword across to the right side of his stomach, the blade was already cutting shallow and had revealed its naked tip, slippery with blood and grease. But, suddenly stricken by a fit of vomiting, the lieutenant cried out hoarsely. The vomiting made the fierce pain fiercer still, and the stomach, which had thus far remained firm and compact, now abruptly heaved, opening wide its wound, and the entrails burst through, as if the wound too were vomiting. Seemingly ignorant of their master's suffering, the entrails gave an impression of robust health and almost disagreeable vitality as they slipped smoothly out and spilled over into the crotch. The lieutenant's head drooped, his shoulders heaved, his eyes opened to narrow slits, and a thin trickle of saliva dribbled from his mouth. The gold markings on his epaulettes caught the light and glinted.

Blood was scattered everywhere. The lieutenant was soaked in it to his knees, and he sat now in a crumpled and listless posture, one hand on the floor. A raw smell filled the room. The lieutenant, his head drooping, retched repeatedly, and the movement showed vividly in his shoulders. The blade of the sword, now pushed back by the entrails and exposed to its tip, was still in the lieutenant's right hand.

It would be difficult to imagine a more heroic sight than that of the lieutenant at this moment, as he mustered his strength and flung back his head. The movement was performed with sudden violence, and the back of his head struck with a sharp crack against the alcove pillar. Reiko had been sitting until now with her face lowered, gazing in fascination at the tide of blood advancing toward her knees, but the sound took her by surprise and she looked up.

The lieutenant's face was not the face of a living man. The eyes were hollow, the skin parched, the once so lustrous cheeks and lips the color of dried mud. The right hand alone was moving. Laboriously gripping the sword, it hovered shakily in the air like the hand of a marionette and strove to direct the point at the base of the lieutenant's throat. Reiko watched her husband make this last, most heart-rending, futile exertion. Glistening with blood and grease, the point was thrust at the throat again and again. And each time it missed its aim. The strength to guide it was no longer there. The straying point struck the collar and the collar badges. Although its hooks had been unfastened, the stiff military collar had closed together again and was protecting the throat.

Reiko could bear the sight no longer. She tried to go to her husband's help, but she could not stand. She moved through the blood on her knees, and her white skirts grew deep red. Moving to the rear of her husband, she helped no more than by loosening the collar. The quivering blade at last contacted the naked flesh of the throat. At that moment Reiko's impression was that she herself had propelled her husband forward; but that was not the case. It was a movement planned by the lieutenant himself, his last exertion of strength. Abruptly he threw his body at the blade, and the blade pierced his neck, emerging at the nape. There was a tremendous spurt of blood and the lieutenant lay still, cold blue-tinged steel protruding from his neck at the back.

5

Slowly, her socks slippery with blood, Reiko descended the stairway. The upstairs room was now completely still.

Switching on the ground-floor lights, she checked the gas jet and the main gas plug and poured water over the smoldering, half-buried charcoal in the brazier. She stood before the upright mirror in the four-and-a-half-mat room and held up her skirts. The bloodstains made it seem as if a bold, vivid pattern was printed across the lower half of her white kimono. When she sat down before the mirror, she was conscious of the dampness and coldness of her husband's blood in the region of her thighs, and she shivered. Then, for a long while, she lingered over her toilet preparations. She applied the rouge generously to her cheeks, and her lips too she painted heavily. This was no longer make-up to please her husband. It was make-up for the world which she would leave behind, and there was a touch of the magnificent and the spectacular in her brushwork. When she rose, the mat before the mirror was wet with blood. Reiko was not concerned about this.

Returning from the toilet, Reiko stood finally on the cement floor of the porchway. When her husband had bolted the door here last night it had been in preparation for death. For a while she stood immersed in the consideration of a simple problem. Should she now leave the bolt drawn? If she were to lock the door, it could be that the neighbors might not notice their suicide for several days. Reiko did not relish the thought of their two corpses putrifying before discovery. After all, it seemed, it would be best to leave it open. . . . She released the bolt, and also drew open the frosted-glass door a fraction. . . . At once a chill wind blew in. There was no sign of anyone in the midnight streets, and stars glittered ice-cold through the trees in the large house opposite.

Leaving the door as it was, Reiko mounted the stairs. She had walked here and there for some time and her socks were no longer slippery. About halfway up, her nostrils were already assailed by a peculiar smell.

The lieutenant was lying on his face in a sea of blood. The point protruding from his neck seemed to have grown even more prominent than before. Reiko walked heedlessly across the blood. Sitting beside the lieutenant's corpse, she stared intently at the face, which lay on one cheek on the mat. The eyes were opened wide, as if the lieutenant's attention had been attracted by something. She raised the head, folding it in her sleeve, wiped the blood from the lips, and bestowed a last kiss.

Then she rose and took from the closet a new white blanket and a waist cord. To prevent any derangement of her skirts, she wrapped the blanket about her waist and bound it there firmly with the cord.

Reiko sat herself on a spot about one foot distant from the lieutenant's body. Drawing the dagger from her sash, she examined its dully gleaming blade intently, and held it to her tongue. The taste of the polished steel was slightly sweet.

Reiko did not linger. When she thought how the pain which had previously opened such a gulf between herself and her dying husband was now to become a part of her own experience, she saw before her only the joy of herself entering a realm her husband had already made his own. In her husband's agonized face there had been something inexplicable which she was seeing for the first time. Now she would solve that riddle. Reiko sensed that at last she too would be able to taste the true bitterness and sweetness of that great moral principle in which her husband believed. What had until now been tasted only faintly through her husband's example she was about to savor directly with her own tongue.

Reiko rested the point of the blade against the base of her throat. She thrust hard. The wound was only shallow. Her head blazed, and her hands shook uncontrollably. She gave the blade a strong pull sideways. A warm substance flooded into her mouth, and everything before her eyes reddened, in a vision of spouting blood. She gathered her strength and plunged the point of the blade deep into her throat.

NOMA HIROSHI

Like Dazai Osamu and many others of his generation, Noma Hiroshi (1915–1991) was deeply interested in Marxism while he was in college. During the war, he was conscripted into the Japanese army and fought in a number of battles. His military experiences are described in his novel *Zone of Emptiness* (*Shinkū chitai*, 1952), which was translated into both English and French within a few years, quickly earning him an international reputation. Noma's short story "A Red Moon in Her Face" (Kao no naka no akai tsuki), published shortly after the war in 1947, suggests as well his interest in experimenting with contemporary European forms of fiction writing.

A RED MOON IN HER FACE (KAO NO NAKA NO AKAI TSUKI)

Translated by James Raeside

There was a kind of expression of suffering in the face of the widow Horikawa Kurako. Not that her face bore that type of so-called unapproachable, elegant beauty sometimes seen in Japanese women, a face that conveys a sense of soft flesh enclosed in a rather cold outline; nor was it the type whose attractiveness derives from the way one feature—eyes or nose or mouth—upsets the harmony of the whole. As a face, it had, if anything, the regularity associated with a run-of-the-mill kind of beauty. Yet, undoubtedly, there was something warped about it, as if, in the midst of burgeoning life, something had been forcibly torn from it, and this had given her face a beauty that was filled with an unusual degree of energy. Suffering appeared in the middle of it, as if working its way out from her wide, white forehead and the under-fleshed area around her mouth, which shifted frequently in response to changes in the world outside.

As the number of occasions on which he looked at her face grew, Kitayama Toshio recognized that its expression was gradually penetrating into the depths of his heart. A little under a year ago he had come back from the tropics and taken a job in a firm belonging to an acquaintance, situated on the fifth floor of a building near Tokyo station, and he often bumped into her in the corridor, in the elevator, or near the entrance to the bathroom. On those occasions, he had discerned this strange kind of pained expression in her face. He became aware that the woman's face worked upon the suffering within his own heart with a spiritual sweetness that was coupled with pain.

He was unable to estimate her age. Or rather, he never wondered about it—that is, from the outset, her age had been hidden from him by her beauty. Naturally, this was because he had gone for a long time without seeing any women from his own country, and also perhaps because, having had a painful experience in the past, he had lived resolving to avoid women in general. Also, he was not aware that she had once been married. He guessed her to be much younger than she actually was, and for that reason he thought it strange that such a youthful face should so clearly preserve and express what lay within—something very rare among Japanese women.

Because she worked at the Yachiyo New Development Company in the office facing his own, she was separated from him by a corridor. The corridor was long and dark with offices of exactly the same pattern along both sides, so the occasions when he met her or brushed past her were very brief, and he did not have the time to inspect her face closely; however, from her face as it floated up in the dark atmosphere of the corridor or when it was before him, sandwiched between a mass of backs in the elevator, he felt an energy of beauty released and directed at him, like that of a landscape close to sunset at the instant of its intensest radiance, when it is just on the point of fading, when the sharply defined line of a mountain range and the line of the horizon glow with that last, strangely powerful beam of light shining from a sky huge with silence. At first he had only been concerned with this aspect of her face, but recently he had come to realize that the quality of suffering in her facial expression had penetrated everywhere throughout her rather small body, clad in a somber, blackish suit, and itself at odds with that face of hers. He also felt that her appearance, seemingly steeped in suffering, was reviving in him memories of a painful experience from his past. Without doubt, that face had a beauty that well matched the suffering he had inside him, but it was impossible for him to understand why her face approached so exactly what was in his heart. However that may be, that face of hers did touch the suffering there. Sometimes, as he was going down the stairs, he would suddenly feel something squeezing him around the chest. He didn't understand what it was at first, but in fact it was the impression of her suffering face sinking deep into his mind. He sensed that the woman's face was at the core of whatever it was that was squeezing his heart. So he fixed his gaze on that face within his breast. His heart ached and he was seized with a vague anxiety; he was plunged into the sensation that the feet under him would no longer respond to his will. Then suddenly, a dark, incomprehensible thunderbolt of emotion passed through his breast. It came whirling up from the deepest recess of his memory, wielding a power that his present strength was completely unable to withstand. And it laid him low.

"Ah, no!" He stopped dead for a moment. "No, no!" He shook his head. Nonetheless, he was rocked by chaotic memories that he had no idea how to dispel. He became aware that the words he himself would not affirm, words denying human life, denying humanity, were forcing their way up from inside him. It was an unendurable moment, it seemed to him that his whole body was lit, from inside to the tips of his fingers, by a dark lightning that passed through him and then was gone.

He told himself, No, it's not true; I don't think that at all, I don't reject humanity. . . . I'm better intentioned than that. I'm a straightforward soul. I have much, much more faith in humanity than that. Yet he recalled the very different impression of day-to-day humanity that he had gained when fighting in the field, and he suffered the attacks of that fanged beast that resides in all human beings. He knew that the tooth marks left by the cruel fangs of his fellow soldiers on the battlefield were still clearly evident in his skin, and, at the same time, that he had left the same kind of tooth marks in the skin of his comrades; he shuddered at the thought of the selfish guise that human beings assume when their lives are in danger on the battlefield.

The reason why the appearance of Horikawa Kurako caused the antihuman voice to arise and the memories of the battlefield to be revived in Kitayama Toshio was that her appearance corresponded to that of another suffering woman. When he saw Horikawa Kurako, he could clearly picture in his mind his own pitiful figure walking through the battle zone, nursing in his heart the image of that other woman.

In the past Kitayama Toshio had taken for a lover a woman whom he could not, for the life of him, love from the bottom of his heart. She was, so to speak, a substitute for his lost love: a woman whom he had loved beforehand, but who had soon left him. This lost love of his had not been particularly wonderful or endowed with extraordinary qualities; it was just his tough luck that he'd met such a woman in the intense and feverish era of youth. Following a pattern of behavior commonly seen in adolescent lovers, he had idealized this woman. Enumerating all her real or imaginary graces, he had placed her on a pedestal. But then, since her family opposed him and he was unable even to overcome that opposition, leaving her uncertain of his ability to make his way in life, the woman had announced she wanted to break things off. Yet even while hating her, he had continued to preserve her image in his heart. Then his next girlfriend had made her appearance. This woman, who worked as a clerk at the munitions company where he was employed, had been in love with him. Unlike his first love, this woman had immediately given him everything. She was sickly with a thin face and skinny neck and hips, but she was intelligent and her upbringing and cast of mind matched his own. Although he'd had the strength to endure the loss of his previous love alone, he was not the kind of person who could bear to be always solitary; nor was he strong-willed enough to forgo the prop to his vanity that he derived from the proximity of a woman who loved him; thus, he also lacked the willpower to back off from her proffered love. Yet, because it had been obtained so easily, he was not able to comprehend that the love of this woman who believed in him completely, who gave him everything, was precious in a way that he would never find again in his lifetime. He had taken her on as a substitute for his former love and that was how he loved her. He looked at her, indeed, with a callous eye. As he touched the skin of her breast, which was weak, even slack, he felt the chill in his own heart. His eyes compared her breasts to those of his former love and the soft flesh they had enclosed. That feeling of something missing, of dissatisfaction, made him think his heart had shriveled inside. It irritated him to realize that there was no sort of an inviting sexuality that drew him to her face, in a way a rather modern face, with its pale, narrow forehead and slightly protuberant cheekbones. When he brought her face nearer, he felt a wave of contempt for the clumsy way she had applied her rouge. Of course it was not as though he habitually thought about her in this cold way . . . but when such thoughts became very frequent, the devoted love she showed for him weighed heavily on him. It oppressed him to feel his body enfolded by the full, passionate feeling that seemed to flow from her heart.

News of her death had come to him while he was in the army, still stationed at home, and only then, as a result of her death, did he realize how criminal had been his pretense of love toward her. For, in the course of the life full of hardship that he was leading as a new recruit, he was finally forced to comprehend how great the value of love was. There was a saying among the enlisted men that you only find out how wonderful your ma's love is after you get in the army, and in his army bunk he too would think of his mother, and of love. He thought of the greatness of one human being loving another. In a certain sense, it's a saccharine, comical idea: a man over thirty, wet with tears, nibbling a bun between the blankets, working out from his everyday life as a soldier—a life strictly bound by training and private brutalities—the belief that the only thing necessary in human life was love, that love alone had value. With his own chilled hands, he stroked his cheeks, swollen and purple where they had been struck by the soles of army boots, and he thought of his mother's soft hands, of the gentle palms of his dead lover. When he was in the field, these thoughts became even more intense—that is, while they were stationed in Japan, there were still some reciprocal feelings of sympathy and pity among the new recruits who all were experiencing the same miseries. In the darkness beside the latrines, they exchanged brief words filled with pity for each other. During life at the front, however, while constantly oppressed by the incoming enemy bullets and by the shortage of food, their mutual sympathy naturally disappeared—of course as far as their attitudes toward officers and senior privates were concerned, but even toward their fellow new recruits. He understood that, in the face of fierce combat, each human being would simply protect his own life with his own strength, console himself for his own suffering, and grasp his own death with his own hands. Just as they all selfishly guarded the water in their water bottles, they desperately clutched the life in the leather bottles of their selves. No man ever gave any of his water to another; no one ever risked his life for the benefit of another. If one individual's physical strength was inferior—even by just a little—to that of his comrades, he rapidly dropped out of the conflict, and death swooped upon him. Giving up your food to another when the entire platoon was starving would mean your own death. And comrades in arms faced each other down over possession of a single item of food.

When in the intervals between the extreme tensions of hand-to-hand com-
bat he thought back briefly over the half of his life he had lived so far, it seemed
to him that, of all the many people he had met, all the colleagues and friends,
the only ones who had really loved him had been his mother and his dead
lover. . . . During a lull in the fighting, in that agonizing silence that de-
scended on the front when an outpost of enemy skirmishers had strangely
ceased firing, he looked ahead through the sights of the 41-caliber field gun,
searching for the clump of trees behind the wide grassfield, which was his next
target; in those moments, it seemed to him that, from out of his past life, the fig-
ures of the two people who had truly loved him rose up tremulously and has-
tened toward him. In the scene as it was displayed in his sights, his dead lover
walked toward him with her large left foot swung outward as she walked, a gait
she had never been able to correct. He felt her appearance penetrate his suffer-
ing heart. Recalling her awkward gait he felt a trembling in his heart—now
brought to the point of exhaustion by heat and fatigue—for he had wounded his
former lover while she was alive, when he used to look down as he walked with
her and inwardly sneer at the way she twisted her left foot. I'm sorry, I'm sorry,
he said in his heart as he faced the enemy. And so, keeping in his breast the im-
age of this lover who had given him all she had without regret, he had endured
the hardship of battle.

He had come to the Southern Front from China. As a junior private, his bat-
tle was not fought with the enemy—it was a battle he fought with fellow Japa-
nese soldiers. Because of the intense heat, the horses all developed saddle sores,
the hide on their backs peeling off in strips. Even when wearing saddle blan-
kets, the horses could not be put to service, so the low-ranking privates took the
place of horses in pulling the gun carriage. They could not march during the
day because of the power of the sun, so most marches were done at night. They
would get up at one in the morning, start off at one-thirty, and set camp at
eleven that same morning. When they set camp, however, the junior privates
had to take care of the horses, check the ammunition, service the guns, and pre-
pare food—they got only about two hours sleep a night. Tired as they were, they
could hardly pull the gun carriages forward at all, so the senior soldiers, the
fourth- and fifth-year privates, would beat the juniors who stood in for the
horses, until, finally, the juniors started to defend themselves against these at-
tacks. To these junior privates, the enemy was not the foreign enemy before
them, but the fourth- and fifth-year privates, the NCOs and officers at their
sides.

Thus beaten by enemies from his own camp, with the image of his lover in
his heart and the traces of the gun carriage over his shoulder, Kitayama Toshio
pulled the gun onward through undergrowth from which geckos called.

"What are you thinking about? You're thinking about that again, aren't
you?" his dead lover had sadly questioned him as, their lovemaking finished, he
remained silent and unmoving. She was well aware that he was dissatisfied with
her. She was sure that, once again, he was thinking of his former lover.

"I'm not thinking of anything," he instantly denied. But his tone of voice was certainly not one of denial; instead, it contained an acknowledgment of her accusation.

In her letters she often wrote to him: "I don't know any other way of living but to love you, whatever you may think of me." Then she wrote, "Some day you too will understand how I feel. Even though I might be dead by then. . . ." So when he thought of her, and her feelings emerged from these banal phrases to pierce his breast, he considered he deserved all the suffering he was undergoing.

Go on, suffer more, he told himself, as he pulled the gun forward under the whips of the fifth-year privates. Fields of sugar cane, set ablaze by Filipino soldiers and now burnt black, stretched out darkly far below. Through a haze of dust stirred by the soldiers, the large red sun of the tropics rose above the line of the cliffs. The soldiers' faces were jaundiced and wracked with fever; their sweat-stained summer uniforms appeared dyed red by the sun's light. The company was stretched out a long way, advancing along the gradually narrowing mountain path in a broken line. From behind came the hoarse voice of the company commander, "Number Two, Number Three, change places." Replacements came up from the midst of the ranks with wordless groans, their gas masks hanging down in front of them while the dust, soaked by the sweat that ran down them, clung like black moss to their jackets.

Handing over the traces of the second gun-carriage shaft, Kitayama Toshio, along with Number Three, Private, Second Class, Nakagawa, a former fishmonger, fell out of line. Yet he had no notion of when he had handed over the traces to his replacement or why it was that he had fallen out of line. The back of his neck was feverish, his eyes clouded, the outline of his heart, jumping in his chest, knocked against his chest wall. Together with Private, Second Class, Nakagawa, he remained standing there as if petrified, but at last they joined the very end of the line. . . . They began to walk, each taking the reins of a skinny, saddleless horse, the bones of whose flanks stuck out, which their replacements had clung to until then. But they no longer had the strength to walk along with the horses. Their feet, inside military gaiters that they had not taken off for ten days, had lost all feeling. And it was as if they were shedding a great quantity of blood with each step they took up the slope.

"What are you doing there!" The lance corporal acting as platoon leader came back to the tail of the line and let his whip fall on their hands as they clutched the horse's reins. "Don't you know the horse will snuff it if you hang on to it like that! We can replace you two, but we can't replace the horse. Now, don't come whining to me about every little thing in this fucking heat."

Wordlessly they looked up at the lance corporal, then, resignedly, they let the reins go slack and walked at a greater distance from the horse. But their feet did not move. It was as though, no matter how deeply they breathed out, dirty air remained in their lungs to choke them. The straps of their gas masks pressing down on their right shoulders seemed to finally stop all breathing. . . . The surface of the mountain, which soaked up the febrile rays of the sun during the day, at night time gave off a burning heat that enveloped the bodies of the troops and blocked their pores with dust and sweat. One might say that it was only the form of the company marching before them and dragging their bodies after it that caused them to carry on walking.

"I can't walk no more," came the voice of the fishmonger, Private, Second Class, Nakagawa from the far side of the horse's body, which was pulling him. This was the same declaration that he had made umpteen times before, and his voice bored into the exhausted mind of Kitayama Toshio. His strength worn completely down, Nakagawa had now lost all the energy necessary to move his heavy-boned frame. "This time, I've really had it. I just can't walk no more." Still, he continued to walk for another thirty minutes, dragged along by the horse.

The platoon was advancing up Mount Samat[1] and, if they did not proceed at a forced march, they would inevitably come under fire from the well-provisioned, well-armed enemy advancing from the right. So they continued to march, the platoon commander giving no order to rest.

"I'm going to let go. I'm letting go." From the voice of Private Nakagawa, Kitayama Toshio sensed that his comrade's strength was completely spent. The ends of his words became increasingly faint, and these pitiful words, originally spoken in a tone of appeal to Kitayama Toshio, had now lost this tone of one appealing to another and seemed rather to be words addressed to himself, perhaps showing that, at the end of life, his conscious mind was ranging around his entire lifetime—and the words made their way into the very depths of Kitayama Toshio's heart. Yet he had no strength to do anything for his comrade in arms, be it only a simple act of encouragement, such as a pat on the shoulder. Rather, if he had begun to make such a gesture, then he would have lost the strength to keep his own body moving, only to perish himself. Steeling himself against the entreaty in Private Nakagawa's voice, he walked on.

"I'm letting go." And then Private Nakagawa's hands slipped from the horse's reins, and he remained unmoving, his knees bent. He had chosen his fate—to be buried under the thickly lying sand. As if to show that his body had at last been set free by death, after being dragged along for so long in ropes of slavery, he shook his head slightly over the sand and then fell. Private, Second Class, Nakagawa: slow-witted, with a weak memory, continually beaten by the senior privates, ended his life on a path on Mount Samat. And, just to save his own life, Kitayama Toshio abandoned his comrade to his fate. By the time he was demobilized, his mother was no longer in the world.

On a day on the verge of spring, he left the office with a fellow worker named Yugami Yuko. Homeward-bound workers mingled together at the entrance of the elevator. Next to the tobacco kiosk, the XX company was holding a special

---

1. Mount Samat is on the way from Lingayaen Gulf to the Bataan Peninsula, the scene of an important engagement during the Japanese conquest of Luzon in 1942.

sale, and a crowd had gathered in front of a bare table piled with household goods. As they parted the crowd and headed toward the entrance, Yugami Yuko, indifferent to those around her, called out in a loud voice, "Horikawa san!" at which, among the knot of people around the newsstand to their left a single woman's face turned. It was the face, shrouded in suffering, of Horikawa Kurako. With her back to the bright air outside the building, her faintly smiling face floated amidst the crowd.

"Are you on your way home? Let's go together," Yuko said, coming up to her. Then she introduced her to Kitayama Toshio.

The three of them, surrounded by people hurrying homeward, walked toward Tokyo Station. Flanked by her companions, Yugami Yuko was the most cheerful of the three: although she had lost her husband in the war and was looking after a child by herself, she seemed to be stepping out in life with the same firm tread with which she walked on the street. Her thick hair, hanging down over her navy blue jacket, ornamented her full shoulders.

On her left Kitayama Toshio, although only halfway into his thirties, looked older. In his way of carrying himself one could detect that kind of indifference born of a wandering life and the traces of suffering that naturally went with long years spent in the army. Despite this, one could also sense the inward strength of one who had been able to come through that army life and the rigors of combat. His gait as he dragged his long legs was like a soldier's.

On the right, Horikawa Kurako was that day wearing a spring suit of rather bright shades, with a sky-blue stripe that seemed to gently dissolve into the evening light still lingering in the station square; she seemed somewhat closed in on herself in contrast with Yugami Yuko's completely open, easygoing manner—and she walked with short steps, her head held down.

When they had got to the line at the ticket window, Yugami Yuko displayed the large cloth bundle hanging from her right hand, showing it to neither of her companions in particular but holding it straight out in front of her.

"I've got this today."

"What is it?" asked Horikawa Kurako.

"I'm off to sell it now—it's a skin, a bear." From one edge of the cloth wrapper Yuko pulled out the clawed paw of some black animal. Mischievously she waggled the paw of the small bear two or three times, then burst out laughing. Horikawa Kurako laughed along with her.

"A skin, is it?" asked Kitayama Toshio, with a pang in his breast at the thought that Yugami's livelihood was sustained by this comical bear's paw.

"Yes, they say I should able to sell it for 4,000 yen; it's a bit small, so the price is a lot less. People kept saying 'Sell it, sell it,' so finally I've decided to. I've really got nothing else left to sell."

"It's the same with me, I'm selling off my things so I can eat," said Horikawa Kurako. Then she turned a smiling face toward Kitayama Toshio.

"So you're in the same boat too? It's terrible, isn't it," said Yugami Yuko.

"Still, at least you had some things to sell," said Kitayama Toshio. Even if his tone was cold, it was because he had been startled at the way a curtain had suddenly been lifted on the two women's lives, and he could not find the right words.

"But you know, it can't go on like this forever. I can only hold out for another year. Right?" She turned her face toward Horikawa Kurako seeking agreement.

"Yes," Horikawa Kurako shook her head. "I'm really getting depressed about it too." Then she pulled in her chin and on her face appeared the shadow of that deep anxiety with which she looked on life.

The train was horribly packed, and the three of them became separated as they stood crushed by the crowd. Within the tight press of people, Kitayama Toshio reflected on the two women striving to earn a living, and on the similar circumstances that darkened the path that lay before him. His friend's company, where he worked, dealt in metal goods—tableware and such, even extending to things like children's tricycles—but the supply stocks had almost run out, and it had become very difficult to keep the business going. Then again, although he had previously worked in a munitions factory, his six years in the army had robbed him of his abilities as an office worker.

Horikawa Kurako got off at Yotsuya. The train emptied a bit and Kitayama Toshio and Yugami Yuko met up again and stood near the central door.

"She's pretty, isn't she?" observed Yuko.

"Yes," said Kitayama Toshio, in the voice of one lost in thought.

"Don't you think so?"

"Yes, she's pretty. She's very pretty," he said hastily. But he did not have the exact words to express the melancholy that he had sensed in Horikawa Kurako. It was not prettiness. It was not beauty. It was something that strangely squeezed at his heart, squeezed it and made it tremble violently.

"Really, I always think I would like to have seen her when she was young. You know, somehow I'm not attracted to good looks in men anymore—my eye is always taken by attractive women."

"Is that so?"

"You know, she is the same as me."

"The same?"

"Yes, her husband lost his life in the war, you know."

"Is that so?" he said with apparent unconcern, but he could not continue. He saw the figure of Horikawa Kurako flash suddenly before him. Her face was resurrected directly in front of his eyes. And he felt that strange, strength-filled beauty in that face of hers forcing itself straight at his heart. It was then, for the first time, that he clearly understood the source of the sadness in her face.

As Yugami Yuko told it, Horikawa Kurako's wedding had been the result of a love match, and she had lost her husband in the third year of their marriage, after he had been conscripted. They had loved one another, had been perfectly happy, and her happiness had been destroyed by the war. Recently, Yugami added, there had been some talk of Horikawa remarrying, but it appeared that she was still very hesitant to make up her mind and do it.

Having parted from Yugami Yuko at Shinjuku, Kitayama Toshio walked along the back street that led off from the front of the station. The electricity substation near his lodgings had been burnt down, and when he reflected that, even when he got back, there would be no lights and he would have to spend weary hours in his dark room, he lost all desire to go home. He went into a little café, ordered a coffee and a croquette, and ate the supper that he had cooked using the electricity at work. Ordering another coffee, he lit a cigarette. He had continued to think about the two widows. It was those who had suffered from the blows of war to whom he now felt the closest. He remembered the black bear's paw with its claws. His face was half-smiling but inside he was in deep pain, and the smile disappeared without having spread across his face. He recalled the face of Horikawa Kurako and thought how her husband surely must have been deeply in love with her. And then, that she must have loved her husband, that she had returned his love to the same degree. But now that she had lost what she had loved, what was there in her life to sustain her? Now that it had lost its object, where could that love try to flow? Was it like the lingering light of evening, which is greater than the white brilliance of midday when it sets the air of the whole sky fiercely aflame before fading away? It must be her blighted love that conveyed the twisted quality into her face, while the beauty touched with madness that sometimes radiated from her face must arise from the lonely conflagration of her love.

Kitayama Toshio left the café and went back into the throng of people milling around the row of food stalls in front of the station. The odor of cheap fried oil hung in the air, and people, only their faces illuminated by feeble lanterns, were working their jaws. Suddenly his eye was caught by a man in front of a stew-stall kitty-corner to him, who was lifting his bowl to his mouth. Looking at the thin face of this young man clad in a pair of narrow-legged cotton army trousers, he thought, "He's hungry. He must be working as a day laborer somewhere." He remembered the fliers he had seen on telegraph poles by the city ward office advertising jobs: XX yen per day, lodging also available.

"Really, how does he manage to keep going? Even if he sells off his possessions for food, he's clearly got nothing left to sell . . . and with that body of his, his wages can't be enough . . . although my own strength is not much to speak of." He looked in the direction of the man's vacantly working mouth. It was thick-lipped and it glistened red and moist above the plate. Then the man's mouth turned into the out-thrust snout of a pig he had clubbed to death when in the army, and then from some remote corner of his body came an unbearable emotion, accompanied by a sensation of burning heat. "Ah, no, no!" he said to himself, beating down the emotion as he urged his legs onward. "It's a pig, a pig!" Something continued to yell from inside him, arising like a feverish mass from deep within his body. In his head the pig's lips continued to make chewing motions. That bastard fifth-year Private Matsuzawa who grabbed my water bot-

tle off me at Lingayen Gulf . . . my mind set only on rations. . . . No! No! . . .
in his head, the moist lips of the pig continued to make their chewing motion.
That guy's mouth is a pig's, my mouth is a pig's . . . chew chew chew . . . ah,
he thought. He suddenly stood still, closed his eyes hard, and shook his head.
When the pig's mouth had disappeared from inside his head, a dark flame be-
came visible in the pitch blackness of his field of vision. Then he slowly opened
his eyes and continued to walk. The hot, dark thoughts that had thrust their way
up from inside his body had already withdrawn, like an ebbing tide. As he
walked, he mentally examined the region of his heart, from which those horri-
ble thoughts he found so hard to drive away had boiled up and where flecks of
emotion still remained after their departure, like black flames.

"However much this emotion may be a rejection of humanity, it is only the emo-
tion of an instant. Apart from that at other times I am as usual: a walking, breath-
ing, eating human being who vaguely affirms humanity," he thought. Yet, as he
walked on, he also reflected that this human being who ate and walked was also
certainly one who knew no love. If they were on the battlefield, all these people
would only protect themselves, as I did myself. They would fight over food ra-
tions, wouldn't they? They would abandon their comrades, wouldn't they? . . .
He began to think of his mother, reportedly burned to death in the air raids. A
mother's love is said to be blind. Yet what human being, apart from a mother, is
able to love another human being? On the battlefield, who would have spared
some of their own rations and given them to another? No one but a mother. And
yet even mothers might be doubted. In his mind, the figure of his mother which
had risen up before his eye changed to that of the woman who had loved
him. . . . He reflected upon his dead lover. He thought of how, as an individual
being, she no longer existed. And then, that it was only her love that he needed.
Did there have to be a war that took the lives of many millions of people in order
for me to understand the value of her love? Moving through the gaps between
the people he reached the edge of the crowd, then turned back into it. Then at
last, becoming chilled, he went home to his dark boardinghouse.

Kitayama Toshio would sometimes go to drink tea with Yugami Yuko and Hori-
kawa Kurako on their way home from work. Later on, he went with Horikawa
Kurako alone. Naturally, he did not consider the feeling he had for her to be
love or anything like that. It was true that his heart was drawn to her beauty. Yet
it wasn't exactly like the heart being drawn, either. It was rather that her appear-
ance linked him to his own past, made him clearly comprehend the miserable
first half of his life. He found it painful to meet her, but that pain was necessary
to him. Of course if it had been pointed out to him that some feeling of love was
mingled in his heart, he would probably have acknowledged it, but it was not
for that reason that he sought her out. Moreover, he knew that the woman's
thoughts lay strictly with her dead husband.
    "I gather that you were very happy?" he observed to her one day.

"Yes, really happy," she replied, then added in a decisive tone, "I can definitely say that I made my husband happy. Even though he's dead, I have no regrets on that score. I did absolutely everything I could for him. Of course I too was really happy then."

"Even in these times, there must be some people who can say the same, I suppose."

"He was an unhappy person. He had suffered a lot from family problems. But I'm sure that the three years he lived with me were really happy ones."

"And then he went into the army, right?"

"Yes."

"Was he an officer?"

"No, he went in as a private."

"Oh? The Southern Front, was it?"

"Yes, the south. He died of disease over there."

"It must have been very tough for him to leave you."

Horikawa Kurako replied in a slightly embarrassed, but decisive and clearcut tone. "Yes, he said it was just like a holiday at the government's expense, but I knew very well what he was really feeling."

"I suppose you must have."

"After he died, people kept telling me how sorry they felt for me, but it's my husband I have to feel sorry for. Nobody seems to think that about the dead. But that's the only way I can see it."

". . ."

"In the end, once you're dead everything's over, isn't it? It's over."

". . . Yes."

"Although I suppose he must have been contented if it was a death he chose for himself."

"Everyone around me seems to be in the same boat."

"You mean Yugami san?"

"Yes."

And then, to this woman who had spoken of her past to him, he told the story of his past love.

"I thought for sure you must be someone who'd had a very sad experience," she said. The two of them then left the tea shop and, saying she had some shopping to do, she walked off toward the station.

For a while he stood looking after her. Her back view disappeared and then reappeared among the busy crowds passing to and fro in the square in front of the station.

"What exactly is that person trying to sustain in her life? Those hands that once warmly embraced her face are now gone, aren't they?" he thought as he watched her. "Why is it that her face has to become beautiful as a result of her unhappiness?" Unaware of how bizarre this question of his was, he stood staring fixedly after her. At which he felt from within his own heart or from that woman's figure, he couldn't clearly tell which, a melancholy mood flowing out and settling over the whole square. It was as if it quietly descended along with the soft light of the sunset from a sky grown wider through the destruction of tall buildings, and it entered the breasts of each of those many people who had lived through the unhappiness of the war.

One day a friend who had been demobilized with Kitayama Toshio from the South Pacific campaign came to visit him. He was a soldier who had been at the university and was one of the last new recruits to be sent out to join his company in the South Pacific from a posting in Japan. When he had first arrived from Japan, he had been nicely plump, but in less than a month the cruel heat had rapidly wasted him, and Kitayama Toshio had often looked after him in his debilitated state. Regarded as an "intellectual," he would crumble with unusual rapidity under the punishments of the senior soldiers, and he did not possess the kind of bad faith that would attempt to buy them off with money and gifts. After demobilization, as one might have expected, he got a job at a small company near Hamamatsuchō through a senior classman from his university, but occasionally he would come to visit Kitayama Toshio to get his discontent and grievances off his chest.

"So, I've finally caught you! Do you know how many times I've come by here recently? I've really been downcast at always seeing your light off when I get to the fruit store on the corner. Just picture me, will you—reluctantly dragging my feet as I make my way home again." So said Kataoka Saburō adopting his habitual position, back propped against the wall.

"Huh? Looking at how well-fleshed you are, I'm not going to shed any tears for you, even if it is spring."

"She really runs her life so well."

"You don't want to speculate at all about the emotions of one who has come countless times to unburden his heart to his old friend?"

"The penniless emotion of Suzuki Daisetzu,[2] perhaps?"

"Yes, recently I've been completely impoverished and detached. You, however, you have a very 'attached' look, haven't you? You're out every evening— have you started a love affair?"

"Hum? Love, eh?" Kitayama Toshio hesitated. "But are there any women in Japan capable of love?"

"Whether there are or not is really beside the point—men will, after all, love women. Even though we lost the war, men will want women and women want men!"

"So can you make love with that ample figure of yours?"

"Certainly. When I start to make love, I'll rapidly slim down." They grilled a sweet potato on the electric stove and began to eat.

"I'm finally broke, too," said Kataoka Saburo. "So, starting next month, I'm starting a side job."

---

2. Suzuki Daisetsu (1870–1966) was a celebrated scholar and popularizer of Zen Buddhism.

"Huh?"

"Shall I put some your way?"

"Translating, is it?"

"What? It's black market stuff."

"Hmm?"

"Well, yes, it's dealing in medical supplies, so I can do it even while I'm working. You're feeling the pinch yourself, aren't you?"

"Yup, I'm really up against it. But I'd be no good at dealing."

"That's probably true." The pair fell silent.

After a while Kataoka Saburō said, "The other day I met Yamanaka on my way home—all our friends are scratching around for a living!" Yamanaka was, of course, another soldier demobilized with them.

"What's he up to?"

"What's he up to, you say? He's selling chocolate. You know, those chocolate bars. He buys them up and then takes them round the country villages."

"Yamanaka does?"

"He does. But he's not stupid, you know. That Yamanaka is doing way better than the rest of us with his chocolate bars. He buys them in at 7 yen, 50 sen a bar and sells them to the little country grocery shops at 8.50—he says he's making 3,500 yen a month. But on the day he started up in the chocolate business, where do you think he tried first? He set his sights on Atami, which is flooded with new yen.[3] That was way off target, and he didn't sell one. But when he was walking up the hill to the station with his pack on his back, he apparently thought of the fate of Kiso Yoshinaka."[4]

"Yoshinaka?"

"Right. Yoshinaka in the end was seriously wounded and told his retainers that the metal of his armor, which he used to make nothing of, seemed to weigh him down, right? Well, Yamanaka apparently felt as though each single one of those bars of chocolate he was carrying on his back was made of steel, and that if you bit one you would break a tooth—so that was the reason he couldn't sell any!"

"He did, eh?"

"You're not laughing, are you? I guess my humor doesn't work on you. . . . Anyway, all our friends are in a bad way. After demobilization, they came home to find their houses had been burned; they had nothing to wear. Now their landlords are planning to throw them out of their lodgings again. All positions are filled; what are they gonna do? . . . The other day, in these freezing February

---

3. New yen refers to the yen devalued by the American Occupation government in February 1946.

4. Kiso Yoshinaka was a valiant general of the Minamoto clan during the war between the Minamoto and the Taira clans. Kiso's fate is described in *The Tales of the Heike* (*Heike monogatari*), chap. 9, sec. 4.

days, they went and rationed out mosquito nets . . . but who has the money to buy them? Even if you bought one, it would soon end up with the black marketeers . . . and the marketeers, being the way they are, go after the stuff rationed out to war victims and buy everything up. . . . What do you think the items rationed out yesterday were? Army pillow covers and children's shoes! . . .

". . ."

"So, I was thinking maybe I should start a love affair of my own."

"You can't carry on a love affair."

"Probably not, eh. . . . I'll always be tubby like this, I suppose."

"What do you eat these days?"

"Potato croquettes off the stall."

"Croquettes? I like them too, but I don't get fat."

"That's because you're in love."

They both laughed.

Kitayama Toshio didn't particularly think he was in love. But Horikawa Kurako was necessary to him. When he was face-to-face with her, he felt for the first time that in the breast of the human being before him stirred the same anguish as in his own. When he looked at her face, it was brought home to him that he was already forgetting the suffering he had endured on the battlefield and trying to live a pretty aimless sort of existence. It was true that, when he had first returned to his native land, the extreme changes it had undergone had struck him like a blow to the chest. But now that impression had begun to fade, and he had come to think nothing of the burnt ruins of buildings or the long lines of open-air stalls on either side of the road and the pullulating hordes of people. And so he felt that her suffering face wiped away the fog from his heart.

The two of them often went to Ginza on their way home. She explained that, although she was living at her childhood home, she was sharing the house with relatives who were very straitlaced. So she declared that she would have to go home without fail at eight o'clock. He didn't particularly try to hold her back. It seemed to him that he now wanted to take a new step forward in his life. Yet he did not know how to make that start. If he took that first step, then the weight of the past that hung upon him would be dispelled. But he did not know how to accomplish this.

"Are you managing to survive?" he tried asking her.

"Yes," she said.

"Is everything all right?"

"Yes, I'm fine."

After falling silent for a while he said, "Of course, you have lived a much more straightforward life than me."

"Do you think so?"

"It's a wonderful thing for a human being to make another happy. I haven't met someone like that myself. Naturally, I wasn't able to. It's the fact that you were that sustains you now, perhaps."

It was evening. Above the street spread the clear, spring sky, mixed with yellow. The two of them were sitting by the window on the first floor of a café and had been conversing for a long time. He told her about how, despite his mother's hopes, he had switched from the law faculty to the fine arts department at college and that, although she was concerned that his chances of finding a job on graduation wouldn't be very good, his mother had still willingly allowed him to apply for the transfer. She had devoted her life to him.

"I really would have liked to have been able to see her one more time," he said. Horikawa Kurako was silent, and he became aware that his words had made her recall her husband.

"Naturally, those six years in the army have messed up my life, but I don't think it's impossible for me to get over that . . . I'm going to find something sometime soon. . . . I'm sure there's a kind of strength in me that's rising up. I'm going to achieve whatever I want. Fortunately, the army has physically trained me for that."

He told her a little about the conditions of warfare. And then he said that what had sustained him during the sufferings of battle had not been his learning in the least, but the suffering that was already in his heart.

"When I look at you I want somehow . . . to do something for you in some way. But I'm well aware that it's hopeless. It really is hopeless," she said brokenly, her voice sounding as if she were choking. He was unable to reply. For a while they silently faced each other.

One day when Kitayama Toshio was going up the stairs to the third floor, he came across Horikawa Kurako standing stock-still, bent over at the waist.

"What's the matter?"

"I just tripped here," she replied, turning around to look at him. "I was thinking about something." He saw that unhappiness flee across her face.

They met up on their way home and aimlessly walked in the direction of Kōfukubashi. Horikawa Kurako appeared unusually subdued. While walking beside her, he felt that her attention was not turned at all toward him but had slipped down somewhere deep within her body. It was a windy evening. White dust danced on the road. The planks of the wooden bridge creaked. They walked along the river toward Nihonbashi.

"Is your leg OK now?" he said after a while.

"Leg?" Her hair fell across her face as she turned to him.

"Yes, you tripped on the stairs earlier—you were limping, I thought."

"Yes, it's fine. Recently I've somehow been so absent-minded, and at that time as well I was thinking over so many things I was in a daze."

". . ."

"Before, I didn't use to be like that, but for some reason, I, these days, I've suddenly become so helpless!"

"Hmm? You have, have you?"

"Yes. Is it odd?"

They passed through the crowds in the park and emerged into the Ginza.

"You're always treating me. Today I want you to let me treat you to something."

"You say always, but I only buy you coffee."

"But still, today I've got a little money, you see."

They had a simple meal, and, saying they would like some good coffee, they went into the nearest café they came to. Each had something that they wanted to say to the other, and yet, while thinking they must speak, they remained silent.

"Kitayama san," she said at last, as always avoiding his eyes, which were gazing at her face. "The other day you said you would find something. Do you think you will?"

"Well, not so easily as all that, you know. But I've begun to study again. I've gotten into the mood to study even while doing my job. Even someone like me may be able to become a good person. Once I've become a good person, I'd like to die, that's what I'm thinking."

" . . ."

"It's sort of as though, having lived through that war, if I can't live in that kind of way, it would be better to die."

"I'm sure that good days are coming, too."

"For whom? For the Japanese?"

"No, . . ." she hesitated.

" . . ."

"I, since that time, I've been thinking I should find someone who would be good for you."

"Yes." He broke off, and then was silent for a while, considering the meaning of her words. "Thank you," he said coldly. "But what about yourself?"

"What about me?" Horikawa Kurako drew back her face slightly.

"I heard that there'd been some talk about you marrying again," said Kitayama Toshio, maintaining the same coldness as before.

"Oh. You heard about that?" Horikawa Kurako said, as if oppressed by the iciness in his words.

"I heard."

"But," she mumbled, "But I just can't make up my mind to do it. Kitayama san, do you think I would be better off remarrying?"

"Well yes, perhaps you would."

"Really?"

Thus they sat in the back of the café with a barrier between them, unable to find anything to say. When they headed toward Yurakuchō it was already quite late, well after eight o'clock.

On the platform was a group of made-up women on their way back from a nightclub. Their boisterous laughter rose up under the dim lanterns. The pair moved away from the women and stood side-by-side at one end of the platform, looking down at the dark streets of the city spread out below.

All the trains that arrived were going in the clockwise direction, and though they stood there for a long time, no counterclockwise train appeared.

"How long will her life be able to continue? She said she's selling things to live, so when that's finished, what will she do, I wonder?" He began to consider the woman Horikawa Kurako, standing unmoving beside him, her eyes directed toward the dim lanterns of the city at night. "And I, what shall I do after all? What am I looking for? . . . Do I want love from her? . . . A woman who has lost her beloved husband in the war joining together with a man who has come to know the value of his dead lover's love through the war—it's a bit too much like a story," he thought. He suddenly felt that next to him, a small life was stirring. Within Horikawa Kurako's body, its two small legs sticking out from her small skirt, he felt the existence of that pitiful living being, which carried its suffering within it wherever it went. He felt that, deep within that being, her suffering lay hidden and unmoving like a quiet, well-trained animal. "No, it is not her that I'm looking for. And what she is looking for is not me. She said that there's no help for my suffering. And I, in turn, can't do anything for hers. . . . But when I think that I can't do anything even for this single, pitiful human life, right beside me . . . my existence is mine alone . . . and this person's existence is hers alone—there's no other way I can think, is there?"

Another clockwise train arrived.

"Shall we get on?" said Horikawa Kurako, unexpectedly rousing herself and walking forward.

"What for?" said Kitayama Toshio, while following after her, drawn on by her small back.

"Let's get on . . . at least this will get us there, somehow." She looked briefly back and then, without paying any heed to him, stepped inside the train. It seemed to him that a youthful seductiveness was playing across her face. He boarded the train, bumping into her as he did. Yet once in the train, they hardly spoke.

"Why? Why do you want to get on this one?"

"No particular reason. I just couldn't go on waiting anymore." And there the conversation ended.

A slightly breathless atmosphere had arisen between them. Kitayama Toshio felt a certain air of seductiveness flowing from the figure of Horikawa Kurako as she hung on the leather strap to his left.

"Is your place far from the station?" he said after a while.

"Yes," she said while still looking straight ahead.

"About how many minutes?"

"It takes about fifteen."

"So it's unsafe?"

"Yes." She nodded her head. "Yes, somebody who lives near us was attacked. But that time she only lost her parasol."

"Shall I see you home?" he said. She said nothing in reply, but he saw her head gently, sorrowfully shake from side to side. Then they stood, once again with that barrier between them.

They went through Meguro and Shibuya and arrived at Shinjuku. Kitayama

Toshio, still agonizing about whether he should see Horikawa Kurako home or not, walked with her to the platform of the Chūō Line.

"Shall I see you home?" he said again. As before, she made no reply.

Although the train was deserted, they stood in the doorway looking at each other. He was watching how the wind, blowing through the window, stirred the lock of hair that hung down to the nape of her neck. He observed this small body, leaning a little to the left, this living being with nothing to rely on that was set before him. He sensed that, in the end, she would not be able to get by in the world after the defeat. "Before long she'll be feeling the pinch. . . . After all, even though our salary is supposed to be going up a little from this month, it all goes to food. . . . It must be the same in her company. . . ." And he imagined the contents of this woman's body being gradually reduced, losing the fullness of life, being scattered somewhere like dust.

He could no longer say to her the words that he should. He felt that whatever words emerged from his mouth, they would not reach deep into the heart of this woman before him. There was, without doubt, a great suffering inside this person. And that suffering was trying to thrust down this little woman, to crush her. Yet there is no way I can touch this person's suffering. I don't know the first thing about her. I only know my own suffering, and so I can only concern myself over my own suffering. . . . That's all.

Kitayama Toshio saw that Horikawa Kurako had raised her head and was looking at him. Her white face floated before him, across the dim atmosphere that lay between them. He fixed his eyes directly on her face. . . . On the other side of her face, no doubt, there is an individual suffering that the war has brought about, he thought. He reflected how much he would like to somehow enter into that suffering of hers. If within a person like him there was even a little truth and uprightness left, he would like it to touch her suffering . . . if their two human hearts could directly meet and they could exchange their sufferings, if two human beings could in this way exchange the secrets of each other's existences, if a man and woman could show the truth of themselves to each other . . . it would be then that, perhaps, human life could have a new meaning. . . . But it seemed that this was impossible for him.

The train was already approaching Yotsuya where she would get off. He continued to gaze with fixed eyes at her white face. Then all at once he noticed that there was a small blemish in one corner of her face. This blemish began to strangely unsettle his mind. It was so faint and small as to make it very difficult to judge whether it was actually there or not. Perhaps it was a trace of dust or soot. Or perhaps it was a mole, visible through her white make-up. In any event, the mark made his heart tremble minutely. Driven by an impulse to clearly determine the existence of this spot above her left eye, he concentrated his vision upon it. He stared at the mark. But it was not the mark on her face that was distressing him. He felt that somewhere in some corner of his own heart there was something like a small mark. And he already understood what the meaning of that small spot in his heart was. He gazed toward the mark within his heart. As he did, he realized that this mark was swelling, becoming larger. It became gradually bigger and moved toward his eyes. It was nearing his eyes from the inside. It was coming close to his eye. Ah, he exclaimed inwardly. He saw the area of the mark on Horikawa Kurako's white face gradually widening. A large, round, red object appeared in her face. A large, round, red tropical moon rose in her face. He saw the jaundiced feverish faces of the soldiers; then the broken line of the platoon, stretching into the distance, arose before him.

Kitayama Toshio's body shook with the rattle of the carriage. "I can't walk no more." From out of that vibration, he heard the voice of the fishmonger Private, Second Class, Nakagawa saying, "I'm going to let go, I'm letting go." The rattle of the train arose from the depths of Kitayama Toshio's frame. Some boiling hot thing welled up from the depths of his body. "I'm letting go! I'm letting go!" He felt Private, Second Class, Nakagawa's body leaving him and advancing on toward death. He felt himself thrusting away the body of Nakagawa, Private, Second Class, to his death.

With a rattle the train left the tunnel. Kitayama Toshio silently endured the black memory that welled up from the depths of his body. "There was nothing else for it. There was nothing else for it, was there? I abandoned Nakagawa to his fate in order to preserve my own existence. For my own existence. For my own existence. But that's the only way human beings can live, isn't it?" He went on reflecting, quietly forcing down his emotion. "There was nothing else to do. And I am still the same person as I was then. I'm in the same situation as I was then, and so, of course, I'm the kind of person who will abandon another human being to his fate. Without a doubt, I'm merely protecting my own existence. And I can do nothing for this person's suffering." He felt something like the breath of her heart blowing toward him from the outline of her white face. "I can't enter into this person's life! I am inside only my own life!" He felt that he could not properly respond to this wind that was blowing from her heart. "I just can't. I can't do anything about anyone else's life. Something that is protecting only its own existence just can't protect that of another," he thought.

The train arrived at Yotsuya. The train stopped. The doors opened. He saw Horikawa Kurako's face looking at him. He saw her small, right shoulder inviting him. "Shall I walk her home or not? . . ." "I can't, I can't!" he thought.

"Good-bye," he said, looking down.

"Yes," she replied, instinctively drawing her own face back. Then a pained smile appeared upon it.

She got off and the doors closed. The train moved off. He saw her face on the other side of the glass, searching for him in the train. There he watched her face become distanced from him as she stood on the platform. He saw her face rubbing against the broken glass of the window. He saw his existence rubbing against hers. He felt that between their two existences was a single, transparent sheet of glass, which moved between them at an infinite speed.

OZAKI KAZUO

Ozaki Kazuo (1899–1983) considered himself a disciple of Shiga Naoya, adopting the same kind of deceptively simple style that Shiga used in such works as "The Paper Door" (Shōji, 1911), which appears in volume 1 of this anthology, in which often grave matters are expressed in a subtle and understated way. The following short story, "Entomologica" (Mushi no iroiro, 1948), is perhaps Ozaki's best-known and most admired work among his Japanese readers.

ENTOMOLOGICA (MUSHI NO IROIRO)

Translated by Chris Brockett

A spider once came out and behaved most oddly on the wall of my room. It happened one bright, sunny afternoon late in autumn. The radio had just begun to play classical music.

I have been ill for four years now. Occasionally I get a little better, but all in all the disease seems to have the upper hand. My progress isn't too good from one year to the next, spring to spring, autumn to autumn. It could be that my strength is slipping away imperceptibly. At any rate, I spend most of my time nowadays lying in bed gazing at the boringly familiar rain stains on the cedar ceiling of my spacious eight-mat room.

Although the weather is too cold for other winged insects, the flies still cling to the ceiling. When the sun shines in, they come down and wander across the tatami matting and the veranda. The flies are a nuisance. They settle on my face.

I also see spiders on the walls and ceiling—great mottled gray ones with leg spans easily four inches across. There must be three of them lurking somewhere in my room. They only come out one at a time, but I see them so often I can tell them apart at a glance. The one that acted strangely was the smallest.

The radio had begun to play "Zigeunerweisen." I recognized it instantly as the same big red Victor record of a Jascha Heifetz performance I used to own. I thrust whatever I was thinking about out of my mind; my ears automatically readied themselves in anticipation of the brilliant melody.

Something darted into my hazy line of sight. A spider ventured about a foot from a corner of the room and halted. Then, out of the corner of my eye, I saw it begin to walk slowly across the wall, moving its legs one at a time with a slightly springing gait. "The Dance of the Spider," I thought for a moment. But it wasn't exactly dancing, or even moving in time with the music. It just wandered around in a clumsy, somehow irritated fashion.

"He's gone and got carried away," I thought in half-disgusted amusement. It was a trifle uncanny. I had heard of cows and dogs being charmed by music—human music, that is—and I had even seen it myself in dogs. But spiders? I found that a bit hard to take. My skeptical eyes remained glued to the spider, determined to see what it would do when the music stopped.

The piece ended. The spider stopped abruptly and disappeared back into its corner with quick noiseless steps. It looked exactly as if it were beating a retreat, slightly embarrassed at having been caught out.

Can spiders hear? I don't know. I once read a book on entomology by Jean-Henri Fabre, but I don't remember if it held the answer to my question. I don't even know if they are equipped with some other sense instead. I am totally ignorant of these matters. Unable to write off what I had seen to chance, I had the queer feeling that spiders weren't to be underestimated.

I once unwittingly trapped a spider for a while. In summer, when I was up and about—I generally feel better when the weather is hot—I needed an empty bottle for some reason. I found what looked like a good one and opened it unsuspectingly. A spider shot out and scuffled into hiding. Only an inch or two across, it was much smaller than the ones in my room, and its slender body was the color of raw meat.

A bit taken aback, I searched my memory. I had had the children wash those bottles at the beginning of spring. They had set them upside down for a day to dry, then stoppered them to keep the dirt out and put them away in an empty box. The spider must have crept in that day.

I doubt the spider gave the matter a thought when the exit was blocked. It would have noticed its predicament some days later when it grew hungry and felt like hunting for food. All efforts would have proved the impossibility of escape, and eventually it would have given up the struggle and waited stoically for its chance. Half a year went by. Then, the moment I removed the stopper, it escaped with a speed that could only be matched by a runner poised for the gun on the starting block.

Something similar happened on another occasion. There is a toilet at the western end of the veranda on the south side of my room. The window above the urinal opens toward the west, so I can gaze through the plum trees at the looming bulk of Mount Fuji when I relieve myself. One morning I found a spider caught between the two sliding window panes. Someone—it could have been me—must have opened the window the night before, shutting in the spider, which had been clinging to one of the panes. There was enough space between the panes so that it wasn't crushed, but the overlapping frames yielded no crack for escape. About four inches across, the spider was the same kind as the ones in my room.

I immediately thought of the incident with the bottle and felt an urge to see how long this one could hold out. I instructed the family not to shut the window. The spider in the bottle had survived for about six months without food on only the air from a tiny gap in the crude wooden stopper. This one was much bigger and plumper. It was going to be a long test of staying power between us.

The Fuji I see from the toilet window changes garb according to the weather and the time of day. In the daytime, in clear weather, the view is uninspiring. But in the middle of the night, under the chill moonlight, the mountain silently emits a dull white fluorescence. And at dawn, while the stars still gleam in the sky, it glows rosily at the summit and a deep mauve at the base.

The spider always stood there, superimposed diagonally on the mountain as if treading its slopes. It never moved. It didn't kick once the whole time I held it prisoner. At times I would be almost ready to give up. I would tap on the window and call out to it; all it would do was flinch resignedly.

After a month or so, I noticed it was thinner.

"The spider in the toilet's getting thinner," I called out to my wife.

"I know. The poor thing."

"I wonder how long a spider can go without food."

"I wouldn't know," my wife replied. She sounded as if she couldn't care less, either. It was a tone that said, "Small things amuse small minds" and "It's certainly no fun for the spider."

"Don't let it out, though," I retorted.

About two weeks later, the spider was clearly emaciated and its color had faded. Then, just before two months were up—only a few days after that other spider took a stroll on my wall—I heard my wife cry out from the toilet.

"Oh, no." A pause. "It got away."

In my somnolent daze I realized she had let it out. But I didn't really mind, so I said nothing.

"Whenever I clean the toilet," my wife explained defensively, "I'm always very careful to move both panes together so it can't get out. But today I forgot and moved only one. I got it half open before I realized, and then it was too late. You should have seen how fast it moved; it was just as if it had been waiting for the chance."

Her words flowed in one ear and out the other. "That's one spider that's lucky to be alive," I muttered. In fact, I'd grown a bit bored with fine test of staying power, and now the matter was settled. If anything, I was grateful the contest had turned out this way.

From the day I was born into this world, I have been running three-legged, tied to a fellow named Death. Unasked, he has accompanied me everywhere for forty-eight years. His mien is decidedly grim these days; it worries me constantly.

I was going on twenty when it first sunk in that the bastard had always been with me. I had just begun to be aware of life, much later than most people. I took my time about such things.

When I was twenty-three, I fell seriously ill for a year. I nearly gave in to him then, but somehow I pulled through, and ever since I've thought him an easy match. Not openly, mind you. He'd be infuriated if I let it show, and that wouldn't do me any good. I wouldn't want him to speed up.

I don't like writing in this pretentious vein, so I'll get to the point. One thing is clear: I've got to go wherever he's going. It makes no difference whether I resist. It's only a matter of time.

With nothing to do but watch the spiders and flies come and go on my ceiling, I give myself over to musing: Nothing is more poignant, more pitiful, than humankind's efforts to escape time and space, to grasp at God or the Absolute or a straw, or anything else that floats by. An instant is a thousand years, the cosmos within the individual, you name it, I bet it's only at conceptual edifice. So why don't we give up? Why mustn't we give up? Look at the magnificent castles in the air built by people who have refused to give up. How exquisite they are!

Getting back to insects, I once read somewhere how a showman breaks in fleas for a circus. He catches a flea and puts it in a small glass sphere. The flea jumps with its powerful legs. But it is surrounded as if by a steel wall. After jumping frantically, it begins to suspect that jumping may be the wrong answer. It tries again. And fails. It gives up and quiets down. The trainer, the human, frightens it. The flea instinctively jumps. But it can't get out. The human frightens it again. The flea jumps. It realizes jumping won't work. With repetition, the flea won't jump no matter what. At that point it is taught tricks and put on show.

I remember thinking it horribly cruel that the insect's innate ability should be changed so easily. One morning an action that had been preconscious and thus beyond question suddenly becomes wrong. Few things, I thought, could be more cruelly inexplicable.

"It's a terrible business," I told a young friend who had made my illness an excuse to come down from Tokyo. "I can hardly imagine the flea's despair when it finds out it's no use. It certainly deserves a bit of sympathy. But then, the flea does rather bury its head in the sand, doesn't it? Perhaps it's born stupid. . . . All the same, why can't it give it another try? Just once, even."

"Maybe the flea thinks it's absolute." My friend grinned. "Thinks it's given it that one last try."

"Maybe. It's a pity all the same." I put on a sorrowful face.

"I came across exactly the opposite story the other day." My friend laughed. "This bee, I forget its name, its wings aren't strong enough to lift its weight. Someone studied all the data on its wing area and the number of beats per second it makes in the air and concluded that the laws of dynamics make it impossible for it to fly. And yet the bee flies quite happily because it doesn't know it can't."

"Hmm. Could be. You know, that's a pretty good story." The thought crossed my mind that dynamics might be suffering from overconfidence. But I was tickled by the notion of something being possible because one doesn't know it isn't. I felt a little less depressed about the flea.

Neuralgia and rheumatic pain aren't supposed to be massaged. When the pain isn't too bad, however, it often subsides with rubbing, so I get my wife or daughter to massage me. If they make it worse, though, the pain is excruciating; the slightest touch is agony, and bystanders can't lay a hand to it.

When it's only stiff shoulders that are the problem, not neuralgia, I indulge myself by grabbing one of the members of the household from her chores and getting her to massage me. I often have my sixteen-year-old daughter do it now-adays. She's almost as tall as her mother now, wears the same size shoes, and has a good bit of strength. Her fingertips are more supple and effective than my wife's, which have been roughened by all the heavy work since we evacuated to the country because of the war. Besides, my daughter makes good use of the time: She uses me as a desk, going over her lessons with a book open on my back while she massages my right shoulder.

Sometimes she talks. Mostly it's everyday chat about school, her teachers, and her friends, so all I have to do is grunt to show I'm listening. But now and then she asks questions. The other day, quite out of the blue, she asked whether the universe was finite or infinite. I felt as though I'd been caught napping.

"I don't know. I'm not sure anyone knows."

"Not even the scientists?"

"I don't think there's any accepted theory. Don't ask me. Your father would like to know even more than you do."

I remembered an article I'd read a while earlier. It said there are an esti-mated hundred million spiral nebulae in the universe, an average of two mil-lion light-years apart. The farthest, at the edge of the universe, is two hundred fifty million light-years from the earth. Each is twenty thousand light-years in diameter. And our solar system is only a tiny component of one of these hun-dred million spiral nebulae. I remembered once having lapsed into sentimen-tality about the vastness of the universe—I must have been in my senior year of secondary school. Now that my sixteen-year-old daughter seemed to have reached the same stage, I felt an urge to reassure her.

"Do you know what a light-year is?" I asked.

"Yes, sir. It's the distance light travels in a year." She deliberately replied as if answering a classroom question.

"Very good. Now then, how many kilometers is that?" I played the teacher.

"Umm."

"Stop that and get a pencil and paper. I want you to do some calculations."

"Let's see, now. The speed of light is . . ."

My daughter came up with a figure about thirteen digits long.

"Help, the zeros have gone off the page," she said.

"Now multiply that by two hundred fifty million." "I can't. It's too astronomical."

"This is astronomy, though."

"Oh yes, so it is. These figures make me feel funny, kind of sad." She let the pencil drop.

We fell silent. Eventually I spoke. "You needn't be surprised at the figures, you know. After all, numbers are a human invention. Everything depends on where you set the unit. Suppose we made a hundred million light-years the unit, call it, say, a super-light-year. Then the radius of the visible universe comes out at two and a half to three super-light-years. That's only two point five or three, you see. But if you were to use atomic units, the zeros wouldn't just run off the page, you couldn't even write them all down in a lifetime."

"Mmm," she answered in a small voice.

"It all depends on the unit. If the universe is finite, then the figure will fit inside the human head, no matter how many zeros there are. But if it's infinite, only . . ."

The word *God* was about to fall from my lips, and I broke off. My daughter was massaging my shoulder mechanically. The question had begun to get under my skin, and I carried on muttering in my head.

Where do we stand in the universe? Where are we stuck in time and space? Can we ever know for ourselves? And if so, would we then cease to be ourselves?

I thought about the spiders and the fleas and that bee, whatever you call it. The two trapped spiders had escaped by chance. I had to be impressed by, while almost resenting, the way they waited patiently for a chance that might never come, and the speed with which they seized it when it came.

The flea is stupid and gutless; the whatsitsname bee is blind and fearless. Which are we? Fleas that abandon all hope even after the glass globe has been removed? Or bees that make the impossible possible by believing? Forget the *we*: Which am I?

I can't match the spider's calm doggedness, much as I'd like to. I don't think I have it in me.

I could never match the blind confidence of the whatsitsname bee. But is that really confidence? Confidence isn't the word if the bee does it unconsciously. It's perfectly natural to the bee, so no one has any right to tell it otherwise.

Perhaps I'm a bit like the stupid, gutless flea.

Does freedom exist? Or is everything predestined? Is my freedom determined by some scenario? Or is everything sheer chance? Does the glass globe exist or not? I don't know. All I know is that someday the three-legged race will end.

What if someone out there is watching my every movement the way I contemplate the spiders and the fleas and the bees? What if someone is trying to control my thoughts and actions the way I trapped those spiders and let them escape? What if I am about to be cruelly enlightened in the same manner as the flea? How do I know someone isn't going to turn around to me, the bee, and say, "You can't fly"? Does that someone exist in the first place, or do we create him? Or do we become him? Nothing tells me the answers.

The flies are a nuisance. Because it's winter, they only come out when the sun is at its height. They make a playground of my face as I lie buried to my chin in quilts.

I have made an important discovery about flies. When they land on my face,

I twitch a muscle or shake my head slightly to drive them away. They immediately return to the same spot. I chase them away again. They fly off and land once more. After three tries, they give up and find somewhere else to go. It happens every time. Flies seem to have the habit of changing their minds the third time round.

"Try it. It's fun," I tell the family.

"That's interesting," they say without really meaning it. No one tries the experiment. They are tacitly telling me they are too busy. Of course, I don't force them to try it, but I grumble to myself, "What do they mean, too busy? Is what they're doing really so important?"

I once pulled off a rare feat. I caught a fly on my forehead. It had landed there, and without particularly intending to drive it away, I raised my eyebrows sharply. A commotion promptly broke out on my forehead. My movement had made a furrow that had snared I don't know how many of the fly's legs. The fly was right there buzzing its wings exaggeratedly in its panic.

"Quick! Someone!" I bellowed, keeping my eyebrows raised to hold the wrinkle in my brow. It made me look doltish. My eldest son came in wondering what the fuss was about.

"Get that fly on my forehead, will you?"

"How? You don't want me to swat it, do you?"

"Pick it up in your hand. It's easy. The fly's not going anywhere."

My son's dubious fingers had no difficulty picking off the fly.

"How about that? Pretty good, huh? Not everyone can catch flies with their forehead. It may go down in history."

"I don't believe it." My son wrinkled his brow and felt it with his hand.

"You're not up to it." I grinned, watching my son as he stood holding the fly gingerly in one hand and rubbing his brow with the other. He's thirteen and in his first year of middle school. A big, healthy lad. He can't produce a decent furrow. Mine run deep, and they aren't confined to my brow.

"What's up? Is anything wrong?"

Everyone trooped in from the next room and roared with laughter at my son's account. "Wow, that's neat." My seven-year-old younger daughter laughed cheekily. They all rubbed their brows in unison.

"All right, everybody out," I said. I was beginning to feel a little disgruntled.

SHIBA RYŌTARŌ

In the 1960s, Shiba Ryōtarō (1923–1996) began writing historical novels and, to interest younger readers in historical subjects, presenting them with psychological roundness and attractive detail based on his background research. Some of Shiba's works were dramatized for film and television, and, as a result, he became perhaps the most popular writer among the general Japanese public in the past twenty-odd years. The story "Daté's Black Ship" (Date no kurobune,

1964), which deals in a most unusual way with the coming of the West to Japan in the nineteenth century, was published in the collection *Drunk as a Lord* (*Yotte soro*, 1975).

DATÉ'S BLACK SHIP (DATE NO KUROBUNE)

Translated by Eileen Kato

1

The man Kazo lived in a back-alley tenement called the Heibedana in Urama-chi 4-chome in the castle town of Uwajima. "In the entire town, you could not find a man more filthy," was the general opinion of him.

Uwajima was the domain of the Daté family, and in it minute differences in social rank were observed with exaggerated care. The townspeople properly so styled were people of substance who lived in fine estates along the main thoroughfares and were privileged to elect town elders. Just beneath them were the tenants of rented houses. Even among these rent-payers, however, were "upper" and "lower" classes. People like Kazo—the "back-alley slum dwellers"—were the lowest of the low.

People spread rumors about Kazo. "His wife ran away from him!" neighbors said. By now this had become almost common knowledge. The man came from Yawatahama, the chief trading port of the domain. He had once been the proprietor of a small shop that sold cereals, but had been unable to make money at it and eventually arrived at the castle town broke. The wife who abandoned him went by the name O-Kuma and was the daughter of a Yawatahama oil dealer. She stayed with Kazo for a year before she could no longer tolerate his shiftlessness and impoverishment. She ran home to her parents' house, leaving a child behind. These were the details of Kazo's discreditable past with his wife.

"You're completely useless when it comes to making money!" his mother told him when she learned that his wife had left him. "I'll look after the child. You go up to the castle town. There at least you may have a chance of feeding yourself on the rice grains that fall your way from passing loads."

Kazo was twenty-three years old when he first arrived in the castle town. Now he was forty-two. He had tried his hand at all kinds of work. For a while he peddled shredded tobacco. One might even say that he attained a certain notoriety for it; people remarked, "For some reason, that Kazo's tobacco stinks!" The secret to any trade is personal charm. If a roll of kimono cloth is sold by a dealer with personal appeal, the fabric itself—even the very pattern—will be enhanced. The converse applied to Kazo: the tobacco he sold, even if it was the same tobacco sold anywhere else, seemed to discourage purchase simply because it had been handled by Kazo. People were inclined to view it as horse dung.

As a matter of fact, people called him "Horseshit Kazo" behind his back. Nor was that his only nickname. Because he was plagued by smallpox, he was also

"Pumice with Eyes and a Nose"—a reference to his pockmarked face. With terrible looks and no way to make money, it would seem he had nothing to recommend him. Moreover, at his present age, it was hardly expected that he would be able to get himself another wife.

But there was one promising attribute this product of the back-alley tenements did have, and that was his amazing skill as a craftsman. One might say that he had the hands of a god, for without any formal training whatsoever, he could look at a thing once and produce an improved version of it. He was exceptionally clever at repairing old, tattered lanterns. When people's lanterns were torn he would promptly fix them. "Kazo, why don't you take up that work and make a living?" urged Seike Ichirozaemon, a wealthy merchant with a home in Honmachi 4-chome. With these words of encouragement and a little assistance from Seike himself, Kazo set up shop. A cedar signboard in front read:

YOUR LANTERNS REPAPERED—KAZO—

But knowing he could not make ends meet just by papering lanterns, he appended under this in small letters:

ANY AND ALL TYPES OF HANDIWORK DONE

Kazo's business was not limited to paper lanterns; he also produced ornamental crafts such as hairpins, lacquerware, and miniature palaces for Doll Festival celebrations. He also made poles for raising streamers on the Boys' Festival. Occasionally he would even find himself repairing a samurai's helmet or suit of armor or sculpting a Buddhist statue. No matter what he undertook to make or fix, he did the job with such mastery that people were astounded by his talent.

Still, not many people brought him work. To every craft its own craftsman. That was common sense for people of the castle town. Few would be so foolish as to entrust precious family heirlooms, such as suits of armor or Buddhist altars, to a jack-of-all-trades, no matter how clever his hands were rumored to be. Thus Kazo continued to while away his days in poverty, unsure where the next meal would come from.

"That Kazo is quite an interesting fellow," Seike often exclaimed. There seemed to be no one else who spoke so kindly of him, and for that reason, Seike's house was the only one Kazo ever visited.

"If it weren't for the Honmachi master," Kazo had often thought, "I'd be no better off than a stray dog."

Whenever Kazo visited the Seike house, he would go in by way of the service entrance, bent over double. Even before the humblest of kitchen servants, male or female, he would grovel and cringe and bow his head low as he made his greeting—"Fine weather we're having!" If the master wanted a word with him, Kazo would go around to the earthen-floored kitchen in the rear of the house and, with one knee to the bare earth, place his hands side by side on the

elevated floorboards and listen. Because of his social standing—or lack thereof—
he never once presumed to gaze upon the face of this great merchant towns-
man, Seike, who had the right to bear both sword and surname.

Such was Kazo's life. Or at least it was until January 31, 1854—the third day
of the new year, the first year of Ansei. Kazo was forty-two years old.

"Kazo!" shouted the big boss from an inner room. Kazo genuflected as usual
on the earthen kitchen floor as Seike spoke.

"I have something very important to say to you, so come on up into the
room. We'll talk over a round of spiced saké."

Kazo stepped up onto the boarded area. Then, bending his knees as low as
they would go, he crossed the floor, being careful not to cause the slightest
squeak. With another step up, he entered an outer room; after passing through
it, he crossed over a line of partition grooves to enter the innermost room where
the master was. He had been coming to this residence for well over ten years,
but this day marked the first time he had been allowed in one of the tatami-
matted rooms.

"You know the house councillor Ko'ori Saemon?" asked Seike.

"I've heard his name."

"We spoke together recently. It seems that in foreign lands they have made
a ship called a steamer that can go without oars and is propelled only by me-
chanical devices."

"Would that be the same sort of ship that anchored off Uraga last year with
a navy commander on board, a Meriken called 'Peruri' or something like that—
the ship they call the black ship?"

"That's it! That's it! The black ship! The ship that practically turned the
country upside down and threw everything into confusion. At that time,
Lord . . ."

"Lord?" Kazo broke in. "You don't mean Ko'ori-Sama, the house councillor,
do you?"

"No, I mean the daimyo. The daimyo said to Ko'ori-Sama, 'Why not build a
black ship like that in our own domain?'"

"Did he really?"

"Ko'ori-Sama discussed the matter with me. He asked me if there was no one
in Uwajima who could take on such a project. Then it occurred to me. I clapped
my hands and said, 'Why, yes, there is! He goes by the name Kazo and runs a
lantern shop.'"

Kazo gulped and then went deathly pale. No matter how skilled a lantern re-
pairman he might be, there was no reason to assume he could build a steam-
ship. But the big boss, great merchant that he was, showed determination.

"There is nothing a foreigner can make that an Uwajima lantern repairman
cannot. Kazo, you can do it!"

Kazo began to shiver and shake. If he did not build it, this master merchant—
supplier to the entire domain—would be discredited, and the house councillor

Ko'ori would fall out of countenance with the daimyo. Crawling out the service door, Kazo made his way down the Honmachi road without even a lantern to light his way. That night, he walked every street that could be called a street until daybreak, trying to think what to do. He occasionally sat down for a rest under the temple gates. At sunrise, he went out to the beach and mingled with a group of fishermen hauling in a trawl and even joined in with them as they sang their trawlers' songs.

"Queer sort of fellow," the fishermen thought. They presented him with one of the fish from their net. Kazo placed it in the breast fold of his kimono and parted company with them that morning feeling rejuvenated.

Trawling is done by means of a pulley. It was seeing the pulley that had put Kazo in such high spirits. The moment he set eyes on it, his imagination took off. It would not be too much to say that Kazo's poverty-stricken life changed its course entirely in that moment.

When he got home, he let down the shutters and posted out in front of his shop an awkwardly written sign: "No one Home." For fifteen days, he stayed holed up in his house, building a strange, box-like contraption. When finally he brought it to Honmachi 4-chome, the master inspected it closely. It was two and a half feet long, one foot wide, and about seven inches deep. Attached to it were four wheels. Based on a design inspired by the pulley, the inside had a mechanical system of several cogwheels, both large and small. If the central axle was turned once, the outer wheels would turn three times. Seike put the device to the test by grasping the axle and turning it. Instantly the box began to move.

"It moves by itself!" cried the master in amazement.

Nor was that all. The box was also equipped with a small, lever-like contrivance that, when lifted, made the inner cogwheels reverse direction. The master tested this too, and sure enough, the wheels began to turn the other way.

"Ha! If this is set into a ship, it will go by itself!" Seike exclaimed in sheer delight. Seike, although Kazo called him "master," was no more knowledgeable about the "self-propelled" black ships than Kazo; they both had learned about them only by hearsay and had no understanding of the theoretical principles or mechanisms involved in their design. Seike figured, though, that they must be driven by some such device as what Kazo had produced.

Saying that he must show Kazo's machine without delay to the house councillor Ko'ori, who would no doubt also be delighted by it, Seike set about "going through the proper channels." It was an extremely punctilious society when it came to matters of personal rank and status.

No denizen of the back-alley tenements, even if he were a genius who had made a great discovery, could hope to be recognized as a fully respectable human being unless his landlord publicly vouched for him. Kazo's box, along with his words recorded on an attached piece of paper, went from his landlord to the town elders, from them to the town magistrate, and finally, from the town magistrate to the house councillor Ko'ori. Ko'ori, in turn, presented it to the daimyo in power at the time, Daté Munenari. "This is extraordinary!" exclaimed Munenari, one of the renowned "wise lords" of the day. He was so pleased he clapped his hands.

2

Here we must say a word about Daté Munenari.

He was not born into a daimyo family. He was the fourth son of a *hatamoto*, a direct retainer to the shogun, by the name of Yamaguchi Naokatsu. Munenari was adopted at the age of twelve into the Daté family of Uwajima, with whom his own family had kinship ties. At twenty-seven, he succeeded to the line of daimyo descended from Daté Hidemune, son of Masamune, and was granted junior fourth court rank, lower grade, with the title "governor of Totomi."

There are many anecdotes concerning this man.

To begin with, when he was eighteen and still known as Heigoro, he lived at the residence of the Daté family in Azabu Ryudocho, and he often visited the Mito residence. The lord of Mito at the time, Tokugawa Nariaki, a man renowned among his peers for his indomitable spirit, took a liking to the lad, and made him more or less his disciple. Later on in life, when Munenari became active as a kind of daimyo-turned-*shishi* (most of the pro-imperial, anti-bakufu patriots called *shishi* were drawn from lower samurai ranks), people attributed it to Nariaki's influence. It was at about this time, at any rate, when Munenari was eighteen, that the following story takes place.

On one of his visits to the Mito residence, it so happened that the vassals were in the garden gathering into two teams, the reds and the whites. They were about to begin a game of *dakyu* polo; the Mito lord Nariaki was the sponsor. In the game of *dakyu*, two teams are mounted on horseback and each man is given a long polo stick. In the middle of the playing field are piles of red and white balls. The players gallop in from opposite ends of the field and, in the great melee that ensues, try to hit the opponents' balls into a designated goal area. The team that succeeds most often wins.

The young Daté Munenari loved athletic contests of this kind and begged Nariaki to let him join in.

Probably because Nariaki thought the boy's participation might add excitement to the game, he made himself captain of the reds and young Munenari captain of the whites. Soon the two teams were fiercely competing, raising great clouds of dust.

In politics, Nariaki was a wily old fox. He displayed that same craftiness on the field that day; when defeat seemed imminent, he surreptitiously picked up one of the last red balls and concealed it between his elbow and hip. The eighteen-year-old Munenari caught him at it, though, and came galloping out of the team captain's enclosure, spurring on his horse at full speed. When he approached Nariaki, he lifted his stick and—psssh!—struck the ball loose.

Then he skillfully scooped it up and galloped away with it, straight into the goal area.

The enthralling sight of Munenari flaunting his team's camp colors as he rode into the goal area, still in his saddle after making so many dangerous moves, was like that of a gallant young warrior in battle. Nariaki's wife, who had watched the game from the sidelines, commented, "Minamoto no Kuro Yoshitsune in his scarlet-laced suit of armor must have looked a lot like that young nobleman," and then earnestly urged the princess, her eldest daughter, to make a match with the young Munenari. Nariaki, too, had high hopes for a marriage after witnessing this. He even had the artist Tachihara Kyosho paint a picture of the gallant Munenari as he raised high the colors of his camp and triumphantly galloped into the goal area. Afterward, Nariaki showed this painting to his daughter on regular occasions. And so it was no surprise that Nariaki's daughter fell in love with Munenari, sight unseen. For a while she even busied herself with wedding preparations. When it came time to exchange engagement gifts, a man by the name of Takeda (a Mito house councillor who later became head of a radical loyalist group called the Tenguto) was appointed envoy and came to the Daté house. But, alas, five days before the wedding, the princess died of illness, and the marriage arrangements came to nothing.

Munenari, who later nicknamed himself "Longface," indeed had a long face. The bridge of his nose ran straight and high, while his mouth formed a firm line. He could well have been called a fine-looking man. And an educated one. He had a love for learning. Among the chief vassals of his clan, not one could boast Munenari's level of cultivation.

Munenari was an adopted heir. When one considers that most of the "wise lords" active in the last days of the shogunate came from households of unexceptional social standing and only became daimyo after having been adopted into great families, it becomes apparent that they all had in common a trait one might call "adopted son syndrome." Munenari was a prime example. Had he been less fortunate, he would have merely been the fourth son of a *hatamoto* and, as such, could never have hoped to inherit even the three thousand *koku* of his own house. Yet owing to a distant connection with the Daté family, he was able to become lord of the 100,000-*koku* Uwajima domain. Naturally, ambition swelled in him. He aspired to tap the power and action of the domain like no one born rightful heir to a daimyo house would. This aspiration, common to adoptive daimyo, revealed itself in his handling of *han* affairs: he vigorously promoted production. But he also had a special feel for social matters and frequently acted as mediator and conciliator in daimyo family feuds. Finally, he was a man with a very kind disposition.

The Shimazu family of Satsuma was riven with internal conflict. The in-house feud stemmed from the lord Shimazu Narioki's seeking to disinherit his legitimate heir Nariaki and supplant him with Hisamitsu, a son born of his jealous concubine O-Yura. This gave rise to a protest movement for which Narioki ordered seventeen of the protesters to commit suicide by ritual disembowelment.

Terrible trouble ensued, and Munenari was called upon by a kinsman of the Shimazu family to act as mediator. He went to see the chief shogunal councillor Abe Masahiro and got him to persuade Narioki to retire, immediately establishing Nariakira as the lawful successor. For this reason, the Shimazu family felt greatly indebted to Munenari. Samurai of the Nariakira faction like Fujii Ryosetsu, Takasaki Sataro, and Takasaki Inotaro never forgot their gratitude to the man. Though they were all active in Kyoto during the final years of the shogunate as agents of Satsuma, they were also agents of Munenari who kept him informed on all important happenings in the capital and sent him regular reports just as if they were his own retainers.

It was the same with the Yamauchi family of Tosa. When the fourteenth daimyo Toyoatsu had fallen ill and died suddenly, not long after succeeding to the headship of the clan, the whole house was thrown into confusion. This was because an heir had not yet been selected. According to bakufu law, if a daimyo died without an heir, his line would be declared extinct, and his lands and castle forfeited. The chief vassals of the Yamauchi family, in utmost secrecy, buried Toyoatsu's corpse in the residence grounds and said only that he was stricken with illness. Then they called upon Shimazu Nariakira to help them devise a stratagem to deal with the bakufu. Nariakira, in turn, had recourse to Munenari, who had great personal magnetism and an uncanny ability to conduct difficult negotiations. Munenari then called on the shogunal councillor Abe Masahiro to repair the delicate situation. The deceased Toyoatsu "lived on" to go into "formal retirement," while Yamauchi Toyoshige (later known by the name Yodo), a youth from a branch family and one highly acclaimed for his intelligence, was quickly made heir. Disaster had been successfully averted thanks to the good offices of Munenari, and the Yamauchi lived on. For as long as he lived, Toyoshige—or Yodo, as history calls him—regarded Munenari as his benefactor.

With only the status of adoptive daimyo of a mere hundred thousand *koku*, Munenari had put in his debt the Shimazu clan of Satsuma with their more than seven hundred thousand *koku*, the Kuroda of Chikuzen with their five hundred and twenty thousand *koku*, and the Yamauchi of Tosa with their two hundred and forty thousand *koku*. In a word, Shimazu Nariakira and Yamauchi Toyoshige both came to be daimyo because of Munenari.

That Munenari should come to occupy a unique position among the daimyo, even though his status was such that he was assigned last place in the Great Hall of Edo Castle, was doubtless due to his tact and versatility in social capacities, as well as to his superior gift for discerning the trend of the times. In the final years of the bakufu, he earned an esteemed place among the "four wise lords," whom patriots throughout the country looked to as saviors. The other such lords were Shimazu Nariakira of Satsuma, Yamauchi Yodo of Tosa, and Matsudaira Shungaku of Echizen.

Tomita Oribe, a retainer of the Sanjo family in Kyoto, went to Edo in the early summer of 1858 to meet with these four sages. Here is what he had to say about Munenari in the character sketch he gave at the time: "The lord of Uwa-jima engages in much debate. He is a somewhat disputatious person."

In 1865, the young Ernest Satow, interpreter for the British, visited Munenari in retirement, and the impression he received does not appear to have been alto-gether positive: ". . . A tall man with strongly marked features and a big nose, re-puted to be one of the most intelligent of his class, imperious in manner. . . ." This is not the Munenari one reads about in records postdating the Meiji Restora-tion; Munenari in those days was an old man so mild in manner that he is de-scribed as the very epitome of a gentleman.

The thread of the story is getting lost.

Munenari had yet another strong trait. This was his love of anything novel. He was quite interested in so-called "Dutch studies." He was even called a "Dutch addict" because he collected whatever Western gadgets he could get his hands on. He aspired to reproduce in his Uwajima domain, in the southwest corner of Shikoku, any new invention of European civilization.

In 1849, after successfully conciliating a feud between the Kuroda family of Chikuzen and the Nabeshima family of Hizen, a package was delivered to his Azabu residence in Edo. It was sent by special courier from Fukuoka in Chiku-zen by Lord Kuroda himself. The message inside read: "In token of gratitude." It was a large gold-lacquered box. When the lid was lifted, a small paulownia box was revealed inside. The lid of this box in turn was lifted to reveal two tiny sticks wrapped in silk. These were matches.

Munenari had heard about matches, but this was the first time he had actu-ally seen one. He showed them off enthusiastically to anyone and everyone at the shogunal palace. "It doesn't matter whether it is against the ground or against a wall; if you rub this small, round, red 'leek-blossom' head against a surface, it will immediately catch fire." This was his way of explaining the match as he went about on his rounds.

The phosphor "lucifer match" was invented in Europe only a few short years before this, so even in Europe there would have been a great many people in rural areas who had never even seen one. If one bears in mind the history of the European match, Munenari's elation was not out of the ordinary. But would it not be kinder of us to put ourselves in his position, to imagine ourselves as the lord of a small provincial domain in the Far East, learning about the match at roughly the same time the Englishman in the streets of London began to light his cigarette with it? If we do this, perhaps we can understand Munenari's ad-miration for the small sticks, and why he felt inspired to produce the same sort of thing in his own domain.

It was in 1849 that Munenari was mesmerized by the two matchsticks. Four years later, in 1853, U.S. Commodore Matthew Perry sailed into Edo Bay, de-manding that the bakufu put an end to its policy of seclusion. The ensuing tur-bulence brought down the final curtain on the era of the shogunate. Throughout those years, "wise lord" Munenari had gradually been formulating an idea: "Wouldn't it be possible to build a warship like Perry's in our own domain?" He discussed the matter with his house councillor back at home, Ko'ori Saemon. The gist of his thinking eventually filtered down to lantern repairman Kazo, a mere eight months after the coming of these "black ships."

3

Munenari happened to be at home in Uwajima Castle when house councillor Ko'ori Saemon presented him with the box on wheels.

"Quick!" he said, after he had peered inside. "Have a self-propelled ship made with this mechanism! The man who built it—what does he do for a living, anyway?"

"He repapers lanterns and things," replied Ko'ori with all seriousness.

This by itself was not a surprise to Munenari. There was no reason why a lantern repairman should not be able to make a battleship, he figured. He was excited, and whenever he became excited, his speech would accelerate until he began to stammer. If his orders were not promptly carried out, he would have no reserve about voicing his displeasure.

As soon as he returned to the staff room, Ko'ori Saemon set about implementing Munenari's order. Through the offices of the town magistrate, he sent a command to Kazo's landlord: "Tomorrow he is to be sent to the domain shipyard. However, he will not be compensated for his services." In other words, Kazo would be a shipwright's helper.

The shipbuilder's shed at the domain shipyard was built on the beach, and the overseer was the superintendent of shipping. Here, under the supervision of various officials, carpenters were constantly engaged in the manufacture and repair of the daimyo's vessels. They had just finished building a new boat when they received orders from the *han* to attach Kazo's mechanism to it. Kazo went to work with the regular shipwrights bustling all around him. The work progressed, and in twenty days' time the basic machinery had been completed. On the model of Perry's vessels, several pairs of wheels, each mounted on an axle, were then installed in the hull. To operate these wheels, all that was needed was for one man inside the boat to turn a wheel about the size of a handcart wheel.

When at last the machine was put to the test, the outer wheels began to turn with a growl and a roar, cleaving the air around them and setting the whole shed shaking. It raised a great gust of wind and churned up the earth below. The terror-stricken shipwrights scattered in all directions.

At last the ship was launched. For her trial run it was decided to have her sail from the shore of the castle town to the offing of the Kabasaki guardhouse and back—a distance of several hundred yards. Twenty officials were aboard, including several captains and the *han* superintendent of shipping for the domain.

The whole thing ended in failure, though. Kazo had no clear understanding of the physical forces exerted on a ship's hull. He had attached his mechanism to an ordinary Japanese vessel, not designed to carry such heavy machinery. Consequently, the ship sank over a foot below its normal waterline, and the outer wheels did not function as they should have. Four men were at work turning the wheel inside the vessel but she just drifted.

Kazo was terrified. He thought of running away from Uwajima, but he lacked the courage to do so, and as was his wont, holed himself up at home. He lowered the shutters and put up a sign on his door that read, "Kazo is not at home." For a few days, he just lay low, like a cur beaten in a fight, almost afraid to breathe. He was racked with hunger. No work had come his way for some time now, and so he had no money to buy food. While he stayed shut up in his shop, he ate or drank scarcely a thing.

But after a few days, his landlord came with an official writ of summons. "Kazo, listen to this!" he exclaimed. "It says you are to go in formal dress to the Management Office." Sure enough, the official summons read: "In connection with work for the domain, you are hereby ordered to present yourself without delay at the Management Office."

Finding this rather strange, Kazo went to consult the Honmachi 4-chome master. The master rejoiced after reading the summons. "Kazo, that earthen floor beneath you puts us on a different level. Come on up to the room. This is tremendous!" He lent Kazo a *haori* and *hakama* and said, "Go immediately," adding breathlessly that if good fortune is not taken when it comes, luck runs out.

At the Management Office, Kazo was called into a room where an official with a sly face like a badger read aloud his appointment. "As pertains to you, you have been appointed shipbuilder with a two-person stipend of five sacks of rice. You will be under the direction of the superintendent of shipping."

Kazo was now a carpenter officially in the employ of the domain. He was not a samurai, but something slightly better than a samurai's lackey. He still did not have the right to take a surname, but that did not matter; for Kazo the lantern repairman who lived in a slum tenement, just to know where his next meal would come from was a high step up in the world.

When he returned to the waiting room, the notary, Furusawa Iemon, a fine samurai, wept tears of joy for the humble tenement dweller Kazo, whom he had never even met before. "This is a most fortunate thing," he said, and gave Kazo a list of the names of officials at the Management Office. "Now go around and thank all of these officials." Though Kazo did not rightly understand what had happened to him, he nevertheless did as he was told and went about making his rounds. When he got back to town, everyone from the landlord on down came to visit him and offer their congratulations.

When he went to Honmachi 4-chome, the master took him by the hand and led him into the guest room. The lady of the house, who normally never showed her face, was there too, along with all her daughters, to celebrate Kazo's good fortune. Even the old clerk, usually so stern, now joined in the festivities, saying, "It's like the rise to greatness of Taiko Hideyoshi."

In fact it was. Under the Tokugawa regime that proscribed all social mobility, in a country town that was like a thick scab on the body politic, a middle-aged man who lived in a slum tenement and who until yesterday had been treated like human refuse, had now been promoted to the status of domain employee and was entitled to draw a regular stipend. This could well be compared to the miraculous rise of Toyotomi Hideyoshi in the Sengoku era.

But for three days after his appointment, his good fortune left Kazo in dire straits. Neighbors and kinsfolk had come to see him and offer their congratulations; each of them came in and sat down, so naturally Kazo had to serve them saké. In Uwajima, when one visited another's house, one did not say "good day" but came right in with a loud long-winded "*Haaii!*" Every time Kazo heard this sound coming from the entryway, he would begin to tremble.

When Munenari gave out an order, the Uwajima domain would usually take administrative action straightaway. A writ had come from the Management Office that was tantamount to a call for Kazo's eviction. "As regards your dispatch to Nagasaki for work on the steamer, you are to set out on the ninth," it read. Kazo had no choice but to obey. Could a battleship be built as easily as a lantern could be repapered? Kazo doubted it. To begin with, he had never seen the so-called "black ships" that had recently arrived off the coast of Uraga, nor could he even imagine what they were like. He considered refusing the order he had been given. By now he was just about able to feed himself; he did not need the help of the *han*. Yet when he thought about the wretched life he had led for the past twenty years, it was not easy to throw away a guaranteed stipend of five sacks of rice. Building a black ship was better than peddling tobacco or repapering lanterns, he concluded. "We'll see what happens after I get to Nagasaki," he told himself. But battleships? For a man of such lowly birth as himself?

There was something terrible in store for Kazo, as he soon found out. At the Management Office he had been told: "As regards the trip to Nagasaki, the honorable Sudo Dan'emon will be in charge. You will follow his every instruction." That very day, Kazo went to Sudo's residence. As soon as Sudo saw him standing there in the front entrance, he roared, "Are you the man Kazo? What brings you to the front entrance?" Kazo was ordered to go around by the garden and to get down with his knees to the ground. He kept his head lowered as Sudo's harangue rained down on him from above.

Later, people informed him that in official circles it was a custom to present, on such occasions, an obligatory contribution of money discreetly hidden in a cake box. But even if Kazo had known this in advance, he did not have a single coin to offer. For his lodgings in Nagasaki, he was told he would stay at the house of one Aritaya Hikosuke, the Uwajima official in charge of *han* commerce. His board and lodging fees would be paid for by the *han* afterward.

On April 6, 1854, humble Kazo set out from the castle town of Uwajima on the splendid mission of researching the mechanics of steamship construction. No one from the domain but a few neighbors saw him off. Sailing from Mikaerizaka to Oura and then on to Yoshida, they anchored at Yawatahama and Kazo visited his aged mother. From Yawatahama, he crossed the straits of Saganoseki, went through Kurume, and then traveled overland to reach Nagasaki.

In Nagasaki, some of the domains had established a *kurayashiki*, a commercial agency, while some had not. Since Uwajima was one of those that had not, a local merchant—the aforementioned Aritaya Hikosuke—was under contract to conduct business on its behalf. Notification had already been sent to Aritaya that Kazo would be coming, and sure enough, he appeared. He proved to be a middle-aged man with his hair tied up in a workman's knot, a traveler's sword in the frayed scabbard at his side, skin that looked as if it had been simmered in soy sauce, and with a face—a hideous face—pitted with pockmarks.

"This country yokel is no samurai. Would he be the lackey?" Aritaya thought to himself as he sized up Kazo's general appearance with meticulous attention. When he opened his mouth, he spoke to Kazo in the rudest manner. It was the sort of language one would employ with the lowest menial.

To Aritaya's surprise, Sudo Dan'emon arrived a short while later. He had followed hard on the heels of Kazo. One manservant accompanied him. Sudo had no special knowledge of ships or machinery; his duty was to oversee Kazo. But all that distinguished him from Kazo was his higher samurai rank, nothing more.

This Sudo, whose haughty demeanor was the very picture of a warrior, took up lodgings in Aritaya's guest room. Having nothing to do all day, he spent his time strolling about town. When night fell, he and Aritaya went to the Maruyama pleasure quarters. Before leaving, though, Aritaya thought it well to ask, "In what manner shall I treat this Kazo of indeterminate status?"

"Kazo? He's here under my supervision to learn about shipbuilding. He's an ordinary townsman who has only recently been called into service by the *han* authorities. I'd therefore like you to run him around no differently than you would a servant."

Since Sudo was the official emissary, whatever he said could be taken as coming directly from the *han*. Aritaya was reassured and said, "I see. I'll pass that on to the household and shop staff."

Apart from Sudo, there were other samurai from Uwajima staying at the Aritaya residence. They were all on official business. Kazo alone was discriminated against, treated no better than a dog or a cat. He was not even called to his three meals in the way the other guests were; for him there was only the beat of the oak clappers. This was the same signal used to call the numerous servants of the house, male and female. When they heard it, they would all assemble in the kitchen to eat. Kazo had to eat alongside them. Sudo's manservant Yoshizo also ate with them, but he was given a higher seat than Kazo.

It never occurred to Kazo to ask, "Is the man entrusted with building a battleship to have a lower place than a mere porter?" For Kazo, a man who from the day he was born had never sat in a place higher than another person, this manner of treatment seemed perfectly natural. But it was definitely unfair, for unlike the Aritaya servants or the manservant Yoshizo, Kazo had to go out every day to conduct his investigations, and there were times when he arrived late for meals, only to find that there was no food left in the kitchen. In fact, Kazo had to go without a meal about once every three days. One evening, when he missed his meal, the pangs of hunger grew so unbearable that he went and bought himself a fish. He was at the sink beginning to prepare it with a kitchen knife when the beldame of the residence dashed in shouting, "You there! What do you think you're doing?" and started reviling him in the most vulgar manner. She hurled abuse at him, accusing him of having stolen the fish from the house supplies, and asked if it was to be tolerated that someone like him should go into other people's houses and use their charcoal without so much as a "with-your-leave . . ." or a "by-your-leave . . ." and so on and so forth. She treated him the way she might a beggar.

The following day, unable to endure any more of it, Kazo refused to pick up the chopsticks from the tray in front of him and eat his evening meal. "Starting tomorrow, I will no longer stay at this house," he said, and shed bitter tears of misery. When the servants heard this, they tried hard to soothe him, but he would not listen. He went off upstairs to the servants' sleeping quarters and lay down to sleep.

At this point, Aritaya Hikosuke arrived home drunk. When his wife told him just what Kazo had said, he rushed straight up the stairs, without even trying to talk sense into his wife, and began endlessly taunting and insulting Kazo, throwing at him questions like, "Kazo! What complaint do you have about your station in life?"

The Uwajima lord Daté Munenari was in Edo at this time. It had not been long since the arrival of Perry's ships, and the country was still in turmoil. As one of the "wise lords," he was engaged with particular zeal in the problem of the shogunal succession.

The Great Hall in Edo Castle had a floor space of about three hundred tatami mats, and it was in the center of this room that Munenari held secret discussions with fellow daimyo. When he and the other wise lords put their heads together, it would be understood, even by prying eyes, that they were in "secret consultation," and there was no fear that anyone could listen in on their conversation. On one particular day, after confiding in Shimazu Nariakira of Satsuma, Yamauchi Toyoshige of Tosa, and Matsudaira Yoshinaga of Echizen about his maneuvers in favor of Hitotsubashi Yoshinobu as shogun, Munenari casually added, "The black ships—I am aiming to have one of those built." At this, the other wise lords were utterly astonished. Munenari could not hide his feeling of triumph. "I have someone investigating their design at this very moment. I've sent one of my own people to Nagasaki to conduct research on their construction. One of these days, the ship will prove useful for coastal defense. I imagine, too, that I will make my journeys to Edo in it."

"This is amazing!" one of the wise lords exclaimed. "But we saw the black ships here only last year! To build one in such a short period certainly must be no easy task. I trust you have an unusually gifted man in your domain. Would he be a Dutch scholar?"

"Well yes, something of the sort," Munenari, being deliberately vague. He saw no good reason to reveal that the man in charge of building the ship was only a lantern repairman. Munenari had never laid eyes on the humble old townsman Kazo, yet was totally convinced of his exceptional talent. But confident though he might have been, he was not unaware of the risks involved in the project. At the time of the proposal, he had said to the house councillor Ko'ori Saemon, "I must eventually report all this to the bakufu and also to the other daimyo. Thus, if Kazo fails to deliver a ship, I will no longer be able to lift my head as I walk the corridors of the shogun's palace." This was true. Munenari would lose face if the plan came to nothing. Moreover, the house councillor Ko'ori—the man who had suggested to Munenari the idea of employing Kazo—would have to ritually disembowel himself. Indeed, Ko'ori was once heard to say jokingly, "If by terrible luck all fails, I will have to commit *seppuku*, won't I?"—an indication that he knew all too well the danger in enlisting Kazo to build a warship, and that he was furthermore ready to face the consequences.

Kazo would not fail. This was Munenari's firm belief and declared conviction. Munenari was a junior fourth rank chamberlain, a successor to the 100,000-*koku* domain of Uwajima in Iyo, and a ninth-generation descendant of Daté Masamune. He was sagacious, of sound judgment in sundry matters, and trusted as a loyalist daimyo by the imperial court. He was the quintessential daimyo. Up until middle age, he had never "seen the whole mackerel," as the saying goes; he had only seen the good bits. He was surprised, of course, when he finally did see the whole fish. His battleship-building enterprise was a grandiose conception, to be sure. But he had no way of knowing that the man charged with carrying out the project was being scolded and ridiculed in the kitchen of his lodging house by the landlord and his wife, that his three meager meals were hardly enough to live on, and that at night he was reduced to sleeping beside common servants.

Kazo was earning a mere subsistence wage. For expenses incurred during his trip to Nagasaki, he was casually given a paltry sum of forty-three *monme*; any expense over and above that, including that of his straw sandals, was "to be entered item by item in a notebook and claim made for the exact cost." This meant that every time he called on scholars or officials in Nagasaki, a precise figure for the cost of the obligatory gifts—cakes, saké, snacks, and so on—had to be recorded and added up. Only then would he be doled out a reimbursement.

The person to whom Kazo had to hand over his list of expenses was none other than Aritaya Hikosuke. This ordinary townsman, who acted as commercial agent for Uwajima, naturally assumed the airs of a domain official as he passed the money to Kazo. Soon, however, Aritaya began to overstep his bounds. Looking at the figures Kazo presented to him, he would open his mouth wide and say, "These straw sandals are one *monme* too expensive. You must be cheating," or "Don't try to fool me! I know cakes don't cost this much! You must be eating some of them yourself." If Kazo tried to defend himself at all, Aritaya would begin to bully him.

4

Kazo's pursuit of knowledge was a rather wretched sort of business. In the temple quarters of Nagasaki, there was a large Jōdo shinshū temple called Kogenji. The chief priest had a serious bent for science, and particularly for metallurgy. It was his hobby, one could say, to invent things. So well known was he for making *buriki*, tin-coated sheet iron (*briki* in Dutch), that the townspeople nicknamed him "the *briki* bonze." Kazo thought that *briki* tinplate would be an essential material for the machinery of his ship, so he asked Aritaya Hikosuke to put in an application for his instruction in the secret formula. Aritaya agreed, and the priest said that he would teach Kazo the art but that the lessons would not be free of charge: one session would cost a full ten *ryo*. It was a substantial investment and would require approval from the *han*. A courier was dispatched to the domain to make the request. He soon returned, letter in hand, and Kazo was able to begin his studies in earnest.

Kazo absorbed all the instruction in one day. Over the course of that day, he and the priest grew closer, and the priest kindly offered to teach him everything he knew about the methods of manufacturing double bellows, hand grenades, and even the detonators for guns.

"How much will that be per item?" Kazo asked hesitantly.

"Half a *ryo* will do," the priest answered in a whisper.

Kazo thought this very odd. When he asked if it were only the fee for instruction in producing *briki* that ran so high, the priest gave him a funny look and said no, not at all, that a class on *briki* production costs only two *ryo*. Kazo probed further and finally learned that of the ten *ryo* he had paid for the lesson, Aritaya Hikosuke had pocketed eight. This Aritaya was a cunning man.

There was a town physician in Nagasaki by the name of Yoshio Keisai. Rumor had it that he had read all about steamship mechanisms in a recent Dutch publication, so Kazo went to see him. Again, Hikosuke acted as go-between. Kazo's first impression of Keisai was that he did not seem to be such a bad fellow, but that like many "Dutch addicts" he was a little superficial.

"All right," Keisai said, "I'll make you a model of a steamship. But I will have to hire some craftsmen. For that I will need eight *ryo*." Kazo happily agreed to pay the fee.

A full month passed, however, and Keisai had not yet shown him the model. Was it complete? The diffident Kazo was worried, but screwed up his courage and went knocking on Keisai's door morning and evening, pressing him to get the job done. Keisai quickly became annoyed.

"A baseborn lout will press demands in a nasty way!" he said in a fit of anger one day. At this, Kazo shut his mouth and abjectly apologized, his forehead pressed to the ground.

Still, Kazo did not give up. He was already on friendly terms with an official of the Nagasaki magistrate's office named Yamamoto Monojiro, who had been a disciple of the late Takashima Shuhan and who was well versed in matters of Dutch-style artillery. This man alone seemed to recognize Kazo's rare gift and was kind to him in many ways. Since Monojiro was quite intimate with Keisai, he undertook to ask him how things stood with regard to the steamship project. To his astonishment, he learned that Keisai had given half of the advance payment to Aritaya Hikosuke and that his own half was already spent. In a word, he had no money left to pay the craftsmen.

Monojiro exploded in anger. "Get on with the job!" he ordered Keisai. "And don't let Kazo be discredited." Keisai could only reluctantly obey.

In a few days' time, Keisai brought Kazo a contraption that was supposed to be a model of a steamship. It was laughable. When Kazo asked questions about its operational principles, Keisai was incapable of answering a single one of them. This did not faze Keisai in the least, however. "You have been sent here on business," he said to Kazo. "The *han* officials will be satisfied with a superficial effort on your part. Take this back to Uwajima; you'll find it will be to your credit."

While Kazo was running about like this, seeming to get nowhere, the fifty days allotted for his trip soon ran out. From the start, it was unreasonable to order a lantern repairman to build a black ship in the space of fifty days. But since he was under *han* orders, there was nothing to be done but try.

"It was all for nothing." When Kazo said this to Yamamoto Monojiro, with tears in his eyes, Monojiro rejoined, "I have encouraging news for you, my friend. Before long, a Dutch battleship will come from Holland. It is a sailing ship, but it will be bringing with it a small steamship. For now you can go home to your domain, but I invite you to come back to Nagasaki to see it." Kazo refused outright, weeping and wailing, saying he'd had enough of black ships and that if all he was ever going to get for his pains was trouble, he would rather go back to Uwajima and repaper lanterns like before. Monojiro then raised his voice.

"Master Kazo, are you not a *kokushi*?" A *kokushi* basically meant a good citizen who put his country before himself. "At the present time there are several men in Japan who are fired with the ambition to build a black ship. Whatever manner of men they may be, they are of no concern to me. You are, though. I have always treated you not as a lantern repairman from Uwajima, but as a *kokushi*. How can a *kokushi* talk in such a spineless, unmanly way?"

Kazo was taken aback. Having no idea what Monojiro's talk was all about, he prostrated himself, kowtowing several times, till finally he made his exit, bending low as he used to do at the master's residence in Honmachi 4-chome.

On the trip home, Kazo pondered over what Monojiro had said to him.

Not knowing the word *kokushi* he took it for *kobushi*, which meant "fist," and was quite pleased with the image. Indeed, it seemed unreasonable to expect that one fist sent to Nagasaki would be able to learn the mechanics of the black ships right away. He decided he would have another go at it.

It was July 4, 1854, when Kazo returned to Uwajima. But after only one short week's rest, the *han* once again sent him off unceremoniously to Nagasaki.

As before, Kazo's supervisor was Sudo Dan'emon. But this time another man went along with him. He was a high-ranking samurai named Yanagawa Sozaemon. "I am the second-in-command of this investigation," Yanagawa said with an air of arrogance as the three of them headed out to the boat from the castle town. The indispensable Kazo was made to carry the baggage of the two men in charge. He brought up the rear, wobbling precariously under the load.

On July 22, the day after the party reached Nagasaki, just as had been predicted, a Dutch ship entered the harbor, accompanied by a small steamer. The rumor of the self-propelled ship soon spread all over town.

Kazo wanted to make a sketch of her engines, but this seemed nearly impossible. At the time, the Dutch were confined to a fan-shaped sandbar called Dejima. According to bakufu law, contact with them was forbidden to all but a few specified officials of the Nagasaki magistrate's office and a limited number of other Japanese of various backgrounds. Entering Dejima was out of the question for this crew.

"Don't worry! I'll think of something," said Yamamoto Monojiro, and he set about devising a strategy.

This Monojiro was a local Nagasaki man whose work involved facilitating communication between the magistracy and two local guilds. If he had some suitable government business, he could go in and out of Dejima more or less at will. His plan was to go in, passing off Kazo as his servant. In order to do this, he had Kazo dress in a servingman's livery, with his straw sandals stuck in his belt.

They went into the Dutch residence compound every day. There was a problem, however: the small Dutch steamer was being guarded like a treasure. It was docked in a sluice, the gates to which were kept tightly locked. No one could even see it. Moreover, the engine had reportedly been removed and was housed in the machinery godown. This engine was all that Kazo was interested in seeing.

In those days, even Holland did not have that many steam engines, so it took extremely good care of the ones it had. Every afternoon at two o'clock, the engine was taken out of the godown for an hour and a half of examination and overhaul by two mechanics. When Monojiro heard this, he used his proficient Dutch to negotiate. "I am anxious to study that engine," he told the Dutchmen. "Would you mind allowing my attendant to make a sketch of it?" The Dutchmen agreed, and Kazo prepared a great ledger. For the next five days, when the time came for looking over the engine, Kazo came with Monojiro and made his sketches. Soon it was complete.

But Kazo had misgivings as to whether the sketches would help produce a seaworthy ship that could churn up big waves in the ocean. Seeing nothing but this engine was like seeing *azuki* beans and flour, and trying to imagine from them what *manju* cakes might be like.

Then a most unexpected event occurred: the Dutch, as a gesture of appreciation for centuries of friendly relations with the Japanese government, offered to take a select few people aboard the steamship for a trial run. When this was announced at the Nagasaki magistrate's office, the chief of police, a high official of the Saga domain, sent word home by way of a messenger and, lo and behold, it was soon given out that the lord of that domain, Nabeshima Kanso himself, would go aboard. In no time, a flood of high officials from other domains came begging for their own place on the ship. In this situation, it became impossible for one of such low status as the bogus servant Kazo, the *han* employee, to go on board as well.

Kazo did not give up, though. Again, he went crying to Monojiro, and as usual, Monojiro had a ready answer: "I'll think up a way for you to get on board. We'll wait until the visitors have left the ship. You'll have to get on board as nimbly as a rat, then run around inside and do what you need to do as quickly and as quietly as you can. There won't be much time."

The day came, and Kazo did just that. In the engine room, with ledger in hand, he scurried around for all the world like a rodent. Having finished all the sketches, he returned to the Aritaya house, where, again, he was lodging, and made clean copies of everything. There were five copies in all—one for the Uwajima *han* officials, another for himself, and three for his kind benefactor Yamamoto Monojiro. When Kazo presented them to Monojiro a few days later, the latter was filled with admiration.

"Not since the time of my late teacher Takashima Shuhan have I seen such a well-drawn engine plan! Kazo, what I am about to ask you, I ask you in my capacity as public official: in certain government circles, they are thinking of building a ship like the one we saw the other day. Do you think you could build one yourself?"

"Well, since I've come this far," said Kazo thoughtfully, "I think I might be able to do it some way or another." Kazo was officially in the employ of the Uwajima domain, but having started as a simple townsman, he had no great sense of *han* identity. Or rather, he saw the bakufu as being above the *han* and naturally thought orders from it should take precedence over those from the domain.

When the *han* official Sudo Dan'emon heard the proposition from Yamamoto Monojiro, he was incensed. "Yamamoto Monojiro, I would have expected more from you. This is an outrage. That fellow Kazo is a *yakko* of our domain."

Sudo had said *yakko*. The word could be used in reference to a menial, but it was also a common word for "slave." Monojiro was startled, and felt like retorting, "Doesn't your 100,000-*koku* domain cry for shame, having only a menial to build its battleships?" but as a Nagasaki official renowned for his mild temper, he decided to hold his peace, saying only that if that were the case, there was nothing to be done about it, and quickly withdrew.

Kazo's allotted time in Nagasaki was up, and so he once again returned to Uwajima. When he came to Nagasaki for third time, it was mid-December 1854, and winter was setting in. This time the *han* had no great expectations of him.

There was another Dutch scholar in Nagasaki at the time. His name was Takeuchi Ukichiro, and he lived in the neighborhood of Sakayamachi. He, too, was a disciple of Takashima Shuhan and for some time had had a reputation as an authority on Western gunnery. When the Dutch steamship arrived in Nagasaki earlier in the year, Takeuchi was ordered by the bakufu through the Nagasaki magistrate's office to take up residence in Dejima and conduct research on the vessel. This man was quite different from Kazo, who had no learning, spoke not a word of Dutch, and even as regards the steamer itself, had merely scampered and scurried around the engine room.

Uwajima's official representative, Sudo Dan'emon, who was then temporarily residing in Nagasaki, had no confidence in Kazo. One day, he happened to run into this Takeuchi in the Maruyama pleasure quarters. He pressed him to give a lecture on steamships to the men of his domain, saying that as soon as he, Takeuchi, gave the word, the Uwajima samurai would come to Nagasaki to hear him. Takeuchi gave a good-natured but evasive answer, which Sudo interpreted as consent. Straightaway, Sudo sent a courier to Uwajima with the news. The Uwajima officials, in turn, immediately selected a number of talented men and sent them off to Nagasaki. In the lineup were Matsuda Gengozaemon, Matsuzawa Kizaemon, Watanabe Sakunoshin, Ninomiya Keisaku, and Kunitomo Chozaemon. With them went Murata Zoroku (later Omura Masujiro), who was not an Uwajima samurai but an attendant physician from another province. Kazo also went along with them as a kind of guide. They all lodged at the residence of Aritaya Hikosuke. As usual, Kazo alone was consigned to the servants' room and made to sleep among the menials.

Sudo Dan'emon was bloated with pride at having located the great scholar Takeuchi Ukichiro. Shrugging off the circumstances with a jocular "Even a stroll through the Maruyama quarters can be viewed as an act of fealty to the *han*!" he set off to see Takeuchi Ukichiro again. But when he reached Takeuchi's residence, he found it full of samurai from other domains. He had been greatly mistaken in thinking that Uwajima had taken the initiative. Several officials of other *han* had apparently already gotten in contact with Takeuchi and had stolen a march on Sudo. The great scholar was already instructing a number of eager learners. The breakdown by domain was roughly as follows: Satsuma, Saga, Kumamoto, Isahaya, Omura, Fukuoka, and Matsue, with Satsuma sending as many as five men.

"I have great difficulty coping with such large numbers," Takeuchi said with a weary look in his eyes. "To refuse would not be proper. I will teach, but please, only one man from your domain."

"Only one man! You must understand, the samurai are all of equal rank. It would be very difficult to pick out just one."

"No, not at all. Your domain has a scholar by the name of Kazo, I don't know his surname, but . . ."

"He has no surname. That fellow is only a common townsman!"

"Townsman or not, it doesn't matter. I've got neither the energy nor the time to take on a beginner with no preparatory study or training. It's impossible. If I can't have Kazo, then I must refuse."

Takeuchi was being so stubborn that Sudo had no recourse but to select Kazo. Sudo had merely sought to enhance his own standing as an Uwajima representative in Nagasaki, but now his efforts proved to be for the sole benefit of Kazo. He must have been beside himself with fury when he realized this. In the past he had often smacked Kazo over the head for trifling matters; his treatment of him from here on out would be much more severe.

"Serves you right!" Kazo might have said to Sudo, had it been in his nature to use such a tone. He meekly kept his tail down, however. Meekness came easy to him; as one from the lowest caste, it was his only strong point.

Kazo began to attend classes at Takeuchi's house in Sakayamachi, but what he was taught was mainly what he already knew. Takeuchi recognized this and said to him, "You, I'd like you to come early in the mornings. I'll teach you before breakfast." Kazo did as he was told, hoping all the while he might be permitted to copy a three-dimensional sketch of the steam engine Takeuchi had drawn. Takeuchi readily lent it to him. Kazo then made a copy of it and returned the original the following morning. From about this time, Takeuchi began to think that Kazo's real abilities were perhaps greater than his own. In any case, his discreet questioning of Kazo on doubtful points became more frequent. Kazo would always answer modestly, clearly, and succinctly.

A few days later, when Kazo appeared for his regular morning lesson, Takeuchi rushed him into a room to show him something. There, in the alcove, was a replica of a steam engine. According to Takeuchi, he had had the thing made according to plans he himself had drawn. He wanted to use it that day as teaching material in his class, but wondered if it would be possible to have it inspected beforehand. Takeuchi was already beginning to take on the role of disciple. After examining the model in minute detail, Kazo said, "I think it's somewhat flawed. I mean, the steam produced by the boiler goes first into the distributor and then into the steam cylinder, where it makes the piston move up and down. That's the principle on which the steam engine works, isn't it?"

"It is."

"The steam blown into the cylinder should be pumped in turns from above and below. If that is done correctly, the piston will move up and down. There should be two pipes to direct the steam from the distributor to the cylinder. But in Master Takeuchi's model, there is only one. The steam is thus blown only in one direction. Because of this, the all-important piston cannot move up and down."

"Hmmm . . ."

Takeuchi pondered over this for a moment. After a short while, he realized that Kazo was right. Then, as if ready to leap for joy, he grabbed Kazo's hand and said, "You—where steam is concerned, you are the greatest man in all Japan! You have no equal. You are the one and only!" Kazo allowed the master to squeeze his hand over and over again, and began to sob. It was not happiness at being called the greatest steam expert in Japan that moved Kazo so deeply, but rather that the kind and gentle Takeuchi had addressed him man to man, like a fellow human being. This was a first for Kazo.

The year was drawing to a close. The other men in Takeuchi's class—the samurai—were all preparing to return to their respective domains. Kazo, however, spent his time visiting as many of those known to have experience with Western technology as he possibly could. His thirst for knowledge was insatiable.

In Nagasaki's Konya-cho, there was a carpenter called Kinshiro. This Kinshiro had formerly taken part in the building of Nagasaki's battery fort. But even after that work was completed, he was still ready to build more. Hearing that this man had gone on to make exact models of Western fortresses, Kazo went to visit him.

Kinshiro was a decent man.

"They tell me you were a lantern paperer in Uwajima. We're all the same, us craftsmen; ask me anything you want."

Astonishingly, this carpenter had even succeeded in making a model of a breech-loading cannon. Breech-loading artillery was still a very recent invention in Europe. In Nagasaki, there were few who knew anything of its design.

Ueno Toshinojo was another Nagasaki man who knew something about Western technology. He had a plan for a reflector furnace. When Kazo heard this, he went to see what he could learn from him. In the course of a few days, he was allowed to copy the plan and was given an explanation of the theoretical principles upon which it was based.

At the end of the year, Kazo returned home accompanied by the same group of samurai with whom he had come to Nagasaki.

On February 28, 1855, Uwajima at last gave notice of its plan to construct a steamship. Personnel appointments were officially announced at that time as well. Murata Zoroku was made technical director for hull construction. Kazo was put in charge of the engine. But this was not exactly how the appointment read. Ostensibly, the director was an important official by the name of Tahara Shichizaemon. Following his name were those of a whole galaxy of men with notably high stipends. Only at the very end, in tiny characters, was it written, "domain employee Kazo." Everyone knew, though, that Kazo would be the de facto director.

The kitchen wing of an annex to a *han* office building was knocked down to create a work yard, and Sakuemon, Kizahyoei, and Choemon—three metal casters—were hired in quick succession to work as technicians.

Kazo was opposed to this. He insisted that tinplate be used for the boiler and that tinplate craftsmen, not metal casters, be employed. But the *han* officials had other ideas: "Tin is not strong enough; the metal casters agree. It is best to make everything of good strong iron." When Kazo continued to protest, they roared at him, "Don't you forget what class you come from!"

Meanwhile, the daimyo Daté Munenari returned to Uwajima from Edo. On the way, he took great pleasure in reading progress reports on the construction of the ship. Upon his arrival, he announced that he would inspect the works. The construction had recently been moved from the annex to the iron foundry. On the day of the inspection, the workplace was swept and cleaned, and the *han* elders and all the important officials under them crammed into the foundry alongside the commissioners, each one trying to get a view of the thing.

The role of guide fell to the amateur Tahara Shichizaemon. Munenari was looking very satisfied as he made his tour of inspection. The indispensable Kazo, however, was not to be seen. Owing to his low station, he was forbidden to set eyes on the great lord, and had been turned out of the workplace. Presently, he huddled with the metal casters in a corner of the yard where the boatbuilding materials were stored. He had to kowtow with his face actually rubbing into the earth like a ground grub.

Thanks to Kazo's strenuous efforts, the engine was finally completed in the winter of 1857. It was a fine piece of work, but Kazo still felt uneasy about it. Would iron be a safe material to use?

The trial run was made on a day when the puddles of water around the construction site were covered with ice. Great bundles of pinewood were briskly fed into the mouth of the furnace. Gradually the water came to a boil, and the pressure gauge began to rise. Kazo had made this meter himself using the knowledge he had acquired from a Nagasaki clockmaker named Tetsuzo. When the pressure reached five pounds, the observers started shouting. An accident had occurred. Jets of steam burst from the iron boiler. It looked like a porcupine with all its needles spread.

"Kazo, stop it! Make it stop!" Tahara Shichizaemon shouted in alarm. Kazo paid no attention, though, and went on feeding bundles of pinewood into the fire, until at last the pressure reached ten pounds and the boiler, as if possessed by an angry god, started spouting vapor in all directions. The group of onlookers began to scatter. Only then did Kazo stop the boiler. "Just as I thought, iron will not do!" he muttered to himself. Not once during all this did he show any expression of fear.

The local samurai were milling around him, hollering at him as if they had gone mad, "*Harakiri!* It's *harakiri* for us, thanks to you!" Odd snatches of their speech reached Kazo's ears as he went about his work. It sounded very odd to him; if he were a samurai, he'd certainly have to commit *harakiri*, but being lowborn Kazo, he was exempt from doing so. "If you commit *harakiri*," he shot back, "will that help us to make a boiler?" It was perhaps the only sarcasm this man uttered in his entire life. After saying it, he was amazed at his own temerity. The samurai were not angry, however; instead, they changed their tone to one of abject entreaty and implored him with subdued voices, "Isn't there anything you can do?" He thought there was not.

"Let's see now! Let's pack tin into the cracks."

"What's that? Tin? Well then, give it a try!" the samurai shouted. Tin was brought, and Kazo set about patching up the boiler.

The following day, the boiler was tested again, but the tin was blown out immediately, and Kazo and the onlookers found themselves in the same situation as the day before. Nothing had been accomplished; the *han* had wasted its money. The commissioner, moreover, felt it his duty to tell the house councillor Ko'ori Saemon that such expenses as building a black ship were an excessive drain on the resources of a small domain and that no more money should be spent on the project. The reputedly stouthearted Ko'ori just smiled a bitter smile and said in a quiet voice, "It's the lord's hobby. There's nothing we can do about it."

Daté Munenari, even after he heard about the fiasco, showed no sign at all of being perturbed, but simply remarked, "It stands to reason. It could never have been expected to succeed." It was the kind of response one could expect from a "wise lord."

Meanwhile, malicious talk centered on Kazo. The officials involved told Munenari that the failure was all Kazo's fault, whereupon Munenari replied, "I'd like to hear from the man himself sometime." The members of his entourage were horror-stricken when they heard this. Only samurai of a high rank were permitted direct, personal contact with the daimyo. If the *han* lord himself were to break with such precedent, it could only bring trouble. Was it not all just for a steam engine? If the clan system were thrown into upheaval for something so frivolous, the entire clan might fall to ruin. Bearing these considerations in mind, the house councillor Ko'ori ventured an objection: "I humbly submit that I think that would not be a good idea."

"You're right," said Munenari with a nod. He himself was a stickler for order. Although Uwajima was in theory of pro-imperial persuasion, Munenari himself strictly abided by shogunal regulations. This explains why, until the final days of the shogunate, only a few people ever absconded from his domain.

Before long, encouraging news reached Munenari. In Satsuma, the daimyo Shimazu Nariakira had ordered the construction of battleships, and all was proceeding apace. One of his ships, moreover, was nearing completion. It was not a steamship, of course, but a sailing ship.

Nariakira had already conceived of building a Western-style ship some two years before Perry's arrival. It was 1851, the year he had succeeded to the headship of his clan. The only reason he had not already beaten Munenari to the task was because the bakufu had, at the time Munenari gave the order to build a ship, only recently lifted its ban on the construction of seaworthy vessels, and so he, Nariakira, was off to a late start.

In any event, Satsuma was one of Japan's largest and most powerful domains. Nariakira's proposal was for a considerable fleet of twelve sailing ships and three steamships. From early on, Nariakira had had his own ideas on national defense. His proposal was that the Kyushu domains move promptly to ensure the protection of the Annam region against the European advance. Doubtless this is what underlay his plan for building such a large fleet.

Nariakira was favored by a number of lucky circumstances. In the same year that he became daimyo, a castaway from Tosa by the name of Nakahama Manjiro drifted ashore and was taken into custody by Satsuma officials. This Manjiro had been in America and had worked as a sailor. Nariakira heard this and ordered a few elite retainers to get out of the man everything he knew about seamanship and navigation and the whole sum of his knowledge about ships and ultimately make him build a sailing ship.

This project of Nariakira's was at last bearing fruit—the *Shohei Maru* was about to be launched. However, it was not a Western-style ship, but a Chinese junk with only a single cannon on board. On that account alone, rival Daté Munenari was set at ease. The race was to build a Western-style vessel—and that meant a steamship.

By the time Kazo was on his first trip to Nagasaki, Shimazu Nariakira, in Edo, had already sent a swift courier home with instructions to build such a ship: it was to be sixty-six feet long, have a fifteen-horsepower engine, and be constructed on the Iso shoreline outside Kagoshima Castle. The confidential information that reached Munenari stated that a foreigner was secretly held in custody in Satsuma and was assigned to direct the construction of the engine.

Hoping he would be able to have his retainers observe the project, Munenari negotiated with Nariakira. Unable to refuse this benefactor who had helped him so much at the time of his succession, Nariakira gave his consent. Without delay, Munenari put Tahara Shichizaemon in charge and sent with him Kazo, the metal caster Kunitomo Chozaemon, and the metal fittings specialist Toyoshichiro.

These men set out from Uwajima on January 8, 1858, and were back in time for New Year's, which fell that year on February 14. While in Kagoshima, they never got to see the all-important foreigner, however, and thus were unable to learn anything from him. Perhaps the Satsuma officials had deliberately hidden him from them. The only thing the Uwajima men had for their pains was the sight of a half-made boiler. This only confirmed what Kazo had suspected all along.

Upon their return, an order was issued: "Complete the steamship before Satsuma completes theirs." The honor and reputation of Munenari as the wisest and most able of daimyo hinged on their ability to carry out this order.

Kazo got down to work in earnest in late March. This time he was given free rein to carry out the work as he saw fit. The entire domain stood behind him.

Construction took about eight months to complete. It was finished in the autumn of 1858. Kazo had all the parts assembled so that by mid-autumn the ship was ready for testing in the shipyard. Tahara Shichizaemon and his subordinates huddled together to closely observe Kazo as he went about hauling fuel to the site. The blackened Kazo worked hard, until finally it was time to stoke the furnace. The fuel caught fire and soon was raging. The water came to a boil, and the steam pressure gauge began to rise. Kazo carried out various operations as he moved in circles about the boiler. At last he opened the valves, and the wheels began to churn. As he steadily raised the pressure, the boiler began to roar and bellow like a wild animal, and the terrible turning caused the entire shed to tremble as if an earthquake had hit it.

At last, success! Tahara Shichizaemon, arms and legs flailing, danced around the boiler a full ten times. Rumors were circulating that Satsuma had by that time already launched five sailing ships, but there was no word of it producing a seaworthy steamship.

Kazo then had the engine installed in the hull of the ship built according to the design and specifications of Murata Zoroku. With this, the boat was complete. At long last, on March 1, 1859, she was put to sea.

On the appointed day, a fierce westerly wind was blowing. It was not possible to have her go very far on the open sea, so it was decided to have her navigate along the coastline, past Rokusobori in the vicinity of the castle, and then on to the Kabasaki guardhouse. Kazo went on board with his legs shaking. Immediately he went down to the bowels of the ship, where he holed himself up in the cramped engine room without once returning to deck. Quietly he lit the boiler and carried out the necessary operations to start the engine. Soon the ship began to move. Turning his head to the side, he looked out the porthole: the castle's Tenshukaku tower seemed to be slowly moving.

"She's moving," he thought, wiping away the beads of sweat that formed on his head. As usual, he was hunkered down in front of the stoke hole. But now he suddenly got down on all fours, trying to maintain his balance. Before long, his body was jerking and shaking and he could no longer stay crouched. Transports of deep emotion and wild joy seemed to tear through his entire being. He inadvertently pissed on himself, but even when his crotch was soaked, he failed to take notice of it.

Munenari was on board above. The *han* elders were there too. Even Kazo's former supervisors, Sudo and Tahara, were aboard for the occasion. But as regards the seaworthiness of the vessel, one may well wonder whether any one of them knew a joy like the joy of Kazo, stuck down there in the bottom of the ship.

Then something strange started to happen. At first, the ship was sailing along with the axles of the wheels in excellent condition and was working up a considerable speed. But as time went on, she began to lose her momentum. She was visibly slowing her pace.

The boiler is too small for the hull. That was the realization that suddenly hit Kazo. Kazo knew that at this rate, she would not be able to navigate heavy seas. But the specific measurements for the engine were ordered by the *han*. They were beyond his control. Within the limits of his station in life, he had given his all to this work. He had succeeded in producing a steam engine. That alone gave him more than enough satisfaction. Whatever might be said now was politics, and naturally, as a mere townsman, Kazo had neither the intellectual capacity nor the habit nor the enthusiasm to give thought to such matters.

He had succeeded.

But just a few days after this joyous occasion, news was received that Satsuma had successfully tested a seaworthy steamship of its own. Moreover, the report stated that it had happened a few days earlier than the testing in Uwajima.

Many of the other domain employees and townsfolk envied Kazo for his success. The metal caster Kyuemon, who accosted him in the street—"Kazo, you're not such a great fellow after all! The Satsuma men have beaten you to it, haven't they?"—was a prime example. Kazo admitted to himself that that was the truth, but then, some ten days later, he had come around to thinking that no, the Satsuma men had not beaten him. Uwajima and Satsuma were different domains. His had not produced a steam engine by concerted organization and the unified effort of the entire *han* administration. Rather, it had done so thanks to the vision of an enlightened daimyo and the ingenuity of an ordinary townsman. That townsman was himself. True, Satsuma was the winner, and Uwajima was only in second place; but there was nothing in that to adversely affect Kazo's own personal honor.

A few days after this, the ship that Kazo had built left the harbor as highspirited as a young puppy. It mesmerized all as it sailed the sea outside the castle town. The boiler seemed to be in excellent condition. But after about an hour, like a feeble old man, the ship slackened its pace. The samurai of the domain all thought it was a failing common to steamships, however, and the reputation of this Uwajima black ship was not in the least bit damaged.

This failing was the only thing that marred Kazo's satisfaction. He wanted to be allowed to make a much bigger boiler, a ship with far greater horsepower. He mentioned this to the samurai physician Murata Zoroku, who had designed the hull. Murata churlishly replied, "That boiler is good enough for a domain the size of Uwajima," and without another word, lapsed into a sullen silence.

After the initial launching of this vessel, a great miracle occurred in the life of Kazo: he was allowed to take a surname. Maehara was the name he chose.

Since the opinion was expressed that his given name, Kazo, lacked dignity, he changed it to Kaichi, the name of his father, who had lived out his life as a dealer of cereals in Yawatahama. This writer fails to see wherein the name Kazo lacks dignity while Kaichi does not.

Kaichi was promoted to the lowest samurai rank and was given a threeperson stipend of nine sacks of rice. He had certainly not become a *bushi* warrior, but for a lantern repaperer, you will agree that his was indeed a most remarkable success story.

His promotion came in the sixth year after the arrival of Perry's ships.

SHIINA RINZŌ

Shiina Rinzō (1911–1973) followed an unusual trajectory as both a person and a writer. Born into a poor family, he began working in a variety of menial jobs in the late 1920s and soon found himself arrested because of his ties to the Communist movement. He recanted his beliefs and continued, in face of increasingly bad health, to write, but he had no success until his existential stories of the early postwar years were published. In 1950, despondent, he decided to become a Christian, and he remained devoted to his new faith until the end of his life. The works written after 1950, which treat the spiritual, rather than the economic, woes of post-Occupation Japan, are generally considered Shiina's best. His story "The Go-Between" (Baishakunin, 1962) looks at the complications and responsibilities of family relations.

THE GO-BETWEEN (BAISHAKUNIN)

Translated by Noah S. Brannen

1

I left my wife in my study where she had come to call me, and I hurried down the stairs. One would have thought that I was a man bent on defending his castle from some brazen intruder. I was. And what's more, I was angry. According to what my wife had told me, Tamio Ikawa had suddenly appeared from the west saying that he wanted to be put up in our house until he found work. He claimed to be the son-in-law of my cousin, but I couldn't even remember having met him, except perhaps once. When I got downstairs, I found that he had already stepped up into the house from the entrance way and, with his back to me, was piling quite a few pieces of baggage up in one corner of the entrance. There were a Boston bag, a suitcase, and two or three bundles tied in large kerchiefs. Though he was twenty-six years old, his back looked so weak that I marveled that he had been able to manage all this baggage from the station to my house. Evidently sensing my presence, he turned to face me. Then he smiled and bowed slightly, as if to say he was confident I would not refuse him. My words came of their own accord:

"I—I'm angry with you."

With my eyes I motioned to a chair in a corner of the entrance. Encountering this unexpected resistance, he dropped his eyes and undulated disgustingly like a jellyfish. He fell exhausted into the chair, making a wry face as if he had met with some swindler. This was to show me, no doubt, how completely worn out he was. Though he came from my own hometown, a rural community, he was dressed like someone from a gangster film. Furthermore, his jumper and mambo pants were new. Probably he had bought them in preparation for his trip to Tokyo, thinking them to be the latest thing here. He didn't have the burned, ruddy complexion common to rural folks; rather, his face wore a sickly, dough-like pallor.

I said, making my displeasure at his unexpected visit as obvious as possible, "I have no idea why you left home in such a hurry, but you could at least have sent a postcard ahead advising that you were coming. Especially since you're no relation of mine."

His body seemed to go out of control again and undulated, this time to the left. I wondered if he had a spine at all. Still he took care not to wrinkle the crease in his trousers.

"Sure," he answered irresponsibly with half-shut eyes, "I couldn't stand it no more, not even one more day. I was fed up with that place. So I thought once I go to my uncle's in Tokyo, somethin'd work out."

I felt a creepy sensation running along my spine. He had no right to address me as "uncle." Until this fellow, Tamio Ikawa, married my cousin (the daughter of an only aunt who still lived in my hometown), he was completely unknown to me. Of course I had heard he came from a nearby village, but I had never been in his home. At the time of the wedding I just happened to be stopping over in the next town; so my aunt asked me to serve as go-between,[1] in name only, at the wedding. At the ceremony I met him for the first time. That was all. Immediately after the reception the couple left for Wakayama on their honeymoon. Evidently the custom of the honeymoon has been adopted today even in the country. So this was only our second meeting. Through his marriage to my cousin Myoko, he could conceivably be called a cousin-in-law, but there was certainly no uncle–nephew relationship, even though I am twenty years his senior.

Trying to control my irritation, I said, "Well, anyway, you'd better go back home. I'll give you the train fare."

He leaned his body far over to the right and then drew up his left trouser leg. I don't know whether or not a crease is important to mambo pants, but there was no mistaking his concern about it. Then, apparently exhausted, he propped his head against the wall on his right. He was still demonstrating how tired he was, for my benefit no doubt. I didn't like his attitude. If I had been in his position, I would have sat up straight, no matter how awful I felt.

"I already have plenty of reason to be angry with you," I said. "You wrote me twice asking for money." (Regret, which I had almost forgotten, began to well up inside me again.) "And though I was under no obligation whatsoever to do so, didn't I send you my hard-earned money? But you never sent one word saying whether you had received it. I didn't put a return address on my letter inquiring about it because I thought you wouldn't want my aunt to know about it.

---

1. The go-between, or "matchmaker," continues to be an important functionary in Japan's system of arranged marriage. In this instance, the narrator simply took this role on the day of the ceremony.

Still there was no word, in spite of the fact that you seemed capable enough of writing quite a long letter when it came to *asking* for the money. 'Now the rice planting is over, and the clean air is blowing across the paddies.'"

He smiled, proud of himself, so I spoke with added emphasis. "You could fill up five or six sheets of stationery with that kind of silly, flowery clap-trap, but you couldn't manage a simple postcard to let me know you got the money. Don't you think that a bit strange? Since I make my living by writing, I read your letter over and over hoping to get a clue to your character which would explain this abnormal behavior. But I couldn't find anything. The reasoning seemed coherent, and you were able to say exactly what you wanted to say." (Again he beamed in satisfaction.) "I'm not praising you! I'm *mad*, can't you see? What else would you expect me to think other than that you obviously looked on me as someone whom you didn't have to bother answering? I don't like to be treated that way. In fact, I consider it a personal insult!"

I stopped talking. He had fallen asleep, in spite of the fact that just now he had smiled that satisfied smile. At best he was sleepy-eyed, but now he was leaning hard against the wall, motionless and breathing evenly. I hesitated, wondering whether to wake him. The nerve, going to sleep on me just when I was getting worked up enough to bawl him out good! On the other hand, he had just arrived from the west and probably really was tired. Dispirited, I got up out of my chair. But I didn't pass up the chance to scrape the chair noisily over the floor. He drew a deep breath like a sigh, but otherwise he didn't stir. Was it the poise of an expert? Or perhaps he had already been asleep and dreaming a moment before when he smiled as I talked. There seemed to be nothing to do but to let him go on sleeping, so I decided to give him ten minutes, but no more. I was determined to see him off to his home that very day. I went into the dining room and found my wife preparing tea for him. In a voice that had been drained of all amiability I said, "He went to sleep on me. Just when I was delivering him a real sermon."

"How about letting him stay here just tonight?" she said, in a noncommittal way.

"But when I sent him the money, you were really the angry one, weren't you? And besides, we don't have a room to put him in."

"But," she hesitated ambiguously, as if at a loss.

With that she went into the kitchen. It was clear that she was thinking of my relatives and that she considered Tamio among them. Upset, I knelt beside the low breakfast table. I looked at my watch. It was 3:40. At 3:50 I planned to wake him, no matter what. I thought of my aunt's home in the country. I tried to imagine the confusion which must have been created by his sudden disappearance.

My aunt's house was surrounded by a white wall just at the place where the road emerges from a bamboo thicket. The maples and pines in the garden, which could be seen over the wall, were always well trimmed. Though I refer to it as my aunt's house, actually it is the house into which she married, where she and her husband still carry on the farm. Their children—two girls—came late.

The second daughter, still only a high school junior, lived with relatives in the city; and the older one, Myoko, now twenty-five, worked at a credit union until she was married. Tamio Ikawa commuted from a nearby village to a fruit factory in the city. As it happened, his factory was located right next to the credit union, and the two of them took the same route home every day. That was how he got to know Myoko. Still, in my hometown this doesn't add up to a marriage. There had to be the consent of parents and relatives. But fortunately for him, he was some distant relative of my uncle; and this, together with the fact that he was an orphan, drew the sympathy of my aunt and uncle and was a big factor in bringing about the marriage. At that time I was, by chance, staying on business near that city and was asked to be go-between (in name only) for the wedding. This was because I had the confidence of my aunt and uncle. Shortly after the wedding I returned to Tokyo.

In May, less than half a year after the wedding, I received an unexpected letter from Ikawa asking for money. He wanted to borrow fifty thousand yen[2] to make a down-payment on a motorbike so he could ride to the factory. He said he would repay the money a little at a time. Apparently the bus schedule made it inconvenient for commuting to the factory. My aunt's domicile is a half-converted farm and she certainly could afford to buy a motorbike, but he explained that he had only recently been adopted into the family (by marriage) and an adopted husband[3] couldn't ask for money. I had sympathized with this boy who was not very good at farm labor and whose position was that of adopted husband. It made no difference that these facts had been recognized and accepted by the parents at the time of the marriage.

My aunt had spoken to me about just this situation: "It don't matter if he's no hand at farming. It's all right if he'll just pitch in now and then when we're real busy. He'll get the hang of it in time."

But in actual fact things didn't go that way, as I discerned from his letter. So I scraped up the money and sent it to him. And this was in spite of my wife's firm objection.

But I never received any word from Tamio that the money had reached him. Uneasy about it, I sent him a letter with no return address written on it. My "uneasiness" was not so much over whether or not the registered letter had reached him as that perhaps my aunt and her husband had found out that I sent him money and that he had fallen into some tight predicament. I wrote, in this letter of inquiry, that I regretted not having sent the money to the factory where he was employed. Of course I would have done so if I had known the correct address. But there was no answer to this letter either. After several weeks had elapsed, my wife pointed out to me the discourtesy of my relatives

---

2. Fifty thousand yen is about $112.

3. The status of an "adopted husband" is an inferior one, in which a man moves into the home of his wife, takes her family name, and agrees to abide by her family's decisions.

in not sending some kind of answer. That night I was so angry that the sleeping pills I had taken had practically no effect at all. But I couldn't stay angry forever. It wouldn't have been good for my health.

Before four months had elapsed, another letter requesting money came from Tamio. This letter enclosed another letter—from his sister-in-law who had reared him. Obviously it was written from a hospital, where she was being treated for a stomach ulcer. The report was that if she did not have an operation, she wouldn't last very long. She had asked Tamio for help, but he was in no position to do anything. So, though it was impertinent on her part to make such a request, she had no place to turn except to me—and after all, I had been the go-between for Tamio. Since it was a matter of life and death, could she please borrow[4] thirty thousand yen for the operation? Tamio wrote a letter to accompany the request and said since it meant the life of the sister who had reared him, he was begging me to help. But he didn't say a word about the fifty thousand yen he had already borrowed.

In my reply I said that there probably was some way to get medical aid, and I enclosed a consolation gift of five thousand yen. There was no acknowledgment, naturally. I took this as a matter of course and held my temper. No doubt the reason I received no word this time was because I hadn't sent the amount requested. Still, deep inside, I couldn't suppress a certain feeling of displeasure.

I got up and went to the front hall. The time was now 3:50 P.M. Tamio was already awake. When he saw me, he grinned and went into the jellyfish act again. Probably the grin was habitual with him and didn't mean a thing, but to me it was disagreeable.

"At any rate you'd better go back home on the night train tonight," I said coldly. "I have absolutely no intention of putting you up here."

He was silent. With eyes closed, he leaned his body far over to the left. Then my wife brought tea, and with that I started up the stairs for my study. As I did so, I heard her saying in a sweet tone of voice, "This is your first time to come to Tokyo, isn't it?"

I stopped halfway up the stairs. I could not understand why my wife was being so sweet to him, and I felt indignant about her attitude. This was because her sweetness canceled the effect of my unyielding attitude toward him. Though I had almost reached the top of the stairs, I descended two or three steps and sat down. I could hear her continuing in that saccharine tone: "Now you realize how hard it is to get around in Tokyo!"

"I came here from Tokyo Station by taxi. We wandered all over till it cost me 'leven hunnerd yen."

"You really were lost, weren't you? Usually it costs about six hundred."

"I had to look ever'where."

---

4. There is a saying in Japan that one should never lend anything that he cannot afford to give away.

"But why did you come to Tokyo so suddenly?"

"Well . . . ," he said in a most doleful voice.

Obviously, that voice was calculated to play on my wife's sympathy. I rushed down the stairs. I had made up my mind, come hell or high water, not to listen to his story, but my wife was innocently ready to hear him out. I knew that once we listened to his story, no matter how worthless it might be, we would be obliged to put him up at least for one night. Then when that was done, it would be hard to deny the fact that he had stayed with us. He would use that as his precedent and stretch it out one day and then another. That was why, no matter what the story, I intended absolutely—that is unconditionally—to deny his request. Whatever the cost, I wanted to strike a blow at his pampered ego. My family and I have carved out our own raison d'être in the face of hard reality. But it was no use; he had already begun to tell his story to her.

"If I went home now, they'd kill me."

"Kill you?" she said, startled. "Why?"

Tamio stole a look at me as I descended the stairs. But my wife, entirely oblivious of me, was wrapped up in the story and insistently repeated her question, "Why? Why would they kill you?"

Again he glanced in my direction. Relief and victory showed in those eyes. From then on, he ignored me completely and enthusiastically began to talk to her.

"The Ikawas are real feudalistic. I work in the factory all day long, but they still shake me at five of a morning and chase me off into the fields. It's harvestin' time now, so I know ever'body's busy; but I get tired out working in the factory all day. And I tole 'em I couldn't do farm work when I married into that family, and they said it wouldn't matter. But they don't remember nothing they said."

Though I hadn't any business there, I wandered out to the kitchen. I knew that since he had managed to get his story out it was all over. Seeing that I was no longer there, he launched into an even sadder yarn. The voice carried to where I was standing idle and made me more despondent.

"It was too much for me," he was saying. "Then four or five days ago, when I complained about it to the old man, I got into a big fight with him. Before it was over, he went out to the barn and come back with a big, long stick. So me, I went 'n got a pole. I figured that made us about equal. You see, the old man he's sixty, but he's in terrific shape. Me, I may be young, but I ain't no good in a fight at all, but it ended up me hitting the old man on the head. The old man, he fell back on his fanny and started grabbin' his head. I guess it was bleeding, I don't know. Anyway, Mom, she calls out the alarm, and Jutaro—my cousin, you know?—he flew in. He took one look at the old man, and then he got mad all over and started at me yelling that he'd kill me for doing that to the head of the family. Jutaro's rough, and I ain't no match for him by a long shot. I ran out and hid myself in the thicket and finally managed to get to my friend's house in town. He hid me for about three days, and I had him go and get the rest of my wages that was coming to me from the factory. But my friend said he couldn't go on hiding me there 'cause they'd be sure to find me and didn't I have a swell uncle in Tokyo? So, he says, why didn't I go there? But I told him that I'd already been enough trouble to my uncle, but he says hadn't my uncle even been the go-between at my wedding? I says yeah, and so here I am."

Then, just like a woman, my wife asked: "But what about your wife?"

"Her? She don't know which end's up."

"Don't you love her?"

"I don't hate her. . . . She got a baby, you know."

"Oh? How old?"

"She's still carrying it. She's five months along."

"Is that so?" my wife exclaimed in great sympathy.

That voice sounded my defeat! How mothers nowadays can be so proud of their weakness for children always amazes me. I went around from the kitchen to the dining room, then over to the stairway, and slowly and deliberately went up the stairs. This was a kind of one-man protest demonstration against Tamio and certainly against my wife. Of course I knew it was futile. I felt like letting everyone do just as he damn-well pleased. I lay down on the bed in my study. I was in no mood to face my desk. No sooner had I lain down than my wife came up. Looking down at me, she said, "How about letting him stay with us just till he finds a job? After hearing his story, how could we send him back?"

I looked up at my wife. She was, as always, in the pink—plump in the tummy revealing her nearly fifty years; nor were the legs which could be seen protruding from below her skirt what one would call slim. Still, there was an indefinable instability about her.

As if giving an order, she said to me, "But what else can we do?"

Finally I answered, "There's nothing else we can do because you had to go and listen to his fool story."

"But that's why he ran away, because he had a story. So, if we didn't listen to it, we wouldn't know anything at all."

"That's just what I'm saying: We weren't obliged to listen to it."

But my words didn't seem to reach her. Already she had made up her mind to put him up. Referring to our oldest son, she said, "Toshiyoshi won't be back for a month, so he could sleep in his room."

"When Toshiyoshi does come home, he'll be mad."

For employment during the school vacation Toshiyoshi had gone to Nagano to make a survey of village farm life.

Then she said, bringing our high school daughter into the picture, "When Toshiyoshi comes home, Reiko and I can sleep together and Tamio can sleep in the dining room where I usually sleep."

"Then Reiko will complain for sure."

As if she had been driven to the wall, she fell silent. She was inordinately weak when it came to children. And our two children absolutely abhorred strangers coming into our home, whether they be relatives or whatever.[5] They couldn't tolerate even the woman who came to help with the housework. She remained silent as I pushed my point further.

"If we were to have him stay at a cheap inn, it'd cost us thirty thousand yen a month, wouldn't it? If that's what you want, then it's all right with me to send him to an inn."

Suddenly her entire expression changed. She sat down, almost throwing herself on the floor, and screamed, "How can you talk like that when we haven't even paid back the money we borrowed at the time when you were sick!"

I recoiled a bit. I guess I had pushed her a little too far. But she kept after me.

"And you're a Christian? Here your own relative has come to you in trouble."

"I don't see any connection between this problem and being a Christian. This is strictly a matter of social mores. Whether or not a person should urinate on the street hasn't anything to do with Christianity."

"I'm not talking about urinating on the street."

"It's the same kind of question."

"You're nothing but a cold-blooded scribbler!" she exclaimed, growing whiter by the minute. "You're the go-between, aren't you? Don't you have any sense of responsibility as go-between?"

"Go-between? But that was only in name—"

"In name only or whatever, at that time you were looked upon as go-between by the Ikawa family and were paid respect as such, weren't you?"

That did it. As far as I was concerned, it made up my mind for me. Perhaps I actually did have some responsibility. But it was hard to see just what that responsibility was.

Then she said, "So you have an obligation to stand between the Ikawa family and Tamio and try to work out some kind of solution."

Suddenly her tone had become gentle. The blood began to flow back into her ashen face. I was nonplussed. I felt I was on unfamiliar ground. She now lowered her voice and said ever so gently: "And it seems his wife is carrying a baby."

A happy little smile faintly crossed her face. There was no help for it, so I replied, "Well then, I'll write a letter to the Ikawas. Maybe they're worried about him."

She hurried down the stairs. I don't know why, but she seemed overeager to me. That Tamio fellow, because he was young and emaciated, had wrapped her around his little finger. I jumped up and took down my entire set of law books. I searched all through them, but nowhere could I find a word written about the obligations or responsibilities of a "go-between." In fact, I couldn't

---

5. The sociological concept of the inviolability of one's home and the traditional attitude toward strangers (*tanin*) are behind this statement.

even find the word. Just as I had expected, all that's needed for a marriage is the mutual consent of the two parties. I thought of the big, red lacquer wedding cup that was placed in the alcove of the Ikawa's house during the ceremony. They explained that some big official had used it many years ago, but I wondered at the time what connection something like that had with the wedding ceremony. A go-between is like that wedding cup—an over-and-above item, the presence or absence of which makes absolutely no difference. If I had any responsibility as a go-between, then it was an "over-and-above" one.

Still, I couldn't make out clearly what my responsibility really was.

2

I sent a letter to my aunt by special delivery. It was a letter of reconciliation, which went something like this: Tamio Ikawa is sorry not only that he has run away to my house but also for what he has done; and he still has a great deal, almost too much, affection for his wife Myoko. What is more, it seems she is carrying their child (I checked all these points with Tamio). So now, out of consideration for my role as go-between, I am asking you to forgive him. I did not overlook adding that my house is small, and we find it very difficult to make room for him. I didn't compose flowery phrases such as "the fresh breeze blows across the paddies," but I think that, while considering their position, I expressed both Tamio's desire and my own very politely.

Five days passed, then a week, and still there was no answer. I could imagine how it might be with the Ikawas, but one would have expected some word from Tamio's wife, who had lived with him for a year and a half. But there was nothing even from her. After ten days I was angry enough to consider sending a telegram to press them for some kind of answer. But when I get angry, I get too angry. This is something I have to watch in myself. So instead, once more I sent letters, this time two—one to my aunt and one to Tamio's wife. I didn't put any return address on them. The result was the same. Five days passed, then six, and still no answer came.

Even apart from their failure to reply, I had fallen into a miserable frame of mind, like one who has been turned out in the middle of the night. I tried to get to my work but couldn't settle down. My own home had become the house of a stranger with no place where I could find peace of mind. Our son's room was a nine-by-nine room right next to my study-bedroom, and this was where Tamio slept. Though I don't have to get up and go to the bathroom downstairs very often, still whenever I tried to get down the stairs, invariably he would be coming up. If he had come on up the stairs, I could have waited for him; but he would always stop halfway up and make no move to come up or go down. On that narrow stairway it was like a game of "I dare you." I wanted to shout out, "Well, either come up or go down!" but I suspected his actions were intentional. I would force my way down the stairs. When I did this he would freeze against the wall like a lizard to let me pass. I tried to give him credit for not doing this on purpose; however, this was the action not of a two- or three-year-old, but of a man already past twenty-five, and I simply couldn't understand it. To me it wasn't an especially funny game.

Even when he was in his room (I guess there must be something wrong with his nose), he was always letting out one big sneeze after another. Each time I would be jolted from the manuscript on which I was intent. How could one who is not only a writer by profession but who has also found in that work his reason to go on living, help getting violently angry at what comes like a threat from the devil? I tried to overcome my reaction first by thinking that a sneeze is, after all, a natural physical phenomenon and that to rebuke the sneezer constitutes a violation of human rights; if my work was upset by a sneeze from the next room, then it must mean that I hadn't been very deeply engrossed in my work in the first place; the reason why a sneeze from the next room sounded so enormous was that the wall was thin, the responsibility for which lay in the fact that it was built cheaply right after the war; but it was no use—no matter what I thought, it didn't help. The bookshelf-side of the room was separated from his room by a very thin veneer board. After the sneezes stopped, he would heave a pitiful sigh, which came like a dramatic announcement of his personal despair of the total universe. When this was over, he would start tossing about in his bed until the whole house shook.

After I had spent about two months in the Keio and Tokyo University hospitals because of a dangerous heart affliction (coronary thrombosis), I recuperated for a year at home. After that experience, and then because occasionally my heart fluttered, I had ordered a bed put in my study so that when I got tired, I could lie down at any time. Since it was better to be sleeping than sitting at my desk upset, I'd crawl into bed. I had been on strong sleeping medicine ever since my attack, but even when I took a stronger dose than the prescription called for, there were many times when I couldn't sleep. Still, sometimes in the daytime I could doze off. At times this wouldn't last more than an hour. But just when I did manage to get off, as if waiting for the cue, the radio would blast out from the next room.

I had encouraged Tamio over and over to go to the employment office. He'd give some vague answer, but all day long he would hang around. From the very beginning he had had no intention to try to find work in Tokyo. One day when I was at the breaking point, I opened the sliding doors to the adjoining room. He was sitting, doing nothing, in the middle of the room, tailor-fashion with one leg under him and one leg stretched out.

"If you're bored, be quiet about it!" I barked. "I'm working. If you're so bored, why don't you go sightseeing in town?"

"Since that time the police picked me up for questioning, I'm scared to go out walkin' any more."

"That time you looked suspicious because you walked about in the same place for so long."

"But I'd get lost if I went anyplace by myself."

"That's why I gave you the map."

"Even with a map I can't make out what's where. . . ."

"Take the sightseeing bus again. My wife took you the other day so you ought to know how to do that."

Then he said reluctantly, "Oh, she gonna take me again?"

"What are you saying? Haven't you got a tongue of your own? I can't have her leaving her housework and going gallivanting all the time. You ought to know by now how many visitors come to this house."

He was quiet a minute. But right away he said in a pitiful tone of voice, "Last night I had such a stomachache I didn't get no sleep at all."

"Why didn't you say something?"

"How could I?" he said as if he had been injured. "This ain't my home. I ain't free to wake you people up in the middle of the night. Boy, I found out last night I don't have no home of my own. Nobody understands me. It's just like everybody had abandoned me. Last night I really cried. You didn't know that, did you, Uncle?"

"I wouldn't have done anything about it if I had."

He looked down. "It was the same at the Ikawas' house. When I asked for something, no matter what it was, they wouldn't hear it. 'Let me just sleep thirty minutes more,' I said. And I had good reason, too. I had to be at the fruit-processing factory in the city by eight, and I worked till six. Then even when I got home, I couldn't relax. I had to help with the rice-hackle and stuff till ten. And by the time we had supper it was after 'leven before I ever got to bed. I ain't very strong. I was worn out when I went to bed. So I asked 'em for thirty minutes of a morning; if they'd've just let me have thirty more minutes to sleep, it would've made a lot of difference in how I felt. Even this little favor was embarrassing for me to have to ask, don't you understand? I just told 'em the honest-to-God truth. Then when I did, Dad and Mom, both of 'em, looked at me like I was a liar or somethin'. And that's not all. The whole village is some kind of relation of the Ikawas—cousins or aunts or somethin'. From the morning I made that request, everyone in the village began to look on me as some kind of swindler. They wouldn't even speak to me when I said hello. It was like the whole village lined up against me. I decided to hell with them and when they called me the next morning, I'd play possum and just wouldn't get up. When that happened, the old man really got mad—and that's when the fight started."

"What was your wife doing all that time?"

"She wasn't no help at all. She belongs to the Ikawas, so she joined the enemy camp." Then, to get my sympathy, he said, "I really found out this time what it means to be an orphan with no home. More 'n an orphan, it's like I was a bastard that don't even know his parents."

I said nothing, but left and went back to my adjoining study. I wanted to inform him that because of his presence here it was I who had lost my home. In despair I let my eyes fall on the blank sheets of manuscript paper which were spread on my desk and which I couldn't for the life of me set my hand to. Then I went downstairs and said to my wife:

"I'm going to accept that lecture series in Osaka."

"But the doctor said you couldn't give any lectures," she answered critically. "Didn't he say that the cardiograph you had the other day wasn't good? And you haven't finished that manuscript."

Her objection was of course due partly to my health and partly to the fact that financially the lectures wouldn't mean nearly so much as writing the manuscript. But she suddenly had a change of heart when I said, "The second day of the lectures is to be near my hometown, so I thought I'd go to my aunt's and settle this problem about that fellow upstairs."

"Fine. Then you could talk over the matter as go-between and come up with a solution. You do that."

Though she had brought it up herself, apparently she had completely forgotten the matter of my poor health. This was no doubt because she had weakened under the opposition of our daughter. Our daughter wouldn't eat supper in the dining room with us but had it in her own room alone because at night Tamio was glued to the television in the dining room. Her criticism of her father and mother was really very simple. It was, "You're just not with it." When my wife asked her what it was we weren't with, my daughter replied as if her explanation were the most logical in the world: "When you're not with it, you're just not with it." She wouldn't look at Tamio or say one word to him but kept herself in her room all the time. The fact that she would have to sleep in the same room with her mother when Toshiyoshi returned from Nagano, from the point of view of her present psychological development, was simply something she couldn't even think about. There was no doubt about it: Tamio's feeling that he was an unrecognized illegitimate child was an actual fact to me and to my family.

Several days later I spoke in the afternoon in Osaka and then set out for my hometown. It was already eight at night by the time I reached the station. Even though it was a small city of about fifty thousand people, there was plenty of activity even at this late hour. They seemed to be making a rotary in front of the station, and cement mixers and trucks were lumbering about noisily. After the rain the night before, the street was one big quagmire. Carrying my traveling case, I finally made it to the bus stop just across the way. But they told me there wasn't another bus for the village for which I was heading. The idea of staying that night in the city flashed across my mind, but on the next day I had to travel to another city about six hours from there to give the next lecture. And my return ticket had already been sent to me by my sponsor, calling for a direct return by air from the next city to Tokyo. I didn't want to waste the ticket by coming back here. At the same time I had a deadline to make on my work which was waiting for me back in Tokyo. I went to the taxi office. There were three men inside a tiny box. When I asked how much the fare would be to my destination, the man at the window said probably about twelve hundred yen, as if he were talking about someone else's business and any amount would do. Somehow I felt uneasy about his answer and even asked if they would think of sending a car that far. When I asked this, the man said disinterestedly, "Well, that's our business."

I thought, if that's your business, you're not very businesslike about it. With his eyes the man at the desk signaled to the man sitting beside him. The other man got up and for some reason or other at the same instant stuck out an unusually long, red tongue for them to see. It didn't appear that the tongue had any connection with the conversation which they had been engaged in up to this point. I felt rather uneasy. I had the feeling that I was going to be cheated on the fare or on something.

Right away the car left the bright street that ran in front of the station and entered a dark country lane. I couldn't help thinking about the long, red tongue which my driver had shown his buddies. He was about forty and didn't appear especially to be a bad sort. And there was a regular taximeter fixed to the steering wheel. Though I had been to the village five or six times, always before I had gone by bus; that was because the bus route ran through the town where I was born. It brought back memories to see the houses in my native village from the bus window. And the bus fare was only sixty yen. This was the first time to go by taxi.

The taxi bounced up and down mercilessly. The road was an unpaved country one, so I had to put up with the bouncing. But since it seemed that I was going to be thrown out of the seat, I had no choice but to hang onto the front seat. I looked out the window but it was pitch dark, so I could see nothing but some houses along the road, or the thicket, or the boundaries of fields which were caught in the light of the headlamps. I thought that by this time I should have seen a certain bridge which I remembered, but it didn't appear. Apprehensively, I reminded him: "It's H—— Village, you know."

"I know," the driver answered with displeasure. "Please take your hand off the seat. It's dangerous driving with you pulling on the seat."

Quickly I let go my hold on the back of the seat behind the driver and caught onto the metal handle which raises and lowers the window. But when we hit a large bump, this was no use to me at all. Still worried, I said, "Haven't you gotten off the road? This is my old home ground, and I know almost all the roads around here."

The driver replied curtly, "This is a new road opened just this spring."

I was silent. I realized that I'd have to leave it to him. I resolved that wherever he took me, I'd just have to deal with the problem when I got there.

But the car arrived right at the entrance to the village, where the bus stop is located. The driver said the car couldn't proceed any further. Remembering how automobiles had driven right up to the front of Ikawa's house at the time of the wedding, I informed the driver about it. But he insisted that the road at the foot of the mountain was narrow and dangerous and that he couldn't drive it at night. Suppressing my anger, I said, "But when I got in, you said you would take me to H——."

"That's right. This is H——."

With this the driver pointed to a sign standing, as it were, in the middle of nowhere. The round-shaped sign illuminated by the headlights clearly said H—— Village. Dejectedly I paid the fare indicated by the meter. It was exactly what the fellow at the window at the station had said—twelve hundred yen. This made me feel out of sorts. After the taxi had backed up twice in order to reverse its direction, it was gone with a sudden burst of energy. About two kilometers down the road there was a faint light burning—evidently a street light left on all night. That would be the light at the entrance of the first settlement in H——, and the Ikawas' house to which I was going was still two kilometers more down the stream which ran along the foot of the mountain. I started walking in the direction of the mountain which could be faintly discerned beyond the settlement that lay immediately before me. I took the road through the dark rice paddies. I don't know just why, but I was fighting mad. I only regretted that I hadn't left my case at the station. The weight of that case made the pointless anger even worse.

Eventually I reached the first settlement. Here and there were houses where a gate light was burning, but it was quiet as death. In spite of the fact that Tamio had said that he had been made to work until ten, this settlement was sunk in deep slumber, and there was no evidence of a living soul. There was not even the sound of a dog barking. I didn't know anyone who lived here. Yet I remembered the houses. Finally the path brought me to the shrine. The street light at the entrance of this village which I had seen from afar was for the sake of this shrine. From here the road ran to the foot of the mountain. On my left a stream flowed from a reservoir; and on my right, which was the foot of the mountain, pine trees sent their branches out over the road. The road was extremely rough; and since it was dark at my feet, time and time again I stumbled, staggering over large rocks on the road. But a car could have made it down this road. I muttered to myself, "Why did that driver stick out his tongue?"

I had the feeling I would never understand why he did it. In the next moment my body doubled, involuntarily, and I found myself in a crouched position on the ground. It was my heart. A pain had seized my chest with such violence that I thought it would tear out my ribs. I could hardly get my breath. Cold sweat broke out on my forehead. I pulled out of my pocket the emergency medicine which I always carried, and; tossing it into my mouth, I went down to the stream, ignoring the danger. My feet slipped, and one foot slid into the stream. But I wasn't aware of it. Nor did I know whether the water in that stream was pure or polluted. With one hand gripping the grass along the bank, I scooped up the water in the other hand and swallowed down the medicine in my mouth. An irrelevant thought crossed my mind: "What in the world am I doing here?" Meanwhile, the dangerous pain in my chest continued unabated.

3

I passed along the road through the thicket and finally came out at the next settle-
ment. I suppose the emergency medicine had taken effect because after I rested for
about twenty minutes, the pain left me without trace. The settlement was deep in
darkness. The mountains which should have been surrounding it were not visible at
all and could only be faintly felt. Here and there a light could be seen. What Tamio
called the village was actually this settlement which was a part of H——. There
couldn't have been more than twenty houses. I rested a bit after coming out of the
thicket and, carefully carrying the traveling case, began to walk on slowly. Of
course, I didn't make the case lighter by handling it daintily, but my mind was
eased somewhat. I felt I was taking every precaution possible under the circum-
stances; if I were to suffer another attack, it would not be because of negligence on
my part. Fortunately Ikawa's house was at the entrance of the settlement. Already
the white wall was clearly visible under the street light. Since the road divided at
this point, probably the village office carried a special budget for this street light.
At the same time, the light was testimony to Shinkichi Ikawa's influence in the
community.

Around the naked light bulb, hundreds of insects had gathered. I looked at
my watch. It still wasn't ten. Yet not only were all the shutters closed on Ikawa's
house beyond the wall, but everything indicated that the people inside were al-
ready asleep. I hesitated a moment, but I went and stood before the front gate. I
couldn't turn back now. Calling out my own name, I knocked on the door of the
gate and asked to be admitted. My fist sounded louder than the door did. At any
rate it was a miserable sound. Such a gate door—like the gates of a castle, thick
and solid, and bolted shut—one wouldn't think necessary in these modern times.
There was no chance that that meager sound of my knocking would ever man-
age to cross the inner garden, penetrate the closed shutters, and still have force
enough left to startle the sleeping ears. Maliciously, I thought it could very well
be that the head of the Ikawa family had a heart constructed like that gate door.
While I was still banging against the door, some chickens that they kept some-
where in a corner of the yard began to cackle in confusion. This encouraged me,
so I kept on knocking to stir up the chickens further. But they wouldn't cackle
any more. I then decided I had no alternative but to act in the manner of a thief
who was attempting to break into the house.

Following the wall, I made my way around to the back. I didn't really intend to
break in like a thief, but I thought surely this house had a weak spot somewhere.
In the dark I stepped off the path and stumbled, but finally I found the Achilles'
heel. There was a sliding door in the rear beside the well. I knocked on it. It rat-
tled thunderously as if it would break to pieces any minute. A light went on, and
someone came down to the kitchen. I breathed a sigh of relief. The door slid
open, and a black shape appeared in the entrance. It was my aunt. Tying a narrow
sash to her pin-striped kimono, in a startled voice she called my name: "My, my!
Is it Juntaro? My, my! Well, come on in."

"Forgive me, at this hour—"

"You can apologize later. If you had let us know, we would have had the front door open and waiting for you."

I was led through a large dirt-floor kitchen to a tatami-mat room.[6] This seemed to be the guest room where I was always taken. Directly all the house was up, and a lot of commotion began. From the kitchen the sound of a fire being lighted could be heard, and there was the continuous sound of someone going in and out of the storage room. Of course the whole household should have consisted of only three—my aunt and uncle and the oldest girl, Myoko, leaving out the daughter who was staying in the city. Cursorily I looked about the room. Nothing had been changed. In the alcove a porcelain statue of one of the seven gods of luck had been placed, and on the walls above the sliding panels the two or three nondescript pictures still hung as before. On one wall was a picture of the Emperor and Empress; on another were a picture of my uncle in his youth in soldier's uniform (he had been an army sergeant), a certificate of decoration of the eighth order, three decorations including a medal for soldiers who served at home, and a certificate of appreciation received from the Farmers' Cooperative in recognition of this "progressive" farm. I had always before looked upon all this a little patronizingly, thinking that it expressed my uncle's childish patriotism, and it had still continued unchanged. But now I couldn't help thinking of what Tamio had said about "feudalism" as it was reflected in these framed pictures and documents. Still, I thought of my uncle as modern and not, as Tamio did, feudalistic.

Just then the chickens in the front yard started cackling noisily. At the same time my aunt's rebuking voice could be heard: "Even if we wring off the chicken's head now, it won't be ready for tonight."

My uncle answered simply, "Shall we pluck it tomorrow, then?"

Evidently the chicken had already been killed. Finally the sound of footsteps, coming from the direction of the storehouse into the back dirt-floor room, could be heard; and eventually my uncle appeared from the room which corresponded no doubt to the sleeping room. Probably because he dressed in such a hurry, his sash was carelessly tied. Just as Tamio had said, though he was over sixty, he had the robust body of a farmer. When I had finished saying formal greetings to him; I told him about my trip and that I had to leave by nine the next morning.

"Then we can't have a very leisurely visit, can we?" he said, obviously genuinely disappointed. "You're a busy man, so it can't be helped, I suppose. But the mushrooms are late this year, and I thought I'd like to take you mushrooming because they've just begun to come out the last day or so. We hardly ever find mushrooms in November."

---

6. Kitchens in rural houses often have dirt or concrete floors; other rooms are floored with thick woven straw mats called *tatami*.

My uncle's attitude was, as always, full of goodwill toward me. He didn't seem at all like a person who would neglect entirely to answer my letters. And my aunt, who brought me beer, was just like my uncle. When she heard from my uncle about my plans, tears filled her eyes as if she were saying goodbye to someone she'd never see again. Then my uncle, as if he had got hold of himself finally, welcomed me:

"I'm sorry we have only one bottle of beer. But we'll have some warm saké for you in a minute. If you had come a little earlier, I'd have gone to the city on the bicycle and bought some fish." Then he called out to my aunt, who had gone into another room, "Mother! You had some cans, didn't you?"

Without making obvious what I was doing, I examined my uncle's head. His salt-and-pepper gray hair was cropped short, but there didn't seem to be any scar indicating that Tamio had hit him. Then he yelled in the direction of the other room, "What happened to the saké? Isn't it hot yet?"

Up to this point I had let the couple go on with their preparations for entertainment without saying anything, but at this point I blurted out, "It's late, and I'm forbidden to drink saké by my doctor."

"You can't believe everything the doctor says. And a drink or two won't hurt you." Again he yelled short-temperedly, "What's the matter? Hurry up with that saké!"

Hurriedly my aunt came bringing the saké bottle with fish which looked as if it had come out of a can.

"You kept calling for me to hurry so it's not very warm, and the fish ain't well prepared. Please forgive us."

Finally I decided to broach the subject and said, "To tell the truth, the reason why I've come at such an hour has to do with Tamio."

My uncle put his saké cup down so quickly it hit the table with a bang. The smile he had been wearing vanished as if it had never been there, and his face became hard as granite. My aunt, still holding onto the tray, sat down as though her spine had dissolved. My uncle's voice changed noticeably, and he said tensely, "I have nothing to say on the subject of Tamio. If you must ask, then ask her."

Then, without another word, he left and went into the adjoining room. Surprised, I said to my aunt, "Did you get my letter?" But my voice trembled a little. I too had received an embarrassing shock brought on by the sudden change in the attitude of my uncle. As if my manner had upset her, she explained:

"He still thinks you're on Tamio's side. A moment ago he thought you really understood and that was why you came here in the middle of the night."

"I'm not on either side," I said meekly. "So I'm not *against* anyone, either. It's just that my wife said that out of my duty as go-between, even if I were go-between in name only, I had the responsibility to do something to bring about a reconciliation between the Ikawas and Tamio, and that's why I'm here. I myself feel that no matter what differences of opinion there are, there is a way to live together on friendly terms. That's what I wrote clearly in my letter, but for some reason or other I have not yet received an answer."

"I think your letter's over at Masakichi's or somewheres."

"Masakichi's?"

"They're Granddaddy's[7] cousins-in-law." Then, gaining momentum, she continued, "You know, he's employed by the railroad. When you came here year before last, didn't you meet him? He's been transferred to another city. He don't get home more'n once a week. So I think your letter got stopped over there."

Surprised, I said without thinking, "So my letter is making the round of all the relatives?"

"Whatever's the business of the head-family is the business of all. If they don't all decide, then there's all kinds of trouble afterward. We got your special-delivery asking for an answer, but right now's fall and the busiest season on the farm. And we have to show your letter to Granddaddy's brother way over in S—— City and talk it over with him. And we haven't got time to go way over there. Even Granddaddy couldn't have sent you an answer unless all the relatives agreed."

My head began to ache. I inquired, "When Tamio came here in the first place, did you take that complicated a procedure? I knew nothing about it if you did."

"At that time we just had a conference with the main relatives."

"Couldn't you do that this time too?"

"But this time he's not coming to us. We're deciding whether or not to turn him out, you know. This has to be done by all the relatives. When you turn someone out, then ever'body gossips about it. Comin' together is simple, but separation's not so easy. It can't be decided by two or three."

"Well, up till now what is the opinion of those who have seen my letter?"

"Well, the fact is, he hit Granddaddy on the head with a stick. There's those 'at says he oughtta be let die in the ditch." And then, for some reason, she wiped her eyes and said, "And in spite of all that, Juntaro, some of 'em's saying, we can't understand you'd take sides with a rapscallion like that and turn against us."

"All I've done is to try to bring about a reconciliation. Tamio himself has repented, so couldn't Uncle just bend a little and try to get along? It seems that Myoko is going to have a baby, so wouldn't it be for everyone's happiness if they got along? This is all I am saying. Before, I was a go-between in name only, I suppose. But after this separation over a quarrel, I think it's necessary for me to become a real go-between."

"Yes, but people are saying all sorts of things. We've tried to tell 'em that you don't know nothing about it at all."

The wall clock struck. I saw by my watch it was indeed midnight.

"I can't understand why my letter had to be circulated, but I would like to know what you yourself think about all this."

---

7. She calls her husband "Granddaddy" out of a mixed feeling of intimacy and respect.

My aunt was silent. Then she wiped her eyes again. I couldn't understand why she was crying. I lost the will to question her anymore, and poured out some cold saké. She said in a small, hoarse voice, "Myself, I married into the Ikawa family."

Then, as if she had reached some decision, she got up saying, "You're tired. I'll put down your bed. Get a good night's sleep."

She began to put down my bed. It was new, bright-colored bedding, and I could easily imagine that this was bought for the newlyweds, Tamio and his wife. This thought gave me a strange sensation, and I asked almost in a whisper, "Where is Myoko?"

"She's here," my aunt answered in an embarrassed tone. "I told her to come in and just say hello, but she said she didn't want to be seen."

"But she's not a child any longer; she must be a fine woman of twenty-three."

"That's right," my aunt answered noncommittally.

As usual I took my sleeping pills and crawled into the bedding which had been spread on the floor after the table was taken away. The wadding was soft, and the material of the quilts felt good against the skin. But that good feeling turned into a strange, tingling sensation. It was because, no doubt, the couple, after returning from their honeymoon, had slept at least two or three nights in this bedding. There was the feeling of soft warmth in it which could have been the body warmth of the newlyweds themselves. I couldn't help but be disgusted with myself. First of all, I couldn't for the life of me figure out why I had come here at all. I had some kind of simple notion at the bottom of my mind that my coming would be enough to bring about a solution to Tamio's problem. Not only did I think I had the confidence of my aunt and uncle, but I was trusting that if we apologized for Tamio's rough behavior, eventually the question of separation would be decided by the young couple themselves. Moreover, up until now, I thought I was capable of working out the solution to any problem of estrangement, wherever it happened, anywhere in the world. But the situation I now faced seemed of an absolutely different nature. Tamio had used the word "feudalistic," but even that wasn't adequate to describe the monolithic structure of this rural community. If it had been truly feudalistic, then wouldn't it have been impossible to recognize Tamio and Myoko's love for each other and so take him into the house? The community was based on blood relations, and, as it happened, in this settlement relatives made up the major part. Though they called this the head-family, my uncle didn't have the feudal lord's rights as far as I could tell from what my aunt had said. But still, my uncle probably couldn't forget that it was he who was hurt by being struck with the stick; yet he himself couldn't make a decision regarding Tamio. The point was that Tamio had quite simply and decisively extricated himself from that monolithic society.

Still half asleep, I sensed it was morning and bounded out of bed. The sleeping medicine hadn't worked very well. I seemed to have been dreaming profound dreams one after the other, but I completely lost them the moment

I woke up. Once awake, I couldn't afford to go on recalling dreams. It was already light outside. I picked up my watch from beside my pillow and looked at it. It was already after six. Quickly I changed into my clothes. No doubt hearing me move about, my aunt came in.

"Are you already awake? Why don't you sleep a little longer?"

"I have to get the nine o'clock train from the city."

"You can't stay a little longer?"

"No, I can't," I said definitely.

My aunt seemed perplexed as she left and walked quickly in the direction of the kitchen. Taking a wash basin, I went out to the front yard. I knew that there was clean water from a mountain stream in the corner of the yard. The family had said that even when the well was dry this little spring never ran dry. We were surrounded by mountains, but there were rice paddies as far as one could see, and the harvest seemed almost finished. Everywhere I could see the cut rice hanging on the rice racks. The sound of rice-hackle machines and motors moving them, cutting off the heads of rice, could be heard from different directions. I washed my face with the spring water. Then I noticed a woman who had just come around the corner of the house and stopped, startled. She looked for a moment as if she were going to run and hide on the other side of the house. But we were too close. It was Myoko. She appeared to have been working in the paddies and had a towel tied about her head. She was fatter than the last time I saw her. I checked myself for fear my eyes would focus on her stomach.

"Good morning."

Hurriedly she took the towel from her head and bowed curtly. She seemed more womanlike than before. Though she no doubt worked in the fields, her face was not suntanned.

"Tamio's staying with me," I said, testing her reaction. But she only looked down with her head bowed. Since her mouth appeared to be moving, she no doubt was saying something, though it was inaudible.

"Why didn't you come out last night?" I asked.

She twisted her body and looked toward the rice paddies as if she were about to run away. I had to hurry if I meant to talk to her.

"You like Tamio, don't you? They say you're going to have a baby, and . . ."

She turned around as if she had given up the idea of trying to escape, but still she continued to stare at the ground without answering.

"Then you don't like Tamio?"

But she continued silent with her eyes fixed on the ground. Irritated at her attitude, I pressed her for some answer.

"Then, are you thinking you'd just as soon be separated?"

She continued to keep her silence. Yet she had begun to fidget with the hem of her apron.

"You don't have to talk to me if you don't want to," I said, angry with her. "I'm up against it myself. I came here thinking that, if I could do anything as a go-between, I would try one way or another to get you two together again. And

I went to a lot of trouble to do it, too. In spite of all that, last night my uncle treated me as if I were his enemy. But I thought I could get you to say something, since, after all, I'm looking after your husband. My house is small, not like your house here. And because of this, I can't even do my own work. When I consulted law books, I found that a go-between has no legal responsibility; but I came here anyway out of moral obligation. Perhaps I've been too conscientious. I haven't done this expecting any thanks from you, I just want to hear one word from you—one word which will let me know what you are thinking."

At this point Myoko seemed to say something to herself. With mixed emotions of contempt and pity I asked her again, "What's happened to the girl who year before last, when we went out gathering bracken, put a snake in my canteen and when it startled me as I started to take a drink, she had to hold her stomach because she laughed so hard? Can't you laugh like that any more?"

For an instant there was the flicker of a smile, but she quickly repressed it and finally spoke in an embarrassed manner: "It's up to them."

"Up to them? I'm not asking *them*; I'm asking you. I'm asking you if you love Tamio or not."

"So I said it's all up to them."

"I'm talking about you—whether you love him or don't love him. Are you going to have them decide even that for you?"

"If I let them decide, then—whether I love him or not—it's not my responsibility."

I looked at her, bewildered. I couldn't understand it. I wondered whether there was something wrong with me. Seeing my aunt appear at the entrance of the house, as if knowing she would be reprimanded for talking with me, Myoko trotted off in the direction of my aunt and disappeared into the house. I didn't know whether I should believe what was happening or not. My aunt looked at the girl and me with a dubious expression, but that was all. In a pleasant voice she called to me: "It's not much, but breakfast is ready. Are you ready to eat?"

I returned to my room. When I looked at what was on the table, I lost my appetite (which hadn't been much to start with). Heaped on a large dish was an enormous quantity of rice balls. They were made out of cooked glutinous rice pounded lightly and smeared with bean paste. But my aunt hadn't served them to make fun of me; obviously, with good intentions, she had gotten up early and prepared them especially for me. Suppressing a sigh, I said, "But I can't eat all these."

"Now, a child could eat ten or twenty of them."

Finally I got one down, but I just couldn't bring myself to eat a second. Again my aunt wiped her eyes. Somehow or other she had mixed up my physiology and my psychology.

"You can't eat my cooking anymore," she said as if she had been deeply hurt. "I can see that Tamio has been buttering you up and now has you on his side."

I explained at length that it was nothing but that I just didn't have any appetite, but she became more and more gloomy, like a person suffering from some mental depression, and only continued to wipe her tears and repeat over and over the same complaint.

"Ain't I your only aunt? And you let yourself be taken in by Tamio and can't be on our side."

I explained emphatically that it had nothing to do with Tamio at all. But it had no effect whatever on her. Since there was no escape, I took one more rice ball and put it on my plate. But I couldn't eat more than a third of it. Then my aunt, as if she had made up her mind, said, "Well, there's nothing we can do— even if you do think we are in the wrong."

I left my aunt's house hurriedly—not that I was afraid that if I stayed longer, I'd be murdered with her rice balls. But it was almost 7:30, and the walk to the bus stop would take at least forty minutes. Since there were only two buses an hour, I didn't want to miss the eight-twenty. The leave-taking with my aunt was unpleasant, but that couldn't be helped. As I was leaving through the front gate, my uncle returned, walking with dragging steps, dressed in his work clothes. I politely thanked him. But he, as though he wasn't the same uncle I had talked with last night, said, in a weak voice, "Oh, then you're off."

That was all he said. For whatever the reason, the power had drained out of him.

Again I carried the heavy suitcase and walked slowly down the narrow country road. I feared another heart attack—so much so that when I reached the incline, I took a long rest. There I could see all the people working in the fields and every house in the settlement. That village had its own identity as a unified community and its own distinctive social field of influence.

I thought, "They are satisfied and at peace, in their way." But though I had made the effort to come here, I had not only failed to unite Tamio with the village, I had left bad feelings there. Perhaps that is the fate of an arbitrator, and yet . . . I felt I could never visit there again, at least until the Tamio matter was settled.

4

When I arrived home in Tokyo I was ready to explode out of my anger and despair. I finally reached the house only to discover my wife was not at home. Apparently she had gone out shopping. I went on upstairs to my study; but upon opening the sliding doors, I was met with a scene that left me frozen in the entrance, speechless. My bed had been put away, and there Tamio was lying on the floor. Seeing me, he grinned and began slowly to get up. Three or four of my books were carelessly scattered about on the mat floor. I highly valued the books on my shelf, and I disliked having them touched even by my wife. Before I knew it, I spoke out in a voice trembling with rage: "Whose permission did you have to come into my room like this?"

Tamio answered, grinning either in contempt or in an attempt to disarm me: "Toshiyoshi came back from Nagano, so Aunty said since Uncle was gone I should use your room."

"I don't want anyone using my room," I said with finality, angry at my wife's arranging. "And let me make this clear once and for all, though I may be your cousin-in-law, I am *not* your uncle. I don't wish to be lightly referred to as 'Uncle.'"

Crestfallen, he answered, "I understand."

He was so dejected that I lost heart, and though this was my own room, I sat down in the doorway as if it belonged to someone else. When I did this, I felt—strangely—as if he and I were cohorts lined up against the Ikawa family. I had gone to the village to seek a reconciliation between the Ikawas and this Tamio who was before me here. It was nonsense for the Ikawas to look upon him and myself as fellow conspirators against them. But in a way I felt as though we were just that.

Somewhat against my better judgment, I said in a most restrained tone, "I stopped by the Ikawas."

Then, out of embarrassment, he smiled and asked the obvious: "They were mad, weren't they?"

"Yes, I guess they were mad, but they wouldn't kill you as you suggested. They are only deliberating what to do about you."

"But, Uncle," he started to say, and then flinched and corrected it to my surname, "it's been more than half a month, Mr. Hayashi, since you sent the letter."

"You didn't send me an answer even when I sent you money. But the Ikawas plan to answer my letter. The answer has been delayed because they're circulating my letter among the relatives and getting everyone's opinion. Isn't this proof that they are going to answer it? It'll be a responsible answer."

Clearly showing his distrust of me, he said, "You can't count on it. Even if they decide on separation, I'll never sign my name to it. Even if they bring it to court, I'll fight feudalism to the end."

"Court? I don't think they would do anything that foolish.[8] What I think is that if you'll just go to them and bow your head and say I'm sorry, everything will be all right. The Ikawas aren't such bad people."

Then, unexpectedly, Tamio yelled out violently, "Did you really go to that place?"

He no longer tried to hide his distrust of me. Nor did I make any attempt to control my anger: "It wasn't a question of going or not going; I had to go, didn't I?"

"I can't believe it. If you did go, you ought to have at least got one word from Myoko."

---

8. A court action would bring disgrace to the family. In this society, a marriage could be dissolved without recourse to the courts if the family had never registered it. More than likely, the marriage would not be registered until after the birth of the first child.

"Myoko only said that she'd left everything up to them where she was concerned."

"I can't believe it . . . that Myoko didn't say anything to me. You've gone over to their side, and you're all trying to get rid of me. You belong to the Ikawa line anyway."

I was shocked by Tamio's attitude of not wanting to believe me. I thought of how I had gone to the Ikawa house in spite of my heart attack. But even if I could have gotten through to Tamio to tell him what trouble I had been through, he had already made up his mind not to believe me. And, after all the effort to try to get him to understand, if he still refused to believe me, that would have made me even angrier. This, of course, was what he wanted. He probably had thought that I would bring someone from the Ikawas to get him—if not Myoko, then at least one of the relatives.

I said, in an effort to pour cold water on his fancy dreams, "You're not only expelled from the Ikawa family, but you're also shut out of the entire village. You're even more an orphan than you thought you were. You ought to realize the seriousness of your situation. I'm the only person who could help you get back to that village. If you won't trust me, then there's nothing even I can do. I'll just have to leave you alone. First of all, I am a go-between in name only. I have no obligation to try to bring you back together with the Ikawa family. The reason I went to that village was that we can't have you continuing to stay on with us. And I guess I did sympathize a little with you."

"I know I'm being a lot of bother to you, but Aunty said it was a lot of help to her to have me here."

"Help? What help could you be to us?"

Trying to avoid the question, Tamio was silent. But only for a moment. Soon he said vigorously, "You're blind because you're related to the Ikawas. The Ikawas are more to blame than me. My crime is a personal crime in hitting the old man on the head in a fight—that's all. Not liking to work on the farm—that's my own private affair. But the crime the Ikawas committed can be called a social crime. Don't you think so? Nowadays, isn't feudalism a social crime? A person like you, Mr. Hayashi, you got a responsibility to wipe out that kind of thing, I've seen your name in the Who's Who register that lists men of culture."

With that word I felt I had regained my rights and said, "There are feudalistic men of culture, you know."

"Are you saying you are one of those feudalistic men of culture?"

"No, I call myself a Christian, though."

As if beaten, Tamio was suddenly silent. He didn't seem to know whether a Christian was feudalistic or progressive. I could certainly sympathize with him, because a Christian is neither feudalistic nor progressive but a different variety entirely. Unfortunately Tamio didn't keep his silence long. Suddenly he burst out again, "If you're a Christian, then you ought to know whether my sin is greater or the Ikawas' sin is greater."

"Both of your sins are about the same."[9]

Angrily he yelled, "Are you on their side? Or are you on my side?"

"I'm not on either side. And I'm no one's enemy either."

"What are you then, a bat?"[10]

"A bat?" I said, aroused. "I understand everyone's side. Especially Myoko's. What I'm saying is that I can't really sympathize with you."

Then he muttered contemptuously, "Just like a go-between. When they're arranging a marriage, doesn't the go-between always talk on both sides like that? Something that can be taken well by either side?" Holding his head in his hands, groaning in the manner of an actor, he sighed, "Ah! It's all over. There is nothing left for me but to die."

I stood up and went downstairs in such a way as to show that I would have no more to do with him. I wanted to show him that his histrionics had had no effect whatsoever on me. I sat down on the floor of the dining room and began to sip cold tea. I didn't want to bother with heating water. The place was quiet—our daughter hadn't come home from school. Like a captain whose ship has lost its direction, I muttered to myself, trying to come to a decision: "What am I supposed to do now?"

My wife came back from shopping with a load of bundles. She said in high spirits, "Are you back? Since I had someone to watch things for me, I went to the department store shopping. It's convenient to have Tamio when I need to go out."

I poured out my restrained anger: "Why did you put Tamio in my room?"

"It wasn't being used." Her tone was nonchalant. Then she asked, "How was it? Did the Ikawa family come to terms?"

Without answering her question, I said, "Are the children happy with having someone else live with us?"

"Toshiyoshi is complaining."

"How about Reiko?"

"She's acting strange and will have nothing to do with him. When she meets him in the morning, she doesn't even say good morning. She just ignores him."

My wife began to spread out on the mat floor the things which she had bought. Bundles of different sizes, wrapped in department store paper, were spread out in all directions. Then she opened a box which looked as if it might contain a dress shirt. Instead, it contained an undershirt and shorts. I grew angry at my wife's extravagance.

---

9. The word *tsumi* is used to mean both "sin," in the Christian sense, and "crime," in the legal sense. Obviously, Tamio is using it in the legal sense, and the narrator is using it in the Christian sense.

10. A fairy tale refers to the bat as a detestable creature that belonged to neither the bird kingdom nor the animal kingdom but went from one to the other, spreading ill will between them until he was consigned to the kingdom of darkness.

"Why did you buy that underwear? Didn't I tell you that I could get by this year with last year's underwear?"

"These aren't for you," she said. "It's gotten cold, and Tamio only brought summer underwear with him, so I went out and bought these for him."

"That scoundrel hasn't any use for something like this."

"But he's a relative of yours. And you were go-between for him."

"I'm not go-between anymore."

"Can you do that? At a time like this?"

Then I said, provoked, "The truth is a man can't be a go-between. Only God has judicial rights to that role."

"I really don't understand you," she said. (We had been married for twenty years.) "If you understood that all along, you should never have accepted the position in the first place. And you even had to enlist some Mrs. —— who was around to act as your wife for the occasion."

What she said was true. The one responsible for getting me into this situation was none other than myself. Of course there was the fact that I had been staying about a month in the city nearby. If that had not been so, then I'm sure my aunt would never have sent for me to come all the way from Tokyo just to be the go-between. But the responsibility for becoming a go-between in name only and then treating the role lightly was, whatever one says, my own. In the end, everything boils down to me—to the fact that I exist. And when it comes down to me, no one can be held responsible for this fact but God. Of course my mother and father might have given birth to me, but even they could do absolutely nothing about the fact that I exist.

"It may be God himself who joined enemies," I answered. As if proud of her victory over me because I was now silent, she stood up and quickly went upstairs, carrying the new underwear. I'm not a man to be jealous; yet I was put out at hearing the joyful footsteps of my wife climbing those stairs. And, furthermore, she certainly took her time up there. I was imagining that probably she had Tamio strip naked and was seeing whether the underwear she had bought for him fitted properly. In general, my wife is incredibly naive. So, even if she should come to fall for a young, nondescript male like Tamio, nothing would be likely to happen. From time to time I had already, with a chuckle, forgiven her of that unconscious, lightheartedness which couldn't really be called lightheartedness. She, who got so angry when he didn't acknowledge receiving the money, changed suddenly once she met Tamio. Even so, I didn't hold it against her. Anyway, I couldn't suppress a feeling of uneasiness that she was taking so long to come back down. Finally, when she did come down, I involuntarily raised my voice to her and said: "Who do you think he is, some sort of prince? He's more like a parasite!"

But she was unmoved. She smiled happily and said, "How would you like to take a trip?"

"A trip?" I said, hardly able to control my voice.

"That's right. You're always saying you can't work in Tokyo, aren't you, and you like to take your work to some quiet place in the mountains. How about going to the hot-spring resort where you went last year? You say it's warm there and quiet, and you can get a lot of work done."

"But I don't want to take a trip just now."

"You're not only cold, but you're cruel too," she said, looking on me with pitying eyes. "I was just speaking with Tamio now. He said he'd find a job where he could live in, but until he found one—though it was a lot of trouble for us—would we put him up. So until he finds a job, wouldn't it be better for you to go to that spa you like so well and do your work there?"

"It'd take him ten years to land a job."

"Ten years?"

"I'm asking you if it'd be all right for me to stay at that inn for ten years."

"You're impossible!" she said, truly stupefied. "He says that you've gone to the Ikawas and that it's no good, so he doesn't care just so he can find a job where he can live in. And right now workers are needed everywhere, so it shouldn't take him more than ten to twenty days."

I thought, well if that's the way it is, then that's the way it is. It was regrettable, but that couldn't be helped. I couldn't believe that Tamio would actually do what he said he would do, but the idea to go to the hot-spring resort to do my work wasn't a bad idea. In a sense I didn't want to surrender by leaving my own house, but I couldn't bear giving up my freedom just because I was particular about being head of the house. So I said in a melancholy tone to make her feel in my debt, "Well, since there's no alternative, I'll go. And if Tamio doesn't get out and look for a job, then give him a good slap on his behind and send him out looking."

I went upstairs to get my bag. Needless to say, the feeling of reluctance was very strong. When I opened the door, Tamio, as if he had nothing in the world to do, was looking out the window. When he realized that it was I who had come in, he was startled and trembled all over. But, as usual, he grinned at me in that impenetrable way. Since I hadn't taken out my travel gear, all I had to do was to get the bag and go downstairs. But at least I had to put in manuscript paper for my work. Without a word I went over to my desk; as I did, he spoke to me in a voice full of excitement, "Mr. Hayashi, I . . ."

I turned to look back at him. He quickly said once more in a nervous manner, "Mr. Hayashi, I . . ."

"If it's to thank me for the underwear, forget it," I said, irritated. "That was my wife who went out and bought it on her own."

Then he said, blood rushing to his blank, white, excited face, "No, that's not it. I've written a novel."

I answered as if I had been insulted, "A novel!" Involuntarily I looked down to the top of the desk. On *my* manuscript paper which was spread on top of *my* desk *his* writing had been scrawled. I found, leafing through it mindlessly, that it was only three pages. Then he said jubilantly, "I haven't thought of a title yet."

But I had read the first line, "The fresh breeze is blowing across the pad-dies." Tearing the masterpiece loose from the manuscript pad, I tore the pages into four big pieces! He looked at me dumbfounded. I said to him, "The fresh wind isn't necessarily always blowing across the paddies. Right now the harvest is over, and they're in the midst of threshing the grain. How about thinking just a minute about yourself, young fellow?"

Protesting, he dropped his eyes. Evidently he had been wounded by my abrupt action; not only had I not admired his masterpiece, I had torn it in shreds. But I didn't care. More or less pushing him out of the way, I left the room and without another word went downstairs. I couldn't help feeling wretched because I was unable to get my own work done.

The train from Tokyo Station was not as crowded as I had expected. And the hot-spring resort in Izu was where I had been going for several years, so I knew it well, a quiet place where there were only two inns. The resort was in a spot near the ocean located in the shadow of a mountain; since it was inconvenient to reach, it was not likely to get too popular, thus making it a perfect place to work. Yet this trip, understandably, was not the happy affair it usually was. Bored, I bought an evening paper from the girl who came through selling them on the train. But I threw it down as if it had been a snake, because the word "separation" jumped up at me from the front page.

I muttered to myself, "Let *them* handle it!"

Looking out the window, I saw that it had become dark. If the train arrived on time, I would have exactly ten minutes to catch the bus at the other end. The Japan Railroad, living up to its world reputation, arrived punctually at 6:50. I boarded the only bus which, looking for all the world like the typical country bus, was waiting in front of the station. The ten-odd passengers all seemed to be from this area, and they were joking with the conductress and driver. It was a peaceful, cheery sight. I looked out at the sea which was too dark to see from the bus window, for we were traveling along the bank of the ocean. Twice I watched a lighted ship sail past. One ship was small, but the other was rather large and looked like a luxurious chandelier. I was pacified by its beauty. All unpleasant memories seemed to fade far away. Just then someone spoke to me. The conductress said in her dialect, "How far are you going, sir?"

I had forgotten to buy my ticket; so, taking my wallet out of my pocket, I said, "To the K—— Spa, please."

"The K—— Spa?" She spoke in a noticeably loud voice as if reproving me.

Then for some reason she looked back. The ten passengers in no time at all had dwindled until there were only two middle-aged women who also looked as if they were local people. These two, on hearing the girl's voice, began to whisper to each other—ominously, I thought. You would have thought I had committed some great crime. Apparently reassured by the attitude of the two middle-aged women, the girl turned back to me and said, "This bus doesn't go to K—— Spa."

"But the schedule said," I began, quickly opening my bag, "that it *does* go to K—— Spa."

Then she said, "Did you get on the bus without looking at the sign on the front?"

"But I always take this bus—"

"The K—— Spa caught fire last month and burned down."

"Both inns?"

"Yes, both of them burned to the ground. So there's nothing there at all anymore."

The news shocked me terrifically, but then I realized that it wasn't as if I were about to be killed. I asked the girl if there was some other place where I could stay. She went to ask the driver. The bus stopped, and the two middle-aged women, looking at me as if I were some spectacle, got off. When the bus began to move again, the conductress came back and said to me, "Get off at the next stop. There's an inn there."

All I wanted was an inn to put up at. If I could just stay one night there, then I could plan all over again some suitable place to go. I thanked her and got off at the next stop. She said very politely, "It's just up the mountain there."

I thanked her again. But when I got off and looked toward the mountain that pressed against the sea, there was no road up the mountain to be found. I was going to ask the girl the way again, so I turned back, but the bus had already left and was far down the road. All that could be seen was a flickering red taillight.

I looked all around, but all I could discover was the mountain pressing on me. There were no lights indicating houses where people lived; there was nothing but the sound of the surf. I just stood there awhile, completely at a loss. Finally, thinking that surely someone would come along, I decided not to go walking around in circles. This seemed to be the wisest plan.

With nothing else to do, I went over to the concrete guard rail, which was there for the purpose of preventing automobile accidents. The road was so high that I could vaguely make out only two or three large rocks on the breakwater far below, but it was too dark to see the line of the shore. "This is the devil's place," I muttered.

I felt the shock of my own words. On the other hand, there was something in me, too, which denied that they had any meaning. I started to light a cigarette, thinking that I would wait forever, if necessary, for someone to come along. But the wind blowing off the sea was strong. And no matter how hard I tried, I couldn't get it lit.

SHŌNO JUNZŌ

Despite his fame, Shōno Junzō (b. 1921) is a bit unusual for postwar Japanese writers in that he has continued to describe the life around him in his native Osaka and the surrounding region in central Japan rather than becoming a part of Tokyo's literary circles. "Evenings at the Pool" (Pūrusaido shōkei, 1954) launched his national career and already shows the insight and compassion of his best work.

EVENINGS AT THE POOL (PŪRUSAIDO SHŌKEI)

Translated by Wayne Lammers

At the pool, a series of spirited final sprints were in progress.

Chestnut-tanned swimmers hit the water in rapid succession, chased by the shouts of their coach.

One girl pulled herself up beside the starting block and collapsed on her stomach, her back pumping up and down as she struggled to catch her breath.

At that moment a commuter train came around the gentle curve of the tracks skirting the school grounds beyond the pool. Salarymen returning from work crowded every car, hanging onto the straps. When their view opened up as the train emerged from behind the school building, the blue of the water stretching across the face of the new pool and the swimsuited figures of the girls resting on the concrete deck leaped into their eyes. We may imagine this scene cast a measure of comfort upon the hearts of the sorry, wilted workers besieged by the heat of the day and a thousand private woes.

A single tall man stood watching the animated practice from the far end of the pool. He had the air and features of a gentle, easy-going man. He wore swimming trunks, and a cape hung from his shoulders.

The man's name was Aoki Hiroo. He was an old alumnus of this school, and his two sons were now enrolled in its elementary division. He had long worked for a certain textile company, most recently as acting section head.

In the open lane at one side of the pool, Mr. Aoki's boys frolicked like two happy puppies. The older boy was a fifth grader, the other a year younger.

The Aokis had first appeared at the pool four days ago, and they had returned each evening since. Mr. Aoki and the coach knew each other by sight, and the coach had agreed to let the boys practice their swimming so long as they didn't get in the way of the swim team.

Every so often, Mr. Aoki would dive smoothly into the water and do a slow crawl to the other end of the 25-meter pool. He was quite an accomplished swimmer. Lest he distract the swim team, though, he mostly just stood at the side of the pool while his boys played in the water by themselves. Now and then the boys would ask him something, and he would give them a pointer or two about their form, but the rest of the time he gazed at the intense training of the girls with a look of quiet admiration.

After a while, Mrs. Aoki appeared at the pool gate leading a large, white, bushy-haired dog. When he finally noticed her several minutes later, Mr. Aoki immediately called to the boys, now engaged in a contest of who could send a bigger splash into the other's face. The boys did not dawdle. They leaped from the pool and raced for the showers.

After changing into his shorts, Mr. Aoki went to thank the coach, ensconced as usual in his chair at the center of the starting blocks, and then followed the boys out of the enclosure. Mrs. Aoki smiled and bowed to the coach from where she stood at the gate. She handed the dog's chain to the older boy and started off down the street, walking side by side with her husband. The family lived only two blocks away.

As he gazed after the Aokis disappearing into the shade of the Chinese tallow trees, the coach felt a wonderful warmth fill his heart.

Now that's living, he thought. That's really living the way we all should live. Going home together for a family dinner after an evening dip at the pool. . . .

In the deepening shadows, the Aoki family walked homeward down the paved street with their large, white, bushy-haired dog leading the way. Awaiting them at home was a bright and joyous table, and a summer's evening full of family fun.

But, in fact, it was not so. What really awaited this couple was something quite different—something neither the children nor the neighbors nor anyone else could be told.

It was hard to know just what to call it—this thing that lurked at home.

A week ago, Mr. Aoki had been let go from his job. The cause: embezzling company funds.

Now each evening, after the children went to bed, husband and wife were left to face each other alone. Stretched out on deck chairs on the patio beneath the wisteria arbor, neither said a word. Their only motions were to wave their fans in pursuit of an occasional mosquito hovering near their legs.

Mrs. Aoki was a smallish woman of trim build. When she came down the street in her red sandals with her hempen shopping bag over her arm, she was the picture of youthful buoyancy. Sometimes she could be seen with her dog in tow, eating ice cream at the coffee shop near the station; sometimes she could be seen running races with her boys and laughing gleefully when she won.

But her husband's firing had come as no small blow to her. It was like the punch that sends a boxer down on one knee in the ring.

"What in the world for?" she had asked with rounded eyes when her dazed husband came home and told her he'd been fired.

Before this, he had seldom returned home until near midnight. Sometimes he was out even later and had to come all the way home by cab. But she'd gotten used to that and thought nothing of it anymore.

His explanation had always been the same: he was entertaining clients. That could hardly be *every* night, though, so a lot of those times he must have been entertaining just his own sweet self. As a matter of fact, she had no way of knowing where he went, or what he might be doing.

But what good would it do to make an issue of it? Since all those late nights didn't seem to bother him, and since they didn't seem to have any ill effects on his health, she figured she should count her blessings.

As far as his work itself was concerned, he had never had much to say, nor had she ever bothered to ask. So when he told her he'd been fired, all she could do was wonder what on earth could have happened.

"I borrowed some money," he explained (the amount was equivalent to about six months of his salary), "and they found out about it. I was planning to pay it back, but, before I did, they found out."

Common sense said he should have had to pay the money back even if it meant selling his house, but in this case the company had decided to forgive the debt in exchange for his immediate resignation.

How could this happen? Mrs. Aoki wondered. After working for a company for eighteen years, to suddenly get fired just like that. If only it could be a joke— a practical joke her husband was playing on her because nothing ever seemed to faze her. How happy she would be if that were all it was!

But, in fact, she had known from the instant her husband walked in the door that it could be no mere joke. The ominous cloud hovering over him had told her instantly that something serious had happened.

"There's nothing you can do?"

"Nothing."

"Didn't you ask Mr. Komori to help?"

"He was the angriest."

On the board of directors, Mr. Aoki had been closer to Komori than anyone else. Mrs. Aoki had visited his house several times and enjoyed long talks with his wife.

"Maybe I could go and apologize," she said.

"It's no use. Everything's already been decided."

She fell silent, and, after a few moments, began to weep.

Soon the initial shock passed, and she was able to regain a certain calm. But then something akin to terror came to her all over again when she thought of how easily their secure, worry-free lives had crumbled to nothing.

It could almost be called spectacular.

This is what life is like, she thought.

When she looked rationally at what had happened, she had to admit it was not at all beyond imagining. Her husband had never been a particularly conscientious worker. Nor could you call him a man of strong character. Indeed, she had seen him make time, against all obstacles, for the sake of entertainment and drink. Who could ever have guaranteed that he would not make a mistake?

Even if some of the time he had gone out on company business other than entertaining clients, there had to be limits. And on his salary, he could hardly afford to go out much at his own expense. She had been a fool to take it so casually, and to never once question what was going on.

It had probably never occurred to her husband that things could get out of hand

and lead to a crisis. He had a tendency not to take things very seriously to begin with, which, no doubt, was exactly what had led him to his ruin. If he had truly intended to pay the money back, it wasn't such a large sum that he couldn't somehow have done it. Her husband must never really have felt in his bones what a serious business his work was.

On the other hand, in fifteen years of marriage, it had never once occurred to her that she should be worried about her husband's ways. She could not recall ever having reminded him how important his work was, and that he must never take it lightly.

When she reflected on her marriage like this, she realized for the first time just how foolishly and carelessly they had spent the time they shared as husband and wife. And suddenly the successful man who had risen all the way to acting section head only to be fired began to look like an absentminded half-wit. Her husband might be fun-loving and a bit of a heavy drinker, but these qualities were counterbalanced by his good work—wasn't that how she'd reassured herself? Hadn't she described her husband to her school friends exactly that way? Now she was furious with herself for it.

How in the world could a man thrown out of a job at the age of forty rehabilitate the family name? How in the world would he balance his accounts in this life?

Her head filled with questions that made despair raise its head with every turn of her thoughts. But they were not questions she could simply push from her mind and ignore.

An amazingly large, yellow moon emerged from among the leaves of the sycamore tree in the yard. As she gazed at it, an almost inaudible sigh escaped her lips.

The children were delighted by their father's unexpected vacation. The older boy begged to go hiking in the mountains, while the younger wanted to go on an insect-hunting excursion.

"No, your father is tired and needs to rest at home," their mother headed them off.

Her husband smiled weakly. "That's right. Daddy just wants to rest right now," he said, "so please don't ask me to take you anywhere far away this time."

The boys reluctantly withdrew their requests. In exchange, beginning on the third evening, they dragged their father out to the new pool that had been built at the school. The high school girls' swim team was in training camp for an upcoming meet, so normally the Aokis could not have used the pool.

To tell the truth, Mr. Aoki had no energy for stripping down to his trunks and diving into a pool. He really didn't feel up to anything but lolling about on the tatami with his long legs and arms thrown out every which way. It was Mrs. Aoki who'd insisted he take his swimsuit and cape and get out of the house for a while.

"If all you do is lie around like that, the next thing you know you'll get sick as well. Go swimming. It'll help get you out of your doldrums."

Mr. Aoki had always been fond of athletics. In his student days he had played on the volleyball team, and on Sunday mornings and such he often played catch with the boys in the street out front. During the college rugby season, he liked to take his wife and boys to see the games. And he'd started going to the beach with the boys when they were barely toddlers so he could teach them how to swim.

The first evening, when her husband and the boys had not returned by the time dinner was ready, Mrs. Aoki went to fetch them, and she found her husband quite changed from when she had watched him leave the house tagging along after the boys. Standing with folded arms, he gazed intently after the swimmers as they slowly pushed their kickboards across the pool, beating the water into foam behind them. He didn't even notice her arrival.

Can you believe this man? she muttered inwardly, not knowing whether to feel shame or pity.

On the second evening she bought a box of chocolates as a thank-you to the coach and a treat for the swimmers. She called her husband to the fence and asked him to take it to the coach.

Her husband took the chocolates to where the coach sat at the center of the starting blocks and gave them to him with an amiable smile. The coach beamed back.

"Okay!" he boomed. "Whoever betters their record gets one of these chocolates from the Aokis. Come on! Let's see what you can do!"

All around him swimmers sprang to life, and several shouted back:

"That's mean!"

"Give us a chocolate first, and then we'll beat our records!"

Mr. Aoki looked on contentedly, still smiling.

The coach opened the box to pass out the chocolates, and the swimmers quickly pressed in on all sides. Clamoring noisily, they took their pieces, called "Thank you" to Mr. Aoki, and tossed them into their mouths.

Why doesn't he hurry up and come on back? Mrs. Aoki thought, but her husband continued to stand among the swimmers. Eventually, the coach held the box out to him and asked, "Would you like one?" Even her husband had sense enough then to say "No thanks" and excuse himself, and he finally returned to the far corner of the pool where his boys were playing.

Was he a big kid, or a fool, or what? Mrs. Aoki wondered as she watched him come.

When the Aokis started home in the gathering dusk, the swimmers by the pool turned toward them and called out in a chorus of charming voices:

"Goodbye! Thanks again!"

Looking rather embarrassed, Mr. Aoki returned an awkward wave.

The leaves of the Chinese tallow trees glowed an eerie green in the lingering light of the evening sky. As the family walked along beneath those leaves, Mrs. Aoki sensed the gloom slowly returning to her husband's face. Even as she pretended not to notice, she could feel her own face sagging into much the same expression.

The two boys walked ahead, pulling the dog behind them. Now and then they would call out the dog's name. The energy in their voices grated on Mrs. Aoki's nerves.

"Talk to me," she said. "All this silence only makes it more depressing."

"Yeah, I guess you're right," he said, as though noticing for the first time. "But what shall I talk about?"

"The bars," she said.

He stared at her in bewilderment.

"Tell me about the bars you go to a lot."

"There's not much to tell, really."

"Never mind that, just tell me about them. You know, now that I think of it, you've never said a word about the places you go—your favorite bars and what-not. So come on," she said, putting more cheer in her voice, hoping to raise both of their spirits. "Tell me about the places with the pretty girls where you spent all that stupid money."

She was being deliberately flippant, but her husband grimaced. It brought her a twinge of pleasure.

"There were lots of places," her husband said, recovering himself.

"Start in wherever you like, then, and take them in order."

So, in the light of the moon filtering through the wisteria over the patio, Mr. Aoki began with a place he frequented when he didn't have much money.

Two sisters ran the bar—the older one beautiful but brusque, the younger not at all pretty and very slow mannered. The place always looked as though it had gone out of business two or three days before, but if he went on inside and perched himself tentatively on one of the bar stools, the younger sister would soon emerge from the room in back. The way she came out invariably had a "Who cares?" sort of air about it.

He would half expect her to tell him they were closed, but she would sluggishly duck under the counter. After tidying up a bit, she would finally turn around to face him. At first he had thought she must be in a bad mood, or maybe she wasn't feeling well, but he soon learned this was just her normal way.

For example, if a patron were to say, "No matter when I come, this place has about as much life as an empty depot in a cowboy movie," she would break into a broad, happy smile.

The older sister was much the same—except that she seemed to care even less than the younger and wouldn't come downstairs at all unless she had gotten herself into a really good mood.

As a bar, it made for a very odd atmosphere. If someone came charging in the door ready to party, he'd likely be thrown so completely off balance by the dull and indifferent reception, he'd be stopped dead in his tracks, unable either to forge ahead or to back out.

The bar's drawing card was its cheap prices. Of course, for the patrons to be willing to put up with such indifferent service, the prices would quite naturally *have* to be low.

But Aoki did not frequent the bar solely for its prices. For him, the real attraction of the bar was the older sister. The very first time he went there with a friend, he'd been struck by the older sister's resemblance to the French movie star M, with her worldly looks and otherworldly air. In her beautiful features, he found something a tiny bit scary, but he also found something supremely romantic. What would it be like to go for a stroll down deserted nighttime streets with a woman like this? he wondered, and from that moment forth a vague desire arose in his heart. Before long, his wish was fulfilled.

He bought tickets to an international swimming competition in which a famous American swimmer was scheduled to appear, and he gave one of the tickets to this sister to see what she might do. He hadn't really expected her to come, but when he arrived, she was already there.

Afterward they went from one bar to another, then hailed a cab and drove aimlessly around the late-night city streets. It wasn't a "stroll," but he could say that he had gotten his wish.

As they drove, the girl told him in a somber voice about living with her father in Harbin as a child. In the summer he would take her to the Isle of the Sun, where they mingled with Russian families for a day of fun on the banks of the muddy Songhua River. On the way home they stopped at a restaurant facing the promenade along the river, and at a table right in front of the orchestra her father would drink mug after mug of beer while she chewed on black bread. Together they gazed at the river in the twilight.

The girl spoke with her cheek pressed against Aoki's shoulder. Now's the time to kiss her, he thought, only half listening to her story. But what if he tried to kiss her and she got angry? That would ruin everything. Too worried about what terrible thing might happen if she got angry with him, he could not bring himself to do it.

Never again had another such opportunity presented itself. Several times he had wasted expensive tickets to the ballet or the symphony, hoping for a second chance. But as Aoki continued to observe the girl over the next few months, he came to understand that she had not been her usual self on the night of the swimming competition. If he were ever to have a chance, that night had been it.

In the days and months since, she had become like a castle with mirror-slick walls offering no holds to grasp. Each time he saw that miraculous smile of hers, he'd be filled anew with a longing to somehow make her his own. But he could not gain the faintest hint of what she might be thinking. Were her sights set on marriage, or did she not care? Had someone else already won her heart, or was she available?

Especially frustrating were the days when she knew perfectly well that

Aoki was waiting but still chose not to come downstairs. Times like that, he was left sipping drearily at his beer as he carried on an awkward, slow-moving conversation with the younger sister.

Even worse was when neither of the sisters appeared, and a prune-faced old lady took their place. If the disgruntled Aoki asked the sisters' whereabouts, old Prune-face would tell him the older one had a visitor upstairs and the younger was in bed with a bad toothache, or something of the sort. In a fit of irritation Aoki would sometimes settle in on his stool for an even longer stay than usual, drinking to the old woman's pouring. The old woman must have felt sorry for him at times like this: she would only charge him for one beer even when he had had three.

By probing Prune-face for information, Aoki managed to verify the sisters' claim that the older sister had no patron or lover, and that they'd opened the bar on money from their father. He got her assurance, too, on the occasion when she said there was a visitor upstairs, that the man was merely a friend of their father's and not anyone of questionable repute. Still, it irked Aoki to no end to think that the girl was alone in her room with another man, talking hour after hour about whatever it might be.

Actually, all the men who frequented this bar were, like Aoki, in thrall to the beauty of this older sister. The others, like Aoki, had all felt the same cold shoulder turned against their yearnings; and yet none felt able to make a clean break and give the girl up, either, so they kept drifting back for one more visit. Whenever Aoki happened to find himself with another of these men at the bar, they both could tell immediately by the other's behavior. From this, too, Aoki knew it was nothing but foolishness to keep coming back, but he still couldn't bring himself to turn his steps away once and for all.

One thing never ceased to puzzle him, though. How was it that a bar with so rare a beauty in the home could remain in such a fearsomely depressed state no matter when he went? Why had he never once seen the bar draw a large, boisterous crowd?

What Mr. Aoki told his wife was not exactly as written here, but it covered roughly the same ground.

"That's it?"

"Uh-huh."

Mrs. Aoki let out a little laugh. "You never told me anything like that before."

"Well, if I'm always getting jilted . . ."

"But I don't suppose you always were, were you?" she shot back.

His throat tightened.

"Never mind," she went on. "You don't have to tell me. I know you won't tell me the truth anyway, so forget it."

How could she have been so dense? she wondered. The news that her husband had been fired for embezzling money had put her in such a state of shock that she'd been going around as if in a trance.

There's another woman! My husband spent all that money on another woman!

It had hit her like a thunderbolt as she listened to her husband's story. A violent quaking seized her heart, but she took care to hide it, and when her husband was through, she moved swiftly to head off any further confessions of a similar kind.

The story her husband had told her meant nothing to him. The secret he had to guard was something else entirely, and the story of the girl who grew up in Harbin and looked like the French movie star was nothing more than a smokescreen. She knew this instinctively.

If she were to press him, her husband would no doubt entertain her with other stories about women—stories to make her think he was being open, while in fact steering clear of any real danger. But she would not fall for that.

The things that didn't really matter he could speak of with abandon. But behind them all there was something this man would not touch with the tiniest tip of a needle.

A Medusa's head.

She must not attempt to see it. She must not pursue. She must quietly pretend to suspect nothing at all.

"Talk to me," she had said, but not in her remotest dreams had she anticipated this result. When she'd suggested he tell her about the bars he went to, she really *had* thought it might help raise their spirits. But look what had happened instead! Quite without intending, she'd built herself a trap, and she hadn't even realized it until after she'd thrown herself into it.

The next evening, Mr. Aoki once again went off to the pool with the boys, and as she prepared dinner at home Mrs. Aoki wondered how long these curious days would go on. Their household kitty would be exhausted in two weeks. Their savings account had long been empty—they were both the kind who spent whatever money they had. So once they used up what was on hand, they would have to start pawning their possessions. Would that get them through another six months, perhaps?

Her own family had prospered in the foreign trade before the war, but they'd fallen on hard times since. As for her husband's side, his three brothers all subsisted on the meager wages of civil servants and salarymen. She'd never given it the slightest thought before, but this crisis had awakened her to the fact that she and her husband were like orphans, without any family they could turn to for help in times of need.

Were it not for the children, they might somehow manage. If Mrs. Aoki went out and got a job, she no doubt could fill at least her own stomach—though, lacking any skills, she'd have to be prepared for the worst. But with two grade-school-age boys at home, any such plan was out of the question.

That meant that unless her husband succeeded in finding a new job, their family of four could no longer stay together. But where on earth was he likely to find an employer willing to take in and provide for a married man of forty who'd been fired from his job and thrown out onto the streets?

Mrs. Aoki tried to recall what kinds of things had gone through her mind while preparing dinner just one week before, but she could not remember a single thing.

Somewhere along the line, for some unfathomable reason, her whole world had been transformed. How could a single bolt from the blue have twisted the course of their lives so completely awry, leaving them to suffer such undue pain and fear? What sort of god had permitted this catastrophe to occur?

The motions she was going through now, lighting the stove or taking the frying pan off the heat: what meaning did any of this have? Why did her hands go on working so busily as though nothing were amiss? Why did she still find herself going through the same routine motions she had gone through day in and day out for as long as she could remember? Was the whole thing just some bizarre mistake?

All of a sudden she felt like everything was collapsing into an ever more incomprehensible jumble.

That night, after the boys were in bed, Mr. Aoki sipped at some whiskey and told his wife this story.

In the building where I work, there's a mail chute next to the elevator on each floor. It's essentially a long square tube running all the way from the ninth floor down to the first. The side facing the hallway is clear, so you can watch from the outside as your letter begins to fall. Sometimes when you're walking by, you see a white envelope drop soundlessly through the chute from ceiling to floor; or you see several, one after the other.

The hallway happens to be very dim, and it can give you quite a start to see one of these flashes of white go by when there's no one else around. I'm not quite sure what to say it's like. It's like a ghost, maybe—like some strange, lonely spirit.

One step away, in all the offices along the hallway, is a world where you don't dare let down your guard for a single moment. That's why you get such a start when you emerge into the hallway, to go to the bathroom or something, and you see one of those white flashes.

Some mornings, when I have something I need to get done early, I arrive at work before the normal starting time. I glance around the office, looking at all the empty chairs waiting for the people who usually work there to arrive. Each chair, in the absence of its occupant, seems to assume the shape of its occupant's head, or the way he moves his eyes, or the turn of his lips when he speaks, or the curve of his back as he hunches over his desk.

The patent leather seat where the occupant will soon plant his bottom shines like it was polished with oils that oozed from his body. It's as if, through the years, each man's indignations and frettings and gripes and laments, or his incessant fears and anxieties, have been slowly secreted from his body in the form of an oil. At least that's how it always seems to me.

Each chairback, too, uniquely bent by the press of its occupant's own back, seems to express that man's feelings about his workplace. Willy-nilly, day after day, he's had to come into this office and set himself down on that same desk chair. Is it any wonder that something of his heart might transfer itself to the chair?

I look quietly down at my own chair as well, thinking, Ahh, what a pitiable chair. What a poor, wretched, acting section head's chair . . .

And I wonder: When have I ever sat here without feeling afraid? If someone behind me suddenly clears his throat, it practically startles me right out of my seat.

I know I'm not the only one who trembles in such constant fear. I can see it in the others' faces as they arrive for work. The few who come in looking cheerful and contented must really be happy. They're the fortunate ones—the ones who've been blessed. But the vast majority aren't like that, and they show it in the expressions they have on their faces the moment they push open the door and step into the office. What is it they're so frightened of? Is it some particular person? Is it the company executives—their section head or department head, or the president himself, perhaps? That may be part of it, certainly, but it can't be all. It can only be one of several elements, for those very section heads and department heads come in the door with the exact same look on their faces.

But again, what is it that so frightens all these men? It is neither a particular group of individuals, nor anything else you can really put your finger on. It haunts them even at home, in their time for resting and relaxing with their wives and children. It enters even into their dreams and threatens them in their sleep. It's what brings them the nightmares that terrorize them in the middle of the night.

Sometimes when I gaze around at the vacant chairs and desks, and at the hat stands with their empty hangers here and there, I find myself getting all choked up. Everything I see takes on the image of someone who works there, and seems to have so much to tell me.

"My old lady came on to me again last night with tears in her eyes, begging me, please, please, it's okay if my pay is low and we're always on the verge of going broke, just watch my temper and don't do anything rash and never forget how important my work is. She cried and pleaded with me on and on like that, you know, and hey, it really made me stop and think."

Pressed up against one desk is the chair of the man who spoke these words to me. Every time I look at that chair, I remember how he started in with a simple remark about making ends meet at home and wound up with this doleful lament. I remember it as clear as day—the tone of his voice and his embarrassed smile and everything. . . .

There Mr. Aoki's story came to an end.

His story about the bar had been an eye-opener as well, but Mrs. Aoki now asked herself whether her husband had ever said anything like this about his anxieties at work before. Little had she imagined that he was going off to work feeling like this every day. How could she have missed it all those years? What in the world had they talked about in a decade and a half of living together in the same house as husband and wife?

Even if her husband never got home until midnight and then had to hurry off to work as soon as he got up the next morning, how could they have spent that many years together and never spoken about a single important thing? Even with his long hours, they'd always made a point of going somewhere as a family on Sundays. But what had her husband spoken of, and what had she asked him about, in the time they actually spent together? Never once had it entered her mind that her husband might hold such feelings about his work at the office. She'd always simply assumed that he stayed out late every night because he enjoyed a good time, and she'd thought nothing more of it than that.

He had tended to be out late every night from the time they first got married, so apparently that image of him had become etched in her mind at the very beginning. Their regular Sunday outings compensated for the lack of any kind of family life from Monday through Saturday, and she had always thought it more satisfying that way than if he came home earlier during the week but then had to go in on Sunday as well, leaving her to while away another dull day at home.

Having listened to her husband's story tonight, she now understood why he never came straight home after work even when he had no clients to entertain. It was the deep anguish he felt about his life as a working man. And she understood, too, that he hadn't felt he could find comfort for that anguish at home. Facing his wife and children apparently only increased his pain, while the women at the bars and cabarets let him forget it.

In that case, what had she been to her husband all this time? she suddenly wondered. If their marriage had not been one of fulfillment and trust and mutual support, then what had she been doing all this time?

But she also wondered: if her husband had never told her about the anxiety and pain he experienced in his job, didn't that just go to prove that he had been unburdening his heart to someone else all along? And wasn't it that very someone who was really to blame for their present troubles?

When her husband had told her about the sisters at the bar, the image of a woman had come before her like a flash of revelation. She shuddered at the terrifying reality of that image and tried hastily to push it from her mind, but it would not leave her.

At first she had found it a little bewildering to have her husband get up in the morning only to stay home all day, but by the time a week had gone by she began to think she preferred it this way.

If only their family could always live like this, she thought, without her husband having to go off somewhere to work every day! If only they'd been born in ancient times when this was how everyone lived! Having nothing to do, the man grabs his club to go on a hunt. He tracks down his prey, leaps upon it, and battles it to its death. He carries his trophy home on his shoulders and hangs it over the fire as his woman and the children gather about to watch it cook. If only their lives could be like this—how much happier they would be!

Instead, every morning the man dons his suit and rides the commuter train to a distant workplace, and every night he returns home sullen and spent. Wasn't this the very prescription for an unhappy life? To Mrs. Aoki, it had certainly begun to seem so.

In the darkness, her husband seemed lost in thought.

"You can't get to sleep?" she asked.

"No, no," he said in haste, "I was just starting to drift off." After a pause he added, "I guess it's because of that long nap I took."

"Shall I do some magic that'll help you sleep?"

She brought her face directly before his and edged slowly closer until their eyelids almost touched. It was not magic; it was a special caress she'd invented. With their eyelashes touching, she began blinking her eyes, stroking his eyelashes with the up and down of her own. It brought an odd sensation—like the rapid-fire chatter of two tiny birds absorbed in conversation, or like the last stage of a Japanese sparkler when the tiny ball of fire on the tip starts shooting snowflake sparks in every direction.

In the darkness, she went on blinking her eyes. The motion of her eyelids comforted and soothed, but she could not keep them from also questioning, reproaching.

Mr. Aoki decided to start going to work again.

His vacation of ten days was over. He'd had to call an end to it when the boys began to ask, "How long do you get to take off?"

He also had to consider the suspicious glances some of the neighbors had begun to cast his way. One of the ladies had even asked Mrs. Aoki some rather prying questions at the grocery.

Secrets like this had a way of spreading with astonishing speed. Though none of his former colleagues lived nearby, you could never tell where one of the neighbors might hear something through the grapevine.

But his more immediate concern was the boys. Since he had told them that he was on vacation, he could not simply go on lolling about the house forever; and in any case, he needed to start looking for a new job. Thus, Mr. Aoki decided to resume leaving the house every morning at the same time as he used to leave for work.

The first day, after her husband had gone, Mrs. Aoki suddenly felt limp with exhaustion. In her mind she saw the figure of her husband walking aimlessly through the city streets beneath the late summer sun. The pangs of her husband's anguish as he trudged uneasily along the bustling street, ever fearful that he might meet someone he knew, seemed to pierce her own heart.

She imagined him gazing up at the screen in the darkness of a movie theater where he'd gone to escape being seen. Or she imagined him sitting on a bench at a department store, watching the mothers who had brought their children to play on the rooftop playground.

But then these images abruptly broke up, to be replaced by a vision of her husband quietly climbing the stairs to an unfamiliar apartment building. Her blood turned to ice.

"No! Don't go there. Don't, don't, don't!" she screamed, but her husband continued his slow ascent. "Stop!" she cried. "If you go there, it's all over. It's all over."

The vision returned again and again no matter how many times she tried to drive it away.

Evening came, and Mrs. Aoki found herself in the kitchen once again. Like a person who has come down with a fever, a feeling of listless fatigue weighed heavy on every corner of her body.

In the street out front the boys jabbered back and forth as they played catch.

"They're incredibly fast!"

"Mexican Indians."

"They can chase antelopes all day and not even get winded."

"The tribe's name is Tarahumara. Ta-ra-hu-ma-ra."

"I sure wish they'd come to Japan sometime."

Disjointed snatches of the boys' conversation came to her between pops of the ball.

Will he come home? she wondered miserably. I just want him to come home safe and sound—that's all. I don't care if he doesn't have a job, I don't care about anything else, just so long as he doesn't abandon this family.

She took a match and lit the gas burner, then reached up to get a pan from the shelf.

"Just so long as he comes home . . ."

A quiet hush hung over the pool.

The ropes separating the lanes had been removed, and in the middle of the pool bobbed a lone man, only his head showing above water. The interscholastic swim meet would begin tomorrow, so today's practice had been cut two hours short and the swimmers sent home early. Now the coach was picking up debris from the bottom of the pool with his toes.

The evening breeze sent a rush of tiny waves rippling across the surface of the water from time to time.

Soon a train slid into view along the tracks beyond the pool, and the eyes of the passengers returning from work took in the quiet scene. The usual girl's swim team was gone, and a man's head bobbed all alone on the surface of the water.

TAKEDA TAIJUN

Takeda Taijun (1912–1976) is a relatively unusual postwar Japanese writer in that his chief literary influences and inspiration came from China rather than Europe. Although he began his studies of Chinese literature at Tokyo Imperial University in 1931, he left the following year, turning his full attention to left-wing activities. After he was drafted into the army, he served in China and then worked in Shanghai as a translator immediately after the end of the war in 1945. Takeda's many works rely on his wide knowledge of Buddhism (his father was a Buddhist priest) and his own sense of guilt concerning the activities of his countrymen in China during the war years. "The Misshapen Ones" (Igyō no mono, 1950) touches on many of these themes.

THE MISSHAPEN ONES (IGYŌ NO MONO)

Translated by Edward G. Seidensticker

Not long ago, I dissented from the views of a certain philosopher. A most earnest thinker on all subjects, he was, though ten years older than I, a good ten times as impassioned. His devotion to art was fanatic, and he was possessed of an intense longing for other-worldly beauty. He may perhaps be counted among those I am fond of. (I cannot, it is true, believe that I really am fond of anyone.)

I do not know why a philosopher of his standing should have directed those impassioned remarks at me, no more than a drunkard; but he somehow took me for a young man worth talking to. People who have something to pour out, whether in anguish or in joy, always seem to imagine appropriate powers of understanding in the listener.

I was cool and quiet, a sand pit sucking in all the glistening drops. We were in a teahouse of dubious nature, clammy and cold for such an establishment. A further difficulty was that Hanako, the girl I was living with, worked there. I only had to wait until eleven, when she could leave. I knew how to get along in the world: be moderate in everything, and yet suggest from time to time that the balance can be upset. Though making it seem that I was but sitting there impassively, I contrived to assume a variety of dramatic expressions, and all the while I was reassuring myself. Why, I had plenty of room yet for living. For a long while yet, in pleasure and pain, I would crawl ahead in my way, into infinity.

But now the philosopher was striking out with question after rapid question. His eyes blazed with something very much like hatred, and his voice was tense with anguish and bitterness. At first it seemed to be advice, good, human advice, on my attitude toward women and particularly on my treatment of Hanako. The philosopher called her the Virgin Mary, he likened her to Gretchen. He had bought her a muffler for two thousand yen and given her five thousand in cash (when asked if there was nothing she wanted, Hanako had come up with a phonograph as the most expensive thing she could think of, and he had given her the money for it), and he had taught her to say "Bon soir, monsieur," and "Au revoir." Hanako made the five thousand yen her capital for commodity speculations and in no time worked it up to ten thousand and lost it. Witness to all this, I felt a certain reticence before the philosopher. More than ever like a pit, I took in the glowing words.

Although there were moments when she seemed like the Virgin Mary or Kannon the Merciful to me too, they were moments of delusion and fleeting excitement. Fearful of expending a vitality of which I had not too large a store left, I had surrendered to the tenets of biology, and made it a policy not to use expressions like "Mary" or "Kannon" or "My life" when other people were around—indeed not when the two of us were alone in the dead of night.

"It seems that you do not understand what love is," said the philosopher.

"Oh, I understand."

"Does it make any difference to you whether you hurt the woman you love? Have you ever once thought how your behavior and your general attitude have made her weep?"

"Certainly I have."

"What is love, then?"

"A mistake. It is built on a mistake."

"Well, then." The philosopher turned his face slightly away, as from some repulsive amphibian creature. "What about Goethe's love?"

"The same thing, I would say. Not that I know much about Goethe."

The philosopher, an admirer of Goethe, was evidently dazed by the revelation. His face was twisted in an excess of knowledge and an excess of passion, and below the spectacles the cheeks twitched with impatience to convert the benighted person before him.

"If love is what you say it is, then what is hate?"

"Very much the same thing."

"Hate is a mistake too? Hate is built on a mistake?"

"Well." I was tired of the conversation, though I gave him no hint of the fact. "I believe that human beings are incapable of understanding one another. And because they can't understand one another—with that as a condition—love and hate exist."

"You don't believe in love, then?"

"And what exactly do you mean by believe?"

"To feel. To feel with a certainty in your whole body and soul."

"Oh, I have my feelings. They are very unstable things, though. Very strange and very unreliable. I hardly know what to say when you ask me if I believe in love."

I do not remember what came next. He interrogated me as the guardian of a barrier gate might interrogate a suspicious traveler, and I seem to have given an appropriate answer to each swift, burning question. I do not of course mean a correct answer. I only mean that I managed to make the pieces fit. Finally the philosopher began to shout.

"What do you think of hell? Does it exist for you, or does it not?" It was as if he were flinging red-hot rivets at me.

"Oh, I imagine there is a hell."

"And do you think you will go there?"

"Me? No, I'll not be going," I answered pleasantly, as though we were discussing an outing.

"Well, then." The philosopher's face was suddenly radiant. He seemed to have made his point. "I suppose not, I suppose not. But *I* am going to hell. *I* will go to hell."

I found it hard to understand why he cried "hell" so proudly, why he seemed to fall into a state of rapture, warm with the rays of ultimate truth. He cried "hell" and waved a long, thin hand to the skies, like that Satan of the arts who danced before Dr. Faust.

"To hell? You are going to hell, sir?"

"I am. It is a terrible thing, but I am doomed."

"Really?"

"Really." He said it with greatest eagerness. "I am filled with sin and guilt. Not that you would understand. It is a terrible thing, but there it is. A fact."

"Oh, I hardly think so. Imagine it, going to hell."

"I am going to hell." He smiled triumphantly, to brush away my damp sympathy. But in fact I was not sympathizing at all. I had made the remark with what I hoped would suggest the sureness of a prophet. I wanted to protest the ease with which he sent himself to hell.

"You are going to heaven."

"Heaven?" His brow clouded.

"Whatever you say, you are going to heaven."

"What makes you so sure?"

"Because we are all going to heaven. It's settled."

He gasped, and looked at me with loathing. No doubt he felt like a university professor who has just been told by a first grader that the one or two figures written large on the blackboard are the end of all calculations.

"It's settled," I said, "and there's nothing you can do about it."

It had been long since I last used the word "heaven." "Heaven" simply came to me when my adversary cried "hell." Like a favorite plaything, polished to a glow with the oil from this hand, it came rolling into a useless dialogue between two men brought together by a woman.

The terror of plunging into hell more swiftly than the swiftest rocket, throat straining with the primeval cry of life, flames of guilt crackling in the ears—this he had sought to establish in the name of science and art. He fell silent. His expression must be described as one of extreme displeasure. The eyes were aflame. He seemed to be gnashing and grinding at the puffy, slug-like thing called heaven, which had broken the speed of his fall.

Forgive me, O Philosopher! I did not mean to block your way. Because I was once a specialist in heaven (I realized the fact only a week later), I spoke carelessly. In my youth, I was for a time a priest in a certain pietist sect that offers salvation to those who throw themselves at the mercy of the Lord Amida. It was for this reason that I carelessly (though I pile caution upon caution) resorted to low trickery: I sent everyone off to heaven.

"The Misshapen Ones" is a chapter in my chronicle of heaven.

I became a priest because I am wavering by nature and because at the time there was no sign of anything better to do. I was neither weary of the world nor possessed of an overpowering zeal. I took the easiest road. To all appearances an eager young socialist of nineteen, quick to take something up and as quick to weary of it and flee, I would not have found it necessary to run off in such haste toward heaven if I had not been born and reared in a temple.

A boy who has a lively curiosity in things high and low, who tells himself that he has nothing to lose, that he has nothing else to do, that he won't last long in the work anyway—take such a boy, and he will become a fishmonger if his father is a fishmonger, and a landlord if his father is a landlord. And so I became a priest by trade.

On the afternoon of the day I decided to enter the seminary, I went to the barbershop and had my head shaved. My hair had been long and uncombed, as became a young socialist. Now it was gone, and I felt no particular sorrow for it. Certain peculiar physical sensations, however, went with having a shaven head. I stroked the top of my head and passed my hand down over my face, and there was no difference whatsoever. The whole was smooth, the head where grew my hair had disappeared. On the crown, the skin was young and fresh, a tender pink, the skin of a baby who has not known the winds of the world. Intelligence, packed inside, could no longer rely on a protective coating of hair. It seemed to shrink back in shame, and, at length resigned, to give itself up to the skies.

Already I was something different. I was already separated by an immeasurable gulf from those who prosper in the world, have women and families, become famous, build the nation. Probably I would never be one of them again. I would be a faintly repulsive something, a human being and something besides. See, it had begun. Father, who had been affectionately, almost obsessively, sharpening his razor at a strop fastened to the pillar, had stood up, and there he was, looking at my blue-shaven head in the mirror as at a squid left to die in a corner of an aquarium.

"All right," I said to no one in particular.

That evening I loaded my bedding into a cab, put on a white cotton kimono, a black cotton kimono, and a drab surplice, and passed through the big red-brown gate of the seminary. Inside the door, I changed the footwear of the world for rough straw sandals. I went first to the instructors' quarters. A burly priest, the proctor in charge of the novices, was warming himself over charcoal embers.

"Well, well. You got here." He smiled maliciously. He had a remarkably fine physique, and he was swarthy to the point of blackness. The white teeth he bared at me were vicious. "Don't think it'll be like a skiing trip. It'll be rough."

"Don't have to worry about me."

I had gone on skiing trips with the big fellow, who would have been the ideal model for a portrait of a malevolent priest. Simple and blunt, he had been left as a boy in a temple on the Chiba coast, and he had once had a quarrel with the young bucks of the disorderly fishing village. Having taken up the challenge, he returned to the temple for a shotgun and fired one shot into the crowd. He was barely conscious of what he had done, but from then on the fishermen showed him the respect due a grown man.

I had never heard him read a sutra, but I would see him, stately as an elephant, walking back and forth between the Great Hall and the office, which gangs of ruffians sometimes invaded. I found his physical strength most pleasing, and the freebooting arrogance that went with it.

"You'll never make a priest, but do your best while you're trying." He spoke like the good proctor, then reached for a saké bottle. "It's still early. Have a drink."

"I'll do what's to be done. Don't have to worry about me." I drank it down with the bravado of the novice at arms who appears at a rival field demanding a match. "Is Mikkai still here?"

"Mikkai? He's still here. He'll probably be in with you. Why?" He looked at me sharply.

"Well, you see," I said secretively, "I'd like to talk to him."

A Chinese priest had been at the temple for about a year. He said nothing and wrote nothing. He lived in silence, as if feeble-minded, and he had the room off the kitchen. No one knew whether he belonged to esoteric Shingon or to Zen, or perhaps to a newer Mahayana sect.

"Chinamen are funny even when they're priests," the other priests would say. No one bothered to investigate his character or his thought. Interest seemed to focus rather on matters like this: "Prince Chichibu, there's a real Buddhist for you. Always has a rosary in his pocket, they say." Or this: "The general in command of the First Division comes straight from this temple."

But I was different. I longed for something vast, dim, ineffable, that corner of the universe in a Chinese landscape where the clouds gather, beyond endless masses of rock and water and forest.

I was immoderately fond of anyone from the continent, student or Chinese cook. Students always seemed to have secret missions toward building a new Orient, and Chinese restaurant keepers had heaps of money and treasure, and slim-waisted beauties hidden away in secret chambers. Perhaps even this ordinary priest had been dispatched by the Kuomintang or the Communists, then preparing to resist the Japanese.

The next evening I sat opposite Mikkai on the bare wooden floor of the kitchen. Great clouds of steam rose to the high roof. One of the kitchen hands had taken the lid from the rice cauldron, and, humming a popular song, he was stirring the rice with a ladle as big as a baseball bat. Another, a red devil in the firelight, had opened the oven door and was pushing fiercely at a log. The rough kitchen bands were sons of impoverished rural temples. Unable to afford even a technical-school education, they had gone to work as servants, and they awaited the day when they too would be high priests. And they disliked the well-fed sons of flourishing city temples.

"Could you let me have a little sauce?" I asked one of them.

"What for? Can't do it unless you give me a good, clear reason." The sleeves of the dirty white kimono were pushed up to the shoulders, and a white rag was twisted around his head. He looked peevishly up at me from beside the cauldron. "We've got work to do, you know. Can't go waiting on every last one of you."

"I know. It's for this." I took out a box of sushi tied up in a white cloth. "You can have some too, if you like it."

"Well, as long as you can give me a reason." Turning to hide the pleasure that had spread over his face, he poured me a generous cup of sauce.

Fish and meat were forbidden in the seminary. My family was afraid I would run away, however, and frequently sent a houseboy under pretext of inquiring after my health to bring me the dishes I liked best. He had forgotten soy sauce, which I had to have before dividing the spoils in one of the dormitory rooms.

A priest perhaps twenty-five or twenty-six had been silently watching the exchange from a dark corner.

Though it was March and still chilly, he was dressed, rather sloppily, in a gray linen Japanese kimono. His neck and hands and feet were remarkably long and thin, as though he had somewhere misplaced a part of them. The skin was smooth and a muddy yellow, and on neither the crossed legs protruding from the kimono nor the hand holding the chopsticks was there more than a trace of hair. He had a certain stiffness about him, as of one not quite acclimated to the place. His hair was perhaps an eighth of an inch longer than that on my own shaven pate. The long face, wholly without harshness or angularity, was cocked to the side, and one felt, as he picked at the food before him, that his spirit was focused on some point at a slight remove. There was more of the priest in the man than in any Japanese priest I had ever known. The grease and clamor of the world had worn away, one sensed, and the contemplative marrow had been put in order. "Mikkai, I believe." He nodded a series of short, abrupt nods, and from his full mouth came a series of affirmative monosyllables neither Chinese nor yet quite Japanese. The wide-cut Chinese eyes turned a careful gaze on me. "I'm one of the novices in the seminary. There is something I would like to talk to you about." He wondered if I would wait until he had finished eating, he said in obscure Chinese. I had known enough Chinese students to understand at least that much, and to guess that he was from the south of China, probably Canton or Fukien.

Back in the dormitory, I hurried through my share of the sushi. When I arrived at the kitchen again, pencil and notebook in hand, I found Mikkai putting away his tray. He invited me to his room, and there, seated before me, he answered my questions.

He was evidently working at his answers, but there was no suggestion of obsequiousness in his manner. It was gloomy, rather, and a little dispirited, as if he found it a trial to be with this rude young Japanese and the strong scent of man he brought with him.

"To what sect do you belong?" I wrote in Chinese that was neither literary nor colloquial.

"I am at the moment training myself in Buddhism. I cannot say that I belong to any one sect. Because I am in your temple, I am now studying the Buddhism of the Pure Land," he wrote.

"This means that you are investigating the Heaven of the Pure Land?"

"It does. I am studying that heaven."

"And may I further inquire whether that heaven exists in this world or the next?"

"It exists in the next world."

"It is not in this world?" I wrote.

"It is in the next world precisely because it is not in this. Has this fact not been settled by the sect to which you belong?" He looked at me with a strange, wry smile.

"This is a matter of personal belief: It has nothing to do with what any sect has decided." I was aroused, and wrote rapidly. "Even if there is a heaven to come, I think it a dull, useless sort of heaven. Is it not the duty of priests to build a heaven in this world?"

"Alas, that is not possible. Therefore, we go to the Heaven of the Pure Land."

"I have no interest in the next world. I am only interested in this world."

"You would seem to be a socialist." He toyed with the pencil for a moment, then wrote deliberately: "If you are a socialist and so dislike the next world, may I ask why you found it necessary to become a priest?"

I began to feel uneasy lest, having gratuitously started an argument, I find myself reprimanded for a lack of theological thoroughness, and exposed in all my inadequacy. But what did it matter—I gave the pencil a stronger push. "I cannot really be called a socialist. But I have a great dislike for heavens to come."

"Very well, very well," he muttered, a soft, sad smile on his lips. "Boys of seventeen and eighteen understand nothing," he wrote. "They all think as you do. But"—he carefully underlined this last sentence—"some day you will turn back to heaven."

A wave of horror and revulsion swept over me. On the glowing face, as smooth and spotless as an eggshell, there floated an expression of sorrow and charity, and he looked at me with the calm of the sages.

To heaven? Me to heaven? If it was already decided, then what was left for me? Where were the sorrows of youth, the pleasures, the racking anguish, the melting joys? Yes, and this too: this model exhibit of contradictions, this human-not-human something in white and black, made such through the good offices of the unknown world outside and its own amoebic squirmings? Where were its sinking shame and all its deeper sensations?

Was it not really too neat—and so nihilistic—too clear, like the transparent crack in the glacier? Too physical, too natural, too patly given? I am human. You too are human, Mikkai. Would it not be well to press yourself upon life, to stumble against it and fall and roll in it, to be encompassed by it?

"And did you have the moxa treatment on your head?" I wrote. In the last years of the Manchu Dynasty, when corruption and lassitude were extreme, the moxa treatment was ordered for the priesthood. To evade taxes and other civic duties, people were posing as priests, and only those who were prepared to endure the pain of the moxa were officially recognized.

Mikkai bowed silently. On the stubbly head there were six clear marks about the size of pennies, like spots of bare ground left by flower pots on a well-tended lawn. Here and there the skin was slightly crinkled, strangely luminous. I felt impossibly alone before those six man-inflicted scars.

"No doubt you have a keen sense of social right. That is as it should be," he wrote, oblivious of my feelings. "But you should occasionally focus your thoughts on the universe. In the universe there are millions and hundreds of millions of stars. Our world is but one of them. Among these numberless stars, one or another is always exploding and disappearing in dust. Every moment and every second, with every breath we take, we are in the embrace of enormous exploding and dispersing and vanishing forces. If then, there is a Buddhist truth, it must be able to bear immense upheavals, destruction, and annihilation, in the womb of this universe. Ah, it would be well for you to think of the terrible difficulties of bearing so much. The heavy, cold, hard, infinite difficulties. This *heaven to come* which you so dislike is no more than one slight hint your elders found as they wandered lost among the difficulties. You have not suffered as your elders. You are unable to envision the heaven they came upon to assuage their sufferings."

I knew that I was not suffering in the least, and I was not prepared to argue.

A drum announced the beginning of the evening services. I left Mikkai's room.

In the dormitory, a string of four ten-mat rooms and two eight-mat rooms with partitions removed, life bustled on and took little notice of Mikkai's heavy Buddhism. Among the novices were a man in his forties who had taught English in a girl's school, and a dry-goods merchant approaching sixty who had felt the urge to become a priest when he failed in business; but most of us were not past our middle twenties, and most of us were either sons of priests or employees of temples. Since life would be secure once we returned to our temples, the seminary, its air untroubled by employment problems, was sunnier than most schools. All eighty of us, however, had lived lives in which fleshly appetites played their usual part: and now we were plunged into a regimen from another age, that we might become "Pathfinders in the Three Worlds."

With continued abstinence, problems of sex became pressing. There were those who, looking back on the days we had passed, would comment upon those problems in purposely loud voices, moved I suppose by a sort of inverted hypocrisy.

Still celibate myself, I had never before given such unmixed attention to the matter of "woman." On the battlefield, when one has known woman, enforced celibacy joined to a fear of death can turn a man into an animal. Here, enveloped in the masculine smell from eighty white kimonos, my white-stockinged feet crossed as I lay in the sunlight and stared at the ceiling, I sometimes felt that every young pore was sighing out for woman. Woman might in fact be heaven.

Every shining material particle, glittering like the scale of a fish, bore down upon me with the weight and softness of the Garland of Truth. I could throw myself into my studies with a concentration in no way inferior to Mikkai's. No doubt it would be worth while to push my way down the road toward bearing the difficulties he spoke of. But as long as there was woman, I thought, and as long as I felt this burning, I could never be a real priest.

Shortly after the Meiji Restoration, the Government gave priests permission to marry and to eat fish and meat. A result was that I myself came to be, and would one day go to heaven. But at nineteen, I found it impossible to think of me the priest trembling with pleasure in my warm bed. I saw no Buddhism there, only happiness.

I had been strongly drawn to the high priest in the main Kyoto temple of the sect. Though I had only seen his picture and knew very little about him, I was drawn to him because through the whole of his long life he had never sullied himself with woman. When, therefore, my uncle planned to visit him, I asked to be taken along. It was the year before I entered the seminary.

The high priest was tiny, tiny—swaddled in a scarlet robe. He seemed to be less sitting in the wicker chair than floating weakly up from the enormous folds of cloth. On the thin white neck above the pure white collar, a delicate face tilted precariously. The skin, never exposed to the sun, was startlingly white, here and there splotched pink. He leaned slightly forward, and only the crown of the head, which carried but a trace of white hair, suggested his hundred and three years. The crown of the head, terribly shriveled and winkled, said enough of the wondrous accumulation of months and years.

My uncle and I pressed forward, as though for a better look. The eyelids moved very slightly above the clear ash-colored eyes. A weak, wandering, glance was turned toward us.

In the dim light at the end of the audience room, gold dust glowed softly on the flower-and-bird paintings of the sliding doors, Through the open doors, a cool wind blew in over the darkly polished veranda from the lotus pond below the hill, and in the summer light the outer half of each face was turned a greenish white.

My uncle, in Western clothes, knelt in a position of the deepest reverence. He brought his mouth to the high priest's ear, and spoke in affectionate tones, mentioning my name and the name of a mutual acquaintance, now dead, and describing the relationship between us. The ears were apparently sound. A slight change passed over the eyes. The mouth moved, and a hoarse voice emerged. It continued for some time. I did not catch the meaning, but my uncle nodded repeatedly.

The mouth opened a little and closed, and the thin lips were a translucent white, washed of the last traces of man. The emotions implicit there had quite lost the smell of flesh. The whole of him was bleached white, one might have said, white and clean.

A thing by way of ceasing to be human was deposited here inert, surrounded by us in whom there was still action, my uncle and myself and the attendant priest. The shifting tones in the ash-colored eyes and the low incoherent words that came from the twisted lips held him tenuously to his surroundings. So, in any case, the matter seemed to me.

"Well, we mustn't tire you." My uncle glanced at the attendant priest, even though our five minutes were not yet up. The casters squeaked, the chair moved lightly off, and the two of us went out to the veranda. My uncle's plump cheeks were aglow with the pleasure of having met the one man in all Japan whom he admired.

Several priests were lounging about the office. They wore white *tabi* and modified clerical dress, but in the shrug of a shoulder or the wave of a wrist one caught something worldly, something very neat, for instance, my own fleshliness. Because of the clerical dress, that something of the world seemed stronger—and because of the impression left by the bleached old man, unresisting as a dead tree.

"And how is he holding up?"

"He seems to be failing fast."

"If he dies now there'll be one fine battle. He'll have to last a bit longer."

Knowing that my uncle pursued the same trade, they talked freely.

Outside the great temple, the streets of the old capital lay before us as though shot down by the rays of the midsummer sun. A streetcar, vaguely yellow, wobbled uncertainly down the tracks.

"What did you think of him?" asked my uncle.

"Not bad at all."

"Oh?" He was pleased. "There's no one else like him. Probably there never will be."

Two middle-aged women passed us. One of them turned to look at me. "They get gaudier and gaudier in Tokyo," she said. I had on a new brown suit and a red necktie. In the white sunlight of that quiet street, the combination must have been dazzling. The women had of course not understood our conversation, nor had they suspected our calling. What would they have thought if they had, I wondered.

We passed a public bath. Strings of azure and green beads, a sort of half-curtain at the door, were swaying in the breeze. From inside came a vigorous splashing and the clack of wooden bucket on wooden floor. Suddenly I thought of the tiny body under those scarlet folds. I thought of the sagging flesh and the wrinkles, the protruding bones, the curve of the bony back and hips. It came to me with intense dearness, the perfect priest's body, the ultimate in bleaching and aging.

"It won't do. It just won't do." From somewhere came the voice, and I felt my own naked body inside the suit and underwear and shoes. I was possessed there in the street by the sensuality of my own muscles, springing and swelling as I walked and stopped and walked again, writhing and coiling and caressing one another; and by the touch of those other muscles, for which they called out.

Some of the novices had known far worse hardships than I, and their experience of woman was no doubt far richer. They talked of it energetically.

"And on Number 606," someone would say as if announcing a race, "the man who did it too often."

Or: "I want to sleep with a white woman once. Just once. I wouldn't care if

I died afterward." If he squirted water from a rubber ball to emphasize the words, it added to the titillation.

Sometimes there was a strain of cruelty in the wantonness. It was particularly noticeable in Anayama, a strongly built youth one of whose legs was a little bad. His father was an impoverished workman, and Anayama himself had been left, as good as abandoned, with relatives in a temple. It was very near my own, and it was remarkably small and poor for a Tokyo temple. Anayama had gone through childhood with scarcely a decent meal. He bitterly disliked the novices from more fortunate temples.

The rich boys, with their messengers from home and their steady flow of supplies, were naturally the center of attention. I was one of them. Anayama looked upon us with contempt and anger. We had never known hardship, we were pampered brats. When, occasionally, he slipped out in the middle of the night and came back drunken and violent, it was as much from rebelliousness as from dammed-up lust. I had no trouble sensing the malice in the cold, hard gaze Anayama turned on my smallest movements.

One night I awoke choking from a dream of a burning building. I looked up. A whitish smoke was indeed trailing over the quilts and the row of sleeping heads. There was little smoke by the window, where I lay, but great white billows were rising from the big iron brazier toward the center of the room. Anayama and two cronies, who seemed to have come home drunk, were roistering in the thickest of the smoke. They had kindled a fire to amuse themselves, apparently, and to intimidate the other novices. Afraid of the violent Anayama, the others were pretending to be asleep.

Anayama's strong back was turned toward us. He staggered over to the sliding door at the veranda, the muscular calf and ankle of his bad leg twisting grotesquely at each step. The sleeves of the black kimono were pushed tidily to his shoulders, and the skirt was bunched at the hips. There was something cruel and at the same time comical about the powerful figure like a bear emerging from a cave ready to test its strength.

"You're going too, Anayama? You're not ready yet?" One of the accomplices rubbed his smarting eyes.

"Just a minute." The skirt of his white under-kimono in one hand, Anayama stood bowed toward the paper-panelled door. He was looking at the lower part of his body. "There. Everything's ready." He brought his head up sharply and thrust his hips forward with a growl. The door rattled but stayed in its groove.

There was a thud as Anayama brought his weight solidly against the door.

His object was not of course to knock the door over. It was to push a hole though with his erect penis. He stepped to one side, growled, and thrust his hips forward again. I thought but could not be sure that I heard the sound of the passage though the paper and low on my own body I felt at each thrust what Anayama must have felt. The darkness from the veranda looked in through a clean circle in the paper panel.

Feigning sleep, I lay counting. "He's done it again." Another growl. "And again. Once more, now. Once more." Sometimes the growling was muted, not because the drunken breathing interfered, but because he had lost himself in his work. Finally it stopped altogether. I could hear only the hoarse breathing.

For all my sexual yearnings, I had a strong dislike for the smutty. I suppose I had not come to the heart of the matter. I had wrapped fleshly beauty in a coating of romantic love.

At first Anayama's performance was revolting. But soon it came to seem more than just obscene. A tightness came over the room. The sticky revulsion disappeared, and the tightness assailed me and seemed to push on through me. I could not call it physically unclean. It smelled of flesh, and it was oppressively heavy.

I closed my eyes and saw the hole dark in the shoji. I did not see it as a genital organ. *That* still had no place in my eroticism, in the feminine Garland of Truth shining before me. But the paper, like white skin, and the hole, meaninglessly black and clean, were there and would not leave. I made no judgment upon them, whether the black stood for defilement or whether it was the focal point of all beauty. The black and the white took on a strangling authority, that was all, and pressed down heavy against my face.

As though remembering his duty, Anayama would occasionally give a growl. There was something coarse in the growling, and at the same time something weak. "Anayama! Still at it?" "Look at him go!" In the beginning his two friends had snickered and urged him on; but now they were silent. The silence was punctuated by the rattling of the door and the breaking of the taut paper. Finally that too stopped.

After a time there was a long, tired sigh from Anayama. Then, in a voice too devoid of art, too beaten, to be called satisfied, he muttered: "Heaven. That's what it is, heaven."

I felt as if the great, heavy, iron door of heaven had fallen before my nose. Or as if a warm void, starless and lightless and without night birds or insects, had spread without limit, and was about to suck up everything. And only the smell of my fevered skin under the quilt, and the unpleasant taste in my mouth, rose up into the void.

Spring was coming. A cobble stone path and steps led for about a hundred yards from the gate up to the Great Hall. There were always beggars and pilgrims on the path, which we took many times each day for six regular services— matins, noon prayers, vespers, and three nocturnal services—and for countless obeisances between. There were women pilgrims too, and simply women out walking. The cheeks and fingertips of women in gay kimonos were rosy. The arms and legs protruding from sweaters and skirts, told of release from the cold. The bright clothes, down to handkerchiefs and gloves, intimidated us like the warning coloration of an insect. Like a flower petal, a parasol slanted and opened. Beads in hand we formed our column and started up the path toward the Great Hall, its tiled roof a burnished silver, and even those among us most given to coarse talk fell silent.

They knew, as if they had discussed the matter and come to an accord, that we were the eccentrics, the misshapen ones. Our smallest act could seem clumsy and comical to the people of the world. Stop and look back at a girl, and that, something as trivial as that, could seem grossly inappropriate, contradictory, unbecoming.

The bell tower and the charnel house, the groves of gingko trees not yet in leaf, the pines, the hillocks covered with dead grass, and, giving color to the ashen space that included them all, white and deep pink peach blossoms. When, small and far away, the figure of a young girl came into the space, it burned brighter and fresher than the peach blossoms or a drop of blood. The world took flame from it and changed color. But in that column of black, even Anayama glowered like a bear in a cave, and fought to keep his thick neck from turning.

With the help of the houseboy from my temple, I left the seminary one evening.

I put on an Inverness and a soft hat, changed straw sandals for wooden patterns, and got into a cab. I alighted at the bright center of the city. In the restaurant, the people of the world were laughing and talking, among the lights and the smells of the world. The lights were bright, the automobiles rushed by, the radios and phonographs sang. I drank red wine and ate a thick cutlet and fragrant ice cream. In the vase was a delicately crinkled carnation, tight against glossy leaves. The silver spoon and fork made pleasant noises against the dishes and glass.

No one would notice that I was an eccentric from a seminary. I turned to the polished mirror and very slightly tipped the soft hat that was my disguise. A shaven strip, not quite face and not quite skull, was exposed. I stared at it as if I were staring at my soul.

A pretty waitress, small and plump—a bud, if she was to be likened to a flower—noticed the strange gesture. In the broad mirror, obnoxiously well polished, she stared in fascination, and the round little hand clutched at the edge of her apron.

"She has reason enough. Reason enough," I muttered to myself; and turned away. The horror in those clean eyes, as if she had seen a leper, was only natural. I was after all a grotesque.

I knew when people would come calling us. In a certain house a certain person dies. A person of this world disappears from this world. Those who are left come to think that we are necessary. They remember that in this world there is a group of aliens who have connections with the other world. They come for us. We take our places like experts beside the corpse. They weep, they are sad. The corpse, no longer of this world, is cooled by bits of dry ice and warmed by the charcoal brazier. In attendance upon it, we seem at home for the first time. People never think of sharing their happiness with us. They come for us when they have sorrows.

In sum, our reason for being is recognized only when the thing called the other world has clouded people's heads a bit. But while people are in this world they hate and dread the other. They therefore hate us specialists in black who remind them of it.

"But to me too this world is a thousand times and ten thousand times dearer than the other. I will give all the other heavens to whoever wants them. This is the one for me."

I wanted to shout it out. I looked around lovingly at the bright center of the world. There the streets were, showing their unconcerned faces as if, whatever Mikkai's teachings, they meant to stand for a hundred billion years. People might suffer, but they clung to these streets, not to be separated from them by a foot or a second. And I too. What relation to these streets, these people, me, were the destruction and annihilation and upheavals Mikkai had going on somewhere always?

To become a specialist in heaven, I returned to the seminary.

The training was almost over. I became involved with Anayama in an incident which, pushed but a little further, would literally have seen me to heaven.

I might give myself up to willful fancies, but for novices from poorer temples, seminary life was not so easy. Some were there on money borrowed from teachers and friends, and others, like Anayama, had been left in temples when small and, after cruelly restricted lives, had been sent to the seminary to work off their indebtedness. From these lower levels of the clergy, so to speak, were several novices who had thrown themselves into seminary life with considerable earnestness. It was the starting point toward independence and toward somehow taking care of parents and brothers and sisters and their own children. Earnestly they went though elementary Buddhism, and on to the technique of bell ringing, the beating of gongs and clappers, the intoning of sutras, and, much the most important, the saying of requiems. At the other extreme, quite indifferent to our duties, were Anayama and I.

My temple owned land and had room for luxury. It made little difference if a son or so played for a while. My relatives were leaders in the government of the denomination, and deans and professors in the denominational university—I was a child of the highest clerical aristocracy. The rich supplies of food and toilet articles that came to me almost every day were distributed to the novices around me. Several were indebted to my family in other ways, and they were careful to see to my comfort. The head novice, who had been generously tipped, would usually consent to look the other way. In short, I was prepared to enjoy the favor of everyone in sight.

I had had some slight acquaintance with barracks and jails, and seminary life was no trial at all. My indifference to duty was as uncomplicated as the escapism of the truant high-school boy.

With Anayama, matters should have been far different.

The others had left for the lecture hall. The floor, a hundred mats spread over it, was slightly ridged and pitted. In the morning sunlight, it stretched away like the side of a lonely hill.

Hidden behind a heap of quilts in the sunlight, I stretched my arms and legs, a little stiff from services the night before. To the rear of the building, a steep hill gave way to a wooded park. In the quiet I could hear the far-off roar of the city and above it the chirping of birds.

I sat up and looked toward the door, at the edge of the mountain of quilts. Anayama, always as ready as I to have a rest, lay glaring up at me.

"Suppose you go die," he said. When I did not answer, he said it more loudly, this time to the ceiling.

"Oh, I'll still be alive for a while."

"So will I," he retorted irritably. "Go on out and die. There's no reason why you shouldn't. With me it's different. I've got things to do yet."

"What've you got to do?"

"Nothing a child would understand. All sorts of things."

He was five or six years older than I, but he looked a good ten years older. Nihilism from long persecution had thrown one more shadow over the already murky pools of rebellion and lust.

"Just children. You go around saying you'll do this and that, and never get around to doing anything. There's nothing I haven't done. But I'll invent things to do if I have to."

"What do you think a preacher can do?"

"Why you . . ." He threw a pillow and an ashtray at me. "Looking down on us because you read all the answers in a book somewhere. But that's not the way things come." He started toward me. Then, reluctant to show his bad leg, he stood with the other leg thrust forward and bawled at me as if someone had touched a match to him. "What would a spoiled brat like you know about me and what makes me run and the plans I've got?" The powerful back swatted the floor again, and he lay face-up.

Thus we approached our final clash. It came when the proctor hit one of the novices.

The hitter was the big priest I had gone skiing with, and the hit novice was one of Anayama's cronies. The drum would boom, and the novices would straighten their clothes and start for the lecture hall. Some of the less earnest had a way of being late. The novice in question was that day late with two or three others. He had become friendly with Anayama and made use of Anayama's violence, and he was shrewd in a way Anayama was not. The proctor reprimanded him in the hall. He turned and flung back an answer. The proctor floored him.

The head novice, with Anayama standing beside him, reported on the incident after dinner that evening. He had taken part in left-wing activities in the denominational university, and he was a clever talker.

"It is not just X here who got hit. It is of all us. If he was late too often, why didn't they point the fact out quietly? How do they justify violence in this holy seminary? And on the part of a man who should be our leader? And what of the language he used—like a sergeant dressing down his platoon. We might as well say that he used the same language on every one of us. He insulted everyone of us. And unless we protest, he will show his contempt by using force time after time.

"This meeting has been called at the suggestion of Anayama," he added.

Anayama was silent. It was pressure from Anayama, however, that forced the head novice on. The latter only wanted to see these last days safely through. He therefore made it clear that the idea was Anayama's. We sat in a cluster, our faces a little tense. The head novice called out sharply to those who found their own conversation more interesting than the meeting, and thus made it clear that the matter was serious.

Comments were requested. One of the older novices stood up. "We should march out tomorrow in a body. It is meaningless to go on. We will march straight out of the place, not just because one corrupt instructor hit one of us, but because we must induce reflection throughout the top levels of the clergy. We will go back to our temples and there put ourselves through rigorous training. The time has passed for old, worn-out methods. Now is our chance to show the strength of the lower orders that are the pillars of the sect.

"Really, they've gone too far." He looked around for support. "Have you ever heard of anything quite like it? They have no idea how young people suffer and how country temples struggle to get by."

I knew this harassed person well, with his pale face and his dry, rustling skin. I knew that he belonged to the dissident faction. There were two main factions in the sect. One, now in control of the organization, was led by a man who had studied in Germany, who knew Sanskrit, and who had revived the teachings of primitive Buddhism. It was, if one must give it a label, the new, cosmopolitan faction. The dissident faction was led by priests who looked to the Mahayana scriptures in Chinese translation, and sought thereby to preserve the traditions of the sect. It could be called the old, national faction. I did not know which was right, but I knew at least that the struggle was between old and new, national and cosmopolitan. The statement we had just heard was but a small outcropping of a basic disagreement.

The head novice stood up again. He offered us an oration on the social environment in which our sect found itself. The grandeur of his style was somewhat disproportionate to the size of the incident, but the young novices were excitable and listened with attention.

"Christianity is gaining," he said. "The political situation shows signs of increased tension. On the left and on the right are accumulations of power large enough to crush our denomination at a blow, and right here before us they are joining battle. Bloody incident follows bloody incident. The times are as they were when the founder of our sect, disgusted with hidebound priests who fawned upon authority and thought only of warming and fattening themselves, began a new religious movement for the common people, driven mad by hunger and deprivation."

Like an elegant leader of the French Revolution, he waved away a clinging sleeve with a flick of the wrist. He became intoxicated with his own eloquence.

"Are we to survive or are we not to survive? Having come upon these degenerate latterday happenings, we of the younger clergy must squarely face the issue. One blow of this hand, one kick of this foot, can decide the fate of our whole denomination. The violent incident we have just witnessed will decide whether we broaden and strengthen our organization and insure the prosperity and independence of our faith, or whether we fall into the ruin we deserve as timeservers and betrayers."

An elbow against the brazier, Anayama was smoking and looking bored and sullen, and somehow apart from the rest of us. When the oration was over, he glanced up. "I should have taken a poke at him. I should have just gone and taken a quiet poke at him."

"I beg your pardon?"

"I'll just run over and hit him. I don't need any help."

I sat in the back row with my eyes lightly closed. I was still in this world, deposited in the very center of it, no choice in the matter. It was a chilly fact, and an itchy fact.

And since there were human beings in that world too, there could be no doubt that they took their quarrels with them. I opened my eyes a little, and had evidence of it in the motions of people in black and white that passed through the two lines of skin and two rows of eyelashes. I had come to feel that if there was right, it lay beyond the realm in which I could act; and the beautiful too was with the impossible. If, then, there was either right or beauty in the scene, bathed in orange light, that came creeping through my half-closed eyes, it was where I could not reach it, could not touch it, perhaps could not envision it. There would be no sense either in joining the commotion or in running away from it.

I must recognize that there was also a certain cunning in my position, the cunning of one who flees to a quiet refuge in times of turmoil. For an instant I inclined very slightly toward Mikkai's view of the universe.

"But it's the proctor they're going to hit. The big fellow." Suddenly the thought came to me. I was looking in another direction while my skiing companion was on the way to being hit. That small fact opened my eyes. It was a sensually repellent fact. I must at least stop the plans to hit him.

Another novice stood up. He had been most diligent in studies and rituals.

"I have doubts about making a hasty decision," he said timidly. "How would it be if we were to call him here? He may apologize, and he will have things to say for himself, and we can make our decision afterward."

Everyone agreed. The head novice and two others went for the proctor, and came back to report that he would be with us in a moment.

We heard a heavy step far down the hall. A threatening step, which approached at double the usual speed of the proctor. One of the twenty white doors at the veranda was shoved roughly open, almost torn from the groove, and the swarthy face and the massive black-wrapped body appeared. He seemed to have come from the bath—his face and neck were flushed. There was defiance in the folded arms and the feet planted wide apart.

"You had something to talk about? Get it over in a hurry. Who's your delegate?"

"We want an explanation of why you hit X," said the head novice. "Why I hit him?" The face had become an unrelieved crimson. "You want to know why I hit him? You called me here to tell you why I hit him? And what exactly are all of you doing? You call this discipline? There you go straggling along like a line of goldfish droppings, some of you still coming into the lecture hall five and ten minutes after the drum. You think I'll let you get by with it? If you have to hit people to make 'em understand, well, you hit 'em. Straggling along, and straggling along, just like a line of goldfish droppings. Maybe you could brace up just a little?"

"Why did you have to use force?" someone asked in a low voice.

"So you're going to cross-examine me, are you? I did what was right, and I'm not one to be scared by the whole mob of you. Step up, anyone that has a complaint. Step up in a mob, if you want to." He glowered fiercely.

I knew why Anayama was ignoring the challenge. He was making plans for single combat. He would knock the big fellow down and possibly disable him. If Anayama had stood up to land the first blow, the others would have been with him as if afraid to be left out. But Anayama did not mean to waste his time on mass violence. That was too easy, it was childish. Nothing heroic in it, neither the dark taste of conspiracy nor the exquisite taste of blood.

To him there was no question of new and old factions, or of the independence and prosperity of the sect. He only wanted to carry out the conclusions to which the darkness of his days has brought him. There was anarchism in his manner and glance, and his intentions were clear from the gloomy silence he preserved through the rest of the long conference.

Because Anayama did not get up, the moment for attack passed. In the group were some who thought of us, Anayama and myself and the novice who was hit, as worms in the body of the lion. We ignored the rules and showed no respect for authority. Firm believers were in the minority, but one day, quietly, they would become the core of the sect. They feared decay and wanted a purge. And then there were the practical ones who felt that they would get by somehow once they had found their way into the clergy. Their number was the largest. They cared nothing about the incident that was the occasion for the meeting. Time passed, and no new proposals came forth.

A fierce combination of red and black, the proctor stood there like Fudō of the Fires. "Well? Nothing more to say? Why did you send for me, then? At the rate you're going you'll never make priests or rickshaw boys or anything else."

"I wonder if you would mind leaving us," suggested the head novice, who was sensitive to the mood of the assembly.

"Starting tomorrow, things will be harder. If a fist doesn't work, I'll use a club." The proctor cast a savage glance in my direction. "I don't remember when, but there was a night when a person in an Inverness and a soft hat bribed the gatekeeper and went out through the back gate and got into a taxi." Someone snickered. "Whoever he is, his day is coming. We'll find him breaking his vows and maybe killing someone, and the Buddha will see to it that he gets his neck wrung for his trouble. The day is coming, you mark my words. Let him be ready for it. It's coming, and when it does, watch him wail."

(Already evidence was forming to support his prediction.)

"This world is hell. You didn't know it? Go around thinking it's heaven, and you'll get yourself ground to a pulp, skin and bones and all." He turned like a master player and made his exit.

But his words had been too strong a medicine. "We can't let him get away with it." That view gained support. "He thinks right is on his side and he doesn't make the least effort at self-reflection." A proposal from Anayama's friend was being taken seriously: "We'll just have to hit him. That's the easiest thing." And the older novice made his proposal again, and more were inclined to accept it: "We'll leave the temple in a body."

There were several volunteers for the hit faction, and they marched up to take their place before the head novice. The leave-the-temple faction began to prepare a circular letter. "We'll hit him." "We'll leave the temple." The deliberative faction and the activist faction, the legal faction and the extralegal faction. The meeting gathered life, and a pleasant excitement flooded the faces.

At no other time did those youths fettered body and soul in black and white vestments show such vitality. They said what they thought, and they seemed to live again. Held to one narrow path, forced into an antique mold, they seemed to find in the trivial incident an excuse for breaking away just a little.

Drops of rain slanted into the light and ran down the windowpanes, glowing dimly against the darkness that widened out to the park. A frog was croaking at the foot of the hill, a full, yet soft croak. In the warm rain, a female frog would be making its slow way through the underbrush with a male frog on its back.

I looked at all of them in the bright light of the long room, conferring among the braziers and the quilts, and I thought of the groves and something forgotten beyond the lights and voices.

Frogs crawling on all fours, foam on their ugly drab-and-yellow bodies—I saw them with strange clearness. Crawling from clay holes in the breast of the hill and croaking *gué-gué-gu-gu-guru-guru*, they were making their way down the steep, rocky path to the lotus pond.

At the pond, slivers of light were coning through the closed shutters of the tea cottage. Dry lotus leaves, catching sinews of light, were rusting in the wind and rain. The frogs, male and female, slid quietly to the bank, and floated in the water. The one was still mounted on the other, and the backs were shining.

One bright morning, a young man and woman were watching frogs from the stone bridge. The woman wore a kimono and the man wore foreign clothes. "Let's go." The woman pushed gently at the man's shoulder. She too was still watching the frogs. "Please, let's go." She reached for his hand. He nodded, and stood watching.

"See how calm they are about it. How serious." He studied the frogs gravely. "The two of them sinking in the water, and they don't make a move."

"Just doing that."

They started off as other strollers came near. I was watching from beneath a big maple, high up beside the path. I was hidden by the trunk and by clumps of dry grass. Once a foreign man and woman saw me sitting there alone. Hunching their shoulders, they gave a little cry and shook their golden hair.

"We'll take a vote on it. Are there other suggestions?" I heard the unguent voice of the head novice. I came to myself and stood up.

"I have a suggestion." It would not do to let them hit the man. I began talking when I had been recognized by the head novice. "I am opposed both to hitting him and to leaving the temple. If we hit him because one of us was hit, we lose the right to raise the issue. And besides, violence is not good Buddhism. I'm absolutely opposed to taking violent measures." I was conscious of Anayama's gaze. "It would be meaningless to leave the temple. Every one of us wants to be ordained and go back to his own temple as soon as possible. It would do us no good to break discipline now. We would be the losers. We should therefore take over the Great Hall and refuse to move even an inch from it. We should go on a hunger strike like the great Gandhi. We should hold out until we have a promise that violence will not be used again. We should resist by nonresistance."

I had no idea whether Gandhi was Buddhist or a Hindu, but somehow the name Gandhi came to me. There was considerable applause. "A good idea. No need to leave the temple." "No need to hit him." The head novice looked around. "I find much to interest me in what Yanagi has just said. How many agree?" More than half the hands were raised.

"But if you are going to adopt my suggestion, I have one condition: the head novice is to keep watch over the whole class and see that action is united. The policy I have described will be meaningless if, while we are carrying it through, someone hits the proctor." I looked at Anayama, and spoke with emphasis. "Likewise, anyone who leaves the temple is to be punished for breach of discipline."

I repeated the speech I remembered having had from the organizer of a high-school strike. My plan, which would require neither leaving the temple nor launching an attack, pleased the moderates. It meant doing nothing at all. It had almost unanimous support.

The head novice and two others went to consult with the faculty, the proctor excluded. People gathered around me. "We don't eat from tomorrow, then?" "Can we drink water?" "No one can complain if we behave like Gandhi."

Having suddenly won my following, I was feeling expansive. I sat cross-legged in the middle of the assembly. I knew that Anayama's resentment would be doubling and trebling, but I did not sense in that figure lying with its back to me the murderous rage that was to break out two days later.

The other instructors were timider than the proctor, and clever. They took the large view. They foresaw trouble if the novices were to shut themselves up in the Great Hall. If newspapers noticed the incident, the dissident faction would certainly take advantage of it. But most important, there were funerals and other services in the Great Hall every day, and they brought in money.

The very next day the proctor was sent off to do mission work in the provinces. We escaped without going hungry.

At midnight, we were to take our vows before the golden Amida deep within the Great Hall. With that solemn ceremony, unchanged for centuries, we became brothers in the clergy. The ceremony was held in the inner sanctuary (ordinary visitors were forbidden to enter) of the five-hundred-mat hall. Silently, in darkness reaching high to the roof and shut in on all four sides, we would take our vows by the light of the single candle passed from novice to novice as we advanced in turn to the Amida.

A national treasure that had survived a number of fires, the Amida was said to draw souls by a strange power of its eyes. The best of the large Buddhist statues, whether of the Nara Period or the Kamakura Period, have somewhere in their grandeur and warmth a strain not exactly of contempt for the creatures of this earth, but at least of willfulness, as if they were quite free to do what they would with us.

Sometimes, faint on the tight lips, there is a deeply sardonic smile. Sometimes, in the too sharp light from the eyes, there is a rare malevolence. In either case, the sculptor, trembling at the limits of human understanding, at the abyss, in terror perhaps at the inhumanity and the compassion of nature—the sculptor has carved the hard wood and melted down quantities of metal; and around his work, while it is being finished, a record saturated with groans and sobs, and the blood of the weak, spilled as a matter of course, has been made for history.

Some months earlier a nun had killed herself before the Amida by biting off her tongue. She belonged to a cadet line of the Imperial family. The young body, it was said, had fallen across the powerful knee as though crushed by the great, golden band. A white hand was raised a little, suggesting that at the end she had been making some sad petition to Amida.

There was a growing tension as the time approached.

The soft rain that had been falling from the night before had turned into a storm. Before the seminary door, the white spray soaked the dark earth and gathered in puddles and roared down the glistening pavement. The roof over the hallway was pounded and rocked until it was almost impossible to hear an ordinary speaking voice.

"You remember what happened yesterday." It was Anayama's voice, low at my ear. "You know what to expect. When the vows are over, come out in front." The voice was without emotion. "When you hear the drum for the last services, come out on the hill. No mistake about it. You'll come."

"I'll be there," I answered. I glanced at the sallow, stubble-covered face. It was sullen and twisted. Without looking at me, he turned, blackly silent, to take his place in the procession.

Our feet and the skirts of our kimonos were soaked by the time we reached the Great Hall. We climbed the side stairs to the high veranda, where a small door was open. The head novice and one other were standing to the left and right. In silence, they poured scented water over our heads, and touched the palms of our hands with a fine, brown incense powder. We stepped into the hall over a wavering violet smoke from burning incense.

A stout board wall separated us from the Amida, in the room behind which we were assembled. Waiting our turns, we stood in the high, narrow darkness. Our faces and the hands and feet, dim in candlelight from the door, were earth-colored and touched with red. On the walls to either side—the wall behind the Buddha and the white outside wall—there hung respectively two Mandala cycles and a painting of hell.

On each towering Mandala, innumerable Buddhas in gold and five colors covered a deep purple-blue silk ground. Each Buddha, large and small, had a golden halo, and, in an unbroken network, each sat enclosed in a heart or a flower or an ellipse. The number was overwhelming. Packed tighter than insects in a hive, they sat in calm silence, so crowding the surface left and right and up and down that they seemed to bulge over, and could admit not one thing more. They were quite without expression. The coldness gave one a deeper sense of cruelty than the gaping red and green devils among the crackling, leaping scarlet flames in the hell on the other wall. Over the whole surface one felt an essence of indestructible energy, something not to be budged by any lever.

The candle was passed to me, and I stepped forward. Two or three turns and I saw the short flight of stairs that led to the Amida. They creaked as I climbed. I looked up, and before my face like a boulder were the folds on the knee of the statue. Half sliding across the uncarpeted dais, I took my place at the center. I was sitting with the Amida.

The golden Amida, half in light and half in darkness, stared out over a space far above my head. In the candlelight from below, the nostrils had changed shape. The thick flesh was oppressively heavy. The eyes, painted black, were not visible, but the line of the sockets stood out sharply. Those hard eyes were surely open, and looking intently at something. They were eyes that did not for an instant stop their work of seeing, and would forever go on seeing.

They had no glance for me. They were looking in a wholly different direction. And yet even as they ignored me it was as if they had seen the whole of me, and seen through me. I looked up at Amida, and thought: "I am going out and have a fight. You know as much already. I am going out on the hill and behave badly. You have planned that and led the way. Whether I decide to go or not to go, you have decided everything in advance."

The candle moved, and the enormous shadow at the side of Amida fell down on me.

"You have heard any number of complaints. That nun, and young people and old people who have lost relatives, have poured out their tears by who knows how many tons. Here I am before you. I know it is senseless, but I somehow want to have a serious talk. You are not a human being. You are not a god.

You are an ominous, forbidding something. You do not say you are, you do not tell us what secrets you have as a something. Maybe I will be killed, maybe I will kill him. In a little while I may be a renegade and a murderer. You will watch in silence. A something from centuries ago, and from centuries before that, watching us. All right, something, stay with it. I have made up my mind to go out on the hill tonight."

From the darkness below came the dull, muffled sound of a wooden gong. The sound of the wind, too, was muffled.

"No matter how many times a day I call your name, I cannot make a vow to you. But if I live, I will remember, perhaps unconsciously, the something that you are."

That in substance is what I mumbled as I turned, deeply uneasy, to climb from the black dais. I circled the room and walked out, and the cold, wet wind struck my neck.

YASUOKA SHŌTARŌ

Japanese readers often regard Yasuoka Shōtarō (b. 1920) as one of the few Japanese postwar writers to use humor creatively in his stories, despite a debilitating physical illness that sent him back as an invalid from the Manchurian front in 1944. Yasuoka's mother nursed him with great affection, and his eloquent tribute to her constitutes much of the material used in the composition of his best-known novella, A *View by the Sea* (*Umibe no kōkei*, 1959). "Prized Possessions" (Aigan, 1952), the story translated here, is typical of the masochistically humorous stories Yasuoka produced early in his career, evocations of the physical and spiritual deprivations that were either produced or magnified by his war experience.

PRIZED POSSESSIONS (AIGAN)

Translated by Edwin McClellan

"Cleaned out" is what they say, as if poverty were something that cleansed. We—Father, Mother, and I—have been virtually without income for some years now, and I know that it isn't quite like that—empty rooms, cold clean air blowing through, simple living, and that sort of thing. Rather, poverty to me is more suggestive of something warm, sticky, and messy that clings to you; it means disorder and sickly stuffiness. There is nothing at all bracing or simple about it.

Father used to be a professional soldier but, probably because he was a veterinary officer, managed to avoid being accused of war crimes. It is four years now since he returned home safely from the South Pacific. In all that time, he has hardly ever stepped out of the house. Apparently he had some pretty intimidating experiences during internment, for he is still fearful of being beaten up. Mother, by nature a more enterprising and outgoing person, would, it was thought, show her mettle in times like these; and she did indeed get into the business of peddling saccharine, but the venture quickly ended in disaster when our neighbors found out that she had been selling them very questionable stuff at an appallingly high price. Her reputation was ruined for good, it seems; for our neighbors have remained openly suspicious of her whenever they have any dealings with her, such as when it's her turn to help with the local food rationing. She suffers from a terrible inferiority complex now, and is unsure of herself no matter what she does. It's the way she handles money that worries us particularly, of course. She seems to have lost the ability to add and subtract, and when she goes out to do her day's shopping, she hands her purse over to the shopkeeper and asks him to take out the right amount. It's that bad. Then there's my own illness. I got Pott's disease while in the army, and I still haven't been cured. Much of the day I loll about in bed, recuperating, so to speak.

The kind of confusion that can take over a family which has lost all capacity to manage its affairs has to be seen to be believed. Open a drawer in our tea cupboard and you will find, no doubt to your surprise, a saw. That's there because Mother, in one of her weaker moments, imagined that it was a plane for shaving dried bonito. Father, for his part, hoards and jealously guards everything he deems potentially useful as though he were still at the front. Piled up in some strange order on the staggered shelves on the side of the alcove are such items as his veterinarian's saw, scalpel, glass fragments, seeds of unusual plants, his old rank badges, khaki-colored thread wound around a leather bobbin, and so on. Once swallowed up in this whirlpool of rubbish, his handkerchiefs and socks, even his shirts and underpants, are no easier to extract than salt from the sea. I need hardly say there are cobwebs all over the house—on the transom work, ceiling, electric light cords, anywhere you can think of. They are different from ordinary cobwebs, however, in that clinging to them are thin, fluffy bits of white stuff, resembling flowers growing out of mildew. They are in fact bits of angora rabbit fur. Let me say here that even cats I have never liked very much. I have always wondered at those people who seem to adore these impertinent beasts that come and rub their hairy bodies against your skin and stink up the house with their pee. But I have learned that compared to rabbits, they are immeasurably more tolerable.

It all started when one of Father's former subordinate officers—Mother and I didn't know him—dropped in one day to see "the general," as he still called him. We didn't know it then, but in the space of that short visit he managed to put a strange notion into Father's head. The next morning Father, dressed more respectably than usual, went out. Our response to this unexpected event was not without a slight sense of foreboding, but it was on the whole optimistic. Could it be that he had found himself a lucrative job? "He looks quite impressive when he dresses up like that, doesn't he?" Mother said. I nodded solemnly, remembering that in the old days, whenever something important was about to happen, like a promotion or an advantageous transfer, he went out exactly like that, dressed up and not saying a word. But alas, our optimism was without cause. Father returned late that evening hugging a huge box, minus the wrist-watch he had bought in Singapore. Someone had taken it off his unprotected wrist as he coming home. Anyway, that was when those disgusting creatures entered our lives. Just as a truly evil man has the face of an angel, so these rabbits, both the male and female, seemed extraordinarily endearing as they crouched quietly and timidly on the floor, their red eyes shining in the light. Would you believe it, but I found myself saying, "How pretty!" Mother brought out some bread, and each time she held out a little piece, one would gingerly stick its neck out, then suddenly snap at it and hop off with its prize to a corner of the room. They amused and cheered us, these lively little creatures with their pure white bodies. Their presence seemed to brighten up the whole house. Father of coarse was very pleased with himself. "In half a year," he said, "they'll start bringing in eight thousand yen a month." Mother looked like a child who had suddenly been offered an enormous piece of candy. "My goodness!" she said with feeling, her toothless mouth wide open. And as Father proceeded to tell us about his scheme—a year's yield of fur would be so much, which would mean so many pounds of yarn, which in turn would produce so many yards of cloth, etc.—Mother became so ecstatic she laughed uncontrollably. Oh no, she cried out joyfully, Father was being much too modest in his estimate; why, that much cloth would fetch far more than eight thousand yen a month! It was as though she was already seeing piled up around her mountains of cloth and yarn.

I saw out of the corner of my eye a small black ball rolling on the floor. I looked, and found that there were many others just like it all around us. "Shame-less" is the only word to describe it. Every time they jumped up in the air, an-other black ball would pop out from the crotch. There was not a trace of shyness in either face, no show of cringing, as the process continued. I looked at their utterly expressionless faces, at their cretinous red eyes with their vacant stares, and felt a nasty foreboding.

The next day Father began working like a maniac. He was at his most irritat-ing, I had found, when he "worked." Indeed nothing irritated me more. Nor-mally, his "work" meant stripping off the turf in the garden and turning over the soil when the weather was fine, or, if it was wet, making boxes of various sizes and shapes for which there was no conceivable use. Neither activity brought any tangible benefits, obviously, and as a hobby, it made no sense. What particularly mystified me was the energy he put into it. Half hidden in a cloud of swirling dust—we live by the Kugenuma shore, noted for its strong winds and rough seas—he would wield his hoe, giving a crazed, high-pitched cry each time he brought it down. It was like looking at some madman doing an unending dance, and the sight filled me with despair at the loneliness and pointlessness of the effort. One rain, and all he had would be a waterlogged field of sand where nothing would grow. "You're wasting your time!" I would shout at him across the veranda from my bed. "I wish you would stop! Look at all the sand you're sending into the house!" "What did you say?" he would shout back, glaring at me, his hoe held still for the moment above his head. "So what! What if it is a waste of time?"

The coming of the rabbits provided him with a new obsession. He began to construct rabbit boxes. These were classified as nesting boxes, feeding boxes, exercise boxes, and so on, and each new model in a given category seemed more ingenious than its predecessor. The ideas he had picked up when he was making all those purposeless boxes before were now being put to good use. But they were so original that even when it came to a simple thing like lifting the lid off one of them, only he would know how. The sounds of sawing, planing, chiseling, and hammering now reverberated through the house without cease. Meaningless energy found its way through my skull into my brain, leaving no room for anything else.

What sort of a cry a rabbit made was something I hadn't thought about before, but I discovered that it was a squeak—*chū, chū*. It was, I found, a profoundly disappointing sound; and like the Emperor's voice when I first heard it on the radio, it made me feel quite hollow inside. This strange, futile cry I had to listen to all the time; for, fearing the invasion of burglars and stray dogs, Father had put their boxes in the closet at the end of the corridor, no more than three feet away from my pillow. Rabbits, it would appear, sleep during the day and become active at night. At irregular intervals, but never stopping, various sounds reached me as I lay in my bed in the darkness. One moment I would hear their teeth grinding away at the wood, next their feet stamping on the floor, then their droppings or pee going down the drainage system (this was a remarkable affair constructed of tin, designed to meet the rabbit's moving bottom whichever way it was turned).

A typical night for me after the coming of the rabbits went like this. In the middle of the night I awaken from a bad dream. In the dream always, a huge rat has crawled into my bed and is gnawing at either my feet or my head. Being awake is worse than the dream, for then I am assailed by real hobgoblins. From the tips of my toes, embedded in the ticklish wadding of the coverlet, a strange itchy sensation crawls up my legs and finally buries itself in the afflicted part of my spine. Everything I have on me begins to feel terribly constricting. I tear off the plaster cast, then my undershirt, and scratch my back hard, but to no avail. All that the scratching does is to drive the itch farther inside. In a desperate attempt to force it out, I place my fingers on my chest between the ribs and push as hard as I can. As though in response to my anguish, the animals start making more of a din than ever. In the next room there is a duet of snores going on, interrupted by idiotic cries and mutters.

Father suddenly neighs like a horse—he is laughing. He cries out, "Woobik!" He has been saying the same thing in his sleep ever since he returned from the War, and I have come to realize that what he is really saying is, "Want milk!" He was the youngest of nine sons, and was given his mother's milk until the spring of his thirteenth year. At first I was inclined to suspect that he was not asleep at all and that it was a clever ruse on his part to persuade us of his unfitness for work. But I have since changed my mind, having observed the sincerity of his envy as he watches me drink my convalescent's ration of dried milk. His nightly dream, then, is quite authentic, brought on by both an immediate desire and unforgotten childhood pleasures. I'm not in the least shocked by Father's mother fixation, if that is indeed what he suffers from. I find it rather funny, as a matter of fact. True, the picture of Father sucking away at his mother's breast is grotesque, but then, I've always had a weakness for grotesquery. This is not to say that the cry "Woobik!" in the middle of the night does not startle me every time. That the word is nonsensical and I have had to guess at its meaning, albeit correctly, makes it all the more sinister in its suggestiveness.

Made a nervous wreck by this din in the dark, I begin to imagine that my body is about to disintegrate from both outside and inside. The noise becomes unbearable, and I try to pull the coverlet up over my head. But all I succeed in doing is to pull out handfuls of cotton wadding; most of the coverlet remains caught in my legs. The itch in my spine gets worse and worse. It is something, I feel, that rises bubbling like marsh gas out of the debris in my chaotic room—the dust, the rags, the mucus-soaked paper tissues—and seeps into my body. In an attempt to contain the itch that is beyond my reach, I hold my body absolutely taut. I hear again the rabbits crying in the closet, "chū, chū." What an incredibly feeble cry, I think to myself, for creatures that can bang about so.

The rabbits soon produced babies. These thrived under the skilled care of my veterinarian father. He never told us what he had paid for his two rabbits, but we could guess that they represented a considerable financial investment. Every day he would weigh each of the babies, take the mother's temperature, and fuss neurotically over the texture and mix of the food he gave them at regular, short intervals. This exacting routine left him no time for the boxes. The ingenious drainage system, now long neglected, was a shambles. But let alone find the time to fix it, he couldn't even get around to building a compartment for the babies. Inevitably, then, we found ourselves virtually sharing our own quarters with the entire rabbit family. Our house was turned into a veritable animal hut. That was bad enough, but what bothered me far more was that we, all three of us, began to resemble these creatures that cohabited with us. Even before the babies were born, there had been bits of rabbit fur all over the house. But now they literally filled the air, and our heads, covered with the stuff, looked like haloed apparitions emerging from a cloud of smoke. Because he was constantly brushing the rabbits, big and small, Father looked by far the strangest. There was rabbit fur in his nostrils always. As I watched him across the dinner table biting his food with his front teeth, the fur in his nostrils quivering with each breath, I would catch myself thinking of him as being one of them. Mother, too, seemed unable to leave the baby rabbits alone. They revived in her all her maternal instincts, I suppose. All day long she held them in her arms, and would even take them to bed with her, holding them close to her breast inside her kimono, not minding their scratching. In baby language and in hardly more than a whisper, she would repeatedly tell them—I presume it was they she was talking to—stories about me as a baby. Even Father would chide her then. "Hey, those are rabbits, not humans!'

Saucers, bowls, and pans with bits of gruel, fish skin, tea leaves, etc., stuck to the bottom lay on the floor everywhere. Father was to blame for this. Can't let all those good vitamins go down the drain, he said—he seemed to have committed to memory the exact nutritional content of every food he gave the rabbits—and refused to let Mother wash them. But what bothered me even more than the dirty dishes and pans was that while we ate, he would stare shamelessly at our plates to see how much he could hope to salvage for his rabbits. Mother, however, welcomed Father's hoarding of leftovers. Having become slovenly in her old age, she wanted to have as little to do with the kitchen as possible. It was a double blessing for her: she could now stay away from the kitchen sink, and better still, she could serve us any horrid concoction she liked, for the less we ate, the more the rabbits got, and therefore the greater was her husband's satisfaction.

Of course, our house became a haven for bugs and slugs of every description. They crawled about happily here and there in every room, coated with sauce or soybean paste. Mother, now a woman of leisure but with no one else to talk to (her neighbors would have nothing to do with her), became my constant bedside companion. She would lie flat on her back on the floor beside me and play with the baby rabbits or, when she got bored with that, daydream about sweetcakes. "My, that was good!" she would cry out desperately. Yet unlike Father and me, she got fatter by the day. Her belly and face got quite round, and her legs, peeping out of the open folds of her kimono, were as plump as a child's. Her kind of life must excite one's imagination, for she would without warning start describing my future bride. It was like opening some cheap novel in the middle. Anyway, what I found intolerable was that this imaginary bride she was describing invariably became none other than herself. As we lay thus side by side through most of the day, a whole army of flies, attracted to our house from the neighborhood, would eventually congregate around us. Used to the presence of all such creatures, I didn't mind them particularly. But even I was a trifle appalled when I happened once to pass my hand through my hair, and a pair of mating bluebottles flew out and away.

Father was now engaged in an ambitious project. By some mysterious means known only to those who have served long in the army, he had managed to acquire some glass tubes, wire netting, copper wire, and suchlike, and with surprising speed and efficiency had built himself a scientific apparatus. Its purpose was as follows: to extract from human hair a certain nutrient, feed it to the rabbits, and thus accelerate their development. Clearly, the apparatus was no sudden inspiration. I remembered that recently, whenever he clipped his hair, he would carefully wrap up the clippings in a newspaper and put it away among his "treasures" on the shelf. But it soon became apparent that his stock of his own hair clippings was by no means enough for his purpose. He would mutter, ostensibly to himself but quite audibly, "A barber would have lots of hair to spare." What he was trying to tell us, of course, was that he wanted Mother or me to go to a barbershop and ask for some. Having no desire to go on a fool's errand like that, we would look away innocently, pretending not to have heard. He would then hang his head despondently. At such times he looked more like a rabbit than ever. Finally I deliberately told him a lie: "A barber told me today that the prefectural health department had prohibited the sale of hair. A barbershop runs the risk of being shut down if it's caught doing it." The lie was extraordinarily effective. He shook his head in silence several times (which was his way of summoning patience in the face of adversity) and stopped muttering about barbers.

I was mistaken, however, in thinking that he had given up all thought of getting other people's hair. He took to staring at me wistfully, then sighing like a bad actor—"Haaa . . ." And at night, as I lay in bed, he would watch me furtively, waiting perhaps for a chance to creep up to my bedside. And then one night, unable to restrain himself any longer, he blurted out, "What a lot of hair you have!" He scratched his own head wildly as he said this. Instinctively I covered my head with my hands. Oh God, I thought, he goes to sleep earlier than me and wakes up earlier; by four in the morning, he's usually awake; with that beloved chrome-plated scalpel of his, he could shave my entire head clean while I was still asleep. My fear, though fanciful, was not entirely unjustified: I did have a thick head of hair, too thick indeed for comfort. As I put out the light that night and tried to go to sleep, I thought I could see Father bending over me in the manner of a slaughterhouse foreman about to start on a carcass with his skinning knife. From such fantasizing it was easy to fall into wondering whether I had not become one of *them*—one of those stupid, timid, yet shameless animals living with us.

But all my father's hope and hard work came to nought, even more helplessly than a prized potato field that is ruined by a mere two or three days of rain. As though *our* taking in the rabbits had been the immediate cause, angora wool ceased to be marketable. But this should not have surprised us. After all, rabbits were the easiest things to breed, and even without Father's as-yet-unproduced patent medicine they grew plenty of hair. All those plans for selling the fur and spare rabbit babies and making eight thousand yen a month, of winning first prizes at rabbit shows, turned out to have been just empty dreams. But the rabbits survived the crumbling of Father's hopes. They rushed about as wildly as before—no, they were even wilder, for the babies were now full-grown, and Father was too deflated to care what they did—distributing tufts of fur that floated about like ashes of disillusionment. They invaded the alcove and knocked down the scientific apparatus that stood there in vain resplendence, scattering glass tubes and bits of wire all over the room. With these were mingled Father's hair clippings, mostly gray, which the rabbits had got at by biting through the newspaper wrapping.

Mother began to complain incessantly that she'd had to sell all her clothes in order to buy bean-curd remains for them. As she watched them eat, she seemed to see bits of her clothes being munched away. Not long ago, she had joyfully envisaged them as the provider of shawls, gloves, and other finery for herself. The feeble "*chū, chū*" of the rabbits now was constantly being drowned out by the hysterical cries of an aging woman: "How dare you pee there!"

One day Mother came home with a "visitor." This was the first we had had in thirteen months. He wore high boots, and came on a bicycle with a wicker basket attached to it. As he lugged the bicycle in through the front gate, Father and I watched and waited like soldiers in a fort: "Is he friend or foe?" Mother ran up to me and whispered in my ear, "He works for a sausage factory. Don't tell Father." I accepted the information with equanimity. The rabbits had become white elephants, and the sooner they were disposed of the better. Indeed, if the man had cooked a tasty rabbit dish then and there, I would have eaten it gladly.

The meat buyer was led to the veranda, where the rabbits had been brought together. He said ingratiatingly, "What magnificent specimens!" Father, still ignorant of the visitor's identity, acknowledged the compliment with a shy bow and a schoolgirl blush. Perhaps thrown into confusion by this, the meat buyer suddenly reached for the nearest rabbit and picked it up by the skin on its back. He said in a voice so loud I thought I could see the doors shake, "All you laymen get taken in!" The rabbit hung in midair helplessly under the man's bare arm. Its limbs were all drawn in; the fur on its stomach fluttered softly in the breeze. "Laymen wanting to make money on the side always want horses or cows to begin with. But when they find they can't get them, they go for pigs. And when they find they can't get pigs either, they settle for rabbits. That's when the trouble starts. Ordinary domestic rabbits at first, then angoras, then chinchillas and rexes. There's no turning back then. You leave the rabbits, and go on to monsters like nutrias and guinea pigs. When you've reached the guinea-pig stage, you're finished."

We listened to his loud voice, our eardrums shaking, and understood nothing. It was like listening to a foreigner's gibberish. He continued: "Cows ending up as guinea pigs—that's very funny!" He paused, waiting for his own laughter to subside. "Anyway, you've got to be careful. Rabbits are edible, sure, but try eating a guinea pig. Mind you, these angoras aren't that great to eat either."

At that moment the captive rabbit, its taut gray skin showing through the fur, suddenly straightened its limbs out and bit the meat buyer's arm. I felt blood rushing to my head. For some reason all that my eyes saw then were the rabbit and the hand that held it by its back. "Bite him again!" I said to myself. "Son of a bitch!" the man cried out, and swung the rabbit at the pillar on the veranda. Its head made a sickening crunching sound as it hit the wood. But it was not dead as it lay at the foot of the pillar. Its red eyes, wide open but probably unseeing, looked at us. The meat buyer picked it up and threw it into the basket on his bicycle. He then grabbed the others by the ears, one by one, and stuffed them all in. The lid was closed and secured by a cord. Through the mesh the rabbits' white fur appeared, moving, it seemed, with a life of its own. The meat buyer pulled some dirty bills out of his wallet. He turned toward my father, then looked away quickly—did he sense some rabbitlike qualities there?—and handed the bills to Mother.

The man's bicycle was now near the gate, beyond the vegetable garden where mysteriously only those vines that Father planted for rabbit fodder flourished. We stood by the veranda and watched it go, not saying a word to one another.

YOSHIYUKI JUNNOSUKE

Because of illness, Yoshiyuki Junnosuke (1924–1994) escaped military service and, after the war, studied English literature at the University of Tokyo. In a subtle and skillful use of language, Yoshiyuki describes the demimonde of postwar Tokyo as a means to explore hidden sides of the male psyche. His brief story "Personal Baggage" (Kaban no nakami, 1973) offers a glimpse of the confusion between dream and reality.

PERSONAL BAGGAGE (KABAN NO NAKAMI)

Translated by John Bester

The dagger sank deep into my solar plexus, but I felt no pain at all. Then the blade was drawn straight down with a dull sound, like a knife ripping through a piece of thick cardboard.

It was all a dream.

A naked body lay on the ground. The body looked like me. The recumbent form emerged in sharp relief out of the enveloping darkness. It was flattened, as though someone had made off with the guts out of it. The limbs were the proper length, but looked unnaturally thin.

I must hide it, I thought. There was a bag by me, just the right size for carrying around. It stood there as though it had materialized out of the ground. Opening the top I found it was empty, and started to stuff the body inside.

The body was all limp, as though it had been boned. The wound on the belly had gone. I folded one of the legs in four, and got it in the bag.

As I went about this task, I noticed that the body was smooth and slippery to the touch. The skin had an amber glow, like that of a young woman. My own skin is normally dry and scaly as a result of the allergy to which I'm prone. I remembered hearing about a man who had a dog with some stubborn skin complaint. No treatment did any good. But then the dog died—and in a few minutes its skin was as clear as though someone had drawn a healthy epidermis over it with a brush.

The body went into the bag with no trouble. I picked the bag up and made my escape.

But it was me holding the bag, though. And me in the bag, too. . . . A doubt flitted across my mind: what did I have to run away for? Even so, the bag contained a corpse; mere possession of such a bag, I supposed, justified flight.

I started to run, then stopped and switched to a more normal gait. A tall building loomed ahead. I decided to go up to the roof. I'd no idea what I'd do there; I merely felt, acutely, that there was no time to lose.

The elevator hall was deserted. I suddenly realized my arm was tired, and put the bag down on the floor. Before I knew it, there was another, brown bag there beside it, though no one else was in sight. A kind of Boston bag, of exactly the same size and shape as my own. . . .

I pressed the button.

An elevator appeared to my summons and opened its doors. Fortunately it was the automatic type, and empty. The building had twenty stories. Above the button for the twentieth floor, there was another marked "R." I pressed it, urgently. The figures beside the buttons flashed on and off in a swift series, and in no time we had reached the roof.

The doors opened to right and left with an irritating slowness quite unlike the speed the elevator had shown so far, and I emerged onto the roof. At the same moment, I noticed that the bag dangling from my hand had changed into the brown one.

Fear like a pain ran upward from my heels and halted somewhere around my hipbone. I turned round in a panic, only to see the elevator door already completely closed.

I had a brief mental image of the dark purplish sheen of the bag left behind on the hard floor downstairs.

I ran to the elevator and ground my finger into the button.

But the light in the horizontal row of figures above the doors was at "10," where it remained obstinately stuck. Suddenly I noticed, right next to the doors and about the same size as them, a rectangular opening.

Peering in, I saw a slender silvery rod of metal. It ought to have been vertical, but in fact sloped away at a slight angle before disappearing into the darkness below. The angle somehow gave an impression of safety.

Flinging the brown bag away, I put my arms round the silver rod and let myself go.

Down I slid at an angle, accelerating steadily. I felt sure my arms around the rod would be torn off. I had just begun to get really alarmed—I should never have tried it from the twentieth floor—when suddenly the strain on my arms let up.

There was a sheet of corrugated iron beneath my feet. It was moving vigorously, with myself poised on top. Like an elevator, only much faster. . . . And, unlike an elevator, it seemed to be moving horizontally, carrying me steadily away to some destination unknown.

This wouldn't do. At this rate, I'd end up still further away from the purple case.

But suddenly I found myself on a firm floor. By my side, the bag that I'd left behind gleamed darkly. I grasped it by the handle and made my escape again.

I was the one who'd been stabbed. The corpse too, I was sure, had had my face.

Was it really me, then, that was running away with the bag? I decided to go home, hide the bag in a closet, and give the matter some leisurely thought.

But all of a sudden I couldn't remember where home was. Could it mean, then, that the fugitive was someone other than me? If so, then I supposed I should be going back to his house.

Suddenly, I wanted to take a look at my face. But although whatever I looked at showed up light, everything else round about it was dark. No mirror presented itself within my field of vision—not even a windowpane, which would at least have provided a dim reflection.

I gazed at the surrounding houses, trying to remember where my own was. A signboard with the name of the street and district caught my eye. It was nailed to the post of a gateway standing directly in front of me. The name was familiar: yes, a woman I'd once known lived here.

So, after all, it was me who was carrying the bag around.

We'd been pretty intimate, but I hadn't seen her for five years. She was married now, I'd heard, with a kid. I remembered the name of the district, not because of any lingering interest in her, but because it was out-of-the-way. Like "Tearbridge," or "Sprain," or "Dragonsbeard." . . .

She'd have taken her husband's name, of course. What was it, though? The name reached the tip of my tongue and refused to come any further.

For a while, I could make out nothing in the dark. Then the blackness gradually let up, and I saw a house, and the front door opening.

I was standing facing her.

"Quite a stranger. Everything OK?"

No reply.

"You've got a kid, I hear."

"I'm afraid I don't . . . ?"

I took a look around me. Dark all about still, save for the orange light illuminating the woman. She was particularly bright round the edges.

It might be daytime, or it might be night. If it was night, now . . .

"Say, is your—" And I stuck a thumb out at her in the vulgar gesture meaning a husband or lover.

I watched my own behavior with a feeling of surprise. I'd no recollection of ever having behaved like that to a woman before.

So it seemed I wasn't myself after all.

"I mean, of course," I corrected, "your husband—is he at home?"

"No. Actually," very stiffly, "my husband is still at the office."

Her standoffishness shook me a bit; but I pulled myself together and said, "Lend me your compact a moment, will you?"

When we used to go drinking together in the old days, I'd invariably ask her to lend me her compact in order to take a look at my face in the tiny mirror. Since I'm allergic, a flushed face would be a warning signal not to drink any more.

It had been a kind of ritual between us whenever we met. But she gave no sign of recalling it.

I rather fancied the curve of her body from the waist and on down the hips; but this was no time for thinking of such matters.

Was she deliberately behaving distantly? Or was my face that of a stranger? I longed to take a look at myself in the mirror of her compact.

"*Compact*? What a cheek!"

" 'Cheek,' she says. So you want to forget all about the past, do you?"

"What exactly do you mean by that?"

"Are you trying to tell me you don't remember?"

My voice by now was tinged with a mixture of sarcasm and uneasiness.

"Remember? But I've never seen you before today!"

"Really?"

"Yes, really."

The uneasiness grew.

"Let's get this straight, now—does my mentioning the compact really not mean anything to you?"

"No, nothing."

I needed that mirror. I looked around hopefully for a windowpane, but everything round about was pitch black as ever.

Bending over the bag that I'd put down on the ground, I fiddled with the catch. My idea was to hunt out the part of the body that had the face on it, take it in my hands, and turn it toward the woman.

"Is this the same?—" I said, and paused, fumbling irritably with the unyielding catch.

"Oh, I don't need any of those just now," she said. And shut the door briskly in my face.

Don't need any corpses? What exactly did she mean by that? Then I realized.

I'd been going to show her the body's face and ask if it wasn't the same as mine. But the only possible interpretation of her words was that, seeing me bent over trying to undo the catch on the bag, she'd assumed I was a salesman in cosmetics or something.

The thing I couldn't make my mind up about yet, though, was whether I'd really changed into someone she didn't recognize, or whether she was doing it out of spite.

In the years we'd gone around together, I'd suffered from her little digs on quite a few occasions. I was nice enough to her in my own way, but I never saw her except when I myself felt the need. I pleased myself, and this attitude of mine hurt her, I knew.

Her resentment kept its claws well hidden. Sly sarcasms, concealed beneath seeming solicitude or words of praise. . . . But I showed nothing. She must often have wondered whether I'd really noticed her malice or not. Sometimes she would break a date, her failure to turn up being a sign intended to show me that she wasn't my property, to be summoned at will. The same thing happened on many occasions.

Whenever I'd get her into a cab on the way to the usual hotel, the whole interior of the car would immediately be filled with her smell. Not a strong smell; she had no body odor as such. It was her perfume that, warmed by her amber-colored skin, began to drift up into the air. A faint, mild fragrance, it titillated my nostrils. It was the smell, you might almost say, that kept us together so long.

Occasionally, I'd feel it was too strong, and I'd assume she had more perfume on than usual. The first time, I wondered if she was having her period, but there were no signs of it when we got to the hotel. The smell wasn't just strong; there was something faintly rank about it. Even the red of her lipstick looked darker than usual. And there was a subtle difference, too, in the whole atmosphere of her body.

Perhaps she'd gone into business as a call girl? The suspicion, I knew perfectly well, was unfounded, yet it refused to go away. At such times, I thought of myself as sharing her body with another man, or perhaps with several other men.

One day when the signs were particularly strong, the woman and I had dinner at a restaurant near the hotel. I assumed that when we'd finished we'd go straight to our usual room.

But when we got outside she said, "Now I'm going home."

"Why?" I asked just once, then stood there without saying anything more. With an impatient shake of her body, as though I'd had hold of her arm, she started walking. A few moments before, we'd been eating amicably together; nor had I said anything to offend her. I watched her retreating form. From time to time, her body gave a little wriggle as she walked, as though something sticking to her skin wouldn't be brushed off and her own body disgusted her.

She went on without looking round, her figure steadily dwindling into the distance.

"So the time's come again," I thought to myself.

Again I felt myself as one of the many who shared her.

Then, a few days later, she agreed to see me again as though nothing had happened. . . .

The reception the woman had just given me might be her final gesture of spite. I decided to go back over the day's happenings from the beginning.

First, the dagger had plunged into my belly. It hadn't hurt at all. . . . And with this thought I felt a fierce pain, and woke up.

The precise location of the pain, which extended from my stomach down to my abdomen, wasn't clear. I raised myself on the bed and crouched there, unpleasant wisps of the dream still lingering in my mind.

I bared my belly and inspected it; there was no wound, of course. But neither had there been—I recalled with faint distaste—on the belly of the corpse I'd put in my bag.

Perhaps I'd got appendicitis? That would mean a wound again, I thought, gazing at the floor around the bed. I had an odd illusion that the bag with the dark, purplish-brown sheen would be standing there. My own bag, stowed away in the closet, was of a completely different color and shape.

The pain began to fade a bit.

Perhaps I'd got a chill while I was asleep? Or perhaps the accumulated effect of the dream had irritated the nerves of my stomach? Once in the past, when I'd awoken with food poisoning, I'd had a feeling as though I'd been dealt a heavy blow with a stick on the skull, a feeling that went beyond mere pain.

I got out of bed and gingerly started walking. I got out with the intention of going to the bathroom, but found myself instead opening the closet, checking what was inside. My familiar black bag. I took hold of it and shook it. It felt light in my hand; it was obviously empty.

This was entirely predictable, but I felt a mild sense of relief. I went into the bathroom and took a look at my face in the mirror. My usual face, though a bit puffy. I wondered if the face the woman in the dream had seen was my own face or that of some complete stranger.

There was no point in wondering about such things, but the dregs of the dream were still lingering deep down inside me. The pain by now had diminished considerably, but not completely. In deliberate defiance of it, I downed a large glassful of water. I washed my face in cold water. Another day had begun.

POETRY IN THE INTERNATIONAL STYLE

As some of the poems included here indicate, the careers of many prominent poets spanned a variety of periods and influences. Many of the younger poets began their mature work in the two decades after the end of World War II in 1945. Indeed, the number of highly respected poets writing during this time is so great that Hiroaki Sato, the editor of this section of the anthology, was able to include only a few representative works of those who remain most esteemed by the Japanese reading public. Except where noted, the introductions and translations are by Hiroaki Sato.

AIDA TSUNAO

Aida Tsunao (1914–1990) spent six of the war years in China, first working for a civilian unit of the Japanese military. In 1957, he published his first book of poetry, *Salt Lake* (*Kanko*), which describes in simple language the ravages of war. One of the poems, "Legend" (Densetsu), was based on what Aida heard about the Nanjing massacre while he was in China.

LEGEND (DENSETSU, 1957)

When crabs
crawl up from the lake,
we tie them to ropes,
go over the mountain
to the market
and stand by the pebbly road.

Some people eat crabs.

Hung by the ropes,
scratching the air
with ten hairy legs,
the crabs turn into pennies;
we buy a clutch of rice and salt
and return over the mountain
to the lake side.

Here,
grass is withered,
wind cold,
and we do not light our hut.

In the dark
we tell our children
what we remember of our fathers and mothers
over and
over again.
Our fathers and mothers,
like us,
caught the crabs of this lake,
went over that same mountain,
brought back a clutch of rice and salt,
and made hot gruel
for us.

Soon,
again like our fathers and mothers,
we will carry our bodies, grown thin and small,
lightly
lightly
and throw them in the lake.
And the crabs will eat our sloughs
to the last bit
just as they ate
the sloughs of our fathers and mothers
to the last bit.

That is our wish.

When the children fall asleep,
we go out of our hut
and float a boat on the lake.
The lake is half light
and we, trembling,
make love
gently
painfully.

AYUKAWA NOBUO

Drafted into the military in 1942, Ayukawa Nobuo (1920–1986) returned, wounded, from Sumatra in 1944. After the war, he became a member of the Arechi (Wasteland) Group.

IN SAIGON (SAIGON NITE, 1953)

There was no one on the pier
to welcome our ship.
The French town I'd dreamed of
floated on a nameless sea of an Oriental colony
and the body of a young army civilian
who killed himself with a razor blade
was carried out of a hatch, wrapped in white canvas, undulating.
That was our Saigon.
The sufferings of France
were the sufferings of its people
but were the agonies of us soldiers
the agonies of our motherland?
Over a huge ship carrying a Tricolor
was an endlessly clear blue sky
of a defeated nation.
When many friends die
and many more friends keep dying
how beneath the skin of the living
black maggots begin crawling—
the sick soldiers talked voiceless
with the newly dead.
In the bright breeze,
the razor blade that liberated the young soul
set against our thin throats,
the boat with the stretcher
slowly receded into the distance, plowing the green waves.

THE END OF THE NIGHT
(YORU NO OWARI, 1953)

1

You frighten me, you,
like the night beach,
hold close the flow of my blood tide,
you frighten me, you
hook me onto a sharp stake of love,
make my body writhe like waterweed,
and tear it into shreds.
You frighten me, you
mouth vile words of prayer

and keep fondling my breasts, a virgin dead by water.
I put my averted face
on the water of sorrow,
gazing into each of the distant stars, near stars,
ah, that's all.
You are the gentle one, you
cannot keep in your arms
a flowing river, forever.
No matter how you caress my dark hair,
my senses drop away
from water's edge where we meet, flesh to flesh,
and your fingers cannot get hold of anything.

2

The bars shutting us in
are made neither of iron nor of wood
but of raw muscles;
I cannot escape these mobile bars,
however I try.
Your hot blood vessels
entwine my thin neck
and stifle the cry of my formless soul.
I don't know why I've fallen this far,
I don't know,
To us living in this windowless room
as if a day were a year,
there is neither the sun that rises nor the sun that sets,
where on earth
is the horizon for us?
Ah, in my brain
there's only a table turning round and round,
there are only small bones of beastly meat
and a grimy napkin to wipe plates with,
there is neither love nor pity.
As if to look for an invisible exit,
once again
I grope over the wall
and push open your breasts.

3

> A hand of the air pulls at the curtain
> of the bedroom no one knows,
> The face of mist looks in from the ceiling
> on the bedroom no one knows.

What a cold hand you have,
your five fingers are more savage than any weapon,
have poison far more fierce than any snake,
what do you plan to do by killing me?
> Who is it? playing a concertina of bones
> with cold hands of air.

What a pale face you have,
feigning you've given up on everything
you haven't given up on anything, have you,
what do you plan to do if I die?
> Who's that? a pale face of mist,
> with tears of blood.

WARTIME BUDDY (SEN'YŪ, 1963)

My God . . . it sure has been a long time.
I thought that it was all forgotten now. . . .
Twenty years, huh?
You look at me as though you are seeing back that far.
Well, put her there.
So you're still kicking around then . . .
And what a cold hand.

I suppose you can remember then?
—The bloody straits of Johore—
—The scorched hills of Singapore—.

And you can still hear then, I suppose? The echoes of destruction
    on destruction,
The song the cannon roars
Down from the naval station
At some hour of death?

You crick your neck pretending not to understand,
—Like all those little foxes who hide

Between the books, behind the keyholes.
You and I can meet now only in the past.
Is there still some secret there?

Line up under orders right away.
The black forest of bayonets all ranged in place;
Face the enemy: silently attack.
—One evening over, and you're
Dead.
Where did all that firmness go?
How did it die away,
That incarnation of innocence itself
—That you could follow clear to the horizon:
Glory for our country! Love for our fellow countrymen!
This morning too, when you brushed your teeth
In front of the faucet
There was red blood
Mixed in that toothpaste green
And you spat it out.
You respectfully tied your little necktie
And took your little body, warm still
From the end of sleep.
And had yourself packed
Into the streetcar,
Going reluctantly to work:
To get
Just a little something
You have to pull in
Just a little money
Today too
Day after tomorrow, too.

If there's anything to answer, *then* answer.
You, with the guts of a trembling little bride.
You, my wartime buddy.

No matter how much we all lose
How little have you gained.
Huh?
No matter what the liberation
Gained from any enemy
What reparations did you pay?
Eyes, or ears, or hands and feet

Of the unlucky ones who sacrificed:
What did you do for them?

Yeah, my wartime buddy,
Why don't you speak up, just a little?
If you look straight this way, at me,
What is it
That you cannot see?
Everything will be just fine for the shrewd ones
Has really come to mean
Safety at any price and
A backing into indolence
Does everything you get depend upon
Some endless ability for compromise?

Fighting in the sordid realms of profit, loss,
All of you who mimic life so well
Cry in a single voice that
It's a terrible time.

With some dreary bar girl to talk to,
Water turns to wine,
And you grumble that
Desire will not grow more reckless.

Hiding in the trunk of a great tree.
Your sentimental brotherhood
With fawning heads all stuck together
Sleep
And propagate
(within the proper bounds)
And fill your stomachs
And happy dream of heaven
(within the proper limits).

Don't you count up the storms that come?
Fate will size you up in a single flash of light:
It's been a long time coming,
This end of the world.

See you around,
Friend.
This is the first time,

Really,
For us to part
And I want
No idle kiss

Ta-ta.

Translated by J. Thomas Rimer

HASEGAWA RYŪSEI

Hasegawa Ryūsei (b. 1928) became a member of the left-leaning Rettō (Archipel-ago) Group when it was formed in 1952. After spending years as a day laborer, he went on to write poems full of intellectual tension suggesting barely suppressed violence. Hasegawa's first book of poetry, *Pavlov's Cranes (Paurou no tsuru)*, was published in 1957.

PAVLOV'S CRANES
(PAUROU NO TSURU, 1957)

Beating sturdy feathers,
sweeping down the power of flight,
all at once severing, bouncing
the mist in space,
their oars, wings, a single motion,
wading birds by the thousands, their vibrations
begin to echo in the depth of my ear.
Japanese cranes perhaps, demoiselle cranes, or storks,
hard to distinguish,
Pavlov's odd wing beats,
in night's, quiet cerebrum sky,
like the water split aside by pectoral fins
of gleaming fish in flight,
through my skin, continually,
echo, come closer.

From the marshes of despair
they've flown up and away before you knew it;
and betting the night
or heading toward daybreak,
Pavlov's mysterious cranes,
a hundred or so in each group,
have started their energetic move.

Each, its green beak tilted upward,
its weight placed
on the tail of the crane before it,
balancing power,
gliding through the air current,
forming a single line,
they fly.

The spearheading one,
it's a lump of resistance and exhaustion.
But one after another,
they replace the leader,
the leader, one after another,
in neat order, falls back to the end of the flock;
constructing a balance,
drawing a small half circle,
a line of space,
they fly splendidly.

Haven't you seen it:
it's always touched and led
at the surface of the reflex bow.
Night's cerebrum. It's above a sea of *occipital* cerebral cortex.
Betting nihilism
or heading toward daybreak,
Pavlov's cranes by the thousands,
a hundred or so in each group,
migrate as if mounting an assault.
All the hundred birds, beaks tilted upward,
weight placed on the tails before them,
strung together, in dead silence,
never cease.

A TALE OF THE SQUID-FALLING NIGHT
(IKA NO FURU YO NO MONOGATARI, 1960)

I

In one corner of the sea, only there
the waves are torn, glowing.
Where winter moonlight doesn't reach
squid drift.
They are firefly squid, which glow cold.
There where they swarm

the waves waver with innumerable fins,
the fins waver with innumerable lights.
One goes off on the surface of the water,
another turns on a lamp at the dark bottom of the sea
and floats up,
directly like a small meteorite.

The squadron of late-night long-range bombers that darted away
from the island cape
in the direction of Vladivostok
turned their noses, at a sharp angle,
far above the swarming drifting firefly squid, and soon
burst one dozing town after another, a series of dots.
For a while, a sweep
of night shower assaulted the whole area,
beating down splinters of flying fire.
In one corner of the sea, only there
the waves are torn, glowing.
Where the legs of rain don't reach
ghostly fires drift.
Cold phosphorescences
illuminate countless fins.

II

Through the dark,
someone comes,
running along the beach.
Who is it, coming?
The swish-swish of the sand kicked aside
comes closer, closer.
On the boulder, a giant, a cuttlefish, having crawled
on to it, doesn't try to move his body.
Innumerable small dolphins
appear and disappear among the waves,
playing the flute *whew, whew.*
The giant, the cuttlefish lies under his heavy overcoat,
about to breathe his last breath.
His suckers are all opened wide
to the night's briny wind.
He has vomited raw-smelling water out of his coal black jaw.
Through the dark, swish-swishing the sand aside,
surely, a man
comes, running.

Now, he's very close.
he's right there.

III

Under a faint lamp,
until a while ago, were a man and a woman.
On the floor, the oyster shells the man was cracking with a blade
were cruelly scattered,
blood of his fingers clinging to them.

How much time had passed:
the lamp had run out of oil, it was
totally dark there.
On the floor
the entrails the woman grabbed out of squid's bellies she tore
began to emit phosphorescence and burn.
From the entrails piled up
a funnel tube squeezes out,
its tip, burning.

ISHIGAKI RIN

Ishigaki Rin (1920–2004) was born in Akasaka, in downtown Tokyo. From 1934 to 1975, she worked as a bank clerk and so became known as the "bank clerk poet." Her first book of poetry, *In Front of Me the Pot, the Pan, and the Burning Flame* (*Watakushi no mae ni aru nabe to okama to moeru hi to*) was published in 1959, and the second of her four collections, *Nameplates Etc.* (*Hyōsatsu nado*), was published in 1968. The translations are by Janine Beichman.

ROOF (YANE, 1959)

Japanese houses have low roofs
The poorer the family the lower the roof

The roof's lowness
presses me down

Where does the heaviness come from?
I take a few steps back to look:
it's not the blue of the sky
that's above the house
it's a thickness the color of blood

something that keeps me from going forward
something that locks me in the narrowness of this dwelling
and consumes my power

My invalid father lives on top of the roof
my stepmother lives up there with him
my siblings live up there too

When the wind blows I hear the crackling of
that tin roof
so flimsy it might fly away
the barely forty square yards of it
and riding on top I see
a daikon radish
and a bag of rice
and the bed's warmth too

Carry me! says this roof
under whose weight
I, a woman, feel my spring darken

Far off in the distance the sun goes down

SHIJIMI CLAMS (SHIJIMI, 1968)

woke up in the dead of night—
in a corner of the kitchen
the little clams I'd bought that evening
were alive, mouths open—

"At dawn
I'll gobble you up
each and every one"

let out a cackle
like an evil old witch
after that couldn't help it had to
sleep all night with mouth half-open

LIFE (KURASHI, 1968)

To live we must eat—
rice
veggies
meat
air

light
water
our parents
sisters and brothers
teachers
money and hearts too
without all that eating I'd never have lived this long—
I pat my full stomach
wipe my lips
the kitchen's littered
with carrot tops
chicken bones
Daddy's intestines
At forty's twilight
for the first time my eyes overflow with a wild beast's tears

ISHIHARA YOSHIRŌ

Arrested by the Soviet army soon after Japan's defeat, Ishihara Yoshirō (1915–1977) was detained in Siberian concentration camps until Josef Stalin's death in 1953. In 1954 Ishihara caught the attention of the poetic world with the poem "Night's Invitation" (Yoru no shōtai) as a model of "pure poetry," which was ironic because much of his poetry reflects his "extreme experiences." Ishihara's first book of poetry, *Sancho Panza's Homecoming* (*Sancho Pansa no kikyō*), was published in 1963.

NIGHT'S INVITATION
(YORU NO SHŌTAI, 1954)

Outside the window, a pistol shot,
and curtain instantly
set on fire
and so comes the awaited hour:
night, like a regiment,
framed with cellophane—
France,
make peace with Spain,
lions, each of you,
lick your tail.
I suddenly become tolerant,
hold hands
with a person who's ceased to be anyone,
and enclose between our enclosing hands

an accommodating adult's hour.
Oh sure, in the zoo
there's got to be an elephant,
next to it,
there's got to be another elephant.
That the hour that can't but come
comes,
what a splendid thing.
Allow the severed flowers on the table, too,
the act of pollination.
Now how much time
remains
unresurrected?
The night is rolled back,
the chair shaken,
the card flag pulled down,
the crayon melts in the hand,
and the morning comes to make a promise.

ESCAPE (DASSŌ, 1958)

—in a penal colony in Zabaikal
That moment   there was a gunshot,
sunflowers turned
to look at us.
In the brazen silence
as under a blunt instrument swung up
the world deepened
too abruptly.
Those who saw it, say, I saw it.
Where we crouched,
unmistakably from its midst,
footprints like fire ran south
and where they ran out of strength
already stood a man.
Sandy ground of August of Zabaikal
like a vivid regret.
Nostalgia stumbling forward on toes
was mowed down as if ambushed
and the silence was like
a monastery you abruptly faced.
For a second we stood up halfway,
for a second we looked down.
Was what was shot down a Ukrainian dream

or Caucasian gamble?
The muzzle already turned down
as if it was all just that
he lifted his arm
and checked the time.
The midday of merchants
watching a donkey giving still birth.
With the palms that failed to grasp sand and ants
we covered our mouths
with a terrible clatter.
Ask obviously: Is the back of the hand
there to be stepped on?
A black heel mercilessly
now steps on it and leaves.
Obey.
We strike down our anger
as we do a mottled dog.
We now understand
and we recognize.
We flatly obey
before the muzzle still dangling
a hot tongue after a fierce movement.
Beyond the barren bravery
freshly harvested,
after that second, now remote:
Ukraine,
Caucasus.
Into the space between the boots blocking weightily
we throw a shining innocent gold coin
and now
lock our elbows
like a chain of obedience
that never ends.[1]

KATAGIRI YUZURU

While he was a young man, Katagiri Yuzuru (b. 1931) studied at San Francisco State College in 1959/1960. The poetry that he wrote when he returned home to the volatile political situation in Japan was much more political than his later

---

1. During a march, Russian prisoners often were required to form a line of five men, arms interlocked, to prevent escape.

work. The following poems reveal the Japanese people's uneasiness over the renewal of the United States–Japan Security Treaty and, later, the Vietnam War. The poems were written in English.

CHRISTMAS, 1960, JAPAN (1961)

Oh, unto us a child is born
Unto us a son is given who has no thumbs
conceived by the lightning at Hiroshima
when his mother had all her hair off
Behold the ape of god
denied by
those American nuclear specialists at the A, B, C.
One difference between apes and men
is the use of the thumbs.

WHY SECURITY TREATY? (1961)

I live near an air base
where the noise of jet planes shakes
windowpanes of classrooms
and the children's scores in standard tests
are lower than in other school districts
and scared cows and hens give no milk and no eggs
but there is no escape
Japan is a small country
with poor natural resources
and we don't see why
Japan is in danger of being conquered
by communist countries.

I am an Americanized Japanese
who hears Armed Forces Radio Service
which says all men and women are created equal
as the Fourth of July is coming near
and we do not see the reason
why we must be the crew of an aircraft carrier
of another country which flies U2s
and I live near an airbase
that might be another Hiroshima
and Japan is a small country
where mountains are tilled to the tops
which seem beautiful to American eyes
who want to keep Japan as a museum

of old strange cultures
of polite people.

I like American people
they are kind and they gave us chocolate
I like American ways of living
they are so comfortable
I like American education in which
boys and girls work and play together and are happy
I wanted Japan to be a state of the United States
    of America
just after the war
Now I am glad that Japan is not a state of the
    United States of America
where all young men are taken to be soldiers
and many were killed in Korea without knowing
    why
where citizens are deceived into believing
their safety in a nuclear air raid if they hide
quickly.

I am a taxpayer who does not want
to keep such a big army navy air force
as a result of the Security Treaty
in this age of nuclear weapons
I am a teacher of English
who teaches Gettysburg Address
to the third-year students of a high school who are
scared by the fear of being taken as
    soldiers
and sent to another country to defend another
    country
as Japan is involved automatically in a possible
    limited war
as a result of the Security Treaty.

I am wondering why the government
elected by kind people of America
for the kind people of America, of the kind people
    of America
which issues 25-cent stamps of Abraham Lincoln
has been helping authoritarian governments
in Korea and Turkey and in Japan
the government of Kishi Brothers & Company

for Kishi Brothers & Company, by Kishi Brothers
    & Company.
Whenever Kishi went to America and said
Japan and America were good friends
some attempts were made by the Japanese government
to return to the old educational system
to return to the old national religion
to return to the old family system
to return to the old police state
to return to the old militarism
the explosion of which was Pearl Harbor
done by Tōjō and Kishi.

TURN BACK THE CLOCK (1961)

Turn Back the Clock has come to you through the worldwide
facilities of the United States Armed Forces Radio and
Television Service.

Well, Hayato, let's
turn back the clock
to the good old days
when there was no memory of Pearl Harbor
when there was no memory of Hiroshima
when Japan had the strongest army and navy in
the world
when the Japanese believed in spirits and ghosts
and the Emperor as God
when the young men and women got married as assigned
    by their parents and grandparents when the wife carrying
    a baby on her back and
packages in her hands
walked after the husband.

Turn back the clock
says the minister of education
to the good old days of the Ministry of Education
when the bureaucrats controlled every corner of
every classroom
when the purpose of education was
to fit the boys for soldiers
and prepare the girls not to cry
for their husbands killed in battlefields
crying *banzai* for the emperor.

OK, let's
turn back the clock
to the good old days of Imperial Japan
and throw away every reform
imposed on Japan during the Occupation
and make the people feel once again
the superiority of Japan all over the world
and let them have the pride of being servants of
the emperor
and the pride of being servants to the U.S.
and let us produce young patriots
glad to die
and glad to kill
another Asanuma
crying *banzai* for the emperor
and *banzai* for free nations of the West.

Turn back the clock
to the good old days
when Japan and Germany and Italy formed
an anti-Communism league
and was the threat to the peace of the world.
Those things were decided
when Hayato Ikeda and Assistant Secretary of
    State Robertson met
in October 1953.

NAGASE KIYOKO

Nagase Kiyoko (1906–1995) published her first book of poems, *Grendel's Mother* (*Grendel no haha*), in 1930. She took up farming after World War II and, at age eighty-one, published *You Who Come at Daybreak* (*Akegata ni kuru hito yo*).

THE DAUGHTER OF A CONSTELLATION
(SEIZA NO MUSUME, 1946)

The loves of people who press close
late at night
make up the parts of my flesh and body.
The soul flows through them
and I feel bound down
like the mythical daughter of giant heaven and space
who's nailed to heaven with rivets of stars.

The stars at night
are minerals polished since primordial times
by the eyes turned on them from earth pregnant with
   countless fates.
Having attracted joys and sorrows
from the north, from the south,
they're laden with heavy expectations.

Left by myself,
I am someone who flies easily,
But stabbed by those stars,
I feel like a camellia pregnant with numerous buds.

Floating up in me through the dark night,
its intensity about to bloom, filled with honey, pains me.

Heaviness of the blood congestion of the stars!
Which gravity shall I submit myself to?
Where am I reeling toward?
When night condenses second by second,
will not the mythical daughter of heaven
try to sever the silver-frilled ropes between stars
taut for hundreds of millions of years
and to will to hang from space
intently as a blue spider—
cleaving her cold self
from many sickly loving kindnesses,
trusting only gravity
like a weight downward! Downward!

LIGHTING A LAMP AT NIGHT
(YORU NI HI TOMOSHI, 1948)

Just as the silkworm makes her cocoon,
so I make my own night;
weave the night and make a room.
Under a deep violet starry sky,
lighting a lamp for me alone,
I make a small oval world.

The day exists for everyone.
During that time I work, forgetting everything.
At night everyone recedes into the distance.
All visible things become invisible

and for my willful self,
gently, thoughtfully, disappear into the dark.

Within the lonely world for me alone
I gleam as moss and fireflies do.
Hoping to live a good life,
deepening my longing for things beautiful,
I knit several quiet lines
with fingers soiled during the day.

That which filters through my daytime self filled
    with painful heat
and turns it into a transparent drop,
a drop of night world:
a small lonely world where I light my lamp,
an oval world that exists for memory and prayer,
a quiet path between today and tomorrow that I take alone.

SHIRAISHI KAZUKO

Born in Vancouver, Shiraishi Kazuko (b. 1931) was influenced by the African
American jazz musicians who frequently visited postwar Japan. She published
her first book of poetry when she was twenty-one. Her *Let Those Who Emerge*
(*Arawareru monotachi o shite*, 1996) won both the Yomiuri Literary Prize and
the Takami Jun Prize. Shiraishi is one of the few prominent poets who reads po-
ems to the accompaniment of jazz.

THE PHALLUS (DANKON, 1965)

For Sumiko's birthday

God *is*   even if He is not.
Also He is humorous enough
to resemble a certain kind of human.

This time
with a gigantic phallus over
the horizon of my dream
He came on a picnic.
Incidentally
I regret
I gave nothing to Sumiko on her birthday.
I'd at least   like to send

the seeds of the phallus   God brought
into that thin   tiny   lovely voice of
Sumiko   on the line's other side.
Forgive me   Sumiko
for the phallus   has grown larger day by day
until now   growing   in the middle of cosmos
it wouldn't move like a bus that has broken down.
And so
when you want to see
a star-sprinkled beautiful night sky or
some other man
rushing down the highway   with a hot woman
you really must
lean out of the bus window
to take a good peek.
The phallus
begins to stir and if it's near the cosmos
it's good to look at. At such a time
Sumiko
starry sky's   lighting loneliness
midday's   funny cold
affect your innards entirely
and as they say   what's visible you see   and no one
can help becoming insane.
The phallus has neither name nor personality
nor   a date so that
it's only when someone   passes by
carrying it like a festival shrine
that from the racket   sometimes
you know somehow   where it lives.
In that   hubbub
the primeval riots and voids of
oaths and curses of the seeds not yet controlled by God
reach your ear   on occasion.

The so-called God is   prone to be absent.
Instead   He leaves only debt and phallus behind
to go off somewhere   or so it seems.
Now
the phallus left behind   by God
walks   toward you.
It is   young and gay
and so   full of such artless confidence
it somehow   resembles the shadow of an astute smile.

The phallus   may seem to grow in countless numbers
and in countless numbers   walk toward you
but in fact it's singular   and walks alone toward you.
From whatever horizon you see it
it's uniformly devoid of face and word—
that's the kind of thing   Sumiko
I'd like to give you on your birthday.
I would cover your existence   wholly with it and then
to you   your own self would become invisible
and at times
you   would become   the phallus the will itself
and wander   endlessly
until I might hold you in my nebulous embrace.

SŌ SAKON

Sō Sakon (1919–2006) was born in Tobata City in Kyushu, and he graduated from the University of Tokyo in 1945, majoring in philosophy. His poetry collection *Mother Burning* (*Moeru haha*), published in 1967, is regarded as one of the landmarks of postwar poetry. Sō wrote these poems after the death of his mother in an incendiary raid in 1945 to help alleviate his subsequent burden of guilt.

RUNNING (HASSHITERU, 1967)

Running
Through the sea of fire a road of fire
Stumbling like a pier is
Running
On the road of fire
Like a red nail
I am running
Running
Because the flames on the straight road are
Running I am running
Because I can't stop running I am running
Because I am
Running I can't stop running
I'm running
Because I can't stand still I'm running
Beneath my running feet
Before my running feet
Scorching
Burning

Those running are running
Running running
Overtaking those running
Darting between those running
Those running are running
Running
Those

Not running
Are not
Those not running
Are not running
Those running
Run

Run
Those Running
Are not running
Are not
Those who
Ran

Are not running
Are not
Those who

Are not

Mother!

Is not

Mother is not
Running ran running
Mother is not

Mother!

Running
Me

Mother!

Running

I
Am running
I cannot
Not run

Slippery slippery
Slippery
The thing that
Slipped through slithered down slid away
That was
That was
That hot thing that
Slipped through slipping through
Slithered down slithering dorm
Slid away sliding away
It was greasy so greasy so so greasy
Was that
My mother's hand in my own?
My hand in my mother's?

Running

Who
Is it?
Who is it in whose hand?

Running
Looking back
Running
Looking back
Running
Tottering
Hopping on a red hot plate
Hopping looking back at what's behind

    Mother!
    You
    Have collapsed flat on your back
    On the road of fire
    Raising up
    Your face like a summer orange
    Your right arm aloft
    Like the withered branch of a summer-orange tree
    Thrusting out your right hand

Stretching out your right hand
Out toward me

Me
I am hopping on a red-hot plate
A single red nail hopping
Hopping but already
Running
Hopping running
Running hopping

On the road of fire

Mother!
You
flat on your back
Like a summer-orange your face
Burning
Like the withered branch of a summer-orange tree
    your right hand
Burning
Now
Burning

The road of fire

Running
Can't stop running
Hopping running hopping
Beneath my running feet
Before my running feet
Scorching
Burning
Those running are running
Running hopping
Darting between those running
Overtaking those running
Runners are running
Running
Mother!
Running
Mother!

Road burning
Mother!

Translated by Leith Morton

TAKAMURA KŌTARŌ

Takamura Kōtarō (1883–1956) had a long career as a poet, and a number of his best-known and admired works are included in volume 1 of this anthology. After the war, Takamura often looked back at his earlier prowar attitudes and regretted his early enthusiasm for the Pacific War.

END OF THE WAR (SHŪSEN, 1947)

With my studio completely, cleanly, burned up,
I came to Hanamaki, Ōshū.
There, I heard that broadcast.
Sitting upright, I was trembling.
Japan was finally stripped bare,
the people's heart fell, down to the bottom.
Saved from starvation by the Occupation forces,
they were barely exempt from extinction.
Then, the emperor stepped forward
and explained that he was not a living god.
As days passed,
the beam was taken out of my eyes,
and before I knew it, the sixty years' burden was gone.
Grandfather, father, and mother
returned again to their seats in distant Nirvana,
and I heaved a deep sigh.
After a mysterious deliverance
there's only love as a human being.
The celadon of a clear sky after rain
is fragrant in my capacious heart
and now, serene with nothing left,
I enjoy fully the beauty of the desolate.

MY POETRY (ORE NO SHI, 1949)

My poetry doesn't belong to Western poesy.
The two circles are tangent
but in the end never perfectly merge.
I passionately love the world of Western poesy,

but can't deny that my poetry stands on different sources.
The Athenian sky and the underground fountain of Christianity
gave birth to the language and thought patterns of Western poesy.
It is endlessly beautiful and strong and penetrates my insides,
but its physiology of powdered food, dairy products, and *entrecôte*
keeps at arm's length the necessities of my Japanese language.
My poetry comes out of my organs and intestines.
Born at the tip of the Far East, raised on grain food,
and nurtured on yeast, soybeans, and fish,
this soul has a faint fragrance of the remote Gandhara scented in it,
but has been enlightened more by the yellow dust culture of the vast
    continent,
while bathing, as it has, in the purling stream of Japanese classics,
and now, abruptly, marvels at atomic power.
My poetry doesn't exist outside my being,
and my being is no more than a sculptor in the Far East.
To me, the universe is the source of all structures,
poetry their *contrepoint.*
Western poesy is my dear neighbor,
but my poetry moves in a different orbit.

TAKARABE TORIKO

Born in Manchuria, Takarabe Toriko (b. 1933), along with her family, became
part of the large exodus of Japanese refugees after Japan's defeat in 1945. Before
reaching Japan, she lost her father and sister, an experience that haunts her po-
ems. Takarabe published her first book of poetry, *When I Was a Child* (*Watashi
ga kodomo datta koro*), in 1965.

FROZEN (KŌRITSUITE, 1965)

The winter has swallowed all.
The dead have no pain, a Russian writer said.
What color the beeches in the garden were,
how they had no scent and dried up,
I didn't know.

Enclosed by frost and north wind,
the great past sinks into the stove.
The voice calling back
is about to freeze and decorate the winter.
Reindeer disappear.

In my dreams dreams have frozen solid.
Like a beast I scratch with my nails,
scratch both the inside and outside of the door.
Bark, bark, break the door!
The fierce noises of hooves never stop.

In the closed room wood burns.
While wolves howl,
the fire turns into a clutch of ashes,
my hair turns gray,
and is in no time shut in in a dream.

The Sungari[2] stops moving.
The earth begins to freeze.
Eyelashes solidify, the sun appears to list.
A small corpse freezes.
The terrible *moroz*[3] has arrived!

ABOUT FORMS (KATACHI NI TSUITE, 1984)

On June 14 [1972], JAL's DC-8 carrying 86 passengers crashed in Jaitpur, a village 27 kilometers southeast of New Delhi. Bodies and broken parts of the aircraft were scattered widely in the farmland on the bank of the Jumna River, which flows at the edge of the village. Grotesquely contorted bodies, seats still with humans tied to them, a white girl holding a doll, flames. Ambulances rushed to the scene through dust on the riverbed which was so dry that the sand buried the cars up to the hubcaps. . . . Family members of the passengers left for the crash site on JAL's special plane at 10 a.m, on the 15th, which is expected to arrive in New Delhi at midnight. (Excerpted from a newspaper report)[4]

A corner of an old park by the hotel had a yogi.
A sandstorm had made the lotuses in the mud bloom;
his bones and skin
coiled around his lukewarm innards and rigid meditation.
He wouldn't touch salt

---

2. Sungari is the Manchurian name of the Songhuajiang, a tributary of the Heilongiang, or Amur River.

3. Russian for "frost," *moroz* refers to the deadly cold that characterizes the Russian or Siberian winter.

4. The aircraft made a landing error in a sandstorm. Among the passengers was Takarabe's brother Tetsurō, who was on his way to Tehran to take up a business post. He was thirty-six years old.—Trans.

and seemed to wait single-mindedly for the colors to turn limpid.
A human body should go on drying up like that, I thought.
Facing a *jamun* tree,[5]
it should go on drying up,
without reading written words,
without picking up meanings,
simply hoping not to return to being human.

But it's different in Maulana Azat.
Even a yogi's shadow acquires a raw smell.
Bouquets of *pure* lotus flowers,
ominous bats,
unfortunate flesh (though there is no such thing),
words become stereotypical,
things are swiftly carried from form to protyle.
But the philosophy
that protyle is plastic
earns me neither bread nor flower petals.

Maulana Azat abounds with *unfortunate* deaths.
An *ominous* stench strikes me down.
The voice *Don't touch* forces me back to being human;
    I walk without falling
and read the wooden plaques on the coffins.

Male? In charred state
Female: with false teeth, charred
Small man: only half?
Male about 30 years old with fragment of striped shirt
Male: with remnant of dark hair; upper implant
Female: blonde, ring with JCS
Male: fat body, with capped teeth
White female: golden necklace
Male: about 180 centimeters tall, no head
Male: 175 centimeters, Hitsujiya jacket
Male? extremely charred.

They certainly seem to convey forms.
What form,
I find myself thinking.

---

5. Indigenous to India, the *jamun* has a lovely purple-black fruit about the size of a large berry, which ripens around April or May.

I try to touch you with white gloves,
try to pull up the body that ought to be there, and I can't touch you.
Souls aren't written on wooden plaques, they say,
by color, weight, age, male, Oriental. . . .
The question of soul. . . .
Abruptly there's a voice near my brow:
"Do you believe in something formless?" it says.
"No, never.
      It would be odd for a soul not to have a form."

Trees and cows that pass before my eyes wear nimbuses.
Soul and form, violently collapsed,
are seeping into the red sand.
I was *sad* and wouldn't accept anything,
but I could have been *sad* and accepted everything.
Red mud smeared on his body,
a yogi stands on his head and his form grows transparent.
Letting a mantra rise like steam,
trying single-mindedly to rot
in total red.

TAMURA RYŪICHI

A founding member of the Arechi (Wasteland) Group, Tamura Ryūichi (1923–1998) had his first book of poems, 400 *Days and Nights* (*Yonsen no hi to yoru*), published in 1956. His masculine, declarative poems represent one wing of "postwar poetry," and in 1968 Tamura was chosen as the first poet in Shichōsha's paperback series of modern poetry.

4000 DAYS AND NIGHTS
(YONSEN NO HI TO YORU, 1954)

For a single poem to be born,
we must kill
we must kill many things
we shoot dead, assassinate, and poison the many we love

Behold,
just because we wanted the trembling tongue of a single bird
from the sky of 4000 days and nights,
we shot dead
the silences of 4000 nights and the back lights of 4000 days

Listen,
just because we needed the tear of a single starving child
from every raining city, blast furnace,
midday wharf, and coal mine,
we assassinated
loves of 4000 days and pities of 4000 nights

Remember,
just because we wanted the terror of a single stray dog
that sees what our eyes can't see,
hears what our ears can't hear,
we poisoned to death
imaginations of 4000 nights and cold memories of 4000 days

To give birth to a single poem,
we must kill the ones we care for,
it is the only way we can revive the dead,
and we must choose that path

1940S: SUMMER
(1940 NENDAI · NATSU, 1954)

The world at noon
in this painful brightness all that's self-evident about
    people and matters
has left us wounded!
Tongue lolling out like a dog
      "194—
      on the battle front of ferocious sun and violet of fire
      I fell for no reason, but
      my illusion still lives"
      "I'm still alive.
      It's my experience that died"
      "My room is shut in, but
      you cannot deny
      the chair of my memory
      and the window of my illusion"
We scratch this earth with our nails,
beads of sweat on our foreheads like gleams of stars.
We bury our dead experiences.
We dream of a resurrection of our wounded illusions.

Her eyes are filled with the tragic irony of someone
    who has watched only collapses and downfalls.

Her ears hear only the screams of those shipwrecked
   way in the offing.
Her civilization is black, the color that doesn't
   exist in modern painting.
Her gentle lust makes the earth extremely unstable.
Her question provokes a civil war and storms in every soul.
Compared with her illusions all hopes are fleeting.
Her criticism awakes a desert in a city, dead experiences
   in a human, a black space in the world, and
that scar of the future in us!

I will not be wounded any more than this because
to be wounded, for that alone, I've existed.
I will no longer fall because
ruination, that's my only theme.

Thunderstorm! Our eternal summer is crushed with her teeth.

TANIKAWA SHUNTARŌ

Tanikawa Shuntarō's (b. 1931) first book of poetry, *Two Billion Light Years of Solitude* (*Nijū-oku kōnen no kodoku*), was published in 1952. Since then, he has remained one of Japan's most popular and prolific poets, and his poems also are among those most often translated into English. Tanikawa's influence and popularity are enhanced by his ability to engage poetry fans in public sessions.

GROWTH (SEICHŌ, 1952)

Three years old:
I had no past.

Five years old:
My past went as far as yesterday.

Seven years old:
My past went as far as topknots.

Eleven years old:
My past went as far as dinosaurs.

Fourteen years old:
My past was as textbooks said it was.

Sixteen years old:
I stared at the infinity of my past frightened.

Eighteen years old:
I did not know what time was.

DRIZZLE (KIRISAME, 1952)

The Negro singer, for an encore,
sang a Negro spiritual.
(I'm concerned that the MC spoke coldly)

The Negro composer, in the stage light,
introduced himself.
(I'm worried to death about the amount of applause)

Los Angeles, California, has beautiful starry summer nights,
I'm told, but tonight, in Tokyo, a rain like fine mist continues
to fall quietly.

TOMIOKA TAEKO

In 1957, while Tomioka Taeko (b. 1935) was a college student, her first book of poetry, *Courtesy in Return* (*Henrei*), was published. Although she attracted admirers with her sophisticated chattiness, she stopped writing poetry and moved into other genres about the time a collection of her complete poems appeared, in 1973. Since then, Tomioka has written short stories, novels, and plays and, in the 1980s, became established as an important feminist critic.

BETWEEN — (1957)

There are two sorrows to be proud of

After slamming the door of the room behind me
After slamming the door
Of the entrance of the house behind me
And out on the street visibility zero because of the rain
    of the rainy season
When the day begins
What will I do
What am I going to do
To neither
Am I friend or enemy

Who can I ask
This concrete question
I hate war
And am no pacifist
The effort just to keep my eyes open
The sorrow that I can make only that effort

There are two sorrows to be proud of

I am with you
I don't understand you
Therefore I understand that you are
Therefore I understand that I am
The sorrow that I do not understand you
The sorrow that you are what you are

STILL LIFE (SEIBUTSU, 1957)

Your story is finished.
By the way, today,
what did you have for a snack?
Yesterday your mother said,
I wish I was dead.
You took her hand,
went out, walked around,
viewed a river the color of sand,
viewed a landscape with a river in it.
They call the willow the tree of tears in France,
said Bonnard's woman once.
Yesterday you said,
Mom, when did you give birth to me?
Your mother said,
I never gave birth to any living thing.

YOSHIOKA MINORU

In 1955 Yoshioka Minoru (1919–1990) published *Still Life* (*Seibutsu*), which marked another departure for Japan's postwar poetry. This was the advent of a body of poetry that, to use the words with which Yoshioka described the performances of Hijikata Tatsumi, the founder of the avant-garde dance form of Butoh, may be characterized as "grotesque and elegant, obscene and noble, comic and solemn."

STILL LIFE (SEIBUTSU, 1955)

Within the hard surface of night's bowl
Intensifying their bright colors
The autumn fruits
Apples, pears, grapes, and so forth
Each as they pile
Upon another
Goes close to sleep
To one theme
To spacious music
Each core, reaching its own heart
Reposes
Around it circles
The time of rich putrefaction
Now before the teeth of the dead
The fruits and their kind
Which unlike stones do not strike
Add to their weight
And in the deep bowl
Behind this semblance of night
On occasion
Hugely tilt

THE PAST (KAKO, 1955)

The man first hangs the apron from this thin neck
He lacks the past as well as the will
He begins to walk, holding a sharp knife at his side
A line of ants rushes to a corner of his wide-opened eyes
Each time light from the sides of his knife stirs the dust on the floor
Whatever is going to be cooked
Even if it's a toilet
It will perhaps shriek
Will instantly spurt blood from the window to the sun
What is quietly waiting for him now
What gives him the past that he lacks
A sting ray lies motionless on the board
Its mottled back, large and slippery
Its tail seems to hang into the basement
Beyond it, only the rows of roofs in the winter rain
The man quickly rolls the sleeves of his apron
And thrusts the knife in the ray's raw belly
No resistance

In slaughter not to get any response
Not to get one's hands soiled is terrible
But the man bears down little by little and tears apart
    the membranous space
The dark depth where nothing is spewed out
The stars that sometimes appear and fade
Work done, the man unhooks his hat from the wall
And goes out the door
The part which had lain hidden under the hat
The spot where the hook is, which had been
    protected from the terror
From there the blood with time's adequate weight
    and roundness deliberately begins to flow

POETRY IN TRADITIONAL FORMS

After the end of the Pacific War in 1945, when writers were free to write as they chose, new experiments became possible, in both form and content.

BABA AKIKO

Throughout her long career, Baba Akiko (b. 1928) claimed that her principal interests were *tanka* (thirty-one-syllable poem), the history of woman poets in Japan, and the medieval nō theater. In addition to her accomplishments as a tanka poet, Baba has written about both classical and modern women poets and had her contemporary nō dramas performed at the National Theater and elsewhere. The translations are by Hatsue Kawamura and Jane Reichhold.

within me	*waga uchi no*
a monster also stands	*igyō mo tachite*
and walks along	*ayumu nare*
in autumn our words	*aki wa kotoba mo*
sound like a stone ax	*sekifu no hibiki*
called frustration	*zasetsu to wa*
it is generally painful	*ōku kurushiki*
man's way of course	*otoko michi*
I can see my father fishing	*chichi miete chisaki*
for a very small fish	*uo tsurite ire*
in the evening	*yūgure wa*
as sprightly as silver	*ikitaru gin no*
a fish jumps up	*uo agari*
the desire to wander alone	*ryūri no omoi*
shines for a moment	*setsuna kagayaku*
coming from afar	*ginkan no*
from another galaxy	*kanata yori kishi*
some souls	*tamashii no*
are faintly white	*honoka ni shiroki*
dogwood flowers	*yamabōshi no hana*
being alone is fine	*hitori ga ii*
I am fine being alone	*hitori ga ii to*
the white magnolia tree	*hakuren wa*
tosses into the sky	*hana nisanbyaku*
several hundred blossoms	*sora ni fuki agu*

GOTŌ MIYOKO

Readers of Gotō Miyoko's (1898–1978) tanka have always been impressed with her use of the vernacular language, a remarkable accomplishment within the confines of a venerable tradition. Gotō uses this language to convey a deep personal involvement in the creation of her poems. Many of them are autobiographical and describe four generations of women in her family. The translations are by Reiko Tsukimura.

> Whatever she picks up
> seems dangerous to me
> I snatch it
> from my child's hands:
> regret pierces me.

abunai mono bakari mochitagaru ko no te kara tsugitsugi ni mono o toriagete futto sabishi

Humiliation	*kutsujoku wa*
first experienced,	*nigaku tsumetaku*
cold, bitter,	*ui no aji*
yet refreshing,	*atarashiku sae*
permeates my body.	*mi ni shimiwataru*
In the falling	*furikiyuru*
and melting snow	*yuki ni kioite*
fire continues	*moesakari*
to burn in me, now blazing,	*moeiburitsutsu*
now smoldering.	*taenu hono'o ari*
When my heart	*oiseji to*
rebels and refuses	*aragau kokoro*
to grow old,	*aru toki wa*
I push my children away	*kora tōzakete*
and sharpen my nails.	*ware no tsume togu*
Potatoes	*tsuchi ni marobu*
lie on the ground nodding	*jagaimo tagai ni*
to each other,	*unazuki au*
the large ones silent	*ooki wa modashi*
the small speaking aloud.	*chiisaki wa koe shite*

KANEKO TŌTA

Although Kaneko Tōta (b. 1919) began writing poetry along with his father, Kaneko Mitsuharu, Tōta's professional career as a *haiku* (seventeen-syllable poem) poet started after the war, when he could use his war experiences. Reflecting his long-standing interest in diction and other formal aspects of haiku composition, Tōta has also written about methods of composing haiku.

How lovely their mouths,
All of them: a late summer
Jazz combo.

Dore mo kuchi
utsukushi banka no
jazu ichidan

Translated by Donald Keene

How strong they are, the young men,
Even on a day when onions
Rot on the dry beach.

Tsuyoshi seinen
hikata ni tamanegi
kusaru hi mo

Translated by Donald Keene

High school boys
are talking of God, while the snow
keeps piling up on the ricks.

Chūgakusei
kami katari ori
yuki tsumu wara

Translated by Makoto Ueda

The graveyard is burned, too:
cicadas, like pieces of flesh,
on the trees.

Bochi mo yakeato
semi nikuhen no
goto kigi ni

Translated by Makoto Ueda

Like an arm overstretched
and tired, reddish brown smoke
rising from a steel mill.

Te ga nagaku
darushi akachaketa
seikōen

Translated by Makoto Ueda

KATSURA NOBUKO

Married to a haiku poet who was killed in the war, Katsura Nobuko (1914–2004) was able to save her own manuscripts when her Osaka home was firebombed in 1945. These were published four years later. In all, Katsura produced nine volumes of poetry and won important national awards. She also worked as an editor for haiku magazines and did much to support the work of woman haiku poets in postwar Japan. The translations are by Janine Beichman.

a married woman	*hitozuma ni*
and her green peas	*endō yawarakaku*
simmered soft	*nienu*

I bolt the door	*kannuki o*
and glance behind	*kakete mikaeru*
the insects' darkness	*mushi no yami*

one of the lights	*tomoshibi no*
is my house	*hitotsu wa waga ya*
geese fly overhead	*kari wataru*

beneath	*shuntō no*
the spring lantern suddenly	*moto gakuzen to*
I realize I'm alone	*kodoku naru*

I undress	*kinu o nugishi*
beyond the darkness	*yami no anata ni*
iris flowers	*ayame saku*

KONDŌ YOSHIMI

Kondō Yoshimi (b. 1913) was born in Korea and lived in Hiroshima during the war, although he was out of the city when the atomic bomb was dropped. He has a wide range of interests, as his tanka reveal. The poems about the war years were not published until after 1945. The translations are by Makoto Ueda.

a spoon	*makurabe no*
near my pillow	*saji ni muragari*
swarms with ants	*itarikeru*
I kill them all	*yonaka no ari o*
in the middle of the night	*ware wa koroseri*

having grown up	*shūkyō o*
in a culture devoid	*kyōyō to senu*
of religion	*yo ni sodachi*
inspired by what faith	*tatakai yukeba*
am I to fight this war?	*nani shinjikemu*

scissors
cut through my bloodstained
military uniform
with a snipping sound
that is repeated a while

chi no tsukishi
ware no gun'i o
sakinagara
hasami wa shibashi
oto o tatetsutsu

with headlights on
a line of bulldozers
bound for home
comes out of a building site
in the lowering blizzard

hi tomoshite
kaeru haidoki
tsuranarite
fubuki to narishi
sagyōba o izu

casting shadows
on the white riverbed
heavy bombers descend
each looking as though
not a soul were on board

ishi shiroki
kawara ni kage shi
orite yuku
jūbakuki mina
hito aranu goto

MAEKAWA SAMIO

From a wealthy family in Nara, Japan's ancient capital before Kyoto, Maekawa Samio (1903–1990) oversaw his family's interests but never worked. Some of his wartime poetry verged on propaganda, and, buffeted by criticism from other writers and from the collapse of his family's fortunes in the early postwar years, Maekawa stopped writing until 1953, when he again began to compose tanka, working steadily until his death several decades later. His mature work shows occasional humor and great skill in creating fresh and striking images.

Almost without warning,
the belly of the sky grew
cold and now at times
the silhouette of a mournful
bird sweeps over me

itsushika ni
ten no hara hiete
oriori wa
ware ni kanashiki
torikage wataru

Translated by Janine Beichman

if only
I could clean out the inside
of my body
and stuff it with those
green leaves of daffodils!

mune no uchi
ichido kara ni shite
ano aoki
suisen no ha o
tsumekomite mitashi

Translated by Makoto Ueda

monumental	*hijōnaru*
idiot that I am	*hakuchi no boku wa*
I've sent an umbrella	*jitenshaya ni*
to a bicycle shop	*kōmorigasa o*
for repairs	*shūzen ni yaru*

Translated by Makoto Ueda

the day I was born	*umareta hi wa*
all the fields and hills	*no mo yama mo fukai*
were in heavy fog	*kasumi nite*
making it impossible	*haha no sugata ga*
to see my mother	*mirarenakatta*

Translated by Makoto Ueda

on occasion	*tobu tori mo*
even a winged bird	*kemono no gotoku*
has to scamper	*kusa kaguri*
like an animal in the grass	*hashiru toki ari*
after spring has passed	*haru no owari wa*

Translated by Makoto Ueda

MIYA SHŪJI

Miya Shūji (1912–1986) had a difficult childhood: his bookseller father went bankrupt, and he was forced to help support his family after graduating from middle school. Shūji eventually became the secretary of Kitahara Hakushū—a poet whose work is included in volume 1 of this anthology—an experience that inspired Shūji to begin writing poetry. He fought in China during the war, which ruined his health. Shūji retired from his job in 1960 to guard his declining health and to have more time to write poetry. The translations are by Makoto Ueda.

flowering poppies	*keshi no hana*
appear in my fantasy	*maboroshi ni kite*
and fill it with red	*akaku mitsu*
all things that have passed	*suginishi monora*
touch my heart with sorrow	*nabete kanashi mo*

as if it came	*kanashimi o*
to peer into my sorrow	*ukagau goto mo*
a bronze color beetle	*seidōshoku to*

all alone   *kanabun hitotsu*
in the depth of night   *yowa ni kite ori*

stalks growing   *mikidachi no*
straight, green and sharp   *aoku surudoku*
a forest of bamboos   *takemure wa*
occasionally with something   *aru oriori ni*
that makes me panic   *obiyakashi motsu*

like a long   *rōsoku no*
flame of a candle   *nagaki hono'o*
flickering   *kagayakite*
and flaring up for a moment   *yuretaru gotoki*
my youth has come and gone   *wakaki yo suginu*

on the way home   *seikatsu no*
from where I work for a living   *kyō no kaeriji*
I stop to watch   *mitsutsu tatsu*
vegetables at a grocer's   *mizu utareyuku*
being sprayed with water.   *yaoya no yasai*

NAKAJŌ FUMIKO

A tanka poet from Hokkaido, Nakajō Fumiko (1922–1954) became nationally known when, suffering from breast and lung cancer, she underwent a mastectomy and then used this experience in her own writing. The translations are by Janine Beichman.

My breasts are   *ushinaishi*
gone and there is a hill   *ware no chibusa ni*
that resembles them   *nishi oka ari*
in winter withered flowers   *fuyu wa karetaru*
will adorn it   *hana ga kazaramu*

As long as they blazed   *moyuru kagiri wa*
    I gave to him   *hito ni ataeshi*
    my breasts   *chibusa nare*
and never knew when   *gan no sosei o*
the cancer took on shape   *itsu yori to shirazu*

The ocean is stripped   *yorokobi no*
of all joy and deep below   *ushinawaretaru*

the octopus and	*umi fukaku*
its kin, tentacles tightly	*ashi tojite tako no*
closed, will be frozen forever	*rui wa kōramu*

SAITŌ FUMI

Saitō Fumi's (1909–2002) father was a high-ranking military officer as well as a respected poet, and she began writing tanka under his tutelage. Later, her father was implicated in the so-called February 26 Incident, a well-known army insurrection that took place in 1936, which caused considerable difficulties for the family. It was not until after the war that Saitō's work became known and appreciated. The translations are by Hatsue Kawamura and Jane Reinhhold.

a white hare	*shiroki usagi*
from a snow-covered mountain	*yuki no yama yori*
when it came out	*idete kite*
it was killed	*korosare tareba*
with eyes still open	*me o hiraki ori*

a husband paralyzed	*mahi no tsuma to*
my old mother blind	*me no mienu haha o*
on both sides	*sa u ni oki*
the evening of life	*waga rōnen no*
I enter autumn	*aki ni iriyuku*

long hospital hall	*nagaki byōrō o*
going to the end of it	*yukeba owari wa*
an emergency exit	*hijōguchi*
the only brightness there	*soko ni nomi akaku*
glow of the declining sun	*nishibi ga saseri*

the man's name	*hito no na o*
I've forgotten but	*wasure kawa no na o*
not the river's	*wasurezaru*
distant shining	*natsu no o nukite*
in the summer field	*tōku hikareri*

TSUKAMOTO KUNIO

Tsukamoto Kunio (1922–2005) began writing tanka soon after the war. His work was soon singled out for the "purity of his aesthetic sensibility" by his contemporary, the young novelist Mishima Yukio, whose work also is included in this volume of the anthology. Married in 1947, Tsukamoto later contracted tuberculosis and continued his work in precarious health. Along with his success as a poet, Tsu-kamoto has written on tanka, especially those by Saitō Mokichi (some of which appear in volume 1 of this anthology). The translations are by Makoto Ueda.

> in a grove
> of champagne bottles
> someone teaching a class
> on differential and integral
> investment calculus

shanpan no bin no hayashi no kage de toku bibun sekibunteki chochikugaku

> hands picking a rose
> hands holding a shotgun
> hands fondling a loved one
> hands on every clock
> point to the twenty-fifth hour

bara tsumu te · jū sasaeru te · aiidaku te · te . . . no tokei ga sasu nijūgo-ji

> late summer day
> in a country on the brink
> of collapse
> a nail buried in asphalt
> shows its sparkling head

kuni horobitsutsu aru banka asufaruto ni maibotsu shitaru kugi no zu hikaru

> from a flour mill
> to a charity hospital
> then to a butcher's
> power lines extend
> till they reach the withered moor

seifunsho yori nobishi densen jizun byōin to nikuya o tsunagi kareno e

> this May Day night
> on the wet pavement
> a beetle and I
> one pretending to be dead
> the other doing the reverse

Mēdē yo no michi nurete hanmyō wa shi o yosooi ware wa sei o yosoou

on the water
floats a dead warbler
with its eyes closed
its beautiful days of shame
having passed and gone

mizu no ue ni shi no uguisu no mami tojite haji utsukushiki hibi wa sugetari

DRAMA

BETSUYAKU MINORU

Betsuyaku Minoru (b. 1937) was one of the youngest of the many avant-garde dramatists who began his career during the student revolts of the 1960s. While attending Waseda University, he and other students, including the now-famous avant-garde theater director Suzuki Tadashi, became friends and colleagues. They began to produce a political theater of protest, initially against the renewal of the United States–Japan Security Treaty, and this movement continued in one form or another for nearly two decades. Betsuyaku's play *Elephant* (Zō, 1962), written in a style sometimes reminiscent of that of Samuel Beckett, combining poetry and humor, remains the Japanese theater's most powerful treatment of this subject. *The Little Match Girl* (*Matchi-uri no shōjo*), first staged in 1966, represents the epitome of Betsuyaku's style, mixing the familiar (in this case, the Hans Christian Andersen fairy tale) with disquieting ambiguities.

THE LITTLE MATCH GIRL (*MATCHI-URI NO SHŌJO*)

Translated by Robert N. Lawson

CAST OF CHARACTERS

Woman
Her younger brother
Middle-aged man
His wife

Center stage there is an old-fashioned table with three chairs, a little to stage left a small serving table with one chair.

This may be called an old-fashioned play, so it should open on an old-fashioned, slightly melancholy note.

The theater gradually goes dark, without its being noticed. From out of nowhere, a song from long ago, on a scratchy record, faintly comes to be heard. Then, unexpectedly, as if right in the next seat, a woman's voice, hoarse and low, can be heard whispering.

WOMAN'S VOICE: It was the last night of the year, New Year's Eve, and it was very cold. It had already become dark, and snow was falling.

A poor little girl was trudging wearily along the dark, deserted street. She had no hat, nor even any shoes. Until a little while before she had been wearing her dead mother's wooden shoes, but they were too big for her, and, trying to dodge two carriages that came rushing by, she had lost both of them. Her little feet were purple and swollen, as she put one in front of the other on the stiffly frozen snow.

Her apron pocket was filled with matches, and she was holding one bunch in her hand. She had been trying to sell them, but no one had bought a single match from her that whole day. No one had given her so much as a single penny.

From stage right a middle-aged man and his wife appear, carrying evening tea things. They begin to place them on the table, meticulously. In this household the way of doing such things is governed by strict rule, it seems. The wife sometimes makes a mistake, but her husband then carefully corrects it. Various things—taken from a tray, from the folds of their kimonos, from their pockets— are carefully positioned. A teapot, cups, spoons, a sugar bowl, a milk pitcher, jars of jam, butter, cookies, various spices, nuts, shriveled small fruits, miniature plants and animal figurines, and other small things are all arranged closely together. As this is going on, the two mumble to each other.

MAN: Setting a table is an art, you know. If you arrange everything just right, even a dried lemon will show to advantage.

WIFE: The people across the street place the powdered spinach next to the deodorizer.

MAN: Hum, what kind of pretentiousness is that?

WIFE: Right . . . just what I said to them. "Isn't that pretentious?" But listen to what they answered. "In this house we have our own way of doing things."

MAN: Their own way, huh? Well, fine. But, even so, there should be some principle . . . such procedures should be according to rule.

WIFE: That's right. Just what I told them. There should be some principle . . .

MAN: Hey, what's that?

WIFE: Garlic.

MAN: Garlic is for morning. I never heard of garlic for evening tea.

WIFE: But we saw the sunset a little while ago. Don't you always say, "Garlic for sunset"?

MAN: Garlic for sunrise. Onion for sunset.

WIFE: Was that it? Well, then, onions.

MAN: But let's not bother with them.

WIFE: Why?

MAN: They smell.

WIFE: Of course they smell. But is there anything that doesn't? You can't name a thing that doesn't have some drawback. Ginseng may not smell, but it has worms.

MAN: Yes, but those worms are good for neuralgia, you know.

WIFE: I like to eat onions. Then I don't feel the cold. One works for one night. Two for two nights. So three will work for three nights.

MAN: Roasted crickets are good if you are sensitive to cold. I keep telling you that. One cricket for one night.

WIFE: But there aren't any crickets now. What season do you think this is? There's snow outside.

MAN: All right, then, do this. First, heat some sesame oil. Then, after letting it cool, lick salt as you drink it. Lick and drink. Lick and drink. Three times. It works immediately.

WIFE: Isn't that what you do when you haven't had a bowel movement?

MAN: No, then it's soybean oil. In that case you lick and drink four times. You don't remember anything at all, do you?

WIFE: Say . . . over there . . . isn't that cheese?

MAN: Hmm, it seems to be. It wasn't there last night. Well . . . where should we put it? In the old days, we used to put the cheese next to the dried dates, but . . .

WIFE (*picking it up*): I wonder when we got this. It's pretty stale, isn't it?

MAN: Yes, getting hard. Didn't there used to be something called hard cheese? Cheese that had become hard. . . . (*Thinking.*)

WIFE: Look, teeth marks. You took a bite and then left it, didn't you?

MAN: Ridiculous! Let me see. I'd never do an ill-mannered thing like that. Those are your teeth marks.

WIFE: My teeth aren't that sharp.

MAN: I don't know about that . . . but it could have been the cat.

WIFE: Well . . . maybe. In the old days we had a cat. Could it have been Pesu?

MAN: Pesu was the dog. Kuro was the parrot, Tobi was the goat, and the horse was Taro, so the cat . . . could it have been Pesu after all?

WIFE: The cat was Pesu. Kuro was the parrot, Tobi the goat, the horse was Taro, the dog . . . the dog. . . . I wonder if the dog was Pesu . . .

A woman appears stage left.

WOMAN (*quietly*): Good evening.

MAN: Huh?

WOMAN: Good evening.

WIFE: Good evening.

WOMAN: Are you having evening tea?

MAN: Well, after a fashion . . .

WIFE: We never miss having tea in this house, from long ago.

WOMAN: It was that way in my family, too, long ago.

MAN: Ah, well, since you have taken the trouble to come, won't you please join us?

WOMAN: Yes, thank you.

WIFE: Please do. Not just for evening tea, but any time you have tea it's nice to have company. In the old days we frequently entertained.

MAN: Please sit down.

The three of them sit down. The man pours them tea.

MAN: Now then, before tea in your home, I mean before evening tea, do you say a prayer?

WOMAN: Ah . . . I don't really remember.

MAN: Well then, let's skip that. Actually, saying a prayer before evening tea is not proper. You might even say it is a breach of etiquette. Do you know why?

WOMAN: No.

MAN: Because it's not to God's liking. It says so in the Bible. (*To his wife.*) Do you remember?

WIFE: No.

MAN: She forgets everything. Because of her age. Sugar? How many?

WOMAN: Yes . . . well, if it's all right, I'll serve myself.

MAN: Of course. Please do. That's the best way. People should be completely free.

WIFE: In this house we always have guests who visit at night join us for evening tea. Now, after so many years, you are the victim.

MAN: How many years has it been? But you are late in coming . . . which way did you come from?

WOMAN: I came from City Hall.

WIFE: Ah, City Hall! That gloomy building? Don't you agree that it's gloomy?

WOMAN: Yes, it's gloomy.

WIFE: Gloomy!

MAN: Would you like a sweet?

WOMAN: Thank you.

MAN: We have rich things, too, if you'd prefer. By the way, speaking of City Hall, how is that fellow?

WIFE: What fellow?

MAN: That guy who sits there on the second floor and spits out the window.

WIFE: Oh, he died. Quite a while ago.

MAN: Is he finally dead? He was a problem for everybody. As many as thirteen times a day. People avoided passing that place.

WIFE: Well, no one avoids passing there these days. His son is sitting there now, and that young man is very courteous. But did you come directly from City Hall to our house?

WOMAN: Yes.

MAN: Directly here? That is to say, intending to come to our house?

WOMAN: That's right, directly here.

WIFE: Is that so? (*A little perplexed.*) Well then . . . . ah . . . how nice of you to come.

MAN: Yes. You are certainly welcome. We've had very few visitors lately.

WIFE: But what did they say about us at City Hall?

WOMAN: Nothing in particular.

MAN: That we are good citizens?

WOMAN: Yes.

WIFE: Exemplary?

WOMAN: Yes.

MAN: And harmless?

WOMAN: Yes.

WIFE: Well, that's certainly true. We are the best, most exemplary, citizens.

MAN: Last year the mayor went out on the balcony and gave a speech. Then, at the end, he said, "In our city we are pleased to have 362 citizens who are not only good, and exemplary, but also harmless." Those last two are us . . . really.

WIFE: The city tax isn't much, but we pay it right on time. And we don't put out much trash. And we don't drink much water.

MAN: Our ideas are moderate, too. We *are* both, relatively speaking, Progressive Conservatives. Those Reform party people are so vulgar. Neither of us can tolerate that. One of those guys, you know, will yawn without putting his hand to his mouth. Really! In the old days that would have been unthinkable.

WOMAN (*with feeling*): It is really . . . nice and warm here.

WIFE: Yes, isn't it? And refined, too. We aren't rich, but we try not to be unnecessarily frugal.

MAN: Now, to put it briefly, you've been sent here from City Hall.

WOMAN: No, I wouldn't say that exactly.

WIFE: Perhaps we should say, "dispatched."

WOMAN: No, that's not it. I heard about this place at City Hall. Something that made me want to visit you . . . so I came.

MAN: I see. I understand. You say that you heard something about us at City Hall. That made you want to visit us. And so, here you are—visiting us. That's certainly logical.

WIFE (*in admiration*): That makes sense. In short, since you wanted to visit us, you visited us. That's different from saying that you didn't want to visit us, but visited us anyway.

MAN: It's a goodwill visit, isn't it?

WOMAN: I just had to meet you.

WIFE: My, what a sweet thing to say. Another cup of tea? (*Offering tea.*)

WOMAN: Thank you.

MAN: In that case, whatever questions you have, or whatever requests, please just tell us. It is our established policy never to disappoint anyone who has come so far. Why are we so healthy in spite of growing old? Why are we so cheerful? So full of humor? Why, though we aren't rich, are we not unnecessarily frugal? How can we be both progressive and conservative at the same time? Why are we such good citizens? Why, to sum it all up, are we us?

WIFE: Go ahead and ask your questions. He will certainly answer them well, whatever they are about, I'm sure.

WOMAN: Thank you. But for right now it's enough just to be allowed to sit here this way.

MAN: Don't you have at least one of these "questions"? There are usually three questions for every person.

WIFE: And three for me, too.

MAN: And you know the answers already anyway, right?

WOMAN: Really, I . . . just to be sitting here and you have even served me a warm cup of tea. . . .

WIFE: Ah, of course. This lady is interested in the domestic environment . . . our home's unique domestic environment.

MAN: I see. I understand. This so-called family atmosphere takes some doing. Now, the first thing you can't do without for that homey feel is a cat. Second, a fireplace, or something of the kind. Things like whiskey or home-brewed saké, like detective stories or fairy tales, knitting needles and wool yarn, or torn socks and gloves, and, to top it off, some reading glasses . . . right? We used to have a cat, too, but he seems to have disappeared recently. . . .

WIFE: If you'd given us a little notice that you were coming, we could have borrowed one from the neighbor. . . .

WOMAN: Please, never mind about that. I'm happy just to be here, in a warm place, with such kind people, quietly drinking tea. It's very cold outside. It's snowing. No one is out there.

MAN: I can well believe that. It's supposed to snow tonight. Did you walk all the way?

WOMAN: Yes, all the way . . .

WIFE: Poor thing. You must be hungry. Please help yourself to whatever you'd like.

MAN: We always like to help those less fortunate as much as we can. That's our way. . . .

WOMAN'S VOICE (*from no particular direction*): The little girl was hungry now. She was shaking from the cold as she walked. The snow came drifting down on the back of her neck, to fall among the beautiful curls of her long golden hair. But from every window the light was shining, and there was the strong and savory smell of a goose roasting.

That was as it should be, the little girl was thinking. It was, after all, New Year's Eve. There was a small space between two houses. She drew her body into that corner and crouched down there, pulling her little feet under her. Even so, she could not escape the cold. . . .

WIFE (*in a small voice*): Dear, I think that this lady has something she'd like to say to us.

MAN: Is that so? Well then, please don't hesitate. For that matter . . . well . . . if you'd prefer, I could leave. I know that, as they say, women feel more comfortable talking to one another. . . . (*Beginning to stand.*)

WOMAN: No, please. Don't go. This is fine. Really. Just this, just sitting here quietly like this is fine. I'm perfectly happy this way.

WIFE: Well, if you say so. But you went to a lot of trouble to come here, and we'll feel bad if we don't do anything for you.

MAN: Right. We wouldn't want you to think we were so insensitive.

WOMAN: No, really, I wouldn't think anything like that. . . .

WIFE: Ah, well, isn't there something you'd like to eat? If there is, I'd be happy to fix it for you.

WOMAN: Thank you, but not just now.

MAN: Well, just as she says . . . that's fine. She has just arrived, dear, and probably doesn't feel like asking questions or giving orders yet. That's what it is. It's better just to leave her alone. You know what they say about excessive kindness . . . now what is it they say? . . .

WIFE: Maybe you're right. (*To the woman.*) Just make yourself comfortable. We're not in any hurry.

WOMAN: Thank you.

MAN: But, please don't hesitate . . .

WOMAN: Yes . . . well . . .

WIFE: As if it were your own home . . .

WOMAN: Yes.

Man starts to say something, and then stops. There is an awkward silence.

MAN (*suddenly thinking of something to say*): Outside . . . was it snowing?

WOMAN (*nods*).

WIFE (*eagerly pursuing the thought*): Powdered . . . snow?

WOMAN: Yes . . . (*Nods.*)

Silence.

MAN (*again thinking*):

You're tired . . . aren't you?

WOMAN: No.

MAN (*to his wife*): But she must be tired. Why don't you ask her to lie down for a little while? . . .

WIFE: That's a good idea. Why not do that?

WOMAN: No, this is just fine.

MAN: But . . .

WOMAN: Really . . .

WIFE: Well, whatever you think . . .

There is another awkward silence.

MAN: Say, I've got an idea. Why don't you sing her a song?

WIFE: A song? I can't sing . . . not me!

MAN: "Not me?" Did you hear that? She's just being shy. Or too modest. I shouldn't brag about my own wife, but her singing is something to hear. Come on, sing something for her?

WIFE: I can't do that.

MAN: Of course you can. She'd like to hear it, too. Right? Wouldn't you like to hear her sing something?

WOMAN: Yes . . . but . . .

MAN: See! Don't be so shy. Go ahead and sing. After all, she has taken the trouble to come. (*To the woman.*) She's not much good at anything else . . . just singing. But she's not bad at it. She's rather good.

WIFE: I don't have a good voice any more . . . at my age.

MAN: At your age? . . . Listen to that. Just yesterday she was saying that she could still sing pretty well in spite of her age, because she has always taken care of her voice. . . .

WIFE: But I just meant . . . for in the family . . .

MAN: In the family, outside the family, what's the difference? Go ahead and sing. Try that song . . . "The snow is . . . (*Trying to remember.*) The snow is . . . (*Thinking.*) The snow is getting deeper . . . no *keeps* getting deeper. . . ."

WOMAN (*quietly*): I was selling matches. . . .

WIFE: What?

WOMAN: I was selling matches.

WIFE: My, did you hear that, dear?

MAN: What's that?

WIFE: She's selling matches.

MAN: Matches? Ah, I see! Yes . . . I understand . . . finally. About buying matches. Well, it would have been better to have said so sooner, but . . . you went to City Hall to examine the city directory to find the household most in need of matches and that was us. That's what it is! Fine. I can understand that. And we'll buy them. Buy them all. I don't know if you've got a truckload . . . maybe two but we'll buy them all. Here and now. I promise.

WIFE: But we just bought matches. Far too many. Of course, since she took the trouble to come, we should buy some. Yes, let's buy some. But we can't use many.

WOMAN: No, that's not it. I was selling matches a long time ago.

MAN: Ah, a long time ago. . . .

WIFE: Then what are you selling now? If it's something useful around the house, we'll buy some. You've gone to so much trouble.

MAN: That's right. Even if it's a little expensive. . . .

WOMAN: Nothing in particular right now. . . .

MAN: Nothing? . . .

WOMAN: That's right.

WIFE (*a little disappointed*): Oh . . . well . . .

MAN: Ah . . . I see. You were telling us a story about something you remember from when you were small. . . .

WOMAN: Yes, that's it.

WIFE: About selling matches? . . .

WOMAN: Yes.

MAN: How old were you?

WOMAN: I was seven. . . .

WIFE: It was terrible, wasn't it?

MAN: And you can't help remembering. . . .

WOMAN: Well, really, until just recently, I didn't understand it.

MAN: You didn't understand? . . .

WOMAN: It was twenty years ago.

WIFE: You don't say . . .

MAN: And you had forgotten about it?

WOMAN: I didn't understand. Until just recently, I didn't understand at all. I was married and had two children. One, a boy, is four years old. The other, a girl, is barely two. So far as the girl is concerned, everything is fine, but a four-year-old boy requires a lot of attention.

WIFE: Isn't that the truth!

MAN: A boy of four can take care of himself.

WIFE: Nonsense!

WOMAN: People say that two children are too many at my age. But I don't feel that way.

MAN: You're right. Two is normal.

WIFE: They say you haven't really done your duty till you've had three.

MAN: Well, where are those children?

WOMAN: Don't worry about that.

MAN: Ah . . .

WIFE: Are they healthy?

WOMAN: Yes, quite healthy. . . .

MAN: That's good.

WIFE: That's the important thing . . . for children to be healthy.

WOMAN: Then I read in a book. . . .

WIFE: In a book? . . . My . . .

MAN: A child-care book?

WOMAN: No . . . fiction. . . .

MAN: Ah, that's good. When a woman gets married and has children, she usually quits reading books. Especially fiction.

WIFE: What was it about?

WOMAN: Various things.

MAN: Various things, indeed. Those writers of fiction write about all kinds of things, don't they?

WOMAN: Among other things, about a match girl. At first I didn't understand it. I read it again. Then I had a strange feeling.

MAN: Strange?

WOMAN: Yes. After that I read it many times, over and over. . . .

WIFE: About how many times?

WOMAN: Five . . . or more. . . .

MAN: Then? . . .

WOMAN: Then I saw it. I was amazed. It was about me.

WIFE: About you? . . .

WOMAN: Yes.

MAN: It was written about you?

WOMAN: That's right. I hadn't understood.

WIFE: About selling matches? . . .

MAN: . . . about the little match girl? . . .

WOMAN: Yes. It was about me. I was the little match girl.

WIFE: My goodness . . . that one? . . .

MAN: But . . .

WOMAN: After that I remembered many things. Many things gradually became clear. . . .

MAN'S VOICE (*low, in a murmur*): People were starving then. Every night was dark and gloomy. The town was built on swampland, sprawling and stinking. Here and there shops had been set up, like sores that had burst open. Small animals were killed in the shadows, and secretly eaten. People walked furtively, like forgotten criminals, and now and then, unexpectedly, something would scurry by in the darkness.

That child was selling matches at the street corner. When a match was struck, she would lift her shabby skirt for display until the match went out. People made anxious by the small crimes they had committed, people who could not even commit such crimes, night after night, in their trembling fingers, would strike those matches. Directed at the infinite darkness hidden by that skirt, how many times that small light had burned, until it had burned out. . . .

Those two thin legs held a darkness as profound as that of the depths of the sea, darker than all the darkness of that city floating on a swampland gathered together. As she stood there above that darkness, the little girl smiled aimlessly, or seemed empty and sad.

WIFE: Isn't there someone at the door?

MAN: Nonsense! In this cold? Aren't you cold?

WOMAN: No.

MAN: But then, how about that? Seeing yourself revealed in a story gives you a strange feeling, doesn't it?

WOMAN: Yes, very strange. After that I thought about it for a long time. I had suffered greatly. But there is still one thing I can't understand.

WIFE: One thing? . . .

MAN: What?

WOMAN: Why did I do a thing like that?

MAN: A thing like that?

WOMAN: Yes.

WIFE: Selling matches?

WOMAN: Yes.

WIFE: Well. . . .

MAN: Wasn't it because you were poor? I don't mean to be rude, but . . .

WOMAN: Still, to do that kind of thing. . . .

WIFE: You shouldn't be ashamed of that. Everyone did such things then. Those who didn't, didn't survive. Children stole things. After I had worked so hard to make hotcakes for his birthday, they stole them. It was like that then.

MAN: You should forget the things from that time. Everyone has forgotten. I've forgotten, too.

WOMAN: But I want you to think back, to recall those memories.

WIFE: Well, even if you try, there are some things you can't forget. But what good does it do to remember?

MAN: I had to do such things, too. Just as you did, I tried to sell things as a peddler. It's not that important. It's nothing to be ashamed of. Really.

WOMAN: But how could I ever have thought of doing such a thing? I was only seven years old. Could a child of seven think of that kind of thing?

WIFE: That kind of thing? . . .

WOMAN: That kind of . . . of terrible thing. . . .

MAN: . . . what kind of? . . .

WOMAN: I was selling matches.

MAN: Yes, selling matches . . . you were selling matches. . . .

WOMAN: . . . and while they were burning . . .

MAN: . . . impossible. . . .

WOMAN: No, it's not.

MAN: I can't believe it. . . .

WOMAN: But that's the way it was. It was me. I was the little match girl. . . .

WIFE: Ah, . . . you were the one. . . .

WOMAN: Yes, do you remember? That time? . . . that place? . . .

A pause.

MAN: But, well, all kinds of things happened then.

WIFE: That's true. All kinds of things. It was very different from now. No one knew what to do. It wasn't your fault.

MAN: It's nothing to worry about. That was all over long ago. An old story. My philosophy is to forget it. Forget everything. Without exception! Everything. If you don't . . . well, anyway . . . let life go on.

WOMAN: But I can't forget it.

WIFE: Why?

WOMAN: Because I have remembered.

MAN: I see. Yes, there is such a time in life. Just be patient a while. You'll soon forget. But, let's stop talking about it. Say . . . I'll make you forget in three minutes. Do you know the story of the kind weasel?

Woman does not answer.

MAN: How about fixing us another cup of tea, dear . . .

WIFE: Fine, let me do that. It has gotten quite cold.

Taking the pot, she leaves.

WOMAN: Are mother's feet all right now?

MAN: Mother . . . ah, you mean my wife? No, they still aren't good, particularly when it gets cold. But I'm surprised that you know so much. Things like my wife's trouble with her feet.

WOMAN: I don't mind forgetting that story, either.

MAN: Please do. Just forget it. It happened twenty years ago.

WOMAN: But I would still like to know one thing.

MAN: What?

WOMAN: I'm sure that someone must have taught me to.

MAN: To what?

WOMAN: To do such a thing . . .

MAN: Ah well, that's probably true. No doubt.

WOMAN: Was it you?

MAN: What?

WOMAN: Were you the one who taught me to?

MAN: Me?

WOMAN: Yes.

MAN: Me?

WOMAN: Yes.

MAN: Me? . . .

WOMAN: Yes.

MAN: . . . why would I have?

WOMAN: Don't you remember?

MAN: What?

WOMAN: Don't you remember me?

MAN: Remember you?

WOMAN: I'm your daughter.

MAN: You? . . .

WOMAN: Yes.

MAN: Impossible.

WOMAN: There's no doubt about it. I've made inquiries. That's what they told me at City Hall, too. It's the truth.

MAN: It can't be. It's not possible. I don't have a daughter. We did have a daughter . . . but she died. She is dead.

WOMAN: I don't blame you for making me do that kind of thing. I don't bear a grudge. But I would just like to know. That's all. Why was I doing that? If someone taught me to, who was it? I . . . if I thought of something like that all by myself, when I was just seven years old. . . . I can't believe that . . . that would be frightening. Absolutely frightening! I'd just like to know why. It bothers me so much that I can't sleep at night.

MAN: But it wasn't me. My daughter is dead. She was run over by a streetcar. I saw it . . . my daughter . . . right in front of my eyes . . . run over and killed. I'm not lying to you. My daughter is dead.

WOMAN: Father . . .

MAN: Stop it. Please stop it. Your story is wrong. You have things confused somehow. That's it. A misunderstanding. Such things often happen. But a mistake is still a mistake.

The wife appears, carrying a pot of tea.

WIFE: What's going on, dear?

MAN: Well . . . a little surprise . . . she has just claimed that she is our daughter.

WIFE: Oh, my! Really?

WOMAN: It's true.

MAN: Don't be ridiculous! Our daughter is dead. Our daughter was run over by a streetcar and killed.

WIFE: That's true. But if she were living she would be just about this girl's age.

WOMAN: I *am* living. It is true!

MAN: But I saw it happen. I . . . with these eyes . . . right in front of me . . . very close.

WOMAN: I checked on that at City Hall, too.

WIFE: At City Hall?

MAN: Still . . .

WIFE: But, dear, who can say for sure that she isn't our daughter?

MAN: I can!

WIFE: Why?

MAN: Because I saw it. . . . I . . .

WIFE: I saw it, too. But we need to remember the circumstances. Our daughter behaved a bit strangely. She often ran out in the middle of the night. The first time, she was just three years old. A fire alarm sounded in the middle of the night, and, when I looked, she wasn't there. We ran out after her, frantic. The bridge over the river outside the village was down. That child, drenched to the skin, was being held in the arms of a volunteer fireman. A bonfire was burning. I didn't know what to do. . . .

MAN: It happened a number of times. She died after we moved to town, so she was perhaps seven.

WIFE: She was seven.

MAN: I didn't know what happened. My wife shook me awake. It was in the middle of the night and it was raining. That child, still in her nightgown, went running out in the street where the streetcar line was, running in the deserted street. I ran after her. I called to her again and again. Then, just as we turned the corner, there came the streetcar.

WIFE: That's right. It was raining that night . . . I remember.

WOMAN: Don't you remember me?

WIFE (*staring at her intently, then in a low voice*): It's her.

MAN: You're wrong.

WIFE: But that kind of thing might be possible. . . .

WOMAN: It's me.

WIFE: Please, stand up for a minute.

The woman stands, rather awkwardly. She walks a little.

MAN: Just who in the world are you?

WOMAN: The daughter of the two of you.

WIFE (*to the man*): She looks like her.

WOMAN: There's no mistake. The man in charge of family records examined many thick record books. That's how I found out. He said that my father and mother lived here.

WIFE: What do you think?

MAN: I don't believe it.

WIFE: But let's talk about it a little. Then we can see.

MAN: What?

WIFE: Oh, all sorts of things. But even if, let's say, she isn't actually our child, wouldn't that still be all right? She's had such a hard time.

MAN: I understand that . . . but . . .

WOMAN: I . . . I don't blame you, Father . . . for that. . . .

MAN: Blame? . . . Me? . . .

WOMAN: I can forget even that, now.

MAN: You're wrong. It's all a mistake.

WIFE: That's all right. Let's just sit down. We'll sit and talk.

MAN: Yes, let's sit down. Standing won't get us anywhere. And since you went to the trouble to fix hot tea . . .

WIFE: Right. Let's have our tea. After that, we'll have a long overdue parent–child conversation.

The three of them sit down and begin to drink their tea, in a somewhat pleasant mood.

MAN: Well, I don't deny that there's a resemblance. And, if she had lived, she'd have been just about your age. . . .

WIFE: She did live. I can't help feeling so.

MAN: Now, dear, don't say such things so lightly, even joking, because she is quite serious. . . .

WOMAN: What's best is to see that father and mother are well.

WIFE: My, how often have I thought I would like to hear that!

MAN: But dear, I keep telling you, it's all a mistake.

WOMAN: Ah . . . I . . . it is difficult for me to say this, but . . . ah . . . my younger brother is still waiting outside.

WIFE: Younger brother?

WOMAN: Yes.

MAN: You have a brother?

WOMAN: Yes. We agreed that if I found out that you really were our father and mother, I'd call him.

WIFE: But we had only the one daughter.

MAN: She was an only child. Of course, I always wanted a son, very much, but . . . we never had one.

WIFE: Your real brother? . . .

WOMAN: Yes, he is. So . . . your real son.

WIFE: That would seem to follow, but . . . but we really didn't have a son. . . .

WOMAN: It's cold outside, and if it's all right, I wonder if you could call him in? . . . (*Standing and moving off stage left.*)

MAN: But . . . just a minute . . .

The woman reappears, bringing in her brother. She guides him to the small serving table.

WOMAN: See, this is your mother.

BROTHER: Good evening, Mother.

WOMAN: And this is your father.

BROTHER: Good evening, Father.

WIFE: Please sit down. (*Seats him beside the small table.*)

BROTHER: Yes. (*Sits.*)

WOMAN: You were probably cold, weren't you?

BROTHER: No, not at all. . . .

WOMAN: My brother has remarkable self-control. He has sometimes stood in the snow all night long. And he'd never even sneeze. Have some tea.

BROTHER: Yes. (*Taking a large cup, saucer, and spoon from a bag he is holding. The wife, holding the teapot, pours tea into his cup. While handing him the sugar, she observes him closely.*)

WOMAN: He likes tea very much. Two spoons of sugar. Always. Then he drinks slowly. I taught him that. They say it's best for the body, and for the heart, to drink slowly. (*The brother drinks the tea.*)

WOMAN: Aren't you hungry?

BROTHER: No.

WOMAN: But take something. Since you haven't had anything since yesterday.

WIFE: My, since yesterday?

WOMAN: Yes, my brother's self-control is very strong. He has sometimes gone for over three days without eating. But he never says a word about it.

WIFE: Three days? . . . But that's not good for his health. Even Gandhi went only two days at the most. Well, there's not much, but please eat all you want.

WOMAN (*passing the plate of cookies*): Please take one.

BROTHER: Thank you. (*Bows politely, takes one, and eats slowly.*)

WOMAN: Chew it well. The better we chew our food, the better it is for us.

BROTHER: Yes.

WIFE: You are a good sister. And your brother is very polite.

MAN: He's very sensible. That's an excellent quality.

WOMAN: When you are ready, tell father and mother your story.

BROTHER: All right. But it's not necessary.

WOMAN: Why?

BROTHER: I can tell them later.

WOMAN: My brother is very reserved. Shy. Bashful and uncommunicative besides.

WIFE: But that's good. Not to talk too much is excellent in a man.

MAN: Yes, that's true. Real gentlemen usually don't talk much. Still, to say that it is excellent not to talk misses the point. Speaking from my long experience, I would say that you should talk when it is time to talk. To be more precise, then, it is excellent in a man not to talk when it isn't time to talk.

WOMAN: Mother, won't you tell my brother something about when he was little?

WIFE: But, you know, you're confused about that. We never had a son.

MAN: We never had a son. We had a daughter. And she and she died. So there are no children. None. . . .

WOMAN: We can't get Father to believe us. . . .

WIFE: But . . . really . . .

BROTHER: Mother . . .

WIFE: Me?

BROTHER: A long time ago, you suffered from a bad case of asthma. I remember that very well. I used to rub your back. You'd be short of breath, and your face would get red. To see you bent over suffering like that was terrible. When I rubbed your back, that seemed to help, though, and you would go to sleep. . . .

WIFE: My, I wonder if that could be true. . . .

MAN: Did you ever have asthma?

WIFE: No.

MAN: Then this story doesn't fit, does it?

WIFE: But when a person catches a cold they cough a little.

WOMAN: That must be it . . . that mother had a cold, and that's what he's remembering. He has a very good memory. Would you like another one? (*Offering him the plate of cookies.*)

BROTHER: No, that's fine.

WOMAN: You needn't hold back. This is our home.

BROTHER: All right, then. Thank you. (*Takes one.*)

MAN: Now . . . please listen carefully. I want this quite clear.

WOMAN: He remembers everything . . . many things about Father and Mother in far greater detail than I can.

MAN: That's all very well, but . . . now listen! We did not have a son! I want to make that very clear. *Did not have!* That's the truth! We had a daughter. We had a cat. But no son. *There . . . never . . . was . . . one.* Do you understand? All right. Now, saying that doesn't mean that I want to put the two of you out. So please, just relax. Eat as much as you like. Drink as much as you like. I just want to make this one point. It may seem a mean thing to say, but I think it's important to be sure that it's clear. About this . . . this house. It is our home! You . . . are our guests.

WIFE: Dear, don't be so . . .

MAN: I know. Yes, I know. Please don't misunderstand me. And if we agree on that one point, then we might welcome you as if you were a real daughter and a real son. Wouldn't you say that we have welcomed you almost as we might have a real son and daughter?

BROTHER: And Father suffered from neuralgia. Whenever it got cold, he had a pain in his hips. When that happened, he got irritable. Mother, and Sister, you both knew that. So, whenever he had an attack, you'd go out and leave me home alone with him. His sickness was the cause, of course, but he sometimes hit me and kicked me. At first I would yell, "It hurts! It hurts!"—and cry. But I soon stopped that. Because, no matter how much I cried, he still kept on. I just learned to endure it. But, from that time on, my arm bends like this.

Moves his left arm with a jerk.

MAN: I never had anything like neuralgia. . . .

WOMAN: His endurance is remarkable. No matter what happens, he never cries. Here, have another. (*Offering him the cookies.*)

BROTHER: Thank you. (*Taking one.*)

WOMAN: He's just naturally mistreated by everyone. He's hit and he's kicked. But he bears it patiently. He keeps quiet; he crouches down; he rolls up on the ground in a ball. But he doesn't cry.

MAN: I have never once used violence against another person. . . .

WOMAN: But, Father, he doesn't hold it against you. I have taught him that that isn't good. It wasn't your fault. You were sick.

MAN: I had no son.

BROTHER: Father, I don't hold it against you. It was because you were sick. That's what made you do it. Sometimes my arm hurts. When it gets cold . . . just like with your neuralgia . . . there's a sharp pain, right here. But I put up with it. I accept it. Sister said, "Please endure it." So I do. I endure it.

WOMAN: His body is covered with bruises. It's terrible. But he doesn't complain. He puts up with it. Show Father and Mother . . . so they can see just how much you've endured.

BROTHER: Yes, Sister. (*Begins to unbutton his clothing.*)

WIFE: Stop! Please, stop. Don't do that! I understand. I believe you. You probably are our son.

The brother, uncovering his upper body, stands up.

MAN (*standing, solemnly*): I see. You're the one. You were born. I wanted it. I always wanted a son. So you were born. Evidently that's what it is. They say that if you want something badly enough you'll get it, don't they? That was you. And I never knew it at all . . . it's unbelievable. I'm really surprised that you were born. (*Pause.*) This one . . . kept quiet about it, and I never knew it. That's clear. And you . . . you are my daughter. It's no mistake. I thought that you were dead, but you were alive. The little girl I was chasing that evening was someone else. You say that's so, so it must be. It was a dark evening. To me it was just a fluttering white thing dancing in the wind. That wasn't you. You went flying the other way, running somewhere else. And you never came back. That must be what happened. So you are my daughter and son. My real daughter and son. I remember everything. So then . . . what do you want? What now? . . . Since I am your father, what do you want me to do for you? To look at you with affection? To speak to you in a tender, caring voice? Or do you want money? What is it? . . .

WOMAN: Father?

MAN: What?

WOMAN (*quietly*): And Mother. We don't want you to misunderstand either. We didn't come here to trick you, or to beg for anything. We really are your son and daughter . . . that's all. . . .

MAN: Really? And I never knew. (*To his wife.*) Please ask these people to leave. We must go to bed now. We old people become sleepy earlier than you young people do.

WOMAN: Father.

MAN: Get out.

BROTHER: Not so loud. Please. The children have just fallen asleep.

MAN: Children?

WOMAN: My children. The two-year-old and four-year-old I told you about. I had them come in. It was presumptuous of me, I know. But I couldn't leave them out there in the cold. They were already almost frozen. They couldn't even cry. I felt so sorry for them. . . .

WIFE: Please leave.

WOMAN: Mother . . . don't be so cruel. . . .

WIFE: Please go. I beg you. Just go. I can't stand it. I'll give you money. It's so disagreeable. This is our house.

BROTHER: That's all right with me, Mother, but please think about the children. They're sleeping now, but they're very hungry. My sister has nothing to feed them. We kept telling them, as we came, "When we see Father and Mother, we'll ask them for something for you to eat." We barely got them to walk here. My sister is exhausted. Extremely exhausted. We walked for a long time.

WOMAN: But we are finally able to meet you, Mother. We walked a long way. It was very cold. Snow was falling. . . . (*Gradually laying down her head and seeming to fall asleep.*) Just for one look at Father and Mother . . . that's all we were thinking. . . .

WOMAN'S VOICE: To warm her freezing hands the little girl struck the match she was holding. The tiny stick flickered for a moment, enveloping the area in bright light. The ice and snow glittered a purple color. But, then, the match went out. The little girl remained there, crouching all alone on the cold stone pavement, with the wind blowing, freezing.

The woman's head is on her crossed arms on the table.

WIFE: What happened to her? What's your sister doing?

MAN: She's sleeping.

BROTHER: Sleeping. Sometimes she sleeps. Then, sometimes, she wakes up.

WIFE: My, I wonder if she is crying . . . look. . . .

BROTHER: Yes, she's crying. She cries in her sleep. She's very unhappy.

MAN: Will you please wake her up, and leave? Look, I don't say that out of meanness. If you hadn't come with a strange trick like this, if you had come without saying anything, you would have received a warm welcome. Really. But now listen to me. Are you listening?

BROTHER: Yes.

MAN: Please leave.

BROTHER: But my sister is very tired.

MAN: Are you her real brother?

BROTHER: Yes, I really am . . .

WIFE: Since when have you thought that?

BROTHER: What?

WIFE: How long ago did you become aware that she was your sister?

BROTHER: That was quite a while ago . . . quite a while . . .

WIFE: Please try to remember clearly. It's very important.

BROTHER: But even when I first became aware of it, she was already my sister. . . .

MAN: Already at the time you became aware of it? . . . Well, that's not a very reasonable story.

WIFE: There had to be something before that.

BROTHER: There were many things. Many things. Then I suddenly realized . . . she was my sister.

MAN: It sounds like a miracle. . . .

Pause. The brother gets up stealthily, takes a cookie from the table, goes back, sits down, and eats it.

MAN (*lost in thought. To his wife*): Can you remember back to that time? We were sitting somewhere on a sunny hill . . . the sky was blue, white clouds were floating lightly by, there was not a breath of wind . . . perhaps dandelions were blooming. . . .

WIFE (*prompted to reflection*): There was that, too, wasn't there?

MAN (*in the same mood*): And then . . . some large thing was dead . . . alongside the road . . . what was it? . . .

WIFE (*in the same mood*): A cow . . . it was a large, gray-colored cow . . . just like a cloud. . . .

MAN: Ah, was it a cow? That thing . . . just like a cloud . . .

WIFE: How about it, dear?

MAN: About what?

WIFE: These people . . . should we keep them overnight? . . .

MAN: Well, I was thinking that, too. We'll let them stay.

WIFE: I feel sorry for them.

MAN: Right, and people like that, no matter how they seem, they *are* unfortunate.

WIFE: Let's be kind to them.

MAN: Let's do that. Because there's nothing wrong in that.

WIFE: You two. It'll be all right for you to stay here tonight. We'll let you stay.

MAN: Make yourself at home. These other things . . . well, let's talk about them later. . . .

WIFE: Do you understand?

BROTHER: Yes, but that isn't necessary. Don't worry about us. Just leave us alone.

WIFE: Tell your sister, too, to put her mind at ease.

BROTHER: She already knows.

MAN: She already knows.

BROTHER: She told me that a while ago . . . that Mother had asked us to stay.

WIFE: Mother?

BROTHER: Yes.

WIFE: Meaning me?

BROTHER: That's right.

WIFE: So . . . then that's all right.

BROTHER: Is it all right if I take one more?

WIFE: Yes.

He eats a cookie.

MAN'S VOICE: Good evening.

MAN: Good evening.

MAN'S VOICE: I'm a city fire marshal. Is anything missing in your home. Is anything lost? Has anything disappeared?

MAN: Has anything?

WIFE: No.

MAN: It seems not.

MAN'S VOICE: So everything is in order?

MAN: I can't say that absolutely. You see, this is a very poor household.

MAN'S VOICE: How about your fire?

WIFE: It's all right. We haven't gone to bed yet.

MAN'S VOICE: Not yet? But you're not going to stay up all night, are you?

MAN: We'll check it before going to bed.

MAN'S VOICE: Did you notice?

MAN: What?

MAN'S VOICE: Can you hear the breathing of someone sleeping? Two small ones . . .

WIFE: Children. There are children.

MAN'S VOICE: Be careful, please. Tonight is especially cold. Be careful that they don't freeze to death while they sleep. The city authorities are drawing special attention to that danger.

There is the striking of wooden clappers, which gradually fades. Then, "Watch your fire," is heard from afar. The woman raises her head, as if still half asleep.

WOMAN: Father, while I was asleep, how many cookies did he eat?

MAN: Well, one, wasn't it?

WIFE: It was one, definitely. . . .

WOMAN: No, it was two. He ate two. I had counted them. I don't appreciate your letting him do that. Don't you remember, Father, how many times I asked you not to? He knows no limits. If you let him do it, he'll eat far too many. I have only eaten one so far. That's true, isn't it, Mother?

WIFE: Yes, but since there are plenty, don't feel that you have to restrain yourself. . . .

WOMAN: No, I don't mean it that way. I told him about it, but, no matter how often I tell him, he doesn't seem to understand. It's the same with Father. I've asked you so often!

MAN: But I didn't . . .

WOMAN: No, I had spoken to you earlier. But it's not your fault. (*To her brother.*) You're the one. Mother, I hate to trouble you, but would you put these away?

WIFE: Yes, but there are plenty.

WOMAN: It will become a habit. Now apologize to Father and Mother.

MAN: Well, that's all right. Your brother was probably hungry.

WOMAN: Everyone is. Everyone is hungry. But people exercise self-control. You . . . you're the only one . . . doing such greedy things. . . . Well, apologize.

She gives him a jab with her fingers.

WIFE: Please, don't do that! Really, please stop. It's all right. In this house it doesn't matter at all.

WOMAN: Mother, don't interfere. This is our affair. I raised this child. Apologize. Why don't you apologize? Don't you feel ashamed? What did I always say to you?

MAN: Well, I understand your point very well. It's commendable. It's very commendable. However . . .

WOMAN: Apologize!

MAN: Listen . . . will you? Here's another way of looking at it. What you say is sound, but don't tell me that if he gets hungry, it's his own fault. Really. Shouldn't you think again?

WOMAN: Please stay out of it. I'm the one who raised him. I taught him better.

MAN: Yes, I can understand how difficult that must have been.

WOMAN: No, you can't understand. You don't know how much I have done for him. From the age of seven. I have done things I'm ashamed to admit in front of other people in order to raise him. (*To her brother.*) Why can't you understand? Why don't you listen to me? Why don't you do what I tell you?

WIFE: He seems to obey you quite well.

MAN: That's certainly true. Your brother is very courteous.

WOMAN (*becoming more agitated*): I'm a despised woman. It's because I became that kind of woman that you won't listen to me, isn't it?

She twists her brother's arm. He stands up slowly, and then slowly crouches down on the floor.

WOMAN: What did I do that was so shameful? What do you say I did? And, if I did, who did I do it for? Just who did I have to do that kind of thing for? Tell me! Please tell me! Compared to what you have done, what does what I have done amount to? Which is worse? Tell me, which is worse? Tell us. Come on, out with it!

MAN (*to the brother*): You'd better apologize. Please. Apologize. You shouldn't disobey your sister. You know that she's suffered many hardships to raise you. You understand that, don't you? And that she loves you. It's not good not to obey her instructions. That's bad.

WOMAN: Father! Please be quiet for a while! He doesn't understand yet. What I did . . . and who I did it for. And how miserable I have felt about doing it . . . to this very day. (*To her brother.*) Listen! What did I keep telling you? Did I say you could sink so low just because you're hungry? Did I teach you to be so rude in front of Father and Mother? Now apologize! Say "pardon me" to Father and Mother. I say apologize! Can't you see how ashamed I feel because of what you did? Then, apologize. Apologize! Apologize! Apologize!

While saying this, she bangs his head, with a thumping sound, on the floor.

WIFE: Please stop that! It's all right. Really, he doesn't have to. Don't be so harsh.

WOMAN: Please stay out of it! (*Increasingly violent.*) Whose cookie did you eat? Because of you, who won't have any?

WIFE: There are plenty. Plenty. We can't possibly eat them all.

WOMAN: Whose was it? Who won't get any? Please tell us!

MAN: Stop it. I'll go get them immediately. We have plenty. (*Grabbing her arm to stop her.*)

WOMAN: Let go of me, please!

MAN (*becoming angry*): Stop! What in the world is this all about? What are you doing?

WOMAN (*startled, suddenly becoming humble, bowing her head to the man*): I beg you. I'll make him apologize. I'll make him apologize immediately. Please forgive him. He didn't mean anything. He'll apologize right now. He's usually more obedient. He's usually a well-behaved child.

MAN (*a little bewildered*): But that's all right. Because we're not really concerned about it.

WOMAN: I'll have him apologize, though, because I don't feel right about it. And, please, forgive him. He's already sorry about it, too, in his heart. He *is* apologizing. He's crying. It's just that he can't say anything.

WIFE: You . . .

WOMAN: Please forgive me, Mother. I was wrong. I was a bad woman. I did such a shameful thing. . . .

WIFE: That's not the point. It's all right.

WOMAN: No, it's not all right. But please don't say that my brother is bad. He's feeling sorry. Forgive him. He's basically a gentle, courteous human being. He's usually very self-controlled. Please forgive him. I'll make him apologize. Right now. He was hungry. That's all it is. We can't blame him for that. Please don't blame him for that. I'll make him apologize. I apologize, too.

MAN (*approaching her tenderly and trying to lift her to her feet*): That's all right. Let's stop all this. I understand.

WOMAN (*brushing him away*): No, please forgive me. Don't touch me! You must forgive me. I'm a bad woman. Please forgive me. (*Crawling away from him as she says this.*)

MAN: What are you doing? (*Again extending his hand.*)

WOMAN (*retreating in the direction of the wife*): Forgive me, Mother. I did a bad thing. Please forgive me. At least give me your forgiveness.

WIFE: What's wrong?

MAN: What in the world is it? . . .

WOMAN: Forgive me. Father. (*Again retreating from the man.*) Forgive me, Father. Forgive me, please. Matches. Please don't strike the matches. . . .

She bends down on the floor, covering her head, and remains motionless. The man and his wife stand dazed. The brother rises slowly. They stand quietly for a moment. The wife is about to kneel down next to the woman.

BROTHER (*quietly*): Please don't touch her. She's a woman who can't sink any further. That's why she doesn't want to be touched.

He goes to her, hugging her and lifting her to his knee. The man and wife stand bewildered.

WOMAN (*as from afar*): Matches . . . don't strike the matches.

BROTHER (*murmuring*): Father bought matches. Father bought matches. Father bought matches. Every night . . . every night . . . for my sister . . . night after night for my sister. . . .

MAN: No . . . (*To his wife.*) I didn't do that. I never did that kind of thing.

BROTHER: But I don't blame you. Whatever you did, I can't blame you. Because my sister said, "Don't blame him. Don't blame him. . . ."

WOMAN'S VOICE (*low and hoarse*): Then the little girl struck the rest of the matches all at once, in a great hurry. In doing this, she hoped that she would be able to hold firmly to her mother. The matches were burning very brightly, lighting up the whole area, so that it became brighter than daylight. There was never a time when her mother looked larger, or more beautiful. She took the little girl in her arms, wrapped her in light and joy, and went climbing high, high up. There was no more cold, hunger, or fear. The two of them were called up to heaven.

MAN'S VOICE (*stealthily*): Did you notice?

MAN: What?

MAN'S VOICE: You can't hear the children breathing in their sleep anymore.

There is the striking of wooden clappers, which gradually fades. Then, "Watch your fire," is heard from afar.

The man and his wife sit silently at the table, solemnly beginning "morning tea." . . .

WOMAN'S VOICE (*a little more clearly*): It was a cold morning. The little girl, with red cheeks, and with even a smile playing on her lips, was dead.

The New Year's morning sun illuminated that little body. One hand held a bunch of matches, almost entirely burned up. People said, "She must have tried to warm herself. . . ." It was true. This child had been very cold.

KINOSHITA JUNJI

Kinoshita Junji (1914–2006) was the most gifted of the postwar playwrights who wrote about political events in terms of their own humanistic ideals. In this regard, he may be roughly compared with his American contemporary Arthur Miller. The topics of Kinoshita's plays range from the Tokyo war crimes trials to the incidents involving the Soviet spy Richard Sorge in prewar Japan. Kinoshita's interest in the patterns of ordinary Japanese people's lives led him to write a series of plays based on folk themes. The most famous of these is *Twilight Crane* (*Yūzuru*), first performed in 1949 and now one of great classics of postwar Japanese theater. The play has even been performed by nō troupes and used as the libretto for an opera.[1]

TWILIGHT CRANE (YŪZURU)

Translated by Brian Powell

CAST OF CHARACTERS

Yohyō
Tsū
Sōdo
Unzu
Children

Snow all around. In the middle of it, one small, solitary shack, open on one side. Behind it an expanse of deep red evening sky. In the distance the sound of children singing:

Let's make a coat for grandpa to wear,
Let's make a coat for grandma to wear,

---

1. Kinoshita Junji used language for a specific purpose in this play. For the human characters he invented a type of universal country dialect, and for the crane/wife Tsū he used mainly standard Japanese. In performance, the part is played with no suggestion of a local accent.

It is impossible for a translator to invent a country dialect that would serve the whole English-speaking world. Accordingly, I have made the humans' speech a slightly colloquial language, which actors could adapt to a countrified form to suit their audience. I have made Tsū speak correct English, which I hope could be preserved in performance, as she should be distinguished linguistically from the rest of the characters.—Trans.

> Lah-lala lah, lah lah lah,
> Lah-lala, lah-lala, lah lah lah.

The house has two rooms. One (to the right) is closed off by shōji. In the center of the other, visible to the audience, is a square open hearth. Yohyō is fast asleep beside it. The singing stops, and the children come running on.

CHILDREN (*in unison, as if they were still singing*):

> Come out and sing us a song, please do.
> Come out and play some games, please do.
> Come out and sing us a song.

YOHYŌ (*waking up*): What's all this?

CHILDREN:

> Come out and play some games.
> Sing us a song, please do.

YOHYŌ: Are you calling Tsū? She's not in.

CHILDREN: She's not in? Really not in? That's no good. Where's she gone?

YOHYŌ: Where? I don't know.

CHILDREN: Where's she gone? When's she coming back? Tell us, tell us, tell us!

YOHYŌ: You're getting on my nerves! (*Stands up.*)

CHILDREN (*running away*): Ah! Look out! Yohyō's cross. Yohyō! Yohyō! Silly Yohyō!

YOHYŌ: Hey! Don't run away. Don't run away. I'll play with you.

CHILDREN: What'll we play?

YOHYŌ: Well, what shall we play?

CHILDREN: Knocking over Sticks.

YOHYŌ: OK. Knocking over Sticks.

CHILDREN: Singing.

YOHYŌ: OK. Singing.

CHILDREN: Snowball Fight.

YOHYŌ: OK. Snowball Fight. (*As he speaks, he moves into the children's group.*)

CHILDREN: Bird in the Cage.

YOHYŌ: OK. Bird in the Cage.

CHILDREN (*Chanting*): Stag, Stag, How Many Horns.

YOHYŌ: OK. Stag, Stag, How Many Horns. Right, I'm coming. I'm coming.

CHILDREN: Stag, Stag, How Many Horns. (*They run off repeating this.*)

YOHYŌ (*starting to go after them*): (*To himself.*) Hang on! It'll be awful for Tsū to come back and find the soup cold. I must look after her—she's precious. (*Goes back into the house and hangs the pot over the fire.*)

Tsū glides swiftly in from the back of the house.

TSŪ: Yohyō, really, you are not . . . ?

YOHYŌ: Where were you?

TSŪ: I just slipped out . . . you are not supposed to do that . . .

YOHYŌ: Well, I thought it would be awful for you to come back and find the soup cold. So I put it over the fire.

TSŪ: Oh, thank you so much. I will start preparing the rest of the meal for you.

YOHYŌ: All right. So I'm going out to play. It's Knocking over Sticks.

TSŪ: Really—Knocking over Sticks?

YOHYŌ: And then, Snowball Fights. And then, singing songs.

TSŪ: And then . . . Bird in the Cage. And then, Stag, Stag, How Many Horns?

YOHYŌ: Yes, yes. Stag, Stag, How Many Horns. You come too.

TSŪ: I would like to. But I have the meal to prepare . . .

YOHYŌ: Leave it! Come. (*Takes her hand and pulls her.*)

TSŪ: No.

YOHYŌ: Come on. Why not? Both of us will play.

TSŪ: No, no. No, I say. (*Laughing, she allows herself to be pulled off.*)

The children's singing is heard in the distance. Sōdo and Unzu appear.

SŌDO: Her? Is she Yohyō's wife?

UNZU: She is too. He's a lucky so-and-so, suddenly getting a fine wife like that. Nowadays he spends a lot of his time taking naps by the fire.

SŌDO: He used to be such a hard worker—stupid idiot! And now he's got a fine woman like that—in a place like this! Why?

UNZU: Nobody knows when she came or where she came from. She just came . . . But thanks to her, Yohyō doesn't have to do anything now—and he's made a lot of money.

SŌDO: You weren't fooling me, were you? What you told me about that cloth.

UNZU: No, it's true. Take it to the town and you can always get ten gold pieces for it.

SŌDO (*ponders*): And you say she weaves it?

UNZU: Yes she does. But there is one thing. Before she goes into the room where the loom is, she tells Yohyō not to look at her while she's weaving. So Yohyō accepts what she says, doesn't look into the room, and goes to bed. Then the next morning, there it is—all woven, so he says. It's beautiful cloth.

SŌDO: Crane Feather Weave—that's what you called it, wasn't it?

UNZU: That's what they call it in the town. They say it's so rare you'd have to go to India to find anything like it.

SŌDO: And you're the middleman. I bet you're raking it in.

UNZU: Well—not all that much.

SŌDO: Don't give me that. But . . . if that's real Feather Weave, we're not talking about just fifty or a hundred gold pieces.

UNZU: Go on! D'you mean it? What is Crane Feather Weave, anyway?

SŌDO: It's cloth woven from a thousand feathers taken from a *living* crane.

UNZU (*puzzled*): But where could Yohyō's wife get all those crane feathers?

SŌDO: Hmm. This is the weaving room, I suppose . . . (*Without thinking, he goes up into the house and peers into the closed-off room through a chink in the shōji.*) Yes, there's a loom there. . . . Ah! (*Cries out in astonishment.*)

UNZU: What is it? What is it?

SŌDO: Take a look. Crane feathers. . . . Well. That seems to . . .

UNZU: So the cloth could be the real thing.

Pause. Tsū has returned and glides in from the back.

UNZU (*startled*): Ah!

SŌDO (*thrown off guard*): I'm sorry—we shouldn't have come up into the house while you were out. . . .

TSŪ: . . . (*Pause. Watches the two of them suspiciously, with her head inclined to one side like a bird.*)

UNZU: Oh . . . ah . . . we've met—I'm Unzu from the other village—I'm much obliged to your husband for that cloth. . . .

TSŪ: . . . (*Remains silent.*)

SŌDO: Yes, well, what happened was . . . I heard about the cloth from him (*Indicates Unzu.*). . . . I'm Sōdo—from the same village—what I want to know is—pardon me asking—is it genuine Crane Feather Weave?

TSŪ: . . . (*Remains silent. Stays watching them suspiciously; then suddenly, as if she had heard some sound, she wheels round and disappears into the back.*)

SŌDO: . . . ?

UNZU: . . . ?

SŌDO: What do you . . .

UNZU: What was that? We spoke to her and . . .

SŌDO: She didn't seem to understand a single word. . . . Everything about her's just like a bird.

UNZU: You're right. Just like a bird.

Pause. The dusk gradually deepens. Only the flames in the hearth flicker red.

SŌDO (*looking at the crane feathers*): You know . . . there are stories about cranes and snakes . . . how they sometimes take human shape and become men's wives.

UNZU: What the . . .

SŌDO: Come to think of it . . . Ninji from the village had a story like that yesterday . . . he was passing by that lake in the mountains, in the early evening, four or five days ago, and there was a woman standing at the water's edge, he said . . . he thought there was something strange about her, so he kept watching without letting her see him. He saw her glide into the water, and then—she turned into a crane. . . .

UNZU: Eh?

SŌDO: The crane played around in the water for a while. Then it changed back into a woman and glided away.

UNZU: Ah! (*Runs out of the house.*)

SŌDO: Hey! What're you doing, screaming like that . . . (*Instinctively he leaves the house too.*)

UNZU: So . . . so . . . his wife . . . is . . . a crane?

SŌDO: Shut up you idiot! You don't know that! Don't be such a fool as to even mention it. . . .

UNZU: What am I going to do? I've cheated Yohyō, made a lot of money out of him . . .

SŌDO: Don't worry about it. If that's genuine Crane Feather Weave, we can take it to the capital and make us a thousand gold pieces.

UNZU: What did you say? A *thousand*?

SŌDO: And from what you say, Yohyō's gotten quite greedy recently. If we talk about money, he'll listen all right.

UNZU: I suppose so. . . .

SŌDO: So, we've got to get him thinking like us—and he's got to get a steady supply of cloth from his wife.

UNZU: Well . . . yes . . . I suppose so . . .

SŌDO: Look, he's back.

YOHYŌ (*returns, tired and happy*): Got it.

> "Let's make a coat for grandpa to wear"

What's next? Ah . . .

> "Lah-lala, lah-lala, lah lah lah"

That's right, isn't it? . . . Oh, I completely forgot to put the rice on for Tsū.

SŌDO: Heh, Yohyō.

YOHYŌ: What is it?

SŌDO: Forgotten me? Sōdo, from the other village. Unzu—you do the talking.

YOHYŌ: Ah, Unzu. Is there more money for us to make?

UNZU: Bring me some more of that cloth, and you can have as much as you like.

YOHYŌ: No, there's no more cloth.

SŌDO: Why's that?

YOHYŌ: Tsū said there'd be no more after the last lot.

UNZU: You can't have that—not when I'm going to make more money for you.

YOHYŌ: I know, I know . . . but . . . she's very dear to me.

SŌDO: She may be—but you can really clean up if you get a steady supply of cloth from her.

YOHYŌ: All right, all right, but she's always a lot thinner after she's been weaving.

SŌDO: Thinner, did you say? . . . Let me ask you a question. It's about Tsū moving in with you as your bride. When was that? Anything special about the way it happened?

YOHYŌ (*takes a moment to absorb the question*): When was it now? One evening . . . I was about to go to bed . . . she came in and offered to be my wife. (*Chuckles happily at the memory.*)

SŌDO: Mmm . . . I don't suppose . . . you've ever had anything to do with a crane, have you?

YOHYŌ: A crane? Oh, a crane—yes, some time ago . . . I was working in the fields, when a crane came down the path. It had an arrow in it and was in a lot of pain. So I pulled the arrow out.

SŌDO: Did you now? . . . Hmm . . . (*To Unzu.*) It's looking like the real thing more and more.

UNZU (*trembles*): . . . .

SŌDO: And if it is, it's big money . . . . (*To Yohyō.*) You know that cloth . . . well, the cloth . . . Unzu—you do the talking.

UNZU: Uh . . . how shall I put it . . . if you take that cloth to the *capital* and sell it, you could get a thou . . .

SŌDO (*breaking in*): Idiot! Look here, Yohyō, we could make you hundreds of gold pieces next time. Why not get her to weave again?

YOHYŌ: Did you say "hundreds?"

SŌDO: Yes, hundreds. (*To Unzu.*) We could, couldn't we?

UNZU: Yes, yes. Hundreds.

YOHYŌ: Really? Hundreds of gold pieces?

SŌDO: So talk to your wife a bit more . . . (*Notices Tsū, who has been watching them from inside the house.*) Come over here. I'll spell it all out for you. (*Drags Yohyō into the shadows.*)

Unzu follows them. Tsū comes out of the house and watches them go. A shadow of sadness passes over her face. The children come running in.

CHILDREN (*in turn*): She's back!

(*To Tsū.*) Come on, let's play.

Why were you out?

Let's sing songs.

Bird in the Cage.

Hide and Seek.

Songs.

Ring-a-Ring-a-Ring. (*Form a circle round her.*) Come on.

TSŪ: It's dark already. Enough for today.

CHILDREN: No, no. Let's play. Songs.

TSŪ (*vacantly*): Songs?

CHILDREN: Hide and Seek.

TSŪ: Hide and Seek?

CHILDREN: Ring-o-Ring-o-Ring.

TSŪ: Ring-o-Ring-o-Ring?

CHILDREN: Bird in the Cage.

TSŪ: Bird in the Cage?

CHILDREN: Yes, Bird in the Cage. (*They surround her and begin dancing around.*)

Bird in the Cage.
Bird in the Cage.
When, oh when, will you fly away?
In the night, before the dawn,
Slip, slip, slip, you slipped away.
Who's behind you? Guess.
Who's behind you? Guess.
Who's behind you? Guess.

What's the matter? You're supposed to cover your eyes. Why don't you? Aren't you going to crouch down?

TSŪ (*stays standing, lost in thought*): Eh? . . . Oh. (*Crouches down and covers her eyes.*)

The children dance round her singing. All around becomes suddenly dark. Only Tsū is left, picked out in a pool of light.

TSŪ: Yohyō, my precious Yohyō. What has happened to you? Little by little you are changing. You are starting to inhabit a different world from mine. You are starting to be like those terrible men who shot the arrow into me, men whose language I do not understand. What has happened to you? And what can I do about it? Tell me, what can I do? . . . You were the one who saved my life. You pulled the arrow out because you took pity on me—you were not looking for any reward. I was so happy about that. That is why I came to your home. Then I wove that cloth for you, and you were so delighted—like a child. So I endured the pain and wove more and more for you. And then you exchanged it for "money." I see nothing wrong in this—if you like "money" so much. Now you have plenty of this "money" you like, so I want us to live quietly and happily together in this little house, just the two of us. You are different from other men. You belong to my world. I thought we could live here forever, in the middle of this great plain, quietly creating a world for just the two of us, plowing the fields and playing with the children . . . but somehow you are moving away from me. You are steadily getting farther and farther away from me. What am I to do? Really, what am I to do?

The singing has stopped. The lights come up. The children have gone. Tsū suddenly looks to the side and hurries into the house as if she were being pursued. Pause. Sōdo, Unzu, and Yohyō appear.

SŌDO: So you know what you've got to do. If she refuses to do any more weaving, you threaten her—say you'll leave her.

YOHYŌ (*contentedly*): That cloth's beautiful, isn't it? And it's because Tsū wove it.

SŌDO: Sure, it *is* beautiful, so next time we're going to sell it for two or three times as much money as we got for it before. Get it? We are going to sell it for two or three times what we sold it for before. Tell your wife that.

YOHYŌ (*repeating*): We're going to sell it for two or three times what we got for it before. How did I do?

SŌDO: Fine. For hundreds of gold pieces.

YOHYŌ: For hundreds of gold pieces. Right?

SŌDO: Good. So get her to weave it right away. Yes, Unzu?

UNZU: Yes. Get her to weave it right away—tonight.

YOHYŌ: But Tsū said she wouldn't weave any more.

SŌDO: Don't be an idiot. If you sell it for a high price and make a big profit, she'll be pleased too.

UNZU: Yes, yes. She'll be pleased too.

YOHYŌ: Mmmm . . .

SŌDO: There's something else—listen to this—we're going to take you sightseeing in the capital. Unzu will tell you what a great place the capital is.

UNZU: Yes, yes. It's a great place.

YOHYŌ: I suppose the capital must be a great place.

SŌDO: Of course it is. So have you got it? You're going to make a lot of money, and you're having a sightseeing tour of the capital thrown in. Like I've just said, we'll show you lots of interesting things in the capital. Are you with me? Or maybe you don't want to go to the capital.

YOHYŌ: No, I *do* want to go.

UNZU: You want money too, don't you?

YOHYŌ: Mm. I do want money.

SŌDO (*noticing Tsū in the house*): Right. In you go. You know what you've got to do—make her start weaving right away. If she won't, say you're leaving her.

YOHYŌ: . . . mmmm . . .

SŌDO (*pushing Yohyō into the house*): It'll be all right. You're great. (*To Unzu*) We'll get out of sight and watch what happens.

The two of them hide again.

TSŪ (*as soon as the two have disappeared, rushes toward Yohyō*): Yohyō, come into the house, quickly. You are so wet—you will catch a cold. Supper is all ready. You put the soup on the fire for me, so it is nice and hot. Come on, start eating. Come closer to the fire.

YOHYŌ: . . . all right . . .

TSŪ: Please, do eat.

YOHYŌ: All right. (*Eats.*)

TSŪ: What is the matter? . . . Why are you so depressed? . . . You really should not do such things—staying out so late, in the cold. . . . Please do not go away anymore. Please do not talk to any strangers. Please.

YOHYŌ: All right. . . .

TSŪ: Promise me, will you? Whatever you tell me to do, I will do. Whatever it is, I will do it for you. And you have the "money" you like so much. . . .

YOHYŌ: Yes, I've got money. Lots of it. It's in this bag here.

TSŪ: There you are. So from now on, let us live happily together, just the two of us.

YOHYŌ: Yes. I do love you.

TSŪ: And I really love you, too. So please, please stay as you are now, forever.

YOHYŌ: Yes, I love you, I really do.

Pause.

TSŪ: Have another helping. . . . What is the matter? . . . Aren't you going to eat any more? . . .

YOHYŌ: Mmmm . . . look, Tsū . . .

TSŪ: Mm?

YOHYŌ: You've done lots of good things in your life, haven't you? You went to the capital quite often . . . .

TSŪ: Well, not really, just in the sky—(*Pulls herself up short.*) What is it? Aren't you going to have any more food?

YOHYŌ: Mmmm. . . . (*Hesitating.*) look, Tsū . . .

TSŪ: Yes?

YOHYŌ: I want . . . no, I can't say it.

TSŪ: What is it? What is the matter?

YOHYŌ: I want . . . it's no good, I can't say it.

TSŪ: Why? What is it you can't say? . . . Shall I try and guess?

YOHYŌ: Yes, yes.

TSŪ: Well now . . . you want me to make some of those cakes again. . . .

YOHYŌ: No, it's not that.

TSŪ: Wrong? So . . . you want me to sing you a song. Is that it?

YOHYŌ: No. Of course I like your singing. But not today.

TSŪ: Wrong again? So . . . you want me to tell you about the capital again. . . . Yes? I have guessed it.

YOHYŌ: Well, half right, and half wrong.

TSŪ: Really? Half right, and half wrong? . . . So what is it? Tell me.

YOHYŌ: You won't get angry?

TSŌ: Me be angry? About something to do with you? . . . What is it? Tell me, tell me.

YOHYŌ (*hesitates*): I . . . I want to go to the capital.

TSŪ: Eh?

YOHYŌ: I'm going to the capital and I'm going to make piles of money. . . . So . . . I want some more of that cloth. . . .

TSŪ (*startled*): The cloth? You cannot . . .

YOHYŌ (*flustered*): No, no, I don't, I don't need it.

TSŪ: (*as if to herself*): I told you . . . there was to be no more . . . of the cloth . . . and you promised me so faithfully. . . .

YOHYŌ: Yes, you did say that. So I don't need it. I don't need it. . . . (*Tries desperately to stop himself bursting into tears, like a child who has been scolded.*)

TSŪ (*suddenly realizing*): Ah, those men. Those men that were here just now. It was them, wasn't it? Yes, that must be it. They are gradually taking you away from me.

YOHYŌ: What's the matter? . . . Don't get angry. . . .

TSŪ: . . .

YOHYŌ: Tsū . . .

TSŪ (*blankly*): Money . . . money . . . why do you want it so much?

YOHYŌ: Well, if I've got money, I can buy everything I want—all the good things there are.

TSŪ: You will "buy." What does "buy" mean? What do you mean by "good things"? What do you need apart from me? No, no, you must not want anything apart from me. You must not want to "buy" things. What you must do is be affectionate to me—and only me. You and I must live together, just the two of us, forever and ever.

YOHYŌ: Of course—I like being with you. I really do love you.

TSŪ: Yes, you do! You do. (*Hugs Yohyō.*) . . . Please stay as you are, like this, forever. Don't leave me. Please don't leave me.

YOHYŌ: Don't be silly. Who could leave someone like you? Silly, silly.

TSŪ: . . . When I am being held tightly by you, like this . . . I remember how it used to be . . . the whole vast sky around me, without a care in the world, with nothing to worry about. . . . I feel now like I did then. . . . This is what makes me happy now—as long as I am with you, I am happy. . . . Stay with me forever. . . . Please don't go to any far-off places, will you. (*Pause. Suddenly thrusts him away from her.*) You're still thinking about the capital, aren't you? You're still thinking about your "money."

YOHYŌ: Tsū, look . . .

TSŪ: Yes, you are. You are, aren't you? As I thought . . . (*Suddenly agitated.*) No, no, you mustn't go to the capital. You will never come back. You will never come back to me.

YOHYŌ: Of course I'll come back. I will come back. I'll go to the capital, I'll make a big profit on the cloth and—oh, yes, you're coming to the capital with me.

Pause.

TSŪ: Do you want to go to the capital that much? . . . Do you want this "money" so much?

YOHYŌ: Look, everybody wants money.

TSŪ: You want it so, so much? You want to go so much? You like money so much more than you like me? And the capital as well? Do you?

YOHYŌ: What do you think you're . . . you talk to me like that, and I'll stop loving you.

TSŪ: What did you say? You'll stop loving me?

YOHYŌ: I don't love you. I don't. I don't love you, Tsū. You get on my nerves.

TSŪ: Really . . .

YOHYŌ: WEAVE THE CLOTH! I'm going to the capital. I'm going to make money.

TSŪ: That's too much, too much. What are you saying?

YOHYŌ: Weave the cloth! If you don't . . . I'll leave you.

TSŪ: What did you say? You'll leave me? Yohyō, what has happened to you?

YOHYŌ: . . . (*Stubbornly remains silent.*)

TSŪ: Yohyō, Yohyō. (*Grabs his shoulders and shakes him.*) Do you mean it? Yohyō. Were you serious?

YOHYŌ: . . . . I will leave you. So weave the cloth.

TSŪ: Ah . . .

YOHYŌ: Weave the cloth. Weave it now! We're going to sell it for two or three times what we got for it before. For hundreds of gold pieces.

TSŪ (*suddenly very alarmed and flustered*): Eh? Eh? What did you just say? I heard "Weave the cloth now." Then what did you say?

YOHYŌ: I said, for hundreds of gold pieces. We're going to sell the cloth for two or three times as much money as we got before.

TSŪ: . . . (*She tilts her head to one side like a bird and watches Yohyō suspiciously.*)

YOHYŌ: Listen to me. This time the money we get will be two or three times . . .

TSŪ (*screams*): I don't understand any more. I don't understand anything you are saying. It's the same as with those other men. I can see the mouth moving. I can hear the voice. But what is being said. . . . Ah, Yohyō, you've started talking the language that these men used—the language of a different world—that I cannot understand. . . . What am I to do? What am I to do?

YOHYŌ: Tsū, what's the matter? Tsū . . .

TSŪ: "What's the matter?" "Tsū." You did say that, didn't you? You did say "What's the matter?" just then?

YOHYŌ: . . . (*Taken aback, he just gazes at Tsū's face.*)

TSŪ: I heard you correctly, didn't I? You did say that? Eh? . . . Ah, you are gradually getting farther and farther away from me. You are getting smaller . . . Ah, what am I to do? What? (*Out toward where Sōdo and Unzu might be.*) Don't keep doing this. Don't! Stop taking Yohyō away from me. (*Comes out of the house.*) Where are you? I beg you, I beg you. Don't take my Yohyō away from me. (*Turns this way and that.*) Please, please, I beg you, I beg you. . . . Aren't you there? . . . Are you hiding? Come out! . . . Cowards! . . . Louts! . . . Louts, that's what you are. . . . Oh, how I hate you! I hate you. . . . You're taking my Yohyō . . . Come out of there! Come out! . . . . No, no, I'm sorry. . . . I shouldn't talk like that. . . . Please, please, I beg you. I beg you, please. (*Her strength gradually fails, and she sinks down in the snow.*)

YOHYŌ (*comes out to her, fearfully*): What's the matter? Tsū . . . (*Puts his arms around her.*)

TSŪ (*coming to*): Ah, Yohyō.

YOHYŌ: Come, Tsū, let's go into the house. It's cold, in the snow . . . (*Almost carries her to the fireside.*)

For a few moments the two of them warm themselves at the fire, in silence.

TSŪ: You're so anxious to go? You want to go to the capital that much?

YOHYŌ: Look, Tsū . . .

Pause.

YOHYŌ: The capital's beautiful. And just about now, the cherry trees must be in bloom.

Pause.

YOHYŌ: And then there are the oxen, lots of them. Pulling carriages with people riding in them. You've often told me about all this.

Pause.

YOHYŌ (*yawns*): Oh, I'm tired. (*He stretches out and goes to sleep.*)

Tsū realizes he has gone to sleep and puts something over him. She stares at his sleeping face, immobile. Then she suddenly rises and takes a cloth bag from the corner of the room. She empties the contents over the palm of her hand. The bag contains gold coins, and they spill out over the floor. She stares at them. All around suddenly becomes dark; only Tsū and the gold coins remain, in a pool of light.

TSŪ: This is what it is all about. . . . Money . . . money. . . . I just wanted you to have beautiful cloth to look at . . . and I was so happy when you showed how pleased you were. . . . That was the only reason I wore myself down weaving it for you . . . and now . . . I do not have any other way of keeping you with me . . . weave the cloth to get the money . . . if I do not do it . . . if I don't do this, you will not stay by my side, will you . . . but . . . but . . . perhaps I have to accept it . . . if getting more and more of this money gives you so much pleasure . . . if going to the capital is so important to you . . . and if you will not go away and leave me, provided I let you do all these things . . . well, one more time, I will weave just one more length of cloth for you. . . . And then . . . and then you must be content. Because if I weave more, I might not survive. . . . So you take the cloth, go to the capital . . . make lots of money and come home. . . . Yes, come home. You must come back. You must, must come back to me. Then finally we shall be together, the two of us, and we can live together forever, forever. . . . Please let it be like that.

The lights come up.

TSŪ (*shaking Yohyō awake*): Yohyō, Yohyō.

YOHYŌ: Mmm? Ah . . . (*Mumbling.*)

TSŪ: Listen. The cloth. I will weave it for you.

YOHYŌ: Eh? What was that?

TSŪ: I will weave the cloth for you.

YOHYŌ: The cloth? Ah—you'll weave it for me?

TSŪ: Yes, I will weave it. One piece only.

YOHYŌ: You really will?

TSŪ: Yes, really. I really will weave it for you. So you can go to the capital with it.

YOHYŌ: I can go to the capital? Really?

TSŪ: Yes. So you will come back with lots of the money you like so much. And after that . . . and after that . . .

YOHYŌ: Oh—you're going to weave it? I can go to the capital? Oh . . . yes, I'll come back with piles of money. Piles and piles of money.

TSŪ: . . . (*Staring at how pleased Yohyō is.*) So—just one thing—the promise
you always make. You know you must never look at me while I'm weaving.
You know that, don't you? You absolutely must not.

YOHYŌ: No, no, I won't. Ah, you're actually going to weave the cloth for me?

TSŪ: Listen to me. I'm begging you. You must keep the promise, you must.
Don't look in at me. . . . If you do, everything is over between us.

YOHYŌ: Yes, yes, I won't look. Heh—I'm going to the capital. I'm going to make
two or three times the money I made last time.

TSŪ: . . . Don't . . . don't look . . . (*Goes into the other room where the loom is.*)
The sound of a loom is heard. Sōdo leaps out of the shadows. Unzu follows.

SŌDO: We've done it! She's started weaving—at last!

UNZU: All right, but watching her from the shadows, I began to feel very sorry
for her.

SŌDO: You're a stupid idiot. We're about to make a lot of money—it's not the
time to start feeling sorry for people . . . . (*Runs up into the house and goes
to look into the weaving room.*)

YOHYŌ: Hey—you can't do that. You're not supposed to look.

UNZU: Sōdo, you know you're not supposed to look while she's weaving.

SŌDO: Shut up, both of you. If I don't see her weaving, how do I know whether
it's genuine Crane Feather Weave or not?

YOHYŌ: No, no, you can't. She'll get mad at you. Stop!

UNZU: Sōdo, stop!

SŌDO: Let go of me. Let go! (*Looks into the room.*) Ah . . . ah . . .

UNZU: What is it?

SŌDO: Ah . . . have a look. It's a crane. A crane. A crane is sitting at the loom
and weaving.

UNZU: What? A crane? (*Looks in.*) Ah . . . ah . . . it *is* a crane. The woman's
not in there. It's a crane. It's holding a few of its own feathers in its beak and
moving forward and backward over the loom . . . I've never . . .

SŌDO: Well there you are, Unzu. Looks as though we've got it right.

UNZU: I suppose it does.

YOHYŌ: What is it? What's going on?

SŌDO: That's what you're in love with—in there. Right, Unzu, we should have
the cloth by tomorrow morning. We can go home and wait.

UNZU: I suppose we can . . .

YOHYŌ: Heh, you two—what's in there? . . . Isn't it Tsū?

UNZU (*being hustled off by Sōdo*): It's a crane. There's a crane in there.
Sōdo drags Unzu off.

YOHYŌ: A crane? Can't be . . . can there? In the room? . . . I want to have a
look.. No, I mustn't, I mustn't. Tsū will be angry with me. . . . But what's a
crane doing in there? Oh, I do want to have a look. . . . Would it be wrong
to have a look? Tsū, tell me. Tsū, I'm going to have a quick look. . . . No, I
shouldn't, I shouldn't. Tsū said I should not look. Tsū, Tsū. Why don't you

answer? Tsū, Tsū. . . . What can have happened? What's happened? Tsū . . . no answer . . . I want to have a look . . . I want to look . . . Tsū, I'm going to have a little look. . . . (*Finally he looks in.*) Eh? There's just a crane in there . . . no sign of Tsū. . . . Eh? . . . What's happened? . . . Tsū . . . Tsū . . . She's not there. . . . What am I to do? . . . She's not there. She's gone. Tsū . . . Tsū . . . Tsū . . . (*He goes out of the house and disappears offstage, searching for her frantically.*)

Afterward only the sound of the loom is heard. Blackout. Above the sound of the loom a poem is read aloud.

> Yohyō, Yohyō, where do you go?
> Over the dark, snowy plain, hither and thither,
> Searching for Tsū.
> Tsū . . . Tsū . . . Tsū
> Your voice is cracked and hoarse,
> Soon the rays of the morning sun play on the snow,
> Afternoon arrives and it is the same:
> Tsū . . . Tsū . . . Tsū
> Now in the evening, behind the house,
> Today as yesterday the whole sky is a deep, deep red.

The lights come up. The sound of the loom continues. Sōdo and Unzu come in supporting Yohyō, who is in a bad way.

UNZU: Yohyō, are you all right? Pull yourself together.

SŌDO: I didn't believe it—there you were, lying in the snow—why did you go so far?

UNZU: You'd have frozen to death if we hadn't brought you back.

YOHYŌ: Tsū . . . Tsū . . .

UNZU: He's come round. Hey, Yohyō.

SŌDO: Yohyō, pull yourself together.

YOHYŌ: Tsū . . . Tsū . . .

Pause.

SŌDO: Is she ever going to stop weaving?

UNZU: You're right. She usually weaves it all in one night. But this time it's taking a night and a day.

SŌDO: Hmm. Perhaps I'll take another look.

The sound of the loom stops abruptly.

UNZU: It's stopped.

SŌDO: She's coming out!

The two of them panic and jump down from the house. They hide in the shadows. Tsū emerges carrying two lengths of cloth. She looks emaciated.

TSŪ: Yohyō . . . Yohyō . . . (*She shakes Yohyō awake.*)

YOHYŌ (*almost calling, as before*): Tsū . . . Tsū . . .

TSŪ: Yohyō.

YOHYŌ: Tsū . . . (*Realizes.*) Ah—Tsū. (*Embraces her tightly as he breaks into tears.*) Tsū, where did you go? You weren't here and I . . .

TSŪ: I am sorry. I took so long, didn't I? I have woven the cloth. Look . . . here you are . . . the cloth.

YOHYŌ: The cloth? Oh, you've woven the *cloth.* . . .

TSŪ: . . . (*Stares at the delighted Yohyō.*)

YOHYŌ: This is great. It's beautiful. Oh, there're two pieces, aren't there?

TSŪ: Yes, two pieces. That's why it took me until now. So you take the cloth and go off on your trip to the capital.

YOHYŌ: Yes, I'm going to the capital. You're coming with me, aren't you?

TSŪ: . . . (*Weeps.*)

YOHYŌ: Yes—you're coming with me and we'll all go sightseeing.

TSŪ: Yohyō . . . you looked, didn't you?

YOHYŌ: I want to get to the capital quickly. Tsū, you've woven it so well.

TSŪ: I begged you so hard . . . and you promised so faithfully . . . why, why did you look?

YOHYŌ: What is it? Why are you crying?

TSŪ: I wanted to be with you forever—forever. . . . One of those two pieces is for you . . . keep it and treasure it. I put my whole heart into the weaving so that you could have it.

YOHYŌ: Really, this is superbly woven.

TSŪ (*grasping him by the shoulders*): Keep it and treasure it. Take great, great care of it.

YOHYŌ (*like a child*): Yes, I will take great, great care of it, as you tell me to. I always listen to what you say to me. (*Pleading.*) Let's go to the capital together.

TSŪ (*shaking her head*): I shall be . . . (*Smiles and stands up—suddenly she is white all over.*) Look how thin I have become. I used every single feather I could. What's left is just enough to let me fly. . . . (*She laughs quietly.*)

YOHYŌ (*suddenly sensing something*): Tsū. (*Tries to embrace her, but his arms enclose only empty space.*)

TSŪ: Yohyō . . . take care of yourself . . . take good care of yourself always, always . . .

In the distance the children's singing is heard.

> Let's make a coat for grandpa to wear,
> Let's make a coat for grandma to wear,
> Lah-lala lah, lah lah lah,
> Lah-lala, lah-lala, lah lah lah.

TSŪ: I have to say good-bye to the children too. . . . How many times have I sung that song with them? . . . Yohyō, don't forget me, will you. We had only a short time together, but I won't forget how your pure love was all around me or all the days when we played and sang songs with the children. I will never, never forget. Wherever I go, I will never . . .

YOHYŌ: Heh, Tsū . . .

TSŪ: Good-bye . . . good-bye . . .

YOHYŌ: Tsū, wait, wait I say. I'm coming too. Tsū, Tsū.

TSŪ: No, you cannot, you cannot. And I cannot stay in this human form any longer. I have to return to the sky where I came from, alone. . . . Good-bye . . . take care . . . good-bye—it really *is* good-bye. . . . (*Disappears.*)

YOHYŌ: Tsū, Tsū, where have you gone? Tsū. (*Confused, he comes out of the house.*)

Sōdo and Unzu leap out and hold him back.

UNZU (*out of breath, to Sōdo*): Heh . . .

SŌDO (*out of breath*): She's disappeared.

Yohyō is in a state of stupor in Unzu's arms. The children come running in.

CHILDREN (*in unison, as if they were singing*):

> Come out and sing us a song, please do.
> Come out and play some games, please do.
> Come out and sing us a song.

Total silence.

ONE CHILD (*suddenly points up to the sky*): A crane! A crane! Look, there's a crane flying up there.

SŌDO: A crane?

UNZU (*scared*): Ah . . .

CHILDREN: A crane. A crane. A crane. (*Repeating this, they run off following the crane.*)

UNZU: Yohyō, look, a crane.

SŌDO: It looks as though it's having to struggle to stay in the air.

Pause.

SŌDO (*to no one in particular*): We've got two pieces of cloth. That's great. (*He tries to take the cloth that Yohyō is holding, but Yohyō clutches it to himself.*)

UNZU (*absorbed in watching the crane fly away, still with his arms round Yohyō*): It's gradually getting smaller. . . .

YOHYŌ: Tsū . . . Tsū . . . (*Takes one or two unsteady steps as if following the crane. Then stands stock-still, clutching the cloth tightly.*)

Sōdo also seems to be drawn in that direction, and the three of them gaze, fixed on a point in the distant sky. From offstage the sound of the children singing drifts faintly in.

MISHIMA YUKIO

In the West, Mishima Yukio (1925–1970) is best known as a novelist, but in Japan, he is equally renowned as a playwright. Mishima generally used his plays to express his more poetic and literary aims, saving his novels and short stories for his political views. Mishima knew and appreciated Japan's classical theater in its various forms, and among his most successful dramas are his adaptations of traditional nō plays. These short plays, set in contemporary times, use older themes and concerns but with new, and sometimes startling, twists in plot and psychology.

Yuya, published in 1955, is a fresh and ironic version of the original nō play, in which Yuya's protector does allow her to return to visit her ailing mother.

YUYA, A MODERN NŌ PLAY

Translated by Jonah Salz and Lawrence B. Kominz

CAST OF CHARACTERS

Munemori
Yuya
Asako
Yamada
Masa

A room in Yuya's luxurious apartment. On the fourth wall, facing the audience, imaginary glass doors and balcony. A bed in the stage left area. Beside the bed, a telephone. The windows at the back of the stage face the apartment building's inner garden; only the next apartment building's windows can be seen. In the center of the stage, a table with chairs. Stage right, a door as well as a three-sided mirror and other items. A large suitcase sits beside the bed. The room is extremely neat, with a mood of imminent departure.

Spring. At the peak of the cherry blossom season on a tranquil Sunday morning. Yuya, in her traveling clothes, is lying on top of the bed. Munemori is sitting in the easy chair at stage right, having taken off his jacket, and is smoking a cigar.

MUNEMORI (*a successful business magnate, about fifty years old*): So? Well, shall we leave? If we miss that view from the hilltop of that sea of cherry trees today, we'll have to wait until next year. Whichever newspaper forecast you read, they say the blossoms won't last past Sunday. Only the unemployed can afford to go cherry-blossom viewing on weekdays. And so this year's blossoms can be viewed only today. Right?

I will tell you once again: this will be the last chance to see such a magnificent display of cherry blossoms. This year I'm going to cut down half those trees because I have to expand the zoo and rebuild the aquarium and so on. We no longer live in an age when customers can be lured with mere cherry trees. My train has to carry passengers to the amusement park in all four seasons.

(*Looking at his wristwatch.*) It's already eleven o'clock. Come now, come now. We planned to leave here by ten—what if the changeable spring sky turns to rain? Well?

You don't understand, do you, Yuya? What I want to show you are not just any cherry trees (*pats his chest*) these are my trees. I want to show you my cherry trees, in full bloom.

(*Stands up, annoyed.*) To drive there takes at least two hours. Even if we leave now, we'll arrive at one o'clock at the earliest, and even if we leave immediately, it'll take three minutes to get to the lobby by elevator. Then greeting that overpolite doorman will take another ten seconds. And if that chauffeur happens to be dozing in this fine weather, it'll take another three minutes to wake him.

No, I'm not blaming you for keeping the chauffeur waiting or anything like that. I'm just explaining to you that although you may not realize it, at my usual business pace, one split second can mean millions of yen, sometimes even tens of millions of yen. And I'm saying that you lack sympathy for that fact.

I suppose, on the other hand, that it is precisely because you do not know about these things that makes you who you are. He approaches her and looks down at her face. Isn't that so?

(*As he is about to stroke her hair, the bedside telephone rings. Munemori picks up the handset.*) Yes, it's me. Me. Right. I see. Hm . . . Right. Right. Yes, good work. Right. Yes, please do take care of that for me. That's fine. (*Returns the handset.*)

That was my secretary. He's my manager on Sundays. (*He again tries to stroke Yuya's hair, at which point Yuya withdraws from him, sitting up in bed. She is a twenty-two- or twenty-three-year-old beauty, her face pale from sorrow.*)

YUYA: Please don't be offended. I usually adore it when you stroke my hair. But I can't stand it now. I am so full of grief and anxiety to the ends of my hair that I feel as though tears were spilling even from my hair. And so I'm asking you: please don't touch me. My tears are brimming over, so that moving my body even slightly feels like they will overflow. Even though I'm glad that you thought of taking me with you cherry-blossom viewing . . .

MUNEMORI: You see? You always talk to me this way, even when refusing me. Even when you're angry, you use such gentle words. The sort of woman that I have known until now would scream at a time like this, "If you want to go so badly, why not take your wife and children!?"

YUYA (*sadly but with a faint smile*): I suppose there really are women who would speak so bluntly to a man like you.

MUNEMORI: Well? Why aren't you so blunt with me?

YUYA: Because I'm afraid of you.

YUYA/MUNEMORI (*mocking her*): You're so wonderful . . .

MUNEMORI (*laughing*): See? That won't do.

YUYA: Well then, would it be better if I said, "You, who are so wonderful and kind—"

MUNEMORI: "I, who am so wonderful and kind, try to force you, so anxious for your mother, to go flower viewing. Even though you could fly to your hometown in Hokkaido in one short hop, I absolutely forbid you to go." You are right. You are correct.

As I have been telling you all along, of course I do not want to let you go. No matter how sick your mother is, I have my own reasons. I want you by my side for just a day longer. These days, it doesn't matter to me what people think; I even ignore my own family.

However, what I'm trying to do now is offer a compromise. If you go with me on today's excursion, that will be enough. Tomorrow, I'll allow you to return to your mother's side. That's a promise. But you become obstinate and insist on abandoning our flower viewing and fret and pester me about it, saying that you want to go home today. . . . You should think it over. Or we should call someone to sit as jury and judge this case. Who wouldn't recognize the reasonableness of my position?

YUYA: But do you really think that you can take me with you, my face so full of sorrow, and enjoy flower viewing?

MUNEMORI: I keep telling you; I'll be happy.

YUYA (*covering her face*): If you really loved me, you couldn't be happy. You do not really love me.

MUNEMORI: There you go again, talking of "love." I'm speaking of pleasure. Taking you with me cherry-blossom viewing—that will satisfy me, and I will be happy.

YUYA: But what about my grief? I mean, what about my heart? Are you saying that they have nothing to do with it?

MUNEMORI (*forcefully decisive*): You're right. Your feelings have absolutely nothing to do with it. You have a beautiful face. And a beautiful body. To go with a woman like you cherry-blossom viewing—that alone is enough. For pleasure in this earthly life.

Yuya raises her face to Munemori then, startled, quickly lowers it. Pause.

MUNEMORI (*facing away, extremely gently*): Well, will you come? (*Yuya facing Munemori's back, her head bowed, does not answer.*) Well, then, I guess you don't care for me.

YUYA (*facing Munemori again*): You, you also talk of love, don't you? But can't you understand that it is precisely because I care for you that I'm pleading with you this way? If I had no worries at all, how happy I would be to drive, on such a splendid spring day, to look at the blossoms with you!

But worried sick about my mother, my body is about to collapse with grief. If you drag me against my will to go cherry-blossom viewing, however beautiful the blossoms are, they will look like nothing to me; the happier the people are, the greater the contrast they will be to my own unhappiness, and the bright sky will seem no different from night. And in the end, I'm certain that I'll come to hate you. And that's what I am most afraid of. I'd rather visit my mother now, as soon as possible, to make certain that she is all right. Then as soon as I come back, we can go out for a wonderful excursion to look at the flowers!

MUNEMORI: The blossoms won't wait, Yuya. I keep telling you—the blossoms won't wait.

YUYA: A heavy heart, the trees in full bloom—the pleasure of that flower viewing and this deep grief can never become one. . . .

MUNEMORI: Those are things that I'll bring together.

YUYA: At a time like this, there are no pleasures that could comfort me.

MUNEMORI (*taking Yuya's chin*): Take courage, and turn this sad face toward happiness, Yuya. Your face is like the moon, which, when struck by the light, grows bright but, when stricken by grief, is shrouded in shadows. Do not be a prisoner of your love, but boldly throw yourself into happiness. Yes? If you do, your youth will allow you to forget a thing like your mother's illness.

YUYA (*shaking free and lowering her face*): I can't do that! I can't do that!!

Just then, there is a knock from the stage right door. Yuya and Munemori do not move. Another strong knock and then a voice is heard. "It's me, Yuya, Asako." Yuya starts to rise. Munemori gestures for her to wait and then quickly puts on his jacket and opens the door.

ASAKO: Oh, was I interrupting something?

MUNEMORI: Come in.

ASAKO (*Yuya's friend. She lives in the same apartment building. A woman in the same circumstances. Younger than Yuya, her clothing also is flashier.*): Is it really all right to come in? (*She enters.*) Yuya, here's a letter from your Mother. (*She hands it to Yuya, who quickly takes it and opens the envelope.*)

MUNEMORI: How long have you been delivering mail for the post office?

ASAKO: But it's your fault, Mr. Munemori. Yuya's mother fears you like a god. The trains, the amusement parks, the zoos, the banks—she knows that they all belong to you. And she even thinks that it would take just a word from you to censor the mail. And so she started sending important letters in care of me.

MUNEMORI: You really know how to flatter me, don't you?

ASAKO: After all, everyone here knows that Yuya and I are close friends.

MUNEMORI: Anyway, it's delightful to imagine two such beautiful women sharing each other's secrets. And I suppose Yuya also has been useful to you with your intrigues?

ASAKO: Oh, Yuya's no good at all. She's useless. She's just too honest.

During this exchange, Yuya has been reading her mother's letter, weeping bitterly.

MUNEMORI: Come now, show me the letter.

(*Yuya silently hands Munemori the letter. Munemori takes out his reading glasses and puts them on, turns the letter around and starts to read it, then returns it to Yuya.*) Will you read it to me? I'm used to having my really important letters read to me by my secretary. Besides, the handwriting is so faint, it's hard to read. So, please read it—I am listening.

YUYA (*reading the letter*): "As I wrote you in early March, while I feel somehow that I will not be able to greet the cherry blossoms this spring, the northern snow has begun to melt, little by little. And as the clouds in the sky take on the gentleness of spring, I have come to believe that this omen of spring is but an omen of my death. Like the stubborn icicles under the eaves growing thinner and thinner, I grow weaker day by day. I want so much to see you once more before I die." (*Yuya cries.*)

ASAKO (*crying sympathetically, puts a hand on Yuya's shoulder*): Poor thing, poor thing.

YUYA: "I want so much to see you once more before I die. These days, a sort of rainbow often appears in front of my eyes, and dark shadows pass across them. So while I can still see clearly with these eyes, I want to see your face, even for a moment. That's all I want—that's all I have left in this world. Somehow, get permission to leave, and come visit me one last time."

While Yuya, occasionally wiping away her tears, continues reading the letter, Munemori puffs on a cigar, silently staring at her; Asako gradually notices Munemori's manner, and she glares at him.

ASAKO: Well, Mr. Munemori? Yuya is weeping like some charming, beautiful doll, isn't she?

MUNEMORI (*to Asako*): What are you talking about?

YUYA: "Please come visit me once more, / Please come, before this dying cherry trees falls, / Without blossoming in season. / Please fulfill this old nightingale's hope, / Chilled with snow and about to die / Not having seen this year's cherry blossoms."

MUNEMORI: What are you talking about? Amused, I'm listening sympathetically.

ASAKO: No, for you, Yuya is a charming, pretty, sad doll. The beauty of this weeping woman—I wonder what that looks like from a man's perspective? I know what you're thinking: "She's like a cherry tree in the rain"—Right? You seemed happy beneath the haze of that cigar smoke, your gaze changing Yuya into a small, sad, beautiful, sorrowful, doll.

MUNEMORI: Imagine what you wish—I'm sympathetic.

YUYA:

"Please fulfill this old nightingale's hope,
Chilled with snow and about to die."

MUNEMORI (*after a pause*): Is that all?

ASAKO (*taking Yuya's arm*): Yuya. Don't worry. Mr. Munemori said that he sym-pathizes with you. You won't have to go cherry-blossom viewing. You can go home right away!

YUYA (*a faint smile floats to her face*): Really?

MUNEMORI: No, I'm not giving up our flower viewing.

ASAKO: Mr. Munemori!

MUNEMORI: Once I have decided something, it cannot be changed.

Pause.

YUYA (*drying her eyes and mounting a counterattack*): Are you saying that we must go, no matter what?

MUNEMORI: Yes, no matter what.

YUYA: Flowers bloom every year; today is not the end of spring. But if I don't visit my mother now, I may not see her again in this world.

MUNEMORI: This year's blossoms can be seen only this year, Yuya. Today's plea-sures will not come again. "Today" comes only once in a lifetime.

YUYA: Oh! Then what's more important to you, a person's life or a blossom's life?

MUNEMORI: The most important thing for me is this moment. The "today" that is this day. On that point, regrettably, a person's life and a flower's life are equal. And if they are equal, then I prefer something pleasant to some-thing painful, Yuya. After all, even I may die tomorrow.

ASAKO: What? With such a fine physique?

YUYA: It is my mother who is dying.

MUNEMORI: What has that got to do with blossom viewing? Your mother was so proud of your beauty. Her daughter's beauty was her "career"—she went so far as to say that. That shows tremendous forethought, Yuya. If your mother truly believes that, then when her daughter is at the peak of her beauty, turn-ing strangers' heads as she walks beneath the full-blooming cherry trees on my land—if her daughter is to be the glory of that once-in-a-lifetime "today," she would not mind giving up her own life. In any case, because your mother has such a beautiful daughter, she has been able to live so comfortably, has she not?

YUYA: Oh, what a horrible thing to say!

ASAKO: Mr. Munemori, that's too much!

MUNEMORI: Yes, perhaps I have gone too far. But I—how shall I put it—I regret that you have neglected life's pleasures. The thing called pleasure is like death; it calls us from the ends of the earth. Once you are called by that shining voice, that penetrating sound, in the end you must jump up from your chair and go forth.

YUYA: For you, pleasure is a duty, then?

MUNEMORI: Not a duty. No more than death is a duty. No, not a duty. But he who neglects it will be punished.

YUYA: What kind of punishment?

MUNEMORI: A punishment called "regret." That dark, gloomy monster will appear. I hate it to the depths of my heart. To avoid regret, I do not mind spending any amount of money.

YUYA: If I do not go to visit my mother on her deathbed, it will be I who suffers regret.

MUNEMORI: Why should you feel regret? No matter how you look at it, it is my fault. If you blame me, that will be the end of it. If only you would go flower viewing, you and I both, together we would escape that damnable regret.

ASAKO: You will regret that all you had was mere "pleasure."

YUYA: While mine will be an awful regret that will pursue me throughout my life.

MUNEMORI: But both our regrets will vanish together. If you come with me submissively, blindly. Do not think, but follow me, silently—and those regrets will leave this earth. And only the image of a woman beautiful in sorrow, that rare image of her flower viewing, will remain in people's memory.

ASAKO: After treating Yuya like a doll, now you just want to paint her into a beautiful picture, don't you?

YUYA (*weakly*): I do not want to become some picture.

MUNEMORI: Why do you place such importance on your own emotions, Yuya? That's a kind of disease, you know. You get caught up with all sorts of conflicts between your happiness and sadness, but actually it is those conflicts that people enjoy. Opposites can illuminate each other; things that are incompatible can be fused together. This is what we call beauty. A grieving woman viewing cherry blossoms is more beautiful than a cheerful woman viewing them. Isn't that so, Yuya? You are very beautiful. And because of your beauty, you have the power to make two things, two things that are at odds with each other, become one. Going out blossom viewing in your grief—that is the fate that your beauty invites.

(*Approaching the telephone.*) Well, shall we call down to the lobby? To tell them to rouse that dozing chauffeur?

YUYA (*responding quickly*): Wait a moment! I'm begging you, wait a moment! Look! You can view the blossoms from right here. (*And gesturing as though opening the stage-edge doors to the right and left and taking two steps forward "onto the balcony." A railing may be used specifically for this scene.*) Even from the balcony, you can see so many cherry trees. Come here, you can see many cherry trees!

MUNEMORI (*going out on the balcony, standing next to Yuya*): You mean that tiny park's few, measly cherry trees? (*Stretches.*) Oh, but it does feel good out here. The sun warms you up, and the air is refreshing—far better than arguing in that tiny room.

YUYA (*encouragingly*): Yes, it's true. Here I'm sure you can feel refreshed. And now look at those trees. Each branch is filled with blossoms; it's so pretty.

MUNEMORI: Are you talking about those tiny, withered two or three trees, with faded blossoms that look like cotton fluff?

YUYA: But they are beautiful. Bathed in sunshine, they look like silver hair ornaments. Today the park is full of children. A child dressed in yellow. Another dressed in green. Listen, you can hear the sounds, carried by the wind, the squeak-squeak of the swing.

MUNEMORI: The high-arcing swings at my amusement park are much grander. And there are twenty-five of them in all.

YUYA: So many scattered blossoms have stuck to the shoulders of the children riding the swings, and they keep falling. The children love it. Even for the child who has no one to play with, the blossoms will be playmates.

MUNEMORI: You keep repeating, "the child, the child"—it seems as though you have "converted"—so now you want a child?

YUYA: Look, that little girl; that's me when I was a child. With the needle and thread that she's stolen from the sewing box, she threads each fallen petal one by one. But her hands are slow, and the petals are thin. Before she can finish the flower necklace, the day is over.

MUNEMORI: More important, before she can finish that necklace, the petals will rot.

YUYA: On that bench, beneath the cherry trees, there's a pair of young lovers. They sit where the light filtering through their canopy of blossoms softens their cheeks, afraid to embrace lest they just melt away. Hearing the cheerful shouts from the swings, and the bee's heavy buzzing, they gaze forever into each other's eyes, perfectly still.

MUNEMORI: They are young, and on top of that, poor; they sit that way not to be romantic but because they have no choice.

YUYA: Look! That thing that looked like a flower petal—it's a butterfly! It's landed in the black hair of the man. If his hair were greasy with pomade, the butterfly would soon be repelled. So that man must have used only a faint gel, giving off the natural scent of a field.

MUNEMORI: He hasn't got the money to buy even a cheap pomade, so he borrows some of the woman's leftover hair oil and rubs it in.

YUYA: Look! The woman notices the butterfly—she stretches out her hand—oh! the butterfly flew away. Surely the butterfly must be a female, and just as the face of a woman passing by will cast a slight shadow on even the love-blinded heart of a man, the butterfly paints a single brushstroke of wing powder into the man's soft black hair.

MUNEMORI: Imagine the future of the man who marries her, jealous even of a butterfly. I know many men like that. They fill the tiny boxes of their lives with the hollowness of unattained aspirations and the pathetic trust in their wives' faithfulness, becoming the most ridiculous of cowards.

YUYA: There's the full bloom of a truly beautiful cherry tree. The blossoms are wrapping the shadows, and in the miraculous sunlight, each branch in turn is showing off its fountain of blossoms and, among them, seductive dark branches.

MUNEMORI: What a pitiful sight. Pathetic, miserable cherry blossoms.

YUYA (*looking up at the sky*): Oh, those dark clouds appeared so suddenly.

MUNEMORI (*he, too, looks up at the sky*): Damn. I told you so.

YUYA: But the park is still lit by so much sunlight. . . . Oh, it has clouded over. The blossoms have suddenly lost their color. They have turned into white flowers of mourning. In the sandbox black dots appear here and there. It's raining. My cherry blossoms—soaked in the rain. (*Still gazing at them, she begins to cry.*)

MUNEMORI: Why are you crying? Hm?

YUYA: My cherry blossoms are. . . . My cherry blossoms are . . .

MUNEMORI (*pause*): Do you really want to go home so badly? It's already begun to rain—but surely it's only a passing shower. Well, it's all right, I guess. If you want to go home, hurry up and get ready to leave.

Yuya and Munemori return to the room. The balcony handrails are put away.

ASAKO (*hugging Yuya*): Yuya, It's wonderful, isn't it? It's wonderful, isn't it? You can go home! I really wondered if you'd be able to. It's truly wonderful!

YUYA: I'm so happy. I never wanted to leave without getting the proper permission. You understand. I never wanted to escape down a back alley to have to sneak home.

ASAKO: That's what's they mean by "female pride," Yuya. That's the way things are. There, now—I'll help you pack your things for the trip.

Just then, a knock from the stage right door.

MUNEMORI: Come in.

The door opens, and Mr. Yamada, the secretary, enters.

YAMADA (*fortyish and rather servile*): Sir, I've brought her along.

MUNEMORI: You've done well. Tell her to come in.

YAMADA: Well, come in. We've come so far, there's no need to struggle now. Please. (*Pulled by the hand by Yamada, Yuya's mother, Masa, appears.*) Come in. (*A fiftyish, plump, and seemingly energetic woman in Japanese dress. Yuya and Asako are shocked speechless.*)

MUNEMORI (*gently*): Well, Yuya. Greet your mother, who is on her deathbed.

YUYA (*angrily*): Mother! You're . . .

MASA: I know. I don't care how angry you are; there was nothing I could do. (*Points at Yamada.*) This secretary came all the way to Hokkaido to make sure that I was in tiptop shape. And without letting me get a word in edgewise, he forced me on a plane and then dragged me all the way here.

YUYA (*to Munemori*): Why has my mother been telling such lies? I have absolutely no idea. And she's made me worry so much.

MUNEMORI (*to Masa*): So, please calm down and tell us what you wish to. I'm not so vindictive by nature as to summon you here to attack Yuya or anything so petty.

MASA: Yuya, I'm going to tell him everything.

YUYA: Go ahead, spin whatever lies you want to.

MASA: You needn't speak so recklessly, Yuya. Even if it's painful for you now, at a time like this it's better to expose all, the entire truth. In any case, the president sees through everything. A gentleman dislikes lies. He prefers the truth. This is something that I can say from my long experience. But a gentleman, once he's grabbed hold of the truth, is soon bored. . . . (*To Munemori.*) I meant no harm. I never intended to fool you or lead you astray.

MUNEMORI: Excuses are not necessary. Just tell the truth.

MASA: All the letters were written because my daughter begged me to. She's told me that she has an old lover, named Kaoru, whom she wanted to visit, no matter what the consequences.

YUYA: Mother! So, you've been bribed, have you?

MASA (*ignoring Yuya*): Kaoru is in the Self-Defense Forces, so he cannot easily come to Tokyo. If I got sick, then Yuya could say she'd returned home to Hokkaido under the pretense of a condolence visit. Yuya, of course, never intended to stay in Hokkaido. She would handle everything quietly and, when she returned to Tokyo, would continue to receive your patronage. (*Looking over the room.*) After all, no one could throw such a life away so easily.

ASAKO: Yuya, don't give up. Could a real mother betray her daughter in such a filthy way?

YUYA (*contemplating for a moment, she appears to wake up*): This woman is not my true mother.

MUNEMORI: Are you still saying that your real mother is back in Hokkaido, gravely ill?

MASA: Whatever else you say, I am still the mother who bore this child.

YAMADA (*deliberately removes a document in his briefcase*): Well, according to this family register, Masa is not, in fact, Yuya's birth mother! Her birth mother died before Yuya was fifteen years old.

MUNEMORI: All right, I see—then who is Kaoru?

YAMADA: Kaoru really exists, stationed at Chiba Army Base. According to the reports of the private detective agency, this Kaoru has even bragged to his friends in the unit, "I have a woman in Tokyo who has become a wealthy man's mistress, saving up money for our marriage expenses."

ASAKO: Munemori, you're really something, aren't you? You've got your hand in things all over Japan, don't you?

YAMADA: Yes, it's true. That goes without saying.

All contemplate for a moment.

MUNEMORI: Well, now I wonder whether everyone could please leave? I would like to take some time to relish the truth of this affair.

YAMADA (*coaxing Masa*): All right, you've done your part. I think it would be best to leave now.

MASA: Everyone, please excuse the disturbance I've caused. (*Both leave.*)

ASAKO: Yuya, let's go now and talk things over in my room; after that, you can go on your trip. (*Rising first.*)

YUYA (*rising slowly, starts to leave. Turns her head gloomily*): Good-bye.

ASAKO: Well. (*And goes out the door.*)

MUNEMORI (*pause*): Yuya.

YUYA: . . .

MUNEMORI: You know, you don't have to leave.

YUYA (*gradually, a faint smile*): Oh? (*And shutting the door behind her.*) Oh.

MUNEMORI: Come lie down, just as before, on that bed. (*Yuya does as she's told.*) That's right. And now, just as before, put on that same sorrowful face.

YUYA: With nothing to do. Gazing at the balcony. The rain is growing worse.

MUNEMORI (*taking off his jacket, lights a fresh cigar*): So it seems. It looks as though it was not merely a passing shower.

YUYA: It's growing worse and worse. The room's grown dark. Shall we put on some lights?

MUNEMORI: This is fine just as it is, just as it is.

YUYA: I'm sure that there's not one child left in the park. That pair of young lovers is also gone. And that little girl threading petals is gone. The puddles that have formed there are full of dirty, fallen blossoms. And I am sure that those branches, heavy with blossoms, struck by the rain, are stooping and shaking.

MUNEMORI: Shall we be quiet for a little while?

YUYA: Yes. (*Pauses. Yuya takes off her jacket and edges over to stand beside Munemori.*) May I say just one thing?

MUNEMORI: Go ahead.

YUYA: You believed me more than that lying old woman, didn't you?

MUNEMORI: You shouldn't say such foolish things.

YUYA: . . . I don't have to travel anywhere anymore.

MUNEMORI: You might as well stay.

YUYA: Yes, I'll stay here.

MUNEMORI: But can you not, as before, make that sad face?

YUYA: But when I am happy, I cannot make a sad face.

MUNEMORI: What are you so happy about? Well, Yuya?

YUYA: Everything's been settled.

MUNEMORI: Yes, and your mother is healthy.

YUYA: Yes, I have nothing left to worry about; just being with you makes me happy. (*Pause. The room grows increasingly dark.*) The rain is terrible, isn't it? It's a shame we couldn't go blossom viewing today.

MUNEMORI (*gently unwraps Yuya's arm from his neck and then continues gripping her hand, gazing at her face from that slight distance*): But I had a splendid blossom viewing. I had a truly fine blossom viewing.

ESSAYS
ETŌ JUN

Throughout his life, Etō Jun (1933–1999) remained one of the most erudite, and controversial, of Japan's literary critics. His essays on the writings of the great Meiji novelist Natsume Sōseki, some of whose work appears in volume 1 of this anthology, first made Etō famous when they were published in 1955. His reputation grew with his 1962 study of the greatest of the earlier modern Japanese literary critics, Kobayashi Hideo, whose work also appears in volume 1 of this anthology. Etō was extremely devoted to his wife, who died of cancer in 1998, and he committed suicide in 1999.

His essay presented here, "Natsume Sōseki: A Japanese Meiji Intellectual," was written during his stay in the United States in 1962 and 1963. It apparently was written in English and was published in the *American Scholar* in the fall of 1965. As far as we can determine, it has never been reprinted until now.

NATSUME SŌSEKI: A JAPANESE MEIJI INTELLECTUAL

To the Japanese, the literature of the Meiji period (1868–1912) has a certain distinctive quality which sharply distinguishes it from that of the Taishō (1912–1926) and Shōwa (1926–1989) eras. This quality is not easy to define, but I think it is related to the fact that Meiji writers possessed a strong sense of cultural identity as *Japanese* writers—despite, or rather because of, their having been the first Japanese intellectuals to be thoroughly exposed to the influence of the West in every aspect of their life and thought.

No matter how radically they differed from one another in their literary or poetical opinions, Meiji writers shared in the dominant national mission of their time: the creation of a new civilization that would bring together the best features of East and West while remaining Japanese at its core. However they rejected the official values of Meiji society, they never lost their awareness of their responsibilities as writers in the service of their nation. This combined sense of national mission, social responsibility, and cultural identity seems to have died with the two great Meiji writers, Natsume Sōseki and Mori Ōgai. It has not reappeared among the more gifted writers of the Taishō period, or even among the nationalistic writers of the late 1930's and early 1940's, let alone among my sex-obsessed contemporaries.

Meiji writers were much concerned with modern man's focus upon his own ego; but they nonetheless held fast to an ethic of self-restraint, to the conviction that individual efforts should be subordinated to transcendental values. By contrast, both Taishō and Shōwa writers have expressed the doctrine of the unrestrained assertion and expansion of the individual ego. For Taishō writers this assertion of self took the form of a kind of optimistic, easygoing individualism. Marxist writers of the late 1920's and early 1930's expressed it through an aggressive group egoism. Finally, post–World War II writers have reduced this self-assertion to the still narrower theme of unrestrained sexuality. Indeed, contemporary writers' ludicrous seriousness in dealing with sexual themes illustrates more clearly than anything else the thoroughness with which the ethic of stoic self-restraint has been eliminated from the consciousness of Japanese intellectuals during the half century since the end of the Meiji era.

I should like to explore the way in which this ethic of self-restraint was brought to moving literary perfection by an author who was, ironically enough, exquisitely sensitive to the enormous demands of his gigantic ego. The author is, of course, Natsume Sōseki, and the work in question is the novel, *Kokoro* (*The Heart of Things*). Sōseki was not only one of the greatest figures in modern Japanese literature but also undoubtedly one of the best exemplars of the inner struggles of the Meiji intellectual. His *Kokoro* was written in 1914, at the time of Sōseki's full maturity, and expressed so vividly Sōseki's long-standing sense of man's isolation in the egoistic modern world that one is almost tempted to turn away from its ruthless revelation of truth. *Kokoro* at the same time reflects the profound effect upon one of the best minds of Meiji Japan of two highly significant historical incidents—the death of the Emperor Meiji, and the subsequent self-immolation of General Nogi, one of Japan's great military heroes. Another good reason for selecting *Kokoro* for detailed examination is its availability in English in an excellent translation by Edwin McClellan.

Natsume Sōseki (1866–1916) was an unusually versatile and learned man. He was a gifted *haiku* poet, as well as one of the finest creators of Chinese poetry that Japan had produced in many centuries. He was a gifted calligrapher and traditional painter. He was a formidable scholar of English literature, concentrating upon such eighteenth-century writers as Swift, Fielding and Sterne, and for a period of time served as lecturer on English literature at Tokyo University. Sōseki can indeed be said to have been the ideal humanistic Meiji intellectual, of whom it was required to be knowledgeable in three fields of learning—Japanese, Chinese and Western (or *wa*, *kan*, and *yo*)—if he was to be considered knowledgeable at all. But he was, above all, a novelist, and it is as a great novelist that he has cast his spell on the Japanese reading public. Nor has his popularity wavered since his death in 1916; his thirteen novels (along with a number of essays and short stories) constantly find new readers today.

Sōseki was the fifth son in a once well-to-do Tokyo family. (Sōseki's given name was Natsume Kin'nosuke, Sōseki being his pen name.) The unhappiness of his childhood was caused partly by the sharp decline in his family's status after the Meiji Restoration, but mostly by the complicated human relations frequently found in this kind of Japanese family. In accordance with a widespread Japanese custom, Sōseki, as the last child of his aging parents, was adopted at the age of two by a minor local official and his wife. But at the age of eight he was returned to his original family, along with his foster mother, because misconduct on the part of his foster father had led to divorce. Moreover, this same foster father caused Sōseki much difficulty in later life with his demands for money, claiming that Sōseki was still responsible for taking care of him, as a fil-ial Japanese son, since there had been an error in the formalities of Sōseki's re-turn to his original family. The story of Sōseki's unhappy reunion with his foster father is given expression in his novel, *Michikusa* (*Loitering on the Way*), which followed *Kokoro*. Certainly the pain and confusion in identity from these child-hood experiences were to remain with Sōseki throughout his life.

He nonetheless made his way to Tokyo University, where he excelled in his English studies and, upon graduating, taught English in provincial secondary schools until he was sent to England for study by the Ministry of Education. During his two-and-one-half-year stay in London, he began to experience what was to become one of the basic psychological motifs of his life, the problem of identity in a Japanese intellectual studying English literature during the great historical dislocation of his country's radical Westernization. He was later to re-call this experience as follows:

> Since my early childhood I have enjoyed studying Chinese classics, and
> through these formulated a vague definition of what literature was. I as-
> sumed that English literature would be much the same thing as Chinese
> literature. If this turned out to be true, then it would be worth devoting
> my whole life to the study of English literature—and for this simple and
> childish reason I decided to enter the unfashionable English Department
> of Tokyo University. I studied rather hard, but by the time of my gradua-
> tion I was obsessed by a sense of dissatisfaction, by the feeling that in my
> study of English literature I had been deceived. . . . I went to London
> with the same uneasy feeling which I could not overcome no matter how
> hard I studied. . . . My knowledge of English is far from profound, but I
> can at least say that it is by no means inferior to my knowledge of literary
> Chinese. With this equal proficiency in both languages, why do I feel
> such a strong attachment to the one and such a strong dislike to the
> other? I can only suppose that the two languages are fundamentally dif-
> ferent in nature . . . and that the concept of literature in China and the
> concept of literature in England are irreconcilably contradictory. I came
> to this conclusion under a gaslight in the distant city of London many
> years after I graduated from the University. I may well be a childish
> fellow . . . but no matter how immature I may be, the fact remains that I
> cannot find the same kind of comfort and exaltation in English literature
> that I find in Chinese classics.

Had Sōseki been the kind of scholar who, like many of his contemporaries, had been content merely to introduce recent achievements of English scholarship into Japan, he would not have been confronted with this kind of frustration and disillusionment. But he aimed much higher: he wished to compete with, even surpass, the foremost scholars of English literature in the English-speaking world. This is of course an impossibility, or at least it *was* impossible for a Japanese born in the latter half of the nineteenth century. To understand this extraordinary ambition we must take more of Sōseki's family background into account.

Both Sōseki's original and foster families had been local administrators under the Tokugawa shogunate enjoying a social status equal to that of samurai. A boy growing up in two administrative families inevitably received thorough training in Chinese classics embodying Confucian ethics, and in historical studies dealing with problems of government. Sōseki's original concept of literature, like that of many raised under similar circumstances, stressed its public, rather than private, function. The study of English literature became, for him, as much a form of service to his nation as work in government would have been. And a scholar, no less than a government official, would have to compete with Western scholars on an equal basis in order to produce work worthy of the new civilization to be built. Such must have been Sōseki's inner logic. But his illusions were mercilessly destroyed while studying in London. (I treat this problem extensively in my *Natsume Sōseki*.)[1] During this serious personal crisis, something else also appears to have been destroyed—his tie with the implicit value system of Meiji Japan.

For during his two-and-one-half-year stay in England, Sōseki experienced personal despair and profound disillusionment with his national ideal; in the process, Sōseki the scholar gradually disappeared, and Sōseki the writer emerged. Sōseki experienced a painful emergence from his previously all-enveloping Confucianism, and a liberation of his existential self. It was a form of rebirth or awakening which left him with a sense of self that was in the midst of crisis, totally unrelated, undefined and undefended. For it became depressingly clear to him that his own background of Oriental culture left him irrevocably separated from the organic whole of Western civilization. He was thrown back, and indeed bitterly, upon his own cultural identity. And on that ground he found himself grappling with a monster called ego, which he sought to tame by committing himself to creative writing. He evolved an individualistic ethical principle which he called *jiko hon'i*, or egocentric individualism; yet with it all, he remained a Meiji intellectual with a sense of mission and social responsibility. Thus, in 1906, just after concluding his first novel, *Wagahai wa neko de aru* (*I Am a Cat*), he wrote to one of his disciples:

> If you are determined enough to devote your life to literature, you cannot
> be satisfied with a simple aesthetic product. It is true that I, too, am some
> times attracted by aesthetic things with *haiku* flavor, but at the same time
> I feel a strong impulse to engage in novel-writing with the same fervent
> spirit as *the men of high purpose* of the period of the [Meiji] Restoration
> who willingly staked their lives for the realization of their cause.

---

1. Etō Jun, *Natsume Sōseki*, rev. ed. (Tokyo: Keisō shobō, 1965).

The social commitment is there, but he identifies himself, not with the scholar-administrator representing existing authority, but with the revolutionary "man of high purpose" of the Restoration movement.

Like most Japanese scholars who went to England at that time to study, Sōseki originally intended to do his work at either Oxford or Cambridge. But he found the genteel atmosphere of these institutions disappointing, and chose instead University College of London. Even there he found himself unable to sit through what he considered to be mechanical lectures by uninspiring professors. He finally decided upon private lessons from an authority on Shakespeare, Dr. William James Craig, which he continued for about a year. All the while his financial situation was precarious—his grant from the Japanese government barely supported him—and he experienced great personal loneliness, receiving very infrequent mail from his pregnant wife. Nor could he find comfort in London, where he described himself as "lonely as a stray dog midst a pack of wolves."

In a desperate effort to solve both his personal dilemma and his basic intellectual concern with the nature of literature, Sōseki shut himself up in his room to write a book on the psychological and social basis of literature. It dealt mainly with the search for a common denominator between Oriental and Occidental literature, but his state of mind was such that he approached the point of nervous collapse without being able to finish the study (although he did make use of portions of it in his later lectures at Tokyo University, which in turn were eventually compiled in his complete works as *Bungaku ron* [*A Study in Literature*]). He returned to Japan in January 1903, in a state of exhaustion and despair.

He was nonetheless offered a lectureship in English literature at Tokyo Imperial University, the same position previously held by Lafcadio Hearn. And while serving in this capacity during the next few years he was able to reconstruct his shattered identity and at the same time produce several short stories and two of his most popular novels. The short stories have markedly romantic overtones, but at the same time expressed the author's fear of his own irrational, amorphous, but somehow powerful ego. The two novels—*I Am a Cat* and *Botchan*—won him widespread literary fame, and he readily abandoned the academic life in 1907 when offered the position of head of the literary department of *Asahi*, one of Japan's leading newspapers. From then until his death in 1916, Sōseki had his novels serialized exclusively in *Asahi*—with *Kokoro* the third from the last of these, written two years after the end of the Meiji era and two years before the end of his own life.

To examine the problems of egoism and human isolation that Sōseki treats in *Kokoro*, it is necessary to look more closely at his own anguished experiences in London. With the death of the traditional scholar-administrator within him, there was born a lonely, modern man. Yet why did he consider this emergence of the modern ego, despite his own principle of "egocentric individualism," to be bad and ugly? I believe it was mainly because of the survival within him, despite everything, of a private, Confucian value system. According to Confucian ethics in general, and Chu Hsi ethics in particular, the worth of a man's existence is determined solely in terms of his connection with the transcendental *t'ien* (usually translated as heaven). If he is severed from this transcendental source of value, he becomes worthless—virtually nothing. Trained in this strict Chu Hsi tradition, Sōseki could not tolerate the existence of his own exposed ego, entirely separate from any transcendental values. The still more disturbing impression that nothing but individual ego existed in this world caused him further fear and revulsion—resulting in a vehement form of self-condemnation.

Was there any escape from this deadlock? Sōseki sought to solve the problem by raising questions about the kind of human relationships possible for isolated modern man. He told himself that if a modern man were really capable of love, he might then overcome the agony of his loneliness. But the more Sōseki himself craved love, the less he felt love to be possible for him in his existing surroundings. This must be, he thought, because of the fatal human disease of egoism.

Once severed from transcendental values, man becomes the center of the world and, in Sōseki's judgment, can no longer love anyone but himself. Had Sōseki been a Spencerian social evolutionist, following the fashion of the time, he might well have been satisfied with the idea of man at the center of the world. Had he taken the path of pure aesthetics, he would have paid no attention to the impossibility of love. But instead he combined a realistic outlook that could not avoid these unpalatable truths, with a dedication to traditional ethics that could not permit him to accept them. In an effort to resolve this ambivalence, Sōseki felt himself forced to conclude that man's very existence in this world is sinful and dirty and that there are just two alternatives available to overcome these loathsome qualities: the first, for man to assert himself boldly to the extent of eventually falling into a state of madness, the theme of his novel *Kōjin*; the second, man's violent annihilation of his own existence through suicide, the theme of *Kokoro*. If incapable of either of these ultimate solutions, man has no choice but to endure his ugliness and isolation until the moment of his natural annihilation, never forgetting his own sinfulness. Sōseki's attitude toward the human situation is, to put it mildly, a gloomy one—and in this attitude we find the dark shadow that underlies Japan's seemingly rapid and successful modernization.

In *Kokoro*, Sōseki evoked in a masterly manner his theme of man's isolation and incapability of love. Sōseki's approach in this novel is distinctly ethical, his manner of telling the story simple and clear. The novel is written in a style characterized by dignity and restrained beauty, and its effect is profound. I read this novel for the first time when I was twelve years old, and have since reread it at least ten times. Yet with each reading I am amazed to find myself profoundly absorbed, as if discovering for the first time the book's full power and its moving evocation of human suffering.

Structurally, *Kokoro* is divided into three parts: "Sensei and I," "My Parents and I," and "Sensei and His Testament." In the first two parts, which make up about half of the novel, Sensei (literally, "teacher," but also "master" or "mentor," and perhaps best translated by the French *maître*) is described entirely through the eyes of the first-person narrator, a student about to graduate from a university. In these first two portions, Sensei does not impress us as a tragic figure. He in fact appears to be happily married, well educated, highly civilized in every way, and, what is more, a man of means. His only peculiarities, as observed by the student-narrator, are his having no profession and indeed doing nothing, and his rather disturbing custom of visiting the Zoshigaya cemetery alone once every month. Only gradually does the reader gain the impression that something is wrong with this man, and the suspense grows as he is transported into a strange, sad, transparent atmosphere removed from the surface of ordinary life. He is carried, so to speak, about halfway to *the heart of things*. In the final portion, "Sensei and His Testament," which consists of Sensei's long confession prepared just before his suicide and written in the form of a testament to the student-narrator, the reader finally comes to discover Sensei's true identity and the personal tragedy that led to his suicide. The novel's irony lies in the manner in which this apparently well-placed man becomes a miserable victim of a fatal human situation—of egoism, isolation and the inability to love.

The first-person student-narrator—the "I" of the novel—is not just a technical device but something much deeper—perhaps a representation of Sensei's younger and more immature self, or at least of a younger person possessing a spiritual affinity with Sensei. As a student about to graduate from a university, he is also about to be initiated into the dreadful truth of human life. At the beginning of the novel the reader finds him in this state on the beach at Kamakura where he first encounters Sensei. Basking in the sun and in the gaiety of youth, he has, as yet, no realization that he himself will become alienated from other people and from the beauty of nature itself, that he, too, will be unable to escape from the ugliness of human existence.[2] A passage from the opening chapter, as translated by McClellan, reveals the extent to which he feels himself in harmony with everything around him.

> The next day, I followed Sensei into the sea, and swam after him. When we had gone more than a couple of hundred yards out, Sensei turned and spoke to me. The sea stretched, wide and blue, all around us, and there seemed to be no one near us. The bright sun shone on the water and the mountains, as far as the eye could see. My whole body seemed to be filled with a sense of freedom and joy, and I splashed about wildly in the sea. Sensei had stopped moving and was floating quietly on his back. I then imitated him. The dazzling blue of the sky beat against my face, and I felt

---

2. Edwin McClellan explains this point in "The Implication of Sōseki's *Kokoro*," *Monumenta Nipponica* 14, nos. 3–4 (1958–1959): 117.

as though little bright darts 'were being thrown into my eyes. And I cried out, "What fun this is!"

But this "sense of freedom and joy" soon disappears as the student becomes increasingly involved with Sensei. He never wonders why he is so impelled to this reserved gentleman who, for an unspecified reason, so carefully withdraws from the public and social activities proper for a man of his station. But Sensei is fully aware of the reason for the young man's interest in him. It is because the student is, so to speak, his own shadow, a man about to take the path he has already followed with so heavy a heart. Except for Sensei and his calm, attractive wife, there is no mention in the first part of the novel of the student's friends or acquaintances. When the boy returns to his provincial home after graduation, he feels alienated from his conventional parents and from the framework of traditional rural society within which they live; he is already, without realizing it, isolated from other people.

But when confronted with his father's fatal illness, the student unexpectedly experiences strong compassion toward his dying parent—possibly because of the special isolation and loneliness every human being feels in the face of death. In other words, only on his deathbed can the father achieve spiritual intimacy with his "well-educated" son, himself now in the process of experiencing the spiritual half-death of modern man.

Sensei had been made aware of his alienation when, an orphan growing up in a well-to-do family, he was deceived by his own uncle, who had designs upon his inheritance. The realization occurred while he was still at the university, and after severing ties with this uncle, he returned to Tokyo, having sold his properties, determined never to return to his home area again. At this point, however suspicious about the motives of any human relationship, he still has confidence in his own capacity for love and compassion. He thus attempts to help his poverty-stricken friend, K, to continue his studies by permitting him to share his comfortable boardinghouse rooms; and he seeks to make K, an exceedingly serious young man, more "human" through contact with Ojosan, the daughter of the boardinghouse owner, whom Sensei himself has long secretly loved. Sensei admires K's brilliance and religious dedication in search of the "true path," but considers him incapable of tender sentiment. Therefore, when K confides in Sensei that he, too, loves Ojosan, Sensei finds his confidence in his own capacity for love and compassion suddenly faltering. If he is to remain true to K, he must give up his love for Ojosan; if, on the other hand, he is to remain true to his own tender feelings for Ojosan, he must betray his only friend, K. Sensei had previously been a victim of his uncle's egoism; now it is his turn to be an agent of egoism. He decides to play a subtle psychological trick on K by accusing him of inconsistency in his religious stoicism.

I said cruelly, "Anyone who has no spiritual aspirations is an idiot." This was what K had said to me when we were traveling in Boshu. I threw back at him the very words that he had once used to humiliate me. Even my tone of voice was the same as his had been when he made the remark. But I insist that I was not being vindictive. I confess to you that what I was trying to do was far more cruel than mere revenge. I wanted to destroy whatever hope there might have been in his love for Ojosan.

. . . I said again: "Anyone who has no spiritual aspirations is an idiot." I watched K closely. I wanted to see how my words were affecting him. "An idiot . . . ," he said at last. "Yes, I am an idiot."

He stood still as he spoke, and stared at his feet. I was suddenly frightened that in desperation, K had decided to accept the fact that he was an idiot. I was as demoralized as a man who finds that his opponent, whom he has just knocked down, is about to spring up with a new weapon in his hand. A moment later, however, I realized that K had indeed spoken in a hopeless tone of voice. I wanted to see his eyes, but he would not look my way. Slowly we began to walk again.

Informed a week later of Sensei's engagement to Ojosan, K quietly commits suicide, leaving behind no reference to his love for Ojosan. Now Sensei must face the full ugliness of his ego, without apology, despite his success in gaining the hand of the attractive Ojosan. Seeming to be the winner, Sensei is, in reality, a miserable loser, obsessed by a strong sense of guilt and human isolation. But gradually, over a period of time, Sensei becomes aware of the possibility that K himself might have suffered from the same sense of loneliness he now experiences.

Time and again, I wondered what had caused K to commit suicide. At first I was inclined to think that it was disappointment in love. I could think of nothing but love then, and quite naturally I accepted without question the first simple and straightforward explanation that came to my mind. Later, however, when I could think more objectively, I began to wonder whether my explanation had not been simple. I asked myself "was it perhaps because his ideals clashed with reality that he killed himself?" But I could not convince myself that K had chosen death for such a reason. Finally, I became aware of the possibility that K had experienced loneliness as terrible as mine, and, wishing to escape quickly from it, had killed himself. Once more, fear gripped my heart. From then on, like a gust of winter wind, the premonition that I was treading the same path as K had done would rush at me from time to time and chill me to the bone.

This gust of winter wind not only chills Sensei's lonely heart, but his married life as well. For he refuses to share his agony with his wife, whom he has loved, and who loves him, in the ordinary sense of that word. The Western reader may find this behavior odd, but I believe we can say that rather than reflecting cruelty, it stems from Sensei's realization that his wife would find it unbearable to face the dreadful truth of human isolation. His assumption is that peace of mind protected by ignorance is preferable to the agony of confrontation with cruel truth. If her husband's suicide were the result of a simple nervous breakdown, she might, as a girl raised with the stoical standards of her army-officer father, be able to endure it. But how could she endure being informed of all that had happened between her husband and K? In short, partly from pity, partly from fear, and most of all from his inability to believe in the possibility of overcoming his fatal isolation, even with his wife, Sensei avoids disclosing to her the cause of his loneliness. All this is revealed in a meaningful passage from the last part of *Kokoro*:

My mother-in-law died. There remained only my wife and myself. My wife said to me: "In all the world, I now have only you to turn to." I looked at her and my eyes were suddenly filled with tears. How could I, who had no trust in myself, give her the comfort she needed? I thought her a very unfortunate woman.

And again:

My wife once asked me: "Can't a man's heart and a woman's heart ever become a part of each other so that they are one?" I gave a noncommittal answer: "Perhaps when the man and the woman are young." She sat quietly for a while. She was probably thinking of the time when she herself had been a young girl. Then she gave a little sigh.

It is not, however, until the Emperor Meiji's death, and the subsequent self-immolation of General Nogi, that Sensei finally makes up his mind to kill himself. The development of Sensei's decision is described as follows:

Then at the height of the summer, Emperor Meiji passed away. I felt as though the spirit of the Meiji era had begun with the Emperor, and had ended with him. I was overcome with the feeling that I and the others, who had been brought up in that era, were now left behind to live as anachronisms. . . . A month passed. On the night of the Imperial Funeral I sat in my study, and listened to the booming of the cannon. To me, it sounded like the last lament for the passing of an age. Later, I realized that it might also have been a salute to General Nogi. Holding the extra edition in my hand, I blurted out to my wife, "*Junshi! Junshi!*" (he killed himself! he killed himself!). . . . It was two or three days later that I decided to commit suicide.

It is of course clear that Sensei seeks death because it provides him with the only solution to the agony of egoism. But it is also clear that he dies, as he himself explains, "through loyalty to the spirit of the Meiji era"; he commits suicide because he wishes, like General Nogi, to follow the Emperor to the grave. What this dual motivation reveals is that Sensei, like Sōseki himself a Meiji intellectual, needed, even in suicide, a motive higher than a purely personal one. He had to connect his death to the passing of the great Meiji era so that his act would not be merely an escape from the human condition but would relate itself to ethical issues beyond the self. To understand these ethical issues, we must examine the enormous impact on the Japanese made by these two successive incidents—first the demise of Emperor Meiji, and then the *junshi* (self-immolation) of General Nogi and his wife.

Emperor Meiji died on July 30, 1912. To illustrate the way in which news of his death was received in the West, I should like to cite two comments from the *Times* of London. The first is a character sketch, not devoid of a bit of irony, of the Emperor himself:

> His Majesty was a generous patron of art, and if he can be said to have had any passion it was for poetry. Thousands of the impressionist verselets which represent this branch of Japanese literature were composed by him, and well helped to keep green the memory of a ruler whose name must hold high place amongst the best Sovereigns the world has known. In his private life he was essentially a man of sorrow, for out of 13 children born to him only four survive; but on the other hand, he had the supreme satisfaction of seeing his country rise from the rank of a petty and despised Oriental State to the peer of the Great Powers of the Occident.

The second concerns the Japanese response to his death:

> A dense mass of humanity again thronged the great open spaces outside the Palace walls last night, continually moving up to the Emperor's gate, there to kneel in prayer a few minutes and then pass on once more. The crowd was drawn from all classes, and all preserved the highest degree of orderliness and silence, save for the crunching of the gravel under wooden sandals and the low continuous murmur of prayers. It is said that even Christians were to be found among the kneeling crowd. One who looked over the sea of bowed heads outside the Palace wall could not desire better proof of the vitality of that worship of the Ruler.

Even allowing for the fact that the Anglo-Japanese Alliance had just been renewed for the second time in 1911, these comments in the *Times* are impressively favorable, and reveal how highly the Emperor was regarded both at home and abroad.

General (also Count) Nogi and Countess Nogi performed their self-immolation on September 13, 1912, the day of the Emperor's funeral, and the *Times* had this to say about their actions:

General Count Nogi and his wife are said to have committed suicide with short sword at the moment when the gun was fired which announced the start of the funeral procession of the Emperor. The news that Count Nogi and his wife have committed suicide on the day of Emperor Mutsuhito's funeral is a striking reminder of the persistence in Japan of the spirit to which our ally owes her greatness. To this latest manifestation of its profound but stern appeal, the Western world, even if it cannot fully comprehend, must bow in respectful silence. Men like the late Count Nogi were the mainspring of the era of Meiji, or enlightenment, which may be passing in fact as well as in name with the death of the great ruler whom he served.

General Nogi explained in his testament his reason for committing suicide. He did so, he stated, because thirty-five years before, during the Satsuma Rebellion of 1877, while Commander of the Fourteenth Regiment, then stationed in Kokura in Northern Kyushu, he had lost his regimental banner to the enemy. Until the end of World War II the regimental banner was regarded as the incarnation of the Emperor, and was handed by the Emperor in person to each commander at the time a new regiment was formed. Losing the banner to the enemy, therefore, resulted in extreme shame, which could be redeemed only through death. Nogi had then duly asked his superiors to grant him this death. The Chief of Staff, General Yamagata Aritomo, had been inclined to approve the request, but later changed his mind when persuaded by a military colleague that it would be better for Nogi to survive and serve well. Nogi had, since then, been waiting for the proper time for his suicide.

The opportunity seemed to come to him at long last following his victorious return from the Russo-Japanese War of 1904–1905. Nogi had served in that war as Commander of the Third Army, which had engaged in the siege of Port Arthur, one of the bloodiest campaigns in the history of the Imperial Japanese Army. During this 159-day campaign, Nogi lost 59,000 of the 130,000 men he commanded, including his two sons. Upon returning to Tokyo on January 14, 1906, he was given an audience with the Emperor Meiji at the Imperial Palace, and concluded his report with a petition that he be granted death to make up for the loss of such a large number of His Majesty's loyal subjects. One of his biographers records that, upon uttering this request, Nogi's eyes filled with tears as he prostrated himself before the Emperor. The Emperor remained silent for a while, and then said: "Now is not the time for you to die. If you so earnestly wish your death, it shall be only after my own death." Immediately following this audience, the Emperor issued a special edict, praising Nogi's skillful military actions and the loyalty of his men. Nogi finally found the moment for his suicide at the funeral of the Emperor.

Iconoclastic historians, Japanese as well as Western, have recently sought more prosaic interpretations of this heroic incident. These historians prefer to assume that Nogi had simply been manipulated by cunning court politicians, especially by General Yamagata, who wished Nogi to die at this dramatic moment in order to buttress the Japanese morale which had so deteriorated during the years following the Russo-Japanese War. Certainly it can be said that Nogi, like many traditional military men, had been obsessed throughout his life with the idea of heroic death, and that he wished to bring historical glory to his name even at the expense of his life. But I, for one, cannot agree with these iconoclastic historians. For if one is content with this kind of rationalistic interpretation, one is unable to grasp the deep sense of tragedy felt by the Japanese at the moment of General Nogi's death.

Sōseki was by no means the only writer to respond to this manifestation of samurai-like heroism. The first response came from Mori Ōgai who, as a high official in the War Ministry, happened to be on close terms with Prince Yamagata. On September 18, just five days after Nogi's death, and in fact on the day of his funeral, Ōgai completed and submitted to the editor of *Chūō kōron* his first historical short story, *The Testament of Okitsu Yagoyemon*; it was the story of a samurai of the Tokugawa period who committed *junshi* for a reason quite similar to Nogi's. This story marked a turning point in the career of Mori Ōgai as a writer and thinker. For some years prior to the death of Emperor Meiji, Ōgai's attitude toward contemporary Japanese society had been both skeptical and indecisive. He had been repelled by the emergence of so-called naturalist writers; but he had also been critically concerned with the growing power among younger intellectuals of revolutionary ideologies such as anarchism, socialism and Marxism. He would sometimes seem to be liberal, sometimes authoritarian. But upon being profoundly moved by the death of General and Countess Nogi, his conflicts resolved into determined support for traditional ethics. After *The Testament of Okitsu Yagoyemon*, Ōgai produced nothing but historical works—whether novels, research investigations, biographies or dramas—with the one exception of his excellent translation of Goethe's *Faust*.

For Natsume Sōseki, too, the death of General Nogi stimulated a sudden desire for the restoration of his lost identity as the ambitious scholar-administrator who had wanted to do something for the sake of his country. Just as General Nogi had lost his military banner to the enemy during the Satsuma Rebellion, Sōseki had lost his spiritual banner in his lonely campaign in London. From then on, he had been able to live only as an isolated modern man suffering from the agony of egoism and incapacity for love. But the Emperor Meiji's death and General Nogi's *junshi* made him realize that the spirit of Meiji had not entirely died within him. Now the shadow of the entire value structure of this great era emerged from his tortured past, smiling at him like the ghost of a loved one. Perhaps the ghost whispered to him: "Come to me." And Sōseki responded, indicating through his novel's protagonist that a part of himself had died with the passing of the Meiji era. Thus Sōseki wrote *Kokoro* to make it clear that he was on the side of the ghost of the traditional, but somehow universal, ethics—the ethics of stoic self-restraint or antiegoism— even though fully aware that the whole value system of the Meiji era had crumbled long before the Emperor's death, and that a new age was emerging from this chaos—an age in which the unrestrained assertion of the ego would be considered not an act of ugliness but the privilege of younger generations. It should be noted that the rise of these egoistic generations has precisely corresponded with Japan's increasing isolation in the international community.

KAWABATA YASUNARI

Kawabata Yasunari (1899–1972), whose work appears in volume 1 of this anthology, was awarded the Nobel Prize for Literature in 1968. He was the first Japanese author to receive this honor, and he used the occasion of his acceptance address to review his debt to classical Japanese literature during his own literary career.

JAPAN, THE BEAUTIFUL, AND MYSELF
(UTSUKUSHII NIHON NO WATASHI)

Translated by Edward G. Seidensticker

The 1968 Nobel Prize Acceptance Speech

> In the spring, cherry blossoms,
> in the summer the cuckoo.
> In the autumn the moon, and in
> winter the snow, clear, cold.

> Winter moon, coming from the
> clouds to keep me company,
> Is the wind piercing, the snow cold?

The first of these poems is by the priest Dōgen (1200–1253) and bears the title "Innate Spirit." The second is by the priest Myōe (1173–1232). When I am asked for specimens of my handwriting, it is these poems that I often choose.

The second poem bears an unusually detailed account of its origins, such as to be an explanation of the heart of its meaning:

> On the night of the twelfth day of the twelfth month of the year 1224,[1] the moon was behind clouds. I sat in Zen meditation in the Kakyū Hall. When the hour of the midnight vigil came, I ceased meditation and descended from the hall on the peak to the lower quarters, and as I did so

---

1. By lunar reckoning.

the moon came from the clouds and set the snow to glowing. The moon was my companion, and not even the wolf howling in the valley brought fear. When, presently, I came out of the lower quarters again, the moon was again behind clouds. As the bell was signaling the late-night vigil, I climbed once more to the peak, and the moon saw me on the way. I entered the meditation hall, and the moon, chasing the clouds, was about to sink behind the far peak, and it seemed to me that it was keeping me secret company.

There follows the poem I have quoted, and, with the explanation that it was composed as Myōe entered the meditation hall after watching the moon sink toward the mountain, there comes yet another poem:

> I shall go behind the mountain.
> Go there too, O moon.
> Night after night we shall keep each
> other company.

Here is the setting for another poem, after Myōe had spent the rest of the night in the meditation hall, or perhaps gone there again before dawn: "Opening my eyes from my meditations, I saw the moon in the dawn, lighting the window. In a dark place myself, I felt as if my own heart were glowing with light which seemed to be that of the moon":

> My heart shines, a pure expanse
> of light;
> And no doubt the moon will think
> the light its own.

Because of such a spontaneous and innocent stringing together of mere ejaculations as the following, Myōe has been called the poet of the moon:

> O bright, bright,
> O bright, bright, bright,
> O bright, bright.
> Bright, O bright, bright,
> Bright, O bright moon.

In his three poems on the winter moon, from late night into the dawn, Myōe follows entirely the bent of Saigyō, another poet-priest, who lived from 1118 to 1190: "Though I compose poetry, I do not think of it as composed poetry." The thirty-one syllables of each poem, honest and straightforward as if he were addressing the moon, are not merely to "the moon as my companion." Seeing the moon, he becomes the moon, the moon seen by him becomes him. He sinks into nature, becomes one with nature. The light of the "clear heart" of the priest, seated in the meditation hall in the darkness before the dawn, becomes for the dawn moon its own light.

As we see from the long introduction to the first of Myōe's poems quoted above, in which the winter moon becomes a companion, the heart of the priest, sunk in meditation upon religion and philosophy, there in the mountain hall, is engaged in a delicate interplay and exchange with the moon; and it is this of which the poet sings. My reason for choosing that first poem when asked for a specimen of my handwriting has to do with its remarkable gentleness and compassion. Winter moon, going behind the clouds and coming forth again, making bright my footsteps as I go to the meditation hall and descend again, making me unafraid of the wolf: does not the wind sink into you, does not the snow, are you not cold? I choose it as a poem of warm, deep, delicate compassion, a poem that has in it the deep quiet of the Japanese spirit. Dr. Yashiro Yukio, internationally known as a scholar of Botticelli, a man of great learning in the art of the past and the present, of the East and the West, has said that one of the special characteristics of Japanese art can be summed up in a single poetic sentence: "The time of the snows, of the moon, of the blossoms—then more than ever we think of our comrades." When we see the beauty of the snow, when we see the beauty of the full moon, when in short we brush against and are awakened by the beauty of the four seasons, it is then that we think most of those close to us, and want them to share the pleasure. The excitement of beauty calls forth strong fellow feelings, yearnings for companionship, and the word "comrade" can be taken to mean "human being." The snow, the moon, the blossoms, words expressive of the season as they move one into another, include in the Japanese tradition the beauty of mountains and rivers and grasses and trees, of all the myriad manifestations of nature, human feelings as well. That spirit, that feeling for one's comrades in the snow, the moonlight, under the blossoms, is also basic to the tea ceremony. A tea ceremony is a coming together feeling, a meeting of good comrades in good season. I may say in passing that to see my novel *Thousand Cranes* as an evocation of the formal and spiritual beauty of the tea ceremony is a misreading. It is a negative work, an expression of doubt about and a warning against the vulgarity into which the tea ceremony has fallen.

> In the spring, cherry blossoms,
> in the summer the cuckoo.
> In autumn the moon, and in winter
> the snow, clear, cold.

One can, if one chooses, see in Dōgen's poem about the beauty of the four seasons no more than a conventional, ordinary, mediocre stringing together, in a most awkward form, of representative images from the four seasons. One can see it as a poem that is not really a poem at all. And yet very similar is the deathbed poem of the priest Ryōkan (1758–1831):

> What shall be my legacy?
> The blossoms of spring,
> the cuckoo in the hills,
> the leaves of autumn.

In this poem, as in Dōgen's, the commonest of figures and the commonest of words are strung together without hesitation—no, to particular effect, rather—and so they transmit the very essence of Japan. And it is Ryōkan's last poem that I have quoted.

> A long, misty day in spring:
> I saw it to a close, playing ball
> with the children.

> The breeze is fresh,
> the moon is clear.
> Together let us dance the night
> away, in what is left of old age.

> It is not that I wish to have none
> of the world,
> It is that I am better at the
> pleasure enjoyed alone.

Ryōkan, who shook off the modern vulgarity of his day, who was immersed in the elegance of earlier centuries, and whose poetry and calligraphy are much admired in Japan today—he lived in the spirit of these poems, a wanderer down country paths, a grass hut for shelter, rags for clothes, farmers to talk to. The profundity of religion and literature was not, for him, in the abstruse. He rather pursued literature and belief in the benign spirit summarized in the Buddhist phrase "a smiling face and gentle words." In his last poem he offered nothing as a legacy. He but hoped that after his death nature would remain beautiful. That could be his bequest. One feels in the poem the emotions of old Japan, and the heart of a religious faith as well.

> I wondered and wondered when
> she would come.
> And now we are together.
> What thoughts need I have?

Ryōkan wrote love poetry too. This is an example of which I am fond. An old man of sixty-nine[2] (I might point out that at the same age I am the recipient of the Nobel Prize), Ryōkan met a twenty-nine-year-old nun named Teishin, and was blessed with love. The poem can be seen as one of happiness at having met the ageless woman, of happiness at having met the one for whom the wait was so long. The last line is simplicity itself.

Ryōkan died at the age of seventy-four. He was born in the province of Echigo, the present Niigata Prefecture and the setting for my novel *Snow Country*, a northerly region on what is known as the reverse side of Japan, where cold winds come down across the Japan Sea from Siberia. He lived his whole life in the snow country, and to his "eyes in their last extremity," when he was old and tired and knew that death was near, and had attained enlightenment, the snow country, as we see in his last poem, was yet more beautiful, I should imagine. I have an essay with the title "Eyes in Their Last Extremity." The title comes from the suicide note of the short-story writer Akutagawa Ryūnosuke (1892–1927). It is the phrase that pulls at me with the greatest strength. Akutagawa said that he seemed to be gradually losing the animal something known as the power to live, and continued:

I am living in a world of morbid nerves, clear and cold as ice. . . . I do not know when I will summon up the resolve to kill myself. But nature is for me more beautiful than it has ever been before. I have no doubt that you will laugh at the contradiction, for here I love nature even when I am contemplating suicide. But nature is beautiful because it comes to my eyes in their last extremity.

Akutagawa committed suicide in 1927, at the age of thirty-five.

In my essay "Eyes in Their Last Extremity," I had this to say: "However alienated one may be from the world, suicide is not a form of enlightenment. However admirable he may be, the man who commits suicide is far from the realm of the saint." I neither admire nor am in sympathy with suicide. I had another friend who died young, an avant-garde painter. He too thought of suicide over the years, and of him I wrote in this same essay: "He seems to have said over and over that there is no art superior to death, that to die is to live." I could see, however, that for him, born in a Buddhist temple and educated in a Buddhist school, the concept of death was very different from that in the West. "Among those who give thoughts to things, is there one who does not think of suicide?" With me was the knowledge that that fellow Ikkyū (1394–1481) twice contemplated suicide. I have said "that fellow," because the priest Ikkyū is known even to children as a most witty

---

2. By the Oriental way of counting. Sixty-seven or sixty-eight by the Western. A year or two should also be subtracted form Teishin's age, and the count at Ryōkan's death.

and amusing person, and because anecdotes about his limitlessly eccentric be-havior have come down to us in ample numbers. It is said of him that children climbed his knee to stroke his beard, that wild birds took feed from his hand. It would seem from all this that he was the ultimate in mindlessness, that he was an approachable and gentle sort of priest. As a matter of fact he was the most severe and profound of Zen priests. Said to have been the son of an emperor, he entered a temple at the age of six,[3] and early showed genius as a poetic prodigy. At the same time he was troubled with the deepest of doubts about religion and life. "If there is a god, let him help me. If there is none, let me throw myself to the bottom of the lake and become food for fishes." Leaving behind these words he sought to throw himself into a lake, but was held back. On another occasion, numbers of his fellows were incriminated when a priest in his Daitokuji Temple committed suicide. Ikkyū went back to the temple, "the burden heavy on my shoulders," and sought to starve himself to death. He gave his collected poetry the title "Collec-tion of the Roiling Clouds," and himself used the expression "Roiling Clouds" as a pen name. In this collection and its successor are poems quite without parallel in the Chinese and especially the Zen poetry of the Japanese middle ages, erotic poems and poems about the secrets of the bedchamber that leave one in utter as-tonishment. He sought, by eating fish and drinking spirits and having commerce with women, to go beyond the rules and proscriptions of the Zen of his day, to seek liberation from them; and thus, turning against established religious forms, he sought in the pursuit of Zen the revival and affirmation of the essence of life, of human existence, in a day of civil war and moral collapse.

His temple, the Daitokuji at Murasakino in Kyoto, remains a center of the tea ceremony, and specimens of his calligraphy are greatly admired as hangings in alcoves of tea rooms. I myself have two specimens of Ikkyū's calligraphy. One of them is a single line: "It is easy to enter the world of the Buddha, it is hard to enter the world of the devil." Much drawn to these words, I frequently make use of them when asked for a specimen of my own writing. They can be read in any number of ways, as difficult as one chooses, but in that world of the devil added to the world of the Buddha, Ikkyū of Zen comes home to me with great imme-diacy. The fact that for an artist, seeking truth, good, and beauty, the fear and petition even as a prayer in those words about the world of the devil—the fact that it should be there apparent on the surface, hidden behind, perhaps speaks with the inevitability of fate. And the devil's world is the world difficult of entry. It is not for the weak of heart.

> If you meet a Buddha, kill him.
> If you meet a patriarch of the
> law, kill him.

---

3. Again, by Oriental count.

This is a well-known Zen motto. If Buddhism is divided generally into the sects that believe in salvation by faith and those that believe in salvation by one's own efforts, then of course there must be such violent utterances in Zen, which insists upon salvation by one's own efforts. On the other side, the side of salvation by faith, Shinran (1173–1262), the founder of the Shin sect, once said: "The good shall be reborn in paradise, and how much more shall that be the case with the bad." This view of things has something in common with Ikkyū's world of the Buddha and world of the devil, and yet at heart the two have their different inclinations. Shinran also said: "I shall take not a single disciple."

"If you meet a Buddha, kill him. If you meet a patriarch of the law, kill him." "I shall not take a single disciple." In these two statements, perhaps, is the rigorous fate of art.

In Zen there is no worship of images. Zen does have images, but in the hall where the regimen of meditation is pursued, there are neither images nor pictures of Buddhas, nor are there scriptures. The Zen disciple sits for long hours silent and motionless, with his eyes closed. Presently he enters a state of impassivity, free from all ideas and all thoughts. He departs from the self and enters the realm of nothingness. This is not the nothingness or the emptiness of the West. It is rather the reverse, a universe of the spirit in which everything communicates freely with everything, transcending bounds, limitless. There are of course masters of Zen, and the disciple is brought toward enlightenment by exchanging questions and answers with his master, and he studies the scriptures. The disciple must, however, always be lord of his own thoughts, and must attain enlightenment through his own efforts. And the emphasis is less upon reason and argument than upon intuition, immediate feeling. Enlightenment comes not from teaching but through the eye awakened inwardly. Truth is in "the discarding of words," it lies "outside words." And so we have the extreme of silence like thunder," in the Vimalakirti Mirdesa Sutra. Tradition has it that Bodhidharma, a southern Indian prince who lived in about the sixth century and was the founder of Zen in China, sat for nine years in silence facing the wall of a cave, and finally attained enlightenment. The Zen practice of sitting in silent meditation derives from Bodhidharma.

Here are two religions poems by Ikkyū:

> When I ask, you answer.
> When I do not you do not.
> What is there then in your heart,
> O Lord Bodhidharma?
>
> And what is it, the heart?
> It is the sound of the pine breeze
> There in the painting.

Here we have the spirit of Oriental painting. The heart of ink painting is in space, abbreviation, what is left undrawn. In the words of the Chinese painter

Chin Nung: "You paint the branch well, and you hear the sound of the wind." And the priest Dōgen once more: "Are there not these cases? Enlightenment in the voice of the bamboo. Radiance of heart in the peach blossom."

Ikenobō Sen'ō, a master of flower arranging, once said (the remark is to be found in his "secret pronouncements"): "With a spray of flowers, a bit of water, one evokes the vastness of rivers and mountains. To the instant are brought all the manifold delights. Verily, it is like the sorcery of the wizard." The Japanese garden too, of course, symbolizes the vastness of nature. The Western garden tends to be symmetrical, the Japanese garden asymmetrical, for the asymmetrical has the greater power to symbolize multiplicity and vastness. The asymmetry, of course, rests upon a balance imposed by delicate sensibilities. Nothing is more complicated, varied, attentive to detail than the Japanese art of landscape gardening. Thus there is the form called the dry landscape, composed entirely of rocks, in which the arrangement of the rocks gives expression to mountains and rivers that are not present, and even suggests the waves of the great ocean breaking in upon cliffs. Compressed to the ultimate, the Japanese garden becomes the *bonsai* dwarf garden, or the *bonseki*, its dry version.

In the Oriental word for landscape, literally "mountain-water," with its related implications in landscape painting and landscape gardening, there is contained the concept of the sere and wasted, and even of the sad and the threadbare. Yet in the sad, austere, autumnal qualities so valued by the tea ceremony, itself summarized in the expression "gently respectful, cleanly quiet," there lies concealed a great richness of spirit; and the tea room, so rigidly confined and simple, contains boundless space and unlimited elegance. The single flower contains more brightness than a hundred flowers. The great sixteenth-century master of the tea ceremony and flower arranging, Rikyū, taught that it was wrong to use fully opened flowers. Even in the tea ceremony today the general practice is to have in the alcove of the tea room but a single flower, and that a flower in bud. In winter a special flower of winter, let us say a camellia, bearing some such name as White Jewel or Wabisuke, which might be translated literally as "Helpmate in Solitude," is chosen, a camellia remarkable among camellias for its whiteness and the smallness of its blossoms; and but a single bud is set out in the alcove. White is the cleanest of colors, it contains in itself all the other colors. And there must always be dew on the bud. The bud is moistened with a few drops of water. The most splendid of arrangements for the tea ceremony comes in May, when a peony is put out in a celadon vase; but here again there is a single bud, always with dew upon it. Not only are there drops of water upon the flower, the vase too is frequently moistened.

Among flower vases, the ware that is given the highest rank is old Iga, from the fifteenth and sixteenth centuries, and it commands the highest price. When old Iga has been dampened, its colors and its glow take on a beauty such as to awaken one afresh. Iga was fired at very high temperatures. The straw ash and the smoke from the fuel fell and flowed against the surface, and, as the temperature dropped, became a sort of glaze. Because the colors were not fabricated but were rather the result of nature at work in the kiln, color patterns emerged in such varieties as to be called quirks and freaks of the kiln. The rough, austere, strong surfaces of old Iga take on a voluptuous glow when dampened. It breathes to the rhythm of the dew of the flowers.

The taste of the tea ceremony also asks that the tea bowl be moistened before using, to bring forth its own soft glow.

Ikenobō Sen'ō remarked on another occasion (this too is in his "secret pronouncements") that "the mountains and strands should appear in their own forms." Bringing a new spirit into his school of flower arranging, therefore, he found "flowers" in broken vessels and withered branches, and in them too the enlightenment that comes from flowers. "The ancients arranged flowers and pursued enlightenment." Here we see an awakening to the heart of the Japanese spirit, under the influence of Zen. And here too, perhaps, is the heart of a man living in the devastation of long civil wars.

The Tales of Ise, compiled in the tenth century, is the oldest Japanese collection of lyrical episodes, numbers of which might be called short stories. In one of them we learn that the poet Ariwara no Yukihira, having invited guests, put in flowers: "Being a man of feeling, he had in a large jar a most unusual wisteria. The trailing spray of flowers was upwards of three and a half feet long."

A spray of wisteria of such length is indeed so unusual as to make one have doubts about the credibility of the writer; and yet I can feel in this great spray a symbol of Heian culture. The wisteria is a very Japanese flower, and it has a feminine elegance. Wisteria sprays, as they trail in the breeze, suggest softness, gentleness, reticence. Disappearing and then appearing again in the early summer greenery, they have in them that feeling for the poignant beauty of things long characterized by the Japanese as *mono no aware*. No doubt there was a particular splendor in that spray upwards of three and a half feet long. The splendors of Heian culture a millennium ago and the emergence of a peculiarly Japanese beauty were as wondrous as this "most unusual wisteria," for the culture of T'ang China had at length been absorbed and Japanized. In poetry there came, early in the tenth century, the first of the imperially commissioned anthologies, the *Kokinshū*, and in fiction the *Tales of Ise*, followed by the supreme masterpieces of classical Japanese prose, the *Tale of Genji* of Lady Murasaki and the *Pillow Book* of Sei Shōnagon, both of whom lived from the late tenth century into the early eleventh. So was established a tradition which influenced and even controlled Japanese literature for eight hundred years. The *Tale of Genji* in particular is the highest pinnacle of Japanese literature. Even down to our day there has not been a piece of fiction to compare with it. That such a modern work should have been written in the eleventh century is a miracle, and as a miracle the work is widely known abroad. Although my grasp of classical Japanese was uncertain, the Heian classics were my principal boyhood reading, and it is the *Genji*, I think, that has meant the most to me. For centuries after it was written, fascination with the *Genji* persisted, and imitations and reworkings did homage to it. The *Genji* was a wide and deep source of nourishment for poetry, of course, and for the fine arts and handicrafts as well, and even for landscape gardening.

Murasaki and Sei Shōnagon, and such famous poets as Izumi Shikibu, who probably died early in the eleventh century, and Akazome Emon, who probably died in the mid-eleventh century, were all ladies-in-waiting in the imperial court. Japanese culture was court culture, and court culture was feminine. The day of the *Genji* and the *Pillow Book* was its finest, when ripeness was moving into decay. One feels the sadness at the end of glory, the high tide of Japanese court culture. The court went into its decline, power moved from the court nobility to the military aristocracy, in whose hands it remained through almost seven centuries from the founding of the Kamakura Shogunate in 1192 to the Meiji Restoration in 1867 and 1868. It is not to be thought, however, that either the imperial institution or court culture vanished. In the eighth of the imperial anthologies, the *Shinkokinshū* of the early thirteenth century, the technical dexterity of the *Kokinshū* was pushed yet a step further, and sometimes fell into mere verbal dalliance; but there were added elements of the mysterious, the suggestive, the evocative and inferential, elements of sensuous fantasy that have something in common with modern symbolist poetry. Saigyō, who has been mentioned earlier, was a representative poet linking the two ages, Heian and Kamakura.

> Did I dream of him because I
> longed for him?
> Had I known it to be a dream,
> I should not have wished to
> awaken.

> In my dreams I go to him each
> night without fail.
> But my dreams are less than a
> single glimpse in the waking.

These are by Ono no Komachi, the leading poetess of the *Kokinshū*, who sings of dreams, even, with a straightforward realism. But when we come to the following poems of the Empress Eifuku (1271–1342), from the late Kamakura and early Muromachi periods, somewhat later than the *Shinkokinshū*, we have a more subtle realism. It becomes a symbol of a delicately Japanese melancholy, and seems to me more modern:

> Shining upon the bamboo thicket
> where the sparrows twitter,
> The sunlight takes on the color of
> the autumn.

> The *hagi*[4] falls, the autumn
> wind is piercing.
> Upon the wall, the evening sun
> disappears.

Dōgen, whose poem about the clear, cold snow I have quoted, and Myōe, who wrote of the winter moon as his companion, were of generally the *Shinkokinshū* period. Myōe exchanged poems with Saigyō and the two discussed poetry together. The following is from the biography of Myōe by his disciple Kikai:

> Saigyō frequently came and talked of poetry. His own view of poetry, he said, was far from the ordinary. Cherry blossoms, the cuckoo, the moon, snow: confronted with all the varied forms of nature, his eyes and his ears were filled with emptiness. And were not the words that came forth true words? When he sang of the blossoms, the blossoms were not on his mind, when he sang of the moon he did not think of the moon. As the occasion presented itself, as the urge arose, he wrote poetry. The red rainbow across the sky was as the sky taking on color. The white sunlight was as the sky growing bright. Yet the empty sky, by its nature, was not something to become bright. It was not something to take on color. With a spirit like the empty sky he gave color to all the varied scenes, but not a trace remained. In such poetry was the Buddha, the manifestation of the ultimate truth.

Here we have the emptiness, the nothingness, of the Orient. My own works have been described as words of emptiness, but it is not to be taken for the nihilism of the West. The spiritual foundation would seem to be quite different. Dōgen entitled his poem about the seasons "Innate Reality," and even as he sang of the beauty of the seasons he was deeply immersed in Zen.

---

4. *Lespedeza japonica.*

Chapter 6

TOWARD A CONTEMPORARY LITERATURE,

1971 TO THE PRESENT

Chronologies can never be exact. This final period overlaps with that covered in chapter 5, which includes a number of authors who grew up during World War II and, at this time, began writing about their experiences in those years.

In the mid-1960s, however, new factors came into play on the Japanese political scene, just as they did around the world during that troubled decade. Both Japan's efforts to renew the United States–Japan Security Treaty and the war in Vietnam caused significant social upheaval. Younger writers now found themselves alienated not only from the older generation but also from the Japanese government and other sources of authority. This alienation was portrayed best by the young dramatists of this period, like Kara Jūrō and Betsuyaku Minoru, some of whose works are included in this volume of the anthology. Their political and intellectual awareness also formed the impetus for much of the later work of Ōe Kenzaburō, who is the quintessential writer of this period and never wavered in his conviction of the importance of such concerns.

As Japan became more prosperous in the 1980s and early 1990s, some of these political and intellectual issues were muted. Then, as the Japanese economic situation became more precarious, two new kinds of writers emerged. The first has been termed an "introverted" generation, those who turned away from political events in order to examine themselves and the spiritual dimensions, or lack of them, of the contemporary world. Furui Yoshikichi and Ikezawa Natsuki fit this profile best, for in many ways, they uphold the traditions of high literature in an increasingly commercialized society.

The other group, of still younger writers, might be described as "cool." They produced works that pay homage to the popular culture, much of it derived from Western sources. Of these writers, the internationally popular Murakami Haruki remains, to date, the most successful example. Using postmodern literary techniques, these writers seem to maintain that however important the heritage of a hundred years or more of modern Japanese literature may be, they prefer a style that fits their perceptions of the rhythms of their time. To some readers, the future of Japanese literature appears to lie with them. But other highly admired writers who are capable of great passion and commitment in their writing, such as Nakagami Kenji, suggest that the range of contemporary Japanese literature is much wider. This chapter offers examples of the work of both groups of writers.

FICTION

FURUI YOSHIKICHI

Furui Yoshikichi (b. 1937) began his career as a professor of modern German literature, with a particular interest in such twentieth-century masters as Hermann Broch and Robert Musil. Then in 1970 he resigned his teaching position in order to devote himself entirely to his creative work, and since that time he has become well regarded among contemporary writers. Furui's works show a seriousness of ambition and a somber poetry that allow the reader to enter the often subtle and mysterious psychological worlds he is able to conjure up. Furui's story "Ravine" (Tani, 1980) is one of the best of his works that has been translated into English.

RAVINE (TANI)

Translated by Meredith McKinney

Deep in the mountains there is a voice, chanting holy sutras. Drawn by the sanctity of its timbre he wanders among the mountains, seeking, but the owner of the voice is nowhere to be found. When he returns half a year later, the voice is still faintly audible. This time he conducts a thorough search and discovers, at the bottom of a ravine, the meager whitened bones of a man who had [hanged] himself from the cliff by a hemp rope tied around his legs. A further three years pass, and still the chanting has not ceased. Marveling, he this time carefully investigates the skeleton and discovers that the tongue inside the skull remains unrotted, and is even now continuing to chant with unwavering devotion.

Lying rolled in my sleeping bag in the darkness of the little hiker's hut in the ravine, I recalled this old story of the uncanny voice that rose with the sound of the rushing water from the valley floor, a story I had heard in the classroom a good seventeen or eighteen years earlier and forgotten till that moment. It came back to me now, as a chill autumn rain came racing suddenly in from the mountain, beating at the branches of the forest, and shrouded the ravine where I lay in a sound that merged with the sound of the stream's rushing, till it was as if the rain was pouring upward, out of the earth. And it seemed to me then that, from beneath the almost paralyzed quietness that lay wrapped at the heart of the water's roar, the rich and lustrous weight of a chanting voice reverberated with an astonishing clarity. When I listened intently, there was in fact no single voice discernible. But now it seemed to me that the tumble of water noise in the ravine had instead begun to swell with the breaths of many different people.

This was not the first time I had been bedeviled by auditory hallucinations in the mountains. Once, for instance, at the end of autumn on a night wild with wind and rain, I had heard the midsummer song of a cicada. From deep in the forest there emerged that sharp and numbing shrill, and it echoed back also in layer upon layer from the opposite wall of the ravine. The more closely I listened, the clearer it sounded. It must have been caused by a sort of buzzing in the head due to extreme fatigue, but I could not distinguish it from the sounds of the outside world except for the fact that, when I tried raising my head, it abruptly ceased. I believed for a long time that this auditory hallucination was peculiar to myself. But in the hospital just before he died, Koike confided to me that he too had often been troubled by the cry of cicadas in the middle of the night when he was in the mountains. Nakamura also said he could remember such experiences. Though we three had frequently gone into the mountains together in our twenties, this was the first time this had ever been mentioned among us. . . .

Nakamura, lying next to me in his sleeping bag, moved restlessly from time to time and emitted something between a sigh and a groan. He had struck his lower back against a rock that day as we walked, and the pain was apparently still with him in sleep. It was mid-October; the traditional service of the forty-ninth day after death had now passed, and—in memory of the man who, until the morning he finally lost consciousness, had spoken constantly of our mountain walks together—we were performing what could be called a memorial climb for Koike. It had been five years since our last mountain trip together, when we were thirty, and for both of us the lack of any real exercise in the intervening years had caused drastic physical changes. Until that spring, Koike had also lamented his paunch whenever we met, but when I saw him again three months later he had grown thinner than he had been in his twenties. After fifty days of hospitalization he had finally died at the end of summer, his body parched dark with suffering, leaving behind a wife and two children of five and three. Stomach cancer had taken him at this early age.

Thinking about it now, I realized that from our earliest plans for this memorial climb we were swept along on a strange wave of elation at being the survivors of our companion's death. It was almost as if the chill breath of our dead friend were brushing against us. There was an excited lift to our step; we seemed both physically and mentally to regain our youth, and we were somehow entranced with the sense that we, at least, could still climb mountains. We had met up whenever we could in the midst of our heavy work schedules and briskly accomplished the task of planning the trip, each privately fearing that his physical strength might not be up to it, and somewhat ashamed at the precipitate and unrealistic nature of the decision, given that we were men in our mid-thirties, each with a family; and now here we were actually in the mountains, with a climbing schedule such as we used to set ourselves in our twenties, and an equivalent weight of equipment on our backs. The previous day, the first day of the walk, we had indeed felt the effects of our lack of physical training. We had exhausted our fund of energy simply in carrying the rucksacks from the foot of the mountain up the ravine as far as this hut, so that on our arrival it was all we could do to prepare and eat the evening meal, and we rolled into our sleeping bags leaving the dirty plates to lie as they were on the earth floor, laughingly agreeing together over a cup of saké that after all we needn't feel we had to go all the way to the summit tomorrow if this present exhaustion were still with us in the morning. But in the morning we had woken refreshed and had been impatient to be off as we ate breakfast and cleared up. Slinging a light knapsack over our shoulders, we began to climb through the sweet morning scent of the conifer forest, at first gingerly testing our strength, then gradually growing almost ecstatic at how wonderfully firmly we were walking, each familiar motion and each new mountain view bringing back memories for us, until after four hours of drunkenly joyous climbing we found ourselves effortlessly arriving at the summit.

On the way back down, the threat of rain in the sky hastened our steps, and when we reached a rock scree, Nakamura suddenly lost his footing. His foot slipped only slightly on the loose rocks, but he tipped over backward and didn't try to twist around to save himself from falling; instead he continued to slide down a good fifteen feet, his astonished eyes fixed on my face till finally he rolled over onto his side and came to a halt, striking his lower back against a rock with a dull thud. It wasn't a particularly dangerous situation, but it gave me a rather nasty feeling to see Nakamura, who was usually a man of more than average agility, so suddenly passive and unresisting.

"It's not that I was taken by surprise," he explained in bewilderment when he had scrambled back up to where I waited, "it's just that, purely and simply, my body didn't try to save itself."

When night came the ravine suddenly grew chill and a cold rain came rushing incessantly downstream off the mountain we had climbed that day. Night in the ravine differed from the experience of night on a flat plain: even inside the hut, hearing did not function so much horizontally as vertically. One moment the stream's sound would be heard echoing upward into the sky and the next instant something would shift so that it seemed now instead to be pouring down from above. The wind carried in the swelling sea song of the conifer forest up on the ridge, came beating down on the corrugated iron roof of the hut, and passed on into the ravine beyond, and then in a kind of reverse wave the sound of creaking branches came thrusting back up from the path of the wind. Only the weight of the darkness sank ever more intensely. Finally the rain squall swept everything to oneness within its roar, passed over, and was gone, and now in the sudden silence that pierced to the very quick of the skull, one's own consciousness seemed like a tiny yellow light shining meaninglessly in the huge depths of the mountain darkness.

When we had cleared up after the evening meal and sat warming ourselves by the embers, drinking whiskey and dreamily breathing in the fragrant smoke, Nakamura complained that his lower back hurt. We had a joking exchange about it. At our age backache was merely a humorous complaint. The talk turned naturally to the question of our sexuality now that we were reaching middle age. We were in the midst of some licentious talk on the subject when Nakamura suddenly stretched his back and winced, then grinned through the wince. Taking the fact that the fire had died as our cue, we spread our sleeping bags side by side on the wooden platform and lay down, pulling the hoods up over our heads so that only our faces were exposed to the now rapidly chilling air, and spoke for a while of the dead Koike. Our talk became somewhat oppressive.

"The worst thing about going to see him in the hospital was that he kept wanting to touch my body," Nakamura murmured, already drowsy. "He'd suddenly stare at my arm or my chest while I was talking, and then his thin hand would come sliding out toward it. And he'd just keep touching it, with a kind of envious expression. That would have been back during those hot summer days. . . ."

The conversation had grown rather grim, and we stopped talking. The same thing had happened to me many times with Koike. It wasn't so much that he envied our health as that he marveled at it. He would fix his eyes on me intently, as though staring at something incomprehensible—something he couldn't believe without touching it. Finding myself gazed at thus, sometimes stroked by his thin weak hand, I had constantly to fight down an almost unconquerable sense of idiot arrogance at my own survival, a sheer joy at the fact that I wasn't in Koike's place. Nor was that my greatest unkindness toward Koike.

"I'm putting it out," I said to Nakamura, and blew out the candle. The hut was immediately soaked deep in the sounds of the ravine. The faint light that still hung even in the darkness of this night now slowly spread a gray swathe across the floor from the small window, making the plates and water bottles and rucksacks stand out blackly around our bed. Whenever Nakamura twisted his back and groaned, I teased him with a low chuckle, and he laughed grimly back. After some time of this, Nakamura suddenly lifted his head from the sleeping bag and turned an intrepid face toward the door.

"Isn't that someone coming up the ravine?"

The squall had just stopped, and nothing was audible except the sound of the stream, and the occasional fall of a branch.

"Must be my ears," he said lightly, and lay back and began again the low moaning at regular long intervals, until eventually he no longer responded to my chuckle but seemed to have fallen asleep without his moans ceasing. I found then that I seem to have taken over the role of sentinel. I couldn't manage to get to sleep. To induce myself, I imagined the sleep of a timid animal. The instant it hears a sound that has some meaning for it, deep sleep becomes complete alertness. For this to happen, it must first be thoroughly asleep. It's impossible to have that instantaneous reaction to a sound if you hear it through a wakeful doze. The eyes spring open, and it makes a hairsbreadth escaping leap aside from the claws of death. Then, once it has escaped to temporary safety, it immediately falls asleep again, oblivious to the screams of its companions. There is no consciousness of having been saved.

I was beginning to doze off with these thoughts when, from farther down the ravine, I heard the forced breathing of someone climbing a steep slope with a heavy weight on his back. The climber's hot, uncontrollable panting, which seemed to be retching out his very heart with each gasp, was clearly audible in the lulls between the expressionless rustlings of the trees. No sooner did it seem to have approached somewhat than it merged with the stream's sound and disappeared. Then, after a long time had passed, it was there again at just the point it had been before. I had many times had the experience of welcoming a climber who arrived late at night at a mountain hut. Climbers generally follow the principle of avoiding unnecessary intimacy with members of another climbing party, but when someone comes in very late he generally receives a carefully casual welcome from the unknown companions in the hut. They emerge half asleep from their sleeping bags, pretending they just happen to have woken, to stir up the now-dead fire and warm the remains of their dinner for him, sometimes sitting up half the night with him in desultory talk. No, the footsteps were coming no closer.

Then for a while the events occurred within a dream. I sank to sleep with my ears still straining to hear. As I slept, I could still distinctly hear the sound of the stream and Nakamura's moans. In the distance, what could have been an owl's cry stood out as a single point within the hollow darkness. Suddenly the footsteps rapidly approached and came to a halt outside the hut. Nakamura and I lifted our heads at the same moment. The man was having difficulty opening the door from the outside. We went to lend our strength from within and then, suddenly, a tall man had crossed the threshold and stood in the hut gazing blankly about. A single glance told us that he'd lost his way in the dark and spent a long time wandering out there. Nakamura went round behind him and released him from his rucksack, and I stood in front of him to help him off with his anorak. Just at that moment the man opened his eyes and mouth wide, uttered a voiceless cry, and slumped forward against me, and as he clasped my chest with both arms his body began to convulse. I staggered backward holding him, and managed to sit down on the edge of the raised wooden platform behind me, to sustain his weight; then I braced my legs and heaved his sturdy body up. When the two of us had finally succeeded in laying him down between our sleeping bags, his face was already that of a dead man.

"He's dead," we agreed with a hastily exchanged glance, and in a panic we set about trying to revive him. Nakamura knelt beside him, stripped back the sodden shirt and undershirt, and began to rub his blue chest fiercely with a dry towel. I quickly gathered firewood and lit the fire and, for some reason, set about boiling some water in the cauldron. But as fast as we worked, just as rapidly did his appearance transform itself. Nakamura's massaging did not produce even the faintest flush on the man's chest, and when Nakamura began to work up onto the neck, his movements pushed the man's head so it lolled over sideways, and from the mouth and nose now turned toward me, dark clotting blood flowed.

"Come on, let's sleep," said Nakamura, tossing the towel to the floor; he hastily scrambled feet first into the sleeping bag beside the corpse and immediately set up the same regular moaning as before.

We lay there under the weight of the darkness, with the dead man between us. Whenever Nakamura moaned I had the illusion that it was the dead man, and turned to Nakamura to say, "Hey, he's still alive." And each time I did so, that blue face with its bloody nose and mouth laughed straight in my face. Beside me the corpse had the heavy cold weight of an object, and I felt it sinking interminably farther and farther down into the blackness, on its face an eternal grin of somehow mocking agony. The weight of it was being precariously suspended there between our combined breathing on either side. If we once relaxed our strength, the sinking corpse would pull us under with it. I was astonished at the quiet will at work in the very act of breathing. Then suddenly it seemed the roof and the floor had been removed, and we were floating free in space above the ravine, with the corpse slung between us. The sound of the flowing water connected directly with the expressionless weight of the corpse, and the soughing of the branches was now the sound of the monstrous expanse of time itself. In all that ravine, only we spread around ourselves a tiny warmth, within which we lived. I searched the water sounds desperately for the sound of another person—let it be a voice or footfall, a moan, a gasp, even a last dying cry, as long as it somehow, ever so slightly, shook the expressionlessness of the ravine.

And then a chill rain began to fall, and the ravine began to seethe again, and I awoke with the sound of sutra chanting in my ears, and a sense of having been saved.

It must have been the voice of the sutras that Nakamura and I had heard chanted countless times in the interval between Koike's wake and the forty-ninth-day ceremony for the dead, which had sunk deep into my ears and now returned to me as a voice from the depths of the ravine. Yet the voice sounded so vividly human. It was a rich, ponderous voice, almost as if the human flesh itself had been tempered till it rang. It seemed, I thought, like a sound made in imitation of what one would imagine to be the sanctity of the first sound uttered from the silence of one newly dead. Straining my ears, I felt it was still implicit in the sounds of the stream—so indistinguishable from that natural water sound, yet so distinguishably a human voice, with the echo of every human passion within it.

The rain passed over and the ravine returned to a deep quietness, with only the constant sound of the stream. But the quality of that quietness was irrevocably altered for me. From every corner of the ravine's darkness that wrapped me round, there now swelled intimations of all the breathings of the human flesh, which wove a thick silence all about me. There was even the suggestion of the trembling voice of a woman. Of course the only sounds that actually existed were the groans of Nakamura close beside me and my own breathing, and all these other sounds were no more real than the cicada's song on that stormy night, the effect of my small life force pulsing softly in the eardrum or in the capillaries of the inner ear, which merely made deceptive imitation of the countless lives in that vast darkness beyond. Yet it was nevertheless the motion of life, and saying this to myself I called before my mind the image of Koike lying motionless on his hospital bed. . . .

Even after all signs of consciousness had ceased, Koike remained as a merely physical existence, and for two hours more he continued to groan. His wife called Nakamura and me into the hospital room, and we stood against the wall, watching over him, helpless in the face of his suffering. When Koike's breathing had stopped and the doctors had left, Mrs. Koike gently wiped her husband's forehead with a handkerchief, then put the handkerchief to her own eyes and drew a deep sigh. At that moment, the sounds of the distant street came surging into the sickroom. A soft sobbing flowed within the sounds. I didn't so much hear this sound with my ears as greedily gulp it down into my cold chest. Cocooned in the survivor's sense of reprieve, I had not the wherewithal then to grieve at the death of my friend. Nakamura too was leaning heavily against the wall, face up and eyes closed, his shoulders heaving roughly, as though he had just managed to come through a difficult rock climb.

The deep sighing of a woman welled up in the darkness. The white swelling of the throat was implicit everywhere in the dark, unknotting and smoothing the stiffness of death. There was something in the sound that was akin to the sutra-chanting voice. Even the soft creaks of branches in the wind had about them a hint of woman. All the sounds in the world came whispering enticingly in with the sighing, like the soft rustle of clothing in a voiceless room.

As the voice of my dead friend's wife, needless to say it smote my conscience, but it was at the same time some other woman's voice. Koike had also heard that voice. He seemed indeed to keep the enticement of this voice before him right up until the moment of his death. . . . In the early autumn of the year we turned twenty, we three made a rare visit to the seaside. At midday we lay together in the pampas grass of a broad hill that extended out as a promontory above the sea, our bodies soaking up the warm heavy rays of the sun, unable quite to adjust ourselves to the leisurely pace of existence here compared with our trips to the mountains. As we lay there we talked about women, we who as yet knew nothing of them.

Suddenly from the bushes nearby there welled up the sound of a woman's heavy dark panting.

Then followed a gasping cry, naked with painful physicality. We three sat up simultaneously and gazed in the direction of the voice. After a moment, a woman in a white dress emerged onto the road from the shadow of the nearby bushes and came walking past us with long leisurely strides, heel and toe, her arms folded down low on her belly, her back serenely straight. She headed into the sea breeze, half turning to send a vague glance in our direction as she passed, then was hidden again in the shadow of the bushes farther along the road. She appeared somewhat older than we were. It was difficult to imagine how that heavy panting of a moment before could have emanated from such a gaunt body. A tight black belt bit into her waist, and a straw hat hid her face from forehead to nose in deep shadow, with slightly parted lips and a thin pointed chin poking out below it into the sunlight. It was only the chin and lips that seemed to be turned on us briefly; the eyes gazed vaguely at some distant point far beyond our heads. Her neck, arms, and calves were white and luster-less, and the surrounding brightness made them appear somehow clouded and opaque.

We waited for the excitement that the panting had aroused in our bodies to recede, then got to our feet. When we emerged and set off after her, the woman was already far ahead along the gently winding road, on the point of disappearing into the pampas grass. Once we reached there, we had no idea where she had gone, so we stood stock-still, bathed in the light of sky and sea, feeling help-lessly that something more ought to have come of this. I blinked slowly in the sunlight. When I closed my eyes my body seemed a soft transparent red, and on opening them, a darkness like heavy oil filled me. The repetition of this was like a listless breathing.

Even Koike's sudden dash into the nearby bushes provoked no more than a dull surprise in me. I turned my gaze in the direction he had gone, and the top half of the woman's body suddenly swam up above the grass heads, her oddly white and pinched profile turned to us, against the black glittering expanse of the sea. The figure was somehow difficult to get into perspective; she could have been a hundred feet or more away. I watched Koike's mad dash toward her with a sensation of pleasure, almost as if it was my own sexual desire that was plunging headlong at her. The woman became aware of the footsteps behind her, turned quickly toward us, then, with a fierce look, disappeared as if sinking backward.

"You mustn't die!" cried Koike, and he too disappeared, his diving body thrusting the grasses aside. Nakamura and I looked at each other in astonish-ment, then set off after them.

Koike was crouched facing the edge of the cliff, huddled paralyzed like a hunted animal, and tiny shivers ran over his body.

The woman had crossed the low iron railing, and with an almost graceful movement she sank down right at the cliff edge and slowly pushed her legs over the edge, her hectically flushed face all the while turned on Koike with a steady glare.

"Please don't," Koike pleaded, huddling still lower and slowly inching for-ward on his knees two or three shuffles at a time, judging the best moment to spring at her.

For a long time they remained staring at each other, waiting to see whose strength of will would win out and break the balance. Nakamura was preparing to make a simple lunge at her from the side, but this seemed a dangerous move to me and I stopped him. Koike was now gradually relaxing his pose, and the woman seemed to be slowly cringing before him.

He had reached a point where a single step would bring him within reach of the railing to which the woman's hand clung, and suddenly he leapt at it. He missed his moment by the merest breath; the woman released her grip on the rail, slipped over the edge of the rock and disappeared, still in a sitting position, pitching forward with her back arched as if shouldering away the sky.

"Wait!" shouted Koike, straddling the railing, and with his left hand he clung to it for balance while he stretched his right hand down over the rock ledge.

Above the rim of the rock the woman's face, her face only, rose up like a white death mask against the glittering sea.

"What is it, honey?" she said to Koike in a thin clear voice. Then her purple lips seemed to smile.

"Please don't," Koike said thickly, and then he sprang away from her, scrambled back over the railing, and came tumbling over to us on all fours. As he did so, the woman turned her face to the sky and disappeared over the edge of the rock. There was a sense of something like a heavy sandbag sliding down the cliff face, then she was launched into the air with a wild scream that was neither man's nor woman's, which trailed off into a long moan, and finally at a dizzying depth her body thudded dully into the water. Koike put his hands on the earth, twisted sideways, and vomited. Then he shook his head violently from side to side, and soundlessly began to cry above the vomit.

I left Koike in Nakamura's care and ran headlong back down the hill to the fishing village in the inlet below. At every turn in the zigzag road I was afflicted with the sensation that the sea's horizon with its dense light was bearing down upon me. I rushed into the little police station and gave the news, but the officers seemed to be quite used to this kind of event; a group of people was quickly assembled, and they set off in a fishing boat from the pier, chatting together about the last time this had happened, and disappeared round the cliff, the motor making little soft explosions as they went. They took with them a net that looked just like a fishing net, saying they would drag the corpse to shore through the water. After a while Nakamura and Koike both arrived, each looking as pale as the other, and we three stood together in silence gazing at the sea.

"They've gone by boat to get her out," is all I said to them.

"I should just have made a dash for her at the beginning without hesitating," said Koike, in a dull voice.

"There's a strong smell of fish around here," Nakamura muttered, squatting down on the seawall, and then he vomited into the sea. The vomit spread out finely through the clear water and sank, and little fish gathered to sip at it, the sides of their bellies flashing.

Thirty minutes later the boat reappeared from the shadow of the cliff. I peered at the stern, but there was no sign of anything being dragged along behind. The men in the boat were smoking sullenly, in a mood quite unlike the one they had set out in. As the boat approached we craned forward with the urge to see what fearful thing could be seen, and there discovered in the bottom of the boat on the pile of brown fishing net a small wet collapsed shape. We could make out a white calf with the veins standing out blue in it, and an oddly elongated nape of a neck, and then two arms cradling a bowed head.

"She's alive," one of the men said to us, a little dejectedly.

We assumed that she would be, at any rate, close to death, or badly hurt at the very least, but when the boat reached the pier and the men called to her, she lifted her head, pulled the wet hair back from her cheeks with both hands, and setting her hair in order stood up sinuously, with a listless air. Once she was helped onto the rock by both arms, she bent slightly forward, took her wet dress in delicate fingertips, and pulled the skirt away from her body, then with eyes modestly cast down to her bare feet, she began to walk off.

"You're not, you're not hurt?" Koike asked in a shrill voice, stepping backward as she walked past him.

"No thank you, I'm quite all right," the woman replied in the same voice we had heard on the cliff edge, and off she walked between the men in the direction of the police station, her head meekly lowered, casting him not so much as a glance. To the children who came running up, she turned an embarrassed smile.

It was then that a cold fear finally gripped me. That body, with its white death mask of a face, which had been sucked out into space leaving in its wake a somehow hollow sound, that body was still alive. Drenched though it was, it now walked through the quiet fishing village looking like a normal woman. It was even smiling kindly at children. The stink of fish suddenly assaulted my nostrils. The bay, with its downpour of sunlight, went dark before my eyes, and the woman's bare feet as they trod the sand grew harsh and vivid. Behind Koike and Nakamura, who stood there in astonishment, watching her go, I squatted in shadow and softly retched.

Since the woman had in the end been unharmed, it would have been sensible to laugh off our dismay when we recalled it later. This is what we always did after we had emerged from some dangerous situation in the mountains. But, apart from marveling together at the power of her good fortune, we didn't speak further to each other about the event. We got the bus straight back to the town from there and caught the night train home, cutting our trip short by a day. As we sat in the bus, Koike muttered, "You know, it really is a weakness in us, not to have any way of praying in this sort of situation. It means that you end up bearing the brunt of everything yourself, even the things that are too much to bear."

"Well yes, maybe," Nakamura replied. "But when I saw her stand up in the boat back there, I just thought 'Praise be!' That's all I thought. But I think really that was a kind of prayer."

I was about to say what suddenly came into my mind at this, that if I were to pray to anything it would be to the awe-inspiring nature of that woman, that it's to fearful things that one prays; but at the strange image that this idea conjured up I lost my nerve, and I said nothing.

To the end there was a deep reluctance among the three of us to bring up the subject of that day's events. When Nakamura and I were alone together, we did speculate on the nature of this woman about whom we had learned absolutely nothing, on her reasons for suicide, and what might have become of her subsequently. But when with Koike we never spoke of the event. Koike had become a man who could no longer look women in the eye.

It was Nakamura and I who together threw ourselves into bringing this woman-shy Koike together with the woman who subsequently became his wife. Watching frustratedly from the sidelines, misgivings filled us as we saw our friend only flee the more as the attraction grew. It had been our early obtuseness there by the seaside that had put Koike in the position of facing the terror of that event alone. While Nakamura and I had gone on to have for the most part unproblematic relationships with women, Koike alone had been unable in any way to shake off the aftereffects of the event, right into his thirties. Our sense of our own responsibility in this weighed on us. Also, we were feeling somewhat threatened by Koike's lover, the woman who later became his wife. She had become exasperated at how he would dodge aside at the last minute, just when he'd seemed to be reaching for her, and she finally demanded that he introduce her to his best friends so that she could learn more about him and come to terms with things a bit; she got from him the names and workplaces of Nakamura and myself, and one day she telephoned me. Koike had told me firmly that I was to keep out of this, but I could clearly see how attracted he was to her, and when she telephoned me I agreed to go out to meet and talk to her on several occasions. But how could I, who myself couldn't really understand Koike's feelings no matter how he tried to explain them, manage to sound convincing to her on the subjects? Her pride as a woman had been hurt by Koike, and she was haggard with the impossibility of parting from him. The more I tried to explain, the more irritable she became, and she plied me with questions for all the world as if rebuking me. In the end it was I who was convinced by her, by the fierceness of her love, which eventually sealed my lips.

One night, when she was yet again firing questions at me, I finally spoke of the events by the seaside. She listened then with her eyes fixed on mine. "And ever since, Koike has been the way he is about women," I finished, with a sense of really providing her for the first time with a worthwhile explanation. But in fact it served only to infuriate her.

"So that's how you men feel about women, is it?" she demanded, and she shifted sideways to look past me and refused to respond to all my attempts to justify myself. After a while I became aware that everyone around us was taking this to be some kind of lover's quarrel, so I urged her to come outside.

As we walked together toward the station, I glanced at the tearful face beside me, quite preoccupied and apparently unaware of whom she was with, and the weird thought stole over me that if I suddenly embraced her now things could develop into a three-way relationship with my friend, and then that this could actually make the lovers' relationship rather more straightforward. It was of course an impossibility. Even without taking Koike into consideration, if I contrived to get myself alone with this woman, who knew how she might attack me for my earlier blunder. After parting from her at the station, I went on to Nakamura's place and told him the story to date, finishing by saying that as things stood I'd done Koike a bad turn, and that I left the next stage in his hands.

A week later he came to see me, looking glum.

"Look at it how you will, Koike's in the wrong," he began, in typical Nakamura style. "He just carries on the whole time about his own feelings, and he's making no attempt to shake off his fears for the sake of the woman he loves. He just doesn't deserve to get her, he isn't qualified as a man." But there was a certain bewilderment behind his words.

We agreed that we must make every effort to bring the two of them together; it never for a moment occurred to us that this could be construed as uncalled-for meddling.

Luckily, Koike's married life appeared to go smoothly. Each time we met, Koike seemed more open and relaxed, and his wife's former raw, nervous quality now became swathed in a plump fleshiness; her skin bloomed and shone. A child was born. Then, with a timing that seemed almost to be putting that marriage's success to some personal test, Nakamura married, followed by myself.

Five days before Koike died, I called at the hospital. It was another of those days of heavy rain, and the sickroom was imbued with a faintly marshy scent of wet rocks and forest humus. Koike sat me down on a chair by his pillow, and his dark emaciated face looked somehow dazzled as it gazed up at me, while he set about recalling in intricate detail an occasion when the three of us had lost our way in a ravine on one of our climbing trips. This event had occurred more than a year after the event beside the seaside. We had taken a wrong turning on a path that we had been along twice before, and headed confidently up a completely unfamiliar ravine.

As we followed the stream up, the valley sides grew steeper, and we scrambled up a succession of rock ledges we had no recollection of having come across on our previous trips—yet still we resisted the conclusion that we'd come the wrong way, and almost perversely chose to continue. Then, just when we reached a point where it seemed the path along the ridge above might be almost within our grasp, we found our way barred by a fair-sized waterfall. It was only when we'd clawed our way up to a ledge halfway up its side, and gazed at the dismal sight of the rock face above, that we began to think seriously about our position. We had arrived at a place that seemed to be the deep innermost recess of the ravine; within our range of vision there was only the waterfall, its endless stream pouring with a kind of uncanny slowness from somewhere above our heads, the black rocks that hemmed us in on four sides like a bowl, and a sky that was rapidly darkening with clouds. We stood in silence for a long time, gazing up at the rock face. It wouldn't be impossible to force our way up it as we had forced our way up so far, but at this point we had simply lost the spirit to attempt it. We were not so much searching for a way up as privately taking the inner measure of just how much spirit each of us had lost. Koike alone was impatient. His opinion was that, in the case of a nasty place like this, it was the least dangerous option simply to take a deep breath and climb through it without hesitating and that the longer we stood and contemplated it the more our psychological defenses would crumble; he seemed astonishingly unconcerned with the question of whether it was the right path or not. Astonished though I was, I myself was actually still of two minds as to whether we had mistaken the way. After a little while, Nakamura dealt with the question summarily by saying that whatever the case may be, we should retrace our steps to the first fork in the path. Once it was spoken, this seemed the most reasonable option. We went back down the rock face with ropes and returned to the meeting of the two streams in the same amount of time we had taken to come up, then set up our tents there for the night, as the ravine was rapidly darkening. When we emerged from our tents in the morning, it was clear at a glance that we had gone the wrong way at that point. We had turned up a side stream one back from the point where the path branched, and followed it all the way up the ravine that ended in the sheer cliff etched by its waterfall, without noticing our mistake.

"How could we have been so stupid?" Koike demanded fretfully from his hospital bed, almost as if it had happened just the other day, as if that mistake had led to the gravest of consequences.

"It's all too common with ravines, to make mistakes that seem ridiculous later."

"Yes, but we'd done that walk twice before, hadn't we? You'd think among the three of us someone would have realized instantly that that dismal little ravine wasn't the right one."

He spoke accusingly. Resentment focused his eyes on some distant point in space. Then his right hand emerged trembling from beneath the blankets and took my right wrist in a loose grip. His rough dry palm began stroking my arm repeatedly from wrist to elbow. I swallowed down the disgust that rose in me, and a simultaneous disgust at the sudden consciousness that it produced in me of the greasy sweatiness of my own arm, and replied in a carefully calm voice, "It was because we were tired. We'd walked a long way, remember. When you get tired the brain can't make judgments anymore, you make them with your body: We've walked this far, so this must be the point where we turn off, and so forth. And the tireder you are the sooner . . ."

"You turn up a side path." There was a strangely ironic smile at the corners of his mouth as he spoke. "But then there's no option, really. The darkness inside you makes the whole ravine dark, doesn't it. There's no point saying it was brighter or darker last time we came here. Because each time is the first time. Still, that feeling of going up a ravine you seem to know, or maybe you don't after all, that sensation halfway along that you can't go any farther. . . ."

As he muttered, Koike renewed his grasp on my wrist and drew it under the bedclothes toward his flat chest. My face approached his as he pulled me down, and he gazed into my eyes and lowered his voice to a conspiratorial whisper, as though imparting some important secret. "I've remembered! That cairn—remember? The one where the streams met, a bit out of the way, little heap of five or six small rocks, just piled up as though someone had come along a moment or so earlier and thrown it together in passing. A sign, but from its position you couldn't really tell whether it meant 'go straight ahead' or 'turn left here.' Yes, a treacherous bit of mischief. We'd just come down from the right side of the river; that's why that cairn seemed to be pointing up to the left. But I've remembered now. The moment we went left up that stream I thought, 'This is odd. This is wrong.' You thought the same. You did, didn't you."

"Yes I suppose I did," I replied, unable to avoid supplying the answer he was urging on me; and in fact, now that he mentioned it, I did seem to remember that when we first turned off I had a strong impression that this was wrong, but my feet went tramping on in rhythm with theirs without my having the strength to gainsay the other two.

"We were led astray, that's what it was, just because we didn't pay enough attention at that point where the paths divided." There was a certain urgency in his whispering voice. The core of his eyes seemed to blaze up in a wavering flame. "That's why all we could do was to go on in silence, even when we realized the truth later. That's what it was. But I saw, up on that rock ledge, I saw it, drawing us on from above, peering down at us over the edge there, a woman's face. . . ."

"If you saw a woman's face, why didn't you tell us! What sort of a friend are you?" I tried to lighten the moment with a feeble joke, but as I spoke I found myself pulling my hand and face away from Koike. My tug made Koike's face flop upward from the pillow, and he clutched my arm with both hands. A face that seemed to contain equally both laughter and tears, a face that could have belonged to any of the images one sees surrounding the central Buddha in the dark of temple altars; I knew from the experience of my mother's death that that face had the clear marks of death upon it. A cold confusion of fear gripped me and I rose from the chair. Koike stretched his hands to my chest, gripped my shirt and clung there shaking for a long moment, and a heavy groan thrust itself from deep within him.

"You're both with me, we're always there the three of us when we go into the ravine, you were there too weren't you? You're always the careful and perceptive one, Nakamura can make decisions. . . ."

Mrs. Koike flew in and separated us, pulling Koike's hands from my chest and covering me with her back. She shot me a glance, signaling with her eyes as she put a forefinger softly to her temple, then held Koike against her and pressed him down onto the bed with her body.

"I don't want to die, not all alone, I don't want to die!" Koike cried out from beneath his wife's breast. He continued to cry aloud and weep.

His wife put one elbow on the bed, raised herself on her left leg, turning toward me the almost translucent whiteness of the back of her knee, lifted her right leg from the floor and put it on the edge of the bed, and gently pressed her breast to the upturned face of her weeping husband. Then, as she stoked his long tangle of hair with her fingertips, she too began to cry softly.

From within the sound of the rain, a rich sobbing and moaning swelled and died.

"I don't want to die," Koike groaned several times more, as if reminding himself, but—strangely—his wife's sobs seemed to be calming him.

Once his groans had ceased, Mrs. Koike rose from the bed, quietly straightened the hem of her white dress, brushed the hair back from her forehead, turned her somewhat flushed face to me and lowered her eyes, and in a slightly husky voice said, "I do apologize."

Koike's eyes were closed, and he was breathing gently with sleep.

After my agitation, my mind became a blank, and I just stood bolt upright against the wall listening to the sound of the rain. But in the grim face of this death, at the moment when being alive seemed as unbearable as dying, my heart had been strangely touched by the two voices I heard. And it was only now, when the first commemorative ceremony of Koike's death was over, as I lay straining my ears for the sighs and moans of the myriad voices contained within the ravine's sounds all about me, that I at last understood just how my heart had indeed been touched that day.

HIRANO KEIICHIRŌ

Hirano Keiichirō (b. 1975) was born in Aichi Prefecture and grew up in Kita Kyushu. His first novel, *Solar Eclipse* (*Nisshoku*, 1998), set in France on the eve of the Renaissance, was published while Hirano was still a student at Kyoto University and won the Akutagawa Prize in the following year, making him a celebrity overnight and inviting comparisons with Mishima Yukio, who also made a dazzling, youthful debut. Hirano's second novel, *Tale of One Month* (*Ichigetsu monogatari*, 1999), a fable set in the mountains of Yoshino during the Meiji period, was published right after his graduation. In *Funeral March* (*Sōsō*, 2002), Hirano turned again to France, writing about Chopin, George Sand, and Eugène Delacroix. His first volume of short stories, including "Clear Water" (*Shimizu*), was published in 2003, and another collection, *Ripples of Dripping Clocks* (*Shitariochiru toketachi no hamon*), followed in 2004. Hirano now lives in Kyoto.

CLEAR WATER (SHIMIZU)

Translated by Anthony H. Chambers

Clear water is dripping, far away.

The day was unbearable, the sun scattering incessantly from the morning on.

Wondering at dawn where my slumber had gone (it has stubbornly resisted company for a long time), I gazed through the curtains, marveling at the scene outside as if seeing it for the first time.

I'd been running for days through the same absurd speculations, trying to find a convincing explanation for what was happening to me. Of course, I wasn't as serene at the beginning as I am now. Serene—yes, I'm serene. Might this be called resignation? Probably. That is, if resignation requires such a feeling of powerlessness.

Once they sprouted in my mind, those fragments of memory flourished with a robust, botanical speed, like ivy shooting out tendrils.

It was the memory of a sun of long ago, a memory of a day when the gigantic sun that covered everything over our heads drew away from us, even as it scattered its light everywhere. A shabby blue spread gradually through the sky. I felt the sadness of parting. In tears, I gazed futilely at the scene, on and on.

. . . *Memory.* Yes, I said memory. And yet at first I didn't think of it as such. No—to be more exact, I thought of it as a memory at first, then instantly denied that it was:

It must be a fragment of a myth I read someplace and a trace of the arbitrary daydreams it inspired. Or a scene from a movie? Something I envisioned for a novel? Did some stimulus revive a dream that was lost when I awoke? Or simply the dregs of a fantasy I'd amused myself with?

And yet I couldn't accept any of these explanations. Preceding everything else was *the sensation of having remembered* and *that memory's feeling of actuality.*

Getting out of bed, I sat at the table and looked at a box of cookies as I sipped the remains of last night's coffee.

Is there such a thing as an indubitable memory? —I was drawn back to this question. If no material traces remain to confirm what has occurred only yesterday—even just now—then there's endless room for doubt.

For example, here's a cookie. I am now, without question, gazing at this cookie as it rests in the palm of my hand. I eat it. The image of the cookie on my palm lingers in my memory.

Now, without placing anything on my palm, I try to picture the cookie.

(Watching closely, I clenched my fist, then opened it and pictured the cookie there, then closed my fist again.)

Well? Sure enough, an image of the cookie on my palm lingers in my memory. At this point, how can we demonstrate that only one of the two cookies has truly existed? In my memory, the images of the cookies are the same. Maybe the second cookie is the one that existed. Or maybe there were never any cookies to begin with.—

I drank more cold coffee.

—In that case, I should haul in the memories from before and after the event. The memory of taking one cookie from the box, tearing the paper wrapping, and placing the cookie on my palm. After that, the memory of unconsciously rubbing

my fingers together to dislodge the crumbs that clung to my skin. Right—the trou-
blesome part is that these memories are fragments. . . . Are the memories from
before and after reliable? Hasn't the second cookie in fact imitated the first and be-
gun to extend my memory backward and forward, endlessly? . . .

With a slurp, I drained the remaining ring of coffee in the cup, then rose from
the chair and walked toward the west window.

In the final analysis, it's impossible to demonstrate that the first cookie ex-
isted. . . . (I looked back at the table.) Even that coffee cup might be different
from the coffee cup I remember. How can we say that it's the same? Even I . . .

I had a sudden attack of anxiety as I began to think along these lines, and
feeling under some duress, I hurriedly switched conclusions.

And yet it's still clear to me. The fact that it wasn't the second cookie that ex-
isted but the first. Something clings to my memory of the first cookie—a sense of
substantivity, the feeling of actuality at the moment my hand touched the
cookie. This is, after all, something that my memory of the second cookie couldn't
imitate. . . . A feeling of actuality? In the final analysis, that's about all there
is to vouch for a memory.

I despaired at the fragility of my conclusion. And yet this was the conclusion
I'd desired from the first.

Yes, and ironically, this conclusion serves to confirm my memory. For that
memory is better endowed with a feeling of actuality than any other is.

I felt a slight chill in the air as I approached the window. Although I hesi-
tated to look directly outside, I resolutely opened the curtains. Sure enough, the
sun was scattering more fiercely than ever. As my memory grew more certain, I
could perceive the scattering with greater clarity. *Do I propose to doubt my own*
memory? In fact, hasn't the sun continued to scatter, ever since that day?

I put on the wrinkled trousers I'd taken off yesterday, threw a coat over a well-
chosen sweater, and went outside.

My breath was white. A cold wind like a stray cat blew across my feet and os-
tentatiously lifted the bottom of my coat. I thought it strange that the continually
scattering light didn't dance in the wind. At the same time, I thought myself
strange for finding a hackneyed strangeness in such trivia, even now.

As I walked south on Shimogamo Avenue, the figure of a woman came into
view, sweeping leaves under a Chinese maple that had nervously stretched its
branches. She was the sort of woman you see everywhere, dressed in blue work-
clothes and cotton gloves, her frizzled hair tied up at the back of her head. All
at once I felt uneasy. And when I drew closer, sure enough, before my very eyes
she became a tiny sound and vanished.

Then clear water dripped.

Not missing a beat, a man and a woman came walking toward me, holding
a guidebook. Right at my side, they, too, became two sounds and vanished.—

How can I describe the sound? A sound like that of something splitting. And
it was a dull, unpleasant sound, like that of some resilient substance—human

skin, for example, not paper or wood—being stretched to its limit and, unable to go any further, bursting.

Did they vanish, or did I? This was unclear. Perhaps we all vanished.

Wondering when this sort of thing began, I suddenly came up against thoughts of my own death, its whereabouts unknown.

I feared death as much as the next person does. This is because I believed that death would naturally come calling sooner or later. It's laughable, but when I'd stumble at the end of a moving walkway in a railroad station or at an airport, I'd indulge in the idle thought that I might greet death in this ungainly way when, someday, it made its inevitable call. And when I came across a traffic accident, I'd reflect, like everyone else, that death might strike at any moment.

But one day I realized that my own death had long since been lost in time. Death was nowhere to be found, whether I looked to the future or reflected on the past. This is not to say that I believed in my own immortality. Death still exists somewhere. This the clear water teaches me. The spot where the drip lands is none other than death. —But how to reach that point?

I didn't attempt any of the methods of suicide known to the world. I couldn't conceive that doing so would deliver death to me, and first and foremost, I still feared death.

I just wanted to know. Thinking it over, I tentatively concluded that my own death must resemble an easily liquified metal, like mercury. Now it's still in liquid form, in a small, swollen mass. Each time the clear water drips, I'm bathed in splashes of death. Perhaps that's why I can't touch these people.

A boy rode toward me, the stainless-steel mudguards on his bicycle flashing white. He vanished, leaving nothing behind but his vivid, smiling face. The sunlight showed no sign that it might stop scattering.

. . . *Even so, how curious it is that death doesn't do us the favor of congealing at a certain moment. If time tilts just a little bit, death will come flowing to me from nowhere, as though suddenly sliding down a slope. —Would this really happen, though? Might not death pass me by at that moment, and flow away to somewhere out of reach? Or could it be that death, in a liquid state, has already permeated time and moistened the ground at my feet?—*

Another drip.

When I arrived at Kitaōji Street and turned west, a man coming out of a pachinko parlor vanished just as he was about to bump into me. Noise from inside, released for a moment by the automatic door. After that, nothing remained but an unpleasant echo of the usual sound. Walking a little farther, I met a tour group of about fifteen white people. Two blond boys, twelve or thirteen years of age, walked in front of a flag-bearing guide. Gazing at their faces, I reflected that they must still be elementary-school pupils, though they looked rather grown-up; and then they, too, suddenly disappeared. After that, a middle-aged man with black sunglasses and a red face vanished; the tour guide vanished; a dignified elderly couple listening to the guide vanished, . . . a boy clinging to his father's legs; a freckled girl; a young man with the look of a college student peering sourly at a guidebook; an obese man wearing a baseball cap; and, bringing up the rear, a pair of honeymooners trying to load film into their camera—all of them turned into the usual sounds and vanished. I stopped walking and, standing in the middle of the silent street, watched the light continue to scatter. I thought again of my own lost death.

Is death the only thing lost?

The question flitted through my mind. Hadn't my lifetime ceased long ago to be a straight line? Didn't my existence lie scattered all over time and space, like a boxful of toys overturned by a child?

As I passed a bus stop, I heard three sounds in succession and realized, after they'd vanished, that people had been standing there.

Through the window of a coffeehouse across the street, I saw a man and a woman quarreling. An office worker at the next table, a newspaper spread before him, stole curious glances in their direction. A pregnant woman, shopping bag in hand, walked past the shop. Cars ran calmly in the street.

I found it *incomprehensible*. And I was terrified. I felt as though the word *incomprehensible*, which I used without thinking, had abruptly drawn me close to something indefinable. I felt as though I'd unleashed something irrevocable. And because of that, I felt as though I'd comprehended something for the first time.

Crossing at the signal, I reached Kitaōji Bridge, turned right, and walked for a time along Nakaragi Street.

The needles had withered on a row of pines; before them stood a line of naked weeping cherry trees with slender trunks.

Stopping at one of them, I saw a lump of deformed flesh, covered sparsely with feathers. Blood had flowed, then darkened and congealed.

It was a dead pigeon. The feathers, standing violently on end as though the bird had been plucked, fluttered in a breeze so faint I could hardly feel it. Perhaps the feathers had loosened in the decomposing flesh. Each one twisted in a different direction. The barbs spread apart toward the feather tips, and the slightly blurred, bluish gray white looked like the petals of a fringed orchid. Two or three feathers lay scattered about, like fallen blossoms.

I wondered how feathers that'd been so trim and smooth while the bird lived could get this way when it died. The violated delicacy ironically emphasized the weight of the flesh. I felt an inexpressible tightness in my chest. Uncharacteristically irritable and impatient, I descended to the riverbank, as if running away from something. There the vivid green of the corpse's head flickered obstinately in my mind, even though it hadn't bothered me when it lay before my eyes.

And another drip.

I sat at the edge of the water, on rocks embedded in concrete.

I was alone by the river, perhaps because of the cold. There were no signs of the people one usually sees—housewives walking their dogs, young joggers. The foliage season was over. A ceaseless stream of cars came and went on Kitaōji Bridge, Kitayama Bridge, and the Kamo Highway. Connecting with the cherry-lined street, they formed a broad trapezoid that seemed completely cut off from the outside world.

It was eerie how the light scattered on the surface of the Kamo River. The water glittered so brightly I couldn't look directly at it, no matter which direction I faced.

Did reflections of the light that filled the air blend into one mass, or did the light float on the water, merge in successive waves, and gradually spread?

The sun, fragmented, catching its breath again on the surface. The sun, offering itself to the human-reinforced riverbed and moving away with the flow.—

I was crazed by the falling petals of sun, which scattered with ever greater intensity. This continuous scattering produced an indescribable oppression. The sight held something like music. And yet it was an absolutely monotonous music. In its interminable monotony, it was music that deranged the listener's senses, music wrapped in an ever-changing dream. I felt my sense of hearing contract fiercely then endlessly expand in response to these sounds that should not have been audible. I felt my eardrums tense up as though they would split. The sounds of the flowing river were thrust violently aside. There was no longer any noise from the cars. And yet as the silence closed in, my ears grew more fretful. My sense of hearing couldn't grasp the fact that just as there's no silence on the other side of sound, there's no sound on the other side of silence. My hearing suffered from the illusion that sound might be audible even from silence, just as a faint sound is audible if you listen intently. My sense of hearing had nowhere to go. It wandered aimlessly.

And my vision grew strangely clear.

I watched stubbornly for the moment when they touched the surface of the river. Some swayed back and forth like a pendulum as they fell, then settled flat on the surface, revolved two or three times, and drifted slowly away. Some struck the water at an angle, got wet at the edges, were caught by the current, toppled over and drifted away. The moment when each petal touched the face of the water. The moment when each melted in the light and disappeared. Yet all of them were phantoms in the dazzling light. They were lines without line, shapes without shape. My vision came up against nothing. Just as my hearing sought a sound in the silence, my vision found its way only as far as the expanding light.

Each sense was possessed by a blind impulse to break down. Going mad, each trespassed on the others' territory. I was astonished at their perceptivity, for they knew, long before I did, which way they should turn.

The many steps built at distant intervals in the riverbed sent waves lapping at the sashes of light that lay between them, light that drank up the shadows and spread serenely across the water as if it were the surface of a lake. These delicate waves, infinitely diffused, growing farther apart over a complexion that was neither dark blue nor deep green, vanished, flickering, into the brightest light. A water bird—a faint, black shadow—frolicked there. To watch it descend to the surface of the water, turn into a shadow, then resume its original form as it flew up again, was like gazing at a picture scroll depicting the death and rebirth of a phoenix.

I closed my eyes once, forcefully, with the result that my vision was tinged in red, as though it were clouded with blood. The light withdrew for a moment, and the flow of the river was clearly visible. In the hues and curves that floated into view, I pictured a woman's long hair and her skin. Then with each blink, all grew misty and finally vanished in the light that spread again across the river's surface.

—What had I seen? Or wanted to see?

I looked at the heavens. I felt as though I saw, in the dry winter sky, the sun of my memory. The phantom of that gigantic sun, scattering light everywhere as it receded into the distance. Light scattered. More and more it scattered. Even though they say that even snow against the sky looks like dust. The beauty of this light, and the sadness.

. . . As I placed my hands on the ground, preparing to stand up, a collarless dog came tumbling down the opposite embankment. It ran along the river's edge, slid down the bank, plunged into the water as if it'd gone berserk, and writhed about, soaking its hair, which was a bit longer and more ungainly than the fur of a pure-blooded Shiba.

Light gradually smeared his body, which was soiled with leftover food.

"Ah, you, too . . ."

And another drip.

. . . This, too, was a memory. And it was a memory that amounted to nothing. Looking back, I tried to relive it, as I'd done with all my memories. I headed north, following the river, and walked through the streets. I was trying to believe somehow that this was a memory of today, a memory of something that had just occurred. I was trying to believe that among the multifarious memories that overflowed within me, *this* memory was closest in time to me as I am at this moment. Of course it was a fruitless effort. Now I understood. Even if I could believe this, what would be the point? Nothing, nothing at all. Whether it's a memory of today, of yesterday, of one hundred, one thousand years ago, of whatever ancient time, even the memory of that sun. They're all memories. Moreover, they're solitary memories drifting idly in time. Yes, this moment, too, in all likelihood.

Emerging on Kitayama Avenue, I turned west, then, just before Horikawa, south into a residential neighborhood, then east, then north, then west . . . repeating this meander again and again, I came out somewhere on Shichiku Street, and then, again, . . .

Little by little, my foolish ramble was drawing me closer to something. Not, of course, to a concrete place. On the contrary, it was precisely this wandering that revealed the existence of that *something*. People vanished from sight, leaving only a tiny sound in my ears. Cleansed of all color by the light, the world returned to its immaculate form, like that of a midsummer cicada freshly escaped from its shell.

Existence—yes, there was no longer any doubt—*my existence* was being flung into the past. My existence at this moment, as soon as I've spoken, is already a perilous memory. Before the thought has run its course, it becomes a memory and is receding from me. It's too late to name it, even to be conscious of it. My existence can't even be grasped. I'm merely something that's followed around by a swarm of dispersed memories. I'm something that scatters into the past, like unstrung beads. I'm something that—yes, that's it—vainly gathers the fragments of my own existence, which I've called memories, and tries to link them together. How many I must have overlooked! How many I must have picked up by mistake!

The clear water drips, again and again, and the intervals grow shorter. A drip, another drip.

Walking along a row of gingko trees that had dropped their leaves, I returned to Kitayama Bridge. From there I headed south on Nakaragi Street as if drawn by something. Then I encountered the final mystery. Under a single, slender tree, one of that silent row of winter weeping cherries along the Kamo River, lay a small, square heap of unseasonal cherry petals.

I was certain that I saw them. But they weren't petals. Drawing near, I could see the pale, peach-color handkerchief of an unknown woman. A gust of air, kicked up by my feet as I hurried forward, raised the hem slightly, offering a glimpse of the feathers of the dead pigeon I'd seen before. With a gentle flutter, the handkerchief covered them again. . . .

The sun is still scattering.

I stood there forever, gazing at the handkerchief as it wavered now and then. Thinking of the dead pigeon that still lay beneath it . . . that must still have been lying beneath it.

Even now the clear water drips unceasingly behind me.

HOSHI SHIN'ICHI

Hoshi Shin'ichi (1926–1997) was a prolific master of the short-short story form. Many of his works fall into the category that the Japanese call SF (science fiction), whereas others are better described as imaginative mysteries. Hoshi's stories often have a satirical twist combined with a touch of social commentary. This story, "He-y, Come on Ou-t!" (O-i, dete ko-i, 1978), is a prime example of both.

HE-Y, COME ON OU-T! (O-I, DETE KO-I)

Translated by Stanleigh Jones

The discovery of a deep hole has extraordinary impact on life in a small town.

The typhoon had passed and the sky was a gorgeous blue. Even a certain village not far from the city had suffered damage. A little distance from the village and near the mountains, a small shrine had been swept away by a landslide.

"I wonder how long that shrine's been here."

"Well, in any case, it must have been here since an awfully long time ago."

"We've got to rebuild it right away."

While the villagers exchanged views, several more of their number came over.

"It sure was wrecked."

"I think it used to be right here."

"No, it looks like it was a little more over there."

Just then one of them raised his voice. "Hey, what in the world is this hole?"

Where they had all gathered there was a hole about a meter in diameter. They peered in, but it was so dark nothing could be seen. However, it gave one the feeling that it was so deep it went clear through to the center of the earth.

There was even one person who said, "I wonder if it's a fox's hole."

"He-y, come on ou-t!" shouted a young man into the hole. There was no echo from the bottom. Next he picked up a pebble and was about to throw it in.

"You might bring down a curse on us. Lay off," warned an old man, but the younger one energetically threw the pebble in. As before, however, there was no answering response from the bottom. The villagers cut down some trees, tied them with rope, and made a fence which they put around the hole. Then they repaired to the village.

"What do you suppose we ought to do?"

"Shouldn't we build the shrine up just as it was over the hole?"

A day passed with no agreement. The news traveled fast, and a car from the newspaper company rushed over. In no time a scientist came out, and with an all-knowing expression on his face he went over to the hole. Next, a bunch of gawking curiosity seekers showed up; one could also pick out here and there men of shifty glances who appeared to be concessionaires. Concerned that someone might fall into the hole, a policeman from the local substation kept a careful watch.

One newspaper reporter tied a weight to the end of a long cord and lowered it into the hole. A long way down it went. The cord ran out, however, and he tried to pull it out, but it would not come back up. Two or three people helped out, but when they all pulled too hard, the cord parted at the edge of the hole. Another reporter, a camera in hand, who had been watching all of this, quietly untied a stout rope that had been wound around his waist.

The scientist contacted people at his laboratory and had them bring out a high-powered bull horn, with which he was going to check out the echo from the hole's bottom. He tried switching through various sounds, but there was no echo. The scientist was puzzled, but he could not very well give up with everyone watching him so intently. He put the bull horn right up to the hole, turned it to its highest volume, and let it sound continuously for a long time. It was a noise that would have carried several dozen kilometers above ground. But the hole just calmly swallowed up the sound.

In his own mind the scientist was at a loss, but with a look of apparent composure he cut off the sound and, in a manner suggesting that the whole thing had a perfectly plausible explanation, said simply, "Fill it in."

Safer to get rid of something one didn't understand.

The onlookers, disappointed that this was all that was going to happen, prepared to disperse. Just then one of the concessionaires, having broken through the throng and come forward, made a proposal.

"Let me have that hole. I'll fill it in for you."

"We'd be grateful to you for filling it in," replied the mayor of the village, "but we can't very well give you the hole. We have to build a shrine there."

"If it's a shrine you want, I'll build you a fine one later. Shall I make it with an attached meeting hall?"

Before the mayor could answer, the people of the village all shouted out.

"Really? Well, in that case, we ought to have it closer to the village."

"It's just an old hole. We'll give it to you!"

So it was settled. And the mayor, of course, had no objection.

The concessionaire was true to his promise. It was small, but close to the village he did build for them a shrine with an attached meeting hall.

About the time the autumn festival was held at the new shrine, the hole-filling company established by the concessionaire hung out its small shingle at a shack near the hole.

The concessionaire had his cohorts mount a loud campaign in the city. "We've got a fabulously deep hole! Scientists say it's at least five thousand meters deep! Perfect for the disposal of such things as waste from nuclear reactors."

Government authorities granted permission. Nuclear power plants fought for contracts. The people of the village were a bit worried about this, but they consented when it was explained that there would be absolutely no above-ground contamination for several thousand years and that they would share in the profits. Into the bargain, very shortly a magnificent road was built from the city to the village.

Trucks rolled in over the road, transporting lead boxes. Above the hole the lids were opened, and the wastes from nuclear reactors tumbled away into the hole.

From the Foreign Ministry and the Defense Agency boxes of unnecessary classified documents were brought for disposal. Officials who came to supervise the disposal held discussions on golf. The lesser functionaries, as they threw in the papers, chatted about pinball.

The hole showed no signs of filling up. It was awfully deep, thought some, or else it might be very spacious at the bottom. Little by little the hole-filling company expanded its business.

Bodies of animals used in contagious disease experiments at the universities were brought out, and to these were added the unclaimed corpses of vagrants. Better than dumping all of its garbage in the ocean, went the thinking in the city, and plans were made for a long pipe to carry it to the hole.

The hole gave peace of mind to the dwellers of the city. They concentrated solely on producing one thing after another. Everyone disliked thinking about the eventual consequences. People wanted only to work for production companies and sales corporations; they had no interest in becoming junk dealers. But, it was thought, these problems too would gradually be resolved by the hole.

Young girls whose betrothals had been arranged discarded old diaries in the hole. There were also those who were inaugurating new love affairs and threw into the hole old photographs of themselves taken with former sweethearts. The police felt comforted as they used the hole to get rid of accumulations of expertly done counterfeit bills. Criminals breathed easier after throwing material evidence into the hole.

Whatever one wished to discard, the hole accepted it all. The hole cleansed the city of its filth; the sea and sky seemed to have become a bit clearer than before.

Aiming at the heavens, new buildings went on being constructed one after the other.

One day, atop the high steel frame of a new building under construction, a workman was taking a break. Above his head he heard a voice shout:

"He-y, come on ou-t!"

But in the sky to which he lifted his gaze there was nothing at all. A clear blue sky merely spread over all. He thought it must be his imagination. Then, as he resumed his former position, from the direction where the voice had come, a small pebble skimmed by him and fell on past.

The man, however, was gazing in idle reverie at the city's skyline growing ever more beautiful, and he failed to notice.

IKEZAWA NATSUKI

Ikezawa Natsuki (b. 1945) was born in Hokkaido. He studied engineering, and, indeed, his interest in science no doubt helped him create the parallel worlds he contrasts with the banal and commonsense one in which, he believes, we live our lives. After living in Greece for a few years, Ikezawa settled in Okinawa, a personal trajectory representative of those undertaken by the kind of cosmopolitan writers prevalent in contemporary Japan. Ikezawa's strategy often is to indicate through the ingenious incidents that make up his narratives just what a small place human beings occupy in nature. His "Revenant" (Kaette kita otoko, 1990) is part adventure tale and part an examination of the limits of human understanding.

REVENANT (KAETTE KITA OTOKO)

Translated by Dennis Keene

1

Arabesque.

I make a grid of two-inch squares on a sheet of thick B4 Kent paper. Holding my breath, I draw the lines slowly with the sharp, fine point of a 2H pencil and a ruler. Then I draw two circles with a pair of compasses and a 2H lead, placing the sharp end of the compasses on an intersection. From each intersection I draw two concentric circles, then many more, circle after circle, with great precision, at the desk placed in the light from the window. The large circle and the small one next to it touch. The two arcs gradually approach each other and when I see they've touched they draw away from each other again. That's most important. If the grid of squares has been drawn correctly, then that depressing mess when the two arcs cross and intersect at two different points doesn't occur.

Next, using the same compasses, I divide each circumference into six equal parts and join these points to the center, making 60° angles where they meet. A number of lines and arcs intersect and link up in various places, creating a geometrical design. They all seem to be knitting together. I wonder which parts I should link up next. On my desk there are patterns I can copy. I could look at them and do it, but there's a problem: when I'm connecting two points precisely with my ruler I mustn't take my eyes off the ruler because it extends farther than the line I want to draw. When I start to draw the line, I have be quite sure about where it's going to stop or else I'll go too far and ruin everything. A 2H pencil leaves a groove in the paper, so if I make a mistake I can't erase it.

It usually takes two hours just to draw the pencil outline of a pattern. I start at nine in the morning and by eleven o'clock I've completed my design in pencil on the white paper. Then I have to choose the colors. In this kind of work, color is critical, so I don't immediately start coloring the design I've taken so much trouble over, not on the Kent paper at least. What I invariably do is make copies of the original design on rough pieces of paper and try the colors there first, so I can get a sense of how they harmonize. Taste is important when you're choosing colors; it's not like simply drawing lines. So I try several different combinations and pick the best one.

By now it's close to midday. I go off to have lunch, leaving the actual coloring till the afternoon. The quieter patients and the staff use the clinic's dining room. The few really serious cases seem to take their meals in their own rooms.

I wonder if it's true that their doors are locked all the time? The quieter patients seem like perfectly ordinary people to me. They look as if there was no reason to put them in here in the first place. I wonder if that's how I took to them. Still, I'm not going to talk.

The others talk about all sorts of things while they eat their lunch: TV, some newspaper article, their families, things like that. I just eat my food in silence. I have my memo pad ready in case anybody does talk to me, but practically no one tries to these days, though they did at first. Personally, I don't have anything to talk about. I don't watch TV, I don't read the paper, I don't see my family. I keep quiet and eat up all my lunch properly. I eat quickly. Then I hand in the dishes and go back to my room.

Until half past one I do nothing except sit in a chair and look out the window. There are no bars on my window. If, one fine day, I were to walk out the front door saying "Thanks for everything," no one would try to stop me. I mean, that's what I would say if I could speak. I look out the window at the trees, at a white building I can see across the fence and at the distant purple mountains beyond. The mountains I can see here are nothing at all like the ones around the ruins at Oneiros.

At half past one I start painting the pattern on the Kent paper with my watercolor set. I choose one of the color combinations I worked out in the morning and follow that, creating a complicated arabesque design. When I got back to Japan and was put in here, the first thing I remembered was a book I'd bought just before I went away. It was an album of abstract geometrical designs worked out over the centuries by Arab craftsmen as they decorated the floors and walls of their buildings. As Muslims, they were forbidden to portray the human face. The patterns that had originally been done in stucco, tile and alfresco had been reproduced in the album on paper. I had this book sent from my house, got the staff to give me some paper and a set of watercolors and made it my daily routine, every day from first thing in the morning until late in the afternoon, to draw one of those designs. I now have in my desk drawer 155 arabesques of various shapes and sizes.

At four o'clock the doctor and the matron come to see me. I've been classified as a voluntary patient, so I try to keep things straightforward during these visits. Having said that, I should point out that the doctor's questions hardly vary at all from one day to the next, and neither do my answers. Since I always give the same responses, I suppose I could just as well show him what I wrote down on my memo pad the day before, but somehow I can't do that. When he asks "How are we feeling today?" I write on the pad with my 3B pencil "Very well" or "All right" or "Quite happy" and show it to him. If he asks "How's your work getting on?" I reply "It's not really work. I'm just passing the time," or something like that. Then I show him two arabesques, the one I finished yesterday and the one I'm working on today. If the doctor's questions were a bit more searching I'd be happy to write much longer answers, but since everything he asks is strictly conventional I reply in the same way. Recently his visits have seemed pretty routine. Maybe he doesn't think I'm really ill. But the fact is that I really can't speak and I want to get better.

There's always a part of me that wants to get out of here, but in the outside world I know I wouldn't have the courage to talk. I'm incapable of direct verbal communication with people. I have to walk about with a memo pad and write down what I want to say. I always get the design on the Kent paper finished by five or six o'clock. I've only had to carry it over to the next day three times so far. Each time I complete one it looks so beautiful. I'd like to get down on paper the patterns of the desert in northern Afghanistan as I saw it from the helicopter. Instead of using watercolors, perhaps I could get lots of colored stones, tons of them, and make the design by placing the stones one by one on the ground. If one side measured half a mile, I would have an arabesque corresponding to hundreds of square miles of desert. It would take years to complete, working at it every day, spending a lifetime at it. That's the way I'd like to spend my life.

But I could draw thousands of arabesques on paper and still not achieve what I'm aiming at. It doesn't matter how complex and subtle my design is, or what color combinations I come up with, or how careful I am to keep the colors from overlapping, or how well I wash the brush after I'm done, using lots of water to be absolutely sure the colors don't get mixed, or how much effort I make to lay on the colors precisely within the lines drawn by a device with a 2H lead in it: none of it matters because when the design is complete I can never see the face of God in it. Sometimes when I've painted in only a couple of the colors, I seem to glimpse it, but as I fill in the other colors the face gets lost in the pattern as a whole. Maybe I'm going about it the wrong way.

2

I eat my three meals a day as I'm supposed to. And I take them seriously, because food is important. When someone eats, he puts a piece of the outside world inside him. The substance of his own body is gradually altered by this, giving him energy and, therefore, life. What used to be chicken or sardines or broccoli before being eaten is broken down inside his body into tiny particles, which then join up again in a different order, becoming part of himself. Things that are eaten lose their own shape and qualities and merge with the body of the person who eats them.

I didn't produce the kind of report expected of a member of an expedition. Tajil gave a detailed public explanation of the accident before I returned, so everybody knew about that, but in response to all the other questions, to which only I had the answers, I said nothing. I didn't say what the remains at Oneiros were like or why Pierre hadn't come back. I didn't suggest that a second expedition be sent to find Pierre or who should be sent. I didn't indicate whether I'd be prepared to go on such an expedition myself. I made no reply to any such questions. I didn't reply because I couldn't.

The committee that had dispatched the expedition, as well as the TV network I worked for that had sponsored it, put me through a tough interrogation. But whenever the questioning got too tough I tended to lose consciousness, falling into a deep sleep. It really was a deep sleep—in fact almost a coma, clinically speaking—and not some act I was putting on. The EEG printouts showed this quite dearly. I would stay asleep for twenty-four hours and there was nothing I could do about it. After this had happened several times, I lost the ability to speak. All I could manage in response to the questions was to write down my answers. I no longer felt like talking to other people or even asking them for anything. If my meals didn't appear, I was prepared to put up with hunger pangs for hours without complaining. When my interrogators noticed the condition I was in, they gave up their attempts to get at the truth and it was decided to put me in here for medical treatment.

As for what happened to us, our thoughts at the time, our relationship with the place whose existence was the root cause of everything that transpired, our final decision: I could talk to Pierre even now about all these things because there are still things to talk about. It would be part of a conversation that could, in a way, be considered unending. But I can't speak to ordinary people. There's nothing to be said to the average inhabitant of this world.

And so, because I can't speak about the one matter of really vital importance to me, I've abandoned speech altogether and opted for silence. Maybe the decision was made somewhere in the deepest levels of my mind not to talk about these things, followed by some breakdown in my mental power source, so that the decision can't be reversed. The result is that I am now undergoing mild treatment in this clinic every day, though in practice it's more just a sort of convalescence. My daily routine consists only of drawing these arabesque designs. The doctor smiles and says it's most important that the cure be gradual, but he doesn't look too confident about the outcome. However, since I like it here and the doctor seems to feel it's another interesting case, we get on pretty well. That's my situation at present.

The doctor thinks I've experienced something that could be described as shock, which accounts for my not being able to speak. His interpretation is that I must have done something I simply can't put into words, or seen the sort of thing the human eye should never look upon, and that's why I've withdrawn so completely into myself. Soon after I got here, I heard him saying as much to some journalists. The doctor has no idea what really happened. There's nothing surprising about that, either.

I wonder if he thinks I might actually have eaten Pierre. In one very special sense of the word, it could be said that Pierre was eaten, but not by me. I haven't absorbed his body into mine, broken it down and reassembled its various elements so that they combine with mine, making him part of myself. If I had done something like that, could it cause—as the doctor seems to think it could—my sudden inability to speak? But I'm not unable to speak; it's simply that I have decided not to speak because I know it's impossible to offer any acceptable explanation of what happened there.

Tiny unicellular algae absorb sunlight and carbon gas and turn them into energy. Then small animal plankton eat the algae, breaking down the carbohydrates, starches, cellulose, chlorophyll and other higher chemical compounds that have been stored inside them and re-creating them in new forms. Small fish eat the plankton, then large fish and cuttlefish eat the small fish, then even larger fish, like tuna, eat those fish and the cuttlefish and, finally, I eat them. But nobody eats me.

I am algae. Every living thing is algae. My thoughts are only a repetition of algae's thoughts and the thoughts of a small fish and cuttlefish and plankton and tuna at all those different stages, like some massive mental playback. I am algae, small fish, tuna: I contain all of them and have no existence independent of them. I am like a combination of tile, a multicolored mosaic, a pattern of bright stones in the desert, an enormous arabesque. The act of eating is like the act of assembling stones to create a design.

I did not eat Pierre. To say that Pierre was eaten is not wholly inappropriate way of putting it, but it wasn't I who ate him.

3

Seen in the context of the whole, and individual life, with all its thoughts, is perhaps a trivial and pointless thing, just one line in the great design, a single pixel among millions. But for the individual concerned, his own existence overrides and outweighs all other created things put together. Change the subject, change the point of view, and the whole structure of the world alters completely. That alteration is so vast it makes one flinch before it.

Has the world been made for me and am I at its center? Or am I something quite inconspicuous, occupying one tiny corner of it? I prefer not to answer. Either view seems feasible to me.

Pierre and I were talking on the riverbank near the site of Oneiros. We had just finished our evening meal of fish caught in the river, some of the gooseberry-like fruit that grew along the bank, and canned vegetables we'd brought with us in the dinghy.

That day Pierre had encountered his own past.

"I met myself as a child today," he said. "It was wonderful, going back that far into the past."

He spoke in a low voice, gazing into the flames of the fire as if searching for the memory of a pleasure that was already growing vague.

"Who did you say you met?"

"Myself when I was small. I was sitting in the open space there and a child walked toward me out of the music. He sat down beside me and we talked for a while. We said nothing of any importance, but we communicated our feelings perfectly. It was very nice. Then the child smiled and asked me if I knew who he was."

"And?"

"I just looked at his face, and he giggled and said, 'I'm you when you were small.'"

"So you met yourself?"

"He said 'We're all here. All those that aren't in your world are here. We don't exist separately from one another; we're all dissolved into nebulae throughout space. I've only appeared in the shape of your younger self to draw you out like this. I'm not confined in this human form forever.' That's what he said, anyway."

"You heard his voice from out of the music?"

"Not just a voice. The child was really there."

"Ah," I said, feeling suddenly sad. I didn't imagine I'd ever meet myself as a boy. I didn't think I was capable of such an experience. I wouldn't be allowed in that far. It was because it was Pierre that the child had appeared. Pierre and I were different. I'm not quite sure how to put this, but it's as if the shell of my ego is too thick.

"He said this was a relay station," Pierre blurted out after a while, his voice resonating like the voice of Oneiros itself.

4

It all started with a single aerial photograph. During the Afghan war, a Soviet reconnaissance plane was hit in the wing by a ground-to-air missile, but just managed to stay aloft. Virtually out of control, it flew over wild and unexplored mountainous terrain until the pilot was able to get it back over Soviet territory. There it crash-landed and the pilot was killed. The plane's camera happened to have been set on automatic, as became clear later, but the authorities who handed the set of photographs over to a team of special analysts probably assumed they had no significance. The film had been exposed over part of the western Karakoram range, a mountainous region where the borders of the Soviet Union, Afghanistan and Pakistan meet, totally uninhabited and uncrossed by any major air routes. An eccentric geographer had passed near the area a few decades earlier, but there was nothing in his report to interest non-specialists.

The photographs were enlarged and analyzed in detail. One of them showed what seemed to be the ruins of a stone fortress, or at least something man-made, though the theory that it might be a natural feature created by a series of freakish accidents couldn't be ruled out. It lay in a valley whose sinuous windings followed those of a narrow river, which was unusually full of water for this region, and looked like a cluster of buildings covering an area of several hundred square yards. The whole complex stood out sharply from its surroundings. Its shape was more or less irregular and the roads (if they were roads) that ran between the buildings formed a peculiarly intricate network. The general impression was of a small but extremely disorganized town, though even when the photos were blown up as far as they could go it was still impossible to tell whether the whole thing was a natural or an artificial phenomenon.

The site was named the Oneiros ruins after the nearby river. If it represented the authentic remains of some ancient civilization, it was thought that some written record of it might exist. But historians combed through documents relating to the countries in the surrounding region and found nothing conclusive. There was just one thing that was suggestive. An entry in the records of a once-flourishing kingdom to the south stated that during the reign of a certain king a detachment of soldiers was sent to investigate the truth of a tradition that an eternal city of stone could be found along the upper reaches of the Oneiros River. But the entry was so brief it didn't even state whether the soldiers returned or not, or describe what they reported if they did.

This aerial photograph of mysterious ruins attracted worldwide interest, so it wasn't surprising that the idea was soon put forward of sending a team to investigate. The plan was that a small search party should go out first to determine whether or not the remains were genuine, approximately when the complex had been built, and on what sort of scale. When all that had been established, a proper expedition would be mounted. For the quite accidental reason that the television company I worked for happened to be sponsoring the preliminary investigation, I got to be a part of it. I was the only Japanese member of the group; the rest consisted of two Russians, one of whom was the leader, an Indian archaeologist, an Iranian historian and a brilliant young cultural anthropologist from France, Pierre.

The team gathered in Kabul. That was the first time I met Pierre. I found him very reserved for a European, but he didn't make a bad impression on me. He was quiet, never venturing his opinion until asked, and capable of sudden physical activity when it was required. I can remember thinking that I would probably get on well with him.

5

As long as I stay in this clinic I will remain virtually cut off from other people. This means living in just the opposite way to the life embodied by Oneiros, that sustained condition of heightened existence to which ordinary "life" bears almost no resemblance. Is there no other choice, then, than that of either practicing the principle of Oneiros or rejecting it utterly? Is it impossible in ordinary society to make contact with people in a way that even remotely approaches the Oneiros idea?

It probably is impossible. So basic a denial of the concept of individuality leaves no room for compromise. When all becomes one, when the idea of a part or an individual no longer exists, the self must disperse into the whole. But in actual society, where distinctions are retained, to behave according to that principle would be like going naked among people wearing armor. One's skin would be ripped to shreds in an instant.

Because I dread that outcome, I stay in my room and refuse to speak. For all communication, I rely on the written word. If I were to utter even one phrase I would be allowed to leave, but I remain silent.

I once asked Pierre if he thought the site would affect all visitors in the same way. I wondered if it worked automatically, like some kind of machine, sending the same messages to anyone who happened to stand in that open space. Or did it change its methods according to whoever came? If it did react similarly no matter who was there, it could be seen as a kind of trap, the way the Venus's-flytrap catches flies: the insect pops inside and the door automatically shuts. But if the site were a trap, why did it respond in different ways to each of us, to Pierre and me?

It was possible, perhaps, that the people who went there had already been chosen. It's a fact that only two of the six who had originally planned to reach Oneiros actually arrived. Was that purely accidental or was it something the place itself had arranged? I didn't know the answer, nor did I believe I ever would know. I was never sure what role the great eagle played in it all, either. Why should the site, or whatever power lay behind it, linked up somehow across infinite space, go to all this trouble over two men? Why invite creatures who existed as individual organisms to participate in a different order of being? What could have prompted its interest in us? Was it carrying out some kind of selection process? One possible proof of that was that I was now here: I had come back and Pierre hadn't.

Again, can one even begin to talk of a "consciousness" in terms of something so extensive and ineffable? When one small separate organism affects another, it certainly comes into play, but when existence as a whole is involved . . . ? And were Pierre and I important enough to justify the attentions of such a "consciousness"? Did it see us as potential proselytes? Did it need such proselytes among our kind? If, as Pierre maintained, existence on this planet was controlled by some principle existing above it, did it need to go to so much trouble to let us know? Were we worth it? Was I? I didn't know. I still don't know.

6

The rubber dinghy made smooth progress. The river flowed gently and the water was deep enough for the outboard motor not to touch the sandy bottom. Occasionally one caught a glimpse of fish darting through the clear water. Since the engine was low-powered, we weren't moving fast, proceeding upstream at about the same rate as the current was flowing against us. As I sat in the stern steering the dinghy, the pleasant vibration of the engine traveled through the tiller to my hand and made me feel drowsy.

It was the day after the accident, the day Pierre and I set out alone for the place, so naturally images of the disaster still haunted us. Both of us also had serious reservations about the decision to continue with the expedition. We said little to each other, deep in our own thoughts about those who had died, and about Tajil, who had stayed behind by himself.

But that night, camped on the riverbank and stretched out beside the fire, we slept surprisingly soundly. Perhaps it was the good kind of fatigue brought on by our river journey that did it. Then the next morning, after we'd set off upstream again in the pleasantly chilly dawn air, we began exchanging occasional remarks. From the beginning, Pierre and I had got on well and, since we were both aware of that, we tended to work and spend time together. At least that's how it appeared to me then, although when I think about it now the first time we really talked seriously to each other was on that trip up the river.

The river ran through a gently undulating plateau. In the distance could be seen the blackish shapes of hills under a purple sky. Maybe they weren't hills but enormous sand dunes. There was nothing green in the landscape, only parched soil and the river slowly flowing through it. Just as slowly we drifted up the river, pushed on by our feeble yet remarkably noisy engine. Along a strip no more than a dozen yards wide on each side of the river, grass and trees drew sustenance from the water, but beyond that there were only the dry, rocky lines of hills stretching away interminably. Not one spot of greenery was visible in all that vast expanse. Much farther off we could see a range of white mountains. Our destination lay quite close to them.

"I wonder where this water comes from," Pierre said from the bow of the dinghy, looking back at me. He almost had to shout to make himself heard above the noise of the outboard motor.

"There must be some large source of water way upstream."

"What kind of source?"

"Melting snow. Something underground. Maybe a glacier."

"It must be huge to supply this amount of water."

"A lake, maybe. That's why the supply's so steady."

"I wonder how he's getting on."

"Tajil? Just sitting there waiting."

"When will help arrive?"

"Things will start moving when they realize the helicopter is overdue. It'll all depend on how soon they can get hold of another one."

"Should we have waited?"

"No. I wanted to get going. We'll never have another chance like this. We won't be able to do a proper survey, of course, but this was only a preliminary expedition anyway. All we have to do is work out if it's the remains of some human construction or a natural rock formation. Then we go back."

"That eagle's circling overhead again," Pierre interrupted.

"Are you sure it's the same eagle?"

"I'm beginning to think it was maybe that bird that caused the accident."

"The eagle?"

"I didn't want to make a big thing of it at the time, but I thought I saw something like an eagle diving down toward the helicopter, and then it happened."

Now that I thought about it, I could also remember thinking I'd seen something black, high above us, heading straight for the helicopter.

"But how's an eagle going to make a helicopter crash?"

"Exactly. I can't imagine any bird wanting to tangle with something like that."

"Do you think he's following us?"

"A lookout perhaps?"

But we'd grown tired of looking straight up and soon forgot about it.

We stayed in midstream all day, pulling in to the bank as evening fell. After mooring the boat firmly to a tree, we made camp, just as we'd done the day before, gathering dead branches for a fire, brewing up coffee and making supper of canned food and boiled potatoes.

The sense that we'd completed another day of our journey gave some satisfaction. The memory of the accident was bad, but at least we hadn't been sitting about feeling sorry for ourselves. Here we were actually doing something. That helped, as did the knowledge that we'd covered more than sixty miles in two days.

"I wonder what the place will look like," I said, not addressing the remark to Pierre in particular so much as thinking aloud.

"A kind of fortress. Or maybe a town. Buildings made of large stones, clustered around narrow streets," Pierre replied automatically, as if he were describing not a place he knew but one he's read about. "Those streets, which could just be gaps between the rock walls, are very narrow and winding, and there are places where you can't get through. The stones are extremely irregular, so they may not be buildings after all. There are no doors, apparently. There don't seem to be interior spaces. Still, they're buildings for those who know how to use them. And there are a lot of them. What else? There are openings that look like windows, but they're really just holes between the stones, a bit like small wind tunnels."

"How do you know so much about it?"

"I read the relevant literature."

"Come on—there is no relevant literature, certainly nothing that gives that sort of detail. I've read all there is."

"Perhaps there isn't. Still, I don't think I'm confusing the Oneiros site with somewhere else. I'm certain it's just the way I described it."

"Well, we'll know when we get there."

I didn't say any more. We both had an odd feeling about it, but we also seemed to feel it was best to keep such intimations to ourselves. The more we talked, the more distant we'd grown. So we crawled into our sleeping bags and fell asleep by the fire.

On the afternoon of the next day we arrived at the ruins of Oneiros, al-
though we couldn't see them directly from the river. The first thing we came
across was the entrance to the V-shaped gorge running due south from a spot
near the river to the ruins themselves. No water flowed between the steep, un-
broken walls of this narrow defile. We knew the place because its location,
shape and direction matched up exactly with the aerial photograph, so we
stopped there and continued into the gorge on foot after first dragging the din-
ghy up onto the bank. We carried light day packs, since even though the site
appeared to be only a mile or so from the river we had no idea how long it
would take to get there. The only way to find out if it was an easy walk or not
was to walk it.

I was excited that we were finally going to see the ruins, but Pierre seemed
almost downcast. While we were pulling the dinghy up onto the bank and get-
ting ready to set off for the site, I'd had to encourage him before he would actu-
ally do anything. He didn't seem reluctant so much as apprehensive. But I didn't
let his obvious lack of enthusiasm bother me, hurrying on ahead in my eager-
ness to see the ruins with my own eyes.

It took us over an hour to walk that mile or so. The gorge was an ancient riv-
erbed. In the distant past, water must have flowed through it, but it had dried
up and grown wild over the centuries; parts of the cliffs had collapsed and the
way was strewn with jagged rocks and boulders that made the going difficult.
A north wind blew hard at our backs. Since the only source of drinking water
was the river, the camp would have to be set up there and this two-way trek
would have to be made every day until we'd completed our reconnaissance.

The gorge had been leading due south, but now it turned slightly to the
right. From that bend I could see the ruins stretched out before me. The nar-
row valley widened a little at that point, with the cliffs now towering above it
quite perpendicularly and, depending on the angle from which you looked at
them, even appearing to overhang it. And there at the far end of the valley, ex-
tending from one side to the other and blocking the exit, were rows and rows of
stone buildings. It was immediately clear how difficult it would be to pick them
out from overhead. That one photograph had been a truly remarkable piece of
luck, and it was obvious why repeated analysis of satellite pictures had always
failed to confirm what the photo had revealed. There was only a narrow strip of
sky overhead and the site could be seen only from a certain angle. Our search
for the easiest path through the gorge had brought us to a point halfway up the
side of a cliff, so when we first saw the site we were looking slightly down at it.

At that distance, it was still impossible to be sure whether it was a man-made
or a natural phenomenon. My immediate reaction was to sit down where I was,
flooded with a sense of wonder as I absorbed the entire view; but the expression
on Pierre's face was one not of wonder but of fear.

"What's wrong? Does the place give you the creeps?"

"No. I was just thinking that we'd finally made it, that's all."

"But this is what we came for."

"Yes. But I hadn't expected it would have such power."

"What power?"

"I'm not sure. It's just that I feel the place has been controlling us all along, even when we were still far away. It's as if I was drawn here all the way from France, I don't know why. Standing here I can feel it all the more—like a strong wind blowing from that direction."

"The power of darkness?"

"No, not that, just something powerful."

"Come to think of it, you *must* have known about the place already. From here it looks exactly the way you said it would."

"That's another thing I don't understand—where I could have got that knowledge."

"Anyway, let's go and look."

"Yes. We've come all this way, after all. I could hardly turn my back on it and just go home."

It was still hard to tell whether what we were looking at were buildings or rock formations, whether the gaps between them were really pathways or not. Getting closer made it no easier to decide. Since our main task that day was to get a general picture of the whole place, and because it didn't seem especially dangerous, we agreed that if for some reason we lost contact with each other we would meet up in an hour's time at the entrance. We checked our watches and compasses and, with the wind still blowing at our backs, went down into the site.

The passage we used was narrow and winding, sometimes coming to a dead end, sometimes branching off in two or three directions. We went on cautiously, very slowly, watching each step we took and keeping an eye out for landmarks, hardly speaking to each other. The passage floor was pocked with indentations and scarred with peculiar ridges and hollows, making one wonder if it could possibly have been constructed for human beings to walk along. There were step-like formations, but all irregular in height, some as much as three feet high.

Water had obviously eaten away soft areas of the rock, suggesting that the whole site could have been created that way over the centuries. But why had the water stopped flowing through the valley? Again, if water was the active agent, why weren't more of the surfaces rubbed smooth? Only a series of highly unusual natural events could have produced such formations. Then there were these rows of almost square rocks, looking very much as if they'd been lined up next to each other: surely they implied the work of human hands. Not to mention the fact that each rock was roughly the same height, about fifteen feet.

Walking along those passages I had no sense of fear. Pierre also seemed quite composed by now. I wasn't expecting some monster to be lying in wait around the next corner, or a deep pit to open up suddenly before me, swallowing me, or the walls to slowly close in, crushing me. Yet I still had the feeling I'd had from the beginning that there were presences about us, or rather, that the whole place was suffused with the aura of some larger presence. It wasn't that feeling you get when you sense that one or two other people might be near, but an intimation of something drifting, rarefied, diffuse, something at once weightless and transparent. It's impossible to express this in words because whatever it was surrounding me—and Pierre as well, who was walking a few yards behind me—was something beyond description.

And then, when we entered an open space that looked rather like a small town square, the music started.

7

I'd thought the easiest way to give some idea of the mysteriousness of that place would be by starting with the music, but it turns out that that's the hardest thing of all to describe or explain. I'm beginning to think it's impossible to convey a sense of it to someone who hasn't actually heard it.

When we first noticed it, it seemed to have just started. It could, of course, have been going on for some time, our ears having only slowly become attuned. Perhaps that sense we'd already felt of some ineffable presence had been merely this music, faintly heard. Whatever the truth of the matter, both Pierre and I became aware of it at the same moment. He looked at me, raising a finger to signal me to listen, and I immediately understood the meaning of the gesture.

At first I heard only the sound of the wind, but as I listened I realized that countless lesser noises were hidden within that faint, overriding sound. I sat down on one of the small rectangular stones scattered here and there around the open space and Pierre sat on one on the opposite side. The music was like the sound of the wind passing between the stones but it was too complex and changeable to be merely wind; there were rich harmonies within it, numerous clear sounds combining to suggest a depth more profound than that of any natural harmony.

I was absorbed into the music and held entranced by it, as if I were drinking from some deep well of water so crystal-clear I could see right to the bottom, tasting its depths in one pure drop after another. Gradually I became aware that the music was actually made up of voices and that they were ones I'd heard before, belonging to people I knew. But they weren't just voices from my own vividly remembered past, of people I'd actually met; I could hear ones familiar from records and movies, even people I knew only by name and whose voices I had imagined, people from as far back as a thousand years ago. Not that I could distinguish any of these voices from the others; I simply felt a certainty welling up from deep inside me that these were the voices I was listening to.

Then again, perhaps it wasn't just voices I could hear but musical instruments, too. The more I heard, the more convinced I was of this; they seemed so perfect for that place—for me as well. Yet even the idea of instruments is wrong. These sounds weren't produced mechanically; they were simply the outcome of all the varied sounds existing in the natural world. They weren't made by musicians, yet each one had meaning and they formed a harmony among themselves. All things in existence sang out, and men were moved to sing together with them, all resounding at the very heart and center of the universe, all combining with the perfect harmony that prevailed there. And what reached my ears was the pure essence of that music. I heard it then. I still hear it now.

I was listening to sound itself. No one was required to tune it or to play it. It was the sound of whatever lies at the base of everything that exists, including our own existence, and since it was that most basic of all things, inevitably it could know no discord. All this I realized as I sat there without moving, listening to sounds at once far and clear, faint yet plain: that perfect music.

How long it continued I hardly know. As my body measures time, it seemed to go on for a long while, but as the world works, it was an instant. Since eternity is our standard here, and in eternity even the longest periods are moments, I think it must only have been a moment. In terms of my consciousness of time I was no longer the master of my body or my mind. I was not the one judging such things.

I looked up and noticed that the narrow band of sky above us had darkened, and then glanced at Pierre. He'd noticed the same thing and was just standing up.

We said nothing as we picked our way awkwardly along the stony track back to the riverbank. It didn't occur to either of us to try to discuss what we'd heard. There was no doubt that we had both heard the same thing, that we'd been linked by similar cords to the same source of sound. And no doubt he, like me, was feeling overwhelmed by the mystery of this place we'd found.

So we did everything in silence, there on the bank of the river: unpacked our things, lit a fire, brewed coffee and ate our meal of canned food, potatoes and bread. And the reason we didn't break the silence between us was that it seemed to us we could still hear the music in our heads. We wanted to go on listening and not confuse the music with the sound of our own voices.

In that way our first day at the Oneiros site ended. We laid out our sleeping bags on the bank and slept. With nightfall the wind dropped and the stars shone clear in the sky, a great army of stars brandishing the spears of light, shouting with the voices of light, scattering their light indifferently in all directions.

8

We could see the great eagle almost the whole time now. Pierre still maintained that the bird had something to do with the helicopter accident. I didn't know what to believe, but he seemed convinced. People believe what they see; they also think they've seen the things they believe, which is pretty much the same thing. Perhaps Pierre saw deeper into the heart of things than I did. The idea that the site somehow chose the people who were to visit it doesn't seem so unlikely to me now.

For whatever reason, the great eagle circled continuously overhead. He seemed to be watching us, maybe even watching over us. One felt safe with him always there, confident that no mishap, no sudden stumble on the stone steps, would occur while he was there. Yet it also crossed my mind that if we tried to leave he might do something to stop us. But no, I told myself, he'd probably let us go, deciding that he'd misjudged us and that he would be more careful next time.

Just once the eagle did disappear, but not the way a normal bird would. When a bird vanished from sight, one can usually assume that it has flown off somewhere, to the mountains or over the horizon or into some distant cloud. But this one disappeared while I was lying on my back on the riverbank watching him. He simply went higher and higher into the blue sky, flying up and up until he was absorbed into the firmament. He never seemed to move horizontally; like the sun and the moon, he was already so high up he appeared to be almost directly above our heads. And when he vanished he just flew higher, because the only motion he knew was vertical.

9

How did it happen that Pierre and I were the only ones to see the place? The river indicated clearly enough where it was and the photographs the Russian reconnaissance plane had taken provided map coordinates, so its whereabouts were known almost from the start.

The problem for those before us had been the river. The Oneiros River rises in the Pamir mountains and, after gently traversing a dry plateau that is mostly desert, descends to the plain below as a fierce torrent. Not only is the current particularly strong, but the riverbed is a clutter of rocks, making navigation impossible. This fact alone would explain why the site had remained unvisited, except by that one legendary expedition.

In the case of our own expedition, the whole party was to have been ferried by helicopter from Kabul to a point upstream of the rapids, the plan being to continue by boat across the plateau. The site itself was on the far side of the plateau, where the foothills of the Pamirs start. Since it was impossible to transport the whole party plus all the equipment at one go, it was decided to do it in two shifts. On the first trip the helicopter took three of us: myself, Pierre and the Iranian archaeologist, Tajil, together with all the supplies, such as the rubber dinghy and the various stores and provisions. The remaining three members would come on the second trip with the equipment needed for the survey.

We left Kabul airport at seven in the morning. The 250-mile flight took about two hours, the last half of which was spent following the course of the river. Seen from above, the river flowed along a deep, narrow, meandering valley that had carved its way through high mountains. The mountains themselves looked as if they had been hacked out randomly with a gigantic ax. For this reason it was only possible to glimpse the river occasionally, although it was easy to imagine the ruggedness of the terrain it ran through. The mountains were dark gray, rough and gritty-looking. One got the impression that their shape was sustained by the action of equal and opposite forces, one forcing them up and the other pressing them down. As it flew between the twin expanses of the mountains below and the purple sky above, our helicopter must have looked no bigger than a mosquito.

For the last sixty miles, though, we dropped down into the deep gorge cut by the river, flying perilously between cliffs on both sides. The ground was now more than six thousand feet above sea level and our heavily loaded helicopter couldn't even maintain the altitude of the ridge; the pilot had no choice but to fly down into the gully. So we groaned our way along between those towering walls; and if you could forget for a moment that your own life was being put directly at risk, the view was marvelous. Holding my breath, I looked out through the helicopter's plastic dome at the scarred and broken rock faces, at the plants that had managed to find a foothold on them, at the glittering water far below and at the spot where, as it reflected a white sun, the river shone with a powerful, concentrated dazzle.

Pierre had his face pressed against the opposite window as he too gazed down, absorbed in the landscape. He was as fascinated as I was by this uninhabited world, these cliffs never seen perhaps by human eyes before. The expression on his face was enough to tell me that his mind was working in the same way as mine. We both wanted to dissolve somehow into that barren world. We didn't care about leaving proof of our existence on this earth; we wanted to become part of it, dust floating in its air. We wanted our souls to be scattered among its millions of birds, to participate in their existence. These were our feelings as we gazed at the cliffs, and when occasionally we caught a glimpse of a nest, we couldn't help envying the bird its way of life.

But Tajil wasn't that kind of person. I knew this because I'd worked with him while we were preparing for the expedition back in Kabul; it had been clear at once that his was a healthy, practical approach to life. He had traveled this far from civilization because that was the job he'd been given. He had no fear of this empty world and no desire at all to lose himself in it. While Pierre and I went on staring at it, Tajil slept soundly on his hard seat, oblivious even to the racket of the engine and the occasional buffeting by pockets of air.

When we had traveled far up the valley, the pilot gestured downward. Looking, I saw that the gully had opened out; the surrounding mountains seemed less rugged and there was a narrow, flat space on both sides of the river. The water seemed to be flowing more calmly and the white-capped ripples had disappeared from its surface. The pilot asked Tajil, as the man in charge, if it would be all right to land somewhere around there. After a brief exchange with us, Tajil gave him the OK sign.

The helicopter dropped down until it was almost skimming the water, moving slowly forward in search of a flat piece of ground. Within three minutes the pilot had found a suitable-looking place and lowered the skids gently some twenty yards from the river, raising a cloud of dust. We had landed. I got out first and stood on the firm ground while Tajil and Pierre prepared to hand things out to me. Since goods as well as people had to be unloaded, the pilot switched off the engine and got out as well. Several cardboard boxes, the dinghy and the crated outboard motor were handed down to us. The whole operation took about fifteen minutes. Then the helicopter took off again, leaving the three of us behind.

At the spot we'd chosen the riverbed was about a hundred yards wide and, although the cliffs on both sides were still precipitous, the river itself meandered peacefully along the middle of the bed, suggesting that somewhere not too far upstream the ground did indeed become a wide plateau. When we looked back at the way we'd come, the cliffs seemed to be virtually leaning toward each other and we realized just how little space the pilot had had to maneuver in.

I sat down on a large stone.

"How long will we have to wait?" Pierre asked of no one in particular.

"Four or five hours," Tajil said. "All we'll be able to do today, anyway, is just get everything and everybody here and the camp set up. We could sort out some of the supplies, I suppose." And he started lining up the boxes as he spoke.

"What kind of bird is that?" I asked, pointing at a small black shadow in the sky.

"It's big. Probably an eagle," said Pierre. Tajil didn't look up, but just went on with what he was doing.

"I didn't expect to see an eagle in a place like this."

"The whole region belongs to him. All of this is his."

"What does he live on, I wonder?"

"There must be small animals here—rabbits, lizards. And then of course there are other birds."

We heard the noise of the helicopter again shortly after three o'clock. First we heard the engine, then we caught a glimpse of something moving in the shadow of the cliffs, lost it in deeper shadow, then saw it again as the roar of the engine drew rapidly closer and at last, like a bee loaded with honey, the helicopter flew suddenly into the light. The yellow jacket I'd taken off was nearby and I stood up and signaled with it.

At that precise moment, a dark shadow seemed to fall from the upper air toward the helicopter. It could have been just my imagination, I suppose, yet when I strained my eyes to try to make out what it was, the helicopter suddenly wobbled, lurched sideways, went into a spin and crashed into the cliff. For a second it was impossible to believe it had really happened. The helicopter was still at an altitude of three to four hundred feet when it hit the cliff, exploding in a ball of orange flame where it struck, then disintegrating as it started falling. The roar of the explosion burst inside our stomachs as we stood there watching in horror. The main body of the helicopter flared up again when it hit the ground, and one or two small fragments drifted down on it.

We raced toward the wreckage, stumbling over stones and clambering over rocks, but the helicopter had crashed on the far bank and the river was running too high for us to cross. Pierre waded impetuously into it, but it wasn't shallow enough for fording so Tajil and I pulled him back. All the three of us could do was stand at the water's edge and watch the fire blazing only a few dozen yards away. We went on watching to see if anyone emerged from the wreck, but no one did. A strong stench of fuel, charred metal and other smells of burning drifted over to us across the water. We felt the heat on our faces as the helicopter continued to burn for another ten or fifteen minutes, as if it were determined to show that there had been an accident. Then only the blackened wreck remained, licked by an occasional tongue of flame.

After a while Tajil recovered enough presence of mind to start inflating the dinghy. We crossed the river to the scene of the disaster, not because we thought there was anything we could do, but merely as a gesture. Everything had been incinerated and the smell was appalling. Scattered all around were pieces of twisted metal and a number of scorched and smoldering objects, from which blue smoke still rose. We thought the four corpses would be in the biggest piece of wreckage, right in the middle, but it was still too hot to get close. There was absolutely nothing we could do.

Although this was an exploratory trip we were on, it certainly wasn't the kind that could be described as hazardous. We weren't being asked to make a winter crossing of Antarctica on foot. It wasn't even a full-scale scientific expedition, as our task was only to ascertain the existence of a specific site and find out more or less what it was. So we might have expected one of us to break a leg or something, but nobody could possibly have foreseen that we would lose half our party in a single instant and that the three survivors would be left stranded, with no means of getting back.

That night we lit our fire on the other side of the river, as far away from the scene of the disaster as possible, and prepared a simple meal even though no one felt hungry. Then we sat and stared silently into the flames. Tajil said he intended to sit tight until rescuers arrived and, up until that moment, I'd been thinking along the same lines. When the helicopter didn't return to its base that night, another one would be sent to look for us, within a few days at most. Even if, for some reason, that didn't happen, at least the committee in Paris that had organized the expedition and my television company in Tokyo could be counted on to get some sort of research operation under way. We had food, and our surroundings didn't look particularly dangerous, so the best option would be just to wait.

But even while all this was being spelled out, it occurred to me that we might just as well push on with our investigation of the Oneiros site. Obviously, after an accident in which half our party had been killed, nobody would blame us if we called the whole thing off, but we had already come this far and it was only a fairly short journey to our objective. At least we could find out if the place was an authentic ruin or just an accident of nature.

When I thought about it later, I could come up with no reason why I should have tried so hard to get the others to share this point of view. It wasn't any motive of company loyalty that moved me, no desire to fulfill my mission, no urge to achieve something before I returned home. The only thing that concerned me was to shorten the distance between where I was now and where the site lay, as quickly and surely as possible. Maybe it was just that I disliked the idea of waiting here within sight of the burned wreckage of the helicopter. Most things become harder to understand the farther you get from them. All important decisions are made on the spur of the moment, but we forget the true motives of the mind and heart that lie behind them.

Tajil opposed my plan. No matter what I said, he continued to insist that we stay and wait to be rescued. What he really wanted, he said, was to get out of here, to take the dinghy and go back downstream, but since that was impossible we would just have to wait. In his view, going on into the interior with just the three of us and so few provisions was completely insane.

Pierre couldn't make up his mind. Even I had no intention of going on by myself to look for the site, and if Pierre had said he was staying behind I would have had no choice but to follow suit. He said that his inclination was to press on, but added in a low voice that there was one aspect of the present situation that made him hesitate, though he declined to say what it was. We decided to give him until morning to work out what he wanted to do, and the three of us climbed into our sleeping bags. It was bitterly cold that night, but I don't think that's why I found it so hard to sleep. What kept me awake was the sheer inexplicability of the accident, combined with anxiety over what we were going to do next. I could hear gentle snores coming from Tajil's sleeping bag while I lay there thinking I would never get to sleep. But, as it happened, I had reached the limits of fatigue. By the time I became aware of my surroundings again it was already morning and the sun was lighting up the gorge.

As I was getting up, Pierre spoke to me from his sleeping bag.

"I'll go with you," he said.

10

From the day we first heard the music, we devoted all our daylight hours simply to wandering about the site. How many days that lasted I'm not really sure. We camped on the riverbank, waking each morning eager to resume, eating a quick breakfast or even making do with a little water before heading back up the gully. Once there, we would separate to walk around or just sit on a stone listening for the voices, that music, those wordless messages. Sometimes we would make desperate efforts to transmit our own thoughts to the presence that hovered there. At least, that's what I remember trying to do, but whether I spoke or merely concentrated on stimulating some mental energy, whether I gestured, stamped or even danced in that square of stones, I can't recall. Those kinds of details are so utterly absent from my memory it's as though someone had deliberately erased them.

Sometimes the two of us would sit together for a long time in the square. There would be a complete rapport between us then. To an observer, we would just have looked like two young men sitting in silence, but those were the times when the understanding between us was deepest. The important thing was that while we were together, we had a multiple insight into the connections between humanity and whatever it was that the site stood for. We represented two separate vantage points, for our characters were completely different; yet that very difference created a dual scan, a way of really measuring the distance between our world and that other one and, eventually perhaps, of judging whether the gulf could be crossed. Things wouldn't have turned out as they did, I think, if only one of us had gone to the site.

But what actually happened there? What messages did the site send us? I can't say. I can't express it in ordinary language, the language of this world. All I can do is hesitate, and say I no longer understand. We heard music there. The music was more than just voices and sounds reaching us from outside; it came from inside us as well. It was like your own voice rising within you—not the voice of your ego, nothing as trivial as that, but the real self, that microcosm which includes all living things. If I were forced to put it into words, I would say it was like listening to the sound of the blood inside your ears, to the billions of pulses per second flying between the cells of your brain, to the tiny creaking sounds the bones and joints of the body make when they are so perfectly lubricated that they work almost noiselessly, to the rustling of the cells of the whole body. It was as if this whole process had become transparent. In the stirring of the genes, the passage of time itself became visible—that vast expanse traversed by all individual beings since life began. And then you saw all that preceded life, saw across that immense tract of time to the beginning of everything: the dance of atoms as they changed, the brightening of the universe, the explosions of great stars and the flowing forth of the planet, and finally the cooling of the surface of the earth and the birth of life forms in its oceans. To listen to that music was to hear these processes, to absorb them like things physically experienced.

Amid all this, the self did not exist. I was not myself and Pierre was not Pierre. We were diffused throughout a space that wasn't only vast but still expanding, and we filled the whole of it. Our bodies felt as though they stretched to the very edge of the world. We weren't simply the sum total of all living things—far more than that: we were existence itself. We had escaped from the well of the ego at last, scattered in all directions, filling the universe.

When the wind blew, I could hear that sound. The motion of each particle of air carrying the sound I experienced as the rustling of my own cells. Through that movement, the site, like a relay station, transmitted to me the joy of my own existence. There was no need to peer around outside myself, for I was both looking and being looked at. I was a self observing myself, the viewer and the viewed, the clouds and the blue sky. I was the great eagle that sliced through the air and the man sitting on the stone whom the eagle looked down on. I was the man who danced and the boy who lay on the ground sleeping with outstretched arms, and whose arms, as he slept, became the wings of the soaring eagle.

I had no need to be myself. I didn't have to act always as a specific person among strangers whom one treated with the utmost wariness. I was no longer required to be a man of his time, a man with adequate physical and mental skills, who spoke Japanese and passable English and had a decent grasp of mathematics, who had opinions on current affairs, could support himself and had some capacity for judgment, a man with a socially acceptable level of intelligence: in short, an individual personality acknowledged by other people. I didn't have to be that young Japanese man with the above-average ability to get his own way, since the effort to perform that particular role and to sustain it as long as other people were around had become entirely irrelevant. This didn't mean I would be enjoying some idle Sunday of the spirit where one lolled about at home in scruffy pajamas, having given up the struggle for a while. It meant that, since I now coexisted with everything, I was freed from any obligation to make and remake myself. My thoughts could be transmitted to others unhampered by that perpetual concern with what was being thought of me. While I wasn't even conscious that it was happening, my thoughts would be spreading in waves throughout the world and linking up with other waves from countless other epicenters, waves that met to form a single grand design, the splendid arabesque of the universe.

Alongside me, Pierre was going through an almost identical experience, I knew that. We were two overlapping, nearly concentric circles, our centers only a fraction apart, twin sources of consciousness transmitting in the same bipolar moment. His face was mine and he shared my body, unaltered. His entire past was my past, along with the past, present and future of all human beings, from the mothers of the Neanderthals to the newest-born baby. I could sense them all in me; and yet I was still myself. I never stopped being aware that I was myself. That was the difference between Pierre and me.

How many days did we spend like that? I don't know. All I know is that, as the light faded and the narrow strip of sky above the gully darkened, we stumbled away from the place like a pair of music students at the end of a grueling day at the piano. Usually we left at the same time; sometimes one of us had to wait for the other, but never for long. Clearly there was some accord between us, but whether it was something we communicated directly to each other or something the site transmitted to both of us equally through the great eagle, neither of us knew. Anyway, we would arrive at the entrance to the site almost simultaneously, as if at some agreed time, and make our way back down the gully together.

We gradually stopped eating normal amounts of food. Eating had lost its appeal. From the time we got back to camp until we went to sleep we were busy enough just going over the things we'd experienced during the day. But we were like children who had been set too much homework, or given too big a piece of cake to eat, because as we tried to relive those emotions we would find ourselves unable to make sense of anything, and before we knew it we'd be asleep. To say that one can be aware of being in a state of unawareness is absurd, I know, but in this case it is a fair description of how we felt.

Just once I woke up unusually early. Not wanting to disturb Pierre, I went to the river and started fishing. There was some basic fishing gear among our stores, and on our trip up the river I'd thought I'd like to try it out one day. Now I remembered it. Since the kit wasn't for any particular kind of fish, it had as many as thirty different flies and hooks, but, presumably because the river had never been fished and the fish didn't know what was going on, I caught one with my first fly. In fact I had a bite with almost every cast and had caught five trout-like fish before I knew it.

Back at the camp, Pierre had just got up. I showed him my catch and we decided to have it for breakfast. The fish tasted delicious, and I'd actually enjoyed catching them, but we both had the peculiar feeling that we were somehow eating ourselves. I'd experienced something like it on the riverbank: a feeling that I had become the river and was flowing with it, that two separate things were merging. It was as if the walls of our selves had fallen down and nothing separated us from our surroundings. The fish had been part of us, they had left us, and now they had returned. If that was really how things were, the act of eating—however good the taste—seemed a lot less compelling. The result, in any case, was that we ate no more fish.

11

"I was in love once," said Pierre, about three days after we'd arrived at the stronghold, if that's what it was. We were sitting by the fire at our camp near the river, trying to make sense of the confused impressions of the day, half lost in reverie.

"We were in the same year at university. She was a wonderful girl, and I went out of my way to get to know her. We sat next to each other at lectures and talked for hours in cafes. I sketched her face as she sat on a bench in the park and took her home by the most roundabout route. Every day I would plan how we could spend as much time together as possible. The better I got to know her the more I loved her. We'd both been born on a Saturday—little things like that were nice. I suppose it's the same with everybody. None of the other girls in the class meant anything to me—they were grass in the meadow; I barely saw them as individuals. Just this one flower, that's all I saw. She was the one brilliant spot of color in a black and white photograph.

"Then one day, by which time we'd become very close, she told me she had a boyfriend. But she didn't, for that reason, say she couldn't see me any more. She didn't ask me to forget her. She liked me and didn't think it would be wrong to go on just as we were, enjoying each other's company. She said she'd be happy if things could continue. And she said this in all innocence. She wasn't playing any tricks, or being greedy; she was simply following her heart. As for me, I had no intention of letting this stop me from seeing her. I didn't ask her to choose between the two of us, either.

"So we went on as before, going to movies and plays together, eating in this or that little place we'd found, sometimes taking long walks in the country. She hardly ever mentioned the boyfriend, and she never once told me, now that I knew about him, how much she liked him, what sort of relationship they had, how often she met him or what he did. I suppose if I'd insisted she would have told me, but I wasn't prepared to take the risk. I imagined he was probably some graduate student, but I didn't really care who or what he was. I loved her so much that I was afraid if I asked too much I might lose her. Also I was a coward. I had this fear that if I knew too much about him he would become real to me, sharp and clear enough to cause me pain.

"This may sound unbelievable in the case of a young man and woman both around twenty, but right from the start I hardly laid a finger on her. In fact I never really thought that our relationship would go in that direction. The idea of sleeping together seemed so ordinary it was almost distasteful, like setting up some fake household. I felt that way from previous experience. I also thought that if all I wanted was a girl to sleep with, I could always find one if I tried. But she was special, absolutely special. When I think about it now, I can see an element of sour grapes in all that, but at the time I honestly believed she was different from other girls, perhaps because that notion was all I had to cling to. I despised the body, the flesh. I convinced myself that her very existence was so special she was above such things. I also decided not to think about the question of whether she was sleeping with her boyfriend or not.

"The truth is, of course, that going to bed with her was a gamble, for stakes I thought I couldn't afford. But any normal man would have made that bet, wouldn't he?"

As he said this he looked at me, but I didn't reply, simply urging him to go on with his story.

"So it was enough to hold her hand and kiss her briefly. It was an expression of intimacy and nothing more. And it was wonderful, that intimacy, it really was—I'm not exaggerating. I held her hand and thought that if I could feel as close to her as this, what need was there to sleep with her?

"But it was no good. I started to feel ashamed of my own feebleness. Close friendship isn't like passionate love; it shouldn't be an ego trip, it should be steady, unchanging. What I was feeling therefore couldn't be called that. I knew only too well that one part of me wanted very badly to be fully merged with her, inside the same cocoon, to be naked and to hold her, oblivious of time, to press my face into every nook and cranny of her body. I knew that I should be trying to move things along in some way that would lead to this goal, but in fact I did nothing. I chose to go on believing that I was happy just to hold her hand and that I shouldn't even think about any other aspect of her body. You'll think that's childish, no doubt."

He looked at me questioningly, but I shook my head.

"But it was. I was still young, immature. I still believed that a simple, logical argument could win out over my real self. At least I tried to believe that, but the self isn't quite so easily deceived. I was perfectly aware I was suffering from feelings of jealousy and that they were very painful feelings indeed. It would have been strange if I hadn't been aware of it, since it's not possible to suffer an emotion and not actually feel it, and I certainly felt my jealousy. While I was talking to her the shadow of this invisible man would fall between us. She tried to avoid mentioning him, but sometimes we'd be talking about a subject that seemed somehow to hint at him, and for a second he would appear, then just as quickly disappear again. But she was so pure! Her face, her voice, her heart; it was all pure, all beautiful.

"Once she had her hair cut in a new style. It looked so fresh and lovely it was as if some unseen hands—cherubs' hands, if you like—were behind her, holding it like that. But, just as I was about to say something to that effect, everything suddenly went dark. You see, there was somebody behind her, somebody I didn't know. You know how in an eclipse both the sun and the moon are in the earth's shadow? Well, someone was hidden behind her just like that. When *I* thought her hair was lovely, *he* was thinking exactly the same thing. Anyone who looked at her with the eyes of love was bound to think so. Maybe it had happened only an hour ago, or yesterday, maybe it was going to happen in two hours' time, or tomorrow. And seeing her hair shining in the sunlight, I felt she was moving away from me, going steadily farther away, receding and receding toward a place where I wouldn't be able to reach her any more, and I'd be left there alone. Can you understand that?"

I nodded vigorously.

"It was always the same. She quite innocently enjoyed the time she spent with me, and no doubt she enjoyed the time she spent with the other man just as innocently. Yet I never had the feeling that she must be comparing us, though that didn't make the situation any less painful. As I said, it was like an eclipse, in which this lovely planet passed between me and another body. As long as I was with her, this was what I'd have to put up with.

"Yes, I know, it's a common enough story. It's probably been repeated billions of times throughout history. Think about it: all confessions, all confidences, all kinds of novels, all popular songs boil down to this same situation. Gorillas and lions and whales in the icy oceans probably go through the same agonies in their dealings with the opposite sex. Maybe even plane trees, dandelions, mushrooms, those rare cells that Pasteur discovered, cold viruses and things like that all suffer in exactly the same way.

"Anyway, as time went on I came to feel a weird kind of empathy with this shadowy figure I'd never met. He was another version of myself, the other side of me. I had never even seen him. I suppose I may have come across him without knowing it, though even someone as guileless as she was probably made sure that would never happen. I had no idea what sort of person he might be, I only knew he was a dark reflection of me.

"Then an idea suddenly came to me. If I could somehow link myself to his circuit, if we were joined by a single cable and an attempt at some kind of emotional communication were made, then there could be an exchange between two comrades in love. His joys could be communicated to me and mine to him, and the love we had in common would be love equally shared. If that proved possible, all this futile suffering would disappear.

"I felt at that moment the pointlessness of the competition that the two of us, each trapped within himself, were keeping up. I saw our situation from the outside, and it made me realize that we were the victims of a preposterous trick, an elaborate game whose every rule we obeyed. We were shut inside ourselves— not just the two of us, but everybody. We were all urged to compete, given incentives to compete. We were each at the bottom of a tiny bucket, swung crazily right and left and left and right, slaves to that insane motion. That's all it was. And yet if only we could jump out of the bucket, there was a vast and beautiful world, a world of freedom, waiting for us.

"To link up with my rival, to plug into him, would mean making one little hole in the bucket to pass the wire through. Once that was done, all the joy that he experienced could be transmitted to me and life, with all its usual trials, would change. Why not, why couldn't this be arranged? Who had thought up this system of constant competition and imposed it on us, on all the creatures of the world, all equally the victims of this fraud?

"Anyway, what happened next? Well, the girl and I finally broke up. This love masquerading as friendship lasted about a year, then we both got a bit tired of it. Or you could say, there was no clear desire on her part to move on to another stage, to enter the cocoon, and I didn't have the courage to push for it. The shadow man stayed in the shadows. When at the end of that time I went to a provincial university for a year, I made that my excuse for leaving her. I suppose we'd both outgrown each other, but who knows? Maybe if the other man hadn't existed—this man I called a shadow and whom I'd thought of linking up with somehow—if he hadn't been there things might have gone on longer. Maybe we would have lived together. We might have married and had children by now. I suppose as far as she was concerned I was the person she could most readily open her heart to. I don't imagine she'd ever been as close to anyone as she was to me. The fact that I then accepted the existence of another party, in this lunar eclipse type of arrangement I told you about, just shows how bad I am at relationships. So that's my love story, the story of a good-hearted fool in love.

"But you know, if that's all it was, it would just have been an episode that could have happened to anyone. In my case, though, it was a little more serious than that, a little more significant. For me it turned into something representative of every kind of human relationship. Thinking about it afterward, I realized that even before it started I was already on the defensive. There was something lacking in me. I wasn't prepared to follow the competitive ethic, to hide inside the fortress of myself and shoot arrows at a distant enemy or throw stones at him or write him long, threatening letters. I didn't seem to have the will to win by such methods. In fact I didn't play any game that involved winning and losing. I didn't like the idea of losing myself and I didn't like the idea of making someone else lose, either. So I just hung about not knowing what to do, standing back and making way for the other person, then following unhappily after him, but never overtaking him at places where I should have gone ahead.

"I kept thinking how nice it would be if there were no such thing as struggle in the world, if things had been distributed equally beforehand. I thought how easy it would be if there were no distinction between myself and other people, if we all felt our sensations in common, if we all became a single living organism. I wished the shadow man and I could be linked up by that cable, not so we could each have the same girl but so we could both fall back, equally and at the same time, and then combine. The idea of our separate selves would fade while the consciousness of us together deepened.

"I've gone on thinking in that way. I've spent my days reflecting on things I can't discuss with anyone, because in the eyes of this vigorous, censorious society of ours I would look like a defector, a dropout, a nobody. Perhaps I am one."

"Linkage is not allowed," I said. "Connecting people with cables offends the concept of impartiality. It would infringe the anti-monopoly laws. It would impose a restriction on fair, legitimate competition."

"It's the competitive ethic I don't accept."

"And what you were after was a reverse transaction, a deal worked out behind the scenes, if you like," I said. "You were supposed to be in love with the girl, not the man, and the idea of shared happiness with someone you don't love makes no sense. Anyway, all individual entities are in opposition to one another. This is something that precedes ethics; it's the first principle of existence. The fundamental idea behind the universe is that of competition."

"All right," said Pierre. "But suppose that idea is restricted only to our planet? Suppose the whole box of tricks only applies on this star, that we're the only ones who've fallen for this swindle en masse? Who's to say this isn't the one place in the universe that relies on your principle, the one star where the sense of existence is shut up inside each individual so that we're all forced to struggle with one another? I see no reason why not, or why all those nebulae out there shouldn't share each other's thoughts perfectly and live in total harmony."

"You've taken the argument to such heights I've lost track of it," I said. "Anyway, it's pointless making statements that can't be proved. Let's restrict the argument to what goes on here on earth. If you and that man had been able to achieve some kind of joint possession of your girlfriend, her appeal would have vanished instantly. Her real attraction wasn't just inherent; it was the product of a competition she's in with all the other women in the world. You yourself became the person you are by a constant process of improving yourself through competition with other men, other colleagues and, by extension, with all human beings. You measured yourself against other people and worked out how to get ahead of them. If it hadn't been for all those competitors, all those millions of other men, you would've got tired of her right away. You probably wouldn't even have been attracted to her in the first place, and she wouldn't ever have looked at you. The idea of one heart linking up with others and everyone sharing their happiness comes from a loser in the war between individuals, someone who's fled the battlefield.

"And what about linking up with the girl, never mind the shadow man? If you'd ever managed that, she would virtually have become yourself. But how can you fall in love with yourself? How can you make love to yourself? Her whole heart and mind would have been revealed to you, like looking down at a landscape from a plane and seeing everything laid out. What sort of love do you call that?"

Pierre didn't respond; he just looked silently into the darkness, toward the site at the end of the gully. Obviously he hadn't accepted my simpleminded argument. It was hardly likely that he would.

12

When I draw arabesques on Kent paper I am attempting to restore (if only on paper) the order that this world has lost, and I enjoy that, even though I've failed as yet to make the face of God appear in them. Doing it is very close to the experience of sitting among those stones and listening. The drawback is that everything is on a horizontal plane, extending to a limited horizon. I wonder if I'd be satisfied if I could do it in three dimensions, with minute, intricately linked containers of thin, transparent glass, filled with varicolored gases? No, I doubt it.

What I'm looking for is not something complete and self-contained, whether in a two- or three-dimensional form, but something that connects over a much wider area, operating like a small transmitter. The patterns I draw, the colors I fill in between the lines, would be converted into messages sent out into space. I am here, they would say, I am in the here and now, but what I want is to dissolve, to be absorbed into everything else. I want to be everywhere at the same time, to see everything, to rejoice in everything. That is the message I'd like to send.

The site was probably the one place on earth where it was possible to communicate with the upper world, where messages from a world transcending the one we know could be received. Think of it as a relay station for the universal mind.

If I had to choose a metaphor to describe it—something I never even thought of doing at the time—I would choose a first-floor elevator door. Pierre and I stood before the door and watched intently as the lights indicating the various floors went on and off. On the upper floors were Andromeda Junction and Seifert's Galaxy, the source of supernovas, midnight black holes and Ylem Point. The question was, when the elevator came, would we get on or not? The sign would light up, the door would open and pause, but would we take that step inside?

We went on waiting for that moment, unable to make up our minds.

13

The music of Oneiros was a whirlpool of all possible sounds, full of voices, each one distinct even though they were in perfect unison. I heard the voices of old friends, the voice of my dead father, of a singer I used to like and had completely forgotten, of the helicopter pilot who had just died, the thunder of a waterfall hidden deep in the Andes and as yet unheard by human ears, whales singing in the Antarctic Ocean, all the crickets in the world, one by one, and the sound made by every grain of sand sifting past other sand. And I heard my own voice as a child, as Pierre once said he had.

Yet, in the end, my experience and Pierre's were different, fundamentally so. I heard the voice of my childhood self, but it didn't speak to me directly. I simply heard the voice, because all I did was listen. I didn't speak, I didn't sing. At night, when we returned to camp and sat around the fire, talking briefly every now and then about the day's experiences, Pierre's comments always concerned conversations he'd had. Mine tended to suggest I'd been listening to a concert. The people Pierre had these conversations with were never specified; it was more like a thousand people engaging with another thousand via a million different channels, with him possessing one of the sets of a thousand voices. And I should have realized this could only mean one thing: that he'd been drawn into the greater world where the music originated, had entered the state in which separate identities all merge. He'd taken the step inside the elevator.

We now ate practically nothing. When we woke up in the morning our bodies were already in a state of perfect readiness, and a single mouthful of water saw us through a whole day at the site. We said very little to each other. The shared experience of the place had given us a sense of ultimate intimacy; it was as though, having crossed a certain line; we appeared to each other as transparent and insubstantial as air. Oneiros had come to mean a language not made of everyday words, a logic without structure, invisible images. Through these things it taught us about the nature of the universe, the unfolding of space time and how we could enter it. Nobody did this for us. It was simply a matter of standing on the brink of total being and looking at what could be seen there. That privilege was given to us, that was all, and we spent our time there absorbed in what we saw.

In due course, though, I began to sense a change in us two. Whereas I was standing my ground, hesitating to go on, Pierre had unconsciously entered new territory and was moving farther and farther into it. Perhaps this was a gauge of the difference in our characters, or perhaps the place itself had chosen between us and was now fostering that difference. But something had changed.

My eyes seemed to be gradually opening. The site exercised the same power over me during the day and I was still entranced by the sounds, in which I continued to float like a large nebula—at least that's how it felt. But when we returned to our camp at night and sat in silence by the fire looking at the flames, I experienced more than once a kind of shocked realization that this wasn't a place where I belonged. There was something utterly wrong about the whole thing, although where the mistake lay I had no idea. Somewhere in the middle of a long, long calculation, an error had occurred, but I couldn't pinpoint it. Finally, on one of these occasions, while I was sitting there wondering what to do, I looked at Pierre and said suddenly, before I was even aware I was saying it:

"Let's go back."

"What?" he said in amazement, as if this were the last thing he ever expected to hear.

"Let's just go. This isn't the kind of place anyone should stay too long."

As soon as I'd spoken, I realized where the error lay. I knew now what was wrong.

"Why?"

"I think this is a kind of trap, a trap for people's minds. It takes them captive. It leads them away to a different world."

Pierre didn't reply for a while.

"You may be right," he said at last. "Perhaps we *are* being lured into it. But suppose it led to somewhere people ought to go?"

"There's no such place. There's nowhere else we could live but here on earth."

"I don't agree."

"Then you're wrong. What we're being tempted to believe is that there's another way of life, not living wrapped up in our private selves but sharing one existence. And yet the only way we *can* live is enclosed like that, inside ourselves. That's what life is. The essential condition of life."

"But there's no competition here," said Pierre. "Or rather, in the greater world that starts from here there's no distinction between oneself and others. From the moment I was born right up to now, I've always felt utterly alone— shut up at the top of a high tower, with everybody else shut up inside theirs. Even if I shouted at the top of my voice, no one could hear. I used to think, if only we could all come down from our towers and hug and hold hands and dance in the fields below. But nobody knows the way down. Now, after coming here, I've realized at last that the primordial mistake was to separate life into these individual existences. Everything should be interconnected in a single, harmonious state. Somebody, or something, introduced the principle of individual rivalry on this planet—and nowhere else—in order to conduct an experiment in the accelerated evolution of forms of life. It was an appalling mistake, and we're the ones who've been paying for it, with incalculable misery. The life force isn't meant for such brief periods of existence, such perpetual anxiety, such irrepressible feelings of loss. And that's the fact of it."

"You sound as if you're trying to convince yourself. All I suggested was that we go back."

"I'm trying to explain to you the reason I won't be going with you. Why do people console themselves with religion? Because they're alone, because they're all in their solitary towers looking down at the fields below. They want to go down, but there's no way there. The only way of getting out is to jump, which means jumping to one's death. People want an end to strife, to live in harmony and peace, and with that in view they've come up with any number of religious ideas; the trouble is, none of them is very effective. What these people want is what we've experienced here, the sense of being linked to every minute particle of matter in the world, a sense that one's feelings are shared by everything that lives. Isn't that so?

"Look, we've been chosen. On what basis I don't know, but chosen we have been. Those who aren't ready can't come here. Why the choice had to be made in as violent a way as that helicopter crash I don't know either. Maybe it really was just an accident. But now the two of us are here. We don't even need food any more. There's no reason why this shouldn't continue forever. It's a state anybody would envy us—everybody wants to be where we are now. Why should we go back?"

"Because we're human beings, that's why," I said. "Certainly I'm happy, much more than happy, to have been given this glimpse of the world on the other side. But that doesn't alter the absolute condition that's governed all life on this earth since the very beginning: of being alone, being segregated. However strong the temptation, we can't escape it. You said it yourself, the only way to reach the world outside the tower is through death. Your wanting to stay here, in fact, is just a death wish."

"You're wrong. Can't you feel it yourself—this growing sense of integration? We've found a relay station—a route that gets us to the other side without having to pass through death."

"It's *dis*integration in your case. You're being consumed. The things you're made of are slowly being broken down, to be reused in the 'whole' you talk about."

"Everything you say proves that you can only see things from the standpoint of the ego. You talk in terms of 'uses' and 'purposes,' but it's all beside the point. The individual 'I' isn't being used to serve the purposes of the whole. The whole isn't like some enormous individual. The whole is simply everything. The whole is. And the fact that it is is sufficient reason for it."

I remained silent. I felt as if every temptation experienced by man since human life began lay spread out before my eyes. If you believed that man was what he was because he had reached a higher point than where he started, whether one called it a lonely tower or not, then anything that tried to draw him down again was a temptation to be anti-human. Whether Oneiros was a trap made by angels or devils, it was a temptation to abandon the flesh we were made of and it had to be resisted. To give up one's humanity, even if it was to achieve some higher state of being, was a breach of the contract made when we were born on this earth. . . .

But none of this would get through to Pierre. It was nothing but words, mere arguments, stiff and unyielding. Such was the power of this place, in fact, I only half believed them myself, letting them circle idly in my mind. Pierre didn't say any more either, but got into his sleeping bag. Almost at once I heard his quiet breathing. We were at the stage where, fulfilled by the events of the day, we tended to fall very quickly into a deep sleep. Most evenings when I got into my sleeping bag I would instantly lose all sense of where I was, but that night, probably because of my resistance to the effect of the site, I couldn't sleep. I lay there wondering if I really would leave Pierre on his own. Since coming here our lives had grown oddly abstracted. We hardly ate anything, scarcely felt the heat or cold. Apart from the occasional discussion such as we'd just been having, nearly all our waking hours were filled with music and nothing else. Was it right to leave him to go on like this while I returned alone?

I liked Pierre. This wasn't an effect of the affinity the place brought out in us (or at least I didn't believe it was). I liked him because I felt at ease with him in various ways. For someone like me, who usually found it difficult to get on with people, this had turned out to be an unusually strong friendship. I didn't want to leave him here. I realized that doing so would be the same in the end as leaving him to die. It would mean abandoning him to a dreadful, lingering suicide.

Maybe, I decided, I should tie him up inside his sleeping bag and take him downstream by force. If I got the rope around him quickly enough he'd be unable to put up much resistance; then I could heave him into the dinghy, start the engine and set off. Even a short distance from the site, we might find ourselves free of its influence and able to think and behave normally again. But if he really believed that the site was trying to save us, it would look as if I were the one not willing to listen to reason, behaving like a willful child. Was it really Pierre who was the good boy and I the rebel?

Though still uncertain on this point, I made up my mind to carry out my rescue plan. But just as I was slipping out of my sleeping bag, I looked in his direction. To my astonishment, I saw that his body was glowing; the light it gave off was actually shining through his sleeping bag. My whole frame went rigid—all I could do was stare. His body gradually blazed even brighter, seeming to grow larger as well, and then began to rise into the air, slowly and still horizontal, while he went on sleeping. At the same time it became more and more transparent, like the figure of a young god made of fine green-blue glass. It kept rising, stage by stage, into the air. I watched, spellbound. When he was so high I had to look up at him, I could see stars shining through his body, as if it were expanding to embrace the night and to be embraced, the more rarefied and extended it grew. And then, much farther off—a single dazzling point of light in the distant darkness—I saw the eagle flying.

I thought I was the victim of a hallucination, something that wasn't really happening at all. Yet, even if this were an illusion, I took it as a sort of preview, made possible by some minute adjustment of the time scale, of what was actually going to take place in a few days', or a few years', time. Perhaps the site itself was trying to show me what was in store for him if he stayed there. Perhaps it was showing me the basic difference between myself and Pierre. Any number of ideas tumbled through my head, and my mind stood still, lost among them.

After a while the image grew so fine in the air it simply melted away. But when I looked over at Pierre's sleeping bag again, there he was, sleeping quietly as usual. I decided not to take him with me.

The next morning I told him I was going back alone. He didn't comment. I asked him pointedly if it was all right for me to take the rubber dinghy, since it was the only boat we had, and he nodded. He seemed to have decided not to speak. I divided the provisions in two, left him those things I thought he might be able to use, and loaded mine on board. Then I went up to him.

"Shall I come back to get you?" I asked.

"You'd better not. The place isn't right for you," he said in a low, hoarse voice.

I took him by the shoulders and hugged him. There were tears in my eyes. I suppressed the other things I wanted to say and walked to the edge of the river without looking back, then climbed into the dinghy and pushed off. After a little while I did look back and saw him standing on the riverbank, waving. I waved back at him. That was the last I saw of him, standing there on the bank, waving his hand, silhouetted against the sky.

So I went down the river we had traveled up together. By the second day I was back at the place where the helicopter had crashed. I stood on the bank and saw that Tajil wasn't there, but a little way back from the river I noticed a withered tree with a piece of red cloth tied to it, and under the tree was a radio set, carefully boxed and packaged against the unlikely event of rain. It was the kind where you just wound a handle to operate it and had probably been part of the emergency kit of the helicopter that had come to rescue Tajil. I used it to contact the airport at Kabul, and was picked up without any fuss the next day.

After that I was asked to explain why only I had returned and not Pierre. I was asked to explain what sort of place the site was, whether I thought it was of human or natural origin, and how many days I'd spent there. I was asked to explain everything, but I answered none of the questions.

14

Since I began seriously putting all this down in writing, I haven't drawn any more arabesques. I should have done more than 180 by now, and it's possible, I suppose, that in one of them the patterns and colors might have come together perfectly and the face of God appeared. But I've been lazy about that experiment recently. Perhaps it wouldn't be the God I ought to meet. What I need to think about next is some way of getting in touch with the human race again. I have to find a road that will lead me back to the world of other men.

If I show the doctor what I've written, I should be able to speak again. That's one way. Showing it would almost certainly get me out of here. The doctor would pronounce me psychologically normal, capable of conversation with other people, someone who can lead a normal life in accordance with the standards of society. I'd be able to go back to my old job with the television company. I know that what I've recorded here is an extraordinary experience, but it's written in plain language and with a clear enough conscience, so anyone who reads it should be able to understand me, even if Pierre's behavior is beyond them. It can serve as a farewell to Pierre and a declaration of my wish to return to society.

But I'm still hesitating. What I've put down is for myself; it wasn't meant for others' eyes. I wrote it in secret, so other people wouldn't know about it. Whenever I left my room I would hide the manuscript in a drawer underneath my 156 arabesques. I wrote it to put my own experiences in order. I'm like a child who has done his homework but feels no confidence in it and is reluctant to show it to his teacher.

One reason for this reluctance is that I can still hear the music. Even today I can hear it. The clinic has Muzak playing everywhere, but the sounds of Oneiros are always in my ears and drown it out. I first noticed them right after I got back—heard them all the time in fact, so that I was unable to hear anything else around me. It happened while they were questioning me, probing so persistently when I couldn't manage to reply that I lost consciousness; and when to all appearances I was sound asleep and even the EEG showed I was in a coma, I heard the sounds more clearly still. Then the longing to be back there with Pierre filled my chest so that I could hardly breathe. I remembered every detail of each day I spent there—how long it all seemed now!—and in my heart I wept. I wanted to return to those days, walk along that stony road, look up at the great bird overhead, see those torn, scarred cliffs, drink the river water; and as all those memories flooded through me I was helpless. I could do nothing. When my eyes opened on my present emptiness, the sense of loss I felt was almost unendurable.

Even now, at this moment, I feel something close to that, for the music has suddenly begun to fill my mind again. My experience at Oneiros was so overwhelming that I've had great trouble turning the whole thing into something I can cope with. I've been thinking about it for a long time now, thinking in confused, obscure, obsessive, contradictory images about Pierre and about the path that leads back to the totality of things. But I never regretted leaving that place. I was glad I left, glad I left Pierre behind and came back alone, though this was something I found impossible to explain to anyone who didn't know Oneiros. I also found it hard to explain to myself. Perhaps my failure to understand it was a measure of my ignorance of Oneiros itself. That's why I've had to write everything down, struggling to make sense of it. And now I believe I understand.

I imagine Oneiros will always be somewhere near me from now on. Something will happen and I'll hear that music again, remember how I left Pierre and the site behind, and sadness will overwhelm me, for in leaving I made two farewells. Abandoning Pierre was one of them, abandoning the place itself was the other. And yet I don't think I will ever come to feel I should have stayed. I've been over it all so many times now and have never thought that was the road I should have taken. What I did was right and I'm glad I did it.

But my departure from this clinic is another thing. I still don't see myself handing this account to the doctor, thereby declaring myself cured and leaving by the main entrance, as it were. I'm more likely to say nothing and leave by the side door. There's no longer any reason for me to stay, but I still want to spend some time as hidden away as I can be from other people's eyes. So I shall just make one clean copy of this text and leave it on the doctor's desk when I go, in case they get worried and come looking for me. Then I shall take occasional simple jobs that don't require me to talk much to other people, and wander here and there around the country. That's how I'll live.

The music has started again. I look back, I walk the stony road, I hear the voices singing; then it stops and I become myself again. I suppose this is how I may learn to forget Oneiros one day, simply by having this experience over and over again, hundreds and hundreds of times, until I have built an Oneiros within me, whose music I will keep on hearing in my subconscious mind. While my ordinary, everyday life goes on, I'll be remembering that far-off place, thinking of it twenty-four hours a day, even though I will have forgotten it. I look forward to that day.

But now I hear the sounds again. I hear them quite clearly. I can still hear them . . . hear them. . . .

KAIKŌ TAKESHI

Although Kaikō Takeshi (1930–1989) began writing stories in the late 1950s, he did not come into his own as a writer until he was sent to Vietnam and other trouble spots by a Tokyo newspaper. He wrote of his Vietnam experience both indirectly, in his oblique and touching novel *Darkness in Summer* (*Natsu no yami*, 1972), and quite directly, in his probing reportage of that war in *Into a Black Sun* (*Kagayakeru yami*, 1968). His brief story "The Crushed Pellet" (*Tama kudakeru*, 1978) evokes China during that time and a particular friendship.

THE CRUSHED PELLET (TAMA KUDAKERU)

Translated by Cecilia Segawa Seigle

Late one morning, I awoke in the capital of a certain country and found myself—not changed overnight into a large brown beetle, nor feeling exactly on top of the world—merely ready to go home. For about an hour I remained between the sheets, wriggling, pondering, and scrutinizing my decision from all angles until it became clear that my mind was made up. Then I slipped out of bed. I walked down a boulevard where the aroma of freshly baked bread drifted from glimmering shop windows, and went into the first airline office I encountered to make a reservation flight to Tokyo via the southern route. Since I wanted to spend a day or two in Hong Kong, it had to be the southern route. Once I had reserved a seat and pushed through the glass door to the street, I felt as though a period had been written at the end of a long, convoluted paragraph. It was time for a new paragraph to begin and a story to unroll, but I had no idea where it would lead. I felt no exhilaration in thoughts of the future. When I left Japan, there had been fresh, if anxious, expectations moving vividly through the vague unknown. But going home was no more than bringing a sentence to a close, and opening a paragraph. I had no idea what lay ahead, but it aroused no apprehension or sense of promise. Until a few years ago, I had felt excitement—fading rapidly, perhaps, but there nonetheless— about changing paragraphs. But as I grew older, I found myself feeling less and less of anything. Where once there had been a deep pool of water, mysterious and cool, I now saw a bone-dry riverbed.

I returned to the hotel and began to pack, feeling the familiar fungus starting to form on my back and shoulders. I took the elevator to the lobby, settled my account, and deposited my body and suitcase on the shuttle bus to the airport. I tried to be as active as I could, but the fungus had already begun to spread. On my shoulders, chest, belly, and legs the invisible mold proliferated, consuming me inwardly but leaving my outer form untouched. The closer I came to Tokyo, the faster it would grow, and dreary apathy would gradually take hold.

Imprisoned in the giant aluminum cylinder, speeding through a sea of cotton clouds, I thought over the past several months spent drifting here and there. I already felt nostalgia for those months, as though they had occurred a decade ago instead of ending only yesterday. Reluctantly, I was heading home to a place whose familiarity I had hated, and therefore fled. I went home crestfallen, like a soldier whose army has surrendered before fighting any battle. Each repetition of this same old process was merely adding yet another link to a chain of follies. Unnerved by this thought, I remained rigid, strapped to my narrow seat. I would probably forget these feelings briefly in the hubbub of customs at Haneda Airport. But the moment I opened the glass door to the outside world, that swarming fungus would surround me. Within a month or two, I would turn into a snowman covered with a fuzzy blue-gray mold. I knew this would happen, yet I had no choice but to go home, for I had found no cure elsewhere. I was being catapulted back to my starting point because I had failed to escape.

I entered a small hotel on the Kowloon Peninsula and turned the pages of my tattered memo book to find the telephone number of Chang Lijen. I always gave him a call when I was there; if he was out, I would leave my name and the name of the hotel, since my Chinese was barely good enough to order food at restaurants. Then I would telephone again at nine or ten in the morning, and Chang's lively, fluent Japanese would burst into my ear. We would decide to meet in a few hours at the corner of Nathan Road, or at the pier of the Star Ferry, or sometimes at the entrance to the monstrous Tiger Balm Garden. Chang was a prematurely wizened man in his fifties, who always walked with his head down; when he approached a friend, he would suddenly lift his head and break into a big, toothy smile, his eyes and mouth gaping all at once. When he laughed, his mouth seemed to crack up to his ears. I found it somehow warm and reassuring each time I saw those large stained teeth, and felt the intervening years drop away. As soon as he smiled and began to chatter about everything, the fungus seemed to retreat a little. But it would never disappear, and the moment I was the least bit off guard, it would revive and batten on me. While I talked with Chang, though, it was usually subdued, waiting like a dog. I would walk shoulder to shoulder with him, telling him about the fighting in Africa, the Near East, Southeast Asia, or whatever I had just seen. Chang almost bounded along, listening to my words, clicking his tongue and exclaiming. And when my story was over, he would tell me about the conditions in China, citing the editorials of the left- and right-wing papers and often quoting Lu Hsun.

I had met Chang some years back through a Japanese newspaperman. The journalist had gone home soon afterward, but I had made a point of seeing Chang every time I had an occasion to visit Hong Kong. I knew his telephone number but had never been invited to his home, and I knew scarcely anything about his job or his past. Since he had graduated from a Japanese university, his Japanese was flawless, and I was aware that he had an extraordinary knowledge of Japanese literature; and yet, beyond the fact that he worked in a small trading company and occasionally wrote articles for various newspapers to earn some pocket money, I knew nothing about his life.

He would lead me through the hustle of Nathan Road, commenting, if he spotted a sign on a Swiss watch shop saying "King of Ocean Mark," that it meant an Omega Seamaster; or stopping at a small bookstore to pick up a pamphlet with crude illustrations of tangled bodies and show me the caption, "Putting oneself straight forward," explaining that it meant the missionary position. He also taught me that the Chinese called hotels "wine shops" and restaurants "wine houses," though no one knew the reason why.

For the last several years, one particular question had come up whenever we saw each other, but we had never found an answer to it. In Tokyo one would have laughed it off as nonsense, but here it was a serious issue. If you were forced to choose between black and white, right and left, all and nothing—to choose a side or risk being killed—what would you do? If you didn't want to choose either side, but silence meant death, what would you do? How would you escape? There are two chairs and you can sit in either one, but you can't remain standing between them. You know, moreover, that though you're free to make your choice, you are expected to sit in one particular chair; make the wrong choice, and the result is certain: "Kill!" they'll shout—"Attack!" "Exterminate!" In the circumstances, what kind of answer can you give to avoid sitting in either chair, and yet satisfy their leader, at least for the time being? Does history provide a precedent?

China's beleaguered history, its several thousand years of troubled rise and fall, must surely have fostered and crystallized some sort of wisdom on the subject. Wasn't there some example, some ingenious answer there?

I was the one who had originally brought up this question. We were in a small dim sum restaurant on a back street. I had asked it quite casually, posing a riddle as it were, but Chang's shoulders fidgeted and his eyes turned away in confusion. He pushed the dim sum dishes aside and, pulling out a cigarette, stroked it several times with fingers thin as chicken bones. He lit it carefully and inhaled deeply and slowly; he then blew out the smoke and murmured:

" 'Neither a horse nor a tiger'—it's the same old story. In old China, there was a phrase, '*Ma-ma, hu-hu*,' that meant a noncommittal 'neither one thing nor the other.' The characters were horse-horse, tiger-tiger. It's a clever expression, and the attitude was called Ma-huism. But they'd probably kill you if you gave an answer like that today. It sounds vague, but actually you're making the ambiguity of your feelings known. It wouldn't work. They'd kill you on the spot. So, how to answer . . . you've raised a difficult question, haven't you?"

I asked him to think it over until I saw him next time. Chang had become pensive, motionless, as though shocked into deep thought. He left his dumplings untouched, and when I called this to his attention, he smiled crookedly and scratched something on a piece of paper. He handed it to me and said, "You should remember this when you're eating with a friend." He had written "*Mo t'an kuo shih*," which means roughly "Don't discuss politics." I apologized profusely for my thoughtlessness.

Since then, I have stopped in Hong Kong and seen Chang at intervals of one year, sometimes two. After going for a walk or having a meal (I made sure we had finished eating) I always asked him the same question. He would cock his head thoughtfully or smile ruefully and ask me to wait a little longer. On my part, I could only pose the question, because I had no wisdom to impart; so the riddle stayed unsolved for many years, its cruel face still turned toward us. In point of fact, if there were a clever way of solving the riddle, everyone would have used it—and a new situation requiring a new answer would have arisen, perpetuating the dilemma. A shrewd answer would lose its sting in no time, and the question would remain unanswered. On occasion, however— for instance when Chang told me about Laoshe—I came very close to discerning an answer.

Many years ago, Laoshe visited Japan as leader of a literary group and stopped in Hong Kong on his way back to China. Chang had been given an assignment to interview him for a newspaper and went to the hotel where Laoshe was staying. Laoshe kept his appointment but said nothing that could be turned into an article, and when Chang kept asking how the intellectuals had fared in post-revolutionary China, the question was always evaded. When this had happened several times, Chang began to think that Laoshe's power as a writer had probably waned. Then Laoshe began talking about country cooking, and continued for three solid hours. Eloquently and colorfully he described an old restaurant somewhere in Szechwan, probably Chungking or Chengtu, where a gigantic cauldron had simmered for several centuries over a fire that had never gone out. Scallions, Chinese lettuce, potatoes, heads of cows, pigs' feet—just about anything and everything was thrown into the pot. Customers sat around the cauldron and ladled the stew into soup bowls; and the charge was determined by adding up the number of empty bowls each person had beside him. This was the sole subject that Laoshe discussed for three hours, in minute and vivid detail—what was cooked, how the froth rose in the pot, what the stew tasted like, how many bowls one could eat. When he finished talking he disappeared.

"He left so suddenly there was no way to stop him," said Chang. "He was magnificent. . . . Among Laoshe's works, I prefer *Rickshaw Boy* to *Four Generations Under One Roof*. When Laoshe spoke, I felt as though I had just reread *Rickshaw Boy* after many years. His poignant satire, the humor and sharp observation in that book—that's what I recognized in him. I felt tremendously happy and moved when I left the hotel. When I got home, I was afraid I might forget the experience if I slept, so I had a stiff drink and went over the story, savoring every word."

"You didn't write an article?"

"Oh, yes, I wrote something, but I just strung together some fancy-sounding words, that's all. I wouldn't swear to it, but he seemed to trust me when he talked like that. And the story was really too delicious for the newspaper."

Chang's craggy face broke into a great wrinkled smile. I felt as though I had seen the flash of a sword, a brief glimpse of pain, grief, and fury. I could do nothing but look down in silence. Evidently there was a narrow path, something akin to an escape route between the chairs, but its danger was immeasurable. Didn't the English call this kind of situation "between the devil and the deep blue sea?"

Late in the afternoon of the day before my departure for Tokyo, Chang and I were strolling along when we came to a sign that read "Heavenly Bath Hall." Chang stopped and explained.

"This is a *tsao t'ang*, a bathhouse. It's not just a soak in a bath, though; you can have the dirt scraped off your body, get a good massage, have the calluses removed from your feet and your nails clipped. All you have to do is take off your clothes and lie down. If you feel sleepy, you just doze off and sleep as long as you like. Obviously some are better than others, but this one is famous for the thorough service you get. And when you leave, they'll give you the ball of dirt they scraped off you; it's a good souvenir. How would you like to try it? They use three kinds of cloth, rough, medium, and soft. They wrap them around their hands and rub you down. A surprising amount of dead skin will come off, you know, enough to make a ball of it. It's fun."

I nodded my consent, and he led me inside the door and talked to the man at the counter. The man put down his newspaper, listened to Chang, and with a smile gestured to me to come in. Chang said he had some errands to do, but would come to the airport the next day to see me off. He left me at the bathhouse.

When the bathkeeper stood up I found he was tall, with muscular shoulders and hips. He beckoned, and I followed him down a dim corridor with shabby walls, then into a cubicle with two simple beds. One was occupied by a client wrapped in a white towel and stretched out on his stomach, while a nail-cutter held his leg, paring skin off his heel as though fitting a horseshoe. The bathkeeper gestured to me, and I emptied my pockets and gave him my billfold, passport, and watch. He took them and put them in the drawer of a night table, then locked it with a sturdy, old-fashioned padlock. The key was chained to his waist with a soiled cord. He smiled and slapped his hip a couple of times as though to reassure me before going out. I took off all my clothes. A small, good-looking boy in a white robe, with a head like an arrowhead bulb, came in and wrapped my hips from behind with a towel and slung another over my shoulder. I followed the boy into the dark corridor, slippers on my feet. Another boy was waiting in the room leading to the bath, and quickly peeled off my towel before pushing the door open onto a gritty concrete floor. A large rusty nozzle on the wall splashed hot water over me, and I washed my body.

The bathtub was a vast, heavy rectangle of marble with a three-foot ledge. A client just out of the tub was sprawled face down on a towel, like a basking seal. A naked assistant was rubbing the man's buttocks with a cloth wrapped around his hand. Timidly, I stepped into the water and found it not hot, nor cool, but soft and smooth, oiled by the bodies of many men. There was none of the stinging heat of the Japanese public bath. It was a thick heat and heavy, slow-moving. Two washers, a big muscular man and a thin one, stood by the wall, quite naked except for their bundled hands, waiting for me to come out. The large man's penis looked like a snail, while the other's was long, plump, and purple, with all the appearance of debauchery. It hung with the weight and languor of a man with a long track record, making me wonder how many thousands of polishings it would take to look like that. It was a masterpiece that inspired admiration rather than envy, appended to a figure that might have stepped from the Buddhist hell of starvation. But his face showed no pride or conceit; he was simply and absentmindedly waiting for me to get out of the tub. I covered myself with my hands and stepped out of the warm water. He spread a bath towel quickly and instructed me to lie down.

As Chang had told me, there were three kinds of rubbing cloths. The coarse, hempen one was for the arms, buttocks, back, and legs. Another cotton cloth, softer than the first, was for the sides and underarms. The softest was gauzy and used on the soles of the feet, the crotch, and other sensitive areas. He changed the cloth according to the area, tightly wrapping it around his hand like a bandage before rubbing my skin. He took one hand or leg at a time, shifted me around, turned me over, then over again, always with an expert, slightly rough touch which remained essentially gentle and considerate. After a while, he seemed to sigh and I heard him murmuring "Aiya . . ." under his breath. I half opened my eyes and found my arms, my belly, my entire body covered with a scale of gray dead skin like that produced by a schoolboy's eraser. The man seemed to sense a challenge and began to apply more strength. It was less a matter of rubbing than of peeling off a layer of skin without resorting to surgery, the patient task of removing a layer of dirt closely adhering to the body. Talking to himself in amusement, he moved toward my head, then my legs, absorbed in his meticulous work. I had ceased to be embarrassed and, dropping my hands to my sides, I placed my whole body at his disposal. I let him take my right hand or left hand as he worked. Once I had surrendered my body to him the whole operation was extremely relaxing, like wallowing in warm mud. Soap was applied, then washed off with warm water; I was told to soak in the tub, and when I came out, again warm water was poured over me several times. Then he wiped me thoroughly with a steamed towel as hot as a lump of coal.

Finally—smiling, as though to say "Here you are!"—he placed a pellet of skin on my palm. It was like a gray ball of tofu mash. The moist, tightly squeezed sphere was the size of a smallish plover's egg. With so many dead cells removed, my skin had become as tender as a baby's, clear and fresh, and all my cells, replenished with new serum, rejoiced aloud.

I returned to the dressing room and tumbled into bed. The good-looking boy brought me a cup of hot jasmine tea. I drank it lying in bed, and with each mouthful felt as though a spurt of perspiration had shot from my body. With a fresh towel, the boy gently dried me. The nail-cutter entered and dipped my toes and fingernails, trimmed the thick skin off my heels, and shaved my corns, changing his instruments each time. When the work was completed, he left the room in silence. In his place, a masseur entered and began to work without a word. Strong, sensitive fingers and palms crept over my body, searching and finding the nests and roots of strained muscles, pressing, rubbing, pinching, patting, and untangling the knots. Every one of these employees was scrupulous in delivering his services. They concentrated on the work, unstinting of time and energy, their solemn delicacy incomparable. Their skill made me think of a heavyweight fighter skipping rope with the lightness of a feather. A cool mist emanated from the masseur's strong fingers. My weight melted away and I dissolved into a sweet sleep.

"My shirt."

Chang looked at me quizzically.

"That's the shirt I was wearing until yesterday."

When Chang came to my hotel room the next day, I pointed out the dirty pellet on the table. For some reason, only a twisted smile appeared on his face. He took out a packet of tea, enough for one pot, and said that he had bought me the very best tea in Hong Kong; I was to drink it in Tokyo. Then he fell silent, staring blankly. I told him about the washer, the nail-clipper, the boys, the tea, the sleep.

I described everything in detail and revealed in my praise of these men, who knew one's body and one's needs so thoroughly, and were devoted to their work. One might have called them anarchists without bombs. Chang nodded only sporadically and smiled at whatever I said, but soon fell to gazing darkly at the wall. His preoccupation was so obvious that I was forced to stop talking and begin packing my suitcase. I had been completely atomized in the dressing room of the bathhouse. Even when I had revived and walked out of the door there seemed to be some space between my clothing and my flesh. I had felt chilly, and staggered at every sound and smell, every gust of air. But one night's sleep restored my bones and muscles to their proper position, and a thin but opaque coating covered my skin, shrouding the insecurity of stark nakedness. Dried up and shriveled, the ball of dirt looked as if it might crumble at the lightest touch of a finger, so I carefully wrapped it in layers of tissue and put it in my pocket.

We arrived at the airport, where I checked in and took care of all the usual details. When only the parting handshake remained before I left, Chang suddenly broke his silence. A friend in the press had called him last night. Laoshe had died in Peking. It was rumored that he was beaten to death, surrounded by the children of the Red Guard. There was another rumor that he had escaped this ignominy by jumping from the second-floor window of his home. Another source reported that he had jumped into a river. The circumstances were not at all clear, but it seemed a certainty that Laoshe had died an unnatural death. The fact seemed inescapable.

"Why?" I asked.

"I don't know."

"What did he do to be denounced?"

"I don't know."

"What sort of things was he writing recently?"

"I haven't read them. I don't know."

I looked at Chang, almost trembling myself. Tears were about to brim from his eyes; he held his narrow shoulders rigid. He had lost his usual calm, his gaiety, humor, all, but without anger or rancor; he just stood there like a child filled with fear and despair. This man, who must have withstood the most relentless of hardships, was helpless, his head hanging, his eyes red, like a child astray in a crowd.

"It's time for you to go," he said. "Please come again."

I was silent.

"Take care of yourself," Chang said and held out his hand timidly; he shook mine lightly. Then he turned around, his head still downcast, and slowly disappeared into the crowd.

I boarded the plane and found my seat. When I had fastened the seat belt, a vision from long ago suddenly returned to me. I had once visited Laoshe at his home in Peking. I now saw the lean, sinewy old writer rise amid a profusion of potted chrysanthemums and turn his silent, penetrating gaze upon me. Only his eyes and the cluster of flowers were visible, distant and clear. Distracted, I took the wrapping from my pocket and opened it. The gray pellet, now quite dried up, had crumbled into dusty powder.

MARUYA SAIICHI

Maruya Saiichi (b. 1925) uses an interesting mixture of philosophical distinction and iconoclastic humor in his work. He began his career as a writer while continuing to lecture on English literature at two universities. Maruya's scholarly focus is James Joyce (he translated *Ulysses* into Japanese), and he has also translated works by Graham Greene. His first important novel, *Grass for My Pillow* (*Sasamakura*, 1966), is about a man who evades the draft during World War II. Later, Maruya's reputation as a comic commentator on Japanese society was solidified with the publication of *A Singular Rebellion* (*Tatta hitori no hanran*, 1972) and *A Mature Woman* (*Onnazakari*, 1993). The story translated here, "Sable Moon" (Sumiiro no tsuki), was published in 1990.

SABLE MOON (SUMIIRO NO TSUKI)

Translated by Dennis Keene

The young proprietor of the bar cum restaurant that Asakura the translator sometimes patronized had just returned from a medical checkup, and he had an interesting tale to tell. But Asakura found this story peculiarly disturbing, for he started to wonder whether the racketeer the young man said he'd encountered might not be that same schoolboy to whom he'd taught the fine art of street fighting when he himself had been young. Since Asakura was now in his sixties, the time when he'd been young was well over thirty years ago, and recalling so distant a past made him feel distinctly unwell.

Asakura hadn't managed to graduate from university. He'd read economics for a while but had had to quit halfway through, then had taken a variety of jobs before finally managing to make a living as a translator. In fact, he was doing a bit better than that, having done a couple of series that sold well enough to mean that he was in the more prosperous half of the members of his trade. For some time now he'd been in the habit of meeting an American once every two weeks to ask him about things he couldn't work out in the original, and that was how he'd started coming regularly to this place. On those occasions they'd always go first to the restaurant, then on to the bar, but on the evening in question Asakura had been to a party and had come here alone, going straight to the bar.

The bar had room for only four people at the counter, and there already were two there, one a man in his fifties who worked as a Diet secretary, and the other, a man in his forties, who was somebody in television. The young proprietor, in his customary black outfit, was behind the bar and had started drinking as well. Normally he began much later than this, but he'd heard that day the result of his checkup the week before and was celebrating his clean bill of health.

The first part of what he had to tell about his medical experiences was ordinary enough. Apparently there was a choice of two kinds of checkup; one took a day and the other took two, including an overnight stay, and he'd chosen the latter, so when the first day's session was over, he and another man were taken to a hotel. This other man was very soberly dressed in a dark suit with a plain tie, and he looked like a company director, or at least like someone who was destined to become one, although since they didn't go through the formalities of introducing themselves in the taxi, this was a mere assumption on Asakura's part. During the day he'd naturally seen the other man several times, so he knew his face, but it had created no greater sense of intimacy than what you feel for passengers in the same bus. When they had finished checking in at the hotel, however, the middle-aged man suggested that they have dinner together, and the young man agreed. They had neighboring rooms and arranged to meet in the coffee lounge in an hour and a half's time. Apparently people on a medical checkup didn't use the dining room but had dinner in this lounge.

When they were seated at table and the waiter came to collect their meal vouchers, the man in his forties, who looked like a company director, asked casually for the wine list, a request that the waiter just as calmly refused, so the young man felt obliged to make a conciliatory smile and point out that the next day's tests would be invalidated by any alcohol they drank. In fact, he was successful in persuading the other man of this point of view, but the incident made him feel that there must be something odd about him. He presumed he was some kind of alcoholic (which was probably why he was having the checkup in the first place), although the way he behaved during dinner, the topics he chose to talk about, the kind of jokes he made, all were very respectable. Even when he talked about mah-jongg and card sessions, it was just the way any proper member of society would discuss such things. Naturally when he thought about it now, it was a bit peculiar that he hadn't introduced himself even when they were having dinner together, but at the time it hadn't seemed so, presumably because he was still seeing him in terms of a fellow passenger on a bus.

After dinner they went to their respective rooms, and the young man lay on his bed and started reading a detective story in a translation he'd received from Asakura, but just as he was dozing off, the telephone rang. It was from the middle-aged man next door who said there was nothing decent on television and he was bored stiff, and wouldn't he mind paying him a visit. The young man automatically agreed but suddenly felt nervous about the whole thing as soon as he'd put down the receiver. Perhaps the man was a homosexual.

Still, as soon as he'd sat down in the other room, the man smiled and said something to the effect that he needn't worry because men didn't interest him in that way, and then he assumed a quite different kind of smile as he produced a rather large card on which was printed in flashy characters the information that he was vice president of a certain organization, the organization obviously belonging to the mob. The man was a gangster. The organization was located in a certain well-known amusement area, though not the same in which the young man had his own business.

He gave a gasp of surprise, which he managed to transform into an expression of greetings, and mumbled something about himself, producing his own card. The man who had not looked at all like a gangster up to that moment now looked remarkably like one. The face that had recently seemed to be dominated by an expression of social propriety, even if tempered by a certain resoluteness of attitude, had now become swathed in an overall aura of recalcitrance. Confronted by such a face, he was not at all sure what he should talk about, so he talked about his shop. But it did strike him while he was doing so that it would be a bit awkward if this character became a regular customer. Unfortunately, it looked as if the man had something like that in mind because, no doubt out of what he considered politeness, he asked a number of informed questions about what material the bar counter was made of, what kind of pictures were hung on the wall, and then started fulsomely praising a place he'd never seen, until finally telling him not to worry since he'd no intention of dropping in at any time. At this point, a slightly embarrassed expression came over his face as he rubbed his hands together and asked him if he might not perhaps join him in a few hands of cards, and it was quite obvious that that was the reason he'd invited him in.

Naturally the young man declined. He admitted he'd played in high school with a few friends, but he firmly refused the offer of playing with a real professional. But the gangster wasn't prepared to accept this as an answer. He pointed out that if he should happen to leave the hotel, he was bound to have a drink somewhere and that would mess up the next day's tests. The inevitable result would be that the young men in his mob would despise him, which would be very bad for morale, and the only way he could avoid all this happening was by finding some sort of amusement in the hotel. He continued with the peculiar argument that he felt that they had created a certain relationship in these matters because he was the one who'd stopped him from drinking wine. Then he smiled at him very pleasantly and asked him again if he wouldn't join him in a hand. The manner in which he was behaving was very much like a managing director attempting by astute inquiries and gentle persuasion to ascertain and influence how his staff felt about some delicate question. But perhaps it wasn't at all like that when you came to think about it.

At that point, the young restaurateur said he'd finally worked out what was really bothering him: he was scared stiff he might find the existence of alcohol in the room fridge irresistibly attractive if he was left on his own, and the only thing he could think of to keep his mind occupied was gambling. Since he couldn't have had anything to drink the previous night, this would be the second night in a row that he'd had to go without it. This thought quite naturally made the young man feel that he should to be prepared to make a certain degree of sacrifice himself. Finally the whole thing started to seem ludicrous, yet also very moving, almost to the point of sentimental tears. While he was battling with these conflicting emotions, the fact that it would at least make a good story to tell made his mind up for him. He had fifty thousand yen in his wallet and decided he'd play while it lasted. If things went worse than that, he still had his credit cards with him.

The gangster smiled happily and rang room service to buy some cards at the local tobacconist's. He also had three large cushions brought, placed on the carpet, and the two sat there facing each other and played for a couple of hours. Naturally they were playing a Japanese card game and not an imported one. They played "flower cards," one of the more common of the various games of that name. At first the young man was on a winning streak, then things were fairly even for a while until he finally realized he was losing every time, at which the game abruptly came to an end. This meant, of course, that it wasn't real gambling but just complete manipulation by the professional. Still, he seemed satisfied, and the young man had found it interesting enough. After all, he'd managed to get through the whole thing without anything disastrous happening, and it hadn't cost him a penny.

The end of the story was greeted with large shouts of laughter. Naturally various uncomplimentary comments and grunts had been made while the story was being told, but now his customers began to evaluate and question more precisely, which meant only, for example, as far as their evaluation went, that the Diet secretary commented that he was lucky he still had his shop, and the questions were similarly expectable, such as whether the gangster still had all his fingers intact (apparently he did) and whether he were tattooed (since he'd kept his shirt sleeves rolled down, it was impossible to say, but he was quite sure he was), most of these coming from the man in television. At a natural change in the conversation, the Diet secretary got up and said he was up to his ears in work and would have to go, reminding Asakura as he left that he mustn't forget about the coming Sunday. This was the wedding of his daughter, whom Asakura had helped find a job with a publisher, and who was getting married that day to the son of a very rich financier whom she'd gotten to know at a skiing school. Asakura had been asked to attend both the wedding ceremony and the reception afterward.

The young man behind the bar now accepted Asakura's offer of a drink and began to talk about what happened after the gambling session ended. The gangster had phoned the front desk to tell them he'd be in the room next door if anyone called, and there he relaxed and opened up, showing himself to be not just fond of stories but fairly adept at telling them, as he gave various accounts of what went on in the world of business, of the perils of gambling, and episodes from his own life. One of these was about what happened to him when he was in his early teens at school. Apparently his father had been a fairly high-up official in the prefectural office, but despite this, when he was having trouble at school with a gang of four (two older boys and two in the same class) who kept bullying him, he was given by a gangster from Tokyo some useful instruction in the art of handling himself. The result was not only that he managed to beat up the four but also what started him off on his life of crime. If he hadn't been taught the art of street fighting, then he would no doubt have been a different man today, he had concluded in what was no doubt meant to be a jocular tone of voice. The young man himself burst out laughing cheerfully at this point, but Asakura himself didn't even smile, for this final episode had shaken him to the core of his being. In the distant past, when he'd drifted to the Hokuriku area, something like that had occurred between himself and a schoolboy of about that age.

It was in the late 1940s. He'd graduated from high school into a university economics faculty, but he became friendly with a gangster in the street-trading racket whom he'd happened to meet at one of the eating stalls with which he was involved, and he'd been asked by him to help out with a client of his who was having trouble getting his son into university. This meant doubling for the son at the entrance examination, which Asakura did. In fact, he did the same thing a dozen times for various clients. Since this meant he became fairly affluent through the payoffs for this and other profit-making opportunities his gangster friend put in his way, he managed to get himself a woman. But that turned out to be the beginning of his troubles, as she was the mistress of another gangster, the head of a gambling racket. His street-trading friend arranged for him to leave Tokyo, and he went to Hokuriku, where he stayed a few months until word arrived that they were on to him and he'd better go down to Kyushu, which he immediately did, finding work at first on an American base and then going from one job to another. Naturally this meant that he ceased to be registered at his university. The upshot was that he finally drifted back to Tokyo and started to make a living as a translator of detective stories. But a deep impression of one thing that had happened during his wanderings remained with him, and that incident had occurred just before he left the region in Hokuriku where the prefectural offices were.

It was sometime at the end of June or the beginning of July, and he was being treated for ringworm. As he lay behind the white curtain under the mercury lamp, the doctor was talking to another patient, a schoolboy in his early teens who was stubbornly refusing to answer the doctor's questions. It was clear to the doctor from his injuries and the fact that his vision had been noticeably impaired that the boy had been beaten up, but he wouldn't say who had done it. The doctor explained that he wanted to know only in order to make sure it wouldn't happen again, but the boy obstinately refused to open his mouth. It appeared from what the doctor said that the boy's father was a professor at the local university, which didn't quite fit in with the other story. Asakura had caught a glimpse of the boy through the gap in the curtain, so he recognized him when he got outside the doctor's office, called him over and invited him to have a bowl of *ramen* (a great treat for a schoolboy at the time). He managed skillfully to extract the whole story from him, which was to the effect that three classmates of his (that also was a bit different) who'd always been friends had suddenly decided for some reason or other to start beating him up. This was how Asakura came to teach him the secret art of street fighting he'd learned from his gangster street-trading friend, a man normally very uncommunicative. On this occasion, though, he'd been almost eloquent (or at least the precise gesticulations he'd made had been), and it was what he remembered of it that Asakura taught the boy. First of all he told him the basic things one needed to know about street fighting, and then had the boy practice in front of the henhouse of the place where Asakura was staying. Asakura hadn't done much fighting himself (indeed, none at all for some time now), and his behaving as if he were a master of the art came from a simple feeling that he just wanted to help the boy, perhaps out of compassion for his stubborn courage in refusing to snitch on his classmates.

But he was unable to wait for the day when the boy would finally overpower his enemies, for a telegram arrived from Tokyo telling him to leave and go into hiding as soon as possible. So their relationship came to an end, and he had no idea what became of him, never hearing even a trace of a rumor. But the incident had always remained for him one of which he was rather proud in a dissipated youth that, although he didn't go out of his way to conceal, was mostly a subject about which he felt little inclination to talk. But if now the real truth was that the boy had started to go wrong because of what he'd taught him, then it was a totally different matter. Of course, it was still highly doubtful that this gangster and that schoolboy were one and the same person, but even so.

At this point, the man who was somebody in television burst out laughing, and the man behind the bar called out his name, so Asakura was wakened from his reverie. They both were laughing at him. From the situation the story had now reached, it seemed that the gangster had been going on with various recollections of his life when a woman arrived, and although this was a matter of no importance, of course, the young man had found it very hard to sleep, listening apparently for hours to the erotic tones of the woman's voice next door. It was to the sound of the same voice he awoke at daybreak. This was the part that Asakura had missed, and the man in television saw this as direct proof of how deluded Asakura had become, falling into a trance thinking about something else with something as good as that being related. Because he kept on pointedly laughing at him, Asakura was obliged to smile and shake his head and indulge in various bits of repartee before the man also went home and left Asakura as the only customer at the bar.

The young man allowed Asakura to buy him one more drink and asked whether he was going to wear black tie for the wedding reception. Asakura's opinion was that the bride's father's station in life implied that a mere dark suit would not be adequate in his eyes and that he'd worn his dinner jacket only once last year, at a gala concert, anyway, so the young man agreed to wear his as well.

Then Asakura asked a few more questions about the gangster, whether he might have come from the Hokuriku area, how old he looked and so on, explaining that he had the idea that a man he knew might have been the very person who taught him how to fight when at school. But the young man could reply only that he thought he must have been in his forties and he hadn't asked him where he came from, producing a card from his wallet that he handed to Asakura. The name printed on it meant nothing to him, and people in that kind of business were always changing their names for superstitious reasons anyway. While he was thoughtfully looking at the card, the young man cheerfully remarked that he'd never imagined Asakura had any connections with gangsters, and the fact that the very man who had instructed his own racketeer in the mysteries of street fighting might be seated here before his very eyes was one that was apparently a deep source of astonishment. He stretched out his hand and took the card back, then immediately called the racketeer's office. He said it would be quicker to find out for sure rather than just speculate about it.

The boss wasn't in, but surprisingly, only ten minutes later, he called the bar. He always carried a beeper with him, and his office had contacted him. He'd also been given a clean bill of health that day and had gotten drunk celebrating. The two congratulated each other, then got down to the question at issue, until the young man burst out laughing, finally putting down the receiver after they had had a fairly lengthy discussion. Still laughing, he passed on his information to Asakura. What he'd been told about the gangster's reason for starting out on the road to crime had been a total fabrication. He'd taken it from a story in a comic book, in fact. His father had not been an official in the prefectural office but a mere carpenter, and as a boy he'd been the leader of the local gang and had never been bullied by any one at any time, and all his fighting methods were ones he'd worked out for himself. It was perhaps for these very reasons he'd been so struck by the story, and he'd liked it so much that the comic book it was in was one of the few pieces of literature he possessed.

The young man reflected bitterly that he'd been taken in a number of ways that night, and Asakura tried to console him by saying that all sorts of people had trouble with literary thefts of that kind and that the history of world literature was little more than the history of plagiarism. He was thinking not only that it would cheer him up to put the problem on this elevated level but also that no doubt he himself was feeling relieved that no basis of any kind had been found for the large assumption he'd been making. This had produced an almost playful state of mind. But just as he was asking for the bill, the young proprietor recalled how the gangster had told him that the fighting method taught in that story was so gruesome that even he had never felt called on to use it during his long career. Asakura asked what it was, and he said it consisted of grabbing hold of your opponent's ears between forefinger and thumb and suddenly jerking down with all your might. This forced the other to squat down, and when you had him on his arse you hit him in the face, not kicking but lowering your hips and pummeling away.

Asakura had started to stand up but suddenly lost all the energy to do so. He sat down again and ordered another drink, then asked him if he could possibly manage to get hold of that comic book in some way or other, as he really wanted to have a good look at it. The young man seemed slightly bewildered but said he'd try, promising to phone the next morning.

He kept his promise. Three days later Asakura found a large cardboard envelope in his pigeon hole at the block of luxury apartments where he lived, and inside was a rather grubby comic book with a memo attached: "He says he went home specially to get this after an absence of two months. So his wife will have been glad of your curiosity. Perhaps even he was? You never know."

The comic book was part 2 of a series entitled *Yakuza Champion*, and this volume was entitled "Sable Moon." The author's name was Amamiyama Momoyo, a woman writer of whom he'd never heard, but since he had no personal interest in comic books and no son either, it didn't mean she must be unknown just because he didn't know her. Because he didn't have part 1, there were aspects of the story he couldn't quite follow. The whole thing took the form of a narrative related by the daughter of a very powerful underworld boss, who was studying French at university and was also an amateur actress (only in little theaters, however). In a number of places it was rather strange how she could have known about some of the events she described. She had an elder brother, and (naturally enough, seeing who his father was) he'd been causing a lot of trouble since his schooldays. His exasperated father's response to this troublemaking was given in comic form, and that was quite interesting. Anyway, this son gets to know another youth while in reform school, and they meet up again later, but this time as members of rival mobs. The reason that these two who could have sworn eternal friendship are fated to be linked by lifelong enmity is that the sister, the little-theater actress, falls in love with her brother's friend/enemy.

Owing to various odd fluctuations in the time sequence and the fact that one set of recollections tended to fade into someone else's, the plot was peculiarly difficult to work out. The scene in question appears near the end, where it turns out that the actress's lover is the son of an important official in the prefectural office of a large provincial town. Although he is quite a well-built fellow and his grades are not too bad, while he is at school he is picked on by three of his classmates and is continually being beaten up, probably because they object to the intellectual, cultured air he has absorbed from his privileged background. He doesn't tell anyone, of course, because it's unmanly to tell tales. He just has to put up with it, until he gets to know a mysterious stranger who has drifted to this part of the world from Tokyo, and he learns from him how to fight. He is told that when he finds himself alone with the strongest of the opposition, he should suddenly to seize hold of that boy's ears between his forefingers and thumbs, jerk them violently downward, and when the other crouches down with the pain, he should punch him hard in the face. He must aim at the nose; in fact, he must have a picture in his mind of a couple of inches inward from the nose, and strike at that. He mustn't kick, just hit. The other will start crying and beg him to stop, but he must go on hitting. When he's begged twice, he can tell him he must order the other two to leave him alone. If he agrees, then he can let him go.

The man who teaches him all this suddenly has to leave town. Now that the pupil has lost his master, he begins to have doubts about himself, but the three continue tormenting him and finally he makes up his mind. So the high official's son wins the fight and then (at which stage the story becomes a bit odd), the three become his underlings, and the gang of four now start intimidating other schoolboys and behave very badly indeed, until they finally are arrested by the police. The other three show all the right signs of penitence, but our hero refuses to change his attitude, and so he is sent off to reform school despite all his father's pleas and hectic behind-the-scenes machinations. It is there that he meets the son of the great gambling boss, the brother of his future mistress.

There is another jump in time at this point to a scene where the actress asks him if he, scion of the elite, has ever regretted the road he has taken (although a particularly lurid scene of lovemaking takes place immediately before this). He replies that he has no regrets, although he confesses he did feel them just once, for one night only. It was in his early twenties, when he woke up late at night on the day he'd been tattooed and realized he now could never again be accepted into the normal world, never associate as an equal with ordinary people, and for a couple of hours, he wept manly tears. Naturally, while he is making this confession, a picture of the tattoo on his body appears, a horribly false-looking full moon shining behind sable clouds; at which point "Sable Moon," part 2, comes to an end.

Asakura found he couldn't get on with his work that night. He read the story in the comic book over and over again, trying to arouse images of his distant past, but it all became only a mass of suppositions and fantasy. The use of imagination to speculate on the relationship between a work of fiction and real life is generally considered rather juvenile. Certainly aspects of that process in this case turned out to be futile, for he kept discovering mysterious similarities between the spy thriller he'd been doggedly translating every day and this gangster comic. Obviously there was no possible connection between the two, and yet they still seemed to have much too many details in common. It might well be that what had taken place between him and that boy only reflected some transmitted knowledge shared by enough people to assume almost mythological status, and the comic book was merely one of the forms into which that myth had settled. That certainly was possible, although it seemed more likely, surely, that the author had heard the actual story from that boy in one of his later manifestations, maybe when they were in bed together? This seemed even more likely when Asakura was in bed himself, and just before he fell off to sleep, he decided the only thing he could do now was get in touch with the writer herself.

He managed to reach Amamiyama Momoyo on the phone the next night. The voice that responded to his highly ceremonious greetings sounded a little drunk, and also suspicious, but she was reassured when she realized that he wanted only to ask her something about a story she'd written more than ten years ago, and she agreed to meet him. He was a little surprised by the venue she chose for this, the kabuki theater, but she explained that she was going to the matinee performance on the day after tomorrow, and during the second act there was an actor she didn't like, so they could use that period of time. She would meet him in the upstairs lobby on the sofa under the picture of Mount Fuji. She was very busy nowadays and that was the only time she had to spare.

In fact, there were two pictures of Mount Fuji in the upstairs lobby of the theater, but one of them was a commonplace traditional effort, whereas the other was a fairly avant-garde piece showing cherry blossoms blooming profusely under an exaggeratedly elongated version of the mountain. Asakura decided that was the one a drawer of cartoons would naturally have in mind. So he sat on the sofa in front of that one, and hardly before he'd had time to take a breath a middle-aged woman appeared from out of the darkness of the colonnade, briefly bowed, and sat down beside him.

She was probably in her early forties, a little plump; ordinary enough but certainly attractive, and the kimono she wore, dark blue overlaid with a large lattice pattern in gray, plus a greenish sash whose color was accentuated by the thin red supporting band, made her look almost erotic.

Asakura handed over two recent volumes of translations in lieu of a visiting card and explained what he wanted to see her about. There was no partitioning on the ground and first floors, and he could hear the voices of what seemed to be people in charge of some large group that had come to see the play joking away somewhere downstairs, and occasionally the music from the stage reached this far. So to this varied accompaniment he gave a detailed account of the matter in hand and finally asked her if she'd modeled that character in her story on anyone in real life.

She had remained completely silent and motionless while he talked, but at this point she shook her head slowly from side to side, not as a simple negative to his question, however, but more as an expression of the fact that she couldn't answer it. It seemed that at that stage in her career (at that stage in the history of gangster comics, in fact), somebody else wrote the story and she just drew the pictures, using the cinema in order to get the details right. She had no idea whether any of the characters were modeled on anybody but assumed they probably were not. When he asked her about the writer, she said he was of an age that seemed to fit. But he came from Shikoku; his father had been a dentist, but he didn't like the idea himself, so he read literature at university and got a job as a journalist on a trade paper. Or at least that is what he had said.

Even if his age fitted, Shikoku is certainly a long way from Hokuriku, so it didn't look as if he'd based the story on his own experience. While Asakura was thinking about this, the woman must have thought that he looked very disheartened, for she apparently tried to cheer him up by saying that he'd had many acquaintances in the underworld, and perhaps he'd chosen a model from one of them. But this particular path of inquiry immediately ended at that point, for when he said he'd like to meet the author and talk to him, she replied that he'd disappeared after "Sable Moon" and she'd heard nothing of him since. She didn't even know if he was still alive.

Her voice then completely changed in tone, as it took on a tragic melancholy hardly suited to the minor irony of life it was about to relate, saying it was a very good thing he did disappear because the gangster comics had not been selling very well, and when he'd gone she had to write her own stories, romantic ones for schoolgirls, and she'd done very well with those indeed. Asakura had the odd feeling that something else was coming, so he said nothing and she then started vilifying the man in the most unmistakably heartfelt tones, saying he had not just been obsessive about gambling but a filthy liar as well, and a drug addict into the bargain. So that's how it was, thought Asakura, lost in mournful gloom, as she went on to explain that they'd lived together for three years but that he'd often be away for days, even weeks at a time, and there was no knowing when he'd come back. While she was continuing this bitter recital of her misfortunes, she happened to glance at her watch and asked him if he'd like to see the last moments before the curtain fell. It seemed that the man looked very much like one of the actors, and her dislike of this particular actor whom she always avoided was only because of that. So they went downstairs and stood at the back and watched the actors as they left the stage along the raised walkway that leads between the audience to the back and side of the auditorium, and he was able to get a fairly close view of a heavily whitened face, but he didn't have time to ask her if it was this thickly made-up face that resembled the man's or the actor's natural one, for she had disappeared somewhere.

That night, Asakura lay in bed thinking about his life and coming to the conclusion it had been a failure. This conclusive idea took hold and wouldn't let him sleep. Perhaps part of it was that it was raining miserably at the time, and then there was the fact that his interview with Amamiyama Momoyo had produced nothing; in fact, the whole incident had been simply ridiculous. Still, what really seemed to hurt was the thought that something he'd done more than a third of a century ago and been proud of, and which he'd only meant to do good at the time, had turned out to have had a completely contrary effect, ruining the life of a young boy, setting him off on the wrong track. Certainly that might not have happened, but the possibility of its having happened was real, and he had to admit that such a possibility had existed in the act itself when he'd performed it. If that were the case, then what could be said of countless other things he'd done, for as he reflected on his life, on this action and on that, the various human relationships he'd had all seemed to assume one threatening shape, one that spoke only of distress, misfortune, and grief. It was this compound shape in various images of uniform malignance that assaulted and tormented him. He'd pledged himself not to drink anything on this day, but by dawn he felt he just had to have one glass of whisky.

That may well have done him good, since he slept soundly from daybreak onward, and his eyes opened cheerfully on a bright autumn day around noon.

He felt physically well, light in his movements, and the rather later than usual Sunday breakfast tasted wonderfully good. After breakfast he took up his writing brush, carefully dipped it in the ink, and wrote the necessary words on the conventional celebratory envelope.

Dressing up in evening clothes after so long an interval proved to be as much, or more, trouble than he'd expected. First of all, he couldn't find his suspenders and had to hunt all over the place before he did. That took time, and when he finally came to put on his trousers, he seemed to have grown fatter, for they were a very tight fit. His dress shirt looked a bit old and frayed, but he felt he could get away with it. When he put his wallet and notebook into his pockets, however, they stuck out in an unhappily obtrusive way, and his wife said it looked awful, so he took them out again and made do with a few banknotes in his pocket.

He left home carefully on time but started walking very briskly in the direction of the main road, for he was aware that his dinner jacket would be the object of people's attention at this time of day, and he wanted to find a taxi as quickly as possible. What he should have done was stand boldly at the main road and wait for one, but he was feeling embarrassed by the outfit he was wearing and just kept on walking, glancing out of the corner of his eye for a possible taxi and not watching where he was going, and that was where he went wrong. He felt some alien object cling to his left foot, and when he hurriedly looked down he noted a splatter of yellowish lumps on the pavement. It was dogshit and he'd stepped in it. Repressing an oath, he inspected the sole of his elegant Italian shoe, and there was a bright pattern of the muck stained into it.

By chance he happened to be beside a small park, so he walked diagonally to his left a few yards and wiped the sole of his shoe gently on an exposed piece of earth, wet with last night's rain, then moved his foot a little to one side onto a fresh piece and wiped it again. This cleverly removed all the dogshit from that area, and luckily he had got none on the side of the shoe, so he could go on to the wedding reception in the confidence he would be introducing no alien stench into it. Still, he was feeling a righteous indignation at this dog owner who allowed his pet to foul the public highway, when it was simple enough to clean up after it, there being enough giveaway paper accumulating in any household, all that advertising junk that came with the newspaper everyday, when he glanced back at the place he'd met with the disaster and noticed that he seemed not to be the only victim. A boy with a baseball glove tucked under his arm was standing by a small oak tree and trying to scrape the shit off the sole of one of his sneakers by rubbing it on the rectangular stone surround. He didn't seem to be managing all that well. Asakura called out to him and showed by gesturing that he ought to try rubbing it on the soil. The boy went to an area of uneven, rutted ground at the edge of the park, and did as he'd been shown. This method worked and the boy beamed with pleasure. Asakura felt a superior sympathy for the poor kids today who didn't know you had to use real earth for something like that, although it wasn't all that surprising, seeing that practically the whole country was asphalted over nowadays.

Then he quite vividly recalled the feel of the earth on his feet that day all those thirty and more years ago, in that back yard in Hokuriku with chickens running all over the place as he taught that boy the art of street fighting. He'd slipped off his *geta* and was barefoot, of course. This boy here now resembled that other one, in both age and physique, although that could well be some trick his memory was playing, and he looked around for him. The boy was practicing baseball by himself, throwing his ball at the park wall and catching it as it rebounded. He looked profoundly unhappy, even wretched, although he gave no impression of physical delicacy or weakness.

He walked slowly over to him and asked whether he was being bullied at school, because if he was he could teach him how to fight, since he knew a few things about it despite the way he might look now. The boy was certainly taken aback for a moment by being suddenly addressed in this way, but then his face grew animated as he smiled and made a large, positive nod of the head. Asakura nodded back and smiled too, whereupon the boy asked him to shake hands on it, putting out his hand which Asakura shook, thinking as he did so that this was all a lot different from what it had been thirty years ago.

He taught him the basic principles first. You only fight one opponent at a time. That's what fights were about. If you did that, you could always win. That was the first principle. If there were more than one, then you waited till you had their leader alone, got him to fight and beat him, and made him order the others to leave you alone. That was number two. The one who gets in the first blow is bound to win, so it's surprise that counts. Anything will do. Throwing a thermos flask at him, or a handful of coins, or dust or ashes. Everything's fair in a fight. That's number three. Then for number four, he produced the ear-pulling attack.

At this point, Asakura had to get down to practical demonstration, and he thrust out both thumbs in front of the boy's face (they stood for the ears) and made him seize hold of them between forefinger and thumb and jerk suddenly down. It was no good being timid or drawing back as you did it. You had to get your face so close to his you could feel the breath of his nostrils. That was the knack. The other wouldn't be able to help himself; he'd start screaming and have to squat down, and that's when you let him have it in the face. This needed practice, so Asakura started screaming and held the baseball glove down low, lower than his waist. The boy knelt down and punched the glove, went on punching it over and over again.

After this had been repeated a number of times, as Asakura crouched down once more he heard a ripping sound between his legs, and when he felt in that area his right hand encountered a large tear in his trousers. Now he'd done it. Perhaps they'd be able to get it sewn up for him at the hotel, or should he try to find a tailor? But while he was speculating on this question the boy came in again with his relentless attack.

As he went on instructing him, soaked now in sweat, Asakura began to feel as if he himself had returned in spirit to his early teens. It was he who was the boy energetically pummeling at the glove. And the man who stood before him, panting and puffing, urging him on, telling him how good he was getting, what a punch he had, how that last one had really done for him, was simply an old man in a dinner jacket with gray hair, someone he'd never seen before.

MURAKAMI HARUKI

Murakami Haruki (b. 1949) has doubtless become the most widely read contemporary Japanese author in the United States, with his stories (in translation) often appearing in the *New Yorker* and other magazines. A popular writer, in both Japan and elsewhere, Murakami treats ambitious themes with his own brand of laconic humor. A number of his novels are available in English translation, notably *Hard-Boiled Wonderland and the End of the World* (*Sekai no owari to hādo-boirudo wandārando*, 1985) and *The Wind-up Bird Chronicle* (*Nejimaki-dori kuronikuru*, 1994–1995). "Firefly" (Hotaru, 1983), a preliminary sketch for his novel *Norwegian Wood* (*Noruei no mori*, 1987), presents a wry view of student life in Tokyo.

FIREFLY (HOTARU)

Translated by J. Philip Gabriel

Once upon a time—more like fifteen years ago, actually—I lived in a privately run dormitory for college students in Tokyo. I was eighteen then, a brand-new college freshman, and didn't know the first thing about the city. I'd never lived on my own either, and my parents were naturally worried; putting me in a dorm seemed to be the best solution. Money was a factor, too, and the dorm seemed the cheapest way to go. I'd been dreaming of living in my own apartment, having a great old time, but what can you do? My folks were footing the bill for college—tuition, fees, a monthly allowance—so that was that.

The dorm was situated on a generous piece of land on a rise in Bunkyō Ward and had a great view. The whole place was surrounded by a tall concrete wall, and right inside the main gate stood a huge zelkovia tree. Some 150 years old, maybe more. When you stood at its base and looked up, its huge, leafy branches blotted out the sky. The concrete sidewalk detoured around the tree and then ran straight across the courtyard. On either side of the courtyard were two concrete dorm buildings, three stories tall, lined up side by side. Huge buildings. From the open windows, somebody's transistor radio was always blasting out a DJ's voice. All the curtains in the rooms were the same cream color, cream being the color that fades least in the sunlight.

The two-story main building fronted the sidewalk. A dining hall and communal bath were on the first floor, an auditorium, guestrooms, and meeting rooms on the second. Next to the main building was a third dorm building, also three stories. The courtyard was spacious, and sprinklers spun around on the lawn, glinting in the sunlight. Rounding it all out was a playing field for soccer and rugby behind the main building, as well as six tennis courts. Who could ask for more?

The only problem with the dorm (not that everybody *was* convinced it was a problem, though) was who ran it—some mystery foundation headed up by a right-wing fanatic. One look at the pamphlet the dorm put out made this clear. The dorm was founded on a spirit of "achieving the basic goals of education and cultivating promising talent to serve the country." And a lot of well-heeled businesses that agreed with that philosophy apparently helped underwrite the dorm. At least that was the official story. What lay beneath the surface was, like many things there, anybody's guess. Rumor had it the whole place was a tax dodge or some sort of land-fraud scheme. Not that this made a bit of difference to the day-to-day life at the dorm. On a practical level, I guess, it didn't matter who ran it—right-wingers, left-wingers, hypocrites, scoundrels. Whatever the real story was, from the spring of 1967 to the fall of 1968, I called this dorm home.

Each day at the dorm began with a solemn flag-raising ceremony. The platform for the flag raising was in the middle of the courtyard, so you could see it from all the dorm windows. Of course, they played the national anthem. Just like sports news and marches go together, you can't have one without the other.

The role of flag raiser was played by the head of the east dorm, the one I was in. He was fiftyish, tall, an altogether tough-looking customer. He had bristly hair with a sprinkling of gray and a long scar on his sunburned neck. It was rumored he was a graduate of the Nakano Military Academy. Next to him was a student who acted as his assistant. Nobody knew too much about him. He had close-cropped hair and always wore a school uniform. Nobody had any idea what his name was or which room he lived in. I'd never run across him in the dining hall or the communal bath. I wasn't even sure he was a student. But since he wore the uniform, what else could he have been? Unlike Mr. Nakano Academy, he was short, chubby, and pasty looking. Every morning at six, the two of them would hoist the rising-sun flag up the flag pole.

I don't know how many times I saw this little scene played out. The 6:00 A.M. chime would ring and there they were in the courtyard, School-Uniform Man carrying a light wooden box, Nakano-Academy Man, a portable Sony tape recorder. Nakano-Academy Man placed the tape recorder at the base of the platform, and School-Uniform Man opened the box. Inside was a neatly folded Japanese flag. School Uniform handed it to Nakano Academy, who then attached it to the rope. School Uniform switched on the tape recorder.

"May thy peaceful reign last long . . ." And the flag glided up the flagpole.

When they got to the part that goes "Until this tiny stone . . ." the flag was halfway up and reached the top when they got to the end of the anthem. The two of them snapped to attention and gazed up at the flag. On sunny days when there was a breeze, it was quite a sight.

The evening ceremony was about the same as in the morning, just done in reverse. The flag glided down the pole and was put away in the wooden box. The flag doesn't wave at night.

I don't know why the flag has to be put away at night. The country continues to exist at night the same as always, right? And plenty of people are hard at work. Doesn't seem fair those people can't have the same flag flying over them. Maybe it's a silly thing to worry about—just the kind of thought a person like me is likely to fret over.

In the dorm, freshmen and sophomores lived two to a room, while juniors and seniors lived alone. The kind of two-man room I inhabited was cramped and narrow. On the wall farthest from the door was a window with an aluminum frame. The furniture was Spartan looking, but solidly built—two desks and chairs, a bunk bed, two lockers, and a built-in set of shelves. In most of the rooms, the shelves were crammed full of the usual stuff: transistor radios, blow driers, electric coffee pots, jars of instant coffee, sugar, pots for cooking instant noodles, cups, and plates. *Playboy* pinups were taped to the plaster walls, and lined up on the desks were school textbooks, plus the odd popular novel.

With just men living there, the rooms were filthy. The bottoms of the trash baskets were lined with moldy orange skins, and the empty tin cans that served as ashtrays contained four-inch-high layers of cigarette butts. Coffee grounds were stuck to the cups; cellophane wrappers from instant-noodle packages and empty beer cans were scattered all over the floor. Whenever the wind blew in, a cloud of dust swirled up from the floor. The rooms stunk, too, since everyone just threw their dirty laundry under the beds. And no one ever aired out their bedding, so all of it reeked of sweat and BO.

My room, though, was spotless. Not a speck of dirt on the floor, gleaming ashtrays as far as the eye could see. The bedding was aired out once a week, the pencils were lined up neatly in the pencil holders. Instead of a pinup, our wall was decked out with a photo of canals in Amsterdam. Why? The reason was simple—my roommate was a nut about cleaning. I didn't have to lift a finger, since he did it all—the laundry, too, even *my* laundry, if you can imagine. Say I'd just finished a beer; the instant I set the empty down on the table, he'd whisk it away to the trash can.

My roommate was a geography major.

"I'm studying about m-m-maps," he told me.

"Oh, you're into maps, then?" I asked.

"That's right. I want to get a position in the National Geography Institute and make m-maps."

To each his own, I figured. Up until then, I'd never given a thought to what kind of people wanted to make maps and for what reasons. You have to admit, though, that it's a little weird for someone who wanted to work in the National Geography Institute to stutter every time he said the word "map." He stuttered only part of the time, sometimes not at all. But when the word "map" came up, so did the stutters.

"What are you majoring in?" he asked me.

"Drama," I replied.

"Drama? Oh, you mean you put on plays?"

"No, I don't act in plays. I study the scripts. Racine, Ionesco, Shakespeare, guys like that."

"I've heard of Shakespeare but not those others," he said. Actually I didn't know much about them myself. I was just parroting the course description.

"Anyhow, you like that kind of thing, right?" he asked.

"Not particularly," I replied.

He was flustered. When he got flustered, he stuttered more than usual. I felt like I'd done something terrible.

"Any subject's fine with me," I hurriedly explained, attempting to calm him down. "Indian philosophy, Oriental history, whatever. It just ended up being drama. That's all."

"I don't get it," he insisted, still upset. "In m-m-my case I like m-m-maps, so I'm learning how to make them. That's why I came all the way to Tokyo to go to college and had my parents pay for it. But you . . ."

His explanation made more sense than mine. Not worth the effort, I figured and gave up trying to explain my side of the story. We drew straws to see who'd get the top and bottom bunks. I got the top.

He was tall, with close-cropped hair and prominent cheekbones. He always wore a white shirt and black trousers. When he went to school, he always wore the school uniform with black shoes, toting a black briefcase. He really did look like a right-wing student, and most of the others in the dorm tagged him as such. In reality, the guy had zero amount of interest in politics. He just thought it was too much trouble to pick out other clothes to wear. The only things that could pique his interest were changes in the shoreline, newly completed tunnels, those sorts of things. Once he got started on those topics, he'd go on, stuttering all the while, for an hour, even two, until you screamed for mercy or fell asleep.

Every morning, he got up at six on the dot. The national anthem was his alarm clock. Guess the flag raising wasn't a complete waste. He dressed and went to wash up, taking an incredibly long time to do so. Made me wonder whether he wasn't taking out each tooth and brushing them one by one. Back in the room, he smoothed out his towel, hung it on a hanger, and put his toothbrush and soap back on the shelf. Then he'd switch on the radio and start exercising to the morning exercise program.

I was pretty much of a night owl and a heavy sleeper, too, so when he started up I was usually still fast asleep. But when he got to the part where he began to leap up and down, I'd bolt out of bed. Every time he jumped up—and, believe me, he jumped really high—my head would bounce three inches off the pillow. Try sleeping through *that*.

"I'm really sorry," I said on the fourth day, "but I wonder if you could do your exercises on the roof or something. It wakes me up."

"I can't," he replied. "If I do it there, the people on the third floor will com-
plain. This is the first floor, so there isn't anyone below us."

"Well, why don't you do it in the courtyard?"

"No way. I don't have a transistor radio, so I wouldn't be able to hear the
music. You can't expect me to do my exercises without music."

His radio was the kind you had to plug in. I could have lent him my transis-
tor, but it could pick up only FM stations.

"Well, then could you turn the music down and stop jumping? The whole
place shakes. I don't want to complain, or anything, but—"

"Jumping?" he seemed surprised. "What do you mean, j-jumping?"

"You know, that part where you bounce up and down."

"What are you talking about?"

I was starting to get a headache. Go ahead, suit yourself, I thought. But once
I'd brought it up, I couldn't very well back down. So I started to sing the melody
of the NHK radio exercise program, jumping up and down in time to the
music.

"See? This part. That's part of your routine, right?"

"Ah—yeah. Guess it is. I hadn't noticed."

"So—," I said, "could you skip that part? I'll put up with the rest."

"Sorry," he said, lightly dismissing the idea. "I can't leave out one part. I've
been doing this for ten years. Once I start, I do it w-without th-thinking. If I
leave out one part I wouldn't b-be able to d-do any of it."

"Then could you stop the whole thing?"

"Don't be so bossy—ordering people around."

"Come on! I'm not ordering anyone around. I just want to sleep till eight.
Even if I can't sleep till then, I'd still like to wake up the way people usually do.
You make me feel like I'm waking up in the middle of a pie-eating contest. Can
you follow me here?"

"Yeah, I get it . . . ." he said.

"So what do you think we should do about it?"

"I've got an idea! Why don't we get up and exercise together?"

I gave up and went back to sleep. After that, he continued his morning ex-
ercises, never skipping a single day.

She laughed when I told her about my roommate's morning radio exercises. I
hadn't intended it to be funny, but I ended up laughing too. Her laughter
lasted just an instant, and I realized it'd been a long time since I'd seen her
smile.

We'd gotten off the train at Yotsuya Station and were walking along the bank
beside the railroad tracks in the direction of Ichigaya. A Sunday afternoon in
May. The rain had ended around noon, and a southerly breeze had blown away
the low-hanging gray clouds. The leaves on the cherry trees were sharply out-
lined and glinted as they shook in the breeze. In the sunlight was a clear scent

of early summer. Most of the people we passed had taken off their coats and sweaters and draped them over their shoulders. A young man on a tennis court, dressed only in a pair of shorts, was swinging his racket back and forth. The metal frame of the racket sparkled in the afternoon sun. Only two nuns sitting together on a bench were still bundled up in winter clothes. Maybe summer isn't just around the corner after all, I mused, watching them absorbed in a lively conversation.

After walking for fifteen minutes, sweat started to roll down my back. I pulled off my thick cotton shirt and stripped down to my T-shirt. She rolled up the sleeves of her light gray sweatshirt up above her elbows. The sweatshirt was an old one, faded with countless washings. It looked familiar, as if maybe I'd seen it sometime—a long time ago. Maybe my imagination was playing tricks on me. Even at eighteen, my memory wasn't what it had once been. Sometimes *everything* felt like it had taken place a long long time ago.

"Is it fun living with someone else?" she asked.

"I don't know. I haven't been there that long yet."

She stopped in front of the water fountain, sipped a single mouthful of water, and wiped her mouth with a handkerchief she took out of her pants pocket. She retied the laces of her tennis shoes.

"I wonder if it would suit me," she mused.

"You mean living in a dorm?"

"Yes," she said.

"I don't know. It's more trouble than you'd imagine. Lots of rules. Not to mention radio exercises."

"That's right," she said and was lost in thought for a time. Then looked me straight in the eyes. Her eyes were unnaturally limpid. I'd never noticed till then how limpid. It gave me a kind of a strange, transparent feeling. Like gazing at the sky.

"But sometimes I feel like I *should*. I mean . . ." she said, looking into my eyes. She bit her lip and looked down. "I don't know. Forget it."

End of conversation. She started walking again.

I hadn't seen her for half a year. She'd gotten so thin I almost didn't recognize her. Her plump cheeks had thinned out, as had her neck. Not that she struck me as bony or anything. She looked prettier than ever. I wanted to tell her that but couldn't figure out how to go about it. So I gave up.

We hadn't come to Yotsuya for any particular reason. We just happened to run across each other in a train on the Chūō Line. Neither of us had any plans. Let's get off, she said, and we did. Left alone, we didn't have too much to talk about. I don't know why she suggested getting off the train. From the very beginning, we didn't have anything to talk about.

After we got off at the station, she headed off without a word. I walked after her, trying my best to keep up. There was always about a yard between us, and I just kept on walking, staring at her back. Occasionally she'd turn around to say something. Sometimes I could come up with a reply of sorts, but sometimes I couldn't figure out at all what to say. And sometimes I couldn't catch what she said. Didn't seem to make any difference to her. She just said what she wanted to say, turned around again, and walked on in silence.

We turned right at Iidabashi, came out next to the palace moat, then crossed the intersection at Jinbōchō, went up the Ochanomizu Slope, and cut across Hongo. Then we followed the railroad tracks to Komagome. Quite a walk. By the time we arrived at Komagome, it was already getting dark.

"Where are we?" she suddenly asked me.

"Komagome," I said. "We've made a big circle."

"How did we end up here?"

"You brought us here. I just played Follow the Leader."

We dropped in a soba noodle shop close to the station and had a bite to eat. Neither of us said a single word from the beginning to the end of the meal. I was exhausted from the walk and felt like I was going to collapse. She sat there lost in thought.

"You're really in good shape," I said, the noodles finished.

"Surprised?"

"Um."

"I was a cross-country runner in junior high. And my dad liked to hike in the mountains, so ever since I was little I went hiking on Sundays. Even now my legs are pretty strong."

"I never would have guessed it."

She laughed.

"I'll take you home," I said.

"It's OK," she said. "I can get back by myself. Don't bother."

"I don't mind at all."

"It's OK, really. I'm used to going home alone."

To tell the truth, I was a little relieved she said that. It took more than an hour by train to her apartment, and I didn't like the idea of the two of us sitting there side by side on the train all that time, silent as before. So she ended up going back by herself. To make up for it, I paid for the meal.

Just as we were saying good-bye, she turned to me and said, "Uh—I wonder, if it's isn't too much to ask, if I might see you again? I know there's no real reason for me to ask you . . ."

"You don't need any special reason," I said, a little taken aback.

She blushed slightly. She probably could feel how surprised I was.

"I can't really explain it well," she said. She rolled the sleeves of her sweatshirt up to her elbows and then rolled them down again. The electric lights bathed the down on her arms in a beautiful gold. "I didn't mean to say *reason*. I probably should have used another word."

She rested both elbows on the table and closed her eyes, as if searching for the right words. But the words didn't come.

"It's all right with me," I told her.

"I don't know . . . these days I just can't seem to say what I mean," she said.

"I just can't. Every time I try to say something, it misses the point. Either that or I say the opposite of what I mean. The more I try to get it right, the more mixed up it gets. Sometimes I can't even remember what I was trying to say in the first place. It's like my body's split in two, and one of me is chasing the other. There's a big pillar in the middle, and we're running circles around it. The other me has the right words, but I can never catch her."

She put her hands on the table and stared into my eyes.

"Do you know what I'm trying to say?"

"Everybody has that kind of feeling sometimes," I said. "You can't express yourself the way you want to, and you get irritated."

These weren't the words she wanted to hear, apparently.

"No, that isn't what I mean," she said but stopped there.

"I don't mind at all seeing you again," I said. "I have a lot of free time, and it'd sure be a lot healthier for me to go on walks with you than lie around all day."

We left each other at the station. I said good-bye; she said good-bye.

The first time I met her was in the spring of my sophomore year in high school. She was the same age and was attending a well-known private Christian school. One of my best friends, who happened to be her boyfriend, introduced us. The two of them had known each other since grade school and lived only a couple of hundred yards down the road from each other.

Like many couples who had known each other since they were young, they didn't have any particular desire to be alone. They were always visiting each other's homes and having dinner together with the one of their families. We went on a lot of double dates together, but I never seemed to get anywhere with girls, so we usually ended up a trio. Which was fine by me. We each had our parts to play: I played the guest, he the able host, and she was his pleasant assistant and leading lady.

My friend made a great host. He might have seemed a bit standoffish at times, but basically he was a kind person, and fair. He used to kid the two of us—her and me—with the same jokes. If one of us fell silent, he'd start talking to us right away, trying to draw us out. His antennae could instantly pick up the mood we were in, and the right words just flowed out. And add to that another talent: he could make the world's most boring person sound fascinating. When I was talking with him, I felt that way—like my life was one big adventure.

But if he stepped out of the room, she and I clammed up. We had zero in common and no idea what to talk about. We just sat there, toying with the ashtray on the table, perhaps, or drinking water, waiting for him to return. When he got back, the conversation picked up where it had left off.

I saw her again just once, three months after his funeral. There was something we had to discuss, so we met in a coffee shop. But as soon as that was finished, we had nothing to say. I started to talk about something a couple of times, but the conversation just petered out. She sounded upset, like she was angry with me, but I couldn't figure out why. We said good-bye.

Maybe she was angry with me because the last person to see him alive was me, not her. I shouldn't say this, I know, but I can't help it. I wish I could change places with her, but it can't be helped. Once something happens, that's all she wrote; there's no way to change things to the way they were.

On that afternoon in May, after school (actually school wasn't over yet, and we'd skipped out), he and I stopped inside a pool hall and played four games. I won the first one; he took the next three. As we'd agreed, the loser paid for the games.

That night he died in his garage. He stuck a rubber hose in the exhaust pipe of his N360, got inside, sealed up the windows with tape, and started the engine. I have no idea how long it took him to die. When his parents got back from visiting a sick friend, he already was dead. The car radio was still on, a receipt from a gas station still stuck under the wiper.

He didn't leave any note or clue to his motives. I was the last person to see him alive, so the police called me in for questioning. He didn't act any different from usual, I told them. Seemed the same as always. People who are going to kill themselves don't usually win three games of pool in a row, do they? The police thought both of us were a little suspect. The kind of student who skips out of high-school classes to play pool might very well be the kind to commit suicide, they seemed to imply. There was a short article about his death in the paper, and that was that. His parents got rid of the car, and for a few days there were white flowers on his desk at school.

When I graduated from high school and went to Tokyo, there was only one thing I felt I had to do: try not to think too deeply. I willed myself to forget all of it—the pool tables covered with green felt, his red car, the white flowers on the desk, the smoke rising from the tall chimney of the crematorium, the chunky paperweight in the police interrogation room. Everything. At first it seemed like I could forget, but something remained inside me. It was like air, and I couldn't grasp it. As time passed, though, that air formed itself into a simple, clear shape. Into words. And the words were these:

Death is not the opposite of life but a part of it.

Say it aloud and it sounds trivial. Just common sense. But at the time I didn't think of it as words; it was more like air filling my body. Death was in everything around me—inside the paperweight, inside the four balls on the pool table. And as we live, we breathe death into our lungs, like fine particles of dust.

Up till then I'd always thought death existed separately, apart from everything else. Sure, I knew death was inevitable. But you could just as easily turn that around and say that until that day comes, death has nothing to do with us. Life is over here; death is over there. What could be more logical?

After my friend died, though, I couldn't think of death in such a naive way. Death is not the opposite of life. Death is already inside me. And I couldn't shake that thought. The death that took my seventeen-year-old friend on that May evening took hold of me as well.

That much I understood, but I didn't want to think about it too much. This was no easy task. I was still just eighteen, too young to find some neutral ground to stand on.

After that I dated her once, maybe twice, a month. I guess you could call it dating. Can't think of any better word for it.

She was going to a women's college just outside Tokyo, a small school but with a good reputation. Her apartment was just a ten-minute walk from the college. Along the road to the school there was a beautiful reservoir that we sometimes took walks around. She didn't seem to have any friends. Same as before, she was pretty quiet. There wasn't much to talk about, so I didn't say much either. We just looked at each other and kept on walking and walking.

Not that we weren't getting anywhere. Around the end of summer vacation, in a very natural way, she started walking next to me, not in front. On and on we walked, side by side—up and down slopes, over bridges, across streets. We weren't headed anywhere in particular and didn't have any plans. We'd walk for a while, drop by a coffee shop for some coffee, and off we'd go again. Like slides being changed in the projector, only the seasons changed. Fall came, and the courtyard of my dorm was covered with fallen zelkovia leaves. Pulling on a sweater, I could catch a scent of the new season. I went out and bought myself a new pair of suede shoes.

At the end of autumn when the wind turned icy, she began to walk closer to me, rubbing up against my arm. Through my thick duffel coat I could feel her breath. But that was all. Hands stuck deep in the pockets of my coat, I continued to walk on and on. Both of us had shoes with rubber soles, and our footsteps were silent. Only when we crunched over the trampled down sycamore leaves did we make a sound. It wasn't *my* arm she wanted, but someone else's. Not *my* warmth, but the warmth of another. At least that's how it felt at the time.

Her eyes looked even more transparent than before, a restless sort of transparency. Sometimes, for no particular reason, she'd look deep into my eyes. And each time she did, a feeling of sadness washed over me.

The guys at the dorm always kidded me whenever she called or when I went out to see her on Sunday mornings. They thought I'd made a girlfriend. I couldn't explain the situation to them, and there wasn't any reason to, so I just let things stand as they were. Whenever I came back from a date, invariably someone would ask me whether I'd scored. Can't complain, was my standard reply.

So passed my eighteenth year. The sun rose and set; the flag was raised and lowered. And on Sundays I went on a date with my dead friend's girlfriend. What the hell do you think you're doing? I asked myself. And what're going to do next? I hadn't the foggiest. At school I read Claudel's plays, and Racine's, and Eisenstein. I liked their style, but that was it. I made hardly any friends at school, or at the dorm, either. I was always reading, so people thought I wanted to be a writer. But I didn't. I didn't want to be anything.

Many times I tried to talk with her about these feelings. She of all people should understand. But I could never explain how I felt. It was like she said: whenever I struggled to find the right words, they slipped from my grasp and sank into the murky depths.

On Saturday evenings, I sat in the lobby of the dorm where the phones were, waiting for her call. Sometimes she wouldn't call for three weeks at a stretch, other times two weeks in a row. So I sat on a chair in the lobby, waiting. On Saturday evenings, most of the other students went out, and silence descended on the dorm. Gazing at the particles of light in the still space, I struggled to grasp my own feelings. Everyone is looking for something from someone. That much I was sure of. But what came next, I had no idea. A hazy wall of air rose up before me, just out of reach.

During the winter, I had a part-time job at a small record store in Shinjuku. For Christmas I gave her a Henry Mancini record that had one of her favorites on it, the tune "Dear Heart." I wrapped it in paper with a Christmas tree design and added a pink ribbon. She gave me a pair of woolen gloves she'd knitted. The part for the thumb was a little too short, but they were warm all the same.

She didn't go home for New Year's vacation, and the two of us had dinner over New Year's at her apartment.

A lot of things happened that winter.

At the end of January, my roommate was in bed for two days with a temperature of nearly 104. Thanks to that, I had to call off a date with her. I couldn't just go out and leave him: he sounded like he was going to die at any minute. And who else would look after him? I bought some ice, wrapped it in a plastic bag to make an ice pack, wiped his sweat away with a cool wet towel, took his temperature every hour. His fever didn't break for a whole day. The second day, though, he leaped out of bed as though nothing had happened. His temperature was back to normal.

"It's weird," he said. "I've never had a fever before in my life."

"Well, you sure had one this time," I told him. I showed him the two free concert tickets that had gone to waste.

"At least they were free," he said.

It snowed a lot in February.

At the end of February, I got into a fight with an older student at the dorm over something stupid and punched him. He fell over and hit his head on a concrete wall. Fortunately he was OK, but I was called before the dorm head and given a warning. After that, dorm life was never the same.

I turned nineteen and finally became a sophomore. I failed a couple of courses, though. I managed a couple of Bs, but everything else was Cs and Ds. She was promoted to sophomore, too, but with a much better record: she passed all her courses. The four seasons came and went.

In June she turned twenty. I had trouble picturing her as twenty. We always thought the best thing for us was to shuttle back and forth somewhere between eighteen and nineteen. After eighteen comes nineteen, after nineteen comes eighteen—*that* we could understand. But now here she was twenty. And the next winter I'd be twenty, too. Only our dead friend would stay forever as he was, seventeen years old.

It rained on her birthday. I bought a cake in Shinjuku and took the train to her place. The train was crowded and bounced around something awful; by the time I got to her apartment, the cake was a decaying Roman ruin. But we went ahead and put twenty candles on it and lit them. We closed the curtains and turned off the lights, and suddenly we had a real birthday party on our hands. She opened a bottle of wine, and we drank it with the cake, and had a little something to eat.

"I don't know, but it seems kind of idiotic to be twenty," she said. After dinner we cleared away the dishes and sat on the floor drinking the rest of the wine. While I finished one glass, she helped herself to two.

She'd never talked like she did that night. She told me these long stories about her childhood, her school, her family. Terribly involved stories that started with A, then B would enter the picture, leading on to something about C, going on and on and on. There was no end to it. At first I made all the proper noises to show her I was following along but soon gave up. I put on a record, and when it was over, I lifted up the needle and put on another. After I finished all the records, I put the first one back on. Outside it was still pouring. Time passed slowly as her monologue went on without end.

I didn't worry about it, though, until a while later. Suddenly I realized it was 11:00 P.M. and she'd been talking nonstop for four hours. If I didn't get a move on, I'd miss the last train home. I didn't know what to do. Should I just let her talk till she dropped? Should I break in and put an end to it? After much hesitation, I decided to interrupt. Four hours should be enough, you'd think.

"Well, I'd better get going," I finally said. "Sorry I stayed so late. I'll see you again real soon, OK?"

I wasn't sure whether my words had gotten through. For a short while she was quiet, but soon it was back to the monologue. I gave up and lit a cigarette. At this rate, it looked like I'd better go with plan B. Let the rest take its course.

Before too long, though, she stopped. With a jolt, I realized she was finished. It wasn't that she'd finished wanting to talk; her well of words had just dried up. Scraps of words hung there, suspended in midair. She tried to continue, but nothing came out. Something had been lost. Her lips slightly parted, she looked into my eyes with a vague expression as if she were trying to make out something through an opaque membrane. I couldn't help feeling guilty.

"I didn't mean to interrupt you," I said slowly, weighing each word. "But it's getting late, so I thought I'd better get going . . ."

It took less than a second for the teardrops to run down her cheeks and splash onto one of the record jackets. After the first drops fell, the floodgate burst. Putting her hands on the floor she leaned forward, weeping so much it seemed like she was retching. I gently put my hand out and touched her shoulder; it shook ever so slightly. Almost without thinking, I drew her near me. Head buried in my chest, she sobbed silently, dampening my shirt with her hot breath and tears. Her ten fingers, in search of something, roamed over my back. Cradling her in my left arm, I stroked the fine strands of her hair with my right. For a long while, I waited in this pose for her to stop crying. But she didn't stop.

That night we slept together. That may have been the best response to the situation, maybe not. I don't know what else I should have done.

I hadn't slept with a girl for ages. It was her first time with a man. Stupid me, I asked her why she hadn't slept with *him.* Instead of answering, she pulled away from me, turned to face the opposite direction, and gazed at the rain outside. I looked at the ceiling and smoked a cigarette.

In the morning the rain had stopped. She was still facing away from me, asleep. Or maybe she was awake all the time, I couldn't tell. Once again, she was enveloped by the same silence of a year before. I looked at her white back for a while, then gave up and climbed out of bed.

Record jackets lay scattered over the floor; half a dilapidated cake graced the table. It felt like time had skidded to a stop. On her desktop there was a dictionary and a chart of French verb conjugations. A calendar was taped to the wall in front of the desk, a pure white calendar without a mark or writing of any kind.

I gathered up the clothes that had fallen on the floor beside the bed. The front of my shirt was still cold and wet from her tears. Putting my face to it, I breathed in the odor of her hair.

I tore off a sheet from the memo pad on her desk and left a note. Call me soon, I wrote. I left the room, closing the door.

A week passed without a call. She didn't answer her phone, so I wrote her a long letter. I tried to tell her my feelings as honestly as I knew how. There's a lot going on I don't have a clue about, I wrote; I'll try my damndest to figure it all out, but you've got to understand it doesn't happen overnight. I have no idea where I'm headed. All I know for sure is I don't want to get hung up thinking too deeply about things. The world's too precarious a place for that. Start me mulling over ideas, and I'll end up forcing the people around me to do things they hate. I couldn't stand that. I want to see you again very much, but I don't know if that's the right thing to do . . .

That's the kind of letter I wrote.

I got a reply in the beginning of July. A short letter.

For the time being I've decided to take a year off from college. I say for the time being, but I doubt I'll go back. Taking a leave of absence is just a formality. Tomorrow I'll be moving out of my apartment. I know this will seem pretty abrupt to you, but I've been thinking it over for a long time. I wanted to ask your advice, many times I almost did, but for some reason I couldn't. I guess I was afraid to talk about it.

Please don't worry about everything that's happened. No matter what happened or didn't happen, this is where we end up. I know this might hurt you. And I'm sorry if it does. But what I want to say is I don't want you to blame yourself, or anyone else, over me. This is really something I have to handle on my own. This past year I've just been putting it off, and I know you've suffered because of me. Perhaps that's all behind us now.

There's a nice sanatorium in the mountains near Kyoto, and I've decided to stay there for a while. It's less a hospital than a place where you're free to do what you want. I'll write you again someday and tell you more about it. Right now I just can't seem to get the words down. This is the tenth time I've rewritten this letter. I can't find the words to tell you how thankful I am to you for being with me this past year. Please believe me when I say this. I can't say anything more than that. I'll always treasure the record you gave me.

Someday, somewhere in this "precarious world" if we meet again I hope I'll be able to tell you much more than I can right now.

Good-bye.

I read her letter over a couple of hundred times, and every time I did, I was gripped by an awful sadness. The same kind of disconcerting sadness I felt when she gazed deep into my eyes. I couldn't shake that feeling. It was like the wind, formless and weightless, and I couldn't wrap it around me. Scenery passed slowly before me. People spoke, but their words didn't reach my ears.

On Saturday nights, I still sat in the same chair in the lobby. I knew a phone call wouldn't come, but I had no idea what else I should do. I turned on the TV and pretended to watch baseball games. And gazed at the indeterminate space between me and the set. I divided that space into two and again in two. I did this over and over, until I'd made a space so small it could fit in the palm of my hand.

At ten I turned off the TV, went back to my room, and went to sleep.

At the end of that month, my roommate gave me a firefly in an instant-coffee jar. Inside were some blades of grass and a bit of water. He'd punched a few tiny air holes in the lid. It was still light out, so the firefly looked more like some black bug you'd find at the beach. I peered in the jar, though, and sure enough, a firefly it was. The firefly tried to climb up the slippery side of the glass jar and slipped back down each time. It'd been a long time since I'd seen one so close up.

"I found it in the courtyard," my roommate told me. "A hotel down the road let a bunch of fireflies out as a publicity stunt, and it must have made its way over here." As he talked, he stuffed clothes and notebooks inside a small suitcase. We were already several weeks into summer vacation. I didn't want to go back home, and he'd had to go out on some fieldwork, so we were just about the only ones left in the dorm. His fieldwork was done, though, and he was getting ready to go home.

"Why don't you give it to a girl?" he added. "Girls like those things."

"Thanks, good idea," I said.

After sundown, the dorm was silent. The flag was gone, and lights came on in the windows of the cafeteria. There were just a few students left, so only half the lights were lit. The lights on the right were off; the ones on the left were on. You could catch a faint whiff of dinner. Cream stew.

I took the instant-coffee jar with the firefly and went up to the roof. The place was deserted. A white shirt someone had forgotten to take in was pinned to the clothesline, swaying in the evening breeze like some cast-off skin. I climbed the rusty metal ladder in the corner of the roof to the top of the water tower. The cylindrical water tank was still warm from the heat it had absorbed during the day. I sat down in the cramped space, leaned against the railing, and looked at the moon in front of me, just a day or two short of full. On the right, I could see the streets of Shinjuku; on the left, Ikebukurō. The headlights of the cars were a brilliant stream of light flowing from one part of the city to another. Like a cloud hanging over the streets, the city was a mix of sounds, a soft, low hum.

The firefly glowed faintly in the bottom of the jar. But its light was too weak, the color too faint. The way I remembered it, fireflies were supposed to give off a crisp, bright light that cuts through the summer darkness. This firefly might be growing weak, might even be dying, I figured. Holding the jar by its mouth, I shook it a couple of times to see. The firefly flew for a second and bumped against the glass. But its light was still dim.

Maybe the problem wasn't with the light but with my memory. Maybe fireflies' light wasn't that bright after all. Was I just imagining it was? Or maybe, when I was a child, the darkness that surrounded me was deeper. I couldn't remember. I couldn't even recall when I had last seen a firefly.

What I could remember was the dark sound of water running in the night. An old brick sluice gate, with a handle you could turn around to open or close it. A narrow stream, with plants covering the surface. All around was pitch black, and hundreds of fireflies flew above the still water. A powdery clump of yellow light blazed above the stream and shone in the water.

When was that, anyway? And where was it?

I had no idea.

Everything was mixed up, and confused.

I closed my eyes and took a few deep breaths to calm myself. If I kept my eyes shut tight, at any moment my body would be sucked into the summer darkness. It was the first time I'd climbed the water tower after dark. The sound of the wind was clearer than it had ever been. The wind wasn't blowing hard, yet strangely left a clear-cut trace as it rushed by me. Taking its time, night slowly enveloped the earth. The city lights might shine their brightest, but slowly, ever so slowly, night was winning out.

I opened the lid of the jar, took out the firefly, and put it on the edge of the water tower that stuck out an inch or two. It seemed like the firefly couldn't grasp where it was. After making one bumbling circuit of a bolt, it stretched out one leg on top of a scab of loose paint. It tried to go to the right but finding it had reached a dead end, went back to the left. It slowly clambered to the top of the bolt and crouched there for a time, motionless, more dead than alive.

Leaning against the railing, I gazed at the firefly. For a long time, the two of us sat there without moving. Only the wind, like a stream, brushed past us. In the dark, the countless leaves of the zelkovia rustled, rubbing against one another.

I waited forever.

A long time later, the firefly took off. As if remembering something, it suddenly spread its wings and, in the next instant, floated up over the railing into the gathering dark. Trying to win back lost time, perhaps, it quickly traced an arc beside the water tower. It stopped for a moment, just long enough for its trail of light to blur in the wind, then flew off toward the east.

Long after the firefly disappeared, the traces of its light remained within me. In the thick dark behind my closed eyes, that faint light, like some lost wandering spirit, continued to roam.

Again and again, I stretched my hands out toward that darkness. But my fingers felt nothing. That tiny glow was always just out of reach.

NAKAGAMI KENJI

Nakagami Kenji (1946–1992) began his life in a slum and suffered through a series of family crises, including the suicide of his older brother. He began his writing career while working in a factory, and his powerful stories of the lives of people who inhabit the ghettos of the "outcast" class, or *burakumin*, have made him one of the most consistently admired writers of his generation. Less well known, perhaps, are his stories set in historical times, which have a special mythic power that is almost unique among contemporary writers in Japan. "The Wind and the Light" (Sōmoku, 1975) reveals Nakagami's narrative force.

THE WIND AND THE LIGHT (SŌMOKU)

Translated by Andrew Rankin

He met a man in the mountains. It was deep in the hills, about an hour's walk from Odaigahara. The man was crouching down with his back against the base of a tree and breathing with great difficulty, his shoulders heaving. Broken arrows protruded from the thigh and calf of his left leg and blood was seeping from both wounds. One of his eyes was closed up with bloody pus.

The man looked up at him. He showed no surprise, as though he had always known that he would be found. He was like a wounded animal unable to hide itself any longer.

At first he wondered if the man might be a god living here in the Kumano mountains. A great one-legged, one-eyed god.

He stood in front of him.

"What happened to you?" he asked.

The man shook his head in silence.

Perhaps he was an illusion. In the mountains, people often see visions of relatives who have passed away or distant loved ones. He had seen such a vision himself. With the sound of the cicadas rasping and ringing through him, he had seen his dead brother pass right in front of him. That was real, he'd thought, a genuine vision of a human soul.

"What happened to you?" he asked again.

"I got wounded, didn't I?" the man said savagely, and glared at him with a look that seemed to say: Make one false move and I'll tear your throat out.

He knelt down in front of him and offered him the water bottle he kept hanging at his waist. The man gave him another hard glare and then snatched the bottle from his hand. He removed the cork with his teeth and drank. The water spilled from his lips and ran down his chin and neck. Some drops fell on the hairs on his chest through a rip in his tattered and muddied clothes. But it wasn't a rip, he realized. The man was wearing a thick tunic, tied at the front like a judo suit.

He certainly was a strange-looking creature. It was hard to know whether he was human or animal.

The man drank until the bottle was empty, then handed it back. He gave a deep sigh. He tried to rise, but lurched so hard that he stepped on his own wounded foot. Blood spurted out. Putting his back against the tree, he then straightened his legs and stood up. The man was taller than him, he noticed.

The sound of cicadas in the distance. The damp scent of cedar.

"I lost," said the man. His manner had changed since accepting the water. Now he sounded ashamed of his injuries. He shook his head as though his blind eye was bothering him, and pressed his hand to it. "I lost. They beat me good an' proper. It's the end for me," he said. Then he laughed,

"Which way are you headed?" he asked the man. "Are you going to Ise, or back to a village in Kumano?"

"Where would I be going to? There *is* no place for me to go," said the man, shaking his head. "You just tell me where it is and I'll go there. Don't mind where."

The man managed to take one step but wobbled on the next.

He extended his arm as support. The man angrily resisted but then fell down, landing on his backside and knocking his head against the tree. He put an arm around the fellow's waist to help him up. This time he didn't refuse, and meekly allowed himself to be lifted to his feet.

The man stank like an animal. Or was that what people actually smelled like? He remembered the time he'd been hospitalized after catching his leg under a crate at work. Unable to take a wash, it wasn't long before his head, his belly, and his crotch began to stink like a beast.

With the man's arm around his shoulders they made their way together through the trees. Shortly they came out onto a ridge. The cliffside undergrowth shimmered a strident green in the glare of the sun. He heard the man's breathing, a short wheeze following each injection of air into his lungs. He sat him down on a patch of rocky ground.

A gang of crows came swirling up from below the ridge.

The man looked at him.

"Might as well leave me here and be on your way," he said glumly. "Or maybe you'd do me the favor of throwing me off this here cliff?"

He assumed the man felt bitter about not being able to walk by himself. From where he stood he could see the mountains stretching away. There seemed to be no end to them. He knew they had two more mountains to cross before they would find a place with hot water. Given time to sit here and think about it, the man's resentment at being rescued by a complete stranger would only increase. He decided not to waste any more time.

"Let's get going," he said. He lifted the man to his feet and they made their hazardous way down the path that led from the cliffs until they found themselves in another grove of tall cedars. Soon the cliffs were lost behind them.

The hum of the cicadas was punctuated by the breathing of the two men as they pressed on through the trees.

The man kept rubbing his blind eye.

It reminded him suddenly of the pet birds he'd left behind in Tokyo. Just for a moment, it seemed as though they were the illusion.

He'd noticed it just before coming back to Kumano for his brother's memorial service. One of the finches that had left the nest that spring was blind. He had no idea what caused it. Possibly a lack of nutrition while it was a chick, or maybe a stroke of genetic bad luck, with recessive genes just happening to coincide, resulting in this blind finch also being white all over. And yet its father had the usual black-and-white speckles and was as fit as a fiddle. He wondered whether it might be something to do with inbreeding. He'd bought the birds in the pet section of a department store. Later he found out that males and females sold in the same shop often come from the same parents. That gave him a bad feeling. What was he supposed to do? After all, they were just birds, not people. Keeping a blind bird as a pet wouldn't be much fun. And anyway, they were only Bengal finches, not especially pretty to look at or to listen to. Their strong point was that they were as tough as weeds. They were perfectly happy just cheeping and flying about and weren't bothered by a bit of hardship. If there was a nest box available they laid eggs and raised the chicks and three months after hatching the chicks were grown up.

The blind albino finch was perched on the wire netting. Should he kill it? He gave it a poke. When he touched its beak it scurried out of reach. He'd lost count of how many finches he had altogether. The cage he'd built specially for them was three feet high and three feet wide and the perch inside was crowded to the limit. The blind bird wasn't strong enough to shove its way in with the others. It fell straight down and landed, quite by luck, on the food tray. Its eyeballs were a cloudy white.

It was a beautiful little finch.

It perched a second time on the netting and just sat there dopily as though it was looking at something. After a while it turned and fluttered down to the food tray. It pecked at the food and drank some water and then flew up and perched on the netting again. It repeated this routine endlessly.

He kept wondering if he should kill it, pretend it had never existed.

He slipped his hand inside the cage. The finches panicked and scattered. Three sides of the cage were boarded up with planks and when the birds slammed into them they fell spiraling down. Others hid behind the nest boxes.

The blind bird was in one corner of the cage. It extended its neck and peered cautiously around, ready to take off at any second. He snatched it up in his massive hand. The finch made frantic efforts to flap its wings, as though it knew it had been caught by something vastly bigger than itself. It wriggled vigorously as it tried to escape. The glare of the sun lay on it.

He began to squeeze.

The little finch struggled. If he squeezed any further he would crush its frail bones and it would die. He'd killed some of the budgerigars like that before. They were the weakest. He kept on buying new ones and they just kept on dying. They'd be full of energy when he left for work in the morning, but by the time he got back their feathers would be puffed up and they'd be tottering about, unable to climb onto the perch. He tried everything. He warmed the cage. He forced medicine down their throats. He kept the cage by his bedside at night, and heard the birds' wings tapping the sides of the cage as they made unsuccessful attempts to fly. At some point he would fall asleep. When he awoke, the birds would be dead. He couldn't bear to watch them vomiting all the time and in obvious pain, so he ended up crushing the life out of them with his bare hands. It wasn't exactly euthanasia. He just didn't want to have to watch them suffer. It was enough that human beings, with their human knowledge, their self-awareness, should suffer. But the blind finch he held in his hand now was too small for that, too indifferent to its own blindness. He put it back in the cage.

He was a big man. To others, he didn't look like the sort who would be interested in raising finches. Seeing him looking after these fragile creatures with his great rough hands, people often said he was like the "gentle giant" in the fairy tale. There was something funny, something eccentric, about a man his size taking care of little birds and their nests. It was almost heartwarming. At least, it would have been if the birds weren't plagued by death and deformity.

The blind finch sat on the edge of the food tray. It didn't try to eat. It just sat there, its neck extended, its wings tucked tightly against its body, gazing at him with its sad white eyes as though it were praying to something, calling to something. The healthy birds jostled for room on the perch or gripped the netting. The blind albino finch stayed in the center, the others darting wildly around it, pecking at the food and drinking the water, as if some magnetic force were given out by the white bird's feathers.

At one time, he had tried separating Goldcrests into two cages: one for males only, and one mixed. The mixed cage had one male and four females in it. He knew they were laying eggs, but he thought, what's the point, and he left them there. They were such cowardly birds. One sound would send the whole cage into a commotion. He glued paper over the netting so that they couldn't see outside, but it made no difference. One sound was all it took. The birds erupted into a wild frenzy. The chicks they'd spent such a long time rearing were kicked out of the nest or trampled on. The chicks died.

So many had died that way. They looked like hairy caterpillars. Others fell and died with flecks of blood on their heads. When he cleaned out the mixed cage with the five birds in it he removed all the eggs. He tossed a couple straight into the garbage can without even bothering to crack them open. He picked up another. Might as well take a look, he thought. He cracked the shell. He saw red flesh wriggling inside. He gasped.

The beat of a tiny heart, exposed to the open air, twitched in the palm of his hand.

He hadn't meant to kill it. It was a mistake. Just a mistake.

Forgive me. Buddha, god, whoever you are, forgive this wretched sinner. Forgive me for what I've done to this naked, skinless lump of life.

Never had he felt the light of the sun so strongly on him. It seemed to burn him, scorching his body as though it was his own life that had been laid bare. His own life, squirming, pulsating, exposed to the sun and the air.

He had broken eggs accidentally like that four times before. Of course, even if they had hatched, the chicks might have been blind or deformed. But he felt he was sharing the experience of the falconer in the *Hosshin-shū* who looks on helplessly as a living thing appears from the belly of a dog he has fed to his hawk, a life too young to have grown fur, something made up only of red skin and flesh. It was not the blood that horrified him, nor the red flesh. It was the life itself, the small, squirming, immaculate life formed in the darkness of its mother's belly, that horrified him.

The sound of the cicadas swept over him in waves. He heard the man's sharp breath, and his own, like tens of thousands of people inhaling and exhaling. The man weighed heavily on his shoulder as he carried him along. Beads of sweat trickled into his eyes.

He began to feel as if he was the one being led through the mountains by this man. It was his eye that was sightless, his leg that was injured.

The dense cedars continued endlessly. The sun was directly above, but the light was obscured by canopies of branches.

I was the one born blind. I was the one hidden in a darkness that was abruptly shattered and exposed to the sun. It was me, my flesh, squirming in the light.

Shakily, he walked on.

Passing around a patch of bare rocks he came across a spring. A grassy slope descended gently away from him. He let the injured man down by the water.

"Just leave me here," said the man. "Why d'you try and help me?"

He didn't answer. He took a sip from the bubbling spring and poured water over his head and onto his chest. Forgetting himself for a moment, he lay down on his stomach and thrust his head under the flow and splashed the water over himself again and again.

The man was wheezing badly. He filled the bottle with spring water and offered it to him, but the man only groaned and shook his head. His chest was pumping.

He emptied the bottle over the man's head. He took the towel he kept tucked into his belt, soaked it in the spring and wiped the man's dusty face, taking care not to touch the clotted blood in his left eye. Then he soaked the towel again and wiped the man's belly and armpits.

"Thank you."

The man reminded him of someone. But who?

He dipped the towel again in water and wiped the area around the broken arrows embedded in the man's leg. The arrowheads were sunk in too deep to be pulled out by hand and both shafts had snapped off. He needed a doctor quickly or it would be too late. But they were still not even halfway over the first mountain.

What had happened? Who could have done this to him?

A solitary kite circled above. There was no sound.

"Right, let's get going," he said.

The man refused to move. The cicadas started to rasp. The man's left eye was blind, his left leg lame. He let out an anguished cry.

Leave me here. Here, sitting in the grass, motionless. Wounds fester and the body grows feverish. Every brush of the wind is agony. Then life ends. The body rots. The crows flock around the corpse. They pluck out the eyes and rip the belly and peck at the flesh. Then they vanish into the sky.

He helped the man to his feet. He set off again, taking the man's weight on his shoulder. But it wasn't him who was walking now: it was one red, shapeless, squirming thing helping another piece of wounded, squirming flesh.

He thought of nothing. He felt nothing.

They made their way down along the line of the cliffs, climbing over damp, mossy rocks and following the faded traces of the mountain path. Now the man seemed almost weightless. The sounds of human breathing had multiplied. He heard a huge number of them, all panting and wheezing, hundreds of pieces of living flesh moving together, the fit assisting the wounded. They were behind him, too. He could hear them all.

The man moaned.

They descended a slope and were soon engulfed by trees again. There was no light. The sun seemed to have been swallowed up by the sky.

Suddenly the man burst into tears.

"Kill me, kill me here!" he cried. "I beg you, kill me!" His voice quavered like a broken flute. "I don't know who you are, sir. But I'm blind and lame. Strangle me, bash my head against a tree, crush my skull with a stone, but for god's sake kill me!"

He set the man down at the foot of a cedar with his back resting against the trunk and tried to calm him. The man extended his sickly colored left leg, bent his right knee, curled up like a spring and struck the back of his head hard against the tree trunk. Then he tried to turn himself about on his knees, but lost his balance and fell over sideways.

"Look at me, I can't even die by myself," he wailed, opening his mouth wide. All his lower teeth were missing.

"Who gave you these wounds?" he asked.

But the man made no reply. He lay on his side and covered his face with his hands to stifle his tears. Had one of the villagers attacked him? Or were his injuries sustained in some ancient battle? Could he be the spirit of some warrior of old, vanquished in battle? He didn't know what to think. He still wasn't sure whether the man was real or imaginary.

If the man had been defeated, then so had he.

If the man had suffered, then so had he.

The big man's cries echoed through the mountains, the volume magnified many times over. Each of these mountains resounded with the voice of this vanquished, one-eyed, one-legged man who was incapable of taking his own life.

He sensed his own body responding to the sound like a musical instrument. He sat down beside him, leaned back against the tree, and listened.

To the treetops quivering and rustling.

To the grasses, drooping from lack of sunlight, shivering in sympathy.

To the cicadas joining in, weeping together.

The whole landscape weeping with him.

For a while he wanted to stay right there. Just to sit and listen, and sense his body, like the red flesh he'd found inside the egg, breaking through and bearing life. There at the very origin of life itself: in that darkness, that light. Mute, deaf, and blind. Unfeeling, unthinking. A vast darkness.

His own bones vibrating to the man's misery, he tucked in his arms and legs and curled up like a seed buried in the earth. There, in that dense grove, amid the moist air and the tears and the scent of cedar, he knew something inside him was changing, and he felt himself lifted up on the wind like spore from the ferns.

He cried with the man, then slept. He woke and cried again.

Are you my brother?

Again, he slept.

It was me. I was the one who blinded him, crippled him, took away his power even to kill himself. It was me. And yet, what am I? Just a lump of flesh, a shape that's come to life?

Then he saw it.

They were holding the memorial service at his mother's house in Kumano. Everyone in the room was kneeling in front of the family altar. They looked so small, with their shoulders hunched forward. The priest was chanting phrases from the sutras and the people attending, many of them friends from the neighborhood, responded in chorus: "*Namu Amida-butsu, Namu Amida-butsu.*" His mother was sitting immediately behind the priest. Beside her were his three sisters, who had traveled from different parts of the country to attend the service. He was there too, sitting with his stepfather and his stepfather's son. Candle flames flickered red and yellow on the altar. The service had already begun.

He was there, in his mother's house, listening to the incomprehensible sutras and murmuring along with everyone else: "*Namu Amida-butsu, Namu Amida-butsu.*" The chanting stopped. The priest burned some incense.

But surely *that* was the illusion? In reality, wasn't he here in the mountains? Yes, he was here, trembling at the sound of a man's cries. Trembling, crying, sleeping, and crying.

He watched his mother. A recent coronary thrombosis had left her face dark and swollen. She repeated the words of the chant and offered a sprinkle of incense.

He wouldn't worry about the man any more. Or about his brother. He didn't care about himself. All he wanted was for his mother to be allowed to die peacefully, like a blade of grass that quietly fades and withers.

Wisps of smoke were rising from the box of incense. His mother handed the box to his sisters and one by one they made their offerings. He did it too. The priest resumed his chanting.

Suddenly it came back to him. His brother, younger then than he himself was now, had sat before this altar for nearly an hour chanting a different kind of sutra. He remembered him saying: "I'm the one who has to go." In the morning they found him dead. He had hanged himself.

After I die, everything will be all right again.

Now, sounding like shamans calling up the dead, his mother and his sisters would mention his brother's name whenever they had a chance. They looked like his blind finch. And since then, just the sight of him seemed to remind them of his brother, as though the two of them had become Siamese twins.

The man had stopped crying. The sun was starting to sink and it was growing cold, but the damp air was still pleasant. The man was leaning against a tree stump and breathing quietly. It felt strange to think that, until moments earlier, his own flesh and bones had been vibrating to the sound of this man's cries.

"One more hour and we'll reach the river," he said. "If we follow that, it'll take us to a village."

"I don't want any more help," replied the man. "Please, either kill me or leave me here."

"But, who *are* you?" he asked.

The man laughed weakly. "What does it matter who I am? I'm just a beggar roaming the hills, a leper. I haven't got a name."

"But I want to help you."

"Then you're a fool!" The man's voice echoed through the darkness. The sun had dropped completely out of sight and the outline of the trees, vaguely visible until just before, had vanished. Drops of moisture were falling steadily from the leaves of the trees.

The man pleaded with him. "I can't bear it, the thought of having to live like this for years and years. Just kill me, will you!" He gave a sudden start. "D'you hear that? They're calling me again, from the village."

Yes, he heard them. Voices of men and women, young and old, calling and calling. And the mountains all rustling together with the waves of voices. The trees shaking and the grasses around his feet stirring restlessly. The ground itself seemed to be moving, making a hollow sound. Suddenly he found it hard to breathe.

"Those voices, they're the reason I can't sleep at night," said the man.

He listened.

It was the voices of his mother and sisters that he heard.

"Go home," said the man. "Go and tell them to forget about me. Tell them to stop blaming themselves. There's no point in Mother grieving now. Our sisters are married, they should be happy. There's no reason for them to suffer. I didn't hang myself to cause them pain, I did it to make them happy. They must forget about me and enjoy their lives."

"But your own pain—your eye, your leg . . ."

"That doesn't matter," came the sharp reply. "You're a grown man now, so I'm asking you—kill me."

He heard his older sister's voice calling to the man: Do you remember me?

He heard his mother crying: The day you hanged yourself they carried you into the house, and when I looked at your face I saw the trickle of blood from your nose. You were such a beautiful boy! Why did you have to die so young? It was my fault for deserting you. I was to blame for everything.

"Here, let me help you," he said. He rose to his feet and reached for the man's arm. "I don't want your help." The man pulled away from him.

The trees trembled and swished. The man let out a harsh cry of pain like a wild animal.

Just then, he thought he sensed someone abruptly stand up beside him and walk away through the trees, crunching on the ground. His mother's voice wafted up again: You were so beautiful. Why did you have to die?

The man roared on and on.

"Forget your brother! I should never have been brought into this world! Forget me!"

As he listened to him roaring out in pain, the image of that tiny, red, wriggling body returned to his mind. A pure, innocent, living thing, knowing nothing, understanding nothing, writhing in the wind and the light. Could that have been his brother reborn?

"Go home and tell Mother. There's no reason for her to suffer. Forget me. Her health is poor, what good is it for her to go on torturing herself, counting the years since her child died? I hear her crying, I hear my little sisters crying. There's no need for them to mourn, they'll spoil their looks. They should get on with their lives, give themselves body and soul to their husbands, and forget their dead brother. Tell them, please, to *live*."

Tears welled up in his eyes. Here he was, sitting on the roots of a cedar in the icy darkness, talking to a brother who died over ten years ago! Had his wounded brother been hiding in the mountains all these years, unable to meet death face to face?

After the memorial service, he'd returned to Tokyo and found the blind finch dead. It had caught its leg in one of the nests in the cage and shriveled to a pulp.

It looked as though it might actually have starved itself to death. He unraveled the thread that was around its leg and placed the bird in the palm of his hand.

He stared at it for a few moments, dry and shriveled and dead.

Now the light of the sun on it seemed strangely kind.

ŌE KENZABURŌ

Although Ōe Kenzaburō (b. 1935) is a thoroughly contemporary writer, in some ways he also represents the last of Japan's long line of intellectually and politically liberal writers. Ōe's writing is powerful, often difficult, and always a critique of the conservative status quo. Some of his better-known novels are available in English, including *A Personal Matter* (*Kojinteki no taiken*, 1964) and *The Silent Cry* (*Man'en gannen no futtobōru*, 1974), as well as newer works like *An Echo of Heaven* (*Jinsei no shinseki*, 1989). Even today, Ōe continues to speak out on a number of important national and international issues. In 1994 he received the Nobel Prize for Literature, and his acceptance speech is the last selection in this volume of the anthology.

"Teach Us to Outgrow Our Madness" (*Kyōki no ikinoboru michi o oshieyo*, 1969) is a shorter work that has long been admired for many of the qualities that made Ōe such a powerful spokesperson for his generation.

TEACH US TO OUTGROW OUR MADNESS
(KYŌKI NO IKINOBORU MICHI O OSHIEYO)

Translated by John Nathan

In the winter of 196—, an outlandishly fat man came close to being thrown to a polar bear bathing in a filthy pool below him and had the experience of very nearly going mad. As a result, the fat man was released from the fetters of an old obsession, but the minute he found himself free a miserable loneliness rose in him and withered his already slender spirit. Thereupon he resolved, for no logical reason (he was given to fits of sudden agitation), to cast off still another heavy restraint; he vowed to free himself entirely and let the sky tilt if need be, and when he had taken his oath and a reckless courage was boiling in his body, still scaly and stinking of rotten sardines from the splash of the rock which had been thrown into the pool finally in his place, he telephoned his mother in the middle of the night and said to her,

"You give me back the manuscript you stole from me, I'm fed up, do you hear! I've known all along what you were up to."

The fat man knew his mother was standing at the other end of the line eight hundred miles away with the old-fashioned receiver in her hand. He even concluded unscientifically that he could hear the whisper of breathing into the other phone as distinctly as he did because no one was near the circuits due to the lateness of the hour, and since this happened to be his mother's breathing, the fat man felt his chest constrict. As a matter of fact, what he was hearing through the receiver he had pressed against his ear, delicate out of all proportion to the massiveness of his head, was his own breath.

"If you won't give me back what's mine, that's all right too!" the fat man shouted in growing anger, having realized his small mistake. "I'll write another biography of Father that's even more revealing, I'll tell the whole world how the man went mad and shut himself up all those years and then let out a roar one day and died where he sat in his chair. And you can interfere all you like, it won't do you any good!" Again the fat man stopped and listened for a reaction at the other end of the line, careful this time to cover the phone with his thick hand. When he heard the receiver being replaced, calmly and for that reason the more adamantly, he went pale as a young girl and returned trembling to his bed, curled up in a ball, pulled the covers over his head despite the stench of the pool, which made him gag, and sobbed in rage. It wasn't only his mother; the loneliness of the freedom he had acquired that morning at the zoo had quite intimidated him, and so he cried in the stinking darkness beneath the covers where he could be certain he was unobserved. It was rage, and terror, and his overwhelming sense of isolation that made the fat man cry, as if the polar bear immersed to its shoulders in brown, icy water had gripped his bulky head in its freezing jaws. Before long the fat man's tears had wet the sheets all around him, so he rolled over, curled up again, and continued to sob. He was able to enjoy this particular freedom, minor but not to be despised, because for several years he had been sleeping alone in the double bed he once had shared with his wife.

While the fat man cried himself to sleep that night, his mother, in the village of his birth, was steeling herself for a final battle against her son. Thus the fat man had no reason to weep, at least not out of the frustration of having had his challenge ignored yet another time. As a child, whenever he began to question her about his father's self-confinement and sudden death, his mother has closed the road to communication by pretending to go mad. It reached a point where the fat man would affect madness himself before his mother had a chance, smashing everything in reach and even tumbling backward off the stone wall at the edge of the garden and down the briary slope. But even at times like these, his sense of victory was tiny and essentially futile: he never managed to make contact. Ever since, for close to twenty years, the tension of a showdown between two gunmen on a movie set had sustained itself between them—who would be first to affect madness and so to win an occult victory?

But late that night, the situation began to change. The very next morning the fat man's mother, resolved on new battle regulations, took to the printer in a neighboring town an announcement she had drafted during the night and had it mailed, registered mail, to the fat man's brothers and sisters, their husbands and wives, and all the family relatives. The announcement which arrived care of the fat man's wife and marked Personal in red ink, but of a nature which obliged her to show it to her husband, read as follows:

> Our flirt whore has lost his mind, but it should be known his madness is not hereditary. It pains me to inform you that, while abroad, he contracted the Chinese chancres. In order to avoid infection, it is hoped you will abstain from further commerce with him.
>
> Signed
winter, 196—

But how much gloomier
  The garden
Seen from the orphanage toilet—
  Age thirty-four!

Uchida Hyakken

Unfortunately, the significance of this text was clearest to the only member of the family who depended on language for a living, the fat man himself. With her pun on his age (he was thirty-four) his mother had tried to shame him, and by adding the verse about the orphanage toilet (he wasn't clear if it was really by the poet Hyakken) she had even insinuated that he was not her real son: the announcement was the product of its author's overriding hatred, a vexatious hatred which no one in the family was equipped so adequately to feel as the fat man himself. One thing was certain, there was no doubting the blood bond between them: like the fat man himself and like his son, her grandson, his mother was fatter than fat. The fat man was confident his wife would not suspect him of carrying a disease he had brought home from the Occident; even so, when he considered that the local printer must have read the announcement and when he pictured it being delivered into the hands of all his friends and relatives, he submerged in a terrible gloom. The effect of which was to impress on him the importance, not to his son perhaps but certainly to his own well-being, of the heavy bond of restraints which (so he had believed) had united himself and the child formerly. The trouble was, ever since his harrowing experience at the zoo, the fat man had doubted the very existence of these restraints and even suspected that his own desire to create and maintain them had led him to repeated feats of self-deception. Besides, once gained, his freedom was like an adhesive tape which could not be peeled away from his hand or heart.

He could not return to what had been. Until that day when it seemed he would be thrown to the polar bear and he was on the verge of losing his mind, the fat man had wandered around, sprawled on the floor, and eaten all his meals together with his son, allowing nothing to separate them. And this permitted him a perfectly concrete sense of the child as primarily a heavy and troublesome restraint which menaced, even as it regulated, his daily life. In truth, he enjoyed thinking of himself as a passive victim quietly enduring a bondage imposed by his son.

The fat man had always liked children; in college he had qualified for three kinds of teaching licenses. And as the time approached for his own child to be born he was unable to sit still for the spasms of anxiety and expectation which rippled through his body. Later, looking back, he had the feeling he had been counting on the birth of his child as a first step toward a new life for himself which would be out of the shadow of his dead father. But when the moment finally arrived and the fat man, painfully thin in those days, nervously questioned the doctor who emerged from the delivery room, he was told in an even voice that his child had been born with a grave defect.

"Even if we operate I'm afraid the infant will either die or be an idiot, one or the other."

That instant, something inside the fat man irreparably broke. And the baby who was either to die or to be an idiot quickly elbowed out of the breakage, as cancer destroys and then replaces normal cells. In arranging for the operation the fat man dashed around so frantically that his own in those days still meager body might well have broken down. His nervous system was like a chaos of numbness and hypersensitivity, and an inflamed wound which had begun to heal but only in spots: fearfully he would touch places in himself and feel no pain at all; a moment later, when relief had lowered his guard, a scorching pain would make him rattle.

The deadline for registering the new infant arrived, and the fat man went to the ward office. But until the girl at the desk asked what it was to be, he hadn't even considered a name for his son. At the time the operation was in progress, his baby was in the process of being required to decide whether he would die or be an idiot, one or the other. Could such an existence be given a name?

The fat man (let it be repeated that at the time, exhausted, he was thinner than ever in his life) took the registration form nonetheless and, recalling from the Latin vocabulary he had learned at college a work which should have related both to death and idiocy, wrote down the character for "forest" and named his son Mori. Then he took the form into the bathroom, sat down in one of the stalls, and began to giggle uncontrollably. This ignoble seizure was due in part to the state of the fat man's nerves at the time. And yet even as a child there had been something inside him, something fundamental, which now and then impelled him to frivolous derision of his own and others' lives. And this was something he was obliged to recognize in himself when his son finally left the hospital and came to live at home. Mori!—every time he called the child by name it seemed to him that he could hear, in the profound darkness in his head, his own lewd and unrepentant laughter mocking the entirety of his life. So he proposed giving his son a nickname and using it at home, though he had difficulty satisfying his wife with a reason. It was in this way that the fat man, borrowing the name of the misanthropic donkey in Winnie the Pooh, came to call his son Eeyore.

He moreover concluded, with renewed conviction, that his relationship with his own father, who had died suddenly when he was a child, must be the source of the somehow mistaken, insincere, unbalanced quality he had to recognize in himself, and he undertook somehow to re-create a whole image of the man, whom he remembered only vaguely. This produced a new repetition of collisions with his mother, who had never spoken about his father's self-confinement and death and had combated him for years by pretending to go mad whenever he questioned her. Not only did she refuse to cooperate; during a stay at his home while he was traveling abroad she had stolen his notes and incomplete manuscript for a biography of his father and had retained them to this day. For all he knew, she had already burned the manuscript, but since the thought alone made him want to kill his mother, he had no choice but not to think it.

And yet the fat man was dependent on his mother to a degree extraordinary for an adult of his age, another truth he was obliged to recognize. Drunk one night on the whiskey he relied on instead of sleeping pills, he was toying with a clay dog he had brought all the way from Mexico when he discovered a hole beneath the creature's tail and blew into it hard, as if he were playing on a flute. Unexpectedly, a cloud of fine black dust billowed out of the hole and plastered his eyes. The fat man supposed he had gone blind, and in his distraction and his fear he called out to his mother: Mother, oh Mother, help me, please! If I should go blind and lose my mind the way Father did, what will become of my son? Teach me, mother, how we can all outgrow our madness!

For no good reason, the fat man had been seized by the suspicion that his mother soon would age and die without having disclosed the explanation she had kept secret all these years, not only for his father's self-confinement and death but the freakish something which underlay it and must also account for his own instability and for the existence of his idiot son, an existence which inasmuch as it presented itself in palpable form, he assumed he could never detach from himself.

The fat man's loneliness that night as he slept in the bed too large for even his bloated body has already been described, but the truth is that still another circumstance can be included as having contributed to it. That the fat man spent all his time in the company of his fat son Mori, called Eeyore, was known to most of the citizens in the neighborhood. What even the most curious of them did not know was that, until the decisive day when he was nearly thrown to a polar bear, the fat man had never failed to sleep with one arm extended toward his son's crib which he had installed at the head of his bed. In fact, his wife had quit his bed and secluded herself in another part of the house not so much because of strife between them as a desire of her own not to interfere with this intimacy between father and son. It had always been the fat man's intention that he was acting on a wholesome parental impulse—if his son should awaken in the middle of the night he would always be able to touch his father's fleshy hand in the darkness above his head. But now, when he examined them in light of the breakage which had resulted in himself when hoodlums had lifted him by his head

and ankles and swung him back and forth as if to hurl him to the polar bear eye-
ing him curiously from the pool below, the fat man could not help discovering,
in even these details of his life, a certain incongruity, as if a few grains of sand
had sifted into his socks. Wasn't it possible that he had slept with his arm out-
stretched so that the hand with which he groped in the darkness when uneasy
dreams threatened him awake at night might encounter at once the comforting
warmth of his son's hand? Once he had recognized the objection being raised
inside himself, the details of their life together, which to him had always seemed
to represent his bondage to his son, one by one disclosed new faces which added
to his confusion. Yet the very simplest details of their life together troubled him
only rarely with this disharmony, and in this the fat man took solace as he grew
more and more absorbed, feeling very much alone, in the battle with his mother.
The fact was, even after his experience at the zoo, that he continued to enact
certain of the daily rituals he shared with his son.

Rain or shine, not figuratively but in fact, the fat man and his son bicycled
once a day to a Chinese restaurant and ordered pork noodles in broth and
Pepsi-Cola. In the days before his son was quite so fat, the fat man would sit
him in a light metal seat which he attached to the handlebars. And how often
he had been obliged to fight with policemen who held that the metal seat was
illegal, not to mention riding double on a bike! The fat man had always pro-
tested earnestly, because he had believed his own claim. Now, when he looked
back from his new point of view, he had to wonder if he really had believed
what he had argued so vehemently, that his son was retarded (precisely because
he so loathed the word itself he always used it as a weapon against the police)
and that the only pleasure available to him, his only consolation, was climbing
into a metal seat attached to the handlebars illegally and bicycling in search of
pork noodles in broth and Pepsi-Cola. Sooner or later his son would tire of sit-
ting on a bicycle halted precariously in the middle of the street and would be-
gin to groan in displeasure, whereupon the fat man himself would raise his own
hoarse voice in the manner of a groan and increase the fervor of his argument,
with the result that the dispute generally ended with the policeman giving way.
Then, as if he had been long a victim of police oppression with regard to some
matter of grave importance, the fat man would announce to his son, staring at
the road ahead with utter indifference to his father's feverish whisper:

"Eeyore, we really showed that cop! We won, boy, that makes eighteen wins
in a row!" and pedal off triumphantly toward the Chinese restaurant.

Inside, while they waited for their pork noodles in broth, Eeyore drank his
Pepsi-Cola and the fat man raptly watched him drinking it. As prepared at the
restaurant they frequented, the dish amounted to some noodles in broth gar-
nished with mushrooms and some spinach and a piece of meat from a pork
bone fried in a thin batter. When it was finally brought to their table, the fat
man would empty two-thirds of the noodles and some of the mushrooms and
spinach into a small bowl which he placed in front of his son, carefully watch
the boy eating until the food had cooled, and only then begin to eat the pork

himself, probing with his tongue for the gristle between the batter and the meat and then disposing of the halved, white spheres, after examining them minutely, in an ashtray out of Eeyore's reach. Finally, he would eat his share of the noodles, timing himself so the two of them would finish together. Then, as he rode them home on his bike with his face flushed from the steaming noodles and burning in the wind, he would ask repeatedly,

"Eeyore, the pork noodles and the Pepsi-Cola were good?" and when his son answered,

"Eeyore, the pork noodles and Pepsi-Cola were good!" he would judge that complete communication had been achieved between them and would feel happy. Often he believed sincerely that of all the food he had ever eaten, that day's pork noodles was the most delicious.

One of the major causes of the fat man's corpulence and his son's must have been those pork noodles in broth. From time to time his wife cautioned him about this, but he prevailed in arguments at home with the same reasoning he used against the police. When his son's buttocks eventually grew too fat to fit into the metal seat, the fat man hunted up a special bicycle with a ridiculously long saddle, and propped Eeyore up in front of him when they rode off for their daily meal.

The fat man had concluded that this bicycle trip in quest of pork noodles and Pepsi-Cola was a procedure to enable his idiot son to feel, in the core of his body, the pleasure of eating. However, after his experience above the polar bears' pool, it no longer made him profoundly happy to separate the gristle from the pork rib with his tongue and inspect the shiny hemispheres; and the joy of appetite in Eeyore, eating noodles in silence at his side as always, communicated to the core of his own body as but a feeble tremor. He wondered sometimes if Eeyore's craving for pork noodles and Pepsi might not be a groundless illusion of his own, if his son had grown so fat because, pathetically, he had been eating mechanically whatever had been placed in front of him. One day when doubts like these had ruined the fat man's appetite and he had left the restaurant without even finishing his pork rib, the Chinese cook, who until then had never emerged from the kitchen, caught up with them on a bicycle which glistened with grease and inquired in a frighteningly emphatic accent whether anything was wrong with the food that day. The fat man, already so deflated that he lacked even the courage to ignore the cook, passed the question on to Eeyore and then shared the Chinaman's relief when his son intoned his answer in the usual way:

"Eeyore, the pork noodles in broth and Pepsi-Cola were good!"

By accumulating numerous procedures of this kind between himself and his son, the fat man had structured a life unique to themselves. And that the structure demanded his bondage to his idiot son long had been his secret belief. But when he reconsidered now, with his experience above the polar bears' pool behind him, he began to see that the maintenance of this extraordinary structure had been most ardently desired by himself.

Until his son began to peel from his consciousness like a scab, the fat man was convinced that he experienced directly whatever physical pain his son was feeling. When he read somewhere that the male celatius, a deep-sea fish common to Danish waters, lived its life attached like a wart to the larger body of the female, he dreamed that he was the female fish suspended deep in the sea with his son embedded in his body like the smaller male, a dream so sweet that waking up was cruel.

In the beginning no one would believe, even when they saw it happening, that the fat man suffered the same pain as his son. But in time even his most skeptical wife came to accept this as fact. It didn't begin the minute the child was born; several years had passed when the fat man suddenly awoke to it one day. Until then, for example, when his son underwent brain surgery as an infant, although the fat man caused the doctors to wonder about him queasily when he pressed them to extract from his own body for his son's transfusions a quantity of blood not simply excessive but medically unthinkable, he did not experience faintness while his son was under anesthesia, nor did he share any physical pain. The conduit of pain between the fat man and his fat son was connected unmistakably (or so it seemed, for even now the fat man found it difficult to establish whether the pain he once had felt was real or sham, and had been made to realize that in general nothing was so difficult to re-create as pain remaining only as a memory) when Eeyore scalded his foot in the summer of his third year.

When his son began to raise not simple screams as much as rash shouts of protest, the fat man was sprawled on his living room couch, reading a magazine; and although behind his eyelids, where his tears were beginning to well, he could see with surrealistic clarity, as if he were watching a film in slow motion, the spectacle of the pan filled with boiling water tilting up and tipping over, he did not rise and dash into the kitchen in aid of his son. He lay as he was submerged in a feebleness like the disembodiment that accompanies a high fever, and chorused his son's shouts with a thick moaning of his own. Yet even then it couldn't have been said that he had achieved a firm hold on physical pain. He strapped his son's heavy, thrashing body into a rusty baby carriage which he dragged out of his shed and somehow managed to secure the scalded foot. And although he groaned heavily all the way to the distant clinic as he slowly pushed the carriage past the strangers halted in the street to watch his eerie progress, he could not have said with certainty that he was actually feeling Eeyore's pain in his own flesh.

However, as he bore down against the explosive thrashing of his son's small projectile of a body so the doctor could bare and treat the blistered foot, the following question coalesced in the fat man's mind: could any conscious state be so full of fright and hurt as perceiving pain and not its cause, and perceiving pain only, because an idiot infant's murky brain could not begin to grasp the logic of a situation in which pain persisted and was apparently to go unsoothed and, as if that were not enough, a stranger stepped in officiously to inflict still another pain while even Father cooperated? That instant, the fat man began through clenched teeth to express cries of pain himself which so resembled his son's screams that they merged with them indistinguishably and could not have shocked the doctor or the nurses. His leg had actually begun to throb (he believed!) with the pain of a burn.

By the time the wound had been bandaged, the fat man himself, at the side of his pale, limp son, was too exhausted to speak. His wife, who had been in the examination room helping to hold the patient down, went home with Eeyore in a taxi, leaving the fat man to return alone down the narrow street which paralleled the railroad tracks, the rope he had used to secure his son coiled inside the empty carriage. As he walked along the fat man wondered why his wife had wrested Eeyore away from him and raced away in a taxicab. If he had put his son back in the carriage and they had returned together down this same street, had she been afraid he might have launched himself and the carriage between the used ties which had been newly erected to fence off the tracks and attempted to escape the pain which now gripped them both by throwing himself and the child beneath the filthy wheels of the commuter express? Possibly, for even if his cries had not reached the ears of the doctor and the nurses, merging with his son's screams, to his wife they must have been clearly audible; for in pinning his son's shoulders she had leaned so far over the table toward him that her head had nearly touched his own. Although he handled the empty carriage roughly, the fat man made his way down the street with excessive care, as though he were favoring a leg which had been just treated for a burn, and if he had to skip over a small puddle he produced an earnest cry of pain.

From that day on, insofar as the fat man was aware, whatever pain his son was feeling communicated to him through their clasped hands and never failed to produce in his own body a tremor of pain in unison. If the fat man was able to attach positive significance to this phenomenon of pain shared, it was because he managed to believe that his own understanding of the pain resonating sympathetically in himself, for example, as resulting from blistered and dead skin being peeled away from a burn with a tweezers, would flow backward like light through his son's hand, which he held in his own, and impart a certain order to the chaos of fear and pain in the child's dark, dulled mind. The fat man began to function as a window in his son's mind, permitting the light from the outside to penetrate to the dark interior which trembled with pain not adequately understood. And so long as Eeyore did not step forward to repudiate his function, there was no reason the fat man should have doubted it. Since now he was able to proclaim to himself that he was accepting painful bondage to his son happily, his new role even permitted him the consolation of feeling like an innocent victim.

Shortly after Eeyore's fourth birthday, the fat man took him for an eye examination at a certain university hospital. No matter who the eye specialist, examining an idiot child who never spoke at all except to babble something of little relevance in a severely limited vocabulary, or to utter noises in response to pain or simple pleasure, would certainly prove a difficult, vexatious task. And this young patient was not only fat and heavy, and therefore difficult to hold, he was abnormally strong in his arms and legs, so that once fear had risen in him he was as impossible to manage as a frightened animal.

The fat man's wife, having noticed right away something distinctively abnormal about Eeyore's sight, and having speculated in a variety of amateur ways on the possible connections to his retardation, long had wanted a specialist to examine his eyes. But at every clinic he had visited, the fat man had been turned away. Finally, he went to see the brain surgeon who had enabled the child whose alternatives were death or idiocy to escape at least from death, and managed to obtain a letter of introduction to the department of ophthalmology at the same university hospital.

The family went to the hospital together, but at first his wife left the fat man in the waiting room and went upstairs alone with Eeyore. Half an hour later, dragging her heavy, shrieking son and obviously exhausted, she staggered back. The examination had scarcely begun, and already the doctor, the nurses, even his wife was prostrate, while Eeyore himself presented a picture of such cruel abuse that the other patients were looking on in dismay. The fat man, furious to see his son in such a state, and menaced, understood why his wife had left him in the waiting room and gone upstairs alone with Eeyore. There was no longer room for doubt that a thorough examination of a child's eyes was an uninterrupted ordeal, rife with some kind of grotesque and virulent terror.

Eeyore was still producing at the back of his throat something like the echo of a feeble scream when the fat man dropped to his knees on the dirty floor and embraced his pudgy body. The hand which Eeyore wound around his neck was moist with the sweat of fear, like the pads on the foot of a cat that had tasted danger. And the touch of his hand infused the fat man with the essence of his son's entire experience during the thirty minutes past (so he believed at the time). Every hollow and rise of the fat man's body was possessed by an aching numbness that followed thirty long minutes in the spiny clamps of medical instruments he had never actually seen: had not Eeyore quieted gradually in his arms until now he was only whimpering, he might have raised a terrific scream and begun writhing on the floor himself.

Unique in his household for her excessive leanness, the fat man's provident wife had taken the precaution of stopping downstairs in hopes of preventing the two of them, himself and his son, from behaving in just this lunatic way.

"They must have been horrible to him," the fat man moaned, sighing hoarsely. "What the hell did they think he is, the bastards!"

It was Eeyore who was horrible: he kept kicking the doctors and the nurses away, one after the other, and he broke all kinds of things, said the fat man's wife. It wasn't that she always tried for fairness or objectivity so much as that she refused to participate in the fat man's paranoia. The fat man listened to her sighing now, mournfully angry at her violent son, and felt that he was included in her attack.

"No, there must have been something wrong basically, otherwise Eeyore wouldn't have been so wild. Think how gentle he always is! And you said the examination had just begun—then how did Eeyore know there was something so bad in store for him that he had to fight that way? There has to be something fundamentally wrong, I mean with the eye department here, and you just missed it, that's all," the fat man said rapidly, forestalling his wife's almost certainly accurate rebuttal and beginning to believe, because he was insisting on it, that there was indeed something wrong with the hospital. He even established arbitrary grounds for the judgment: his son, who had finished rubbing the back of his neck with his sweaty palm and was simply moaning softly at his side, had communicated it to him telepathically.

"I'm going to take Eeyore back up there. We may not be able to get a diagnosis, but at least I'll see what they're doing wrong," the fat man rasped, his round face an angry red. "Otherwise it will be the same business all over again, no matter how many times you come back, and Eeyore's experience here will haunt him like the memory of an awful nightmare without ever making any sense to him!"

"It won't take Eeyore long to forget about it—he's nearly forgotten already."

"That's nonsense, Eeyore won't forget. Do you know that he's been crying a lot in the middle of the night recently? It's frightening enough just that Eeyore's frightened, can you stand to think of him having nightmares he can't make any sense of?"

With this the fat man decisively silenced his wife, who did not sleep in her son's room at night. He then swung Eeyore on to his shoulders with the same emphaticness and marched up the stairs toward the examination room, the dirt from the floor still on his coat. Being able to parade the truth this way, that the existence essential to his pudgy son was not his mother but himself, inspired the fat man with a courage close to gallantry. At the same time, the prospect of the cruel ordeal the two of them might have to undergo left him pale and dizzy, and at each breathless step he climbed his head flashed hot and his body shook with chill.

"Eeyore! we have to keep a sharp watch, you and I, to see they don't put anything over on us," said the fat man, lifting his voice in an appeal to the warm and heavy presence on his shoulders which sometimes felt, to his confusion, more like his guardian spirit that his ward.

"Eeyore, if we can finish this up together, we'll go out for some pork noodles and Pepsi-Cola!"

"Eeyore, the pork noodles and Pepsi-Cola were good!" his fat son lazily replied, satisfied to be riding on his father's shoulder and seemingly liberated from the memory of his experience a while ago.

This seemed to testify to the accuracy of his wife's prediction, and if the fat man had not been spurred by his son's voice he would certainly have lost his courage at the entrance to the examination room and returned meekly as he had come. For not only was a young nurse bolting the door which she had just closed, with the unmistakable intention of locking further patients out, the clock having stuck noon, but when she turned and saw the child riding on the fat man's shoulders a look of panic and protest came over her face, as if she were reencountering a ghost she had finally managed to be rid of, and she scurried behind the door to hide. The fat man, counting on the elitism of a university hospital, announced unbidden and as pretentiously as possible that he had been referred by a certain Professor of Medicine, and named the brain surgeon. The nurse didn't answer him directly; it was unlikely she even considered chasing away by herself the large, fat man who had planted himself in front of the office without even lowering his son from his shoulders. Instead, leaving the door half open, she ran back inside to a dark corner which was curtained off at the rear of the room and began some kind of appeal.

For just a minute, the fat man hesitated. Then he stepped over the lowered bolt and strode to the back of the room, where he encountered a shrill voice protesting behind the curtain in what sounded like uncontainable anger.

"No, no, no! Absolutely not! It would take every man in the building to hold down that little blimp. What's that? He's here already? I don't care if he is, the answer is No!"

This was a point for the fat man's side. With calm to spare, he slowly lowered Eeyore to the floor. Then he thrust his large head inside the curtain and discovered a doctor so diminutive that he looked in his surgical gown like a child dressed up in grownup clothes, arching backward in the dimness right under his nose a tiny head that recalled a praying mantis as he shouted at the disconcerted nurse. The fat man took a long, brazen look, then said with stunning politeness, "I was referred here by Professor of Medicine X. Could we possibly try again, perhaps I can help?"

So the examination began. How can you refuse when the patient's enormous parent interrupts you with that deadly politeness in the middle of shrieking at your nurse? seemed to be the question smoldering in the praying mantis's head as, peevishly ignoring the fat man, he began his examination by shining a pencil light in Eeyore's eyes. It was to increase the efficiency of this tiny bulb that half the room was kept in shrouded darkness. The fat man crouched uncomfortably in the narrow space behind the swivel chair, his arms locked around Eeyore's chest. It made him proud to think that the boy was sitting in the chair at all, although his body was straining backward and continued to shudder, because it was himself, who invariably stayed with his son through the night, who was holding him around the chest. Thirty minutes ago, not realizing that Eeyore's fear of the dark could not be overcome unless it was directed through the conduit between father and son, his wife and the doctor and these nurses must have driven the boy to the desperation of a small animal at bay in this same stage of the examination. But this time, he was able to think with satisfaction, the fat man had observed himself that the darkness in this room was not particularly frightening, and the essence of his judgment had been transmitted to Eeyore through the pressure of his hands and was lowering one by one the danger flags flapping in the boy's dim mind.

Even so, Eeyore was afraid of the pencil light itself and refused to look in the direction the doctor desired, straight into its tiny beam. By tossing his head from side to side and watching out of the corner of his eye, he continued to evade the agitated pursuit of the pencil light in the little doctor's hand. Presently, the young nurse stepped in to help, probably hoping to redeem herself with the doctor. *Garuk! Garuk!* The fat man heard an odious noise and felt Eeyore's body contract with anxiety, and when he looked up in reproof he saw a hair-raising rubber frog, coated with phosphorescent paint which made it gleam in the dark, dancing back and forth in the nurse's hand and croaking horribly, *garuk, garuk, garuk,* as she attempted to attract the patient's attention. The fat man, more in response to the formidable protest rising from his own bowels than to stop the nurse for his son's sake, was about to utter something angrily when Eeyore succumbed to total panic, began to rotate around the axis of his father's arms, and kicked to the floor not only the doctor's pencil light and the rubber frog in the nurse's hand but a variety of objects on a small table diagonally in front of him. Even as he gave vent to a moan of rage in secret chorus with his son the fat man saw in a flash that Eeyore had brought clattering to the floor, in addition to several large books, a bowl of rice and fried eel which seemed to be the doctor's lunch. And from the abnormally rapid pitch of the examination after this, it was impossible to avoid the impression that the little doctor was indeed provoking his intractable patient, and out of anger which derived at least in part from hunger unappeased. This permitted them—the composite of his son and himself—to sample the pleasure of retaliation. At the same time, it was the basis for a very grave fear. Here was a doctor tired and hungry after a full morning of appointments, and now his lunch was in ruins, yet he lacked the courage openly to revile this idiot boy and his corpulent father who flaunted a letter of introduction from Professor of Medicine X—how could the fat man be sure the little man couldn't work some subtle vengeance on his son's eyes? The new terror was accompanied by regret; the fat man withered.

The doctor loudly assembled his entire staff, and when the young patient had been stretched out on a bare, black leather bed, he gave triumphant instructions that all hands were to help to hold the boy down (the fat man just managed to appropriate for himself the task of securing Eeyore's head between his arms and pinning his chest beneath the weight of his whole body), and then jumped ahead to the second, unquestionably more complicated, stage of the examination, though it was clear that the first test had not been completed.

With Eeyore secured so firmly to the bed from head to foot that his only freedom was the screaming which wrenched open his mouth and bared his yellow teeth (it was impossible to train Eeyore to brush his teeth: he was terrified of opening his mouth under coercion from no matter who it came; even if you managed to work the toothbrush between his closed lips, he would act as if it hurt or sometimes tickled him and simply clamp down), the nurse placed at the head of his bed a slender aluminum rod bent into an oblong diamond so as to fashion a kind of forceps. The fat man had only to estimate that the slender, tapered apex of this instrument would be introduced beneath the eyelid and then opened to bare the eyeball for a throbbing pain to spread like fire from his own eyes to the central nerve of his brain. Ignoring him and his panic, the doctor squeezed two kinds of drops into Eeyore's eyes, which, though tightly closed, continued to spill tears like signals of the boy's protest. Eeyore renewed his screaming and the fat man shuddered violently. Only then would the doctor say, by way of information:

"This anesthetizes his eyes, so he won't feel any pain."

When the fat man heard this, the silver shimmer of pain connecting his eyes and the marrow of his brain flickered out. But Eeyore continued to moan, as if he were being strangled to death. The fat man, rubbing the tears out of his own eyes with the back of his hand, just managed to see the doctor insert the slender instrument under Eeyore's eyelid while the boy's moaning surged even higher and then completely bare the eyeball only inches away from him. It was truly a large sphere, egg-white in color, and what it felt like to the fat man was the earth itself, the entire world of man. At its center was a brown circle, softly blurred, from which the pupil, lighted with a poor, dull light, blankly and feebly gazed. What it expressed was dumbness and fear and pain, and it was working hard to focus on something, laboring to resolve the blurred whatever-it-was that kept cruelly bringing back the pain. With this eye the fat man identified all of himself. He was not in pain because of the drug, but there was a numbed sense of terror, or discord, in his heart, and this he had to battle as he gazed up helplessly at the crowd of faces bearing down on him. He nearly began to moan along with his son. But he could not help noticing that the brown blur of the eye conveying only dumbness and fear and pain was including his own face in its scrutiny of the crowd of Eeyore's unknown tormentors. A jagged fissure opened between himself and his son. And the fat man forced the first finger of his right hand between Eeyore's yellow, gnashing teeth (not until after his experience above the polar bears' pool would he recognize that he had done this because he was afraid of that fissure, afraid that if he saw to the bottom of it he would have to confront what certainly would have revealed itself there in its true form, the self-deception impregnating his conscious formulation Eeyore=the fat man), saw wasted blood begin to spurt in the same volume as the tears his son continued to weep, heard the sound of teeth grinding bone and, clamping his eyes shut, began to scream in chorus with his son.

When the fat man had received emergency treatment and descended to the waiting room, his wife reported to him, with Eeyore sitting at her side, still pale and limp but calm again, the little doctor's diagnosis. Eeyore's eyes, as with mice, had different fields of vision; like mice again, he was color blind; furthermore, he could not clearly resolve objects farther away than three feet, a condition impossible to correct at present, because, according to the doctor, the child had no desire to see objects in the distance clearly.

"That must be why Eeyore nearly rubs his face against the screen when he watches commercials on TV!" The fat man's wife valued the practice of maintaining the will in good health at all times, and she spoke with emphasis in her attempt to raise the fat man from his gloom, as if she had discovered even in this hopeless diagnosis an analysis of benefit to herself.

"There are children with normal vision who rub the TV screen with their noses, too," the fat man protested apprehensively. "That little doctor didn't do much of anything, you know, except frighten Eeyore and hurt him and make him cry. In which part of the examination is he supposed to have discovered all that calamity?"

"I think it's true that Eeyore doesn't see distant objects clearly and doesn't want to," said the fat man's wife in a voice that was beginning honestly to reveal her own despondency. "When I took him to the zoo, he didn't get the least bit excited about the real animals, and you know how he loves the animal pictures in this books—he just looked at the railings or the ground in front of him. Aren't most of the cages at the zoo more than three feet away?"

The fat man resolved to take his son to the zoo. With his own eyes and ears for antennae and their clasped hands for a coil, he would broadcast live on their personal band a day at the zoo for Eeyore's sake.

And so it came about one morning in the winter of 196— that the fat man and his fat son set out for the zoo together. Eeyore's mother, anxious about the effect of the cold on his asthma, had bundled him into clothing until he couldn't have worn another scrap; and the fat man himself, who preferred the two of them to be dressed as nearly alike as possible, had outfitted him on their way to the station in a woolen stocking cap identical to the one he had worn out of the house. The result was that, even to his father, the boy looked like an Eskimo child just arrived from the Pole. This meant without question that in other eyes they must have appeared, not a robust, but simply corpulent, Eskimo father and son. Bundled up like a pair of sausages, they stepped onto the train with their hands clasped tightly and, sweat beading the bridges of their noses and all the skin beneath their clothing, a flush on their moon faces where they were visible between their stocking caps and the high collars of their overcoats, enjoyed its lulling vibrations.

Eeyore loved the thrill, which was why he liked bicycles, of entrusting himself to a sensation of precarious motion. But the thrill had to be insulated by the secure feeling that his own never very stable body was being protected by another, ideally his fat father's. Even when they took a cab, one of Eeyore's delights, if the fat man tried to remain inside to pay the fare after Eeyore and his mother had stepped into the street, the boy would disintegrate in a manner terrible to see. If ever he got lost from his father in a train, he would probably go mad. For the fat man, riding the train with his son who was so dependent on him, in the face of the strangers all around them, was a frank and unlimited satisfaction. And since, compared to the feelings he normally identified in the course of his life from day to day, this satisfaction was so pure and so dominant, he knew it did not have its source within himself, but was in fact the happiness rising like mist in his son's turbid, baffled mind, reaching him through their clasped hands and being clarified in his own consciousness. Moreover, by identifying his own satisfaction in this way, he was in turn introducing in Eeyore a new happiness, this time with focus and direction—such was the fat man's logic.

The doctor had suggested that Eeyore lacked the vision to see distinctly at a distance and apparently he was right, for Eeyore, unlike other children, was never fascinated by the scenery hurtling by outside. He took his enjoyment purely in the train's vibration and acceleration, in the sensation of motion. And when they pulled into a station, the opening and closing of the automatic door became the focus of his pleasure. Naturally, Eeyore had to observe this from less than three feet away, so the fat man and his son always stood at the pole in front of the door, even when there were empty seats.

Today, Eeyore was busily concerned with the fit of his new cap. And since his standard was not the cap's appearance but how it felt against his skin, it was not until, after a long series of adjustments, he finally pulled it down over his ears and even his eyelids that he discovered the final sense of stability and comfort. The fat man followed suit, and felt indeed that a stocking cap could not possibly be worn in greater comfort. At the station where they had to change trains, as they walked along the underground passage and climbed up and down stairs, the fat man often was aware of eyes mocking them as an outlandish pair. But far from feeling cowed, when he saw their squat, bulky image reflected in a show window in the underground arcade, he stopped and shouted hotly, as if they had the place all to themselves.

"Eeyore, look! A fat Eskimo father and son; we look really sharp!"

Eeyore's hand functioned as a wall against other people, turning the fat man, who had to take tranquilizers when he went out alone, into such an extrovert. Holding his son's hand liberated him, allowing him to feel even in a crowd that they were all alone together and protected by a screen. Much to his father's relief, as Eeyore shuffled along cautiously, staring down at his feet as if to determine with his poor eyes whether the checkerboard pattern of the passage continued on a level or rose into a staircase, he repeated civilly,

"Eeyore, we look really sharp!"

With the meditation of their hands, which were moist with sweat though it was before noon on a winter day, the fat man and his son were in a state of optimum communication when they reached the zoo at ten-thirty, so the fat man imagined to his satisfaction, exalted by the prospect of the experience still wholly in front of them. So when they approached the special enclosure called the Children's Zoo, where it was possible to fondle baby goats and lambs and little pigs and ageing geese and turkeys, and saw that it was too crowded with children on a school excursion to permit a sluggish little boy like Eeyore to work his way inside, they were not particularly disappointed. It was the fat man's wife who had wanted Eeyore to get within three feet of the animals in the first place, so he could observe and touch them. But the fat man had something different in mind. He intended to defy the eye doctor's diagnosis by functioning as Eeyore's eyes; he would focus sharply on the beasts in the distance and transmit their image to Eeyore through the coil of their clasped hands, whereupon his son's own vision, responding to this signal, would begin gradually to resolve its object. It was the realization of this procedure so like a dream that had brought the fat man to the zoo. Accordingly, after one look at the children brandishing bags of popcorn and paper cups of mudfish as they clamored with excitement in their eyes around the pitiful, down-sized animals in the special enclosure, the fat man turned away from the Children's Zoo and led Eeyore toward the larger, fiercer animal cages.

"Tell me, Eeyore! Who comes to the zoo to see wild animals as friendly as cows! We're here to see the bears and the elephants and especially the lions, wouldn't you say, Eeyore? We're here to see the guys who would be our worst enemies if they weren't in cages!" To this felt opinion the fat man's son did not respond directly, but as they passed the lion cages, like an animal cub born and abandoned in the heart of the jungle scenting the presence of dangerous beasts, he seemed to grow wary, and the fat man thrilled to the feeling that he had been attended and understood.

"Look, Eeyore, a tiger! You see the great big guy with deep black and yellow stripes and a few patches of white, you see him moving over there? Well, that's a tiger, Eeyore is watching a tiger!" said the fat man.

"Eeyore is watching a tiger," his son parroted, detecting the presence of something with a sense of smell which was certainly too acute and tightening his grip on his father's hand while with one poorly focused eye, his flushed moon-face consequently a-tilt, he continued to gaze vacantly at the spot where the bars sank into the concrete floor of the cage.

"Eeyore, look up at the sky. You see the black, bushy monster on the round, brown thing; that's an orangutan, Eeyore's watching a big ape!"

Without letting go of his hand the fat man stepped behind his son and with his free arm tilted back the boy's head and held it against his thigh. Eeyore, required to look obliquely upward, squinted into the glare of the clear winter sky, screwing his face into a scowl of delicate wrinkles which made him look all the more like an Eskimo child. Perhaps it wasn't a scowl at all but a smile of recognition, perhaps he had verified the orangutan squatting uneasily on an old car tire with the blue sky at his back, the fat man couldn't be sure.

"Eeyore's watching a big ape," the fat little boy intoned, his vocal cords communicating their tremor directly to his father's hand cupped around his chin.

The fat man maintained his grip on Eeyore's head, gambling that the orangutan would go into action. It had rained until dawn and there was still a rough wind up high, which gave the blue of the sky a hard brilliance rare for Tokyo. And the orangutan itself was as giant and as black as it could be, its outlines etched vividly into the sky at its back. Furthermore, as the fat man knew from a zoology magazine, this was a lethargic orangutan, for it happened to be afflicted with melancholia so severely that it needed daily stimulants just to stay alive. So this particular orangutan had all the requisites for a suitable object of Eeyore's vision. But unfortunately it appeared that the monkey's melancholia was indeed profound, for though it frequently peered down with suspicious eyes at the pair waiting so forbearingly in front of its cage, it gave no indication that it was even preparing to move. Eventually the brilliance of the sky began to tire even the fat man's eyes, until he was seeing the monkey as a kind of black halo. He finally led

his son gloomily away from the orangutan's cage. He could feel himself begin-
ning to tire already, and he was afraid the feeling might reach his son through
the conduit of their clasped hands. Dreamily he considered the quantity of
drugs the orangutan would consume in a day, and was badly shaken to remem-
ber that he had forgotten to take his own tranquilizers before leaving the house
that morning.

But far from giving up, the fat man renewed his determination to function as a
pipeline of vision connecting his son's brain with the dangerous beasts in the zoo.
Possibly he was spurring himself lest he communicate to his son—echoing his fa-
ther mechanically as he directed his vague, misfocused gaze not at the animals so
much as the sparse grass growing between the cages and the railings, or the refuse
lying there, or the fat pigeons pecking at the refuse with their silly, blunted beaks—
a mood developing in himself of submission to that eye doctor who had performed
all manner of cruelties in his soiled, baggy gown, the smoked meat of his insect's
face twitching with tension, only to deliver his disheartening diagnosis. He was
also resisting the deep-rooted disgust which threatened to stain the twilight of his
son's spirit along with his own head. The truth was that the odor of countless ani-
mal bodies and their excrement had nauseated the fat man and given him the be-
ginnings of a migraine headache from the moment before they had entered the
zoo. An abnormally sensitive nose was certainly one of the attributes which testi-
fied to the blood bond between them. Nonetheless, in defiance of every one of
these baleful portents, the fat man continued to wander around the zoo, gripping
his son's hand even tighter, addressing him with more spirit.

"Don't forget, Eeyore, that seeing means grasping something with your
imagination. Even if you were equipped with normal optic nerves you wouldn't
see a thing unless you felt like starting up your imagination about the animals
here. Because the characters we're running into here at the zoo are a different
story from the animals we're used to seeing every day that don't require any
imagination at all to grasp. Take those hard, brown boards with all the sharp
ridges that are jammed up in that muddy water over there. Eeyore! how would
anybody without an imagination know those boards were crocodiles? Or those
two sheets of yellow metal slowly swaying back and forth down there next to
that mound of straw and dung, how would you know that was the head and part
of the back of a rhinoceros? Eeyore! you got a good look at that large, gray, tree-
stump of a thing, well that happened to be one of an elephant's ankles, but it's
perfectly natural that looking at it didn't give you much of an impression that
you'd seen an elephant—tell me, Eeyore, why should a little boy in an island
country in Asia be born with an imagination for African elephants? Now if you
should be asked when we get home whether you saw an elephant, just forget
about that ridiculous hunk of tree-stump and think of the nice, accessible ele-
phants like cartoons that you see in your picture books. And then go ahead and
say, Eeyore saw an elephant! Not that the gray tree-stump back there isn't the
real thing, it is, that's what they mean by a real elephant. But none of the nor-
mal children crowding the zoo is using genuine imagination to construct a real

elephant from what he observes about that tree-stump; no, he's just replacing what he sees with the cartoon elephants in his head, so no one has any reason to be disappointed because you weren't so impressed when you encountered a real elephant!"

While the fat man continued in this vein, speaking sometimes to himself and sometimes to his son, they made their way gradually up a sloping walk and wandered into a narrow passage which had been built to look like a rock canyon. The fat man talked on, but he was aware of a precarious balance being maintained at the outer edge of his consciousness, now directed inwardly and sealed, by jubilation at having escaped the crowds, and anxiety of a kind that somehow tightened his chest. And all of a sudden there sprang up from the ground, where they had been sitting in a circle, a group of men dressed like laborers, shouting incomprehensibly, and the fat man discovered that he and his son had been surrounded. Even as panic mushroomed in the fat man, he wrested his consciousness away from Eeyore, where it wanted to remain, and cast it outward—not only had they left the crowds behind, they had wandered into a cul-de-sac like a small, stifling valley. It was the back of the polar bears' enclosure; far below, on the other side of a cliff of natural stones piled up to look like mountain rock, was a steep ice-wall for the bears to roam and a pool for them to sport in. To someone looking up from the other side, this place would seem to be the peak of a high and unknown mountain beyond an ice-wall and a sea: the fat man and his son had wandered behind the set of a glacial mountain. This secret passageway was probably used by the keepers to gain entrance to the artificial Antarctic below when they wanted to feed the bears or to clean the pool and the icy slope, though it was hard to believe, judging from the stench, that much cleaning was done. Now that the fat man had his bearings, the stench emanating from the back of the zoo, the animals' side, a very nearly antihuman stench, was assaulting his body like an army of ants.

But who were these men? What were they doing squatting at the back of this passageway? And why had they surrounded the fat man and his son with such fierce hostility for simply wandering in on them? The fat man quickly concluded that they were young laborers who had hidden themselves back here to gamble. From the private room of his one-sided dialogue with Eeyore in which it had been locked, he had only to expand his consciousness outward to discover at once the signs of an interrupted game, so openly had they been playing. In the course of a dialogue entirely personal to themselves, a dialogue which turned about the axis of their clasped hands, the fat man and his son had already invaded too deeply their den, in animal terms, their territory, to avoid a confrontation with the gamblers.

Still gripping his son's hand, the fat man began to back off, at a loss for the words he needed on the spur of the moment. But one of the men was already in position behind him, and another was pummeling him even while he attempted the move. A severe interrogation began, while several pairs of rough arms poked and pushed the fat man around. Are you a cop? An informer? Were you doing all that talking into a hidden mike so all your copper friends could hear you? As he was kicked and punched around, the fat man tried to explain, but what he said only angered the men. You were blabbing a mile a minute just now, and serious too, that's the way you talk to a kid like this? The fat man protested that his son was nearly blind in addition to being retarded, so that he had to explain their surroundings in detail or nothing made any sense. But how could a little idiot make sense of all those big words, and this kid really is an idiot, look at him, he don't look as if he understands a word we're saying! The fat man started to say that they communicated through their clasped hands, then simply closed his punched and swollen mouth with a feeling of futility. How could he hope to make these hoodlums understand the unique relationship he shared with his son! Instead of trying, he drew Eeyore protectively to himself, started to, when suddenly his hand had been wrenched away from the boy's hot, sweaty hand and he had been seized by the wrists and the ankles and hoisted into the air by several of the men, who continued to shower him with threats as they began to swing him back and forth as if to hurl him down to the polar bears. The fat man saw himself being swung back and forth as passively as a sack of flour at this outrageous height, saw clearly, if intermittently, the revolving sky and ground, the distant city, trees, and, directly beneath him, now at the hellishly deep bottom of a sheer drop, the polar bears' enclosure and pool. His panic and reflexive fear were buried under an avalanche of despair more grotesque and fundamental; he began to scream in a voice which was unfamiliar even to his own ears, screams that seemed to him must move all the animals in the zoo to begin howling in response. As he was swung out over the pool on the hoodlums' arms and reeled in and cast out again (the vigor of this seemed to anticipate hurling him all the way down to the polar bear submerged to its muddy yellow shoulders in the pool below), the fat man perceived, with the vividness of a mandala in which, like revelation itself, time and space are intermingled in a variety of ways, the despair gripping him as a compound of the following three sentiments: (a) Even if these hoodlums understood that I'm not an informer, they could easily throw me to the polar bear for the sake of a little fun, just to protract their excitement. The fact is, they're capable of that; (b) I'll either be devoured by a polar bear whose anger will be justified because its territory really will have been invaded, or I'll be wounded and drown in that filthy water, too weak to swim. Even if I escape all that, I'll probably go mad in thirty seconds or so—if it was madness that drove my father to confine himself for all those years until he died, how can I escape madness myself when his blood runs in me? (c) Eeyore has always had to go through me to reach his only window of understanding on the outside world; when madness converts the passageway itself into a ruined maze, he'll have to back up into a state of idiocy even darker than before, he'll become a kind of abused animal cub and never recover; in other words, two people are about to be destroyed.

The tangle of these emotions confronted the fat man with a bottomless darkness of grief and futile rage and he allowed himself to tumble screaming and shouting into its depths and as he tumbled, screaming into the darkness, he saw his own eye, an eye laid bare, the pupil which filled its brown, blurred center expressing fear and pain only: an animal eye. There was a heavy splash, the fat man was soaked in filthy spray, the claws and heavy paws of maddened, headlong polar bears rasped and thudded around him. But it was a piece of rock broken from the cliff which had been dropped, the fat man was still aloft in the hoodlums' arms. He was becoming a single, colossal eye being lofted into the air, the egg-white sphere was the entirety of the world he had lived, the entirety of himself, and within its softly blurred, brown center, fear and pain and the stupor of madness were whirling around and around in a tangle like the pattern inside a colored glass bead. The fat man no longer had the presence of mind to trouble himself about his son. No longer was he even the fat man. He was an egg-white eye, a one-hundred-and-seventy-pound, enormous eye. . . .

Night had fallen on the zoo when the fat man completed his gradual return from a giant eye to himself (he assumed from the savage odor of his skin and clothing, which was like a dirty finger probing in his chest, that he had actually fallen into the pool, and learned only later that he had been splashed by a rock), and began to inquire frantically about his son, who, for all he knew, having become a kind of animal cub, was already dead of frenzy. But the veterinarian (!) taking care of him at first insisted there had been no talk about a small boy, and then tried to use the subject to make the fat man remember what had happened to himself. According to this animal doctor, he had been discovered after closing time when the zoo was being cleaned, weeping in a public toilet in roughly the opposite direction from the polar bears' enclosure, and for several hours thereafter had only mumbled deliriously about his son. The fat man insisted he had no memory of his movements during the nine or so hours of his madness. Then he grabbed the veterinarian and begged him to find the little boy either dead of frenzy already or soon to be dead. Presently an employee came in to the office where the fat man had been stretched out on a cot (there were several kinds of stuffed animals in evidence), and reported that he had himself taken a stray child to the police. His panic unabated, the fat man went to the police station and there reencountered Eeyore. His fat son had just finished a late supper with some young policemen and was thanking them individually:

"Eeyore, the pork noodles in broth and Pepsi-Cola were good!" Asked for proof that he was the child's guardian, the fat man finally had to telephone his wife and then wait in the police station until she arrived to take them home.

It was in this manner that a cruel freedom was enforced on the fat man. It came his way just four years and two months after the abnormal birth of Mori, his son.

The fat man's this-time conscious battle for yet another freedom did elicit a printed notice from his mother, but beyond that the front did not advance; for she would not respond further, and continued to ignore her son's repeated letters and phone calls. She refused to accept the letters, and would not come to the phone when he called.

Late one night after several weeks of this, the fat man renewed his determination and once again telephoned his mother. The village operator took the phone call in standard, formal Japanese, but when she came back on the line after a minute of silence, she addressed the fat man directly by name (since he was the only Tokyo resident to place long-distance calls to this little valley, the operator knew from whom and to whom the call came as soon as she heard the number being called, and would probably eavesdrop, something which occurred to the fat man but which he was too distracted to pursue), and then apologized to him in excessively familiar dialect which conveyed her sympathy and confusion:

"There's no answer again tonight, no matter how many times I ring. She (meaning the fat man's mother, living alone in the family house) never goes anywhere, and it's the middle of the night besides—she doesn't come to the phone on purpose every time you call! That isn't right, you want me to hop over on my bike and wake her up?"

So the fat man asked this special favor of the operator and before long the phone was answered. Not that his mother said anything, merely lifted the receiver and held it in silence. As soon as he had cleared his mind of the friendly operator, who had probably hurried back to the switchboard on her bicycle (professional duty!) and was listening in, the fat man began a somehow persuasive, somehow threatening speech to his silent mother:

"Who did you think was going to believe the lies in that announcement? And sending it to my wife's relatives! Mother, if I'm crazy from a disease I picked up abroad and if the baby was born abnormal as a result, then the baby's mother has to be infected too, isn't that so? But you sent your announcement directly to my wife, the baby's mother, Mother! Now that's all I need to tell me that you don't even believe yourself what you insinuated about my disease and my madness. . . . Or have you gone into that old act about being mad yourself? Well that routine is too old, you won't fool anybody that way. And let me tell you something, if you can pretend to be mad well enough to fool someone again then you're not pretending anymore, you really have gone mad! . . . Mother, why won't you speak? You're hiding my notes because you're afraid if I publish something about Father every one who knows the family will think he was mad, and that his blood runs in all the children, and that my son is the living proof of that, isn't that so? And you're afraid of the humiliation that would be to my brothers and sisters, isn't that so? But don't you realize that pretending to be crazy and advertising that an evil disease has made me mad is going to result in something even worse? . . . Mother, I haven't made up my mind that Father died of madness, I just want to know what really happened. My older brothers were in the army and the others were just kids, so I'm the only one of the children who remembers Father letting out a scream all of a sudden and then dying in that storehouse he'd locked himself in, that's why I want to know what that was all about. You ask why it's only me, only me of all the children who keeps worrying about Father's last years and death, I'll tell you why, Mother, because I really have to know. You used to say to me when you brushed me aside, 'The other boys have important things on their minds, and you ask questions like that!' but to me it is important to know what really happened. . . . Mother, if I don't find out, I have a feeling that sooner or later I'll confine myself in a storehouse of my own, and one day I'll scream all of a sudden and the next morning my wife will be telling Eeyore just what you once told me and nothing more, 'Your father has passed away, you mustn't cry or spit or make big or little business thoughtlessly, especially when you're facing West!' . . . Mother, you must remember a lot about Father. . . . Didn't you ask my wife not to take 'sonny boy' seriously if he started glorifying his father's behavior during his last years? My father happens to have spent his last years sitting in a storehouse without moving, with his eyes and ears covered—didn't you tell my wife not to believe for a minute that he'd done that as a protest against the times, because he wanted to deny the reality of a world in which Japan was making war on the China he revered? Didn't you tell her it was simply madness that made him do what he did? Didn't you even say that Father had been as fat as a pig when he died because he'd been stuffing himself with everything he could lay hands on without moving anything but his mouth, and then insinuate that he had hidden himself in that storehouse because he was ashamed of being the only fat man around at a time when food was so scarce? You tell my wife all that and you won't talk to me at all, you even steal the notes I've made about things I've managed to remember by myself, how can you do that Mother? . . . That morning my wife had the illusion I was about to hang myself, you told her my father was never in earnest; that he knew everything he did was fake, because he told himself he was not in earnest whenever he began something, but he didn't notice the effect it was actually having on him however little at a time, wasn't conscious of it, and that it was too late when he did notice. Tell me, Mother, what is it my father did that was not in earnest? What was too late? . . . Mother, if you intend to continue ignoring me, I have some thoughts of my own: I'll sit down in a dark room just as Father did, with sunglasses on and plugs in my ears, and I'll show you what fat can really be, I'm already a tub of lard, you know, and when I eventually let out my big scream and die, what do you intend to do, Mother, console my wife by telling her again that 'sonny boy' and his father noticed whatever it is they noticed too late? Do you intend to say Foolishness! again, and play the Grand Lady? . . . I've only learned this recently, but it seems my son can get along without me, as an idiot in an idiot's way, and that means I'm free now, I'm as good as liberated from my son, so from now on I can concentrate exclusively on my father; I'm free to sit myself in a barber's chair in a dark storehouse until the day I die just as Father did. . . . Mother, why do you keep repudiating me with silence? I keep telling you, I only want to get at the truth about my father's last years. . . . I don't really care about writing his biography, even if I do write something I'll promise never to have it published if that's what you want, do you still refuse to talk to me? . . . If you won't be convinced that I'm telling the truth when I say I only want to know what really happened, then let me tell you something. Mother, I can write up a biography of Father that chronicles his madness and ends in suicide any time I want, and I can have it published, too. And if I did that, you could spend every penny of your estate on paper and printing and mailing announcements, and people in numbers you couldn't possibly match would believe what I had to say and not you! What I'm telling you is that I don't care so much about getting back my manuscript, I just want to hear the truth from you, because I have to have it, Mother, I need it. . . . Believe me, there'd be no problem if it were the manuscript I needed, I can probably recite it for you right now, listen: 'My father began his retreat from the world because . . .'"

Quietly, but firmly, the phone was hung up. The fat man returned, pale with cold and despair, to his bed, pulled the covers over his head and for a long time lay trembling. And he wept furtively, as he had wept that night after his experience about the polar bears' enclosure. He remembered how long it had been since he had actually heard his mother's voice. This last time it was through his wife that he had finally managed to learn what she had said about his dead father. When it came to talk of his father in particular, he couldn't even recall when last he had heard his mother's voice. When she spoke to his wife, she had apparently referred to his father as "the man." The Man. The fat man was reminded of a line from a wartime poem by an English poet, actually it resided in him always, as if it were his prayer. Like the Pure Land hymns which had resided in his grandmother until the day she died, it was part of his body and his spirit. And the poem itself happened to be a prayer spoken at the height of the very battle in which his father had lost his Chinese friends one after the other. The voice of Man: "O, teach us to outgrow our madness." If that voice is the voice of the Man, then "our madness" means the Man's and mine, the fat man told himself for the first time. In the past, whenever he whispered the poem to himself as though in prayer, "our madness" had always meant his own and his son Eeyore's. But now he was positive that only himself and *the Man* were included. The Man had deposited his massive body in the barber chair he had installed in a dark storehouse, covered his eyes and ears, and tirelessly prayed, "Teach us to outgrow our madness, mine and his!" The Man's madness is my madness, the fat man insisted stubbornly to himself, his son already banished beyond the borders of his consciousness. But what right did his mother have to obstruct the passageway leading from himself toward the Man's madness? The fat man wasn't weeping any more, but he was still trembling so that the sheets rustled, not with cold but rage alone.

Once he had adjusted his perspective in this way, the fat man no longer equated himself and Eeyore, even when he considered the hoodlums' attack above the polar bears' pool. He was even able to feel, precisely because it had liberated him from bondage to his son, that the experience had been beneficial. What kept his already ignited anger aflame was his knowledge that his own mother had so long prevented him, in danger even now of being hurled to a polar bear of madness, from discovering the true meaning of that appeal to which *the Man* may have been so close to hearing an answer at the end of his life, "Teach us to outgrow our madness."

The fat man finally fell asleep, but his fury survived even in his dream: his hot hand was clutched in the hand of a hippopotamus of a man sitting with his back to him in a barber chair in a dark storehouse, and fury flowed back and forth between them as rapidly as an electric current. But no matter how long he waited, the fuming giant continued to stare into the darkness and would not turn around to face the fat child who was himself.

When the fat man woke up, he readied himself for a final assault on his mother and swore to begin a new chronicle of the Man's madness in his last years and to undertake an investigation into outgrowing "our madness," *the Man's* and his own. But once again he was beaten to the offensive. During the night, while he had been weeping and raging and having dreams, his mother had been so prudent as to contrive a strategy of her own, and by dawn had even drafted a new announcement in which she broke a silence of twenty years and spoke of her dead husband. Only two days after his phone call, the notes and incomplete manuscript for the biography in which he had attempted to reconstruct an entire image of his dead father arrived at the fat man's house, registered mail, special delivery. That same week, delayed by only the number of days it had taken the printer to fill the order but unquestionably written the same night as the fat man's call, a new announcement also arrived, addressed to the fat man's wife, registered mail, special delivery:

> Recently it was my duty to inform you that my third son had lost his mind. I must now announce that I was mistaken in this, and ask you kindly to forget it. Apropos this season of the year, I am reminded that my late husband, having had an acquaintance with the officers involved in a certain coup d'état, was led upon its failure to the dreadful conclusion that no course of action remained but the assassination of his Imperial Majesty. It was the horror of this which moved him to confine himself in a storehouse, where he remained until his death.
>
> The cause of death, let me conclude, was heart failure; the death certificate is on file at the county office. Begging to inform you of the above, I remain,
>
> Sincerely yours,
Signed
winter, 196—

> But who will save the people?
> I close my eyes and think:
> A world without conspirators!

Choku

Although she had not appeared much moved by the first announcement, this one jolted the fat man's wife surprisingly. For most of an evening she read it over to herself and only then, having reached no conclusions of her own, informed the fat man that it had arrived and showed it to him. Only when the fat man had read it over to himself and was simply standing in silence with the announcement in his hand did she speak up and disclose the substance of her agitation:

"You remember your mother asked me not to take you seriously if you started glorifying your father's last years? Do you think she decided to bring all this to light because you've finally made her begin to hate you with your attacks on her? Do you think your mother had made up her mind to renounce you, and this is her way of saying, imitate your father all you want, nothing you do is her responsibility any more?"

Since the shock which the fat man had received himself came from an entirely different aspect of the announcement, he could only pursue his own distress in silence. The minute he read it he had sensed that this blow, like the blow he had received through Eeyore, was aimed at something fundamental in himself and could be neither countered nor returned. For several days he tried to discredit his mother's account of his father by checking it against what he remembered from his childhood and what he had heard. But among all the details he had collected in order to write the biography, he could find nothing which mortally contradicted the announcement.

His grandmother had said more than once that his father had been attacked by an assassin with a Japanese sword and that he had managed to escape harm by sitting perfectly still in the dark storehouse without offering any resistance. The assassin was probably one of the band which had been associated with his father through the junior officers in the revolt. And he must have been a man with no more stomach than his father for an actual uprising or for individual action in the next stage of the revolt. He had tracked down a craven like himself to the place where he was living in self-confinement, and brandished his Japanese sword and threatened emptily, but that was all he had ever intended to do.

Then there was the drama commemorating a certain coup d'état, one of the fat man's reveries since his youth, in which the widows of the junior officers who had been involved, old women now and incarcerated in a rest home, playing themselves as young wives thirty-five years earlier, attacked with drawn daggers a man seated with his back to them in a barber chair, "the highest Authority to have abandoned the insurgents; or—a private citizen who sympathized politically, provided funds, and was generally in league with the junior officers until the day of the revolt, finally betrayed him, dropped out of the uprising, and spent what remained of his life hiding in a storehouse in his country village." The idea undoubtedly had its distant source in things the fat man had been told as a child, probably in such a way as to hint even that long ago at the contents of his mother's announcement. At any rate, he must have known vaguely that there was some connection between his father and that attempted coup, for he had spoken about it to his wife. It was on a stormy night some time ago, and he had been relating a perfectly normal memory which had renewed itself in him, of his father telling him as a child, on another stormy night, that life was like a family emerging from the darkness, coming together for a brief time around a lighted candle, and then disappearing one by one into their own darkness once again.

For a week, the fat man studied his mother's announcement and pored over the notes and fragments of manuscript which he had written for his dead father's biography. And then early one morning (he hadn't been to sleep at all; that entire week he had slept only four or five hours a night and, except for quick meals, had remained in his study) he went into the garden in back of his house and incinerated a sheaf of pages which contained every word he had written about his father. He also burned a picture card which had been thumbtacked above his desk ever since he had brought it back from New York, of a sculpture, a plaster-of-Paris man who resembled his father as he fancied him, about to straddle a plaster-of-Paris bicycle. He then informed his wife, who was out of bed now and getting breakfast ready, that he had changed his mind about a plan which until then he had opposed. It was a plan to get eyeglasses for Eeyore and to place him in an institution for retarded children. The fat man knew that his wife had gone back to that eye doctor without his permission and persuaded him to prescribe a special pair of glasses, probably by groveling in front of the little man, which she was secretly training Eeyore to wear. The fat man had been severed from his son already, they were free of one another. And now he had confirmed that, in the same way, he had been severed from his dead father and was free. His father had not gone mad, and even if he had, insofar as there was a clear reason for his madness, it was something altogether different from his own. Gradually he had been giving up his habit of bicycling off with Eeyore to eat pork noodles in broth; and although, as he approached the age at which his father had begun his self-confinement, his tastes had inclined toward fatty things such as pigs' feet Korean style, he was losing once again almost all positive desire for food.

The fat man began taking a sauna bath once a week and sweating his corpulence away. And one bright spring morning he had come out of the sauna and was taking his shower when he discovered a swarthy stranger who was nonetheless of tremendous concern to him standing right in front of his eyes. Perhaps his confusion had to do with the steam fogging the mirror—there was no question that he was looking at himself.

The man peered closely at the figure standing alone in the mirror and identified several portents of madness. Now he had neither a father nor a son with whom to share the madness closing in on him. He had only the freedom to confront it by himself.

The man decided not to write a biography of his dead father. Instead, he sent repeated letters to *the Man*, whose existence nowhere was evident now, "Teach us to outgrow our madness," and jotted down a few lines which always opened with the words "I begin my retreat from the world because . . ." And as if he intended these notes to be discovered after his death, he locked them in a drawer and never showed them to anyone.

SHIBUSAWA TATSUHIKO

Shibusawa Tatsuhiko (1928–1987) was a friend of Mishima Yukio and an advocate for the work of the avant-garde Butoh dancer Hijikata Tatsumi. He also was a scholar of French literature, a translator of Sade into Japanese, and a writer on art and medieval demonology. Shibusawa's unusual stories made him a well-known figure in artistic circles. "Fish Scales" (Gyorinki, 1982) is a historical fantasy set in the Tokugawa period.

FISH SCALES (GYORINKI)

Translated by Anthony H. Chambers

According to the *Nagasaki Annals*, an activity called *visspel* was popular early in the nineteenth century among the snobs who gathered in the Kabashima district of the city.

Vis means "fish" in Dutch, and *spel*, "play." The compound *visspel*, however, probably originated in Japan. Inhabiting the sea off the province of Bizen, where Nagasaki is located, was a fish called *torobotchi* in the local dialect. When one of these was released in a bottle of water and a drop of vinegar added, the fish would go berserk, changing from one color to another like a chameleon as it thrashed around, until finally, flourishing bright red scales, it would jump from the bottle. To amuse oneself by watching this was called *visspel*. Silly, perhaps; but *visspel* was also a game. Sometimes, we are told, a number of *torobotchi* would be released together in a large glass bowl; each of the aesthetes in attendance picked a fish of his own, and the one whose fish leaped highest and farthest was proclaimed the winner. No doubt betting was involved. To be charitable, perhaps we should say this was an appropriate game for recluses in a tranquil age; but probably they would have been hard put to wring such a stupid game from their heads had they not been bored to death.

Incidentally, the name of the fish is believed to be of local, Bizen origin; but some, including the author of the *Annals*, think it was originally a Dutch word.

"That reminds me. Back when I used to visit you often—was it five years ago?—we recluses spent all our time on *visspel* when we gathered together. I often thought of it after I returned to the capital."

The painter Fujiki Yūkō spoke nostalgically to his host, Nishijima Hakuyō-sai, as, on his first visit to Nagasaki in some years, he accepted his old friend's invitation and made himself at home. A man of about forty, he was lean as a crane. Hakuyōsai, a bald, corpulent interpreter for the Dutch traders who operated in Nagasaki, was Yūkō's senior by about twelve years.

Glancing behind him, Hakuyōsai caught the eye of his wife Chiyo and looked uncomfortable; but he said lightly, "I had second thoughts and gave up *visspel* completely."

"You don't say! And you used to enjoy it so much. What brought about this change of heart?"

Hakuyōsai smiled grimly. "It's a cruel pastime, when you think about it. You make sport of living fish and, though you may not actually kill them with your bare hands, you force them to thrash about until they're half dead. They say that the greater loss is taken by him who enjoys watching a killing, not by him who commits it; and *visspel* is the very portrait of that greater loss. Such a pastime is best given up. I've turned from fish to keeping birds. There's no cruelty in that."

As Hakuyōsai seemed reluctant to go on, Yūkō said nothing more about *visspel* and let it appear that he'd forgotten the subject. Catching up after a five-year separation, the two men moved easily from one topic to another.

Hakuyōsai's children came in to pay their respects. A boy and a girl, they looked very young in relation to their father's age. The girl carried a large birdcage. Yūkō recalled what his friend had said about keeping birds.

"Hello, Uncle. Have you been well? It has been a long time."

"How you've grown since I saw you last! You were such children then. How old are you now?" he asked the boy.

"I'm *negen*," he replied gravely.

Yūkō was lost for a moment. Translating quickly in his head, he seemed to remember that *negen* was "nine."

In this household, even the children used Dutch effortlessly. Though he'd known this five years before, Yūkō was startled anew. Perhaps it would be more accurate to say that he was flabbergasted.

Born into a family of hereditary priests at the Kamo shrines in Kyoto, Yūkō, even as he matured, could not put aside the artist's brush he had loved since childhood. While he was studying Japanese-style painting in the capital, a chance encounter sparked an appreciation for Western art, and when he was just past thirty, a desire to learn the process for making copperplate prints drew him irresistibly to Nagasaki. It was at this time that he met Hakuyōsai. Having benefitted from the personal instruction of Yoshio Kōgyū and languidly succeeded to his forefathers' profession as a Dutch interpreter, Nishijima Hakuyōsai was even then the boss of the sybaritic snobs of Nagasaki. During his stay in Nagasaki, Yūkō had looked to Hakuyōsai for guidance in everything, from his first lessons in Dutch to the proper behavior for a customer at the Maruyama pleasure quarter. Given the intimacy of their relationship, then, Yūkō should not have been surprised by a simple *negen* from the mouth of a child. The feeling of disbelief that filled him was perhaps due to the five intervening years of separation.

Yūkō had drifted into an emotional reverie, but now the seven-year-old girl held her birdcage up to his face.

"Look, Uncle. Isn't this an unusual kind of *vogel*? Do you know what they're called?"

Inside the cage, two small, green birds with red dots on their breasts and tailfeathers hung upside down from the perch, asleep. It seemed odd that birds would be comfortable in this position. As a painter of flowers and birds, Yūkō was curious and took a close look.

Delighted, the children laughed. "I'll bet you don't know, Uncle. If you don't know, just say so. We'll tell you."

Chiyo checked their high spirits with a wave of her hand. "How rude you are! You mustn't make such a commotion. Mr. Fujiki has only just arrived from the capital, you know, and it has been such a long time."

Hakuyōsai had been looking on with pleasure as he smoked a silver pipe. Now he spoke up. "As the children said, Mr. Fujiki, these are truly unusual birds. You can see that they're in the habit of sleeping upside down. I'm told they're called 'sugar birds.' They were brought recently on a foreign ship from the islands south of Macao and Luzon. Now, what was it the Dutch call sugar birds?"

"*Parkiet, parkiet*," cried the children in unison.

Hakuyōsai beamed with delight, making no effort to disguise his fondness for them. "That's right, that's right. *Parkiet*. Kōtarō and Oyone, you both remembered. Well done!" Turning to Yūkō, he said, "I've taken a great liking to these birds. I've been looking askance at the world for a long time, but I've never looked at it upside down. I may see the world through Dutch eyeglasses, but I'm not as queer as these birds are. According to a man named Kuyder, there's a race on the other side of the globe called Antipodae, who live upside down, suspended from the earth. These are the Antipodae of the bird kingdom. Maybe if we looked at the world upside down, we'd see things we can't normally see. But what I really wonder is what these birds dream about as they sleep upside down. Their dreams may contain secrets that we would never imagine. I'm sure it must be so. There's no basis for my theory, of course. Please laugh if you like."

That night, Yūkō, escorted by the children, settled into the second-floor room that had been allotted to him and in which he would sleep. The Nishijima house commanded a magnificent view: the twinkling lights of the harbor could be seen from the hall outside his room.

As befit the home of a disciple of Yoshio Kōgyū, Hakuyōsai's house had carpets in every room; and the shelves in Yūkō's room, in particular, were cluttered with rare objects from Holland. A spyglass, an astrolabe, cut-glass containers, ivory carvings, surgical instruments, and objects whose function was not immediately apparent lay in a jumble. Yūkō remembered that there'd been an alcove resembling a fireplace in the back wall of the room, in which the large bowl used for *visspel* had rested impressively; but the alcove had been plastered over, and a Gobelin tapestry was hanging there discreetly to hide the alteration.

Exhausted from his journey, Yūkō stretched out on the damask quilt that had been provided for him and immediately fell asleep. He had a dream.

In his dream, Yūkō was a *parkiet*. He didn't feel like a *parkiet*, but he was perched high in a tree and some children were looking up at him, shouting, "*Parkiet, parkiet*." "I'd better act like a *parkiet*, then," he said to himself, in a mood to humor them. Steeling himself, he dangled from the branch by his feet.

He found he could easily hang suspended in space. Pleased with himself, he thought he was doing pretty well; but after he'd been hanging that way for some time, the blood gathered in his head until it was more than he could bear and, far from acting like a *parkiet* any more, he forgot about appearances and cried out. At that moment, he awoke.

Lighting the lamp by his pillow, he sat up and sighed with relief. It had been a dream. Then the door slid open quietly and a girl came into the room. She appeared to be about twelve years old. She had thick eyebrows and an intelligent face, and her hair was drawn back into a bun; an everyday silk kimono hung from her narrow shoulders.

Yūkō remembered as soon as he saw the girl's face. How could he have forgotten? It was Yura. Yura, Hakuyōsai's eldest daughter.

Hakuyōsai had three children, the eldest being Yura. That day the two younger children had come to gather to pay their respects, but Yura hadn't appeared. Yūkō had neither thought it odd nor asked Hakuyōsai about it. Somehow he'd forgotten that Yura ever existed.

Maybe she'd been away from home—visiting relatives, or at a lesson—when her brother and sister came. Probably it bothered her that she hadn't paid her respects, and so she came, belatedly, in the middle of the night to the room where he slept. Or was this a continuation of his dream? As he turned these thoughts over in his mind, he was already speaking to the girl reflexively.

"Well, well. Miss Yura. It's been a long time, hasn't it? You haven't changed at all in five years."

The girl, however, making no reply—indeed, not even looking toward Yūkō, and seeming to ignore his presence completely—walked slowly across the carpet until she came to an abrupt stop in front of the wall at the back of the room, the wall that contained the plastered-over alcove, and for a moment placed one hand on the Gobelin wall-hanging. Then she turned on her heel, walked past Yūkō, who watched in a daze, and with quiet, unhurried steps left the room. She closed the sliding door behind her. Only about a minute had passed from the time she entered the room until she left it. Yūkō, though, felt as if a fearfully long time had elapsed.

The room was dim in the faint lamplight, the shapes of things hazy; but it seemed to Yūkō that there'd been a strange brightness around the girl and that he'd been able to make out clearly the arrow-feather pattern on her kimono. Yūkō was awake the rest of the night, assaulted by doubts.

The next morning, Yūkō was still asking himself whether he should tell Hakuyōsai. The girl's appearance was too vivid for him to keep folded up in his breast, and something would not permit him to discuss it as a fleeting vision. And even if it were a vision, no one could go so far as to deny the existence of Hakuyōsai's eldest daughter, whom Yūkō had known, and who asserted her firm reality in his memory. Where had Yura been? Why hadn't Yura appeared during the day with her brother and sister? Yūkō thought that this, at least, would give him ample pretext for questioning Hakuyōsai.

Yūkō began casually, with a smile. "Your story must have stuck in my mind—last night I dreamed I was a *parkiet*."

"I envy you. I'm always wishing for such a dream, but I've never had one. And did you make any interesting discoveries when you dreamed upside down?"

"No. With my head down I was suffering too much to do any dreaming. I was in quite a fix. Only—I don't know whether it was because I turned into a *parkiet*, but unexpectedly I was able to meet your elder daughter, Miss Yura. I'm embarrassed to admit that I don't know whether I was dreaming or not, but Miss Yura came to my room."

Hakuyōsai's face abruptly clouded over. Yūkō, who hadn't foreseen that his words would be so disturbing, regretted his rashness.

Hakuyōsai was apparently unable to reply immediately; but the story he finally told, sadly and with frequent pauses, was roughly as follows.

"About four years ago, shortly after you returned to the capital, Yura died. The child who entered your room, therefore, was not of this world. To tell the truth, she's appeared often before. It's taboo in our family to speak of this, and so I must ask you not to say anything to my wife. She seems to feel partly responsible for our daughter's death, for to this day she's constantly reproaching herself."

"Chiyo is?"

"Yes. I know very well that she wasn't responsible, but at the time it must have affected her deeply. It's understandable."

Rather than quote the exact words in which Hakuyōsai related the circumstances of Yura's death, the author believes it would be better to use indirect discourse, and so would like to retreat four years into the past and shift the story to a different time.

The date is four years earlier.

In those days, Nishijima Hakuyōsai's house in Kabashima was as lively as a gambling hall. Day after day the no-account intellectuals who loitered around Nagasaki—students *manqué* of Western science—would gather there and, presuming on their portly host's generosity, throw themselves into *visspel* revels. For young men who had come to Nagasaki for instruction, but had abandoned academics and were too ashamed to go back home, the house was an oasis that allowed them for a moment to forget their fecklessness. Fujiki Yūkō, who'd recently returned to Kyoto, had been one of the young men who frequented the house; but as he was somewhat older than the others and came from a good family, he'd always received special treatment from his host.

Placing the glass bowl on a low, round table, four or five men would sit around it in a circle and gaze intently at the four or five fish swimming in the bowl. Silver scales flashing, the fish swam back and forth as though possessed. Suddenly their silver scales turned gold, then vermillion, crimson, yellow, cobalt, emerald, azure, indigo, and green—the dizzying display of mysterious transformations never ceased for a moment. Finally, when the fishes' excitement reached its climax, they would strike the surface of the water with their tails and leap high in the air, one after another, writhing, and the force would carry them clear out of the bowl. They looked as though transformed into shafts of light, glittering in the seven colors of the prism. The piquancy of *visspel* reached its peak here, and the spectators were intoxicated.

Occasionally a sluggish fish would betray expectations by failing to change color quite so dazzlingly, or by being too weak to jump all the way out of the bowl. When bets had been placed, the person who selected such a fish was the loser; developing an eye for choosing vigorous fish was considered the secret for success in *visspel*. It was customary to pick one's fish while it was still swimming in the holding tank.

According to one theory, it wasn't vinegar that was added to excite the fish, but nitric acid, which was also used to make copperplate illustrations, and the manufacture of which was prohibited by the government. Vinegar was only a cover to hide the chemical's real identity from the world. This theory of the author of the *Nagasaki Annals* is, however, rather hard to believe.

One day, when some people had gathered as usual at Hakuyōsai's house for *visspel*, two children came slipping into the room. They were Hakuyōsai's daughter Yura and a boy of about the same age. Hakuyōsai himself must have been away from home, perhaps at the government office in Dejima, because he didn't like children to intrude upon *visspel* gatherings and forbade them even to watch.

Sitting quietly on Western-style chairs behind the adults, the two children gazed with apparent interest at the fish swimming madly around inside the glass bowl. There's no need to introduce Yura here; her companion was a boy who turned up now and then unexpectedly at Hakuyōsai's house, though no one knew where he came from. With some misgivings, the family let him in, because he was cute and well-dressed. When asked his name, he said simply that it was Jūichirō. He never gave his family name. When asked about his home, he replied that it was in Aburaya. Reticent as he was, the boy made himself right at home. He and Yura became friends and played happily together, with the result that his comings and goings were tolerated at Hakuyōsai's house.

Chiyo, however, frowned upon Jūichirō's visits, because she suspected that he was the child of a mistress her husband kept in Aburaya. In fact he wasn't, but the idea had become so firmly rooted in Chiyo's mind that she seemed absolutely convinced that it was so.

During a pause in the *visspel* competition, one of the young men in the group turned to look behind him. For fun, he said, "Miss Yura, would you like to try?"

"Yes." Yura rose calmly and joined the group. The young men stared in disbelief at her performance. They realized that it had been a serious mistake to underestimate her simply because she was a child. Each of the fish that Yura selected from the holding tank and released in the bowl was violently energetic and writhed with superabundant vigor as it leapt high above the surface of the water. Not only that—the leaping fish would describe an arc in the air and fly directly to Yura, as though drawn by the force of her personality. Each time it was the same. The spectators were astounded at her eye for choosing the right fish.

"This is amazing. The fish leap straight to Miss Yura. She must have the kind of personality fish like."

"Maybe she's a reincarnation of the Sea Princess."

"She'll end up marrying a fish, no doubt about it."

They spoke without reserve to cover their chagrin, though of course they couldn't make obscene jokes in front of the children.

Then Jūichirō, who'd been looking on, suddenly reached out and snatched up the fish that was lying before Yura, having just leapt from the bowl. To everyone's astonishment, he sank his teeth into the fish. One of his front teeth broke and tumbled onto the table, as though he'd bitten a hard object. At the same moment, he spit out something from his bloodied mouth—a steel pellet. It was obvious that Jūichirō had located it inside the fish with his teeth and taken it into his mouth. Jūichirō's gory lips curved into a disagreeable smile.

As Hakuyōsai confirmed later, the pellet, though very small, had the same shape as the pointed knobs found atop railing posts and stone lanterns. It might also have been called onion-shaped. One of these pellets was found in each of the four fish that had been selected by Yura and had jumped from the bowl.

It was like some sort of riddle; no one knew what was going on. The moment Jūichirō bit into the fish and spit out the pellet, Yura, her face red with anger, left the room brusquely. Jūichirō followed and disappeared. The young men saw nothing particularly scandalous in what had happened; but it was a bizarre incident, and it had occurred when they brought a child into the game in their host's absence. Loath to be blamed for it, they wasted no time leaving the Nishi-jima house.

Since everyone was keeping quiet, several days passed before Hakuyōsai learned of the incident. In the meantime, he was happily surrounded by the young men who frequented his house. But one day, when a careless fellow let the story slip, Hakuyōsai immediately felt anger smoldering inside him. One cause of his irritation was, of course, that his daughter had disobeyed him by getting involved in *visspel*; but the bigger cause was his suspicion that Yura, incited by Jūichirō, was keeping something from him. Though he was an indulgent man, Hakuyōsai wouldn't tolerate lies and secrets. That's not to say that he knew exactly what she was hiding. What did the little pellets in the fish mean? He tried asking Yura in a roundabout way, but she said she didn't know and acted as if nothing had happened. Jūichirō, for his part, abruptly stopped coming to the house. With one thing and another, then, Hakuyōsai had almost forgotten the incident, when, away from the house one day, he happened to run into Jūichirō.

The afternoon sun was beginning to sink toward the horizon as Hakuyōsai emerged from his mistress's residence in Aburaya. A child's voice came from a clump of grass at the roadside, close to his heels.

"Mr. Nishijima, where were you?"

Looking back, he saw Jūichirō. Though the boy was only a child, Hakuyōsai felt at a disadvantage, having just come from the gate of his mistress's house. He hemmed and hawed. He thought it possible that Jūichirō had been lying in wait for him. The child, however, went right on as though he'd forgotten his question.

"Shall I tell you something interesting?"

"Yes?"

"It's Miss Yura. She's a crafty one."

Hakuyōsai was surprised to hear this from a boy who was usually so reticent. "Why, what makes you say that?"

"There's a Dutch *magneetsteen* (magnet) in your house, isn't there? Miss Yura thought of using it to attract the fish in the bowl."

"What's that?"

"It's true. She was hiding the *magneetsteen* under her apron during the *visspel*, but no one noticed. They're blind as bats. It was Miss Yura who got the fish to swallow the steel balls, too."

"Surely not!"

"But it's true. Those fish are so greedy they'll swallow anything you drop into the holding tank. They don't care if it's steel or what have you."

At a loss for words, Hakuyōsai asked himself whether it would really be possible to attract fish with a magnet. Once at an *electriciteit* show booth in Osaka he'd seen a paper doll dancing attracted by electricity; but it was hard to believe that the same thing could be done with steel balls and a magnet. Fish were full of life. And was his magnet that powerful? Was it the property of those steel balls to be drawn so readily by the magnet?

Looking the child straight in the eye, Hakuyōsai suppressed his agitation and asked, "Where did those steel balls come from?"

Jūichirō replied boldly, with a snicker. "They're from the clock on the second floor of your house. Take a look when you get home. The clock is square, with a kind of roof, and there's a little onion-shaped ball decorating each corner of the roof. They come right off if you unscrew them."

"Was that your idea?"

"Oh, no, not mine. It was Miss Yura. I just watched."

"Watched, and didn't stop her?"

"She wouldn't have listened if I tried to stop her. She was fascinated by the way a *magneetsteen* attracts steel. She couldn't wait to test its power. I don't know why she was so preoccupied with it."

Hakuyōsai paused for a moment before putting the next question. He was afraid it was a silly thing to ask.

"This may be beside the point, but why did you come to play at my house so often?"

"To put it simply, it was because I liked Miss Yura. Like a fish being drawn to a magnet. That's why you come to Aburaya, isn't it? I'm sick of women now, though."

Jūichirō spun around and hurried away, as though he'd said all there was to say. Hakuyōsai was about to call out, "Wait, who are you? Where did you come from?" but he swallowed the words. Jūichirō's face as he turned, bathed from behind in the rays of the afternoon sun, looked just like pictures of a demon child Hakuyōsai had seen in Western books.

Hakuyōsai started home with heavy steps. He was mortified, but there was nothing he could do. He felt as though he were watching a drama unfold in a world beyond his reach.

The moment he got home, Hakuyōsai climbed briskly to the second floor, without speaking to anyone, and examined his cherished Spanish clock. As Jūichirō had said, the four decorative balls were gone, leaving holes where they had been. He opened a desk drawer to look for the *magneetsteen* a foreign ship captain had given him. He prayed that it would be there, but, sadly, it too was missing. Then it's true, he thought, feeling thoroughly beaten.

Hakuyōsai didn't intend to question his daughter himself. He couldn't remember ever having done so. And so it was only natural that, after agonizing over it, he finally decided to give his wife this onerous role; he had no ulterior motive. Chiyo wasn't a woman to let her emotions run away with her; Hakuyōsai was confident that she'd never blame or reproach her daughter unjustly.

When asked by her mother, Yura stubbornly insisted that she knew nothing about the magnet. It wasn't her fault that it was missing. Maybe a burglar had broken into the house. She'd never thought of luring fish with a magnet, nor did she believe that such a thing was possible. It was too preposterous. She'd seen *visspel* that day for the first time—it was clear, wasn't it, that she couldn't possibly have played tricks with the steel balls? Who on earth had made up this groundless story, Yura countered, and who had come to her mother telling tales?

Her mother, not thinking it appropriate to mention Jūichirō's name, spoke brusquely, in spite of herself, "It doesn't matter who, does it? You should be taking a good look at yourself."

"But it *does* matter who. I must know the name of the person who told on me."

At her wits' end, her mother said, "It was Jūichirō."

"Jūichirō told you that?"

"Not me, but your father. Your father happened to meet him on the street the other day."

Deeply shocked, Yura seemed unable to speak for a few moments. Finally, she said passionately, "It's a lie. Jūichirō would never say such a thing, it's a lie."

"Then you don't believe what your father says?"

Without answering, Yura turned on her mother. "I know very well that you don't like Jūichirō. But don't expect me to believe it when you say Jūichirō has been telling on me."

"Do you trust Jūichirō that much?"

"No, I don't trust him at all. But he liked me. No one tells tales on someone he likes."

Yura's egocentric logic was more than her mother could handle, and she was steadily losing control of the situation. Suddenly Yura rose, weeping. Pulling free when her mother tried to restrain her, she rushed into her bedroom and buried herself under the quilts. Her perplexed parents thought that her excitement would probably run its course by the next morning.

Yura's sobbing and hiccups continued, however, and grew worse as the night deepened. She began to have convulsions that shook her whole body, and finally she lost consciousness. Then, as her parents watched, the twelve-year-old girl arched her body backward and stopped breathing.

There's no need to describe her parents' grief. After that, her mother grew gaunt and haggard, tormented day and night by self-reproach and remorse for having wounded her daughter by accusing her unjustly. Hakuyōsai, too, was tortured by vague feelings of contrition. He realized in retrospect that there was no evidence to support Jūichirō's story, and no one could say whether Yura had actually taken the *magneetsteen* from her father's desk or removed the steel balls from the clock and fed them to the fish. Had Yura done anything to be censured for? Even that wasn't clear, but—as Yura's parents realized now, to their despair—their daughter had been sacrificed because of the meddling of a dubious, mysterious boy.

Fujiki Yūkō, after listening to Hakuyōsai's long account, was too stunned to speak for a time; but then, as if he'd just thought of something, his painter's eyes began to flash. The movements of the girl who had visited his room the previous night came back to him vividly.

"Mr. Nishijima, you mentioned some steel balls that were fed to the fish. Are they still here in the house?"

"Yes, they are. I screwed them back where they belonged, and I'm still using the clock. It's in the next room. Shall I remove one of them and bring it to you?"

"Please do, by all means. I have an idea."

With the ball in his hand, Yūkō led Hakuyōsai up to the second floor, to the room he'd slept in, the room in which the girl's ghost had appeared. Placing the ball on his palm, he quietly slid the door open and, as the girl had done the night before, walked slowly across the carpet toward the wall at the back of the room.

About three feet from the wall, the ball on Yūkō's palm suddenly flew in a straight line and attached itself to the Gobelin tapestry hanging there. With a start, the two men looked at each other.

"Tell me about this wall."

"As you know, there used to be an alcove here, but after Yura died we plastered it over. There was no need to keep the bowl when we gave up *visspel*." Hakuyōsai's voice quavered.

"Last night I saw Miss Yura touch this wall-hanging with her hand. You said she'd appeared often before. Did she always do that?"

"Yes, she always put her hand there."

"Did you think of looking inside the wall?"

"That never occurred to me."

"What would you think of breaking into the wall and taking a look inside?"

"I have no objection, of course."

When they made a hole in the wall and reached in, they found, right where the girl had placed her hand, a horseshoe-shaped *magneetsteen* embedded in the plaster. Despite the dust and rust that covered it, Hakuyōsai recognized it as the one he'd been given by a Dutchman.

"Mr. Fujiki, I don't understand. How did the *magneetsteen* get plastered in here? Did Yura hide it? No, that couldn't be. We plastered the wall after her death."

Hakuyōsai buried his head in his hands. Giving him a sidelong look, Yūkō said sardonically, "Whether Miss Yura hid it or not, it's certain at least that her ghost wanted to show us where the *magneetsteen* was. She couldn't rest in peace until we found it. But what really bothers me is that boy Jūichirō. Did you ever meet him again, Mr. Nishijima?"

Hakuyōsai opened his eyes wide with horror and looked as if he were about to faint. "Certainly not! Never again. I even wonder if I wasn't having a nightmare when I met him. I can't believe that it really happened. Mr. Fujiki, please don't frighten me that way."

The magnet they'd just found, and the steel ball, rested on the table in the room where they were talking. The two objects clung firmly to each other, as if determined never to be separated again. Yūkō fancied that they looked like the souls of the two children.

It's probably not necessary to add that, after the magnet was found in the wall, Yura's ghost never again appeared in Hakuyōsai's house.

SHIMA TSUYOSHI

Shima Tsuyoshi (b. 1939) is one of several pen names used by the native Okinawan writer, playwright, and historian Ōshiro Masayasu. It literally means "the island is strong." Many of Shima's works focus on the brutal fight for Okinawa at the end of World War II. In this story, "Bones" (Hone, 1973), which was published just a year after the United States returned control of Okinawa to the Japanese government, he turns his attention to the continuing repercussions of that struggle.

BONES (HONE)

Translated by William J. Tyler

The work crew had arrived at the construction site and was taking a break when a yellow safety helmet swung into view at the foot of the hill. The man in the helmet was moving at a fast clip as he made his way up the dirt road that cut through the pampas grass. Right behind him was an old woman. She relied on a walking stick, but she dogged him like a shadow.

The construction site was situated atop a stretch of foothills from which one could see the entire city of Naha in a single sweep. Long, long ago the area had been covered in trees, and many a tale had been told about the ghosts who resided in the dark, densely wooded hills. But that was until the war. The heavy naval bombardment from offshore had leveled the *akagi* forests down to the last tree. And then came the postwar expansion of the city that had altered the way the land looked down below once and for all. It was as though the whole area had been painted over in colors that gave it a bright, gaudy look.

The denuded slope was like a half-peeled papaya. The top had been lopped off, and from there to the road a quarter of the way down the hill, the red clay was exposed to the elements. According to the notice posted at the construction site, the hilltop was slated to become the site of a twenty-story luxury hotel.

The five men in the work crew were from Naha City Hall. Sitting under the shade of a giant banyan tree, they gazed at the city as it stretched before them. The plain was flat and dry and looked as though it had been lightly dusted in a silvery powder. The August sun had risen to a point in the sky where it was now almost directly overhead.

As the light danced over the whitecaps that broke against the coral reef lying offshore, it seemed almost playful. It was as though the sun had come to make fun of the men and the bored, fed-up expressions they wore on their faces. Meanwhile, some forty to fifty feet from the tree sat a big bulldozer. It was resting quietly for the moment, but the prongs on the shovel were pointed this way. It was just about there, too—the spot where the bulldozer was parked—that the bones had turned up the day before.

The man in the yellow safety helmet nodded in the direction of the assistant section chief as he approached the work crew from city hall. He was the man in charge of the construction site, and the company name, "TOA ELECTRIC," was embroidered on his breast pocket in fancy gold letters. They glittered in the sunlight.

"Well, where are the bones?" asked the assistant section chief, a round-shouldered man. He had grabbed a shovel and looked as though he was ready to get to work right away.

"I hate to say it, but there's been a new hitch." As the construction boss turned and looked behind him, the metal rims of his glasses seemed to flash as they caught the light of the sun.

There was the old woman—her neck thrust forward, her withered chin jutting out prominently into the air. She was out of breath from keeping up with the man in the yellow safety hat as they had climbed the long incline.

"So where is it, this spot you're talking about?"

There was a razor-sharp edge to the man's voice as he turned to address the old woman. With that, she lifted her walking stick and pointed it at the men from city hall.

"That's it there. I'm sure of it. Because the tree marks the spot. Any place from the tree to where you've got your bulldozer parked over there is where you'll find 'em. Yes sir, underneath it's nothing but bones. I know 'cause I saw it all with my own two eyes. There's no mistake. I'm absolutely certain of it."

The construction boss could hardly believe what he was being told and turned to the assistant section chief with a look of total incredulity. "I never thought I'd have a mess like this on my hands. It wasn't until this morning that these people let me know there was a *graveyard* up here."

The construction boss introduced the old woman to the assistant section chief. She was the former owner of the property, and her family name was Higa. Higa Kame. Her given name sounded the same as the word for turtle, and the boss could not help feeling there was something tortoise-like about the old woman's appearance.

The turtle woman cut him short. "No, Mister, this is no graveyard. We just dug a hole and threw the bodies in. That's all there was to it. We were in the middle of a war here on the island, and nothing more could be done."

"But that's exactly what I needed to hear from you. Why in hell didn't you say something about graves before now? Letting heavy-duty equipment sit idle even for one day costs a fortune. We're taking a big loss."

The anger in the man's voice was countered by an equally furious look from the old turtle woman. Her aging, yellowed eyes had peaked into small triangles, and her lips were tightly pursed. The assistant section chief tossed his shovel aside. He knew trouble and could see it coming now.

"What kind of numbers are we talking about here?" he asked uneasily.

"Thousands. The mayor had us gather up all the bodies from around here and put them in a pile. There were so many you couldn't begin to count 'em. . . ." The old woman waved her stick in the air as if to make her point. Doubtless she was having trouble expressing herself in standard Japanese and felt the need to emphasize what she had to say.

"That many, huh?" A look of despair crossed the assistant section chief's face.

"There were so many bodies they wouldn't fit in the hole. Later on we used gasoline to burn them and then buried the ashes. The mayor said he'd look after the upkeep of the site, but then we never heard another word from him. Poor souls. There was no one to care for them when they died, and now their bones have been completely abandoned."

"That's not how I heard it. No siree, that's not the story I was told."

The frustration and anger in the construction boss' voice was almost palpable as he spat out the words in his own local Osaka dialect from mainland Japan.

No, that was not the story.

It was a line from the script recited to him by the people down at city hall. But the line was supposed to be delivered by them to him, not by him to someone else.

It was yesterday when he had phoned them from the construction site to say unmarked graves had been uncovered on the hill and that the company was asking city hall to step in and deal with the problem.

"Unmarked graves are the responsibility of the Health and Physical Education Section," he was told. "They're the ones to handle it."

But then again, if he was talking about the bones of war dead, "Well, *no, that was another story* altogether."

"Where's a phone around here?" The assistant section chief seemed to have decided on some plan of action and needed to report it to the office.

The boss took the lead as the two men headed up the red clay slope of the hill. The others remained seated on the ground, watching the boss and the assistant section chief disappear into the distance.

The first to speak was the oldest member in the group. He was wearing a pair of rubber work boots. "Ma'am, when you say 'bones,' are you talking about the bones of mainland Japanese?"

The turtle woman inched her way under the big banyan tree. Her lips were in constant motion. It was as if she were chewing on something or muttering to herself.

·"Hell, what does it matter whose bones they are? They all died in the big battle. Japanese. Americans. Men. Women. Even little babies got killed while they were still sucking at their mothers' breasts. We dumped them all together into this one big pit."

"You mean there really are thousands of bodies buried under here?" This time it was the fellow with only one eye who spoke. He could hardly believe what the old woman had said.

"They talked about putting up a memorial stone. That's what the mayor told us, and that's why my father planted this tree to mark the spot."

Without thinking, the men let their eyes scan the tree that branched overhead. Now that she had mentioned it, there was something strange about a banyan tree growing here. But there it was, standing in the middle of a field of pampas grass. It had been free to grow as it pleased, and, tropical plant that it was, it had shot up to a height of ten yards. From its boughs hung a long red beard of tendrils that reached all the way to the ground.

"That means it's twenty-eight years old." The one-eyed jack blew a puff of smoke from his lips. He sounded impressed at the thought of how much the tree had grown.

"And, ma'am, that means when you got the boss here to buy the land you pretended not to know about the bones, right?" This time it was the youngster in the group who spoke up. What with a crop of whiskers on his chin, he looked like a hippie, and there was a smart-alecky grin on his face.

"No, idiot. The reason the company got the property was . . ." The old woman sprayed the area with the spittle that flew from the gap between her missing two front teeth. "It was all because of that dumb son of ours. He let the real estate agent pull the wool over his eyes. We tried to educate him. We tried to get him to understand what sort of property it was and that it ought not to be sold, but he never got the point."

It was not long before the assistant section chief and the construction boss were back. They both looked agitated.

"We've got no choice. We're the ones who will have to step in and deal with the problem, and that's that. The government is ducking it at both the national and prefectural levels, saying there's no budget. Or no manpower. That means we're elected for the job. So let's get to work." The assistant section chief turned to his men and addressed them in a voice that was more mature than expected for a person his age.

But no one moved. The men continued to sit, smoking their cigarettes and wearing the same dull expression that had been on their faces all morning. The construction company boss studied them with a forlorn, even helpless, look. "Just how many days is this going to take, anyway?" he asked.

"Hmm, I wonder. After all, these are the only men we could muster from the city's Disinfection Unit. With such a small crew, there's no telling how long it might take," replied the assistant section chief.

The construction boss walked in a circle, trampling the thick clumps of summer grass underfoot. It appeared he had some sort of plan in mind. Suddenly he stopped in his tracks and looked up, turning the full force of his charming baby face on the crew. "First, I must ask you men not to let anyone from the newspapers get wind of what's happening here. Once the press gets to shouting about it, we'll have a real mess on our hands."

The assistant section chief had a questioning look in his eye as he closely studied the construction boss' face. He seemed to be stumped and not fully prepared to digest what the boss might say next.

"We don't want any news to get out that will damage the future image of the hotel."

The assistant section chief nodded in agreement. Clearly, something in the boss' argument had impressed and persuaded him.

But by then Hippie-Beard was already on his feet. "Here we go again. And whose ass are we wiping this time? I can't believe we are going to do this." His heavy, gong-like voice resonated in the air. Yet if he was being sarcastic, his remarks seemed aimed at no one in particular.

"It's a helluva lot better than having to dig up undetonated bombs," piped up One-Eyed Jack.

All the men from city hall knew what he was talking about. They also knew he had a history of dropping explosives overboard in the ocean to catch fish illegally, and this was how he had lost an eye.

"Anyway, we start work right after lunch," announced the assistant section chief.

But Kamakichi was in no hurry, and he was the last member of the crew to get to his feet. The shadow that the big banyan tree cast on the ground had shrunk to nothing by now. In the distance, the cicadas were droning away. The mere thought of what was about to unfold was enough to make Kamakichi depressed. And, try as he might, he could not help feeling this way.

It was a little past noon the following day when the first bones began to surface. The men had been digging all morning, and until then the only noticeable change had been in the color of the soil as it turned from red to gray. As they dug deeper, they began to find some white things that looked like pieces of broken clamshells scattered in the powdered soil. Perhaps they only imagined it, but the earth seemed to give off the odor of rotting flesh.

"It's like the old woman said. The upper layer is all ashes."

The assistant section chief directed his crew to spread a canvas tarp along the edge of the pit. Kamakichi and the man in the rubber work boots were put to work doing the sorting. When each spadeful of dirt and ash was shoveled out of the hole, their job was to pick out the pieces of bone and put them in a burlap bag. Because the small, cremated pieces of bone had been reduced almost to a powder, it was impossible to identify any of them as belonging to a particular part of the human anatomy. Kamakichi closed his eyes. It was with a sinking feeling of dread and disgust that he forced his hands to sift through the piles of ashes.

The work went at a livelier pace once whole pieces of bone began to emerge from the pit. The gloomier the job became, the more it seemed, paradoxically, to raise the men's spirits. From out of the ashes came two round objects about the size of Ping-Pong balls.

"*What're these?*" When Kamakichi showed them to the man in the boots, Rubber Boots laughed and thrust them in the direction of Kamakichi's crotch.

"Fossilized balls."

All at once the men roared with laughter.

"No, no. It's not right to laugh at the dead. They're all bodhisattvas now, you know." The assistant section chief looked very serious, befitting his position of responsibility, and there was a mildly admonishing tone in his voice. "That's the hinge ball where the femur attaches to the hipbone."

"I bet you were born after the war," said Rubber Boots to Kamakichi.

Kamakichi felt as if the older man was trying to make fun of him. As for the war, he had no memory of it. "I was two when the war ended."

"Why, it's practically the same thing. If you ask me it seems like, ever since the war, we've all kept on living here in these islands by picking our way through a huge pile of bones. That's what's kept us going."

"Back then, nobody batted an eye at the thought of sleeping with a corpse," chimed in One-Eyed Jack.

Rubber Boots went on with what he was saying. He spoke with the authority of an older person who was the senior member of the work crew. "I was in the local defense forces when I was taken prisoner. One day I discovered a patch of big, white daikon growing in a field not far from the POW camp. But when I went to dig them out of the ground, I found they were growing on top of a huge mound of bones."

"Did you eat 'em?" asked Hippie-Beard.

"Of course I did. What do you think?"

Once again the men roared with laughter.

"It's the dead protecting the living," said One-Eyed Jack. The tone of his voice was almost reverential.

"This here banyan tree is a lot like us. It's had good fertilizer." Rubber Boots stretched himself upward from the waist and craned his neck to peer up at the tree.

"It's the same for everybody here in Okinawa," added One-Eyed Jack, sounding almost as if he were making excuses for himself.

"That may be true, but what about the others? You know, the ones who've used their fellow Okinawans as bonemeal to feed off them and make themselves rich and fat." It was Hippie-Beard speaking up again. He had been born after the war but was determined not to let this conversation pass without putting in his two cents.

"So just who is it you're talking about?" One-Eyed Jack had turned serious.

But now Hippie-Beard got flustered, at a loss to explain.

As Kamakichi sorted out the pieces of bone, he could feel the gorge rise in his throat, and he had to swallow hard from time to time just to be able to keep working. He felt oddly out of place amid the lively banter of the other men in the work crew. What they were saying struck him as terribly disrespectful, even blasphemous, toward the dead. At the same time, he kept trying to tell himself that the bones were just objects, no different from what one might find in an archaeological dig of an old shell mound.

In the afternoon, as the men began to let their pace slacken, all at once the old woman silently reappeared, as if out of nowhere. They welcomed her back, trying to joke with her about the job they were doing. But she would have no part of it. She hunkered down next to Kamakichi and began to study the pile of bones. As always, her mouth was in constant but wordless motion.

"Hey, ma'am. Afterward we want you to do a good job of saying prayers for the dead buried here to rest in peace. Otherwise, there'll be hell to pay if so many lost souls get out and start wandering all over the place." The assistant section chief seemed to be in an uncharacteristically jocular mood.

But the old woman said nothing, and presently she began to help Kamakichi sift through a pile of ash. She worked with the deftness of a farm girl trained to sort beans of different sizes. As her fingers sifted, her mouth in ceaseless motion began to form words that she muttered to herself. "You poor, poor things. Whose bones are you, here in this miserable place? Look what's become of you. Who were your parents? And who were your children? It's all so sad."

Her mutterings were like a pesky gadfly that flitted about Kamakichi's ears. As he watched the deft movements of the old woman's withered hands, suddenly he was reminded of his mother. And then he remembered the three stones she had told him about. She said she had collected them at the bottom of the precipice at Mabuni. That was the place where Japanese soldiers had jumped to their deaths rather than surrender to the enemy at the end of the Battle of Okinawa. But he knew that the story about the stones was no more true than the inscription "June 23rd," the last day of the battle, that was written on the back of his father's mortuary tablet as the date of his death in the war. He recalled the photograph placed on the family altar of his father dressed in the uniform for civilians in the Okinawa Defense Corps. His father had been taken from his job at the town office and conscripted into this citizens' army, which was supposed to be the island's last line of defense. It had all happened so very long ago that, to Kamakichi, it seemed like some ancient, mythical tale that had no connection with him now.

Just as the men were about to finish for the day, the construction boss showed up. The straps of his safety helmet were, as always, tied firmly in place, and there was a folding ruler in his breast pocket.

"Looks like it's going to take a lot longer than expected." There was an arch look on his face as he peered down at the men in the pit.

"Look at it, will you? There are thousands of bones down here." Such was the cheerless reply the assistant section chief shouted back from the bottom of the hole.

Hippie-Beard shoveled a spadeful of bone and ash over the edge of the pit. "Wiping the ass of people who make a mess starting a war is no picnic, you know."

"This area here will be the front of the hotel's stroll garden," announced the construction boss as he walked around the pit one more time. "The landscape design is going to be quite elaborate."

"The view will be wonderful," said the assistant section chief, picking up on what the boss said and complimenting him.

"That's why, starting tomorrow, if it's okay with you, we'll get to work with the heavy equipment in the area next to your crew. As things stand now, we're way behind schedule, and it's time to start construction on the hotel."

"That's fine with us," replied the assistant section chief without a moment's hesitation.

That night Kamakichi sat drinking *awamori* at an *o-den* restaurant in Sakae-machi. It was his first night out in quite a while. But he had no appetite. It was almost as though his stomach were no longer his own. The mutterings of the old turtle woman continued to resound in his ears no matter how hard he tried to tune them out. Little by little, and long before he realized it, he had drunk himself into an alcoholic haze. He thought of his father, and the memories came back fast and furious, without letting up.

The bulldozer went to work in the area adjacent to the pit on the crew's third day at the site. The loud, ferocious roar and the perpetual cloud of dust it generated assaulted the men mercilessly. Their mouths filled with grit, and they began to feel sick. It was as though something had swept them up in the air and was shaking their internal organs violently. To make matters worse, what had been the sole source of pleasure in their lugubrious task was now denied them because the bulldozer obliterated all possibility of conversation. Indeed, it stamped out anything they tried to say in much the same way it trampled the weeds growing on the hillside. The men now fell into a dark, sullen mood, and as the temperature climbed and their fatigue increased, they became wildly careless wielding their shovels. As they spit and tried to clear their parched throats, they felt a rising anger directed in equal parts at the steel-monster bulldozer and the idiocy of the assistant section chief.

The old woman was back again to help, having arrived in the morning. On the one hand, the din generated by what she called "the bull" made it impossible to hear her and thereby saved Kamakichi from having to listen to her gadfly-like mutterings. On the other hand, the lack of conversation or any other diversion left him all the more vulnerable to his private fantasies about the bones, causing him to withdraw into ever-deeper introspection.

It was a little past noon when the men began to uncover bones in the shape of whole skeletons. If not apparent earlier, it was now all too clear that excavating the gravesite would be far more time consuming than originally anticipated. The bones were solid, each one a heavy weight. In addition, buried along with them were all sorts of paraphernalia. Metal helmets. Army boots. Canteens. Bayonets. The mouth of the pit looked like a battlefield strewn with the litter of war. All the bones had turned a rusty red. Collarbones. Shoulder bones. Thighbones. Rib bones. Tailbones. Skulls. One after another, bones like those Kamakichi remembered seeing in high school science class were chucked over the edge of the pit. Each time he went to pick one up, he could not prevent his mind from clothing it in fantasies about the living human flesh to which it had once been attached; and when he went to toss it in the burlap bag, he could not avoid hearing the dry, hollow sound it made. At times it seemed to him as if the bones were quietly laughing, their laughter not unlike the sound of a stone rolling over and over, or of a cricket chirping.

A skull cracked in two right before his eyes. As he looked at the jagged edges, he felt he was about to be sick. He had been suffering from a hangover since morning and was sure his stomach was about to go on a rampage. In the midday heat, his head felt terribly heavy.

A tattered pair of army boots was slung over the edge of the pit. As Kamakichi went to set them aside, he saw a perfect set of foot bones inside. Each and every white piece of bone was intact, arranged in five neat little rows. As he began to pull them out, he heard one bone that had stuck to the boot's inside sole snap and break off with a crisp, popping sound. He felt his fingers go numb. And suddenly, his chest began to heave. The nausea swept over him like a great wave that rose from his stomach and then surged forward.

The old woman was collecting skulls from which she painstakingly wiped the dirt. No matter what skull she picked up, it always seemed to have the look of a living human face. Although everything else had turned a rusty red, the teeth eerily retained their original shining white. It was if they were alive and wanted Kamakichi to know how hungry they were. He remembered the words his mother had said so many times. "War is hell. And, in that hell, no one escapes becoming a hungry ghost." She, too, had known what it was to fall into that hell and live among the hungry ghosts. Once, at the bottom of a dark cave at Makabe, she had taken a fistful of dirt and stuffed it into her little boy's mouth. Kamakichi was just a baby. He would not stop crying, and this was the only way she could silence him. She had seen a Japanese army officer silhouetted in the light at the mouth of the cave. His sword was drawn, and she knew that meant he would kill the child if he did not stop crying. And so it had become her habit to say to her son, "That's what war is like."

Doubtless these bones had been on the verge of starvation when the people died, and even now they wore a hungry look. Kamakichi's hands ceased to move, and kneeling there in front of a skull, he mentally traced on it what he could remember of his father's face.

Just then a canteen came rolling over the edge of the pit. Casually, Kamakichi picked it up, then realized he could hear water still splashing inside. He felt as if his face had been dashed with cold water, and a terrible chill ran down his spine.

At the 3:00 P.M. break the assistant section chief asked if the men had come across any gold fillings. The engine on the heavy-duty equipment owned by Toa Electric had been switched off, but still the men made no effort to reply. "It's amazing. All these bones and not one goldcapped tooth in the lot. I wonder why." The answer to this question he had posed like some mysterious riddle was patently obvious, but something kept the men from speaking up. It required too much energy.

That was when Kamakichi happened to notice a flat piece of bone sitting right in front of him. It was shaped like a spatula, and a fragment of rusted metal protruded from its surface. When he picked it up and looked at it closely, he could see that a sharply pointed blade had pierced all the way through to the other side. "It must have hurt like hell," he said, muttering almost to himself. Even he was shaken by the implication of his own words.

What was that? Suddenly he was overcome by a hallucination that his father was lying right next to him. Yes, there he was, lying on his side. Kamakichi had never thought much about his father until now. It had always seemed natural for his father not to be around. Except once—and that was when he had gone for an interview at the bank and they had rejected him for the job. He had resented being a son with a father who had never been more than a fleeting figure—a ghost—in his life.

Before anyone knew it, the construction boss was back, standing around and talking with the assistant section chief. It appeared they were discussing the next step in the project. Since there was no sign that "the bull" was about to start up again, the men in the city hall work crew stretched out and decided to relax for a while.

"Cut it down?" They could hear the high-pitched voice of the assistant section chief.

"The landscape people will be here tomorrow to do their survey, and we can't wait any longer. We're way behind schedule."

"But what a waste. You can't just cut down a tree as big as this one. And didn't you say this spot was going to be part of the hotel garden?"

"But that's exactly why it's in the way. Besides, it's only a local tree that grew here naturally. We'll be bringing in coconut and fern palms as part of the garden's motif."

The assistant section chief made no attempt to question the construction boss further.

"Since it has to be cut down, we might as well do it now," the construction boss said. "Then, starting tomorrow, we'll put up a tent over there for shade at break times."

"Damn it. This is an outrage! It's out-and-out violence, that's what it is. Now you've gone too far." Suddenly Hippie-Beard had leapt to his feet.

Startled by the young man's voice, everyone started to get up. But his expected protest did not last. And, looking as cool as could be, the construction boss ignored him.

"Our company has no intention of doing anything to inconvenience you."

Just then, the old turtle woman pushed her way through the men and stepped to the front of the group.

"Well, Mr. Bossman. You say you're going to chop down the banyan tree? And just who do you think it belongs to? That tree there was planted by my father. What's more, it has come to be possessed by the spirits of thousands of dead people. That's where their spirits live. Don't you have any common sense?"

There was something of the shamaness about the old woman. Her raised eyebrows floating high on her forehead and her old, yellowed eyes coated with moisture gave her the look of a woman possessed.

"I can't say I know much about the customs in these parts," said the construction boss. "Besides, the title to the land has already been transferred, and . . ."

"I'll never permit it. Never. Because this tree here is my father's. Don't you have any appreciation for all the hardship and suffering people had to go through in the past?"

"We can't allow you to interfere with our job. No matter what you say."

The men continued to stand where they were, silent and expressionless.

The construction boss' face was full of anger as his eyes surveyed, one by one, the row of apathetic faces before him.

At last the assistant section chief spoke. "Isn't it possible to move the tree somewhere else?"

"There'd be no problem, if it were all that easy. But look, I only work for somebody else, just like you."

The turtle woman stepped between the two men. "Look here, you. If you so much as lay a finger on that tree, there will be a curse on you wherever you go in Okinawa, and, before you know it, bad luck will come crashing down on that head of yours."

Kamakichi leaned back against the banyan tree as he studied the withered nape of the old woman's neck. Given his druthers, it was a scene he would have preferred never to have witnessed. How much better it would have been if he had averted his eyes and looked the other way. He felt his head grow feverish, and from time to time a knot tightened in his chest that made him feel as if he were going to be sick at any moment.

The surface of the banyan tree was rough to the touch, and it hurt when he rubbed his back against the trunk. Still, there was something about the tree that made him feel cool and refreshed. It made him think of his father again.

For no apparent reason he reached up and tore a single leaf from the branch overhead. Almost automatically his fingers went to work, and after trimming off the edges, he rolled the leaf up. Then, pinching one end of the rolled leaf between his fingers, he blew through it as hard as he could. The piercing screech it made took everyone by surprise. Even the construction boss' yellow safety helmet appeared to flash and—bang!—explode in the bright sunlight as he turned toward the sound of the whistle.

SHIMIZU YOSHINORI

Shimizu Yoshinori (b. 1947) began his writing career producing science-fiction novels and juvenile literature. In 1981 he hit his stride with the publication of the first of many amusing popular pastiches on such varied topics as college entrance examinations and the pitfalls of using a Japanese word-processing program. Shimizu even tried parodying classic works in both his native and Western literary canons. This story, "Jack and Betty Forever" (Eien no Jyakku & Betti, 1991), is typical of his satirical dig at the rigid norms of Japanese social interaction.

JACK AND BETTY FOREVER (EIEN NO JYAKKU & BETTI)

Translated by Frederik L. Schodt

Jack stared at the woman's face and felt time go into reverse inside his brain. She had a sophisticated, intelligent look, and sparkling brown eyes. She was no longer young, but she was still attractive and in full possession of her feminine charms.

Why, it's Betty, he thought fondly, as his speech control center regressed some thirty years. Words he would have normally used in conversation—the *Say, you're Betty, aren't you?* sort of thing—failed him, and he found himself reverting to the quaint speech patterns of his junior high school days.

"Are you Betty?" he asked.

A look of surprise spread over the woman's face when she heard this. And then her speech also became quaint, as if she, too, were overcome by nostalgia.

"Yes, I am Betty," she said.

"Are you Betty Smith?"

"Yes, I am Betty Smith."

There was no mistaking it. Her speech was filled with overtones of a time long past.

Then she asked him a question.

"Are you Jack?"

"Yes, I am Jack."

"Are you Jack Jones?"

"Yes, I am Jack Jones."

Thus, after meeting on the street for the first time in thirty years, the two of them began their odd conversation.

"Ah, it is so good to see you again," said Jack.

"Yes," said Betty. "I still have many memories from the old days."

"Are you single?"

"Yes, I am single."

"Let us drink a cup of coffee, or a cup of tea."

"Yes, let us do that."

Jack invited Betty to a local coffee shop. When they were inside, he asked, "Is this a table?"

"Yes," she answered, "this is a table."

"Is that a sofa?"

"No, that is not a sofa. That is a chair."

"Please sit down."

"Thank you."

"May I sit down, too?"

"Yes, you may sit down."

Just when Betty had reached the age when she would have gone to a good high school, her family had moved from the suburbs of Chicago to Utah. That was why Jack hadn't seen her since then. He was filled with fond memories. It had been thirty-four years. Both of them were now fifty years old.

"What do you do?" Betty asked, wondering what sort of work Jack did.

"I am a lawyer," he replied.

"That is a good job."

"Two months ago, however, I lost my job."

"Oh, that is too bad."

"I was a lawyer for an automobile manufacturer. The company went bankrupt because of increased imports of Japanese cars."

"That happens often, doesn't it?"

Jack suddenly assumed an ironic expression. "Do you remember," he asked, "that when we were in junior high school there was an English-language textbook for Japanese people modeled after us?"

"Yes. I remember it well. They used our names for the title."

"And because of that, at our school we deliberately started speaking English in a way that was easier for Japanese people to understand."

"Yes. I still find it hard not to speak like that."

"And now, thirty years later, I lose my job because of some Japanese who learned English from that same textbook."

"It is too bad."

Jack decided to change the subject. It was too depressing to talk about this when meeting an old friend.

"Where do you live?" he asked.

"Two weeks ago, I began living in Chicago again."

"What do you do?"

"I work at the Women's Liberation Association." Jack was a little surprised. Could the pretty young girl he remembered really be a militant in the Women's Lib movement?

"Are you married?" he asked.

"I used to be married," she said. "However, I live alone now."

"Did you and your husband divorce?"

"No. He died."

"I am sorry to hear that."

"He went to Vietnam right after we were married."

"Oh. Was he killed there?"

"No. He came back from Vietnam. However, he developed a mental illness. One day he barricaded himself in a supermarket and shot eight people to death with a gun. Then he was shot to death by the police."

"Oh, I am sorry to hear that."

"That is all in the past, however."

"How have you been?"

"I have been fine. And you?"

"I have been fine. Do you have any children?"

"Yes, I have one son. He is a high school student."

"Do you live with him?"

"No, he lives with my mother. Do you remember my mother?"

"Yes, I remember your mother. When I was twelve, you introduced me to her."

"She still remembers you."

"How is she?"

"She is fine."

"How is your father?"

"He died."

"Oh, I am sorry to hear that."

"His store went bankrupt when McDonald's entered the neighborhood. He was driven to despair, and one day after he had been drinking, his car ran off the road into a canal and he drowned."

An awful lot can happen to a person in thirty years, Jack thought. He wished there something they could do about their speech patterns, though.

"Does your son play baseball?" he asked.

"No, he does not play baseball."

"Does he play football?"

"No, he does not play football."

"Does he play the piano?"

"No, he does not play the piano."

"What does he do?"

"Sometimes he does drugs and rapes women."

An awkward silence ensued.

After a while Betty asked Jack a question.

"Are you married?"

"I used to be married. Now, however, I am single."

"Are you divorced?"

"Yes, I am divorced. After the courts took away our child, who was born from an artificially inseminated surrogate mother, we stopped getting along."

"Is your mother well?"

"No, she died two years ago."

"How is your father, who used to be an engineer?"

"He is in an old folks' home, but he is fine."

The conversation was strained. The awkward quality of their speech was one reason, but the subject matter was also putting a damper on things. Life wasn't quite as bright and cheery as they had imagined as children. Both Jack, who had once had such rosy cheeks, and Betty, whose eyes had been so clear and beautiful, were now middle-aged, and living in a harsh reality.

Jack tried to think of something more entertaining to talk about. "I remember your two older sisters," he said.

"I remember them, too," Betty answered.

"Jane was the oldest sister."

"Yes, Jane was the oldest."

"She was a teacher."

"She still is a teacher. She has been teaching all her life and she is still single. Sometimes people call her an 'old maid,' and she has a fit."

"Your next oldest sister was Emily. She was a university student."

"Yes, and after graduation she worked at a computer company."

"That is a good job."

"She became neurotic, however, and committed suicide."

The conversation came to a halt.

To ease the awkwardness, Jack said the first flattering thing he could think of.

"The clothes you are wearing are very beautiful, aren't they?"

Betty looked suspicious for a second, but then suddenly seemed to realize this line of conversation was much easier. She relaxed, and replied, "Thank you."

"That shirt is one of the most beautiful shirts I have ever seen," Jack continued.

"I bought it at a supermarket in the town where I used to live in Utah."

"What is that shirt made of?"

"This shirt is made of cotton."

"What is that skirt made of?"

"This skirt is made of acrylic fiber."

"You are not wearing a jacket."

"No, I am not wearing a jacket."

"Why are you not wearing a jacket?"

"It is too hot to wear a jacket today."

It is *too—to—*. It was such a familiar construction.

"I think so, too."

"I have never experienced such a hot day."

"This is one of the hottest days in memory."

"Lincoln was one of the greatest men in the history of the world."

"You are one of the most beautiful women in America."

"That is one of the most obviously flattering remarks I have ever heard in my life."

They had evidently reached a dead-end with the construction *One of the most—in—*.

Jack was wearing a jacket, so he said, "On a day this hot, I usually take off my jacket as soon as I get home."

"You probably take off your jacket to feel cooler."

"As soon as I take off my jacket I will feel cooler."

Jack regretted this line of conversation. It led nowhere.

"Where is the house that you now live in?"

"I live in a room in an apartment building nearby."

"Where is it?"

Betty pointed outside the window, and said, "Go east on this street, and turn left at the third intersection."

"I will."

"Then turn right at the second intersection and go a little farther. You should see a white building on the left side."

"I will probably see it."

"I live there."

Jack had absolutely no idea where she lived. But apparently it wasn't far away.

Betty suddenly changed the subject. She, too, seemed to want to get away from this stilted conversation.

"Whom do you admire?" she asked.

"I admire Neil Armstrong and John F. Kennedy."

Jack sensed a slight disappointment in Betty.

"Whom do you admire?" he asked.

"I admire George McGovern and Buckminster Fuller," she answered.

I'd better not discuss politics with this woman, Jack decided. Fuller, he knew, was the scholar who was practically a guru to the hippies who had made the *Whole Earth Catalog.* McGovern was the presidential candidate who had been supported by yippies, and lost. He and Betty apparently had very different politics and philosophies. He decided to steer clear of those subjects, and stick to something safer. The only problem was that they were both speaking so oddly that he didn't know what to talk about. He blurted out a silly sentence that no normal person would ever use in such a situation.

"This is a window," he said.

Betty, as if relieved, replied in the same vein.

"This is a floor," she said.

The two of them smiled, and exchanged some safe conversation.

"I have a pen."

"I have a receipt from the dentist."

"I have a short pencil."

"I have a shaver to remove unwanted hair."

"Is this your suppository?"

"No, that is not my suppository."

"Where do you keep your birth control pills?"

"I keep them in my handbag."

"Who are your favorite actresses?"

"I like Meryl Streep and Sissy Spacek. Who are your favorite actresses?"

"I like Brooke Shields and Phoebe Cates."

Our tastes are completely different, Jack thought. *She goes for career over looks, while I go for the precocious Lolita types.* But at least this line of conversation was easier.

"Do you speak French?"

"Yes, I speak a little French."

"Do you speak Tagalog?"

"No, I do not speak Tagalog."

"Do you have some butter?"

"No one takes butter with them when they go out."

"Which do you like better, Calvin Klein underwear or medicine for whitlow [fingernail or toenail] infections?"

"Does anyone really like that stuff?"

It was apparently not a good idea to be too nonsensical.

"What do you think of the influence, either direct or indirect, that existentialism as defined by Jean-Paul Sartre has had on the collapse of democracy in the United States of America?"

"I don't know. What do you think?"

"I don't know, either."

Jack grinned, trying to gloss over the situation.

"What time is it now?" he asked.

"It is one forty-five," Betty said.

"Is that fifteen minutes before two o'clock?"

"Yes, it is."

"What do you like to eat for breakfast?"

"I like orange juice, eggs, milk, buttered toast, and tofu pie."

"What do you eat for lunch?"

"I usually eat sandwiches and milk, or tuna and avocado sushi."

"What do you eat for dinner?"

"I usually eat vegetables, meat, milk, and bread and butter, but now I am fasting for health reasons."

"How many months are there in a year?"

"There are twelve months in a year."

Their senseless conversation quickly reached a dead-end. All of a sudden Betty said nostalgically, "I remember your younger brother. His name was Bill."

"Yes, his name is Bill."

"He invited me to his birthday party when he was seven."

"Yes, I remember it."

"I gave him a birthday present. It was a story book."

"Yes, it was."

"I remember him well. He was a cute little boy with fat cheeks. He was a charming boy, the type everyone loves."

Jack choked a little, but managed to reply, "He used to be the type of boy everyone likes."

"How is he?"

"He is not well."

"Is he sick?"

"He is in the hospital with AIDS."

Betty blinked in surprise and hurriedly changed the subject.

"I remember your little sister," she said. "Her name was Mary."

"Yes, her name is Mary."

An uneasy expression appeared on Betty's face.

"When I was in seventh grade, she was two years old."

"Yes, she used to be two years old."

"She was a very cute little girl."

"Yes, she was very cute."

Betty was at a loss for words. She turned toward Jack with a worried look, as if searching for something. And then, in a trembling voice, she asked, "How is she?"

Jack shrugged and said, "Who knows?"

Betty, having come this far, felt she had to probe further.

"Well, how is she doing?"

"When she was in her late teens she decided she wanted to become a movie star."

"Oh, I see."

"Then she appeared in several hard-core porno movies."

"Oh."

"After that I suddenly lost contact with her. I haven't heard a thing from her since."

"Oh, no."

"According to some people, she is working as a massage girl at a Japanese geisha house. But another theory is that she married an Eskimo, had thirteen children, and now spends her time busily skinning seals."

As if trying to smooth things over, Betty suddenly said in a ridiculously loud voice, "Let us talk about our old school."

"It was on a hill in the suburbs of Chicago."

"Yes, it was. It was a beautiful hill covered with grass."

"The principal's name was Mr. Brown."

"No, the principal's name was Mr. Hill."

"We are probably both correct."

"There was a teacher named Mr. Johnson."

"There was also a teacher named Mr. Rivers."

"There was also a teacher named Mr. Green."

"One of our classmates was named Dick."

"One of our other classmates was named Kate."

"It was a beautiful, peaceful school. I remember it fondly."

"I remember it fondly, too."

"I wonder what the school is like now?"

Jack shrugged again.

"The school is torn down now," he said. "They built a nuclear power plant on the hill."

"Oh, no."

"There was a little accident there last year, and they almost had a 'China Syndrome.'"

Noticing a gloomy look in Betty's eyes, Jack decided to change the subject. *I'm not having any luck with this conversation today,* he thought.

"Do you remember going to the bird show with me?" he asked.

A happy expression appeared on Betty's face.

"Why, yes," she said. "There was a bird show in the park. I liked birds, so the two of us went to the show."

"Do you remember the beautiful parrots there?"

"Yes, I do remember them. They were very beautiful parrots."

"Do you remember the big swan there?"

"Yes, I do remember the swan. And I also remember this. In front of one of the parrots you said, 'I think this is the most beautiful of all.' "

She was right. Jack could recall as clear as day how he had felt then. He had been very young, and he had actually wanted to say something different. He really couldn't have cared less about the beautiful parrot. And he hadn't even been thinking about the graceful swan. He hadn't invited Betty to the bird show because he wanted to watch birds. He had just wanted to go somewhere, anywhere, with her.

I was in love with Betty then, he thought. *In fact, I was in love with her the whole three years we were together at school, from the moment we introduced ourselves to each other with "I am a boy," and "I am a girl." But I was so naive then. During the whole three years, I never did manage to tell you how I really felt, Betty. I never kissed you, or even hinted that I loved you.*

All we did was go to the bird show together.

But, hey, I wasn't looking at the birds. When I said that one bird was the most beautiful, I really meant something completely different. I really meant that of all the girls at school, Betty, you were the most beautiful. That you were the most attractive girl in the whole wide world. You were far more charming than any old parrot or swan. I really believed it.

Jack could recall his first true love as clear as day. At the time he had thought that he might have had a chance with her in high school, but soon after that she had moved and disappeared. It had been a time when young people were more innocent than they are today, but he had already been interested in the opposite sex. He had later played around with a few girls, eventually been caught by one of them, gotten married, and then. . . . Perhaps if he had spent his youth with Betty, he thought, they might have fallen in love with each other.

Jack stared at Betty's face, right before him. It was true that she was no longer young, but she still exuded a refined beauty.

"What is the matter?" Betty asked.

Jack thought about trying to seduce her. They were both single, and there was nothing stopping them. Besides, as a single, middle-aged man, he was used to having a little fun. He should just act as he normally would in such a situation, he told himself.

But today he couldn't. His speech had reverted to patterns of thirty years ago, and all he could think of saying was *I want to have sex with you.*

He knew that wouldn't work. He knew she wasn't going to answer *Yes, I want to have sex with you too.*

He smiled forlornly. "It's . . . it's nothing," he said.

TAKAHASHI TAKAKO

Like many others, Takahashi Takako (b. 1932) is a postwar Japanese writer with a great interest in French literature, particularly in the novels of François Mauriac. In 1971, after her husband, himself a novelist, died, Takahashi began traveling to Europe, mainly to France. Partly because of the influence of the writer Endō Shūsaku, Takahashi was eventually baptized a Catholic. In the mid-1980s, she stopped writing for a while to become a nun but later resumed. Her writing often has a Jungian sense of the interpermeable borders of human personality. The story translated here is "Invalid" (Byōshin, 1978).

INVALID (BYŌSHIN)

Translated by Van C. Gessel

She was in the habit now of asking him how he was feeling. He always had something wrong with him somewhere, and he was so frail, it was evident that he carried some affliction inside him.

"How are you feeling?" She spoke the words into the receiver for what seemed like the thousandth time.

"Uh, not very good," he answered for the thousandth time. Over the telephone, his *uh* sounded like an *ugh* . . . which made him seem like a whining baby.

She asked the ritual question. "Where don't you feel good?"

"I've kind of got a cold." As evidence, he sniffled a couple of times.

"Oh, you're right, that's your nose, isn't it?" She had grown playful.

She could almost picture the white tip of his nose on the other end of the connection. It narrowed to a slender point, and it was cold. But from that protuberance he exhaled air, the faintly warm artifact that provided her the only contact she had with the interior of this man, this other person.

"I can almost see your nose," she laughed.

"You can?" He sounded a bit out of sorts. Perhaps she was having fun at his expense. He was in no mood for that. He had a cold and felt lousy.

"Is that all? Is your nose the only problem?" She knew as she spoke that she was turning rapacious.

"My throat hurts a little, too."

"Do you have a cough?"

Instead of answering, he hacked twice into the mouthpiece. The membranes in his throat must be several times more sensitive than a normal person's, she thought. But what shape was he in down in the deepest, unseeable parts of his body? She wanted to see and know the colors, the shapes, the feel and everything else about him.

"Cough again."

But this time he was silent. He must have sensed that she was toying with him.

One morning as he lay flat on his back, she had tightened her hands around his throat. He did not move or speak; he let her have her way with him. But soon after she loosened her grip, some kind of artifact welled up from inside him, like the sound a clock with failing springs makes just before it chimes. She held her breath and watched as the sound seeped from his mouth, and finally he had begun to cough.

"I've just been listening to Erik Satie." He changed the subject.

"Really? Even though you're not feeling well?" It seemed very peculiar to her.

"His *Gymnopédies* are marvelous, aren't they?" He raised his voice a bit when he said "marvelous."

She seemed to be able to hear the clear, indolent melodies. Moments earlier the music had filled the square, white space of his room and coursed over his body. She wanted to hear through the telephone the vestiges of sound that were tinged with the fragrances of his flesh.

"Imagine being able to listen to music when you aren't feeling well." She was caught up in the idea. In what manner did music insinuate itself into the interior of a man who had caught a cold? How were music and illness reconciled inside him? There probably were no answers to these questions. It all boiled down to the fact that she didn't think anyone sick could listen to music, whereas he was someone who could.

"Strange," she ventured.

"What is?" he asked in a stupefied voice.

"You are. Your insides are."

He invariably refused to follow her lead when she became this difficult.

"Do you have a fever?" The questioning resumed.

"A slight fever." There was no way of knowing how many times he had been prompted to utter that line.

"How does it make you feel?"

"That's enough."

"No, I want to know. Please tell me."

"I feel heavy." He was still able to respond pliantly.

"Where? Your head? Your whole body?"

"Everywhere."

"Really? Everywhere." With the fever as her probe, she wanted to penetrate his entire body. Then she could understand him better. "Then it's a fever and your nose and your throat. That's all that's bothering you." She presented her conclusions definitively, like a physician. But unlike a doctor, she did not analyze his symptoms. She wanted to experience his body in the same way that he experienced it.

"My stomach doesn't feel very good." He finally parted with the information grudgingly, as though he were uncovering a private treasure.

"Really!" Her spirits soared: she had been handed another clue. Unrepentant, she resumed the interrogation.

"What's wrong with it?"

"I feel sort of nauseated." This, too, was a speech he had repeated innumerable times. Strangely, though, the phrase did not seem worn no matter how many times he uttered it. On each and every occasion, he was in fact ill, and he was making a sincere effort to describe his condition. For her part, too, she listened to his complaints with an ever-fresh anticipation.

"Did you throw up?"

"I felt sick to my stomach in the middle of the night last night."

"But you didn't throw up, did you?"

"Lately I feel sick to my stomach every night."

"You just feel sick? I wonder why?"

"I've been this way for years. I just get nauseated sometimes."

"I know. It's peculiar, isn't it." It frustrated her that she could not get her hands on the nausea that nested within him. That inability began to seem like a grand enigma to her. If he had gotten sick because he'd eaten some spoiled food or had too much to drink, then there would be a physiological explanation for it. But evidently these attacks washed over him for no clear reason. It was a nausea that had recently come to roost within his body in the middle of the night, a nausea that could not be eradicated because they did not know its source, a nausea that seemed to be the riddle that was himself.

She was reminded of an earlier experience: then, too, he had contracted a cold. He complained of a sore throat, so she gave him a lozenge, a brown troche made of medicinal herbs. He took one in his hand, placed it in his mouth, and began to suck. He was sitting on the windowsill at this time, and as she stood over him, for no reason at all she put her hand on top of his head. A strange reverberation rumbled through her hand. So she placed her ear on top of his head where her hand had been. There could be no doubt: a peculiar echo sounded in her ears, as booming as if it had been amplified through a loudspeaker system. The situation was so ludicrous she began to laugh. It was the sort of sound that made her want to ask someone what it might be. She wondered if perhaps a pair of dice was rolling around inside his skull cavity. The more intent she became, the more she was convinced that she was listening to the riddle of his inner workings, a sound like rolling dice that could not possibly come from inside a person's head. And yet she was certain that if she asked him to take the lozenge from his mouth, the riddle would be all too easily solved.

Wouldn't it be possible to unravel the mystery of his illness in the same way? If that happened, she was certain that she could unravel the man himself from within.

"You're a strange person." After the third time she said that, she hung up phone.

The more greedily you try to understand people, the less you understand them.

On the other end of the connection she had just cut, though it was separated by several miles from where she sat, a conduit direct and invisible to the eye had been formed by virtue of the conversation that had passed between them, and she could hear the opening strains of an Erik Satie piece coming from the opposite pole. The sound came from a white room in a tall apartment building. Because the walls and ceilings and even the clothes closet were stark white, a somehow hypnotic languidness filled the room. And his prized stereo system was pumping the white room with the clear, indolent tones of the first of Satie's *Trois Gymno-pédies*. The sound was like an ivory mah-jongg tile clattering in a glass of white wine, a wine of course not Japanese but a vintage that had slept in the dark confines of a European cellar for more than a century. Decadence had distilled in the bottle, but it contained not a single impurity, resulting in a decadence peculiarly clear in color. Several quick drinks from the glass and it is evident that this is decadence, but a languorous sensation surges through the body and mind. Even in that lilt of intoxication, the cold ivory tile continues to clatter back and forth in the glass. There is no more trace of emotion: only sensation. That is Erik Satie. The man slides effortlessly into the very center of the music. And, yes, his illness resembles its melody. Now he turns away from the stereo and walks through the white room toward his bed. From the highway comes the dull echo of passing automobiles, and through his fifth-floor window, the brightness of an afternoon sun in a cloudless sky shines mercilessly, and at midday he cloisters himself in the white room with his maladies, and tilting his languid, slightly feverish head in the direction of the music, he stands stiffly next to his bed. Suddenly he is gripped with apprehension, as though he has completely forgotten everything that was just said over the telephone. The faint light of some vague existence has just opened a yawning pit before him. His illness is not solely to blame. As if to shield himself from that abyss, he focuses his ears on the music. With his innately keen sense of hearing, his ears can capture each of the sounds that make up a Satie composition as though they were concrete objects. "Superb," he thinks but does not say aloud, and comforted by the thought, he collapses onto the bed. Although the heat is turned up high, he feels a chill throughout his body and burrows under the covers. The white ceiling and white walls abruptly drop in on his eyes. Erik Satie floods the room. The lethargy that emanates from his ailing body joins with the flow of the lethargic music. Superb. Yet somehow unsettling. As if he is waging a battle between the two conflicting sensations, he thrashes his heavy, slightly feverish head back and forth on the pillow.

Relying on the imaginary conduit created by the telephone line, she watches the movement of his head, the only clues available to her.

"An Other," she mutters, then corrects it to, "The interior of an Other." She walks to the stereo in her own room. "Maybe. Maybe not."

In her record cabinet she has an Erik Satie, a present from him. But she takes out Saint-Saëns's Third Symphony instead. The stereo components he has assembled for her are smaller than his. She places Saint-Saëns on the turntable and sets the needle. It begins with a low melody that suggests a dark, desperate passion. She feels as though she is suddenly being abducted. To where? Yes, to inside herself. This symphony drags her with a fury into the depths of herself. The phone conversation that has just concluded is distant now—the man, his illnesses, everything about him hangs motionless like a star in the heavens, and she is brought face to face with the subterranean tempest that is her own interior. From inside her the first movement of the Saint-Saëns raises a blackly swirling storm. Unexpectedly the music thunders out, and spurts of blood or lava gush out, whether from Saint-Saëns or from herself she cannot say. Her entire body gyrates with sensations that are either joy or torment. And in the very lowest regions an immeasurably deep tempest coils like a serpent. So long as this music continues, she will not be able to be free of it, will not be able to return to life in human society. But it doesn't matter. This is what she is.

This is the kind of woman I am, she says to him.

I know that; I've heard it so many times.

No, I'm talking about what I'm like inside.

I've heard that, too. You're like a tempest, right?

But do you understand what I'm feeling now? Can you feel it exactly as I'm feeling it? To call it a storm—that's just an expedient. It's something that I can only try to describe in words like "tempest." It's indescribable, dark, fierce, pathetic, an incredible yearning. Even if you were here listening to this music with me, you couldn't comprehend what it opens up inside me. I could never make you understand it in a million words.

When the symphony ended and she stopped the record, she felt the kind of exhaustion that follows after a violent shock has passed through the body.

At some point in her life she had started listening to every word that emerged from the lips of anyone she conversed with. It was not some strategy she had adopted, but a habit she had unconsciously developed. Even as she strolled the paths of conversation alongside those who spoke with her, she was careful not to miss a single word that went into the forging of those paths. By paying close attention to the process of selection whereby one particular word was chosen over any other, she came to know her speakers very well. While it was true that everyone let slip an occasional discordant word, even those words—or, rather, those very words themselves—revealed something about that person's internal workings and served as the means by which she understood them thoroughly. In short, by tracing back each separate word that emerged from an individual, she was able to experience the interior that was the source of those words.

Her aim in speaking with others was to get to know them even better than they knew themselves. Her antennae were extended into realms of which others were not even aware.

But even these abilities ran into a solid wall of resistance in the presence of her rapacious feelings for this man.

He phoned to complain of a new malady, and again her spirits soared. This was a new clue about him.

Just as words emerge from a person's interior, sickness comes from the same source.

Even though he was young, his back had begun to ache. She strongly recommended that he be tested at an orthopedics ward, and it was decided she would meet him there.

When she reached the front door of the hospital, the dazzling whiteness of the newly constructed building made her hesitate for a moment. It had been a long time since she had set foot in a medical facility. The image of hospitals she carried in her mind was of places black and dismal and rife with shadows, with walls and corridors and ceilings and doors painted in terminal colors, as if they had been infected by the patients who passed by them. But here she was surrounded by shiny, polished colors; the entire building was dominated by a feeling of smoothness so overpowering it seemed likely that she would slip and fall if she were not careful, or that a patient might drop the illness he had carried in with him.

She noticed him sitting on a sofa in the first-floor waiting room, his back toward her. She had quickly glanced around and scooped him up with her eyes from among the crowd of waiting patients. Only the spot where he sat seemed to have a halo of life hovering over it.

"How is it? How's your back?" she asked, beaming.

He was holding the examination forms that the receptionist had given him, and he seemed just to be waiting for her to arrive before he hurried up to the orthopedics ward. He stood up as soon as she spoke to him.

"What's wrong with your back?" She continued to press him as they walked side by side through the meeting hall on the first floor. She had to be careful not to smile.

"I can't describe it," he responded dourly and would not look at her. They stood beside one another on the wide steps of the escalator leading to the second floor.

"Try to describe it anyway." She noticed a cluster of dandruff flakes on the back of his navy blue blazer and brushed them off with her hand, muttering to herself about men who live alone and pay no attention to their backs.

"Well, let's see," he said. Since she was older than he, whenever she badgered him he tried to comply and answer.

Apparently they had at least an hour's wait in the corridor outside the orthopedics ward. A godsend seemed within her grasp: she could spend that time asking him anything she wanted about his afflictions.

"I fell down skiing when I was a child. Ever since then my back hurts sometimes." He lit a cigarette.

"Really? You ski? I didn't know that."

"I tried it for only a little while."

"I should think so. You never struck me as a sportsman. No, you mustn't ever get involved in sports. You were born an invalid, after all." She realized the remark was peculiar, but she made no attempt to retract it, and he did not try to challenge it. That was the nature of the relationship that had developed between them.

"This time, though, it seems to hurt a little differently." He apparently had accepted the fact that having come ailing to a hospital, there was nothing to do but talk about his illness.

"How is it different?" She was insistent. She had come so far with him. But she was not tormenting him with her questions: she was the one in agony. There was no way she could escape this agony if she could not find out just how his back hurt him.

"It's a throbbing pain."

"Where?" She started to lift up the tails of his blue blazer, but since others were watching, he stopped her. Patients were jammed together in the sofas that lined the corridor.

"Right around here." After he pushed her hand away, he placed his own hand on his back near the waist.

"Where?" She ducked her head and gazed searchingly at his back. He must be talking about the flat, fleshless crevice between his slender waist and his buttocks.

"It's so bad I can't walk."

"But you walked here, didn't you?"

"I just had to endure it."

"Endure it? How much endurance did it take?"

"I told you I can't describe it."

"Don't try to fool me. Anybody can say he can't describe it."

"But it hurts!" He would say no more after that outburst.

"For one thing, I have no idea how much pain you're in. For another thing, I have no idea how much you've had to endure the pain. There isn't any way I can understand that until somebody invents some kind of machine to measure what goes on inside a person's feelings. So I don't know who's in more pain— the person who screams that he's in pain, or the one who quietly endures. Does the man who screams have no threshold of endurance, or does he cry out because he's suffering infinitely more pain than the man who puts up with it? Does the man who grits his teeth remain silent because he has the ability to bear up against excruciating agony, or can he endure because he really isn't in all that much pain . . . ?"

She went on in a low voice, even though in reality she wanted to shout her questions to the whole world.

"I'm sorry." She realized what she was doing. "And you in so much pain." In fact she was in pain inside, too. It was a pain that would probably not subside until the world provided some answers to her questions.

She looked around at the patients. Unlike other social gathering places, here each individual was crouched inward, focusing only on himself. It was obvious at a glance that some were invalids, while others on the surface looked no different from someone who might be seated beside you on a train. But all of them were equally turned inward now. Probably because their illnesses lay inside. There was just one woman, a plump, red-faced housewife, who was playing noisily with two young children: that single spot in the building seemed to be suspended in midair. She looked as though she had gone insane. What was she doing here? Was she waiting here for a husband or relative or girlfriend? Everyone else in the corridor seemed to be submerged in thought and indifferent to the vibrant clamor. They were thinking that since they had to wait here, there was nothing else for them to think about except that they had to wait here.

Finally his name was called. She stood up to go into the examination room with him, but he motioned for her to remain, so she sat back down on the sofa. He vanished behind the thin cream-color plastic door, leaving her with the impression that he had disappeared from the planet. The substance of the pain he bore had been snatched away from her on the opposite side of that fiercely hygienic door. She had come here with the intention of being present as the doctor examined him. The thing she most wanted to know was being stolen away from her by the doctor at this very moment. She wanted to become a doctor herself and grope her way through his organs and bones and muscles one by one, until she could lay her bare hands on the illness tucked deep inside.

He came back out, carrying his blue blazer over his arm and an examination chart in his hand.

She sprang to her feet. "How did it go?"

Uh was all he said. It was that same whining voice that sounded like an *ugh* over the telephone.

"Is it bad? Or nothing to worry about?" She walked beside him down the corridor.

"I have to have a blood test and then some X-rays." That must be why he had removed his jacket.

"They're going to take your blood? I'd like to watch. I wonder what color it is?" Her eyes widened.

"Stop it. You're too greedy," he said peevishly.

"I'm too greedy? You figured that out, did you?"

"I've never met a woman like you." He gave a quick chortle and hurried to the room for the blood test, where again he disappeared behind a door.

When he came back out, his right sleeve was rolled up, and he held a piece of cotton against the inner part of his forearm. Blood trickled from beneath the white cotton. Her eyes locked onto it.

"They found out once when I had a blood-precipitation test that I have unusually thin blood." The remark came out randomly as he walked toward the X-ray room.

"Unusually thin?" Again she looked at the bloodied cotton ball against his arm.

"Yes. They tell me that's just the opposite of a healthy person's."

"I'm sure it's beautiful thin blood." She narrowed her eyelids and tried to picture the color of the fresh blood that coursed through his white body. There must be some correlation between the whiteness of his skin and the viscosity of his blood.

He was swallowed up behind the door of the X-ray room. She paced aimlessly up and down the corridor. Several different examination rooms had been clustered together, making it a simple matter to make the rounds of the entire floor. The alienation she had felt from the sparkling slipperiness of the new building when she first came in had largely subsided. In fact, the wards were decorated with chains of red flowers; a large plant that resembled a palm tree had been set out in the center of the second-floor meeting hall; and flower arrangements had been provided in each room. The whole building had been made whitely, inorganically bright, as if in the hope of neutralizing the diseases that people carried so protectively inside themselves.

She walked in front of the receptionist's office outside the X-ray room. Through the receptionist's glass windows, she could see into the dark X-ray chamber. She crouched down and thrust her head forward, struggling to see into the room. She could make out the faint reflection of the man's naked upper torso and head. The X-ray machine must be pointed at his ailing back. He had to change postures and positions over and over again. They seemed to be taking pictures from a variety of angles. In that dark room packed with imposing metal instruments designed to peer into the interior of the human body, he looked as though he was being forced to perform some sort of ridiculous gymnastic movements. He bent over at the waist, twisted his torso, leaned forward, leaned back, lay on his side—in the course of these twists and turns, for even a fleeting moment would his illness bare its flat, expressionless face?

Several days later a large envelope was sent to her address via registered mail. In response to her eager request to see his X-rays, he had come up with some pretext and gotten permission to borrow them from the hospital. They seemed to have taken scores of pictures that day, but he had sent her only three—one taken directly from behind, one at an angle from behind and one straight on from the side. All were of only the waist area of his body. She first examined the picture taken from behind. Seen in this manner, his bones appeared surprisingly slender. His vertebrae were stacked one upon another like jewels, culminating in the gem of his tailbone. It lay in the spot where there were vestiges of a tail from the time when human beings were animals. His pelvis, too, looked surprisingly small, as though it belonged to a child.

She lined up the three photographs beside one another, narrowed her eyes and studied them one by one, then stepped back and took them all into her field of vision. The internal structure of the body she knew so well from without emerged grayly and dimly before her. These diagrams, with their white cross-stripes and black caverns—the more carefully she examined them, the less she was sure what they signified. Even so she waited; waited in the hope that somewhere in the depths of those translucent slides that purported to display the human body, a flat, expressionless face would make its appearance.

He had enclosed a letter. —*As I told you on the phone the other day, they can't say anything for certain, as you can see from the enclosed. They can't determine the source of my back problems from these photographs. They tell me it's called "back pain." And that's it.*

Back pain, she muttered, and smiled to herself. They had searched for the cause of his back pain and had given it the name of "back pain." If the back was having problems, anybody could come up with a name like "back pain."

Through the photographs, she blankly turned her eyes upon his interior. *They can't say anything for certain.* The words came back to her like an echo.

TAWADA YŌKO

Although Tawada Yōko (b. 1960) was born and raised in Tokyo, she has lived in Germany since 1982, received a master's degree in German literature from Hamburg University in 1990, and writes in both Japanese and German. Her story "The Bridegroom Was a Dog" (Inumuko iri, 1993, trans. 2003) won the Akutagawa Prize, and in 1996 Tawada was awarded Germany's Adelbert von Chamisso Prize, given to outstanding foreign writers. Her collection *Where Europe Begins* (*Yoroppa no hajimaru tokoro*, 1988) contains stories written in both German, as was the title story, "Where Europe Begins" (Wo Europa Anfängt), and Japanese.

WHERE EUROPE BEGINS (WO EUROPA ANFÄNGT)

Translated from German by Susan Bernofsky

1

For my grandmother, to travel was to drink foreign water. Different places, different water. There was no need to be afraid of foreign landscapes, but foreign water could be dangerous. In her village lived a girl whose mother was suffering from an incurable illness. Day by day her strength waned, and her brothers were secretly planning her funeral. One day as the girl sat alone in the garden beneath the tree, a white serpent appeared and said to her: "Take your mother to see the Fire Bird. When she has touched its flaming feathers, she will be well again." "Where does the Fire Bird live?" asked the girl. "Just keep going west. Behind three tall mountains lies a bright shining city, and at its center, atop a high tower, sits the Fire Bird." "How can we ever reach this city if it is so far off? They say the mountains are inhabited by monsters." The serpent replied: "You needn't be afraid of them. When you see them, just remember that you, too, like all other human beings, were once a monster in one of your previous lives. Neither hate them nor do battle with them, just continue on your way. There is only one thing you must remember: when you are in the city where the Fire Bird lives, you must not drink a single drop of water." The girl thanked him, went to her mother and told her everything she had learned. The next day the two of them set off. On every mountain they met a monster that spewed green, yellow and blue fire and tried to burn them up; but as soon as the girl reminded herself that she, too, had once been just like them, the monsters sank into the ground. For ninety-nine days they wandered through the forest, and finally they reached the city, which shone brightly with a strange light. In the burning heat, they saw a tower in the middle of this city, and atop it sat the Fire Bird. In her joy, the girl forgot the serpent's warning and drank water from the pond. Instantly the girl became ninety-nine years old and her mother vanished in the flaming air.

When I was a little girl, I never believed there was such a thing as foreign water, for I had always thought of the globe as a sphere of water with all sorts of small and large islands swimming on it. Water had to be the same everywhere. Sometimes in sleep I heard the murmur of the water that flowed beneath the main island of Japan. The border surrounding the island was also made of water that ceaselessly beat against the shore in waves. How can one say where the place of foreign water begins when the border itself is water?

2

The crews of three Russian ships stood in uniform on the upper deck playing a farewell march whose unfamiliar solemnity all at once stirred up the oddest feelings in me. I, too, stood on the upper deck, like a theatergoer who has mistakenly stepped onstage, for my eyes were still watching me from among the crowd on the dock, while I myself stood blind and helpless on the ship. Other passengers threw long paper snakes in various colors toward the dock. The red streamers turned midair into umbilical cords—one last link between the passengers and their loved ones. The green streamers became serpents and proclaimed their warning, which would probably only be forgotten on the way, anyhow. I tossed one of the white streamers into the air. It became my memory. The crowd slowly withdrew, the music faded, and the sky grew larger behind the mainland. The moment my paper snake disintegrated, my memory ceased to function. This is why I no longer remember anything of this journey. The fifty hours aboard the ship to the harbor town in Eastern Siberia, followed by the hundred and sixty hours it took to reach Europe on the Trans-Siberian Railroad, have become a blank space in my life which can be replaced only by a written account of my journey.

3

Diary excerpt:

The ship followed the coastline northward. Soon it was dark, but many passengers still sat on the upper deck. In the distance one could see the lights of smaller ships. "The fishermen are fishing for squid," a voice said behind me. "I don't like squid. When I was little, we had squid for supper every third night. What about you?" another voice asked. "Yes," a third one responded, "I ate them all the time too. I always imagined they were descended from monsters!" "Where did you grow up?" the first voice asked.

Voices murmured all around me, tendrils gradually entwining. On board such a ship, everyone begins putting together a brief autobiography, as though he might otherwise forget who he is.

"Where are you going?" the person sitting next to me asked. "I'm on my way to Moscow." He stared at me in surprise. "My parents spoke of this city so often I wanted to see it with my own eyes!" Had my parents really talked about Moscow? On board such a ship, everyone begins to lie. The man was looking so horrified I had to say something else right away. "Actually I'm not so interested in Moscow itself, but I want to have experienced Siberia!" "What do you want to experience in Siberia?" he asked, "What is there in Siberia?" "I don't know yet. Maybe nothing to speak of. But the important thing for me is traveling *through* Siberia!" The longer I spoke, the more unsure of myself I became. He went to sit beside another passenger, leaving me alone with the transparent word *through*.

4

A few months before I set off on my journey, I was working evenings after school in a food processing factory. A poster advertising a trip to Europe on the Trans-Siberian Railroad transformed the immeasurably long distance to Europe into a finite sum of money.

In the factory, the air was kept at a very low temperature so the meat wouldn't go bad. I stood in this cold, which I referred to as "Siberian frost," wrapping frozen poultry in plastic. Beside the table stood a bucket of hot water in which I could warm my hands at intervals.

Once three frozen chickens appeared in my dreams. I watched my mother place them in the frying pan. When the pan was hot, they suddenly came to life and flew out the kitchen window. "No wonder we never have enough to eat," I said with such viciousness even I was shocked. "What am I supposed to do?" my mother asked, weeping.

Besides earning money, there were two other things I wanted to do before my departure: learn Russian and write an account of the journey. I always wrote a travel narrative before I set off on a trip, so that during the journey I'd have something to quote from. I was often speechless when I traveled. This time it was particularly useful that I'd written my report beforehand. Otherwise, I wouldn't have known what to say about Siberia. Of course, I might have quoted from my diary, but I have to admit that I made up the diary afterward, having neglected to keep one during the journey.

5

Excerpt from my first travel narrative:

Our ship left the Pacific and entered the Sea of Japan, which separates Japan from Eurasia. Since the remains of Siberian mammoths were discovered in Japan, there have been claims that a land bridge once linked Japan and Siberia. Presumably human beings also crossed from Siberia to Japan. In other words, Japan was once part of Siberia.

In the *Atlas of the World* in the ship's library I looked up Japan, this child of Siberia that had turned its back on its mother and was now swimming alone in the Pacific. Its body resembled that of a seahorse, which in Japanese is called *tatsu-no-otoshigo*—the lost child of the dragon.

Next to the library was the dining room, which was always empty during the day. The ship rolled on the stormy seas, and the passengers stayed in bed. I stood alone in the dining room, watching plates on the table slide back and forth without being touched. All at once I realized I had been expecting this stormy day for years, since I was a child.

6

Something I told a woman three years after the journey:

At school we often had to write essays, and sometimes these included "dream descriptions." Once I wrote about the dream in which my father had red skin.

My father comes from a family of merchants in Osaka. After World War II, he came to Tokyo with all he owned: a bundle containing, among other things, an alarm clock. This clock, which he called the "Rooster of the

Revolution," soon stopped running, but as a result, it showed the correct time twice each day, an hour that had to be returned to twice a day anyhow. "Time runs on its own, you don't need an alarm clock for that," he always said in defense of his broken clock, "and when the time comes, the city will be so filled with voices of the oppressed that no one will be able to hear a clock ring any longer."

His reasons for leaving the land of his birth he always explained to his relatives in a hostile tone: "Because he was infected with the Red Plague." These words always made me think of red, inflamed skin.

A huge square, crowds of people strolling about. Some of them had white hair, others green or gold, but all of them had red skin. When I looked closer, I saw that their skin was not inflamed but rather inscribed with red script. I was unable to read the text. No, it wasn't a text at all but consisted of many calendars written on top of each other. I saw number-less stars in the sky. At the tip of the tower, the Fire Bird sat observing the motion in the square.

This must have been "Moscow," I wrote in my essay, which my teacher praised without realizing I had invented the dream. But then what dream is not invented?

Later I learned that for a number of leftists in Western Europe this city had a different name: Peking.

7

Diary excerpt:

> The ship arrived in the harbor of the small Eastern Siberian town Na-chodka. The earth seemed to sway beneath my feet. No sooner had I felt the sensation of having put a border, the sea, behind me than I glimpsed the beginning of the train tracks that stretched for ten thousand kilometers.

That night I boarded the train. I sat down in a four-bed compartment where I was soon joined by two Russians. The woman, Masha, offered me pickled mushrooms and told me she was on her way to visit her mother in Moscow. "Ever since I got married and moved to Nachodka, my mother has been *behind* Siberia," she said. Siberia, then, is the border between here and there, I thought such a wide border!

I lay down on the bed on my belly and gazed out the window. Above the out-lines of thousands of birches I saw numberless stars that seemed about to tumble down. I took out my pocket notebook and wrote:

When I was a baby, I slept in a Mexican hammock. My parents had bought the hammock not because they found it romantic, but because the apartment was so cramped that there was no room for me except in the air. All there was in the apartment was seven thousand books whose stacks lined the three walls all the way to the ceiling. At night they turned into trees thick with foliage. When a large truck drove past the house, my Mexican hammock swung in the forest. But during the minor earthquakes that frequently shook the house, it remained perfectly still, as though there were an invisible thread connecting it to the subterranean water.

8

Diary excerpt:

When the first sun rose over Siberia, I saw an infinitely long row of birches. After breakfast I tried to describe the landscape, but couldn't. The window with its tiny curtains was like the screen in a movie theater. I sat in the front row, and the picture on the screen was too close and too large. The segment of landscape was repeated, constantly changing, and refused me entry. I picked up a collection of Siberian fairy tales and began to read.

In the afternoon I had tea and gazed out the window again. Birches, nothing but birches. Over my second cup of tea I chatted with Masha, not about the Siberian landscape but about Moscow and Tokyo. Then Masha went to another compartment, and I remained alone at the window. I was bored and began to get sleepy. Soon I was enjoying my boredom. The birches vanished before my eyes, leaving only the again-and-again of their passage, as in an imageless dream.

9

Excerpt from my first travel narrative:

Siberia, "the sleeping land" (from the Tartar: *sib* = sleep, *ir* = Earth), but it wasn't asleep. So it really wasn't at all necessary for the prince to come kiss the Earth awake. (He came from a European fairy tale.) Or did he come to find treasure?

When the Creator of the Universe was distributing treasures on Earth and flew over Siberia, he trembled so violently with cold that his hands grew stiff and the precious stones and metals he held in them fell to the ground. To hide these treasures from Man, he covered Siberia with eternal frost.

It was August, and there was no trace of the cold that had stiffened the Creator's hands. The Siberian tribes mentioned in my book were also nowhere to be seen, for the Trans-Siberian Railroad traverses only those regions populated by Russians—tracing out a path of conquered territory, a narrow extension of Europe.

10

Something I told a woman three years after the journey:

For me, Moscow was always the city where you never arrive. When I was three years old, the Moscow Artists' Theater performed in Tokyo for the first time. My parents spent half a month's salary on tickets for Chekhov's *Three Sisters*.

When Irina, one of the three sisters, spoke the famous words: "To Moscow, to Moscow, to Moscow . . . ," her voice pierced my parents' ears so deeply that these very same words began to leap out of their own mouths as well. The three sisters never got to Moscow, either. The city must have been hidden somewhere backstage. So it wasn't Siberia, but rather the theater stage that lay between my parents and the city of their dreams.

In any case, my parents, who were often unemployed during this period, occasionally quoted these words. When my father, for example, spoke of his unrealistic plan of founding his own publishing house, my mother would say, laughing, "To Moscow, to Moscow, to Moscow. . . ." My father would say the same thing whenever my mother spoke of her childhood in such a way as though she might be able to become a child again. Naturally, I didn't understand what they meant. I only sensed that the word had something to do with impossibility. Since the word "Moscow" was always repeated three times, I didn't even know it was a city and not a magic word.

11

Diary excerpt:

I flipped through a brochure the conductor had given me. The photographs showed modern hospitals and schools in Siberia. The train stopped at the big station at Ulan-Ude. For the first time, there were many faces in the train that were not Russian.

I laid the brochure aside and picked up my book.
A fairy tale told among the Tungus:

Once upon a time there was a shaman who awakened all the dead and wouldn't let even a single person die. This made him stronger than God. So God suggested a contest: by magic words alone, the shaman was to transform two pieces of chicken meat given him by God into live chickens. If the shaman failed, he wouldn't be stronger than God any longer. The first piece of meat was transformed into a chicken by the magic words and flew away, but not the second one. Ever since, human beings have died. Mostly in hospitals.

Why was the shaman unable to change the second piece of meat into a chicken? Was the second piece somehow different from the first, or did the number two rob the shaman of his power? For some reason, the number two always makes me uneasy.

I also made the acquaintance of a shaman, but not in Siberia; it was much later, in a museum of anthropology in Europe. He stood in a glass case, and his voice came from a tape recorder that was already rather old. For this reason his voice always quavered prodigiously and was louder than a voice from a human body. The microphone is an imitation of the flame that enhances the voice's magical powers.

Usually, the shamans were able to move freely between the three zones of the world. That is, they could visit both the heavens and the world of the dead just by climbing up and down the World-Tree. My shaman, though, stood not in one of these three zones, but in a fourth one: the museum. The number four deprived him permanently of his power: his face was frozen in an expression of fear, his mouth, half-open, was dry, and in his painted eyes burned no fire.

12

Excerpt from my first travel narrative:

In the restaurant car I ate a fish called *omul'*. Lake Baikal is also home to several other species that actually belong in a saltwater habitat, said a Russian teacher sitting across from me—the Baikal used to be a sea.

But how could there possibly be a sea here, in the middle of the continent? Or is the Baikal a hole in the continent that goes all the way through? That would mean my childish notion about the globe being a sphere of water was right after all. The water of the Baikal, then, would be the surface of the water-sphere. A fish could reach the far side of the sphere by swimming through the water.

And so the *omul'* I had eaten swam around inside my body that night, as though it wanted to find a place where its journey could finally come to an end.

13

There were once two brothers whose mother, a Russian painter, had emigrated to Tokyo during the Revolution and lived there ever since. On her eightieth birthday she expressed the wish to see her native city, Moscow, once more before she died. Her sons arranged for her visa and accompanied her on her journey on the Trans-Siberian Railroad. But when the third sun rose over Siberia, their mother was no longer on the train. The brothers searched for her from first car to last, but they couldn't find her. The conductor told them the story of an old man who three years earlier, had opened the door of the car, mistaking it for the door to the toilet, and had fallen from the train. The brothers were granted a special visa and traveled the same stretch in the opposite direction on the local train. At each station they got out and asked whether anyone had seen their mother. A month passed without their finding the slightest trace.

I can remember the story up to this point; afterward I must have fallen asleep. My mother often read me stories that filled the space between waking and sleep so completely that, in comparison, the time when I was awake lost much of its color and force. Many years later I found, quite by chance, the continuation of this story in a library.

The old painter lost her memory when she fell from the train. She could remember neither her origins nor her plans. So she remained living in a small village in Siberia that seemed strangely familiar to her. Only at night, when she heard the train coming, did she feel uneasy, and sometimes she even ran alone through the dark woods to the tracks, as though someone had called to her.

14

As a child, my mother was often ill, just like her own mother, who had spent half her life in bed. My mother grew up in a Buddhist temple in which one could hear, as early as five o'clock in the morning, the prayer that her father, the head priest of the temple, was chanting with his disciples.

One day, as she sat alone under a tree reading a novel, a student who had come to visit the temple approached her and asked whether she always read such thick books. My mother immediately replied that what she'd like best was a novel so long she could never finish it, for she had no other occupation but reading.

The student considered a moment, then told her that in the library in Moscow there was a novel so long that no one could read all of it in a lifetime. This novel was not only long, but also as cryptic and cunning as the forests of Siberia, so that people got lost in it and never found their way out again once they'd entered. Since then, Moscow has been the city of her dreams, its center not Red Square, but the library.

This is the sort of thing my mother told me about her childhood. I was still a little girl and believed in neither the infinitely long novel in Moscow nor the student who might have been my father. For my mother was a good liar and told lies often and with pleasure. But when I saw her sitting and reading in the middle of the forest of books, I was afraid she might disappear into a novel. She never rushed through books. The more exciting the story became, the more slowly she read.

She never actually wanted to arrive at any destination at all, not even "Moscow." She would greatly have preferred for "Siberia" to be infinitely large. With my father things were somewhat different. Although he never got to Moscow, either, he did inherit money and founded his own publishing house, which bore the name of this dream city.

15

Diary excerpt:

There were always a few men standing in the corridor smoking strong-smelling Stolica cigarettes (*stolica* = capital city).

"How much longer is it to Moscow?" I asked an old man who was looking out the window with his grandchild.

"Three more days," he responded and smiled with eyes that lay buried in deep folds.

So in three days I would really have crossed Siberia and would arrive at the point where Europe begins? Suddenly I noticed how afraid I was of arriving in Moscow.

"Are you from Vietnam?" he asked.

"No, I'm from Tokyo."

His grandchild gazed at me and asked him in a low voice: "Where is Tokyo?" The old man stroked the child's head and said softly but clearly: "In the East." The child was silent and for a moment stared into the air as though a city were visible there. A city it would probably never visit.

Hadn't I also asked questions like that when I was a child? —Where is Peking? —In the West. —And what is in the East, on the other side of the sea? —America.

The world sphere I had envisioned was definitely not round, but rather like a night sky, with all the foreign places sparkling like fireworks.

16

During the night I woke up. Rain knocked softly on the windowpane. The train went slower and slower. I looked out the window and tried to recognize something in the darkness. . . . The train stopped, but I couldn't see a station. The outlines of the birches became clearer and clearer, their skins brighter, and suddenly there was a shadow moving between them. A bear? I remembered that many Siberian tribes bury the bones of bears so they can be resurrected. Was this a bear that had just returned to life?

> The shadow approached the train. It was not a bear but a person. The thin figure, face half concealed beneath wet hair, came closer and closer with outstretched arms. I saw the beams of three flashlights off to the left. For a brief moment, the face of the figure was illumined: it was an old woman. Her eyes were shut, her mouth open, as though she wanted to cry out. When she felt the light on her, she gave a shudder, then vanished in the dark woods.

This was part of the novel I wrote before the journey and read aloud to my mother. In this novel, I hadn't built a secret pathway leading home for her; in contrast to the novel in Moscow, it wasn't very long.

"No wonder this novel is so short," my mother said. "Whenever a woman like that shows up in a novel, it always ends soon, with her death."

"Why should she die? *She* is Siberia."

"Why is Siberia a *she*? You're just like your father, the two of you only have one thing in your heads: going to Moscow."

"Why don't you go to Moscow?"

"Because then you wouldn't get there. But if I stay here, you can reach your destination."

"Then I won't go, I'll stay here."

"It's too late. You're already on your way."

17

Excerpt from the letter to my parents:

> Europe begins not in Moscow but somewhere before. I looked out the window and saw a sign as tall as a man with two arrows painted on it, beneath which the words "Europe" and "Asia" were written. The sign stood in the middle of a field like a solitary customs agent.
>
> "We're in Europe already!" I shouted to Masha, who was drinking tea in our compartment.

"Yes, everything's Europe behind the Ural Mountains," she replied, unmoved, as though this had no importance, and went on drinking her tea.

I went over to a Frenchman, the only foreigner in the car besides me, and told him that Europe didn't just begin in Moscow. He gave a short laugh and said that Moscow was not Europe.

18

Excerpt from my first travel narrative:

The waiter placed my borscht on the table and smiled at Sasha, who was playing with the wooden doll Matroshka next to me. He removed the figure of the round farmwife from its belly. The smaller doll, too, was immediately taken apart, and from its belly came—an expected surprise—an even smaller one. Sasha's father, who had been watching his son all this time with a smile, now looked at me and said:

"When you are in Moscow, buy a Matroshka as a souvenir. This is a typically Russian toy."

Many Russians do not know that this "typically Russian" toy was first manufactured in Russia at the end of the nineteenth century, modeled after ancient Japanese dolls. But I don't know what sort of Japanese doll could have been the model for Matroshka. Perhaps a *kokeshi*, which my grandmother once told me the story of. A long time ago, when the people of her village were still suffering from extreme poverty, it sometimes happened that women who gave birth to children, rather than starving together with them, would kill them at birth. For each child that was put to death, a *kokeshi*, meaning make-the-child-go-away, was crafted, so that the people would never forget they had survived at the expense of these children. To what story might people connect Matroshka some day? Perhaps with the story of the souvenir, when people no longer know what souvenirs are.

"I'll buy a Matroshka in Moscow," I said to Sasha's father. Sasha extracted the fifth doll and attempted to take it, too, apart. "No, Sasha, that's the littlest one," his father cried. "Now you must pack them up again."

The game now continued in reverse. The smallest doll vanished inside the next-smallest one, then this one inside the next, and so on.

In a book about shamans, I had once read that our souls can appear in dreams in the form of animals or shadows or even dolls. The Matroshka is probably the soul of the travelers in Russia who, sound asleep in Siberia, dream of the capital.

19

I read a Samoyedic fairy tale:

> Once upon a time there was a small village in which seven clans lived in seven tents. During the long, hard winter, when the men were off hunting, the women sat with their children in the tents. Among them was a woman who especially loved her child.
>
> One day she was sitting with her child close beside the fire, warming herself. Suddenly a spark leapt out of the fire and landed on her child's skin. The child began to cry. The woman scolded the fire: "I give you wood to eat and you make my child cry! How dare you? I'm going to pour water on you!" She poured water on the fire, and so the fire went out.
>
> It grew cold and dark in the tent, and the child began to cry again. The woman went to the next tent to fetch new fire, but the moment she stepped into the tent, this fire, too, went out. She went on to the next one, but here the same thing happened. All seven fires went out, and the village was dark and cold.

"Do you realize we're almost in Moscow?" Masha asked me. I nodded and went on reading.

> When the grandmother of this child heard what had happened, she came to the tent of the woman, squatted down before the fire and gazed deep into it. Inside, on the hearth, sat an ancient old woman, the Empress of Fire, with blood on her forehead. "What has happened? What should we do?" the grandmother asked. With a deep, dark voice, the empress said that the water had torn open her forehead and that the woman must sacrifice her child so that people will never forget that fire comes from the heart of the child.

"Look out the window! There's Moscow!" cried Masha. "Do you see her? That's Moscow, *Moskva*!"

> "What have you done?" the grandmother scolded the woman. "Because of you, the whole village is without fire! You must sacrifice your child, otherwise we'll all die of cold!" The mother lamented and wept in despair, but there was nothing she could do.

"Why don't you look out the window? We're finally there!" Masha cried. The train was going slower and slower.

> When the child was laid on the hearth, the flames shot up from its heart, and the whole village was lit up so brightly it was as if the Fire Bird had

descended to Earth. In the flames the villagers saw the Empress of Fire, who took the child in her arms and vanished with it into the depths of the light.

20

The train arrived in Moscow, and a woman from Intourist walked up to me and said that I had to go home again at once, because my visa was no longer valid. The Frenchman whispered in my ear: "Start shouting that you want to stay here." I screamed so loud that the wall of the station cracked in two. Behind the ruins, I saw a city that looked familiar: it was Tokyo. "Scream louder or you'll never see Moscow!" the Frenchman said, but I couldn't scream any more because my throat was burning and my voice was gone. I saw a pond in the middle of the station and discovered that I was unbearably thirsty. When I drank the water from the pond, my gut began to ache and I immediately lay down on the ground. The water I had drunk grew and grew in my belly and soon it had become a huge sphere of water with the names of thousands of cities written on it. Among them I found her. But already the sphere was beginning to turn and the names all flowed together, becoming completely illegible. I lost her. "Where is she?" I asked, "Where is she?" "But she's right here. Don't you see her?" replied a voice from within my belly. "Come into the water with us!" another voice in my belly cried.

I leapt into the water.

Here stood a high tower, brightly shining with a strange light. Atop this tower sat the Fire Bird, which spat out flaming letters: M, O, S, K, V, A, then these letters were transformed: M became a mother and gave birth to me within my belly. O turned into *omul'* and swam off with S: seahorse. K became a knife and severed my umbilical cord. V had long since become a volcano, at whose peak sat a familiar-looking monster.

But what about A? A became a strange fruit I had never before tasted: an apple. Hadn't my grandmother told me of the serpent's warning never to drink foreign water? But fruit isn't the same as water. Why shouldn't I be allowed to eat foreign fruit? So I bit into the apple and swallowed its juicy flesh. Instantly the mother, the *omul'*, the seahorse, the knife and the volcano with its monster vanished before my eyes. Everything was still and cold. It had never been so cold before in Siberia.

I realized I was standing in the middle of Europe.

TSUSHIMA YŪKO

Tsushima Yūko (b. 1947) is the daughter of the novelist Dazai Osamu, some of whose work appears in volume 1 of this anthology. Not unlike her father,

Tsushima explores her own shifting psychologies in her stories and novels, which have found a wide readership in Japan and earned her many important literary prizes. Two of her novels, *Child of Fortune* (*Chōji*, 1978) and *Woman Running in the Mountains* (*Yama o hashiru onna*, 1980), as well as a collection of stories, have been translated into English. Her story "That One Glimmering Point of Light" (Hikarikagayaku itten o, 1988) recounts a remarkable incident in a relationship between mother and son.

THAT ONE GLIMMERING POINT OF LIGHT
(HIKARIKAGAYAKU ITTEN O)

Translated by Van C. Gessel

By the time we realized a quarrel had started, it was already too late to do anything. We heard in the same moment a shrill cry like the wail of an infant and a low, husky shout, and then it looked as though one of the women's bodies was suddenly crumpling before our eyes. The body collapsed face-down to the ground, and though we noticed a pool of red spreading quickly around her, it didn't occur to us right away that anything serious had happened; we merely looked on blankly at the woman's disheveled body.

—*She's dead.*

—*Stabbed in the chest.*

—*With just a single stroke. What terrible luck!*

—*And what a mess the other woman's gotten herself into—I mean, stabbing someone with a knife.*

—*What's going to happen, now that someone has died?*

Whispers from the onlookers filled the air.

We were at a park with a lake, not far from my house. A group of women who had graduated from a girls' high school were getting together for the first time in some while. Both the stabbed woman and the attacker were members of that class.

Still unable to believe that the stabbed woman could really be dead or that a person could die so easily over something so trivial, we became conscious of the attacker and shifted our gaze toward her. She stood silently beside the dead woman, her back hunched over as though nothing—not her eyes or ears or any other organ—was functioning any longer. The only change was in her complexion, which had turned a pale green. The word "murder" came to mind. All avenues of escape were now closed to her. So many people had witnessed what she did, after all. The blood drained from my face as well, and my legs began to shake. How could a simple argument escalate into something so awful?

When we were in high school, the assailant was often said to resemble an actress of the day, and she herself was very proud of her well-featured face. She seemed rather stuck-up, an impression exaggerated by the wealth of her family, and she often seemed like a show-off. Even after she married and had children, that impression did not seem to change much. But just now this woman had been transformed into something utterly different, a person deprived of contact with any other human being in the world, a solitary existence stripped even of her name. The transformation was overpowering to me and to the other women, rendering us incapable of movement. All we could do was continue watching the woman from the sidelines. Even if we had wanted to help her by acting as though nothing had happened, now that a person was dead, that wasn't an option for us. And yet faced with this sudden death, we had no idea what our initial response should be.

It felt as though a very long time passed. I wondered whether there was something we should have done immediately in order to save the life of the woman that we had decided was already dead. But by now it was too late. The woman's body had already started to change color and been transformed into a corpse.

The murderer suddenly straightened up and her features hardened. She first looked in our direction, and we stiffened, fearing she might make some sort of appeal to us. But her eyes never focused on us onlookers. Instead, she tried to lift up the corpse at her feet all by herself. Even though she was able to get both arms around the torso, she was unable to lift the body. Her face flushed red, but still she could not get things to go her way. After examining the situation several times, she picked up both legs of the corpse and began dragging it with all her might. The corpse seemed very heavy—the woman hunched over and clenched her teeth, and even though she was putting every ounce of force into the endeavor, the corpse moved only a little at a time. We continued to watch the woman; it never even occurred to us to try to stop her, much less to help her. The woman, too, had utterly forgotten that there were people around her.

When she struggled her way to a spot a little way away from us, she placed the corpse to one side and began digging a hole in the ground with both hands. She dug single-mindedly, but since she had no tools, she made little progress. Just what was she planning to do with the corpse? We couldn't imagine what she was thinking.

Having dug the hole—or perhaps it would be better to say that all she had done was stir up the top layer of the soil—the woman seemed to have decided she was finished and stopped digging. She dragged the body to that spot and studiously began to sprinkle soil over it. Once the corpse had disappeared from sight she firmed up the mound with the palms of her hands and rose to her feet. A look of relief washed over her face as though she had now finished handling a bothersome situation, and after vigorously shaking the dirt from her palms she scurried away, still oblivious to those of us who continued to observe her and even appearing to have already forgotten all about the corpse.

Feeling deflated, we watched her retreat into the distance until we could no longer see her.

—Does she think that she somehow hid it by burying it in a place like that?
—She's made up her mind that nobody saw her.
—If you make up your mind that nobody saw you, that's what happens.
—Now what?
—Hmm.
Once again the voices whispered back and forth.
—I don't imagine she'll want to come back here again.
—She probably assumes she's basically taken care of everything.
—Yes, but if she'd just chosen some other place . . .
—She wasn't in any state of mind to worry about the location.
—Well, for her, she did what she could . . .

When the onlookers had finished exchanging views, they seemed to have decided that there was nothing more to do but to let matters take their course. Some went over and sat down on benches; some headed toward the pond. They moved away in groups of three and four in the most casual of manners. For a few moments I, too, began to feel at ease, as if a great burden had been removed from my shoulders, but when I glanced toward the new earthen hill that the woman had left behind, my thoughts turned to the alteration that would take place in the corpse beneath the ground, and I felt ill. Perhaps if this were a place I didn't frequent I wouldn't have felt so concerned about it. But unfortunately this park is very close to where I live, and I look up at this grove of trees almost every day, and sometimes I even have to walk through here. I was sure that each time I passed by I would think about the corpse's transformation, and I would continue to worry about when the body would be discovered, just as if I had buried the corpse there myself. The longer it lay undiscovered, the less conspicuous the mound of earth would become, soon becoming indistinguishable from any other location, and it's not unimaginable that I might thoughtlessly plant my foot right into the center of the spot. The feeling of that decomposed corpse beneath the earth being crushed!

I felt suddenly nauseated, and I had to ask a person beside me:
—But, doesn't someone have to report this to the police? We know right where this spot is . . .

The woman turned to me with a vacant expression as though she had not understood what I was asking.
—There'll be problems if we don't notify the police right away. Since we all saw what happened, surely we can't just do nothing!
—Why not? She gaped at me and asked in a soft voice.
—Well, for starters, there's a dead person over there. . . .
—It's all right. We can leave things as they are. We all saw it, didn't we? That's enough. We're not the ones who will discover the body. Someone else will do that. Listen, somebody is sure to find it and notify the police, and the police will do all sorts of investigating. We don't have to go out of our way to do anything. Time no longer has any meaning for the dead, for one thing. See? That's how it is.

She flashed a smile and walked away.

So that's how it is. Recalling the scene I had witnessed, I felt as though I could now accept what had happened.

One night I took my two children to see flying squirrels in the forest. It had been a hot day in midsummer. Someone had told me that if you went to that forest at night, you'd have no trouble seeing the squirrels flying from tree to tree in search of food. The location was about two hours from where we lived in Tokyo. We decided to set out right away. That was the summer four years ago, the last summer my younger child spent in this world.

For a long while I had wanted to see in person, with my own eyes, the wild squirrels darting through the skies in a nighttime forest. I had watched them in a zoo, but you really can't say you've seen a flying squirrel if all you've seen is some of them curled up asleep. Since I knew only life in the city, the thought of squirrels gliding through the air seemed almost mystical to me. But I wonder whether I would have actually felt like going to see them had it not been for my son, the younger of my two children. From the time he first became aware of the world around him, his fascination with unusual living things—loaches and goldfish of every type, green caterpillars, spiders, earthworms, water beetles, water scorpions, and other aquatic creatures, along with frogs and newts, liz-ards, and snakes—merely intensified with the passage of time. His curiosity wasn't limited to insects and animals: he was mesmerized by plants with pecu-liar ecologies such as cacti, spherical lake-jewels, and carnivorous plants. He became engrossed in learning about the universe, about human and animal anatomy, about the atom—about, ultimately, anything and everything that was strange and mysterious.

Once I realized his inclination toward such things, it was natural for me as his mother to notice and point out to him things that would delight him, whether I saw them on television or as I walked along the street. If the item wasn't particularly expensive, I'd end up buying it for him. And his reaction never disappointed me: he would always come flying, eyes flashing, to see what I had gotten him. I was certain he'd be thrilled by seeing the flying squirrels glide through the trees. My heart leaped when I heard about them, and I knew I had to let my son see them.

He was eight years old. As he grew he showed some real promise, and I wanted to provide him with a variety of useful experiences. We went camping and set off on a ten-day vacation—all in all a very active summer. When I told him about the flying squirrels, without a moment's hesitation he made up his mind that he wanted to go see them. My daughter, four years older than her brother, announced she would go with us ("If he's going, I'm going too!"), less out of interest in the squirrels than driven by a sense of competition with him.

If we left Tokyo on an express bus around three in the afternoon, we would arrive at our destination no later than six. As we ate dinner there, we would wait for darkness to envelop the forest. Evidently the squirrels emerge from their nests and do their most vigorous flying for about an hour, starting around 7:30. I was surprised to learn that the squirrels do not build their dwellings hidden away deep in the heart of the forest. With the trees in the forests today being used as a source of wood, virtually all the hundred-year-old trees have disappeared. But flying squirrels live only in the hollows of older trees. Several trees of at least one hundred or two hundred years in age can always be found within the precincts of a Shinto shrine located in an inhabited area. Realizing that, the squirrels had settled into the groves of trees surrounding the shrines, and at night they set out for the mountain forests that were their native domain. Because their gliding operates on the same principle as that of a parachute, they are limited in the distance they can fly. They leap from a high point on one tree to a lower point on the next tree; then they climb that tree and leap from its highest point toward another tree. The goal of these squirrels is to continue this process until they reach the mountains, but since the distance between the shrines and the mountains is covered with both fields and highways, at certain points they are forced to scramble across the unfamiliar ground just like moles. In the process, some are attacked by dogs; others run over by automobiles. That's the situation into which the flying squirrels have been driven in modern times, we were told.

In the local villages, primarily at the schools, action was taken to protect the squirrels. They even set up an organization to encourage as many people as possible to come and observe the squirrels, during which time they could explain their present plight and solicit funds. It was a local person involved in such activities who helped us pick the day and time and gave us directions to the shrine in the grove where the flying squirrels could be seen.

As the express bus finally approached our destination, the mountain forests visible through the window had caught the light of the setting sun and had begun to divide into segments that glittered almost blindingly and segments that were sinking into dark shadows. My emotions seemed to be pulled deeply into those shadows, and when I realized that I was not starting home with my children, but in fact had not even arrived at our destination, I was struck by the irrational fear that I had thoughtlessly dragged my children into a frightening situation. The mountains—really, just gently rolling hills—could no longer be seen. The bus continued through the flat country landscape, which was rimmed with a succession of meager farm plots at the base of the hills and nothing at all worth seeing. Fortunately my son, who always suffered from motion sickness, slept through the entire ride thanks to the medicine I had given him.

After we climbed off the bus, we got into a taxi and proceeded to a school near the shrine. Already more than a dozen people like us had gathered to see the squirrels. Boxed dinners were handed out to each of us who had ordered them, since we were told there were no restaurants or inns nearby. After we ate, we looked at the school's exhibits of the moles and field mice that inhabit the area. Then, in a tiered classroom we listened to a lecture about the flying squirrels, complete with maps and slides. The group of spectators was made up mostly of children who had come with their middle-school class, families, and elderly people with plenty of time on their hands. They all listened with unexpected composure to the school-like lecture, and a few of them even took notes. My children, perhaps fascinated to be in a classroom after dark, sat rigidly and paid close attention to what was said.

After the lecture, T-shirts, books, postcards, and bookmarks were sold to support efforts to protect the squirrels. My children, believing that one was expected to buy such things, hounded me until I bought something for them: for my daughter, a T-shirt, and for my son, a book on frogs—which had nothing to do with squirrels!

A little after 7:30, we finally set out for the forest. They told us we were free to use flashlights along the way, but that they absolutely had to be turned off when they gave the signal. Flying squirrels are very cautious, and if they have even the slightest indication that humans are lurking nearby, they refuse to come out of the tree hollows. The squirrels did not, however, respond to red light, and so a couple of them were brought along with us. We were asked not to make loud noises and to be very quiet when speaking.

All it took was the walk along the path to the shrine for me to be terrified by the intensity of the darkness. My sixth-grade daughter walked casually ahead of me, so I didn't worry about her, but I clutched the hand of my second-grade son more tightly than necessary and kept whispering insistently to him: "Don't let go! If you run off by yourself, it's so dark here that once you've wandered away you'll never find your way back!" "If you aren't careful, you'll fall in the river!"

I am continually haunted by the fear of becoming separated from my children and never see them again for as long as I live. Having lost sight of my husband around the time my son was born, I had to get a job, and often I had to leave my children with others. Perhaps that was the source of some of my fears. What if I were involved in some kind of accident right at the time I was supposed to pick up my children and didn't show up on time? What if something unexpected happened to their sitter and she disappeared somewhere with them? Suppose we were headed for the busy downtown area of the city, or off to some friend's house, or starting on a trip—what if we were separated from one another in an eddy of strangers in some unfamiliar place? I could never free myself from the fear that my children might wander endlessly inside a maze with no exit.

It will happen someday. There's no way you can avoid such a calamity. That murmuring voice has echoed without ceasing somewhere inside my body from the moment I became a mother. It has now been four years since my son, on the eve of his graduation from second grade, was suddenly snatched away from me by an unexplained death. My immediate thought was *There—what you've always dreaded has finally happened!* But I couldn't link that thought to the unfathomable phenomenon called "death," and I am never for a moment free from suffering over the situation that he is simply "missing." Even now, four years after it happened, I'm fine in the light of day, but after I fall asleep at night, I remain in constant dread of the possibility that I might someday, somewhere, be separated from my two children.

The sign was given, and in unison we turned off our flashlights. In their place, the red lights were switched on. Whispering voices passed along the reminder that we needed to avoid making any noises.

Shrinking back from the deepening blackness, I abruptly hugged my son to me and whispered, "Where's your sister? When she's not right here next to me, I have no idea what's going on."

"Shhhhh! We can't talk! She's right over there, so don't worry!" he answered in a subdued voice.

The group silently collected at a spot behind the shrine where we had been told we would have a clear view of the tree hollows where the squirrels live. Two small spotting scopes and some binoculars were provided for us.

Our guide directed the red lights toward the grove of trees within the shrine precincts. Evidently the squirrels' nests were in more than one location. He shined the two lights back and forth and then quickly waved the onlookers over and whispered: "Look, you can see the eyes of the squirrels shining red. If you look closely you'll see. You can see two red points of light right next to each other." His words were passed along to those standing in a spot a little separated from us.

"Where?" "That tree right in the middle, apparently." "There's two of them!" "Two? Ah, I see them!" "You can see some over there, too!" "Oh, they've gone back into their nests!" The time we had waited for with anticipation had finally arrived, and every member of the group was excited. Jostling against one another, we tried to pick out the red points of light in the darkness.

I was equally anxious, and I asked a person who happened to be standing next to me, "Where do you see them? Which tree?" She indicated with her finger. When I finally located the glittering lights, I quickly pointed them out to my son. Wondering where my daughter was, I glanced around. Someone beside her had shown them to her.

"Wow! They're really flashing!" In his excitement, my son spoke at normal volume. Immediately he gave me a look that said he had realized his blunder, and he shrugged his shoulders. Then, in a deliberate whisper he asked, "So, why are their eyes like that?"

"Probably because they're reflecting the light that's shining at them. Their eyes seem to shine with the same intensity as the light that's directed toward them."

"Why do they look like they're shining?"

"I wonder. . . . Maybe it's because they're creatures of the night. But it really is strange, isn't it? I wonder why they glimmer like that."

They were tiny red dots of light, literally no larger than a pinhole. If you didn't use binoculars, you couldn't even tell that there were two of those dots side by side. Because of the darkness it was difficult to determine how far we were standing from the squirrels, but I imagine it must have been a considerable distance. The points of light were so tiny you normally couldn't even see them, but once you did catch sight of them, it was surprising how intense the light really was. Even knowing that they merely reflected the light shone on them from without, a person couldn't help but be captivated by the almost dazzling glimmer of those tiny red lights. That tiny, red, unapproachable, all-too-brilliant glimmer.

When they informed us that the squirrels had started to emerge from their nests, everyone pushed and shoved and peered into the scopes and binoculars to help one another identify the creatures scrambling from their nests and climbing up the tree trunks. Initially we were able to pick them out as well. We were told that nearly thirty of them were living in this forest. So long as the winds and rain were not severe, every day about half the squirrels would watch for the darkness of night to settle in and then set out together for the mountains.

Once all the squirrels had emerged from their nests, we hurriedly shifted to a location on the opposite side of the shrine. We were told that the squirrels, who had climbed to the very top of the old hollow trees, would at last begin to fly. The bank of a stream flowing along the opposite side of the grove was the best place to observe the gliding of the squirrels. The guide made his way around the group, excitedly whispering to the onlookers, "They'll start flying from right up around there. Yes, right up there. It happens very quickly, so watch carefully!" A young man who appeared to be his assistant directed the red lights toward the upper branches of the old trees, which seemed to be the starting point for the gliding.

I passed the guide's words along to my son: "He says it's right up there. And that they move very quickly, so you've got to watch carefully!" Eagerly we waited for the squirrels to start flying. At some time along the way, my daughter had come back beside me. We were now farther from the grove than we had been earlier. The clump of old trees created a black wall up into the heights of the sky. I couldn't determine just where or how the bodies of those tiny creatures would glide across those dark shadows. I stared at the spot where the red lights were shining until I was seized by a light-headed, drowsy feeling and an infantile sense of loneliness mounted within me.

"Look! They're flying! They're flying!" someone called, and even though every subsequent cry came in suppressed tones, the entire group was in a frenzied state. "There went one! I saw it!" the voices kept repeating, and cries of wonder and even laughter sprang up here and there. And the excitement continued: "There's another one! Now one over there!" Apparently any number of them were launching into flight, one after another. But I still hadn't seen a single one gliding through the sky. Each time a cry sounded, I would quickly shift my eyes toward the indicated spot, but whether I couldn't make out the figures or whether I had looked too late, I couldn't locate any movement whatsoever. I had no idea what sort of movement I should be watching for. If there were just something tangible to rely on, no matter how tiny, it would be easier to get a glimpse of the gliding shadows, but I couldn't even imagine what to look for, so I just let my eyes float aimlessly around the blackness of the forest.

"Wow! That one was huge. Huge!"

Yet another cry. Just as the voice erupted, I had the feeling that something had glided past my eyes, but when I strained to see if that might have been it, I could no longer see anything.

Excited voices were exchanged just to my side: "That one really flew really far!" "I saw it. Very clearly."

"Did you see that one?" I asked my son, whose hand I still clutched.

"I did. I saw it! It went whooshing by. Did you see it, Mom?"

"I'm not sure."

"But there's so many of them. How could you not see them? I've seen a whole lot of them!"

"Really?"

He nodded proudly.

It was so strange to me—how could all those other people see the squirrels? Had they actually seen the flying figures? And was I expected to say that I had seen them, too? I felt that I should, in a way. But the truth was that I had not seen one single thing for sure, and I could hardly bring myself to declare that I had. I didn't know where I should look. I didn't have a clue to what my eyes should be following. I couldn't see a thing. Even so, something had darted past my eyes. But I could not catch its movement.

Today, four years later, I'm having an equally difficult time locating my son. I feel like he's standing beside me. But he's not. This must be him, I think, but there is just something lacking. Even though it would be perfectly natural for him to be at my side, it is only the feeling that he is there, and I cannot draw him into my arms.

As I walked around searching for my son, I remembered someone who had looked after him when he was an infant, so I stopped by the apartment building where we had been living back then. Just as I had expected, I had forgotten and left him there. He had reverted to being a baby who hadn't even learned to crawl. And when I tried to pick him up, he burst into tears. He had forgotten my face.

Our new house was finally finished, and as we were putting things away, I wondered what my children were up to and looked into their room. It was a large room for both my daughter and son to share. Boxes were stacked up, still unopened, and items had been piled on top of the built-in bed. *Don't just play, you've got to get this place straightened up*, I scolded them, then began helping them put things away. Then, thinking I had better finish up the kitchen before working on the children's room, I told them, *I'll be back in a little while, do some things by yourselves* and went back to the kitchen. I heard no reply, and I had no idea what my son was doing in his room. During the long interval when he had been separated from me, he had gone back to being a child scarcely able to talk. That thought saddened me. But then I thought how fortunate we were to be able to live together again and realized I shouldn't be complaining.

I went into a building on a corner lot and remembered that I had once left my son with someone at a house that formerly stood on that lot. Many years had passed. With the house no longer there, I wouldn't have any way to locate him. The people working in the building wouldn't have known where the former residents had ended up. I wonder how my son is getting along as he matures? Even if I did happen to run into him sometime, how close would he feel to this mother of his? Would I even recognize him at first glance? It's hard to imagine what he would look like as an adult. He was so young when we were separated.

Walking along the street, I discovered a frog. It was a tiny frog, but when I examined it closely, it appeared to be a very unusual type of frog. The rear half of its body was encased in triangular tubing just like a turban shell, and when I removed the tubing, a pale green snake, tinier than an earthworm, was curled up inside. It was disgusting, but I knew I had to catch it and show it to my son, so, almost frantically, I caught it up in a piece of tissue paper. It pleased me to think how happy my son would be, but for the life of me I couldn't remember where to take it so that I could give it to him.

Where is he? I know he's around somewhere, but I don't know where. I don't even know why that's the case. It makes perfectly good sense that he would be right at my side, but when I turn my head, he disappears.

One year, we went to look at some greenhouses, nearly a dozen of which, large and small ones, had been built on a slope in a place famous for its hot springs. A route was marked to view the greenhouses, but they were linked together by a complex web of trails that soon made you lose track of where you were walking. The children raced ahead on their own, and I lost sight of them. Entranced on the one hand by the beautiful glass rooms—one for cactus, another for gorgon plants and water lilies, another for ferns, yet another for bougainvilleas—that enticed you one after another into a dreamlike trance; on the other hand I was stricken with anxiety and wandered around in search of my children.

Just as though I still continue to wander from one glass house to another, I continue to torment myself in my dreams, dragging somewhere along behind me a sensation of sweetness as I try to locate the figure of my son.

Would you please tell me the truth?

Two years after my son died, I finally had to ask that question of a certain person.

It's simply that I want to know what really happened. I'm not agonizing over it, and I haven't started feeling uneasy about it again after all this time. It's just that I don't like leaving things up in the air, and I'm quite confident that it won't bother me in the least no matter what actually occurred. It's OK either way. It isn't at all important. I'm just saying that oddly enough, because it's not important, I can't feel any relief until I understand it with total clarity.

Knowing the kind of person you are, I wanted if at all possible to resolve this without asking you. No matter how much I asked you not to worry, that it's just a matter of curiosity, you would undoubtedly worry about me and show me all kinds of sympathy. But I've made up my mind to ask you, even though I hate to, because you're the only person I can ask about this. After it happened, my boy was taken to the hospital, and when I realized that we wouldn't be coming home from the hospital right away, I worried about finding someone to take care of my daughter, so I called you. You came right away, but by then he was past all medical help. You stayed with me through that entire night. When morning came, the people from the police who had been hovering around the previous night disappeared. And not a single person from the police has bothered me since. But what about you? I think if the police were seeking testimony, you who were beside me that entire night would be the one person they would think of. And so the only way I can clear up my clouded emotions is to ask you directly, since you're the one who was placed in that position.

I know I seem too persistent, but I'm just asking to know the simple, honest truth of what happened. I can't help feeling that something is missing, and as I've wondered what that could be, I've come up with one little concern. It's occurred to me that out of concern for my feelings you have kept something from me. There's a police box very close to where I live, and every time I pass by there, I have the strangest feelings: Why am I allowed to walk outside so freely? Why am I allowed to decide on my own what I eat each day, who I talk to, where I go, and everything else I do? You can please put out of your mind any ridiculous notion that I'm suffering from any guilt over my son. That's not it at all. I know very well without anyone having to tell me how stupid it is to punish myself in that way. But—how shall I put this?—maybe I could just say it feels like there's something missing. Basically I'm haunted by the feeling that there's something I haven't been told.

Are you sure you weren't questioned as a witness by the police, either that night or on some other day, about my daily activities, my relationship with my son, and the details of my life? "Do you think she's the sort of person who might go into a fit of rage and kill her own child?" Or "Are you sure she didn't frequently spank her children?" I know you wouldn't give any answer that might harm me, and I know for myself, while I may have been a poor excuse for a mother, that I honestly loved that boy and that I rarely scolded him in earnest— that's very clear to me, since it's me I'm talking about. Are you sure the police didn't listen to your unwavering answers and as a result abandon their suspicions that it might have been murder? I just can't help but feel that's the case. I'm very clear in my understanding that I didn't kill him with my own hands— all I have to do is search my memory to know that. But what about other people who weren't there to see what happened? It was, after all, so sudden—such an inexplicably strange way to die. It was such a bizarre course of events, so totally unbelievable to think that one moment he's soaking in the bathtub, and the next moment his body is floating faceup in the hot water with a wide grin on its face. I can't imagine there is anyone who would believe that's what really happened. Isn't it perfectly natural that the police, of all people, would suspect foul play at my hands? Because, after all, not one person actually saw what happened to him in that one fatal moment. Not even my daughter realized how terrible it was until I picked him up out of the bathtub and laid him out on the floor of the changing room.

In any case, the police never asked me a thing that would suggest they suspected he had been murdered. In fact, they even showed me sympathy. How is it that the police of all people would be so quick to believe what I told them? It just can't be. Don't you think they took your testimony and examined his body in great detail, and then at some point in their investigation they dismissed all suspicions about me? Or is it that maybe they haven't completely stopped suspecting me, and I'm being watched as I go throughout the day? Sometimes I think that might be what's going on. Of course, I don't keep thinking such things seriously.

I'm the only one who can be absolutely sure that I didn't kill my boy. Because I realize that, it seems almost inevitable that the police should suspect me. Are you sure you weren't interrogated and have continued to conceal it from me? On that night, or on some other day? There's no more need to hide it. Please tell me what really happened. I beg you.

I still don't have the answer to my question.

As I puzzled over what I should do, I realized that I couldn't ask in person, so I started writing a letter. I rewrote it over and over, and tore up every one. No matter what I wrote, it's impossible for me to believe that I could get an answer that would satisfy me. And so I'm still unable to ask the question, regardless of what the answer might be. Recently I've started thinking that perhaps it's OK not to know. It's very likely that none of the things I worry about actually happened and that nothing has been kept from me.

YOSHIMOTO BANANA

Yoshimoto Banana (b. 1964) is one of the most popular writers in Japan today, thanks to a large audience of young female readers. She is the daughter of Yoshimoto Ryūmei, an influential leftist intellectual who was a leader in the student uprisings of the 1960s. Yoshimoto achieved almost immediate acclaim with the publication of her first story, "Moonlight Shadow" (Muunraito shadou), in 1986. The following year, her first novel, *Kitchen* (*Kittchin*), became a sensation in both Japanese and its translation into many foreign languages. The story in this volume, "Newlywed" (Shinkon-san, 1991), is unique in that it appeared in serialized form on hanging posters inside Tokyo commuter trains.

NEWLYWED (SHINKON-SAN)

Translated by Ann Sherif

Once, just once, I met the most incredible person on the train. That was a while ago, but I still remember it vividly.

At the time, I was twenty-eight years old, and had been married to Atsuko for about one month.

I had spent the evening downing whiskey at a bar with my buddies and was totally smashed by the time I got on the train to head home. For some reason, when I heard them announce my stop, I stayed put, frozen in my seat.

It was very late, and I looked around and saw that there were only three other passengers in the car. I wasn't so far gone that I didn't realize what I'd done. I had stayed on the train because I didn't really feel like going home.

In my drunken haze, I watched as the familiar platform of my station drew near. The train slowed down, and came to a stop. As the doors slid open, I could feel a blast of cool night air rush into the car, and then the doors again closed so firmly that I thought they had been sealed for all eternity. The train started to move, and I could see the neon signs of my neighborhood stores flash by outside the train window. I sat quietly and watched them fade into the distance.

A few stations later, the man got on. He looked like an old homeless guy, with ragged clothes, long, matted hair, and a beard—plus he smelled really strange. As if on cue, the other three passengers stood up and moved to neighboring cars, but I missed my chance to escape, and instead stayed where I was, seated right in the middle of the car. I didn't have a problem with the guy anyway, and even felt a trace of contempt for the other passengers, who had been so obvious about avoiding him.

Oddly enough, the old man came and sat right next to me. I held my breath and resisted the urge to look in his direction. I could see our reflections in the window facing us: the image of two men sitting side by side superimposed over the dazzling city lights and the dark of the night. I almost felt like laughing when I saw how anxious I looked there in the window.

"I suppose there's some good reason why you don't want to go home," the man announced in a loud, scratchy voice.

At first, I didn't realize that he was talking to me, maybe because I was feeling so oppressed by the stench emanating from his body. I closed my eyes and pretended to be asleep, and then I heard him whisper, directly into my left ear, "Would you like to tell me why you're feeling so reluctant about going home?"

There was no longer any mystery about whom he was addressing, so I screwed my eyes shut even more firmly. The rhythmical sound of the train's wheels clicking along the tracks filled my ears.

"I wonder if you'll change your mind when you see me like this," he said.

Or I thought that's what he said, but the voice changed radically, and zipped up into a much higher pitch, as if someone had fast-forwarded a tape. This sent my head reeling, and everything around me seemed to rush into a different space, as the stench of the man's body disappeared, only to be replaced by the light, floral scent of perfume. My eyes still closed, I recognized a range of new smells: the warm fragrance of a woman's skin, mingled with fresh summer blossoms.

I couldn't resist; I had to take a look. Slowly, slowly, I opened my eyes, and what I saw almost gave me a heart attack. Inexplicably, there was a woman seated where the homeless guy had been, and the man was nowhere to be seen.

Frantic, I looked around to see if anyone else had witnessed this amazing transformation, but the passengers in the neighboring cars seemed miles away, in a totally different space, separated by a transparent wall, all looking just as tired as they had moments before, indifferent to my surprise. I glanced over at the woman again, and wondered what exactly had happened. She sat primly beside me, staring straight ahead.

I couldn't even tell what country she was from. She had long brown hair, gray eyes, gorgeous legs, and wore a black dress and black patent leather heels. I definitely knew that face from somewhere—like maybe she was my favorite actress, or my first girlfriend, or a cousin, or my mother, or an older woman I'd lusted after—her face looked very familiar. And she wore a corsage of fresh flowers, right over her ample breasts.

I bet she's on her way home from a party, I thought, but then it occurred to me again that the old guy had disappeared. Where had he gone, anyway?

"You still don't feel like going home, do you?" she said, so sweetly that I could almost smell it. I tried convincing myself that this was nothing more than a drunken nightmare. That's what it was, an ugly duckling dream, a transformation from bum to beauty. I didn't understand what was happening, but I knew what I saw.

"I certainly don't, with you by my side."

I was surprised at my own boldness. I had let her know exactly what I had on my mind. Even though the train had pulled in to another station and people were straggling on to the neighboring cars, not one single person boarded ours. No one so much as glanced our way, probably because they were too tired and preoccupied. I wondered if they wanted to keep riding and riding, as I did.

"You're a strange one," the woman said to me.

"Don't jump to conclusions," I replied.

"Why not?"

She looked me straight in the eye. The flowers on her breast trembled. She had incredibly thick eyelashes, and big, round eyes, deep and distant, which reminded me of the ceiling of the first planetarium I ever saw as a child: an entire universe enclosed in a small space.

"A minute ago, you were a filthy old bum."

"But even when I look like this, I'm pretty scary, aren't I?" she said. "Tell me about your wife."

"She's petite."

I felt as if I were watching myself from far away. What are you doing, talking to a stranger on a train? What is this, true confessions?

"She's short, and slender, and has long hair. And her eyes are real narrow, so she looks like she's smiling, even when she's angry."

Then I'm sure she asked me, "What does she do when you get home at night?"

"She comes down to meet me with a nice smile, as if she were on a divine mission. She'll have a vase of flowers on the table, or some sweets, and the television is usually on. I can tell that she's been knitting. She never forgets to put a fresh bowl of rice on the family altar every day. When I wake up on Sunday mornings, she'll be doing laundry, or vacuuming, or chatting with the lady next door. Every day, she puts out food for the neighborhood cats, and she cries when she watches mushy TV shows.

"Let's see, what else can I tell you about Atsuko? She sings in the bath and she talks to her stuffed animals when she's dusting them. On the phone with her friends, she laughs hard at anything they say, and, if it's one of her old pals from high school, they'll go on for hours. Thanks to Atsuko's ways, we have a happy home. In fact, sometimes it's so much fun at home that it makes me want to puke."

After this grand speech of mine, she turned and nodded compassionately.

"I can picture it," she said.

I replied, "How could you? What do you know about these things?" to which she smiled broadly. Her smile was nothing like Atsuko's, but still it seemed awfully familiar to me. At that moment, a childhood memory flitted through my head: I'm walking to school with a friend, and we're still just little kids, so we're wearing the kind of school uniforms with shorts, instead of long pants. It's the dead of winter, and our legs are absolutely freezing, and we look at each other, about to complain about the cold, but then we just start laughing instead, because we both know that griping isn't going to make us any warmer. Scenes like that—smiles of mutual understanding—kept flashing through my mind, and I actually started having a good time, on my little train bench.

Then I heard her saying, "How long have you been down here in Tokyo?"

Her question struck me as terribly odd. Why had she said it like that, "down here in Tokyo"?

I asked her, "Hey, are you speaking Japanese? What language are you using?"

She nodded again, and replied, "It's not any language from any one country. They're just words that only you and I can understand. You know, like words you only use with certain people, like with your wife, or an old girlfriend, or your dad, or a friend. You know what I mean, a special type of language that only you and they can comprehend."

"But what if more than two people are talking to one another?"

"Then there'll be a language that just the three of you can understand, and the words will change again if another person joins the conversation. I've been watching this city long enough to know that it's full of people like you, who left their hometowns and came here by themselves. When I meet people who are transplants from other places, I know that I have to use the language of people who never feel quite at home in this big city. Did you know that people who've lived all their lives in Tokyo can't understand that special language? If I run into an older woman who lives alone, and seems reserved, I speak to her in the language of solitude. For men who are out whoring, I use the language of lust. Does that make sense to you?"

"I guess so, but what if the old lady, the horny guy, you, and I all tried to have a conversation?"

"You don't miss anything, do you? If that were to happen, then the four of us would find the threads that tie us together, a common register just for us."

"I get the idea."

"To get back to my original question, how long have you been in Tokyo?"

"I came here when I was eighteen, right after my mother died, and I've been here ever since."

"And your life with Atsuko, how's it been?"

"Well, actually, sometimes I feel like we live in totally different worlds, especially when she goes on and on about the minutiae of our daily lives, anything and everything, and a lot of it's meaningless to me. I mean, what's the big deal? Sometimes I feel like I'm living with the quintessential housewife. I mean, all she talks about is our home."

A cluster of sharply delineated images floated into my mind: the sound of my mother's slippers pattering by my bed when I was very young, the trembling shoulders of my little cousin, who sat sobbing after her favorite cat died. I felt connected to them, despite their otherness, and found solace in the thought of their physical proximity.

"That's how it feels?"

"And how about you? Where are you headed?" I asked.

"Oh, I just ride around and observe. To me, trains are like a straight line with no end, so I just go on and on, you know. I'm sure that most people think of trains as safe little boxes that transport them back and forth between their homes and offices. They've got their commuter passes, and they get on and get off each day, but not me. That's how you think of trains, right?"

"As a safe box that takes me where I need to go, and then home?" I said. "Sure I do, or I'd be too scared to get on the train in the morning—I'd never know where I'd end up."

She nodded, and said, "Of course, and I'm not saying that you should feel the way I do. If you—or anyone on this train, for that matter—thought of life as a kind of train, instead of worrying only about your usual destinations, you'd be surprised how far you could go, just with the money you have in your wallet right now."

"I'm sure you're right."

"That's the kind of thing I have on my mind when I'm on the train."

"I wish I had that kind of time on my hands."

"As long as you're on this train, you're sharing the same space with lots of different people. Some people spend the time reading, others look at the ads, and still others listen to music. I myself contemplate the potential of the train itself."

"But I still don't understand what this transformation's all about."

"I decided to do it because you didn't get off at your usual station and I wanted to find out why. What better way to catch your eye?"

My head was swimming. Who was this being, anyway? What were we talking about? Our train kept stopping and starting, slipping through the black of the night. And there I was, surrounded by the darkness, being carried farther and farther from my home.

This being sitting next to me felt somehow familiar, like the scent of a place, before I was born, where all the primal emotions, love and hate, blended in the air. I also could sense that I would be in danger if I got too close. Deep inside, I felt timid, even scared, not about my own drunkenness or fear that my mind was playing tricks on me, but the more basic sensation of encountering something much larger than myself, and feeling immeasurably small and insignificant by comparison. Like a wild animal would when confronted by a larger beast, I felt the urge to flee for my life.

In my stupor, I could hear her saying, "You never have to go back to that station again, if you don't want to. That's one option."

I guess she's right, I thought, but continued to sit there in silence. Rocked by the motion of the train and soothed by the rhythm of the wheels below, I closed my eyes and pondered the situation. I tried to imagine the station near my house and how it looked when I came home in the late afternoon. I recalled the masses of red and yellow flowers whose names I didn't know out in the plaza in front of the station. The bookstore across the way was always packed with people flipping through paperbacks and magazines. All I could ever see was their backs—at least, when I walked past from the direction of the station.

The delicious smell of soup wafted from the Chinese restaurant, and people lined up in front of the bakery, waiting to buy the special cakes they make there. A group of high school girls in their uniforms talk loudly and giggle as they walk ever so slowly across the plaza. It's weird that they're moving at such a leisurely pace. A burst of laughter rises from the group, and some teenage boys tense up as they walk past. One of the boys, though, doesn't even seem to notice the girls, and walks on calmly. He's a nice-looking guy, and I'd guess that he's popular with the girls. A perfectly made-up secretary passes by, yawning as she walks. She isn't carrying anything, so I imagine that she's on the way back to the office from an errand. I can tell that she doesn't want to go back to work; the weather's too nice for that. A businessman gulping down some vitamin beverage by the kiosk, other people waiting for friends. Some of them are reading paperbacks, others are people watching as they wait.

One finally catches sight of the friend she's been waiting for and runs to greet him. The elderly lady who walks slowly into my field of vision; the line of yellow and green and white taxis at the taxi stand that roar away from the station, one after another. The solid, weathered buildings nearby and the areas flanking the broad avenue.

And when I began to wonder what would happen if I never went back to that station, the whole image in my mind took on the quality of a haunting scene from an old movie, one fraught with meaning. All the living beings there suddenly became objects of my affection. Someday when I die, and only my sod exists, and my spirit comes home on a summer evening during the Bon Buddhist festival, that's probably what the world will look like to me.

And then Atsuko appears, walking slowly toward the station in the summer heat. She has her hair pulled back in a tight bun, even though I've told her that it makes her look dowdy. Her eyelids are so heavy that I wonder whether she can actually see anything, plus she's squinting now because of the glaring sun and her eyes have narrowed down to practically nothing. She's carrying a big bag instead of a shopping basket. She looks hungrily at the stuffed waffles in the little stall by the station, and even pauses for a moment as if she were going to stop and buy one, but then she changes her mind and walks into the drugstore instead. She stands for a long while in front of the shampoo section.

Come on, Atsuko, they're all the same. Just pick one. You look so serious! Shampoo is not something worth wasting time on. But she can't decide and keeps standing there, until a man rushing through the store bumps into her. Atsuko stumbles and then says she's sorry to the man. He bumped into you! You're not the one who should apologize. You should be as hard on him as you are on me.

Finally, Atsuko finds the perfect shampoo, and she takes it up to the cash register, where she starts chatting with the cashier. She's smiling sweetly. She leaves the store, a slender figure of a woman, becoming a mere black line as she recedes into the distance. A tiny black line. But I can tell that she's walking lightly, though slowly, and drinking in the air of this small town.

Our house is Atsuko's universe, and she fills it with small objects, all of her own choosing. She picks each of them as carefully as she did that bottle of shampoo. And then Atsuko comes to be someone who is neither a mother nor a wife, but an entirely different being.

For me, the beautiful, all-encompassing web spun by this creature is at once so polluted, yet so pure that I feel compelled to grab on to it. I am terrified by it but find myself unable to hide from it. At some point I have been caught up in the magical power she has.

"That's the way it is when you first get married." Her words brought me back to my senses.

"It's scary to think of the day when you'll move beyond the honeymoon stage."

"Yeah, but there's no point dwelling on it now. I'm still young. Thinking about it just makes me nervous. I'm going home. I'll get off at the next station. At least I've sobered up a bit."

"I had a good time," she said.

"Me too," I replied, nodding.

The train sped forward, unstoppable, like the grains of sand in an hourglass timing some precious event. A voice came booming out of the loudspeaker, announcing the next stop. We both sat there, not saying a word. It was hard for me to leave her. I felt as if we'd been together a very long time.

It seemed as if we had toured Tokyo from every possible angle, visiting each building, observing every person, and every situation. It was the incredible sensation of encountering a life force that enveloped everything, including the station near my house, the slight feeling of alienation I feel toward my marriage and work and life in general, and Atsuko's lovely profile. This town breathes in all the universes that people in this city have in their heads.

Intending to say a few more words, I turned in her direction, only to find the dirty bum sleeping peacefully by my side. Our conversation had come to an end. The train sailed into the station, slowly, quietly, like a ship. I heard the door slide open, and I stood up.

Incredible man, farewell.

POETRY IN THE INTERNATIONAL STYLE

Deciding which poets belong in the previous chapter and which in this chapter is rather arbitrary, since many of those active in the 1960s are still writing, and some of the poets represented here are, in calendar terms at least, their contemporaries. But the fresh currents running in the poetry composed during the most recent decades are immediately evident, and more women poets have gained lasting prominence. Furthermore, the loose, even slangy, language now sometimes found in poetry reflects both the influence of popular culture and an easy freedom of expression, often highly personal, that suggest new possibilities for both self-revelation and humor. Much of this poetry is truly cosmopolitan, contemporary verse that only by chance happens to be written in Japanese. Except where noted, the selection, introductions, and translations are by Hiroaki Sato.

FUJII SADAKAZU

Fuji Sadakazu (b. 1942) is a rare postwar poet who has also established his reputation in a different field: classical Japanese literature. He has published several books of poems, most notable among them *Purify!* in 1984.

IN THE LAKE (MIZUUMI NI WA, 1982)

Why, then, is it that the history of fishery
the lake
tends to go outside
the mainstream of history?
the lake
to put it simply
the lake
the industry called fishery
the lake
characteristically goes down
as productivity goes up
the lake
yes, in lakes
this is especially notable
the lake
as soon as nets come out that can catch a lot of fish
the lake
overfishing results in no time
the lake

and fishery
tapers off
the lake
and so
the lake
studying the life of the Japanese fisherman
the lake
as far as coastal fishing is concerned
the lake
inevitably leads to the clarification
of the process in which it declines and vanishes
through the process of the advancement of productivity of society
the lake
that is
the lake
according to forecasts made from studies
the lake
on condition that the productivity of society stagnates
the lake
we can recover
the lake
our lakes
the lake
where fish
and fishermen
live together
the lake
quietly bringing down a fire
the lake turns
into the waves
that lap the beach
the lake
behind the mirror is the lake
a friend of the pond
a relative of the marsh
the father of the spring
the lake
fish
the lake
must live there
the lake

—Partly of quotations from the historian Mr. Amino Yoshihiko.

ISAKA YŌKO

Both the mother and the grandfather of Isaka Yōko (b. 1949) were writers, and she began composing poetry in high school. After graduating from college, Isaka became a teacher of Japanese at various private girls' schools. Her first volume of poetry was published in 1979, and since then she has written four more books of poetry. The translations are by Leith Morton.

FINGERS (YUBI, 1979)

When I was little
My father extended his index finger
And I grasped it with my hot five fingers and walked
Letting the landscape of the days go past
His index finger possessed perhaps
Slightly more speed

Men tangle me up slowly
In the hollow in the palm of my hand heat accumulates
And exudes some moisture
I bend my five fingers
After folding them so they do not overlap
I size them up
By the degree of heat and moisture
As the years pass
My fingertips have become dry

FATHER'S PIANO (CHICHI NO PIANO, 1984)

It seems that
The melody was interrupted by his perversity
My father is sitting in front of the keys
With his kimono skirt awry
Assuming what is communicated to me by my father is
Simply the husk
The blank spaces between sounds
Can usually be filled in by the imagination
From the vines in the wisteria trellis
Fruit shaped like small gourds hang
The autumn breeze blows
But he will not pick a single one
From his white hair
Only that kind of clumsy belief is suspended
This happened over and over again so

Every time I open the shutters in the morning
I allow the noise to escape
Loose things rotten things
Smelly things are
For example hiding beneath the furniture
The sound passes along the slippery corridor
Knocks on the door
With nowhere to stop
Leaps over the plates
Every morning
With a tongue like top-quality ham
My mother eats it up

ITŌ HIROMI

Itō Hiromi (b. 1955) published her first book of poems, *Sky of Grass and Tree* (*Sōmoku no sora*), in 1978 and since then has published poems notable for their explicit descriptions of sexual relations, pregnancy, childbirth, and child rearing. Itō is known for her incantatory readings.

UNDERGROUND (TSUCHI NO SHITA, 1985)

I was related by marriage and so in August
I paid a visit to their graves. Connecting via the Bullet train with
      the Chūgoku Expressway
I left Tokyo and my relatives
Behind. The cemetery provided a breeding-ground for light-
      brown stick insects, green stick-insects, blister-beetles and
      mosquitoes. Black Prince cicadas and Green Grocer cicadas
      breed there. My mother (in-law)'s
Unvarnished plain wooden memorial tablet is still on top of the
      gravestone Exactly where my father (in-law)
Had placed it when the ashes were interned.
My father (in-law)'s
Movements are slow. So slowly it was irritating
He washed the grave. The neighboring grave
Was that of siblings separated by less than a year who died last
      year and this year. The earth
Heaped up in the shape of two coffins was protected
By a wooden roof. The roof was discolored by weathering
The heaped-up earth was loose the pair of
Six-year olds beneath were in the process of decomposition.
      Children's yellow school

Umbrellas were thrust into the soil. I speculate
About the two six-year olds' real names from the single
    character taken
From their real names in their Buddhist names given posthumously.
My father (in-law)
Trampled the stick-insects underfoot and continued to
Wash the grave. Tokyo, my family, my father (in-law)
And my husband all think that
I will be buried in this grave.

Translated by Leith Morton

GLEN GOULD GOLDBERG (1988)

A photograph of Gu Gu sitting in a chair
A curved photograph
A photograph of Gu Gu staring
A photograph of Gu Gu squatting
A photograph of the back of a chair
A photograph of Gu Gu stretching backwards
A photograph of Gu Gu staring
A photograph where Gu Gu is resting his chin on his hands
A photograph in which Gu Gu's cheeks, mouth, shaven hair
    are distorted
A photograph of Gu Gu staring
A photograph of Gu Gu's dog
A photograph of Gu Gu peeping
A photograph of a finger staring
I can hear a singing voice
Gu
Static
Foreign static
A photograph of a chair staring
Gu Gu
A photograph of a gurbed chair
A photograph of a binger staring
The chair is doing penance, no doing genance
Gense doing genance
A gotograph of a finger

Translated by Leith Morton

SEXUAL LIFE OF SAVAGES (MIKAIJIN NO SEISEIKATSU, 1985)

*Rorschach[1]

"This is a female sex organ, isn't it?"
I was asked.
"It looks like the line connecting the female sex organ and the   rectum,"
I replied.
"And there should really be above this a hole from which the piss
    comes out."
"But I wonder if such a line exists."
"Yes, it does,"
I replied.
"There is a similar line between my navel and my sex organ."
"That's different."
"But they are about the same color."
"Well, then, what is the line for, I wonder, the line connecting the
    female sex organ and the rectum."
I couldn't answer this question.
"Look, there's nothing that isn't necessary."
"But, then, how about the pubic hair and armpit hair?
"How about doughy earwax and the underarm odor resulting from   it?
"I'm told that if your earwax is doughy, you are 90% likely to have   a
    strong underarm odor.
"How about slimy blue snot?
"All those things that are dear to me with which I always want to
    fiddle are not necessary and can only be thrown away.
"There are even those who don't have such things."
"Let me say this is really a female sex organ."
"But to me it only looks like the line connecting the female sex
    organ and the rectum."
"Let me tell you it *is* a female sex organ."
"But I am more fascinated by the line connecting the female sex organ
    and the rectum."
"Let me tell you it *is* a female sex organ."
"But I find the line connecting the female sex organ and the rectum
    more pleasant."
"Let me tell you it *is* a female sex organ, and its entirety links up
    with a male sex organ.
"The portion you insist is a female sex organ is the clitoris.

---

1. Evidently a subtitle, this, along with the asterisk, is part of the poem. The title itself is taken,
Itō told me, from the anthropologist Bronislaw Kasper Malinowski's book of the same name.

"That's where you get the pleasant sensation.
"You are somewhat biased toward the rectum,
"you are embarrassed,
"you are, let's say, about the female sex organ,
"you are, let's say, somewhat repressed about the female sex organ,
"when you were small,
"did you have anorexia,
"or did you have bulimia,
"do you menstruate?"
        "I am a pregnant woman."
"Are you having sex?"
"I am.
"But my stomach moves.
"Even while we're doing this, it is hiccupping.
"Its regular stimulation of my intestines bothers me.
"I have confirmed that all children are turds
"and that they are born like turds."

SHINKAWA KAZUE

When she was a high-school student, Shinkawa Kazue (b. 1929) was introduced
to poetry by the popular songwriter and professor of French literature Saijō
Yaso. Shinkawa then went on to create a large body of "elegant and sinuous"
work, as one critic put it, as well as poems for children. Her complete poems
were published in 2000.

THE DOOR (TOBIRA, 1959)

Whenever a deadline approached
I would grow even more reticent
and making my workroom stagnant as the dark bottom of the sea
let my fish scales glow quietly by a rock all day.
At such a time
you would come down the hall with your infant steps,
stop in front of the stubbornly closed door,
and call your mother's name with a tireless passion:
Mama! Mama! Mama!

Watching silently from inside
the blue-green handle turn, click-click,
your mother's eyes would begin to see, with painful clarity,
a rabbit caught in clairvoyance,
your small figure on tiptoes holding onto it.
In the end I'd lose

and open the door wide.
You'd quickly run up to me,
brightly scattering the cries of a brave soldier
taking back a prisoner, how innocent of you!

You call the swivel chair covered with faded velvet Mama
and turn my world like a top.
You call a pen Mama
and tell me to draw
on the blank margins of my lined sheet
lots and lots of choo-choo trains.

One day
out of a very gentle feeling
I kept company with you from morning, all day.
You were in a terribly good mood
and were twice as good a boy as usual. Yet,
remembering I don't know what, suddenly you tossed off your toys,
ran to the study where I wasn't, that day,
and called out:
Mama! Mama! Mama!

Listening to your voice
I felt oddly lonely.
For you
what was wanted was always behind the door.
The person who'd open the door after your repeated calls
and pick you up had, for you, the reality of mother.
Listening to your voice
I gradually became unnerved.
In time I became inorganic
and standing close behind you
raised a pitiful cry:
Me! Me! Me!

When the two of us
violently pushed the door open
I definitely saw, I thought:
seated in the old swivel chair,
facing a lined sheet spread on the desk,
and drawing one picture after another
of the matchbox choo-choo train you liked, weeping,
a profile of the real me—

"WHEN THE WATER CALLED ME . . ."
(MIZU GA WATASHI O YONDA TOKI . . . , 1977)

When the water called me
my body spilled from the log bridge
and before I took another breath was held in the river's arms.
I flowed. The water sang.
—Your red clothes, wet, open,
    are beautiful like a water flower.
    Let me give this flower to the water god
    as soon as possible.

But at that moment
with a voice stronger than water's someone called me.
I opened my eyes a little. It was the riverbed
and a fire was burning.
—We can't offer this healthy girl
    as a sacrifice to the water.
    We'll just give her clothes to him.
    Come, burn like me.
    Totally naked, you enchant me.

Myself enchanted, I stared at the fire.
My body became hot and my life caught fire.
My girlhood of "shoulder fabric"
flowed away, along with my clothes, in the hometown river;
I left a red flower, first sign of womanhood, abloom on a pebble
and began to walk.

Sometimes even now, far or near,
the water tries to lure me with his sweet song.
And each time I freely release my clothes to him
and become naked.
I make a fire and from near it
start out once more as if for the first time.

TAKAHASHI MUTSUO

Mino, My Bull (*Mino atashi no oushi*, 1959) was Takahashi Mutsuo's (b. 1937)
first book. Its topic was homosexual love, a subject he pursued for a number of
years, with his "Ode" (Homeuta, 1971) being perhaps his greatest achievement.
Takahashi has also written distinguished haiku and tanka, winning prestigious
prizes in those genres as well.

THE TERRIFIED PERSON (KYŌFU SURU HITO, 2000)

The universe in which we are will disappear someday—to think
this is terrifying.
As long as it has an end, the universe must have had a beginning;
and before it began it must not have existed—to think this is
even more terrifying.
We are living in the universe that once did not exist and
will not exist in time—to think this is terrifying.
This universe has no meaning and our living in this meaningless
universe has no meaning—to think this is terrifying.
Only our feeling terrified is the substance of our existence—to
think this is terrifying.
The fact that the terror ends is the same as the fact that
the terror did not begin—to think this is fatally terrifying.
I plead with you. Please make this terror grow and multiply until this
meaningless universe becomes full. Please do not stop doing so.

TO THE TERRORIST E. P. (TERORISUTO E. P., 2002)

The first year of the new millennium of turmoil, at year's end,
    in front of a fire,
I turn the pages of a photo album showing you in old age, in exile:
With a cane, back straightened, you gaze into the labyrinth
    of winter water;
under a large, glittering tree of summer, you stand, hair unkempt,
    with lovers napping in the background;
on your 81st birthday, surrounded by toasting glasses, you are
    expressionless.
One photograph shows a shelf where papers are stacked carelessly,
with a copy of a portrait of you in your prime, beard black,
    placed also carelessly.
You in those days, filled, filled with power, were a terrorist of words.
On the radio in a country that was enemy to your country, you kept
indicting your country for having corrupted itself into a stock
    exchange.
You were arrested, incarcerated, and driven out by your country.
Your forehead has bundles of deep wrinkles like the surface of earth.
With a voice as hoarse as the wind blowing across the frozen marshes
you say, as if spitting it out:
My life has been a great waste,
poetry, movements, everything, everything has been a waste.
But, if you are to speak of waste, Creation itself,

in particular, the birth of mankind and the history that followed,
    has been the greatest waste,
more than waste, an irredeemable typographical error.
Thirty years since you left us with a great sense of absence,
the arrogant stock exchange of your country
has kept swelling, thousands, tens of thousands of times.
The two Towers of Babel sucked in two iron birds and exploded.
What exploded was probably Earth itself.
It will take time for us to realize this
and when we realize this, we'll no longer be here.
We'll no longer be here, Earth will no longer be here,
nor, of course, will your photo album nor you in the photo album
wandering by the water.
But your words of warning will keep ringing
as an echo of memory no one will hear
across the marshes of the Galaxy where the stars died out.

TATEHATA AKIRA

Tatehata Akira (b. 1947) launched his poetry-writing career with the prize-
winning collection *Runners in the Margins* (*Yohaku no runner*, 1991). His latest,
fourth, collection, *Dog at Zero Degree* (*Reido no inu*, 2004), also won a prize.
Most of Tatehata's poems are written in prose. A well-known international art
critic and curator, he served as the Japanese commissioner for the Biennale di
Venezia in 1990 and 1993 and as the artistic director for the Yokohama Trien-
nial in 2001 and the Busan (Korea) Biennale in 2002. He is the director of the
National Museum of Art, Osaka.

THE STRUCTURE OF THE EGGPLANT
(NASUBI NO KŌZŌ, 1992)

Goddamn! I had told you eggplant isn't a "color," hadn't I? Born between
formalist and imagist, the eggplant must have gone through its own pain-
ful experiences. In the event, if you knowingly explain it as "structurally,
the camouflage of a leisurely shrimp," I can't dismiss the matter as simple
ignorance. To be sure, the eggplant has never had bones in its insides.
But what about it? Because it doesn't have bones, it must camouflage it-
self with adornments—with that kind of short-cut thinking, how do you
propose to understand the troubles the eggplant had to go through for so
long? I'm too appalled for words is what I am. You all observe only the
surfaces with the "good eyes" of which you are so proud and simply de-
light in describing them. And with that, you think you saw through the

eggplant's inner mechanisms. You feel you've conferred corporate status upon it. Before you know it, you switch a vegetable to fish or shellfish. Listen, fellows, despite its appearance, the eggplant is an individualistic vegetable. Each of them has its own "good history." If a vegetable were no more than a "color" or a "form," as you say it is, Tokyo Tower would be a carrot, Rokuharamitsuji Temple a tomato. If you brandish the myth of the eye and say everyone's the same, goddamn, you might as well destroy me with straw arrows and lotus guns!

THE PUMPKIN'S GALLSTONE
(KABOCHA NO TANSEKI, 1992)

Well, I suppose many of you won't believe this, but the pumpkin had a gallstone. The surgery was a success, so you should be relieved, but it's a mystery how the pumpkin developed a gallstone. There are many things you can't explain about human life, and this goes to show the pumpkin's life is similar. Surrounded by philistines, he (or she?) nonetheless grew up healthy. I don't imagine something like a gallstone would affect him too much, but anyhow he experienced surgery like *mankind*. From his sickroom the setting sun was beautiful, and it was just about that time that everyone came to see him. On his bed, half of him bathed in the sun, his normally wrinkled body deepened its shadows, as though his moderate personality had added some weightiness. "The stone's right here," he'd say. "Looks like a mushroom, doesn't it?" Those who came to see him were relieved by these accommodating words. But some fools would respond unthinkingly, "A mushroom in a pumpkin, you say?" This would make him frown suddenly. "I don't understand that myself. Seems contrary to the promise made at birth," he'd mutter, and clam up. "Well, you know, *mankind*, too, has a mushroom type of gallstone," someone would try to soothe him, but too late. It was the silence of the stern pumpkin staring at the huge setting sun. The visitors who happened to be in that spectacle all felt solemn, or so they said. In fact, it couldn't have been something that touched a taboo, but I wouldn't second-guess. Looking at a pumpkin's gallstone and the beautiful setting sun, anyone would become somewhat philosophical.

YOSHIMASU GŌZŌ

Beginning with *Starting Out* (*Shuppatsu*, 1964), Yoshimasu Gōzō (b. 1939) has created a body of poetry notable for its sweeping vision and minute attention to words and their associations. The following poem is from his book "*Snowy Island*" *or* "*Emily's Ghost*" ("*Yuki no shima*" *aruiwa* "*Emily no yūrei*," 1998), which won the Education Minister's Prize.

WALKING ALL BY MYSELF, MY THOUGHT'S / GHOSTLY POWER—
(TADA HITORI ARUKU SHIKŌ NO / YŪREI NO YŌ NA CHIKARA—,
1998)

On the road to the AFUNRUPAR [*ahun-ru-par*]= to the "AFUNRUPAR formed
   as I hadn't even imagined" (*Research Reports on Northern Cultures*, 11th Issue,
   March, 31st Year of Shōwa)
I had started walking all by myself perhaps because of the power of just one word
   "*only*"
Blade of grass (as *terrify*ing as, . . . the wraith of a *word's* ending . . .) *ly-lily*,
   language's spirit's
stalk forming "an invisible beautiful curve" (Chiri Sachie-san, *James Joyce*) which in
   the footpath of my imagination (Ms. Mayama Taka-*san* et al., Itako-*san*)
made flowers bloom *itana*, . . . blowhole *itana*, . . . bowhead *isana* (Dr. Chiri
   Mashiho), . . . blowhole *itana*, . . .

Why is (the entrance = solitude)
(Am I trying to walk past the road *par*) in me,
      (or am I just passing by it, . . .) Drooping his head
a wooden buddha in rags or something like that, . . . giving a sidelong glance
   at the beautiful lightly made-up top of Zaō from the window of Hotel Castle,
next to "Sokolow's crane," without giving a side-glance "walking past / passing
   by,"
"This is B-class, . . ."

I walked up to the window, peered out, and was listening to the mysterious "n't"
   in "You've learned A for B, have, n't, you, . . . ?"
which "beautiful Zaō" smiling whispered
unable to pronounce it, . . .
In the window of the bus heading to the airport, "*ru*," "*ru*," *ru*," . . . floated up
   "Mount Moon"
May have been the figure/form like the ghost of AFUNRUPAR
That in me too, there was a street "*ru*" like this of the universe, . . . was surprised

Let's do something, yes, let's dance like this, like Emily

(*Watashi wa jibun no seimei o ryōte de furete mita*
   I felt my life with both hands
(*Soko ni aru ka dō ka tashikameru tame ni*
   To see if it was there
(*Watashi no tamashii o kagami mi chikazuketa*
   I held my spirit to my Glass,
(*Motto hakkiri sasetakute*
   To prove it possibler—

. . . . . .

. . . . . .

(*Guruguru jibun no sonzai o mawashite*
    I turned my Being round and round
                    (Niikura Toshiichi-san, *Emily Dickinson—Fuzai no Shōzō,*
                            published by Taishūkan shoten, p. 18)
She really turned round and round didn't she Emily
"Many cloud peaks collapse and the moon over the mount" (Bashō-san)   The old
    gentleman's (and his slowing counting eyes) voice . . .
I proved . . . , by myself, isn't it?

"Collapse and, possibler, . . ." We, too, "stack" new word/s, and "tilt" them
E(SachiE)h?, a dead dog supports the Moon Mountain, his legs stretched out
    side by side, . . .? ("On Wakabayashi Osamu," by Mr. Koizumi Shin'ya, Yamagata
    Museum of Arts, October 23, '97) ("The Moon and Immortality")
Somehow there's a smell
                    of rubbing (rasping),
                                        the universe becomes aware of
Probably, collapse
                    and ballooning (possibler)
                                        "Silver Heel,"
                                                I wish the Sea of Japan
        had a name like that,
Emily's *ly,* "Silver Heel," Chiri Sachie-san

(*Soshite marude tampopo no sode ni yadotta*
    And made as He would eat me up—
(*Itteki no shizuku o nomihosu yō ni*
    As wholly as a Dew
(*Watashi o nomihosu kakkō o shita*
    Upon a Dandelion's Sleeve—
(*Sokode watashi wa aruki hajimeta*
    And then—I started—too
(*Suruto umi wa sugu ato o ottekite*
    And He—He followed—close behind—
(*Sono gin no kakato o*
    I felt His Silver Heel
(*Watashi no kurubushi ni kanjita*
    Upon my Ankle—Then my Shoes
(*Sorekara watashi no kutsu ga shinju de afureta*
    Would overflow with Pearl—

. . . . . .

. . . . . .

(*Umi wa hitori mo chijin ga inairashiku*
   No one He seems to know—
(*Ōkina manazashi de watashi o ichibetsu shite*
   And bowing with—a Mighty look—
(*Shirizoite itta*
   At me—The sea withdrew—

(Niikura Shun'ichi-san, from the same book, p. 23)

And bowing (again it's B), . . . So the sea too bowing withdraws, its body, as it goes
   away
How's that

Scent of Ishikari (Inkari no ka), although I am a B-class poet, I've *begun* to learn
   "And bowing. . . ." . . . .
At a place called *Chambre* in Sapporo Station (within its building), waiting for the
   connection (*P.M.3.00~3.30*),
though I wanted to drink dark/lager beer, "someone has taken this mountain path"
   (*Orikuchi Shinobu-san's tanka*)
"Being inside the building was for some reason *terrifying*, . . ."
I prick up my ears to, *at*, the footfalls of an ancient old Ainu's crane. My ears next
   to, . . .

(Angels rent a house next to us / no matter where we move
Terrify! Crane's bed,——

(*Massuguni seyo, mattoresu o*
   Be its Mattress straight—
(*Manmaruku seyo, sono nakura o*
   Be its pillow round—
At the entrance to the two B's lying side by side, clouds, slowly, collapsed/broke

"*C!*"
"*C?*"

POETRY IN TRADITIONAL FORMS

In the past two decades, increasing experimentation with form, combined with less formal diction, has brought a contemporary feeling to the traditional haiku and tanka forms.

KATAYAMA YUMIKO

Katayama Yumiko (b. 1952) began her career as a pianist and helped support herself by giving piano lessons. One couple whom she taught wrote haiku as a hobby. At their suggestion, she began to write haiku, and soon poetry became her main interest. Katayama has since published four collections of her poetry, as well as an anthology of modern haiku written by women. She sees her art as describing "things that are not noticed except by haiku poets," those moments that can make her readers "a bit happier and better to be alive." The translations are by Makoto Ueda.

prolonged	*rakuseki no*
aftermath of a falling stone—	*yoin o nagaku*
the mountain sleeps	*yama nemuru*
post-blossom foliage—	*hazakura ya*
differently white	*shirosa chigaete*
salt and sugar	*shio satō*
no poem to poverty	*mazushisa no*
in this age of ours—	*shi to wa naranu yo*
an eggplant flower	*nasu no hana*
falling	*yakusoku o*
like broken promises	*tagaeshi gotoku*
spring snow	*haru no yuki*

MAYUZUKI MADOKA

The daughter of a haiku poet, Mayuzuki Madoka (b. 1965) began her career as a television reporter. Her interview with the poet Sugita Hisajo, a sample of whose haiku can be found in volume 1 of this anthology, deepened her interest in writing poetry. A thoroughly contemporary woman, Mayuzuki is more likely to mention a polo shirt or sunglasses than those traditional objects favored by more classically inclined poets. The translations are by Makoto Ueda.

Mother's Day—	*haha no hi no*
I end up making	*haha o nakashite*
my mother cry	*shimaikeri*
mannequins	*manekin no*
whispering among themselves—	*sasayaki aeru*
hazy spring night	*oboro kana*
now the trip is over—	*tabi oete*
my summer holidays	*yori B-men no*
start their B side	*natsuyasumi*

TAWARA MACHI

Hugely popular, Tawara Machi (b. 1962) has become the spokesperson for what is termed *shinjinrui*, "the new human species," a breed of young Japanese who, to their parents at least, seem to inhabit a whole new country. As a high-school student, Tawara enjoyed acting in plays but took up poetry as an avocation while an undergraduate student at Waseda University. With the publication of her anthology *Salad Anniversary* (*Salada kinenbi*) in 1987, when she was only in her mid-twenties, she became one of the best-known young literary figures in Japan and has continued to write for her large public ever since.

> That single word
> I let slip the chance to say
> floats like a leaf
> in hot pepper soup,
> so bitter my eyes water.

hitotsu dake iisobiretaru koto no ha no hatōgarashi ga horohoro nigai

Translated by Edwin Cranston

> At breakfast
> coffee smells so good
> on my table—
> what's this about a life
> with only room for love?

kōhī no kaku made kaoru shokutaku ni ai dake ga aru jinsei nante

Translated by Edwin Cranston

I remember
your hand, your back,
    your breathing,
the white socks left
where you took them off.

omoidasu kimi no te kimi no se kimi no iki nuida mamma no shiroi kutsushita

                    Translated by Edwin Cranston

"Phone me again."
"Wait for me."
Always always
you make love
in the imperative.

"mata denwa shiro yo" "mattero" itsu mo itsu mo meireiki de ai o iu kimi

                    Translated by Edwin Cranston

Your room—I'll never be here again
    don't let them spoil   the milk   the onions

mō nido to konai to omou kimi no heya
    kusarasenaide ne   miruku   tamanegi

                    Translated by Edwin Cranston

This is how it starts—
but perhaps I had it wrong:
    this is how it ends,
the night that let itself be held
so lightly in our embrace.

hajimari to omoitakeredo oshimai to naru ka mo shirenu yoru o dakareru

                    Translated by Edwin Cranston

Out of paper and writing I construct my heart;
    you'll probably get it in the mail.

kami to moji de boku no kokoro o kumitateru
    kimi ni wa tabun todoku to omou

                    Translated by Edwin Cranston

Heart turned clear as ice
by a conversation I had no desire
to hear
I kept the washing machine going deep into the night.

kikitaku wa nakatta hanashi ni kokoro saete
shin'ya mawashite iru sentakki

Translated by Edwin Cranston

Your disappearing figure,
a little too cool—
it's always the man
    who sets off on a journey.

Tabidatte yuku no wa itsu mo kotoko nite kakko yosugiru senaka mite iru

Translated by Juliet Winters Carpenter

Changing trains
as if folding up
an umbrella—
I return
to my hometown

oritatamigasa o tatande yuku fū ni kisha norikaeta furusato ni tsuku

Translated by Leza Lowitz, Miyuki Aoyama, and Akemi Tomioka

Fireworks, fireworks
watching them together—
one sees only the flash
the other,
the darkness

hanabi hanabi soko ni hikari o miru hito to yami o miru hito narabi ori

Translated by Leza Lowitz, Miyuki Aoyama, and Akemi Tomioka

DRAMA

Since the 1970s, performances of contemporary drama have continued to be popular, not only in Tokyo, but also in Osaka, Kyoto, and Nagoya. Dramatists like Shimizu Kunio and Kara Jūrō, who began on the fringes and whose work is included in this section, have now found themselves part of the mainstream, with their plays sometimes televised and their complete works published by major publishing houses. In addition, the acceptance of the avant-garde has made it possible for drama companies to support and encourage a more generally popular, commercial drama, and these plays often experiment without losing their audience. Of these dramatists, Inoue Hisashi is without doubt the most successful and most innovative of his generation.

INOUE HISASHI

Inoue Hisashi (b. 1934) is one of contemporary Japan's most popular satirists and dramatists. His numerous novels and plays range over a wide spectrum of themes, from a retelling of the famous forty-seven *rōnin* story to a recent drama set in 1945 when the atomic bombs were dropped on Japan.

Inoue's continuing interest in the comic novels of the Tokugawa (Edo) period (1600–1868) may have prompted him to compose his one-character play *Makeup* (*Keshō*), first staged in 1983 and now a mainstay of the Japanese stage.

Nowadays, most visitors to Japan see a performance of kabuki in its grandest and most classic form, with all male actors. But since kabuki's inception in the seventeenth century, until well into the postwar period, more modest, often bowdlerized, versions of these dramas, staged by groups of itinerant players, have visited towns and villages throughout the country. Women often participated in such productions, and the troupe pictured here played in just such a performance.

MAKEUP (KESHŌ)

Translated by Akemi Horie

The forlorn dressing-room of a rundown little theater. A large makeup mirror downstage left of center for the troupe leader; however, the mirror cannot be seen by the audience. In fact, all this play actually needs is an actress to play the actress-manager; makeup equipment, costumes, and a wig for her to transform herself into a "yakuza" hero named Isaburō the Brave; twenty or so "enka" songs; and the active imagination of the audience.[1]

---

1. The wig specified by the author is *ichō-honke-binmushiri*, the type of hairstyle popular among young *yakuza* during the latter half of the Edo period (1600–1868).

As the light comes on in silence, a woman is seen taking a nap in front of (from the audience's viewpoint, the other side of) the mirror. According to what she herself believes, she is Satsuki Yōko, the forty-six-year-old actress-manager of a traveling theatre troupe, "The Satsuki."

Nothing much takes place for a while. Only Satsuki Yōko tossing about vulgarly from time to time. At her third or fourth toss, an "enka" song becomes audible in the distance. For example, Suizenji Kiyoko's "What Would You Do If You Were a Man." At this sound, Satsuki Yōko springs to her feet as if she had been yanked up by a string from the ceiling.

Here we go, they've started letting in the audience. (*Giving a quick glance in the direction above the mirror.*) Damn, what a black sky for a July evening and it's not even six yet! Can't afford rain now, not on a Saturday night when we're hoping for good business. Hold on for another 40 minutes or so, won't you? Till the curtain's up?

Apparently there is a window diagonally above the mirror. She places a Dunhill cigarette between her lips and lights it with a gold-plated lighter. She takes one deep breath as she gazes at herself in the mirror and blows the smoke out at her reflection. Thereupon an apprentice of the troupe, visible to her but invisible to the audience, brings tea.

Ta.

She takes a sip, and chances to look at the boy's face.

Hey, your makeup is much too thin, love. For heaven's sake, paint your face solid like a wall, won't you? Once you get into the habit of putting on sloppy makeup, you're finished as an actor in our business.

As she moves about stage-right checking the makeup of other actors:

Start getting stingy with the makeup, and you end up exposing your rotten old faces; you just can't imagine how many troupes like us have gone bust on that account.

It seems that she is using the space according to the following principles. First, she believes that ten or so members of her troupe are present stage-right; so when addressing them she will look toward this direction. Second, the right wing of the stage that we see apparently functions simultaneously as the wing of the stage on which she is about to perform. Third, she will soon produce on her left an invisible man from a TV channel; in her conversation with him, she will direct her face and mind toward stage-left. Further, the "enka" songs will be heard continuously throughout the performance, and the selection of these songs must be made with great care. In the main, lively, rhythmic songs with upbeat feelings must be chosen. Under no circumstances should a morose and melancholy piece like Misora Hibari's "The Sorrowful 'Saké'" be played. Indeed the selection of the "enka" medley, played to attract the audience, is one of the important tasks of the troupe leader. In other words, the songs played are mostly her own favorites; thus she will from time to time sway her body to the music. One final point: as far as the "enka" songs are concerned, the audience can also hear them.

Let me remind you once again, if I may, this is our opening night here. I want you to give it everything you've got and try like hell out there. I myself have decided to appear in all the numbers tonight, from the opening play to the Grand Song and Dance Finale; my strategy is to captivate the first-night audience with the full blast of my performance, so with any luck they'll spread the word and bring in a good crowd for the rest of the week. So keep up with my pace as best you can, will you? As you know, this theater is going to be knocked down in ten days; apparently a block of flats is going up instead. This means we've got to gird up our loins and try all the harder, wouldn't you say? Who's that? Who gave that silly laugh just now? What's so funny, darling? Eh? . . . as the boss is a "lady," mightn't it cause me a bit of discomfort with a tight loin-cloth cutting into my crotch? Honestly, it's only a figure of speech— you're asking for a good hiding, love! Seriously, if the very last finale of this theater should end up with a poor house, the name of Satsuki Yōko will be mud; the good name of the Satsuki troupe will be lost forever. So I'm asking every one of you to pull your weight and try your hardest to jam-pack the house every night; I'll be putting my life on the line, too. Then luck will surely come our way; great theaters like the Shinohara Enbujō and the Mokubakan will come rushing to buy us out. So, do your damnedest, this could be your great beginning. Now, as for my speech of greeting to the audience, I'll do it right after the second play as usual. (*She practices her speech.*) "Ladies and gentlemen, welcome, welcome to our performance tonight. Thank you very much for coming so eagerly on our first night, despite our long absence from these parts. I know it is impolite to address you from up here on stage, but my heart is at your feet and I would like to express our deep gratitude. Although we are already halfway into tonight's performance, may I take the opportunity of this interval to say a few words of greeting. Tonight is the all-important opening night, and with your kind indulgence we have so far performed the opening play *Isaburō's Parting* and the second piece *The Tale of the Hairdresser Shinza* without mishap . . . fantastic? Was it really fantastic? Oh, thank you, thank you. And now what remains is *The Golden Stage of Song and Dance*. . . . For the finale, we are presenting our special number, *Fukagawa*: we shall all dress up as handsome young dandies and erotic geisha, and enchant you with our titillating beauty. So I hope you will all make yourselves comfortable and enjoy the show right to the end. Once again, we thank you very much for coming to our performance tonight. . . ."

She has been smoking as she rehearses her speech, but now stubs out the cigarette in an ashtray. She did not like the speech.

God, that was pretty feeble, I must say. (*She thinks a little.*) "Welcome, welcome to our performance. It is twenty years since my husband Satsuki Tatsutarō II passed away in his prime at the age of thirty-one. Perhaps some of you may remember the incident; twenty years ago, my husband died suddenly on this very stage of this theater while performing. . . ." Mind you, if anyone says "I remember," he's a big liar. True, the man disappeared twenty years ago all right. But the real truth is that he ran off with one of his fans and the mistress of some ironmonger[2] in Ryōgoku, heroically abandoning his sinking ship. "Dying on stage. Indeed, ladies and gentlemen, it must have been a most gratifying end for my husband, born actor that he was." The bastard was handpicked by my dad Satsuki Tatsutarō I to marry me; so naturally he was, shall we says, an above-average actor. However, character-wise, ugh, what a worm! "That was the period when film stars like Kinnosuke, Chiyonosuke and Yūjirō were in their prime, and television was invading our homes with terrifying speed. The theaters were empty wherever you went—the full houses we had had in the fifties seemed like a dream, and troupes like us were going bankrupt one after the other, one yesterday, two today and three tomorrow. . . ." (*Glowering at the invisible mirror.*) Can't see a damn thing in this mirror, for some reason. "Needless to say, we, the Satsuki troupe, were no exception; at the best of times our audience was twenty to thirty and we were living from hand to mouth. We were so broke, we were grateful for the cigarette butts you left behind, which we collected and smoked each night after the performance. Then came the untimely death of my husband; when your luck runs out, bad luck really does pile up on you; as they say, 'You stumble, only to find yourself in the dung heap.' " Would you believe, within ten days the number of Satsuki members went down from fifteen to a bare three. Still, if they had simply run away, I could have forgiven them. But, damn them, they pinched the precious costumes and wigs my dad had collected over the years, as a kind of farewell present; it turned out that I'd been acting with a gang of thieves all those years. To cap it all, I had a baby boy, three months old. I tell you, I really felt I had no way out but to kill myself and the boy right then. "But, thank heavens, you were with us; our small but eager, warm-hearted, and appreciative audience were with us." Mind you, there were some greasy ones too. "Yeah, I'll buy a block of fifty tickets, so let me do what I want with you for the night," one oozed. How could I refuse? "It was the warm support of such audiences that kept the Satsuki Troupe going during those difficult years. We are eternally grateful." Shall I cry here? "It is impolite to address you from up here on stage but my heart is at your feet and I would like to express our deepest gratitude. We are already halfway into tonight's performance, but may I take the opportunity of this interval to say a few words of greeting? Tonight is the all-important opening night, so we have opened our performance with my hit, *Isaburō's Parting*. This is my favorite, favorite play. I've had the pleasure of performing it for you hundreds of times, but every time I play the part I cry, and I've cried again tonight. The second piece, *The Tale of the Hairdresser Shinza*, was my husband Satsuki Tatsutarō II's star turn, indeed he was performing this

---

2. The Japanese here is *tetsuzai-tonya* (iron material wholesaler). The text indicates that Satsuki's husband ran off with two people: "a fan" and "the mistress of a wholesale ironmonger" (*hiiki-kyaku to Ryōgoku no tetsuzai-tonya-san no nigō to*).

very play when he was struck down on this stage twenty years ago. Tonight, to commemorate his death, I, Satsuki Yōko, have played his part to the best of my ability. And now what remains is *The Golden Stage of Song and Dance.* . . ." Okay, okay—that will do for the speech.

Looking toward a specific point stage-right.

Who's that—who's snoring at this time of day? Nakamaru, my dear. Mr. Ichikawa Nakamaru. Grandpa Nakamaru. (*Shouts.*) Nakamaru! For heaven's sake, how could you drift off so shamelessly like that, just before the curtain? Don't forget, it's up to you and me to hold the audience's attention in *Isaburō's Parting.* If you have time to snore, shouldn't you be going over the scene a couple more times? Look, this is the first time you've ever played the part of Isaburō's mother; I hoped you'd take it a little more seriously. . . . Wipe up your dribble. And will you please redo your makeup, around the mouth? (*Sotto voce.*) Really, makes you wonder, doesn't it? We had to ask him to help out from today because we're a bit short-staffed, but what a promising start! "Yes, I have been acclaimed as the best mature female impersonator in the Kantō region," he says. First-rate when it comes to self-promotion, I must say.

At this point, her attention is caught by something in the wings stage-left. She looks toward it, and then speaks in the direction of stage-right.

Toshi, there's someone there. You mustn't let people into the dressing-room before curtain up. You know the dogsbody's duties include guarding the dressing-room against intruders. We just had our costumes pinched at the Oshima Theater in Kawasaki, remember? The chappy looked so impressive I thought he was a journalist from some magazine; then, before you know it, he runs off with a basket full of costumes. . . . Eh? Someone from TBS Television? He says he'd like to talk to me after the show, so you let him in?

Turns toward stage-left.

Oh my, let me introduce myself: I am Satsuki Yōko.

She takes something deferentially. It looks like a card.

Mr. Koyama. Well, very pleased to meet you.

Toward stage-right.

Toshi, dear, why didn't you tell me sooner that we have a guest?

In the direction of stage-left.

You don't mind waiting until after the show? It would be better afterward because it concerns a serious matter? A serious matter, I see. My heart is already going pit-a-pat with excitement, like a little girl's.

Toward stage-right.

Toshi, darling, how about opening a bottle of beer for our guest? And could you run along to the front of the house to get us some *oden*[3] to go with the beer? Well, just oden might be a bit lonely. Add a plate of grilled

---

3. *Oden* is a traditional Japanese dish of cooked vegetables and fish. In performance, this could be replaced by sushi, a more widely known Japanese dish.

squid. . . . Wait a minute, Grandpa Nakamaru, I didn't ask you to go along. Just imagine, an old woman in white makeup parades across the stalls carrying a grilled squid in front of her—the audience will have a fit! You're an old hand and I'm sure you don't need a lecture on the actor's ABCs but, for heaven's sake, our job is to sell dreams—you can't walk about the stalls in your makeup and costume. Eh? You want to wait for your cue in the wing? That's why you were going out? Honestly, Grandpa; come here a minute.

Her eyes move. They follow his movement which stops at her side.

Nakamaru, dear, I don't like to say this, but have you really ever played a female part before? The way you just walked over here—you were concentrating so hard on pointing your toes inward that you forgot all about your knees. I tell you what, why don't you put a sheet of paper between your knees and try to walk without dropping it. That's the basic technique for walking like a woman. For goodness sake, don't just stand there looking gormless— try it. Here, take this tissue. Now, as you walk about, listen very carefully. We've already gone over[4] the scene of *Isaburō's Parting* twice. If an actor can't get it right after two rehearsals, there isn't much hope for him in our kind of theater; I'm afraid he'll have to go legit.[5] So, remember, *Isaburō's Parting* is made up of three scenes. The first scene is almost entirely mine. There lives in the sea-town of Chōshi a clan of yakuza gangsters called the Yamagen. The chieftain is Yamamoto Gengorō and I am—that is, Isaburō is—the heir to the clan. Yakuza they may be, but the Yamagen are one of that rare and honest breed of gangsters, made up from top to bottom of saint-like characters. Well, one day Isaburō, on his old man's behalf, pays a visit to Katori Shrine in Sawara, in neighboring Shimousa Province. When the rival Isetatsu clan find this out, however, they seize the opportunity to raid the Yamagen. The Isetatsu is an upstart yakuza clan in the same town, and naturally they're all villains. Caught unawares, and with the invincible Isaburō away, alas, not a single man of the Yamagen survives this vicious raid. And now the old chieftain lies drawing his last breath. . . . At this point the curtain rises. As soon as the curtain's up, Isaburō, who learned of the fatal news on his way home, comes rushing back, crying out "Father!" The old man, with his dying breath, says:

---

4. *Kuchidate-keiko* is a mode of rehearsal still practiced in the traditional popular theater, by which the lines and plot of the play are learned orally, without a written script, from the head of the troupe.

5. The Japanese here is *shingeki* (new theater), which is the Japanese counterpart of the legitimate theater in the West. The *shingeki* produces "serious" foreign and native plays by such authors as Shakespeare, Chekhov, and Beckett, or Abe Kōbō and Inoue Hisashi, and naturally allows plenty of time for rehearsal. For the relation among the traditional Japanese theater, kabuki, and the new theater, see A. Horie-Webber, "Modernisation of the Japanese Theatre: The Shingeki Movement," in *Modern Japan: Aspects of History, Literature, and Society*, ed. William G. Beasley (London: Allen & Unwin, 1975).

(*The lines from the scene of* Isaburō's Parting *that appear several times in the following are for the most part based on a seven/five—or sometimes five/seven, seven/seven—syllabic rhythm.*)[6]

"I've been waiting for you, Isaburō. My life, like a rice cake in summer, won't last till the night. Don't bother attending to my wounds but listen, listen carefully to what I have to say. It's about your origin . . . you are not my real son. Some twenty-odd years ago, the slave-trader Denkichi gave me a babe-in-arms for five ryō of gold, and that child was you; you are my adopted son. What? You knew that? Then you also know where your real mother lives? Ah, that you don't know. I heard on the wind, she now makes a humble living alone at the Numata pass in windy Jōshū province, serving tea and selling straw sandals to travelers. Don't trouble yourself with avenging me. Forget the Isetatsu, but leave here at once. Here, this is the talisman that was tied around your neck as a baby; it's the talisman of the goddess Kishibo of Iriya. And 20 ryō—my farewell gift to you. Take care, Isaburō, and look after your mother well. Ah . . . how detestable is the yakuza life!"

She becomes the chieftain halfway through, and here she/he dies. But she rises immediately.

Good grief, what a long speech, bloody unnatural on his deathbed. That's how countless "popular" theaters went bust in the past. However, that's that for the moment.

She looks toward stage-left.

Really, there are a lot of scenes like that in Shakespeare? You don't say. Uh . . . Shakespeare . . . Shakespeare. . . . Ah, him, he's the big shot in the legit theater, isn't he? Don't they ever go bankrupt, playing scenes like that? They don't? Aren't they lucky to have such tolerant audiences.

She begins to put on her costume.

Toshi, this (*a piece of her costume*) stinks. It hasn't been washed. Toshi. . . . Where is everybody in this play? Actually, Isaburō does avenge his Yamagen foster-father. He dashes over to the Isetatsu headquarters all by himself and kills everyone in sight. In the process, he ends up also killing a crooked sheriff, Isetatsu's crony, and becomes an outlaw. This is the second scene; it centers around sword-fighting. Then comes the scene at the tea-hut on the Numata pass. Grandpa Nakamaru plays the old woman at the tea-hut, that's right, Isaburō's natural mother . . . you know that, do you? Well, then why do you need to wait in the wings before the curtain's up? That's what I wanted to ask you. Really, Grandpa, couldn't you just relax and wait in the dressing-room? The wings are too crowded; you can't hang around there without a good reason.

---

6. The traditional syllabic rhythm of Japanese verse is 5/7 or 7/5, as in the thirty-one-syllable waka (5/7/5/7/7) and the seventeen-syllable haiku (5/7/5).

She puts on a wig at about this point. With the wig on she now looks very much "the abandoned son."

In the third scene, Nakamaru, dear, you are already on stage when the curtain rises. As the lights come up, you are seen sprinkling water in front of your tea-hut. The water accidentally hits the feet of Isaburō, who happens to be passing by. The old woman apologises profusely and offers him tea. Your line here is: "Three miles to a saké shop and two miles to a tofu shop, this is a remote mountain hut, sir; I have nothing much to offer you but a cup of brewed tea. If you don't mind that, won't you please relieve your thirst. . . ." Got it? You must time this line exactly. Without your tea, Isaburō will just have to pass by the hut and be gone. Can you try that line?

She listens to his line as she puts on her costume, and responds to it.

"You speak the same dialect as mine, ma'am. Aren't you from the sea-town of Chōshi?"

She listens to the line spoken by the other.

"They say dialect is the passport of your homeland, and, just as I thought, you too come from Chōshi. How good to hear that familiar Chōshi accent in these strange parts. But I wonder, why should anyone brought up in sight of the ocean want to live in a remote mountainous place like this? There must be some deep reason. . . . Well, old mother, by some providence our paths have crossed here, and what's more we come from the same town; I'd like to hear your story. . . . Somehow I crave to hear it. As you see, I am a rolling stone; come tomorrow, I shall be gone from the Numata pass. Even if I wanted to repeat your story, I should have no one to tell it to. I shall forget it as soon as I hear it. So you can pretend you are just talking to a wall. . . ."

Suddenly, toward stage-left.

Well what is this "serious matter" you wanted to talk about? As Isaburō says, "Somehow I crave to hear it. . . ." I know, you'd like me to appear on television. That's it, isn't it? Of course I will. It's great publicity. How about the whole Satsuki troupe appearing all together, wham . . . ! Oh, just my-self? Well, in that case, let's see, first my close-up appears on the screen, with a big caption across the top saying something like "20 YEARS OF HARD-SHIP! NOBLY THE ACTRESS/MANAGER BORE IT ALL"; then the music, ta-ra. . . . No? A reunion on the morning show!? But reunion with whom? Tagami Haruhiko! Oh, I've heard of him. He's the laddie who started out with the New Music Group, then broke away to become an actor, isn't he? I know the name and the face—I do at least read the gossip magazines, you know. I see, he's just got a big part in a prime-time TV drama, so, to boost publicity, you're setting up a real-life reunion drama on the morning show? Well, that's very nice for him. But personally, I don't know Tagami Haruhiko. And if I don't know the boy, it couldn't be a reunion, could it? What a funny idea. Are you really from TBS television?

To stage-right.

Grandpa, that long speech about her life you just tried—there were several important items missing. Would you please include all the points, in the right order, and speak clearly: (1) I was married to a fisherman in Chōshi twenty-three years ago; (2) I got pregnant right away and had a baby boy; (3) about that time, my husband, as if possessed by devils, suddenly began to go astray; (4) three years later he was stabbed to death by a yakuza in a fight over gambling; (5) furthermore he left behind as much as thirty ryō in gambling debts; (6) to pay off those debts, I was sold to a hostelry in Jōshū Province as a prostitute; (7) I had no choice but to hand my baby over to a go-between; she promised to have him adopted by a respectable foster-family; (8) two years later, I was bought out by a haberdashery merchant from Numata and became his second wife; (9) immediately I started looking for the go-between, but she was nowhere to be found; my second husband went to Chōshi to look for the child several times, but he couldn't discover his whereabouts; (10) eight years ago, my second husband died; I seem to have rotten luck in my choice of husbands. I folded up his shop and set up the tea-hut here. With the panoramic view from here, I feel as if I could see my home town, Chōshi, though of course one can't possibly see it. . . . So there are ten points all together. Unless you mention all ten in the right order, it won't do, you know.

She has almost finished dressing herself for the part. It only remains to put on the straw sandals. While she draws the sword out and in of the scabbard:

And for the closing lines of this long speech about her life, please remember to highlight every word like a jewel. "Sir, you've been such a good listener that I seem to have revealed all my shameful past, despite myself. Now let me warm up a bottle of homemade sweet saké for you. There are some baked rice-cakes, too. It's cold in the mountains, and an empty stomach doesn't help, so won't you have something before you go. . . . What's the matter, sir, are you crying?"

Toward stage-left.

Child? Yes, I had a boy. He was adopted by a respectable family. We were living literally from day to day then, often without enough to eat. So much worry that my milk dried up in the end, and he was put into care at some Christian orphanage in Bunkyō district; yes, I remember now, it was called the Orphanage of the Holy Mother.

Toward stage-right.

"To tell the truth, my circumstances are just like your son's: I too was sold to a stranger as an infant, and I don't know if I have a brother or a sister, or even any relative at all; that's why I was so moved by your story. But by some good fortune my foster-father was a kind man, like a Buddha but with a dagger at his side and a tattoo on his back: he cherished me and raised me like his own. All the same, ma'am, I bear a grudge, I hate the mother who abandoned me."

She listens to a line from the other (probably very short), and responds:

"But why did she bear me at all if she was so ready to abandon me? . . . Your son would probably say the same."

She listens and responds.

"I would rather have been killed than abandoned. The mother kills her child in desperation, unable to bring herself to give it away: that is the mercy of a true mother, isn't it?"

Looks toward stage-left.

What—wasn't my boy adopted by the Yokoyama Electrical Shop in Hachiōji? Honestly you do go on with your silly questions; can't you find anything better to do? The nurseries don't tell you the details of where your child went; that avoids any trouble between the adoptive and natural parents later on. The matron said to me, "Don't worry, your child will be adopted by a respectable family. But if you want to change your mind, this is the time: Will you take the child back or send him away?" I cried and cried for a whole half-day till my tears dried up, feeling half-grateful and half-dejected. But, just supposing—mind you, it's a big "if"—supposing someone or other's child really was adopted by the Yokoyama family, what of it? . . . I see, the Yokoyamas had a child of their own in time and, not unexpectedly, began to ill-treat their adopted son. Well, well . . . and what happened next? . . . The boy left home when he turned fifteen and he's been missing ever since. Ah, it's a heartrending story even for a stranger. But this boy Tagami Haruhiko eventually came up in the world, and became a star, isn't that right? So the story has a happy ending, three cheers!

Toward stage-right.

" 'How can you tell a motherless child'; do you know that children's song? It goes on, 'He stands in the doorway, sucking his thumb.' In the dusk, you watch the circle of children playing together, squatting in the doorway, sucking your thumb, crying because you are left out . . . that's a lonely feeling for any child. . . ."

Turns toward stage-left.

A photo? Tagami Haruhiko always carried an old photo next to his heart, all the while eking out a living from one downtown restaurant job after another? A photo of a mother holding a baby? And it shows the corner of something like a costume box in the background? Are you seriously suggesting the mother's face in the picture somehow resembles mine? Come on, mine's a very common face with eyes looking like almonds; how can you be sure? I see, the mother's face in the photo is rubbed off? Because of the boy's caressing and stroking it every day? You really make my heart bleed! What—? Nonetheless you can see the character *tsuki* on the costume box in the background? Look, just because the box has *tsuki* written on it, it doesn't mean that it says *Sa-tsuki*. It could be *tsuki-mura* or *tsuki-gata*. . . .

She looks toward stage-right, at some distant point. She raises her hand to respond, and shifts her eyes to the point at stage-right where Ichikawa Nakamaru is supposed to be.

Did you hear what Toshi just said, Grandpa? With a bit of a last-minute rush, we may have a full house tonight. Isn't that wonderful? What a break! "Even a mourning child, bereft of his mother, has some mementos left to remember her by, like her tattered kimono or a straw sandal with a broken strap. But for an abandoned child, like myself, there was not even a shadow of a memento . . . it was heart-breaking."

Toward stage-left.

Me, frightened? Frightened of what? Of being reproached by my abandoned son? I'll tell you, what I am really frightened of is rain at curtain time, that's the only thing. Now, would you mind not disrupting our rehearsal, please?

Toward stage-right.

"Indulgent parents who coax the crawling child to stand and the standing child to walk . . . how I longed to find parents like that somewhere, some day. Night and day, in the frosty morning and the stormy evening, I used to pray to the gods, to Buddha, to the Sun and Moon, joining my tiny hands like maple leaves. . . . Then, as I came to realize that my wish would never come true, I turned blasphemous: the gods don't exist; Buddha is the most merciless villain of all; may the Sun burn itself out and the Moon drown herself. . . .

The old woman of the mountain tea-hut cries at this point, Grandpa Nakamaru; she really does break down pathetically. Isaburō is taken aback, "Well, well, I got carried away. Your son will be different, he is not a ruffian like myself; he couldn't possibly speak such harsh, hurtful words. However much he might reproach you at first, that will pass. I assure you, he will soon be crying out 'Mother' even as he rebukes you, for his hatred is only skin-deep, while his heart is crammed with voices saying 'I've missed you; I've longed for you.' Deep down he is sure to be thinking, 'She must have had some powerful reason to abandon her child.' The old poem says: 'Though there are a thousand different bonds of love in the world, none is stronger than that felt by a mother for her child.' It's cruel to blame the mother who had to sever that bond and abandon her child. She must have suffered ten times more than I. . . ." The old woman of the tea-hut who doesn't realize that her own son, having poured out all his resentment, has just called her "Mother," says, "How happy, how happy I'd be if my son felt the same way. Sir, thanks to you, the heavy weight pressing on my heart these twenty years is lifted. It's amazing how lighthearted I feel now; even my body feels lighter. Well, it's time for saké, yes, time for saké. You must have a sip of my homemade saké. Won't take long, it'll be ready right away." Left alone, Isaburō ponders, "Because of the murder of that sheriff, I am a homeless fugitive, fleeing today eastward, tomorrow westward. Were I to declare myself openly, I'd cause more trouble for my mother; she would be caught up in my crime.

Forgive me, mother, I had no other way to reveal myself. What's this . . . a money-box. Good, in go twenty ryō and my precious talisman, and farewell. (*She strikes the first note of "ki."*)[7] I take my leave (*the second note of "ki"*)." *She strikes a dramatic pose or "mie"*[8] *as the departing Isaburō, but immediately glares toward stage-left.*

Indulging myself? Me, self-indulgent, how? Eh? I'm punishing myself by playing the abandoned son who rebukes his mother? I don't know what the hell you're talking about. . . . I see, I'm purging myself within the safe framework of the play, am I? And I even let the son forgive his mother in the end? That's how I'm indulging myself? That's why I play this part so often, just to ease my conscience? Why don't I come out of the play to face reality, and confront Tagami Haruhiko? Well, thanks very much, but it's none of your business. Those were terrible days—the audience didn't turn up; the troupe members had to be fed; the debts were piling up, and that damned husband I was relying on ran out on me; there was no other way. (*Having been exposed, she is now very agitated.*) Gouged by loan-sharks, harassed by men, I cried, I bled; I crawled in order to survive. (*Realizing that she has let herself go too far she tries to get a grip on herself.*) Well, everyone, our guest is leaving. Will someone escort him to the front? . . . What's the matter? Could someone please take our guest. . . . (*She explodes.*) Where is everybody in this play!? (*Returning to a normal tone.*) Toshi, dear, open the window, let's have some fresh air.[9] (*As her eyes follow the departing TBS man.*) . . . It wasn't a matter of throwing away an object, but a child, your own baby you had borne in pain; a mother had to be deadly resolute to go through with it. And having gone through with it, how could any mother be so shameless as to go along to a reunion, just because the child has come up in the world? How could she dare face her. . . . (*Suddenly.*) My son was adopted by a family in Iwamisawa, Hokkaidō. He graduated from high school, got a job at the Iwamisawa railway station . . . and died in an accident. When I rushed to his bedside, he looked at me and said, "Life is like that, isn't it, mother." He smiled sadly, and died. At that moment a shooting star fell from the sky outside the hospital window. *A sad "mie." At this moment, some indescribable sound is heard. It sounds like "ki" and then it doesn't. She stops the tape, and makes an announcement herself loudly, "Thank you very much for waiting. Tonight's first play by the Satsuki*

---

7. *Ki* is a traditional percussion instrument, which makes a sound by clapping together two hard rectangular pieces of wood. In the traditional theater, this sound is usually heard at the beginning and end of the performance.

8. *Mie* is a pose like those observed in a kabuki performance.

9. The Japanese here is *Shio maitokure* (Sprinkle some salt), meaning "Purify the bad atmosphere left by the man from the TBS." Traditionally, salt has been one of the most common purifying agents used for ritual purposes. For example, before a sumo wrestling match (which is said to have been performed originally for the purpose of divination), the wrestlers still purify the ring by sprinkling salt on it.

troupe, Isaburō's Parting, *will commence shortly." Then she starts a new tape, this time of rather old-fashioned melodramatic music, for the opening of* Isaburō's Parting.

She looks into the mirror, then as she walks slowly toward stage-right, carrying a straw hat:

Grandpa Nakamaru, and everyone, I'm counting on all of you. Let's give them a heck of a performance.

She halts at the wing stage-right; when the music stops, she runs off, the straw hat held high over her head. After a few seconds:

"Father!"

The lights dim slowly.

Toward the end of the interval, during which the curtain does not fall, the last few lines of Isaburō's Parting *become gradually audible from the direction of the right wing, that is, the direction of the stage on which it is being performed.*

". . . Because of the murder of that sheriff, Isaburō is a homeless fugitive, fleeing today eastward, tomorrow westward. Were I to declare myself openly, I'd cause more trouble for my mother; she'd be caught up in my crime. Forgive me, mother: I had no other way to reveal myself. What's this . . . a money-box. Good, in go twenty ryō and my precious talisman, and farewell *(the first note of "ki").* I take my leave *(the second note of "ki")."*

The sound of "hyōshi-maku" (a crescendo "ki" clapping which slows down as it becomes louder) suggests that she is ending her performance with a great "mie." Scattered applause. A few whistles and shouts from the audience—for example: "Bravo, Yōko!" "Satsuki, you made me cry!" "Keep it up, Yōko!" "You're the greatest!" For some reason, all the voices are male.

Soon she comes back to the dressing-room in Isaburō's costume. She wears a wreath made out of thousand-yen banknotes and her straw hat is filled with paper-wrapped tips thrown down onto the stage by the audience. She lights a cigarette and takes a deep breath:

What an enchanting audience.

She enjoys the moment. The medley of "enka" begins.

I'd forgotten how wonderful it tasted. A smoke after a job well done—it's heavenly.

She takes off the wig and looks at a point stage-right.

Nakamaru, darling, you were pretty good too. Well, actually, more than "pretty good"; you really did respond splendidly to my impassioned performance. I do thank you for that. However, I'll have to have those tips[10] in your kimono sleeves, if you don't mind. No use trying to hide them now, dear. I saw three packets thrown in your direction. Haven't you noticed I've got eyes in the back of my head? You can't cheat me. As the head of the troupe I'll take

---

10. *Ohineri* are paper-wrapped tips thrown onto the stage by the audience, still a common practice in the traditional popular theater.

all three of them. I'll look after all the tips until we finish here, and then distribute them fairly among us. Haven't you worked in the popular theater long enough, dear? I'm sure you are familiar with the back-stage custom that tips from the audience are handled by the head of the troupe. So why pretend innocence. Really, one can't drop one's guard even for a moment nowadays.

She has been watching her straw hat reflected in the mirror as she touches up her makeup, but:

Wait a minute, Grandpa, how many packets did you just put in the hat? Three? That's all you have? Don't lie to me, darling. You only dropped two in, not three. Please put the other one in too, like a good boy. That's it, well done, thank you. Toshi, keep them somewhere safe, will you? And what's happened to my tea? You haven't brought a hot towel yet, either. Toshi . . .

She looks around the dressing-room, but freezes like a pinned butterfly as she looks at a point to her left. She stays frozen for a considerable time, but eventually she begins to move in response to the "figure." They appear to be locked in silent confrontation for a while, trying to place themselves in a more comfortable physical position. But soon the "figure" seems to park himself at a point stage-left (where the man from TBS was apparently seated in the first act). Toward stage-right:

Toshi, I recognize this young man. Haven't you all seen his face on TV or in the magazines?

Toward stage-left:

You're Tagami Haruhiko, aren't you? I thought so. Good gracious, I'm surprised the audience didn't make more fuss. (*She turns toward the mirror.*) We watch as well, you know; we watch the audience from the stage like hawks. You see, we have to spot at a glance those customers most likely to throw us a tip, and strike a dramatic pose as close to them as possible. But I didn't see your face there. . . . I see, you were watching secretly from behind the food stall? Ah, no one would have seen you, then.

As she chatters away, she touches up her makeup, pretending to be calm. But she reveals her true feelings in her shaky hand and in the way she does her makeup. She tries to retouch her eyebrows but she ends up drawing one on her forehead, when Tagami Haruhiko says something.

What's that? You'd like to see the talisman I've just used on stage? (*She laughs.*) You won't find it by looking around there. That talisman and the striped purse I used at the end of that scene are my important props: I usually bring both of them back to the dressing-room myself. (*She laughs again.*) Look, the only thing you'll find among the tips in that straw hat is the purse. The talisman is my most precious prop of all . . . or, rather, my blessed guardian, a crutch for my heart to lean on. So, when I'm not on stage, I keep it like this (*takes it out from her breast*) right in here. This talisman of the goddess Kishibo never leaves my body, not even for a moment.

Suddenly she seems to be grabbed by her left arm.

For heaven's sake, don't be so rough!

But the "figure" on her left is strong, and she is dragged off the stool in front of the mirror. She fights for her talisman, trying not to let the "figure" have it.

You'll break the string, you're pulling my head off! Look, I'm not going to run away from you or hide, am I? What? The pouch of my talisman looks just the same as yours? (*She looks intensely at the talisman shown her by the "figure."*) It's true, the string as well, the same strands of purple, orange and white. . . . Then, then . . .

She snatches her talisman away as she withdraws, and sits down with her hands placed on the floor before her.

Supposing it is, what about it? . . . Twenty years ago, you were left at the Holy Mother Orphanage in Bunkyō district; it was early December; you were just three months old. Your natural mother left with you that Kishibo talisman, together with a photo. And that Kishibo talisman looks the same as mine.

She sits with her face turned aside as if she were avoiding a sandstorm. Painfully:

Mother . . . !?

She does not move for a while. Or rather she cannot move. Tears fill her eyes, and seem to dissolve away the defensive armor she has worn up to this point.

Forgive me . . . I know, you can't possibly forgive me but please, Tatsuo, I beg you. These past twenty years, there were days when the cocks didn't crow but there wasn't a day I didn't think of you. I thought of you the whole year round, without a break. If my heart were made of bamboo, I'd cut it open to show you the inside. . . . On cold autumn mornings when dead leaves fell in the wind, I was afraid that you might catch cold and in my mind I'd place my hand on your forehead; on hot summer nights, I'd worry that you might be kicking off your blanket, so in my heart I'd tuck you in. . . . Tatsuo is your name. Your father's and grandfather's stage name was Tatsutarō, so we took "tatsu" and combine it with the "o" in "hero." The matron of the orphanage said, "It's a fine name but the people who adopt him might want to give him a different name. And of course he will be officially registered as the son of his adoptive parents." Since you didn't recognize your real name, I suppose they did change your name after all, as the matron said. Of all the troubles in life, poverty is the worst; because of it I couldn't do many things a mother would do for her child. But I'm proud that at least I gave you a luxurious and exuberant name. If I had been your adoptive mother, I wouldn't have changed your name, not your name; because it's a fine name. . . .

She moves back three feet or so while remaining seated.

Don't glare at me like that. Please, don't be angry with me. If I'd known you were here, I wouldn't have told the man from TBS that I didn't know you. . . . Besides, now you're finally shooting up to stardom, I didn't want to hold you back by suddenly intruding into your life. For me it was enough to know that the darling baby I bore in pain has now grown up to be a fine young man. So, I was just going to watch you from a distance, to fast and pray to the goddess Kishibo that your popularity may last forever. That's why I sent the man from TBS away. . . .

Her face lights up as if electricity has just passed through her body.

Never mind? You no longer bear a grudge against me!? It's been hard for you, but I must have suffered a hundred, a thousand times more? . . . How sweet you are!

Her voice cracks with emotion and she draws closer to her "son."

But it's you who've really suffered; it must have been a thousand, no, a million times harder for you. You can do whatever you like to me. Beat me, if that will clear away your anger. Yes, beat me, beat me, beat me until my face is swollen like a goblin's.[11] Tatsuo . . . !

She embraces her "son" and breaks involuntarily into a lullaby that she used to sing to him.

". . . Sleepy, sleepy, sleeping babe,[12] a crab's just crawled up your arse." Whenever I sang this lullaby, you used to get very excited. . . . "Even though I fish it out and throw it away, it crawls back once again. . . ." You don't remember it; you were only a few months old at the time. "Once again I fish it out, then boil it in a pan and eat it up." I was frightened. A reunion of mother and son after twenty years—it sounds good, but I didn't know what to say to apologize; anyway I was sure you'd never forgive me. That really frightened me. So I was determined not to go along with what the man from TBS was saying. If I'd known you were so kindhearted, I'd have listened to him more readily. He was a good man and I was wrong not to listen to him. . . . "Though the crab's been thoroughly boiled, it still stinks to high heaven."

As if tapped by someone, she looks up over her right shoulder:

What's that, Toshi, love? Time to get ready for the next show? No, I haven't forgotten; though I think I'm going to hold the curtain for ten minutes or so.

Looking toward stage-left, sternly:

What's that, Nakamaru? The audience'll get restless if they're kept waiting too long? Who's worried? Don't forget, we have a food kiosk by the stalls

---

11. The Japanese here is *Yotsuya-Kaidan no Oiwa-san no yōna kao ni shiteokure* (Make my face like that of Oiwa in *Yotsuya-Kaidan*). *Yotsuya-Kaidan* is a popular kabuki play by Tsuruya Nanboku (1755–1829), in which the heroine, Oiwa, being slowly poisoned to death by her husband, haunts him after her death, appearing with a horrific face deformed by the effects of the poison.

12. The Japanese word is *neko*, a pun with the double meaning of "a sleeping child" and "a cat." Hence, the last phrase of this lullaby is *Yoku nita kani-nanoni, dōnimo neko-kusai* (Though the crab's been boiled thoroughly, it still stinks like a polecat). Because the pun cannot be conveyed in English, it is translated without any reference to a cat.

just for that reason. If they get bored, they'll buy something to eat; that's the whole attraction of our sort of theater, didn't you know? I'm sure the kiosk woman will come around after the show to thank us all for taking an extra long interval; just wait and see. Yes, that's it.

She moves away from her "son" and speaks to the members of the troupe stage-right.

I can weave all the details of our tearful reunion into my speech to the audience. (*Rehearses her speech, pretending the troupe members are her audience.*) "Ladies and gentlemen, welcome, welcome to our performance tonight. Will you please accept our sincere apologies for the unusual delay in starting our next number, *The Tale of the Hairdresser Shinza*. But, ladies and gentlemen, there was a very good reason for this very long delay. That's right; during that long interval, a real-life drama, just like the one we performed for you earlier tonight, was unfolding in our dressing-room before our eyes. Indeed, as they say, 'Truth is stranger than fiction.' In the dressing room of this very theater, Satsuki Yōko has just been reunited with her long-lost son, after twenty years. Tears, tears, tears . . . we were drowning in our tears; the mother held her son's hands, the son clasped his mother's shoulders, and we cried to our hearts' content. Yōko is a true child of the theater, born, bred and schooled in the dressing-room; moreover, she is sworn to her father's credo: 'Come fire or flood, the curtain must go up.' She should have raised the curtain on time, no matter what was happening in the dressing-room, a reunion of mother and son, or a double suicide, the whole place awash with blood. That being said, ladies and gentlemen, Satsuki Yōko is only human, daughter of a mother and mother of a son; she could not keep to her father's credo. To compensate, if you'll excuse this impertinent expression, I shall now bring my son on stage and have him say a few words of greeting to you. 'The son of a frog is a frog; the son of an actor is an actor'— my son, ladies and gentlemen, is none other than the rising young television star Tagami Haruhiko. . . ."

Toward stage-left:

It's all right to say something like this, isn't it? You will come on stage beside me and speak to the audience, won't you? Just a few words will do. You will? Wonderful! This is going to cause a real riot; they'll turn the place upside down. And tonight is only the beginning; I'll bet all the papers and TV shows will be full of our story for a while, I'm sure of it. . . . (*Continues with her speech.*) "Quiet, quiet! Ladies and gentlemen, please be quiet. I would like to say just one more word before I bring Tagami Haruhiko on stage: it's about what finally proved he was my son. (*She grins at the audience coyly.*) Yes, you'd like to know, wouldn't you? My son, that is, Tagami Haruhiko, had two mementos of his mother, a photo and a talisman of the goddess Kishibo. But aren't I a bad mother, I didn't remember the photo at all. The only thing I remembered was the talisman . . . it's all coming back now—it was early December, twenty years ago; I was taking my son to the Orphanage of the Holy Mother in Bunkyō district; on my way I stopped at the Kishibo Shrine in Iriya to pray to the goddess, the blessed patroness of children and child-bearing, and got two talismans wrapped in identical pouches: I put one around the neck of my baby and the other around my own. . . ."

She is crying, and after a while she wipes her tears with the back of her hand:

I'll probably end up crying on stage too.

To stage-left.

If I start crying, don't mind me but just come on stage. What, darling? You'd like to see my talisman once again? Why not.

She hands it over to her "son" stage-left, and sits in front of the mirror.

In any case, it's really about time we raised the curtain for the next show.

However, she is so happy that she can't help looking at "her son" stage-left with a big smile. Turning to stage-right, toward the members of her troupe.

Look at him, take a good look at him, everyone. This is my child. Isn't he beautiful—so handsome!? Even I, his mother, could fall for him. What's that, Nakamaru dear? For my son, he doesn't look a bit like me? (*Laughing.*) Well, it's like the duck giving birth to a swan, wouldn't you say? (*Repairing her makeup.*) Well, my darling Tatsuo. . . . No, better call you Haruhiko, hadn't I? Well, now that we've finally met, shall we set up house together? Frankly, for all her vigor, Satsuki Yōko is a little tired: I made my debut in the spring of my sixth year; it's been forty years since, and I haven't had a single day's break; I'm really worn out, body and soul. Sure, I'll earn as much as I can cashing in on The Reunion of Mother and Son for six months or so. But beyond that, well . . . can't you guess? You must have a nice girlfriend. . . . Not at the moment? But you'll soon find one. The girls won't leave you alone. With that handsome face of yours, it'll be more difficult avoiding them than breaking into the Bank of Japan. First a girlfriend; then along comes a baby—that'll be my grandchild! How I'd love to hold my grandchild in my arms! And to babysit for him! All my life, I've been like a floating leaf on the river, drifting here and there; every day was like crawling naked through a thorny hedge or walking on the blades of swords; I'm tired to death of it. My dream of dreams is (*she speaks with deeply felt emotion*) to sit on a sunny veranda with a grandchild in my arms, "Sleepy, sleepy, sleeping babe, a crab's just crawled up your arse. . . ."

She looks toward stage-left as if a bomb has just been thrown at her:

The talismans don't match? Yours is a Kishibo talisman from Zōshigaya?

She smiles coyly.

Iriya and Zōshigaya. Not much difference; they're both Kishibo talismans, aren't they? That's good enough for me.

At this moment, there comes the sound of demolition from the direction of stage-left. And the voices of demolition workers. "Hurry up, luv, you've got to hand over the dressing-room." "If you don't move out, you'll get hurt, you know." "We can't finish the job till we knock down the dressing-room." "Oh, heck—What shall we do?" "She keeps repeating the same old act, all by herself—doesn't she get tired of it?" "Hey, Satsuki, come on out!" "Yōko, if you'll just come out, you'll be the greatest!"

The sound of demolition continues. She looks toward stage-left:

Tatsuo, where are you going? If it's the loo, it's to the right of the stage-door.

She sees him off. From now on, she no longer recalls her son. Or rather, she has forgotten all the events in her "real life" since reaching this point in her opening night at this theater. That is to say, she is a lonely, mad woman who only remembers these happiest ten minutes or so of her life, and is repeatedly reliving alone the events leading up to this blissful moment.

Hey, Nakamaru, I've just had a flash of inspiration. Why don't we do a sequel to *Isaburō's Parting* instead of our next number. Don't worry, it'll be a great hit. Can we go over the lines quickly while we touch up our makeup? Don't miss a single word. Ready? Pay attention.

She touches up her makeup as she rehearses the lines but she merely messes it up by, say, painting one cheek red, drawing a cross on her forehead, or painting the tip of her nose blue.

Toward the end of the scene, I try, that is, Isaburō tries to leave the tea-hut after putting twenty ryō and his talisman in the money-box, doesn't he. But the old woman, that's the one you are playing, who we thought went off to warm up some saké, turns out to be listening to his confession. So she rushes out and clings to Isaburō. "I never guessed . . . you are my son . . . !" Isaburō is taken aback; he stands speechless, stunned at this unexpected turn of events. Now, from this point on, the stage is all yours for a while, darling. It's a very good part. "When I recall the countless words of rancor you spoke earlier, my blood runs cold and I feel as if I'm being torn apart. . . . I realize nothing I say now can make amends, but still, forgive me, Isaburō." The old woman of the tea-hut joins her hands in supplication. "I beg you, with all my heart; there were days when the cocks didn't crow but there wasn't a day when I did not think of you; every day I would take out my talisman—look, exactly like yours—and caress and stroke it, praying for your happiness. . . ." The old woman takes off her talisman and hands it over to Isaburō. For that, we need another talisman, don't we? Toshi, dear, can you get us another talisman? Toshi! . . . (*She explodes.*) Why doesn't anyone come!? . . . Why . . .

Sounds of demolition work.

Now the audience is starting to riot. I'll have to go on ahead of you, Grandpa. "So you are a notorious sheriff-murderer on the run. All the more reason, then, for you to take refuge in this tea-hut. They say, rumors die in seventy-five days and in one hundred days the wind will clear the sky. From that day on, you can mend your ways and lead an honest life.[13] And then, take a wife. Then I can retire happily, living out the rest of my days looking after my grandchildren. I know it's wishful thinking but take pity on a mother who cannot help dreaming. . . ." At this moment, Isaburō reels back: "In heaven's name, does God exist no more? The talismans don't match! Mine is from the shrine in Iriya, but this is from Zōshigaya, west of Iriya. Everything else fits perfectly but the talismans themselves do not. . . . Well, old mother, the wise old saying says life wouldn't be life if one could fulfill all one's wishes. We have to learn to accept it. Now I must be on my way." Isaburō starts to make his exit, but at the sight of the old woman so distressed, so lost in her grief, he cannot bring himself to leave . . . no, no, better still, he is drawn back to the tea-hut; listen, Grandpa, this is your big moment. Play the scene with such feeling that we know, if the old woman is left alone, she will go mad and die.

She has completed her "grotesque" makeup. The mad woman picks up her straw hat, cape and sword:

The last line is mine: "Old mother, wipe away your tears; they say, every time you grieve, you shorten your life by three days. Well, ma'am, how about this: Isaburō is seeking a mother who abandoned him and you are seeking a son whom you abandoned; so if we become mother and son, we'll fit each other happily, like a broken cup pieced together. I'll mend my ways and lead an honest life. I'll carry water and cut wood for you; I'll take a wife and raise a family; I'll rub your back when you grow old. Won't you let this Isaburō do what your son would do for you?"

She becomes the ecstatic mother:

"Isaburō . . . !"

She becomes the ideal son:

"Mother . . . !"

Amid the noise of demolition, the mad woman is at the zenith of her happiness. The lights slowly dim.

---

13. The Japanese here is *nan aratamete*, meaning "change, renew or reform one's appearance" with regard to the hairstyle and the type of kimono worn. The phrase makes sense in the context of the Tokugawa period, when the kimono and hairstyle of the *yakuza*—even though they were townsmen (as distinct from members of the military or peasant classes)—were different from those of the *katagi* townsmen. *Katagi ni onari* means "become a *katagi*." *Katagi*, the opposite of *yakuza*, refers to the law-abiding and correct way in which ordinary townsmen lived.

KARA JŪRŌ

Kara Jūrō (b. 1940) considers himself to be primarily an actor. Nonetheless, his politically charged plays have become famous not only in Japan but also in many other countries around the world where his troupe has traveled. Most were composed to be staged not in theaters but in Kara's famous outdoor "red tent," which can be moved from place to place. Despite the subsequent political and economic changes in Japan, Kara has maintained a close relationship with his admiring public and, like Betsuyaku Minoru, continues to write plays of contemporary significance. *The 24:53 Train Bound for "Tower" Is Waiting in Front of That Doughnut Shop in Takebaya (24-ji 53-pun no "Tō no shita" yuki no densha ga Takebayachō no dagashiya no mae de matteiru)*, published in book form in 1976, gives a glimpse of his work, in which he provides opportunities for his performers to show the range of their acting skills.

THE 24:53 TRAIN BOUND FOR "TOWER" IS WAITING IN FRONT OF THAT DOUGHNUT SHOP IN TAKEBAYA (24-JI 53-PUN NO "TŌ NO SHITA" YUKI NO DENSHA GA TAKEBAYACHŌ NO DAGASHIYA NO MAE DE MATTEIRU)

Translated by Coudy Poulton

A Play in One Act

CAST OF CHARACTERS

An Old Woman
Old Man A
Old Man B
The Man
The Old Woman's Son
A Man
A Woman
A Tramp

The stage is dark. Here and there, on the steps leading to a certain tower, are candles burning. In the gloom, around the staircase one can dimly make out two or three shapes laid out under straw mats. To the left is a small two-wheeled wagon with a wooden frame on it. From upstage left an old woman enters, carrying a candle in her hand.

OLD WOMAN (*muttering a nursery rhyme to herself, she slowly makes her way across stage*): Canary, canary, forgotten her song. What's to be done? Cat got her tongue? Shall we whip her with a willow cane? Or dump her out back in the bamboo lane? Oh, no, that wouldn't do, that would be wrong. . . .

Then, uh, then, what comes next? Hey! How's it go? Canary, canary, forgotten her song . . . .¹ (*Exits.*)

Two old men shuffle out on tottering legs, tapping their canes. One old man has tucked a briefcase under one arm.

OLD MAN A: I say! What a muggy day it is!

OLD MAN B: I say! What a muggy day it is!

A: What did you say?

B: I said, "I say! What a muggy day it is." What did you say?

A: I said, "I say! What a muggy day it is."

B: Grab hold me shoulder. Mind you don't fall.

A: Grab hold me shoulder. Mind you don't fall.

B: Almost there.

A: Yup. Almost there. Eh? Whazzat?

B: That? (*Points over the heads of the audience.*)

A: Jeez, it's tall.

B: Almost there now. (*Clutches his briefcase to his chest.*)

A: What you got there?

B: Important stuff. A whole briefcase full.

A: Like what?

B: Citations from the Fire Department, a certified copy of my birth certificate. Et cetera, et cetera.

A: What the hell do you need those for?

B: I'm taking 'em with me.

A: To the cemetery, are you?

B: These are my pride, I'll have you know. Did I ever tell you how I stopped that fire from spreading? One quick call saved the day.

A: When was this?

B: Oh, a long time ago.

A: Like when?

B: Oh, well, when I was a young lad.

A: Were they grateful?

B: Indeed they were. Said I was (*with emphasis*) a great man.

A: Who?

B: Why . . . me, of course.

A: What's so great about you?

---

1. The old woman is reciting (with some mistakes) the lyrics to a popular children's song written by Saijō Yaso (1892–1970). The lyrics were first published in *Red Bird* (*Akai tori*) 1, no. 5 (1918). They were later set to music by Narita Tamezō (1893–1945). The translation is quite free. The original is as follows: *uta o wasureta kanariya wa / ushiro no yama ni sutemasho ka / ie ie sore wa narimasenu. / uta o wasureta kanariya wa / sedo no koyabu ni ikemasho ka / ie ie sore wa narimasenu. / uta o wasureta kanariya wa / yanagi no muchi de buchimasho ka / ie ie sore wa narimasenu. / uta o wasureta kaanriya wa / zōge no fune ni gin no kai / tsukiyo no umi ni ukabereba / wasureta uta o omoidasu.*

B: Everything.

A: Yes, but just what, exactly?

B: Well, my sense of social duty, for starts. Said I was a veritable guardian of humanism. Et cetera, et cetera.

A (*again looks up*): Jeez, it's tall.

B: I was a great man, yessiree. Society thought so. So did me family. Yup.

A: Think you can make it that far?

B (*squinting as he gazes up*): Uh huh.

A: Shall we, then? Grab hold me shoulder. Mind you don't fall.

B: Shall we, then? Grab hold me shoulder. Mind you don't fall.

As the two old men exit left, the old woman reenters.

OLD WOMAN: What comes next? How'd it go, then? Just what comes next? Hey. You know, "Canary, canary, forgotten her song"? . . . (*Ruffles through one of the piles of straw matting.*) Jeez, you're a sight. Bloody awful. Remind me how that song went, the one about the canary. (*Wakes the sleeping man. He sits up. Half his face is covered in blood.*)

The stage goes dark. A sinister tune on the guitar is heard. Suddenly, there is what sounds like a peal of loud, metallic laughter that falls away into a long, trailing wail. Then, we hear the echo of the hoarse laughter of the two old men; that also falls away. Next, a lusty voice chuckles as if pleased with itself, then falls away like the other voices.

A spotlight shines at right. The man, wearing a tall hat, is standing in front of the wagon.

THE MAN: Good evening. You finally made it, I see. What's that? Me? Why, I . . . We see each other all the time, surely. I always call to you. And you, you look away. Give me a tap on the shoulder one of these days, why don't you? Yes, I live around here. Been here for ages. Change for the metro line in front of that doughnut shop in Takebaya, take the train bound for "Tower" on platform 13, and you're there in no time! Mind you, it doesn't leave till rather late. The 24:53 is the emptiest. Platform 13. Bound for "Tower." Ah, the wind's up. That ain't good, not if you're looking for lost souls. . . . Look there, can you see it? (*Points.*) There, she's about to jump. A woman. Look! (*Cackling laughter trails downward.*) Well, then. Back in a bit. (*Begins to pull his wagon toward offstage, then presently doubles back. Irresponsibly.*) In this town everybody's happy to die. Everybody dies laughing.

Darkness. More sinister guitar music. Again, a spotlight shines at right, this time illuminating the old woman, who is carrying a naked man—her son—on her back.

OLD WOMAN: Canary, canary, forgotten her song. What's to be done? Cat got her tongue? Shall we whip her with a willow cane? Or dump her out back in the bamboo lane? Oh, no, that wouldn't do, that would be wrong. . . .

Canary, canary, forgotten her song . . .
Canary, canary, forgotten her song . . .

The man appears.
THE MAN:

> But if that canary, who's forgotten her song,
> Could sail away on a moon shiny sea . . .

OLD WOMAN: A moon shiny sea? Could sail away on a moon shiny sea?
THE MAN: Pluck her feathers and naked she shall be.
OLD WOMAN: . . . Could sail away on a moon shiny sea. Pluck her feathers and naked she shall be? You sure you got that right? That's not the way it goes. Hey.
SON (*looking up*): Mama.
THE MAN: The kid's still kicking.
SON (*pointing no place in particular*): Over there, take me over there.
THE MAN (*to the son*): Care for a lift?
OLD WOMAN (*ignoring her son*): No way! She'd die without her coat on.
SON: Let's go back, back to that town.
THE MAN: Who'd survive a fall like that? Fucking miracle.
OLD WOMAN (*to her son*): Where? Back where?
SON: Twilight Town.
THE MAN: Sail away on a moon shiny sea!
OLD WOMAN: Let's try again, shall we? Canary, canary, forgotten her song . . .
SON: Hey, mama. You know what I remember most from that town? It was that summer, an evening that summer. I was coming back from the bath and the wind chimes were tinkling. It was eight days before the ambulance came took Gran away. . . .
OLD WOMAN:

> Could sail away on a moon shiny sea,
> Pluck her feathers and naked she shall be.
> Canary, canary, forgotten her song. . . .

Must have *really* forgotten the song, that canary.
THE MAN: Speak for yourself, why don't you. Song, hell. You've forgotten your own *son*. Right—this time I take him.
OLD WOMAN: Away on a moon shiny sea. Across the sea to the sea on the other side. Now, what kind of sea would that sea be? Hey, you. If the canary crossed that sea to the other side, maybe then he'd remember.
SON: And I said, "Good evening!" in a small voice. Said "Good evening" to the lady next door.
OLD WOMAN: The other side? The sea on the other side?
THE MAN: Ain't nothing there on the other side. Across the moon shiny sea there's nothing but more sea, the color of lead. Nothing but minerals. Sink like a stone there. Hurry! Hurry up, now! We got a job to do.

SON: That was the night of the day the morning glory market started. My little brother was crying with the mumps, but I dragged mama outside.

THE MAN (*giving the son a shove*): Huh!

OLD WOMAN: The sea on the other side is cold. Try to remember, canary.

Just then, a man enters from right, looking surprised.

A MAN: Uh, excuse me but it seems I caught the wrong train. Could you tell me the name of this place? But what's that tower I see there? That grand, magnificent tower. Could this place be the Acme of Salvation that the man at City Hall told me about?

THE MAN (*going toward a man*): I see, you're looking for the Acme of Salvation, are you? You came to the right place. Folks 'round here also call it Rest Haven. But how the hell did you find your way here, anyway?

A MAN: I boarded the wrong train, meant to take another one. Then I realized I was headed in the wrong direction, but never mind—it was right I came this way after all. To be sure I went the other way, but you might say it was lucky I did.

THE MAN: Lucky?

A MAN: Am I wrong to say that? Wouldn't you say I was lucky? The lucky truth is I made a lucky mistake.

THE MAN: Where exactly were you headed to begin with?

A MAN: Fact is, my sister told me about it—what was it called now? Twilight Town? Something like that. . . . Meant to board the train at Platform 3 but I guess I got my digits mixed up, hah, hah, hah. . . .

THE MAN (*also laughs*): That was mighty careless of you!

A MAN: Odd how you don't hear any voices here, just laughter.

THE MAN: Well, this is the instant nirvana everybody's been looking for.

A MAN: Now you mention it, uh, you know, I could hear people laughing, ever since I set foot in this place—two, three people in all, maybe. At first I thought they were close by, but then one voice seemed real far away. I had no trouble getting here, but then it was as if I hadn't arrived at all yet, like somebody'd posted a sign saying No Entry.

THE MAN: Not at all. The train brings everybody here. All sorts these days, if you catch my drift. . . . This is the end of the line.

A MAN: Maybe you know, but I was searching for something, for a new, a better life. Like, money. . . . Just joking! (*Laughs feebly.*) —For years now, the weather's been just brutal. Foul air, a cold wind blowing. The man in the street, folks at home, the whole town, even folks you can't tell are unhappy just by looking at them—just everybody's been bloody miserable.

THE MAN: No one's got any miserable memories in this town.

A MAN: Well, well! Now what kind of lifestyle do folks practice here then?

THE MAN: No magic, I assure you. Folks just climb that there tower. Then they fall . . . asleep.

A MAN: I believe I was telling you that I was searching for something new, a better life for myself. And quite by chance I ended up here. I was on the point of throwing it all away, the dreary commute, the abacus at the workplace. Then my little sister told me I ought to go to Twilight Town. She urged me to go back there and find myself. So on two, three days' holiday I had coming to me, I took off, just like I was making a short trip to the country. But, well . . . I thought to myself, when I get to Twilight Town, damned if I won't remember nothing but lousy memories of how poor we used to be there. Good thing I came here. City of Joy—no, of Laughter. . . . That's not it, either. Acme of Salvation, did you call it? . . . Spa for the Soul. But something's bugging me. So folks climb to the top of that tower to laugh, but where does everybody go after that?

THE MAN: They just laugh, and then . . .

A MAN: And then?

THE MAN: Then . . . you forget everything.

A MAN: My old life? You're quite the lyricist, aren't you? (*Gazes up at the tower.*) You can hear their voices from down here, can't you?

THE MAN: Up on the tower there.

A MAN: What did you say that tower was for?

THE MAN: The Tower of Deliverance. Or. . . . In any event, all my job entails is taking you to the top.

A MAN: You're most kind. You must be from City Hall.

THE MAN: Tch!

The two exit.

   The old woman and her son appear in a spotlight. The guitar plays "*Memories.*"

SON: Let's go back to Twilight Town, mama.

OLD WOMAN: Away on a moon shiny sea. Across the sea to the sea on the other side. Now, what kind of sea would that be? Just what kind of sea d'you think that'd be? Got any idea?

SON: Someplace as far as you can go. If you don't go as far as you can, you'll never get there.

OLD WOMAN: If you don't go as far as you can, you'll never get there?

SON: Like, we go bumpety-bump, bumpety-bump, all the way to that town. There, kindness. . . . —Mama, next time I'm gonna take the stairs.

OLD WOMAN: You're going to take the stairs.

SON: Yes, I'm going to *walk* down.

OLD WOMAN: I see, you're going to walk down.

SON: Today's the first Thursday in September. Hey, mama! Did'ya see that?! Halley's comet, just shot across the sky!

OLD WOMAN: Eh? Where?

SON: To the west, way across the sky over there!

OLD WOMAN: To the west, way across the sky over there . . .

SON: Sh! Be quiet! I can hear it, way off to the west, a kind of rumbling—the Ineffable Universe.

OLD WOMAN: I can hear it! I can hear it!

SON: Be careful! Mind that kid on the bike.

OLD WOMAN: Mind that kid on the bike. Whoa! Be careful!

SON: The tofu man's blowing his bugle.

OLD WOMAN (*smiling*): The tofu man's blowing his bugle.

SON: Ah! Fireworks!

"Boom, boom! Kaboom! Boom, boom! Kaboom!"—This sound is provided either in the form of sound effects, or alternately, the old woman and her son can make the noises themselves.

SON: That was the Mauve Feathered Mantle.

OLD WOMAN: There's another one! The White Narcissus, that one.

SON: The White Narcissus, was it?

OLD WOMAN: Looks like a festival they're having here.

SON: It's a festival they're having here, all right.

OLD WOMAN: Ah! There goes another one! Look! There, over there! Shinji.

SON: Shinji. Why, that's my name. Shinji.

OLD WOMAN: Be careful! Mind that kid on the bike.

Enter the man, from stage left.

THE MAN (*irresponsibly*): In this town, everybody climbs the tower laughing. In this town, everybody laughs as they climb up. (*As if put out, he hurries them along.*) OK, time for you to climb, and this time I want to hear you laugh. Up there on the tower there's no moon, it's as black as night, but don't you worry, I'll tell you where to put your feet. Right now, let's be on our way. No need to talk, nothing you need to remember neither. So long as you prepare yourself for a good long sleep, before you know it, you'll be splitting your sides with laughter. And then, you take off. You put a spring in your right big toe and leap into a dark so dark it's like the darkness in a picture from the dark ages. You'll be a citizen of a world of silence. In that place, every living thing goes hard and cold and turns into some kind of mineral or other, like those ferns or dragonflies squashed in layers of red mud or granite. That's right, you'll turn into a citizen of a world of silence. Right you are, then! You're almost there, all you have to do is make it to the top of that tower. Forget your sweet memories, forget the past. Any time now, you'll start laughing, full of the joy of a good sleep! And I, I'll watch over you, witness to your laughter. The last laugh. (*He pulls apart the old woman and the son. The old woman falls over, leaving the son as he was.*)

OLD WOMAN: Shinji, let's go back again. To that town. It was summer, wasn't it? A summer evening. When you came back from the bath, the wind chimes were tinkling—when was that, anyway? How many days before the ambulance came took Gran away?

SON (*kicks the old woman*): Get lost, you fucking hag!

OLD WOMAN (*disappears into the gloom until we can only hear her voice*): I was raising the blinds when you said "Good evening!" to the lady next door. Just like that, "Good evening!" in a small voice.

THE MAN:. Why, tell me, do we need to go back to all that, when we know memories have a way of repeating themselves as something miserable? Right, now. Get outa here! (*To son.*) And you, climb!

OLD WOMAN (*voice only*): That night, I recall, was the night of the day the morning glory market started. Yoshio was crying with the mumps, but you dragged me out, saying "Let's go! Let's go!"

THE MAN: Soon you won't need to speak. You won't need no memories neither.

From up on the tower there is a peal of laughter.

WOMAN'S VOICE (*from offstage right*): Brother!

With the sound of her voice, both the old woman and the man disappear completely from view. All we can see in the dim light is the silhouette of the son and the cart. The woman is standing, holding an open umbrella.

WOMAN: Wait! Didn't you forget your umbrella? It rains in that town, you know. Until the first Thursday in September, a really cold, sleety rain that makes you go all numb. So cold you can't feel your hands. That's what I told Mama, and she said, Go fetch the collapsible umbrella, but I said you oughta take the nice big one with the bamboo handle instead. I was *really* insistent. Remember? Then you forgot to take the marble. What a twit you were, forgetting your marble when you knew you had to show it instead of your ID when you entered town. What train did you get on, anyway? You must've caught the wrong one. Where on earth did you go? Show me a sign, brother! I'd feel a whole lot better if you did. Anybody here heard an oboe? When you got to the other side. You said you'd blow me a note or two.

A tramp is seated at her feet—this man is actually the man who was pulling the cart in disguise—but she hasn't addressed her inquiry to him.

TRAMP (*a bit drunk*): "As the parrot said to Silver" . . . No, that's not it. How's it go, then?

WOMAN: (*noticing the tramp crouched under her*): Did you say something?

TRAMP (*as before, paying her no attention*): "As the parrot said to Silver" . . . No, that's not it. How's it go, then?

WOMAN: Have you been here long? Happen to hear an oboe?

TRAMP: Uh uh. Heard nothing. —Hoowhee! —As the parrot said to Silver, Why, I don't hate you. But that eye of yours ain't gonna get better. —Nope, ain't heard a thing.

WOMAN: In that case, you didn't happen to see a man, did you? Nobody on the train?

TRAMP: No money, did ya say? I'm loaded. . . . But that eye of yours ain't gonna get better, and that hook of yours, why, it don't bleed.

WOMAN: My brother wasn't there?

TRAMP: Your brother? We-e-ll. As the parrot said to your brother. . . . Shit, am I drunk! (*Slaps his cheeks with the palm of his hands.*) Nope. Ain't got a clue. Never seen your brother.

WOMAN: He's *my* brother.

TRAMP: Your brother, is he? I see. Nope, can't say I seen your brother. Seen nobody but perverts here. "As the parrot said to Silver"—now, what the hell did the parrot say to Silver, anyway? —Shit, I'm coming down. Nope, ain't seen him, your brother, that is. Seen nobody but perverts here.

WOMAN: What kind of perverts you talking about?

TRAMP: The kind who climb up that tower in the town yonder.

WOMAN: Tower? What town?

TRAMP: As the parrot said to Silver, Why, I don't hate you. Yeah, that's it! I remember now. —Why, I don't hate you . . .

WOMAN: What tower where!?

TRAMP: But that eye of yours ain't gonna get better, and that hook of yours, why, it don't bleed. As the parrot said to Silver . . . As the parrot said to Silver . . .

The tramp disappears into the gloom, leaving the woman with the umbrella standing alone in the spotlight, gazing up at the imaginary tower.

At right, the two old men can be seen slowly ascending the staircase.

OLD MAN B: I've fulfilled all my duties and responsibilities as a citizen of Tokyo.

OLD MAN A (*with grave emphasis*): Duties and responsibilities.

B: That's right. As a citizen of Tokyo.

A: A humanist—what's that mean, anyway?

B: Someone who's . . . radiant.

A: Radiant. . . . Who're we talking about here?

B: Why . . . me. That's who.

A: Like when was this?

B: Oh, a long time ago. I was a young lad then. Didn't I tell you? how I stopped that fire from spreading? One quick call saved the day.

A: You sure you told me?

B: I never told you? Is that so. —They sure were grateful. Said I was (*with grave emphasis*) a great man.

A: Great? Who was great?

B: Why . . . me, of course.

A: What's so great about you?

B: Everything.

A: Yes, but just what, exactly?

B: Well, my sense of social duty, for starts. Said I was a veritable guardian of humanism.

A: Humanism?

B: That's right. Humanism.

A: Humanism . . . now what the hell would that be?

B: Well, a humanist is someone who's . . . radiant.

A: Radiant? Who're we talking about here?

B: Why, me, of course.

A: Like when was this?

B: Oh, a long time ago. I was a young lad then. Didn't I tell you? how I stopped that fire from spreading? One quick call saved the day.

A: You sure you told me?

B: Whoops-a-daisy! Grab hold me shoulder. Mind you don't fall.

A: Whoops-a-daisy! Grab hold me shoulder. Mind you don't fall.

B: So! I never told you . . .

A: Not a word. You never tell me anything.

The two slowly disappear into the gloom.

B (*voice only*): Almost there now.

A (*voice only*): Yup, almost there.

B: Quite the trooper, ain't you?

A: You're quite the trooper, too.

Their voices completely fade away.

OLD WOMAN (*voice only, heard faintly in the darkness*): Shinji, come back. It's Twilight Town. Way off, way, way off, on the other side . . .

The son appears, and begins to climb the staircase.

SON: Away on a moon shiny sea. Across the sea to the sea on the other side. Now what kind of sea would that sea be? Hey, mama? What would a canary do over there? That's where I'd like to go.

VOICE: Shinji, let's go back to that town on the other side. Twilight Town.

SON: The cold sea is the color of lead. The cold sea is the color of lead. Canary, canary, forgotten her song. What's to be done? Cat got her tongue? Shall we whip her with a willow cane? . . .

VOICE: Say it's summer. A summer evening . . .

SON: Or dump her out back in the bamboo lane? Oh, no, that wouldn't do, that would be wrong. . . .

VOICE: There's a festival there, in that town. . . .

SON: But if that canary, who's forgotten her song, could sail away on a moon shiny sea. . . .

VOICE: Be careful! Mind that kid on the bike.

SON: Pluck her feathers and naked she shall be. And puke up blood for you and me!

VOICE: For God's sake be careful! Mind that kid on the bike!

SON: Pluck her feathers and naked she shall be. And puke up blood for you and me! (*Disappears.*)

A man proceeds to climb up the steps.

A MAN: 9901, 9902, 9903, 9904, 9905, 9906, 9907 (*Gazes around briefly, then once again looks down and continues to climb.*) 9908, 9909, 9910, 9911, 9912, 9913 . . . (*Stops.*) 9913, 9913, 913 . . . 13, 13, 13. It was the train on platform 13 I boarded. Shit! Who was it told me to catch the train bound for Twilight Town? The one that was leaving at four in front of that doughnut shop. Who was it told me now? 9913, 9914, 9915. But how come it's so dark here? Surely, after climbing all this time . . . 9916, 9917, 9918. . . . Hang on. I seem to have forgotten something. What the hell was it, then? I know, I know, I said. What did I say I knew? 9919, 9920, 9921, 9922. . . . (*Suddenly.*) I got it. I was searching for something, for a new, a better life. I'm sure that's what I said. Searching for a new, a better life! Huh! (*Pleased with himself, he repeats the phrase.*) I was searching for a new, a better life! Hah, hah, hah, hah, hah, hah, hah. . . . Ain't that something. (*Joyfully resumes his climb.*) 9923, 9924, 9925 . . . 9926. . . . So, that train leaving from the doughnut shop at four o'clock— what was its destination, anyway? I was told to catch that train. So where was that train headed? Where was I supposed to be going? . . . 9927, 9928, 9929. Hang on. That train was leaving from the doughnut shop at what time? Where was it headed? Who told me? Who? (*Angrily.*) Nobody told me! 9930 . . . 9931, 9932, 9933. . . . Nah, nobody told me nothing. 9934, 9935, 9936, 9937 . . . (*He disappears, leaving behind only a voice counting numbers.*)

Sinister guitar music drifts down from on top of the tower. Suddenly, metallic-sounding laughter is heard, followed by the hoarse laughter of the two old men, sounding like a duet that trails off, leaving only the sound of the guitar. About the time that a man disappears, the woman and the man appear in a spotlight at stage left. The man is gazing up at the imaginary tower. The woman is standing slightly off to the side and facing the audience.

WOMAN: Did you hear that? Did anybody hear an oboe?

THE MAN (*still gazing aloft*): Just like those ferns or dragonflies, squashed in layers of red mud or granite—

WOMAN: He should've blown it by now.

THE MAN: Shut up. Just . . . shut up—

WOMAN: So, you didn't see him catch the train here either then. The four o'clock, platform 3—

THE MAN: In pursuit of something, giving up on life—

WOMAN: He was supposed to have gone to that town.

THE MAN: Leaving all memory behind—

WOMAN: Took time off work.

THE MAN: To go climb the tower.

WOMAN: His boss was really persistent, he said. Kept asking Where you going? Don't waste your time.

THE MAN: Climb up the tower and laugh. Just laugh—

WOMAN: I'll go find what I've lost. I'll run as far as I can go, I'll take that train. That's what he said, my brother.

THE MAN: That tower ain't no mirage, you know. That town neither.

WOMAN: Somebody, please. Somebody blow the oboe for my brother. He said he would when he got to the other side. He was going to take the train on platform 3.

She disappears, all but for a silhouette holding an umbrella.

THE MAN (*abruptly turning to address the audience in familiar tones*): I live there. Have done so for years. —Guess you might call me a civil servant. Take the train from platform 13 in front of that doughnut shop in Takebaya. The one at 24:53 is the emptiest, but anytime's fine, just call me and I'll give you a helping hand. —But if you don't call me with all your heart and soul, I'm afraid you'll never see me. The quickest way is go to City Hall. They'll give you a letter of reference, with a certificate of resident status. (*As if struck with a wonderful idea.*) Hey folks! We're accepting tour groups, so step this way! Let's all climb together! (*Pointing.*) See the tower? Up we go!

There is a ring of raucous laughter. Guitar music plays. The man turns into a motionless silhouette. Only a marble, held in the hand of the woman standing upstage, continues to glimmer.

Curtain

SHIMIZU KUNIO

Shimizu Kunio (b. 1936) has been an active dramatist since his student days, when he began to write plays protesting the contemporary political situation in Japan, particularly the Kishi government's attempts to renew the United States–Japan Security Treaty in 1960. The director Ninagawa Yukio has staged Shimizu's plays both in Japan and abroad, and some of his plays are available in translation.

One of Shimizu's most political and most shocking dramas is *When We Go Down that Heartless River* (*Bokura ga hijō no taiga o kudaru toki*), written in 1972, which won the Kishida Drama Prize in the same year. The play is a dark extended metaphor dealing with the purges within one of the factions of an extremist group, the United Red Army (Rengō sekigun). This infamous incident was a turning point for the larger Japanese public, who were understandably shocked by the group's actions. As a result, many turned away from overtly political activities. Although the play does not mention the political situation directly, the interrogations and their results are suggested in a series of dark reflecting mirrors.

WHEN WE GO DOWN THAT HEARTLESS RIVER
(*BOKURA GA HIJŌ NO TAIGA O KUDARU TOKI*)

Translated by J. Thomas Rimer

CAST OF CHARACTERS

Poet (the younger brother)
Older brother
Father
A group of men crowding around a public lavatory

Dark night. A lonely public bathroom somewhere in the city. From time to time, at the back of the scene, the headlights of passing cars dimly illuminate the area.

The translator would like to thank Sachiko Howard for her assistance in preparing this translation.

This is a spot where, it is rumored, men collect, in a coquettish fashion, to seek out other men. One man abruptly walks in. Without glancing to the right or to the left, he hurries into the bathroom. Trembling, he urinates. At that point, a woman, dressed in Japanese-style clothing, enters the men's area. The man, in the middle of his business, is startled. The woman (a man wearing women's clothing) is not at all ruffled but opens his kimono and, standing in the stall next to the man, begins to urinate. Without taking his eyes off the man's face, the man dressed as a woman sends him an amorous glance. The man takes his eyes away and, zipping up his pants, leaves hastily. Looking disappointed, the man dressed in woman's clothes takes off his wig to let the air cool his head and leaves.

The toilet is empty. A flash of headlights. A young man rushes in. Thrusting his head into the front of the toilet, he begins to wail. These laments from the young man fill the darkness of the night. . . . Then he notices on the shelf in front of him a bunch of red roses that someone has evidently left behind. Picking them up, he kisses them lightly; suddenly he begins to chuckle to himself and, in a melancholy fashion, tears the bouquet to pieces, scattering the flowers around. When the flowers are gone, he tosses away the stems and, thrusting his hands inside his pockets, leaves.

Again the scene is empty. From somewhere or other, the sound of a guitar can be heard. The poet (actually, the younger brother) appears.

POET: This lavatory is filled with some sort of premonition. There's nothing special about the way it looks. And there's something sort of nostalgic about the faint stench, something almost arrogant in the way it proclaims itself. Day after day, it never stops its conversations with all those who come here, one after another. . . . And it's no simple reflection of the relation of a poet to his times. The real work of a poet is to tie up the hidden elements of the present. You might say that the poet must seek out and discover the real truth of these times. Now do you have any complaint with that! The evening is fully attired in its swindles. The streets themselves are a rebuke. And this lavatory as well. And under the cherry trees, too, in their full bloom, the poet said, many dead bodies are buried. And then in addition, under this public toilet, the poet also said, there are dead bodies buried as well.

The poet now goes inside the lavatory, where he slowly begins to stroke the walls and posts. Two men soundless enter the lavatory. Then another. Then three more, then still another . . . in an instant, the lavatory is filled with some ten men. The poet, startled, looks around him. The men say nothing. . . . A sense of tension. In a nonchalant fashion, their glances intertwine as they seek a response. The poet tries to sneak away quickly. The men concentrate their glances. The poet is rooted to the spot.

POET: Brother! My big brother! Where are you?

He manages to go into one of the stalls, locking the door. At that moment, two men enter, carrying a coffin made of unfinished wood. In the darkness, it almost seems as though the coffin were carrying itself. Greatly startled, the men run away. The coffin, it appears, is startled as well and comes to a halt. Silence prevails. In the next instant, the men quietly melt away into the darkness. The two men shouldering the coffin come closer to the lavatory. Then, with a sigh of relief, they put the coffin down.

FATHER: Who are they, that crowd?

BROTHER (*with a self-satisfied look*): Ah, some sort of all-night party, no?

FATHER: In a public toilet?

BROTHER: If you are surprised at that, imagine how they felt when they saw us!

FATHER (*as he glances at the coffin*): Well, it's not as though we were carrying a refrigerator or a TV or something. . . .

A sound comes from the closed toilet door.

FATHER: There's someone there . . . !

They both stoop down and look inside the lavatory.

BROTHER: That's him! I'm sure I heard him. Over that way. (*The door of the toilet opens, and the poet stealthily peers out.*) Is that Tōru? It must be Tōru . . . it's me, your older brother.

POET: What were those guys up to?

BROTHER: What do you mean, those guys?

POET: That crowd that was just in here.

BROTHER: They've completely disappeared.

POET: Really? Aren't you tricking me?

BROTHER: Now, would I go and trick you?

The poet, checking that no one has remained, comes out. He abruptly clutches his father's throat.

POET: Curse you and your dirty tricks! You came here thinking to stuff me in that cage, didn't you! Die!

FATHER: He . . . help !

BROTHER: Stop that! (*With all his might, the older brother pins down the poet.*) That's wrong! You always exaggerate!

The poet quickly springs up.

POET: Yeah, it was wrong of me . . . Papa . . .

The father massages his neck.

FATHER: Well, I'm fed up with the whole thing . . .

POET: Fed up?

FATHER (*evasively*): I'm completely exhausted.

POET: Is the coffin as heavy as all that?

FATHER (*to the older brother*): Well, you're the one who wanted to be a dutiful brother and wanted us to meet up with this crazy one. Well, as of tomorrow, I'm out of all this altogether.

POET: Altogether? "Altogether" refers to a quality of absolute truth, don't you think? Eh, Papa?

FATHER: Try to understand what I mean however you want.

POET: Absolute truth is a firebrand. An enormous bonfire. That's why we squint our eyes and try to flee without getting very close. That's because we fear of getting burned by the fire, don't you understand?

BROTHER: And it's not just that those burns will leave traces on our skin. They leave ugly scars on our souls as well.

POET: Be that as it may, human beings are like tiny pendulums, swinging between tears and smiling faces. . . .

BROTHER: Yeah, or to push these analogies, like a bunch of organs for eating, for sex, smeared with shit, all bound up together.

POET: Is that any way to talk when you come after a poet? (*He suddenly appears to be afraid.*) Well, now you're angry with me, aren't you? You're offended, aren't you?

The older brother suddenly strikes at him.

POET (*without thinking, returning the blow*): Hey, I'm the one who did wrong. You know what good reflexes I have. Try hitting me again.

BROTHER: No, that's fine.

POET: Come on, come on, hit me again!

FATHER: Why don't you come right out and say what you want? I'm fed up with all this.

The poet again pounces on his father.

POET: Shut up! Die!

The father tries to wriggle out as hard as he can.

FATHER: Ah! Somebody is coming!

The poet, startled, takes his hands away.

POET: Who is it? Those guys, I bet. Give me a hand, Brother.

The poet opens the lid of the coffin and quickly hides inside. The father immediately sits on the lid. No one comes.

FATHER: My military tactics were successful, don't you think?

BROTHER: It's not a good idea to fool him like that.

FATHER: I'm tired, completely exhausted. Imagine, a man in his fifties, doing all this. Now let's think this thing through. There aren't really any dead bodies piled up under this lavatory, are there?

BROTHER: Remember, he's a poet.

FATHER: Ridiculous! He's crazy! You've always pampered him too much. So his symptoms have gotten worse and worse.

BROTHER: I haven't pampered him. But inside, you know, I'm still the same older brother to him.

FATHER: You mean, something of the manliness and strength of an older brother?

BROTHER: Sure, manliness and strength . . .

FATHER: You're not the problem. But your younger brother treats me like a piece of shit. By now, if he weren't my own kid . . .

BROTHER: What do you mean, "by now . . ."?

FATHER: You . . . you . . .

BROTHER: Do you mean just like a year or so ago? Shall we wring his neck?

FATHER: Don't talk like that.

A short silence.

FATHER: That time, you should have used a leather belt.

BROTHER: Yeah, that's why I told you to give me your belt. But you refused; you said you didn't want your pants to fall down.

FATHER: Well, after all, I didn't want to kill my own child with my bottom half exposed. And you didn't put your whole strength into it, even though you were a great success as a boxer.

BROTHER: You used too much strength, like some old man hanging on a street-car strap. That's why I got pulled around myself and fell forward. . . . If you want to wring someone's neck, then your force has to be perfectly balanced. That's what Archimedes said, after all. . . .

FATHER: Archimedes . . . ?

The coffin begins to rattle around.

BROTHER (*with a start*): Did we open a hole for air?

FATHER: Nope.

The younger brother suddenly gets up from the coffin. The father, however, uses his body to keep the lid on.

BROTHER: Father . . .

FATHER: Don't worry. It's all right.

He forces the older brother to sit down.

FATHER: If anyone asks what we are doing, we just say that we're sitting here. That's all.

BROTHER: You mean, just sitting here . . . ?

FATHER: Sure. Just sitting here.

BROTHER: But, I mean . . .

FATHER: What a quiet night, don't you think? And look, how the stars are shining. . . .

The coffin is unexpectedly silent. A heavy silence.

BROTHER: . . . Now what . . . ? It's all your fault. It was no big deal to carry this coffin around like this night after night, as long as you thought of it as some kind of training to condition our bodies. . . .

He begins to whine and snivel.

FATHER: Stop that wailing. You don't really feel sorry for that fool; you're just crying because you can't go back to the way things were before. Do you think that you can go on living in the middle of those useless delusions? Well, say a sweet good-bye to all of that.

BROTHER: Shit! It's not just him you'd like to kill. You'd like to take me on as well.

FATHER: Stupid fool! Calm down!

The two rise, glaring at each other. At that moment, the lid of the coffin is pushed up with great force, knocking over the two of them. The poet lifts himself up so that his upper body is visible.

POET: I had a dream. A short one, hard to understand. I wondered to myself if I were having a nightmare. . . .

The father and the older brother look at each other.

BROTHER: If you put it that way, then a little . . .

POET: But I realized something. What is knowledge! Ever since a class society emerged, there have been only two kinds of knowledge in this world. One can be called the knowledge of class warfare, and the other, the knowledge of the struggle for production. Natural science and social science represent a crystallization of those two sorts of knowledge; philosophy is a synthesis of our knowledge of nature and our knowledge of society. (*He suddenly faces the audience.*) Well, and what other kinds of knowledge are there? Just tell me what other kinds there might be!

FATHER (*disappointed*): Ah, it's all started again.

POET: Huh?

FATHER: They're all gone.

POET: Ah, is that so? You aren't trying to fool me?

FATHER: Still, if that's the way it is, won't they come back?

POET: Those guys are like snakes, with their sinuous passions. What kind of disguise did they have tonight?

FATHER: Disguise?

BROTHER (*poking at his father*): Of course they were disguised.

POET: Should I try to guess? How about the people who work for the city sanitation department?

BROTHER: Yeah, that's it!

FATHER: You guessed just right!

BROTHER: They asked two or three questions about the cleanliness of the public lavatories in the city. . . .

POET: Hey, wait a minute. What day is it today?

FATHER: Ah . . . Wednesday, isn't it?

POET: If it's Wednesday, they are not city sanitation people. Shouldn't they be guards, covered with tears from weeping?

Father and brother are puzzled.

BROTHER: If you say so . . . That's the right kind of atmosphere. . . .

The poet suddenly begins to crawl on the ground.

POET: Look! Red roses!

Father and brother look. Red roses have fallen as if overflowing with blood.

POET: Here! I finally found what I was looking for. So it's here, brother. Here, underneath this public toilet, where the bodies are piled up, like islands of roses.

FATHER: What a bunch of nonsense! The drunks must have dropped these.

The poet enters the lavatory.

POET: Listen. Listen, brother. It's exactly what I expected. Yes! hey, listen carefully.

BROTHER (*straining his ears*): Huh?

POET: Well, don't you hear it? That weeping, that wailing that seems to crawl along the ground?

BROTHER: Whose is it?

POET (*in a tone of irritation*): It's those young guys. Destroyed by love.

BROTHER: Destroyed by love?

POET: That's right. They are nameless knights, defeated by love in a battle of roses.

FATHER (*suddenly pulling out a pocket flask and taking a swig*): A battle of roses? If you're talking about World War II, I know what that is, of course, but . . .

POET: Look! Now you can see for yourself! The islands of roses! Look, brother, how they spread out before us!

BROTHER: But, you . . . I can't see. . . .

POET: Never mind that. Even if you don't see anything, it's all right. After all, you're not a poet. You're an athlete. You use your muscles, not your head . . . well, let's start digging.

BROTHER: Digging?

POET: We're going to dig up the islands of roses.

FATHER: That's a laugh. If you do something like that, you'll get arrested for destroying public property.

POET: Public property? (*Suddenly an expression comes over his face as though he were searching for something from the distant past.*) Public property . . .

The father suddenly peers through the darkness.

FATHER: Quiet!

BROTHER: That trick! Not again!

FATHER: You fool, someone is really coming.

The poet again tries to jump into the coffin. Just as they did before, the father and the brother lift it up. The poet falls.

POET: Shit! Where are you taking my barricade!

The two don't answer.

FATHER: What should we do?

The two pick up the coffin and then try to dump it into the public toilet.

BROTHER: Is it a man or a woman?

FATHER: It looks like a man who looks like a woman.

BROTHER: Whichever it is, hurry up and decide!

FATHER: Ah, the shirt is a flowered pattern.

BROTHER: So it's a woman.

FATHER: So you think, but it's a man.

The two lift the coffin and try to shove it into the woman's toilet. Because they are nervous and clumsy, they have difficulty pushing it in.

BROTHER: Shit!

Gathering their strength, they force the coffin in. A deafening roar. A crack appears in the forward wall of the lavatory, and a piece of the wall falls down. White smoke.

In the back, a door of one of the toilets opens with a bang. Two naked men, carrying their pants and shirts, rush out; they rush off in a state of fear and confusion. From the fissure in the cracked concrete, half the coffin, its unfinished wood glowing white, sticks out of the wall in an eerie fashion. The man in the flowered shirt who has turned up quietly moves toward the coffin. He evidently is nearsighted. He almost brushes against it. Bowing his head, he takes out a cigarette and lights it. Suddenly:

MAN: A coffin!

He rushes away like a frightened rabbit. The father and the brother stand staring into space. Suddenly they realize that they can no longer see the poet. Wide-eyed, they begin to search frantically for him. At that moment, the poet staggers out from a pile of debris; the lid of the coffin has clattered open. With a start, the poet runs to the corner of the lavatory steps as though he were frightened. Automobiles pass behind him. Headlights flash on and off. The poet's head floats up in the light.

POET: Yes!

Nervously, he straightens his body and assumes a position of respect as though he were about to be interrogated. Then, suddenly facing the darkness, he begins to speak as though answering.

POET: Yes . . . yes . . . yes. My evening meal, did you say? Yes, it was delicious, and I enjoyed it very much. In particular, I'm very fond of that dried fish. And the meat was nice and fatty, and it was cooked just about the right amount. And then . . . yes, I had some of the tea, too. Well, yes, it was rather lukewarm, but my own mouth's pretty sore so, so that's just about the way I like it. Yes, it was really good. It's true, though, that there was a faint odor of disinfectant . . . but it wasn't anything you'd notice. I suppose it's creosote. And sure, you're absolutely right, afterward I ate a caramel to take away any bad taste. That caramel was really good. It's true, though, that sometimes when I bite down, my upper and lower jaws stick together, which is really bothersome. But today I discovered a way to avoid this. At the minute when I bite down—no, actually the moment after I bite down—I kind of bend the muscles on one side of my face, and the candy doesn't stick to either side. Then I can go right on chewing, you see, without any difficulty. Actually, I can show you now how it works, if you like . . . (*suddenly becoming obstinate*). My name is Fukao Tōru, age twenty-one . . . (*irritated*). My name is Fukao Tōru, age twenty-one . . . other than that I have nothing to say (*with a mocking laugh*). How ridiculous this is. That you, brother, would get involved. If you are planning to cheat me, it's useless. Let me be honest about this. I intend to say absolutely nothing about this matter. It's not a question of hiding anything or not hiding anything. I feel no necessity whatsoever to speak (*irritated*). How many times do you have to be told this? I will say nothing. I am firmly resolved to say nothing. (*He shakes his head furiously.*) It's no good. I will keep quiet. I have my own sense of justice . . . no matter how much you threaten me about keeping quiet, it's useless. As far as I'm concerned, is this bad or not. . . . I don't care, there's no connection. Concerning myself, I've made a firm decision. I will not speak. I will not. I will not speak!

The poet ferociously holds his head with his arms. The brother quietly moves behind him.

BROTHER (*gently*): That will be the end of today's interrogation.

The poet looks up with hollow eyes.

BROTHER: I say, that will be the end of today's interrogation.

The father approaches too.

FATHER: Now that he's calmed down, let's get him home.

Lifting him under his arms for support, the brother and the father begin to lead him away. Suddenly, the poet pushes the two of them away and runs to hide in the public lavatory.

FATHER: What are you doing?

The poet shouts from inside the lavatory.

POET: Who are you, you two?

BROTHER: Who are we? It's your older brother and your papa, can't you see?

POET: Stop telling lies! My father? My brother? You make me laugh. I know you're in disguise. Next you'll be telling me that you are some sort of sanitation workers.

FATHER: Now what's going on?

BROTHER: I think he's still all mixed up in his head.

FATHER: Well, whatever state he's in, it's scary that he can't even remember our faces. Why just tonight, we were sitting together, the three of us, drinking beer and eating our dinner. . . .

POET: Where did we do that?

FATHER: Why of course, in our apartment, where do you think? In the dining room, where we keep that Buddhist altar for your mom.

POET: Here in the dining room?

FATHER: What's that?

POET (*irritated*): If this is the dining room, then where is Mom's altar?

FATHER: No, no, here, this is the public lavatory.

POET: Look, you two, your story is full of holes. If we were really a family, of course we would be in the dining room. Then why would we be in a public lavatory at this hour? Don't you think there is something strange about this? This goes beyond common sense.

BROTHER (*to the father*): Well, you started to talk about all this; he's all mixed up.

The father goes over to the coffin.

FATHER: Look at this! What do you think it is?

POET: It looks like a box to me.

FATHER: Well, it's not just that.

The poet quietly comes closer.

POET (*startled*): A coffin!

FATHER: Oh, come on. You're surprised at this? You made us make this for you. Your papa and your brother. Even though we've never made anything more than shelves, weekend carpenters that we are. . . . You said that you needed it, no matter what . . .

POET: A ridiculous object? A coffin is not a ridiculous object. It is a holy object in which to bury the dead. What is ridiculous is the fact that this coffin is here, near this filthy public lavatory. That's what's ridiculous. It would be better to say that there's some kind of dangerous, criminal situation involved here. You are up to some scheme, the two of you, aren't you?

FATHER: Stop making jokes. You're the one who started this.

POET: No, no, I see it, you're plotting something. There is something that you'll try to do. It's some kind of trap. Some kind of crafty, cunning trap, that's what it is. You are planning something weird that will take place here, in the middle of everyday reality. You want to blur and confuse the image of us poets, so filled with rich emotions. It's a cunning trap to lead us to defeat. I'm right on the mark, aren't I? If you thought you could trick me, well, you won't get away with it. Go away!

The poet hides himself again.

FATHER: He's just like Amaterasu shutting herself up in the dark cave. Whenever the going gets rough, he just disappears. Just let it go.

BROTHER: Just let it go, you say, but do you mean to just abandon the whole thing?

FATHER: The trouble, you know, is that from his point of view, he doesn't acknowledge his family connections. Above and beyond that, why does he insist that we are related?

BROTHER: I certainly don't intend to abandon him.

FATHER: Well, until now you've been doing just that.

BROTHER: Stop saying such things!

FATHER: Yeah, well, just don't pretend that there isn't a problem. That's the worst habit of your generation. Not abandon him? What a joke! It's just because you're not completely ready yet to give up. Inside that crazy head, you still have some old image of the way things were before, one that you can't give up.

BROTHER: Yeah. That's exactly it.

FATHER: So go on then, give it up.

BROTHER: This is really disgusting. I won't give it up. As long as we are hanging around public lavatories, that makes me a hero, in his eyes, at least. So do we really have to put up with being tired of him?

FATHER: Shit! He, too, has really gotten all mixed up inside that head of his.

The brother moves closer to the lavatory.

BROTHER: Hey! Tōru! . . . Come on out. Hey, it's your brother. . . . (*He sud-*

denly takes up a boxing pose.) Hey! Come on! We used to do this before, remember?

He does some footwork. Silence from the lavatory.

BROTHER: Are you scared? You're afraid of my "straight punch from the right," and that's why you are hiding, aren't you? Punch, punch, jab, jab! (*He continues his shadowboxing.*)

FATHER (*peevishly, he takes out his pocket flask and drinks*): It's useless, you know. If you act like that, it's a real waste. . . .

The brother, paying no attention, continues his shadowboxing.

BROTHER: Punch, punch . . . hey, you coward, come on out and fight fair and square! (*As he continues his shadowboxing, the brother kicks his father.*) Papa, stop drinking and get ready to play the referee, just like always. Hey, Tōru, Papa's all excited about being the referee!

FATHER: That's a big joke.

BROTHER: Punch, punch, jab, jab! . . .

The poet peeks out from the lavatory door.

POET: Hey, brother. (*The brother suddenly whirls around to face him, and the poet also adjusts his pose.*) Are you really my brother?

The brother somewhat nervously adjusts his pose.

BROTHER: Sure, I'm your brother, that's who I am.

POET: Why do you seem to have suddenly gotten older like this?

BROTHER: Older?

POET: And who's that disgusting old man?

FATHER: What do you mean? I'm your Papa.

POET: That's not true. You are trying to trick me. If you are in some sort of disguise, then you should have picked a better one!

The poet hides himself again.

FATHER: Shit! I really started to think that we were in disguise. But if I'm in disguise, then where can you find the real me?

The brother drags over the father to face him.

FATHER: What are you doing?

BROTHER: Come on, hit me!

FATHER: Hey, I'm the referee, remember?

BROTHER: Come on, no griping . . .

Without thinking, the father returns the brother's jab.

BROTHER: Yeah, that's the idea.

FATHER: Hey, don't do this for real now!

The two exchange hooks. The father begins to carry out some light footwork.

FATHER: Somehow, it seems that my body's gotten lighter.

Hitting his stride, the father throws a series of punches. The brother fiercely begins the count. He swings at the father.

FATHER: I said, don't take this seriously now, huh?

BROTHER: Hey, he's peeking out. Keep hitting me.

FATHER: Here we go.

The father throws himself into the punching. The brother delivers a string of strong punches. The father suffers a "knockdown." The brother suddenly turns in the direction of the poet.

BROTHER: Yeah! Come on!

Without thinking, the poet comes out into the open. An exchange of punches.

BROTHER: Oh, you are good. But you are still not on top yet. Keep up your guard on the left. . . . Here's a punch! And another!

The brother continues striking in a composed fashion. Suddenly, one of the poet's punches strikes home. The brother begins to fight back in earnest. The poet attacks in a bloodthirsty manner. The fight begins to get serious. The brother is driven back up against the wall. The poet keeps attacking relentlessly.

POET: Die, dammit, Die! Die!

Blood spurts from the brother's face; he collapses. Lifting his bloodied hand in a gesture of victory, the poet stares at him. Suddenly, he turns to face the audience directly.

POET: Who is it? Who is it out there? I know there's a whole bunch of you who would like to put me into a cage. But I won't let you do it. (*He shows his bloodied fist.*) Look. I won't hide. So show yourselves to me. Reveal to me your real selves! Why? Why won't you show me? I'm showing myself to you. . . . Please, I ask you, show yourselves.

The poet falls to his knees and beats the floor. Then suddenly he seems to be aroused from his frenzy. He lifts his head.

POET: You're laughing, aren't you? Someone is laughing. . . . There's a wind. . . . Hey, it's my brother. I know it's you. . . . Where are you hiding? And even you, you're acting like them, too? Where are you? Don't just take it out on just me. Don't separate me from the others. I'm already an adult, you know. . . . I know. You're going to come at me from behind, push me down. Or if not that, you'll suddenly throw a rope around my neck and you'll hang me, like a cat. It seems like the time you tried to dunk me into the river. Give it up, please give it up. You know I don't know how to swim. If it is anything else, I could endure it somehow. But don't separate me from the others.

Now the brother dizzily rises. His face is bloody. The poet turns to look at him.

POET: Brother . . .

The brother collapses again on the ground. The poet rushes to help him up.

POET: Get ahold of yourself, brother.

BROTHER: I'm OK. Everything's just fine.

POET: Who was it? Who was it who did this to you?

BROTHER (*astonished*): Who did this . . . ? Why, you . . .

POET: It must have been them. Yes, it must have been. Don't you think so, brother?

BROTHER (*realizing that it is no use*): Yeah, sure. It was them.

POET: Damn! Let's give it to them. An eye for an eye. Where do you think they made off to?

BROTHER: Never mind now.

POET: Don't talk like that. And remember what you always tell me. If someone attacks you, you have to strike back. And if only one person is on the attack, why even a little flame, if it's kept burning, it can sometime burn up a whole field.

BROTHER: Wait a minute now. I should have taught you this too. In a revolution, or a revolutionary war, attack is important, but so is defense, and so is retreat. Defense for the sake of attack, retreat for the sake of advance, flank attack for the sake of a direct assault.

POET: So do you mean that, well, we should wait?

BROTHER: Wait, carry out ambush attacks, counteroffensives. Just like in boxing. Countdown blows, to the death!

POET: Were there lots of them?

BROTHER: I don't know. After all, they attacked out of nowhere.

POET: Just what I figured. If that hadn't happened, then, brother, then there wouldn't have been a body of the dead enemy, two bodies . . . ah, a dead body.

BROTHER: Nonsense. That's Papa.

POET: You look like you're still drunk. Get up.

BROTHER: Don't. Just let him sleep.

POET: But remember, you said that even a single person could mobilize the masses. Isn't that right?

BROTHER: Now look carefully. There's Papa over there. Do you really think that he would have the courage to fight the two of us? He's just a greasy old pig.

POET: Look at Papa. He must be having a bad dream. Look at the tears streaming down his face.

BROTHER: I guess he must be dreaming about his little garden.

POET: His little garden?

BROTHER: Papa's always talking about those stupid things he remembers, you know. In the tiny garden, the little flower stand for roses . . .

POET: Yes . . . yes, I remember. He would always walk around with these pips in his pocket: Charleston, or Super Star, or Victory Rose . . .

BROTHER: When was it, don't you remember, that because you wanted to please him, you bought a flower pot and secretly planted one of those pips?

POET: No seedling ever sprouted.

BROTHER: That's right. However long you waited, nothing sprouted. . . .

POET: However many days I waited, nothing came up. . . .

BROTHER: It was a fraud.

POET: That's right. Papa fobbed off a fake pip on me. . . .

A short silence.

POET: I hear footsteps.

BROTHER: . . . it's the sound of the wind.

POET: You're wrong. It's footsteps.

BROTHER: The sound of the wind.

POET: The sound of the wind.

A short silence.

POET: How long do we have to wait?

BROTHER: Are you uneasy?

POET: Don't be ridiculous. You can stop treating me like a child.

A short silence.

POET: How peculiar . . . once before I waited like this. . . . Yes. And I was with you.

BROTHER (*for some reason he flinches*): With me?

POET: When was it? I don't rightly remember. . . . I was certainly waiting for someone. . . . I was extremely nervous . . . and while I was waiting, you suddenly said, "This stinks. . . ." Don't you remember?

BROTHER (*shaking his head*): I don't remember anything.

POET: Well you certainly said it. "This stinks." And then you laughed. A big horselaugh. "You really are a brat. . . ." Yes, you were so cruel then. I was so nervous I pooped in my pants. And you threw me into the river. Even though you knew that I couldn't swim . . . and yet I wanted to laugh. Force myself to laugh. Even though my head went down in the water time after time, I wanted to laugh. And do you know why? Because I didn't want to be abandoned by my older brother. . . .

BROTHER: That's enough. Besides, I didn't abandon you. I mean, look, here we are, still together.

POET: Yes, I understand. . . . You didn't abandon me. . . . But still, who were we waiting for? At that time, who were we waiting for?

BROTHER: I've forgotten . . . I've forgotten everything.

POET: But why? I know that I got thrown into the river, but the memory of all that isn't really so terrible. . . . I can't really remember, but there was something, well, happy about it, too. . . . I was in such a state of nerves . . . and so awful, so terrible. . . . I just can't remember, but at that time, who were we waiting for? And what happened?

BROTHER: Hey, I told you to cut that out!

The brother pushes the poet away.

POET: Brother . . .

BROTHER: Go home! Go home just as fast as you can! When you're here, you're nothing but a nuisance. You're in the way. You're a drag. Hurry up and get lost! And you think you want to help me? And just what is it that you think you could do? I'd like to hear what you think that might be.

POET (*shrinking back*): That's horrible. Horrible, what you said.

BROTHER: Stop using that sugary voice. And stop taking that attitude that you don't want to be abandoned.

POET: Then tell me. What is it that you want me to do?

BROTHER: Don't you think you know? I told you to use your own judgment and act accordingly.

POET: I don't understand. I will do anything, anything, for you . . .

BROTHER: You'll do anything? Is that right? You'll do anything I want you to? Fine, turn into a horse.

POET: A horse?

BROTHER: Yeah. A horse. With four legs. See? You can't do that. They say, don't they, that even a baby kitten has its pride. But then look at Beethoven. A really superior man must pass through sorrow in order to achieve his sense of joy.

The poet suddenly begins to crawl on the ground.

POET: So, come on, come on, and ride me.

BROTHER (*shrinking*): It's a joke. Stop it.

POET: It's fine, just get on and ride. I just remembered something that Solomon said. Before man may attain his glory, he must be smitten with suffering.

BROTHER: If you give this up, I'll play the horse. (*The brother begins to crawl on the ground.*)

POET: Brother . . .

BROTHER: It's an order. Get on and ride me. Suffering acts as a spur to action. And it is only in the midst of action that we can feel the reality of our own lives. So then. Get on and ride.

The poet straddles his older brother's back. The brother suddenly gets up to rush away but soon gives up, exhausted.

POET: Are you all right?

BROTHER: Yeah, I'm fine. Remember, true comrades are not afraid of hardship and do not try to escape it. In fact, they are able to conquer it, destroy it. . . . (*He falls down in a pitiful fashion; then suddenly, he springs up again.*) I'm a fool. I'm the worst there is. Take me off to the slaughterhouse!

POET: What on earth are you saying?

BROTHER: Don't worry about it. Take me off to the slaughterhouse! (*Saying this, he wraps a rope around his own neck.*) Stop hesitating. Pull!

The poet pulls at the rope. The brother groans as if in pain.

POET: I hate this, letting me become the horse; it would be much more convenient if I just let myself be killed.

BROTHER: What do you mean, it would be much more convenient?

POET: Yes, that's right. So take me to the slaughterhouse.

BROTHER: Given the way you are, I'm not surprised that you're so difficult! Do you think that I could stand turning that role over to you? Come on, pull. Wasn't it Camus who said that if we aren't disappointed in life, we cannot love life?

POET: What a terrible thing to say.

BROTHER: Pull harder!

POET (*weeping*): You are . . . really so cruel.

BROTHER (*groaning*): Ah . . . the pleasure that flutters and burns in the midst of disappointment. . . . Pull harder . . . harder. . . .

The rope breaks. The two somersault and fall over. The father dizzily opens his eyes.

FATHER: Who was it? Who was the guy who overturned my flower stand . . . ?

A moment of stillness. The brother springs up.

POET: Is that a river?

BROTHER: A river . . .

The poet sits up, too. The father tries to match the dialogue of the two brothers with his gestures.

BROTHER: Hey! You can hear it, can't you? There's a river flowing . . .

POET (*afraid*): Remember, I can't swim. . . .

BROTHER: There's some kind of commotion. . . . I can hear them, shouting or something, on the bank on the other side. . . .

POET: I think somebody's died.

BROTHER: Somebody's died?

POET: Well, there's certainly a lot of noise and confusion.

BROTHER: You're wrong. It's just an amusement park over there.

POET: Just an amusement park?

BROTHER: Yeah. Just the kind of place where we play like fools with our dear little children. . . .

POET: Well, that doesn't sound so bad. Shall we go on over?

BROTHER: I hate that sort of place. What I like in an amusement park are the fountains. That's all. Especially when they can change color with the lights.

POET: Behind the fountain, in the dusk, so full of expectation . . .

BROTHER: And under the night sky, a little outdoor stage . . .

POET: Confound it all . . . what gorgeous confusion.

By now the two men have risen. In a twinkling, the brother has picked up a slight rhythm with his body and feet.

BROTHER: 1-2, 1-2-3-4, 1-2 . . .

The poet as well, following along with his brother, begins to dance on this mythic outdoor stage. Lights flash off and on. The two, picking up on the rhythm, move with light steps. Suddenly the father too, from the side, joins them, although he can't quite keep up. The three move together. They begin a ridiculous, foolishly comic dance. . . . Soon they change to a sort of unreliable set of steps. At this point, a crowd of men appear from the shadows, or the dark recesses of the lavatory, or from the toilets. They stare at the three. As the three notice, their steps become progressively smaller and smaller, so that eventually they are clicking only their fingers. The men stare with piercing glances, sometimes bewitching glances, at the three. The three spontaneously retire.

POET: It's those punks.

FATHER: Punks? It's just an outdoor summer party. They've just had too much beer to drink, that's all.

POET: Papa, you don't understand. You always fall asleep just when the most important things happen. That's why you don't know what *is* going on! These are the ones who attacked my brother.

FATHER: You . . . and that blood . . . what happened after I fell over?

BROTHER: Nothing. Nothing happened at all. . . . I just took his punch, I guess.

POET: My punch? What do you mean by that?

BROTHER: This playful dream is definitely over now.

POET: Playful dream?

The brother taps the poet on the shoulder.

BROTHER: It's just a joke. We joked around so much before, don't you remember? Playing around, a lot of jokes. Yeah, blow your nose . . .

POET: This has no connection with blowing my nose!

BROTHER: And this has no connection to those guys. . . . And it's not the ones you're thinking about. They're just a lonely bunch, just like us.

POET: What a lie!

The poet tries to run away; the father and brother restrain him.

POET: Let me go! Why is it? I waited when you told me to wait. Defense for the sake of offense, retreat for the sake of advance, guerrilla warfare for the sake of real warfare . . . it's all a bunch of lies, isn't it? At that time, in fact . . .

BROTHER: That time?

POET: Yes. I remember . . . that time I was waiting patiently. Under the shadow of a tall post, in the shadow of thick concrete. . . . I was so nervous I pooped in my pants waiting. . . . Five hours, yes, five long hours. . . . And you were the one who told me, "Relax. We won't permit any failures. You take aim to the right, I take aim to the left. And don't shake. You can count, count sheep. How's that? Relaxed now? When you are relaxed, you can shout to your inner self that the Tree of Freedom . . . the Tree of Freedom . . ."

BROTHER: The Tree of Freedom can grow only if bathed in the blood of the Tyrant.

POET: And then you yelled out, "Light the torches! Our actions, those torches that we burned, will enchant a new generation!"

FATHER (*with a horselaugh*): What a cheap comedy! If it's just words you are worried about, I can yell out all sorts of fancy things. "My sons, my two sons, the future is beautiful, glittering in rosy colors."

POET: Shut up, you drunk. I bet my money on my brother's words. Everything about my brother. . . . And while I was waiting, I remembered. . . . I was so afraid, but I went on out to fight.

The poet breaks lose from the other two and makes a run for the public lavatory.

FATHER: Hey! Son.

BROTHER: Stop this!

Suddenly a knife glitters in the poet's hand. He rushes toward the shadow of a man standing in the shadows of the trees. Silently, the shadow disappears. The poet, nervous, moves to another clump of trees. The shadow soundlessly disappears and then silently reemerges. The poet, confused, turns his head.

POET: Brother? Where are you?

Without thinking, the father and the brother hide in the shadow of some pampas grass.

POET: . . . Why won't you come out? I'm to the right, you're to the left, right? . . . Brother!

Suddenly a group of men come flooding out of the lavatory and surround the poet. He is frightened. The men say nothing, but their eyes glitter.

POET: Brother. . . . Come and help me! Help me! Help!

As he cries out, he is thrust into the middle of the group of men. Saying nothing, the men step aside. With all his might, the poet manages to flatten himself against the wall of the urinal. As he rises and tries to defend himself again, they close in on him like a swarm of insects. In an instant, hands reach out and shred his clothing. His body exposed, the poet is now nearly naked. . . . The brother now comes bounding out.

BROTHER: Wait!

The men turn to look at him.

POET: Brother . . . !

BROTHER (*to the men*): Let him go. I want you to do this for me. This guy is really peculiar. He's crazy in the head. I mean, crazy!

POET: What? What is this? I'm crazy?

FATHER: Yes, exactly. You're crazy. (*to the men*) So we ask this of you. Just pay no attention to him.

POET: This is a lie! I'm not crazy, or anything like that. My brother is making it all up. I'm not crazy, not at all. I'm not . . .

During this time, the men release him and vanish soundlessly. The poet is now left, in rags, in the public toilet.

POET (*weeping*): What you did is terrible, Brother. The same was true then . . . you certainly treated me as though I were crazy. . . . But what is it that I did? I did exactly what you told me to. Wherever, whenever, I always followed your wishes. And yet now you want to treat me as though I were crazy, insane. I feel betrayed. Horribly betrayed. . . . Why have you done this to me? I want you to tell me. (*He beats on a crumbling wall of the lavatory.*) I don't understand. I don't understand at all.

At this moment, the wall begins to crumble, and the coffin of white wood falls forward. From inside, a tide of red rose petals pour out. . . . Occasional light from passing headlights. Silence. The father, somewhat dizzy, approaches the scattered rose petals.

FATHER: Roses . . . my rose stand . . . that stand for roses in that little garden I have dreamed about for so long . . . if only I could plant more superstars, or Charlestons . . . say, it wouldn't be a bad idea to make a fence of roses. (*Looking back at the brother.*) What do you think? Not such a bad idea, huh? Make a kind of bamboo shelf and then train roses to grow along it. White and yellow ones . . . make it full of blooming roses . . . (*The brother does not respond. The father, as if awakening from a dream, has an exhausted expression on his face.*)

FATHER: What is it? Why are you looking at me like that? . . . I feel afraid . . . have I done something to make you angry? It was your fault. You went too far. There are limits to everything, you know. Take that garden, for example. I don't even need ten yards square. Even smaller than that is all right. Even half that size. . . . if I could just have a tiny little stand for my roses. . . . And that's why you should help me realize my dream . . . now, it's not a question of a lot of money, you know. With two people working at it, it wouldn't take all that many years.

BROTHER: I hate this.

FATHER: Hate this?

BROTHER: Yeah, I mean, no thanks. . . . You know I have a duty to look after him.

FATHER: What's this all about? You really haven't given up yet, have you? The idols have been smashed. Even inside *his* crazy head. Your idol has been broken to pieces.

BROTHER: I get what you're saying. I understand. About my idol being destroyed . . . but does that mean I should just abandon him?

FATHER: So, that's how you want to put it. "Does that mean I should just abandon him?" But just who is abandoning whom? What you're afraid of is that he has abandoned *you.*

BROTHER: That's right. You've got it exactly right. And I don't want to be abandoned by him!

A short silence.

BROTHER (*staring hard at the knife*): Just two minutes. For just two minutes. I was confused. That concrete pillar suddenly became icy cold, it felt like to me. I wonder why it was that I suddenly felt a cold shiver? . . . ridiculous, it's all so stupid. The coldness of the pillar seemed to pull me, drag me off my feet. It held me up for two minutes. Just two! (*He suddenly begins to giggle.*) So then, you think that I have a bad character? . . . that I am venal? . . . Isn't it a bit like getting a quick glimpse into the mouth of some hussy and spotting the gold teeth? . . . Isn't it a little like your mother giving a friendly smile when she's in your old man's bed? . . . Just two minutes, two short minutes. By the time I realized what was happening, this guy had come running . . . he rushed in like he was crazy or something . . . everything was confused . . . he was really afraid . . . so then, I suddenly realized he was crazy. . . . He was really strange in the head. Really strange. I demand a psychiatric evaluation!

POET: I deny this. I absolutely refuse to have this evaluation. . . . I am certainly not crazy. Not in any way.

FATHER: Listen, you . . .

The brother and the father turn to look. In an instant, as though he has just had some sort of spasm or attack, the poet curls up in a corner of the steps, hugging his knees as though he were in the midst of some phantom interrogation session.

POET (*shaking his head furiously*): I don't know why, but I don't understand. I don't know why my brother would say that about me. . . . If that's what you want to know about, ask my brother. I don't like to talk, I don't like to talk about anything. . . . But I will say just one thing. If my brother is saying things like that because he wants to try to save me, that's a big mistake. He's making a big mistake. Please tell him that. . . . (*suddenly laughing in a low voice*) Now I understand. Now I think I know more or less what it is that you want to say to me. It's easier to just say that I'm crazy. Yes, it's not bad to put up a fraud that I'm out of my mind. . . . But it's not like that. . . . If you ask why not, there's no reason why I should tell *you*! This is a problem between the two of us, my brother and I. A problem within our own little world. . . . So, please give it up. Can't you bring yourselves to understand? I'm not going to say any more. There is no need for me to say another word. And it's wrong to frighten me. A waste of time. (*He pushes out his hands as though he had been put in handcuffs.*) So, take me away. I prefer to be by myself. Then I can stare at the stains on the walls and ceiling. Take me back. Please, take me back as fast as you can!

The brother reaches gently from behind and takes hold of the poet's hands.

BROTHER: So then, let's go. Today's interrogation is finished. . . .

The poet rises. He suddenly looks around.

BROTHER: What is it?

POET: There's somebody staring at me. . . .

BROTHER: Somebody . . . ?

POET: Yes. Somebody . . .

The poet again looks around. Startled, he goes about, pointing at the clumps of trees and the wall of the lavatory.

POET: Look! There! . . . and there!

Suddenly, from the dark shadows of the trees and the shadow of the lavatory, the men, having now removed their pants and transformed themselves into naked youths, peek out. The father and the brother apparently see nothing. The two stare out into the darkness.

BROTHER: Where? Where do you see somebody?

FATHER: I don't see anything . . . I don't see anybody . . .

The brother and the father stroll around in the shadows of the lavatory and the trees.

POET: Well then, come on out, all of you. Don't hide yourself away in places like that, come out and show yourselves. . . . Come on, come close to me.

The naked youths begin to show their white faces from between the trees.

POET: So that's it. It's you. . . . I've been looking for you all this while. . . . So come on, pull yourselves together. Why do you have such pale faces? After all, there's a whole bunch of you, so why don't you say something? . . . I've been looking for you for so long. No, that's the truth. I've been looking for that archipelago of roses you created. So don't put on any poses, and don't be so shy. Hey!

Dizzily, the poet approaches the trees and tries to take hold of the young men. They quickly fade into the darkness.

POET: Why are you running away? Why are you avoiding me? It's wrong to keep the archipelago of roses to yourselves. Remember, I'm part of your group, too. That's true, you know. (*The poet approaches another clump of trees. The young men disappear.*) Hey! (*The poet runs from one clump of trees to another, and as he does so, the youths sit down in the middle of the rose petals still strewn all over.*) Shit. I can't control *them*. And as for this archipelago of roses. . . . It's cold. So cold. Damn. With this many roses blossoming, why is it so cold? . . . Is it spring now? . . . or is it winter? . . .

As the poet looks over his shoulder, something moves inside one of the toilets.

POET: Who are you, hiding in there?

The poet opens the door with a bang. As he does so, the brother, who has white makeup on his face like that of the youths, is crouching there. He gives the poet a kind of fawning, weak laugh.

POET: You. . . . So then, you are the only one who stayed behind and didn't escape with the others. Well come then. Come here then.

Suddenly he notices the knife in the brother's hand.

POET: Hey, what's that? Don't you know—that's a dangerous weapon you are holding there. (*The brother, noticing the knife, nervously tries to hide it. The poet deftly takes hold of the brother's arms.*) Hold on. Hand it over. This is too hard for you young guys, you know. That's because you don't know how to use it. Hand it over. If you really want to use it, I'll show you how to use a knife. It's not all that hard to do. You just have to get the knack of it. You always seem to aim for the side of the chest. But better give that up, because the chance of failure is too great. What you need to do is to aim at the nape of the neck. (*He taps on his neck.*) See, right here. In this place . . . why are you hesitating like that? Just give a good thrust!

With all his determination, the poet pulls the brother's arms in closer. The knife touches the nape of the poet's neck. Blood! The poet, as he rolls his body over, leans on the wall, collapses, then slides down.

BROTHER: Hey . . .

The father comes running out of the shadows.

FATHER: Stupid! What is all this?

The two rush over.

BROTHER: Hey! Are you all right?

FATHER: It's your papa!

The poet pushes the two of them aside.

POET: Who is it? Who are you?

The brother and the father fall silent.

POET (*with a cold laugh*): Well, that's a pretty feeble disguise you're wearing. Is today a holiday? That's why you've disguised yourselves as my father and brother. Well, give it up. Because if you keep disguising yourselves too often, then you won't know any longer who you really are.

FATHER: Listen, son . . .

POET: That's enough. Just leave me alone. When I'm alone, I just like to stare at the stains on the ceiling. . . . Let me disappear!

The poet rolls himself into one of the toilets. A moment of silence. The brother and the father call into the toilets.

BROTHER: Hey!

FATHER: Hey!

BROTHER: Where are you?

FATHER: Where are you?

BROTHER: Come on!

FATHER: Come on!

Yet the sound of the poet's voice does not come back to them. A long silence. Light from headlights occasionally appears and then fades. The father suddenly begins to touch himself all over, searching for something.

FATHER: . . . It's not here . . . it's not. Those rose pips are gone . . . could I have dropped them someplace? . . . I'll have to go and buy some more. . . . Shit, I was really cheated this time. . . . Maybe for once I should take a new lease on things, buy some pink ones. (*During this time, the brother slowly rises and enters the toilet. His figure disappears.*) Or then, maybe yellow climbing roses, should I get those? . . . Sterling Silver, roses like that, those aren't bad . . . come to think of it, in a tiny garden, those climbing roses might be best. Exactly. In a little garden of five or ten yards square, climbing roses are exactly what you want.

The brother now appears from the toilet. On his back is tied the dead body of his brother, bound there with a strong rope.

FATHER: Son, you . . .

BROTHER: Let's take off.

FATHER: Take off? Where to?

BROTHER: To another public lavatory of course.

FATHER: So he's dead, is he? So what are you talking about? We don't have to.

BROTHER: Shut up! You have a big mouth. Don't say a word. The connection between a poet and his society is not a direct one. Rather, his task is to seek out the hidden areas of that society, to find the real significance of his period, if you will. And so in the evening, dressed in a gorgeous disguise, on the street, in the lavatory, just as this poet said, there are buried underneath the cherry blossoms in full bloom a mound of dead bodies. And as he said again and again, there are piles, piles of bodies buried in the depth of night, underneath the public toilet. . . .

FATHER: Give up this ridiculous farce. I can see right through it. You say all this stuff, but what does it really mean? He's dead, right? And so you will be an outcast forever.

BROTHER: That's a lot of crap. Why do you say a thing like that? What right do you have to say that I'll be an outcast forever? Remember what he himself said. This was a problem just between the two of us. A problem in the realm of existence we share . . . making an outcast, being an outcast, it's not that simple. . . . None of it is your business.

FATHER: This is crazy. You're really crazy. You abandoned him. And you were abandoned by him. What more is there to it?

BROTHER: Shut up. Don't say another word. You're fast asleep in those damned roses of yours. . . .

FATHER (*clinging to the brother's legs*): Come. Come on. Let's go home. To our home.

BROTHER: Damn you! Die!

He shakes off the father, who rolls down onto the spilled roses and stops moving.

BROTHER (*in the voice of the poet*): When was it? I don't remember very well. . . . I was waiting for someone. . . . And I was so nervous . . . and you told me that it stunk . . . you remember, don't you brother? (*He reverts to himself.*) Yeah, I do remember, I remember. (*Reverting to the poet again.*) And you were so cruel to me then. I was so nervous that I pooped in my pants, and you wanted to throw me into the river. Even though you knew that I couldn't swim. . . . And yet I wanted to laugh. Force myself to laugh. and do you understand why? Because I didn't want you to abandon me. (*Back to the brother.*) Shut up now. I didn't abandon you. And that's why we're together now, isn't it? (*Returning to the poet.*) I understand. I understand that you didn't abandon me. But we were waiting for someone, weren't we? We were waiting . . .

Suddenly from the trees and the shadow of the public lavatory can be heard giggling voices. The brother turns his head sharply.

BROTHER: Who is that over there? . . . it's those guys. Look. We aren't hiding ourselves any more. So you shouldn't hide either. Show who you are.

The brother rushes toward a clump of trees. As he does so, the figures of the men disappear. He rushes to another clump. They vanish again. He goes to still another. And they disappear. The brother now is exhausted.

BROTHER: Shit. And I'm so thirsty . . .

He goes into the public lavatory and fastens his mouth on the faucet attached to the basin. But no water comes. He gives up and leaves the lavatory. Suddenly he stops and strains his ears.

BROTHER: Someone is crying . . . or the wind . . . or no, maybe it's the sound of water. . . . It's the river. The river, flowing. . . . A terrible smell . . . it's really hideous . . . maybe there are the dead bodies of some animals floating along down . . . a cat, maybe, or a pig, maybe even a human corpse . . . what gorgeous confusion, so filled with shame and dishonor . . . anyway, let's try to get to the riverbank. But who cares anyway? But my throat is parched dry. You really cling to me, don't you? Well, don't shake yourself free. If we can manage to get safely to the riverbank, you and I will take a boat. Even if the boat is weak and frail, like a butterfly in October, we'll still be able to row on out. . . .

The brother, seeking the river in the darkness, moves out toward the seats in the theater. He vanishes into the darkening path with his brother still tied onto his body. Suddenly, at that moment, the white wooden coffin in the toilet glimmers faintly white. Then darkness.

    Curtain

ESSAY

ŌE KENZABURŌ

Ōe Kenzaburō (b. 1935), whose story "Teach Us to Outgrow Our Madness" (Kyōki no ikinoboru michi o oshieyo) appears in the fiction section of this chapter, was awarded the Nobel Prize for Literature in 1994, the second Japanese writer to receive this honor. Unlike Kawabata Yasunari's address, which also is included in this volume, Ōe's acceptance speech is not on aesthetics but on the ambiguous role of Japan in the contemporary world and the legacy of its own troubled history. Ōe's sense of engagement and responsibility as expressed here marks him as a contemporary figure. His observations thus seem to be a fitting conclusion to this anthology, in which we, as its editors, have tried to trace, through literature, Japan's cultural and artistic path from its opening to the West in 1968 to the present.

JAPAN, THE AMBIGUOUS, AND MYSELF
(AIMAI NA NIHON NO WATASHI)

Translated by Hisaki Yamanouchi

During the last catastrophic World War, I was a little boy and lived in a remote, wooded valley on Shikoku Island in the Japanese archipelago, thousands of miles away from here. At that time there were two books that I was really fascinated by: *The Adventures of Huckleberry Finn* and *The Wonderful Adventures of Nils*. The whole world was then engulfed by waves of horror. By reading *Huckleberry Finn* I felt I was able to justify my habit of going into the mountain forest at night and sleeping among the trees with a sense of security that I could never find indoors.

The hero of *The Wonderful Adventures of Nils* is transformed into a tiny creature who understands the language of birds and sets out on an exciting journey. I derived from the story a variety of sensuous pleasures. Firstly, living as I was in a deeply wooded area in Shikoku just as my ancestors had done long before, I found it gave me the conviction, at once innocent and unwavering, that this world and my way of life there offered me real freedom. Secondly, I felt sympathetic and identified with Nils, a naughty child who, while traveling across Sweden, collaborating with and fighting for the wild geese, grows into a different character, still innocent, yet full of confidence as well as modesty. But my greatest pleasure came from the words Nils uses when he at last comes home, and I felt purified and uplifted as if speaking with him when he says to his parents (in the French translation): "'Maman, Papa! Je suis grand, je suis de nouveau un homme!'" ("Mother, Father! I'm a big boy, I'm a human being again!")

I was fascinated by the phrase "je suis de nouveau un homme!" in particular.

As I grew up, I was to suffer continual hardships in different but related realms of life—in my family, in my relationship to Japanese society, and in my general way of living in the latter half of the twentieth century. I have survived by representing these sufferings of mine in the form of the novel. In that process I have found myself repeating, almost sighing, "je suis de nouveau un homme!" Speaking in this personal vein might seem perhaps inappropriate to this place and to this occasion. However, allow me to say that the fundamental method of my writing has always been to start from personal matters and then to link them with society, the state, and the world in general. I hope you will forgive me for talking about these personal things a little longer.

Half a century ago, while living in the depths of that forest, I read *The Wonderful Adventures of Nils* and felt within it two prophecies. One was that I might one day be able to understand the language of birds. The other was that I might one day fly off with my beloved wild geese—preferably to Scandinavia.

After I got married, the first child born to us was mentally handicapped. We named him Hikari, meaning "light" in Japanese. As a baby he responded only to the chirping of wild birds and never to human voices. One summer when he was six years old we were staying at our country cottage. He heard a pair of water rails calling from the lake beyond a grove, and with the voice of a commentator on a recording of birdsong he said: "Those are water rails." These were the first words my son had ever uttered. It was from then on that my wife and I began communicating verbally with him.

Hikari now works at a vocational training center for the handicapped, an institution based on ideas learned from Sweden. In the meantime he has been composing works of music. Birds were the things that occasioned and mediated his composition of human music. On my behalf Hikari has thus fulfilled the prophecy that I might one day understand the language of birds. I must also say that my life would have been impossible but for my wife with her abundant female strength and wisdom. She has been the very incarnation of Akka, the leader of Nils's wild geese. Together we have flown to Stockholm, and so the second of the prophecies has also, to my great delight, now been realized.

Yasunari Kawabata, the first Japanese writer to stand on this platform as a Nobel laureate for literature, delivered a lecture entitled "Japan, the Beautiful, and Myself." It was at once very beautiful and very vague. I use the word "vague" as an equivalent of the Japanese *aimaina*, itself a word open to several interpretations. The kind of vagueness that Kawabata deliberately adopted is implied even in the title of his lecture, with the use of the Japanese particle *no* (literally "of") linking "Myself" and "Beautiful Japan." One way of reading it is "myself as a part of beautiful Japan," the *no* indicating the relationship of the noun following it to the noun preceding it as one of possession or attachment. It can also he understood as "beautiful Japan and myself," the particle in this case linking the two nouns in apposition, which is how they appear in the English title of Kawabata's lecture as translated by Professor Edward Seidensticker, one of the most eminent American specialists in Japanese literature. His expert translation—"Japan, the beautiful, *and* myself"—is that of a *traduttore* (translator) and in no way a *traditore* (traitor).

Under that title Kawabata talked about a unique kind of mysticism which is found not only in Japanese thought but also more widely in Oriental philosophy. By "unique" I mean here a tendency toward Zen Buddhism. Even as a twentieth-century writer Kawabata identified his own mentality with that affirmed in poems written by medieval Zen monks. Most of these poems are concerned with the linguistic impossibility of telling the truth. Words, according to such poems, are confined within closed shells, and the reader cannot expect them ever to emerge, to get through to us. Instead, to understand or respond to Zen poems one must abandon oneself and willingly enter into the closed shells of those words.

Why did Kawabata boldly decide to read those very esoteric poems in Japanese before the audience in Stockholm? I look back almost with nostalgia on the straightforward courage he attained toward the end of his distinguished career which enabled him to make such a confession of his faith. Kawabata had been an artistic pilgrim for decades during which he produced a series of masterpieces. After those years of pilgrimage, it was only by talking of his fascination with poetry that baffled any attempt fully to understand it that he was able to talk about "Japan, the Beautiful, and Myself"; in other words, about the world he lived in and the literature he created.

It is noteworthy, too, that Kawabata concluded his lecture as follows:

My works have been described as works of emptiness, but it is not to be taken for the nihilism of the West. The spiritual foundation would seem to be quite different. Dōgen entitled his poem about the seasons "Innate Reality," and even as he sang of the beauty of the seasons he was deeply immersed in Zen.

Translation by Edward Seidensticker

Here also I detect a brave and straightforward self-assertion. Not only did Kawabata identify himself as belonging essentially to the tradition of Zen philosophy and aesthetic sensibility pervading the classical literature of the Orient, but he went out of his way to differentiate emptiness as an attribute of his works from the nihilism of the West. By doing so he was wholeheartedly addressing the coming generations of mankind in whom Alfred Nobel placed his hope and faith.

To tell the truth, however, instead of my compatriot who stood here twenty-six years ago, I feel more spiritual affinity with the Irish poet William Butler Yeats, who was awarded a Nobel Prize for Literature seventy-one years ago when he was about the same age as me. Of course I make no claim to being in the same rank as that poetic genius; I am merely a humble follower living in a country far removed from his. But as William Blake, whose work Yeats reevaluated and restored to the high place it holds in this century, once wrote: "Across Europe & Asia to China & Japan like lightnings."

During the last few years I have been engaged in writing a trilogy which I wish to be the culmination of my literary activities. So far the first two parts have been published, and I have recently finished writing the third and final part. It is entitled in Japanese *A Flaming Green Tree*. I am indebted for this title to a stanza from one of Yeats's important poems, "Vacillation":

> A tree there is that from its topmost bough
> Is half all glittering flame and half all green
> Abounding foliage moistened with the dew. . . .

"Vacillation," lines 11–13

My trilogy, in fact, is permeated by the influence of Yeats's work as a whole.

On the occasion of his winning the Nobel Prize the Irish Senate proposed a motion to congratulate him, which contained the following sentences:

> . . . the recognition which the nation has gained, as a prominent contributor to the world's culture, through his success . . . a race that hitherto had not been accepted into the comity of nations.
>
> Our civilisation will be assessed on the name of Senator Yeats. Coming at a time when there was a regular wave of destruction [and] hatred of beauty . . . it is a very happy and welcome thing. . . . [T]here will always be the danger that there may be a stampeding of people who are sufficiently removed from insanity in enthusiasm for destruction.

The Nobel Prize: Congratulations to Senator Yeats

Yeats is the writer in whose wake I would like to follow. I would like to do so for the sake of another nation that has now been "accepted into the comity of nations" not on account of literature or philosophy but for its technology in electronic engineering and its manufacture of motorcars. Also I would like to do so as a citizen of a nation that in the recent past was stampeded into "insanity in enthusiasm for destruction" both on its own soil and on that of neighboring nations.

As someone living in present-day Japan and sharing bitter memories of the past, I cannot join Kawabata in saying "Japan, the Beautiful, and Myself." A moment ago I referred to the "vagueness" of the title and content of his lecture. In the rest of my own lecture I would like to use the word "ambiguous" in accordance with the distinction made by the eminent British poet Kathleen Raine, who once said of Blake that he was not so much vague as ambiguous. It is only in terms of "Japan, the Ambiguous, and Myself" that I can talk about myself.

After a hundred and twenty years of modernization since the opening up of the country, contemporary Japan is split between two opposite poles of ambiguity. This ambiguity, which is so powerful and penetrating that it divides both the state and its people, and affects me as a writer like a deep-felt scar, is evident in various ways. The modernization of Japan was oriented toward learning from and imitating the West, yet the country is situated in Asia and has firmly maintained its traditional culture. The ambiguous orientation of Japan drove the country into the position of an invader in Asia, and resulted in its isolation from other Asian nations not only politically but also socially and culturally. And even in the West, to which its culture was supposedly quite open, it has long remained inscrutable or only partially understood.

In the history of modern Japanese literature, the writers most sincere in their awareness of a mission were the "postwar school" of writers who came onto the literary scene deeply wounded by the catastrophe of war yet full of hope for a rebirth. They tried with great pain to make up for the atrocities committed by Japanese military forces in Asia, as well as to bridge the profound gaps that existed not only between the developed nations of the West and Japan but also between African and Latin American countries and Japan. Only by doing so did they think that they could seek with some humility reconciliation with the rest of the world. It has always been my aspiration to cling to the very end of the line of that literary tradition inherited from those writers.

The present nation of Japan and its people cannot but be ambivalent. The Second World War came right in the middle of the process of modernization, a war that was brought about by the very aberration of that process itself. Defeat in this conflict fifty years ago created an opportunity for Japan, as the aggressor, to attempt a rebirth out of the great misery and suffering that the "postwar school" of writers depicted in their work. The moral props for a nation aspiring to this goal were the idea of democracy and the determination never to wage a war again—a resolve adopted not by innocent people but people stained by their own history of territorial invasion. Those moral props mattered also in regard to the victims of the nuclear weapons that were used for the first time in Hiroshima and Nagasaki, and for the survivors and their offspring affected by radioactivity (including tens of thousands of those whose mother tongue is Korean).

In recent years there have been criticisms leveled against Japan suggesting that it should offer more military support to the United Nations forces and thereby play a more active role in the keeping and restoration of peace in various parts of the world. Our hearts sink whenever we hear these comments. After the Second World War it was a categorical imperative for Japan to renounce war forever as a central article of the new constitution. The Japanese chose, after their painful experiences, the principle of permanent peace as the moral basis for their rebirth.

I believe that this principle can best be understood in the West, with its long tradition of tolerance for conscientious objection to military service. In Japan itself there have all along been attempts by some people to remove the article about renunciation of war from the constitution, and for this purpose they have taken every opportunity to make use of pressure from abroad. But to remove the principle of permanent peace would be an act of betrayal toward the people of Asia and the victims of the bombs dropped on Hiroshima and Nagasaki. It is not difficult for me as a writer to imagine the outcome.

The prewar Japanese constitution, which posited an absolute power transcending the principle of democracy, was sustained by a degree of support from the general public. Even though our new constitution is already half a century old, there is still a popular feeling of support for the old one, which lives on in some quarters as something more substantial than mere nostalgia. If Japan were to institutionalize a principle other than the one to which we have adhered for the last fifty years, the determination we made in the postwar ruins of our collapsed effort at modernization—that determination of ours to establish the concept of universal humanity—would come to nothing. Speaking as an ordinary individual, this is the specter that rises before me.

What I call Japan's "ambiguity" in this lecture is a kind of chronic disease that has been prevalent throughout the modern age. Japan's economic prosperity is not free from it either, accompanied as it is by all kinds of potential dangers in terms of the structure of the world economy and environmental conservation. The "ambiguity" in this respect seems to be accelerating. It may be more obvious to the critical eyes of the world at large than to us in our own country. At the nadir of postwar poverty we found a resilience to endure it, never losing our hope of recovery. It may sound curious to say so, but we seem to have no less resilience in enduring our anxiety about the future of the present tremendous prosperity. And a new situation now seems to be arising in which Japan's wealth assumes a growing share of the potential power of both production and consumption in Asia as a whole.

I am a writer who wishes to create serious works of literature distinct from those novels which are mere reflections of the vast consumer culture of Tokyo and the subcultures of the world at large. My profession—my "habit of being" (in Flannery O'Connor's words)—is that of the novelist who, as Auden described him, must:

> . . . , among the Just
> Be just, among the Filthy filthy too,
> And in his own weak person, if he can,
> Must suffer dully all the wrongs of Man.

"The Novelist," lines 12–14

What, as a writer, do I see as the sort of character we Japanese should seek to have? Among the words that George Orwell often used to describe the traits he admired in people was "decent," along with "humane" and "sane." This deceptively simple term stands in stark contrast to the "ambiguous" of my own characterization, a contrast matched by the wide discrepancy between how the Japanese actually appear to others and how they would like to appear to them.

Orwell, I hope, would not have objected to my using the word "decent" as a synonym of the French *humaniste,* because both terms have in common the qualities of tolerance and humanity. In the past, Japan too had some pioneers who tried hard to build up the "decent" or "humanistic" side of ourselves. One such person was the late Professor Kazuo Watanabe, a scholar of French Renaissance literature and thought. Surrounded by the insane patriotic ardor of Japan on the eve and in the throes of the Second World War, Watanabe had a lonely dream of grafting the humanistic view of man onto the traditional Japanese sense of beauty and sensitivity to nature, which fortunately had not been entirely eradicated. (I hasten to add that Watanabe's conception of beauty and nature was different from that of Kawabata as expressed in his "Japan, the Beautiful, and Myself.") The way Japan had tried to construct a modern state modeled on the West was a disaster. In ways different from yet partly corresponding to that process, Japanese intellectuals tried to bridge the gap between the West and their own country at its deepest level. It must have been an arduous task but also one that sometimes brimmed with satisfaction.

Watanabe's study of François Rabelais was one of the most distinguished scholarly achievements of the Japanese intellectual world. When, as a student in prewar Paris, he told his academic supervisor about his ambition to translate Rabelais into Japanese, the eminent, elderly French scholar answered the young man with the phrase: "L'entreprise inouïe de la traduction de l'intraduisible Rabelais" (the unprecedented enterprise of translating into Japanese [the] untranslatable Rabelais). Another French scholar answered with blunt astonishment: "Belle entreprise Pantagruélique" (an admirably Pantagruelian undertaking). In spite of all this, not only did Watanabe accomplish his ambitious project in circumstances of great poverty during the war and the American occupation, but he also did his best to transplant into the confused and disoriented Japan of that time the life and thought of those French humanists who were the forerunners, contemporaries, and followers of Rabelais.

In both my life and writing I have been a pupil of Professor Watanabe's. I was influenced by him in two crucial ways. One was in my method of writing novels. I learned concretely from his translation of Rabelais what Mikhail Bakhtin formulated as "the image system of grotesque realism or the culture of popular laughter": the importance of material and physical principles; the correspondence between the cosmic, social, and physical elements; the overlapping of death and a passion for rebirth; and the laughter that subverts established hierarchical relationships.

The image system made it possible to seek literary methods of attaining the universal for someone like me, born and brought up in a peripheral, marginal, off-center region of a peripheral, marginal, off-center country. Coming from such a background, I do not represent Asia as a new economic power but Asia marked by everlasting poverty and a tumultuous fertility. By sharing old, familiar, yet living metaphors I align myself with writers like Kim Chi Ha of Korea, or Chon I and Mu Jen, both of China. For me the brotherhood of world literature consists of such relationships in positive, concrete terms. I once took part in a hunger strike for the political freedom of a gifted Korean poet. I am now deeply worried about the fate of those talented Chinese novelists who have been deprived of their freedom since the Tiananmen Square incident.

Another way in which Professor Watanabe has influenced me is in his idea of humanism. I take it to be the quintessence of Europe as a living entity. It is an idea that is also explicit in Milan Kundera's definition of the novel. Based on his accurate reading of historical sources, Watanabe wrote critical biographies, with Rabelais at their center, of people from Erasmus to Sébastien Castellion, and of women connected with Henri IV from Queen Marguerite to Gabrielle d'Estrées. By doing so he hoped to teach the Japanese about humanism, about the importance of tolerance, about man's vulnerability to his preconceptions and to the machinery of his own making. His sincerity led him to quote the remark by the Danish philologist Kristoffer Nyrop: "Those who do not protest against war are accomplices of war." In his attempt to transplant into Japan humanism as the very basis of Western thought Watanabe was bravely venturing on both "l'entreprise inouïe" and the "belle entreprise Pantagruélique."

As someone influenced by his thought, I wish my work as a novelist to help both those who express themselves in words and their readers to overcome their own sufferings and the sufferings of their time, and to cure their souls of their wounds. I have said that I am split between the opposite poles of an ambiguity characteristic of the Japanese. The pain this involves I have tried to remove by means of literature. I can only hope and pray that my fellow Japanese will in time recover from it too.

If you will allow me to mention him again, my son Hikari was awakened by the voices of birds to the music of Bach and Mozart, eventually composing his own works. The little pieces that he first produced had a radiant freshness and delight in them; they seemed like dew glittering on leaves of grass. The word "innocence" is composed of *in* and *nocere*, or "not to hurt." Hikari's music was in this sense a natural effusion of the composer's own innocence.

As Hikari went on to produce more works, I began to hear in his music also "the voice of a crying and dark soul." Handicapped though he was, his hard-won "habit of being"—composing—acquired a growing maturity of technique and a deepening of conception. That in turn enabled him to discover in the depth of his heart a mass of dark sorrow which until then he had been unable to express.

"The voice of a crying and dark soul" is beautiful, and the act of setting it to music cures him of this sorrow, becoming an act of recovery. His music, moreover, has been widely accepted as one that cures and restores other listeners as well. In this I find grounds for believing in the wondrous healing power of art.

There is no firm proof of this belief of mine, but "weak person" though I am, with the aid of this unverifiable belief, I would like to "suffer dully all the wrongs" accumulated throughout this century as a result of the uncontrolled development of inhuman technology. As one with a peripheral, marginal, off-center existence in the world, I would like to continue to seek—with what I hope is a modest, decent, humanistic contribution of my own—ways to be of some use in the cure and reconciliation of mankind.

BIBLIOGRAPHY

GENERAL READINGS

Fiction

Birnbaum, Alfred, ed. *Monkey Brain Sushi: New Tastes in Japanese Fiction*. Tokyo: Kodansha International, 1991.

Birnbaum, Phyllis. *Modern Girls, Shining Stars, the Skies of Tokyo: Five Japanese Women*. New York: Columbia University Press, 1999.

Cohn, Joel R. *Studies in the Comic Spirit in Modern Japanese Fiction*. Harvard–Yenching Institute Monograph Series, no. 41. Cambridge, Mass.: Harvard University Press, 1998.

Colligan-Taylor, Karen. *The Emergence of Environmental Literature in Japan*. New York: Garland, 1990.

Copeland, Rebecca L. *Lost Leaves: Women Writers of Meiji Japan*. Honolulu: University of Hawaii Press, 2000.

Copeland, Rebecca L., and Esperanza Ramirez-Christensen, eds. *The Father–Daughter Plot: Japanese Literary Women and the Law of the Father*. Honolulu: University of Hawaii Press, 2001.

Cornyetz, Nina. *Dangerous Women, Deadly Words: Phallic Fantasy and Modernity in Three Japanese Writers*. Stanford, Calif.: Stanford University Press, 1999.

Fairbanks, Carol. *Japanese Women Fiction Writers: Their Culture and Society, 1890s to 1990s*. Landham, Md.: Scarecrow Press, 2002.

Fowler, Edward. *The Rhetoric of Confession: Shishōsetsu in Early Twentieth-Century Japanese Fiction*. Berkeley: University of California Press, 1988.

Fujii, James A. *Complicit Fictions: The Subject in Modern Japanese Prose Narrative.* Berkeley: University of California Press, 1993.

Gabriel, Philip. *Mad Wives and Island Dreams: Shimao Toshio and the Margins of Japanese Literature.* Honolulu: University of Hawaii Press, 1999.

Gatten, Aileen, and Anthony Hood Chambers, eds. *New Leaves: Studies and Translations of Japanese Literature in Honor of Edward Seidensticker.* Ann Arbor: Center for Japanese Studies, University of Michigan, 1993.

Gessel, Van C. *Three Modern Novelists: Sōseki, Tanizaki, Kawabata.* Tokyo: Kodansha International, 1993.

——, ed. *Japanese Fiction Writers, 1868–1945.* Vol. 180 of *Dictionary of Literary Biography.* Detroit: Gale Research, 1997.

——. *Japanese Fiction Writers Since World War II.* Vol. 182 of *Dictionary of Literary Biography.* Detroit: Gale Research, 1997.

——. *The Sting of Life: Four Contemporary Japanese Novelists.* New York: Columbia University Press, 1989.

Gessel, Van C., and Tomone Matsumoto, eds. *The Shōwa Anthology: Modern Japanese Short Stories.* Vol. 1, *1929–1961.* Tokyo: Kodansha International, 1985.

——. *The Shōwa Anthology: Modern Japanese Short Stories.* Vol. 2, *1961–1984.* Tokyo: Kodansha International, 1985

Goossen, Theodore W., ed. *The Oxford Book of Japanese Short Stories.* Oxford: Oxford University Press, 2002.

Heinrich, Amy Vladeck, ed. *Currents in Japanese Culture: Translations and Transformations.* New York: Columbia University Press, 1997.

Hibbett, Howard, ed. *Contemporary Japanese Literature: An Anthology of Fiction, Film, and Other Writing Since 1945.* New York: Cheng & Tsui, 2005.

Hijiya-Kirschnereit, Irmela. *Rituals of Self-Revelation: Shishōsetsu as Literary Genre and Sociocultural Phenomenon.* Cambridge, Mass.: Council on East Asian Studies, Harvard University, 1996.

——, ed. *Canon and Identity: Japanese Modernization Reconsidered: Transcultural Perspectives.* Berlin: Deutsches Institut für Japanstudien, 2000.

Hirata, Hosea. *Discourses of Seduction: History, Evil, Desire, and Modern Japanese Literature.* Harvard East Asian Monographs, no. 242. Cambridge, Mass.: Harvard University Press, 2004.

Japan PEN Club, comp. *Japanese Literature in European Languages: A Bibliography.* Tokyo: Japan PEN Club, 1961.

Karatani, Kōjin. *Origins of Modern Japanese Literature.* Translated and edited by Brett de Bary. Durham, N.C.: Duke University Press, 1993.

Katō, Shūichi. *A History of Japanese Literature.* Vol. 3, *The Modern Years.* Tokyo: Kodansha International, 1983.

Keene, Donald. *Appreciations of Japanese Culture.* Tokyo: Kodansha International, 1981.

——. *Dawn to the West: Japanese Literature of the Modern Era.* Vol. 1, *Fiction.* New York: Holt, Rinehart and Winston, 1984.

——. *Five Modern Japanese Novelists.* New York: Columbia University Press, 2003.

——. *Modern Japanese Literature: An Anthology.* New York: Grove Press, 1956.

——. *The Pleasures of Japanese Literature.* New York: Columbia University Press, 1988.

——. *Some Japanese Portraits*. Tokyo: Kodansha International, 1988.

Kleeman, Faye Yuan. *Under an Imperial Sun: Japanese Colonial Literature of Taiwan and the South*. Honolulu: University of Hawaii Press, 2003.

Kokusai bunka kaikan, ed. *Modern Japanese Literature in Translation: A Bibliography*. Compiled by the International House of Japan Library. Tokyo: Kodansha International, 1979.

Kornicki, Peter F. *The Reform of Fiction in Meiji Japan*. London: Ithaca Press, 1982.

Kuribayashi, Tomoko, with Mizuho Terasawa, eds. *The Outsider Within: Ten Essays on Modern Japanese Women Writers*. Lanham, Md.: University Press of America, 2002.

Lewell, John. *Modern Japanese Novelists: A Biographical Dictionary*. Tokyo: Kodansha International, 1993.

Lippit, Noriko Mizuta. *Reality and Fiction in Modern Japanese Literature*. White Plains, N.Y.: Sharpe, 1980.

Lippit, Noriko Mizuta, and Kyoko Iriye Selden, eds. *Japanese Women Writers: Twentieth Century Short Fiction*. Armonk, N.Y.: Sharpe, 1991.

Lippit, Seiji M. *Topographies of Japanese Modernism*. New York: Columbia University Press, 2002.

Mamola, Claire Zebroski. *Japanese Women Writers in English Translation: An Annotated Bibliography*. New York: Garland, 1989.

Matthew, Robert. *Japanese Science Fiction: A View of a Changing Society*. London: Routledge, 1989.

McDonald, Keiko I. *From Book to Screen: Modern Japanese Literature in Film*. Armonk, N.Y.: Sharpe, 2000.

Mertz, John Pierre. *Novel Japanese: Spaces of Nationhood in Early Meiji Narrative, 1870–88*. Ann Arbor: Center for Japanese Studies, University of Michigan, 2003.

Miller, J. Scott. *Adaptations of Western Literature in Meiji Japan*. New York: Palgrave, 2001.

Mishima, Yukio, and Geoffrey Bownas, eds. *New Writing in Japan*. Harmondsworth: Penguin, 1972.

Mitsios, Helen, ed. *New Japanese Voices: The Best Contemporary Fiction from Japan*. New York: Atlantic Monthly Press, 1991.

Miyoshi, Masao. *Accomplices of Silence: The Modern Japanese Novel*. Berkeley: University of California Press, 1974.

Molasky, Michael S. *The American Occupation of Japan and Okinawa: Literature and Memory*. London: Routledge, 1999.

Mortimer, Maya. *Meeting the Sensei: The Role of the Master in Shirakaba Writers*. Leiden: Brill, 2000.

Morton, Leith, ed. *Seven Stories of Modern Japan*. Sydney: Wild Peony, 1992.

Mulhern, Chieko I., ed. *Japanese Women Writers: A Bio-Critical Sourcebook*. Westport, Conn.: Greenwood Press, 1994.

Murakami, Fuminobu. *Ideology and Narrative in Modern Japanese Literature*. Assen: Van Gorcum, 1996.

Napier, Susan J. *Escape from the Wasteland: Romanticism and Realism in the Fiction of Mishima Yukio and Ōe Kenzaburō*. Harvard East Asian Monographs, no. 33. Cambridge, Mass.: Harvard University Press, 1991.

——. *The Fantastic in Modern Japanese Literature: The Subversion of Modernity*. London: Routledge, 1996.

Ōe Kenzaburō, ed. *The Crazy Iris (Nan to mo shirenai mirai ni) and Other Stories of the Atomic Aftermath.* New York: Grove Press, 1985.

Petersen, Gwenn Boardman. *The Moon in the Water: Understanding Tanizaki, Kawabata, and Mishima.* Honolulu: University of Hawaii Press, 1979.

Pollack, David. *Reading Against Culture: Ideology and Narrative in the Japanese Novel.* Ithaca, N.Y.: Cornell University Press, 1992.

Powell, Irina. *Writers and Society in Modern Japan.* London: Macmillan, 1983.

Prindle, Tamae K. *Made in Japan and Other Japanese Business Novels.* Armonk, N.Y.: Sharpe, 1989.

Rimer, J. Thomas. *Modern Japanese Fiction and Its Traditions: An Introduction.* Princeton, N.J.: Princeton University Press, 1978.

——. *Pilgrimages: Aspects of Japanese Literature and Culture.* Honolulu: University of Hawaii Press, 1988.

——. *A Reader's Guide to Japanese Literature.* 2nd ed. Tokyo: Kodansha International, 1999.

Rimer, J. Thomas, and Van C. Gessel, eds. *Modern Japanese Literature.* Vol. 1, *From Restoration to Occupation, 1868–1945.* New York: Columbia University Press, 2005.

Richie, Donald. *Japanese Literature Reviewed.* Tokyo: ICG Muse, 2003.

Rubin, Jay. *Injurious to Public Morals: Writers and the Meiji State.* Seattle: University of Washington Press, 1984.

——, ed. *Modern Japanese Writers.* New York: Scribner, 2001.

Sakaki, Atsuko. *Recontextualizing Texts: Narrative Performance in Modern Japanese Fiction.* Harvard East Asian Monographs, no. 180. Cambridge, Mass.: Harvard University Press, 1999.

Sas, Miryam. *Fault Lines: Cultural Memory and Japanese Surrealism.* Stanford, Calif.: Stanford University Press, 1999.

Schalow, Paul Gordon, and Janet A. Walker, eds. *The Woman's Hand: Gender and Theory in Japanese Women's Writing.* Stanford, Calif.: Stanford University Press, 1996.

Schierbeck, Sachiko Shibata. *Japanese Women Novelists in the 20th Century: 104 Biographies, 1900–1993.* Copenhagen: University of Copenhagen, Museum Tusculanum Press, 1994.

Schlant, Ernestine, and J. Thomas Rimer, eds. *Legacies and Ambiguities: Postwar Fiction and Culture in West Germany and Japan.* Washington, D.C.: Woodrow Wilson Center Press, 1991.

Shea, George Tyson. *Leftwing Literature in Japan: A Brief History of the Proletarian Literary Movement.* Tokyo: Hosei University Press, 1964.

Slaymaker, Douglas. *Body in Postwar Japanese Fiction.* London: Routledge, 2004.

Snyder, Stephen, and Philip Gabriel, eds. *Ōe and Beyond: Fiction in Contemporary Japan.* Honolulu: University of Hawaii Press, 1999.

Stewart, Frank, and Leza Lowitz, eds. *Silence to Light: Japan and the Shadows of War.* Honolulu: University of Hawaii Press, 2001.

Suzuki, Tomi. *Narrating the Self: Fictions of Japanese Modernity.* Stanford, Calif.: Stanford University Press, 1996.

Swann, Thomas E., and Kinya Tsuruta, eds. *Approaches to the Modern Japanese Short Story.* Tokyo: Waseda University Press, 1982.

Tachibana, Reiko. *Narrative as Counter-Memory: A Half-Century of Postwar Writing in Germany and Japan*. Albany: State University of New York Press, 1998.

Takamizawa Junko. *My Brother Hideo Kobayashi*. Translated by James Wada and edited, with an introduction, by Leith Morton. Honolulu: University of Hawaii Press, 2001.

Tanaka, Yukiko. *Women Writers of Meiji and Taishō Japan: Their Lives, Works and Critical Reception*. Jefferson, N.C.: McFarland, 2000.

Treat, John Whittier. *Writing Ground Zero: Japanese Literature and the Atomic Bomb*. Chicago: University of Chicago Press, 1995.

Tsuruta, Kinya, and Thomas E. Swann, eds. *Approaches to the Modern Japanese Novel*. Tokyo: Sophia University Press, 1976.

Ueda, Makoto. *Modern Japanese Writers and the Nature of Literature*. Stanford, Calif.: Stanford University Press, 1976.

——, ed. *The Mother of Dreams and Other Short Stories: Portrayals of Women in Modern Japanese Fiction*. Tokyo: Kodansha International, 1986.

Vernon, Victoria V. *Daughters of the Moon: Wish, Will, and Social Constraint in the Fiction of Japanese Women*. Berkeley, Calif.: Institute of East Asian Studies, 1988.

Walker, Janet A. *The Japanese Novel of the Meiji Period and the Ideal of Individualism*. Princeton, N.J.: Princeton University Press, 1979.

Washburn, Dennis C. *The Dilemma of the Modern in Japanese Fiction*. New Haven, Conn.: Yale University Press, 1995.

Washburn, Dennis C., and Alan Tansman, eds. *Studies in Modern Japanese Literature: Essays and Translations in Honor of Edwin McClellan*. Ann Arbor: Center for Japanese Studies, University of Michigan, 1997.

Yamanouchi, Hisaaki. *The Search for Authenticity in Modern Japanese Literature*. Cambridge: Cambridge University Press, 1978.

Drama and Poetry

Beichman, Janine. *Embracing the Firebird: Yosano Akiko and the Birth of the Female Voice in Modern Japanese Poetry*. Honolulu: University of Hawaii Press, 2002.

Downer, Leslie. *Madame Sadayakko: The Geisha Who Bewitched the West*. New York: Gotham Books, 2003.

Fitzimmons, Thomas, ed., with Yoshimasu Gōzō. *The New Poetry of Japan: The 70s and 80s*. Translated by Christopher Drake et al. Santa Fe: Katydid Books, 1993.

Goodman, David G. *Japanese Drama and Culture in the 1960s: The Return of the Gods*. Armonk, N.Y.: Sharpe, 1988.

——, trans. *After Apocalypse: Four Japanese Plays of Hiroshima and Nagasaki*. New York: Columbia University Press, 1986.

Harada, Hiroko. *Aspects of Post-War German and Japanese Drama, 1945–1970: Reflections on War, Guilt, and Responsibility*. Lewiston, N.Y.: Mellen, 2000.

Havens, Thomas R. H. *Artist and Patron in Postwar Japan: Dance, Music, Theater, and the Visual Arts, 1955–1980*. Princeton, N.J.: Princeton University Press, 1982.

Heinrich, Amy Vladeck. *Fragments of Rainbows: The Life and Poetry of Saitō Mokichi, 1882–1953*. New York: Columbia University Press, 1983.

Japan Playwrights Association, ed. *Half a Century of Japanese Theater*. Tokyo: Kinokuniya, 1999–2005. [Ongoing series of translations of plays from 1950 to 2000]

Japan Society and Japan Foundation. *Japanese Theater in the World*. New York: Japan Society, 1997.

Keene, Donald. *Dawn to the West: Japanese Literature of the Modern Era*. Vol. 2, *Poetry, Drama, Criticism*. New York: Holt, Rinehart and Winston, 1984.

Klein, Susan Blakely. *Ankoku Butō: The Premodern and Postmodern Influences on the Dance of Utter Darkness*. Cornell University East Asia Papers, no. 49. Ithaca, N.Y.: East Asia Program, Cornell University, 1988.

Lueders, Edward, and Naoshi Koriyama, trans. *Like Underground Water: The Poetry of Mid-Twentieth Century Japan*. Port Townsend, Wash.: Copper Canyon Press, 1995.

Morton, Leith. *Modernism in Practice: An Introduction to Postwar Japanese Poetry*. Honolulu: University of Hawaii Press, 2004.

——, ed. *An Anthology of Contemporary Japanese Poetry*. New York: Garland, 1993.

Ooka, Makoto, and Thomas Fitzsimmons, eds. *A Play of Mirrors: Eight Major Poets of Modern Japan*. Rochester, Mich.: Katydid Books, 1987.

Ortolani, Benito. *The Japanese Theatre: From Shamanistic Ritual to Contemporary Pluralism*. Rev. ed. Princeton, N.J.: Princeton University Press, 1995.

Poulton, M. Cody. *Spirits of Another Sort: The Plays of Izumi Kyōka*. Ann Arbor: Center for Japanese Studies, University of Michigan, 2001.

Rimer, J. Thomas. *Toward a Modern Japanese Theatre: Kishida Kunio*. Princeton, N.J.: Princeton University Press, 1974.

Rolf, Robert, and John Gillespie, eds. and trans. *Alternative Japanese Drama: Ten Plays*. Honolulu: University of Hawaii Press, 1992.

Sato, Hiroaki, and Burton Watson, trans. and eds. *From the Country of Eight Islands: An Anthology of Japanese Poetry*. Seattle: University of Washington Press, 1981.

Scholz-Cionca, Stanca, and Samuel L. Leiter, eds. *Japanese Theatre and the International Stage*. Brill's Japanese Studies Library, vol. 12. Leiden: Brill, 2001.

Senda, Akihiko. *The Voyage of Contemporary Japanese Theatre*. Translated by J. Thomas Rimer. Honolulu: University of Hawaii Press, 1997.

Shields, Nancy K. *Fake Fish: The Theater of Kobo Abe*. New York: Weatherhill, 1996.

Suzuki, Tadashi. *The Way of Acting: The Theatre Writings of Tadashi Suzuki*. Translated by J. Thomas Rimer. New York: Theatre Communications Group, 1986.

Takaya, Ted, trans. *Modern Japanese Drama: An Anthology*. New York: Columbia University Press, 1979.

Ueda, Makoto. *Modern Japanese Poets and the Nature of Literature*. Stanford, Calif.: Stanford University Press, 1983.

Wilson, Graeme, ed. *Three Contemporary Japanese Poets: Anzai Hitoshi, Shiraishi Kazuko, Tanikawa Shuntarō*. London: London Magazine Editions, 1972.

5. EARLY POSTWAR LITERATURE, 1945 TO 1970

Fiction

Abe Kōbō

The Ark Sakura [*Hakobune Sakura maru*]. Translated by Juliet Winters Carpenter. New York: Knopf, 1988.

Beyond the Curve [*Kābu no mukō*] *and Other Stories*. Translated by Juliet Winters Carpenter. Tokyo: Kodansha International, 1990.

The Box Man [*Hako otoko*]. Translated by E. Dale Saunders. New York: Knopf, 1974.

The Face of Another [*Tanin no kao*]. Translated by E. Dale Saunders. New York: Knopf, 1966.

Iles, Timothy. *Abe Kōbō: An Exploration of His Prose, Drama, and Theatre*. Fucecchio: European Press Academic Publishing, 2000.

Inter Ice Age 4 [*Daiyon kanpyōki*]. Translated by E. Dale Saunders. New York: Knopf, 1970.

Kangaroo Notebook [*Kangaru nōto*]. Translated by Maryellen Toman Mori. New York: Knopf, 1996.

The Ruined Map [*Moetsukita chizu*]. Translated by E. Dale Saunders. New York: Knopf, 1969.

Secret Rendezvous [*Mikkai*]. Translated by Juliet Winters Carpenter. New York: Knopf, 1979.

Woman in the Dunes [*Suna no onna*]. Translated by E. Dale Saunders. New York: Knopf, 1964.

Agawa Hiroyuki

Citadel in Spring [*Haru no shiro*]: *A Novel of Youth Spent at War*. Translated by Lawrence Rogers. Tokyo: Kodansha International, 1990.

Ariyoshi Sawako

The Doctor's Wife [*Hanaoka seishū no tsuma*]. Translated by Wakako Hironaka and Ann Siller Konstant. Tokyo: Kodansha International, 1978.

Kabuki Dancer [*Izumo no Okuni*]. Translated by James. R. Brandon. Tokyo: Kodansha International, 1994.

The River Ki [*Kinokawa*]. Translated by Mildred Tahara. Tokyo: Kodansha International, 1980.

The Twilight Years [*Kōkotsu no hito*]. Translated by Mildred Tahara. Tokyo: Kodansha International, 1987.

Enchi Fumiko

Masks [*Onnamen*]. Translated by Juliet Winters Carpenter. New York: Knopf, 1983.

The Waiting Years [*Onnazaka*]. Translated by John Bester. Tokyo: Kodansha International, 1971.

Endō Shūsaku

Deep River [*Dīpu ribā*]. Translated by Van C. Gessel. New York: New Directions, 1994.

Five by Endo: Stories by Shusaku Endo. Translated by Van C. Gessel. New York: New Directions, 2000.

Foreign Studies [*Ryūgaku*]. Translated by Mark Williams. London: Peter Owen, 1989.

The Girl I Left Behind [*Watashi ga suteta onna*]. Translated by Mark Williams. London: Peter Owen, 1994.

Samurai [*Samurai*]. Translated by Van C. Gessel. New York: Harper & Row, 1982.

Scandal [*Sukyandaru*]. Translated by Van C. Gessel. New York: Dodd, Mead, 1988.

The Sea and Poison [*Umi to dokuyaku*]. Translated by Michael Gallagher. London: Peter Owen, 1972.

Silence [*Chinmoku*]. Translated by William Johnston. Tokyo: Tuttle, 1969.

Stained Glass Elegies: Stories by Shusaku Endo. Translated by Van C. Gessel. New York: Dodd, Mead, 1985.

Volcano [*Kazan*]. Translated by Richard A. Schuchert. London: Peter Owen, 1978.

When I Whistle [*Kuchibue o fuku toki*]. Translated by Van C. Gessel. New York: Taplinger, 1979.

Williams, Mark. *Endō Shūsaku: A Literature of Reconciliation*. London: Routledge, 1999.

Wonderful Fool [*Obakasan*]. Translated by Francis Mathy. London: Peter Owen, 1974.

Hayashi Fumiko

Ericson, Joan. *Be a Woman: Hayashi Fumiko and Modern Japanese Women's Literature*. Honolulu: University of Hawaii Press, 1997.

Fessler, Susanna. *Wandering Heart: The Work and Method of Hayashi Fumiko*. Albany: State University of New York Press, 1998.

Floating Clouds [*Ukigumo*]. Translated by Lane Dunlop. New York: Columbia University Press, 2006.

I Saw a Pale Horse [*Aouma o mitari*] *and Selected Poems from Diary of a Vagabond* [*Hōrōki*]. Translated by Janice Brown. Ithaca, N.Y.: East Asia Program, Cornell University, 1997.

Hotta Yoshie

Judgement [*Shinpan*]. Translated by Nobuko Tsukui. Osaka: International Research Institute, Kansai Gaidai University, 1963.

Ibuse Masuji

Black Rain [*Kuroi ame*]. Translated by John Bester. Tokyo: Kodansha International, 1969.

Castaways [*John Manjirō hōryōki*]: *Two Short Novels*. Translated by Anthony Liman and David Aylward. Tokyo: Kodansha International, 1987.

Liman, Anthony V. *A Critical Study of the Literary Style of Ibuse Masuji: As Sensitive as Water*. Lewiston, N.Y.: Mellen, 1992.

Salamander [*Sanshōuo*] *and Other Stories*. Translated by John Bester. Tokyo: Kodansha International, 1981.

Treat, John Whittier. *Pools of Water, Pools of Fire: The Literature of Ibuse Masuji*. Seattle: University of Washington Press, 1988.

Waves [*Sazanami gunki*]. Translated by David Aylward and Anthony Liman. Tokyo: Kodansha International, 1986.

Inoue Yasushi

Chronicle of My Mother [*Waga haha no ki*]. Translated by Jean Oda Moy. Tokyo: Kodansha International, 1982.

The Counterfeiter [*Aru gisakka no shōgai*] *and Other Stories*. Translated by Leon Picon. Rutland, Vt.: Tuttle, 1965.

The Hunting Gun [*Ryōjū*]. Translated by Sadamichi Yokō and Sanford Goldstein. Rutland, Vt.: Tuttle, 1961.

Journey Through Samarkand [*Seiiki monogatari*]. Translated by Gyō Furuta and Gordon Sager. Tokyo: Kodansha International, 1971.

Lou-lan [*Rōran*] *and Other Stories*. Translated by James T. Araki and Edward Seiden-sticker. Tokyo: Kodansha International, 1979.

The Roof Tile of Tempyō [*Tenpyō no iraka*]. Translated by James T. Araki. Tokyo: University of Tokyo Press, 1975.

Tun-Huang [*Tonkō*]. Translated by Jean Oda Moy. Tokyo: Kodansha International, 1978.

Wind and Waves [*Fūtō*]. Translated by James T. Araki. Honolulu: University of Hawaii Press, 1989.

Ishikawa Jun

The Bodhisattva [*Fugen*]. Translated by William J. Tyler. New York: Columbia University Press, 1989.

The Legend of Gold [*Ōgon densetsu*] *and Other Stories*. Translated by William J. Tyler. Honolulu: University of Hawaii Press, 1998.

Kita Morio

Dr. Manbo at Sea [*Dokutoru Manbō kōkaiki*]. Translated by Ralph F. McCarthy. Tokyo: Kodansha International, 1987.

Ghosts [*Yūrei*]. Translated by Dennis Keene. Tokyo: Kodansha International, 1991.

The House of Nire [*Nire ke no hitobito*]. Translated by Dennis Keene. 2 vols. Tokyo: Kodansha International, 1984, 1985.

Kurahashi Yumiko

The Adventures of Sumiyakist Q [*Sumiyakisuto Q no bōken*]. Translated by Dennis Keene. St. Lucia: University of Queensland Press, 1979.

The Woman with the Flying Head [*Kubi o tonda onna*] *and Other Stories*. Translated by Atsuko Sakaki. Armonk, N.Y.: Sharpe, 1998.

Matsumoto Seichō

Inspector Imanishi Investigates [*Suna no utsuwa*]. Translated by Beth Cary. New York: Soho Press, 1989.

Points and Lines [*Ten to sen*]. Translated by Mariko Yamamoto and Paul C. Blum. Tokyo: Kodansha International, 1970.

The Voice [*Koe*] *and Other Stories*. Translated by Adam Kabat. Tokyo: Kodansha International, 1989.

Mishima Yukio

Acts of Worship [*Mikumano mōde*]: *Seven Stories*. Translated by John Bester. Tokyo: Kodansha International, 1989.

After the Banquet [*Utage no ato*]. Translated by Donald Keene. New York: Knopf, 1963.

Confessions of a Mask [*Kamen no kokuhaku*]. Translated by Meredith Weatherby. New York: New Directions, 1958.

Death in Midsummer [*Manatsu no shi*] *and Other Stories*. Translated by Edward Seidensticker. New York: New Directions, 1966.

The Decay of the Angel [*Tennin gosui*]. Translated by Edward Seidensticker. New York: Knopf, 1974.

Forbidden Colors [*Kinjiki*]. Translated by Alfred H. Marks. New York: Knopf, 1968.

Nathan, John. *Mishima: A Biography*. Boston: Little, Brown, 1974.

Runaway Horses [*Honba*]. Translated by Michael Gallagher. New York: Knopf, 1973.

The Sailor Who Fell from Grace with the Sea [*Gogo no eikō*]. Translated by John Nathan. New York: Knopf, 1965.

Scott-Stokes, Henry. *The Life and Death of Yukio Mishima*. New York: Farrar, Straus & Giroux, 1974.

Silk and Insight [*Kinu to meisatsu*]. Translated by Hiroaki Sato. Armonk, N.Y.: Sharpe, 1998.

The Sound of Waves [*Shiosai*]. Translated by Meredith Weatherby. New York: Knopf, 1956.

Spring Snow [*Haru no yuki*]. Translated by Michael Gallagher. New York: Knopf, 1972.

Starrs, Roy. *Deadly Dialectics: Sex, Violence, and Nihilism in the World of Yukio Mishima*. Honolulu: University of Hawaii Press, 1994.

Sun and Steel [*Taiyō to tetsu*]. Translated by John Bester. Tokyo: Kodansha International, 1970.

The Temple of Dawn [*Akatsuki no tera*]. Translated by E. Dale Saunders and Cecilia Segawa Seigle. New York: Knopf, 1973.

The Temple of the Golden Pavilion [*Kinkakuji*]. Translated by Ivan Morris. New York: Knopf, 1959.

Thirst for Love [*Ai no kawaki*]. Translated by Alfred A. Marks. New York: Knopf, 1969.

The Way of the Samurai [*Hagakure nyūmon*]. Translated by Kathryn N. Sparling. New York: Basic Books, 1977.

Wolfe, Peter. *Yukio Mishima*. New York: Continuum, 1989.

Yourcenar, Marguerite. *Mishima: A Vision of the Void*. Translated by Alberto Maguel, in collaboration with the author. New York: Farrar, Straus & Giroux, 1986.

Noma Hiroshi

Dark Pictures [*Kurai e*] *and Other Stories*. Translated by James Raeside. Ann Arbor: Center for Japanese Studies, University of Michigan, 2000.

Zone of Emptiness [*Shinkūchitai*]. Translated from French by Bernard Frechtman. Cleveland: World, 1956.

Ozaki Kazuo

Rosy Glasses [*Nonki megane*] *and Other Stories*. Translated by Robert Epp. Ashford: Norbury, 1988.

Shiba Ryōtarō

Drunk as a Lord [Yotte sōrō!]: Samurai Stories. Translated by Eileen Kato. Tokyo: Kodansha International, 2001.
Kukai the Universal [Kūkai no fūkei]: Scenes from His Life. Translated by Akiko Takemoto. New York: IGC Muse, 2003.
The Last Shogun [Saigo no shōgun]: The Life of Tokugawa Yoshinbobu. Translated by Juliet Winters Carpenter. Tokyo: Kodansha International, 1998.

Shiina Rinzō

The Go-Between [Baishaku nin] and Other Stories. Translated by Noah S. Brannen. Valley Forge, Pa.: Judson Press, 1970.

Shōnō Junzō

Evening Clouds [Yūbe no kumo]. Translated by Wayne P. Lammers. Berkeley, Calif.: Stone Bridge Press, 2000.
Still Life [Seibutsu] and Other Stories. Translated by Wayne P. Lammers. Berkeley, Calif.: Stone Bridge Press, 1992.

Takeda Taijun

This Outcast Generation [Mamushi no sue] and Luminous Moss [Hikari goke]. Translated by Yasuburo Shibuya and Sanford Goldstein. Rutland, Vt.: Tuttle, 1967.

Yasuoka Shōtarō

A View by the Sea [Umibe no kōkei]. Translated by Karen Wigen Lewis. New York: Columbia University Press, 1984.

Yoshiyuki Junnosuke

The Dark Room [Anshitsu]. Translated by John Bester. Tokyo: Kodansha International, 1975.

Poetry

Saitō Fumi. *White Letter Poems.* Translated by Hatsue Kasamura and Jane Reichhold. Gualala, Calif.: AHA Books, 1998.
Shiraishi Kazuko. *Let Those Appear [Arawarere monotachi o shite].* Translated by Samuel Grolmes and Yumiko Tsumura. New York: New Directions, 2002.
———. *Seasons of Sacred Lust [Seinaru inja no kisetsu]: The Selected Poems of Kazuko Shiraishi.* Edited, with an introduction, by Kenneth Rexroth. Translated by Ikuko Atsumi et al. New York: New Directions, 1978.
Tamura Ryūichi. *Dead Languages: Selected Poems, 1946–1984.* Translated by Christopher Drake. Rochester, Mich.: Katydid Books, 1984.
———. *Poetry of Ryuichi Tamura.* Translated by Samuel Grolmes and Yumiko Tsumura. Palo Alto, Calif.: CCC Books, 1998.

Tanikawa Shuntarō. *At Midnight in the Kitchen I Just Wanted to Talk to You: Poems by Shuntaro Tanikawa.* Translated by William I. Elliott and Kazuo Kawamura. Portland, Ore.: Prescott Street Press, 1980.

——. *On Love.* Translated by William I. Elliott and Kazuo Kawamura. Santa Fe, N.M.: Katydid Books, 2003.

——. *62 Sonnets and Definitions: Poems and Prosepoems.* Translated by William I. Elliott and Kazuo Kawamura. Santa Fe, N.M.: Katydid Books, 1992.

——. *With Silence My Companion.* Translated by William I. Elliott and Kazuo Kawamura. Portland, Ore.: Prescott Street Press, 1975.

Yoshioka Minoru. *Celebration in Darkness: Selected Poems of Yoshioka Minoru.* Translated by Onuma Tadayoshi. Rochester, Mich.: Katydid Books, 1985.

——. *Lilac Garden: Poems of Yoshioka Minoru.* Translated by Hiroaki Sato. Chicago: Chicago Review Press, 1976.

Drama

Abe Kōbō

Friends [*Tomodachi*]. Translated by Donald Keene. New York: Grove Press, 1969.

The Man Who Turned into a Stick [*Bōni natta otoko*]. Translated by Donald Keene. Tokyo: University of Tokyo Press, 1975.

Shields, Nancy K. *Fake Fish: The Theatre of Kobo Abe.* New York: Weatherhill, 1996.

Three Plays by Kōbō Abe. Translated by Donald Keene. New York: Columbia University Press, 1993.

Endō Shūsaku

The Golden Country [*Ōgon no kuni*]. Translated by Francis Mathy. Rutland, Vt.: Tuttle, 1970.

Kinoshita Junji

Between God and Man: A Judgment on War Crimes, a Play in Two Parts [*Kami to hito tono aida*]. Translated by Eric C. Gangloff. Tokyo: University of Tokyo Press, 1979.

Requiem on the Great Meridian [*Shigosen no matsuri*] *and Selected Essays.* Translated by Brian Powell and Jason Daniel. Tokyo: Nan'un-do, 2000.

Mishima Yukio

Five Modern Nō Plays [*Kindai nōgaku shū*]. Translated by Donald Keene. New York: Knopf, 1957.

Madame de Sade [*Sado kōshaku fujin*]. Translated by Donald Keene. New York: Grove Press, 1967.

My Friend Hitler [*Wagatomo Hittora*] *and Other Plays of Mishima Yukio.* Translated by Hiroaki Sato. New York: Columbia University Press, 2002.

6. TOWARD A CONTEMPORARY LITERATURE, 1971 TO THE PRESENT

Fiction

Furui Yoshikichi

Child of Darkness [*Yōko*] *and Other Stories.* Translated by Donna George Storey. Ann Arbor: Center for Japanese Studies, University of Michigan, 1997.

Ravine [*Tani*] *and Other Stories.* Translated by Meredith McKinney. Berkeley, Calif.: Stone Bridge Press, 1997.

Hoshi Shin'ichi

The Spiteful Planet and Other Stories. Translated by Bernard Susser and Tomoyoshi Genkawa. Tokyo: Japan Times, 1978.

Tales of Japanese Science Fiction and Fantasy. Translated by Robert Matthew. Brisbane: University of Queensland Press, 1981.

Ikezawa Natsuki

A Burden of Flowers [*Hana o hakobu imoto*]. Translated by Alfred Birnbaum. Tokyo: Kodansha International, 2002.

Still Lives [*Sutiru raifu*]. Translated by Dennis Keene. Tokyo: Kodansha International, 1997.

Kaikō Takeshi

Darkness in Summer [*Natsu no yami*]. Translated by Cecilia Segawa Seigle. New York: Knopf, 1973.

Into a Black Sun [*Kagayakeru yami*]. Translated by Cecilia Segawa Seigle. Tokyo: Kodansha International, 1980.

Panic [*Panikku*] *and Runaway* [*Rubōki*]: *Two Stories by Takeishi Kaiko.* Translated by Charles Dunn. Tokyo: University of Tokyo Press, 1977.

Maruya Saiichi

Grass for My Pillow [*Sasamakura*]. Translated by Dennis Keene. New York: Columbia University Press, 2002.

A Mature Woman [*Onna-zakari*]. Translated by Dennis Keene. Tokyo: Kodansha International, 1987.

Rain in the Wind [*Yokoshigure*]. Translated by Dennis Keene. Tokyo: Kodansha International, 1990.

Singular Rebellion [*Tatta hitori no hanran*]. Translated by Dennis Keene. Tokyo: Kodansha International, 1986.

Murakami Haruki

After the Quake [*Kami no kodomo-tachi wa mina odoru*]: *Stories.* Translated by Jay Rubin. New York: Knopf, 2002.

The Elephant Vanishes [*Zō no shōmetsu*]: *Stories by Murakami Haruki*. Translated by Alfred Birnbaum and Jay Rubin. New York: Knopf, 1993.

Hard-Boiled Wonderland and the End of the World [*Sekai no owari to hādoboirudowandārando*]. Translated by Alfred Birnbaum. Tokyo: Kodansha International, 1991.

Kafka on the Shore [*Umibe no Kafuka*]. Translated by Philip Gabriel. New York: Knopf, 2005.

Norwegian Wood [*Noruwei no mori*]. Translated by Alfred Birnbaum. Tokyo: Kodansha International, 1989.

Norwegian Wood [*Noruwei no mori*]. Translated by Jay Rubin. New York: Vintage, 2000.

Rubin, Jay. *Haruki Murakami and the Music of Words*. London: Harvill Press, 2002.

South of the Border, West of the Sun [*Kokkyo no minami, taiyō no nishi*]. Translated by Philip Gabriel. New York: Knopf, 1999.

Sputnik Sweetheart [*Supūtoniku no koibito*]. Translated by Philip Gabriel. New York: Knopf, 2001.

Strecher, Matthew Carl. *Dances with Sheep: The Quest for Identity in the Fiction of Murakami Haruki*. Ann Arbor: Center for Japanese Studies, University of Michigan, 2002.

Underground [*Andāguraundo*]. Translated by Alfred Birnbaum and Philip Gabriel. New York: Vintage, 2001.

A Wild Sheep Chase [*Hitsuji o meguru bōken*]. Translated by Alfred Birnbaum. Tokyo: Kodansha International, 1989.

The Wind-up Bird Chronicle [*Nejimaki-dori kuronikuru*]. Translated by Jay Rubin. New York: Knopf, 1997.

Nakagami Kenji

The Cape [*Misaki*] *and Other Stories from the Japanese Ghetto*. Translated by Eve Zimmerman. Berkeley, Calif.: Stone Bridge Press, 1999.

Snakelust [*Jain*] *and Other Stories*. Translated by Andrew Rankin. Tokyo: Kodansha International, 1998.

Ōe Kenzaburō

An Echo of Heaven [*Jinsei no shinseki*]. Translated by Margaret Mitsutani. Tokyo: Kodansha International, 2000.

A Healing Family [*Kaifuku suru kazoku*]. Translated by Stephen Snyder. Tokyo: Kodansha International, 1996.

Hiroshima Notes [*Hiroshima nōto*]. Translated by David L. Swain and Toshi Yonezawa. New York: Marion Boyars, 1995.

Japan, the Ambiguous, and Myself: The Nobel Prize Speech and Other Lectures. Tokyo: Kodansha International, 1995.

Nip the Buds, Shoot the Kids [*Memushiri kouchi*]. Translated by Paul St. John Mackintosh and Maki Sugiyama. New York: Marion Boyars, 1995.

On Politics and Literature: Two Lectures. Berkeley, Calif.: Doreen B. Townsend Center for the Humanities, 1999.

A Personal Matter [*Kojinteki na taiken*]. Translated by John Nathan. New York: Grove Press, 1969.

The Pinch Runner Memorandum [*Pinchi rannā chōsho*]. Translated by Michiko N. Wilson and Michael K. Wilson. Armonk, N.Y.: Sharpe, 1994.

A Quiet Life [*Shizuka na seikatsu*]. Translated by Kunioki Yanagishita, with William Wetherall. New York: Grove Press, 1996.

Rouse Up, O Young Men of the New Age [*Atarashii hito yo mezameyo*]. Translated by John Nathan. New York: Grove Press, 2002.

Seventeen [*Sebuteen*]: *Two Novels*. Translated by Luk Van Haute. New York: Blue Moon Books, 1996.

The Silent Cry [*Man'en gannen no futtobōru*]. Translated by John Bester. Tokyo: Kodansha International, 1974.

Somersault [*Chūgaeri*]. Translated by Philip Gabriel. New York: Grove Press, 2003.

Teach Us to Outgrow Our Madness [*Warera no kyōki o ikurinobiru michi o oshieyo*]: *Four Short Novels by Kenzaburō Ōe*. Translated by John Nathan. New York: Grove Press, 1977.

Wilson, Michiko. *The Marginal World of Ōe Kenzaburō: A Study in Themes and Techniques*. Armonk, N.Y.: Sharpe, 1986.

Tawada Yōko

The Bridegroom Was a Dog [*Inumuko iri*]. Translated by Margaret Mitsutani. Tokyo: Kodansha International, 1998.

Where Europe Begins. Translated from German by Susan Bernofsky and from Japanese by Yumi Selden. New York: New Directions, 2002.

Tsushima Yōko

Child of Fortune [*Chōji*]. Translated by Geraldine Harcourt. Tokyo: Kodansha International, 1983.

The Shooting Gallery [*Shateki*] *and Other Stories*. Translated by Geraldine Harcourt. New York: Pantheon, 1988.

Woman Running in the Mountains [*Yama o hashiru onna*]. Translated by Geraldine Harcourt. New York: Pantheon, 1991.

Yoshimoto Banana

Amurita [*Amurita*]. Translated by Russell F. Wasden. New York: Grove Press, 1997.

Asleep [*Shirakawa yofune*]. Translated by Michael Emmerich. New York: Grove Press, 2000.

Goodbye Tsugumi [*Tsugumi*]. Translated by Michael Emmerich. New York: Grove Press, 2002.

Hard-Boiled [*Hādoboirudo*] *and Hard Luck* [*Hādo rakku*]. Translated by Michael Emmerich. New York: Grove Press, 2005.

Kitchen [*Kitchin*]. Translated by Megan Backus. New York: Washington Square Press, 1993.

Poetry

Takahashi Mutsuo

A *Bunch of Keys: Selected Poems*. Translated by Hiroaki Sato. Trumansburg, N.Y.: Crossing Press, 1984.
Poems of a Penisist. Translated by Hiroaki Sato. Chicago: Chicago Review Press, 1975.
Sleeping Sinning Falling. Translated by Hiroaki Sato. San Francisco: City Lights Books, 1992.

Tawara Machi

Salad Anniversary [*Sarada kinenbi*]. Translated by Juliet Winters Carpenter. Tokyo: Kodansha International, 1989.

Yoshimasu Gōzō

Devil's Wind: A Thousand Steps. Translated by Brenda Barrows and Marilyn Chin. Oakland, Mich.: Katydid Books, 1980.

PERMISSIONS

Grateful acknowledgement is hereby made for permission to reprint copyrighted material. Every attempt has been made to trace copyright holders. The editors and the publisher would be interested to hear from anyone not acknowledged appropriately.

Ariyoshi Sawako. "The Village of Eguchi," translated by Yukio Sawa and Herbert Glazer, *Japan Quarterly* 18, no. 4 (1971): 427–442. Reprinted with permission of the estate of Ariyoshi Sawako.

Baba Akiko. Five poems, translated by Hatsue Kawamura and Jane Reichold. From *Heavenly Maiden Tanka: Akiko Baba*. Copyright © AHA Books, 1999.

Betsuyaku Minoru. *The Little Match Girl*, translated by Robert N. Lawson. From *Alternate Japanese Drama: Ten Plays*. Copyright © University of Hawai'i Press, 1992.

Enchi Fumiko. "Skeletons of Men," translated by Susan Matisoff, *Japan Quarterly* 35, no. 4 (1988). Reprinted with permission of the estate of Enchi Fumiko.

Endō Shūsaku. "Mothers," translated by Van C. Gessel. From *Stained Glass Elegies*, copyright © 1959, 1965, 1973, 1979 by Shusaku Endo, English translation copyright © 1984 by Van C. Gessel. Reprinted by permission of New Directions Publishing Corporation.

Etō Jun. "Natsume Sōseki: A Japanese Meiji Intellectual," *American Scholar* 43, no. 4 (autumn 1965): 603–619. Reprinted with permission of the estate of Etō Jun.

Furui Yoshikichi. "Ravine," translated by Meredith McKinney. From *Ravine and Other Stories*. Copyright © Stone Bridge Press, 1997.

Gotō Miyoko. Five poems, translated by Reiko Tsukimura. From *I Am Alive: The Tanka Poems of Gotō Miyoko.* Copyright © Katydid Books, 1988.

Hoshi Shin'ichi. "He-y, Come on Ou-t!," translated by Stanleigh Jones. From *The Best Japanese Science Fiction Stories.* Copyright © Barricade Books/Dembner Books, 1989.

Hotta Yoshie. "The Old Man," excerpt from *Shadow Pieces,* translated by P. G. O'Neill, *Japan Quarterly* 13, no. 3 (1952).

Ibuse Masuji. "Old Ushitora," translated by John Bester. From *Salamander and Other Stories.* Copyright © Kodansha, 1981.

Ikezawa Natsuki. "Revenant," translated by Dennis Keene. From *Still Lives.* Copyright © Kodansha International, 1997.

Inoue Hisashi. *Makeup,* translated by Akemi Horie, *Encounter* 22, no. 5 (1989): 3–18. Reprinted with permission of Inoue Hisashi.

Inoue Yasushi. "The Rhododendrons of Hira," translated by Edward Seidensticker, *Japan Quarterly* 2, no. 3 (1955): 322–347. Reprinted with permission of the estate of Inoue Yasushi.

Ishikawa Jun. "The Jesus of the Ruins," translated by William J. Tyler. From *The Legend of Gold and Other Stories.* Copyright © University of Hawai'i Press, 1998.

Kaikō Takeshi. "The Crushed Pellet," translated by Cecilia Segawa Seigle. From *The Shōwa Anthology.* Copyright © Kodansha International, 1985.

Kaneko Tōta. Three poems. From *Modern Japanese Haiku: An Anthology.* Copyright © University of Toronto Press, 1976. Reprinted with permission of the publisher.

Katayama Yumiko. Four poems, translated by Makoto Ueda. From *Far Beyond the Field: An Anthology of Haiku by Japanese Women.* Copyright © Columbia University Press, 2003. Reprinted with permission of the publisher.

Kawabata Yasunari. "Japan, the Beautiful, and Myself," translated by Edward Seidensticker. Copyright © The Nobel Foundation, 1968.

Kita Morio. Excerpt from *Doctor Manbo at Sea,* translated by Ralph F. McCarthy. Copyright © Kodansha, 1987.

Kondō Yoshimi. Five poems, translated by Makoto Ueda. From *Modern Japanese Tanka: An Anthology.* Copyright © Columbia University Press, 1996. Reprinted with permission of the publisher.

Kōno Takeo. "Final Moments," translated by Lucy North. From *Toddler-Hunting and Other Stories.* Copyright © 1961 by Kōno Takeo. Reprinted by permission of New Directions Publishing Corporation.

Kurahashi Yumiko. "To Die at the Estuary," translated by Dennis Keene. From *Contemporary Japanese Literature: An Anthology of Fiction, Film, and Other Writing Since 1945.* Copyright © Alfred A. Knopf, 1977.

Maekawa Samio. Four poems, translated by Makoto Ueda. From *Modern Japanese Tanka: An Anthology.* Copyright © Columbia University Press, 1996. Reprinted with permission of the publisher.

Matsumoto Seichō. "The Stakeout," translated by Daniel Zoll, *Japan Echo* 12, Special Issue, "Literature in Postwar Japan," 1985, pp. 14–22. Reproduced by permission of the publisher.

Mayuzuki Madoka. Three poems, translated by Makoto Ueda. From *Modern Japanese Tanka: An Anthology.* Copyright © Columbia University Press, 1996. Reprinted with permission of the publisher.

Mishima Yukio. "Patriotism," translated by Geoffrey W. Sargent. From *Death in Mid-summer and Other Stories*. Copyright © 1966 by New Directions Publishing Corporation. Reprinted with permission of New Directions Publishing Corporation.

Miya Shūji. Five poems, translated by Makoto Ueda. From *Modern Japanese Tanka: An Anthology*. Copyright © Columbia University Press, 1996. Reprinted with permission of the publisher.

Murakami Haruki. "Firefly," translated by J. Philip Gabriel. Copyright © 1984 by Haruki Murakami. Reprinted by permission of International Creative Management, Inc.

Nakagami Kenji. "The Wind and the Light," translated by Andrew Rankin. From *Snakelust and Other Stories*. Copyright © Kodansha International, 1998.

Noma Hiroshi. "A Red Moon in Her Face," translated by James Raeside. From Noma Hiroshi, *Dark Pictures and Other Stories*, translated and with an afterword by James Raeside, Michigan Monograph Series in Japanese Studies, Number 30 (Ann Arbor: Center for Japanese Studies, The University of Michigan, 2000). Translation copyright © 2000 Center for Japanese Studies. Used with permission.

Ōe Kenzaburō. "Japan, the Ambiguous, and Myself." Copyright © The Nobel Foundation, 1994.

Ōe Kenzaburō. "Teach Us to Outgrow Our Madness," translated by John Nathan. Copyright © 1977 by John Nathan. Used by permission of Grove/Atlantic, Inc.

Ozaki Kazuo. "Entomologica," translated by Chris Brockett, *Japan Echo* 12, Special Issue, "Literature in Postwar Japan," 1985, pp. 9–13. Reproduced by permission of the publisher.

Saitō Fumi. Four poems, translated by Hatsue Kawamura and Jane Reichold. From *White Letter Poems*. Copyright © AHA Books, 1998.

Shiina Rinzō. "The Go-Between," translated by Noah H. Brannen. Reprinted from *The Go-Between and Other Stories* by Rinzo Shiina, copyright © 1970 by Judson Press. Used by permission of Judson Press, 800-4 JUDSON, www.judsonpress.com.

Shima Tsuyoshi. "Bones," translated by William J. Tyler. From *Southern Exposure: Modern Japanese Literature from Okinawa*. Copyright © University of Hawai'i Press, 2000.

Shimizu Yoshiyori. "Jack and Betty Forever," translated by Frederik L. Schodt. From *Jack and Betty Forever*. Copyright © Kodansha International, 1993.

Shōnō Junzō. "Evenings at the Pool," translated by Wayne Lammers. From *Still Life and Other Stories*. Copyright © Stone Bridge Press, 1992.

Takahashi Takako. "Invalid," translated by Van C. Gessel. First appeared in *Manoa: A Pacific Journal of International Writing*, Fall 1991, published by the University of Hawai'i Press.

Takeda Taijun. "The Misshapen Ones," translated by Edward Seidensticker, *Japan Quarterly* 4, no. 4 (1957): 472–498. Reprinted with permission of the estate of Takeda Taijun.

Tawada Yōko. "Where Europe Begins," translated Susan Bernofsky. From *Where Europe Begins*. Copyright © New Directions, 2002.

Tawara Machi. One poem, translated by Juliet Winters Carpenter. From *Salad Anniversary*. Copyright © Kodansha International, 1989.

Tawara Machi. Two poems, translated by Leza Lowitz, Miyuki Aoyama, and Akemi Tomioka. From *A Long Rainy Season: Haiku and Tanka*. Copyright © Stone Bridge Press, 1994.

Tsukamoto Kunio. Six poems, translated by Makoto Ueda. From *Japanese Modern Tanka: An Anthology.* Copyright © Columbia University Press, 1996. Reprinted with permission of the publisher.

Yasuoka Shōtarō. "Prized Possessions," translated by Edwin McClellan. From *Contemporary Japanese Literature: An Anthology of Fiction, Film, and Other Writing Since* 1945. Copyright © Alfred A. Knopf, 1977.

Yoshimoto Banana. "Newlywed," translated by Ann Sherif. From *Lizard.* Copyright © 1995 by Ann Sherif. Used by permission of Grove/Atlantic, Inc.

Yoshiyuki Junnosuke. "Personal Baggage," translated by John Bester, *Japanese Literature Today* (1976): 4–8. Reprinted with permission of the estate of Yoshiyuki Junnosuke.

OTHER WORKS IN THE COLUMBIA ASIAN
STUDIES SERIES

TRANSLATIONS FROM THE ASIAN CLASSICS

Major Plays of Chikamatsu, tr. Donald Keene 1961

Four Major Plays of Chikamatsu, tr. Donald Keene. Paperback ed. only. 1961; rev. ed. 1997

Records of the Grand Historian of China, translated from the Shih chi of Ssu-ma Ch'ien, tr. Burton Watson, 2 vols. 1961

Instructions for Practical Living and Other Neo-Confucian Writings by Wang Yang-ming, tr. Wing-tsit Chan 1963

Hsün Tzu: Basic Writings, tr. Burton Watson, paperback ed. only. 1963; rev. ed. 1996

Chuang Tzu: Basic Writings, tr. Burton Watson, paperback ed. only. 1964; rev. ed. 1996

The Mahābhārata, tr. Chakravarthi V. Narasimhan. Also in paperback ed. 1965; rev. ed. 1997

The Manyōshū, Nippon Gakujutsu Shinkōkai edition 1965

Su Tung-p'o: Selections from a Sung Dynasty Poet, tr. Burton Watson. Also in paperback ed. 1965

Bhartrihari: Poems, tr. Barbara Stoler Miller. Also in paperback ed. 1967

Basic Writings of Mo Tzu, Hsün Tzu, and Han Fei Tzu, tr. Burton Watson. Also in separate paperback eds. 1967

The Awakening of Faith, Attributed to Aśvaghosha, tr. Yoshito S. Hakeda. Also in paperback ed. 1967

Reflections on Things at Hand: The Neo-Confucian Anthology, comp. Chu Hsi and Lü Tsu-ch'ien, tr. Wing-tsit Chan 1967

The Platform Sutra of the Sixth Patriarch, tr. Philip B. Yampolsky. Also in paperback ed. 1967

Essays in Idleness: The Tsurezuregusa of Kenkō, tr. Donald Keene. Also in paperback ed. 1967

The Pillow Book of Sei Shōnagon, tr. Ivan Morris, 2 vols. 1967

Two Plays of Ancient India: The Little Clay Cart and the Minister's Seal, tr. J. A. B. van Buitenen 1968

The Complete Works of Chuang Tzu, tr. Burton Watson 1968

The Romance of the Western Chamber (Hsi Hsiang chi), tr. S. I. Hsiung. Also in paperback ed. 1968

The Manyōshū, Nippon Gakujutsu Shinkōkai edition. Paperback ed. only. 1969

Records of the Historian: Chapters from the Shih chi of Ssu-ma Ch'ien, tr. Burton Watson. Paperback ed. only. 1969

Cold Mountain: 100 Poems by the T'ang Poet Han-shan, tr. Burton Watson. Also in paperback ed. 1970

Twenty Plays of the Nō Theatre, ed. Donald Keene. Also in paperback ed. 1970

Chūshingura: The Treasury of Loyal Retainers, tr. Donald Keene. Also in paperback ed. 1971; rev. ed. 1997

The Zen Master Hakuin: Selected Writings, tr. Philip B. Yampolsky 1971

Chinese Rhyme-Prose: Poems in the Fu Form from the Han and Six Dynasties Periods, tr. Burton Watson. Also in paperback ed. 1971

Kūkai: Major Works, tr. Yoshito S. Hakeda. Also in paperback ed. 1972

The Old Man Who Does as He Pleases: Selections from the Poetry and Prose of Lu Yu, tr. Burton Watson 1973

The Lion's Roar of Queen Śrīmālā, tr. Alex and Hideko Wayman 1974

Courtier and Commoner in Ancient China: Selections from the History of the Former Han by Pan Ku, tr. Burton Watson. Also in paperback ed. 1974

Japanese Literature in Chinese, vol. 1: Poetry and Prose in Chinese by Japanese Writers of the Early Period, tr. Burton Watson 1975

Japanese Literature in Chinese, vol. 2: Poetry and Prose in Chinese by Japanese Writers of the Later Period, tr. Burton Watson 1976

Scripture of the Lotus Blossom of the Fine Dharma, tr. Leon Hurvitz. Also in paperback ed. 1976

Love Song of the Dark Lord: Jayadeva's Gītagovinda, tr. Barbara Stoler Miller. Also in paperback ed. Cloth ed. includes critical text of the Sanskrit. 1977; rev. ed. 1997

Ryōkan: Zen Monk-Poet of Japan, tr. Burton Watson 1977

Calming the Mind and Discerning the Real: From the Lam rim chen mo of Tson-kha-pa, tr. Alex Wayman 1978

The Hermit and the Love-Thief: Sanskrit Poems of Bhartrihari and Bilhaṇa, tr. Barbara Stoler Miller 1978

The Lute: Kao Ming's P'i-p'a chi, tr. Jean Mulligan. Also in paperback ed. 1980

A Chronicle of Gods and Sovereigns: Jinnō Shōtōki of Kitabatake Chikafusa, tr. H. Paul Varley 1980

Among the Flowers: The Hua-chien chi, tr. Lois Fusek 1982

Grass Hill: Poems and Prose by the Japanese Monk Gensei, tr. Burton Watson 1983

Doctors, Diviners, and Magicians of Ancient China: Biographies of Fang-shih, tr. Kenneth J. DeWoskin. Also in paperback ed. 1983

Theater of Memory: The Plays of Kālidāsa, ed. Barbara Stoler Miller. Also in paperback ed. 1984

The Columbia Book of Chinese Poetry: From Early Times to the Thirteenth Century, ed. and tr. Burton Watson. Also in paperback ed. 1984

Poems of Love and War: From the Eight Anthologies and the Ten Long Poems of Classical Tamil, tr. A. K. Ramanujan. Also in paperback ed. 1985

The Bhagavad Gita: Krishna's Counsel in Time of War, tr. Barbara Stoler Miller 1986

The Columbia Book of Later Chinese Poetry, ed. and tr. Jonathan Chaves. Also in paperback ed. 1986

The Tso Chuan: Selections from China's Oldest Narrative History, tr. Burton Watson 1989

Waiting for the Wind: Thirty-six Poets of Japan's Late Medieval Age, tr. Steven Carter 1989

Selected Writings of Nichiren, ed. Philip B. Yampolsky 1990

Saigyō, Poems of a Mountain Home, tr. Burton Watson 1990

The Book of Lieh Tzu: A Classic of the Tao, tr. A. C. Graham. Morningside ed. 1990

The Tale of an Anklet: An Epic of South India—The Cilappatikāram of Iḷaṇkō Aṭikaḷ, tr. R. Parthasarathy 1993

Waiting for the Dawn: A Plan for the Prince, tr. with introduction by Wm. Theodore de Bary 1993

Yoshitsune and the Thousand Cherry Trees: A Masterpiece of the Eighteenth-Century Japanese Puppet Theater, tr., annotated, and with introduction by Stanleigh H. Jones, Jr. 1993

The Lotus Sutra, tr. Burton Watson. Also in paperback ed. 1993

The Classic of Changes: A New Translation of the I Ching as Interpreted by Wang Bi, tr. Richard John Lynn 1994

Beyond Spring: Tz'u Poems of the Sung Dynasty, tr. Julie Landau 1994

The Columbia Anthology of Traditional Chinese Literature, ed. Victor H. Mair 1994

Scenes for Mandarins: The Elite Theater of the Ming, tr. Cyril Birch 1995

Letters of Nichiren, ed. Philip B. Yampolsky; tr. Burton Watson et al. 1996

Unforgotten Dreams: Poems by the Zen Monk Shōtetsu, tr. Steven D. Carter 1997

The Vimalakirti Sutra, tr. Burton Watson 1997

Japanese and Chinese Poems to Sing: The Wakan rōei shū, tr. J. Thomas Rimer and Jonathan Chaves 1997

Breeze Through Bamboo: Kanshi of Ema Saikō, tr. Hiroaki Sato 1998

A Tower for the Summer Heat, by Li Yu, tr. Patrick Hanan 1998

Traditional Japanese Theater: An Anthology of Plays, by Karen Brazell 1998

The Original Analects: Sayings of Confucius and His Successors (0479–0249), by E. Bruce Brooks and A. Taeko Brooks 1998

The Classic of the Way and Virtue: A New Translation of the Tao-te ching of Laozi as Interpreted by Wang Bi, tr. Richard John Lynn 1999

The Four Hundred Songs of War and Wisdom: An Anthology of Poems from Classical Tamil, The Puṛanāṇūṛu, ed. and tr. George L. Hart and Hank Heifetz 1999

Original Tao: Inward Training (Nei-yeh) and the Foundations of Taoist Mysticism, by Harold D. Roth 1999

Lao Tzu's Tao Te Ching: A Translation of the Startling New Documents Found at Guodian, by Robert G. Henricks 2000

The Shorter Columbia Anthology of Traditional Chinese Literature, ed. Victor H. Mair 2000

Mistress and Maid (Jiaohongji), by Meng Chengshun, tr. Cyril Birch 2001

Chikamatsu: Five Late Plays, tr. and ed. C. Andrew Gerstle 2001

The Essential Lotus: Selections from the Lotus Sutra, tr. Burton Watson 2002

Early Modern Japanese Literature: An Anthology, 1600–1900, ed. Haruo Shirane 2002

The Sound of the Kiss, or The Story That Must Never Be Told: Pingali Suranna's Kala-purnodayamu, tr. Vecheru Narayana Rao and David Shulman 2003

The Selected Poems of Du Fu, tr. Burton Watson 2003

Far Beyond the Field: Haiku by Japanese Women, tr. Makoto Ueda 2003

Just Living: Poems and Prose by the Japanese Monk Tonna, ed. and tr. Steven D. Carter 2003

Han Feizi: Basic Writings, tr. Burton Watson 2003

Mozi: Basic Writings, tr. Burton Watson 2003

Xunzi: Basic Writings, tr. Burton Watson 2003

Zhuangzi: Basic Writings, tr. Burton Watson 2003

The Awakening of Faith, Attributed to Aśvaghosha, tr. Yoshito S. Hakeda, introduction by Ryuichi Abe 2005

The Tales of the Heike, tr. Burton Watson, ed. Haruo Shirane 2006

Tales of Moonlight and Rain, by Ueda Akinari, tr. with introduction by Anthony H. Chambers 2007

Traditional Japanese Literature: An Anthology, Beginnings to 1600, ed. Haruo Shirane 2007

MODERN ASIAN LITERATURE

Modern Japanese Drama: An Anthology, ed. and tr. Ted. Takaya. Also in paperback ed. 1979

Mask and Sword: Two Plays for the Contemporary Japanese Theater, by Yamazaki Masakazu, tr. J. Thomas Rimer 1980

Yokomitsu Riichi, Modernist, by Dennis Keene 1980

Nepali Visions, Nepali Dreams: The Poetry of Laxmiprasad Devkota, tr. David Rubin 1980

Literature of the Hundred Flowers, vol. 1: Criticism and Polemics, ed. Hualing Nieh 1981

Literature of the Hundred Flowers, vol. 2: Poetry and Fiction, ed. Hualing Nieh 1981

Modern Chinese Stories and Novellas, 1919–1949, ed. Joseph S. M. Lau, C. T. Hsia, and Leo Ou-fan Lee. Also in paperback ed. 1984

A View by the Sea, by Yasuoka Shōtarō, tr. Kären Wigen Lewis 1984

Other Worlds: Arishima Takeo and the Bounds of Modern Japanese Fiction, by Paul Anderer 1984

Selected Poems of Sō Chōngju, tr. with introduction by David R. McCann 1989

The Sting of Life: Four Contemporary Japanese Novelists, by Van C. Gessel 1989

Stories of Osaka Life, by Oda Sakunosuke, tr. Burton Watson 1990

The Bodhisattva, or Samantabhadra, by Ishikawa Jun, tr. with introduction by William Jefferson Tyler 1990

The Travels of Lao Ts'an, by Liu T'ieh-yün, tr. Harold Shadick. Morningside ed. 1990

Three Plays by Kōbō Abe, tr. with introduction by Donald Keene 1993

The Columbia Anthology of Modern Chinese Literature, ed. Joseph S. M. Lau and
Howard Goldblatt 1995

Modern Japanese Tanka, ed. and tr. Makoto Ueda 1996

Masaoka Shiki: Selected Poems, ed. and tr. Burton Watson 1997

*Writing Women in Modern China: An Anthology of Women's Literature from the Early
Twentieth Century*, ed. and tr. Amy D. Dooling and Kristina M. Torgeson 1998

American Stories, by Nagai Kafū, tr. Mitsuko Iriye 2000

The Paper Door and Other Stories, by Shiga Naoya, tr. Lane Dunlop 2001

Grass for My Pillow, by Saiichi Maruya, tr. Dennis Keene 2002

For All My Walking: Free-Verse Haiku of Taneda Santōka, with Excerpts from His Diaries, tr. Burton Watson 2003

The Columbia Anthology of Modern Japanese Literature, vol. 1: *From Restoration to
Occupation, 1868–1945*, ed. J. Thomas Rimer and Van C. Gessel 2005

STUDIES IN ASIAN CULTURE

*The Ōnin War: History of Its Origins and Background, with a Selective Translation of
the Chronicle of Ōnin*, by H. Paul Varley 1967

Chinese Government in Ming Times: Seven Studies, ed. Charles O. Hucker 1969

The Actors' Analects (Yakusha Rongo), ed. and tr. Charles J. Dunn and Bungō Torigoe
1969

Self and Society in Ming Thought, by Wm. Theodore de Bary and the Conference on
Ming Thought. Also in paperback ed. 1970

A History of Islamic Philosophy, by Majid Fakhry, 2d ed. 1983

Phantasies of a Love Thief: The Caurapañcāśikā Attributed to Bilhaṇa, by Barbara
Stoler Miller 1971

Iqbal: Poet-Philosopher of Pakistan, ed. Hafeez Malik 1971

The Golden Tradition: An Anthology of Urdu Poetry, ed. and tr. Ahmed Ali. Also in paperback ed. 1973

Conquerors and Confucians: Aspects of Political Change in Late Yüan China, by John
W. Dardess 1973

The Unfolding of Neo-Confucianism, by Wm. Theodore de Bary and the Conference
on Seventeenth-Century Chinese Thought. Also in paperback ed. 1975

To Acquire Wisdom: The Way of Wang Yang-ming, by Julia Ching 1976

Gods, Priests, and Warriors: The Bhṛgus of the Mahābhārata, by Robert P. Goldman
1977

Mei Yao-ch'en and the Development of Early Sung Poetry, by Jonathan Chaves 1976

The Legend of Semimaru, Blind Musician of Japan, by Susan Matisoff 1977

Sir Sayyid Ahmad Khan and Muslim Modernization in India and Pakistan, by Hafeez
Malik 1980

The Khilafat Movement: Religious Symbolism and Political Mobilization in India, by
Gail Minault 1982

The World of K'ung Shang-jen: A Man of Letters in Early Ch'ing China, by Richard
Strassberg 1983

The Lotus Boat: The Origins of Chinese Tz'u Poetry in T'ang Popular Culture, by Marsha L. Wagner 1984

Expressions of Self in Chinese Literature, ed. Robert E. Hegel and Richard C. Hessney
1985

Songs for the Bride: Women's Voices and Wedding Rites of Rural India, by W. G. Archer; ed. Barbara Stoler Miller and Mildred Archer 1986

The Confucian Kingship in Korea: Yŏngjo and the Politics of Sagacity, by JaHyun Kim Haboush 1988

COMPANIONS TO ASIAN STUDIES

Approaches to the Oriental Classics, ed. Wm. Theodore de Bary 1959

Early Chinese Literature, by Burton Watson. Also in paperback ed. 1962

Approaches to Asian Civilizations, ed. Wm. Theodore de Bary and Ainslie T. Embree 1964

The Classic Chinese Novel: A Critical Introduction, by C. T. Hsia. Also in paperback ed. 1968

Chinese Lyricism: Shih Poetry from the Second to the Twelfth Century, tr. Burton Watson. Also in paperback ed. 1971

A Syllabus of Indian Civilization, by Leonard A. Gordon and Barbara Stoler Miller 1971

Twentieth-Century Chinese Stories, ed. C. T. Hsia and Joseph S. M. Lau. Also in paperback ed. 1971

A Syllabus of Chinese Civilization, by J. Mason Gentzler, 2d ed. 1972

A Syllabus of Japanese Civilization, by H. Paul Varley, 2d ed. 1972

An Introduction to Chinese Civilization, ed. John Meskill, with the assistance of J. Mason Gentzler 1973

An Introduction to Japanese Civilization, ed. Arthur E. Tiedemann 1974

Ukifune: Love in the Tale of Genji, ed. Andrew Pekarik 1982

The Pleasures of Japanese Literature, by Donald Keene 1988

A Guide to Oriental Classics, ed. Wm. Theodore de Bary and Ainslie T. Embree; 3d edition ed. Amy Vladeck Heinrich, 2 vols. 1989

INTRODUCTION TO ASIAN CIVILIZATIONS

Wm. Theodore de Bary, General Editor

Sources of Japanese Tradition, 1958; paperback ed., 2 vols., 1964. 2d ed., vol. 1, 2001, compiled by Wm. Theodore de Bary, Donald Keene, George Tanabe, and Paul Varley; vol. 2, 2005, compiled by Wm. Theodore de Bary, Carol Gluck, and Arthur E. Tiedemann; vol. 2, abridged, 2 pts., 2006, compiled by Wm. Theodore de Bary, Carol Gluck, and Arthur E. Tiedemann

Sources of Indian Tradition, 1958; paperback ed., 2 vols., 1964. 2d ed., 2 vols., 1988

Sources of Chinese Tradition, 1960, paperback ed., 2 vols., 1964. 2d ed., vol. 1, 1999, compiled by Wm. Theodore de Bary and Irene Bloom; vol. 2, 2000, compiled by Wm. Theodore de Bary and Richard Lufrano

Sources of Korean Tradition, 1997; 2 vols., vol. 1, 1997, compiled by Peter H. Lee and Wm. Theodore de Bary; vol. 2, 2001, compiled by Yŏngho Ch'oe, Peter H. Lee, and Wm. Theodore de Bary

NEO-CONFUCIAN STUDIES

Instructions for Practical Living and Other Neo-Confucian Writings by Wang Yang-ming, tr. Wing-tsit Chan 1963

Reflections on Things at Hand: The Neo-Confucian Anthology, comp. Chu Hsi and Lü Tsu-ch'ien, tr. Wing-tsit Chan 1967

Self and Society in Ming Thought, by Wm. Theodore de Bary and the Conference on Ming Thought. Also in paperback ed. 1970

The Unfolding of Neo-Confucianism, by Wm. Theodore de Bary and the Conference on Seventeenth-Century Chinese Thought. Also in paperback ed. 1975

Principle and Practicality: Essays in Neo-Confucianism and Practical Learning, ed. Wm. Theodore de Bary and Irene Bloom. Also in paperback ed. 1979

The Syncretic Religion of Lin Chao-en, by Judith A. Berling 1980

The Renewal of Buddhism in China: Chu-hung and the Late Ming Synthesis, by Chün-fang Yü 1981

Neo-Confucian Orthodoxy and the Learning of the Mind-and-Heart, by Wm. Theodore de Bary 1981

Yüan Thought: Chinese Thought and Religion Under the Mongols, ed. Hok-lam Chan and Wm. Theodore de Bary 1982

The Liberal Tradition in China, by Wm. Theodore de Bary 1983

The Development and Decline of Chinese Cosmology, by John B. Henderson 1984

The Rise of Neo-Confucianism in Korea, by Wm. Theodore de Bary and JaHyun Kim Haboush 1985

Chiao Hung and the Restructuring of Neo-Confucianism in Late Ming, by Edward T. Ch'ien 1985

Neo-Confucian Terms Explained: Pei-hsi tzu-i, by Ch'en Ch'un, ed. and tr. Wing-tsit Chan 1986

Knowledge Painfully Acquired: K'un-chih chi, by Lo Ch'in-shun, ed. and tr. Irene Bloom 1987

To Become a Sage: The Ten Diagrams on Sage Learning, by Yi T'oegye, ed. and tr. Michael C. Kalton 1988

The Message of the Mind in Neo-Confucian Thought, by Wm. Theodore de Bary 1989

The Columbia Anthology of Modern Chinese Literature, 2d ed., ed. Joseph S. M. Lau and Howard Goldblatt